EVIL INTENTIONS OMNIBUS

Find Me A Villain

The Cost of Silence

Crime in Question

Also by Margaret Yorke

SUMMER FLIGHT
PRAY LOVE REMEMBER
CHRISTOPHER
DECEIVING MIRROR
THE CHINA DOLL
ONCE A STRANGER
THE BIRTHDAY
FULL CIRCLE
NO FURY
THE APRICOT BED
THE LIMBO LADIES
NO MEDALS FOR THE MAJOR
THE SMALL HOURS OF THE MORNING
THE POINT OF MURDER
DEATH ON ACCOUNT
THE SCENT OF FEAR
THE HAND OF DEATH
DEVIL'S WORK
THE SMOOTH FACE OF EVIL
INTIMATE KILL
SAFELY TO THE GRAVE
EVIDENCE TO DESTROY
SPEAK FOR THE DEAD
ADMIT TO MURDER
A SMALL DECEIT
CRIMINAL DAMAGE
DANGEROUS TO KNOW
ALMOST THE TRUTH
SERIOUS INTENT
A QUESTION OF BELIEF
ACT OF VIOLENCE
FALSE PRETENCES
THE PRICE OF GUILT
A CASE TO ANSWER
CAUSE FOR CONCERN

Featuring Patrick Grant

DEAD IN THE MORNING
SILENT WITNESS
GRAVE MATTERS
MORTAL REMAINS
CAST FOR DEATH

Collected short stories

PIECES OF JUSTICE

EVIL INTENTIONS OMNIBUS

Find Me A Villain
The Cost of Silence
Crime in Question

MARGARET YORKE

timewarner
paperbacks

A *Time Warner* Paperback

This omnibus edition first published in Great Britain by
Time Warner Paperbacks in 2004
Evil Intentions Omnibus Copyright © Margaret Yorke 2004

Previously published separately:
Find Me A Villain first published in Great Britain in 1983 by
Hutchinson and Co. Ltd
Published by Arrow in 1986
Published by Warner Books in 2000
Reprinted 2000
Reprinted by Time Warner Paperbacks in 2002
Copyright © Margaret Yorke 1983

The Cost of Silence first published in Great Britain in 1977 by Hutchinson
Published by Arrow Books in 1979
Published by Warner Futura in 1996
Reprinted by Time Warner Paperbacks in 2002
Copyright © Margaret Yorke 1977

Crime In Question first published in Great Britain in 1989 by
Century Hutchinson Ltd / Mysterious Press UK
Published by Warner Books in 1998
Reprinted 2001
Reprinted by Time Warner Paperbacks in 2002
Copyright © Margaret Yorke 1989

The moral right of the author has been asserted.

*All characters in this publication are fictitious and any
resemblance to real persons, living or dead, is purely coincidental.*

All rights reserved.
No part of this publication may be reproduced, stored in a retrieval
system, or transmitted, in any form or by any means, without the prior
permission in writing of the publisher, nor be otherwise circulated in any
form of binding or cover other than that in which it is published and without
a similar condition including this condition being imposed on
the subsequent purchaser.

A CIP catalogue record for this book is available from the British Library.

ISBN 0 7515 3655 5

Printed and bound in Great Britain by Clays Ltd, St Ives plc

Time Warner Paperbacks
An imprint of
Time Warner Books UK
Brettenham House
Lancaster Place
London WC2E 7EN

www.TimeWarnerBooks.co.uk

Find Me A Villain

In tragic life . . .
No villain need be! Passions spin the plot:
We are betrayed by what is false within.

George Meredith

1

Rain fell from the leaden sky. It dripped from the few dead leaves which remained on the trees, and from the spiky hedgerow brambles. Water collected in pools on the paths through the copse, and the tall withered grasses drooped under their burden.

There was no wind.

A mile from the copse, lorries sped past on the new by-pass. No one stopped here now, but once, not so long ago, lovers had carved their names on the trees and ramblers had kept open an unofficial footpath through the undergrowth. In the meadows beyond the copse, cattle grazed peacefully.

It was a heifer who disturbed the covering of earth and leaves over the body. More venturesome than her sisters, she leaned against a post that had worked loose in the fence round the field and pushed it over, catching a leg in the wire as she crossed into the copse. She gave a bellow of pain, but moved on, and soon three others from the herd followed. They trampled the leaf-strewn ground and nibbled at shoots as they passed. It was some hours before their escape was discovered and they were driven back into the field. By then they had moved past the shallow dip where the body lay, but their passage had shifted the soil and leaves, exposing a foot to which still clung shreds of the dead woman's pale, patterned tights. There was no shoe.

Rain went on falling, pattering on the rotting leaves and woodland soil, dripping from the trees, trickling into the shallow grave.

2

When she smiled, she reminded Nina of a cat. Her eyes seemed slanted, and they glinted green. There were lines etched round them. At any moment, Nina thought hysterically, she would lick a paw and begin to wash her whiskers. She was gazing into the eyes of Nina's husband with an intensity which was, to the woman watching her, obscene. Her claw – no, her hand – rested on his jacket sleeve as they sat at a small table in the restaurant.

Nina had expected her to be young, but she wasn't, though her hair hung straight to her shoulders in youthful style and the dress she wore was pleated and ruched like those sold in boutiques catering for teenagers. Martin was smiling into those green, slitty eyes; his was, Nina thought, an inane, fatuous grin. She peered at them both from the shelter of the round felt hat she wore, holding the menu before her face as a screen.

Nina felt like a character in a gangster film as she sat there, in semi-disguise, watching her husband and his mistress lunching together. She had waited in a telephone box near Martin's office and had followed him when he emerged. In dark glasses and an old raincoat, with her hat pulled well down, she had walked along the road behind him as he strode away from her, Nina knew, for ever. The woman, whose name was Caroline, had appeared from the other direction and the two had embraced, for all to see, on the public pavement. Passers-by had to alter course to avoid them. Then, arms linked, heads turned to talk to each other, faces almost touching, they had walked on and entered the restaurant.

Nina felt physically sick as she stood on the pavement outside. She walked past, then turned back and went into the restaurant. She sat at a table separated from theirs by a screen which was festooned with climbing plants. She had been there before, with Martin, and knew that concealment would be possible behind this barrier. Watching them, Nina saw that she need not fear recognition. Martin had eyes only for Miss Kitty-Cat. Even if he were to glance round, he would never expect to see Nina; he would imagine her, if he thought about her at all, at home at Silverlea, still in tears as he had left her last night.

No doubt he'd already described the scene to Miss Kitty-Cat. He would have told her how Nina had wept and stormed and refused to believe that he meant to leave her and marry this other woman who was, it seemed, pregnant by him. At last he'd walked out of the house and driven off in his red BMW, saying that he was sorry to hurt her but

4

there was no point in prolonging their interview.

He and Caroline had met at a party, Martin had said. It was something to do with his work – he was in advertising – and she'd handled the promotion material for a firm whose account he looked after. The affair had been in progress for over four years. Four years! Nina found it hard to take in what he was saying. How many others had there been, before this one, she had demanded, and Martin had not replied. That meant that Caroline was not the first. Nina's instant reaction was sheer, physical jealousy as she imagined Martin in bed with another woman; she felt ill, thinking of it. Then came awareness that what she had thought was good, had believed in and had worked for throughout her adult life, had been a myth. That knowledge was almost more painful. She had loved Martin and trusted him, and had thought that he was as content as she was with their life. How long ago was the first betrayal, she wondered. Now he had met someone who did not intend to let him go.

Martin did not like cats: it was strange that he had fallen for this one, Nina thought. Her throat felt choked; she could not eat or drink anything now, and she rose and left the restaurant. She had seen enough.

A bus stopped just as she stepped on to the pavement, and without looking to see where it went, she boarded it, moving right to the front where there was an empty seat. She sat there, unaware of the route the bus took, heedless of

5

anything except her own misery. Tears flowed down her face. The conductor came to take her fare and she thrust several coins at him, forgetful, even, of what the minimum fare was. After several stops a woman with a large shopping bag came to sit beside her, and Nina, turning her head away, peered out of the window at last. They were in Oxford Street. At the next stop she got to her feet, blundered past her neighbour and left the bus. She walked on, still not heeding where she went, chivvied and jostled by shoppers on the crowded pavement.

It began to rain.

Nina went into John Lewis's and wandered around among the handbags and into the fabric department. Here, in an islanded space, she stood still and endeavoured to regain her self-control. She blew her nose on a crumpled tissue found in the pocket of her daughter Jenny's old school rain-coat which she wore, and which she had borrowed as part of her disguise. Then she walked on through the store and out into Oxford Street again. It was raining harder now. She crossed the road, and when she reached Woolworth's, went in. The only tissue she had was sodden, and she could not find her handkerchief, so she bought a small packet of tissues and wandered on. In a display of pottery objects arranged on a counter, Nina saw a row of painted cats. She halted, staring at them. They were moulded in various postures, and, to Nina's prejudiced eye, they all wore smug, self-satisfied smirks on their glazed faces. Nina's gaze focused on one of them. It seemed to have exactly the same expression as she had seen on Caroline's face earlier.

She bought the cat and carried it out of the store in a paper bag.

Nina walked on in the rain. Drops pattered off the brim of her hat past her nose. Her feet, in her smart black boots, were warm, but her hands, one holding her handbag and the other the Woolworth parcel, were cold. She had left her gloves on the bus. The Woolworth's bag was getting wet and it began to disintegrate. Nina put it in her handbag and walked on. In her mind she was following Martin and Caroline away from the restaurant. Maybe they would go back to her flat now, before he returned to the office. He had spent many nights in her flat, Nina knew, nights when he had said he was at a conference or attending a business dinner. He had left Surrey for good. Last night he had said he had already consulted a solicitor and would be putting the house up for sale. She should have part – he did not say how much – of the proceeds. He would be in touch with their daughters. He would see that she was looked after in a financial sense. He had not explained his feelings at all, although, amid stormy tears, she had wanted to know what she had done wrong, where she had failed. They had been married for twenty-four years. Nina had had no other romance in her life.

On she walked, shivering. She felt dizzy and sick, and at last her own physical distress began to impinge on her mental anguish. She looked vaguely about to see where she was and found that she was almost at the bottom of Bond Street. Piccadilly lay ahead. Nina had no memory of how she had got there, what had made her go in that direction.

Swan and Edgar's, she thought: the snack bar there would have tea, coffee, a sandwich. But Swan and Edgar's was no more. Nina paused on the pavement outside Burlington House. Across the road the clock outside Fortnum and Mason's began to strike, and some tourists stopped to watch. Inside, there would be warmth and shelter. Nina crossed the road and passed through the portals into the fragrant, muted bustle of the grocery department and went on, up the stairs, to the Mezzanine Restaurant, where she looked vaguely round. She felt rather dizzy. All the tables seemed to be occupied, but ahead, at the counter, she saw a vacant seat. She climbed on to it, stowing her packages, and ordered tea and a Danish pastry. When they came, however, she could barely swallow the tea, much less eat the pastry. Her throat seemed to have closed up. She forced some tea down, and the warmth did help a little. I really need a brandy, she thought wryly, and wondered if they would serve her with one at four o'clock in the afternoon. Her recollection of the past hours while she walked the streets was a blur; she was quite shocked to see how late it was.

The spaces on either side of Nina at the counter were occupied, but now one neighbour descended from her tall chair to leave and someone else took her place. Nina barely noticed the movement; her horizon had shrunk to the limits of the counter before her, the cup and saucer, and the plate bearing the glistening pastry, now battered and in disarray after her prods at it with the fork supplied.

Nina's new neighbour settled her handbag in the shelf space under the counter and took off her coat, hanging it over the back of her chair. She knocked Nina's arm as she did so, and apologized.

'So sorry – do forgive me,' she said.

'What – oh –' Nina was barely aware of the contact. 'It's quite all right,' she mumbled.

'These seats are awkward if you're rather short,' said Priscilla Blunt.

'Oh – er – yes,' Nina answered, and prodded her pastry again.

'What a terrible day,' Priscilla Blunt went on. 'Fortnum's is always so reassuring, isn't it?' Now she was taking off a plastic rain hood. She looked round for somewhere to put it, and, finding no handy spot, pushed it under the counter with her handbag.

Nina slowly turned to look at her.

'I suppose so,' she agreed.

She saw blonde-rinsed, freshly coiffured hair from which came a faint scent of expensive hairspray, and a well-made up face that was not in the least feline. Priscilla, whose husband said she was inclined to be too friendly and outgoing, was aware only of a drooping figure in a navy gaberdine raincoat and a round waterproof hat, an entirely respectable person to address. Priscilla often talked to strangers in trains and cafés because she liked to speak her thoughts aloud; she never looked for much response but she was seldom snubbed and would scarcely notice if she were.

Nina needed to blow her nose. She rootled in her handbag for the tissues she had just bought, and to find them took out the packaged cat, which she set on the counter. Because, in her distress, she was not coordinating properly, she had to rummage in the depths of her bag and drew forth other possessions – a zipped make-up bag, her purse, a diary – before she found the tissues. Priscilla could not fail to notice all this burrowing. Nina blew her nose and began putting everything back in her bag.

'Have you got a cold?' Priscilla asked, and frowned. She did not want to catch one, and she drew away from Nina, though germs, of course, abounded in every public place, even Fortnum's.

'No – no, it's not a cold,' said Nina.

Priscilla opened her own bag and extracted her spectacles, which she put on and through which she then inspected Nina. In spite of the lowered brim of the hat, it was obvious that she had been crying; her face was blotched and mascara had run round her eyes.

'Are you feeling all right?' Priscilla enquired.

'I'd got a bit chilled, walking about in the rain,'

said Nina and turned a face of misery towards her.

Priscilla did not like having to notice other people's problems in case she felt obliged to help them, but if confronted with them she would not evade them. She had a lot of energy herself and thought positive action was the remedy for most difficulties; tackling problems head-on and going straight through them enabled, in her view, normality to be swiftly restored behind the upset.

As can be the way with strangers, Nina found herself relating what had happened.

Priscilla wanted to drink her tea and enjoy the slice of coffee cake which she had ordered. She sipped and munched, saying 'Oh dear,' and 'Really?' at intervals, while the tale was told. Nina spoke in a low voice, and disjointedly, but her story was coherent; it was an old one.

'Perhaps he'll come back?' Priscilla suggested, pouring out more tea.

'I don't want him, now,' said Nina. 'Not after this. How could I ever trust him again?'

'Lots of men stray,' Priscilla said. 'It needn't mean a great deal.'

'But it does,' said Nina. 'I hadn't realised – all those years – our married life – I thought that we were happy, but he had other women then. I was a fool.'

'You know about them? These other women?' asked Priscilla.

'He didn't deny it,' Nina said. 'It makes all our life together a – a sham.'

'Awful for you,' said Priscilla vaguely. Then,

more collectedly, for soon she must be on her way and she could not abandon this wretched creature altogether, she asked, 'What will you do?'

'I don't know.'

'Have you a good solicitor?'

Nina hadn't thought so far.

'There's the one we used when we bought the house – twelve years ago, that was. We moved from a small cottage into such a lovely house, Silverlea. It's not far from Oxted,' she said.

'Perhaps he's acting for your husband,' said Priscilla. 'But there must be others. I should consult one quickly, if I were you.'

'Yes. You're right,' said Nina.

'And what about a job? Find something to occupy yourself,' said Priscilla. She already knew that Nina had two daughters, both grown up, one married and one in her second year at university.

'What can I do?' asked Nina. 'I'm not trained for anything.'

'Didn't you work before you were married?'

But Nina had married Martin fresh from secretarial college, and Sarah had been born within a year. She had never used her office skills.

A dim warning thought came into Priscilla's mind as she recalled her own son's matrimonial difficulties.

'If you earn, it may prejudice the settlement you get,' she said. 'Your husband must provide for you.' Her only son, now married for the second time, was having to provide for his first wife, though there were no children.

12

'He said he'd see I was looked after,' Nina said.

Priscilla had asked for her bill and had taken her purse from her handbag. Now she drew a card from it and gave it to Nina.

'I've had an idea,' she said. 'My husband and I are going away at the end of next month, to South Africa. It's partly business, partly pleasure. We'll be away two months. We had a Spanish couple who looked after our house in the country, but they have had to go back to Spain because of some family trouble; and there won't be time to get and train a new couple, and make sure they're trustworthy, before we go. We don't want to leave the house empty for so long, and I was going to engage a house-minder. There are agencies where you can find such people – they're often retired policemen, I believe.' She laughed. 'You could mind our house,' she said. 'We wouldn't want you until just before we go, so you'd have time to sort out your own afrairs. And we would say that what we paid you was expenses, so that there would be no question of it affecting your entitlements.'

'But you don't know me! You know nothing about me,' Nina said.

'On the contrary, I know a lot,' said Priscilla. 'And I'm sure you can provide a character reference – the vicar – a JP from where you live – someone like that who has known you for some time.' She gave the card to Nina. 'If I haven't heard from you by Thursday, I'll go to the agency,' she said. 'Tell me your name.'

Nina supplied it.

13

'Good,' said Priscilla. She laid notes and some coins on the plate bearing her bill. 'Do finish your tea,' she said. 'And think over my idea. It would give you a chance to recover and make a long-term plan.' And help me too, she thought, for there was no doubt about Nina's utter reliability; anyone who looked like that, dressed so dowdily, just had to be respectable and honest.

Nina helped her into her coat and handed her her umbrella.

'Thank you very much,' she said. 'I'll think about it.'

When the stranger had gone, Nina poured herself out another cup of tea and ate several mouthfuls of her pastry. She was feeling better.

She looked at the card the other woman had given her.

Mrs Leonard Blunt, she read, and an address in Berkshire: The Hall, Netherton St Mary, near Murford. Nina hadn't heard of it. She put the card away in her own notecase.

When she asked for her bill, she found that Mrs Blunt had paid for her.

Now she would have to get in touch with her, if only to thank her for that.

3

There were lights on when Nina reached home that night.

Rain was still falling as she drove her Metro from the station, swishing through puddles that had formed in the lane. Each house in this neighbourhood was set in an acre or more of land, with trees around to ensure seclusion. You seldom saw another person, except by design; there was no village near, no community feeling, and the nearest shop was two miles away.

The house should be empty, dark: who was there? Was it Martin? Had he come back? Could he have changed his mind after all? Her stomach began churning as she stopped the car on the concrete path outside the garage, but then the front door opened and Jenny came running towards her.

'Mum – where on earth have you been?' she asked. She looked pale and harassed.

'In London,' said Nina. 'What are you doing here, Jenny?'

Nina had not gone straight home after she left Fortnum and Mason. She had walked round the corner into the Haymarket, and had sat in the darkness of a cinema for several hours. She had not wanted to go home at all, but in the end it seemed the only thing left to do.

'But you haven't seen Daddy. He told me he hadn't seen you,' said Jenny.

Nina had got out of the car and the two began to hurry towards the house through the rain.

'Did you ring him?' Nina gasped. How had Jenny known where to find him after he'd left the office?

'No. I've been to see him,' said Jenny. 'I had this mad letter from him, so I went to find out what it was all about.'

'Come inside,' said Nina, shushing Jenny ahead of her into the warm house, as she had done throughout the girl's life. Martin had said he was telling the girls his plans; had he already written to them before speaking to her?

It seemed so. It did not occur to Nina that Martin might have acted thus in order to force himself into tackling her, something he had kept putting off.

'Mum, it's awful. I'm so sorry,' Jenny said. She turned to her mother and for a moment they clung together in the hall, Jenny dressed in blue jeans and a loose sweater, her mother still in the old school gaberdine. Jenny suddenly realized what she was wearing. 'Good heavens, you've got my old school mac on,' she said. 'Why on earth–?'

'It would take too long to explain,' said Nina, undoing it. She had taken her hat off in the car; at

16

least Jenny hadn't seen the full disguise. 'Have you had any supper?' she asked.

'No. I wasn't hungry, somehow,' said Jenny. 'Have you?'

'No, but I had tea at Fortnum and Mason's,' said Nina.

'Did you? You were going it a bit, weren't you?' said Jenny. 'That's great.' She stood back to examine her mother, whose face seemed to have suddenly developed new lines and sags.

'Then I went to the cinema,' Nina said.

'Really?' Jenny began to smile. 'I wish Dad had known,' she said. 'He thought you'd be moping about the place drenched in tears.'

'I was,' Nina admitted. 'It was a terrible shock, Jenny. I simply had no idea. Had you?' she asked.

'No,' said Jenny. 'I thought he might have gone temporarily off his head – had a brainstorm – something like that, but he seems to mean it.'

She'd caught an afternoon train to London after reading her father's letter, and had gone to the address which he'd put at the top of the page. She'd found him there with this woman, Caroline, who was plain and bony, and quite old. Caroline had kept touching him. As she moved across the room to fetch a drink for him – Jenny had refused even tea – drawing the curtains – switching on the electric fire – it had seemed to Jenny that she sought excuses for passing close to him, resting her hand on his arm, brushing against him. The flat was Caroline's but her father was clearly very much at home there.

Jenny had clenched her fists and spoken harshly.

'What about Mummy?' she'd asked. 'What are you going to do about her?'

'She'll be looked after,' he'd said evasively. 'The house will fetch a lot of money and she'll be entitled to part of it.' There was no need to mention the mortgage repayment which would eat into whatever sum was obtained.

'But she's got to live somewhere,' Jenny had said. 'It's so cruel of you, Daddy.'

'These things happen,' her father had said. 'I'm sorry to hurt her, of course, but it can't be helped.'

'Couldn't you just – couldn't you – well—'

'Carry on as we've done?' her father had finished the difficult sentence for her.

'Mmm.'

He'd told her, then, about the baby, which hadn't been mentioned in his letter. Jenny had felt rather sick. She'd left at once and come straight home, expecting to find her mother in need of consolation. Instead, the house was empty and her mother's car was not in the garage. There was nothing on the kitchen diary to indicate where she might be, and when an hour passed and she still did not return, Jenny had telephoned her sister, Sarah, to see if their mother was with her.

But Sarah did not know where she was. She had received a letter from their father, too, almost a replica of the one he had written to Jenny, and had at once telephoned their mother, but there had been no reply. She had been worried, Sarah confessed, and they had decided that Jenny should telephone various friends in the district to see if anyone knew where she had gone. Jenny had done so, but with no success.

Now, the telephone rang as Nina was taking off the gaberdine raincoat.

'Answer it, Jenny, would you?' she asked. She hung the raincoat up in the downstairs cloakroom and there, in the mirror above the basin, saw how distraught she looked, her face grubby from where the mascara she had put on from habit had run, her lipstick not restored. She washed her face and was patting it dry on the big, mushroom-coloured towel when Jenny called to her.

'It's Sarah. Will you talk to her?'

'Oh,' said Nina. 'Of course.' She tried to hide her dismay; at the moment she didn't feel strong enough to talk to her elder daughter, whose personality was rather overpowering. She always knew what was best for everyone else, including her son and her husband as well as her mother.

Jenny was pleased to see, as Nina took the telephone receiver from her, that she looked more like herself now, with her hair combed, though her face shone after its wash; normally her mother was always well made up and her complexion matt; it had frightened Jenny to see her in disarray.

That Caroline had rotten skin, Jenny thought: she'd got acne scars all over her face. How could Daddy fancy her, after Mum?

'Yes, Sarah?' Nina was saying into the telephone. 'How are you, darling?'

'Never mind that,' said Sarah. 'What about you, Mother? Where have you been? We've been so worried. You shouldn't have gone off without letting someone know where you were.'

'I've simply been to the cinema,' Nina said. Why should she, she thought rebelliously, have to account for her movements to Sarah? Why should Sarah be trying, now, to put her in the wrong? Martin had done it, too, telling her she was dull; that she bored him.

'The cinema?' Sarah was saying. 'At a time like this?'

'Why not?' Nina asked. 'I'd no dinner to cook for your father. What else was there to do?'

'Well – see a solicitor, for one thing,' said Sarah. 'Jeremy's found the name of a good one, who goes in for this sort of thing.'

What sort of thing, wondered Nina. Adultery? Betrayal?

'Very kind of him,' she said, managing not to point out that most solicitors closed their offices at five o'clock or so.

'You're not to worry, Mother,' Sarah instructed. 'We'll organize you. You'll always have a home with us.'

'That's kind of you, darling,' said Nina. 'But I've made no plans so far.'

'Well, of course not. It's all so sudden,' said Sarah. 'I want you to know that Jeremy and I are thoroughly shocked. We're right behind you, one hundred per cent.'

'I'm glad,' murmured Nina. She saw that the

conversation would not be swiftly concluded and gestured to Jenny, who was standing at the foot of the stairs watching her, to bring her a chair. Jenny did so, and made winding-up signals indicating that Sarah was getting into gear for a peroration. Nina winked at her and Jenny grinned.

'Yes, darling,' she heard Nina meekly agree, as she went into the dining room, and thereafter heard more such short utterances as she took glasses and bottles from the sideboard. She reappeared by her mother's side and handed her a full tumbler.

'Brandy and soda,' she said.

Gratefully, Nina took the glass and drank half of its contents at a gulp. It gave her dutch courage.

'Sarah, dear, you're both so kind. Please thank Jeremy,' she said, cutting into her elder daughter's flow of speech. 'I'll ring you tomorrow. It's too late now to go on talking. Jenny and I haven't had supper yet. We all need time to think about what's happened. He's your father still, after all, and he still feels the same about you and Jenny, remember.'

But what did that feeling amount to? He'd admired the girls for their prettiness when they were small, and had been quite indulgent, but he'd taken small part in their various activities. 'That's girls' stuff,' he'd often said, and 'You girls deal with that,' bundling them all together, dismissing them, going off to play golf or to business commitments, or so he had said.

'He's ashamed,' Jenny said, when Nina had hung up. 'Perhaps he does love us – but then, what is love?' She gave a huge sigh.

Nina knew that the concern both her daughters, in their different ways, were showing for her at this moment was love, in one of its forms.

'It's like soup – comes in a good many varieties,' she said, lightly. 'Now, Jenny, you must be starving. Shall we have scrambled eggs?'

In the kitchen, over scrambled eggs – six between them – Nina said that Sarah intended to organize her.

'Don't let her,' said Jenny. 'She's already got her eye on some cottage in the village for you to buy – she thinks Daddy will give you the money. She means you to take up full-time grannying. She said it will make you feel wanted.'

'It's kind of her,' said Nina. 'And I'm sure she could do with some help.'

'Very likely,' said Jenny. 'But she loves telling people what to do, Mummy. You know that – I've seen you crumple when she gets into her stride. She saps you. If you once get under her thumb you'll never escape. Just like Jeremy – but he needs it. She's pregnant again, did you know? Her and Caroline. Isn't it awful? They'll be sort of twins, yet an uncle, or aunt. Or something. I think it's disgusting.'

Nina knew that Jenny's warning was apt. If she once let Sarah start arranging her life, she would be committed and unable to withdraw.

'You're too young to give up, Mum,' Jenny went

on. 'Look at Daddy, starting all over again, and he's older than you.'

'It's different for men,' Nina said.

'I don't see why it should be,' said Jenny. 'You just show him.'

'Well, I've got a job,' Nina said, suddenly making up her mind. 'It's only temporary, but it's a start.'

'Have you really? Why, that's great,' Jenny said. 'What is it? How did you find it?'

Nina did not describe the circumstances of her meeting with Mrs Blunt.

'I went to see about it today,' she said primly. 'Before the cinema. The details aren't arranged yet. I don't start for several weeks.'

'That'll give you time, then,' said Jenny.

'Time for what?' asked Nina.

'To pack up the house and all that. Daddy's got a buyer for it. Someone he knows through work. I suppose he can sell it over your head?'

'I don't know,' Nina said. 'I'll have to find out. It's his house – it's in his name.'

'Mum, you're not a bit liberated are you?' said Jenny gently. 'You've got your rights, you know.'

Nina had never thought about that before; she had been content with her role, a background one, supporting Martin, running his home smoothly.

'There's you, Jenny,' she said. 'You need a home – I'll only go where there's room for you too, in your vacations.' She'd only accept Mrs Blunt's offer if that was agreed between them, Nina resolved. She rose and went to fetch her handbag.

From her notecase she took the card Mrs Blunt had given her and gave it to Jenny. 'That's where my job is,' she said.

'How grand,' Jenny said.

Nina had taken a tattered parcel out of her bag and set it on the drainer.

'She's nice, this Mrs Blunt,' she said. 'I'm to be a house-minder.'

'Whatever's that?' Jenny asked.

Nina was pleased to be able to tell one of her daughters something she did not already know. She explained.

'You don't need any special training,' she ended.

'How much will you be paid?' Jenny asked.

'That's to be decided,' Nina said.

'Well, don't worry if you can't have me there,' Jenny said. 'I can always go to Sarah – or to Alec's,' she added, lightly.

Nina had not yet met Alec, who was a year ahead of Jenny at university.

'I'm not quite sure if the job goes on until Christmas,' Nina said. 'Exact dates are to be arranged.'

'Well, don't let me be a problem,' Jenny said. 'I'm sure it will all work out. It's funny,' she went on.

'What is?'

'Well – you and Sarah. You both did the same thing – married so young, I mean – yet you're very different.'

It was true that both Nina and her elder daughter had married at nineteen and had their first

24

baby at once. Both had immersed themselves in domestic, maternal life.

'I don't think Jeremy's very like Daddy,' said Nina.

Jenny, however, thought that he was: he was a rather selfish young man who intended to be well looked after.

'Sarah doesn't let herself be pushed around,' she said. 'She's much tougher than you are, Mum. She knows what she's doing.'

'And I didn't, at her age?' Nina asked.

'Well, girls didn't then, did they?' Jenny said, kindly. 'Things were different. Marriage was all the rage, wasn't it?'

It was true. When Nina left school, girls expected to work for just a few years, until reprieved by marriage and children. She had considered no other future and when Martin had singled her out, was elated.

'Yes,' she said.

She began collecting up their plates.

'See – there you are, automatically clearing up. You're conditioned to the domestic scene,' Jenny said, but she was laughing. 'Leave that, Mum. You look shattered. I'll see to it.'

'Put them in the dishwasher,' said Nina. 'They can wait till tomorrow.'

'I will. I'm not two years old, you know,' said Jenny.

'No,' said Nina. 'Thank you, Jenny.'

'Go on up and have your bath,' Jenny said, waving her out of the room.

'I'm so glad you're here, Jenny,' Nina said, at the door. 'Thank you for coming. But you must go back tomorrow. You mustn't miss your lectures.'

'I'll go if I'm satisfied that you're all right,' Jenny said. 'Now, off with you!'

Nina went. Jenny heard her going slowly upstairs. Usually her mother, who was small and compact if a little overweight, moved briskly, with small, rapid steps. Jenny began clattering the dishes so that she could not hear the slow, dragging tread on the polished stairs. Then she noticed the parcel on the drainer and picked it up. The half-rotted paper fell away from it, revealing the cheap pottery cat.

What an odd thing for her to buy, Jenny thought, and put it on the dresser where it wouldn't get knocked over.

4

Nina would take from the house everything that was hers – her clothes, her books – mainly cookery books and works on home management or needlework. She made a neat list of the contents of the linen cupboard and packed up half for herself. She set out the crockery and kitchen utensils and catalogued all of them, then packed up what she wanted in large cardboard cartons from the supermarket. She needed no garden implements and those would offset any balance in her favour so far. The furniture was to be split by agreement and attention to value, as arranged by Mr Drew, the solicitor whom she had consulted, and Martin's lawyer.

Nina had found Mr Drew by means of the yellow pages in the telephone directory. She had seen him the day after her trip to London. A stranger, she had decided, would be a better choice than a solicitor recommended by some friend, or by Sarah's husband. Mr Drew was an elderly young man of thirty-two who advised her that she had rights and, when she explained about her house-minding job, said she should not move

27

out of Silverlea just yet. Nina insisted that Martin had said she would be looked after. She trusted him, even without a written promise, and would not agree to Mr Drew registering the house to protect her interest.

Mr Drew's desk was stacked with neat piles of paper and several folders. He looked at her sagely across the top of them. He had pale-blue eyes and a small, fair moustache.

'You trust him,' he repeated. 'Well, I hope you won't be disillusioned.' Trusting Martin, he implied, had brought her to this office.

'He isn't mean,' said Nina.

'Wasn't,' corrected Mr Drew. 'You say this woman is pregnant. He'll be needing money, Mrs Crowther. Certain sums are your due, of course, but errant spouses are often reluctant to pay.' Much of Mr Drew's income came from this sort of tangle and the pursuit of entitlements.

'He's already got a buyer for the house, it seems,' Nina said. 'I'd like everything settled as soon as possible. Divorce can be quite quick these days, can't it?'

All things being equal, yes, Mr Drew agreed, but her future must be safeguarded. Years when she might have been building up her own lucrative career had been spent caring for husband and family, he pointed out; why should she lose now? His job was to see that she didn't, he added, not telling her that in his experience, and despite his skill, in the end she would. He saw that she was determined to take this temporary job. At least she was not due to begin it just yet, which would give him time to start striking bargains with the opposition. She must make a new will at once, he told her meanwhile. He would have it prepared straightaway, and she could sign it the very next day.

'But I've never made a will,' Nina said. 'I've nothing to leave.'

'Your jewellery – your clothes. You have a car?' Mr Drew suggested. 'And eventually, what money we win from the sale of the house. If anything happened to you, it would all revert to your husband, and I'm sure you would prefer your daughters, for instance, to have it.'

He was right. Nina meekly agreed and went home to telephone Mrs Blunt.

That Sunday, Sarah, her husband Jeremy, and their son Sebastian arrived for lunch. Each evening, till then, Sarah had telephoned urging Nina not to give up. Her father would come to his senses, she said, and return. Nina refused to discuss his conduct or her plans on the telephone, and refused, too, to accept Sarah's repeated invitations to stay.

'My solicitor has advised me not to go away,' Nina said slyly, enjoying using Mr Drew in this way.

Hence the visit.

Sarah had told Jeremy, who was a computer systems analyst, that they must go and talk sense to her mother.

Jeremy, a balding young man with an incisive brain, narrow horizons and a strong sense of self-preservation, knew when to submit. A good lunch, at least, was a certainty at Silverlea. They strapped Sebastian into his seat in the rear of their Peugeot and arrived in Surrey with good appetites for the roast lamb and blackberry and apple pie which Nina had prepared.

Jeremy had brought a bottle of sherry as an expression of sympathy and a bottle of wine for lunch. He loomed gravely over Nina in the kitchen as she dished up the vegetables while Sarah potted Sebastian. Nina's plight was, in his opinion, worse than if she had been widowed, for then she would have been cushioned by Martin's insurances, and there would have been grief, but not humiliation.

'I'm awfully sorry about all this, Nina,' he said. 'And we do want you to move near us. If it's really final, I mean.'

Sarah, entering the kitchen, overheard, with approval, these words.

'There's plenty you could do, Mother,' she said. 'Sebastian would love to see more of you. And this one, of course.' She patted her not-yet-bumpy stomach.

'I'm sure there are lots of ways in which I could be useful,' Nina said. 'But I might decide to go round the world before settling down. I've never had a chance to, before.'

Jeremy stared at her. He had no great perception of mood and could not interpret hers. Perhaps she had already been at the sherry?

'This job you mentioned,' he said. 'What is it?'

'I'm to work for Leonard Blunt,' Nina said, with perfect truth. 'You know who I mean? He's the chairman of Blunt's – the grocery chain.' Mrs Blunt had explained this when Nina had telephoned to accept the post. Leonard's father had founded the business with a chain of bakeries which had expanded first into tea shops and later into a network of supermarkets which now extended nationwide and whose turnover was vast.

'Good gracious,' said Jeremy, impressed, and added hastily, 'I mean, well done.'

Sebastian, who had come into the room with his mother, now noticed, on the dresser, the pottery cat Nina had bought in Woolworth's.

'Nice pussy,' he said, trying to reach it.

Sarah moved it out of range.

'I haven't seen that before,' she said. 'Where did you get it? It's rather crude, isn't it?'

'It caught my eye,' Nina said. 'Does it remind you of anyone?'

They'd met Caroline, she knew; they had gone to London the day before though they hadn't had time, yet, to describe their encounter. Nina, in any case, did not want to hear about it.

'It's just a cat, isn't it?' Sarah said, frowning. 'A pottery cat in rather poor taste.'

'Yes,' agreed Nina. 'That's all it is, my dear.'

Driving home in the evening after an excellent lunch, a short walk on the common and a large tea, Sarah felt baffled.

31

'She seemed very strange, didn't she?' she asked Jeremy.

'She looked very tired,' Jeremy said.

'She was making jokes,' Sarah said. 'She's never done that. Or not much.'

Jeremy had to agree that wit was not Nina's predominant characteristic.

'Well, she seems to have found a suitable job, at any rate,' Sarah said. 'Though I can't think what she'll really be doing. She's got no business experience at all. Perhaps she's to be some sort of receptionist. She always looks nice, after all. She dresses well, and she knows how things should be done.' She sighed. 'I can't understand Daddy.'

But Jeremy could. Just occasionally – not very often – he wondered what it would be like to be married not to Sarah, who was pretty, capable, even-tempered and affectionate, though, unlike her mother, rather untidy, but instead to come home to a tiger in disguise. It might not be very comfortable, he thought; it would only be a delight during a fit of fever in the blood: but it would be exciting. Perhaps Caroline was a tiger.

A fling would be possible, Jeremy thought, looking ahead: a minor fling, on a trip abroad, maybe, when Sarah could never find out, just to prove one's blood was red, but not this sort of thing, which was very sordid. Oh, no! He took his left hand from the steering-wheel and laid it on Sarah's thigh. She was always willing, as long as Sebastian was safely asleep, and sometimes, still, even eager. He loved her.

With such a name, Nina had expected Netherton St Mary to be a typical English village, with thatched cottages, a duckpond and friendly inhabitants.

She had lived all her life in suburban Surrey, where her father had been a doctor in general practice. He had volunteered for the RAMC during the war but was rejected on health grounds; as a civilian doctor he worked, in those years, for very long hours and dealt with bomb casualties as well as day-to-day ailments. Her mother was involved with the Red Cross and ran First Aid courses. An elderly maid looked after the house, and as Nina grew older she learned, automatically, to cook and to clean as she helped Gertrude. Her older brother was sent to boarding school, but Nina, after some years at a kindergarten, went to a private day school where she shone at nothing but was content. Her mother continued, after the war, with her voluntary work, which she had enjoyed, and Nina, who was fifteen when Gertrude retired, took over many of the responsibilities of running the household. Her happiest hour of the day was when her father came home to the evening meal she had prepared. She enjoyed protecting him from importunate patients and hated it when he had to go out to calls at night. He died suddenly, of a heart attack, when she was seventeen.

Nina and her mother settled down uneasily

together. Her brother was now at medical school and seldom came home. Nina left school and began a secretarial course. When she met Martin at a party, and he singled her out, she found him different from the boys she had known all her life – her brother's friends. He was older, more self-assured. Martin was drawn by her freshness and lack of sophistication.

After their marriage, her mother moved into a flat in Eastbourne where she lived in contentment for fifteen years. Then, to the amazement of her son and daughter and of her friends, she married a widower whom she had met when she went on holiday to the Algarve, where he had a villa. They lived there still, in perfect harmony.

Nina had written to tell her mother that she and Martin had parted, and her mother had replied kindly, hoping that the rift was only a temporary one and inviting her to stay. Time and distance might be helpful, she suggested. Nina replied calmly, saying that there was no hope of a reconciliation and perhaps she might come for a visit later on. She and Martin had been out there once, for a week, and her mother and her husband had come over for Sarah's wedding, but not since. Her husband was now rather frail, and the journey was very tiring for him.

Driving to Netherton St Mary on a cold day at the end of October, Nina reflected on her mother's reckless act in marrying, in her sixties, a man she scarcely knew. Hearing about it, Nina's friends all told worrying tales of other such matches hastily contracted between lonely survivors with nothing but their bereaved states in common, and which had not turned out well. But this one had; her mother was happy.

She must have been lonely in those Eastbourne years, Nina thought, but she had never complained and she had worked tirelessly for various good causes in the manner Sarah now thought appropriate for Nina herself. How much courage had it required to make that fresh start, Nina wondered now: as much as she needed herself at this moment?

She had had a second meeting with Mrs Blunt, in London, in the Blunts' Knightsbridge flat. Here, Nina was told about her duties, which included looking after a well-behaved, docile black Labrador dog. There was no cat. Mrs Blunt said her son, as a child, had an asthma-provoking allergy to cats so they had never kept one. The dog was present during the interview. He wagged his tail and gazed benignly at Nina.

'He'll be company for you,' said Mrs Blunt. 'I must warn you that the house is rather isolated.'

Mrs Blunt had been surprised to find Nina, at this encounter, no longer dowdy; but the impression she had of her reliability was unchanged.

Nina's neighbour and friend, Felicity Wainwright, listened to an account of the interview when Nina returned and said that it sounded fantastic. It would do Nina good to have a touch of high life.

'Bully for the Blunts,' she said. 'I expect he rose

35

from behind the counter cutting up cheese to his present eminence.'

'It must have been the bakery counter, not cheese, since it began with buns,' said Nina.

'Did you meet him?'

'No.'

'Oh well, she seems nice. That's the main thing,' said Felicity.

Felicity had been wrathful on Nina's behalf when she heard about Martin's defection. She had undertaken to tell the rest of their circle, couples living in similarly secluded, expensive houses in the area, the bare facts. She'd made her husband check the credentials of Mr Drew, Nina's solicitor, and he had confirmed that the yellow pages had led her to a dependable representative of an impeccable firm.

Felicity offered practical help. Nina's summer clothes and her personal possessions were stored in her attic, although by the time Nina left for Netherton St Mary no final arrangements had been made about the house or its contents. Martin, through his solicitor, had indicated that the sale was going ahead, but, as contracts had not yet been exchanged, Nina expected to return, however briefly, after her job ended.

Mrs Blunt proposed that Nina should receive a cheque at the start of her time at the Hall.

'To cover expenses,' she said. 'Then, at the end, we'll give you a present – quite a substantial one,' and she named a figure. 'In that way you won't be obliged to declare a wage, which might prejudice your alimony.'

She was to draw on the contents of the Blunts' three deep freezes, where bread and other food supplies were stored along with fruit and vegetables from the garden, and was to charge anything else to the Blunts' accounts with local shops. All bills were to be sent to Mr Blunt's secretary who would telephone once a week to make sure that there were no problems. If any arose, Nina was to consult the secretary, or Mrs Jowett who lived at the Manor House. She and Mrs Blunt had been at school together, Nina was told.

Surveying her new surroundings on that cold, grey day, Nina thought it was rather like moving into a Hollywood film. The house, however, was neither as large nor as old as she had expected. It was a late Victorian gothic building, solidly built and expensively modernized so that it lacked no aid to comfort and convenience. The sense of unreality which Nina had felt ever since the course of her life had so suddenly altered grew stronger as she walked round with Mrs Blunt. She had found the way without difficulty, following instructions sent by Mr Blunt's secretary to take the slip road from the motorway and go through Murford. Nina was not a confident driver; she had passed her test years before, it was true, but she never drove on long journeys or on motorways; Martin did that. Hers were the school and shopping trips along local, familiar roads. She had felt quite a sense of achievement, entering the village at last without taking any wrong turning.

'We'll leave you lists and things,' Mrs Blunt had

said, arranging that Nina should arrive a few hours before the Blunts themselves departed for London, where they would spend the night before catching their plane. 'And Dan Fenton will be up to do the garden. He's got real green fingers. I found him when our old boy retired. His own garden's a dream, but doesn't give him enough scope so he loves ours. It's saved him, I think, poor man. His life has been tragic.'

'Oh?' Nina thought interest was expected.

'His only daughter was killed – shot in a bank raid not long before he and his wife came to this village. His wife never got over it and she died soon after they moved.'

'Oh dear,' said Nina. 'How very sad.'

Her friend Felicity had looked the Blunts up in *Who's Who*. Leonard, she had told Nina, was sixty-eight, and Charles, the only son, had been born in 1942.

'Mrs Blunt must be about sixty-eight too,' Felicity said, but Nina disagreed. She looked much less: nearer fifty, she said.

'Well, she must be older than that, to have a son of that age,' Felicity pointed out. 'We're not much older than him.'

'I feel antique,' Nina had sighed.

'Poor old thing. You'll buck up,' Felicity said. 'Rot Martin.'

'We never quarrelled,' said Nina. 'Odd, isn't it? All that was going on, and I never knew.'

'A quarrel can clear the air,' Felicity said.

But the hardest thing for Nina to bear was the

knowledge that for years she had trusted in something that didn't exist – had, possibly, never been there at all.

And now she was at The Hall, Netherton St Mary, its custodian for the next two months, alone in the house while the rain still fell outside, the keys in her care. The Blunts had been driven away in a large limousine.

Mrs Blunt had shown Nina all over the house while her husband, a short, cheerful man with sparse sandy hair, made some final telephone calls. He explained the complex locking system to her, making sure she understood. The various lists were handed over, and Rory, the dog, was patted and told to look after Nina. He looked very melancholy when the Blunts had gone.

There were fourteen bedrooms in the house. Nina went round once more and counted them. Some were in the attic, including the flat where the Spanish couple had lived. Nina was glad she had not been instructed to sleep up there, under the eaves. She had been allotted the yellow spare room, one of the nicest, with its own bathroom and a view across the fields.

'You can try out every room,' Felicity had said. 'Who's to know, when they've gone? I expect you'll meet everyone in the village.'

Like Nina, she had never lived in a rural village, and her impressions of life in one had been gleaned mainly from the novels of Agatha Christie. She thought Nina would have quite a social time.

Driving through Netherton St Mary, on that first day, Nina had felt doubtful of this. The place was larger than she anticipated. Several streets radiated from the main Murford road, and though there were some old buildings, she saw modern houses too. Her instructions were to bear right by the Black Swan, go past the Baptist Chapel and turn right again, then continue for half a mile until she came to the decontrolled sign. Now she would find herself driving along beside a high stone wall which marked the Hall grounds.

Tall iron gates were set between high stone pillars on which crouched carved lions. Nina had driven slowly up the well-kept drive which ended in a gravel circle around a rosebed in front of the house.

Mrs Blunt had said it was isolated, she reminded herself. That was why she was needed; otherwise, they would have locked the place up, she thought, and put the dog into kennels. But now she felt as lonely as if she were marooned in a desert. There was no other dwelling for at least three-quarters of a mile.

Nina put a great many lights on all over the house and went into her room to unpack. She hung her clothes in the fitted cupboard and put photographs of the girls and of Sebastian on the walnut chest. She unwrapped the pottery cat from several layers of tissue paper and looked at it consideringly. Then she put it in the bathroom, on the window-sill. Leaving the landing light on, she went downstairs and into the study, which Mrs

Blunt thought she might find cosier to sit in than the drawing-room. In any case, the television set was kept there.

Rory, the dog, lay uneasily beside her as she tried to watch television. He kept lifting his head and gazing mournfully round, seeking his master and mistress, Nina supposed, but she could not help wondering if he was hearing unusual sounds and several times she got up to check all the doors and windows. The wind had risen and the earlier soft rain became heavy, lashing the latticed panes audibly in spite of the double-glazing.

For the first time in her life, Nina was alone in unfamiliar surroundings. She had lived in only three homes: her childhood one, the small house she and Martin had bought when they were first married, and Silverlea. She had not expected to feel so strange. Was it the size of the house, with its lofty rooms, that made her uneasy? Was it the responsibility of being in charge of so many valuable pieces of antique furniture and a collection of Meissen arranged in a Chippendale cabinet in the drawing-room? How long would it take her to settle down?

She turned up the television and tried not to think of the weeks ahead. The news on ITN had just ended when the telephone rang.

It would be Jenny or Sarah, wanting to know how she was getting on. Both had said they would ring her often, and both had promised not to tell their father where she was. Nina hurried to answer.

When she lifted the receiver and gave the number of the Hall, no one spoke. All she heard was a shuddering sigh.

5

Nina slept badly that night, her first at the Hall. She had said, 'Hullo? Hullo?' into the telephone several times, and stated her own number, all the while aware of a listening presence at the other end of the line although the sigh was not repeated.

'Who do you want to speak to?' she asked, deciding not to say that the Blunts were away. At last, when there was still no answer, she hung up.

A few minutes later the telephone had rung again, and once more no one spoke. There was no sigh this time, but Nina hung up instantly.

There had been no obscene remarks. Anyone's breathing could be audible on a telephone. It was a mistake, a wrong number, Nina told herself as she let Rory out for a final run. She was glad he was with her in the house, sleeping in his basket in the lobby beyond the kitchen.

Didn't burglars sometimes telephone to discover if a house was occupied before robbing it? Well, if her caller was a burglar, he'd know the Hall was not empty. But would a burglar dial the number twice? And if it was a straightforward wrong number, wouldn't the caller apologize?

She lay in bed, trying to sleep but starting awake at every sound, real or imagined. Her bedside clock seemed to tick very loudly. The heating system made a few ticking sounds. Outside, the wind still blew and the rain beat down.

Nina's single bed was soft and comfortable. She drew the primrose-coloured blankets and printed sheet around her shoulders. She was not accustomed, yet, to sleeping alone, although Martin had often spent nights away or come home late. Lying there, tense, she imagined him now, beside Caroline, and felt bitter hatred for them both. Would she ever stop feeling like this?

At last she turned on the light and looked at the time. Though she felt as if she had lain there for hours, it was only half-past twelve. Nina turned off the light and lay down again, trying to calm her racing brain, but at half-past one she gave up and went to the bathroom. Reflected in the huge mirror that filled one wall, she saw herself, in her pale green nightdress, moving about, getting a drink, swallowing two of the sleeping pills the doctor had reluctantly given her when she told him that she could not sleep. The pottery cat on the window-sill seemed to watch her movements, smirking at her.

Nina got back into bed. Her mind was haunted by images of Martin and Miss Kitty-Cat, intimately linked. How about his snores? What did

Caroline think about them, Nina wondered, with some malice.

She tried to turn her mind away from its obsession with her own distress and think about the village, Netherton St Mary, into which she had come, trying to recall what she had noticed as she drove through that afternoon. There was the pub, she remembered, and a shop or two; the long stretch before the decontrolled sign and the gateway to the Hall. She'd explore it all tomorrow.

At last the pills worked, and in the morning, when she woke, it was nearly half-past eight. Nina was still drowsy from the drug. The room was unfamiliar and her heart began to pound as she struggled to remember where she was.

The dog, she thought, remembering. He'd be bursting, poor thing. She swung her legs out of bed, pulled on her dressing gown and slid her feet into her slippers, then drew the curtains back. The rain had stopped, and a thin, wintry sunlight filtered downwards between clouds.

Rory rose to greet her as she came into the back lobby. He stretched and wagged his tail, not seeming desperate at all. His muzzle was grey; he wasn't a wild young dog, eager to be off hunting or courting, she thought gratefully. Though she had never liked dogs much, for they shed hairs and had messy wet feet and often sniffed at you quite rudely, she was glad to see him. They'd settle down together, she decided, patting him before opening the back door to let him out into the garden.

The air smelled damp. A bottle of milk stood on the step, and later, by the front door, she found a heap of letters on the mat. That seemed civilized enough, considering the distance from the village, Nina thought. At Silverlea the milk never arrived before noon, and the post not until ten o'clock. Her spirits rose. Would a paper also come?

She hadn't asked about them, and they weren't mentioned on Mrs Blunt's list. No doubt they took *The Times*. Martin always read it on the train. Nina thought it dull. She rather liked the gossip in the *Mail*.

She was sitting at the kitchen table eating bran flakes, the only cereal she could find, when the telephone rang. Immediately her fears of the night returned, but this time the caller was Sarah. Nina's heart warmed with gratitude as she gave a falsely reassuring report. In the background, as they talked, Nina could hear shrieks from Sebastian, due at playgroup later that morning. Sarah said she couldn't linger; she had to go to the ante-natal clinic after dropping Sebastian.

Nina felt guilty as she replaced the receiver. Poor Sarah had a lot to do; she might, in her pregnancy, feel tired and ill and in need of help, yet here was her own mother over seventy miles away from her, employed by a stranger.

But I had no help when the girls were small, Nina thought defensively. She'd washed and ironed and cooked and sewed, practising thrift, grateful as time went on for various aids Sarah had had from the beginning, such as an efficient washing machine and an electric mixer. But she'd been content. She'd wanted nothing more.

Yes, and look where it's got you, she told herself, returning to her cereal. She'd thought herself secure, but there was no safety anywhere. A wave of terror filled her. She might be only halfway through her life; certainly, in the ordinary run of things, there were many years ahead of her. What further blows lay waiting?

As if he sensed her sudden panic, Rory padded towards her, paws clattering on the tiled floor. He laid his head on her lap and stared at her mournfully.

'All right, boy,' she said. 'We'll go for a walk as soon as I've tidied up.'

Though there was no witness, she felt she must keep the house so spick that if Mrs Blunt suddenly walked in unannounced there could be no criticism of her custodianship. She'd do specific tasks each day, make a routine.

Scouring the sink after she had washed the breakfast dishes, Nina thought of the hours she had willingly spent in the same way at Silverlea. She'd seen Martin off each morning with a smile and a wave from the door; when he returned in the evening, dinner was already organized and the girls, when small, were almost ready for bed. Later, they were settled with their homework, pleased to see him but not expecting much communication. There had been anxieties – childish ailments, Jenny's adenoids and Sarah's appendicitis, and, at first, money had been short, but they had supported one another, or so Nina had thought. Martin had shown interest in the girls' guinea-pigs and later paid for riding lessons; then there had been worries about exams. They'd been, she'd believed, united as a family. At what point had the betrayal begun? Years ago, when Martin had started coming home late from the office, pleading extra work?

She shook herself. There was no point in going over it all again. If Miss Kitty-Cat had not got pregnant Nina might be still unaware of her existence. Perhaps Caroline had planned the baby to force Martin to act. Nina had asked him that, savagely, during their dreadful scene, but he'd ignored the question.

She went upstairs to make her bed. The room was so pretty. Just think where you might be, she told herself. You're lucky, living here in luxury. You might have had to live in digs and be a cleaning woman, with your lack of skills. Martin could have cut off all support. Men often did, Mr Drew had said, frowning over the fact that she had given Martin written consent to sell the house. Meanwhile, he was making her a small allowance.

Mr Drew warned that because Nina had made no contribution towards the purchase of the house, nor had a job after her marriage and thus no salary to put towards the mortgage, she might, in the end, get much less than she was expecting.

Nina's mind went on squirrelling round unhappily while she got ready to take Rory out. She had put her coat on and was tying a scarf round her head when a bell pealed piercingly through the house.

It was not the telephone. The front door? Nina went there and opened it, but no one stood on the step. The bell rang again, and Rory gave a loud bark from the rear of the house. Nina hurriedly locked the front door again and secured the various bolts, then went to the lobby by the kitchen and opened the back door.

A woman in an olive-green padded anorak stood on the step. She had tousled grey hair and a weatherbeaten face with the threads of broken veins giving her a florid look. There were women who looked like that in Surrey; you saw them about with dachshunds or corgis on leads.

'Mrs Crowther?' the woman said, and stepped into the house. Nina saw she wore green wellington boots. The visitor looked at Nina's beige suede coat and her printed headscarf. 'Going out?' she asked. 'I'm just in time, then. My name's Heather Jowett. I came to collect you for a good walk. I'll show you some of the best ways to go with Rory. Get your boots on – it will be muddy after the rain. I'll wait here – I don't want to dirty your floor on your first day here.'

This was the woman whom Mrs Blunt had mentioned, the one with whom she had been at school, Nina remembered. But surely they weren't contemporaries? Mrs Jowett looked at least fifteen years older than Mrs Blunt. She glanced down at her own legs. She was already wearing boots, but they were fashionable black leather ones, zipped and with small heels. She hadn't worn wellington boots for years.

'Oh – er,' she said doubtfully, as Rory made snuffling sounds and licked Mrs Jowett's hand in a welcoming manner, clearly her friend. Perhaps she had been head girl when Mrs Blunt was the lowliest junior.

'I'll show you a splendid field walk,' Heather said, and smiled. Her face changed, its harsh lines dissolving. She had vivid blue eyes.

'I won't be a minute,' said Nina, and hurried off to the cloakroom where she had seen a row of boots neatly arranged. The smallest pair was still too large for her, but she stuffed the toes with Andrex from the roll in the lavatory and soon rejoined Mrs Jowett, who had moved outside and was surveying the garden with Rory beside her, leaving the back door open.

Nina carefully checked the various processes as she locked the back door and put the keys in her pocket. If she neglected any part of the ritual, a bogus meter reader might call and force an entry.

'I'm glad Priscilla took my advice,' said Heather as they strode off down the drive at a brisk pace. Nina's heels rubbed up and down in the too-large wellingtons as she stepped out.

'Oh?' she said, wondering if she should put Rory on the lead. He seemed to be walking meekly enough beside them at the moment, but if she were alone she would not have left him free.

'I said she should find someone to live in the house when Jose and Maria left,' said Heather. 'It's better than leaving an isolated place like this unoccupied, and better for Rory than kennels. I couldn't have him you see, much as I'd have liked to.' Why not, wondered Nina silently. 'After all, anyone could break in and no one would notice,' Heather went on. 'Except possibly Dan, that's the gardener. You know about him, don't you?'

The man whose daughter had been shot, Nina remembered. She said that Mrs Blunt had mentioned him, and commented on the size of the village.

'It's grown a lot lately,' said Heather. 'In the building boom a few years ago people sold spare land – fields and tennis courts and things – to developers, and there are several new estates where young people live. I rather like seeing babies about, but there was a time when one knew everyone in the place. It's not like that now.'

'Where do they all work?' asked Nina. 'Do they go to London?'

'Some do, but there's a big industrial area in Droxton – that's about twenty miles away. It used to be a quiet market town, like Murford.'

They were walking along the lane now, away from the village. Nina plodded on in her boots. Her new friend, who was quite tall, took long strides. Heather soon turned off the lane down a track where, after all the rain, deep puddles filled the ruts made by tractor wheels. Now, Rory ran on ahead.

'He'll get covered in mud,' said Nina.

'It won't hurt him. A big dog needs plenty of

exercise and he doesn't get enough with Priscilla,' said Heather. 'Have you done much house-minding, Nina?'

'Not a lot,' Nina answered.

'It must be rather fun,' said Heather. 'No heating bills to pay – no rates. Everything found.'

'Yes,' Nina cautiously agreed.

'We never go away,' said Heather. 'Not now. We spent a lot of time abroad when we were younger. My husband was in the army, you see.'

'Oh.'

They were walking along the headland of a ploughed field. Damp, heavy clay clung to Nina's feet so that every step involved lifting a weighty clump of earth. Her companion seemed unaware of any difficulty. Country life, thought Nina: she'd liked the idea of a friendly village, she reminded herself, and here, certainly, was a friendly neighbour.

Suddenly Heather stopped, rummaged in her pocket, and bent down by the hedge. To Nina's amazement she had drawn forth some small bulbs and a pocket knife. She carefully cut some holes in the turf near the hedge and planted the bulbs, shabby tweed skirt stretched over her lean hips, legs in thick wool tights set wide apart.

'Snowdrops,' she said, replacing the turf and treading it down. She cut another piece and planted more. 'I must put some scillas in here too.'

When she stood up again, she noticed Nina's astonished expression and explained, 'I always have something to plant in my pocket – bulbs or seeds, sometimes seedlings or a sapling, or a rooted cutting, depending on the season. Man is destroying his environment. This field was once divided into four, but now the hedges have been grubbed out to make it simpler to harvest. Windbreaks have gone. Wild flowers have been lost. I replace them whenever I can.'

Nina's surprise had become approval.

'What a good idea,' she said. 'But isn't it expensive?'

'Money's relative,' said Heather. 'One person's necessity is someone else's luxury. I collect nuts and acorns from the woods, so they cost nothing, and I save seeds from my own garden. Even the bulbs are some I've thinned from clusters of my own. To plant just one fine tree – one that reaches maturity – is worth doing, I consider.'

'I'm sure you're right,' said Nina.

She warmed to her companion as she trudged on, her mud-laden feet growing heavier by the minute. How far were they going? She tried to remember their route as they turned right and left, skirted a copse, clambered over stiles. Several times they stopped for further planting sessions. Nina's tight skirt hampered her when they climbed a gate which was securely locked, but Heather, in her pleated tweed, stepped nimbly over. They walked through a herd of steers who blew and snorted as they passed among them, something Nina would never have dared on her own. Rory's free running was controlled; he never moved far from them, and although he paused to gaze into the face of a steer which bent to inspect him, he soon moved on.

'He's a good dog,' Heather said. 'He's too old, now, to run away, and he's well disciplined. You won't have any trouble with him.' It was she who had undertaken the role of his controller during the walk, issuing the few commands required. Nina would never have allowed him all this freedom.

They did not talk much, but the silence was not uncomfortable. Now and then Heather indicated spots where trees – sometimes diseased elms – had been felled, or varieties of wildlife had once flourished. They paused on a humpbacked bridge over a fast-flowing stream which, said Heather, joined the river which ran through Murford further on; sometimes these low-lying fields were flooded after rain.

'It's like a lake,' she said. 'We often skated here, in icy spells.'

Who were 'we'? She'd mentioned a husband. She must have children too, Nina decided.

'The Manor's over there,' said Heather at last, and pointed across ploughland to a hollow where a large brick house with a grey roof was visible, among trees. She glanced at her watch. 'I'll go straight on home now – I must get back. You'll be able to find your way to the Hall again, won't you, Nina? Just follow this hedge the way we've come, go over the stiles and past the wood, and you'll be back within sight of the path where we started.'

Nina was far from sure she could manage this,

and it seemed as if she must still walk several miles, but it wouldn't do to protest.

'I'm sure I'll find the way,' she said. 'Thank you.'

'Goodbye,' said Heather, and again the expression of great sweetness came over her face as she smiled. 'We'll walk again,' she said.

Nina watched her stride away, hands thrust into her jacket pockets. What a weird woman, but she was nice. She fitted into Nina's expectations about the inhabitants of Netherton St Mary by being eccentric with her flower-planting.

Rory displayed a wish to follow Heather. Nina called him sternly, and was relieved when he turned back towards her and trotted on beside her. She began to rehearse in her head how she would write to the girls about Mrs Jowett – whom perhaps she must think of, even address, as Heather, since the older woman had called her by her first name. 'A kind woman who has lived here in the Manor House for many years,' she would tell Sarah. Jeremy would like the touch about the Manor. 'A funny old thing in green wellies who's into nature,' she would say to Jenny, 'and not at all stuck-up.' She'd hurried off rather suddenly, after she'd looked at her watch, rather as if she'd remembered leaving the iron on, or a saucepan on the stove.

Nina would have to get some wellingtons of her own. These were most uncomfortable and she was sure they would have rubbed holes in her tights.

At last she and Rory reached the Hall again, and Nina wiped her boots on the grass by the side of the drive in an attempt to rid them of some of their mud. On she trudged, and when she reached the house she saw a bicycle parked by the back door and a distant figure on the lawn, sweeping leaves. Rory left her, running towards the man who, with a besom brush like a witch's broom, had swept drifts of beech leaves into neat piles.

This must be Dan Fenton.

Nina walked slowly over the grass to meet him. She wondered how often he came. He was a big man, dressed in a stone-coloured anorak, with dark corduroy trousers tucked into ordinary black wellingtons. His feet were large. He paused in his sweeping to talk to the dog, bending to pat him. He did not realize, at first, that Nina was there, seeming totally absorbed in talking to Rory and fondling his ears, but then he sensed her presence and, straightening up, touched his cap.

'Good morning,' Nina said, shying from using his first name straight away, yet feeling 'Mr Fenton' would be too formal.

'Ah – good morning, Mrs Crowther,' Dan said.

'Rory and I have been for a walk,' said Nina. 'He's got rather muddy, so I suppose I'd better rub him down.' She'd only just thought of this, and had a sudden memory of her mother's Jack Russell; he'd had to be bathed in the kitchen sink, a task she had deplored, hating the woolly smell of wet dog.

'Mrs Blunt keeps a towel for him in the boiler room,' said Dan. 'I take him out for her sometimes, when she's busy.'

'Oh – do you? Thank you,' Nina said. 'We went over the fields. Mrs Jowett kindly called for me.'

'Oh yes – she likes a good walk,' Dan said. 'That's when she's not busy in the garden. She gets out of the house, one way and another, when the colonel's painting.'

'Painting?'

'He's an artist. Has a room there fixed up as a studio,' said Dan. 'Mrs Jowett takes the paintings off and sells them.' He smiled faintly. 'A neighbour of mine used to help in the house, but not any more.'

Nina longed to know why not, but knew she must not encourage gossip.

'Yes – well, I'd better see to Rory,' she said, repressively. 'Come along, boy.'

The dog looked enquiringly at Dan, who nodded to him and told him to go along.

'He's an obedient dog,' said Nina.

'Yes. Mrs Blunt isn't one to stand nonsense,' said Dan, returning to his sweeping.

Nina could believe it, not from dog, man or woman.

In the boiler room she found a large, brightly patterned towel with which she dried Rory's wet paws and coat. She cleaned Mrs Blunt's boots before putting them away, and sure enough there were holes in the heels of her tights. She went upstairs and changed them. By now she was longing for a cup of coffee, and she put the kettle on when she came downstairs.

What about Dan? He'd expect one, wouldn't

he? The jobbing gardener they'd had at Silverlea had always been given coffee and a slice of cake, mid-morning. He'd expected to come into the kitchen for this refreshment, and Nina had quite enjoyed chatting to him as she worked there. Did the same apply in a mansion?

Cautiously, Nina decided to take a mug of coffee out to Dan in the garden today. She could be more friendly later, when she had settled in; after all, it wasn't her house.

Dan was grateful. He took his cap off and scratched his head when he had taken the mug from her.

'I put sugar in,' said Nina. Workmen, in her experience, always took two, if not three spoonfuls.

'Thank you,' said Dan.

He was very bald, she saw, though there was strong grey hair that curled above his ears, and he had thick, bushy eyebrows.

'I'll bring the mug in before I go,' he said.

'Oh – yes,' said Nina, and turned to walk back to the house. There couldn't be a lot to do in the garden at this time of year, she thought. At Silverlea, they'd had no help in the winter. The jobbing gardener had put in bedding plants in spring, and mowed. Nina had snipped dead heads from roses and cut blooms for the house. Martin, when he was young, had seemed to enjoy gardening but he'd done less and less latterly. Nina had never done much outside although she liked arranging flowers and had even been to classes to learn how to do it more skilfully. She'd been to occasional cookery demonstrations, too, but she had never wanted to learn German, as Felicity had done, or take any sort of job, even a voluntary one, apart from rare fund-raising ventures for charities. She'd always been busy. After all, Jenny had been at home until last year.

How swiftly things could change! Only weeks ago she had been at Silverlea, taking the continuing pattern of her life for granted. Where would she be a year from now?

Again the large, strange house felt alien. She wished that, after all, she had invited Dan to have his coffee in the kitchen.

6

Death sometimes comes too suddenly for any goodbye. So it had been on a day, seven years ago now, when a young bank clerk had gone to work as usual. A few hours later she was dead, shot as she waited to be admitted past the inner security door on her return from lunch. Two masked robbers had held up the small branch and had got away with money being drawn for wages by men from a local firm, one of whom had been wounded. The girl had tried to run for it, to raise the alarm outside. The police caught the villains within days; they were still in prison but, with remission of their sentences, would not serve much longer. Dan Fenton thought that this was not punishment enough for murder.

Ellen, his wife, had never recovered from her daughter's violent death. Afterwards, she had become sad and silent and had sought refuge in religion, going to chapel twice on Sundays and praying a great deal in between, but none of it had brought her comfort. Dan had taken early retirement, hoping that would help, for they had long planned to move to the country and keep bees, but

Ellen had died soon after they came to Netherton St Mary, simply fading away after a minor illness.

'She turned her face to the wall,' the doctor said. 'She had no stamina left.'

So now Dan lived alone in the pebble-dashed villa in Chestnut Crescent. It was one of a group that were built in a period of expansion between the wars, soundly constructed and with a large garden. Neither Dan nor Ellen had had the heart, when they bought it, to pursue the search for something more picturesque. Dan had done the house up inside, following, after Ellen's death, the scheme that she had limply approved, applying white vinyl paint over the purples and oranges of the previous, rather younger, owners. The couple who had moved next door a year ago, found him reserved. They felt sorry for him, and often the young wife, when she had been baking, would bring him some scones warm from the oven, or a slice of moist fruit cake.

He didn't, in the end, go in for bees. The neighbours might not have liked them, and now there seemed no point. Instead, he set up a tank for tropical fish and tried to get absorbed with them; they were company of a sort, and undemanding, not moping when he went out for the day, as he regularly did.

He had tamed the neglected garden, and grew vegetables which won prizes at the Netherton St Mary horticultural show. His neighbours, to whom he gave lettuces, tomatoes, beans and cauliflowers in return for their cakes, were proud of his success. Priscilla Blunt, presenting the awards, had noted how annually he won most of them, and made enquiries. Thus it was that she had arrived on his doorstep one day to ask if he would be interested in taking on the garden at the Hall.

Now Dan spent a great deal of his time there, keeping only the vaguest record of the hours he worked, for to him, they were the best ones of the day. His life revolved around the two gardens, his tank of fish, and his weekly trips to London.

Dan had made one of his journeys to London a few days before Nina arrived at the Hall. This was an extra visit, a pilgrimage to his daughter's grave on the anniversary of her death. To reach the vast cemetery where she was buried involved two changes on the underground and he had to wait some time for the second train. As, at last, he walked the last quarter of a mile up the hill, he stopped at a florist's. His choice of flowers for her had become part of the ritual: virginal white chrysanthemums now, spring flowers on her April birthday. If she had not been killed, by this time she might have been married, with children. Dan sighed, thinking this, as he stepped past headstones in the graveyard.

It was very quiet on this rainy day. He saw no other visitors, although a burial was in progress near the boundary wall. Dan stood by the simple tombstone which had weathered from its first early purity. His were the only flowers that rested there. Who else remembered her, he wondered sadly.

He stayed there some time, deliberately trying to call back her memory, finding it difficult, now, to picture her face. He remembered various birthdays: her first little bicycle: the day she cut off her long, fair plaits against her mother's wishes.

At last he felt that it was time to go. The rain still fell, spattering the path. His flowers would soon be faded, Dan knew, walking slowly back to the gate and into the road. He went on down the hill to the tube station.

Sometimes, on his days in London, he went to Euston or St Pancras; sometimes to King's Cross; sometimes Liverpool Street. Though the stations varied, there was almost always someone to be found.

He always picked the youngest girl he saw.

Today, in the buffet at Euston, Dan ate a ham sandwich and drank a cup of railway tea. There were several girls in the busy place; he noticed two at one table; at another table, a girl was on her own. She had shoulder-length dark hair, and smooth, plump cheeks. While she ate a pie, she kept her gaze fixed on her plate.

Dan watched her covertly. Soon, she rose, picked up a small case, and went off through the glass doors on to the station concourse.

Dan followed.

Twenty miles from Netherton St Mary, Police Constable Peter Downes was driving along on patrol, a happy man. He was enjoying his freedom, alone in the car after completing his probationary period in the force, and other spells of patrol duty with a more experienced officer.

His task today was to cover a large area of the division watching for crime and criminals, noting any suspicious activity, guarding the Queen's Peace and ensuring the preservation of law and order. In his career thus far, he had met a variety of incidents – a good deal of drunk and disorderly conduct, domestic disputes, vandalizing juveniles. He had been present at several road accidents, controlling the traffic at the scene, comforting the injured, measuring skid marks and reporting the facts. A patient civilian clerk at Murford Police Station had taught him how to write his reports clearly. Now he was fully trained to protect the populace. His awesome appearance, pink-cheeked and with a wispy fair moustache adorning his youthful upper lip, would be enough, it was hoped, to deter potential villains from their felonious intent who might see him passing.

It was Saturday morning, and Downes kept his eyes open for wandering schoolchildren with time on their hands who might be tempted to broach open windows and unlock doors in their quest for diversion. Downes knew that seventy-seven per cent of all crime was preventable, being the result of opportunist activity.

He drove over Droxton common and past a warehouse, its gates secure. A car ahead of him dropped its speed as the driver noticed him in the rear-view mirror and Downes smiled to himself at this proof of the effect of his presence.

His was the nearest car when headquarters received a 999 call from two ten year-old boys who had been to the spinney on the bypass looking for conkers. He was the officer sent to investigate what they had found, half-buried among leaves.

The boys were waiting for him by the telephone box from which they had made their call. One was white-faced and shaky; the other was already on the mend and would soon be enjoying his brief notoriety, but it was his friend who had actually discovered the body. Downes sent them off to wait at a distance while he approached the spot they had indicated, and verified for himself that it was, indeed, the remains of a human leg and foot which protruded from the leaves.

He felt a sour taste in his mouth as he noted the time and called in to report, stepping back from the spot where the body lay, anxious to disturb nothing that might be remotely a piece of evidence. He was too old, he reminded himself, to throw up at the sight of a corpse. He took the boys back to his car where all three waited until reinforcements arrived.

Nina had gone up the village with Rory that Saturday morning. She'd half expected Heather Jowett to come round again and had loitered a little before setting off, but the old woman did not appear.

Old woman: if she was the same age as Mrs Blunt, she wasn't really old, Nina reminded herself, and before she tied a scarf over her own fair hair she searched for grey strands and fresh wrinkles on her face. She had lost weight lately, and there were new lines on her forehead. Below her eyes were pouchy bags that had not been there three months ago.

Today, she wore her own neat boots for she did not intend to walk over fields. She buttoned up her suede coat and set forth with Rory on his lead, carrying the letters she had written to both the girls the night before, and the mail that had arrived that morning for the Blunts, redirected, as she had been instructed, to the London office for forwarding. Her notes to the girls were short. In addition to describing her walk with Heather, she had told Sarah how well equipped the Hall was and mentioned the size of the grounds. Jenny, she thought, would be more interested in the description of the study with the rows of neatly shelved books – the complete works of Dickens, among others, so that Nina would have no excuse not to repair notable gaps in her reading. She kept the tone of her letters light and she did not refer to the telephone calls.

There had been another call the evening before, at much the same time as the first one. Again, no one was there when she replied. She'd spoken quite sharply.

'What do you want?' she'd snapped, and when no one answered had slammed down the receiver, trembling with a mixture of fear and anger. Now, walking up the road in daylight, with the dog, her idea that the caller was a burglar wanting to know if the house was occupied seemed silly. A child, perhaps, had picked up the telephone and dialled at random. But no child would do that at twenty minutes to eleven at night, surely? And no child would dial, by chance, the same number twice.

She had lain awake in bed wondering what to do. Perhaps she should tell the police. After all, she was responsible for the house and they might have ways of tracing such calls. She had got out of bed and gone round checking all the doors and windows and had left several lights burning to deter thieves. Once again, she needed a pill before she could sleep.

She might ask Heather's advice about what she should do, Nina thought: if she met her, that was: she didn't think she could call on her so soon, if at all, unless there was a real emergency; she really should wait to be invited. Nina passed a lane leading off the main road and decided that it must be the way to the Manor. Cars passed as she walked along, and a bus stopped further down the road. The activity was reassuring. She met, separately, two old men with dogs on leads – one had a spaniel, one a shaggy black mongrel. The men kept their gaze on the path before them, and Rory ignored the dogs. Nina went past a block of former almshouses, now privately owned, built of brick with slate roofs, then the Baptist Chapel which she had noticed when she arrived, a rough-cast building with texts printed on posters pinned in a frame on each side of the open iron gates: *Mark ye the Way*, said one, and *God Sees You*, warned the other. The next houses were small detached ones of individual design, about fifty years old and not, to Nina's eye, attractive. She was looking for thatched roofs, leaded windows, beams, but she saw little that was picturesque on her way to the post office, which was part of a terraced block in the main street. She needed stamps for her letters and had to wait while earlier customers were served with sweets and toys, which the shop also sold. She had missed the outgoing mail, she saw, when at last she was able to put her letters in the box that was set into the post office wall. On Saturdays the only collection was at ten-fifteen.

There had been no near letter-box at Silverlea, but the postman would always take ready-stamped letters when he delivered, if you left them for him. Nina, then, had written few letters apart from those to her mother. The post had not seemed important and most of what came was for Martin, often bills or circulars. The thought that her letters to the girls would not start on their way until Monday was frustrating. She could telephone Sarah, but it wouldn't be easy to get in touch direct with Jenny.

Don't be silly, she said to herself. You don't need to speak to the girls.

She crossed the road to look at the few shops on the other side. There was a grocer, a butcher and a greengrocer. They were all busy. Further on was a garage with petrol pumps and a workshop. That was lucky, thought Nina. Her Metro was fairly new and was in good order, but she was glad to know that there would be help at hand if it went wrong. Martin had been quite good at simple mechanics and had usually been able to cure the non-starting of the car she had had before. She didn't mean to use the Metro much; she'd walk a lot with Rory.

She walked on past a pub, the Black Swan, where the road forked, the main road going on to Murford through which she had come after leaving the motorway when she arrived. Now she took the other spur, a lesser road which led past, at last, some pretty cottages with tiled roofs and a few larger houses, old ones, set back behind hedges or low walls. Further on was a telephone box on the corner of a curving road, Chestnut Crescent, which seemed to be a collection of plain, squarish pebble-dashed semi-detached houses. Nina walked past the turning and came to a field in which several ponies were grazing. A drive led to a farmhouse some fifty yards from the road. Beyond the farm, at what must be the end of the village, stood the church, an old stone building with a Saxon tower. Nina hesitated, but now Rory drew her on, tugging gently at his lead. He led her towards the wooden gate, green with lichen.

Nina opened it and went up the path to the door of the church.

It was locked.

How odd, she thought. Weren't churches meant to be always open as places of sanctuary? She turned away and wandered into the churchyard. There were old tombstones set in the grass, the names often worn and hard to decipher. Flowers were laid on some graves, and in a corner there was a new one, the ground humped and covered with a heap of withering wreaths. Worms, thought Nina, and shuddered. She glanced at the names on some of the tombstones and saw that families were buried together in groups. She noticed several Jowetts, and stopped at one. Rory slumped down on the ground beside her as she read the inscription: *Robin Jowett 1942–1963 R.I.P.*

Could that be Heather Jowett's son? Nina felt shocked. What had caused his early death? She turned away, suddenly cold, and left the churchyard with its overhanging evergreens, its yew hedges and its silent memorials, walking briskly back towards the village.

Passing the newsagent's, on impulse she went in and bought a paper.

'You'll be from the Hall, then,' said the newsagent, who was a plump man in a green overall.

Nina was pleased at this recognition, which went with her theory that everyone knew one another in a village.

'Rory and I are old friends,' the man explained, bending to pat the dog. 'He used to come in with Jose. I'm afraid we can't deliver up there. It's too far – the boys don't have time before catching the school bus. There's only the Hall along that way.'

'Well,' said Nina, rallying. 'I have to take Rory out every day. I can fetch my paper then, if you'll keep it for me.' It would give shape to her day to have this task.

It was agreed. The newsagent asked how she was settling in, and Nina said, 'Quite nicely, thank you.' She felt reluctant to leave the warm shop and the friendly newsagent, but she could think of no way of prolonging the conversation. She and Rory left the shop and walked home. The wind was getting up, and leaves from the gutters scurried past them as they walked on. Nina tied her headscarf more tightly and Rory slunk along, tail down, his back to the wind.

She spent most of the evening watching television, even dropping to sleep for half an hour during one dull programme. On the evening news, the local programme reported the discovery of a woman's body in a copse near the Droxton by-pass. The body had not been identified, but it had lain there some time and the police were treating the enquiry as a case of murder.

How dreadful, thought Nina, switching channels. She had seen Droxton on a signpost in the village earlier; Mrs Jowett had said it was twenty miles away.

There was no mystery telephone call that night. She listened for it, expectantly, but there was no ring, and, although the wind grew stronger in the night, blowing a gale by two in the morning, she slept soundly, without a pill.

There seemed to be no good reason for getting up the next morning. There was no one to send off to school, no one hurrying to the office, no breakfast to cook. But there was Rory, always Rory. Nina, who had drowsed off after waking early, forced herself to get up and go downstairs.

The wind almost tore the door from her grasp when she opened it to let Rory out. A cluster of leaves blew in round her feet, and across the lawn she could see twigs and small branches from the trees. She turned on the radio and learned that there had been much damage during the night, with trees blown on to power and telephone lines, and across roads.

Nina already knew the lights were working. She lifted the telephone and heard the dialling tone.

Rory soon returned to the house, scrabbling at the door to be admitted. Nina was getting quite fond of him and she patted him warmly when he came in. She had breakfast in her dressing gown, almost succumbing to the temptation to get back into bed. She'd seldom had breakfast in bed at home; she knew Sarah did, quite often, at her own insistence, not Jeremy's. Sarah had said that her father was the original male chauvinist pig and she had no intention of letting Jeremy go the same way. When Nina defended him, saying her own role had been responsibility for domestic chores as her share of the partnership, Sarah had laughed shortly.

'That lets you off the hook, Mother,' she'd said. 'That way you don't have to try.'

Nina hadn't understood.

Now, she wondered if Martin would help Miss Kitty-Cat, who perhaps was suffering from morning sickness? Nina hoped it was very bad, and would last through the whole nine months. Swilling the water round the basin, she looked at the pottery cat on the bathroom window-sill. It seemed to watch her as she moved, its simper ever wider. Now, at that instant, Martin might be making love to that woman.

Disgust and jealousy nearly overwhelmed Nina then. She felt almost giddy, and picked up the cat in her two hands, holding it above her head, about to dash it down on the bathroom floor. But it wouldn't break on the soft carpet, she thought, laying it down again. How foolish she was being! Anyone watching her would think she was mad. Perhaps she was, a bit, she thought. Her heart thudded uncomfortably as she went back to her room and brushed her hair.

How was she going to manage, here on her own all day, and for nearly two more months? How could she pass the hours?

I must take it a day at a time, she thought, sitting down at the kitchen table, her head in her hands. Today is Sunday. I'll deal with that first – not look ahead. Then, gradually, the weeks will

73

pass. She could go to church this morning. But church, except at Christmas and Easter, had never been part of her life.

If she were back at Silverlea, if nothing had happened, she'd be preparing lunch for Martin, who might have gone to the golf club. Even in bad weather, like today, he often went there for a drink with his cronies.

She'd have to eat something for lunch herself, she supposed. There was sure to be a chop in the freezer.

During the night Dan had heard the wind rising, gusting round the eaves. Ellen had hated the wind; she had feared the banshee wail it made when it blew from the north-east and came howling down Chestnut Crescent. She'd lived long enough to hear it there more than once. Dan remembered that now, lying in his bare room at the front of the house. He no longer used the bedroom at the back, where she had died; it was pervaded too much by memories and he had equipped the other more appropriately for his bachelor existence. It was starkly furnished, austere, but had all that a man required for an ordered life: a narrow bed, a plain wardrobe, and a chest of drawers on which were placed neatly his hairbrush and comb; he took pains with what hair remained to him, and went to the barber regularly.

When he got up, he could see signs of storm

damage even in his own garden; twigs lay on the lawn and a bough had blown down from a plum tree. He wondered about Mrs Crowther up at the Hall, in a big house that was strange to her. No doubt she was used to such places, earning her living by caretaking in them, as he imagined she did. Nevertheless, when he had cleared his own garden of debris, he decided to make sure that she was all right.

It was too windy to go on his bicycle, and he seldom took his small car on such a short trip. He set off on foot, a big, broad man in boots and anorak, a tweed hat on his head and a scarf round his neck. The wind caught at him as he went past the telephone box at the end of the road. A single car passed him, but he met no one walking. He stopped at the newsagent's to get his own paper and to consult the newsagent about taking one up to the Hall. Mrs Crowther had asked for the *Sunday Express* to be kept for her, he was told.

Papers tucked under his arm, he went on up the road. He kept his mind busy with thoughts of the present, not of the past. When he was occupied in the garden – his own, or the challenging one at the Hall – he forgot everything but the job in hand, and he enjoyed using his strength to dig the beds and clip the hedges. He had enough mechanical skill to keep the large mower at the Hall in good order, and he liked cutting logs, laying turves, and the harder tasks, as well as growing plants from seed. He enjoyed climbing a ladder to pick apples and putting them into racks in the stables. He'd nailed fine wire mesh round the apple racks to frustrate the mice who had always made merry in there before he worked at the Hall.

A large branch, blown from a tree by the gate, lay across the drive entrance. Dan dragged it to one side. It would cut up nicely into logs for the study fire. He glanced at the telephone lines and the electric cable that led to the house from a pole outside, although most of the village now received its power from lines under the ground. Everything looked all right.

The closed windows of the house glinted dully as he approached. It was a gloomy sort of place viewed from outside, Dan always thought, though the interior had been done up in such style that it was quite light and airy. He knocked on the back door and heard Rory give a low bark. Soon the door was opened an inch or two, and Nina peered out. Leaves and dust blew past Dan into the lobby.

'Come in,' Nina said, still baulking at calling Dan by any name and surprised to see him on a Sunday.

Dan stepped inside, taking off his tweed hat.

'Good morning,' he said. 'I came to make sure you were all right after the storm in the night. And I picked up your paper on the way.'

'Oh, that was kind of you,' Nina said. She was glad he had come.

'I'll fetch you in some coal and logs,' he told her. 'You'll be needing them for the study fire.'

'Well – yes. I'd been using the electric heater,' said Nina. Perhaps fetching in fuel was part of his work? It didn't appear on Mrs Blunt's list.

'Though really, with the central heating, it seems extravagant to burn something else,' she added.

'That's a big draughty chimney in there,' said Dan. 'You need a bit extra now winter's coming.'

It seemed natural, when he had brought in the fuel, to offer him coffee. He sat at the kitchen table stirring the sugar round in his cup, his anorak hanging over the back of his chair. He had left his boots in the back lobby and padded across the floor in his thick grey socks. The collar of his cream-coloured shirt, over which he wore a green crew-necked sweater, was spotless. He was not quite the sort of man you expected to find employed as a gardener, Nina thought, sitting opposite him with her own cup of coffee.

'You haven't always done gardening, have you?' she asked.

'Only as a hobby,' said Dan. 'It's my second career, you could say, now I'm retired.'

'I suppose this is my second career, too,' said Nina. 'House-minding, I mean.'

'Do you like it?' he asked.

'It's all right, so far,' said Nina.

'Here, you mean? Or is this the first time you've done it?' said Dan.

'Both,' Nina answered.

'I see. Somehow I thought you were used to it,' said Dan. 'You're not nervous? It's a big place to be in, alone.'

Nina denied any nervousness, but she thought of the telephone calls. Should she mention them to him?

'Are you on the telephone?' she asked, instead.

'No. There's a box at the end of the road, if I need to make a call,' said Dan. 'I've no one wanting to ring me up now. I've lost touch with folk from where I lived before.'

Nina remembered his sad circumstances, described by Mrs Blunt, and felt she had better head the conversation into a safer area. She mentioned the shops, and how many there were.

'It's easier than at home – where I used to live, I mean,' she said. 'We had none at all near.'

She was sorry when he left.

The gale continued to blow all day. In the afternoon, Nina read the paper. A short paragraph reported the discovery of a woman's body the previous day near the Droxton by-pass but gave no more details than she had learned from the television news. Later, she turned the set on and watched a romantic film which made her feel sad; she was glad to have Rory there, lying on the rug in front of the fire that Dan had lit. Rory had no proper walk that day, just a series of runs in the garden.

The telephone rang again that night, at twenty minutes to eleven, and again there was just a single sigh when Nina answered.

7

The body lay on the mortuary table. Little flesh was left on the small bundle of bones.

Police Constable Downes stood by the table, his one aim not to keel over. As the officer who had first seen the body after its discovery, it was his duty to confirm that it was the one found in the copse where, before its removal, it had been photographed from every angle. The area had been staked out and measured, and the surrounding woodland and meadows were still being sifted for evidence as to the identity of the dead woman and the method by which she was killed.

There was no doubt about it being a woman, but at this stage little more was known. The first doctor at the scene had been the police surgeon, whose task was formally to certify death, and to deduce that this was unlikely to have been a natural event. The forensic pathologist who was examining the corpse had been to the scene and made notes before permitting the body's removal. Now, as he worked, he spoke into the tape-recorder nearby, his particular method of noting details as he carefully inspected the remains.

Downes swallowed hard and gazed at the ceiling, trying to ignore the various smells. There was no rule to say you must watch. He thought about going to Spain, maybe, when he had leave, on a package tour, and perhaps finding some juicy young bird. But this body, this mass of bones and fibre, had once been that – a warm, living human being, able to laugh and make love. Whilst he fought his nausea, Downes also knew that he would not be happy until whoever had reduced her to this pitiful state had been found and punished. For there was no doubt at all that she had been killed: the pathologist had found a fracture of the hyoid bone in the neck, a typical injury in a case of strangulation, as if being covered in leaves wasn't enough on its own. She was very young, too; certainly no more than twenty-five and probably nearer sixteen, the experienced doctor remarked. Tests would affirm the exact age more precisely. Some dental work had been done, and was now recorded; if a possible identity for her was discovered, a chart comparison would confirm it one way or the other, but at the moment there was nowhere for the police to start their search. No handbag, purse, jewellery or other personal possessions had yet been found. All that was certain, apart from her age, was that she had fair hair, worn shoulder-length, and was about five foot two. Her clothing, which the doctor had painstakingly removed in fragments, must be analysed and might offer a lead; she was wearing an Indian print cotton dress. She had been dead between two and three months; the doctor hoped to pin that down more accurately later.

Some technicians were watching the post-mortem. One of them made a light remark in an aside, and Downes felt his own tension slacken. That was it, he thought; think of something trivial – no disrespect meant to the dead – or you might not be able to take it. There would be more of this sort of thing for him in the future, he knew, and he'd have to be tough, get used to it.

Later that day he told his sergeant he'd like, in time, to put up for the CID.

Nina had decided she must report the mysterious telephone calls to the police. She had slept very badly again, spinning various theories in her mind about the anonymous caller, even imagining it was Martin purposely trying to frighten her, though he didn't know where she was and even if he did, was unlikely to act like this as she was cooperating with his wishes over the divorce and the sale of the house. He was anxious for everything to be settled rapidly, so that he and Miss Kitty-Cat could be married before the birth of their baby.

The gale was still blowing, and heavy rain lashed the windowpanes. The scene outside was grey and depressing and even Rory looked dejected when she greeted him that morning. He was soon back from his run in the garden.

Nina looked up the number of the nearest

police station in the directory. There was one at Murford, she saw. She picked up the telephone, to find it dead.

It had been working at ten-forty the previous night, when the caller rang.

The feeling that now she was really cut off from the world outside was frightening. Although it meant no more anonymous calls could be made to her, she could not summon aid if she needed it. She must report the telephone out of order at once. Nina made herself a cup of instant coffee and drank it standing up as she tied on her headscarf and buttoned her coat, not waiting to have any more solid breakfast. She called Rory to her, and, taking her folding umbrella, set off.

Her umbrella blew inside out before she had reached the end of the drive, and she left it there, behind a shrub, to retrieve on her return. She should really have taken the car, she supposed, but Rory had to have exercise and he had not had a proper walk the day before. They splashed down the road together, the dog showing little enthusiasm for the expedition. They met the old man with the spaniel whom she had noticed before. The man's head was down as he faced the gale.

In the telephone box by the corner of Chestnut Crescent, she dialled Faults and reported the telephone at the Hall out of order. Faults told her that the gale had brought down numerous lines and seemed gloomy about a speedy repair but promised to do what it could. Then Nina dialled

Murford Police Station. A woman answered, and when she said why she was ringing, passed her on to a man. She felt foolish as she described what had happened – the regularity of the calls at twenty minutes to eleven each night and then the silence. The voice at the other end spoke kindly but said it was a matter for the telephone people. Her calls could be intercepted by the exchange; this soon discouraged mischief makers, he said. Nina uttered her theory that the caller might be interested in finding out if the house was empty, to be told thieves rarely made that sort of call at night, only by day. They'd be more likely to come and look themselves, at night, he said, not very reassuringly, Nina thought. Lights on in the house and other signs of occupation were what they would notice, he added. He repeated his advice to ask the telephone exchange to help if the calls continued; the nuisance would soon stop then, he declared.

Nina was disappointed. She'd somehow expected to be told that the line would be bugged and the offender caught, but as he was silent, perhaps that wouldn't be easy. She and Rory turned back, stopping at the newsagent's on the way. Dan had already been in, she was told, and collected her paper.

He'd come in his car. She saw a small green Ford parked by the back door as she approached the house, her collapsed umbrella under her arm. Dan was sitting inside the car, and he got out as she drew near. He told her he'd come to fetch in her fuel, but as she was out and the house was locked up, he hadn't been able to do it.

'I never thought you'd go out in this weather,' he said.

Nina explained about the telephone being out of order. She thought of mentioning the calls, but Dan had cut in.

'I never saw you,' he said. 'In the village, I mean. I came right by the box.'

She'd had Rory inside it, with her, lying by her feet.

'Well – thank you for getting my paper,' she said. 'Come in and I'll make some coffee.'

Dan could do nothing outside in such weather, and when he had fetched in the logs and the coal, and had his coffee, he left. Nina took the paper into the study by the fire and read some gossip about the Royal Family and the latest film world romances. On an inside page there was a piece about the by-pass murder, as the paper now called it; the body had not been identified yet. Since the reporter had few facts to use in his story, he was forced to speculate, and drew comparisons between the discovery of other corpses in woods in recent months, and this one. A body had been found in a Sussex wood a year ago, and another in Epping Forest some time later; both victims were young girls, and their killer had never been found. They had been strangled.

Nina turned the page over and started to do the crossword.

Guy Jowett was washing his hands at the kitchen sink. He dried them carefully on a paper towel. Then he washed them again and dried them once more on another piece from the roll suspended near the sink.

He took two cups and saucers from the cupboard, peering at them closely, and ran hot water into the plastic bowl in the sink, squeezing into it a generous amount of Fairy Liquid. He washed the cups and saucers thoroughly, and dried them on paper towels too, then put them on the kitchen table. Next he washed his own hands again before scalding the teapot and replacing it on the Aga beside the simmering kettle. He liked to do what he could to help Heather, who worked so hard and was out now, taking his paintings to a dealer she'd found in Droxton who would sell them. She'd soon be back, bringing scones from Anne's Pantry. Guy, himself, had not been to Droxton for years.

He looked forward to the scones. Heather assured him the shop where she got them was very clean. Heather's own baking produced some-what leaden results; cooking was not one of her talents.

He heard the car just as he was setting out butter and honey.

Guy moved to the sink again and ran the taps, then, making a big effort, turned them off. He had already, he knew, washed thoroughly.

Heather brought an aura of cold, damp air into

the kitchen with her. They moved towards one another and kissed lingeringly.

'It's stopped raining,' said Heather. 'But it's still blowing hard. I passed Nina Crowther out walking with Rory, and asked her in for tea.'

'Who's Nina Crowther?' Guy asked.

'Oh darling, you know! The woman who's looking after the Hall while Priscilla and Leonard are away,' Heather said. 'I've told you about her – I went to see her the day after she arrived.'

'Nina Crowther,' Guy repeated. 'Looking after the Hall?' he added, questioningly.

'While they're in South Africa. You remember,' said Heather. 'Their Spaniards have gone and they don't want to leave the place empty. She's nice – Nina, I mean. I think she's rather shy, so I'll go and meet her. You make the tea.'

As the rain had stopped at last, Nina, out walking with Rory, and curious about the Manor House, had decided to look for it. She was embarrassed when a car coming up the road behind her stopped and she saw Heather inside. Heather had simply wound down the window and said, 'Come in and have a cup of tea – the next house on your left round the bend,' and driven off.

A hundred yards on, Nina came to a gateway. A short drive, gently curving, led to a square house built of mellow brick. It had long sash windows under its slate roof. The proportions were perfect; Nina thought she had rarely seen anything so immediately attractive. It made the Hall seem almost vulgar, by contrast. She started up the rutted drive and saw Heather coming towards her, in the familiar tweed skirt and boots.

'What a beautiful house,' said Nina.

'It's been in Guy's family for ever,' said Heather. 'We're doing our best to preserve it. Come along in.'

'What about Rory?' asked Nina.

'He'll wait for you in the porch,' said Heather. 'Like he does when Priscilla comes round.'

Nina found it odd that Rory was not admitted into the house, and, indeed, that Heather, so much an outdoor person, had no dog of her own. She hoped Rory wouldn't catch a chill.

Heather led her round to the back door, where she took off her boots. Nina wondered if she should do the same, but hers were not in the least muddy. Heather went ahead into the house and Nina, following, wiped her feet well on the mat inside. Heather had gone on into the kitchen, in her stockinged feet, and Nina, behind her, saw a tall old man with silver hair standing near the Aga holding a large brown teapot.

'This is Guy,' Heather introduced them. 'Darling, here's Nina – from the Hall. Remember?' She rested her hand briefly on Guy's arm and the old man set the teapot down.

'How do you do?' he said gravely, and held out his hand.

Nina had pulled off her gloves as she entered the house. She took his proffered hand, thinking the gesture quaint and formal, but agreeable, as she touched his palm. It felt soft and cool.

Guy Jowett wore a beautifully cut tweed jacket with leather patches on the elbows and leather binding round the cuffs. His old brown brogues gleamed.

'Let me take your coat,' he said. His voice was deep and slightly hoarse. Nina thought him the most distinguished-looking man she had ever met. She allowed him to help her off with her coat which he bore away down the passage, leaving Nina alone in the large kitchen. The room had charm, she thought, but was scarcely labour-saving. The sink was an old porcelain one, with wooden draining boards each side. A hod of coke stood by the Aga. The quarry-tiled floor was polished, and on it stood two bright fibre mats, one by the sink and one by the stove. In the centre of the room was a scrubbed deal table with a checked gingham cloth covering one end where tea things were laid.

Heather had vanished in search of some shoes, but Guy soon returned.

'Do be seated,' he said, waving vaguely at a chair by the table, and as Nina obeyed, he said, 'Excuse me,' and went to the sink, where he ran water into a bowl and washed his hands very carefully, soaping them well. Nina watched him dry them on a paper towel. Then he opened a paper bag that rested on the dresser and took from it some scones which he put on a plate and placed in the low oven. All his movements were slow and careful. Then, to Nina's amazement, he washed his hands again.

He was still doing this when Heather returned. She wore flat black shoes, and had brushed her hair.

'Sit down, darling,' said Heather.

She handed the old man a clean towel which she took from a drawer, and a shadow crossed his face as he accepted it and began drying his hands, paying particular attention to the cuticles, pushing them back, as Nina had noticed he did with the paper towel earlier. His hands were very white; they were narrow, with long, tapering fingers. He turned to Nina and smiled.

'Where did you say you lived?' he asked.

Before Nina could reply, Heather came forward and put the large teapot down on a mat on the table. She set down another cup, saucer and plate, and a knife, then pulled forward a third chair to join the two already at the table.

'Milk and sugar, Nina?' she asked.

'Yes, please,' said Nina. She felt rather light-headed and was bewildered by Guy's behaviour, but as she accepted a scone she remembered that she had forgotten to have any lunch, and now that she thought of it, had had only coffee before going down to telephone that morning. After reading the paper and becoming depressed by its news, she had vacuumed several rooms at the Hall and polished the dining-room furniture. By then the light had begun to fail and she had decided to take Rory out. She had not wanted to sit idly; it still seemed strange not to be centring her day round the time when Martin came home in the evening for dinner.

'You've got two daughters, haven't you?' Heather said, when everyone was settled with tea and scones. 'Tell us about them. What do they do?'

Nina began in a deprecating way, meaning only to speak briefly, but it was as if a dam had burst. Words poured from her as she described Sarah, Jeremy and little Sebastian, and Jenny's college course. Heather smiled and nodded, saying 'Really?' and 'How interesting,' at intervals, and Guy silently ate three scones, smiling at Nina now and then. Nina talked so much that she forgot her own scone, though she paused to drink her tea.

'I'm sorry,' she said at last, suddenly aware that neither of her hosts had uttered more than a few words. 'What about you? Have you a family?' Too late, she remembered the tombstone, and her heart began to beat loudly.

But Heather answered calmly enough.

'Our daughter, Rosemary, is married to a soldier and they're stationed in Germany at the moment. She has a son and a daughter.' She talked a little about her grandchildren, and poured out more tea, smiling at her husband and laying a hand briefly on his shoulder as she passed on her way to refill the teapot. Nina finished her scone and took another when Guy offered her the plate.

'They're delicious,' she said, which was true, though she knew her own were better.

'I bring them from Droxton whenever I'm

90

there,' said Heather. 'They're one of our treats.'

'We have lots of treats,' said Guy. 'We celebrate sunny weather with extra time in the garden. When it rains in the winter, we light the fire early and sometimes have toast for tea.'

'We have sherry on birthdays and anniversaries,' Heather said, pouring Nina more tea.

'Extra time in the garden?' Nina asked, puzzled.

'Yes. We have our various tasks, you see – Guy has his painting to do and I have the house and the garden, but we both like sitting at ease in the sun, when there's time.'

'Have you a large garden?' asked Nina. It seemed a safe question.

'We let the fields, as the Blunts do,' Heather said. 'That leaves us about three acres of garden. Much of it's orchard.'

'That's a lot to look after,' said Nina. Surely they had a gardener?

'We manage,' said Heather. 'We let a lot of the grass go to hay and a local girl with a pony comes and takes it away. But we grow a lot of vegetables – we're entirely self-supporting in the matter of fruit and vegetables.'

They were very hard up, Nina realized.

'Of course, Priscilla has the paragon Dan to look after the garden at the Hall,' Heather was saying. 'How are you getting on with him? I imagine you've met?'

'He seems very nice,' Nina said. 'He brought me in coal and logs.'

'Ah,' said Heather, nodding.

'Good, good,' said Guy. 'So he should. Knows his job, doesn't he? An excellent gardener.'

'Indeed he is,' Heather said. 'Are you sure you won't have more tea, Nina?'

Nina sensed she was being gently dismissed. She rose.

'Thank you so much,' she said. 'I must go – poor Rory—'

They lent her a torch, for it was quite dark outside and there were no street lights in this part of the village. Tears fell down Nina's cheeks as she walked home with Rory. She'd talked and talked. They'd never ask her again. She wept on, with shame, as she walked round the Hall drawing the curtains.

In the dining-room, she looked at the sideboard where decanters of sherry and whisky, gin and port, stood arranged. Sherry for birthdays and treats, the Jowetts had said. But it wasn't her birthday, and she mustn't start tippling the Blunts' liquor. She went upstairs and fetched the *gros point* she was working for Sarah, to cover her dining-room chairs, and turned on the television.

At the Manor, Guy said to his wife, 'What a lonely woman. Who did you say she was?'

The telephone at the Hall did not ring that night. It was still out of order.

In Chestnut Crescent, Dan Fenton drew the living-room curtains to shut out the dark evening. He paused by the tank of tropical fish and noticed one

92

specimen motionless among the plants at the bottom: the glass catfish, faking dead again. It constantly did so.

He'd done his housework that day. He had a routine, cleaning all round on a Monday, as Ellen had done, and putting his washing through the machine.

He dusted Ellen's bedroom, never used now. All her frippery things were gone; he'd bundled them off, tied in plastic sacks, to the Oxfam shop in Droxton afterwards. The vicar had wanted to take them for the church jumble sale but Dan wouldn't have that; he didn't want anyone local to wear Ellen's clothes, or a pair of her shoes. Her feet had been pretty and neat, small and high-arched. He liked dainty feet on a woman.

Nina Crowther had small feet too, he'd noticed. He wondered why she had taken on such a lonely sort of job. Was she a widow? Mrs Blunt hadn't said anything about her, except for telling him her name. He'd enjoyed sitting in the kitchen with her over their coffee, though he'd taken care not to stay long. She was a pretty woman, soft and gentle, he thought, as Ellen had been.

Dan sighed, remembering his wife. The couple next door, the Morrises, had asked him why he didn't take in a lodger; he'd got the large room going spare, they'd said, and it would be company; but Dan was accustomed, now, to his solitude. His days were planned out, his routine rarely varied.

That evening he sat by the fireside, spectacles on, and opened the paper.

GLADE DEATH LINKED WITH WOODLAND MURDERS ran the headline across the centre page. There were grainy photographs of two young girls, previous victims of an untraced killer, and a shot of a police car parked by some trees.

Dan had missed the television report of the body's discovery on Saturday, though he had seen the short paragraph in the Sunday paper. Now he read an expanded version of what Nina had seen in her paper, including the theories of the reporter following the case.

He fetched the kitchen scissors and cut the article out of the paper. Then he took it upstairs to the tiny third bedroom where there was a cheap, scratched desk, an upright chair and an old typewriter, and clipped it into a file which he took from a drawer. The file already held a number of newspaper cuttings.

Dan returned downstairs and sat by the fire, hands folded across his stomach, until it was time for the radio news. There was no mention of the body, nor was it referred to on the television news later.

The girl was unnamed. Her family – her mother, her father – did not yet know she had met a sudden and violent death. Their shock was still to come.

He sat there, motionless, all the evening.

8

After the gale, leaves lay thick on the ground at the Hall. Nina wondered if Dan would come to sweep them up, but by ten o'clock he had not arrived so she decided to go down to the shops in the village. There was the paper to fetch, and she might buy a few things at the grocer's. Little and often for shopping, she thought, not the weekly forays to Sainsbury's that she'd made before: that way, she would talk to someone each day, even if it was only the newsagent or the grocer.

Dogs were denied admittance to the grocer's, a notice on the shop door declared, and quite right too, Nina thought, tying Rory's lead to a railing nearby. Mr Goody, the grocer, was about thirty-six, a pale man with sandy hair and a sallow skin. Nina watched him slice her bacon on to his hand, then lay the slices on some paper beside the machine. With that same hand he took the money she gave him and handed her her change.

Nina walked on to the newsagent's and collected her paper. Now she had spoken to two people today. As she passed the last buildings before the long stretch of road that led to the Hall, she met the old man with the spaniel again; he still gazed at the ground ahead of him, as he always did, the dog pulling at the lead. Nina's pace slowed. She didn't want to go back. Yet at Silverlea, she'd always been glad to get home with her shopping and on with the next task – preparing dinner, sewing, whatever it was. Often someone would come in to coffee, or she would pop round to a neighbour, yet the friendships she had thought were strong had melted away when Martin left and only Felicity seemed to care. People blamed her, Nina thought, for not being able to keep her husband. It did not occur to her that they feared her condition might be infectious.

Near the Hall gates she saw a man coming towards her from the other direction, where she had walked with Heather Jowett on that first morning. He wore a sheepskin coat and a tweed cap and black, not green, wellington boots. Nina soon recognized Guy Jowett. He raised his cap gravely when they met.

'Good morning,' cried Nina, delighted to see him. Three conversations today, she thought: not bad.

'Good morning,' said Guy.

Rory stood wagging his tail but Guy made no move to pat him or speak to him.

'Could you tell me the time?' Guy asked.

Nina looked at her watch.

'It's five past eleven,' she said.

'Oh – not lunch time, then,' said Guy.

'No – not for ages,' said Nina, surprised.

'Thank you,' said Guy, raising his cap once more. 'Good morning,' he added, and walked off.

His boots, Nina noticed, were covered in mud; he must have come round by the fields. She had the feeling he didn't remember meeting her before.

She was cleaning the silver coasters from the dining-room when the telephone rang some time later. She was glad to know it was working again and wondered if the caller would be Leonard Blunt's secretary making the regular calls she had been told to expect. But it was Heather, who wanted to know if she had seen Guy.

'I've been to the dentist in Murford,' she said. 'He was in the studio when I left, but now I can't find him anywhere.'

'I met him about an hour ago,' Nina said. 'He asked me the time. He was just near the gates, going towards the village.'

'Oh dear,' said Heather. 'Where can he have got to?'

'He seemed to be out for a walk,' Nina said. 'The weather's much better today – perhaps he just felt like having some exercise.'

'But he's been gone so long, if you met him all that time ago,' said Heather.

'Why are you so worried? Do you think he might have had an accident?' Nina asked. People did fall down dead sometimes, without warning, and very nice for them too, thought Nina, though a shock for their families and whoever found them. Had Guy collapsed somewhere? 'Shall I come down and help you to look for him?' she suggested. It would be nice to have something useful to do.

'Oh, would you, Nina? Would you just come to the house and be here, in case he comes back, while I go and look for him? Would you have a look round the Hall grounds first, in case he's wandering about there? If you find him – if you meet him on your way – bring him back here with you. Be firm. Don't let him fob you off. I'll go towards Stokebourne – as I didn't meet him on the way back from Murford, he must have gone somewhere else. I'll leave the house open, so that if you find him, you can bring him indoors.'

She was talking as though Guy were a child, Nina thought, and remembered how he had washed his hands several times the day before, and the vague way he had looked at her this morning, forgetting they had met. Was he ill?

She took Rory into the garden to help her search, for if the old man lay unconscious somewhere the dog might see him before she did, but though they traversed every path and looked in all the outbuildings, no one was there.

Nina locked Rory into the house and then got into her car and drove to the Manor, looking out for the tall figure who had walked, she remembered now, rather shamblingly when they had met earlier, but she did not see him. She went slowly up the rutted drive of the Manor and parked at the side of the house, in the yard. The garage doors were open and Heather's Mini had gone. Nina decided to take a look round the garden; he might have returned across the fields, and, apart from that, she was curious to see the garden.

The cultivated section was well kept, but here and there were some weeds or some withered growth that had not been cut back, something not to be seen at the Hall. As Heather had said, a large area was put down to grass but there were rose beds and a mixed border close to the house, and beyond an old brick wall, as mellow as the house, was a vegetable garden planted with cabbages and sprouts, and with a fruit cage well wired round in which were raspberries, currants, strawberries and gooseberry bushes. Fruit trees – peaches, perhaps, or plums, Nina didn't know – were trained against a south-facing wall.

Nina went back to the house. Should she search it, to see if he had come back and was up in the studio? She had, so far, seen only the kitchen, and now she wandered into the front hall. A long-case clock ticked away the minutes. Worn rugs covered the polished floor. Nina opened one of several closed doors and saw the drawing-room, a square room, light and airy, with a threadbare carpet on the floor and chairs and a sofa in faded covers. The room was chilly. A fire was laid in the hearth. She closed the door, and was wondering where to go now when she heard a car outside.

Heather had found Guy. He got out of the passenger seat as Nina came out of the house.

'Oh, good morning,' he said to Nina, and raised

his cap, as he had before. 'Have you come to lunch? I'm so sorry we're late.'

He was looking at her again as if they had never met, but this time he smiled, very sweetly. His manners were certainly wonderful, Nina thought; such old-world charm almost made up for his poor memory.

'Nina's just dropped in for a minute,' Heather said briskly, coming round to take his arm. 'Come along, darling.'

She led him indoors. Nina stood aside to let them pass. Guy began taking off his sheepskin coat. Beneath it, he wore his old tweed jacket and a checked shirt with a regimental tie. A worried expression came over his face.

'I've got myself dirty,' he said, looking down at his boots. 'I must bath and change.'

'Just take off your boots and wash your hands, darling,' said Heather. 'That's all you need do. We'll have some sherry. I'll get you some.'

'But it isn't a birthday,' Guy said.

'No, but it's a celebration,' said Heather.

'I'll go, then,' Nina said, but Heather seemed not to hear her. She might have offered me some sherry too, Nina thought, aggrievedly, going back to her car, but Heather had been oblivious of anything except Guy, who had been lost and was found, a cause for rejoicing.

Nina forgot about lunch when she reached the Hall, but she made herself a cup of instant coffee which she drank in the study. The fire took some reviving, though the heap of ashes, which Dan had said need be cleared only once a week or so, was warm. She wondered why he hadn't come that morning.

For a while, sitting there, she looked at the paper. Then she turned on the television, something she had never done in the afternoon at Silverlea except during the Wimbledon tennis fortnight. After a time, in the warmth, she dozed off, and was woken by the back door bell. Perhaps it was Dan?

But it was Heather who stood on the step, in her usual green husky jacket. Her car was parked outside. She looked exhausted, her face grey beneath its network of veins.

'Oh – come in,' Nina said. 'Come and sit down – would you like some tea? Or coffee?' Though really, Nina thought, eyeing the other woman, brandy might be more appropriate.

'Coffee, please,' said Heather. 'But I mustn't be long. Guy's asleep.' She'd given him two tranquillisers today with his lunch, instead of the normal one, the powder extracted from the capsules and mixed up in the mashed potato. They, and the sherry, would ensure that he slept soundly this afternoon. 'I've come to apologize,' Heather went on, following Nina into the kitchen. 'You must have thought me so rude, this morning.'

'Oh – not at all,' said Nina, blushing. She bustled about with cups and the jar of instant coffee.

'Guy's rather forgetful, you see,' Heather said. 'He'd gone some distance down the Stokebourne road before I found him. I'm always afraid he'll get run over. He often can't remember where he is.

I try not to let him go out alone, and the mornings are usually safe, when he's painting, but sometimes he gives me the slip.'

'Well, you had to go to the dentist,' Nina pointed out.

'Yes. I should have had an afternoon appointment, though,' Heather said. 'He always has a sleep then. But I'd had toothache, you see, and had to go when the dentist could fit me in.'

Nina had made the coffee. She picked up the tray on which she had set two pretty cups, the milk in a jug, sugar, and some biscuits.

'Let's take this into the study,' she said, standing back for Heather to go first.

'He's been better lately,' Heather went on, when they were sitting by the fire. She put two lumps of sugar in her cup.

'Oh,' said Nina encouragingly, unable to think of a comment.

'You mustn't mind if he doesn't always recognize you,' Heather continued.

Nina remembered the handwashing she had seen. Surely that wasn't just forgetfulness? He'd seemed almost obsessed by the need to be clean. He'd wanted a bath when Heather brought him home. It reminded Nina of something, some character in a play.

'He has dreadful dreams,' Heather was explaining.

Lady Macbeth! That was it! She'd been haunted by dreams and tried to wash blood from her hands. Surely Guy had no evil past like hers?

102

'It was the war, you see,' Heather said. 'He got over it – he was all right, until we retired. Then he had time to think. It all came back to haunt him.'

'Oh,' said Nina, inadequately. She did not understand. 'What shall I do if I meet him out walking again?' she asked. She had an idea, and added, 'Shall I try to persuade him to go home – pretend I'm walking that way myself and go with him?'

'Oh, would you, Nina? Or bring him in here and settle him down, then let me know – ring up?'

'Of course,' Nina said.

'It's best if he doesn't wander round the village. Some of the new people don't know about him – who he is. A small boy brought him home once.'

A tear trickled slowly down Heather's lined and weatherbeaten face.

'He won the DSO during the war,' she said.

Dan had had something more urgent to do that morning than go to the Hall. He backed his small Ford into the road and headed out of the village, past the church towards Stokebourne and on down the Droxton road. When he reached the new roundabout outside the town he took the by-pass, driving down its full three-mile length and parking beyond it in a gateway near the old road which was now fenced off, apart from a small area that was used as a lay-by. Here, a lorry was parked, the driver asleep.

Dan climbed the fence and walked along the

old road, his tweed hat pulled firmly down so that the fresh wind which still blew, though the gale had dropped, would not tug it off.

He reached a point from which he could see the copse. Traffic on the by-pass went steadily past, sometimes a group of vehicles boxed behind a slow-moving leader, sometimes just a single car. He had seen a police car parked beside the verge as he drove by himself. *No parking* cones had blocked a track entrance nearby. That would be the direct route to where the girl's body was found, now that this road was closed.

They'd be busy down there, still, Dan knew. As he watched, he saw distant figures moving about and the white of a police car parked by some trees. They'd be hoping to find a handbag, a scarf – something personal that would point to the dead girl's identity.

There would be no such lead, Dan knew. This killer was careful. The other two girls found in woods, his earlier victims, as the papers had surmised, had been identified only by patient detection, the piecing together of evidence about their appearances with facts relating to girls missing from home.

Dan turned and went back to his car. He drove into Droxton, where he went to the pet shop and bought some live food for his fish, as a treat; you couldn't get it in Murford and he usually got some when he came over this way. Then he went to a pub where he had half a pint and a pie for his lunch.

He drove past Chestnut Crescent when he returned to Netherton St Mary, and on to the Hall, for he hadn't taken in any coal or logs that day and he felt a need to make sure that Mrs Crowther was all right. You never knew what might happen to someone living alone if they felt depressed, and besides, he wanted to see her.

Mrs Jowett's old Mini came out through the gateway as he approached. Dan would have liked to help the Jowetts with their garden. He would have done it for nothing, for he knew they could not afford to pay. It was well known in the village that Mrs Jowett only bought the cheapest cuts of meat and no delicacies. But he knew their pride would not permit them to accept his labour for nothing, and besides, if he did not charge them, how could he charge the Blunts? He needed more money than his pension brought in; his trips to London and all they involved were often expensive, and costs were rising all the time.

Mrs Crowther seemed pleased to see him. She said she'd just had a cup of coffee with Mrs Jowett, but she had another with him.

'She's a nice lady, that Mrs Jowett,' said Dan. 'Sad about the son.'

'I've seen his grave,' Nina said. 'What happened?'

'He was killed in a sailing accident,' Dan said. 'He was with Charles Blunt. They were great friends as boys, it's said in the village. There are folk still here who knew them in spite of all the newcomers, like me. The Jowetts were away a lot, though, with the colonel serving overseas and that.'

'How dreadful,' Nina murmured.

'Yes,' Dan agreed.

He liked sitting there, facing her across the table, domestically. He liked the grave look she now wore, contemplating the Jowetts' past.

Today, he'd stop for a second cup, if she offered him one.

9

Nina was settling down. Mr Blunt's secretary had telephoned, showing concern, after the lines had been down, lest she had been perturbed by being incommunicado. Nina had assured her that she was unworried and mentioned that the gardener had been round regularly. The secretary rang again within a few days, with further enquiries; this time, they had quite a chat. A telex had come from the Blunts, now in Johannesburg, and Mr Charles had spoken to his parents on the telephone only yesterday. They were enjoying their trip and the weather was good. Nina did not mention the mystery telephone calls as there had been no more, and the conversation relieved her sense of isolation. The strangeness was wearing off and in the daytime she felt quite at home, but the evenings were drawing in, and were difficult; she was often depressed then, and she kept the radio on continuously, carrying it round the house to whatever room she was in, listening to plays and talks and quizzes, even concerts, but it was the sound of the human voice she really sought. She watched a great deal of television.

Every day, Nina went into each room in the house making sure that all was well, pulling the curtains morning and night and cleaning the rooms in rotation, though that was not officially part of her job. She had realized that Priscilla and Leonard occupied separate bedrooms. A linking door connected them. Priscilla's room had a thick cream carpet, apricot curtains and bedspread, and some beautiful antique furniture – a sofa table used as a dressing table and a regency *chaise longue*. Leonard's room was blue – dark blue walls and lighter blue carpets, curtains and bedspread. On the walls hung framed photographs of groups of young men at college, a rowing eight, some men in naval uniform. In Priscilla's room there were photographs of a boy in various stages of growth. He was dark-haired and smiling. This must be Charles. Nina inspected one of him as an adult man which stood alone on a walnut tallboy. He looked cheerful. She knew he was the managing director of the firm. No doubt, by now, he was married and had a family, Nina thought, but she had seen no pictures of grandchildren. Mrs Blunt had referred only to his role in the business, not to his private circumstances.

Wondering about the Blunts kept Nina's mind from dwelling on Martin and Caroline, although when she woke every morning she always thought of him, her hand automatically stretching out to find him beside her. Bitter anguish still filled her when she thought of Caroline's cat-like face, the claws clutching at Martin. Did she scratch? Maybe she bit, too. Sometimes Nina dreamed about them, and would wake in the night, crying, but by day it grew easier to control her misery.

What was she to do when the Blunts returned? Panic swept over Nina when she thought of the future, but she tried to be calm. She could advertise for further house-minding posts, or Mrs Blunt had said there was an agency, to whom she could apply. Felicity had pointed out that she would have a reference after this job, a significant one, since the Blunts were people of consequence.

Mr Drew had no news of the money she was due to receive from the sale of Silverlea, but these things always took time. Nina had signed various papers to do with the divorce. As they had agreed – by post, through the lawyers – on so much, it should be straightforward. She stamped her insurance card each week, as instructed by Mr Drew who said she must look ahead, for if Martin were to die, Caroline would receive the widow's pension. Suppose she were ill herself, Nina would think, waking at night, sweating: the girls would see that she was looked after, she consoled herself, but it was another thing to dread.

Almost every day Dan Fenton came. Nina missed him on the days when he did not appear. He seemed to find plenty to do outside, brushing down the yard, digging, and sweeping the leaves which still fell. He came in for coffee every day, prolonging their chats and even helping with the crossword, which she did as a way of sharpening her wits. He always went home at one o'clock. Nina wondered about his lunch. It would be easy to cook him a meal; she'd like to, it would remind her to eat herself. She had little appetite these days and often forgot about meals; she was losing weight and her skirts hung loosely round her.

One day she met Guy Jowett again, this time near the post office. He raised his hat as they passed in the road but did not stop. Nina hurriedly bought her stamps and posted her letters, not stopping for her usual few words with Mrs Fox, the postmistress, aptly named as she had red hair and a sharp pointed face. She hastened up the road behind Guy and followed him all the way back to the Manor, waiting to make sure he had gone right into the house.

She had her own green wellington boots now, bought in Murford, with thermal soles to keep her feet warm, but she had not bought a padded anorak; she still wore her own suede coat unless it was raining hard, when she borrowed Priscilla Blunt's Burberry from the cloakroom. They were much of a size, apart from their feet. Whenever she went to the village she met the two men with their dogs whom she had noticed on the first expedition with Rory. Nina was always ready to say 'Good morning' in the friendly fashion she thought was part of village life, but the men plodded on, heads down, never looking at her. It seemed as if they spent the whole day circling round the village.

She asked Dan about them one day.

'Their wives don't want them hanging about the place, getting in their way,' he said. 'They've been used to having the house to themselves, you see, by day. Then the husband retires and they've lost their castle.'

'Oh,' said Nina. 'That's awful! Is it true? What do they think about, walking around like that?'

'Nothing much, I'd say,' said Dan. 'Maybe they're hoping their number will come up on the pools. They do a bit of gardening in the better weather; it's easier then.'

'You haven't got a dog,' Nina said.

'No, just some tropical fish,' said Dan. 'A good few of the wives go to Bingo. They have meetings in the village hall regularly. Very popular they are, I'm told. I go to the Black Swan now and then, on a Saturday, and hear the news there.'

'Oh yes?' Nina listened with interest.

'Then there's the Silver Club,' Dan went on, sitting back in his chair, his booted feet on a piece of newspaper, the technique he and Nina had evolved so that he did not have to sit intimately with her in his socks.

'The Silver Club? Are they collectors?'

'No. They're the senior citizens – silver hair, you see,' said Dan. 'They play paper games and whist and have talks, and cakes to eat, like a kids' party, really, once a month or so. All old ladies except for three fellows brave enough to join.' He chuckled. 'Some of them come from Stokebourne, and even Cerne St Mary – they're too small to have Silver Groups of their own. It's quite a business getting them here – some good ladies drive them. Two or three of the drivers are older than their passengers, but they're of a different sort, you see – doing good, not having it done to them.'

'It sounds grim,' said Nina.

'It isn't. It's good for them all, whichever kind they are,' Dan said. 'It gets them out, meeting folk. Most of them are alone all day, the rest of the time. They have coach outings, too. Some of them would never get away, otherwise. Off to London to theatres, and to the seaside. Marvellous.'

Nina tried to picture herself in twenty years' time as a member of a Silver Club. Or would she be an elderly ministering angel instead of the recipient of mercy? The idea appalled her, yet she could see what Dan meant about its benefits: she had discovered already the enervating effect of isolation.

When Dan said he would not be coming the next day, her heart sank.

'I'll leave you some extra fuel,' he said. 'And I'll be in on Saturday.'

She wanted to ask where he was going, but did not like to pry.

Her spirits soon improved, however, for that evening Jenny rang to announce she was coming for the weekend. She'd arrive fairly late the next day.

'How will you get here?' asked Nina. 'You're not to hitch-hike.'

'Oh Mum,'came the cry, and Jenny went on, 'I knew you'd say that. I've found out about the trains.'

'Have you enough money?' Nina asked. She and Martin had always insisted that neither girl should ever hitch: money for taxis and buses and trains was money well spent, Martin had always said.

Jenny intimated that she had enough but would not be above accepting a refund.

She planned to catch the last train to Murford, which Nina said she would meet.

With something definite, now, to do, Nina ran upstairs to make up a bed for her in the green room which Mrs Blunt had said she might use. It was near enough to share Nina's bathroom. She put out a towel for Jenny, and as she did so, stuck out her tongue at the smirking pottery cat on the window-sill.

That night, at twenty minutes to eleven the telephone rang, and when she answered, again there was just a sigh. It was nearly two weeks since there had been such a call.

The police in Droxton were continuing their work on the murder case. A sketch of the girl whose body had been found in the copse near the by-pass was prepared. It was based on her skull measurements and the way her teeth were arranged in her jaw and was mainly guesswork, but the victim's hair had been shoulder-length, and fair, and her Indian print dress was described. Her underclothing and tights had come from a multiple store. The likeness was circulated through every division in the country, but Detective Superintendent Wilshaw, head of the division which included Droxton and in charge of the murder investigation, knew that the imagined features might bear only a very slight resemblance to the girl as she was in life, and the chances of it leading to an identification were not high. There was no one missing in the area whom it could be, but the collator, in touch with other forces, might learn of missing women with similar characteristics. Dental records could lead to a positive identification, if that happened; it was the only hope, so far. Forensic tests on the girl's garments might, even after so long, produce traces of her killer; there could be an alien hair, for instance; but without a suspect to match them against, they would be useless, and without a name for the girl, the search for her killer could offer no hope of success.

Meanwhile, he might kill again.

10

The man had come up to Christine as she was leaving the station buffet. She had noticed him earlier, sitting at a table not far from hers and reading a newspaper while he drank his tea. He was quite old, and very respectable-looking.

She and her friend Lynn had left Manchester together rather on the spur of the moment. Originally, their plan had been to come to London in a few weeks' time, when they might be able to get seasonal work over Christmas in one of the big stores. Extra staff were sure to be needed then, and if they seemed bright and willing, as they were, they would be taken on, the girls felt sure, in preference to other applicants for any jobs that were going. They wouldn't be too choosy at first, they had decided, about what jobs they did. Anything would be more exciting than staying on at college, where they were both learning office procedures. Christine was fed up at home; she kept having rows with her stepmother, and trying their luck in London was her idea. They'd start off at a hostel and get a room – even a flat – later. They'd both brought their savings, and Christine had got hold of some other money which she hadn't yet told Lynn about.

On the train, Lynn felt ill. She'd been a bit queasy before leaving home, but once the journey began she grew steadily worse, and spent much of the time in the toilet compartment. When they arrived, she was green.

'I'll have to go back, Christine,' she said, on the platform. 'I really will – I feel awful.'

'You'll be all right when we get to the hostel. They'll give you something, fix you up in no time,' Christine said, but her heart sank at the sight of her friend's face.

Lynn was thinking with dismay of how much the trip had already cost, and what she must now pay to go home, but she held on.

'I can't go through with it, Christine,' she said. 'Not feeling like this. I'll come later. You get fixed up and let me know where you are. I'll only hold you up.'

For a moment Christine thought of turning back too, but that would solve none of her own problems.

'Will you be all right on the train?' she asked.

Lynn nodded. She'd never been as keen on this scheme as Christine, for things were easier for her at home, and indeed, at the prospect of returning to the distracted but effective care of her busy working mother she already felt better. It would take some time to save enough money to come again.

116

When Lynn had gone, Christine felt very uneasy. In front of her friend she had acted boldly, pretending there was nothing to fear. Now, alone, she must find the way to one of the hostels on the list they'd made in the library at home from the yellow pages of the London telephone directory. Standing on the busy concourse with her suitcase, Christine could not decide which address to try. Which was the nearest to where she was now, she wondered. Who could she ask?

At Euston station there was an advice bureau for just such people as Christine, but she failed to see the sign as she walked towards the exit. The station was bustling with people leaving London for the weekend. Christine turned back, and, to postpone resolute action, went into the nearby buffet where she put her case down by a corner table and lined up to buy a cup of tea and a bun.

He saw her several places ahead of him in the queue and he picked her out at once as a possibility, a lost girl on her own acting big, faking courage. It was almost too easy, he thought, watching Christine eat her bun.

He followed her from the buffet and spoke to her as she hesitated outside, looking at the various direction indicators. He told her he worked at a nearby hostel which was nice and friendly and would have a vacancy for her. Christine had no qualms as she set off with him on the last journey of her life.

Only a few people got off the late train at Murford that Friday night. Jenny was first through the barrier, where her mother was waiting.

'Haven't you any luggage?' were Nina's first words when they had hugged briefly. Unexpected tears pricked her eyes at the contact and her voice was gruff.

'Everything I need's in here,' Jenny said cheerfully, indicating the plastic carrier bag she held. She wore jeans and a duffle coat.

'I hope you've brought a toothbrush,' said Nina, motioning her out to the car.

Jenny tossed her carrier on to the back seat and stretched out her thin legs as Nina started the engine. The beam of her headlights picked up a man who was walking towards the car park.

'Hullo, that's Dan,' said Nina.

'Dan?'

'Dan Fenton, the gardener. I must have told you about him,' said Nina. She pulled up beside him and wound down her window. 'Do you want a lift?' she asked.

'Oh – good evening, Mrs Crowther,' said Dan, and he lifted his hat. 'No, thank you. My car's here.'

'This is my younger daughter, Jenny,' Nina said. 'She's come down for the weekend.'

'Hullo,' Jenny called, across her mother.

'That's nice,' said Dan. 'I'll be along in the morning, Mrs Crowther.'

'Oh good,' Nina said. 'I'll see you then. Good-night.'

'He only just caught the train,' said Jenny as they drove off. 'He was in the same compartment as I was – he came running along as the train was leaving, and just managed to get on.'

'So that's where he goes when he doesn't come to the Hall,' said Nina. 'I wonder what he does in London? Perhaps he's got an old mother, or something.' He was a bit old himself to have a mother still, Nina thought; the 'or something' was much more likely. She vaguely imagined a blowsy woman with jet black hair and carmine lips, hung about with beads and bangles. 'Take notice of Murford, Jenny. We're almost through it.'

'What's Murford got, then?' asked Jenny, peering through the windscreen.

'Not a lot. It's a market town – cattle sales and things. I'm surprised it's still got a station. It connects at Droxton with the main line to the Midlands.'

'Have you turned into a country bumpkin, Mum?' Jenny asked. 'I mean – cattle sales!'

'Well, I haven't been to one, if that's what you're thinking,' Nina said. 'But I've got some green wellies. They're uniform here.'

'That's a start,' Jenny said. 'You could do worse than take up country crafts. You're so good at sewing. You could make patchwork and things. Start a business.'

Nina thought this sounded rather an ambitious

scheme. She concentrated on the road, aware of lights behind her, though not too close: probably Dan.

'Shall I drive?' offered Jenny, as they trundled along at forty miles an hour.

'If you do, we'll have to put on the L plates,' said Nina. 'It's not worth stopping now, it isn't far. We'll go out somewhere tomorrow – that would be nice – and you can drive then.'

'OK,' Jenny said. 'When you've paid me my train fare, I'll take you out to lunch in a pub. I bet you haven't been anywhere since you got down here.'

'I've been to tea at the Manor,' said Nina.

'Big deal,' said Jenny. 'I can't wait to hear about it.' But she gave her mother no chance to describe the event, prattling on about her own activities – the societies she had joined and her work. Nina listened with half an ear, concentrating on the road. She felt proud of her busy, confident daughter.

The following lights turned off as they went through Netherton St Mary, and Jenny was silent as they drove on out of the village to the Hall.

'It is a bit out of things, isn't it?' she said.

Nina turned in at the Hall gates.

'A bit,' she agreed. She felt oddly proprietorial as they approached the house. 'You get used to it,' she added.

'Cor, what a heap!' exclaimed Jenny when she saw it. 'Bit gloomy, isn't it? Like a junior cathedral.'

'It's very comfortable inside,' said Nina. 'But I agree, it's not very beautiful.'

Rory was pleased to see them. He snuffed and sniffed round Jenny, wagging his tail and licking her hand.

'I'm starving, Mum,' said Jenny. 'Have you got any food?'

They'd had scrambled eggs the last time they'd had supper together at Silverlea, Nina remembered. She took the big frying pan out of the cupboard and had just laid some rashers in it when the telephone rang.

'I'll go,' Jenny said. 'Where's the phone?' She rushed from the room pursuing the sound.

'No!' Nina called after her. It was later than his usual time, but she knew who was calling. She hurried out, hoping to stop Jenny from answering, but she was too late.

Jenny, in the hall, was talking crossly into the instrument.

'Who do you want? Who's there? Hullo?' she kept repeating, and then said to Nina, who stood watching her, 'There's no one there.'

'No, there isn't. Hang up,' ordered Nina.

Jenny stared at her, surprised at her peremptory tone, but she obeyed. Nina went to the telephone and put her hand on the receiver. She waited a few seconds, then lifted it and listened. When she heard the dialling tone, she laid it on the table. Her hand shook.

'Mum!' Jenny cried. 'What are you doing?'

'I've been getting these calls,' Nina said, trying

to keep her voice steady. 'Calls with no one there. Some fault in the exchange, I expect, but anyway, if it's off the hook, we can't get any more.'

'No obscene remarks?' said Jenny.

'No.'

'Breathing, though. I heard that,' Jenny said.

'Yes,' admitted Nina.

'How long has this been going on?' Jenny demanded.

'Oh – it only happens now and then,' Nina said. 'Not very often.'

'What have you done about it?'

Nina told her what the police had said.

'I haven't reported it to the exchange yet,' she said. 'He hasn't rung for a bit.' But there had been a call the night before. Did it come in cycles, this madness?

'I'll fix him,' said Jenny. 'Just leave your nutty caller to me.'

'What do you mean?'

'All you need is a whistle. We'll get one tomorrow. I expect there's a sports shop in Murford or somewhere that sells them. All you do, when he rings again, is blow very loudly. That'll finish his nasty little game. With luck, it'll give him a headache, and it might even burst an eardrum,' said Jenny with relish.

'That seems a bit drastic,' Nina suggested.

'Well, it serves him right,' Jenny said. 'He's not ringing from a callbox, is he? No pips.'

'No,' said Nina. It was odd to think of someone, somewhere, standing in a building dialling

122

the number of the Hall, perhaps from a living-room, or a deserted office.

'Poor Mum, with a weirdo to deal with,' said Jenny. 'It's a good thing I'm here, isn't it?'

'Yes, dear, very,' said Nina. 'Heavens – your bacon. It'll be cinders.'

But all was well. Nina pulled the pan to the side to cool it before breaking the eggs into it.

'I think I'll have some too,' she said, adding a third egg to the two she had put out for Jenny. She fetched two more rashers, laying them alongside the others.

'Good idea,' said Jenny. 'You've lost weight, haven't you? Mind you, it's an improvement,' she added. 'You were getting a bit of middle-aged spread.'

Tears pricked Nina's eyes again. Children set you up and then put you down sharply, without a pang, she thought, but they told you the truth. Sitting at the table with Jenny she found it hard to remember when she had last eaten a proper meal.

Having Jenny there was wonderful, but she must not say so too effusively; neither of the girls favoured displays of emotion. And she'd better not get too accustomed to her company, Nina thought: it would make letting her go at the end of her visit so painful.

In the morning, Nina had been up some time before, wearing a loose, shaggy sweater over her nightdress, Jenny appeared. She came into the kitchen yawning and stretching, her fair, silky hair unbrushed and her face still shiny with sleep. To Nina, she looked about fourteen.

Nina was making pastry. Jenny loved treacle tart.

'Kettle's on the boil, and coffee's in that cupboard,' Nina said, pointing.

'Oh Mum, things haven't changed. That's what you always said at home,' Jenny said.

'Well, this is home now,' said Nina. 'But take care. None of the things are ours.'

'Except that frightful cat in the bathroom,' said Jenny. 'That's yours, isn't it?' She'd seen it at Silverlea. 'Wherever did it come from? It's not your style at all.'

Nina was tempted to tell her the truth. They'd laugh, and Jenny would say 'Let's blow whistles in its ears and Caroline will go deaf,' or something like that. But Caroline would soon be married to Jenny's father, and Jenny would have to get on with her.

'It's a sort of joke mascot,' she said. At any time she could smash the cat, boil it in a pan, harm it somehow and vicariously torment her supplanter, Nina told herself. 'Would you like some porridge?'

'Just toast, thanks,' said Jenny. She wandered about the kitchen assembling her breakfast, pouring milk into her coffee, making herself several slices of toast which she loaded with butter and marmalade. She sat at the table to eat, watching her mother rolling the pastry.

'You enjoy cooking don't you?' she said.

'Yes – when I'm not in a rush and when there's someone to cook for,' said Nina.

'But you're never in a rush,' Jenny said. 'You're always so well organized. Dad's mad. I bet that Caroline can't cook for peanuts. She's as thin as a lath – well, I suppose she isn't by now,' she amended.

'I bored him,' Nina said flatly.

Maybe she had, after twenty-four years, Jenny thought, uneasily, but there must be more to it than that.

'Well—' words like loyalty, duty, came into her head, but they were not part of her everyday language and she would have been embarrassed to say them aloud. 'I think it's rough,' she said.

Nina decided to change the subject.

'When Dan comes, I thought we'd ask him to lunch,' she said, trimming pastry from the rim of the tin. 'There's plenty of food and he may be glad of something hot.'

'We were going to go to a pub,' said Jenny.

'Well, we can go out to tea instead,' Nina replied. 'I haven't asked Dan before,' she added. 'It never seemed a very good idea, somehow – just the two of us – though he's only the gardener.'

'Very prudent, Mum. You don't want to give him ideas, do you?' said Jenny. 'Stick to your middle-class values.'

'Don't be silly, Jenny,' Nina rebuked her. 'And

125

you'd better get some clothes on. He'll be in soon for his coffee and you're not decent.'

'Yes, I am,' said Jenny. 'I'm covered all over.'

'Well – he may not be used to young girls,' said Nina.

'Hasn't he got a family?'

Nina told her what she knew of Dan's sad history. Jenny was shocked.

'What a thing,' she said. 'Poor bloke. Are you sure he won't do for you, Mum?'

'You're outrageous,' said Nina, but she laughed.

'You mean because he's just the gardener?'

'No, of course not, and anyway he was something else first, I'm not sure what,' said Nina.

'Your prejudices are showing,' said Jenny.

'Not at all,' said Nina. 'There never could be anything like that between us. It's out of the question.'

'You mean, you don't fancy him,' said Jenny bluntly.

'Exactly,' said Nina. 'Since you put it so crudely.'

Dan wouldn't stay to lunch, although he was grateful for the invitation. He accepted a slice of hot treacle tart and bore it away on a plate wrapped in foil, which he put in his bicycle basket.

'Nice old boy, but I see what you mean,' said Jenny, when he had gone. 'And he is a bit old for you, Mum.'

They took Rory out in the afternoon. Jenny was

surprised by the modern buildings in the village, the explosion of houses.

'Before long the village and the Hall will join up,' she said.

'I doubt it. The land in between belongs to the Blunts, and they won't need to sell it,' said Nina. 'They let it to a farmer.'

'And these Jowetts – the flower-planting person – where do they live?' asked Jenny.

'We'll go past their house,' said Nina.

Thin sunlight shone on the Manor as they reached the big gates. One hinge was broken, and the open gate sagged; dead leaves lay at the sides of the drive, waiting, presumably for Heather to sweep them up. Didn't Guy help her at all, wondered Nina.

'It's lovely,' said Jenny. 'Big, though. What happens after they're dead?'

'Jenny!'

'Well, what does? Will a film star buy it, or something?'

'I've no idea,' said Nina. 'They've got a daughter – their son died. It would be a pity if it went out of the family – they've had it for generations. But they won't be dying just yet; they're not even seventy – well, he may be, but she's not, though she looks it. People quite often live to be ninety or more, these days.'

'Two old dears rattling round in there,' said Jenny. 'I bet they don't keep it properly.'

'It needs a few things done to bring it up to date, certainly,' Nina said. 'But they do keep it properly – the garden is beautiful and the house is very clean. I hope you don't think they should be turfed out and the place given over to a bunch of drug-taking drop-outs?'

'No, no. Cool down,' Jenny soothed her. 'I just thought it was a bit pathetic.'

'It isn't,' said Nina, but there was something in what Jenny said. Though there was much to admire in the way the Jowetts hung on to the place, with, she assumed, Guy's army pension their main source of income, it must be an exhausting struggle. 'The house is their whole life,' she said, with more conviction.

'You said the old boy paints. Have you seen any of his pictures?' asked Jenny as they turned back.

'No. He sells them, though, so they must be good,' said Nina.

Walking back, they passed the chapel, with fresh texts now framed, one showing an apple cut through to reveal the core rotting. The legend said *God sees the inside*.

'Ugh,' said Jenny. 'How beastly. I hate the idea of a Prying One up above.'

Nina thought anyone who might be up above had long since washed their hands of the problems below.

Jenny hadn't forgotten about the telephone call, and after their walk they went to Murford to buy the whistle, leaving Rory in the house. Jenny watched as Nina carefully carried out the locking ritual. A mixture of pity and admiration filled her;

her mother must be lonely in this huge place with only the dog for company – and she'd never been keen on dogs. The telephone calls were a worrying complication, yet she hadn't complained and, Jenny guessed, would not have mentioned them had it not been for Jenny answering one of the calls herself. She was showing spirit and mettle Jenny had not realized she possessed. She remembered a fall she had had as a child, when she had cut her leg very badly. Blood had poured from the wound, frightening her more than the pain. Her mother had been utterly calm, bathing the injury, then deciding it needed stitching and taking her off to have it done. When they reached home afterwards, the wound dressed, Nina had vanished upstairs, reappearing later ashen white. She had been very sick, she'd admitted. What would happen when this job ended? Would there be some sort of collapse then? The patchwork idea she'd suggested so lightly wasn't so far out, Jenny thought; her mother should have work of some kind. Apart from the independence it would bring, it would give her an identity of her own, even if Daddy did go on paying up. Jenny didn't trust Caroline not to make him find an excuse to cut off funds; she'd think the past years of marriage counted for nothing, but that wasn't right, not after so long, and when you remembered that women of her mother's age often lacked training. It wasn't enough to hope that Mum might, in time, meet some nice widower who would look after her. That wasn't the answer, not any more: a woman must be able to stand on her own feet.

They fixed the L-plates on the Metro and Jenny drove them to Murford.

'You must have some more proper lessons,' said Nina. 'I'll give you some for Christmas if you like. You should be able to take your test before long.'

Daddy had sent her a cheque for a course; conscience money, Jenny had thought, banking it. She didn't tell Nina about it.

They found a shop that sold sports gear; it stocked whistles. After buying one, they went to the Primrose Café for tea, where they each ate a large toasted teacake with strawberry jam. Nina had not eaten so much in so few hours since she came to the Hall. She felt better, though whether that was due to food or the company, she didn't know; perhaps it was both. When they returned to the Hall she got out of the car and waited while Jenny put it away in one of the several spare garages. They were both walking round to the back door, over which a light shone, when a tall figure suddenly loomed before them.

Jenny gave a startled shriek, but Nina managed to swallow hers, for she recognized Guy Jowett almost at once.

'Oh!' she gasped. 'Good evening.'

'Good evening, madam,' said Guy. 'Are you visiting Mrs Blunt?'

Nina sensed Jenny tense beside her. She put out a hand and pressed her daughter's arm warningly.

130

'The Blunts are away,' she said. 'But won't you come in for a glass of sherry? I'll telephone your wife and invite her to join us.'

'Oh – very well. Away, did you say?' said Guy. 'Are you sure? How long for?'

'Some weeks,' replied Nina. She walked on towards the house, the keys already in her hand.

Jenny stared curiously at the tall old man in the light that shone from above the back door as her mother undid it. Whoever was this?

'Come in,' said Nina, opening the door. 'This is my daughter Jenny. Jenny, this is Colonel Jowett from the Manor.' Nina was grateful to Dan for supplying her with this detail of martial rank, not disclosed by Heather, so that she made a correct introduction. She turned to the old man. 'Do come in,' she repeated. 'Jenny, you'll find glasses and a decanter of sherry in the dining-room. Please bring them to the study – four glasses.' Then she turned to Guy. 'Let me take your coat,' she said.

Guy allowed her to help him remove it, and gave it to her, with his cap.

'I must wash,' he said abruptly, and he headed along the passage to the cloakroom. Of course, he would be familiar with the house, Nina realized; he must often come here. She was recovering from her fright. She went into the study and stirred up the fire which had died down while they were out.

Jenny soon came in with the drinks tray.

'He's in the cloakroom,' Nina said. 'We'll get

131

him settled, then I'll ring Heather and she'll come to collect him.'

'Is he quite gaga?' asked Jenny.

The use of so brutal a word shocked Nina.

'I think he's ill,' she said. 'He's rather a dear. I like him.'

They waited ten minutes for Guy to return. Jenny was sure he had collapsed in the lavatory, but Nina had remembered his elaborate hand-washing ritual at their first meeting.

Jenny had to admit that he was a handsome old man as he smiled at her, accepting his sherry. Now, he seemed to know who Nina was, calling her by name and understanding that Jenny was her daughter. Nina left them together while she telephoned Heather, and Guy began to ask Jenny about her university course with apparent comprehension of her replies. When Nina returned, they were discussing *Hamlet*. Jenny was sitting on the floor in front of the fire and Guy was leaning back in a deep armchair, completely relaxed.

'He wasn't mad,' he was saying. 'It was a pretence, to get away with murder. Not such a bad idea.' Then he added, 'I've got a grand-daughter much your age. A little younger, perhaps. She isn't at university – doesn't plan to go there. She's mad on horses. It's not surprising, I suppose. Her mother was just the same.'

'I grew out of them,' said Jenny gravely.

'Her mother hasn't,' said Guy.

It seemed quite an interruption when Heather

arrived. She'd been on the point of going out in the car to seek her wandering spouse when Nina had rung. Her relief at finding him was evident; she eagerly took the glass of sherry Nina gave her.

Sherry was one of their treats, Nina remembered.

11

'He is rather an old charmer,' said Jenny, when Heather had taken her husband away. 'There's something about men of that generation – that type. I can see why you're taken with him, Mum.'

'Don't be ridiculous, Jenny,' said Nina. 'I'm not taken with him, as you put it. I'm sorry for him. He must have been a fine, active man, once.'

'He seemed perfectly sensible, once we were indoors and he'd got his drink,' said Jenny. 'It's pretty awful for her, though, if she has to keep chasing round after him all over the place.'

'I suppose he can't stray very far, if he's on foot,' said Nina. 'But it's getting dark early now – he might have an accident.'

After their supper they sat in the study with the television turned on to an old, indifferent film. Nina did her *gros point*, paying little attention to the screen, and after a time Jenny grew bored and began to examine the bookshelves.

'Golly, look! Here they all are when they were young!' she exclaimed.

'Who?'

'The Jowetts, and it must be the Blunts too. Fascinating! Come and see, Mum. Lots of old snaps,' said Jenny.

She was sitting on the floor inspecting a photograph album.

'Where did you get that?' Nina asked. 'Put it back.'

'Why? It's not private,' said Jenny. 'It was on the shelf, beside Thackeray. Just look at their clothes! Those skirts! Here, Mum,' and she got up and put the open album on her mother's lap, on top of the embroidery canvas. 'It's pure Noel Coward!'

Nina saw a print of some young people standing in a row, smiling self-consciously. The women's hair was waved, and their straight skirts were worn well below the knee. In some photographs they held tennis rackets. On most pages their names were neatly printed beneath, so that it was easy to learn that Guy was the slim young man with thick, dark hair, and Heather the tall, pretty girl beside him, her features strong even in youth.

'Don't they look happy?' said Nina, intrigued despite her words to Jenny. 'Here's Mrs Blunt – and this must be him – Leonard. He doesn't seem to come into many – I suppose he was the photographer.'

Priscilla Blunt, when young, had a soft, warm expression as she gazed at the camera. She had worn that look in Fortnum and Mason's as she listened to Nina's sorry tale, though her face had lost its smoothness and she was elegant now, rather than pretty.

There were pictures of the Hall, with a pre-war Austin saloon parked outside the front door. Jenny went on looking through the albums, while Nina returned to her sewing.

'Here are the children,' said Jenny suddenly. 'Look, Mum. The Jowetts and the Blunts, with two boys and a girl.' She read out the names. 'Robin, Charles and Rosemary.'

Nina, who was threading her needle with sage-green wool, became interested again and looked at the album. Three small children sat on a rug with a toy horse on wheels beside them. In the black-and-white photograph, slightly faded now, all wore pale clothes and looked excessively neat.

'Robin Jowett died when he was only twenty-one,' said Nina. 'His grave's in the churchyard.'

'How awful,' said Jenny. 'What happened?'

'A sailing accident, I believe,' said Nina.

Jenny did not ask her how she had learned this.

'Rosemary must be the horsey daughter,' she said, turning a page. 'What about Charles? I suppose he makes buns, like his dad.'

'Yes.'

'Nice to walk into such rich shoes,' said Jenny.

'I'm sure his father worked hard to acquire them,' Nina said, somewhat tartly.

'Yes – well.' Jenny inspected further snapshots. 'They are rather fun,' she said. 'Here are the children getting older. Look at those caps the boys are wearing!' She tittered at the sight of the two small boys in large tweed caps.

Nina could remember her own brother in one like that.

At last Jenny put the albums away, saying that she felt sleepy.

'It's all the country air,' she said. 'Don't forget the whistle, Mum, if your funny friend rings up tonight. It's here by the telephone. Just blow it as hard as you can.'

Nina said that she would. She sat on for some time after Jenny had gone upstairs, expecting the telephone to ring, but it didn't. At last she, too, decided to go to bed. She folded her sewing away inside its bag, plumped up the cushions and glanced round the room before switching out the light. The fire had burned right down, but she put the guard across.

Jenny had replaced the photograph albums, but one of them stuck out from the shelf, breaking the neat line. Nina went to push it back, but instead, she removed it, and began looking through it. In the centre of this one were some wedding photographs of Leonard and Priscilla, in 1938. 'Peace in our Time!' was written below. Those were the Prime Minister's words, said after Munich. Nina had seen Neville Chamberlain on television so often, when old news reels were shown, that she thought she remembered the original occasion, but as she was only a year old at the time, that was hardly likely.

She leafed on through the album and soon saw

photographs of Guy and Leonard in uniform, one an army officer, the other in naval uniform with the words Sub-Lieutenant Leonard Blunt, R.N.V.R., printed below. There were prints of Priscilla in uniform, too; she was a Red Cross nurse; but after that, apart from a few snapshots of Rosemary Jowett, at first in a pram and then as a toddler, there was a gap which covered most of the war years. The history continued with the photographs Nina had already seen. She moved on to another album, her attention caught. Had Jenny noticed what she now saw? Surely not, or she would have said so. Nina felt, still, that in a sense she was prying, but as Jenny had said, the albums were kept openly on the shelf, and certainly photographs were not as private as letters.

There were a number of prints of the three children, Charles, Robin and Rosemary. Nina scrutinized them. She had not imagined the likeness between the two boys; it was pronounced, and it persisted through the years. There they were as young men, standing beside an old Morris Minor, both of them grinning. By now, Robin was taller than Charles, just as Guy was taller than Leonard, but they were still very alike.

The sequence of albums ended after 1963, as though with Robin's death photography had ceased to be a hobby, but there were earlier albums here, which Jenny had not opened. They went back another generation, and Nina saw women in long skirts, with wide, shady hats, standing outside the Hall. There were ancient cars, a chauffeur in leggings, a pony and trap. So the Blunts had been here a long time: that was a surprise to Nina; perhaps they had built the house. She picked out Leonard's parents, and some brothers and sisters. What had become of them, she wondered: were they still in the firm? Families were larger then. The ink beneath the entries had faded, and often it was hard to read the names.

It was getting late when she came to the last album. Nina glanced through it, intrigued by the history it revealed. She looked at her watch when she returned the book to the shelf and saw that it was after half-past eleven. He had never rung so late; she felt sure it would be all right tonight.

In the morning it rained.

On Sunday morning, while Nina was busy preparing vegetables for lunch, Jenny slipped off to the study where, if she used the telephone, she could not be overheard. She had promised to ring Alec, to pronounce on her mother's condition. If she seemed all right, Alec would come over to collect Jenny. He was aware that there might be problems; Jenny might even have to find a callbox to use; but he had promised to wait near the telephone until half-past ten. After that, he'd give up.

While the number rang, Jenny idly turned the pages of the telephone directory. There were the Jowetts – Lt. Col. G.R., she read, The Manor House.

Someone answered the telephone and went off to fetch Alec, who had been standing nearby only minutes before. Jenny turned back through the directory, and the name Fenton suddenly stood out from the page. Fenton, D.E., she read, and a Netherton St Mary number. Then Alec came to the telephone and she closed the directory.

The shining whistle glinted at her throughout her conversation.

Jenny found her mother receptive to the idea of one extra for lunch even though he might be late; she was glad that Jenny would have a lift back.

'I'll bring him next time I come,' said Jenny. 'If that's OK. I thought I'd better not, the first time, as it isn't our house and all that.'

Nina gave permission. She'd clear it with Leonard Blunt's secretary on the telephone, and another time, if she took such a post, it would have to be part of the deal.

'Tell me about Alec,' she added.

'Oh – it's not serious,' said Jenny lightly. 'He's a biologist.'

'Oh – he can talk, then,' said Nina.

This made Jenny laugh. She'd been out for some time with a budding mathematician who was by nature morose. Neither Nina nor Martin had managed to extract more than monosyllabic replies from him when he came to Silverlea.

Nina wanted to beg Jenny not to stick exclusively to Alec, but she knew the modern way was to cling to a partner, once found, or you were considered a social outcast. It seemed to her that, paired in this fashion, it was almost as difficult to break away as to leave a marriage. The so-called freedom of this generation was a myth.

Alec turned out to be short and merry; he had a mop of curly hair which, if he'd been a girl, Nina would have thought was permed. Perhaps it was. He wore corduroy trousers, not jeans, and a tie.

Nina saw by the tie that he had made an effort, wanting her to approve of him. She warmed to him instantly. He'd brought a bottle of wine, and he stood up when she entered the room. Without being asked, he revealed that his father was a farmer who had five hundred acres in Cornwall on the edge of a real village, not a developing one like Netherton St Mary.

When the young people departed that evening, Nina felt bleak. The house seemed so silent. She called Rory to her, and he, who had been wandering round looking melancholy after the car had gone, laid his head on her knee and made a sad howling sound.

Nina, at this, could not hold back her tears any longer. She wept for ten minutes while the dog looked at her sadly.

At last she was able to make an effort to pull herself together. She went off to wash her face, then tried to settle with the paper, but she could not concentrate. There were only the God-spots on television and she did not want to watch them. She went over to the bookshelves and took down one of the later photograph albums, spreading it open at a page showing the two boys, Charles and

Robin, aged about twenty. Then she hunted back through the earlier ones to the first photographs showing Guy Jowett as a young man.

Robin Jowett resembled his father. He had dark hair, straight, well-defined eyebrows and deep-set eyes. Charles Blunt, though shorter and more sturdily built, was also dark. He had the same thick, straight brows over deep-set eyes.

It's chance, Nina thought: the figures in the photographs were, after all, small. She looked again at the Blunts' black-and-white wedding photographs, taken when they were young. Leonard's hair, which she remembered as thin and sandy, looked fair. Both of them had gently arched brows.

It proved nothing. Even so, she could not stop thinking about it.

That night the telephone rang at twenty minutes to eleven, and she heard the soft sigh of her unknown caller.

The whistle, placed by Jenny near the telephone, winked up at her. Nina picked it up, took a deep breath, hesitated for a moment, for it seemed a ridiculous action, then took another deep breath and blew hard. She put the receiver back without waiting for any reaction and went up to bed feeling extremely shaky. But Jenny would be pleased and if it worked she need not ask the telephone exchange to intervene.

12

Lynn felt better as her train drew in to the station, but her stomach had started churning again by the time she got off the bus at the corner near her home. If her parents had found the note she had left in her room, there'd be a row.

Her parents owned a newsagent and tobacconist's shop on the edge of the city. It was a lucrative business, with low overheads as both her mother and father worked there full time, and there was a flat above, where they had lived years ago, which was let at a good rent. Their day, however, was long, and both were always tired in the evenings.

Lynn and her friend Christine had both left school that summer and had enrolled on the same business course, but Christine had dropped out after the first week. She spent her days in coffee bars, and most afternoons met Lynn in time for the two girls to go home together. Lynn was not enjoying her course, which had been her parents' idea; they thought a knowledge of book-keeping would help her when she started to work in the shop. Lynn didn't look forward to that; she wanted to do something more exciting – be a model, work in a dress shop – and she had let Christine talk her into their escapade. She had planned to telephone her parents that night, when she and Christine were installed in their hostel, to spare them worry. She often went out in the evenings, to a disco with Christine or to the home of some other girl, but her parents always knew where she went and she was never late home.

Christine's was a different case. Her mother was dead, and her older brother and sister were married. Her father had recently married again and his wife, Iris, was young. Christine felt Iris usurped her mother's place, and the girl was incapable of responding to her new stepmother's friendly overtures. She was rude and uncooperative. Her mother had been a good cook and home-maker, but Iris was not, and the meals she prepared were mainly fry-ups or came out of tins. The house, once neat, was neglected and grubby. Christine had taken a pride in looking after her father and keeping the place clean after her mother's death. Now she was not needed. Lynn had sympathized with her wish to start a new life.

Walking up the path to the house where she lived with her parents and younger brother, Lynn planned to accept whatever scolding, and even punishment, she received without complaint. She'd think hard before running away again.

As she entered the house – she had her own

key – she heard the radio playing. Lights were on in several rooms, but there was no one at home. Lynn went upstairs at once to her own bedroom. The note was still there, on her pillow, where she had left it. Heart thumping, she tore it into tiny pieces and flushed them away down the lavatory. In the kitchen, propped by the bread bin, was a note with her name on it. It said that her grandmother had had a bad fall and broken her leg. Her mother and father had gone to the hospital and might not be back till late.

She'd been reprieved! Lynn couldn't believe her luck, though she was sorry about her grandmother, of whom she was fond. Never had the house felt so safe and welcoming! She even felt hungry. She made herself scrambled eggs on toast and a cup of tea, went upstairs and had a bath, and was in bed when her brother, Neil, came back from the neighbour's where he had spent the evening.

In the morning, Christine's father came round to see if by any chance his daughter had spent the night at Lynn's, as she sometimes did. He was not on the telephone, so she couldn't have rung to say that she wouldn't be home.

Lynn was asked if she knew where Christine was.

She knew she was safe, for she'd seen her arrive in London, but she didn't know where she was; not exactly. She barely hesitated before giving her answer, for she could still save herself.

'I don't know where she is,' said Lynn.

'Christine's got other friends besides Lynn,' said Iris Potter when her husband returned after seeing Lynn's parents.

'She's never stayed away without telling us,' said Frank.

'Maybe she's doing it on purpose to make us worry,' said Iris.

'Now, why would she want to do that?'

'Well, Frank, she doesn't go much on me, does she? You can't deny that.'

'She'll come round,' Frank said, uncomfortably, but he found Iris's theory credible, though it angered him. They were both nice girls. Why couldn't they get on? He'd often heard Christine make hurtful remarks to Iris, and, in private, he'd scolded her for it. If Iris was right, she'd be back in a day or two. She'd want money, for one thing.

Iris discovered her money had gone from the tin where she kept what Frank gave her that afternoon, which was her Saturday off. She'd planned to buy a new dress from La Boutique, but she couldn't do that anyway, with Frank so upset; it wouldn't be right. She didn't tell him about the money. When Christine came back, she'd ask her about it and make her repay it. She'd enough of her own to manage with, meanwhile.

Frank was sure Christine would return on Sunday; she'd want to get ready for college next day – wash her hair, all that. Over the weekend he'd been to see several of her school friends to find out if anyone knew where she was, but no one could tell him. It was not pleasant, admitting to the parents of other youngsters that she'd gone off without a word. People went 'Tch, tch,' and looked sympathetic, but Frank was sure they blamed him for her disappearance. If he hadn't remarried – and a girl young enough to be his daughter – it wouldn't have happened, he inferred. None of the youngsters told him that Christine had dropped out of college, though several of them knew.

He searched for a note in her room, and saw that the suitcase he'd bought her for a school trip to France a few years ago had gone. He could find no washing things, nor a hairbrush. In a way these discoveries were a relief for this meant her departure was planned; she hadn't been whisked by magic from the streets, or so he thought then.

He took Monday morning off from work and went to the college to confront her himself. He was there for over an hour, for when she did not appear he made enquiries, and soon found that she had not been in for some time.

What had she been doing? What did it all mean? He didn't know where to start looking for her now. Perhaps, he thought hopefully, she'd gone to her married sister or brother? He should have thought of that before. Both lived some distance away. He couldn't get hold of them till the evening, since both couples were out at work all day, so he went back to his own job, meanwhile. That evening he rang both families from a telephone box. When neither had any news, he went to the police.

Police Constable Young came round to the Potters' house to collect a photograph of Christine and to find out what she had been wearing when she left home. At the police station, Frank had not been able to give a certain description of her clothes, though she usually wore jeans and an anorak unless she was off to the disco, and sometimes even then. Iris might know which of her clothes were missing, he thought.

'That will be Christine's mother,' said Young. He was a big, slow-moving man with a high bald forehead and pale eyes. Facing him, Frank was glad they were both on the same side; he thought it would be hard to get past that penetrating gaze with a lie.

He explained about his new wife.

'And did they get on? Her and Christine?' Young asked.

'Well,' said Frank, and was silent. His tone was a reply, and Young, who had heard this sort of story before, prodded him gently.

'It's quite usual to have trouble with kids, when a parent marries again,' he said. He'd been married twice himself. His first wife hadn't been able to accept the demands of the job, with its unsocial hours and sudden spells of overtime. She'd taken the kids, when she left.

Frank admitted that Christine had not taken kindly to Iris.

'Mind you, Iris has been very good – very patient,' he said. 'But she's not like Christine's own mum.'

When Young saw Iris, he felt a twinge of envy, quickly suppressed as disloyal. His second wife was a tough, sturdy woman his own age who had been married before to a soldier who was killed in Northern Ireland. She had grown strong herself, while alone with her two children, and she was a good sort of wife for a policeman; he'd been lucky to meet her. But she hadn't the looks of Iris.

Young noticed a pile of ironing on the kitchen dresser, the unwashed dishes heaped in the sink. Well, it didn't do to set too much store by that; he'd seen a lot worse. He went up to Christine's room with Frank and Iris. Iris looked among Christine's clothes and said that a lot had gone, including a green wool skirt and the mock fur jacket Frank had bought her for her sixteenth birthday.

'So she's planning to be away some time,' said Young. 'What about money?'

Frank thought she spent most of her pocket money on clothes and cosmetics, though there were her fares to college, of course, and her meals. He gave her as much as he could, but she wasn't likely to have a lot put by.

'How will she manage, if she's skint?' he asked, his worried face sagging. 'She'll be—' he couldn't bring himself to say what she might be forced to do.

Iris put a hand on his arm.

'She's got some money, love,' she said. 'There was some in the dresser drawer. I keep a bit there. It's gone. There was nearly a hundred pounds.'

Frank was furious.

'She stole it – she took your money,' he said, and as he rubbed his hands across his face Iris saw him through new eyes. He looked really old.

'I expect she felt it was yours. She knew it came from you,' Iris said. 'That wasn't like stealing.'

'It was stealing,' Frank insisted.

'Let's have a list of her friends,' said Young. 'She may have told someone her plans.'

Frank said he'd already asked them, but Young said they must be asked again. He began writing down their names. He told Frank that most youngsters who went missing turned up quite soon; they learned their lesson and came back home. Only a few were never heard of again.

Lynn couldn't think why Christine hadn't phoned on Sunday. She couldn't be job-hunting on a Sunday. Had she already found new friends and was too busy with them to remember her old ones?

Lynn went to college on Monday. If she worked hard, she thought guiltily, her grandmother, who was still very ill, would get better. She bent industriously to her studies that day, but during breaks her thoughts returned to Christine. Was she already at work in a shop? Christine had said that a job in a shop, or even as a waitress, could lead to all sorts of things. An agent passing through might notice you as just the type he was wanting, and sign you up. Such a case had been written about in a book she'd read. In Christine's vocabulary, books and magazines were synonymous. She'd read a good few in her truant hours.

Lynn saw Christine's father at the college that morning. She expected to be sent for and questioned about her friend, but that did not happen.

On Monday evening she and Neil were at home watching television. Their parents had gone to the hospital after closing the shop – her mother had been there for most of the day – for her grandmother's condition had deteriorated. When the doorbell rang, Neil went to open it. They had been told to be careful when alone in the house; although the area was a quiet, respectable suburb, break-ins could happen anywhere, and at any hour.

A uniformed woman police officer stood on the step, and at first Neil thought she brought news about their grandmother, but Lynn knew why Woman Police Constable Dixon had called as soon as she entered the house, and her stomach lurched.

After years of working at the same level as her male colleagues on cases of drunken disorder, theft, and even riot control, WPC Dixon was now, like other women police officers, specializing in work with children, assaults on women, and domestic problems, as had been typically the woman police officer's role for years until the Equal Opportunities Act decreed that there were no differences between male and female officers. First she established why Lynn and Neil's parents were not at home. As Lynn explained, Beryl Dixon perceived her unease, and suggested that Neil might care to make them all a cup of tea while she and Lynn had a chat.

'What do you want to talk to her about?' Neil asked, squaring his shoulders and looking tough. 'She's not done nothing wrong.'

'No, I'm sure she hasn't,' said WPC Dixon. 'I'm not here about anything like that. I want to talk to her about Christine Potter. You're close friends, aren't you, Lynn?' she added, and when Lynn nodded, continued to Neil, 'Lynn probably knows a good deal about where she spent her time and who her friends were. She's missing from home, you know. You do know that, don't you?'

'Yes. Mr Potter came round,' said Neil. Reassured that his sister was not about to be arrested, he went off to the kitchen, and WPC Dixon suggested to Lynn that they might sit down while the kettle boiled. In the living-room, she sat on the sofa and watched Lynn turn off the television and subside into a chair as far away as possible.

'Now, Lynn, you do know something, don't

you?' said WPC Dixon. 'Did Christine go off with a boyfriend?'

Lynne's mouth had gone dry.

'No.'

'But you do know where she went?'

Lynn looked anywhere but at the police-woman.

'Well? I suggest you tell me before your brother comes back,' said WPC Dixon. 'All we want to do is find her, Lynn. Make certain she's safe. If she is, there's no need to worry.'

This made sense.

'She went to London,' said Lynn, in hoarse tones.

'I see. You know that for certain, do you?'

Lynn nodded.

'Do you know when? Was it on Friday, the day she didn't go home? She didn't go somewhere else first?'

'No – it was Friday,' said Lynn.

'But you didn't tell Mr Potter when he came asking?' said WPC Dixon. 'Why not?'

Lynn swallowed.

'He said, did I know where she was. I didn't, exactly. She said she'd phone up, but she hasn't,' she said.

'Did you know her plans? Had she any friends in London? Somewhere to stay?' asked WPC Dixon.

'She'd got some addresses of hostels. She wrote them down from the yellow pages in the library,' said Lynn.

'Do you know which ones she meant to try?'

'Not really. She just wrote them all down,' said Lynn. 'We – she said there were plenty.'

WPC Dixon noticed the slip. Lynn knew more about Christine's disappearance than she was willing to say, but she may have made a pact with her friend to keep her secret. Antagonizing the girl would not help to trace Christine.

'You can't tell me any more?' the policewoman asked as Neil came in with the tea. 'Do you know which train she caught, for instance?'

Lynn told her.

WPC Dixon noted it mentally. In the absence of the girl's parents, she had written nothing down. She stayed for a cup of tea; a few more minutes would make little difference in the hunt for Christine, who was probably safely installed in a hostel in London while her father made himself ill with worry. It was important to establish a friendly feeling between herself and these two young people.

When she had gone, Lynn rounded on Neil.

'Don't say anything,' she warned him. 'Don't tell Mum and Dad she was here.'

'But it was about Christine,' said Neil.

'Never mind. You're too young to understand,' said Lynn. 'No one likes the police at their house.'

Neil thought it would be bad tactics to say that, even though it was dark, a neighbour might have noticed the police car outside. If he told, Lynn would get back at him, he knew. There were lots of ways she could do it, like telling her mother that he came home from school by the canal path, which he was forbidden to do in case he got into a fight and fell in, as had happened to one of his friends. There were plenty of ways in which he transgressed against parental rules and which Lynn had discovered.

He agreed to keep quiet.

13

Nina received a letter from Mr Drew, the solicitor, on Monday morning. Though bearing a first class stamp, and postmarked with Friday's date, it had taken the whole weekend to make its way to Netherton St Mary. It contained hard news, and Nina knew it would have spoiled her time with Jenny if she had read it sooner. The sale of Silverlea was not going ahead: Martin intended to live there himself and was moving in quite soon. Nina couldn't help wondering if this had been his plan all along, but he must have discovered that she was no longer there and perhaps that had influenced him. He had, through his own solicitor, agreed to release capital to her; indeed, if he did not, the court would order him to do so and he could be forced to disclose his assets in order to arrange a fair sum. Unless there was a quick, satisfactory response, Mr Drew would take the matter to court, but some delay was inevitable and much depended on how Martin planned to raise the money.

Nina had to concede that Mr Drew's doubts about Martin's intentions had been justified, but what she minded most was the thought of Caroline occupying the house which had been her own home for so many years.

When she took Rory out, she walked glumly along with her head down, just like the old men she met daily walking their dogs. She almost collided with Heather Jowett outside the grocer's, where most days now Nina went for some small purchase. She and Mr Goody were quite friendly by this time. She had grown used to his hand going straight from the cheese and the ham to the till.

'Sorry,' said Nina, who had been about to tether Rory to the railings outside the shop.

'My fault,' said Heather. 'I wasn't looking where I was going. Nina, thank you for retrieving Guy the other night. I was going to ring you. Has your daughter gone?'

'Yes.'

'You'll be missing her. Come and have tea this afternoon,' said Heather. 'I can't stop now – Guy hasn't settled this morning, I don't know why. You didn't meet him, did you?'

'No.'

'He's in an odd mood. Perhaps he caught a chill that night. Anyway, it would be nice if you came. We don't see many people.'

Nina accepted. Since the Jowetts regarded shop-bought scones as a treat, how would they react if she made them a cake and took it round, she wondered. She'd love to do it, but perhaps it would be wrongly interpreted. It would be dreadful to offend them, and really she hardly knew them.

Perhaps, after all, she didn't need to buy anything from Mr Goody today, she thought, turning away. There was food left over from the weekend, and Rory's tinned supply of Blunt's branded dogfood stretched along a whole shelf in the larder. Her purpose had really been to exchange a few words with another person.

Dan had brought her paper. When she got back, she sat in the kitchen reading it. By coincidence, there was an article on the woman's page by a bright thirty-year-old journalist advising divorced women – of whom the journalist was one – to retrain for a career. But what was the good of such counsel to her, Nina thought. With so much unemployment, who would take on an older woman? And train for what? Was she capable of going to college now? Could she live like Jenny while she learned something or other? What could she usefully study?

Dan found her sitting there when he came in for his coffee.

'Well, now,' he said, feeling embarrassed, for he saw that she had been crying.

Nina jumped up, dabbing away at her face with a handkerchief.

'Oh – sorry, Dan, I'd forgotten the time,' she said.

'You'll be missing Jenny,' he stated.

Nina accepted this excuse for her tears.

'Yes,' she said.

'She'll be back to see you soon,' said Dan.

He wanted to comfort her. He wanted to put his arms round her, draw her close, feel her softness, her hair brushing his cheek.

Instead, he sat down with his cup of coffee.

Guy's paintings were so bad.

Nina stood in the small attic room which he used as a studio, trying to think of a kindly comment. She had small confidence in her own artistic judgement, but these scenes, with the crude colours, the trees and buildings geometrically arranged like sentinels, offended her eye. If she had not been standing beside the artist as she looked at the work on the easel, Nina would have thought it had been done by an eight-year-old child. Vivid blue sky surmounted a landscape dotted with dark trees; there was an orange-coloured church in the centre of the picture, with a donkey, its limbs stick-like, its ears exaggeratedly large, standing nearby. Looking round the room, Nina saw other paintings stacked against the walls, presumably waiting for Heather to take them away for sale. All were vivid scenes with the same sort of dark trees, harsh orange or terracotta buildings with scarlet roofs, and overhead, always, the brilliant sky.

'Where is it?' she asked, of the work on the easel. Surely this wasn't England?

'It's Italy,' said Guy, standing back to squint critically at his masterpiece. 'The camp was over in this direction,' and he pointed away from the canvas.

'The camp?' said Nina.

'Guy was a prisoner in Italy during the war,' said Heather.

'I began painting then,' said Guy. 'Several of us took it up to while away the time between escapes. Others studied for degrees. Painting's a relaxing occupation. I decided to take it up again when I retired. Now it pays the bills.'

Who on earth would want these paintings, Nina wondered.

'How long does a picture take you?' she asked.

'Oh – a week or two. It depends,' said Guy.

'Do you use photographs?'

'The photographs are in here,' said Guy, tapping his head.

Nina nodded, and searched her wits for further comment. She was saved by Heather, who said it was time for tea as the kettle would have boiled by now. Asking to see Guy's work had seemed an obvious request to make in a conversational lull after she arrived. She had been taken to the drawing room, where a smoky fire burned in the grate, so her advent was being treated as an occasion. The room was cold, however; draughts whistled in through the windows and past the long curtains. Guy had seemed pleased with Nina's interest; he had led the way up the stairs, along an icy passage whose floor was covered in threadbare brown Wilton carpet, and up a further flight of stairs, lino-covered, to the top floor and this north-facing room which must once have been, Nina supposed, a maid's bedroom. Would the children have slept up here too, she wondered, in a nursery suite under the eaves, cut off from their parents, banished with a nanny? Guy's studio contained nothing except his bench, easel, a high stool and other equipment, and a calor gas stove.

As they left the room to go downstairs, Guy stood back by the door, holding it for the two women. He followed them out, closing the door. There was something about him that touched Nina's heart. He had no idea that his work was worthless. Yet it couldn't be, she reminded herself: it sold.

'I must wash,' said Guy abruptly, in the hall. He turned off into what must be the cloakroom.

'Can I help you?' Nina asked Heather.

'No. You go and sit down,' said Heather. 'I won't be a minute with tea – I must just get Guy a clean towel.'

Nina wandered back to the drawing room, where she rescued the ailing fire by judiciously moving some of the logs into better positions. There were radiators in the room; she touched one and found it stone-cold. Heating oil was very expensive; perhaps having the central heating on was another Jowett treat, Nina thought, and sat down in an armchair. It sagged, badly in need of re-upholstering.

Minutes passed.

Nina remembered Guy's elaborate washing ritual as she had witnessed it at their first meeting;

she thought of the time he had spent in the cloak-room at the Hall on Saturday. What was behind this obsession with washing?

She had almost decided to go in search of her hostess when she heard a clunking sound outside and Heather came in, pushing an ancient tea-trolley. Nina sprang to help her before the milk spilled and, between them, they steered it to harbour in front of the fire.

'Ah – that's burned up well,' said Heather. 'I knew it would,' and she looked with satisfaction at the fire. Much of the heat was disappearing up the wide chimney. 'Sit down, Nina. Guy's just coming.'

He entered as she spoke, smiled vaguely at Nina, and sat in an armchair at one side of the hearth.

Heather had made some hard little rock buns. Guy, balancing his plate on his bony knee, cut his bun exactly in half, then split it. He spread it carefully with a minuscule amount of butter and cut it again, this time into bite-sized pieces suitable for a small infant. Then he frowned, laid his knife down on the plate and put the plate on the small table beside him, where Heather had placed his tea. He looked at his hands, holding them out before him, pale and long-fingered. He started to rise.

Heather got up and pushed him gently back into his chair.

'It's all right, darling,' she said. 'You've washed.'

'Oh – yes,' said Guy. He sat back, and then, as if

162

nothing unusual had happened, suddenly began to talk. He described hiding in Italy, in the Apennines in the snow; visits from partisans who brought food; the intense cold; finally, with the improved weather, the hopeful though ill-advised southerly trudge towards the advancing armies.

Nina listened, amazed. His voice grew stronger as he talked, and, animated, he seemed younger. All of a sudden, as suddenly as he had begun, he stopped talking and began to eat his bun.

'More tea, Nina?' said Heather calmly, and asked about Jenny's plans. They discussed the disillusionment young people must feel when, after having high hopes, they failed to find jobs at all, much less any post worthy of higher education and qualifications.

'It was different when we were young,' Heather said. 'We weren't brought up to have careers outside the home, and the war, when it came, channelled our energies – gave us a cause in which we believed. You're younger, of course, Nina,' she added. 'But you must have regarded marriage as a career too.'

Nina agreed that she had, but did not add that this thinking had been the biggest mistake of her life.

Guy had finished his bun. He stood up.

'I'm a little tired,' he said. 'Please excuse me,' and he turned to Nina, bowing slightly as he looked at her vaguely. 'I'll go up and lie down, now,' he said, rubbing a hand over his forehead. He had gone very pale.

'Very well, darling,' said Heather, also rising. 'I'll come up with you.'

Nina stood, too.

'I'll go,' she said. She was horrified at the sudden change in Guy. He had talked sensibly, compellingly, about his war experiences and now, once again, he had become a lost soul; moreover, he looked it.

'No – stay. Have another bun. I won't be long,' said Heather. She took Guy by the arm and led him from the room.

There were only two buns left: one each for Guy and Heather tomorrow, thought Nina. They were not very nice, but to Guy and Heather they counted, no doubt, as a treat. She collected up the china, wheeled, with difficulty, the heavy old trolley out to the kitchen, and by the time Heather returned had washed everything up, put it away, wiped down the sink and the top of the stove and rinsed out a milk bottle.

She had just dried her own hands – there were no rubber gloves – when Heather came into the room. She took the towel from Nina, folded it up and put it in the drawer from which Nina had seen her take one and hand it to Guy on her first visit.

'But it's damp – I've just used it,' said Nina.

'Doesn't matter. He won't notice – he'll think it's clean,' Heather said, 'I have to do things like that all the time.'

Nina could think of no reply.

'You like him, don't you?' said Heather. 'I know you do.'

'Yes – of course,' Nina was shocked by the question but her answer was prompt.

'Everyone does,' said Heather.

'I didn't know he'd been a prisoner of war,' Nina said, tentatively.

'He was recaptured trying to get through to our armies,' said Heather. 'He was sent to Germany. He had an awful time there. He's never really got over it – a long forced march, friends shot. Even I don't know the whole story. He has nightmares about it, still. It's strange, Nina. Things that happen when you're young – that you think you've forgotten, or at least have come to terms with – like someone's death, for instance – can come back years later, as a sort of haunt.'

Was she haunted by her dead son, wondered Nina.

'I dream about my father, sometimes,' she said. 'He died years ago.' It was all she could offer as comment.

'Guy's sleeping now,' Heather said. 'He didn't sleep much last night. When he talks like that – which he hardly ever does – he gets tired.'

'Is it good for him to dwell on the past so much?' Nina asked. She was thinking of the paintings.

'I think it is. He didn't live through all his hurt and grief – fear, too – at the time. He's doing it now,' said Heather. 'He had to pick up the pieces – go on with his active life after the war. He pushed it away then and he's having to face it now. One can't always run away from uncomfortable thoughts.'

'Will he sleep long?' asked Nina.

'Yes. He's had some pills,' Heather said. 'He missed his after-lunch nap today.' He hadn't eaten the baked custard in which she'd dissolved his tranquillizers. When she saw his mood, she'd popped them into his tea, with the sugar. She'd put the powder in his cup before bringing in the trolley, stacking another cup on it as concealment.

'How do you manage?' The words burst from Nina and as soon as they were uttered she wished them unsaid.

Heather looked surprised.

'We've had a wonderful marriage,' she said. 'Sorrows, of course, but one can't escape those. So much joy, too.' Her face softened. 'He wasn't always forgetful and ill. What worries me is, how would he cope if I was ill, or if I died first? Rosemary wouldn't be patient enough to look after him. Still, I'm tough – I keep well,' she added, and smiled.

And you do the garden, and plant your bulbs and scatter wild flowers round the countryside, Nina thought. Some people might call you dotty too.

'I expect you miss Mrs Blunt,' she said.

'In a way,' said Heather. 'I don't know many people in the village now that it's got so large. They seem to come and go so fast. Their jobs change. We used to have friends all over the county, but with petrol so expensive and so on, one can't keep up the social round now. Anyway, there isn't time, and it's not easy for Guy. He can't adjust – he can't get used to the village being full of modern houses with people rushing off to their offices in Slough, or wherever they go, leaving those estates almost deserted. I meet a few of them. I still manage one or two committees.'

'Please let me know if there's anything at all I can do, the rest of the time I'm here,' Nina said earnestly. 'I can shop, or be here in the house, if you have to go out,' she added. 'I've plenty of time.'

'Thank you,' said Heather, but she knew there was nothing anyone could do.

Departing in her car, Nina felt that her own problems were comparatively straightforward. She had only herself to worry about, and now she knew she would survive.

14

The Metropolitan Police searched for Christine Potter at every hostel listed in the yellow pages. No girl of that name had asked for a bed. When her photograph was shown, no member of staff at any hostel recognized her as having booked in under a different name. As the time passed, Christine Potter was still missing.

The police enquired at Euston station, where the train she was on, according to Lynn, had ended its run. It was unlikely that she had left it before her intended destination, although she might have met someone persuasive during the journey. The ticket collector who was on the barrier could neither confirm nor deny that she had passed through. In a mass of travellers leaving the platform, who would recognize a particular girl unless there was something unusual about her? In the station buffet, however, the enquiring constable was luckier. A cleaner could not be sure which day it was, but he had seen a girl like the one in the photograph. He added, however, that one young girl, these days, was much like another. You often saw these girls on their own, in their furry coats, with their bags. The cleaner, whose job was to wipe the tables and clear the crockery, had an idea the girl may have left with a man. Perhaps it was not the same girl, the cleaner added, but there was a man who came there often, and talked to girls. He was able to describe this elderly man.

The collator had come up with a possible name for Detective Superintendent Wilshaw's unidentified body. One Maureen Betts, aged sixteen, had left Newcastle last August and had never been heard of again. She had worn, when last seen, an Indian print dress; she was fair-haired, and five foot two inches tall. At the time of her disappearance railway staff at Newcastle had seen a girl resembling Maureen, wearing an Indian dress and high-heeled sandals, waiting for the London train.

Her dental records were sent for comparison with the chart of the teeth of the girl found near Droxton.

The other two girls who had been found in woodland graves, and whose killer had not yet been caught, had both run away from home, one after a row with her parents, the other as the result of some whim. It seemed as if the Droxton body was that of a girl who had run away too, and now a fourth girl, Christine Potter, had vanished after leaving home. The chance that all these cases were linked was high, and fears for Christine increased. Every police force in the country had her photograph, and patrolling officers were asked to display extra vigilance in searching for her. In woodland areas, it was stressed, unusual activity should be noted. Christine's photograph was shown on television in an appeal for information, and it appeared in the newspapers under the headline: HAVE YOU SEEN THIS GIRL? Details about her were added, and the girl herself was asked to come forward if she was safe.

Her father and Iris were scarcely able to speak to each other, so far apart had they become since she disappeared. Frank, unable to sleep, was drinking to keep himself going. Iris, sure that he blamed her for Christine's flight, was frightened and miserable.

Marrying Frank had, to Iris, meant security. He was even-tempered and kind, with a good job, and they'd had a lovely fortnight in Spain for their honeymoon. Iris had wanted to settle down. She worked in a supermarket where most of the female staff were married. Shopping there was easy. Her own mother had fed the family from tins and on convenience food and it had not occurred to Iris that there were other ways, though Frank had once or twice wistfully asked if they couldn't have a roast on a Sunday, and what about apple pie? She produced the apple pie, from the supermarket; it only needed warming through; but a roast was beyond her. They'd had a frozen lasagne, though, as a change.

She'd learn, Frank had thought. She was still very young. They'd met at the supermarket, where he was a regular customer on late-night shopping Fridays, and he often went to her till. Iris, at the time, had a boyfriend who was giving her the run-around. Finally he dropped her, and Iris, vulnerable, had become interested in Frank who was always so pleasant, paying his bill from a wad of notes drawn out of his pocket. She'd begun to wonder why he did the household shopping.

Iris was pretty, and Frank looked forward to his weekly meetings with her at the check-out. Once, when she wasn't there, he felt quite let down, and the next week he waited outside for her until the store closed, then invited her to the Bull for a drink. She accepted, and it went on from there. In her company, Frank was rejuvenated. Neither had looked very hard at all that was involved, and Frank had wanted to make sure of her before a younger man cut him out. He had expected Iris to have the household skills of his dead wife, and he hadn't foreseen the trouble with Christine.

While the television screen displayed the missing girl's photograph, Frank sat drinking in front of the set and Iris didn't know what to do. He'd suddenly turned into an angry, elderly stranger. She went up to bed alone, and lay curled in a ball beneath her new printed apricot sheets, weeping with guilt and fear.

'There's another young girl missing, I see,' said Nina to Dan on Friday. 'I wonder if there's a connection with that poor girl they found near

Droxton. The police seem to have found out who she was.' She had been looking at the paper while she waited for the kettle to boil for their coffee. 'Maureen Betts, she was called. Only sixteen. How horrible.'

Dan was not making his usual Friday visit to London this week. While the hunt for Christine Potter went on, the railway stations would be staked out, and any girls planning to leave home might be postponing their departure.

'They get it into their heads that the streets of London are paved with gold,' said Dan. 'Coming up thinking glamour jobs grow on trees, even these days.'

'What happens?' Nina asked. 'I suppose they meet a – a pimp, or something.'

'Oh, somebody sweet-talks them,' said Dan. 'Offers them a nice place to stay and when they get there it's a brothel – something like that. They know no better than to go along, though they must all have been warned of the dangers dozens of times.'

'This Christine has probably been killed too,' said Nina. 'Otherwise, surely she'd have come forward. It's dreadful – such a waste.'

Dan was stirring his coffee and crumbling his digestive biscuit. Normally, he ate it quickly.

'Yes,' he said. 'They never think harm will come to them. People always think violence happens to others.'

'Dan, I'm sorry, I shouldn't have brought the subject up. I'm sure you'd much rather not talk about these things,' said Nina. 'It must be painful for you.'

'No, no, Mrs Crowther,' said Dan, who still addressed her like this, although Nina had been using his first name for some time. 'Facts are facts,' he added.

'Even so—' Nina made a gesture with her hand as she tried to think of the right response.

'It's all right. Everyone's afraid of mentioning Susie,' said Dan. 'No one ever does. Perhaps I should talk about it to someone.'

Nina remembered Heather's words about facing the past.

'Susie,' she repeated. 'A nice name. Was she like you?'

Dan took a worn leather wallet from his pocket and from it extracted a faded snapshot. Silently he handed it to Nina. A smiling teenager looked at her from the scuffed print. She had curly hair and a small, straight nose. Nina thought she did look like Dan, and said so.

He was pleased.

'People said they could see it,' he admitted. 'I've other pictures at home. Better ones. There's one taken a month before it happened. She'd been a bridesmaid.'

'I'd love to see them,' said Nina warmly.

'Would you?' Dan brightened. 'Would you come round, Mrs Crowther? Come to tea, perhaps? Or even –' he paused, summoning courage, 'to supper?'

Nina was startled. She'd meant him to bring his

photographs with him one day, to the Hall. How should she answer? She didn't want to snub him.

'Tea would be lovely,' she said. 'Thank you. May Rory come to your house?'

'Oh yes,' said Dan. 'Of course.'

Visions were flashing through his mind, superimposing themselves rapidly one upon the other. In the first, Nina sat in the chair that once had been Ellen's, her soft fair hair haloed by the nearby lamp, a glass of sweet sherry beside her. This was succeeded by a scene at the dining-table, places laid for two, roast chicken before them, or even, he thought, growing bold, a pheasant – the butcher in Murford sold them and Dan was sure he could cook one with the aid of his cookery encyclopaedia. They'd talk, and he'd show her the photographs. She'd notice his tank of fish and he'd tell her about them. Then he'd bring her home in his Ford – he forgot that she would probably have come in her own car – and he'd ask her to come again. Next time, she'd say that she would be cook; she'd wear his big apron and he'd see her soft arms – fair-skinned they'd be, for she was so fair – bare to the elbow, for she'd roll up her sleeves to protect them as she worked.

The shutter closed on this fantasy, to be followed by one where she sat drinking tea and eating a slice of cake with Rory at her feet. Her hair would still touch the back of the chair, and he'd still be able to ask her again.

'Will you come on Sunday?' he asked. 'Your daughter won't be here again so soon?'

'No,' said Nina. 'Not just yet. I'd love to come. Thank you.'

She needn't stay long, she thought, clearing away his cup while he went back to prolong his work in the garden on the chance of another chat with her before leaving. He was mending a fence that the gale had damaged. There was always something to do in a garden.

A farmer near Bedford noticed some tyre marks when he was walking along a track on his land that afternoon. It was a public footpath, but at that time of year was not used a great deal. It was not suitable for cars, yet a vehicle had been along there recently. The tyre marks showed distinctly where the ground was damp and muddy. They ended abruptly. The car had reversed out, he thought. There had been very little rain since the previous week when there were gales and storms, but even so the driver was lucky not to get stuck.

Broken twigs at the side of the path caught his eye. The undergrowth was beaten down where someone had blundered through it to the spinney beyond. Cursing under his breath, imagining at best empty beer tins deposited among the small trees and bushes, but more likely larger items of rubbish, for people thought nothing of using your land as a tip, he followed the trail of damage.

He saw the piles of leaves heaped up higher than the surrounding area. Because he was expecting to find an old cooker, a chair, or a broken bicycle, his reactions were slow, and at first he did not connect what he saw with the recent appeals in the press. He took little notice of missing girls. He bent and moved some of the leaves from the long, low mound. There was freshly turned earth beneath.

He still thought only of rubbish, dumped by someone tidier than usual who'd taken the trouble to bury it, but he burrowed a little at the side of the mound. He touched something cold, and moved more earth away. His fingers felt other fingers, the cold, dead touch of a human hand.

15

On Sunday morning the Jowetts set out to church. When Matins were held in Netherton St Mary they never missed, but they did not attend family services, where children ran freely about the aisles and played in the chancel, and strange, jolly hymns were sung. The vicar was shepherd of a far-flung flock, for the parish had been combined with Stokebourne and Cerne St Mary, and, on his motor-bike, he travelled from one to the other. He was a short, sturdy man, a youthful forty, keen on cricket, and he mortified himself by playing it a great deal during the summer for various village teams he had helped to organize. The mortification came from being unable to watch better matches on television when obliged to field long-stop on the village pitch.

Guy couldn't get on with the fellow, as he grumblingly put it, and had given up reading the lesson, a duty he and before him his forebears had undertaken, with rare breaks during wars and the like, for generations.

Heather endured the services. At least, during them, she knew where Guy was, and could let her mind stray, even doze unobtrusively during the long, uncompelling sermons. Sometimes she gazed at the commemorative plates on the wall, several referring to the Jowetts from long ago, and she would think of the grave outside, where Robin lay. Occasionally, she would yearn to lie there too, tranquil at last, but she must survive Guy, for his fate, if she were not there to protect him, would be grim.

As the vicar exhorted them to be like little children and trust their troubles to the One Above, Heather, seated beside her own elderly child who was fidgeting restlessly, turned her thoughts to the greenhouse, where, although she could not afford heat, she raised seedlings, and rehearsed in her mind what must be done with the plants wintering there.

Most of the congregation came to church by car, but unless it was wet, Guy and Heather walked.

'This generation will lose the use of its legs,' said Guy testily as they left, Heather in her old camel coat and green felt hat, Guy in his British warm. He made this remark every time they went. On the way back they kept to the side of the road while the cars of worshippers who were not going on to the pub dashed past.

'Why do we go to church?' Heather said suddenly as they turned down their lane. She put her hand through Guy's arm.

'To set an example,' said Guy firmly.

It's habit, thought Heather. Neither of us believes in all that any more, but Guy still sees himself as the squire, with a role to perform. She sighed.

'I don't suppose anyone notices,' she said. 'Not even the vicar.'

There was sherry, however, when they got home, and hand of pork, already in the oven. Afterwards, Heather sent Guy off for his rest while she sat down in the drawing room with the paper. They lit the fire early on Sundays, and today it was drawing well. With her chair pulled close to the hearth, she was warm. Soon, she slept.

When she woke, the light was fading. She got up and went to see if Guy was still sleeping. Their bedroom was above the kitchen and was warmed by the Aga.

She must wake him, or he wouldn't sleep tonight.

Heather opened the bedroom door and went in.

Guy was not there, and the bed was undisturbed. It looked as if he had not rested at all. But he'd had his pills; she'd mixed them into his sprouts. The familiar dread swept over her as she rushed upstairs to see if he had gone to the studio, but it was empty. Heather hunted all over the house. Sometimes he went to Robin's room, and would sit there in the cold, gazing at nothing.

He was not there today. He was nowhere to be found. She ran round the garden, hair blowing wildly, calling his name, seeking him in the dusk, but without success. Before going out in the car to search for him, she telephoned Nina, as she would have telephoned Priscilla, in case he had gone to the Hall, but there was no reply.

Walking up the path to Dan's front door, Nina felt self-conscious. The young man from the adjoining house was washing his car and looked at her curiously as she and Rory arrived.

'Good afternoon,' said Nina, nodding austerely.

'Hullo,' said the young man. He smiled pleasantly. Nina was sure he was wondering what lay behind her visit. He'd tell his wife about her, she thought uncomfortably, and they'd laugh. It didn't matter, she told herself; she knew few people in the village, and she would be leaving before long.

Dan was watching for her, and the door opened before she could ring. He was wearing a suit. It was a good suit, dark grey and well cut, and with it he wore a pale blue shirt and a narrow maroon tie. He looked quite unlike the handyman who fetched coal every day at the Hall and brought logs in to pile by the hearth. Nina was taken aback; her gracious condescension was, perhaps, misplaced.

He took her coat and put it on a hanger which he hung in a cupboard under the stairs.

'I noticed your neighbour washing his car,' said Nina, unable to think of a better opening remark.

'Ah yes – young Tom. They're a nice couple,' said Dan. 'Sometimes I baby-sit for them.'

'Do you?'

'Why not? It's only next door. I watch their television instead of my own,' said Dan. 'They're good to me – they give me cakes and puddings.'

They were standing close together in the narrow hall. A faint, fresh scent came from Dan: aftershave, Nina recognized, with a pang.

'Come along,' Dan said, quite masterfully, ushering her into the long, narrow living-room which ran the whole width of the house. A large tank of fish occupied a table at one side of the room, and a bright fire blazed in the hearth. Rory wandered about looking for a spot for himself and finally slumped down on the hearthrug. Nina, not yet at ease, had already walked past the fish so she looked through the french window at the garden. She saw a neatly pared lawn, tidy beds planted with a few rose bushes but mainly given over to fruit and vegetables. Bright green netting was draped over the winter greens to protect them from marauding wood pigeons.

'What a model garden,' she said.

'Yes. It doesn't take long to keep neat,' said Dan. 'Now you can see why I was pleased to have the chance of looking after the Hall garden. I've plenty of time. It's a pleasant second career.'

'What was your first one?' asked Nina, genuinely curious.

'I was a civil servant,' he replied. 'Do sit down.'

What sort of civil servant, Nina wondered, taking the wing armchair he was indicating. She decided that it would be impertinent to ask.

The tea things were laid on a long coffee table. There were pretty bone china cups and saucers, decorated with delicate flowers. When Dan went out to make the tea, Nina looked at the bottom of one cup; it was Spode. He soon returned, carrying a plate of hot scones as well as the teapot. Rory was given part of a scone, though Nina said she didn't give him titbits at meals. She found herself telling Dan how anxious she had been about undertaking the care of him, but how fond of him she had grown.

'I've never really lived in the country before,' she said. 'We called it the country, in Surrey, where I used to live. There are lots of nice houses with big gardens, and there are woods and common land, but not many real villages.'

'Netherton St Mary used to be an agricultural village,' said Dan. 'I mean, the old cottages were the homes of farm workers and so on. Not now. Most of them have been done up for commuters. There aren't too many of the real village folk left. Still, I like to see the youngsters about, like the Morrises next door. But they come and go. They change their jobs.' He stopped talking while he poured out the tea gravely, with concentration, then asked her about Jenny and Sarah. After that, conversation faltered. Nina had eaten a slice of excellent fruit cake as well as a scone. He had made both, it transpired. He was a better cook than Heather Jowett seemed to be, she thought wryly. Now it was time to get to the purpose of her visit, and then she could leave.

'Your daughter,' she said. 'You were going to show me some photographs.'

He had been waiting for it; the albums were ready on the sideboard. At his suggestion, they moved to the sofa, where they could sit side by side as he turned the pages. Nina remembered the other albums she had looked at the week before, the likeness she thought she had seen, as she admired photographs of Susie as a baby; as a solemn, plump toddler with bucket and spade on a beach; as a serious schoolgirl; and as a bridesmaid in a long yellow dress. She saw pictures of Dan's wife, Ellen, a round-faced woman with a mild expression.

'I've got a lot of newspaper clippings, too,' Dan said. 'From when she died, you know.'

Nina feared he meant her to see them. She had run out of comment – 'Oh, what a sweet little girl', and 'Where was this taken?' and so on, and felt unequal to the change of emotion the grim newspaper reports must evoke.

'I'm sure it must upset you to look at them,' she said.

'It does,' Dan agreed. 'But I have to, sometimes. I can never forget.'

He wanted to show them to Nina; he wanted to tell her the whole story. She was so calm and sympathetic, so soft and feminine, sitting there beside him. But now she was standing up, speaking to Rory, saying that she must go home. The moment had passed.

Nina, however, was not going home. She was returning to a large, empty house where she constantly answered the telephone to a ghost who never spoke.

Dan wanted to drive her back; he didn't mind Rory in his car at all, he said, but Nina replied that the walk would be good for them. It wasn't raining, and Rory needed the exercise. He'd see her home, then, Dan suggested: walk with her. But Nina said this wasn't necessary. She had brought a torch, which she'd need for the last part of the way, where there were no street lights. She left, thanking him for the tea, fearing he would insist, hurrying off before he could put on his coat, her footsteps echoing as she hastened away.

Dan felt flat, let down, as he turned back to the house. It seemed empty, now she had gone. A cushion on the sofa was crushed where she had leaned against it, and he imagined her scent hung on the air. He left the cushion as it was to remind him that she had really been there, in the room. Slowly he set about clearing away the tea things and washing them up, putting away the good china he never used when alone.

Nina met a few people on their way to chapel as she hurried back to the Hall. She didn't like the last part of the journey. In Surrey she would never have walked home from anywhere, except Felicity's or one of the other close neighbours. She drove to the shops and the houses of friends, and never went out of Silverlea's grounds on foot after dark. She liked lighted ways and people about unless she was in her own safe home. But her home had, in the end, turned out not to be safe after all and was no longer hers. Walking along, Nina thought of Caroline, who would be heavy, now, with her pregnancy. Did Martin still love her, desire her? Would she, perhaps, have a son?

I smothered him, Nina thought suddenly. I made him everything – there were the girls, of course, but Martin was really the centre, to me. What a burden I must have been! One human being can't be the whole of life to another, it's asking too much. She felt tears rise to her eyes as she walked on with her troublesome thoughts. She was doing a lot of weeping these days. Rory seemed to sense her distress and he snuffled beside her, pressing against her leg. A few cars passed, and one cyclist who made her jump, coming up behind her and pedalling past in the dark. She'd been silly not to let Dan come with her, she thought. The truth was that she hadn't wanted to be seen walking along with him. She hadn't even wanted her car to be noticed outside his house, which was why she had walked there.

Why not, she asked herself, and knew that the answer lay in some difference she perceived between them. Yet what did it matter, even if it existed? And hardly anyone in the village knew who she was, anyway. Besides, what, precisely, was her own status? She was a house-minder and Dan was a gardener, but he had been a civil servant and he possessed good china and a well-cut suit, and used aftershave.

With Martin appearances had mattered; they had mattered among their friends, too. Possessions had been important. One had to watch one's figure, and it was essential to give elegant parties. When all that was torn away, what was left? Who cared, now, if she wore the knitted two-piece that was three years old? All you needed as a house-minder in Netherton St Mary were a padded anorak, slacks and green wellies, she thought, turning in at the Hall gate.

She had left lights burning, but she was relieved to let herself into the house at last. Because she came in by the back door she did not find Heather's note for over an hour, for she went straight to the study to stoke up the fire. Then she turned on the television for company. She went upstairs at last, to hang up her coat and wash her face, for she had done some more crying sitting in front of the television. In the bathroom, she looked at the pottery cat, still smirking on the sill, and called it a few names aloud, the worst she could think of. If she dropped it in a river or pond, perhaps Caroline would fall into the canal near her flat or meet some other watery fate. In her mind, she rehearsed the doorbell ringing, and Martin revealed on the step, returned to his senses, begging forgiveness. Part of her, in this dream, cast herself eagerly into his arms; but another part, the emerging cold, independent part, stood back and slammed the door.

Walking downstairs again, planning to have a glass of the Blunts' sherry to cheer herself up, Nina noticed the square of paper on the mat by the front door.

4.40p.m. Guy missing again, she read. *Please ring*

if you've seen him. Have looked round outside. Heather.

Oh dear, Nina thought. Then she felt a spurt of excitement. There was something urgent to do, if he were still lost, for she must help to find him. But Heather's note was written some time ago and by now he might have turned up. The first thing to do was to find out.

There was no reply when she telephoned the Manor. Did that mean that Heather was still out searching for him? Nina hadn't noticed her car as she walked back from Dan's, and surely, if Heather had recognized her in the darkness – and she might, because Rory was with her – she would have stopped. She may have been searching further afield. Nina stood by the telephone wondering what was the most effective help she could give. Then she decided. She fed Rory and told him to guard the house, locked him in, and went out to the garage, leaving a great many lights on in the house as well as those outside.

She drove straight to the Manor. Lights were on there, too, but no one came when she pressed the bell. She tried the door and found it unlocked. Nina went in to the house and called out, but there was no reply. She called several times and looked in the downstairs rooms, but the place was deserted. Heather had abandoned thoughts of security, Nina thought, for she must often have to leave the place open like this while she went off searching for Guy in case he came back on his own. Presumably she knew his favourite spots, and if he liked a particular walk she would search there. Was she combing the bridle paths in the dark?

Nina had brought a torch. She walked round the side of the house to the yard where Heather kept her Mini in a garage which must once have been part of the stables. Nina saw that the doors stood open and the car was out. As at the Hall, there were considerable outbuildings here, and these were really old. She felt curious. Besides, she thought, justifying the exploration she wanted to make, Guy might have wandered back and be in one of the sheds or whatever they were: dairies, perhaps, or still-rooms. She opened a door and looked in, shining her torch.

The room revealed was long and narrow, with whitewashed walls. There was a saddle horse at one side of it, with three saddles on it, a small felt child's one and an old, worn leather one with knee rolls. The third was a strong, well-arched one. Nina touched them. The leather was dry. Wasn't saddlery very expensive these days? Why didn't the Jowetts sell them? Even a few pounds for the three would be a help, buy some treats, several bottles of sherry at least. But the daughter was keen on horses, she remembered, and the granddaughter too. She saw some bridles, with rusting bits and curb-chains, hanging from hooks on the wall. At the rear of the room a staircase ascended to some sort of loft beyond. Nina, so nervous at the Hall, felt no fear here; she was too much intrigued by the Jowetts and their lives. She mounted the stairs. A door at the top was locked, but the key was there. Nina turned it and went into the room, shining her torch around. She saw a light switch by the door. It would hardly be working, she thought, but when she pressed it, the light came on, a single low bulb hanging from the raftered roof.

Nina saw a row of galvanized bins. They were for corn, of course, she thought, and opened one, expecting it to be empty. She peered in, her body coming between the light and the bin, and, not believing what she was seeing, she shone her torch inside.

The bin was filled with canvases. Nina reached in and lifted one out. It was a landscape with dark, rod-like trees protruding from a vivid background. Next to it, a smaller grey painting depicted tiny human figures standing in groups with huts in the background and, to the front, rolls of what was meant, she supposed, to be barbed wire. There were more of the same, and some English landscapes with fields of cut corn standing in stooks. How old-fashioned, thought Nina; today, it was instantly harvested by those monster machines you met on the road in the summer.

All the bins were filled with paintings. There were several trunks and boxes in the loft too, and they also contained paintings. A door in the far wall opened into a further loft. There was no light in here. Nina shone her torch round and saw some more pictures covered in sacks and black polythene bags. There were a few bales of straw here, and some musty hay, and in one wall was a solid door secured by a strong wooden bar that dropped into sockets. Slowly Nina worked out its function: when open, hay or straw could be dropped directly into the yard below, or conversely, pitched up from a cart, to be stored.

She went back the way she had come, turning off the light and locking the door at the top of the stairs. She walked past the dry, cobwebby tack. Heather didn't sell the paintings at all, for no one would buy them. She hid them here, so that Guy wouldn't know. Meanwhile, he went on buying expensive canvas and paints, and Heather somehow deceived him into believing that he had been paid. She must fiddle the housekeeping to do it, unless he left all the budgeting to her. Nina felt stunned by what she had discovered.

She crossed the yard and returned to the house. Heather had not come back, and neither, it seemed, had Guy. What could she do? Perhaps Guy had been hurt or was ill, and Heather had taken him to the doctor, or even to hospital? She might even, Nina supposed, have asked the police to find him, but would they bother much about an old man? They couldn't do a lot in the dark, whoever was lost, she thought, old man, child or young girl.

She went into the house and searched for some paper so that she could leave Heather a note. In the kitchen, she found a pad and a stubby pencil on the window.

Sorry to miss you. Found your note and called in

*7.30 but no one at home. Telephone if I can do anything.
Nina*, she wrote. That would do, even if Guy was
the one to find it. She left it on the kitchen table.

She drove slowly back to the Hall, looking carefully along the road in case the tall figure was
somewhere about, but she met no one.

16

The whistle had proved effective; Nina's mystery caller had not telephoned since she blew it a week ago. But that evening Nina wished the telephone would ring; she wanted to hear from Heather that Guy had returned. Unable to bear the uncertainty any longer, at half-past nine she dialled the Manor, but there was no reply. After that she rang again at half-hourly intervals, but when there was still no answer at eleven o'clock, she decided there was no point in staying up, for Heather, unless in real trouble, would be unlikely to ring so late. Guy had doubtless returned, and Heather was probably too busy looking after him to answer the telephone.

Before she went to bed, Nina took down one of the old photograph albums and glanced through it again. There were the boys, as like as the brothers she felt convinced they must be. There was Guy, a dark, handsome, smiling man. Odd things had happened during the war and contraception had been uncertain before the Pill. Men had been away for years, but it was Guy who had been the prisoner of war. Where was Leonard Blunt then?

Had he been at sea? What form had his naval career taken? The albums provided no answer to that. Marriage was a strange, private affair which no outsider could understand. When the Jowetts and Blunts were young, people divorced less easily than today. What had happened between the two couples then? They all seemed to be close friends now, and Heather and Guy appeared to be devoted to one another. Heather must love Guy dearly to deceive him over the paintings, and there was no doubt that he was utterly dependent upon her. Apart from a wish to understand, Nina felt great concern for them.

As she got ready for bed, she thought about her own future. She must decide where to go when the Blunts returned. She could put an advertisement in the *Lady*, seeking another house-minding post. Now that the telephone calls had stopped, she was sleeping better; it was not a demanding job, and one lived in comfort, since those willing to pay for the service had well-equipped homes, but it was solitary, and offered no great challenge. As a career for the rest of her life, it lacked allure, but it might see her through for a while. She didn't want to plant herself on Sarah and Jeremy for more than a night or two; and with Martin and Caroline due to move into Silverlea, she couldn't visit Felicity or any other friends in the area; it would be painful for her, and embarrassing for those who now had to accept Caroline – as they would, and quickly, Nina knew. Turning it round in her mind, Nina switched out her light and snuggled under the bedclothes, drifting towards sleep.

Some time later a small sound made her start up, wide awake, heart thumping. She clutched the blankets round her. What had she heard? It couldn't be Rory; he was shut into the back lobby by the boiler, where he spent every night, and it wasn't a barking noise. He'd bark, wouldn't he, if an intruder had entered the house? She could hear her own alarmed, rapid pulse pounding in her ears. Were there burglars downstairs? She was here to defend the house, so she ought to find out, but what she had read about robberies came into her mind. She'd be mugged, if she surprised them. Let them take the silver and Meissen; it was certain to be insured.

But the craven nature of these thoughts made her ashamed. How could she face the Blunts and say she had done nothing to protect their possessions? She could slip along the passage to their bedroom and ring up the police from that extension, then lock herself in until help came.

She'd better not put on her bedroom light in case there was someone outside, even now, on the landing, although the sound she thought she had heard had seemed to come from somewhere deep in the house, not near. She always kept a torch on the bedside table, and she switched it on, waiting tensely for her bedroom door to burst open and masked raiders appear. Nothing happened. She got out of bed, put on her dressing gown and slippers, then moved quietly to the door. Gingerly, she turned the handle and opened it, peering cautiously out. There wasn't a sound. Had she imagined the noise? She would look pretty silly if she called the police and it was a false alarm. But perhaps what she heard had been the burglars departing? Although, if so, they'd been quick; she hadn't been in bed very long – less than an hour.

The landing and hall lights were on, as she left them every night. Nina went down the wide front stairs clutching the torch, which would be a weapon of sorts, if required. She listened outside the dining-room door and could hear no sound from within. Greatly daring, she opened the door. The room was in darkness and she switched on the light. All was tranquil. No thieves were there and the silver was still on the sideboard. The drawing-room was empty, too, and undisturbed. She must have imagined the sound.

At the end of the passage was the study. A burglar would surely make off with the valuable objects in the dining-room and the drawing-room before trying his luck in here, she thought, but she had better make certain. She turned the handle of the study door.

The first surprise she received was the fact that the light was on. Because the passage was lit, she had not seen the bar of light under the door. She must have forgotten to turn it off when she went to bed, she decided, reaching out for the switch. Her heart seemed to stop as a figure, invisible when she opened the door because the high back

195

of the wing armchair, where he sat, was turned towards her, rose as she entered the room.

'Where is he?' asked Guy, advancing towards Nina with arms outstretched. 'Where is our son?'

Nina felt sick with shock as Guy approached, but she knew there was no need to be afraid of him. She took a step forward round the side of the chair. In the soft light from the shaded wall fixtures, her fair hair shone round her small head like a halo.

'Hold me again, my darling,' said Guy.

His mind must have snapped completely. Did he think she was Heather? Nina concentrated on taking some deep breaths to steady her racing heart. What could she say to him? Robin, his son, was dead.

Now Guy was close to her, arms wide. Nina hesitated, then took a small step backwards.

'Oh, don't go away again,' said Guy. 'Please.'

In a detached way, Nina had already recognized in Guy the wreck of a once sexually attractive man who was still handsome. Now, as he reached for her, she made a conscious decision not to retreat for fear of confusing him even further. To her own astonishment she felt a faint, half-forgotten physical flutter as he touched her. It was not difficult to let him put his arms round her, enfold her against him. He was so tall that the top of her head came level with his chin. She felt soft kisses on her hair, and a gentle hand stroked it.

'You were always such a little thing,' he said. 'Such a naughty little thing.'

He thought she was Priscilla! Nina's heart thundered as she tried to think how Priscilla would answer.

'It was so long ago,' she said. 'Sit down, Guy.'

'Charles has to be told,' said Guy. 'There are things I must ask him to do. Duties to the future.'

'Yes, my dear,' said Nina. 'We'll talk about it.' Though her pulse was still racing, she felt calm. She must avoid disturbing him even further. She took his two hands in hers. They felt very thin and soft as she moved them away from her body. 'Sit down, Guy,' she repeated.

'Yes,' said Guy, and drew her back with him towards the sofa. His hands were still linked with Nina's as he subsided into it, pulling her with him.

'I'm too heavy,' she protested, as he held her so that she sat on his lap.

'You never used to be,' said Guy. 'Please stay, my darling.'

Nina thought his old thigh bones might crack. She felt ridiculous and had a wild urge to giggle. She had never sat on any man's knee since her father died; such a posture had not been part of her life with Martin. As the impulse to laugh died, she felt a wave of panic. Surely he wouldn't want –? Her mind refused to pursue this thought.

But Guy had drawn her to him. He tucked her head against his shoulder. She felt light, passionless kisses on her hair.

'Charles,' he said. 'Where is Charles? I must talk to him. It's important. I keep ringing up and some strange woman answers the phone – never you, never Charles. Not even Leonard.'

Now Nina's poor, overstrained heart began battering away again in her chest.

'You've been ringing up?' she gasped.

'Yes. When poor Heather is having her bath. Then some strange thing happened – my ears – I had a headache,' said Guy. 'I forget.'

Guy was the phantom caller! And she, with the whistle, had made an assault upon him – this poor, foolish, harmless old man. Aghast, Nina made a fractional move towards him.

'Why do you want to speak to Charles?' she asked softly.

'It's Heather. He must take care of Heather,' said Guy. 'And the house. I want it to stay in the family.'

'I'll tell him,' said Nina. 'Don't worry, Guy.'

'Promise?'

'Yes,' Nina said.

'Ah,' said Guy. 'Good.'

She felt him relax as she lay there against him, keeping very still, letting him hold her. Gradually her own tension eased and she felt oddly comforted, though she began to fear that he would get cramp. His grasp round her slackened and his breathing grew slower. He had fallen asleep.

Nina must somehow get herself off his lap without waking him. Heather must be told he was safe; she would be frantic with worry by now. But what if he went rambling on like this, about Charles, when he went home? And the telephone calls – if only she'd known! At least she could somehow have humoured him; she wouldn't have been afraid, and she wouldn't have blasted his ears with the whistle.

Very gently she moved his arm, limp now, and heavy, from around her, and slid her own body down sideways, on to the sofa away from him. He stirred slightly, turning his head, and gave a little moan, but he did not wake. He must have been wandering about for hours, she supposed, and was exhausted. Where had he been? Hiding here, in the house, while she was out and while Heather was searching for him? How had he got in? She knew she had locked up properly. Had he loved Priscilla all these years, continuing their affair under Heather's nose? That was an awful thought, but such things happened. Yet his present concern seemed to be for his wife – and, she remembered, the Manor.

It was Heather who mattered now. Nina got to her feet and stood looking down at Guy. He had moved a little, resting more on his side, and she bent and lifted his long legs, laying them on the sofa. He did not wake. Nina went upstairs and fetched two blankets which she brought down to the study. He had not stirred. Gently, she unlaced his heavy brogues and slid them off. He grunted, but slept on. Nina draped the blankets over him, tucking them round him, her hand lingering a little, caressingly, as a mother would with a child.

Then she went upstairs to telephone Heather from the bedroom extension where she would not disturb Guy.

What if Heather were still out, searching? As she dialled the number, Nina worried about the course to take, but the telephone was answered after a single ring.

'Oh, thank God,' Heather said, 'I'll come round at once and collect him.'

Nina had said she had woken up and come downstairs, thinking she heard a noise, and that Guy was asleep in the study, implying that she had found him like that. She couldn't begin to relate their conversation to Heather.

'Why don't you leave him?' she said now. 'He looks as if he'll sleep all night.' If Guy were to be woken suddenly, what might he not say? He might become more disturbed than ever. Nina had a strong desire to protect Heather from discovering what she was sure had, so far, been kept secret from her. 'I've already put some blankets over him,' Nina went on. 'His clothes are quite dry and the room is warm. You must be exhausted, yourself. Why don't you go to bed now and come round in the morning?'

'He mustn't be left,' Heather said. 'I'll come round and stay in the study with him.'

'I'll do that,' Nina said. 'I can make a bed from the two armchairs – you're too tall to do that comfortably. I'll be all right. You'd do better to have a good night's sleep yourself in case he's a bit confused tomorrow, when he finds where he is.'

'It's not your responsibility,' said Heather.

'It won't hurt me,' Nina said.

'Oh Nina – you tempt me,' said Heather. 'I'm so cold and tired – I've been out over the fields with a torch. God knows where he's been. How did he get into the Hall?'

'I've no idea,' said Nina truthfully.

'Perhaps you left something unlocked,' Heather said.

This was no time to insist that she knew she had not. Nina let it pass.

'You have a bath and a good hot drink,' she advised. 'Take some pills, if you've got any. You needn't worry about Guy – I won't let him escape.' Her own firm, authoritative tone amazed Nina, who had seldom before, in her life, taken a lead.

Heather gave in.

'Very well. I'll be round first thing if you don't ring before,' she said. 'You will ring, if he wakes?'

Nina crossed her fingers.

'Yes, of course,' she said.

'I don't know how to thank you,' said Heather.

As she hung up, Nina thought that Heather might feel less grateful if she knew that a blast from a whistle blown by Nina had given Guy a headache and led – for surely it must have done – to this increased deterioration.

She fetched a pillow and blankets from her own bed and took them downstairs. Before turning out the study light she made up the fire, quietly, blessing Dan for leaving such a good supply of fuel in the house. Nina looked at Guy as he lay shrouded in blankets, a bundle on the large sofa. A lock of his hair had fallen over his face. He looked stripped, defenceless. An immense pity surged in Nina. It was hard to picture him as a bold adulterer, yet he was. She remembered Priscilla Blunt at their three meetings: neat, petite, composed – kind, too, showing sympathy for Nina. Was it the sympathy that sprang from her own guilt? Nina saw that she and Priscilla could be described as physically alike. Perhaps her arrival had disturbed Guy – revived old memories. Yet the first telephone call was made before they had met. He might have had an emotional parting from Priscilla Blunt before she left on her trip. Nina thought she would never learn all the answers. She turned out the light and clambered into her makeshift bed, which was snug and comfortable. The flickering firelight cast shadows round the room. In an odd way, it was nice not to be alone.

She woke to find Guy gazing at her. He was sitting up straight at one end of the sofa, his hair brushed, the blankets she had arranged over him tidily folded, his feet neatly together. The curtains had been drawn back, and the morning light poured in.

Nina blinked at him, surfacing, remembering.

'Mrs Crowther, please don't be alarmed,' Guy said when he saw that she was awake. He struggled to his feet, and then, fearing his height might make him appear to loom threateningly over her, sat down again. 'I seem to have been here some time,' he added.

'Er – yes,' agreed Nina. 'All night, really.'

She put her hands to her hair, patting it, trying to make it lie down, and he smiled at her.

'Your hair looks nice. In fact, you look charming,' he said, and an almost impish expression crossed his face, so that he seemed to shed years.

'Yes, well, thank you,' said Nina. How to extract herself in a seemly manner from the nest made by the two chairs was her immediate problem. She felt with her toe, under the blankets, for the edge of the chair on which her legs rested, and gave it a kick. It moved away, and she stood up in a smooth movement, making sure her dressing-gown was effectively fastened across her, a hand at her throat.

Now an alarmed look had come over Guy's face.

'I hope I didn't – I hope nothing—' he floundered.

'You don't remember?' asked Nina.

'No,' said Guy. Then he asked, hesitantly, 'Was I looking for my son?'

'Yes,' said Nina.

'How foolish of me. He's dead,' Guy stated firmly. 'Robin died in a sailing accident when he was a young man.' He gazed steadily at Nina as he said this.

'I know,' she said. 'It's very sad.' Could he really have forgotten their interlude in the night?

'Heather will be anxious,' he said. 'I must go

home, but I didn't want to leave without an apology to you for whatever—' he waved a vague hand.

'I telephoned her last night,' Nina said. 'She had been out looking for you and was very tired. We arranged that she would come round and collect you this morning. I promised to stay with you, in case you woke during the night.'

He accepted this explanation without comment.

'You're sure I haven't – I didn't – that my conduct—?' Guy wanted reassurance.

'Nothing improper happened,' said Nina primly, but well might he ask, the bad old man.

'I slept well,' he said. 'So did you, I think. You looked enchanting, when I woke up. You still do, in your pretty dressing-gown.'

Nina was suddenly aware of her bare feet. She looked round for her slippers, kicked off last night.

'I went upstairs and had a bath in Leonard's bathroom,' said Guy. 'I found a spare razor.'

'Oh – did you? I didn't hear you go,' Nina said.

'I tried to be quiet,' Guy said.

She'd been certain she'd wake if he stirred. What if he'd left the house? He might have got lost again.

She found her slippers and put them on.

'Breakfast,' she said. 'What do you normally have? An egg?' Perhaps an egg, like a scone, was a treat?

'A boiled egg would be nice,' said Guy. 'I'll prepare it, and one for you, too, while you dress. I know where everything is in this house.' He paused, and went on, 'Including a spare set of keys.' He took them from his pocket and showed them to her. 'I'll let Rory out,' he added.

He'd lapse again, Nina felt sure as she went upstairs. This sharp grasp of events must be just temporary; perhaps, after a sort of collapse, he improved – a seesaw effect. She had the feeling that he had not totally forgotten what had happened during the night. Did he remember the promise he had extracted from her?

They had slept late, she discovered. It was after nine by the time they were eating their eggs and drinking their coffee. Guy had capably laid the table in the kitchen, and made toast. They were just finishing their breakfast when Dan arrived with the paper. He looked very surprised when he came into the kitchen and found them both there, and the eager expression he had on his face died away.

He can't imagine we slept together, thought Nina. But we did, literally, she told herself, almost giggling aloud.

It was none of Dan's business.

17

It was after ten o'clock when Heather arrived. She came racing up the drive, scattering gravel on either side and watched disapprovingly by Dan, who had lit a bonfire at the end of the garden and was out fiercely raking up stray loose twigs and rubbish. Flames crackled and sparks soared into the sky as he added the withered tops of michael-mas daisies and hardy chrysanthemums to his pyre. His first shock at seeing Guy in the kitchen began to disperse as he recognized the probable innocence behind his presence in the house. The colonel was known to be vague and forgetful. Perhaps Mrs Jowett had been away for the night and Mrs Crowther had been looking after him, as a child would have to be cared for in its mother's absence.

The night before, after Nina's call, Heather had taken two of Guy's tranquillizers and a hot whisky. Only then had her shivering stopped. She had been severely shocked by Guy's prolonged disappearance; always, before, if he had not returned home on his own, she had managed to find him fairly soon. She had confidence in Nina's efficiency, and knew that after one of his escapades Guy always slept soundly for hours, exhausted by whatever demon had driven him out to roam around. It made sense to get what rest she could, Heather had decided. The drug, to which she was not accustomed, and the whisky, took effect, and she slept heavily, waking late. Automatically, Heather reached out for Guy in the morning, but she was alone in the large four-poster bed. Her head was muzzy. It took her some minutes to wake up properly and recall what had happened. Then, in haste, she swung her thin, muscular legs out of the bed and scurried along the landing to the chilly bathroom to splash cold water on to her face. She brushed her teeth, dressed quickly in her shapeless everyday skirt and sweater, thick patterned tights and stout shoes, and went out to the car.

She entered the Hall without ringing, by the back door, and found Guy and Nina sitting together in the study in peaceful silence. Guy was reading the paper and Nina was working at some embroidery. When Heather burst into the room, Nina slipped out to let them get their reunion over in privacy.

She went upstairs to fetch Guy's coat, which she had found that morning when she went round the house drawing back the curtains. It was lying on Priscilla's bed. The cushions on the chaise longue in her bedroom were crushed. Guy must have waited there for the house to be quiet before going down to the study. Nina had drawn the curtains early that afternoon because she was going out to tea, otherwise she might have found him sooner. He must have been up there while she ate her solitary supper, had her bath, thought herself alone. Though she wasn't afraid of Guy, it was alarming to know that he had been there all that time. She wondered about the set of keys he had shown her, unnerved to think they existed. No doubt he used them to visit Priscilla when Leonard was up in the London flat. Had the Spanish couple known what was going on? Probably not, in their remote flat at the top of the house.

She watched the Jowetts drive off; both seemed calm. What would happen now? Would Guy paint more useless pictures for Heather to conceal? As he left, he had taken Nina's hand and pressed it, gazing into her eyes, nothing feeble or confused in either his touch or his direct regard. Replaying the moment in her mind, Nina recognized his charm. This was the man who had terrified her with his telephone calls.

When they had gone, Nina found it hard to settle down for the rest of the day. Dan was silent when he came in for his coffee; she had to call him from the garden, though now he usually came in promptly at eleven without being summoned.

Offering him a digestive biscuit, Nina said, 'I enjoyed coming to tea with you yesterday,' in an effort to mollify him.

Dan had spent the evening before weaving a plan to invite her to the cinema. There was a good film on in Droxton, one that had had acclaim and seemed suitable to watch with someone you didn't know well: so many films, these days, could be embarrassing under such circumstances. They could have a meal first, at the Star Hotel, which was staidly respectable and had a reputation for good food. Now, he would not risk a rebuff. An intimate of the Jowetts, she had moved away from him.

He made no reply to Nina's remark, so she asked a question about something that was, to her, more important.

'Does Charles Blunt come down here much?' She couldn't find out from anyone else in the village.

'Not a lot, no,' said Dan.

'What's he like?' Nina pursued.

'Pleasant enough.' Dan made an effort. 'He's been married twice,' he said. 'There was a divorce. It was all in the paper. Sandra, next door, was quite interested – gossip, you know. His new wife's half his age. They haven't been married long.'

A chip off the old block, thought Nina.

'Any children?' she asked.

'I don't think so,' said Dan, and went on abruptly, 'I'm going to London tomorrow. I'll bring you in plenty of fuel today.'

'Isn't Friday your usual day?' Nina asked.

'Yes, but I didn't go up last week,' said Dan. 'I suppose I can please myself, go when I like.' He'd decided to go to the bus station at Victoria to avoid the police. Plenty of people travelled long distances by coach as well as by train, and he'd found young girls at the terminal there, before.

'Of course – I'm sorry,' said Nina.

But her apology did not placate him.

'You can always go down to the Manor for company,' he said.

How prickly he had become, Nina thought. She shrugged. What did it matter? She'd soon be leaving here anyway; a few ruffled feathers were of no account. She made no reply, turning away from him, taking her cup to the sink. On her mind was the problem of Charles, and what to do about the promise Guy had extracted from her on Sunday night. He'd probably forgotten all about it by now, but if not, what was to prevent him from getting in touch with Charles himself? Couldn't he write? Or did Heather intercept his mail?

There was no need, she decided, for any immediate action.

In the car going home, both Jowetts behaved as though nothing out of the ordinary had occurred. They discussed the weather. The sun was out, filtering palely through the trees to which, since the recent gales, only a few leaves still clung.

'We'll have a treat today,' Heather said, stopping at the newsagent's. 'I'll see if they've got a *Times* left.' They couldn't afford it now, and took a paper only on Sundays, relying on the television and the radio for the news.

Guy waited while she went into the shop and

took her turn to be served. People were buying their magazines and paying accounts. Heather kept glancing anxiously out to make sure he was still in the car. There was no spare *Times*. Heather rejected the *Sun*, which was all that remained, so the newsagent rummaged about in a pile of papers at the back of the shop and produced a *Mail* he'd intended to read himself, which she took. It might help to keep Guy quiet for a couple of hours.

She expected him, when they reached the Manor, to go straight to the cloakroom or to the kitchen sink to wash, but he did not. He took off his coat, hung it up, and then went into the drawing-room where he sat in his usual chair. The room was cold, with the heating off and the fire unlit, and to go there at this hour was never part of the weekly routine. This was painting time. However, Heather stopped by the grate and began to clean out the ashes.

'You shouldn't be doing that, my dear,' Guy said. 'Why haven't we got some help in the house? What happened to that woman – what was her name?'

'Oh Guy, you know she had to leave and we decided to manage without,' said Heather.

'Well, it's not right. You ought to have help,' Guy said.

Protesting would be useless. Heather couldn't have anyone in the house who might discover how vague Guy had become, but she promised to look about for someone. He'd soon forget.

'That's a nice woman Priscilla's found,' Guy said. 'Pretty, too. Why isn't she with her husband?'

'They've parted, I think,' said Heather. 'Surely I told you?'

'Hmph,' said Guy. Perhaps she had. He forgot such a lot these days, but oddly, today, his memory was sharp.

Heather went out of the room to fetch kindling. When she returned, he had put on his glasses and was glancing at the paper, though he had already read Nina's. He looked up as she stooped to her task, briefly seeing not a tall, scrawny woman in an ill-fitting skirt and loose, slightly matted sweater, with untidy grey hair framing a weather-beaten face, but a thin, leggy girl, full of spirit but shy, whom he had met when he went to a ball in that perilous time just before the war. No young person, now, could understand the mood of those days: the excitement; the danger; the challenge.

'We were brave,' he said aloud.

'Brave? Who?' asked Heather.

'Our generation, when we were young,' said Guy. 'I'm sorry, Heather.'

'Whatever for?' said Heather. 'Darling, don't talk like this. We've been wonderfully happy.' She stood up, rather stiffly, and went over to perch on the arm of his chair, laying her hand on his knee. 'I've never loved anyone else,' she said. 'You know that.'

He did. He wished he could say as much.

He'd met Priscilla at the same ball. Leonard,

whom Guy had known all his life, was also there and it all began then, for the four had often met at the same social functions after that night. Guy had enjoyed watching Heather's shyness dissolve as she felt his charm. He had tried its effect on Priscilla, too, but she had soon seen which of the young men was the better prospect. Leonard already had his foot on a high rung of the ladder to his father's position; Guy, in the army, seemed to have no great ambition. Priscilla turned Guy down and married Leonard; three months later, Heather and Guy were married.

'We might get a dog,' Guy said, as Heather rose from the chair and returned to the grate. 'That labrador of Leonard's seems to give no trouble. It would be company for you, on your walks.'

'But Guy—' Heather felt the pulse in her throat flutter with fear. They'd had dogs in the past, and a cat too, who was intended to deal with the mice in the stables but spent most of his time in the house. When Guy developed his passion for cleanliness, he had refused to allow an animal into the house. 'They cost a lot to feed,' said Heather lamely. It would not do to remind him of his earlier attitudes.

She went out to the kitchen to see about lunch. He was, though apparently calm, in a mood she did not recognize. Would he go wandering off again? Could she find some excuse to hide his shoes? She didn't want to consult the doctor, who had years ago prescribed tranquillizers and renewed the prescription without any trouble when she telephoned, for she feared what he might say.

As always, she must just take each day as it came, she decided. He'd refused to take the pills the doctor had ordered. 'Quack's nonsense,' he'd said. So Heather had evolved her own method of seeing that they were swallowed, and ensuring, at the same time, an hour or two free from worry herself, while he slept.

Though relieved to have a name for the body found buried near the Droxton by-pass, Detective Superintendent Wilshaw was pessimistic about finding whoever had put her in her leafy grave. But now there was a new and similar victim, one whose body had been discovered only a week after she left home and disappeared. This time, clues might be found which would lead to the killer. There could be a connection between the two cases, and Wilshaw made contact with his opposite number in charge of the other case. If the police investigating Christine Potter's death made an arrest, it might be possible to prove the same person had killed Maureen Betts.

Frank Potter had been taken to the mortuary to identify his daughter. He had seen the sad little corpse, tidied up now, doll-like. He felt numb, totally unable to accept the fact of her death. No one said, in his presence, that girls of her age should not travel alone to London without having somewhere to stay. No one suggested that Frank had provoked her flight. Girls did these things, said the police officer who showed him the body. They made mountains from problems that could be resolved if only the girl and her parents could discuss them; perhaps they existed only in the young person's head, products of a too-active youthful imagination.

She had been strangled. The hyoid bone in her neck was fractured. At this stage, no one was going to volunteer the information that she had been sexually assaulted, but when Frank asked, he was given the answer.

The pathologist had learned a lot from the body. More information would follow when his report was complete but already the police knew that it had been moved after death. Hypostasis showed that it had lain on its side, probably with the legs drawn close to the chest. The theory was that Christine had been taken from the place of her death to the copse in a van or the boot of a car. If the vehicle could be found, it might reveal traces of Christine's presence – fragments of clothing, hair.

Enquiries in the area where she was found had brought results and the police were investigating every report of cars seen near the spot at the approximate time when she may have been taken there. Quite a lot of cars had travelled that way, and some had parked. A blue Cortina, the easiest type of car to steal, had been seen in a lay-by near the place on the night of Christine's disappearance, and a blue Cortina had been stolen from a street not far from Euston that same afternoon. Eventually, if necessary, all blue Cortinas registered on the computer would be tracked down and their owners questioned, but the stolen car might be found first.

There was another lead for the police to pursue: the man who had been seen at the station talking to young girls so regularly. His photofit picture had been prepared with the help of several witnesses and would be circulated to the police forces throughout the country. It would be issued to the media too. The police had something to go on now: the scent had not had time to grow cold.

Frank was taken home in a police car. When he arrived, the house was empty. Iris had taken all her clothes from the bedroom; her washing things were gone from the bathroom. Most strange of all, the place had been cleaned and polished from top to bottom until it shone, and there were flowers, a great mass of small pink chrysanthemums, in the lounge.

18

Nina had grown used to Dan's early arrival with the paper and she missed him on Tuesday morning. Later, she took Rory down to fetch it, and went on to the Manor. She was concerned about the Jowetts.

The house lay in a pool of winter sunlight as Nina walked up the drive between the potholes. Rory flopped down in his usual spot in the porch as she rang the bell. When Heather opened the door, she wore a flowered apron over her skirt and sweater, and looked harassed.

'Oh – Nina – I'm just doing out the kitchen,' she said. 'Come in.'

'I came to see if everything was all right,' Nina explained, following Heather through the hall to the kitchen, where the chairs were upended on the table. A tin of red polish, a kneeling mat and some rags lay on the floor.

'Goodness – what a job,' said Nina, who remembered this chore from her childhood but not since, when cork or lino tiles, cleaned with a squeezy mop, had been her own experience. 'How often do you do it?'

'Once a week,' Heather said. 'I was going to come round to see you later today, Nina, to thank you for what you did. It was so good of you. You must have been very frightened when you found Guy. I suppose he stayed in some other room, while you were still up and about.'

'I suppose he did,' Nina agreed.

'Of course, he's known the house all his life,' Heather said. 'Perhaps he had a sleep in one of the bedrooms – like Goldilocks.'

'Yes,' said Nina. 'I didn't think of searching the house.'

'Why should you?' said Heather. 'He's been very quiet, ever since we got back. Quite rational – very thoughtful – not that he wasn't before,' she added quickly.

Nina thought that there was no great difference between Martin's betrayal of her, and Guy's conduct. But Guy had not left Heather; he had not broken her life. He had implied that Heather had no idea of the truth about Charles. To discover it now would be devastating for her, Nina knew; more so, even, than Martin's defection had been to her. Yet, for the rest of Heather's life, the risk of finding out would exist. Did Leonard know the truth? It might be something he did not want to admit, even if he suspected it, Nina thought, and knew that she would join their conspiracy of silence.

She gave Priscilla's bedroom a really good cleaning that afternoon to remove any trace of the visitor.

Dan still seemed to be sulking on Wednesday, so Nina decided not to ask him about his day in London. She could think of nothing at all to say as they drank their coffee together. She was feeling depressed herself, for she had received a letter from Felicity which disclosed that Martin and Caroline had already moved into Silverlea. Felicity was refusing to invite them to her house, but most of the rest of their circle were welcoming them, and someone had given a party for them. No one seemed to know that they weren't married yet, except Felicity, but anyway, that sort of thing didn't matter these days. Felicity's husband said that they would have to accept the position, but Felicity meant to hold out.

Nina was grateful for Felicity's partisan stance, but knew that it could not last. It was as if she had died, she thought.

Caroline had won it all now: Martin, the house, and Nina's former position in the district.

Jenny seldom saw television. She was usually at a meeting or working in the evenings. She did not read newspapers very often, either, in her university life, except those concerned with campus affairs and run by the students. On Wednesday, she found a copy of the evening paper on a chair in a café where she was waiting for Alec, and glanced at it idly. On the front page she saw a photofit picture of a man the police wanted to trace.

His face reminded Jenny of someone, but she could not think who it was. Those made-up pictures were weird, not really like the person at all. Different people gave different descriptions of the same person.

Alec arrived and she forgot about it, tossing the paper down on the bench beside her as he sat down opposite her, his new infant beard giving his face, in her opinion, an air of distinction.

The blue Cortina stolen from the street near Euston the day Christine Potter disappeared had been found in a parking lot in Luton. Before it could be reunited with its owner, it was taken away for examination by police forensic scientists. Even before their tests began, a long, light brown hair had been seen on the floor of the boot. This would be matched with the dead girl's hair, and the police hoped they would find further clues. There might be fingerprints not belonging to the owner or anyone else with a legitimate right to be in the car. More probably, careful inspection might produce a thread from the driver's clothing, or, on the floor by the pedals, earth from the area where Christine's body had been found. Soil particles might cling to the tyres or the car's underside. However, even if such evidence were to be found, tracing the man who had stolen the car, unless there was a fingerprint and he had a record, would be difficult. They needed a name, a man they could bring in to question, whose clothes could be examined for traces from Christine. It might require more than a photofit picture to identify him.

Extra vigilance would be enforced at the big London railway terminals. Plain clothes officers would mingle with the crowds. Meanwhile, the photofit pictures had been widely circulated. Somebody, somewhere, would recognize the man.

Three years ago, on her sixtieth birthday, Heather had received a most generous gift from Priscilla. It was a large chest freezer, into which she could put her fruit and vegetables grown during the summer. Until then, Heather had still bottled fruit and salted beans.

'I don't know how you exist without one,' Priscilla had said, waving away Heather's thanks.

For the same celebration, Rosemary had given her a food processor. Guy's gift had been a painting of the garden; she had hung it in their bedroom.

On Thursday, for a treat, Heather took some raspberries out of the freezer, and some mince, which she bought in bulk from a butcher in Murford. That afternoon she was going to a charity committee meeting in the village. She was the president of the association, and today she intended to resign. She had, until now, felt it her duty to make this effort for the welfare of others, and she enjoyed the brief escape from her normal routine. She liked meeting the brisk women, some her own age, but most of them younger, who worked more actively for the cause. She had been chosen as figurehead years ago, because she lived in the Manor. That had less significance these days, particularly since functions had ceased to be held there. Guy no longer wanted people even to use the garden for fêtes, though once he had thought it an obligation to open the grounds.

Guy ate all his lunch. The pills were in his helping of the mashed potato on top of the shepherd's pie which Heather had made from the mince. He went off to bed for his nap, and Heather, in her old maroon tweed suit, drove away in the Mini. It was making a most disturbing noise, a rattle from somewhere deep inside. It would be very serious indeed if the Mini needed some costly new part. Well, she couldn't worry about that now, Heather decided, parking outside the large, comfortable modern house where lived the committee chairman who would take the meeting after she, Heather, had graciously asked her to do so. She'd resign at the end, when the business had been concluded.

There would be tea, later. Heather would have some before going home. There were always delicious cakes on these occasions. She longed to smuggle some into her handbag to take back to Guy, but hadn't the nerve.

Guy was soon asleep. The room was warm, the bed his familiar one, and he had eaten a filling, if not very exciting lunch. The raspberries had been a pleasant surprise. Heather made most of the crop into jam and tended to reserve the ones she froze until after Christmas when, she said, everyone needed a tonic.

Then the dreams began. There were shots, screams, terror; and somehow Robin was there, in the prison camp. Guy started awake, but as he struggled to surface from the drugged muzziness, the past would not retreat. He saw Robin and Charles in the water, the upturned boat hitting Robin's head, the boy going under. Why Robin? What fate had decreed which boy should survive?

Guy sat up in bed, seeing again the cottage near Amesbury where he and Heather, with Rosemary, then a baby, had lived while Guy was stationed nearby. Leonard was away at sea, and Priscilla had come to stay for a few days' leave from her London hospital. One afternoon Guy came home unexpectedly early to find her alone, asleep in the garden. Heather and Rosemary had gone to another child's birthday party in the village. That chance was all that they needed.

Leonard had leave some weeks later, but when Charles was born, allegedly prematurely, was again at sea. He did not see the baby until Charles was six months old, by now a sturdy child. Leonard, a robust man himself, would expect his son to be strong, even if he had arrived early.

Guy, by now in North Africa, heard of the baby's birth from Heather but did not think much about it. A few months later Robin was born, and within a year Guy had been wounded and captured. His parents still lived at the Manor, and Heather and the children spent the rest of the war there. Priscilla and her son joined Leonard in Scotland when he had a spell ashore, and remained there for the rest of the war.

Guy continued in the army after the war, apparently none the worse for his experiences. At first the family were based at the Manor, and when Guy was posted abroad Heather and the children followed. During the years they had a number of overseas postings, but in between would return to the village. Guy's father died not long after the war, and soon his mother decided that she could not cope with the place any longer. She went to live with a widowed sister, but she died a year later. Two sets of death duties in such a short space of time seriously depleted the Jowetts' estate, and Guy let the Manor whenever the family was not using it. Meanwhile, Leonard had returned to the firm as soon as he left the navy. He was responsible for its rapid expansion when conditions improved. At first he and Priscilla lived, with the small boy Charles, a few miles outside Slough, where the firm's offices were at that time. Then old Mrs Blunt died, and Leonard's father, who was still working, had no heart to remain at the Hall. He found a flat in Datchet, and the young family took over the house in the country. There were long spells when the Jowetts were away from Netherton St Mary, but in between, the two households saw a great deal of each other, and the friendship between Charles and Robin developed.

Guy, the would-be painter, noticed the likeness, and hoped earnestly that no one else would do the same. His suspicion that Charles was his son was confirmed one evening during dinner at the Hall. Heather was pregnant again, and this was, to the Jowetts, dismaying. Money was tight, and they had not planned a third child. Rosemary was due to go to Heather's old school, where she and Priscilla had met, Robin to Guy's; the expense of a third set of fees was daunting.

'It's you and Leonard who should be having the big family,' Heather had said. 'You've got this big place and you can afford it – you should have four or five.'

'I wish we could,' Leonard said, 'we seem to have lost the knack.'

At that moment, Guy had felt Priscilla's gaze on him. Over the years, she had become more assured, developed an elegant style and transformed herself into an effective wife for a dynamic tycoon, as Leonard was proving to be. Now, Guy met her stare. It was hard, steady, and told him the truth.

Well, he had thought at the time, but for their interlude Leonard would have no heir. Later, Heather miscarried, and much later still, Robin had drowned.

Now, Guy remembered all this, struggling against the muzziness induced by his pills, fighting the fear of his dreams. You pay, he thought, and not only you, but others, innocent people who don't deserve to suffer. Heather had lost her son, and her third child, also a boy. Since his retirement, he'd thought about it all a great deal. It had preyed on his mind and lately he had become obsessed with the need to make sure that Charles would look after Heather, and preserve the house that had meant so much to the Jowetts for so many years. He could buy it – he had plenty of money now – and live there till his parents died. It and the Hall could become – as in fact they had been for years, in a way – interdependent. That woman at the Hall had said she would get in touch with Charles, but she might forget her promise. Guy decided that he must do it himself, since his attempts to get hold of Priscilla on the telephone had failed. She, after all, should bear some responsibility.

Guy got out of bed and padded across the floor in his socks to the chair where his neatly folded trousers were laid. He put them on, and took his tweed jacket with its leather patches from its hanger. He had put on no weight since it was made by his Savile Row tailor fifteen years before. Guy brushed his white hair, opened the door and went out of the room.

'Heather?' he called when he reached the foot of the stairs. If he was going to use the telephone to ring up Charles in his office, he must make sure Heather would not find out. She would query the bill, when it came, he knew. He'd think up some story – say he'd rung the bank – the Jowetts banked at Coutts – find an excuse. She often went out in the afternoons, if only into the garden to work. He must help her more – give up these afternoon sleeps; he was, after all, only a year or two older than Leonard, who was still so active.

Guy went round the garden looking for Heather. She wasn't there. Perhaps she'd gone out in the car. He walked on to the yard and saw the garage doors were open, the car gone.

The fresh air had cleared his head and he remembered now that she'd gone to a meeting. There was plenty of time to telephone London. Committees always talked for hours. Guy paused in the yard, the ghosts from the past still with him.

Years ago, there had been horses here in the stables. He and his sister, a widow now and living in Edinburgh, had ridden; Rosemary and Robin had had a pony. Guy's father had hunted, and so had Guy, long ago. His father's horse was a big chestnut with a temper that matched his colour. Here, in the tackroom, Joe, the groom, had once worked, cleaning the saddles, rubbing in saddle soap, telling Guy tales of the past.

Guy opened the tackroom door. He hadn't been in it for years; the hay in the loft had made him sneeze and he kept away.

There were the saddles, the soft one he'd used as a boy, the felt one for the children when they were tiny, and wasn't that the one he had used on Bimbo, a grey who could jump any fence? Guy ran his hand over the dry leather. What a state they were in! He was shocked. Some tattered rosettes, trophies from shows, hung on the wall near the bridles. Guy moved across to the stairs at the back of the tackroom and slowly began to climb them. At the top, he saw the key in the door, and unlocked it.

Here, in the loft, he had had his first sexual experience with Kitty, a girl from the village who worked in the house as a maid. They were both about seventeen. She'd laughed when he had an attack of sneezing. Kitty had later married the gardener and they'd emigrated to Canada. Guy smiled, remembering her plump, eager body and laughing face. There had been no harm in it; it was natural, he thought, a happy initiation.

Guy walked across to the row of bins where once oats and bran had been stored. He lifted a galvanized lid.

He saw the paintings inside the bin.

19

Jenny was finding it hard to attend to the lecture. Her mind strayed away from the subject of Milton and she started to think of the weekend ahead. She had decided to visit her mother. Had there been any more telephone calls? Was her mother all right, alone in that huge house? Jenny was worrying about her. She'd lost so much weight – what if she were ill? Jenny found the idea frightening.

Alec wanted to drive her to Netherton St Mary and it would be fun to be there together. They hadn't however, got round to letting Nina know their intentions, and now something was wrong with Alec's car. It needed a new part, he'd said, which he'd fit on Saturday; they'd go down then, if that was all right with her mother.

It was while she was thinking about this that Jenny remembered who the photofit pictures she had seen in the evening paper the previous day reminded her of: Dan Fenton. Jenny felt quite cold, sitting there in the lecture hall on her functional chair.

As soon as the power to move returned to her

limbs, she gathered up her possessions and scrambled her way out of the room, mumbling excuses but earning frowns from the lecturer. She hurried along the corridors to the vestibule where there was a pay-phone for the students' use, rummaging in her purse as she went for some money. Then she couldn't remember the Hall's number, and had to find her diary, submerged in the depths of her bag, where it was written.

The number rang and rang, but there was no reply.

So she could not warn her mother. What should she do now?

Jenny replaced the receiver and went to get her coat, dragging it on as she hurried out of the building, her bag of books trailing from her arm. There was no time to look for Alec, whose support would have been a help.

There was a police station less than a mile away; she'd been past it often enough on her bike. Going there to report the matter in person would be better than dialling 999. She was terrified. The fact that the man went after young girls wouldn't protect her mother; the telephone calls proved that. She pedalled swiftly off.

That afternoon, Nina prepared for her walk with Rory. In spite of buying her green wellington boots, she had not been over the fields since that first day with Heather. She decided to go that way today, since it hadn't rained for several days and the ground would be reasonably dry. She must justify owning a pair of uniform boots.

Rory was pleased at their choice of route, running on ahead, but not far, looking up now and then to make sure she was near. They passed the spot where Heather had planted the snowdrops. The sun was sinking now in the short winter day. From the spot where she and Heather had parted on that first morning, Nina looked down at the Manor.

She saw a plume of smoke billowing into the air, drifting away from the house. It rose from the source close to the hedge at the end of the garden. This was the bonfire season; Heather must be having a bonfire worthy of Guy Fawkes himself. Guy Fawkes: Guy. The connection made Nina somehow uneasy. Surely it was a massive amount of smoke for a garden bonfire?

She walked towards it, putting on speed, going as fast as she could over the springy turf, and soon she could smell the smoke, an acrid smell, not the pleasant, soft smell of an ordinary bonfire.

Approaching the garden, Nina saw a gate in the fence. These were the Jowetts' fields, she supposed; the ones they let. She turned towards the gate. It would take her into the garden, and if Heather was, after all, simply burning her rubbish, Nina would say she had seen the fire and come over.

The gate led into the vegetable garden. Nina followed a path that ran along near the hedge towards the fire. She could hear it crackling now, and flames leaped up high in the sky. Nina turned a corner and saw a figure who stoked the fire, his long legs taking scissor strides as, his back towards her, Guy Jowett gathered together the canvases on the pyre. It was a weird, satanic spectacle, the tall man, pitchfork in hand, raking stray fragments up from the edge of the fire and adding them to the blazing mass. As she drew near, Nina saw him cast an entire canvas on to the fire. She realized, then, what he was doing. Somehow he had discovered what Heather had done with his work, and was destroying it. Did Heather know? Had she helped?

This was some private rite. Nina had no place here, as a witness. She had put Rory on the lead as they entered the Manor grounds, and now she drew him towards the house, hoping to slip away with him, unobserved. She walked quickly through the yard and saw the garage empty, its doors wide. The loft doors, above, appeared to be closed.

Nina felt rather disturbed to think that Heather was out while the incineration went on. Didn't Guy sleep in the afternoons? She walked down the drive and out into the lane, where she turned left, away from the Hall. She'd walk on for a bit, she decided, take a turn round the village and then come back to the Manor to see if Heather was there. There had been something wild, demoniac, about that figure, capless, just in a jacket, stirring the flames. Yet he couldn't hurt himself, surely? And there was no risk of the house catching fire, though the flames had been leaping high: the bonfire was well away from the house and the outbuildings. Guy had the right to do as he chose with his own creations.

Nevertheless, Nina felt uneasy as she walked towards the village. She turned at the end of the lane into a road which would, she thought, take her back to the Black Swan. Then she could circle round again, past the Manor.

She thought she knew where all the village roads went, but to her surprise Nina found that this one, along which she had not walked before, led into Chestnut Crescent, where Dan lived. This was rather annoying. The last thing she wanted, now, was to meet Dan. She hurried on, Rory padding beside her, and round a bend in the road saw ahead, parked outside Dan's house, a police car. As she walked towards it the door of Dan's house opened and two policemen came out. With them was Dan. They got in the car together and drove away. Nina, who had slowed down as they appeared, stared after them. Her first thought was that she hoped Dan hadn't seen her; her second was to wonder what reason the police could possibly have for taking Dan off in the car.

She slowed up, passing his house, looking at it curiously. Had it been burgled, his precious fish stolen, perhaps? As she hesitated on the pavement outside, the door of the next house opened and a young girl came out, holding a baby. This was the neighbour Dan baby-sat for, Nina supposed, moving on.

'Excuse me – Mrs Crowther – Mrs Crowther,' the girl called after her, and Nina stopped. The girl came hurrying down the path, though she wore no coat, and the baby was clad simply in a pink stretch suit. 'You are Mrs Crowther from the Hall, aren't you?' the girl said at the gate.

'Yes,' Nina acknowledged.

'I thought so – I saw you the other day – Sunday – when you came to tea. Dan often talks about you – he thinks the world of you,' said the girl.

'Oh,' said Nina, not certain how to take this.

'The police took him away,' said the girl. 'Did you see? Just now. Oh, I do hope he's not in some trouble.'

'Why should he be?' asked Nina. 'I expect it's about something quite simple – I thought perhaps his house had been broken into.'

'They wouldn't take him away, if it had,' said the girl. 'At least, I don't think so. Oh, Mrs Crowther, I'm dreadfully worried about him – I'm so glad you came by. Would you come in for a minute?'

Nina saw that she must, if the girl and her baby were not to catch cold. She urged the girl back to the house and went up the path behind her.

'What about Rory?' she asked, at the door.

'Oh, bring him in,' said the girl. 'He's a love isn't he?'

Nina followed her into the house, the mirror-twin of Dan's. The living-room, like his, looked over the garden, but across this one, in the fading light, flapped a line of washing, mainly nappies. The girl laid her baby in an armchair, propping her up with a cushion. The infant smiled round benignly.

'Thank goodness she's still young enough to be dumped,' said the child's mother, and picked up the newspaper which lay on another chair. 'Have you seen this?' she asked.

Nina had not looked at the paper that day. She took it from the girl. Across the page were photofit pictures of a man wanted by the police in connection with the killing of Christine Potter. She stared at them, slow to see the implication.

'It is like Dan, isn't it?' said the girl. 'That one.' She pointed. There were three versions, and one, Nina had to concede, did resemble Dan. She stared at it, and then at the girl; then back at the paper again. 'It can't be him,' said the girl, her voice shaking a little. 'He's so kind and gentle. You should see him with Amanda.' This was the baby, obviously. 'It must be some awful coincidence,' the girl insisted.

The mysterious trips to London, thought Nina; the sulkiness which she, in her vanity, had attributed to Guy's presence at the Hall on Monday. She felt sick.

'But his own daughter was killed,' she told the girl. 'Shot in a bank raid.' She tried to speak calmly.

'It could have made him flip, I suppose,' said Sandra Morris sadly. 'Couldn't it?'

Heather hummed under her breath as she drove home. She had had one tea at the committee meeting and would be in time for another with Guy. She had enjoyed her sojourn in the luxurious, warm home of the chairman. The women reminded her of the army wives she used to know. They had displayed regret at her resignation, which was nice. She could not know that earlier there had been lobbying aimed at applying pressure to get her to go: someone should, it had been suggested, voice the thought that it was wonderful of Mrs Jowett to find the time to come when she had so much to cope with at home, and that she mustn't hesitate to say if she wanted a rest. An active faction of the committee wanted Priscilla Blunt to become the president; she was rich, on the ball, had better contacts, and, moreover, would allow the Hall to be used for various functions.

'You must admit Mrs Jowett's pretty eccentric, wandering around planting flowers all over the place, and her husband's completely dotty,' said the leader of this group.

'I like Heather Jowett,' said a dissenter. 'And I think planting flowers is a good idea. If you ease her out, I go too.'

As the rebel was the treasurer, her loss would be grave. It had been decided to leave the subject for the moment, and now Heather herself had taken the initiative. When she had gone, most of the committee expressed their delight, and resolved to invite Priscilla Blunt to take her place.

The treasurer went angrily home, where she exploded to her husband as soon as he came back from his office. She might still resign, she said; it was disgusting.

Unaware of all this, Heather drove into the garage and turned off the ignition. She got out, and closed the garage doors. It was dusk now, almost dark. As she walked towards the house she smelled smoke, a strong, odd smell, not like an ordinary fire. She sniffed. It must come from somewhere nearby, yet the Manor had no close neighbours. No one else's bonfire ever blew their way.

She dropped her handbag on the ground and began running down the garden. She saw smoke spiralling up from a heap of ashes on her bonfire spot.

Who could have set the fire but Guy? She called him, but there was no reply, and she couldn't see him in the garden. What had he been burning?

She knew the answer before she looked down and saw, on the edge of the dying fire, a last curling wisp of singed canvas and a fragment of stretcher from a frame, but she had to confirm it. She turned and ran back to the yard, a lanky, ungainly figure loping along in her maroon suit and the lacy tights Rosemary had sent her last Christmas. She opened the tackroom door and ran up the stairs. Because Guy never came up here, she no longer removed the key unless her family were visiting, and now the door was open. Heather rushed into the first loft, which was in darkness. She turned on the light and saw that the lids of the bins were raised. The door beyond, leading into the hayloft, was closed. Heather was very frightened as she opened it.

At first she did not see Guy there, in the dark. He was sitting on a straw bale on the far side of the loft, and, as she burst in he stood up, taking a step away from the sudden interruption. Guy had pulled the outer doors to, but he had not secured them. When he stepped heedlessly back, they parted behind him, and with one loud cry he fell to the ground below.

20

'Did you tell the police about Dan?' Nina asked the girl.

'No. I didn't look at the paper until after Tom had gone to work,' she said. 'And he only glanced at the sports page, so he didn't see it. I thought it must be just a coincidence.'

Nina was rallying.

'It probably is,' she said. 'The police must have come about something else.' She thought of her pleasant sessions with Dan at the Hall over coffee, his courtly good manners when she had tea at his house. It couldn't be true. Yet weren't some of the most vicious murderers mild and quiet at home? 'He'll be able to tell the police where he was when that girl was killed,' she said. 'An alibi,' she added, remembering Felicity's diet of thrillers.

Sandra, shocked by the episode, was reluctant to let Nina go. Apart from anything else, she had trusted Dan with her precious infant. Nina stayed until she was calmer, but she refused a cup of tea. She was still anxious about Guy and wanted to make sure things were all right at the Manor.

Nina had no torch as she approached the Manor

for the second time, and it was getting dark, but her eyes had adjusted and she could see well as she reached the gate. Lights shone from the lower windows of the house, and she almost turned back then, but there was something about them – the number that were on, the fact that the curtains were not drawn, that made her uneasy. She went a little way up the drive, and soon saw that the front door was open.

Nina hurried on, then, and when she reached the house, stepped inside, loudly calling Heather. No one answered. Were they both down at the bonfire? She'd smelled it on the air as she came down the drive.

Nina hurried out again and round the side of the house to the yard. The exterior lights were on, and she found them there, both in the yard, Heather crouched over Guy's inert form, holding his hand and stroking his hair and murmuring to him.

Nina dropped on her knees beside them, releasing Rory's lead. The dog gave a small keening sound and stood off at a distance. Nina laid a hand gently on Heather's arm, not wanting to startle her.

'Heather – it's me – Nina,' she said. 'What happened?'

Heather turned a ravaged face towards her.

'He fell,' she said, and looked upwards.

Above their heads, the loft doors stood open.

'Is an ambulance coming?' Nina asked. 'Have you telephoned?'

Heather nodded. She'd run in to call it, turning on all the lights as she rushed through the house to the telephone. Then, coming back to him, she had put her own jacket over the upper part of his body and was shivering herself, both from shock and the night air.

The cobbles Guy lay on must be so cold, Nina thought, but moving him might make his injuries worse. He was deeply unconscious, and now she saw, with a sinking heart, that his head was turned at an odd angle. One arm was twisted beneath him. She took her own coat off and put it over his legs.

'I'll go and get some blankets,' she said. 'The ambulance might be a few minutes getting here.'

'Oh – good thinking,' said Heather, her voice steady. 'No – I'll go – I'll be quicker. Stay with him, Nina.' She relinquished his hand and lumbered away.

The keys, Nina thought suddenly: the keys to the Hall. What if Heather were to find them? Quickly she felt in Guy's jacket pockets, hardly expecting that they would still be there, but they were, wrapped up in a handkerchief. Nina dropped them into her own pocket before Heather returned.

She stayed with them both till the ambulance came, and when it had driven away, with the two of them inside it, Nina went into the house to close it up. She'd get her own car and follow them to the hospital for they would need help. The daughter must be got hold of, and someone must look after Heather.

She forgot about Dan, his plight driven from her mind by the more immediate claims of the Jowetts.

Later that evening Jenny and Alec arrived at the Hall in a car they had borrowed, an aged Hillman Imp. Its maximum speed was sedate, and Jenny had been steadily growing frantic as they ground up hills in low gear.

'Don't worry, Jenny. I'm sure everything's all right,' Alec kept saying, as he had from the moment she told him her fears and described her interview with a police constable who was, at first, unbelieving, but soon decided to shift the responsibility for action on to the sergeant's more experienced shoulders. After that, she had tried to ring her mother again, but got no reply. In the end, because she was so worried, Alec suggested they should abandon their lectures for the rest of the week and go to Netherton St Mary at once, assuming he could borrow a car as his own was not roadworthy.

'We'll have to tell the police Mum's missing,' Jenny said, as they went down the Droxton by-pass.

The loss of her normal cool self-possession was having a powerful effect on Alec. He wanted to scoop her into his arms and apply masculine comfort. Instead, he must coax the rest of the distance out of the Imp.

'She's not missing,' he said. 'She's probably

gone out to tea, or to the Women's Institute – it's all go in these villages, you'd be surprised. You don't have to worry about this Dan – the police took what you said seriously. They won't hang about. It's a murder case, after all.'

'You don't have to tell me,' said Jenny, shuddering.

The old car ground up the drive of the Hall at last, and Jenny was reassured by seeing lights on, the ones outside and a thin line beside some of the curtains, but there was no reply when they rang the bell except for some barking within the house.

They went round to try the back door, and here the barking was louder.

'Rory, good boy, where's she gone?' Jenny asked the dog through the stout wood of the door. A few snuffling sounds answered her, and another bark.

Alec had wandered away to the garage.

'Her car's out,' he reported. 'So you can calm down, Jenny. She hasn't been abducted – she's probably gone out to dinner. Now, who are her friends?'

'I only know about the Jowetts,' said Jenny.

'Well, let's go to their place and see if she's there,' said Alec.

Jenny agreed to this sensible plan and they returned to their elderly car, turned it round and set off again.

'You wouldn't think bad things could happen in a place like this, would you?' said Jenny. 'I mean, a peaceful old village.'

'I guess you would,' said Alec. 'Witches being

burned, that sort of thing. Human nature doesn't change much – it just demonstrates differently.'

This was not a soothing response, and Jenny did not speak again except to direct him to the Manor. Here, also, lights were on, both outside the front and back doors, in the yard, and in the house, where Nina, so security-conscious, had drawn the curtains and left some lights burning to discourage prowlers. But her Metro was not parked outside and there was no reply to their repeated knocking and ringing.

Alec went into the yard and tried the garage doors. They were not locked and he saw the battered Mini inside. He shut the doors and sniffed the air.

'They've been burning rubbish,' he said. 'Old tyres or something. Smells a bit weird.'

Jenny had no time for any thoughts not relating to her mother's disappearance.

'Never mind about that,' she said. 'What shall we do?'

'The only other person you know of here is this Dan Fenton, right?' said Alec. 'Where does he live?'

Jenny shivered.

'He won't be there – he'll be in prison, I hope,' she said.

'We'd better make sure,' said Alec. 'Where's his house?'

'I don't know,' said Jenny.

'Well, you know he's on the telephone. There'll be a callbox somewhere, for sure. Let's look him up,' he said.

A few minutes later they parked the Imp by the callbox on the corner of Chestnut Crescent. They had no torch, so Alec removed the tattered local directory and took it to the car. They turned the pages and there was the entry: Fenton, D.E. with the Netherton St Mary number.

'Jenny, this D.E. Fenton doesn't live in Netherton St Mary. It's a Stokebourne address,' said Alec. 'I expect there's one telephone exchange for several of these villages. It's like that at home.'

Jenny stared. She read the line above his pointing finger. Fenton, D.E, 18 Hill View, Stokebourne.

'Oh, Alec, what have I done?' she gasped.

'The right thing,' said Alec robustly. 'You thought the photograph in the paper was like the man and your mother told you he pops up to London quite a bit. But he can't have been your mother's mystery telephone caller.'

He got out of the car and returned the directory to the box.

'We'll go and ask where he lives at the pub,' he said. 'They may know. Perhaps he's a regular.'

They drove back to the Black Swan, where the publican described how to find Dan's house and they realized how close to it they had just been. The publican was not sure which number it was in Chestnut Crescent, but they would know it by the green gate and the neat rosebeds in the front garden, he said.

Alec was longing for a beer and a sandwich, but he knew Jenny was in no mood for delay. They drove back the way they had come.

Dan's house was the only one in the Crescent with no lights on. For form's sake, though very relieved, Alec walked up the path and rang the bell. Jenny followed, loitering behind him, telling herself things like this didn't happen in England: your mother didn't just vanish.

Alec, who had been wondering how to phrase his request for information about where Nina might be to Dan, if he were at home, now felt a keen desire to know what had happened here today.

'I'll ask next door if they know anything,' he said, walking up the path and through the nearest gate – luckily, and quite by chance, choosing the Morrises and not the neighbours on the other side, who had seen nothing of the afternoon's events.

Tom Morris opened the door, and Alec asked if he knew where Dan was.

'Well,' said Tom. 'That depends.'

He had expected the press to be outside, after what Sandra had told him. It could only be a matter of time before television crews and reporters were there with their cameras and microphones, wanting the villagers' opinions about their neighbour, and the prospect appalled him. This young man with his wiry curls and wispy beard might well be a journalist.

'It's my mother we really want to know about,' Jenny said, stepping forward. 'Mrs Crowther – Nina. She's living at the Hall at the moment.'

'Oh – my wife saw her today,' said Tom, his

defensive manner dispersing at once. 'Come in and she'll tell you.'

Twenty minutes later eggs and bacon were being cooked for Alec and Jenny by their new friends, and Jenny was relaxing in the knowledge that her mother had been in this very house minutes after Dan was driven off in a police car.

While they were eating their meal, having described their search round the village, Tom told them that Colonel Jowett had been badly hurt in some sort of accident. He'd met the ambulance hurrying through the village, siren wailing and blue light flashing, on his way home from work. Such a sight was rare in Netherton St Mary. One of their neighbours knew it had been to the Manor.

'Mum will be helping, if she can,' said Jenny. 'She likes the old colonel. So do I, come to that.'

'Well, let's find out,' said Tom. He understood Jenny's anxiety, even though she knew, now, that her mother had not been strangled. If Dan Fenton had been somehow mixed up with that murder, the thought that he had lived next door, visited them, been alone with the baby, was terrifying. Reassurance all round was needed, and he dialled the hospital's number.

After some delay, Nina was traced and brought to the telephone. Jenny almost burst into tears at hearing her voice.

'I was so worried – Dan Fenton – those photographs in the paper,' she said, incoherently. 'They're just like him.'

Nina had quite forgotten Dan.

247

'I know,' she said. 'It must be a mistake. He's not that sort of man at all.'

How did one know, wondered Jenny. She saw that this was no time to confess her own possible part in his detention. Her mother, meanwhile, was turning her mind to practical matters.

'You'll be wanting beds, you and Alec,' she said. 'And you can't get into the Hall. I don't know how long I'll be here, Jenny. Things aren't too good and I can't leave Heather. You could come and collect the keys.'

'Hang on for a tick,'said Jenny, and turned to Alec. 'We're to go and get the keys and let ourselves in,' she said.

'You're not,' said Tom firmly. 'Your mother may be at the hospital all night, and you're staying here. We've got a spare room. Only one,' he added, grinning.

'Are they sure?' Nina said, when the invitation was relayed. 'Oh, how kind. There's going to be rather a lot to do here, Jenny. The daughter to ring in Germany – that sort of thing. I'm afraid there's not much hope.'

Alec was smiling away to himself as the conversation was concluded. He would have his chance to comfort Jenny, at last.

21

Though she had slept for only a few hours, Nina woke the next morning charged with energy. There were tasks ahead, but they were the kind she knew she could manage, concerned mainly with domestic organization.

In a room along the passage lay Heather Jowett. Guy had died just after midnight, without regaining consciousness, and Heather, after shedding about five tears, had allowed Nina to bring her back to the Hall. She had accepted a mug of hot milk and one of Nina's sleeping pills, laughing shakily and saying she'd soon be a junkie, since this was the second time in a week she'd gone to bed doped.

The hospital had warned Nina that there would have to be an inquest. She must let Charles Blunt know what had happened, and someone must decide whether his parents should be told of the death of their friend. Heather, when she woke, might think of this herself, Nina realized.

What a thing to learn of the death of your lover while you were sunning yourself in South Africa, Nina thought. What a shock.

Would Priscilla mind very much?

Heather woke when Nina drew back the bedroom curtains. She stirred and stretched in the unfamiliar, very soft bed. She was in a strange room, and daylight was filtering in through heavily latticed windows.

Guy was dead. She remembered at once, and experienced a dreadful sense of total desolation.

'You've slept, that's good,' Nina was saying. 'I've brought you some breakfast. Please try to eat something.'

Like a capable nurse, she helped Heather to sit up in bed, propped up her pillows and offered her a peach bedjacket which she had found in a drawer in Priscilla's bedroom.

'Oh – Nina—' Heather fought for her self-control.

She looked so old, Nina was thinking, with pity.

'Come along,' she said aloud. 'Look – there's just some toast. I didn't think you'd want much more.'

On the bedside table rested a tray. It was laid with delicate china on a linen traycloth. There was a shining silver spoon in the saucer, and a small silver toastrack with crustless slices cut into triangles. Heather had seen nothing like it for years as the tray was laid across her knees.

'I hope you like coffee,' said Nina.

'Yes,' said Heather. 'Perhaps it will wake me up. I feel so stupid.'

Nina poured out a cup of coffee and added hot milk. There was sugar in a small bowl. Heather took some sips. Then she began spreading butter on to a slice of toast. The tiny silver knife felt, in her inept grasp, as heavy as a small shovel; all her strength seemed to have gone. There were two little pots, one filled with honey, the other with marmalade, each with its miniature spoon. Nina had enjoyed setting a tempting tray.

'How lucky for me that you were here, Nina,' said Heather. 'You've been so kind.'

'Mrs Blunt would have been more help,' said Nina.

'She wouldn't have done so much,' said Heather. 'She'd have told me to pull myself together.'

'You don't need to,' said Nina. 'You haven't collapsed. Perhaps you should, but not just yet, not till I've told you about Rosemary and when she arrives, that sort of thing. Now, eat some toast and when you've finished your breakfast, why don't you have a bath? It will refresh you. There's loads of hot water. Would you like me to fetch you some clothes from the Manor?'

'Oh no, Nina. What I had on yesterday will do,' said Heather. 'Once I'm dressed, I must go. There will be people I should ring. Guy's sister in Scotland. And others.'

'Well, of course. We'll see about all that later on,' said Nina. 'Your daughter will be here this afternoon and you'll want to be on your own then.'

'She'll be very upset,' said Heather. 'She hadn't realized how he'd been failing.'

During the night, Nina had spoken on the telephone twice to Rosemary, once with the news of the accident, later to say that Guy was dead. Her husband had rung the Hall early this morning giving the arrival time of Rosemary's plane.

'There are things I must do before she comes,' said Heather. 'I must clear up—' her voice trailed away. She meant that she wanted to make sure no evidence remained of Guy's destruction of his work.

Nina was wondering if Rosemary knew her father's paintings were hidden away and decided that she did not. She thought of the wild figure she had seen by the bonfire, the frantic piling of canvas on canvas. If she had come forward then, made her presence known, could she have persuaded him to go into the house, have managed to calm him? Could she have prevented the accident? Nina knew she would often have to face this thought. But now her mystery telephone caller was dead and she would never let anyone know that he had frightened her in such a manner. She would tell Jenny that the whistle had ended the nuisance – as it had. It was after that episode that Guy had grown quiet, less confused: the lull before the final storm, and again Nina wondered how much she was to blame. Had the whistle triggered off the final tragedy?

'He loved you so much,' she said abruptly, not good at expressing emotion. 'He told me so, on Sunday night when he stayed here.' It wasn't a lie;

Guy's main concern had been for his wife's protection after his death.

'I wish you'd met him when he was young,' said Heather. 'He was so handsome – so gay, in the old sense of the word – there's no other word with quite that meaning. He could dance divinely, and he rode so well. The war changed everything. Afterwards, he didn't get on well in the army. The carefree part of him seemed to shrivel up and it had quite gone by the time he retired. Then, at first, he helped in the garden and so on, and he was on the District Council, but he lost his seat and that upset him, and a few years ago he got this obsession about keeping clean. You must have noticed, Nina. Odd – he'd stopped that in the last few days. Though he was so quiet, he was much more like his old self.' She did not mention his paintings.

Nina saw that she must be careful not to let slip that she knew the nature of the rubbish Guy had been burning. At the hospital, Heather had simply said that he'd been clearing the loft and must have forgotten to fasten the outer door when he went up to make sure he'd brought it all down. She'd gone up there to look for him; he hadn't heard her coming and, startled, had stepped backwards.

'He was still a fine-looking man,' Nina said. 'I liked him so much, and I'll never forget him. Jenny liked him too,' she added, and went on smoothly. 'She's here now – Jenny. She's come for the weekend with her boyfriend.'

The two had arrived at the Hall while she was

preparing Heather's tray. Their overnight hosts had given them one breakfast already, but now they were having more coffee and toast in the kitchen. Alec had offered to meet the Jowetts' daughter at Heathrow. Rosemary's husband was to follow as soon as he could. Alec thought Mrs Jowett should get in touch with her solicitor promptly for the police would want to find out just how the accident had happened. When Nina said he seemed to know a lot about this sort of thing, he replied that a fatal tractor accident had happened on a farm owned by a friend of his father's, and he remembered that the unavoidable formalities which followed had been very distressing to the family. Nina thought how sensible Alec was, and was grateful for his support.

She left Heather to finish her breakfast and went downstairs to the kitchen to tell the young people that it looked as if she would cope with the day ahead fairly well. When she entered the kitchen there was a small scuffle as Jenny and Alec sprang apart. Both looked happy and beaming. Nina felt an odd lurch in her stomach, part a pang, because Jenny was adult now and experiencing feelings appropriate to her age, part a sort of envy because one aspect of her own life seemed to be over, and yet she sensed that there was a whole area of it she had never properly understood.

'Don't mind me, you two,' she said, with a smile.

'You've got a super daughter, Mrs Crowther,' said Alec. 'Takes after you, doesn't she?'

'I'm not such a good cook,' said Jenny, and added, 'yet.'

At this light-hearted moment, the back door opened. In came Dan, carrying the paper.

His appearance startled them all, and he was the one who spoke first.

'I'm sorry to be later than usual. I hope you weren't waiting for the paper. There were things I had to see to before I came,' he said.

The astonished silence in the kitchen seemed to last for minutes before Nina managed to say, in her usual calm voice, 'Well, I'm so glad you're here, Dan. We're busy today. Mrs Jowett stayed here last night – she isn't up yet. I don't know if you've heard, but Colonel Jowett had an accident yesterday and I'm afraid he died during the night in Murford Hospital.'

Dan hadn't heard. Talking about it carried them over the awkwardness off Dan's recent predicament – presumably, since he was here, now resolved – and soon he was sitting at the table having toast and coffee too. Breakfast at Droxton Police Station had not been quite so appetizing.

Nina basely left them to it, saying she must see if Heather was ready for her bath. Upstairs, she could adjust to her surprise at his prompt release. But then, she'd said all along that he could have had nothing to do with the death of that girl. She'd been proved right, for otherwise the police would never have let him go. Would they? She felt rather relieved that Alec was here, however, and that Jenny was not alone with Dan just now.

She went along to Priscilla's bathroom and turned on the water, adding bath oil from a bottle among many on a deep shelf She had already put out an immense towel with a dense, soft pile. Heather came tottering along the landing just as Nina was going to see how she was faring.

'Are you sure you feel all right?' she asked. Heather looked grey.

'Shaky, but I'll manage,' said Heather. 'Silly, isn't it?'

Nina did not think so at all.

'I'll be nearby,' she said. 'Give a shout if you want anything.' She did not quite like to suggest that Heather should leave the bathroom door unlocked.

While she had her bath, Nina stayed on the landing outside, fearing she might faint, slip, anything. Without warning, overnight, Heather had been transformed into a widow and would, rightly, receive much sympathy. She, Nina, would soon be a divorcée, hideous word, and in her case, a woman scorned, though she knew not all divorced women were the same. Some of them had done the scorning and it must feel a great deal better to be, not the rejected, but the one who did the rejecting. Even so, sympathy and understanding would be pleasant instead of the critical disapproval Nina expected to attract.

I'm being too prickly about it, she thought, and it's only just begun. She leaned her arms on the landing window-sill, brooding, gazing out at the garden as reassuring splashing sounds came from the bathroom.

Below, two heads appeared, one covered in a shabby tweed hat, the other bare, a mass of wiry brown curls like an aureole around the skull. Dan and Alec, walking down the garden, stopped a short way from the house. Alec seemed to be asking Dan a question, and Dan, as he replied, made a large gesture with his arm. The movement lifted his old anorak at the back. Nina saw that his corduroy trousers were slack and made folds over his shrunken buttocks; the boy's jeans, beneath his sweater, were filled tightly with young, firm flesh.

The two men moved across the garden. Had the police really suspected Dan of killing that girl? How many people had noticed his resemblance to the photofit picture? Who had told the police about the likeness? What did he do in London?

Nina brooded on Dan and his secret life for a while, and then her thoughts turned to Alec, who might become her second son-in-law. It wouldn't happen, if it ever did, for a long time; the pair were still so young, and they were a modern couple, less conventional than Sarah and Jeremy.

Nina had not thought of Sarah for at least twenty-four hours. She must telephone her tonight, she thought with guilt, as she heard Heather's bathwater running out. Now she could safely leave her sentinel post. She collected the breakfast tray and went downstairs.

While Heather was dressing, Nina went into the study and dialled the number of Blunt's London offices. She must do this task herself, and before Heather came down and heard her. When the switchboard answered, she asked to speak to Mr Charles Blunt, and explained who she was. Rather to her surprise, she was put straight through – she had thought she might be intercepted by Leonard Blunt's secretary.

Charles Blunt seemed to expect her to have a problem. He sounded pleasant; his voice, to her relief, was not at all like Guy's.

'What can I do for you, Mrs Crowther?' he asked.

'I'm afraid I have some bad news,' Nina said, and plunged in. 'Colonel Jowett had a fall late yesterday afternoon. I'm sorry to tell you he died during the night. Mrs Jowett is here now.'

'Oh, my God,' said Charles, and there was a moment's silence on the line.

It's his father, thought Nina. I've just told him his father is dead. Does he know that it's his father? The words spun round in her head while she waited for him to speak again. When he didn't, she did.

'He can't have known anything about it,' she said. 'He stumbled from the hayloft door and broke his neck. He never regained consciousness.' No need, now, to mention the other injuries; he'd hear about them soon enough.

'I'll come down,' said Charles. 'They'll need some help. Let me see. Let me look at my book.'

'Their daughter is on her way,' Nina said. 'She arrives at Heathrow late this morning.'

258

'I'll have her met and brought down,' said Charles. 'Can you give me her flight number and time of arrival?'

They were on a piece of paper in front of Nina. She read them out.

'I've got a meeting this morning, and as it's too late to see poor Guy, I suppose I may as well go ahead with that. I'll come on afterwards. How is Heather?'

'Under the circumstances, wonderful,' Nina said. 'But very shocked, of course. She'll be better when her daughter arrives, I expect.'

'Yes,' said Charles, sounding doubtful. 'Can you cope meanwhile, Mrs Crowther?'

'Of course, Mr Blunt,' Nina said, primly. 'I'm very sorry about it. I liked Colonel Jowett.'

'So did I,' said the voice, taut now, on the line. 'It's lucky you're there, Mrs Crowther,' Charles went on. 'Please give Heather my love and say I'll see her soon. Tell her not to worry – I'll deal with everything.'

'I'll tell her,' Nina promised.

As she replaced the receiver, she thought that Heather would be relieved to know that big business was hers to depend upon, and it would be much nicer for Rosemary to be wafted here in a firm's car rather than be met by a young man she didn't know, who would have had to have come in Nina's Metro since the Imp had seen better days. She went into the kitchen making plans in her head. Charles would need a good dinner, and she'd better cater for Heather and Rosemary too.

In case they preferred to eat at home, she'd make something in a casserole – but good – that could be divided and taken with them. And Charles might decide to stay overnight. There was a lot to plan.

'Mum, you're swinging into action, aren't you?' said Jenny, grinning at her. 'You like a challenge, don't you?'

'When it's the sort I can handle,' said Nina. 'I can cope with the domestic variety. I'm not good at other kinds.'

'I think you are. I think you've been pretty good these last weeks,' Jenny said. 'It can't have been much fun, especially at first when it was all so strange. And there were those scary telephone calls. Have you had any more?'

'One, and I blew the whistle,' Nina answered. 'There have been none since then.'

'That's something, then,' said Jenny. 'I'll go and tell Alec we don't have to go to the airport. He's helping Dan with something. Poor chap, he spent all night at the police station being grilled about those murders, but he said the police are satisfied that he didn't do them.' For a moment she was tempted to confess her own part in his arrest, but she resisted. She felt ashamed enough as it was. She knew Alec wouldn't give her away.

'I wonder where Charles Blunt sleeps when he stays here,' said Nina. 'There's no way of knowing which was his room.'

The Hall would be full of people this evening. She hummed a little, in the kitchen, planning, and had to remind herself that the gathering was more in the nature of a wake than of a feast.

22

Detective Superintendent Wilshaw and his officers in the Droxton CID, and their colleagues
in other forces, were checking Daniel Fenton's
accounts of his movements on the days when various girls had died. He had willingly surrendered
specimens of his hair and blood, and allowed his
fingerprints to be taken, but Wilshaw knew that
matching them with evidence from the body of
Christine Potter – swabs, hairs – was just a formal-
ity. The man was not responsible for that murder,
although he had admitted being in London and at
Euston station on the day she vanished. They had
been able to check his account of his movements
and to eliminate him.

'Poor bugger,' said Wilshaw's sergeant, who
had returned to Chestnut Crescent and removed
from the upstairs room Dan's collection of newspaper cuttings. 'Obsessed with these young girls,
eh?'

They'd asked him, in the night, if he had been
making mystery telephone calls to the Hall. He'd
looked astonished, denying it instantly. Wilshaw
had believed him. He'd been upset to learn that

Mrs Crowther had been having this trouble and hadn't told him about it. The police did not reveal the source of their tip-off. Oddly enough, no one in the district had pointed out to them the resemblance between Dan and the photofit pictures: those who noticed it thought it just a coincidence, subconsciously reckoning that the killer came either from London or some rough spot, not a peaceful rural area.

In the days after Guy's death, few people in Netherton St Mary, apart from Dan himself, gave much thought to the murder enquiry. A stabbing in Devonshire, where a suspicious husband had returned unexpectedly from a business trip and found his wife in bed with a neighbour whom he had killed with the carving-knife, had pushed it from the headlines. Later, if there was a dearth of stirring news to report and no arrest, the press would whip up rage against the police for failing to find the murderer with headlines such as MAKE OUR DAUGHTERS SAFE.

Wilshaw, when Dan confessed his reasons for going to London so often, had shared his sergeant's pity for the man. He was glad they had been able to release him quickly, before the village had realized where he was, and why. Mud stuck and he would have suffered still more. He'd been through enough.

Police Constable Downes, the first officer on the scene when a decomposed female body was found near the Droxton by-pass, was one of the officers who examined the Manor hayloft and surrounding area, preparing evidence for the coroner. With him was a detective constable.

'There was some old rubbish stored here,' Heather told them, repeating what she had said at the hospital. 'He must have decided to get rid of it while I was out. He just stepped backwards, when I entered the loft looking for him, and vanished.'

Her firm mouth trembled as she spoke.

'I see,' said the detective constable.

He examined the loft door, which was secured with a wooden bar and some metal bolts, making careful notes. She could have pushed the old man, he knew: one shove would be all that was needed. Such things happened.

'My mother is most distressed, officer,' Rosemary said. 'Does she have to go through all this?'

'Now dear, you know the constable is only doing his duty,' Heather reproved her. 'Is there anything more I can tell you?' she asked.

They'd better examine the bonfire, the two constables decided, and with Heather to lead the way, set off down the garden. They saw just a heap of fine ash: Heather had made quite certain of that, and had put away the garden cart which Guy had used to transport the paintings.

The old man was probably tired, the constables concluded, and had been resting in the loft before fastening the door, though it was odd enough to sit there in the dark. It was their duty to make certain of the truth about the death, but after careful inspection of the scene, they were sure it was an accident.

Charles Blunt was concerned about how Heather would live. The Manor was hers, with no capital transfer tax to be paid on it in her lifetime, but how would she keep it up on the income from her army and state widow's pensions? This was all she would have, Rosemary had said. He had been round the house and was dismayed by its lamentable state. There'd been some odd paintings in an upstairs room; he knew Guy dabbled a bit, but what a shame the old boy had no great talent. They were rather awful daubs. Still, it had given him something to do during the last years.

The house needed repairs. It needed modernization, too; it was habitable as it was only if you were tough; but it was worth a lot of money, enough to keep Heather in comfort for the rest of her life. Wouldn't she be better in some cottage in the village, less isolated? She wouldn't want to move away from her friends.

He'd have to talk to Rosemary about her mother's plans. Irritably, he thought how tiresome Rosemary still was, so arrogant and bossy. She'd been like that as a child, parading her seniority over him and Robin, condescending to them both. He sighed, aware of guilt, even now, that it was he who had survived their shipwreck. He'd swum around and around, looking for his friend in the sea, but Robin had never come to the surface. Only later was his body found. It was ironic that both Robin and his father had met sudden deaths.

Before returning to his new wife in Virginia Water, Charles indicated that all the resources of the Hall were at the disposal of the bereaved ladies. Rosemary had refused his offer to help with the funeral. James, her husband, and she would see to it all, she had said.

Charles hoped the dear old boy would have a good send-off with a rousing hymn or two, something martial.

Guy was buried in the village churchyard. The inquest had been opened and adjourned, enabling the arrangements to go forward and giving the police time to prepare a careful case for the coroner.

The church was filled. Representatives came from every organization he or Heather had been connected with through the years, including the treasurer of the charity from whose presidency Heather had resigned on the day of Guy's death. There were older people from the village, come to show their respect, and among the family mourners, his sister from Scotland and his granddaughter, the horsey one. Priscilla and Leonard Blunt, nearing the end of their trip, had cut it short to return in time to join the congregation. Priscilla went off to the church looking restrainedly chic in her mink coat over a plain black dress. What must she feel, wondered Nina, watching her go. She would have liked to be there herself, but it wasn't quite her place. She didn't see Heather until afterwards, when everyone came to the Hall for a buffet lunch provided by the Blunts and produced by Nina. The widow wore a navy-blue coat and hat which she must have owned for years. Her grey skirt dipped at the back beneath the hem of the coat. Nina wished she could have got her hands on the coat, let it down or added a false hem, before the service.

Dan, in a dark suit, was at the Hall to help with the lunch. He had volunteered, saying that Nina couldn't manage alone.

Nina knew that she could. This was an area where she had no fears. Nevertheless, she was glad of his support. It was odd to exist behind the green-baize door, now that the Blunts were at home. They'd invited her to eat with them, but somehow or other, she hadn't felt easy about it. Priscilla had suggested she use the television set from the flat in the attic in the evening. She could have it in her bedroom. Nina had done this: she couldn't intrude on their evenings in the study. It seemed that they did not use the drawing-room a great deal in the winter, finding the study snug, with its open fire.

Nina and Dan ate cold salmon in the kitchen while the sounds from the rest of the house grew steadily more cheerful. Charles Blunt had brought them a bottle of hock, and his mother came out, too, to make sure that they were eating. She reported the atmosphere in the kitchen was cosy.

'Maybe they'll get together – make a match,' said Rosemary. 'She seems a pleasant woman. It would solve your problems, wouldn't it, Priscilla? To have them working for you as a couple, I mean. Though I suppose Dan's getting on a bit, now.'

Unaware that they were being bracketed in this manner, Dan and Nina drank their wine and enjoyed their food. Nina felt rather badly about getting so much pleasure from preparing the meal when the occasion was a sad one.

'You should take it up,' said Dan. 'Catering, I mean. There are plenty of folk like the Blunts who'd pay well to have their parties done, and suchlike.'

'I'd enjoy it,' said Nina. 'But I wouldn't know how to begin.'

'How much longer are you staying?' asked Dan.

'I'm not sure. I was to have stayed another two weeks, but they came home early,' said Nina. 'They may want me to leave, now the funeral's over.' She hadn't thought that far ahead herself. She could go to Portugal, she thought: have a little holiday with her mother; but Christmas was coming. She'd never had Christmas without the girls before. Last year, Sarah and Jeremy had come to Silverlea. She'd seen Sebastian unpack his stocking.

'Mrs Crowther – Nina—' said Dan. 'I want to tell you something. It's about that business – you know – when the police took me in the night Colonel Jowett died.'

'But I know already, Dan,' Nina said. 'They made a dreadful mistake.'

'You didn't think I'd killed that girl, then?'

'Of course not. I knew it was quite impossible,' Nina said firmly.

Dan refilled their glasses.

'You trust me, do you?' he said.

'Yes – of course,' Nina said again. 'Why do you ask?'

'I want you to know the truth,' Dan said, twiddling his wine glass, his expression bleak, avoiding her gaze.

'What do you mean?' Nina felt a flutter of fear. What was she going to hear? Was he the killer, after all? The police did make mistakes, let villains walk free, and they hadn't arrested anyone else for that murder.

'When I go to London,' said Dan, 'I talk to young girls at stations. I go up to them, if they're alone and look at all lost, and ask if they've left home and want somewhere to stay.'

'Do you?' Nina's heart began to thump unevenly against the dark grey dress she had selected as appropriate attire today.

'Yes,' he said.

There was a pause. Nina reminded herself that the house was full of people. She was perfectly safe, whatever he might confess.

'If they say they have run away, and haven't anywhere to go,' he went on, still not looking at her, 'I try to persuade them to go back home. I point out that unscrupulous people could come and talk to them, just as I've done, and entice them away, saying they know of a flat or a room, and they might never be heard of again. I tell them what happened to Susie, when she ran away.'

'But she didn't!' Nina exclaimed. 'She was shot in a bank raid.'

'She wasn't,' said Dan. 'We made that up, Ellen and I. We couldn't bear the truth, you see.'

'I don't understand,' Nina said, but her panic was dying down. She'd always known he wasn't a killer.

'A girl was killed in a bank raid. I didn't show you the newspaper cuttings, or you'd have seen it wasn't Susie, whose photographs you'd been looking at. She was someone else's daughter,' said Dan. 'Ellen and I pretended she was ours, because we couldn't accept that Susie had run away and been murdered by a maniac. They caught him, that one,' Dan added. 'He's still in prison, but I suppose they'll let him out one day. I told the police about it and they checked. Of course, as the superintendent said, it didn't mean I hadn't turned into a sex murderer myself,' he added and almost smiled. 'But in the end they were satisfied. I could tell them the names and addresses of some of the girls I'd been able to persuade to go home. There are a few – not many – who listen. Most of them walk away.' They said rude things like 'Get lost, Dad,' and worse.

'Well, you've warned them, anyway,' Nina pointed out.

'Yes,' Dan sighed. 'The day that girl disappeared, I took one home – went with her all the way, on the train. Sometimes I telephone their parents or a friend to meet them.' He always paid their fares back – went with them to buy the tickets and saw them on to the train. 'I'm going on with it,' he said. 'Even if I only succeed with one more girl, it's worthwhile.'

'Of course it is,' said Nina. She was horrified. 'Was the shot girl's name Susie too?' she asked. 'Did that give you the idea?'

'No,' said Dan. 'But the bank raid happened just after the trial. Ellen and I were feeling so dreadful. I mentioned one day that it would be easier to bear if she'd been shot, like that other poor girl. We wouldn't have felt so ashamed.'

'Why did she run away?' she asked.

'We never knew,' said Dan. 'You see, she just disappeared. There was no chance to explain. Perhaps we were too strict, but then one must have rules.'

'Yes,' said Nina.

'When we moved here,' he went on, 'it was easy to tell the bank story when people asked if we'd a family. Everyone was so sorry. The shooting hadn't happened all that long before – the trial was over, of course, and the men sent to prison. The police caught them, all right. They often do, in the end.'

'Didn't anyone notice about the names being different?' asked Nina.

'Not many people talked to us directly about it. It's the sort of thing that's spread round behind

271

your back, you know, to be tactful,' he answered.
'But one person did. I said she was Ellen's child by
an earlier marriage. One lie soon leads to another,
you see, and in the end I denied my own daughter.'

What a sad little tale, Nina thought.

'I'm so sorry,' she said.

'I'm glad you know what really happened,' said
Dan. 'I wonder if they've finished out there. Shall
we clear the dishes?'

That evening, Nina received two propositions.
The first was from Priscilla Blunt, who suggested
that she should become the resident housekeeper
at the Hall, with her own flat – that occupied by
the Spanish couple – a wage appropriate to her
ability and such a position, and a daily woman to
help with the cleaning.

The second offer came from Charles.

'I know my mother's put her idea forward,' he
said. 'I promised to let her get in first.'

He had come out to the kitchen after dinner,
bringing Nina a glass of Cointreau. They had
pressed her to join them for the meal, but she'd
refused. Now he sat down at the table, bidding
her do the same. Nina, who had been loading the
dishwasher, obeyed.

'My idea is that you should cook our lunches at
the office – the directors' lunches, I mean. We have
a girl who does it now, but she's leaving – wants
to go abroad, cook her way round the world, or

something. She's looking for someone to take her place, but I'd sooner it was you than a girl – someone mature, I'd prefer – who won't leave us on a whim just as we've all got used to one another.'

'But I'm not qualified,' said Nina. 'I've never done that sort of thing. I haven't got a diploma.'

'You're a bloody good cook, and an excellent hostess,' said Charles. 'And you don't lose your head in a crisis. You'd be a great help with foreign visitors – we get lots of them, now we're exporting and setting up stores overseas. You know we don't only make buns?'

'Yes.' Nina had to smile at this.

'There are seven of us, regularly,' he said, 'and often a guest or two. Sometimes my father's there.'

'I'd have to live in London,' Nina said.

'No, you wouldn't, if you didn't want to. You could commute. I do, after all. You could live in Marlow, say – or Datchet, like my grandfather,' said Charles.

But he wasn't really your grandfather, Nina thought. She knew so much about them, such a big secret. She couldn't stay on in this house, with Priscilla, weighted with such knowledge.

'Think about it, Nina,' Charles urged, and as he looked at her, his eyes were Guy's. She saw the charm – felt it, too – noticed the long, mobile mouth, though the smooth, well-shaven face was fleshy and Guy had been so lean. Hadn't everyone noticed the likeness? She'd come fresh to it, she realized, from outside, and had had the facts that confirmed it thrust at her. People saw what they wanted to see, she supposed: when Sebastian was born, members of both families had declared him the image of this one or that.

Charles was mentioning terms. To Nina, they sounded like the wealth of Arabia.

'Come and see us, before you decide,' he invited. 'Have a look at the kitchen – meet the rest of the board – hear about us from Angela – that's the girl who's leaving. Let's make it Tuesday. Mother plans to keep you here as long as she can, but it's time you had a day off and I'll tell her we've got a date. Come to lunch,' and he smiled at her.

Why not, Nina thought.

'If your mother won't mind,' she agreed, and added, 'I won't be accepting her offer, though I'm very grateful to her.'

'Believe me, the favour would be all on your side,' said Charles.

But he was wrong. Priscilla had held out a helping hand when they met that day in London. She could have ignored Nina's distress, but instead she had offered her an opportunity which had led to this moment. If Nina accepted the position at Blunt's, she would be able to rent a room – even a small flat – until Mr Drew had concluded his wrangling with Martin and extracted some sort of settlement.

In her heart, Nina knew that she was going to lose over that. Eventually, she would get some money, but it would be nothing like half the value of Silverlea, for on paper Martin had managed to make a poor financial showing. Promises, from him, were worthless, she had learned, and she hated him now with a deep bitterness she was sure would never diminish. In destroying their life together, he had demonstrated that it was based on an illusion – her illusion, but she felt a sudden surge of defiant confidence as she contemplated Charles' suggestion – a feeling similar to what she had experienced when, to thwart Sarah's plans to organize her, she had resolved in the beginning to come to the Hall. She would accept the job. She need not commit herself to it for ever; if it didn't work out, she could leave when she had been there long enough to gain a reference. It wasn't, as her idea of marriage had been, a contract for life.

She smiled back at Charles as she worked this out.

'I'm sure I'll be able to persuade you,' he said lightly. 'I'll look forward to that.'

He got his way in most things, Nina decided: like his mother.

There was no need for any action over the promise she had made to Guy, for Rosemary and her husband were going to take over the Manor. Rosemary's husband would soon be retiring from the army, and he planned to start a light-engineering business; suitable premises were available in Droxton and he had a potential partner. They would pay Heather a realistic rent for the Manor.

The day before she left the Hall, Nina went to say goodbye to Heather. She had rented a one-room flat near Watford for three months, with an option to renew, and was starting at Blunt's the following week, to work alongside the departing Angela for a few days.

'You'll be all right, Nina,' Heather said. 'I'm glad things have worked out for you.'

'What about you?' Nina asked. 'Will you find a house in the village?'

'No. I'm going to Cornwall,' said Heather. 'I lived there as a girl, and I want to go back to my roots.'

'Won't you miss your friends?'

'What friends?' asked Heather. 'Without Guy, there's no one.'

'Well – the Blunts,' Nina said. Heather was also putting a distance between herself and family – her daughter and grandchildren: but she was used to them, with their army life, being out of close reach.

'I've lived in Priscilla's shadow for a large part of my life,' Heather said. 'Now I can get away. I couldn't before, because of the Manor. Do you know, I almost hate it now – the Manor, I mean. In the end it killed Guy, and it took so much out of us both. I miss him, Nina. It's lonely at night.' She looked at Nina with her large, still beautiful eyes. 'You understand, I know.'

'Perhaps – in a way,' said Nina. She still missed Martin, but he had hurt her so badly that she no longer wanted him. If they were shipwrecked together on a desert island, she told herself fancifully, she would stalk off to the far side of it, immune to his blandishments.

Or would she? She shivered, not sure.

'I want to get away from Priscilla,' Heather said. 'She's always done everything better than I have – she was cleverer at school, and so pretty. But Guy chose me, and nothing can alter that.' Her lined face glowed as she spoke. 'I don't want her to go on patronizing me – giving me expensive presents – that sort of thing.'

'I'm sure she doesn't mean to patronize you,' said Nina. 'She's very kind.'

'When it suits her,' said Heather, and laughed shortly. 'I'm being disloyal to a lifelong friend, Nina.'

But the lifelong friend, decades ago and for who knows how long thereafter, had been disloyal to Heather, Nina reflected.

'It doesn't do to look back too much,' Heather was saying. 'One should remember only the good things, and let the rest go. That's a wise philosophy.'

'Yes,' said Nina. Was it possible that Heather knew the truth and chose to ignore it?

'Come and stay, when I get my cottage,' said Heather.

'I'd like to,' said Nina.

In the morning, she checked her room to make sure she had left nothing behind. Bare of her possessions, the pretty bedroom with its yellow furnishings looked impersonal again, yet here she had wept bitterly; lain terrified, frightened of burglars and anonymous telephone callers; wished malice towards Caroline.

She'd forgotten the pottery cat. It sat on the bathroom window-sill, a silly grin on its painted features. Was it really like Caroline? Nina found that she could not recall the girl's face at all.

How stupid, she thought, picking up the cat. She couldn't leave it here, but it was no longer of any significance. She must have been a bit round the bend to invest it with any, she decided, putting it into her handbag. She'd get rid of it in the dust-bin when she went to fetch Dan, who had said he would bring down her cases.

But first she had something to do.

She found Priscilla in her study at her desk. Leonard had gone to the office. Nina was glad she would continue to see him; his genial kindliness must be part of a massive tolerance if he knew the truth of the past. She had enjoyed her lunch at Blunt's, where everyone had treated her like a guest, not a future employee. Charles, saying farewell, had taken her hand and held it for a moment. Nina had remembered, with a sudden stab, Guy on the night when he had surprised her. There might be more surprises ahead, she thought, not certain quite what she meant. The idea was faintly exhilarating.

'Ah, Nina,' said Priscilla. 'Ready to go?' She held out an envelope. 'Your cheque.'

'Thank you,' said Nina, taking it from her.

'I hope it hasn't been dreadfully boring for you here,' Priscilla said. 'I mean – I know there was the accident – that was terrible – but it must have been dull.'

'Oh no – not at all,' said Nina. Her gaze strayed from the elegant figure at the desk to the window. Dan was out there, busy with something. In Priscilla's absence he had been briefly suspected of murder; and in this very room, Nina herself had spent one extraordinary night about which even Heather did not know every detail. Priscilla had no knowledge of these events, had probably not even heard that a murdered girl had been found near the Droxton by-pass, knew nothing of the telephone calls which had been meant for her, not Nina.

'I knew the Hall was in good hands,' Priscilla continued graciously. 'It was lucky for both of us, wasn't it, that we met that day in London?'

'It was for me,' said Nina. 'You'd have found someone.' People like Priscilla always did. 'Here are the keys you gave me,' she added, handing them over. 'And here—' Nina put her hand in her jacket pocket, drawing out the set of keys she had taken from Guy when he fell. 'Here are these,' she went on. 'Colonel Jowett had been unwell before the accident – rather confused. He came up here several times, and once he let himself in. Mrs Jowett knew he had been in the house – she came to collect him – but she thought I'd left the door open. She didn't know about these keys and I've no idea where he found them.'

She held them out to Priscilla.

'Oh,' said Priscilla, accepting them. 'I see.'

There was no more for either to say. The only safety lay in silence, and it was Nina who, after a moment, broke it.

'May I call Dan to fetch my cases?' she asked.

'Certainly,' said Priscilla, laying both sets of keys on her desk. She stared at them, and then, as Nina turned away, opened a small drawer and dropped one set in. Nina left her sitting there, pen in hand, trying to pick up the threads of the letter she had been writing.

Dan stacked Nina's possessions into the Metro. Her green wellingtons went into the boot; she'd need them when she visited Heather. He shook her hand and wished her luck. He'd never see her again, he knew, as he watched the car slowly move forward. She was the only person, apart from the police, who knew the truth about Susie.

But Nina was not thinking of Dan; there was something she'd meant to do, she remembered, some unfinished business which the matter of the keys had driven from her mind. What was it?

Then she remembered the cat.

She stopped the car and opened her handbag, which was resting on the passenger seat beside her. Dan, meanwhile, came up to the car and was beside her as she drew out the small, garish object. She wound down the window.

'Dan, would you drop this into the dustbin?' she said. 'I forgot about it.'

He took it from her, through the car window, looking at it curiously.

'What is it?' he asked.

'Just a silly mascot I had,' Nina said. 'I don't want it any more. It isn't of any importance. I meant to throw it away before leaving.'

'Very well,' he said. 'I'll see to it,' and, holding it in his hand, he watched her drive off.

As she passed the front of the house Priscilla came to the window and waved, and Nina waved back, driving slowly, careful of Dan's gravel.

She'll never be certain of how much I know, Nina thought.

Perhaps one day Charles should be told: when they were all dead – Leonard, Heather and his mother. Or should he? Did it really matter?

Guy and Martin had been alike in their conduct, but Martin had, in the end, acknowledged his action and his responsibility, whereas Guy had drifted on, acting a lie, ending unable to wash his conscience clean.

There wasn't much to choose between them, Nina thought, driving past the Baptist Chapel. Heather, when she moved away, would leave the ghosts of the past and be happy; Nina must do that herself: try not to dwell on what couldn't be changed. It wouldn't be easy: she knew that black days, and more probably nights, lay ahead.

Leaving the village, she put her foot down and drove on fast, towards the by-pass.

Dan waited until the car was out of sight, then turned back to the garden. He put the pottery cat in his pocket. It was odd, ugly, gaudy, everything Nina was not, and a strange thing for her to have owned, but it was all that he had of her.

A policeman walking along a quiet street behind the Bayswater Road noticed a white Cortina parked at a meter, with a man having some small difficulty in opening the door. The man was stout, not young; he wore clerical dress, with a dog-collar. If it had not been for his respectable attire – particularly the collar – the constable would have questioned him about the car and whether in fact it was his. But vicars didn't steal cars.

They didn't, he reflected, as automatically he made a note of the number, very often drive large Cortinas, cars with commodious boots. A Cortina car had been stolen and used to move the body of Christine Potter some weeks ago now, he remembered, and radioed in.

A check was made on the computer, and the white Cortina proved to belong, not to a parson, but to a man whose address was in Kent. It turned out that he was a sales representative.

The police decided not to pick up the thief at once. They trailed him around the streets, and he parked the Cortina near King's Cross station.

The bogus vicar was watched as he followed a young girl who carried a suitcase out of the refreshment room, and arrested as he spoke to her.

The Cost of Silence

'As a rule, the game of life is worth playing . . .'

Dean Inge

1

From the window above the shop Emma watched all that went on in the square. She saw the motorists going to work, and the school buses; the scooters and motor-bikes and the few cyclists. She saw retired men escaping from domestic imprisonment and housewives bound for the shops. At night, when the traffic on the main road slackened and she lay in bed reading a romance from the library, she would put down her book and listen; then she would hear an occasional car, the roar of a motor-cycle, the late bus from Muddington, and sometimes, in the distance, the barking of dogs out for a last run. The night sounds excited her, reminding her that there was another world beyond the restrictions of her own.

Norman watched the passers-by too, but it was the women he noticed. Mrs Hallam, smartly dressed, with two miniature dachshunds on long red leads, was always early. Later came Mrs Costello, with her wild white hair, shabby sheepskin coat and fat spaniel, relics all of better days spent in a small manor house amid seven acres. That was before her husband shot himself, leaving her little but debts. By the time young Mrs Armitage appeared with Simon in his pram on

7

her way to Bodger's Self-Service the morning was nearly over.

Norman Widnes had run the ironmonger's shop since his father's sudden death from a heart attack; by then his mother's illness had begun. At first she helped him, and for a long time she kept the books, but gradually she was able to do less and less, until she took to sitting upstairs by the window watching what went on outside.

That was five years ago, before it all happened. Now there were just the two of them, and it was Emma who sat there, perpetually waiting.

Once again, Jamie Renshaw was late for school because the Alsatian that lived in Foster Avenue was waiting to gobble him up. Though he had turned back and gone all the way round by the square, he still wasn't safe, for a small white dog stood in the road opposite the ironmonger's shop. He held his breath as he went past, and it ignored him.

Miss Baxter was cross when she found him sitting at his desk in the classroom after assembly.

'That's twice this week you've been late, Jamie,' she said. 'And it was three times last week.'

'I'm sorry, Miss Baxter,' Jamie mumbled, head bent, inspecting the scratches on top of his desk.

It was better to be in trouble at school than eaten alive by a wolf. Sometimes in the afternoons, his mother and baby sister met him, and they would all pass the Alsatian then; his mother always admired it, saying she would like one the same. Jamie lived in dread of this wish's fulfilment, but luckily his father said such big dogs needed a lot of exercise and it wasn't fair to

8

keep them in towns.

Across the square in Old Bidbury, facing the shops, Mrs Minter lived in a small Georgian house separated from its neighbours by a footpath which led over fields to the railway. Until recently, she had run an antique business in New Bidbury with a friend, but when the lease of the premises ran out the friend retired with her share of the capital, and now Mrs Minter was seeking a new interest for hers. Meanwhile, unused to having time to spare, she had taken to walking miles in the district, and as she walked she noticed everything. She often saw the Alsatian which alarmed Jamie Renshaw; it usually stood outside the home of its owner, Paula Curtis, a sculptor, and it barked at all who passed.

The house next door to Paula's was empty and had been up for sale for months; it was built in mock Tudor style, with false beams superimposed, and stood in a glade of straggly cupressus trees from among which protruded the agent's board. People saw over it and were dashed by the need to replumb and repair; they sighed over the tangled garden and did not come back. It was still for sale, Mrs Minter saw, on Thursday morning. As she went past the Alsatian barked at her, and from somewhere nearby came the sound of a child crying, but Mrs Minter was only dimly aware of it because the dog made much more noise.

'Jamie Renshaw was late for school again today,' said Felicity Baxter that afternoon.

It was early closing day, when Norman went off in his van after shutting the shop to see to his business affairs, finishing his round at Felicity's

9

flat which was on the top floor of an old house in a residential area of the town beyond the railway line.

Today he had arrived before she got home; he had brought some daffodils and arranged them in a jug. She had to admit that he was a very considerate lover, but now she disengaged his hands from round her waist, her mind still at school with the children. It had not always been like this: once she had been impatient and eager; but now she had to unwind first.

Norman, absorbed in his second life when he pretended that he lived with Felicity all the time, was willing to show interest in Jamie.

'I don't know him,' he said. 'At least, not by name – by sight, perhaps.'

'He lives in Lincoln Close. His father used to bring him to school but he comes on his own now. It's not far, and he's old enough, but I wonder—'

She had moved away from him while she talked and was now in her bedroom, her voice coming to him through the open door. He caught glimpses of her as she passed back and forth putting her coat in the cupboard, and sitting on the end of her bed to take off her boots. He half rose, tempted to go in after her, but she reappeared before he could do more than start the action and he sank back. Things could be better if you waited for them, a reflection with which he often consoled himself as he stood in Emma's room listening to her heavy breathing in the night.

Felicity was still talking about Jamie.

'There's a new baby,' she said. 'He may be a bit

jealous, you know, after being the only one for so long. But she must be a year old by now, if not more.'

'Perhaps his mother's just late sending him off,' Norman suggested. 'Now that she's busier.'

'Trust you to think of the simple solution,' said Felicity, coming back into the room. 'You could be right.'

She smiled at him. She was feeling better now; the slight headache she'd had all day had lifted.

Norman forgot about Jamie Renshaw and kissed her. They were almost the same height.

'You,' she said, suddenly filled with affection for him.

Norman wrapped his arms round her sturdy body in its Shetland sweater, crushed her to him so that he could feel the softness of her breasts against his chest, and said, 'Don't ever leave me, Felicity. I don't think I could bear it if you did.'

Felicity, responding to him, postponed, not for the first time, the moment when she told him that this was exactly what she intended to do.

Mrs Minter had guessed about Norman and Felicity. She had often seen him walk past her house down the footpath to the fields and the railway line; she walked that way herself when the weather was good. Once she had seen him cross the cutting and enter one of the large old houses that backed on to it. Most of these houses had been turned into flats, and on another occasion she had seen Felicity drive up to the same house in her red Fiat.

He could, of course, be visiting someone else, but Mrs Minter felt sure it was Felicity, whom she had met at an open day at the school. Because of her new-found leisure she had become more involved in local life and had enlarged her acquaintance. Like most people in Old Bidbury, she had been surprised when Norman married Emma almost immediately after his mother's death. Within a year, Emma had had a stroke which had left her partly paralysed. She spent all day on a sofa propped up so that she could look out of the window. With her good arm she could switch on the electric kettle which was kept on an asbestos pad on the floor beside her, operate the radio and the television, and she even managed a little simple embroidery in very large stitches. She could hobble about with a walking aid, and had an immense appetite for food, so that by now she was gross, eyes sunk in folds of flesh, her once red hair streaked with white. Over four years had passed since this had happened, and two years ago Norman had begun to look just a little less defeated; that was when it had started with Miss Baxter, Mrs Minter thought. But with no hope for the future, wouldn't the girl tire of it, eventually?

2

On Friday morning Norman was stocking the till with the day's float when there was a squeal of tyres outside.

Through the glass door of the shop he could see a white mongrel terrier standing in the road, and a small boy, looking petrified, on the kerb at the far side. A Ford Cortina had stopped, and as Norman watched the driver got out and began scolding the child.

Norman slid the catch up on the door of the shop and went over.

'What's up?' he said, interrupting the flow of words pouring from the driver.

'Little wretch stepped off the kerb right in front of me – I had to swerve to avoid a dog – I might have killed him,' raged the man. 'Is he your kid?'

'No. On your way to school, are you?' Norman asked the boy.

'Yes,' said Jamie Renshaw, ashen-faced.

'Your car'll block the traffic, left there,' Norman pointed out to the driver.

Muttering, the man went back to it, and Norman turned to the child.

'Are you Jamie Renshaw?' he asked.

'Yes,' said Jamie, showing no surprise at Norman's omniscience.

'This isn't your best way to school, is it?'

'No. But I can't go along Foster Avenue because of the wolf,' said Jamie.

Norman understood at once.

'Mrs Curtis's Alsatian,' he said. 'You'll be late.'

'I know, but I have to go the long way round,' said Jamie.

'No, you don't,' said Norman, making a quick decision. 'I'll go with you.' It wouldn't take long.

They strode off together, small, slight man and very small boy, back the way Jamie had come along Funnel Lane, into Lincoln Road and round to Foster Avenue.

The Alsatian was there, sniffing round a lamp-post, and he barked at them, but Norman knew it was habit and not hostility. He took Jamie's hand and they marched past. The dog approached, sniffed at them, then lost interest.

'He should be kept in,' said Norman, aware that his companion was trembling. 'But he won't hurt you.'

Jamie was not convinced, but a hundred yards on his courage returned.

'Thanks very much, Mr Widnes,' he said, and sped off up the road to the school.

Well, one small mystery was now solved, Norman reflected: the reason for Jamie's unpunctuality had been discovered. He would be able to tell Felicity about it.

'That mongrel will cause an accident one day,' Emma said, when he returned. She had seen the incident from the window, and knew that the white dog was let out daily when its owners left for work and abandoned until their return at night.

'There's no law about keeping dogs under control, more's the pity,' said Norman. 'That Alsatian should be kept in too.'

'Rub my back, Norm, before you go down, there's a love,' Emma asked him, so he rolled her over, took out the talcum and for nearly five minutes gently massaged the huge rolls of flesh over her spine. She did not get dressed until Mrs Bowling arrived to help her.

When Norman went down to the shop again, his assistant, Madge Pearce, was weighing out nails for the Alsatian's owner, Mrs Curtis. Madge had replaced a youth who had left the shop because he never stayed anywhere longer than three months. Norman had been doubtful about employing her, for she had only just left school, but he had never had a more willing helper. She was a stout girl with persistent acne, and, plain herself, was not repelled by Emma. If things were quiet in the shop she would go up and chat to her. She had once even washed her hair when Mrs Bowling, who usually did it, was away with flu.

Mrs Curtis's dogs, outside in the station wagon, were barking in chorus while Madge carefully tipped out nails into the scoop on the scales. She owned four besides the Alsatian.

'Good morning, Mrs Curtis,' said Norman.

'Morning,' said Paula Curtis. 'Got to fix a broken fence.'

'Oh,' said Norman. 'Is it a big job?' Perhaps this explained the Alsatian's freedom.

'No – won't take long,' said Paula, and went off, a squat figure in grubby corduroy trousers, a duffle jacket and rubber boots. Norman saw her toss the parcel into the back of the wagon among the dogs. A small child with a white face and dark, untidy hair peered out of the side window. She sat on the rear seat, with the Alsatian perched beside her. The other dogs were behind, their heads leaning over her. Norman imagined their breath, strong-smelling, and the long, rasping tongues.

'I shouldn't like to be sat there, among them dogs,' said Madge, expressing just what Norman was thinking.

'She doesn't seem to mind,' he said. 'The kid, I mean.'

'Used to it, I suppose,' Madge remarked. She loved Norman dearly. He never teased her, wouldn't let her carry the heavier goods although she was just as strong as he was, and was always so polite even when telling her what to do. Madge's life had been transformed from the day she entered his employment for she knew she was needed. Who wanted to hang about giggling at the bus stop, waiting to be noticed by some spotty boy, when their days were spent with Mr Widnes? Madge occupied her evenings in washing her hair and putting anti-pimple cream on her face, or reading the magazines passed on to her by Emma.

As Norman watched Madge hurry forward to attend to a new customer, he was thinking that the weekend was coming, and with it Emma's birthday. He would not be able to see Felicity on Saturday night, as he usually did, when Emma thought he was at The Grapes.

Felicity was cutting up fragments of cloth for the children to make into collages. Everyone enjoyed this activity and while the children worked busily

16

at their designs, Felicity was able to let her mind stray from the task in hand.

What a coward she had been, the day before. Once again, when her mind was made up to tell Norman that it must end between them, he had disarmed her. It was unfair of him to make capital of his dependence on her; everyone knew that his domestic life was a strain, tied as he was to an invalid wife much older than himself. People said Emma could not live for long; but how long was long? It might be years. Any permanent future for Felicity with Norman could be only a remote dream, and she was not even sure if it was something she wanted. Meanwhile, her involvement with him was denying her other opportunities – not that there were many in Bidbury. That was, perhaps, why she had slipped into this in the first place. They had met, in the most banal way, when she went into the shop to buy a hand-drill and fitments to put up some shelves. He had told her the best place to buy timber, and after that, whenever she went into the shop, they would discuss what other improvements she planned. Then, one Thursday afternoon when it was raining, he had passed her in his van. She was walking back from school because her car was in dock. Norman had given her a lift; she had asked him in, and so it had begun.

She soon found that the impression of diffidence he gave was misleading; as a lover he was assured and tender. She had invited him into her flat the day their affair began because she was bored and lonely, but she wanted more from life than this limited relationship. Next Thursday she would stick to her resolve and tell him so.

'Perhaps Mrs Curtis will mend her fence over the weekend and keep that dog in,' said Emma, when Norman told her about Paula Curtis buying the nails.

'Maybe he'll be at home for once and do it for her,' said Norman.

'I'm sure she's well able to do it herself,' said Emma. 'She's very capable. She's got to be. He's not like you.'

She stretched out a podgy hand to Norman, the fingers like sausages. She wanted him to caress her. Before she could utter the direct invitation, Norman got up and switched on the television.

'You watch *Nationwide* while I get supper,' he said.

He went out of the room, across the landing to the kitchen, and Emma, propped on the large sofa, gazed after him sadly, not deceived.

Automatically, she popped a chocolate cream into her mouth. Dr Barrett scolded her, every time he came, for eating such a lot; she'd dig her grave with her teeth, he said. But what else was there for her to enjoy?

In the kitchen, Norman was filled with shame. A kiss was little enough to give. He would make amends later, he resolved, neatly dicing cold chicken so that Emma could eat it with a fork. He gave great thought to their meals, refusing Emma the steamed puddings and the pastries that she loved. Mrs Bowling, who cleaned the flat and cooked their mid-day meal every day, brought in sweets and biscuits on the sly and hid them among Emma's possessions. Norman knew it, but he had not the heart to prevent it. He salved his conscience by providing salad and fruit and lean meat, and was, himself, extremely thin.

Sometimes, usually at three in the morning when he could not sleep, Norman would acknowledge that if Emma grew still heavier and threw more strain on her heart, it would all come to an end; if he really wanted to avoid this he would confiscate the hidden titbits and forbid Mrs Bowling to provide more. Perhaps, though, he needed Emma as much as she needed him; at his lowest ebb he would remember how it all began, when his mother was so ill and Emma had suddenly arrived, full of an irresistible warmth. There had been magic then.

It didn't do to look back too far. Some things were best forgotten: those blue capsules, for instance, emptied into that final drink.

Norman took Emma her tray. Then he bent and kissed her cheek, feeling the soft texture of her skin against his lips.

'There, dear. Doesn't that look tasty?'

He laid his own place at the table, where later he would do the books. They kept the television on, so there was no need for conversation.

3

Madge loved Saturday. It was the busiest day of the week in the shop and she was on the go the whole time. Mr Widnes could never manage without her, she was happily certain.

This Saturday she had brought Emma an African violet for her birthday. Emma was delighted with it, and it was on the window-sill beside her when Madge went up at half-past ten for tea.

The electric kettle stood on the floor and Emma had switched it on, but her arms were so flabby that pouring the water was difficult for her. Madge made the tea and while it stood she fetched Emma a chocolate biscuit from the tin they secretly kept in Emma's capacious sewing-bag. She was making a tapestry cushion in large, simple stitches; Mrs Bowling, who would be arriving soon, had sent for the wool and canvas from a magazine.

'Norman will catch us one day,' said Emma, crumbs sticking to her chin.

Madge ate a biscuit too, just as guiltily, for she knew it was bad for her spots.

'Never mind,' she said. 'He wouldn't be really cross.'

'Don't you believe it,' said Emma. 'You don't know him like I do.'

For her lunch Madge brought sandwiches and ate them in the store-room while the shop was closed, or on fine days in the small garden where Norman grew vegetables. Up in the flat Norman, Emma and Mrs Bowling would consume mince, liver, steamed fish, or other such non-fattening fare. Mrs Bowling came every day except Sunday and stayed until three. On Thursdays, early closing day, she stayed until ten-thirty so that Norman could have the proper break which Emma insisted he needed. Mrs Bowling and Emma spent these evenings playing cards.

Before he met Felicity, Norman went to the cinema on Thursdays; now he still pretended that he did so, reading up about what films were showing in New Bidbury and in Muddington in the local paper. At first, lying about them to Emma was difficult, but now it was quite easy and in any case she never showed much curiosity.

Norman and Madge, between them, kept the shop clean. Madge lived across the railway and came to work on the bus. Her father was an electrical fitter who travelled about mending and servicing washing machines and vacuum cleaners, her mother worked in the dry-cleaner's in New Bidbury, and her brother Reg at a local factory. Madge, the butt of teasing at home from Reg and from both boys and girls at school, loved the privacy of her lunch hour at work. She never thought about anything particular then unless it was the next task she would perform in the service of Mr Widnes, but she was aware, though she could not have defined it, of her own utter contentment.

This Saturday she missed her usual bus and so walked home down the path past Mrs Minter's and over the railway. Her mother had said she should not go that way after dark, but Reg had mocked and said that no one was going to bother to do old Madge; whoever would want to?

'That's enough,' their father had frowned. He was ashamed of his daughter's plainness, but he felt an irritated affection for her.

'Ah – there you are, Madge,' said her mother that evening. 'You're late, dear.'

Madge explained that she'd helped Mr Widnes cash up and empty the till. There was ever such a lot of money in it.

'What does he do with it over the weekend?' asked Reg, who was cleaning his boots before going out for the evening.

'That's his business,' said Madge. Why should she tell Reg about the safe in the wardrobe upstairs?

'Stuffs it under his old woman, maybe,' said Reg. 'It'd be safe enough there. Whoever'd move her?'

Madge bristled angrily.

'Mrs Widnes is ever so nice, poor thing,' she snapped.

'It's very sad, as we know,' said the mother in a soothing voice. She hated their squabbles. 'Now come on, you two. Sit down. Tea's ready.'

'Where's Dad?' asked Madge.

'Out,' said their mother flatly. 'We won't be waiting.'

She knew that he'd found a new woman; there

were too many temptations in his kind of job.

'How'd he come to marry her? That Widnes?' Reg was asking between mouthfuls of sausage and chips. 'Old enough to be his mum, isn't she?'

'No.' Mrs Pearce could remember seeing Emma in the shop in those early days. 'Much older than him, yes, but not that old. She was a good-looking woman.'

Emma had been stout then, but handsome; she'd had thick red hair, bright eyes, and a way with her that made you like her at once. Harry, Mrs Pearce's husband, had admired her a lot. It seemed that she and Norman's parents had met years before, on holiday, the story went. Emma, passing through Bidbury, had seen the name Widnes over the ship and called on impulse. When she saw how ill Norman's mother was, she'd moved in and taken the household in charge. She'd been recently widowed herself, it was said, so it answered a problem for her too.

Almost immediately, things changed. Norman stopped looking like a wraith himself; his mother grew more cheerful and was certainly more comfortable, until, after nearly a year, she died.

There had scarcely been time to wonder what Emma would do now before the wedding was a fact.

On Saturday evenings Emma encouraged Norman to go round to The Grapes. Nowadays, though, he spent only a short time at the pub and then went to Felicity's flat. However, because this Saturday was Emma's birthday, he had to stay at home. Jack Phelps, who ran the local garage, was coming with his wife to spend the evening.

Felicity went to the cinema with Elsie Dawes, another teacher, and afterwards, in a pub, they discussed their plans for Easter. While they were talking some youths came into the bar, swaggered up to the counter and noisily ordered their drinks.

'They've seen too many television commercials about the manliness of drinking beer,' said Felicity sourly.

'Hope they don't make a scene,' said Elsie, who was comfortable where she was and wanted another rum and coke before she went home.

The youths were full of physical energy; even their hair, long and carefully styled, seemed to crackle with vitality. They postured and preened themselves like young cockerels.

'Easy enough to break a window,' one said, and Felicity, startled, began to listen to them.

'Someone'd see. There's always folks about. Besides, it wouldn't be kept in the till,' she heard.

One of the boys noticed her looking their way and nudged the speaker.

'Bit old for us, them birds,' he said. 'Been plucked already.'

Amid titters the youths began to discuss where they would go in search of more promising talent.

'Silly kids,' said Elsie, but she spoke tolerantly.

Felicity found them frightening. They were not necessarily lawless, merely misdirected – the sort of young men who could prove heroic in an emergency, such as war. It sounded, now, as if they might be contemplating some sort of break-in. She wondered if the police ought to be warned. She was still wondering when Reg Pearce and his friends left the pub.

'They're taking Emma out,' said Mrs Minter.

It was Sunday, and she was standing by the window pouring out sherry for Mrs Costello, who had come to lunch after going to church. Mrs Minter never went to church but Mrs Costello always did, partly from habit and partly because it helped to pass the time. She vaguely hoped, also, that in some afterlife there would be a chance for her to ask Charles why he had not told her about his financial troubles instead of killing himself and leaving her to face them eventually, but alone. Though it had happened ten years ago, she was still haunted by the memory of finding him in the field below the house, the gun he used for shooting rabbits by his side.

'Emma Widnes? Going out?' Mrs Costello said.

'Yes. I thought they'd given up taking her,' said Mrs Minter.

Mrs Costello joined her at the window. Across the square a large old Rover was drawn up outside the ironmonger's, and Emma, supported on one side by Norman and by an older, burlier man on the other, was tottering through the wide entrance of the shop.

'However did they get her down the stairs?' wondered Mrs Minter.

'That's Jack Phelps, from the garage,' said Mrs Costello. 'They must be going for a drive.'

'Well, Norman is marvellous,' said Mrs Minter. 'He seems to be devoted to her.' Though what about his trips across the fields to see the school-mistress? She gave Mrs Costello her sherry. 'Here you are, Jane. I'll just have a look at the joint.'

They were having half a shoulder of lamb. She knew that Mrs Costello did not bother to cook properly for herself, and unless invited out was likely to start drinking and forget about food. In an exasperated way she was fond of the older woman, and felt obliged to keep an eye on her.

Mrs Costello and her spaniel lived in a small, old house wedged between Bodger's Self-Service and the greengrocer, two doors away from Widnes' Stores. Her garden was longer than Norman's and ran right down to Lincoln Road at the end, where there was a way out through a wicket gate. In summer she had the finest show of flowers in the district, the one factor she had brought to Bidbury from her former life. She worked in the garden constantly while Pedro rootled about beside her. Mostly, she and Pedro were companionably silent, but sometimes she would talk to him, and he only yapped in protest when he was left alone.

Now she stood at her friend's window and shamelessly watched while the great bulk of Emma Widnes was levered into the car. Norman got in beside her, and Jack Phelps, wiping a hand across his heated brow, clambered behind the steering wheel. As they drove off, Mrs Costello saw a white, moon-like face peering out of the side window.

She wondered where they were going, and how they would ever get Emma upstairs again.

Norman wondered the same thing. Emma had not been out of the flat since the summer. Jack Phelps, a kindly man, had suggested the outing as they celebrated her birthday the previous evening.

Well, here they were, driving off. They'd somehow got her down, a step at a time, and somehow they'd get her up again.

The pale sun, low in the wintry sky, shone as they left the square. Three youths who had been sprawling on the seat in the bus shelter saw them go.

'She does go out, then, of a Sunday,' one remarked. 'How long'll they be, I wonder?'

They all got up and slouched over the road to peer in at the window of Norman's shop. Oil heaters, rolls of wire netting, garden tools and so forth were to be seen within, and several tiered columns of saucepans. The till was clearly visible on the counter at the rear.

Reg Pearce had only been showing off his knowledge when he aired the subject in the pub the night before. In theory it would be quite a laugh to see if they could grab the loot, but it was more the lark of trying it that appealed to him than getting the money. He had a good job, and plenty left in his pay packet after his mother had received her share.

He supposed it did no actual harm to look at the shop, however; it didn't mean they'd try anything.

Norman, beside Emma in the car, patted her soft white hand.

'Well, dear. All right, are you?'

Emma looked out at the scene beyond the warm box of the car, hiding a sigh. She had exchanged one prison for another. They would drive to some country pub, bring her a drink to the car, and then drive home again. Jack Phelps had suggested the trip on impulse when the weather forecast was good. If all went well and she seemed to enjoy it, they'd do it again, and a further huge effort would be required from her.

'Lovely, dear,' she said. She clasped Norman's hand and held it against her vast thigh. 'You're good to me, Norm.'

In the mirror Jack Phelps saw Norman look away from her out of the window, his face white and strained, his jaw set.

'Spring's coming,' said Mr Phelps cheerfully. 'There's lambs in the valley. We'll go that way, shall we?'

Emma's heart was thumping uncomfortably and she felt rather breathless. Still, they meant to be kind, taking her out like this; it would never have done to refuse. And it was nice having Norman beside her, close, like they used to be.

'Lovely, Jack,' she gasped.

The boys could see no easy way into Norman's shop from the front. It was wedged between the newsagent's and the greengrocer's, and the shop was the only entrance.

'Maybe there's a way in at the back,' said Terry.

'Oh – let's leave it,' said Reg. 'What's the point?'

'Don't know till we try,' said Mick Green.

They slouched off across the square and down Funnel Lane into Lincoln Road. Here, the gardens of the buildings on one side of the square ended in fences varying in solidity. They walked along, whistling. Mick Green, the biggest of the three, ran his hand along the palings; he picked up a splinter off one, and made a fuss about it. Reg, with large, grimy fingers, prised it out.

Behind Bodger's Self-Service there was a drive-in, and Bodger's van could be seen there; also, beside it, was Norman's small green van. His name was neatly painted on its side. If he kept it there, it must mean his shop had no back entrance, reasoned Mick.

Then they saw Mrs Costello's gate, a wicket one in her fence. Mick was through it in a flash, and making his way up the garden.

Suddenly a high, irate barking came from the house. Pedro, shut in while his mistress was out, was defending the property.

Mick dashed out again at speed, and the three boys ran up the road, laughing.

'No good, you see,' said Reg, very relieved.

'There's ways of making dogs quiet,' said Mick.

'Bet you can't do it – get in and get the loot,' said Terry.

'How much?' asked Mick.

4

'**O**ur children must learn to relate to nature,' said Lydia Renshaw in the voice she had used when she taught home economics before her marriage. 'It's particularly important when they're growing up in an urban environment.'

Geoffrey, intent on the *Sunday Express*, did not look up.

'Mm,' he said.

'You're not listening,' Lydia accused.

'I am – it's important that the children appreciate nature,' he said, masking a sigh. Lydia's earnestness started operating the moment she awoke each morning.

'Relate to, not just appreciate,' she said. 'We ought to get a puppy. You'd like that, wouldn't you, Jamie?' she asked her son. 'Perhaps it could be your very own.' Luckily she did not wait for an answer but swept on. 'Animals communicate on a different level from us. Learning to live with them is a special art. It deepens the meaning of life.'

Jamie heard his mother in an agony of fear.

'There's Claire now, too,' she pointed out. 'The sooner we get a dog the better – they can all grow up together.'

'Why?' asked Geoffrey. 'It's different for people

who are alone, like poor Mrs Costello, who needs a dog for company, but we don't. We've got one another.'

Jamie felt like cheering at these staunch words.

'I'm going to wash the car. Coming to give me a hand, Jamie?' asked Geoffrey, abandoning the paper.

Thankfully, Jamie followed him into the garden.

'I don't like dogs very much, Dad,' he confided as they bent to sponge the bumper of the Vauxhall.

'What? Don't you?' To Jamie's dismay his father did not look pleased. 'Not afraid of them, are you?'

'Oh no! No, of course not,' Jamie said hastily.

He wasn't really: only of big, fierce ones, he told himself. But all dogs had a way of sniffing at you that he didn't really like.

'Because if you are, we must get one as your mother says,' his father told him. 'To get you over it. Can't have that sort of thing.'

That Sunday night, Norman lay wakeful in bed, unable to stop his racing mind as it played back to him a film of the day. Somehow, after her outing, they had got Emma up the stairs, but she'd had to pause halfway for over ten minutes, getting her breath back, and when they reached the top she'd looked very blue. It hadn't been worth the effort; he knew that short of a miracle she would never come down again.

'You're very good to me, Norm,' she'd repeated. 'Fat, useless old bag that I am.'

'Don't talk like that,' he'd answered, wanting to

31

add that he owed her so much, but the words wouldn't come out.

Who owed whom what, he wondered now, staring up in the darkness at the ceiling, and when did payment cease? His door was propped ajar, so that if she called out in the night he would hear her. They'd lain in here together when his mother was dying, listening, the two of them, in the same sort of way. Only when she had sunk into a heavy drugged sleep had they felt free from restraint. Norman was confident that she'd never suspected them.

Those had been wild months. Looking at Emma now, it was difficult to believe it had not been some fantasy. With Felicity he had a much calmer relationship, but under it, never mentioned, was a sense of futility. He was paying now for what happened years ago, binding him and Emma irrevocably together.

Emma was awake too. Her heart thumped and her breathing was difficult, but she had taken her pills and soon she would drowse off. It would take her days to get over this morning's expedition.

Norman was very patient. How would things have turned out for him if she had not arrived in his life when she did, Emma wondered. He'd been so ardent; Emma could still smile, remembering him then, but soon tears would come to her eyes to think that it was all over. She could sense his reluctance now whenever he so much as kissed her. Once, it had been so different.

Norman never left the sleeping tablets within her reach: her heart pills, yes, but not the barbiturates.

'I don't want an accident,' he had said.

It had not been an accident four years ago, and what had happened before could happen again. He would come to it in the end, she was certain.

Paula Curtis cut up the dogs' meat on the drainer in the kitchen. She had a large knife in one big red hand; the other, holding the raw meat, was stained with blood. Around her in the kitchen were ranged her canine pack, in an expectant semi-circle. Excited whimpers came from the Alsatian and the collie. Her two bulldogs leaned forward on their stumpy front legs, panting. Only the Labrador which belonged to Guy, her husband, was absent.

'Well, my boys, hungry then, are you?' Mrs Curtis inquired of them, chopping away. 'All in good time, my lovely lads.'

She went on talking while she portioned the meat into five bowls. Somewhere among them rested a small cabbage, and a chicken divested of its polythene bag, semi-thawed. A half-full bottle of milk was nearby.

A stream of saliva issued from the Alsatian's mouth; his jaws were open, the large pink tongue curling forward, huge white teeth revealed.

'Just a minute more, my pets,' Paula said. 'Greedy boys, then.'

Her voice was crooning. When she had finished preparing the bowls, she set them on the floor in a row; each dog went to his own and sat before it, waiting to be told he might eat. Paula crossed to the back door, opened it, and went out to call the missing Labrador.

'Go on, my boys,' she said to the others,

33

returning, and waited by the open door till Boris padded in and went over to his own bowl.

Paula picked up the chicken, put it in a meat tin, opened the refrigerator and took out some dripping wrapped in crumpled foil; she sniffed it, and then, with the knife she had used for the dogs' dinner, cut off a lump which she arranged on top of the bird. It slid off the slippery wet breast, so she picked it up in her fingers and wedged it over the bone. She wiped the knife across the thighs of the bird before putting it, unwashed, away in a drawer; the roasting tin went into the oven.

After this, Paula stood watching the dogs while they ate. Their jaws made a chumping, slopping sound. After some time another noise penetrated her consciousness: the crying of a child.

She ignored it for over ten minutes, but it grew louder and louder, and at last, exasperated, Paula went out of the kitchen and down the passage to what had once been a breakfast room. The floor was covered in dirty worn linoleum, and the room contained a cheap deal table, several unmatched chairs, a large marrow bone, gnawed white, a chewed-up rubber ball, and a child's cot in which a small girl, wearing only a sweater, stood up shaking the bars and crying hysterically. The blankets on which she stood were stained, and now they were saturated too.

'Damn you, you filthy little beast!' Paula put her two strong hands round the child's chest and plucked her from the cot. 'This is what happens when dogs foul their beds,' she said, and seizing the sodden blanket, she rubbed the child's contorted little face against the wet wool. Then she took the child, held face downwards under one arm, along the passage to the lavatory. It was quite bare except for the pan and washbasin. She thrust the child inside and closed the door upon her.

Paula's husband, Guy Curtis, ran an import and export business based in London, but he spent a great deal of time abroad, chiefly in South America.

He had met Paula at a party in London; he was between women at the time, and her muscular body, gaunt face and deepset brown eyes had intrigued him. He learned that she was a sculptor, but it was some time before he saw her work and realized that she was quite ungifted; at least, in his view. She turned out models of animals, woodenly posed, which were cast by a middle-man and sold to tourist shops as souvenirs; and she lived on a houseboat with her dogs. Without really meaning anything very much, he embarked on an affair with her and was trapped into marriage by the oldest trick of all. One of his friends warned him that she only wanted a permanent meal ticket and that was why she had let it happen, but Guy thought it was bad luck on any child to be born illegitimate. After their marriage they bought the house in Bidbury because it was convenient for London, had space for her animals, and a ready-made studio shed in the garden. The baby, when it arrived, was a thin listless little thing who cried a lot. Guy found her pathetic, and at the same time such attraction as Paula had held for him vanished, so most of the time he kept away. But he did not think seriously of ending the marriage legally; having a wife was a protection from other women who became too demanding. Laura grew from a crying baby into a whining, charmless little girl, and because she did not know him, she cried whenever they met.

Children were better not fussed, Guy thought, when he bothered to consider his daughter at all. He gave her mother a generous allowance and thought no more about his responsibility.

Lincoln Close, where Jamie Renshaw lived with his parents and small sister, was a small development of modern houses south of the square in Old Bidbury. To the north, New Bidbury had grown up round an industrial area with a modern shopping centre and colonies of housing estates. Next to the Renshaws lived the Armitages. Kenneth Armitage worked for a New Bidbury firm which made office equipment; he was an ambitious man, active in local affairs and now a councillor. Sarah Armitage was always behind with her household tasks because she got side-tracked by dipping into books, playing with her small son, Simon, or simply day-dreaming. She kept meaning to undertake something constructive, but the most she had managed was to enrol, this winter, in a weekly yoga class.

Among Kenneth's activities was bellringing, which he had done as a boy. In Old Bidbury the team practised every Wednesday evening for two hours, and sometimes they rang peals which lasted far longer, forcing those who lived near the church to turn up their radios, play their records loudly, and shut all the windows. Kenneth regarded this interest as a relaxation; his council

36

work was his civic duty; his hobby was carpentry, and he attended an evening class in it one night a week. He was thus frequently out in the evening. Sarah's yoga meant that there was now another evening in the week when she need not sit, tense and bad-tempered, with Kenneth. She was lonely when he was out, but she was uncomfortable when he was not.

This Sunday Kenneth had, as usual, rung the bells morning and evening, and in the evening for once he attended the service; he sat next to a nice-looking girl with a pleasant voice and had let his own reedy tenor go, hoping that she would admire it, but she'd given no sign.

When he got home, Simon was asleep, cold supper was laid in the dining recess, and Sarah was practising the shoulder stand upstairs in the bedroom.

Kenneth was annoyed not to find her eager for his return. He poured out two sherries and sat sipping his in the living area which was furnished with G-plan pieces and had Athena prints on the walls. Kenneth was well satisfied with the marks of material success around him, but less so with his wife, who was not living up to the expectations he had of her when he invited her to take up the post. His worldly ascent was assured, but what about her? He feared that Sarah would always be lagging behind.

He called up to her that her sherry was waiting, a note of asperity in his voice. What could she be doing?

Sarah, chin pressed into her chest, stared defiantly at her legs which were in the air. She was beginning to feel rather uncomfortable and would have to return to a more normal position soon, but she had decided to assert herself. She would not run meekly down just because he called: let him wait.

With luck there would be a good play on television, so that they need not try to communicate, for their conversations always became either arguments or instructional lectures from Kenneth.

Emptying her mind, in approved yoga fashion, she adopted the plough posture, feet touching the floor over her head, and stayed in the position some minutes.

She went down at last, past Gyp, the Airedale, who lay on the floor outside Simon's room, and when Kenneth asked what had delayed her she looked at him coldly.

'I was busy,' was all she said.

Mrs Costello, after her lunch with Mrs Minter, had a nip of brandy when she got home, then a snooze. After that she let Pedro out into the garden and joined him there, weeding among the vigorous shoots which the bulbs were sending up. She was rather surprised to see a large, obviously male, footprint on the path by the gate to Lincoln Road, where the ground was damp and the grass worn thin so that only a few sprigs showed in the earth. Perhaps it was the mark of the dustman who had called on Thursday, she thought vaguely, and forgot about it, working on, kneeling on the ground, until dusk fell.

5

On the Monday morning after Emma's outing in the car, Madge arrived at the shop to find Norman outside it with a small boy.

'Ah – Madge,' he said as soon as he saw her. 'Go in, will you, please, and open up when it's time. I'll not be long,' and with no further explanation he set off with the little boy down Funnel Lane.

Madge obediently went into the shop, snibbed the door shut behind her, and hung up her coat in the back lobby. She pulled down her new bright green sweater, bought specially to impress Norman but since it would be covered up all day unlikely to be noticed, and put on her clean overall. Then she set to, and was just ready at nine, the floor swept, the counter-top shining, to open the shop. She started to dust the stock next; trade was seldom brisk first thing on a Monday, though some travellers usually came that day. Norman soon reappeared.

'Mrs Widnes didn't call down, did she?' he asked.

'No,' said Madge. 'Shall I pop up?'

'I'll go,' said Norman. 'She wasn't too well in the night.'

'Oh dear,' said Madge, and watched him go upstairs.

That morning the Alsatian had once again deflected Jamie. When Norman took him past, it had stood watching, not even barking this time. No one could say it was vicious or menacing; it appeared almost indifferent. It was not even in the roadway, a danger to traffic; it was just alarming to look at, especially if you were rather small.

'Why don't you go and see Mrs Curtis about it?' Emma suggested when Norman told her that he had taken Jamie up the road again. 'Ask her to keep it in.'

'Perhaps I will. Or the kid's parents might.' Norman was sponging her pale, clammy face. 'Or I could offer to fix the fence for her. Though the gate is always open – if she closed that it might help to keep the dog in, fence or no fence.'

'You let her mend her own fence, Norm,' said Emma. 'You've enough to do without that. Once start it, and you don't know where it would end. She might have you round there every five minutes.' Emma did not trust what she knew of Paula Curtis.

'Now, is that likely, dear?' Norman asked her. 'As if I'd let her take advantage of me.'

'You're soft-hearted,' said Emma. And might be an easy target, she thought but did not say aloud.

Norman was not interested in analysing his own nature; he was more concerned with Emma's condition. From time to time she had turns like this, and there were pills she took. He gave her one, with a drink, and later that morning when he went up for his tea she seemed better.

*

40

Felicity was pleased to find Jamie punctual again; she knew nothing about Norman's part in this achievement for they had not met since the first time it happened. She had spent Sunday cleaning the flat and washing her hair, then scrutinizing advertisements for teaching posts abroad. The sensible thing was to put as many miles as possible between herself and Norman. He would manage perfectly well without her, or if he could not, would soon find somebody else.

Because she had nothing else to do and enjoyed singing, she went to church on Sunday evening, where, without knowing who he was, she sat next to Kenneth Armitage. During the sermon, which was exceedingly dull, she remembered the youths in the pub and their conversation, and wondered again if she should tell the police what she had overhead. But by Monday she had forgotten it again.

Mrs Costello went to the laundrette on Monday as part of her weekly ritual. She took her washing in a large polythene bag and watched it spin round. It was a way of passing the time, although most people left to do other things while the machine ran.

Mrs Bowling came in and bundled the Widnes washing into one machine and her own into another, before bustling back to the shop. She was a brisk little woman, over sixty now but still energetic; her husband was a ticket collector at New Bidbury station.

'How's Mrs Widnes?' asked Mrs Costello, detaining her.

'Bit poorly today – she went out for a car drive

yesterday and it was too much for her, poor soul,' said Mrs Bowling, who privately thought that Mrs Costello looked none too good either, though that might be due to the gin. Mrs Bowling knew she consumed a fair bit of it, for she often saw her coming away from the off-licence with a couple of bottles in her string bag. It must cost so much, Mrs Bowling thought; no wonder the old woman looked half starved – she couldn't be spending enough on food.

Mrs Costello hung her tumble-dried washing round the kitchen. Then she set off with Pedro to walk to New Bidbury, where she bought some knickers at Marks and Spencer's, red nylon ones with black lace edging at the knee. Next, she went to W.H. Smith's and looked at magazines. While she did this, Pedro kept getting his lead tangled among the other shoppers causing a good deal of exasperation. She bought two paperback thrillers and a biro; she was always losing them when she fell asleep over the *Daily Telegraph* crossword, but seldom thought of searching for them under the cushion of her armchair. Next she turned down a wide arcade that linked the big stores to a row of smaller shops, among them a health shop and the dry-cleaner's. As she approached, she heard a child crying hysterically, and outside the cleaner's she saw a small girl standing on the pavement sobbing in total despair. She was facing the cleaner's window, but she was too small to see over its solid base.

'Have you lost your mummy, dear?' asked Mrs Costello. She transferred Pedro's lead to the hand which held her shopping bag and took the child's hand with the other.

Immediately, the crying stopped.

'Is she in there? Your mummy? In the shop?' asked Mrs Costello.

But the child was unable to answer.

Mrs Costello thought of finding a policeman, but decided to make her own inquiries first. With difficulty, hung about as she was with child, shopping and dog, she opened the door of the cleaner's and said to a woman who stood by the counter, 'Is this your little girl?'

'Yes – and you leave her alone,' snapped Paula Curtis. 'She's to wait outside. You mind your own business.'

Mrs Costello, shocked, backed out of the shop. Inside, Mrs Pearce, Madge's mother, who was serving Paula, looked horrified.

The child began to cry again, and Mrs Costello bent down, dumping her bag, to console her. Pedro, stumpy tail wagging, stood by, displaying goodwill.

Paula came furiously out of the shop.

'I told you to leave her alone,' she said, caught Laura roughly by the arm and dragged her away, scolding her loudly as they went. Mrs Costello stared after them, appalled; it took her a few minutes to gather herself together and go into the cleaner's with a shabby tweed skirt that needed their attentions.

Lydia Renshaw was always busy with dress-making, running up curtains or chair-covers, making jewellery from bits of quartz, or other such projects. Her industry made Sarah Armitage, who lived next door, feel inadequate, but she was grateful for Lydia's friendship.

43

On Monday afternoon Sarah, Simon and Gyp, the Airedale, were all at the Renshaws. The smell of freshly baked bread filled the house, and now Lydia sat crocheting while Sarah, feeling decadent because idle, lounged in a large armchair. The two babies sat on the floor among bricks and toys, playing solitary games in harmony together while their mothers talked. At least, Sarah supposed that they talked. They each, it was true, took turns to speak while the other listened, but Sarah felt they merely made sounds, not contact.

'I must be going round the bend,' she thought distractedly when Lydia's voice suddenly ceased and it was her turn. What had Lydia been saying?

She uttered the first words that came into her head.

'Why don't you get a dog?'

Lydia looked rather surprised. She had been talking about organically grown vegetables and pure food, subjects dear to her heart. But she rallied.

'We mean to,' she said. 'It's important for the children.'

Sarah knew that she needed Gyp for herself. When, as nowadays constantly happened, she found herself wondering what on earth she was doing living with a man who thought only of his status, civic affairs and bellringing, and for whom she felt nothing more than anxious impatience, it was Gyp who kept her in touch with reality. She'd had him long before she had Simon. Kenneth had never objected to him; it was proper to keep a dog – it rounded off the family circle of man, wife and two children, with pet by the hearth: that was his blueprint. Simon had obligingly arrived on schedule; it would soon be time, according to Kenneth's plan, to indent for his sister. What would happen if a brother arrived, Sarah wondered, or worse, no second child? Or wouldn't God dare to defy Kenneth?

'How did you meet Geoff?' she asked now.

Lydia hid her surprise at Sarah's inconsequentiality and crocheted on.

'I've always known him,' she said. 'We lived near each other.'

'Oh. The boy next door.'

'A mile away,' said Lydia. 'I never took much notice of him, though, till a tennis club dance.'

She'd gone with someone else, and Geoffrey had suddenly revealed that he was jealous.

'Are you ambitious for him?' Sarah demanded. 'I mean, do you want him to get on the board of his firm? Shall you have the boss to dinner?'

'Yes, yes, and yes,' said Lydia. 'Why do you ask?'

She thought that Sarah seemed very much on edge. Surely she wanted the same things for Kenneth?

'I just wondered if you ever got fed up,' said Sarah.

'Why should I?' asked Lydia. 'I've nothing to complain of.'

The night before, Sarah and Kenneth had gone to bed not speaking. Her gesture of independence had misfired, for when she finally came downstairs she had knocked her sherry over. Kenneth, wearing a patient expression, had insisted on clearing up the mess and had cut himself on a piece of glass. He had said she was obviously in one of her clumsy moods. Then he had reminded her to put out a clean shirt for him in the morning and to check the buttons. She'd furiously demanded to know whether he had ever yet been left without a clean shirt or found one with a button missing, and had flung the pile of neatly folded shirts at him.

She was to blame for the row, and she had not apologized. She longed to pour all this out but feared that Lydia would not be sympathetic; besides, she must keep up the pretence that all was well at home: it ought to be, for she had everything a girl was supposed to want. To confess otherwise was to admit failure, and it was her failure, not Kenneth's.

'Where did you and Kenneth meet?' Lydia inquired.

'On holiday in Italy.'

Kenneth had seemed different then, in his bright patterned shirt and blue shorts: he was lively and attentive. He showed her round churches and told her all about them; he was a good swimmer and encouraged her to be bolder. Translated back to England, he had seemed less attractive in his city suit, but he had continued to take her to art galleries and museums. They were free in England, she had noted at the time, and suppressed the reflection as base. After they married his instructions were concentrated on housekeeping matters and how she should mould herself to suit his own social and business aspirations. She often wondered, now, why he had wanted to marry her when she was so far from his ideal, and could not know that at the age of thirty-three he had begun to fear no passable girl would accept him; he had pursued many a one, only to be snubbed in the end.

'How romantic,' said Lydia. 'And was he dashing and ardent?'

'I suppose so.' Sarah had no great experience by which to judge.

'Keeping all that up would be very uncomfortable,' said Lydia. 'It doesn't last, does it? Friendship does.'

'I suppose you're right,' said Sarah.

But what if there was no friendship, and the ardour was all spurious?

'Where's Jamie?' she asked, to escape from such uncomfortable thoughts. 'He's late, isn't he?' She liked Jamie, who often looked as worried as she constantly felt.

'Yes, he is, rather,' said Lydia, seeming unconcerned. 'I expect he's day-dreaming somewhere on the way home.'

As she spoke, the back door opened. Jamie was trained to come in that way and change his shoes in the kitchen. In a few minutes he entered the room in his socks, carrying his sandals.

'Hullo, Jamie,' said Sarah.

'Hullo,' said Jamie hollowly.

His mother told him to put his sandals on, and he sat down on the floor to obey. That afternoon he had passed the Alsatian; it had meant loitering about until some more children came along Foster Avenue. He'd tagged on behind them and gone breathlessly past, but he still felt a bit sick with the fear he had felt.

Gyp looked up at him; his square face stared genially at Jamie as he put on his shoes. The snag about Mrs Armitage, who was otherwise one of Jamie's favourite people, was Gyp; but Jamie trusted her, and so he knew that Gyp would not

47

bite him. I'm not really afraid of dogs, he told himself firmly, remembering his father's threat to buy one if he was. To prove himself, he went over to the hearth, put out a tentative hand, and gingerly patted Gyp's back. The dog gave him a perfunctory lick, then laid his head down again on his paws and resumed his staring session with the fire.

Only Sarah noticed Jamie's tense expression as he carried out this self-imposed challenge.

6

After school that afternoon Felicity went to the shop. Norman immediately handed on to Madge the customer he was looking after and came over to her. His obvious pleasure at seeing her made Felicity's resolution falter; she picked up a china mug and looked at the mark on its base.

'I want to talk to you,' she began. The mug had been made in Stoke-on-Trent.

'I'm sorry about Saturday. It couldn't be helped,' said Norman.

By this he took away the initiative. He was looking at her intensely; there was nothing abject about him.

'You've never met Emma, have you?' he asked. 'She'll be having her tea now. Come on up.'

'No – Norman, I couldn't!' Felicity was horrified.

But Norman had turned to Madge, who had finished with her customer.

'Mrs Widnes has got her tea, hasn't she, Madge?'

For every afternoon Madge went upstairs and made it for her.

'Yes, Mr Widnes. I took it to her ten minutes ago,' said Madge. And had slipped her some custard cream biscuits from the hidden tin to reinforce the permitted slice of crisp-bread.

'I'm taking Miss Baxter up to see her,' said Norman. 'You carry on down here.'

'Norman, no—' Felicity was still protesting, but in muted tones, because of Madge.

'Come along.' Norman paid no heed, and swept her out of the shop. There was a lobby at the back, with the entrance to the store-room on the left, and on the right the narrow, steep staircase. 'This way,' Norman directed, propelling her before him.

'Norman, no! I didn't come for this,' said Felicity, stopping halfway.

He put his hands on her waist. 'I know. But it had to happen one day,' he said.

She didn't agree, but he would not let her escape.

At the top of the stairs there was a long landing, off which led several doors. One was open.

'I'll go first,' said Norman.

Why is he doing this, thought Felicity wildly, but she had no time to wonder any longer, for he had gone through the open door and it was beyond her to turn and flee. Her feet seemed to have become stuck to the patterned carpet on the landing.

'Oh, Norman, there you are,' said a voice, none too clearly.

'Yes, dear. And I've brought a visitor. Miss Baxter from the school,' Norman said. He turned to Felicity. 'Come along in.'

Like one hypnotized, Felicity obeyed.

The room she went into was quite large, with a good deal of furniture crammed into it: a dining table, several armchairs, a sideboard, and a huge sofa by the window on which reclined a woman who looked as if she were made of lard. Tiny eyes were sunk in white folds of flesh; several chins rested on her chest so that she appeared to be neckless. A female Humpty Dumpty, Felicity thought hysterically, as she noticed the tiny feet in smart bronze patent shoes protruding from under a soft rug spread over Emma's legs. She's vain about her feet, Felicity registered. The ankles were covered: perhaps they were swollen.

Norman had crossed to the sofa and bent to kiss Emma's forehead. Over her head he looked compellingly at Felicity, who slowly stepped forward.

Emma stretched out a hand.

'How nice of you to call,' she said regally.

Felicity took the extended hand and felt the limp touch of podgy fingers.

'Do sit down,' said Emma. 'Norman—' she waved a hand, still in queenly style, and Norman picked up the kettle. A tea-tray rested on a table close to Emma. Staring, unable to utter, Felicity watched Norman top up the teapot; she saw crumbs on a plate.

'I'll get a cup,' said Norman, and he left the room.

Emma, with another imperious gesture, indicated a low chair that faced her, and Felicity sank slowly down upon it. Now that the situation confronted her, she was appalled.

'You've been at the school some time, Miss Baxter, haven't you?' Emma was saying. 'I've seen you in the square. You've got a little red car. I know so many people by sight, but not to talk to. Though I did, of course, before I was ill.'

Her voice was slighly slurred, and she spoke slowly, but there was no difficulty about understanding what she said.

'Three years,' Felicity gasped, in reply.

'You like it? You'll be staying?'

Felicity plunged.

'I like it, yes, but I plan to move soon,' she said. 'Probably overseas.'

'I see.' Emma nodded, and as Norman returned with a clean cup and saucer she said, 'Miss Baxter tells me she's leaving soon to go abroad.'

Norman set the cup steadily on the tray, poured out Felicity's tea and gave it to her. He hasn't asked if I take sugar, Felicity thought absurdly, so Emma will realize that he knows I don't. There was none on the tray.

She looked at Norman and then she looked at Emma, and she suddenly felt so icily cold that her teeth began to chatter. She clamped them together, accepting the cup and saucer from Norman and willing her hand to remain steady.

For Emma knew. Her acceptance showed on her face.

She's always known, Felicity realized. Perhaps not that it was me, but that there was someone. There had to be.

'I expect Bidbury gets a bit dull after a time,' Norman said in an even voice.

'Not dull, really. Limited,' said Felicity.

She sipped her tea, calmer now. It was fantastic to be sitting here like this, with the pair of them. Norman had drawn up a chair for himself close beside his wife; he looked completely unperturbed.

'Norman likes children. He'd have made a good

teacher. But he'd the shop coming to him,' said Emma. 'And his mother needed him.' She looked at Felicity. 'Now he's saddled with me. And we've no family.'

All the time she spoke the two beady eyes watched Felicity closely. It's as if I were an insect on a pin, and she was devising ways to torment me, thought the girl.

'Don't talk like that, dear,' Norman said. 'You know I regret nothing – nothing at all – except about your health, of course,' and he laid his hand on Emma's arm, pressing it. She held up her plump hand and he clasped it firmly.

Felicity felt rather sick.

He loves her, she thought, half in horror, half fascinated.

'I went out for a drive yesterday,' Emma said, in a lighter tone. She had proved her point.

'How nice,' said Felicity.

'It was. But to do it again, we'd need the fire brigade,' said Emma and laughed. Her fat body shook, huge breasts wobbling above the rug drawn over her knees. 'I got stuck on the stairs.'

'Well, here you are,' said Felicity feebly.

'Yes.'

For ten terrible minutes more Felicity sat there, making small talk. At one point Norman left them, to see if all was well below with Madge, and while he was gone Emma remarked on how good he was.

'He was broken up when his mother died,' she said. 'It was a mercy, though, when it happened. She'd suffered so much.'

And Emma had moved in just when Norman was at his most vulnerable, Felicity thought. Why

53

had they married? An affair, yes – but to marry him, with nearly twenty years between them, the wrong way round – it was obscene.

As if she could read her thoughts, Emma said, 'I wasn't always like this, you know. That's me, over there,' and she nodded towards a photograph that stood on a bookcase across the room.

Felicity, still mesmerized, went over to look at it. It showed Norman looking plumper than he did now; and his hair, which had begun to recede, was quite thick. Beside him was an extremely good-looking woman who, even in a black-and-white photograph, looked full of vitality.

'It was lucky the stroke didn't kill me, wasn't it?' Emma said softly. 'Or don't you think so?'

Felicity did not have to answer, for Norman came back then, but Emma would not let her leave yet. She began to ask about her work.

'Has Norman told you about Jamie Renshaw?' Emma asked.

'No. How could he have?' Felicity seized her chance to strike back in her own defence. 'What about Jamie?'

'He's afraid of an Alsatian he meets in Foster Avenue on his way to school.'

Felicity looked at Norman and saw him nod.

'Yes – it's true. He's been avoiding the dog by coming this way, up Funnel Lane and round by the main road,' he said.

'Norman discovered what was happening, and has taken Jamie past the Alsatian a couple of times,' Emma said.

'So that's why Jamie's been late so often,' Felicity exclaimed.

'The dog's quite gentle. But he does look rather fierce,' Norman said.

'Norman can't bear anyone to be unhappy,' said Emma. 'He tries to please everyone.'

Mrs Costello could not get the thought of the wailing child outside the cleaner's shop out of her mind. So upset was she that she went straight round to tell Mrs Minter about the incident.

Mrs Minter was making marmalade.

'I don't see what you can do about it now, Jane,' she said, slicing rind. 'You don't know who the woman was, do you?'

'No. She was like a harpy – hair all over the place and one of those shaggy coats, all fronded,' said Mrs Costello colourfully. 'As a matter of fact, I had the feeling I'd seen her before, but I don't know where.'

Mrs Minter was appropriately shocked at the tale, but she also welcomed the chance of a crusade for Mrs Costello; it would be a positive action, and might deflect her from the gin on which she spent so much of her meagre income.

'You might see her again, if you keep a look-out,' she said. 'If you see anything else like that, perhaps you could report her to the police or the NSPCC.'

'Yes, I could,' agreed Mrs Costello. 'Well, I do go into New Bidbury quite often – I go to the library twice a week, not to mention the fish shop.' For frozen fish was the only sort obtainable in Old Bidbury and Pedro liked cods' heads, as a change from Meatimix. 'I'll remember.'

'That's right,' said Mrs Minter encouragingly. 'Good luck.'

'You want to get rid of me,' said Mrs Costello.

'I don't, but I must write some letters this evening and I want to get the marmalade done first,' said Mrs Minter. 'You're welcome to stay and chat to me while it boils. I'll make some tea.'

But Mrs Costello was feeling the need for something stronger than tea, so she went away.

'That your old man's?' asked Harry Pearce, picking up a man's jacket on a wire hanger and still in the cleaner's plastic bag.

'Yes. One of the dogs got hold of it,' said Paula Curtis. In fact Guy had thrown the garment out, and she had adopted it to wear herself.

'Mm. Thin fellow, isn't he?' Harry remarked, holding it against his own burly torso. He wondered if Edna had dealt with her at the cleaner's. The thought amused him: two more different women you couldn't find – Edna so neat, rather prim, and utterly virtuous; Paula as crude as any man.

'Fed the dogs, have you?' he asked.

'Can't you tell? Look at them.'

They lay about the kitchen, replete; the bulldogs asleep; the Alsatian immobile but all the time watching the humans; the others dreaming, whimpering now and then.

'What about the kid?'

'She's off too. Hours ago. She never wakes.'

She did, but far off in Paula's bedroom they would not hear her.

'Come on, then. What are we waiting for.'

He pushed her before him upstairs. It was a bit of luck, this one, coming just as he'd tired of his last little sideline, which was how he described them to himself. He'd never met anything like Paula before. There had been plenty of others, and there would be more, he hoped; getting about as he did in his van all over the district he met lonely and frustrated women often enough, though not all of them, however desperate, gave him the nod. It was never worth pressing, however much you fancied them. But this one was different. He never thought he'd go for a slut – and she was one, for all she called herself a sculptor, making clay models in her shed in the garden. She was wild; and though he knew, obscurely, that it wouldn't last for long, at the moment he couldn't get enough of her.

When he went home that night, Edna, who seldom took any notice when he got back so late, stirred as he slid into bed beside her.

'Where have you been, Harry?' she mumbled. 'Petting some dog? You smell of it.'

She was a bitch. Edna was right.

Every Monday, after taking her dachshunds for their early morning walk round the streets, Rose Hallam spent the morning scouring the house from top to toe. Privately her husband Bob, who was manager of a bank in New Bidbury, wished she were less perfect a housekeeper; he felt guilty if a speck of mud fell from his shoe to the pale carpet, or if he did not put away a book he had been reading. But Rose never nagged; it was just a compulsion.

Since she'd taken on her new job at Marguerite's, a boutique in the town, she'd been better, however; he'd once actually noticed a film of dust she'd missed along a picture and had exulted. She was happier now, but he wished she could come out from behind the barrier of her shyness and make friends of her own. He was, by nature, cheerful and gregarious; he enjoyed golf, which he often played at weekends, but he felt guilty at leaving Rose alone then. She depended on him for companionship and for attracting other people to them both. The little dogs were something he suffered in silence. He loved Rose, and so he understood her need to croon over them as if they were human babies, but the fact that she needed them so much made him feel that he had failed her.

'Well – seen anyone today?' he asked, kissing her, when he came home on Monday evening.

'I talked to Sarah Armitage,' said Rose. 'We met when I was out with my boys for their walkies.'

Bob tried not to wince at how she said this.

'That's good,' he remarked.

'I don't think she's very happy,' said Rose. 'She seems rather nervy.'

'Oh darling, surely she's all right,' said Bob. The Hallams were older than the Armitages and the Renshaws, and lived in a larger, more expensive house; they were barely acquainted. Bob knew, however, about Kenneth Armitage's bank account and his modestly comfortable position. 'They've got a nice house – young Armitage will do well.'

'That isn't everything,' said Rose. 'Kenneth may be the trouble. He's got a mean look – and he's smug. I wonder if he's kind.'

Bob felt unable to answer this, and was anyway not much interested in the Armitages' matrimonial relationship, although pleased that

Rose seemed to have made some sort of friendly contact with Sarah.

'What's for dinner?' he asked, and the Hallams settled down to a tranquil evening with sherry before their meal, *Panorama* on television, and then a game of backgammon, which they had recently taken up.

That evening after leaving the shop, Madge had just crossed the square when a figure loomed at her from the kerbside: Mick Green, one of her brother Reg's friends.

'Hi, Madge,' he said.

'Hi yourself,' said Madge, who had no time for Mick.

'Like a lift? I've got the bike.' Mick owned a powerful motor-bike.

'No, thanks.'

'You scared?'

'Course I'm not scared.'

'Well, then.'

'I'd rather walk.'

'Stuck up, are we?'

'In a hurry.'

'Get on the bike, then.'

'No.'

'I'm going round your way. Going to see Reg.'

'He won't be home yet.'

'Yes, he will. Gets home same time I do. Come on, Madge.'

'No,' said Madge, and she pushed past him, hurrying towards the bus stop.

'Get you,' Mick said to her retreating back. He knew few other girls who would refuse such an invitation. But then most girls weren't like Madge.

He wanted to ask her where the money was kept overnight in Widnes' Stores. He'd thought she'd be easy.

He'd have to find some other way to get the information out of her.

7

Every morning now, Jamie came into the square, and Norman, watching for him, suspected that he no longer went to Foster Avenue first; but anyway the Alsatian was always there.

On Thursday, when Jamie had run on to school, Norman turned in at Paula Curtis's gate.

The Alsatian followed him up the drive; it began to growl softly, then to bark. Norman felt slight apprehension but walked resolutely on, and then a black Labrador approached. It snuffled and snorted at him, waving its tail and lifting its lip in a sort of grin. More noisy barking began as the bulldogs joined in, and the collie tore round the side of the house towards him.

The uproar was fearful, and Norman was relieved when Paula appeared, calling the dogs to order. They fell back, the collie, hackles up, crouching beside her, snarling.

'Mrs Curtis – sorry to intrude,' Norman said. 'Er – have you managed to mend your fence yet?'

'No – there's no hurry for it. It's been down for months,' said Paula.

'Er – your dog – it's always in the road,' Norman said. 'This one.' He pointed to the Alsatian.

61

'Hector? Yes, he does wander,' said Paula. 'But the fence makes no difference – it's the one next to Oak House, that's empty, which is broken. Hector goes out of the gate.'

As her gate was almost permanently open it was only surprising that the whole pack wasn't out in the road, Norman thought.

'Some of the children going to school are afraid of him,' he said.

'Lord – he wouldn't hurt a fly,' said Paula. 'He practically shares Laura's cot. I shut the others in the orchard. Tell the kids not to be so silly.'

'Could you keep him in till the children have passed?' Norman asked.

'I could try, but I won't remember,' Paula said.

Norman had to leave it at that. It was really up to Jamie's parents to complain, but if the dog had hurt no one it was probably impossible to compel Mrs Curtis to keep him in; each dog was allowed his bite, in law.

He went back to the shop feeling somewhat defeated and wondering what would happen if the collie got out; it had looked really vicious.

After the shop closed at one o'clock he went off on his usual weekly errands, hurrying through them so that he would arrive before Felicity at her flat. What she had said to Emma about going abroad was just talk: she couldn't have meant it, he told himself. But how long could things go on like this? There must be an end.

He caught himself up. Such thoughts were forbidden. He had tried not to admit them as he watched his mother dwindle away, and Emma was not dwindling. She was becoming not only physically larger but emotionally more demanding. Sometimes he hated her for her encroachment on his freedom.

But he deserved to pay some price, after all.

He could see that last drink of his mother's as if it had just been prepared: her invalid food, a sort of pre-digested gruel, and mixed into it all those pills – the blue cases pulled off and the powder stirred in with the sugar. She'd said it tasted very bitter, and had screwed up her face, but she had swallowed it. He had almost hoped she would vomit it up, but she hadn't.

Next day she was dead.

He had married Emma at once. Spouses could not give evidence against one another, if anyone should ever ask about that night.

But nobody did.

Madge did not like Thursdays, for then she was parted from Norman for the afternoon. On the other hand it gave her a chance to wash her hair and apply a face-pack attack to her acne without risk of ridicule from her brother. Her mother was at home then, too, for the cleaner's was also closed; she used the time to bake and clean, and often Madge helped, but this week she decided to go shopping in Muddington, twelve miles away, where early closing was on Wednesday and the market was held on Thursday. Her new green sweater didn't go too well with her jeans, and she planned to get some matching trousers.

She caught the two o'clock bus and was in Muddington market before three, strolling among the stalls. She did not see Mick Green as he followed her to the bus stop, and she did not see him at Muddington when she got off the bus. He had travelled faster on his motor-bike. She did not notice him following her round the market, either.

He had decided that this might be a better way to spend the afternoon than at his bench in the factory.

Norman's calls took longer than he expected and Felicity was home before he arrived. It had been raining, and her wet raincoat hung on a peg inside the door, making him aware of her live presence before he saw her.

Her hair, where it had escaped from her scarf, was damp.

'How did you get so wet?' he asked, holding her.

'I had to walk home – the car wouldn't start,' she said. 'Jack Phelps is going to fix it – it must be the damp.'

Norman was reminded sharply of the first time he had come here, when again it had rained and her car had been in dock. He held her closer, but Felicity pushed him away. She must, today, make him realize that she meant what she had said to Emma, but the moment he touched her she felt herself weaken. She could not understand why he had this power; he was nothing to look at – thin, sandy-haired, not much taller than she was, and when she analysed their relationship she knew that it was their loneliness which had, in the beginning, drawn them together; yet they had shared rapture, even love.

It would be difficult to leave him.

He had brought éclairs for tea, and produced them now, in a paper bag. They had got slightly squashed and the cream was splurging out.

'I got these – I love them,' said Norman.

'And you can never have them at home because they'd be bad for Emma. I know,' said Felicity in a bitter voice.

'Darling, that's unkind,' Norman protested.

'Do you expect me to be kind, after what you did on Monday?' Felicity snapped, giving way to her angry resentment. 'That was a filthy trick to play, taking me to see her.'

'She enjoyed it. She doesn't meet many people,' Norman said.

'And what about me? I didn't enjoy it at all – I felt terrible,' stormed Felicity. 'But I don't matter, do I ?'

'Oh, Felicity, you do – you mean the world to me,' cried Norman. 'But you've seen Emma now – you've seen the sort of life she has – be generous.'

He tried to put his arms around her again, but Felicity angrily pushed him away.

'You love her,' she accused. 'I could tell that you do, seeing you with her.'

Before, she had never let herself consider such a possibility. She had convinced herself that Norman, in a mad moment of folly, unbalanced after the strain of his mother's illness and death, had been ensnared by a much older woman who had wanted him because of the security offered by his thriving business.

'She needs me,' Norman temporized.

'Of course she does. You're her life-line. And you're wonderful with her. But it isn't hard for you – you're so kind-hearted, I know you are – you couldn't be cruel to – to a wasp,' said Felicity wildly. 'But you're cruel to me.'

'Yes, I am.' Norman's whole body suddenly

sagged with dejection. 'I'm cruel to visit you like this, hole-in-the-corner, when you deserve so much more.'

'Oh—' Felicity raised both her hands in the air. 'That's not cruel – I went into this with my eyes open – no – you're cruel because—'

'Because I don't love only you,' Norman said quietly. 'Because I'm tied to a fat, ageing woman, and not just by duty. But I hate touching her, Felicity. God help me, but I find her repulsive now.'

He could barely utter the treacherous words.

Now, he had said, qualifying the statement. It was through Emma that he had learned how to bring delight as a lover, and she still wanted him to touch her. With icy clarity Felicity knew the truth.

Later, in bed, Norman said: 'You won't really leave, will you?'

Felicity, with her face against his shoulder, would not waver.

'Yes, I will, Norman,' she said. 'As soon as I can.'

But Emma might die: what then? Had he thought of that? She looked ill enough for anything to happen.

'No,' he was saying. 'No, I won't let you.'

'What does the doctor say about Emma?' Felicity asked, turning her face away from him.

She had a right to be answered.

'Her heart's not too good,' Norman said. 'She could have another stroke at any time. But she could live for years. She's not in any pain – she doesn't suffer at all.'

'She does. She knows about us,' said Felicity.

Norman drew back from her, shocked.

'Oh no, it's impossible,' he said.

'She does. I could tell. She's clever – she knew I hated meeting her. She spends her life watching other people – she saw we weren't just acquaintances. She must have suspected you had someone, Norman. She guessed it was me. Perhaps you meant her to – perhaps that's why you took me up there. To demonstrate your power over both of us. Perhaps you are cruel after all. You meant to hurt us both.'

'I never want to hurt Emma,' Norman said. 'She must never, never suffer.'

8

Two-year-old Laura Curtis was accustomed to being thrust into the garden while her mother was working. She would trot round the shrubbery, sometimes getting lost but finding her way back to the house in the end. She cried a lot, because she was hungry, or because she had fallen over, or was cold; but no one ever came to see what was wrong and she usually stopped from exhaustion. Sometimes she played, lethargically, with a stick or some stones. She had no toys. Boris, the Labrador, usually pottered about near her. She was used to the dogs, accepting them as part of her daily surroundings; they licked her impartially as if she were a puppy belonging to all of them, and none, not even the collie, had ever snapped at her or hurt her. But Boris was the one she loved; she would cling to him, arms wrapped round his neck, and one day when she saw him disappear through the broken fence adjoining the house next door it was natural for her to follow.

The garden seemed much the same as her own, though in fact it was wilder, with tangled shrubs and uncut grass. She and Boris wandered about in it contentedly; no one disturbed them. Her mother, in her studio shed, did not know where they were. There was a pond beyond what had once been lawn, and Boris drank some of the water from it; Laura squatted beside him, holding on to his coat, peering in. She saw herself reflected, and saw also a fat goldfish swim from under a lily leaf and then vanish again.

When Boris padded back to the gap in the fence, she followed.

Lydia Renshaw believed in experiencing life as richly as possible, and at all levels. Her creed included keeping Geoffrey in mint condition, so far as she could, in order that he should fulfil himself at work and at home. She fed him on wholesome food, was ready whenever he was at home to discuss politics, their children, or any other theme, and performed with conscientious energy in bed.

She was physically robust, had conceived and borne Jamie without any trouble, and had been chagrined that it took her five years to become pregnant again. However, now that she had Claire there was no possible ground for any self-reproach. When Geoff got his next rise they would move out of town and notch up another rung climbed. She played badminton one night a week and went to upholstery class on another. Geoffrey would not take up any evening classes, not even a language course; he liked reading and listening to records, and willingly stayed in with the children whenever she went out. She had recently taken up bridge, and he encouraged this too, though refusing, for his own part, to follow her lead. Each maintained that the other should be free to develop as an individual; they worked at their marriage with enthusiasm. Or Lydia did, and Geoff submitted; she never suspected with what relief he saw her depart for her various activities, knowing that for two hours or so he need make no effort to keep pace with her.

On Thursday afternoon she went to post a letter, and met Mrs Costello out walking with her spaniel.

'Well, Claire!' Mrs Costello bent over the pram and loomed at the baby, who looked startled at this sudden red face appearing, but did not cry. 'Aren't you getting a big girl, then?'

Claire was too young to reply, and Mrs Costello swept on, saying, 'May I walk a little way with you, Lydia?'

Mrs Costello tended to tag on to people she met when out for a stroll. Lydia, who had experienced this before, felt a glow of virtue at being consciously kind to a lonely old lady as she agreed. Before they had gone far together, Mrs Costello had related the tale of the wailing child outside the cleaner's, satisfactorily horrifying Lydia.

'But I don't know who she is – the mother,' said Mrs Costello as they walked past the end of Paula Curtis's garden.

'She must live in New Bidbury,' said Lydia. 'She couldn't come from round here.' Old Bidbury parents, the inference was, were too enlightened for such conduct.

Mrs Costello, however, believed that people could batter babies anywhere.

That evening, Mrs Minter went to see Mrs

Costello. She found her sitting by the gas-fire with a half-empty glass beside her and the television on. Mrs Costello turned the sound down but let the picture flicker on.

As usual, exasperation at her friend's lack of order filled Mrs Minter. The small room was crammed with large pieces of furniture which had come from Mrs Costello's former home and which she refused to sell in spite of her impoverished plight, though some were quite valuable. They were part of her, she said, and she could not bear to be separated from them.

'You could get smaller pieces which would fit into the room, and have cash over,' said Mrs Minter. 'I'd help you to get the best prices.'

But Mrs Costello stubbornly refused. Mrs Minter still hoped to make her change her mind, and raised the subject whenever Mrs Costello was in fair spirits, which seemed to be less and less often. Tonight the older woman looked very gaunt, sitting in a huddled posture, and somewhat sozzled by now. She had lost a lot of weight recently. Widowhood was not easy for her, but it was not only the loneliness; she felt guilt too, and it would never quite wear off. She had met Charles Costello just after the first war; they had fallen in love, married, and had some golden years. Their two sons were killed in the second war and things had never been quite right after that, although Jane Costello had not realized just how wrong they were. If she had, perhaps Charles might still be alive.

Mrs Minter accepted her own widowed state more robustly, though she sometimes wondered whether, if Hugh had lived, they would have grown bored with one another by now. Their few years together had been happy; he had been killed at the very end of the war, stepping on a mine when her son Derek was just a few months old. She had never found anyone else she could contemplate seeing every day for the rest of her life.

This evening, when she had refilled her own glass and given Mrs Minter some sherry, Mrs Costello disclosed that she had something on her mind.

'I met Lydia Renshaw today,' she said. 'I told her about that little girl I saw crying outside the cleaner's in New Bidbury – you remember, Kitty.'

'Yes.'

'Lydia didn't know who she was.'

'How could she? She didn't see her.' Really, Jane could be exceedingly stupid at times; her brain must be atrophying from too much alcohol.

'True.' Mrs Costello got up and wavered across the room to the table where she kept her drink readily available. 'Drink up, Kitty, and have another,' she said, pouring herself some more gin.

'One's quite enough for me,' said Mrs Minter in a prissy tone. 'I must go. What are you having for supper, Jane?'

'Oh – I shan't bother about it,' said Mrs Costello. 'I'm not hungry.'

'Don't be silly. You must have something. I suppose you've run out of food again,' said Mrs Minter, and went bossily out into the kitchen to look.

There was a slice of stale bread in a bin, a cube of dried cheese, a bottle of milk and two eggs in the refrigerator. In the larder she found a small tin of baked beans and six large ones of dog food. There were also two tomatoes. What could be done about this? She could not undertake to feed Jane Costello every day. However, tonight she would. She went back to the sitting-room carrying Mrs Costello's sheepskin coat.

'I see you've got plenty for Pedro and nothing for yourself as usual, Jane,' she said. 'Come along. I've got some home-made soup and pâté.'

'I don't want anything,' Mrs Costello protested, but in the end she gave in. Mrs Minter had to wait while Pedro was fed, and they left him behind, tucking in heartily to his jellied lumps of Meatimix.

A shaft of light showed behind the curtains of the flat above Widnes' Stores as the two women crossed the square.

'It's Mrs Bowling's night there. They play cards every Thursday while Norman's out,' said Mrs Costello. 'I wonder where he goes? Round the pubs, do you think?'

'I've no idea,' said Mrs Minter shortly. She would utter aloud no surmise about Norman's extramural activities.

'How sad it is,' said Mrs Costello. 'I don't know how he manages. It must have been so dreadful for him seeing his mother in that state. I've often wondered if he helped her on her way. She died so suddenly, in the end. Perhaps Emma knew, and he had to marry her to make her keep quiet.'

Mrs Minter stopped abruptly in the middle of the road and looked at her friend's face, haggard in the light from the street-lamps.

'Jane, what a thing to say!' she exclaimed.

'It could be so,' Mrs Costello insisted, swaying slightly. 'I'm telling you, Kitty, most murders happen at home. It's well known.'

'You read too many thrillers.'

For Mrs Costello got through several every week.

'It could have happened,' she repeated. 'The papers are full of such things. I wouldn't blame him. There must have been plenty of drugs in the place – an extra big dose would do it, and no one would ever suspect.'

Such an idea had never crossed Mrs Minter's mind.

'I hope you don't talk like this to anyone else,' she said sternly. 'It's slanderous.'

'Perhaps he'll kill Emma one day,' said Mrs Costello, unperturbed.

Madge had spent nearly an hour that afternoon wandering round Muddington's market looking at garments hung on rails, trying on coats she had no intention of buying, and examining slacks. She inspected cheap jewellery laid out on trestles and lockets on chains that swung from hooks, bought an apple and ate it, and finally drifted into the town itself where there were several shops selling clothes geared to the teenage market, in dark caverns with pop music blaring loudly. There were few trousers wide enough to contain her splendid hips and thighs, for most were cut to fit androgynous shapes with minimal flesh, but at last she found a pair which, by holding her breath in tightly, she could just zip up over her stomach; once inside, she had the fashionable poured-in look.

She paid for them, and as she left the shop with her parcel it began to rain. There was half an hour before her bus left, so she went to a café and bought a cup of tea and a large Danish pastry. The place was frequented mainly by young people; a juke-box played, and the air was hot and steamy, the smell of sweat mingling with the damp as more people came in for shelter off the street. Madge had been there only a few minutes when a youth pushed through the cluster of people at the counter and squeezed against the girl sitting opposite to her, forcing her to make room for him.

'Do you mind?' said the girl, but she moved up.

'Hi, Madge, how's things?' said Mick Green.

Madge looked at him over her cup of tea and did not reply.

'Having a nice afternoon, are you?' Mick asked her cheerily.

Still no reply.

'Aren't you pleased to see me, then?'

Madge deliberately set down her cup, picked up her pastry and took a large bite. She chewed steadily, looking all round the room – anywhere but at Mick, with his impudent grin and piercing blue eyes. It did not occur to her that their meeting was not accidental; she just wished he would go away; perhaps he would if she ignored him.

'How's Reg?' he asked.

Madge finished her mouthful, turned her gaze upon him, and said austerely, 'If you was at work, like you ought to be, then you'd know.'

'Oh – I felt like a day off,' said Mick airily. 'Doesn't do to be a slave to routine. That's what you are, aren't you? A slave to that berk, Widnes.'

Madge was stung to defence of her beloved.

'I'm not a slave. I work proper hours, and get paid regular, and Mr Widnes is ever so kind,' she said.

'Tied, isn't he, with his missus like that?'

Madge would not answer.

'Don't you want me to talk to you?' Mick asked her. He turned to the unknown girl beside him, put his hand on his chest, and adopted a mournful expression. 'She's breaking my heart,' he declared.

The girl giggled.

'Get on,' she said.

If she hung about, and the spotty-faced cow opposite went on like this, maybe he'd give up and make a play for her instead.

'It's the truth. I've been following her round all the afternoon waiting for a chance to talk to her, and now she won't let me.'

Could it be true? Boys had followed Madge before, but only to mock her, and usually with their mates in attendance, spitting with laughter. Not boys like Mick, though. He could take his pick of girls; he would not waste time chatting her up if he didn't want to.

Madge had no cause to suspect Mick of any motive other than the obvious one: he wanted a bit of fun. She had been treating her pimples and trying at intervals to diet away some of her fat, mainly to be a worthier handmaid to Norman. Could it be that her efforts were succeeding and that she had acquired whatever mysterious attribute it was that she had previously lacked? Madge was no exception to the generalization that within every ugly duckling lurks a hidden swan. Her prickly resistance began to crack. Mick, accustomed to girls, noticed the slight flush on her pallid face and saw the absent-minded way she laid down her half-eaten pastry.

'Have another of those, Madge,' he said. 'I'll have one too. I'll be back,' and he got up to go to the counter.

Madge thought about leaving while he was gone, but suppose he meant what he'd said? She would like to be certain.

'Don't you fancy him?' the other girl asked, curious.

'No,' said Madge bluntly, but was not sure that it was exactly true. A rather odd feeling was going through her, such as she had experienced some-times in the cinema during emotional scenes. It was not a sensation Norman's proximity ever aroused; her passion for him was utterly chaste: he was remote, on a pedestal, untouchable, sanctified.

Mick had gambled that Madge would remain. He returned with a plate of cream cakes, his own tea and another cup for her. It was rather like treating a kid, he thought, putting the bait down before her.

He asked about the shop, and what she did all day, and where the stock was kept, how many doors there were to the premises and if Norman went out much, skilfully inserting the questions among remarks about what was in her parcel and the current pop scene, and playing her choice on the juke-box. The other girl acknowledged defeat and left, baffled by Mick's apparent liking for the dough-faced girl. When she had gone, Mick drew his chair forward and engaged Madge's sturdy legs between his under the table. The funny feeling hit her again. It was nice, in a frightening sort of way, but she still did not trust Mick, and when he asked how much the shop took in cash she clammed up.

'Don't be so nosey, Mick,' she said. 'It's none of your business.'

'Sorry, I'm sure,' said Mick. 'I was just interested,' and he rubbed his leg against hers.

Madge was flustered. She had hitherto dodged the odd groper, and had never understood why other girls spent so much time thinking about sex. Surprise and excitement outran her alarm. She did not approve of Mick, but she did not know why; now she discovered the charm of a rogue. Madge was seldom the recipient of another person's undivided attention; Norman, in the shop, sometimes gave it to her, and so did Emma, and in her gauche way she returned their interest with simple loyalty. Now Mick, whom some would describe as a good-looking youth, was concentrating on her, and her slow response began.

When she discovered that while they were talking the bus had gone, and Mick suggested the cinema, her protestations were quickly overcome.

While Madge was with Mick Green, Paula Curtis was out in her studio. The bulldogs, the collie and the Alsatian were with her, called in from the orchard where they had been roaming. They lay in a semi-circle on the floor, heads on paws, while she built clay up on a wire frame, making the foundation for a new model of the Alsatian's head. She worked at the clay, moulding it with her strong thumbs, the shed warm from a convector heater turned full on.

In the corner of the studio there was a divan piled with cushions and a rather grubby purple blanket; here, Paula lounged and smoked when she was resting.

Harry Pearce saw the light on in the shed and came there to her. The divan smelled faintly of dog, he noticed. It did not put him off.

In the house, Laura cried herself to sleep at last, and Boris, the Labrador, lay outside the door of her room.

9

Jamie knew that at seven years old he should need no escort to school. However, he had an idea and he put it to Norman as soon as they were on their way the next morning.

'If I had a bike, I could ride past that dog, very fast,' he said.

'Well – maybe you could. But you haven't got one, have you?'

'No. But it's my birthday soon. I might be given one. I could try asking,' said Jamie.

'They cost a lot,' Norman pointed out.

'Everything does,' said Jamie with a worldly air.

'Your dad might pick up a secondhand one, I suppose. But I wonder if you'd be allowed one – there's a fair bit of traffic around this way now.'

'I'd ride very carefully,' said Jamie earnestly.

'Well – no harm asking,' said Norman.

They passed the Alsatian, and Jamie ran on up the road while Norman went back to the shop, smiling to himself. He enjoyed their meetings, though there was really no need for them; but dogs did turn savage sometimes, and children had been attacked. Norman meant to ask Felicity to speak to Jamie's parents about the problem, but the need to make her change her mind about leaving Bidbury had driven it out of his head. And he hadn't succeeded in persuading her. She'd go, meet someone else, marry, have kids and forget him. For her happiness, it was what ought to happen, but he could not bear to think of it.

He was preoccupied with his own affairs when he returned to the shop and did not notice Madge's pallor, nor the fact that she would not look him in the eye. It was Emma who pointed out, later in the day, that Madge was not herself.

After the cinema, Mick had taken Madge to a pub and bought her vodka and lime; she liked its innocent taste and drank several without any coaxing. They had sat in the back row at the cinema, and before long Mick had distracted her attention from the screen; his roving hand excited her until her normal common sense dissolved. The idea she had of him was all wrong, she decided, clinging to his arm as they walked down the street.

Mick wondered how he would live this down with his friends, one or two of whom had seen him with Madge and made a few cracks about reject models and so forth, which Madge, if she heard, failed to understand. His behaviour in the cinema was automatic; it was what you went there for; but he knew now how Madge could be made to help him win his bet.

She was too young to be legally drinking in the pub, and it added to her reckless feeling. When she was really giggly they left, and Mick took her, on the back of his bike, to Muddington sports ground, where he knew from past experience that they should be safe from disturbance behind the pavilion. The cold air sobered Madge up slightly, and when he backed her up against the wall and it became clear what would happen, she was frightened. She struggled quite hard, but he told her it was too late now. Afterwards, frantically pulling her jeans round her trembling body, she turned to run off, but he caught hold of her.

'How do you think you'll get home? The last bus has gone,' he said. 'I'll take you on the bike.'

Madge felt dirty, and she wanted to get away from him as fast as she could, yet his grasp on her arm, though firm, was not unkind.

'It's never all that good the first time,' he said, for he saw that she was shaking. He wanted her brought low, so that she would do as he said, but he had expected to achieve this by binding her to him physically for as long as was necessary. Her obvious shock and distress surprised him, but he did not interpret it as an affront to his powers; it was merely the result of her being such a silly kid.

She felt so sore that she wondered whether she would be able to mount the bike, but she did, and was obliged to cling to him as they roared out of the town. He stopped at the lorry-drivers' café on the main road and bought coffee for both of them.

'Can't take you home in that state,' he said. 'What'd your mum say?' Besides, he had not finished with her.

Madge drank the coffee and felt a little better. She could not look at Mick, and she thought that everyone in the café would know exactly what had happened just by looking at her.

He sent her out to the washroom, and she washed her tear-stained face and her hands at the chipped basin. She could do nothing about the rest of herself until she got home. There was no escape from Mick; she couldn't walk to Bidbury, and as it was, by this time of night her mother would be doing her nut because she was not back.

Mick had washed and tidied himself too. His crisp curls were in place and he was talking to the blonde behind the counter when Madge appeared. He'd got two more cups of coffee.

'That Norman Widnes, where you work,' he said. 'Where's he keep his cash?'

Madge did not answer.

'I asked you a question. Where does he keep his money?' Mick demanded.

'In the bank,' said Madge, in a mumbling voice.

'I mean his day's takings. When he empties the till. He doesn't leave it full at night, I'm sure. Where does he put it?'

'I don't know.'

'Has he got a safe?'

No reply.

'You haven't seen one?'

Madge had first noticed the large steel box in Emma's wardrobe when she fetched her best pair of bronze court shoes from it at Emma's request. She set her lips firmly and did not answer.

'I asked you if you'd seen a safe,' Mick repeated.

'No,' said Madge. 'Perhaps there isn't one.'

But she was not a good enough dissembler; Mick was not deceived. He said no more then, but he stopped the bike when they were out in the country and took her into a field, and he did not let her alone until she had told him.

Afterwards, she vomited, and Mick, disgusted, had to wait until she had recovered somewhat before he could take her home. He told her mother she must have eaten something that disagreed with her, for she'd been ever so sick; he was sorry they were so late, but he'd been looking after her, and wasn't it lucky they'd met?

Mrs Pearce, who had been worried almost out of her mind because Madge was so late, ended up by thanking him for being so thoughtful. Madge's father, who might have guessed that things were not quite as Mick said they were, was not at home. Mick gambled on Madge herself being too ashamed ever to reveal what had happened; if she did, he would laugh and say she was a silly kid who had imagined it all. After all, who would want to lay a hand on such an uninviting bit of goods?

Madge expected daily to hear that Widnes' Stores had been robbed. She could never tell Norman, nor anyone else, what had happened, even though she knew she should. Mick's assessment of her was shrewd; she felt totally degraded. Her whole body ached and on Friday she moved about like an old woman. Norman and Emma decided she must be having period pains; Norman treated her extra gently and felt that otherwise the most tactful thing was to pretend not to have noticed, though Emma thought he should send the girl home.

On Saturday Madge looked better; she had gone to bed early the night before, carrying on the pretence of a stomach upset. Her mother gave her bismuth and two aspirins, and she did in fact sleep, though she cried for ages first. In the morning the soreness was easier, and occasionally she was able to forget, just for a few minutes, what had happened.

She had also lost her new slacks, abandoned in their parcel behind the sports pavilion.

Mick was not going to rush it. He had to plan. It seemed that Emma was left alone at times, though not for long.

He spent Saturday afternoon with his friends tearing along the roads on their motor-bikes, cutting up the motorists. Later, they went to a pub.

'Not forgotten about that job, have you, Mick?' asked Terry as they lounged against the bar.

'Nah – got to set it up, haven't I?' Mick answered.

Terry had done some thieving, and Mick had been with him when they'd found a back door open in a Muddington side-street, just asking for them to step in and grab what they could. They'd nabbed a transistor radio, which Mick still used, and some cash. Terry had done a few other jobs; he'd been caught once, and put on probation. Mick, before he got the bike, had lifted an occasional car for the ride home and dumped it, but he had never been charged with anything. The challenge of getting something for nothing appealed to him; it was a shame to let an opportunity slip, and if someone was mug enough to leave stuff around for the taking, they deserved to lose it.

'Might be a good bit there,' Terry said, in his experienced way. 'Them small shops – ruddy gold mines. Like some help?'

But Mick thought not. He'd taken it on as a bet,

hadn't he? Besides, now he'd got interested in the planning.

Reg, who had noticed a dark-haired bird across the bar and was trying to get her to look at him, did not hear this talk. He did not refer to Mick's rescue of Madge, either. He'd suffered plenty of ribbing in the past because his sister was so plain; trust her to go puking all over Muddington. It was decent of Mick to see to her, and too embarrassing to mention.

Late on the Saturday night Guy Curtis arrived back in Britain from South America. He had not told Paula he was coming, for he planned to go straight to his small London flat, but after he cleared customs he changed his mind. In just over an hour he could be in Bidbury: why not go, and see what sort of a welcome he got?

He collected his car from the long-stay garage where he had left it, and set off, arriving at half-past one in the morning.

The house was in darkness. He opened the back door, which was not locked, and went in through the kitchen. At once the Labrador got up and came over to him, wagging his tail and snorting with pleasure. There was no sign of the other dogs, though their empty feeding bowls were ranged across the floor. Guy patted Boris and walked into the hall. An odour of rather unsavoury stew clung to the house, and a smell of wet dog. He supposed the rest of the pack would hear him and start barking, but they might keep quiet if they recognized his tread. He went upstairs and looked into the room in which he expected to find Laura asleep. It was empty, and contained no cot. Guy continued on, and opened the main bedroom door.

He was not really surprised at what he found, and he did not stay to investigate.

As he went back through the house the four dogs who were in the dining-room began to bark. Guy could not know that they had been shut in there so that Harry could leave without them hurling themselves at his legs. They had not got used to him and would go for him if Paula was not there to call them off; jealous, she had said in her mocking way.

Guy got into his car and drove away. It was stupid to arrive in the middle of the night; Paula was not likely to change her habits. But things must be tidied up – he'd come some other time and have it out with her – see what she planned to do. He ought to find out how Laura was, he supposed.

He was dimly aware of a child's high cry above the barking of the dogs as he left, but it was not surprising that she had woken up with all the noise.

Being caught in the act was not in Harry's plans. It had never happened before. As soon as he heard the car drive off he leapt out of bed, flung on his clothes, and departed. To the astonishment of his family he spent all Sunday at home, and as the weather was fine he worked in the garden, industriously planting broad beans and preparing the ground for seeds.

Edna, as usual, did the washing. With going out to work all week she liked to get that done on Sunday. Madge helped her take it to the laundrette round the corner in the plastic bags she kept for the purpose. The girl looked peaky; she hadn't got over her stomach upset yet – she'd scarcely touched her dinner.

Harry did not go out that evening. Edna knew the signs; he'd sickened of whatever woman he'd been running, or she of him, and would find his pleasure at home for a time. It wouldn't last, though. He'd be off again as soon as some fresh bit of skirt took his fancy.

But at least that doggy smell might leave him now.

Mrs Costello, that Sunday morning, was woken as usual by Pedro getting off the end of her bed and shuffling to the door, whining to go out. Without him she might easily sleep all morning. She let him into the garden, brought the paper in, and sat in her shabby dressing-gown at the kitchen table reading the gossipy bits and drinking four cups of instant coffee one after the other. Then she got ready for church, where she tried to imagine herself back in the past with Charles and the boys around her.

For lunch she warmed up the remains of a frozen shepherd's pie left from the day before. She had several glasses of sherry, too, and afterwards she slept. Then she took Pedro out. She'd meant to string cotton round the poly-anthus to keep the birds off, but she didn't get round to it, although it was a fine afternoon. She had a new thriller from the library and started to read that when she returned from her walk, but she couldn't concentrate, so in the end she put the television on and spent the evening with that for company.

Because the weather was so fine, the Renshaws drove into the country that Sunday afternoon and went for a walk in the beech woods. The ground was drying out after the rain and it was soft and springy on the leaf-strewn paths through the trees. Jamie ran on ahead of his parents. The sunny afternoon had brought others out too, and there were a number of walkers in the woods, some with dogs. Jamie fell back and walked beside his parents after a red setter had pranced about in front of him waving its tail and inviting him to play. He put a hand on Claire's pushchair and said he would push her. It was hard work propelling it over the bumpy ground. As they came from one copse into a clearing they met the Armitages. Sarah was pushing Simon and Kenneth was throwing sticks for Gyp, who was over-excited and kept uttering sharp barks.

The families went on together, and Kenneth began asking Lydia about the badminton club, which he thought of joining. It was a blow to learn that it met on the same night as the bellringers, but Lydia suggested that he might take up bridge instead. Unencumbered by either pushchair, they walked in front, while Sarah and Geoffrey, with the children, gradually fell behind. Gyp realized the games were over and calmed down; they met other dogs who came to investigate him, and he sniffed at them in return, but none was unduly hostile to him except a bull terrier which growled formidably. Gyp, no hero, bounded back in alarm, and as he did so Jamie looked thoroughly scared. Sarah noticed his grip tighten on Claire's chair, and he almost tipped her over.

She and Geoffrey at first communicated through the children, comparing their rates of growth and accomplishment, but then Sarah noticed some pussy willow, and Geoffrey pointed out wood anemones. Soon they were talking about wild flowers in general; Geoffrey had found edelweiss in the Alps, and Sarah dreamed of seeing asphodels in Greece. Lydia and Kenneth drew further and further ahead, and by the time they reached the cars, which were parked near one another, had been waiting for some time. They, too, had found plenty to talk about, and Lydia had invited the Armitages to dinner the following Thursday.

10

Rose Hallam, out with her dachshunds, soon noticed Norman and Jamie together, and she quickly realized that their meetings were not accidental.

It seemed rather strange to her that they should walk down Funnel Lane every morning, and it was at the back of her mind when by chance she met Mrs Costello in New Bidbury one afternoon. Mrs Costello had toured the shopping centre, looking out for the woman with the victimized child; she regarded it now as a duty to search for the pair. She had grown tired, and gone to the library for a rest, leaving Pedro tied up outside, for dogs were not admitted. Rose recognized him when she tethered the dachshunds while she popped in to see what books the library had about Sicily, where she and Bob were thinking of going for their holiday.

Mrs Costello had subsided on one of the rexine-covered benches, but when she saw Rose she got up and followed her out of the building. They untied their dogs and started up the road in company. Rose thought Mrs Costello looked exhausted and suggested that they should call in at The Honeypot for tea, where the proprietress knew that if she banned dogs she would lose a lot of custom, and admitted them as long as they were small and could be stowed away discreetly.

Mrs Costello promptly devoured two toasted teacakes, some sandwiches and a large slice of cream cake, while Rose merely nibbled a biscuit. The poor old thing must be starving, Rose thought. She chatted away while Mrs Costello munched on, telling her about Marguerite's sale, the new spring fashions, and thus to trade in general, small shopkeepers in particular, and so to Widnes' Stores.

'Funny, isn't it,' she said, 'how Norman meets little Jamie Renshaw every day? They go down Funnel Lane. Have you noticed them? Jamie must be going to school. He shouldn't pass the square.'

Mrs Costello had not seen them. She and Pedro did not go out until later.

'How odd,' she said. 'But then Norman leads a very peculiar sort of life.'

Rose agreed that it could not be easy.

'I never knew why he married her,' said Mrs Costello. 'I've always thought she must have some sort of hold over him.'

Rose laughed.

'She was attractive, in a blowsy sort of way, I remember,' she said. 'The age difference probably didn't matter then. After all, a younger wife could have had an accident and ended up an invalid too. It happens.'

'I didn't mean that sort of hold,' said Mrs Costello, stirring her third cup of tea. She was feeling better now after her intake of carbohydrate. 'I was thinking that she might know something about him he wouldn't want spread around.' She sipped her tea while Rose looked perplexed. 'His mother died very suddenly in the end, didn't she?'

Rose did not understand the inference at first.

'People do die suddenly,' she said at last, startled and shocked.

'That's as may be,' said Mrs Costello. 'The house would have been full of powerful drugs. It would have been easy enough.'

Although Rose had been the one to raise the subject of Norman's conduct, she thought this was going too far and headed Mrs Costello off the subject by offering her another cake. That night, though, she told Bob.

'Hm. Poor old Mrs C. must be going a bit gaga, starting that sort of rumour,' he said. 'Though I suppose it's not altogether so fanciful. How does one know what one would do in such a situation, after all? Mrs Widnes might have asked Norman to give her an overdose.'

'All the more reason to keep quiet, if she did,' said Rose. 'But surely Emma wouldn't have blackmailed him into marrying her, would she?'

'You've only to read the newspapers to see that stranger things happen every day,' said Bob.

Whenever she got the chance, Madge took to peering inside Emma's wardrobe to make sure the safe was still there. She made little excuses to go to the bedroom to fetch a library book, a clean handkerchief, or Emma's solid cologne stick with which she wiped brow and wrists throughout the day. She had an idea that Mick might manage to steal it without the theft being noticed for several days, but it was a silly thought really for Norman put the takings in it every evening when he cashed up and it would be missed at once, even if Mick left no other sign of his visit. Each time Madge looked, she would touch it, as if it were some sort of talisman.

'Madge is very restless,' Emma remarked after some days of this. 'She used to like sitting here chatting, but now she's for ever bobbing about looking for errands. I believe she's losing weight, too.'

It was true. Madge had not entirely stopped eating, but the craving she shared with Emma for rich, sweet things had gone, and she only pecked at the meals her mother provided.

Sarah had to miss her yoga class because it was the only night possible for the Renshaws' dinner party. Naturally hers were the arrangements that had to be scrapped: nothing could be allowed to interfere with Kenneth's commitments. What with them, and Lydia's bridge, badminton and upholstery, it was quite tricky to fit it in at all. Simon was to go too, to save a baby-sitter; Sarah, in any case, was not organized for finding one.

'You must ask Lydia about it,' Kenneth instructed. 'I'm sure she never needs to refuse an invitation for want of one.'

Sarah nearly retorted that as they never went out together they had hitherto not felt this lack, but it was not worth the effort. She looked at him as he walked about their bedroom buttoning up his clean shirt, and thought how ridiculous he seemed, with his pale legs exposed under its lavender hem.

When they arrived at the Renshaws', Simon, in

the carry-cot which he had now outgrown, was put on the floor in Claire's room. He would not be safe on a bed, for if he woke and sat up he might topple the whole thing over. He was sleepy, and lay there placidly enough.

Jamie was still awake; his bedroom door was open and Sarah could see him sitting up in bed, reading. She looked in to say good night before going downstairs to join the others.

His wallpaper was crimson, with jungle animals striding about all over it. Maroon curtains printed with bears hung across his window.

Sarah was startled by all this vivid display.

'Good gracious, Jamie, are you going to be a lion-tamer when you grow up?' she asked.

'Mum chose it,' said Jamie. 'I wanted ships, but she said animals are living.' He looked at the wall beside him with distaste. 'I don't like them,' he confided. 'They look real.'

In the dim light from his bedside lamp, they did. Sarah imagined how they might seem to swell and move if he let his mind dwell on them.

'They're only pictures,' she said. 'Nothing to worry about.'

'I know. But telling yourself things doesn't always cure you,' Jamie said.

Sarah found it sad that he should have discovered this truth so early in life.

'It helps,' she told him.

Geoffrey put a large drink into her hand when she came into the sitting-room, and then the Hallams arrived.

Lydia had decided that while she was about it, she would make it a real party. She wanted to cultivate the Hallams who could be useful friends; she had first met Rose at a charity coffee morning, and if she could ever persuade Geoffrey to take up golf, such a socially helpful hobby, Bob Hallam could be the means of getting him into the club.

Kenneth was delighted when he saw the other guests; his worry now was that Sarah might let him down. He saw, with disapproval, that she was accepting a second drink from Geoffrey, who had made some sort of cocktail; it tasted innocent, but Kenneth knew already that it was not, after only half a glass. How foolish: surely there would be wine with dinner? Sherry was the proper drink to offer. His opinion of Geoffrey took a downward turn.

Sarah suddenly began to sparkle. At dinner she found that Rose was interested in yoga, so they talked about that. Then Geoffrey, when he had finished carving the capon, remembered that they had discussed flowers before, and revived that subject. Sarah held forth knowledgeably; she had planned to read biology at university, but marriage to Kenneth had changed all that. Bob said she should read for a degree at home; she might enrol with the Open University. Everyone except Kenneth thought it a splendid idea, and Sarah pretended that she might actually do it, though she knew she would never make the effort.

Through all this talk, Kenneth wore a boot-faced look; the conversation kept excluding him, and he made several efforts to get into it, only succeeding when he mentioned bellringing. But even then Sarah took attention from him by complaining that Simon had not been able to get to sleep the evening before because of the weekly practice.

'You should hear Kitty Minter about the bells,' said Rose. 'One of these Wednesdays you'll find she's been up the tower and cut the ropes. She hates them. It's all the overtones, of course.'

'What do you mean?' asked Lydia.

'The echoes. The sound reverberates – it's like when you hold the pedal down on a piano and sustain several notes in discord,' said Rose. 'Some people are very susceptible to it – others don't notice. That's why people are so sharply divided about bellringing.

'You ringers don't hear them properly your-selves, when you're up the tower,' Bob pointed out.

'People can be killed by the noise,' said Sarah, who had read *The Nine Tailors*.

'It's a pleasant sound heard from a distance, but I don't think I'd like it if I lived next to the church,' said Bob.

He thought it a selfish hobby, since it was practised by only eight or so people and afflicted discomfort upon many involuntary listeners, but he did not want to wreck the Renshaws' party by antagonizing a fellow guest, so he kept this opinion to himself.

'Likes and dislikes are funny things, aren't they?' said Sarah, too animated by her sudden social success to be discreet. 'Animals, for instance. Some people don't like them.'

She had intended to mention Jamie's wall-paper, but she lost her chance. Bob seized the opportunity to lead the conversation away from the controversial bells.

'That's another of Kitty's hates,' he said. 'I do

like Kitty – she's so direct – never hesitates to say what she thinks, however unpopular her view. She says there are far too many dogs in Bidbury.'

'There are too many big dogs, that's certain,' Geoffrey said. 'It's one thing in the country – but it isn't fair to keep big dogs in urban areas.'

Sarah wondered if Gyp qualified as large.

'Jamie doesn't like dogs, does he?' she said.

At this both Lydia and Geoffrey looked startled.

'Why do you say that, Sarah?' Geoffrey asked her.

'Didn't you notice on Sunday, when Gyp ran towards him from that bull terrier? He looked quite scared,' Sarah said. 'And he knows Gyp – he shouldn't be afraid of him.'

Rose, busy dissecting a wing of the capon, did not see the horrified glance which Lydia and Geoffrey exchanged at this disclosure.

'Why does Jamie meet Norman Widnes on his way to school every morning?' she asked. 'I've noticed them in the square. Norman takes him to school, I suppose.'

'What do you mean, Rose? Jamie doesn't go through the square to get to school. He goes along Foster Avenue. It must be some other child,' said Lydia.

But Rose knew Jamie.

'It's Jamie all right,' she said. 'And he comes into the square every morning at a quarter to nine.'

'He isn't late for school,' said Lydia, still disbelieving. 'Or if he is, we haven't been told.'

'I expect Norman just likes a stroll before he opens the shop,' said Rose but she had clearly unnerved her host and hostess by her remark.

After this the evening was less successful and the conversation often faltered. When they got home, Rose said that in spite of the shock her disclosure had been, she was glad that Geoffrey and Lydia now knew, and Bob agreed.

'After all, if anything was wrong and I hadn't told them, I'd feel terrible,' she argued.

'I'm convinced, dear,' Bob said. 'But it's not very likely that Norman would meet him openly, if it was.'

'Nothing may have happened yet,' said Rose. 'He may be preparing the way.'

Kenneth, removing his lavender shirt, accused Sarah of drinking too much and losing her self-control. He reproved her for fifteen minutes. Sarah knew he was right, but it was Jamie, not herself or Kenneth, whom she had betrayed.

11

'Don't say a word to him,' warned Geoffrey, the next morning.

As they cleared up after the party, he and Lydia had grimly discussed what there could be between Jamie and Norman. Geoffrey's main concern was with the character of his son: the boy had been revealed as afraid of dogs; he might easily be weak in other ways too.

For once Lydia's placidity deserted her. No child of hers could be permitted fear of animals and he must be cured forthwith, but she thought Jamie too young to have developed the other sort of tendency. Conceding this, Geoffrey pointed out that he was not too young to be debased.

Jamie left for school with fair eagerness, and now that Lydia thought about it, this was a recent development. Breakfast had been rather a silent affair until Claire livened it up by depositing some of her cereal on the floor and Jamie had then tried wondering aloud whether, if he saved and saved, he might manage to buy a bicycle.

'We'll see about that,' said Geoffrey curtly into the *Guardian*.

When he departed, Jamie was followed by his father who wore an old raincoat and cap. Lydia at once grabbed Claire and rushed round next door to Sarah.

'Geoff's following Jamie to see what he and Norman Widnes get up to every morning,' she gasped. 'He's gone off in a sleazy old mac like that private eye on television. Here, take Claire. I'm going to see what happens.'

And before Sarah could speak she had rushed from the house. Sarah, through the window, saw her back the car out of the drive and set off up the road.

When Jamie turned up Funnel Lane, Geoffrey loitered in a gateway at the end of it. Just as Rose had said, after a while he reappeared with Norman. The two seemed to be talking earnestly with Jamie hopping along, waving his arms about as he spoke. Geoffrey seldom saw his son so animated at home, and he felt a physical ache at the sight which he was honest enough, even in his anxious state, to recognize as jealousy.

He hid behind some laurel bushes, hoping the householder would not emerge to flush him out. Jamie and Norman went past and turned up Lincoln Road. Geoffrey fell in behind. There wasn't much time for anything to happen if the child was to be punctual at school; but there was that empty house on the way, with the overgrown garden offering cover enough for all sorts of activity. If Jamie were five minutes late probably no one would mind very much.

As the two ahead turned into Foster Avenue, Geoffrey saw Norman take the little boy's hand. He broke into a trot to pursue them faster, closing the gap as he rounded the corner himself. They were walking along sedately, hand in hand.

Geoffrey did not notice the dog until Norman and Jamie stepped into the road to avoid it; then, after another few yards, Jamie let go of Norman's hand and ran on, without a backward glance.

Norman began walking back the way he had come, and when he reached the corner found a very angry man waiting for him.

'You meet my son every morning,' Geoffrey accused. He tried to be calm; on the evidence of this morning it was unlikely that anything had happened – yet.

Norman's sole instinct was to defend Jamie from possible charges of cowardice.

'That's right,' he said genially. 'It takes but a few minutes of my time.'

'Why?' thundered Geoffrey. 'You have no right to do it. I forbid you to speak to the boy again.'

Norman, bewildered, stared at the other man. It had taken him a moment to absorb the fact that here was Jamie's father; it took more before he understood what was now implied, and when he did, he took a deep breath in an effort to control his own immediate fury.

'Mr Renshaw, your lad is scared of that Alsatian dog, which stands in the way every morning,' he said. 'It seems gentle enough, granted; but the boy was coming round by the square every morning to avoid it, and being late for school.'

'That's a neat excuse,' said Geoffrey, seething.

'It's the reason,' said Norman.

'Why didn't you come and tell me, then, instead of meeting him?'

'Because he thought you might be angry – and he was right, you are,' said Norman, who had discussed this course with Jamie only the day before.

'How long has this been going on?' Geoffrey demanded.

'About a week,' said Norman. 'I hoped he'd get over it, given time. And I've asked Mrs Curtis to keep her dog in, but it's made no difference. Perhaps she'll listen to you, if you ask her. Now, if you'll excuse me, I must get back to my shop,' and he swept past Geoffrey and stalked on up the road.

A moment later Lydia, in the car, drew up beside Geoffrey.

'Well?' she said, as he got into the car. She had parked near the school and watched Jamie arrive.

'He's afraid of that dog – up there – the Alsatian. So Widnes said,' Geoffrey told her. 'What an excuse.'

He went off late to his office unable to decide which of the reasons he preferred to accept.

It was no good trying to protect Jamie now, Sarah knew. His secret was out, and she was basely relieved that Rose had shared her responsibility for its disclosure.

'It's not so awful. He'll grow out of it,' she said, when Lydia related what had happened.

'Geoff thinks there's more to it, on Norman Widnes' part,' said Lydia.

Sarah felt wise, a most unusual sensation for her.

'Norman Widnes is all right,' she stated.

'Well – why didn't he come and tell us about it?'

'Who? Jamie? Children often don't tell their parents things,' said Sarah.

'No – Norman Widnes. Geoff would have taken Jamie by car again,' said Lydia. But would he? He might have said that Jamie must conquer his fear.

'Or I'd have gone with him,' she added.

'Would you?' asked Sarah.

'Of course – you'd have Claire for a few minutes, wouldn't you, while I popped along? It takes such ages bundling her into her outdoor clothes,' said Lydia, rubbing her forehead.

'Would you like an aspirin?' asked Sarah. She could not get over seeing Lydia brought so low.

'No – I'm all right. Thanks, though, Sarah.' Lydia made an effort. 'Well, I suppose we must decide what to do.'

'What did Geoffrey say to Norman?'

'Minced him up properly, I think,' said Lydia.

'He'll have to accept what Norman said, surely,' Sarah said. Geoffrey liked wild flowers and Mahler; he must be capable of understanding a sensitive little boy. It was not as if he were like Kenneth.

'I'll get a dog. I'll get one today,' Lydia decided, reviving at the thought of some positive action. 'You must come with me, Sarah. We'll go into town.'

'You can't get one just like that,' Sarah protested, dismayed at such an impulsive plan. 'You must talk to Geoff about it. Didn't you say you were going to wait until you move to the country?'

'That's Geoff's idea. He thinks we need more space. But you manage Gyp all right.'

Sarah found time to note that this was the first commendation she had ever received from Lydia.

'I get a bit worn out,' she confessed. 'I feel he must have a walk every day, whether I want one or not. Sometimes when it's pouring with rain I hate it. And pushing the pram with him on a lead

104

is hard work – he often heads off in a different direction to where you want to go.'

'We needn't have such a big dog. A spaniel, perhaps, or some sort of terrier,' said Lydia. 'It must be Jamie's responsibility to look after it. Animals exist on another level of consciousness from ours, and he must learn to relate to it.'

She was recovering, Sarah saw.

'If you got a small puppy, perhaps he'd get used to it as it grows,' she said slowly. 'But there's the training, and everything.' It seemed to her very wrong to impose the task and duties of dog ownership on a reluctant child. 'I'm not keen on Alsatians myself – and if you're as small as Jamie they must look pretty alarming,' she said. 'Even Gyp's big enough to knock him over by leaning against him, without meaning any harm.'

'I'll ring Geoff and see if he thinks I should get a puppy this afternoon,' said Lydia, as if Sarah had not spoken.

It was unlike her to voice indecision at any time.

'I should leave it for now,' Sarah advised. 'There's the weekend ahead – think about it. If you do get one, you must go into it carefully. You can't rush into having just any old puppy.'

This was good counsel, and Lydia went off, with Claire tucked under her arm, saying she would ponder well. Sarah was left feeling stimulated by all the excitement and her own unusual role as sage. She wondered how Norman felt about Geoffrey's insinuations.

He ought to be very angry.

He was. He came into the shop with a set face and stumped out to the store without a word to

Madge or a customer who was buying a torch, and he could be heard out there noisily shifting boxes about for ten minutes. Then he went upstairs to Emma. She had seen him striding across the square with his fists clenched by his sides and a furious look on his face.

That black look frightened her. In spite of all that had happened, she had never seen it before.

That afternoon Lydia met Jamie at school. They did not refer to the morning's events, but they walked down Foster Avenue and when they drew near the gate where the Alsatian usually stood, Jamie took hold of the handle of Claire's pushchair and began to look anxious.

The dog was not in sight, but as they passed the gateway he came bounding out, huge tail waving, tongue bared as he barked at them, several short, sharp sounds, deep in his throat, and Jamie quailed.

'He won't hurt you,' Lydia said firmly, facing facts, but she was not so foolish as to recommend patting a strange dog. 'It's like wasps,' she explained as they went on, the dog now stationary, watching them. 'They don't hurt you if you leave them alone. You must learn to understand all living things and make them your friends.'

Understanding wasps was not easy, Jamie knew, nor were they friendly. One had stung him severely only last September.

Mick Green had seen a smart leather coat with a fur collar that he fancied. He was tired of his studded jacket; there was no class to it, and besides, it was tight across his shoulders, for he had filled out since he bought it. But he couldn't lash out on the coat right away; it cost over sixty pounds. If he wanted it quick, and he did, he'd have to get hold of some cash.

12

Once a week Dr Barrett came to see Emma. On Friday afternoon he called, and told Norman that her blood pressure was up.

'She must lose some weight,' he said.

Norman did not see how this could be done.

'I watch her diet very strictly,' he said.

The doctor believed him, but was sure that Emma somehow got hold of contraband food, and he could not altogether blame her. It was his duty, however, to issue a warning.

'Well – you understand the position,' he said.

Later, Norman spoke to Madge.

'If Mrs Widnes wants you to buy chocolates for her, Madge, you mustn't,' he said. 'It may seem unkind to you, but the doctor says she's too heavy and it puts a strain on her heart.'

Madge blushed guiltily and bent her head over the tray of scouring pads she had been tidying. She had never bought anything for Emma, though; she had merely given her what Mrs Bowling had already hidden.

Just before closing time, Mick Green entered the shop.

Madge's heart gave a lurch when she saw him saunter in, hands in pockets, leather jacket undone to display a grinning wolf mask on the chest of his purple singlet. He behaved as if they had never met. After inspecting some pocket knives arranged on a revolving stand, he chose one and was served by Norman. Whistling, waiting for his change, he peered past the counter to the lobby beyond, where on the right, as Madge had told him, the stairs ascended to the flat above. Up there, in a small steel safe, the weekend takings would be placed.

Madge felt rather sick when he had gone, and was glad that it would soon be time to go home.

'What upset you this morning?' Emma at last asked Norman.

The shop was closed, the curtains were drawn in the flat, the television was on, and Norman was sitting at the table making up the books.

In the end, he told her about Geoffrey Renshaw's imputation.

'Is that all?' Emma was relieved. 'Well – send him up to me, that Mr Renshaw,' she said, and laughed, the huge, coarse laugh which made her whole frame vibrate. 'There's nothing like that about you, and I should know.'

Once, Norman had loved to hear her cheerful laughter; now, he had to hide a shudder. He went on totting up figures.

'What are you going to do?' Emma asked. 'You won't take the boy again, will you?'

'I haven't thought about it,' Norman said. His brain felt overloaded with all its problems: Emma; Felicity; and at the moment, Value Added Tax. Jamie was another on the list.

'Poor little lad,' said Emma genially. 'It seems a shame.'

His parents did not mention the subject to Jamie, but when he was in bed that night they talked of nothing else. Lydia said that in future she would take him to school, and walk him past the dog until familiarity cured him.

'He must conquer this,' Geoffrey said. 'He really must.'

They decided to buy him a dog for his birthday next month, and in the meantime promote in him a state of wanting one.

'He really wants a bike,' Lydia said. 'But that will have to wait.'

'The roads are far too dangerous,' said Geoffrey.

Pedro, snuffling about in the garden among the early crocus on Saturday morning, heard a voice calling to him softly from the roadway.

'Good dog, then. Come along, boy,' it said, and Pedro smelled a familiar meaty odour.

Investigating, he found the gate to the road open, and an enticing scent beckoning him out. A little trail of Meatimix, sprinkled on the ground, led from the gate to the pavement, and he shuffled along, licking up the morsels as he went.

'Good boy,' said Mick, as he emerged. No one was in sight, and in seconds he had gathered up the heavy dog and bundled him into the back of a small green van he had borrowed without its owner's permission from a street in New Bidbury earlier that morning. He drove off with the dog, towards the country.

Pedro had not barked once.

That same Saturday Kenneth Armitage went out for the day with the bellringers. They were visiting a church on the other side of the county to ring the fine set of bells in its tower. When he had gone, Sarah relaxed. She had plenty of time to prepare for Sunday so that it might pass without discord; she could catch up on the ironing; she might even read a novel. But first she had a mission: Kenneth had instructed her to call at Widnes' Store and buy some rawl-plugs, for he wanted to put up some shelves in the small bedroom he used as a study over the weekend. He was good at doing odd jobs about the place and spent much of his spare time on home improvements.

Sarah knew that she might easily forget this errand if she did not do it at once, so she set out in the morning. As she came into the square she met Mrs Costello, who looked distraught.

'Oh, Sarah, have you seen Pedro anywhere? He's disappeared,' the old lady said.

Sarah hadn't. She was shocked by Mrs Costello's appearance: her face was pinched and blue; her wild hair more unruly even than usual; and she wore no coat, so that the keen wind cut at her thin body which was wrapped in a long, shapeless cardigan.

'I've looked everywhere,' said Mrs Costello. 'There isn't a sign of him.'

'You'll catch cold, Mrs Costello. Do go home and get a coat at least,' Sarah said. 'Have you looked thoroughly in the house? Perhaps he's got locked into a cupboard or something.'

The dog was old; he wouldn't stray far, Sarah thought. He might have collapsed somewhere in the house or garden – and his mistress would soon collapse too, she feared.

In the end, Sarah persuaded Mrs Costello to turn back to her own cottage, which she had left unlocked. Sarah parked Simon's pushchair in the hall and tied Gyp to the banister rail, then went with the old lady all over the small house and garden, but saw no sign of Pedro. The gate into Lincoln Road was closed, and she did not notice a small trace of Meatimix on the ground near it.

'He sleeps in my bed,' said Mrs Costello, taking Sarah into her room, where there was a smell of elderly dog and grubby garments.

'Mrs Costello, do come and sit down and let me make you some tea,' begged Sarah. 'Then we'll decide what to do.'

She felt that really they ought to call the doctor, but tea, to begin with, might help. Mrs Costello began to cry when they were in the kitchen, and Sarah hunted about until she found some brandy in a cupboard among a heap of empty gin bottles. She poured what was left in the bottle into a glass and gave it to Mrs Costello, who looked better after she had swallowed it.

It was, however, a great relief when Mrs Minter walked in through the front door and took brisk command.

Mick, watching the area, had seen Mrs Costello out walking with the dog and had realized that he was not fierce; it was his warning barks that made him a threat. If dumped, he might find his way home, so some distance from Bidbury Mick stopped his van and dragged Pedro by the collar into a field. The dog made no attempt to escape, although he was bewildered at being tugged along in so unmannerly a way; he tried to ingratiate himself by licking his captor's hand.

Mick had no trouble in finding a stone large enough to smash the dog's thin skull at a blow.

He abandoned the van in Muddington, and thumbed a lift back to New Bidbury where he lived with his parents in a block of council flats.

His motor-bike had stayed at home throughout the operation.

Lydia said, 'How would you like to go to the safari park tomorrow, Jamie?' There was one about thirty miles away. 'Wouldn't it be fun?'

Geoffrey stared at her. She had not mentioned this idea to him. They were having lunch in the kitchen. Claire sat in her high chair waving a spoon around and occasionally stirring her porridge-like mess of minced meat and vegetables; Jamie, until now, had been enjoying his baked potato and fresh salad with cottage cheese, although he would have preferred sausage and chips.

'Would we have to get out of the car?' he asked cautiously.

'You'd want to, to see the animals better.'

Jamie was silent. He imagined himself having to stand amid a pack of hungry lions, and his mother did not think of explaining that the public were not allowed to get out of their cars where the animals were dangerous.

'Man and the animal kingdom have special links,' she said. 'You must start to understand about them.'

Geoffrey's spirits, already low, sank further still. If only she could be less intense about all this.

'Years and years ago,' Lydia went on, in a *Listen With Mother* voice, 'man provoked the animals to become attackers. There's an African legend which tells that man and the animals used to live as friends till the gods sent man the gift of fire, and then the animals fled.'

'Fire came when the iron age men struck flints,' said Jamie, earning his father's silent admiration.

'I said it was a legend. Lots of legends have some truth in them,' Lydia said patiently. 'Well – we'll go, then, unless it's a very wet day.'

'Wouldn't it be better to wait a month or two, till the weather's more settled?' Geoffrey suggested. He had brought a complex report home from the office and planned to study it in peace over the weekend.

'It will be more crowded then,' said Lydia.

Geoffrey, helping himself to more grated carrot, gave up.

Father and son, at bedtime, both prayed for rain.

Mick had learned from Madge that the back door of Widnes' Stores, beyond the lobby, was glass-paned, and led into the small garden which ran alongside the greengrocer's. That in turn, was next to Mrs Costello's. Two men lived above the greengrocer's, Madge had said, but they kept no pets and were seldom seen around. The greengrocer lived in New Bidbury. The rooms over Bodger's Self-Service were used for stock. Mr Bodger had a house in Wilberforce Road.

Mick had thought about forcing Madge to steal a key or get an impression in soap from one, but had given up that idea; he had already taken her to the limit. She had admitted that Norman sometimes left Emma alone for short periods, and every Saturday night went down to The Grapes. Emma had told her so.

On Saturday evening Mick rode his motor-bike into the square and stopped opposite the shop, revving the engine and staring about him. Two girls were in the bus shelter, and he aimed a few remarks at them, though the force of what he said was wasted because of the noise from the bike's exhaust. Nostrils flaring, like a wicked knight on a snorting palfrey, he roared off and circled round to Lincoln Road at the back of the shops. His plan was not complete in all its details; if he left the bike in the road someone might notice and remember it after the robbery; it might even get nicked. He had seen an empty house somewhere nearby that morning when he came in the van and took the dog. At the time he'd noticed it as a possible hide-out. He cut the engine and wheeled the bike up its driveway, where he hid it among the bushes. He'd time for a smoke before going into action.

Mrs Costello refused to have supper with Mrs Minter that evening, for Pedro might come home and it would be dreadful if he couldn't get in. She propped the garden gate open a little way, and she left the back door ajar, just in case she did not hear him.

*

115

'Will you be all right if I slip out for an hour or so, dear?' asked Norman, as he always did on a Saturday.

Their evening meal had been steamed plaice with tomatoes and greens, followed by fresh young rhubarb gently stewed with sweetener instead of sugar. Norman still felt hungry, and so did Emma, but there was a large slice of Dundee cake in the drawer of her bedside table and as soon as Norman had gone she could eat it without fear of discovery.

'There's a good film on television,' she said. 'I'll be happy enough with that.'

Norman got her to bed before he left, putting the portable colour television set close enough for her to reach the controls, and arranging the telephone beside her, in case of emergency.

He did go to The Grapes; he always did when he said he would, in case she telephoned. Though they would tell her he had left, her trust in him would remain; she would think he had gone for a walk. Norman refused to accept Felicity's theory that Emma knew about them.

She had never yet needed to ring The Grapes.

Mick was surprised to find Mrs Costello's garden gate unlatched. He was sure he had closed it properly after abducting the dog. All was quiet, but a light burned at a downstairs window. Mick went silently up the path and approached the house, drawn by the orange oblong to peer in from the shelter of a large shrub which grew close by.

He could see the old woman dozing by the fire; her thin, knobbled legs, in woollen stockings, were thrust before her, and her feet, in worn felt bedroom slippers, rested on a low stool. Mouth open, she looked as if she might be dead. The room was full of heavy furniture which to Mick's eye looked hideous; there were some china objects about the place, but he saw no glint of silver, so he decided not to pay Mrs Costello a personal visit. When he noticed the back door propped open against a brick he hesitated, but only for a few seconds; he had come to do Widnes' Stores, where he was sure of several hundred pounds. Best stick to that and not lumber himself with stuff that might be hard to sell and anyway could be traced.

By means of the coal bin he was able to slide

over the wall and into the greengrocer's garden. There was a light on in the flat above the shop, and Mick could hear music. It wasn't pop: more like that Radio Three stuff; but it should mask any noise he might make below.

It was more difficult to find a way over the fence, which was an interwoven one. Mick worked his way along it, testing it, and then, finding a hurdle that seemed less firm than the rest, decided that a good shove might bring it down.

In fact, it took several attempts before the fence gave with a splintering crash which seemed to Mick as loud as a thunderclap overhead. He paused, motionless, but nothing happened.

At that moment Norman was settling Emma with the television, and the loud title music which heralded the film drowned the noise in the garden.

When nothing happened, Mick moved forward into Norman's plot. He was in dead trouble now if anyone came out of the shop, but he was bigger than that Widnes: a kick where it hurt most, and then the boot – that would do it. He'd be ready, too, expecting trouble; the other wouldn't.

He moved closer to the building, until he could see the glass-paned back door which Madge had described. Beside it was the store, built on to the original structure but entered from within, through the lobby which he had seen from the shop that morning.

After a while the light came on in the lobby and Mick saw a figure moving to and fro. If Norman were going out, he had to leave by the shop entrance for there was no other way into the street, but all the same it was a relief when the light went out. That meant he'd either returned upstairs or left the place, closing the door from the lobby into the shop behind him.

Madge had sworn that there wasn't a burglar alarm; but even if there were, Mick could be away across the gardens before anyone saw him.

He went up to the back door and with his gloved fist knocked out the glass in one of the panes. He put his hand inside and turned the key. The door still did not yield, so it must be bolted. Mick had forseen this, and had brought a hacksaw with him. He had bought it in New Bidbury that morning before nicking the van – not at Widnes' Stores, where its purchase might be remembered. It didn't take him long to saw through several of the struts supporting the rest of the glass, which soon shattered, until there was a hole big enough for him to climb through. He made quite a lot of noise, but no one noticed.

While she watched the Saturday film, Mrs Minter cleaned the silver. She felt guilty when she sat idly; now indulging herself by watching an old film which starred James Mason, she was not entirely wasting her time.

The Hallams were coming to lunch the next day, and she must persuade Jane Costello to come too; she was bereft by the loss of Pedro and would hardly be cheerful company, but perhaps the dog would have turned up by then.

The film was interrupted at a poignant moment by the commercial, and for some seconds bowls of glutinous-looking Meatimix were drooled over by a small girl with a Yorkshire terrier clasped in her arms. Both dog and child slavered. How nauseous, thought Mrs Minter, polishing hard at a Georgian coffee-pot. Then she rebuked herself; she had grown too intolerant; her disapproval of the current dog cult was, perhaps, because she had rejected all love herself. But, she reflected, she had not rejected human love: it had rejected her, for Hugh had been killed and her son Derek, whom she had brought up to be independent, was in Canada, so she had to manage alone. To use an animal as a *raison d'être* was not her way.

But Jane Costello was different, and to be pitied. She needed Pedro, and apart from his constant yapping he was, Mrs Minter had to admit, an amiable dog.

There was now a cat on the screen, lapping up Pussipi. Mrs Minter thought of the tons of protein consumed by domestic pets all over the globe and then of the starving humans: it didn't make sense. To take her mind off it, she got up then and there to telephone Jane Costello about tomorrow's lunch.

The telephone rang and rang in Mrs Costello's house, but there was no reply. Perhaps she had gone out again, wandering about looking for Pedro. Mrs Minter sighed. If there was still no answer later she would go across.

The commercials had ended, and Mrs Minter returned to her television. Her acquaintances who thought her so down to earth would have been surprised if they could have seen the dreamy pleasure with which she watched James Mason, an actor she had always admired, performing in a romantic costume drama.

*

120

Norman was in and out of The Grapes in ten minutes. He drank half a pint of bitter and bought a bottle of wine; his weekly routine. As he hurried down the path beside Mrs Minter's house he sucked a peppermint. It was not nice for Felicity if he arrived reeking of beer. How sordid it was, he thought as he hurried along: the secrecy; the haste. There was never enough time – never time to talk, never a whole night, and all because so long ago he had been obsessed by Emma.

He remembered the doctor's warning. Too often now he found himself thinking that she might not live much longer.

According to Madge, Emma watched television every night, so Mick should be able to get into the bedroom without being heard. The safe was portable; he could carry it down and break it open in the garden. He went upstairs softly, his gloved hand stretched before him to feel the way.

At the top, light filtered out on to the landing from a half-open door on the right, and he could hear voices coming from the television. James Mason, at present delighting Mrs Minter, had been giving Emma much the same nostalgic pleasure.

Surely Madge had said that the living-room, where Emma would be, was on the left? The bedroom, his goal, was on the right. She must have got it wrong, the silly bitch: couldn't tell right from left.

Mick tried the door on the left. It was securely closed, but it opened without a sound as he turned the knob and gently pushed. He had brought a pocket-torch, and he shone it round.

It was the living-room. Madge had not been wrong. But it was empty. Mick looked quickly through the cupboards and found Mrs Bowling's housekeeping purse in a drawer. There was a five-pound note and some loose change in it, which he took.

Then he went on to the landing and peered through the crack of the open door. He had to get in there to find the safe. He had never imagined that Emma might be in bed, and mentally he cursed Madge for not telling him. It was hardly likely that he would be able to creep in under cover of the sound from the television and help himself, but he was not going to be put off now: the woman was helpless, after all.

Cautiously, he pushed the door a little wider, and saw Emma.

He had a shock. She was a hideous sight: a great white bloated face and reddened lips. One of her more courageous endeavours was the daily task of painting on a facial mask to keep herself pretty, as she put it, for Norman, and she had not yet removed it, though cream and tissues were beside her. She wore a lacy-knit bedjacket which had fallen apart over her huge breasts; they lay half exposed, like great sagging melons, but even in the dim light cast by one lamp and the reflected colours from the television screen, ivory white. Mick stared at her, repelled.

She seemed to be heavily asleep. High on drugs, most likely; she was sick, wasn't she?

Purposely, Mick made a small sound, knocking against the wall with his foot. Emma did not stir.

He'd be able to get in and out without her noticing. He knew just where to find the safe.

He crossed to the wardrobe, opened it, and as the door squeaked slightly turned to look at the woman in the bed, but she never moved. The big metal box was just where Madge had told him it would be, on the floor, beyond several pairs of shoes. He lifted it, but though it was heavy it could be carried. He'd never be able to open it without some sort of tool, but there would be plenty of them below, in the shop or the store.

Mick pulled the safe out, careless now in his excitement, and he scraped it against the side of the wardrobe. Just then, Emma woke, and Mick, with the safe held to his chest, saw her gazing at him with small, pig-like eyes sunk in the fleshy folds of her face. She opened her mouth and a weird groaning sound emerged.

Mick did not pause to remind himself that she was completely helpless. He acted on impulse, and repeated what he had done earlier to Pedro, for he already held the weapon.

In fact, Emma died from a gigantic coronary attack brought on by shock, seconds before he crashed the safe down on her head.

14

Wide awake in bed, Jamie worried about the morrow. From his wallpaper and curtains the jungle beasts gazed down upon him, and he imagined their eyes, shining bright, boring into him, seeking the tastiest bits to devour. He had heard other children describe tigers brushing against their car, and apes playing with the radio aerials. Suppose his mother made him touch an ape?

He got out of bed and looked out of the window at the night sky. Would it rain? There were no clouds; he could see a sliver of moon and some distant stars. Below, the french window opened and his parents came out on to the small paved patio. Their voices floated up to him.

'He'll be thrilled to have a dog of his own,' said his mother. 'It will be the best birthday present we could give him. He must look after it himself right from the beginning – take it out before he goes to school, feed it, and so on.'

They moved away before his father answered, the sound of their voices fading, and Jamie leaned against the window sill feeling rather sick. A dog of his own! How would he bear it?

He remembered some puppies that had

belonged to a friend of his – or rather, the mother dog had. Then these puppies had been born. But their eyes were shut and they were bald-looking. He didn't like them much. Next time he saw them he'd been given one to hold. Its racing little heart had alarmed him, thudding against his hand, and its pink, distended belly had quivered disturbingly. Then it had peed all down his sweater and he hadn't thought it a joke, as his friend had done.

He got back into bed and lay panicking. How could he tell his parents that he didn't want a dog? It would cost a lot – as much as a bike, probably. If it was his, perhaps he could sell it. He could give the money back to his parents. But it was ungrateful to sell a present. Perhaps he could give it to a blind man; his parents wouldn't make a blind man give it back.

Jamie's mind raced round in a ferment while his well-intentioned parents, all unknowing, planned to take him close to breaking-point.

In the distance Jamie heard a motor-bike racing down some local road, but he paid it no attention. His mind was on his own small, tormented universe.

Felicity put a Mozart Piano Concerto on the record player and tried not to look at the time. What sort of life was this, coming back to a solitary room and spending her Saturday nights waiting for the hurried visits of someone else's husband?

She thought of the sweeping mountain ranges of the Canadian Rockies. Out there she might find someone prepared to devote at least a good part of his life to her.

She started a letter to the headmaster of a school

in British Columbia, but had got no further than the first paragraph when she heard Norman's key in the door. As always, despite her intellectual efforts at resistance, a surge of pleasure filled her. He had managed to get away; she was not alone; he needed her.

'Aren't you going out then, Madge?'

Reg Pearce looked at his sister with distaste. What a drab piece she was, all pasty-faced and pimply.

'No.'

Madge was slumped at one end of the small settee in the front room, watching a film on television and sucking a sweet. Her jaws moved rhythmically and her eyes followed James Mason. He was old now: even when that film was made he couldn't have been young, not really, but he was nice in a way. Watching him helped her not to think of her own miseries.

Maybe if he helped her a bit, Reg thought, she'd brace up. She didn't seem to have even any girl friends; if he took her out, someone might give her a few ideas about how to go on. He'd no definite plans for the evening – just the idea of going to the bowling alley or finding some of his mates around town. He'd decided to give Mick Green a wide berth; Mick wasn't serious about busting into Widnes' Stores, Reg was sure, but just in case he was, Reg didn't want to know. It was too close to his own doorstep.

'Like to come out with me?' he asked Madge now. 'We could find a few of my mates, maybe.'

Madge could only think that one of his mates was Mick Green.

'No, thanks, Reg,' she said. 'I don't go for your kind of crowd.'

'Suit yourself.' Reg felt snubbed but also relieved. 'I certainly don't want to be lumbered with you, you ugly pudding,' he said, and departed, whistling.

Their mother had heard this exchange.

'Oh Madge, why didn't you go with Reg?' she asked. 'He'd look after you.'

Madge had begun weeping at Reg's last remark.

'I don't like his mates – they're a rude lot,' was all she could manage to say.

Norman left Felicity later than he intended. They had fallen asleep, and he had woken with a start and a rush of guilt. Gently he eased himself out of the bed, trying not to waken her, but she roused as he finished dressing and watched him with a soft tender expression on her face. He could do that to her – make her look like that, he thought with pride.

She reached out an arm to him and he kissed her.

'Till Thursday,' he said.

Knowing nothing of the letter to Canada, which she finished after he left, Norman hurried along the road, crossed the railway and went up the path past Mrs Minter's house. It was almost eleven o'clock when he entered the square and walked over to the shop.

As soon as he opened the door into the lobby and felt the cold air whistling in through the broken glass in the back door, which had banged shut when Mick left, he knew that something had happened. Sick fear caught him in the stomach.

'Emma,' he called, racing up the stairs. 'Emma – I'm back, dear,' and he entered her room.

As Mrs Costello still did not answer the telephone after the film ended, Mrs Minter crossed the square and rang the bell.

There was no answer at the door, either. Jane might be ill – she had been in a very low state earlier. On the other hand, she might merely be in bed, loaded with gin. There was nothing for it but to find out. She knew that the back door would have been left open for the wandering Pedro. Pausing only to go home and collect a torch, Mrs Minter was soon covering the same ground that Mick had gone over earlier. Like him, she saw Mrs Costello sleeping in her chair. She was snoring, and bending over her, Mrs Minter soon knew the cause of her slumber.

It was over an hour later when, having got her difficult, gin-sodden friend upstairs and into bed, Mrs Minter left by way of the front door, her mind full of the need to do something about the old woman. The squalor of Mrs Costello's bedroom had brought home to her the depths to which she had now sunk.

Across the square, outside Widnes' Stores, a police car was parked. Its blue light was turned off, and Mrs Minter paid little attention to it, supposing it to be a patrol keeping an eye on the local night life. Then a second police car, a dark saloon, drew up behind the first. As Mrs Minter opened her own front door she saw two men in plain clothes get out and go over to the hardware shop.

Norman Widnes must have been burgled. How dreadful – just his luck; some people perpetually attracted misfortune.

She did not learn until the next morning the full horror of what had happened.

The scene in Emma's bedroom was grim enough to shock even the most hardened policeman. Detective Superintendent Beddoes and Detective Inspector Cudlipp from Muddington CID, summoned by the constable who had arrived after Norman's telephone call to the police, took in the details.

Emma's body lay sprawled, the face contused and battered, the skull crushed. A gash slit one cheek and her eyes stared glassily at them. There was blood on the bedclothes and on the carpet, but there was no sign of the weapon that had done the damage. The wardrobe door hung open, but it was not until the police asked Norman where he kept his money that he realized the safe had gone.

He sat on an upright chair in the sitting-room telling the superintendent how he had found Emma, just as he had already told the uniformed constable who had arrived first. He had been to The Grapes and then for a walk, he said. He often went for walks. He had walked in the fields by the railway, and along the streets.

'In the dark?' asked the superintendent.

'Yes.'

'Alone?'

'Yes.'

'Till eleven o'clock?'

'Yes.'

While he talked, Norman's heart pounded and there was a strange sort of humming in his ears. He had neither wept nor raged. He simply could not believe what had happened.

The police photographer arrived, and then the divisional surgeon. While they worked, Norman continued to sit in his chair, staring before him. He protested when he realized that they were going to take Emma away, wanting her to remain in her own bed at least for the night, as a mark of respect. It had to be like this, the superintendent said.

'There'll be no crowd to see her go now, Mr Widnes,' said Detective Inspector Cudlipp. 'It would be different by morning.'

She was an awkward burden to get down the narrow staircase in death, as she had been in life two weeks before.

'What time did she die?' Norman asked at last, when it was done.

'We'll have to wait for the doctor to tell us that,' said Detective Superintendent Beddoes.

But the body was cool already. The killer must have come and gone some time before Norman arrived home. Inquiries at the houses on each side of the shop had produced nothing. Detective Sergeant French said that two men in a flat over the greengrocer's shop were having their Ovaltine nightcap when he called; they had been listening to records most of the evening and had heard no unusual noise; there was always a fair amount of traffic along the road on a Saturday night. The single-storey newsagent's shop on Norman's other side was empty at night. The thief had chosen his target well, and since the safe

130

had disappeared, he must have had some means of escape – a car parked in some side-street, for instance.

The full forensic investigation and detailed inquiries in the area were postponed until daylight, and Norman was told that he would have to leave the flat for what remained of the night.

'But why?' he asked. 'I won't go into Emma's room – I understand that nothing must be touched.'

He was desperate to be left alone: he needed solitude to absorb the frightful truth about what had happened; Norman had no instinct to turn outwards for comfort in disaster.

Cudlipp patiently explained that the thief might have left traces of his visit in other parts of the flat. The only obvious signs were in Emma's room and downstairs, where the break-in had occurred, but there might be fingerprints and other evidence elsewhere.

'Have you some friends where you could go?' he asked.

Norman had no time for friends and so had few of them. He thought of Mrs Bowling and her husband: he could not ask them in the middle of the night after such a terrible event; Mrs Bowling would be shocked enough when she heard the news as it was. Then he remembered kind Jack Phelps, who had taken Emma out for her last drive. Jack and his wife would take him in.

'We'll let you back as soon as we can, Mr Widnes,' Cudlipp assured him when the horrified Phelps had instantly agreed.

Norman, alone at last in the Phelps' spare bedroom after they had spent more than an hour discussing the tragedy over cups of tea and brandy, did not even undress. He lay on the bed staring at the ceiling, thinking that Emma had been lying dead in the violated flat while he was with Felicity.

Meanwhile Mick Green had been drinking with Terry in The Rising Sun in New Bidbury and trying to look as if nothing unusual had happened. He knew, though, that he could never claim his bet.

But he'd got the loot, and what a lot; over five hundred pounds in cash. There'd been a wad of cheques too, which were a dead loss. But he'd never dreamed of finding such a sum of money. He could do plenty with that.

He felt no more regret for what he had done to Emma than for the death of the spaniel. Both were in the way and he had dealt with them.

15

God did not listen to either Jamie or his father, and the sun shone brightly on Sunday morning. At breakfast Lydia chatted eagerly about their forthcoming outing, bobbing up and down from the table to attend to preparations for the picnic – boiling eggs, heating home-made soup, even finding time to bake fresh rolls.

Jamie grew quieter and quieter. He ate his muesli and apple, and obediently amused Claire while his father, who was grimly resigned now, went to check the car. Leading Claire by the hand, Jamie, in desperation, pursued Geoffrey and suggested that his sister was getting a cold; perhaps they should put off their trip?

'Is she?' Geoffrey inspected his daughter, who teetered before him on stout limbs destined to develop as sturdily as her mother's. 'Come on, Claire, let's look at you.'

He held out his arms, and with a shriek of joy Claire cast herself adrift from Jamie and lurched over the space between them into his safe embrace. This was what life was all about, thought Geoffrey, his heart warmed by love for the plump child. He looked at Jamie, who was very pale and whose eyes behind his glasses were slightly pink. Weedy little boys could develop into stalwart men and it was his duty to support Lydia's plans for the children. She was a wonderful mother – sensible and never emotional; what was the use in being fey, like Sarah Armitage?

What on earth had made him think of Sarah like that? Geoffrey banished the image of her pale face and addressed his son.

'Claire's all right. She's teething,' he said. If they put the trip off now, they would only have to do it another weekend instead. 'It will do us all good to have a day out. Lend a hand there, will you, with the pump?'

He put Claire into the car where she would be safe and then, kind, affectionate father that he was, spent at least an extra ten minutes attending to the tyres so that Jamie might learn how to test pressures and work the foot-pump.

Lydia brought out rugs and the picnic basket. Then she took Claire away to get ready, telling Jamie to wash and put on his anorak.

Jamie followed her into the house. His father went into the cloakroom to wash the dirt and grease from his hands. Jamie took a deep breath. If his parents could just understand that he didn't like animals, surely they wouldn't waste their money giving him a dog? If he could explain it all to his grandmother, perhaps she would convince them. He went upstairs, collected his anorak but also emptied his piggy-bank of all his savings, seventy-five pence, then went into the kitchen where he found a carrier bag and piled into it apples, bananas and one of his mother's wholemeal loaves. There were no biscuits or sweets in this house. Then he was off, through the front door and running down the road as fast as he could.

Geoffrey, still in the cloakroom, never heard him go.

For Sunday breakfast Paula Curtis gave her daughter some milk and a slice of bread and dripping. Laura was hungry, so she ate it all up. Then, unaccustomed to such heavy food, her stomach revolted and she vomited.

Paula's instinct was to slap her and put her to bed. But it was a fine morning and she had arranged to take one of the bulldogs over to a breeder on the far side of the county with whose bitch he was to mate, so instead she followed the slap by wiping the vomit off the child with the dish-cloth, zipping her into her ski-suit, and bundling her out to wait by the car, telling her to stay there while she shut the house and rounded up the dogs.

The telephone rang while she was locking the back door, and after a moment's hesitation she went in to answer it.

It was Guy. He wanted to see her to discuss the future and said he was coming over right away.

Paula was angry. He'd left it long enough if it was last weekend's episode that was on his mind. She didn't inquire about his activities and she expected the same treatment in return; besides, she did not want to change her arrangements for the day. He never considered her convenience, she told him, turning up without warning at any hour, so why should she now alter her plans because of a sudden whim of his? He must come another time.

She rang off, very annoyed. Things suited her this way, for Guy gave her enough money and seldom came near her. Since his appearance last weekend Harry had not been back and that was another cause for resentment; Paula had not yet tired of Harry. She returned to the car with her mind distracted, and when Boris, the Labrador, did not answer her call she decided to go without him.

Her route did not go near the square, so she did not see the police, and had driven several miles before she realized that Laura, like the Labrador, had been left behind. Even then she did not immediately turn back for she was reluctant to abandon her plans. The child would be all right, damn her; she'd wander about the garden with Boris. They spent hours together every day and came to no harm.

In the end, though, she did turn round, first stopping at a telephone box to let the owner of the bulldog bitch know she would be delayed.

At a quarter to nine Mrs Minter went across to see how Mrs Costello had survived the night and found part of the square cordoned off. Two police cars were parked outside the ironmonger's, and as she walked past she met Mrs Bowling, who was sobbing.

'Oh, isn't it dreadful, Mrs Minter?' she wept. 'I can't hardly take it in. Poor, poor thing.'

'Why? What's happened?' asked Mrs Minter. 'I thought there must have been a burglary.'

Mrs Bowling had heard the news from the paper-boy and had gone round to the shop at once. She had found Norman absent and the place full of police. A detective sergeant was about to call and question her, for Norman had told them that she worked there. Her fingerprints had to be eliminated from the various sets identified in the flat.

'Oh, how dreadful!' Mrs Minter exclaimed, when she had heard all this. 'And Norman was out, was he?'

'Yes. He goes to The Grapes most Saturdays – never for long, mind you – devoted, he was – and then for a stroll. She was never left for long. I'd have gone in, if I'd been asked. Then she might still be alive,' mourned Mrs Bowling. 'I'll never forgive myself.'

'It wasn't your fault,' said Mrs Minter bluntly, 'And if you had been there, you might have been attacked too.'

This theory silenced Mrs Bowling, and Mrs Minter, trying to collect her own thoughts, went on to see Mrs Costello.

She found her friend up, dressed in a fawn woollen dressing-gown, bewilderedly watching the plainclothes policemen who were systematically inspecting what seemed to be every inch of her garden.

Heading for the bus stop, the first point on his journey to his grandmother, Jamie came into the square at a brisk trot. When he saw the police blocking the way he turned tail and fled back down Funnel Lane, heart pounding in fright. Like many a minor miscreant he was overcome by his own guilt at the sight of the law.

By instinct he padded blindly round the corner

and into Foster Avenue; then he faltered, for the dog would be there.

But it wasn't. Miraculously the road was clear. Jamie ran along it, but slowed when he reached the Alsatian's usual spot and looked up the drive. All was quiet.

The next house was empty. Blank windows stared out above the cupressus. Jamie was used to seeing the 'For Sale' sign outside.

He had to hide somewhere. An empty house seemed a good place. When he found the conservatory door unlocked, as it had been left by a careless viewer the day before, he could not believe his luck.

The police soon found the safe in daylight. It lay in a clump of rhubarb, where Mick had dropped it. Bloodstains, dry now, indicated the use to which it had been put, and the lock had been broken with a large wrench taken from Norman's store-room. It too lay in the garden, and was taken away to be tested for fingerprints. The broken fencing and sets of footprints going in both directions showed the route of the intruder.

Mrs Costello, when she had drunk the strong coffee and eaten the toast insisted on by Mrs Minter, felt a little better. She stood in the garden and watched as the CID men patiently quartered the area. Mrs Minter had explained her own footprints leading from the gate. More, those of a man, were very distinct, and a detective was making a plaster cast of one of the sharpest. Fragments of clothing had been found on the fence between the greengrocer's garden and Norman's, and there was a strand of cotton thread on a bush near Mrs Costello's window.

'He stood here,' said the policeman who had found it as he carefully sealed it in a polythene bag, and did not add, watching you, but Mrs Minter, looking at the scuffed ground nearby, understood.

'But killing Emma Widnes—' Mrs Costello kept repeating.

'Come along in, Jane, and have some more coffee,' said Mrs Minter, unwilling to admit that she, too, felt so shocked that she needed some herself.

'Hooligans. Brutes. Beasts,' said Mrs Costello, and then suddenly added, 'I suppose it was the thief who killed her?'

'Of course it was,' said Mrs Minter. 'Who else could it have been?'

'Norman might have done it. I always thought he killed his mother,' said Mrs Costello. 'I told you so, too.'

'Jane! For goodness' sake!' Mrs Minter, appalled, cast an anxious look at the young detective constable who was calmly continuing his search for clues among the shrubs. 'That's nonsense. Come inside.'

Mrs Costello allowed herself to be led indoors. Left alone, the policeman was thoughtful as he worked, and later he told Detective Sergeant French what the old woman had said.

As soon as Jamie was missed at home, Lydia went round to ask if either of the Armitages had seen him. Kenneth, who was just leaving for his bell-ringing stint before morning service, said he would look out for Jamie and departed, astonished that a woman as well organized as Lydia should have mislaid a child.

'It's extraordinary,' Lydia said. 'I can't understand where he's got to – we'd planned this lovely trip to the safari park and he was longing to go.'

'Was he?' Sarah asked.

'Of course.'

Lydia was not yet worried, just cross and puzzled.

They searched the Armitages' garage and garden shed, and stood on the tiny lawn calling him by name, but in vain. Geoffrey, meanwhile, had inquired at the other houses in the close and then taken the car to search the neighbouring roads. After Lydia had gone home, Sarah saw him return alone; she picked up Simon and went round to see what they planned to do next.

'There's been some trouble in the square,' Geoffrey said. 'There are several police cars up there. I think someone has broken into Widnes' Stores.'

'Did you ask the police if they'd seen Jamie?' Sarah asked.

Geoffrey hadn't. It seemed too soon to take what was just a naughty prank so seriously.

'We'll give him half an hour,' he said. 'Then, if he's not back, we must do that. I'll go round the roads again.'

Sarah did not see that there was anything to be gained by delay; as he left in the car she knew that in their place she would have been frantic.

'Well, at least there's no rubbish tip nearby where he might have got into an old refrigerator,' she said, and at this Lydia did show some anxiety.

'You don't really think anything can have happened to him, do you, Sarah?' she asked.

'No, of course not,' said Sarah. 'He's just hiding somewhere. He'll turn up when he's hungry.'

But she did not altogether believe it.

By this time the church bells were adding their clangour to the growing tension.

'Damn that bloody noise,' said Geoffrey, returning. He now looked very worried. 'You'll have to know what's happened,' he added. 'Mrs Widnes is dead. There was a robbery at the shop last night and whoever did it killed her. I've told the police about Jamie and they're sending someone round.'

The police constable to whom Geoffrey had somewhat sheepishly told his story had taken it very seriously. He had gone into the shop and emerged with an older man in plain clothes who, after hearing what Geoffrey had to say, sent him home to find a photograph of the boy and be ready to make a formal statement. As Geoffrey left, a message was already being relayed to police headquarters.

'They'll soon find him,' Sarah said. 'He can't be far away.'

Lydia had been to Jamie's room making sure his anorak had gone.

'He took his piggy-bank money,' she said. 'He might have caught a bus.'

Or hitched a lift.

Soon after nine that morning, Detective Inspector Cudlipp and Detective Sergeant French called to question Madge. Though they were in plain clothes, Mrs Pearce knew at once that they were policemen and her first thought was that Reg had had an accident with the motor-bike. He was still

141

asleep upstairs, it was true, but he might have hit something on his way home last night. It couldn't be anything to do with Harry; for once, she had known all his movements for the past twenty-four hours, and he had even taken her out for a drink the evening before. He was already in the garden raking over the seed-bed, the model of domestic rectitude. It wouldn't last, but while it did she meant to make the most of it.

So when the police asked for Madge, she was astonished.

'We'd better come in, if you don't mind, Mrs Pearce,' said the inspector, who was a thickset man of about her own age, with a craggy face and prominent pale blue eyes.

'Well, of course.'

Madge had been finishing her breakfast in the kitchen. She had not eaten much, just a few cornflakes, and she came into the living-room yawning, hiding her mouth with her hand.

'Well now, Madge,' said the inspector. 'You work at Widnes' Stores, don't you?'

Madge nodded. The world began to spin. Here it came.

'Would you mind telling me where you were last night? Between nine and ten o'clock?'

Madge managed to answer.

'Here. Watching telly,' she uttered.

'That's right – she was here all evening,' said Mrs Pearce, edging protectively forward. What a question to ask. What could be behind it? 'There was that James Mason film. Why do you want to know?'

'I'm afraid I've got some bad news for you,' Cudlipp said.

142

Mick had done it: he had busted into the shop; the waiting was over.

'The premises were raided last night. Money was stolen and Mrs Widnes is dead.'

Madge heard the first words. As she fainted, she thought she imagined the rest.

Her mother, bending to tend the lumpy body of her fallen daughter, was thinking that in fact Madge had been alone in the house during the film, for she and Harry had been at the pub. The girl wasn't involved, of course, and no one would suspect for a moment that she was; but on the other hand her presence at home couldn't be proved.

When Kenneth had finished his bellringing and the worshippers were safely inside the church, he stopped in the square on the way home to find out what was going on.

His face, when he returned, was grave, but there was no one there to witness his solemn entrance. Nor was there any smell of roasting meat.

Impatiently, he went round next door, where he found his wife with Lydia and Geoffrey in the kitchen, untouched cups of coffee before them, and the two small children crawling round their feet. His role of informant was rudely snatched from him as he was told all that was known, and of the visit of a woman police constable to take particulars of Jamie's disappearance. She had only just gone. Barely waiting for the tale to be done, Kenneth seized his chance to be alarmist.

'I don't want to upset you,' he said, desiring to do just that. 'But you must be ready to face a most

143

serious situation. A murderer may be at large in the district. Whoever killed Mrs Widnes must be insane. If he met Jamie wandering about he may have abducted him to use as a hostage.'

'Oh no,' said Geoffrey at once. 'He'd be miles away by now. People who assault helpless women don't – don't kidnap little boys.'

'There was no need to attack Mrs Widnes,' Kenneth pointed out. 'She couldn't have prevented the robbery. There's a maniac at large, but you must do your best to keep calm.'

The house smelled funny: damp and musty. Jamie wrinkled his nose and shivered. He would have to wait for a bit – till it was dark – before he could set out for his grandmother's. He was sure he had enough money for the bus, though it was quite a long way; it took nearly three hours by car. You went to Muddington to start with, and then to Gloucester. He recited her address to himself. It was lucky he'd thought of the food; he needn't be hungry while he waited. Jamie was very conscious of the need for regular nourishment since the preparation of wholesome meals took up so much of his mother's attention.

The conservatory was not a very interesting place. He opened the door that led into the house beyond, and went in somewhat timidly, but there was nothing to be seen except empty rooms. His confidence grew as he investigated; most of the doors were open and he had no fear of something nasty lurking to pounce. The floors, dusty boards, creaked here and there as Jamie walked along. The stairs had dark edges and pale centres, where the treads had been stained on either side of a carpet strip. The bath was funny, on feet, and with an orange mark under the taps. He tried the water, but only a few brownish drops emerged.

From one of the bedrooms he looked out over the garden. It was wild, like a forest, full of trees and bushes. He'd go and explore. There might be food – nuts or fruit. He decided to make his headquarters in the biggest bedroom where there was a fireplace and a window seat, and he dumped his plastic carrier of provisions there. It was at the back, away from the road, although that was not something he took into account. Then he went out into the garden.

There was a lot of long grass, still dew-laden, and his shoes and socks soon got wet. There were fruit bushes, but no fruit at this time of year. There were old windfall apples on the ground, however; most were eaten away or rotten, but some were still sound. He ate one, to be going on with, luckily chancing to choose a sweet one.

Then he beheld a terrible sight.

He had come through the trees into a clearing, and before him was a pond. A little child, much the size of his own sister, was standing in the water and a big black dog seemed to be trying to eat her.

Jamie then acted, within his own terms of reference, with courage equal to that of any holder of the Victoria Cross. He sped over the grass, small face set, eyes blazing behind his spectacles, and with one hand pushed at the dog in an effort to get him away from the child, while at the same time hauling her out of the shallow water with the other.

'Go away, go away,' he hissed at Boris.

Boris, thankful for help in his attempt to save Laura from her own recklessness, relinquished his grip on her clothing and turned to Jamie with a delighted grin on his whiskered face. His tail wagged to and fro and he snuffled with pleasure.

Jamie's heart was beating so hard that he felt it would thump its way right out of his chest. The dog did not seem to be attacking him, but nevertheless he still tried to shoo Boris off. Laura had begun to cry; she was accustomed to Boris's methods, and now looked from him to Jamie in perplexity, not used to comfort from a human.

'There, there, little girl.' Jamie had no doubt that the bedraggled creature was female. 'Don't cry. We'll go into the house, you'll be safe there, and then you can tell me where you live.' For this empty house could not be her home. 'What's your name?'

But Laura was unable to say. She allowed him to take her hand, though, and they trotted off together up the garden, Boris following behind. Jamie cast anxious glances over his shoulder at the black dog, but he certainly did not seem savage. He had heard of dogs rescuing humans; Saint Bernards, for instance. It dawned on him that the dog could have been trying to pull Laura out of the water.

By the time they reached the house he was scarcely afraid of Boris at all; he was nicer to look at than Gyp, not so tall, though fatter, and his coat was smooth. He had a kind face, too, while Gyp's was a curious box-shaped one with a squared-off jaw.

Boris followed the children into the house and up the stairs, which Laura took ages to climb, step by step, hanging on to Jamie. He realized that she must be older than Claire, who could not stand for long alone; this little girl could walk properly and was taller, though she was skinny-looking. She had stopped crying.

'Lie down, boy,' instructed Jamie when they reached his headquarters, and Boris obeyed.

Jamie felt a surge of power. He was a king, with a kingdom and two subjects. He pulled off Laura's wet boots; her socks and trouser ends were very wet, and so was her bottom. He sighed; Claire was like that too. Solemnly he undressed her down to her vest and sweater and spread her wet garments out to dry, then put her back into her ski-suit minus her damp, grey pants.

She rubbed her eyes and said, 'Boy.'

Jamie was delighted.

'I'm Jamie,' he said. 'What's your name?' She might answer now.

But Laura had exhausted her vocabulary.

She could be hungry. He gave her a banana, peeling it for her and breaking it into pieces which he fed her one by one, as his mother did with Claire. Laura wolfed it down. Perhaps she would go to sleep, he thought; Claire slept a good deal. He cast about for a bed. There was nothing in the room, so he took off his own anorak, coaxed her to sit on it and wrapped it round her. Boris, who had been lying perfectly still while all this went on, now got up and sidled over to the children.

Jamie panicked for a moment but did not show it beyond a tremble in his voice as he stoutly said, 'Good boy,' and waited to see what would happen.

Laura put her hand on the dog's neck and he settled down beside her. She leant against him, grubby cheek on his coat, and began to suck a grimy finger. Both lay still.

She seemed all right. Jamie decided to have a look round the house for anything to add to their comfort. There might be a rug somewhere, or at least a sack. He walked all over the house once more, this time looking in cupboards. He found a pile of old newspapers and thought that if only he had a match he could light a fire; there was plenty of wood in the garden. There were some old curtains bundled in a cupboard in the scullery; they smelled rather nasty, but they were better than nothing, so he carted them upstairs. They'd do as coverings or to lie on. Then, just to be on the safe side, he went down and bolted the doors through which they had entered the house.

A police constable, coming along the drive a little later looking for the missing boy, tried the doors and found them bolted. He checked the ground-floor windows and looked in the out-houses and garage, but saw no trace of occupancy nor any sort of disturbance.

Jamie, upstairs, saw him and crouched down out of sight, an anxious eye on Laura and Boris in case they made a noise, but they were silent. Soon the policeman went away.

16

Madge's faint lasted for only seconds. Before long she was sitting on the settee allowing her fingerprints to be taken, while her mother made some fresh tea.

She answered Detective Inspector Cudlipp's questions in a flat voice.

Yes, she did know where the money was kept.

She knew who had taken it, too, and who had killed Mrs Widnes, and she wanted to tell the policeman, but her throat closed and she could not do it. And perhaps it wasn't Mick after all; perhaps he'd told someone else about the safe and they'd done the job. For would even Mick have done such a dreadful thing as a murder?

She remembered his hands, and his hard, cruel words, and she knew that he would.

Although she could not follow a religion in whose name fearful inquisitions had been held and bloody wars waged, and which was still an excuse for bigotry and violence, Mrs Minter admired the architecture and the music it had inspired and would never question the faith of others. Accordingly she encouraged Mrs Costello to stick to her routine and go to church that morning. It would keep her occupied for an hour, and out of the way of the police.

Muttering that this murder business would interfere with the search for Pedro, Mrs Costello departed, wearing the wreck of a persian lamb coat and with her wild hair tethered under a scarf.

Mrs Minter went home to prepare lunch for her guests; despite what had happened, one had to eat, but she expected her party to be somewhat glum. She was laying the table when the doorbell rang.

One of the policemen she had seen earlier stood on the step: a balding man with sandy hair, in plain clothes.

'Detective Sergeant French, madam. Could I have a word?' he asked.

She let him in, and saw him cast a swift glance round; his expression, however, remained impassive.

'About Mrs Costello,' he began. 'Rather an – er – excitable lady, would you say?'

'She's upset at present, sergeant. Her dog disappeared yesterday.'

'Ah – I heard about that. Unfortunate. Ladies get attached to their pets.'

He looked about, expecting there to be one here too.

'I haven't got a dog, sergeant,' said Mrs Minter. 'There are far too many of them about as it is.'

'Quite. Well – Detective Constable Adams heard Mrs Costello refer to the death of Mrs Widnes senior – the mother of Mr Norman Widnes, that is. Before I ask Mrs Costello just what she meant, I thought I would see if you could explain.'

'It was a thoughtless remark and best forgotten,'

said Mrs Minter promptly. Now what had Jane started?

'I can easily check up on when Mrs Widnes senior died, Mrs Minter, and in what circumstances, but it would save time if you would tell me what you know. You've lived in Old Bidbury some time, I believe.'

'Twelve years. Well – anyone will tell you – Mrs Widnes was ill for a long time and suffered a great deal.' Mrs Minter paused.

'Yes – well, she was ill?' French prompted.

'In the end she died suddenly. Mrs Costello very foolishly said that her son might have given her some sort of overdose.'

'Had she grounds for such an allegation?'

'None at all. Mr Widnes was devoted to his mother and he was just as devoted to his wife,' said Mrs Minter firmly. 'I'm very sorry for him, poor man.'

'His wife was a helpless invalid?'

'Almost helpless. She could move about a little. She was in no pain. She read, and played cards, and watched what went on in the square from her window.' Mrs Minter looked sharply at the sergeant. 'I don't know what's in your mind, but I've heard that Emma Widnes was hit over the head. Norman would never do anything so cruel. If you think there's something in Mrs Costello's silly remark about his mother's death, and that having done it once he then helped Emma along too, you're quite wrong. Her killing must have been a brutal business. You're looking for a thief, aren't you? Someone who has committed robbery with violence – violence ending in murder.'

'We're looking for a thief, yes,' said French.

But what if Norman had come in, found the place ransacked, and seized the chance to get rid of his fat, ugly wife, throwing the blame on the burglar? If such an outrageous thought could enter her own mind, Mrs Minter realized, the sergeant was capable of having it too. But perhaps he did not know about Felicity.

In fact French thought that the flaw in this theory was Norman's affection for his wife, which was emphasized by everyone; he appeared to have no motive at all for wanting to be rid of her, and it was certainly no mercy killing.

Police inquiries in the neighbourhood went on methodically throughout the morning. No one seemed to have heard or seen anything unusual.

The landlord at The Grapes confirmed that Norman had been in the night before. He stayed not much above five minutes, had a beer, bought a bottle of wine and left: his normal Saturday pattern.

'Was he going straight home?' enquired Detective Sergeant French.

'Why not ask him?' parried the landlord.

French was thinking that if he, himself, went out walking for a couple of hours he would prefer not to carry a bottle of wine around with him.

'Thought he might have mentioned it. Took a bottle back to the wife every weekend, did he? *After* the evening meal?'

'Perhaps it was for Sunday?' suggested the landlord.

He knew Norman didn't go straight home, and hoped his guess about what he was up to was right; he didn't know who the woman was, and he wasn't going to put the idea into the heads of the police – or of anyone else, come to that. The poor bastard had had a raw deal all round and didn't need his troubles adding to. It wasn't as if he could have had anything whatever to do with last night's dreadful business.

Emma's death was reported on the radio at one o'clock. Felicity began to pay attention only when she heard the words 'Old Bidbury'.

'. . . robbery, near Muddington,' said the announcer. 'A hardware shop in the town was robbed, and the owner's wife was attacked. Mrs Widnes, an invalid, who was aged forty-nine, is dead . . .' The BBC did not yet know that further drama had struck Old Bidbury and two children were missing.

Felicity sat down, feeling suddenly giddy.

'Felicity! What's wrong? You look as if you'd seen a ghost!' exclaimed Elsie Dawes, who had invited herself to lunch, a thing she often did on Sundays, and then, 'Oh – the news – didn't you know? The square is swarming with police. I thought you'd have heard.'

'I hadn't,' said Felicity faintly.

'Well, it's ghastly, of course. Poor old bag – she was bashed on the head, I believe,' said Elsie. 'Not a friend of yours, was she?'

'I had met her,' said Felicity. God, how awful!

'Rather a bloody business,' said Elsie.

Felicity could eat no lunch. Afterwards, at Elsie's suggestion, they went out in the car to visit a stately home. On the way, Felicity posted her letter to the Canadian school.

*

'And so your opinion is?' inquired Detective Superintendent Beddoes.

He and Detective Inspector Cudlipp had been going through the statements about last night's crime. Cudlipp had passed on the hearsay from Mrs Costello about Norman's mother.

'I think, like Mrs Minter – a reliable sort of woman, French says – that it's wild gossip on the part of an eccentric old soul who's upset at the loss of her dog,' said Cudlipp. 'But I'll have a word with the doctor. It's the same one – Dr Barrett – who'd been looking after the second Mrs Widnes.'

'Do that,' agreed Beddoes. 'Everyone seems of the opinion that Widnes was a devoted husband,' he added.

'Yes, sir.'

'What do you think?'

'There's been no suggestion at all otherwise,' said Cudlipp. 'But what a strange pair.'

'She didn't always look like that, Fred, and for better or worse, you know. I've seen stranger attachments. He may have still pictured her in his mind as she was once – handsome, according to the photographs we saw. And he was certainly shocked when we got there.'

'True enough.' Cudlipp began gathering the papers together. 'Well, if we can get any sort of lead to the villain, we should get something on him from forensic. There were the footprints and the bits of his clothing. And he might have picked up some wisps of blanket, not to mention blood.'

'Widnes could have faked the whole thing,' said the superintendent slowly.

'Oh no, sir. His footprints don't match up.

Though he'd time. No alibi since he left the pub. Walking around with a bottle of wine for over three hours – a likely tale.'

'Of course he wasn't walking around all that time,' said Beddoes. 'He's got a woman. That was probably how he managed to stay devoted to his wife.'

Cudlipp reflected, as often before, that his own cynicism was only exceeded by that of his superior. Both had seen too much of the misery that could fester under an apparently untroubled surface.

'There's Madge Pearce,' Cudlipp said. 'The girl who works in the shop. Her prints were on the safe.'

'But Widnes didn't think she knew about it, did he?' Beddoes said.

'That's right, sir. It seems she did errands for Mrs Widnes, though – fetched things for her, like shoes from the wardrobe. That was how she saw it.'

'What sort of girl is she?'

'Very plain, sir, and spotty. She passed out when she heard what had happened. Only sixteen,' said Cudlipp.

'Well, she's not the lady in the case, then.'

Cudlipp's face showed what he thought of this flight of fancy.

'Could she have been an accomplice of the villain?'

'I doubt it,' said Cudlipp. 'No boyfriends, her mother said – not that sort of girl at all.'

Surely most girls were that sort, thought Beddoes.

'Well, bear it in mind,' he said mildly. 'And see

155

what you can find out about Widnes' side activities.'

The Widnes tragedy dominated Mrs Minter's lunch-party conversation.

'But did you know that Jamie Renshaw has disappeared?' said Rose Hallam, when the first flurry of talk about the killing had died down. The Hallams were among those Geoffrey had called on to ask if they had seen him.

'Derek disappeared once,' said Mrs Minter. 'When we were going to do something he didn't want to do – he hid until it was too late to go. It was very frightening. I was furious.'

'Jamie's a funny little boy,' said Rose. 'Geoffrey said he's scared of dogs – Norman Widnes had been taking him to school for over a week, it seems, to avoid some Alsatian he meets on the way.'

This talk of dogs upset Mrs Costello again, and she went into a new lament about Pedro.

'What's happening to Bidbury?' she cried. 'First Pedro – then Emma Widnes – now Jamie Renshaw. Who'll be next?'

Mrs Minter thought these disasters varied in degree. She said so, and added that Pedro might reappear, and Jamie certainly would.

'Things do go in threes, don't they, though?' said Rose.

'Let's hope not, or not to a pattern,' said Bob. 'I hope you're right about Jamie, Kitty. But suppose he hitched a lift with someone – he could be miles away by now.'

All through the roast pork they speculated about where Jamie might be.

'At least he didn't disappear from outside school, enticed away by a stranger with sweets,' said Rose.

She was clearly very upset by Jamie's disappearance, and as she helped Mrs Minter to clear away the dishes, told her in the kitchen about the dinner party at the Armitages'.

'I had to tell them about Norman. Just in case,' she said, wanting Kitty Minter's assurance that she could not have been in any way to blame for what had happened.

Norman sat with his head in his hands staring at the carpet. Brown and orange swirls meandered over a darker brown background. He had never liked it.

What now?

The police were still busy down in the shop and storeroom, though they had finished upstairs. He supposed they would find the killer in the end. It was strange that none of Emma's jewellery had gone; she had several quite valuable rings, but her dressing-table drawer hadn't been touched. Norman thought thieves always looked there first. What had made this one go to the wardrobe? It was almost as though he knew where to find the money. Perhaps he had forced Emma to tell him where it was, before he killed her.

As he sat there, Mrs Bowling came in, having heard that he was back. Because she did not know what to say to him, she put the kettle on to make some tea, plugging it in just as Emma had always done, near the sofa, then clucking to herself and bearing it off to the kitchen, the proper place for boiling kettles. There was no longer any point in hiding Emma's food supplies, and she put some cake and four custard cream biscuits on the tray when she took the tea to him.

'You must keep up your strength,' she said, pouring them each a cup.

She'd been crying, Norman saw. She'd been very fond of Emma. Everyone who knew her had been fond of her.

One spouse may not give evidence against another. Well, that was over now. The secret, guarded in silence for so long, was safe for ever.

'You're not the only one in trouble,' Mrs Bowling said, as they sipped their tea. 'Though I expect he'll soon turn up.'

'Who will?'

'Young Jamie Renshaw. He's gone missing.'

17

'Laura – where are you?' called Paula, and added, 'Damn the child,' when there was no answer. She had expected to find Laura and Boris in some corner of the garden but there was no sign of either of them.

The gate had been left open; they could have wandered into the road.

Paula was cross. The thought that Laura might have had an accident did not enter her mind. She regarded the child as an ill-behaved puppy which still urinated where it shouldn't and had not yet learned to come to heel. For a few weeks after her birth Paula had felt a primitive affection for her, but when she cried or needed tending this soon wore off; now she was just another animal to be looked after, and one that gave Paula more trouble than any of the dogs.

Boris was Guy's dog, not hers.

Guy had been annoyed when, on the telephone, she had refused to see him. She didn't know where he was speaking from. He could have come over, found the dog and the child on their own and taken them both off, just to spite her. Well, she'd give him no satisfaction. He could get on with it. When Laura had whined and wet herself a few times, he'd bring her back; in fact, she didn't really mind if he kept her, but he wouldn't – she'd be too much trouble.

She telephoned the bulldog bitch's owner again and announced that she could bring her own dog over, after all.

When their mother was out of earshot, Madge, who had been very quiet ever since the detectives' visit, asked her brother where Mick Green lived.

Reg immediately made some snide comments and she had to endure baiting as to why she wanted to know before he would tell her.

'He's not your style, Madge,' he said. This was what came of Mick taking the trouble to bring her home the other night; now she was stuck on him. Well, if she went to see him she'd soon get snubbed for her pains.

'I've got a message for him from a friend of mine,' Madge said, her pallid face filling with colour as she told the lie.

All morning she'd been determining her action. If she saw him, she might know whether he looked guilty or not. Better still, she might discover that he was in bed with flu or something, so that he couldn't possibly have done it. She thought she would be safe from him herself, in daylight. Besides, his mum and dad would be at his place. She imagined them as solid citizens, like her own parents, who had their differences but presented a united, authoritative front to their children.

She didn't know what she would say to him, if he was there.

But he wasn't, when she called that afternoon. The door was opened by a thin little woman with wispy greying hair who looked very frail. She also looked very surprised at seeing Madge. Other girls had been round asking for Mick in the past, but none was like this one.

She told Madge that he'd gone out on the bike. She didn't know where, nor when he'd be back.

Madge walked away towards the park in the centre of New Bidbury. Daffodils were in bud, and the trees were pale with opening blossom; children ran about and pregnant mothers let their coats fly open, away from their distended stomachs. Madge sat on a bench feeling sour and wretched: everything was terrible and she was sick at heart thinking of the tragedy for which she was, in her own mind, responsible.

She went home at last, to be greeted by a hug from her mother and a slice of freshly baked sponge cake.

'That'll make you feel better, dear,' said Edna, all concern, for Madge did look ill. 'Maybe you'd better not go to the shop tomorrow. It'll hardly open, as it is.'

'I'll have to,' said Madge. 'Mr Widnes may need help.'

She couldn't just stay away, without a word; he might be counting on her.

After tea, seizing a moment when she was alone in the living-room, she took a sheet of notepaper and an envelope from the drawer where her mother kept them and went up to her room, where she wrote a short letter in large uneven capitals. Then she went along to the post office, bought some stamps from the machine and posted it. She did not realize that there would be no collection from the box till the next morning.

*

On Saturday night, after finding his friends, Mick had spent a lively time. They'd gone to Muddington with some girls. He'd flashed some of the money he'd stolen around a bit and that had won him the best bird; they'd ended up in a field on the way home – the very spot where he'd stopped with Madge. It made him laugh to think of that. This one was a bit different; though the field was chilly it had been very satisfactory. It was well into the early hours of Sunday morning before he got home; he felt no sense of guilt, and slept soundly.

Mick had grown up in the council flat in New Bidbury where he still lived. As a small boy he'd played on the scuffed grass in front of the block; later he'd haunted the streets and alleys around, with never enough to do in his spare time. His mother worked in a supermarket and his father in a factory, where at present he was on night shift.

On Sunday morning his mother brought him a cup of tea in bed, as she always did at weekends, because it helped to put him in a good mood and she was afraid of him. As he drank it, Mick remembered that he had killed a woman. She must be dead. No one could survive such an injury. At the time he'd panicked for an instant; then, calm had returned. He had picked up the safe in his gloved hands, taken it downstairs, found a wrench in the store and broken it open out in the garden, by the light of his torch which he'd propped on a stone. He'd hurled the safe away from him into the darkness. At no time could anything have been seen from the road in front of the shop.

His friends, and particularly the girl he'd got

hold of, wouldn't remember what time he'd joined them even if the fuzz did get around to asking. They'd say he'd been with them all night. There was nothing to link him with the crime at all: except Madge.

He finished his tea and got up. The radio was on but the news was long since over. He couldn't ask his mother if the killing had been reported.

'Well, Mick, going out today, are you?' his mother asked.

When she looked at Mick she felt amazement that something so large and full of vitality could have had its beginnings within her own frail body.

'I'll please myself,' said Mick. 'And I'll have some more tea. Are my eggs ready?'

As the major contributor to the household budget he expected, and got, servility from her.

'Just coming,' said his mother, flustered. Sundays were the worst problem in her difficult week, for if Mick were at home he played records loudly or watched telly, disturbing his father, and the two would often have a row. Several times they'd nearly had punch-ups; but Mick was bigger than his father, who had an ulcer and was a whiner, and got the best of things without using blows. Mick's sister had married and left the district at the first opportunity, so that Mrs Green was left fighting a lonely battle between the two men. 'Had a nice evening, then, did you?' she asked Mick, sliding rashers, eggs and sausages on to a plate.

'What's it to you?' growled Mick, taking the plate without any thanks.

'I only asked,' said Mrs Green.

'Keep your nose out of my affairs,' said Mick.

His mother did not answer. She took the pan to

the sink and made a great business of washing up. Silly cow, thought Mick, hearing the clatter. He'd only to open his mouth and she squirmed.

He spent the morning tinkering with his motor-bike and came back into the flat just in time to hear the one o'clock news on the radio. When he heard the announcer's grave voice telling the world about the death of Emma Widnes, Mick felt amazement that he should have provoked so important an item.

He left the flat the moment the meal was over and went off on the bike. He must see Madge – he'd tell her the crime had nothing to do with him and she must forget about their conversation – it had all been a lark. However, if she did try to shop him no one would believe the silly bint – there was no evidence – it would be her word against his. There was nothing to worry about; he'd just chat her up a bit – she might be upset still, or else she might be beginning to hanker for a bit more of the same, in which case he'd give it her.

When he reached Madge's house she was out. Reg was there, though, and he told Mick that she'd asked for his address. They joked about it. Then Reg told him that Madge was pretty cut up about what had happened at the shop.

'Lucky it was just a joke about you giving it a going over, Mick,' said Reg, relieved to find that Mick was quite his normal self, which he wouldn't have been if he'd been mixed up in something like that.

'Cor – yes,' agreed Mick. 'Good thing I didn't try it at the same time as that other fellow.'

They left together, Reg roaring up the road behind Mick, who was wondering exactly why

Madge should have wanted to know where he lived.

He'd have to fix her, that was for sure.

Detective Inspector Cudlipp found Dr Barrett in his garden, working a hoe through the ground where he planned to sow early peas. Though he had not been called to Emma in the night, the doctor knew what had happened to his patient.

Cudlipp asked about her general condition and Dr Barrett confirmed what the inspector already guessed: that her heart might have failed at any time; that she could have had another stroke; or that she might have lived for years, though her ever-increasing bulk was against her.

'She'd come to terms with her condition. She was content, in a limited way,' said the doctor. 'Lucky to have such a good husband. What a terrible way to die.'

'What about Mr Widnes' mother? You looked after her too, didn't you?' asked Cudlipp.

'Yes, I did.'

Dr Barrett told Cudlipp that the arrival of Emma had transformed Mrs Widnes' last months. Norman had done all that a man could to make his mother comfortable, but Emma had proved an excellent nurse.

'You expected her death?'

'It was inevitable but one never knows quite what to expect in these cases,' said Dr Barrett.

'She did die naturally?' Cudlipp asked.

Dr Barrett looked at him over the top of his half-spectacles.

'What are you suggesting, Inspector? That I helped her?'

'Not you, no,' said Cudlipp.

'Who, then? Not Norman?'

'Why not? Out of pity, you understand, though it's still a crime.'

The doctor leaned on his hoe and surveyed the inspector thoughtfully.

'I don't think so,' he said. 'If he did, it was a merciful act, but no, I think not. I signed the death certificate.'

'It's not impossible.'

'No. But very unlikely.'

'Why do you say that?'

Dr Barrett answered at once.

'It would be too positive an action for Norman Widnes. He's kind, but he lacks drive, dynamism, what you will. He's not one to strike out for himself.'

'I'm not suggesting that this was for himself – it was for his mother,' said Cudlipp.

'For himself too. He was tied.'

'Well, he's free now,' said Cudlipp. 'I wonder what he'll do with his liberty.'

' 'Find himself another cage, I imagine,' said Dr Barrett. 'People's natures don't change, you know.'

After their belated lunch on Sunday, Kenneth took Gyp for a walk. He had not been gone long before Geoffrey came round, and Sarah, who had stayed at home in case the Renshaws needed help, saw at once that there was still no news of Jamie.

'The police ought to be hunting for him, not the murderer,' she said. 'He's alive, after all. It's too late to help poor Emma Widnes.'

'I expect they can handle more than one case at a

time,' said Geoffrey mildly. Then he added, in a voice that Sarah could hardly hear, 'We *believe* he's alive.'

'Oh Geoff, of course he is! You mustn't even think of anything else,' said Sarah.

'Well – suppose that freaky theory of Kenneth's about holing up isn't so freaky after all. Suppose by some odd chance Jamie had found the murderer hiding out somewhere.'

'The timing's all wrong for anything like that,' said Sarah. 'The murder was last night. Whoever did it will be miles away from here by now. Jamie's only been missing a few hours. He'll soon be found, you'll see.'

'It's awful to be so helpless,' said Geoffrey. 'Lydia's sitting right by the phone. I had to get out for a few minutes.'

He supposed that Lydia's constant criticism of Sarah as disorganized was just, but he liked a bit of disorder himself. Now that Kenneth was out – Geoffrey had seen him go – Sarah had somehow rendered the usually rather antiseptic-seeming sitting-room into a homelier place merely by having some knitting lying on a chair and a crumpled *Observer* on the floor. Kenneth would never leave a newspaper in any other condition than pristine. Despite his anxiety, Geoffrey smiled at Sarah, sank down in the chair facing her, stretched out his legs, and sighed, 'God, that's better.'

Sarah could not think what he meant.

'Would you like some coffee?' she asked.

'Yes, please,' said Geoffrey. 'I couldn't eat any lunch. We nibbled at our picnic – wholemeal bread and cottage cheese.'

'Our roast lamb wasn't ready on time,' said Sarah. 'And the potatoes were hard.'

'Why worry?' said Geoffrey.

You try saying that to Kenneth, thought Sarah. She went through to the kitchen and rattled about. Geoffrey heard her drop a cup and swear, and he went out to see what had happened.

'Broken?' he asked.

'Yes, damn it.'

'Best Rockingham?'

'No. Cornish ware from Widnes' Stores,' said Sarah.

'Get another. No need to confess,' said Geoffrey.

'I'm terribly clumsy,' said Sarah.

'I think you're terribly sweet,' said Geoffrey.

He put his arms round her and gently kissed her mouth. Sarah leaned against him, aware of Arran jersey and a comforting solidity. Then he let her go, and she spooned out their instant coffee.

'What about Jamie?' she asked in a practical voice when they were sitting down again. She would have liked to sit next to him on the sofa, and she would have liked him to kiss her again. Being enfolded in Geoffrey's arms was not in the least like submitting to Kenneth's passionate onslaughts. 'Is there really nothing we can do?'

'Nothing. We must leave it to the police,' said Geoffrey. 'I've got a feeling this dog business is at the bottom of it all – or the animal thing, I should say. You realized that he doesn't like dogs. The way to cure him isn't to thrust them at him. He needs gentle treatment.' He thought for a minute and then added, 'Like you.'

Sarah kept calm. The wisest course was to ignore that last remark.

'Need he get to like dogs at all?' she asked. 'After all, people don't get over disliking tapioca pudding.'

'Fears should be overcome,' said Geoffrey firmly. 'Especially needless ones.'

'Dogs can hurt. They can bite,' said Sarah, but she had a sudden feeling that they weren't really talking about dogs and Jamie any longer.

After their lunch with Mrs Minter, Rose and Bob Hallam decided against calling on the Renshaws with offers of help for fear of being intrusive; telephone inquiries, too, would merely block the lines. They went straight back to their house and were greeted rapturously by the dachshunds.

Bob watched Rose as she caressed them. She wore a smart bottle green outfit she'd been able to buy at a considerable discount as a staff perk from Marguerite's; her hair was slightly dishevelled and her usually pale face faintly flushed from the good meal and the wine. What if they'd had a child who went missing? He knew that Rose would be frantic if one of the dachshunds disappeared; she seemed almost as sorry for Mrs Costello over the loss of her spaniel as she was for the Renshaws. But a dog could soon be replaced with another which at least would look the same. You couldn't replace a lost child.

The revulsion about the way she cuddled her dogs, which he had suppressed for years, suddenly overcame his tolerance. He'd had enough of them; her obsession with them wasn't healthy.

'Come to bed, Rose,' he said abruptly.

She gaped at him.

'What – now? But it's half past three—'

It was years since they'd made love at such an hour.

'What's wrong with that? Gives us plenty of time,' said Bob robustly.

Whatever would people think if they noticed drawn bedroom curtains in the middle of Sunday afternoon, at their age, Rose wondered.

'Well,' she said, and giggled.

She put the dogs out first for a run in the garden.

While he went prospecting, Jamie shut Laura and Boris into the big bedroom together; they could not escape for Laura was too small to open the door. Jamie knew all about the dangers of stairs to small children.

He found a tea chest in the garage and carried it upstairs; though it wasn't very heavy, it was big and awkward for him to handle; it would be useful as a table. Then he brought in a supply of apples from the orchard; with his other stores, they would feed him and the little girl until they could get to his grandmother's. This had now become his goal, but they could not set out until the police hunt had died down. He would have to take the little girl with him; his grandmother would know how to find her mother and father. He didn't know what to do about the dog; he supposed it would have to come too. He quite liked it now.

In the potting-shed he found a sack containing a few old potatoes. They were rather green, but if he baked them they might be all right. He'd need to light a fire, though.

He found a half-empty book of matches on the damp grass by the drive where Mick Green had dropped it the night before.

18

With the discovery of the matches a fire became possible, and Jamie patiently assembled the ingredients. There was some coal in the shed, and he found an old pail with a hole in the bottom which he filled with small pieces. He carried some larger lumps up by hand and got very dirty doing it. But there was a rainwater butt, and he washed in that; doing so reminded him that he was thirsty. It wouldn't do to drink that water; there were insects in it. The pond water would be dirty too. He found an old jam jar, which he rinsed in the water butt, and he tried all the taps in the house to collect any dregs. He understood what had happened – that the mains were turned off – for his father did this at home before they left for their annual holiday. But he could not see how to turn them on again; there were various wheels and taps in different places but nothing happened when he turned them, and one was too stiff to budge.

He put his jam jar on the ground in the open, to catch any rain that might fall in the night. Then he tried to light his fire.

First he crumpled some paper in the grate and arranged dry twigs above it, as his grandmother did; his own home was centrally heated with no open fire. Then he struck a match, but nothing happened. The dew had been heavy in the night and he had wasted several matches before he understood that they were damp; then he almost wept, but what would the little girl think if she woke and found him crying? Warmth might help, and he put the match-book, which now held only five unspent matches, inside his shirt against his body. Holding it in position with his arm across his chest like Napoleon, he went downstairs to the telephone. He'd decided to ring up his grandmother; she might come and collect them all. He thought with longing of her comfortable cottage and the chocolate cakes she made, which his mother deplored. He knew her number; he had rung her before; one of Lydia's tenets was that children should know whom to ring in emergency, apart from dialling 999.

But he could not get through. Several times that afternoon Jamie vainly tried the disconnected telephone. He didn't understand why it wasn't working, except that telephones did go out of order. If he kept on trying, it might be mended in the end.

Norman longed to see Felicity, but it wouldn't be right so soon; however, he could telephone. He dialled her number, but there was no reply.

Now that the police and Mrs Bowling had gone, it was very quiet. He couldn't just sit about the flat, alone.

He took the van and drove out to the country, where he went for a long walk and thought about the past; there was a lot to remember. He knew that there would be a period in which he must exist in a sort of limbo – mourn Emma, wait for

173

the law to take its course and find whoever had so savagely killed her – and at last adjust to his new freedom.

When he got home he felt, suddenly, ravenously hungry. All at once he realized that there was no need, now, to exist on lean meat, salads and fruit; he could eat whatever took his fancy – suet dumplings, potato chips, pastries and cream. He washed and changed; then he went out again, got into the van, and drove to Muddington where he consumed a large and expensive meal at The Rose and Crown.

While he was out, Felicity, back from her Sunday outing, telephoned. She wanted to express some sort of horror and sympathy at what had happened, though she did not know quite how to do it. She was rather relieved when there was no reply. At least she had tried.

When Norman returned, replete, and warmed not only by the food but by a modest half-bottle of claret, he saw a car drawing up outside the shop. From it emerged the formidable thickset figure of Detective Inspector Cudlipp.

'I'd like a word, Mr Widnes,' said Cudlipp, as Norman unlocked the door of the shop. 'If you don't mind.'

'At this time of night? Surely you know everything I can tell you already,' said Norman.

'Just a point or two, as we've the chance,' said the inspector. 'Save me asking you to come round to the station in the morning.'

'Oh, very well,' said Norman.

He led the way upstairs to the flat, and sat down himself in the upright chair he had occupied earlier when making his statement. Detective Inspector Cudlipp remained standing.

'Your mother died very suddenly, Mr Widnes,' he said, without preamble.

'My mother!' The apparent inconsequentiality of this remark took Norman by surprise. 'Not at all. She'd been ill for years,' he said.

'But in fact the end was sudden,' the inspector insisted.

'No one ever knows what to expect in those cases,' said Norman, but his palms had begun to sweat.

The inspector, standing in the middle of the room, suddenly seemed large and hostile. His pale blue eyes gazed steadily at Norman.

'Mr Widnes, there is sympathy for people who end the sufferings of very sick people, but it's still against the law,' he said.

He couldn't know about the capsules. No one did, now.

'What are you suggesting?' Norman asked, speaking carefully.

'I'm not suggesting anything at present, Mr Widnes, I'm establishing facts. Very soon after your mother's death you married your late wife – a woman many years older than yourself.'

'Is that forbidden?' demanded Norman, angry now.

'It's unusual,' said the inspector. 'Did you marry her, or did she marry you?'

Norman did not answer. Why should he tell this man that they had already been lovers for months?

'You were a young man with a good business – she was ageing,' said Cudlipp. 'You gave her security.'

'It wasn't like that,' said Norman. 'You wouldn't understand.'

'Mr Widnes, if you did help your mother on her way it would be difficult to prove it now,' said Cudlipp.

'I didn't help her on her way, as you put it, and what has this to do with finding the devil who killed Emma?' Norman's voice was unsteady.

'Your wife would have known the truth about your mother's death.' Cudlipp went on as if he had not spoken.

'If I'd killed my mother, as you seem to be suggesting, yes, my wife would have known, but I didn't,' said Norman. Now he was really sweating. 'I don't see what you're getting at.'

But he did. What could have put the thought into the inspector's head?

Before Cudlipp could tell him, the telephone rang. Neither man moved, and after several rings Cudlipp said, 'Well, aren't you going to answer it?'

As Norman had expected, it was Felicity. It was just the wrong moment for him to speak to her.

'Yes. Yes, terrible,' he said into the instrument, and turned his back to the inspector. 'Yes – I've been out.' Pause, while he listened. Cudlipp studied the ceiling. 'I know. I suppose they'll find him,' Norman said. 'The police are here now, as a matter of fact. Oh, I don't know. More questions.' There was another pause, and he added, 'No, not for a while. I'll let you know. Thank you for ringing,' and he hung up.

'Who was that?' inquired Cudlipp as Norman came back to his seat.

'Just a friend,' said Norman.

'Her name?'

'I don't see why I should tell you that, Inspector.'

'But it was a woman?'

Norman had fallen straight into the inspector's trap.

'What's wrong with that?' he asked brusquely.

'I'm not suggesting that anything is. Is it?' The inspector's tone was mild but his pale eyes were like ice. 'Well, if you won't tell me her name, I shall have to find out from someone else who your friends are, shan't I?' he said, and on that note he left.

In the intervals of trying to telephone his grandmother, Jamie arranged his resources. The tea chest stood on its side in front of the grate, with the supplies inside it. Three bananas were left, and some bread, and there were lots of apples. He had found some sacks, which could be added to the curtains to act as blankets. Both he and Laura had thick clothes, and Jamie had now discovered that the dog, nestled against, gave out a comforting warmth.

Boris had whined and snuffled by the door for a while, and Jamie had grown nervous again.

'Lie down. Good dog,' he had urged.

At last, resignedly, the dog had gone to a corner of the room and raised his leg, and Jamie, in a flood of shame, had understood. He had used the lavatory himself, and had sternly taken Laura there too, though in her case it was once again too late; it was the proper place, even though it would not flush.

He shared another banana with her, cuddling her on his knee, gave her some bread and some to the dog, and ate some himself. Then, since it was dark by now, he decided it was bedtime and settled all three of them down for the night. They huddled close to one another on the curtains with the sacks drawn over them as coverings.

Jamie fell asleep in the middle of telling Laura the story of the Three Bears, complete with different voices.

That evening Paula drank a great deal of gin and began to feel more and more ill-used. Harry had not been round since the night Guy had come home and she was beginning to think he would never return. Guy himself, who should have been in her bed, had stolen their child. She grew still more maudlin, until at last she decided to telephone Guy in London.

When he answered, she did not at first believe that he had not got Laura. It took Guy some time, too, to understand from her garbled tale that the child and the Labrador were missing. Then he said that he would come down at once, and told her to call the police.

In case she was incapable of doing so, he rang them himself before leaving. It was weeks since he had seen Laura, and he really did not know how far a child of her age could wander.

'You mean you went off for the day in the car, thinking I'd got her?' he demanded, when he reached the house and found Paula sprawled in a basket chair in the kitchen, with a half-empty gin bottle on the table. 'You must be out of your mind.'

Paula was dressed in a loose shirt, a long shaggy cardigan, tight jeans, and had rows of metal chains round her rather grubby neck. Surely she hadn't always looked like this? Guy regarded her with horrified distaste.

'You're not natural,' he said.

'Is that what you think?' She laughed in his face. 'You didn't once,' and she opened her mouth at him, showing her tongue.

He slapped her face.

'Sober up, you bitch,' he said.

Into this domestic scene came the police. A woman constable had already been to see Paula and obtained a description of the missing child. There was no photograph available, and she'd reported that the mother was too drunk to give a clear account of how the child had disappeared; she'd refused to have a policewoman left in the house with her, and seemed bent on getting still more drunk.

'What do you think has happened to Laura?' Guy asked the sergeant who now arrived. 'It can't be connected with the murder, surely?'

'I agree that it's highly unlikely, but we can't rule it out,' said the sergeant. 'Now, Mr Curtis, your version of the events, please.'

Guy described how he had heard of Laura's disappearance, not concealing his disgust at Paula's conduct. The sergeant noted the details down with an impassive expression, but the air vibrated with unspoken condemnation.

After the police car had driven away, Guy remembered that Laura had not been in her usual room when he was last in the house and he went to see where she had been sleeping. When he found her cot in the small ground-floor room and saw the state it was in, he was overcome with rage, shame, and his own guilt.

He came back into the kitchen where Paula still sat at the table, sprawling in her chair and fingering her necklaces. He caught hold of the back of her cardigan and jerked her to her feet.

'My God, I could kill you!' he said. 'And you'd better keep out of my way or I probably will.'

For a moment Paula's eyes flashed and a smile began on her none-too-clean face. Guy recognized the expression and flung her away from him.

'You're obscene,' he said, and rushed out of the house. He got into his car and drove at high speed into the country where he stopped, lurched out on to the grass verge, and was violently sick.

After he had gone a reporter who was covering the story of Emma and who had followed the police to the house, rang the front-door bell. He was able to take a photograph of Paula before she slammed the door in his face. His wait outside had not been in vain; he had a scoop from the murder town for the morning papers.

'You were quite right, sir,' said Cudlipp. 'Widnes has got a woman. She rang him up and he wouldn't say who she was.'

Detective Superintendent Beddoes had been drawing cylindrical doodles on his blotting pad while he listened to Cudlipp's account of his interview with Norman.

'Someone will know who she is. He won't have managed to keep it a secret from everybody. Shouldn't be hard to find out,' said Cudlipp. 'That's where he went with the wine every week. He was on foot, so she must be local. He'd not enough time for anyone further afield.'

The superintendent added fine shading to one of his columns.

'Do you think Widnes tried to kill his wife?' he

asked. 'Saw his chance after the break-in?'

'No, I don't, and for two reasons,' said Cudlipp.

'Well?'

'First, he knew too much about illness to make such a mistake. He'd looked after his mother for years. He'd have seen that the woman was dead.'

For by now the pathologist's report had shown that Emma had died seconds before the blow that shattered her skull.

'And second?'

'I doubt if he could be so brutal – and that's borne out by what Dr Barrett said about him – a kind man, and lacking in drive,' said Cudlipp.

'He might have got carried away,' hazarded the superintendent. 'Lost his head – understandable, if he was in the grip of some great passion,' he added fancifully, drawing a heart on the blotter, and an arrow to pierce it. N.W., he inscribed, and a question mark.

Cudlipp had been watching, from his upside-down view, these artistic forays.

'No, sir,' he said. 'I don't think so, but we could lean on him a bit and take it from there. Best be certain.'

'Do that,' said the superintendent. 'And the thief? He's the one we really want.'

'We haven't any line at all,' Cudlipp admitted. 'No prints. Just the girl's, Madge Pearce's, on the safe, and Widnes' too, of course.'

'Widnes never used a night safe?'

'Couldn't rely on getting out to the bank. Had to stay with his missus. Hundreds of prints in the shop, of course, with the customers – no unexpected ones in the flat. Chummy was careful.'

'And cool.'

'Yes.'

'What's Widnes' mood like now?' asked Beddoes.

'Better,' said Cudlipp, and looked disapproving. 'He'd been having a bloody great meal at The Rose and Crown. I checked. Ate right through the menu – wine and the lot.'

'Like a celebration, eh?'

'You could look at it that way.'

Beddoes scratched out the heart, leaving the initials and the query.

'Find the lady,' he said.

19

Jamie woke when it began to grow light the next morning. As he stirred, Boris moved, stretched, and got up, tail wagging. Laura was still sleeping, so Jamie laid a finger to his lips as if the dog could understand the gesture and softly opened the door. The two went downstairs and Jamie let Boris out, watching while he sniffed about. Soon he came back and padded upstairs, waiting for Jamie to let him into the room where Laura was.

While he was standing on the back doorstep waiting for Boris, Jamie heard the whine of a milk float passing along the road and it gave him an idea. Shutting Boris in with Laura, he went down the drive and peered out into the road. The milk float had disappeared round the corner and there was no sign of the frightening Alsatian. Jamie ran along the road until he came to a doorstep with four pints of milk standing on it. He took one and turned to go; then he changed his mind and took a second: babies needed a lot of milk and he felt very thirsty himself.

He got back to the big upstairs room just as Laura woke, and they had breakfast of milk and dry bread followed by a banana. He and Laura drank, taking turns, from one of the bottles, and then he held it for the dog to lap what was left, half trickling it into his mouth. Boris soon got the idea. Jamie was tempted to open the second bottle but decided to set it aside for later.

Then he tackled the fire. He suddenly felt very cold and Laura's hands were icy.

This time the first match struck, but the paper in the grate was damp and so was the chimney; it smoked furiously. Jamie worked away at it, blowing from below as he had seen his grandmother do and feeding in tiny dry sticks which he had found in the shed. It caught, but only just, and continued to smoke. Now he must watch Laura and not leave her alone in the room with the fire. They would soon warm up.

Jamie began to talk to her, trying to teach her his name.

A massive police hunt for the two missing children began early that morning, and a constable patrolling a country district got out of his car to search the roadside ditches. He went through a gateway and into a field. There he found the body of Pedro. Because the dog's head was shattered he reported it instantly.

Despite her mother's protests Madge insisted on going to work, so Mrs Pearce sent the girl off with sandwiches as usual, and a hearty kiss which was not part of the normal routine.

'Come back if you're not needed,' she said. 'Or come round to the cleaner's. I can always find you something to do.'

Before she left for work herself, she glanced at the newspaper. TERROR TOWN STRUCK AGAIN, she read, and beneath the banner headline saw a picture of the woman whose child had been wailing outside the cleaner's only the week before. It was a good photograph of Paula, and she recognized her instantly.

That old lady would know that it was the same woman too. She might have done the kiddy in – with someone like that, there was no telling. It would be easy to find out who the old lady was; Mrs Pearce distinctly remembered the skirt she had brought in, a hairy tweed, purplish and threadbare. Both of them might be needed as witnesses to what they'd seen. The Pearces were not on the telephone, but Edna wasted no time.

It was Kenneth Armitage who saw the smoke. He was taking Gyp for a run to the corner of Foster Avenue before breakfast, and he noticed it issuing from the chimney of what he thought was an empty house. At first he supposed that new owners had moved in without his knowledge but when he walked on to look there was no sign of an occupant and the 'For Sale' board was still in position. He walked up the path and looked through the downstairs windows. There was no fire visible in any of the grates.

A respectable citizen and councillor, Kenneth rang the police and, to be on the safe side, the fire brigade.

The hardware shop was open. Norman was tidying the stock after the going-over the police had given it. It was business as usual. But there were no customers.

Madge did not know what to say about the

tragedy, but no words were needed. Norman just said that Emma had been fond of her and added that they wouldn't talk about what had happened as it was too dreadful to discuss and the police were getting on with finding out who was responsible.

Outside in the square two workmen arranged barriers round a manhole cover, took it off, put up a little tin hut and disappeared inside to drink tea. They were two plainclothes men who were watching the shop to see what women customers Norman had and if he seemed over-friendly with any of them.

Later, Mrs Bowling arrived, with ingredients for a hot-pot since calories need no longer be counted; she made a baked custard too. She and Norman ate it together while Madge as usual sat in the store with her sandwiches.

'We ought to ask her up,' said Norman. 'There's plenty for her.' He wasn't hungry today.

'If you once start that, you'll have to keep on,' said Mrs Bowling. 'Leave it. Take my tip, it's for the best. She's very upset too – better keep her out of this room for a bit – it's so quiet. She'd feel it.'

It was quiet. It was strange to have no Emma lying there, ponderous, on the sofa.

'You'll be making some changes,' Mrs Bowling stated.

'I suppose I will,' said Norman. 'Not yet, though. We'll carry on the same for the present, if that suits you.'

Mrs Bowling agreed. She could hardly believe that there would be no more smuggled swiss rolls and éclairs; no romances to collect from the library; no Thursday evening card games.

186

'When's the funeral to be?' she asked.

Norman shrugged.

'We can't arrange anything till after the inquest,' he said. 'That will probably be on Wednesday, I've been told.'

Emma would be cremated. Norman wanted no memorial tombstone. As far as was possible, everything must be expunged, as when his mother died, though nothing could obliterate memories; they could haunt for ever.

After lunch Mrs Minter came into the shop and found Madge realigning packs of clothes pegs on a shelf.

'I'm not here to buy anything,' said Mrs Minter. 'I came to express my sympathy to Mr Widnes. Is he about?'

Madge fetched him from the store-room. He was grateful to Mrs Minter for calling.

'We might as well be closed,' he said. 'No one's come in all day.'

Mrs Minter had noticed this. She was rather surprised. She had expected a flood of the curious, but instead they had flocked to the other shops in the square and stood staring over at Widnes' Stores. The two men in the hut over the manhole had been obliged to produce some tools and climb down – or one had climbed down, while his companion kept an eye on what was happening.

'There will be some customers now,' Mrs Minter prophesied. She had heard the onlookers discussing what to do; some thought Norman heartless to open after what had happened, but others admired him for it and there was a lot of sympathy for him.

Mrs Minter was right. When she left, a stream of customers flowed in; some had clearly come to gape at Norman and study the scene of the crime but many more mumbled a few words of condolence. The two detectives outside left their work and sauntered across, talking to one another as they watched who came and went. They noticed Felicity's Fiat slow down while she looked at the shop. Then she parked and got out. When she went inside and began talking to Norman, one of them followed.

To Felicity, Norman looked much as usual; perhaps a little paler. He told her he did not know how the hunt for the killer was getting on.

'Well, at least the lost children have turned up,' Felicity said.

Norman had forgotten all about Jamie. He had never known about Laura's disappearance.

'Two children? Jamie Renshaw—' He did not finish the sentence.

'Another child vanished too – wandered off. They turned up in that empty house in Foster Avenue. They're quite all right. I don't know how the two of them got together – some prank of Jamie's, I think.'

Norman thought vaguely that Jamie wasn't the sort of child to go in for pranks, but he had too much on his mind to worry about that.

'I'll ring you when I can,' he said to Felicity.

She wanted to reply that she was rather busy, but she couldn't do it.

The detective who had entered the shop behind her could not hear the conversation, but the earnest manner of it and the fact that she bought nothing was significant. He bought a torch battery himself, from Madge. Then he left the shop and nodded to his colleague. In a few seconds information about Felicity and the number of her car were being radioed to their headquarters.

Both the police and the fire brigade had converged on the empty house that morning, after Kenneth's telephone call.

The police wasted no time banging on the door. They broke in, not knowing what to expect inside. Upstairs, they found one of the bedroom doors locked, for Jamie, hearing them, had turned the key. He crouched in a corner of the room, his arm round Laura who had begun to cry. The fire which had betrayed their presence smouldered smokily, but the room was still very cold, and although he was frightened to the core of his being, a sense of relief swamped Jamie too.

'Open up. Police,' said the sergeant who had arrived. He did not really expect whoever had bashed Emma Widnes on the head to be lurking inside; chummy wouldn't give himself away by lighting a fire when he had been so careful about fingerprints, but he had a brief fantasy, nevertheless, of finding an adult villain inside the room. Laura's wailing upset this idea, but it was the firemen with their ladder to the window who in fact discovered the identity of the fugitives. It did not take them very long to persuade Jamie to open the door.

By the time Mrs Pearce called at the police station on Monday morning Laura had already been found, but a constable took down the details of the incident at the cleaners. A customer had seen it too, Mrs Pearce added: Mrs Costello of Old Bidbury; she had checked the name on the cleaning ticket.

That evening, since she and Harry were now on good terms until he went off chasing some new woman, she told him about it.

Listening to the story, Harry was sickened. It was a nasty business and he was well out of it. He'd better keep his trap shut, too, or he'd find himself involved in a baby battering case. He was appalled to think that the child, whom he'd never seen, had been lying in that state while he was in the house. He'd heard her crying as he left for the last time, but until then he'd barely been aware of her existence.

In future he'd be more careful.

After a night of anxiety such as she had never before known in her well-planned life, relief made Lydia loquacious. When she knew that Jamie was safe she poured out to the police the whole story of his fear of the Alsatian, his walks to school with Norman Widnes and his father's rebuke to Norman.

The inference was clear, and the report was passed on to Detective Inspector Cudlipp.

'It throws new light on Widnes,' he said to the superintendent.

'You mean he's a kinky character fond of little boys?' asked the superintendent. 'Didn't strike me that way, I must say.'

'Nor me,' said Cudlipp. 'I still can't get over him going out the night after his wife died and gorging himself at The Rose and Crown.'

'A man must eat, and a decent dinner isn't

exactly gorging,' remarked Beddoes. 'I think you'll find there's a discreet widow somewhere in the background, or maybe a divorcée – that's what he'd go for.'

'We'll soon know,' said Cudlipp. 'Nothing's been reported from the shop yet. If there is someone, and she doesn't go to see him, in the end he'll contact her. We've only to wait.'

'Nasty business about that little girl,' said Beddoes.

'Lucky for her she met up with young Jamie Renshaw,' said Cudlipp. 'He took good care of her, it seems. Unlike her mother.'

'Parents,' sighed Beddoes, who had one wayward daughter whom he idolized. 'Some don't care, and some care too much, eh?'

'Right, sir,' said Cudlipp, who laid down strict rules for his own family's conduct and was so far obeyed. 'Someone had stashed a motor-bike in the bushes at that house where the children were found,' he went on. 'It was recent – it could have been Saturday – it hasn't rained since then and the tyre marks were pretty distinct. It was in a sheltered spot under some bushes. Wouldn't have been seen from the road. Might have some bearing. There was a fag end there too, and a spent match.'

The constable who had earlier searched the grounds of the house and tried its doors while the children were inside had atoned for his failure to find them by showing extra zeal when sent to the scene later, and had made these discoveries.

'Well, that's a line anyway, wherever it leads,' said Beddoes.

'It's all we've got,' said Cudlipp.

After they were found, both Jamie and Laura were taken to hospital, but Jamie was allowed to go home, where he was given a bath and put to bed. The police had extracted a somewhat confused account from him of what had happened. It was certain that he had had no contact with anyone, apart from Laura, and that Paula's treatment of Laura was the only offence in law committed against the children.

Geoffrey spent some time talking to the policewoman to whom Jamie had told his tale. That afternoon he went to see Sarah. She was in the kitchen eating a chocolate biscuit while Simon gnawed a rusk.

'Have some tea,' she said. 'And a biscuit. Sorry about the muddle.'

She had been ironing, and a pile of shirts was stacked on the ironing board.

'Isn't Kenneth drip-dry?' asked Geoffrey. Lydia did very little ironing.

'No.'

'You should convert him,' said Geoffrey, and added, 'I'd love a biscuit. Thanks.'

'I'm so thankful about Jamie,' Sarah said. 'It's been awful.'

'Poor little blighter – he's upset about some milk he stole off a doorstep. Thinks he'll be sent to prison for it,' said Geoffrey. 'I feel terrible about the whole thing, Sarah. Bloody guilty. It might all have ended very differently.'

'Well, it didn't,' said Sarah.

'It was all my fault,' Geoffrey told her, bent on purging himself. 'It seems he didn't want to go to the safari park and he doesn't want a dog. We'd decided to give him one, you see, to cure him of his phobia. He heard us talking. The police got all this out of him. Awful to think your child will talk to a policewoman and not to you.'

'Well, he is cured, isn't he?' Sarah said. 'That Labrador was with them all the time. He was very sensible, Geoffrey. You should be proud of him. He kept that other child warm and safe, and fed her too, even if he did pinch the milk. He showed lots of initiative. He looked after the poor little thing better than her own mother did, from what I've heard.'

'That's true,' said Geoffrey. 'Can I have another biscuit?'

Sarah pushed the tin across to him. She thought fleetingly that she and Kenneth never had tea cosily like this together; it had to be cups and saucers and plates, preferably in the sitting-room, never mugs and fingers in the kitchen.

'I suppose every man wants his son to be brave,' Geoffrey said, taking two biscuits out of the tin.

'Are you brave?' Sarah asked him.

'No, I'm not,' said Geoffrey. 'That's why I want Jamie to be – I don't want him to be a weak, craven individual.'

'He's not weak or craven – he's already proved that,' Sarah said. 'If a person's never afraid, they've nothing to be brave about. Jamie must have needed plenty of courage to hang on to that Labrador and not run screaming home, even if the whole business was a misguided affair.'

'He fished the child out of the pond,' Geoffrey

said. 'From what he said, I think the dog may have been trying to haul her out too – it seems he had hold of her anorak. But he was rather confused. We'll understand more when he's had a sleep and can talk about it again.'

'You must make him understand you're not angry,' Sarah said earnestly. 'I think you should let him see you think he acted bravely, even though you were worried to bits.'

'You're right about that,' said Geoffrey. 'And you think we shouldn't get a dog?'

'I do. Maybe a rabbit or a hamster – but only if he wants one. Geoff, some people don't like animals all that much and are still perfectly nice. People are more important than pets, though you wouldn't think so sometimes from the fuss that's made about animals.'

'Lydia thinks, if you don't relate to animals, you're missing a basic human experience,' said Geoffrey.

'Maybe you make up for it some other way,' said Sarah. 'Look at Mrs Minter – she can't stand all the dogs there are around here but she's a perfectly normal person. I admire her, too, battling on by herself without even a canary for company. She must often be lonely.'

'You've got Gyp,' Geoffrey stated, and he thought, you're lonely too.

'Yes. He's company, but I don't treat him as a lap-dog,' said Sarah. 'Simon can't say much for himself yet, can you, poppet?' and she wiped his messy chin with his bib.

Geoffrey reflected that Gyp's conversational powers were strictly limited too, but no more than Kenneth's, probably. He wanted to laugh at this

194

thought, and to share it, but obviously he couldn't with Sarah. What on earth could she see in that pompous oaf, he wondered, and then realized that it wasn't funny at all.

'I'll get Jamie a bike,' he said aloud. 'Then if that Alsatian's still around, he can pedal past, pretty quick. I'll teach him to ride safely.'

'The police run road safety courses, I believe,' said Sarah helpfully, pleased with this idea.

'Yes, I think they do,' said Geoffrey, and added, 'I wish I hadn't bawled poor Widnes out about meeting Jamie. He was being extremely kind, really. I feel pretty ashamed about it now.'

Sarah played with the sugar, digging into it with a spoon.

'You thought you were doing the right thing for your child,' she excused. 'At least you're able to admit to making a mistake.' Kenneth would never admit to a fault.

'Jamie likes you,' Geoffrey said. 'I think you understand him better than Lydia or I do.'

'I'm fond of him,' said Sarah.

They were silent. Between them, unspoken, hung all sorts of confessions and avowals.

'You'll move away,' said Sarah at last. 'Lydia wants to, doesn't she?'

'Yes. But it won't happen yet.'

'You'll go up in the world. That's Ken's aim too. It's all he thinks about,' said Sarah. 'He's going to take up bridge next. He thinks it's useful. I've refused.'

'Lydia plays,' said Geoffrey. 'I don't.'

There was another silence. Sarah piled up hills of sugar and then demolished them.

'That little girl – Laura – what will happen to

her?' she asked.

'I should think she'll be taken into care. She's safe at the moment, in hospital. Curtis nearly tore his wife apart, if seems, when he found out the state the kid was in.'

'He'd have known about it if he'd come home more often.'

'That's true.'

'She's doomed, really, isn't she? That child? One of them will get her and neither of them really wants her.'

'The father may do something about it. Who knows?'

'You never do know, really, do you, what's going on between people?' Sarah said.

Geoffrey took her hand.

'Sometimes you do,' he said.

Soon after half-past five that afternoon, Detective Inspector Cudlipp and Detective Sergeant French arrived at Widnes' Stores. Madge had just left, and as she waited for the bus she saw them enter the shop. They must know the truth about what had happened by now; Mick would implicate her and Norman would never speak to her again: this last reflection loomed larger than any other.

Norman, meanwhile, had taken the policemen up to the flat. The sitting-room smelled of polish, for Mrs Bowling had given it a good going over, and it had an antiseptic, impersonal aura. The sofa over by the window still dominated the room, as it had when occupied by Emma. Her mohair rug, neatly folded, lay on the seat.

'You were in the habit of meeting young Jamie Renshaw every morning and taking him to school,' began the inspector in a tougher tone than he had used even the night before.

'Just recently, yes,' said Norman. This had nothing to do with Emma.

'Why was that?'

'I discovered that he was often late for school. He was afraid of Mrs Curtis's Alsatian – it always stands in the road – and he avoided it by coming round this way. I took him past.' Even to himself, Norman's explanation sounded defensive.

'You didn't tell his parents?'

'I meant to, but I hadn't really had time,' said Norman. 'I spoke to Mrs Curtis, but it made no difference.'

'Curious that you could find time to take the boy along the road, yet not inform his parents.'

'I would have, when I'd time,' said Norman. 'I'm sorry I didn't. The boy mightn't have gone missing if his parents had realized.'

'You could have telephoned.'

Norman looked surprised.

'I didn't think of that – I could have done, I suppose. It just seemed to need the personal touch.'

'Mr Renshaw discovered what had been happening and asked you to stop, however.'

'Yes.' Norman still smarted at the memory.

'Why do you think he did this, Mr Widnes?'

'Ask him,' retorted Norman.

Cudlipp judged that the moment had come to put on some pressure. He fixed upon Norman his icy-blue stare.

'Mr Widnes, having an invalid wife was a great tie,' he said.

'Yes. But other men have sick wives,' said Norman.

'You're free now, however, to enjoy – shall we call it a wider social life?'

'I haven't thought about it,' Norman said.

'You might marry again, for instance.'

'That's an indecent suggestion,' Norman said angrily. 'My wife was brutally killed only two days ago.'

But he had admitted the same thought to himself only hours after Emma's death: he need not lose Felicity.

Cudlipp was continuing.

'Mr Widnes, when you got back on Saturday night and found the place had been robbed, was your wife already dead?'

'Of course she was. You saw her. Those dreadful injuries – thank God at least she must have died at once.'

'You didn't seize the chance to get rid of her, throwing the blame on the thief? She wasn't just lying there shocked – unconscious, perhaps – after the robbery and you finished her off?'

Norman's face reddened with fury.

'Inspector, I loved my wife,' he said. 'I would never have hurt her. What you're saying is horrible. Besides, aren't you forgetting that you found the safe in the garden?'

'You could have put it there,' said Cudlipp.

Norman's guilt about Felicity had already made him evasive, but he had never foreseen this nightmare accusation. He felt trapped.

'Where did you go on Saturday night after you left The Grapes?' Cudlipp asked.

'I've already told you. I went for a walk. I often

do. I often used to leave Emma for an hour or two – she liked me to go out. She had the telephone beside her. She could ring up Mrs Bowling in an emergency, or the doctor.'

'No one's come forward to say that they saw you that night,' said Cudlipp.

'Why should they? It was dark – I don't suppose anyone noticed me. Inspector, a criminal killed my wife – some evil thug – why aren't you looking for him?'

'We are, Mr Widnes, we are,' said Cudlipp, and now he spoke in a softer voice. 'I believe you are acquainted with Miss Felicity Baxter?'

Madge got off the bus and walked up the road towards her home, her mind still with Norman. What had he learned from the police, she wondered dismally. She was sure that Mick would somehow put all the blame on her – and it was her fault, after all. But what else could she have done?

She should have told Norman what had happened. But she hadn't, and now it was too late. Even so, she could have confessed today about her part in the affair; he was so good that he might somehow manage to forgive her. But it had all been so dreadful that she could never talk about it to anyone.

Her thoughts went miserably round in her mind while she trudged on and turned into the quiet road where she lived. Suddenly there was a roar behind her as a motor-bike, driven fast, sped towards her. Madge felt a blow in her back; then she was thrown into the air, pitching on to her head against the kerb.

After the two policemen had gone, Norman sat staring at the wall in a state of dulled incredulity. His anger had all gone, faced with the fantastic allegation that he had murdered Emma.

The police knew about Felicity, and to them it was excuse enough. And there had been times when he had longed for freedom: days and nights when the thought of ministering to that gross body filled him with repugnance: moments when he longed for the chance to live without having to think of her before anything else. Then he would remind himself of the secret they shared, and of the heavy cost of silence.

20

The police had soon traced Felicity by means of her car registration number, and on a map of the area they discovered how easy it was to reach her flat from Norman's shop; the journey on foot across the fields would take less than ten minutes.

After they left Norman, Cudlipp and French went to see her. At first she thought they had come about Jamie Renshaw, and when they asked her if she knew Norman her surprise was genuine. But she answered at once.

'Everyone knows him,' she said. 'Everyone uses his shop.'

'You called there this afternoon without buying anything,' said Cudlipp.

Felicity hesitated. Should she say he was out of whatever she had gone to buy? She did not want to be involved with Norman in his trouble, but her planned walking away from him could not be as coldly calculated as to deny him altogether; besides, she was not naturally a liar.

'I called to offer my sympathy,' she said. 'It was a terrible thing to happen.'

'What do you know about the death of Mr Widnes' mother?' Cudlipp asked.

'His mother?' Felicity's astonishment at this

question showed in her voice. 'Not much,' she said. 'It happened before I came here. Why?'

'You've heard no gossip? No suggestion that she was helped on her way?'

'Never! What a monstrous idea!'

'What's your assessment of Mr Widnes?' Cudlipp continued, unruffled.

'My assessment? Why should I think about him at all?' Felicity demanded. 'I thought you'd come here to talk about my pupil, Jamie Renshaw.'

'No. That's a separate matter,' said Cudlipp. 'Although Mr Widnes has been escorting him to school every morning for at least a week. You knew that, didn't you?'

'Why should I?' Felicity parried, but her heart sank. The police must have found out somehow about her and Norman; it was the only explanation for their presence, and exposure, could only bring trouble.

'You'll be seeing more of him, now that he's free,' Cudlipp stated.

His unblinking stare made Felicity feel uncomfortable, but she answered at once.

'Certainly not. It's got nothing to do with me. And anyway, I'm leaving Bidbury. I've applied for a post in Canada.'

'There's our motive,' said Cudlipp, as he and French left. 'She was chucking him and moving on.'

'We've got to prove they were having an affair. It may not be easy,' said French, who thought Felicity seemed an iron-willed young woman from whom it would be difficult to get any sort of admission.

'We'll soon find someone who saw them

together,' Cudlipp said. 'Just slip back, meanwhile, and look in her dustbin. You might find an empty wine bottle in it. With prints.'

Mick was away from the scene of Madge's accident in seconds, before anyone else arrived. It was lucky she lived in such a quiet street, he thought, zooming off in a cloud of exhaust. He left her lying in a huddle on the pavement; she'd be silent now, all right, and for a good long time, he hoped. Even for keeps.

He had been startled when his mother said she had come to see him. It had to be Madge, from the description. And it tied in with her asking Reg where he lived.

'What a nerve,' he'd said.

'Not your usual sort, I'd say,' his mother remarked, primming her lips.

'Fancies me, she does,' said Mick. 'But I'm not interested – get it? In case she comes again.'

He couldn't think what she had in mind; not shopping him, for sure; she'd never have come to see him if that was it. The reason he'd given his mother must be the right one.

All the same, it was only sense to leave nothing to chance.

Felicity risked telephoning Norman. He must be warned.

'The police came to ask if I knew you,' she said. 'I didn't tell them anything, but somehow they suspect.'

'Does it matter?' Norman asked wearily. He had denied their allegations, but he knew that Cudlipp was not deceived. 'Once this is all over, Felicity—'

'I'll be gone, Norman,' Felicity said. 'I've told you already. I'm leaving Bidbury.'

'But things are different now—'

'No. Sorry. I'm fond of you, Norman, and we've had some good times – but it's over now.' She felt shame at what she was doing, but the sooner the break came after what had just happened, the better. 'I'm sorry,' she said again. She did not want to spend the rest of her life with Norman, and she did not want to see him alone again.

Norman hung up, not answering. There was nothing to say. Neither of them knew that a newspaper reporter had seen the police enter Felicity's flat.

'What about this, then?'

Detective Sergeant French came into Cudlipp's office on Tuesday morning holding by one corner, gingerly, so that any prints would not be smudged, a sheet of writing paper. Printed in large capitals, Madge's succinct message read:

MICK GREEN DID IT.

'Did what?' asked Cudlipp.

'Well, sir, the envelope was postmarked Bidbury,' said French.

'Mick Green. Do we know a Mick Green?'

'Not yet.'

'Better see if we can find one, then. And check for prints. Might give us something.'

'Right, sir.'

French went off to order the routine inquiries which would unearth any local Mick Greens. It was an ordinary sort of name and there might be several. It would all take time, and might in the end prove irrelevant, but that was what got results: the painstaking weaving together of different strands to build up a case. There was just the chance that prints on the letter might match up with those of someone already involved in the attack on Emma Widnes.

There were other letters, too, which had to be investigated, mostly from cranks, but all must be checked.

Meanwhile, Madge lay unconscious in hospital.

The van which Mick had used for the removal of Pedro had been found dumped in a back street in Muddington. Before its owner reclaimed it, the constable making the report on its recovery observed some pale dog hairs in it. He made a note of the fact, but otherwise thought it of no importance.

Another constable, on Tuesday morning, called to tell Mrs Costello about finding the dead dog. Because it wore no collar, and she knew Pedro had been wearing his when he disappeared, she wouldn't believe it was Pedro. He would never wander so far, she insisted, and demanded to see the body.

There was no more doubt then.

There were five Michael Greens easily traced in the Bidbury area, and more in Muddington. Probably there were others not recorded as resident – below voting age, newly arrived, not owners of motor vehicles. Slowly the work of checking them went on.

Meanwhile the wine bottle found in Felicity's dustbin showed Norman's fingerprints. There were others on it too – probably hers, and those of the publican who sold it. Detective Superintendent Beddoes swung to the belief that Norman, returning from his clandestine tryst, had found the place done over and had seized his chance; Cudlipp still maintained that he could not be so vicious, although a circumstantial case against him was developing. The best way to oppose it was to find the thief. Robbery on its own was one thing; robbery with violence was a very different matter.

'That tip-off letter – I wonder who wrote that,' Beddoes mused.

'We'll soon know, sir,' Cudlipp said. 'Might be an accomplice of the thief who doesn't want to be an accessory to murder, but who's too scared to shop him properly.'

They both remembered Madge's prints on the safe together, and both dismissed the thought that she could be concerned so that it was a surprise when they learned that hers, and only hers, were on the sheet of notepaper.

21

When Harry Pearce learned that Paula Curtis had been a customer of Edna's, and that moreover Edna was prepared to testify that she had seen her maltreating the little girl, his unease grew. Paula would discover that he was Edna's husband and the truth about their affair might come out. Edna, at the least, was sure to cut up rough and it could all be very unpleasant.

It seemed like a judgement on his conduct when the police arrived to break the news of Madge's accident. United in anxiety about their daughter, Edna and Harry sat by her hospital bed as she lay bandaged and still semi-conscious. She had no recollection, so far, of what had happened or how she had been struck down.

'She may remember later,' said a nurse.

In another ward of the same hospital, Guy Curtis stood beside a high cot and looked down at the small human that was his daughter. She lay inert, but awake, staring at him apprehensively, quite silent. The ward sister, from whom came an almost visible aura of hostility, stood beside him.

'Malnutrition,' she said. 'Bruising on her body. Chafed skin from wet knickers. This apathy is the result of near starvation.'

Guy felt horrified pity for the plight of the child but she stirred no magic chord of affection in him; yet he was responsible for her existence.

'I didn't know,' he said. 'What will happen now?'

'She'll be here for some time,' said the sister with satisfaction.

'And then?'

'I expect the police will have something to say about the state she was in. It's to be hoped she'll be put into care.'

What could he do about it? He couldn't look after her himself, roving about the world as he did, he thought, with relief. She would be better off with a foster parent than with him.

'I'll come and see her again,' he said. 'Perhaps she'll remember me then.'

But he saw no reason why she should.

No one thought of telling Norman about Madge's accident until halfway through Tuesday morning, when her mother telephoned.

Things were still quiet in the shop. Norman knew from experience that people found it difficult to behave naturally towards the bereaved. This time, because of the circumstances, the effect seemed to be even greater; the few customers who did call were reluctant to look him in the eye.

If he had had time to read the newspaper, he would have understood that there was another cause besides mere diffidence. A reporter who had met Mrs Costello standing in Bodger's Self-Service in front of the pet foods and grieving because she no longer needed Meatimix, had recognized a likely source of gossip. As a consequence of the chat he had with her, he had written a piece suggesting that someone other than the thief could have killed Emma, and adding that Norman's mother had died very suddenly five years before. There was no mention of his mother's illness, nor of any names, and the piece was very carefully worded so that it was not libellous, but the inference was there.

When the shop closed, Norman went to the hospital to see Madge. She woke to find him sitting by her bed, and it was like a dream, until she remembered about Emma.

'Oh, Mr Widnes,' she mumbled. 'I'm ever so sorry.'

Norman patted her hand, thinking she was apologizing for absence from work.

'Don't worry, Madge,' he said. 'Just you get better.' He was so used to sick women that he was not upset at being in a hospital ward among a row of them, only distressed by her misfortune. 'What happened?' he asked.

'I don't know. I was walking along, and that's all I remember,' she frowned. 'Then, next thing, I was here.'

'You don't know what hit you?'

'No – at least—' She hesitated. 'I thought it must have been a car, but now I remember a noise.' She concentrated hard. 'It was a motor-bike,' she said.

Norman thought that when he saw the police again, he would mention this; he would not seek them out, however. On his way home, he went into The Grapes, where he had a beer and a grilled steak in the bar. No one seemed to want to talk to him, and in fact several backs were turned. Even the landlord's manner was cool.

An evening paper lay on the bench seat near him, and Norman glanced at it as he ate. On the centre page there was a picture of a very angry-looking Felicity. The caption below read: *Miss Felicity Baxter, 27, friend of ironmonger Norman Widnes whose invalid wife was brutally attacked after a robbery on Saturday night. Mr Widnes had left his wife alone and found her dead body after spending the evening out. Miss Baxter was photographed outside Old Bidbury Primary School where she is a teacher. She refused to talk to our reporter.*

It was vicious: deadly. Felicity's headmaster had been very angry when he saw the item earlier. And so was Norman, now.

Mrs Pearce saw the paper too, and showed it to her son while they had their tea. The news of Madge was a little better, and the family was easier, with time to think of other things.

'Well, poor sod, I'm not surprised. Are you?' said Reg. 'Stands to reason, doesn't it, married to that old bag.'

'He always seemed so nice,' said Edna Pearce. 'He was ever so good to Madge. Who would have believed it?'

Reg said that in Norman's shoes he'd have found someone with a bit more spark to her than that teacher looked to have, though beggars couldn't be choosers, of course.

All men were the same, thought Edna bitterly, wanting their bread buttered on both sides. She went to see Madge in hospital that evening, arriving just after Norman had gone. Madge mentioned hearing a motor-bike behind her just before the accident, but what with one thing and another, Mrs Pearce did not pass the information on to the police until the next day.

Detective Sergeant French had been looking through the station reports. A lost dog had been found with its head smashed; it had belonged to Mrs Costello from Old Bidbury, over whose garden the intruder had gone on Saturday night. A stolen van found abandoned in Muddington had dog hairs in it: blond ones. The van had now been returned to its owners.

He reported the facts to Detective Inspector Cudlipp who ordered the van to be brought in again. The hairs could be matched with the corpse of the dog, if it had not yet been disposed of, and if the van had not been cleaned. Even if it had, traces might linger. There would be plenty of dog hairs to be found in Mrs Costello's cottage, to provide a match. There might even be prints in the van, with a bit of luck.

'And see if anyone saw a motor-bike entering the garden of the empty house on Saturday night,' Cudlipp added. 'One did, to make those tyre marks. Probably no connection – a courting couple or some such – but we must check it out.'

French already had the matter in hand.

Various Michael Greens had been traced, ranging from a dentist to a retired pawnbroker. None seemed a likely candidate for the role of Emma's attacker, but now that Madge's fingerprints had been found on the letter, a police-woman was at the hospital waiting to take a statement.

Madge, however, could not talk; she had lapsed back again into unconsciousness, away from her problems.

By Wednesday morning the right Mick Green had still not been found. He was not on the electoral roll, and the police had only just started to check motor-cycle registrations.

Incensed by the newspapers' scandalmongering, but nevertheless titillated by the revelation of Norman's acquaintance with Felicity, Mrs Bowling advised him to shut the shop until it had all blown over. People would soon forget, she said; what he needed was a holiday. Things fitted together in her mind now – little remarks of a sad nature that Emma had sometimes made and Mrs Bowling had not understood.

'I can't go away until the police have found whoever did it, Ivy,' Norman said.

And what would be the point, anyway, without a companion? He missed Emma: it was strange not to hear her raucous laugh, see her small pig eyes disappearing into the fat folds of her face as she rocked back and forth at some joke or other. He even missed her appeals for physical contact.

'You don't think I did it, then?' he asked Mrs Bowling.

'As if you could – I'd like to know who gave them that wicked idea,' said Mrs Bowling angrily. 'Not anyone who'd seen you with her – with either of them.'

Norman remembered the capsules: a whole heap of them, carefully saved and emptied, their powder content administered in one mammoth dose. What would Mrs Bowling think if she knew the truth about that? But no one would ever know, now.

Mrs Bowling went with him to the inquest, sitting next to him in court with a proprietorial air, ready to defend him if need be from any attack. All the same, she could not help reflecting, it was strange about that Felicity Baxter; it must be true, or he'd be up in arms about it. He'd kept that dark; he might have kept other things dark, too.

The inquest was opened and adjourned after establishing simply the dead woman's identity. Detective Superintendent Beddoes, with the consent of the coroner, had decided not to reveal the actual cause of death and that it was not in fact a case of murder for the moment. The intent had been there; a would-be killer must be caught.

Detective Sergeant French was a painstaking officer. He had caused casts to be made of the tyre marks in the bushes at the empty house very promptly, in case rain were to wash them away, and a watch was kept to trace motor-cycles which they matched. There were a great many, but it was just possible that the right one might still yield traces of earth from the ground where it had been left. Meanwhile, the search for Mick Green produced one who owned a motor-cycle and lived in a block of flats in New Bidbury.

French went there, with a constable.

Mick was at work, said his mother, who had just returned from her shift at the supermarket, when they knocked at the door. And she did not know where he'd been on Saturday night, she added when asked. He always went out with a crowd, she said, but she never asked where. Yes, he did smoke.

She was not alarmed by the visit; she did not connect it with what had happened at Old Bidbury, although into her mind flicked the memory of Mick as a small boy, thumping his sister's head against a wall as he held her by the hair, because she'd refused to give him some sweets she'd bought. He might have been doing some petty thieving, she thought; he'd got a transistor radio that way, she knew, and one or two other things.

French found out from her where Mick worked. When he got back to the police station and learned that Madge Pearce remembered hearing a motor-bike approaching just before she was knocked down, as reported a few minutes before by her mother, the matter became much more urgent.

'We've got to get hold of that bike, sir,' he told Cudlipp. 'That girl may have been knocked down on purpose.'

Cudlipp felt relieved. He didn't like the way things were shaping for Norman.

'Bring Mick Green in,' he said.

That evening a white-faced Edna Pearce was waiting for Reg when he got home. The police had been to question her about her daughter's possible friendship with a Mick Green who was helping them with their inquiries into the break-in at Widnes' Stores.

'Has Mick been seeing our Madge – apart from that night when he brought her home?' she asked Reg.

'Mick and our Madge – not likely,' said Reg, but

his expression was wary. Madge had wanted to know Mick's address, after all; they could have been meeting. 'Why?' he asked.

His mother told him.

Reg was shocked, and he did not attempt to bluff his way out of it. He hadn't seen Mick leaving work that day; usually they rode home at much the same time, but he'd been transferred to a different part of the factory recently and he'd thought nothing of it. Surely if Mick were guilty he'd not have stayed around waiting to get picked up? He told his mother that Mick had talked about robbing Widnes' Stores.

'But it was just fooling,' he added. 'Madge couldn't have had anything to do with it, even if Mick did do the job. But he'd never—' His voice trailed off as he realized just how grave a crime had been committed. Mick would – he was violent: Reg had seen him almost beat the daylights out of a little kid who'd been cheeky one day; the other lads had pulled him off the boy before he'd done him too much damage. He'd forgotten it till now.

'Madge hadn't been herself for a while, before this happened,' Edna said.

Reg knew that this was true.

'But how could she have helped him? She didn't go out that night, did she?'

'I don't think so. But she could have – your dad and I were out ourselves,' she said.

'She might have got him a key or something,' Reg muttered, and then, 'but she wouldn't, would she? She'd not be so stupid.'

'The thief knew where to find the money,' Edna said quietly. 'Madge might have told him.'

22

Above the noise of the factory machines, Mick never heard the two policemen approach. He'd been thinking that he could give this lot up now – move off, go abroad, maybe, like on the TV ads, and lounge under a palm tree somewhere sunny till the money ran out and the fuss over the job had died down. Then, suddenly, there was a solid male body on either side of him, a voice in his ear, and he was being walked quietly away and out into a car before he had time to protest. He shouted a bit then, and when he got to the station he had plenty to say once the questions began. He'd been with a girl on Saturday night, and he gave her name.

He'd made certain she'd support his alibi, so he wasn't really worried. He, Mick Green, was above the law and untouchable.

When the police showed the girl a photograph of Mick and asked her about him, she confirmed what he said; unfortunately for Mick, when the police called her younger sister was at home, and she, too, recognized the photograph. She was one of the girls before whom Mick had been unable to resist flaunting himself outside the ironmonger's shop on Saturday evening before he hid the motor-bike at the empty house. The younger girl was certain and in the end her sister admitted that she might have made a mistake about what time she met Mick.

The police found Pedro's collar in Mick's room, along with several pairs of bikini briefs, an imitation pistol, a varied collection of keys, and some other souvenirs. And a lot of money.

'Well,' Elsie said to Felicity in the staff-room. 'I suppose it's true?' Her tone was sardonic.

'What is?' Felicity glared at her.

'That you'd been having an affair with the ironmonger.'

Felicity thought of denying it, but what was the point? No one would believe her, even if it happened to be true. People liked to think the worst.

'So what?' she said defiantly.

Elsie shrugged.

'Did he do it?'

'Do what?'

'Kill his wife when he saw the chance, after the place was done over.'

'Of course not,' said Felicity.

But was she really so sure? She couldn't believe that he would kill Emma because she, Felicity, had said she was going away. But what was the truth about his mother's death? What had that policeman been getting at? Norman had always been reluctant to talk about it. There was some mystery.

The atmosphere among her colleagues was strained, and the children stared at her with a frank interest which she found unnerving. One or two of the older ones called crude remarks after her as she crossed the playground, and at the end of the day the headmaster suggested it might be wise if she stayed away until things had died down. He would ask for a relief teacher, and perhaps she would consider making a permanent change. She was an excellent teacher, he added, and her private life was her own affair, but not when it impinged on the school.

Felicity was glad to be able to tell him that she had already applied for an overseas post.

Driving home, she suddenly remembered the conversation she had overheard in the pub before all this happened, when a group of youths had swaggered in and discussed what sounded like doing a break-in. She had completely forgotten it until now.

It couldn't have any connection. She struggled to remember what they'd said. Something about breaking a window and money not being kept in a till. She couldn't even remember what they'd looked like, except that they'd been full of energy, and one had worn built-up shoes which she'd noticed particularly. The publican might know them, though, if they were regulars.

She would have to tell the police, just so that they could be eliminated.

Mrs Costello had no reason now to get up in the morning. There was no snuffling damp nose thrust against her sleeping face; no one to open tins for or take for walks; no one to need her.

More terrible things happened than the death of a dog. Murder for instance, like Emma Widnes' death, and the business about the child. But these things had affected other people; Pedro's death was her own, and latest, tragedy.

A noise broke into her thoughts: the front-door bell. Kitty Minter, perhaps, come to nag her. She pulled the sheet over her head but the bell kept on. It might be the police. Now that it was too late, they were taking Pedro's death very seriously and had removed his blanket, which was covered in his hairs. She did not know why they were bothering. It was unlikely that they would seek Pedro's killer when they had a hunt on for someone who had murdered a woman.

The bell kept on ringing. She would have to get up.

She shuffled into her dressing-gown, shoved her thin, veined feet into her slippers, and padded downstairs.

Rose Hallam was at the door, her dachshunds beside her with their leads in a tangle.

'I've heard of a puppy that needs a home,' she said without preamble. 'It's a spaniel – a black one. It's to be put down if one can't be found by the end of the week. Will you come and see it?'

Mrs Costello shook her head.

'I don't want another dog,' she said. 'No one can take Pedro's place.'

Rose, often rather timid, stepped forward until her foot was over the threshold.

'May I come in?' she said. 'You'll get cold standing on the step.' She couldn't let Mrs Costello stand there in disarray for everyone to see. 'You get dressed while I make some coffee,' she added. 'Then we'll go together to look at the dog. Oh, isn't your garden lovely?' She moved to look at it through the window at the back of the hall. 'Snowdrops and crocuses already – you'll soon have daffodils out. It's a very safe place for a puppy, isn't it? You could put a padlock on the gate at the bottom, so that mischievous boys can't undo it.'

Mrs Costello did not take all this in straight away. She still mumbled, 'I don't want another dog.'

Rose smiled at her brightly.

'Go and get dressed,' she said firmly. 'There isn't much time.'

'We've got him,' Detective Inspector Cudlipp told Norman. 'We can prove the break-in and the theft – he'd still got most of the money – and there were strands of his clothing on a bush in Mrs Costello's garden. But there's nothing to prove who assaulted Mrs Widnes.'

Not yet: not unless forensic found something. Cudlipp spared Norman the final irony of hearing that there was new evidence of the robbery being planned in Felicity's hearing.

'You mean you still think I deliberately threw that safe on my wife's face as she lay helpless?' Norman said.

'As it happens, we don't,' said Cudlipp. 'But a clever lawyer, defending his client, could indicate such a possibility.'

'Doubts could be raised about the past, too,' said Detective Superintendent Beddoes, in whose office this interview was taking place. 'About your mother's death.'

'I didn't kill her, any more than I killed Emma,' said Norman. 'Though God knows, I wished for her release.'

Beddoes began doodling again on his blotter,

adding to a fearsome pattern already there. At some point he must reveal that Emma had, in fact, died of a heart attack, but more might be learned from Norman first. The chance of getting any sort of confession out of Mick was slim: he was tough and amoral. But it could be proved that he had stolen the dog, and that he was the most likely person to have killed it. When forensic had finished with his clothing they might find dog hairs and bloodstains, human or canine, and the fact that the dog's head had been smashed, like Emma's, was a coincidence that could be emphasized.

'People may talk,' Beddoes said. 'Some have already. It could be very unpleasant.'

Norman thought that nothing could be worse than it was now.

'Madge Pearce,' he said. 'What about her? She had no part in it, did she?'

'Against her will, yes,' said the superintendent, for by now Madge had come round again and, when faced with the letter she had written, had broken down and disclosed what had happened between her and Mick. 'He forced her to tell him where the safe was kept,' Beddoes said.

'But what did he do?' asked Norman, and then, seeing the other men's faces, understood. 'Oh – God, how awful! Will you charge him for that?'

'I doubt it. I don't think she'd be altogether willing, and he'd deny it – say she led him on,' said Beddoes. 'She may have, in a way, without realizing it. They went to a cinema and a pub together.'

'Is she all right?'

'She'll get over the accident. As to the rest—' Beddoes shrugged. 'It's too soon to say.'

'She must come back to the shop,' Norman decided. 'When she's well enough. If she wants to. She seemed happy with us—' He paused. 'She seemed to like her job.'

'It would be the best thing for her, I expect,' said Cudlipp. Dr Barrett's prophecy was being fulfilled: Norman was preparing to adopt a new burden.

Beddoes had not finished. He drew a hatchet on the blotter before him. Then he asked:

'What happened when your mother died?'

Nothing would ever obliterate the details of that night from Norman's mind. He had entered the kitchen when Emma was mixing his mother's invalid food; she could tolerate little else now, and had grown quite fond of its bland texture, taking it sometimes with fruit flavouring or cocoa added.

On this occasion she had had a good day, even laughing at a programme on television before falling into one of her dozes, and had managed a thin slice of bread and butter for tea.

'You're putting a lot of sugar in it,' Norman had said as Emma stirred the mixture, orange-flavoured tonight.

Emma had gone on stirring.

'It's how she likes it,' she said, and she had taken the drink to his mother. Norman had followed, and heard his mother remark on its bitterness; he had gone from the bedroom back to the kitchen and there, in a screwed-up paper bag in the waste-bin, were a great many empty blue gelatine capsules.

When Emma left his mother's room, silently, he showed them to her.

'Ah yes. I was going to flush them down the toilet later,' Emma said calmly. 'You know it's for the best, dear, and you know you'd never be able to do it yourself. She's had a very good day. Let's hope she keeps them down.'

She had taken the capsules from him and he'd heard the cistern flush.

Later, when she suggested they should marry, she said they both needed to feel safe. They were in it together; each was the other's accessory, and neither, in law, could then be made to testify against the other.

He knew in that instant that her motive had not been mercy.

They had never mentioned the matter again.

'I've nothing to tell you,' Norman said to Beddoes. 'Nothing at all.'

Crime in Question

1

Denis never knocked.

He marched into the house as soon as Yvonne returned from shopping in Leckerton. She was alone. He remembered that the little kid went to a playgroup in the village.

'Come for me cocoa,' said Denis, admitting a blast of raw autumnal air as he stumped along the passage and entered the kitchen.

'You've left the back door open,' said Yvonne. 'And take your boots off.'

The boy raised his eyes to heaven in wonderment at these remarks, but he slouched away to bang the door and leave his boots on the mat. Returning, he did a little jig with his hands over his ears as if he were wearing a Walkman, and capered round the big scrubbed table in a pair of red socks with a hole in one toe before sitting down.

In silence, Yvonne Davies made him a cup of hot chocolate, which was his preferred mid-morning beverage, and fetched a tin from the larder. She cut a slice of sponge cake filled with home-made raspberry jam and put it on a plate before him.

'Ta,' said Denis.

He began to shovel cake into his mouth with one hand, still holding the other over one ear and writhing about as if in response to some ritual beat.

Denis was the jobbing gardener at Ford House. He had applied for the post after seeing it advertised on a card in the village shop, but he did not live in Coxton.

'I'm staying with me gran in Leckerton,' he had informed Yvonne, whose first impressions of the applicant were not encouraging. He had dark, almost black eyes, and a round florid face with a sparse crop of acne. His brown hair was shorn at the back and brushed up in short spikes above his low forehead. He said he was doing casual work before going on a Youth Training Scheme, and that he liked working outside.

Only the last of these statements was true.

'So you wouldn't be staying long?' Yvonne asked.

'No. Sorry,' said Denis.

That suited her. She didn't want the expense of retaining someone through the winter when there would be little to do. Denis's task would be to dig over the vegetable garden, a large neglected area behind a hedge at the side of the house and too much for her to tackle unaided. Yvonne was glad to be living in the country after years in Shepherds Bush, and excited at the prospect of putting things to rights both inside and outside the house, but there was so much to do, and Charles had little time to help. His day was much longer now, with the journey; sometimes she thought he extended it more than he need.

Denis was a stocky, sturdy boy, and digging was straightforward enough. As the only other applicant was a frail-looking man of seventy-three, Yvonne had taken Denis on for the two mornings a week which were all he said he could spare, and today was his third appearance. Yvonne had not been sure he would stay the course, but he was working well, laying the soil in large clods to be broken up by the frost, as she had instructed, and burying all the weeds. If he stayed long enough, she might imprint some manners on the blemished canvas that was his character. The 'ta' this morning was an improvement upon his previous silent grabbing of whatever he was offered.

While he was eating his cake, Yvonne unpacked the shopping and put it away, walking to and from the larder which opened off the old scullery. Ford House had been built near a shallow stretch of the river where there had been a ford before the bridge had been built. It dated from the late eighteenth century, but bits had been added and removed at various times until what was left was a somewhat uncoordinated house. It had been on the market some time before Charles and Yvonne bought it after the asking price was reduced, and it needed renovation which they intended to do gradually when they could afford it. As it was only twelve miles from the motorway, they had thought themselves lucky to have their offer accepted. That was before they discovered that there was an open prison only four miles away to the north.

Buying the house had landed them with a large mortgage to be met from only one salary, and Charles was stretched to his financial limits. They had both been married before, and he had another family to support. Yvonne tried not to resent this drain on their income, but it was difficult. She had never received any money either for herself or for her two children from her former husband, who had disappeared and was thought to be living in Australia.

When she met Charles, Yvonne had been working for an interior decorator for whom she made curtains, cushions and bedspreads. The pay was not very good but she could work at home, travelling back and forth as necessary in her old Mini making deliveries and collecting fabrics. She intended to branch out on her own; there must be local scope for such a service. At last she had plenty of space; a room on the top floor of the house warmed only by a portable gas heater because the ancient central heating did not stretch so far, was her new workplace. She had a large trestle table on which to cut out, and there were shelves for her bolts of material. The ironing board could be kept permanently ready for use, and there was room for Robbie to play with his cars on the floor. In any spare time she could find between commissions, she was making cushion covers and bedspreads to form the basis for her own business.

Denis had finished his cake. Yvonne, as she moved in and out of the kitchen unpacking her shopping, had not noticed his eyes darting about as he wondered what he could pick up which she would not miss. She was too careful; that was the trouble. She never left her purse lying about, nor even the odd coin. He knew where she kept her keys, however; he'd noticed them the first day, hanging openly on the dresser, her car keys and one that opened the front door. They were just asking to be taken.

Denis had not yet decided how best to use them, but he would. You had to take your chance when it came. He'd always done that, ever since he'd seen a pair of brand-new jeans pegged to a clothes line and had liberated them for his own use. He was only twelve at the time. After that he'd done a fair bit of snow-dropping: collecting gear that had been hung out to dry. Some of it he sold to other boys, but most he kept for himself. He liked to look smart, and his mother wasn't too fussy about seeing that he did; when she put on the old washing machine that leaked on to the kitchen floor, she never took any notice of what was in the load and colours got mixed and ran. Denis's sister had sometimes seen to things, but she had gone now, shacked up with a guy who worked as a plasterer. He had his own van and went around working for different builders; self-employed, he was, and Denis admired him for that. Sometimes he went round to see them, and it was Alan who had brought him over to Coxton for the ride on the day that he saw the card advertising this job. That had been in the school holidays when working was a way of passing the time. Denis had told Mrs Davies he was seventeen but it wasn't true. He would be sixteen in November and then he could give up school, where both he and the staff agreed he stood no chance of ever passing an exam. His departure would be a relief on both sides and meanwhile he could simply not turn up sometimes; he'd done it before but not often enough to land himself in serious trouble.

Mrs Davies – for some reason Denis always thought of her in that respectful way – had paid up for new boots for him, for naturally he couldn't go digging in his trainers. Instead of buying them, he'd liberated a pair of wellingtons from a stall in Leckerton market at no cost at all. He'd tried them on when the place was busy and then, still wearing them, had picked up some shoes as if to inspect them while he waited for an opportunity to walk away with his own trainers tucked up under his bomber jacket. The chance had come while the stallholder was busy with two talkative women. He had been tempted to take the shoes too, but that would have been asking to get caught. He had laid them down and walked away.

It was dead easy.

Denis liked that sort of challenge. Why pay good money for things you could get free?

After his first day, when Denis had worn a pair of Charles's boots padded out with extra socks, he was not at all sure that he would come again. It wasn't easy to get over to Coxton without a lift and he was certainly not going to use the bus, although Mrs Davies was going to pay his fare; that was a wicked waste of money. Turning over the heavy soil had been hard work, though there was satisfaction in seeing the area of neatly dug earth slowly increasing. His back had ached a bit, but not a lot. He'd been starving hungry after a very short time, and when she called him to the house for his mid-morning break he had been surprised; he hadn't expected that. For one of her sort, she wasn't bad, and she made great cakes. He supposed she used those packets you got at Tesco's, like his mum had done on good days when he was young. She'd paid him on the nail and advanced him the cash for the boots.

Yvonne had had misgivings about that as she handed the money over, having telephoned a shop in the town to ask about prices. She would be waving it goodbye and the boy would never turn up again. But the next week there he was, and he had given her twenty pence back, saying it was the change.

She had accepted it as a matter of principle, and she had found him an old anorak of Charles's to wear while at work, so that his own wouldn't get soiled.

Charles knew nothing about the deal with the boots. He simply paid for Denis's time and his bus fare.

Denis discovered how near Ford House was to the open prison after his second day's work. On his way to hitch a lift at the crossroads, he decided to take a look round the village and walked down a road he had not been along before. Soon he came to the church, where he saw a group of men in overalls repairing the stone wall which bordered the graveyard. He recognized them at once for what they were, although there was no sign of a warder in charge.

As he passed, Denis had his make-believe earphones attached to his head, his hands cupped, and he was listening in his mind to Michael Jackson. This distracted him from immediately thinking of speaking to any of them. Later, he realized that they might be interested in the pickings up at the big house, all those bits of fancy china he'd seen through the window, dotted about on cupboards and stuff, and she'd probably got loads of jewellery. A con would know how to get rid of it the best way without getting caught, and there'd be a good cut for whoever had set up the job. Denis did not see as a flaw in this theory the fact that the men had already proved fallible enough to be charged and convicted.

The four men busy in the chuchyard repairing the wall had seen Denis go by. They noticed everyone who passed. Interested parishioners, including those who never went to church, came to see what they were doing, and the parochial church council was so pleased with their efforts that it was contemplating asking for prison labour to repair the roof.

The men rode to work on bicycles.

Mrs Bannerman, who lived at Ivy Lodge, had asked for a prisoner to help her plant a hedge. Some villagers had reservations about the presence of these men among them, but she had none. Help was difficult to find in Coxton, and by employing a convict she might, in some small way, make up a little for the past.

Denis had been back in the garden for only half an hour after finishing his cake and hot chocolate before it began to rain.

As soon as what had started as a fine drizzle turned into a downpour, Yvonne called him into the house.

'You can't go on in this, Denis,' she said. 'You may as well give up for today. I'll take you down to the bus stop on the way to pick Robin up from the playgroup.'

Denis had never been to a playgroup. When his mother was at work he was left with a child minder, and he had soon learned to fend for himself. The child minder was an unofficial one who crammed ten small children into her small terraced house, where survival was for the fittest. Once, Denis had been shut in a cupboard for hitting another boy over the head with a wooden engine. There were good moments, though, when the child minder had made them all sit down and watch television and had given them buns and milk. His mother worked at a factory in Leckerton packing small plastic objects into boxes. She spent much of what she earned on drink. Denis's father was a warehouseman. He liked drink too. It made him free with his fists and he had knocked them all about, Denis and his sister Tracy, and their mother, but the rows between husband and wife ended in noisy reconciliations when the children were locked out of the house if they had not already chosen to leave until things quietened down.

Sometimes their mother took men upstairs who were not their father. Tracy and Denis were always locked out then.

The grandmother Denis had mentioned to Yvonne did not exist any more. Years ago the children had spent their school holidays with their grandparents near Ramsgate but that had ended when their grandmother died and their grandfather was now in a home.

Denis got into Yvonne's old blue Mini and watched how she started it up. If ever he was in any sort of motor vehicle, he always studied how it operated. He reckoned he could drive Alan's van as easy as wink and begged to be allowed to try, but Alan always refused.

'What, have you out on the road when you've not got a licence? Suppose you crashed? Think again, Den,' Alan had said.

'Where's the playgroup?' Denis asked.

'At the vicarage,' Yvonne told him. It was run by Amy Parker, the vicar's wife, who was a former teacher; two other mothers took turns to help her.

They drove through the village and as Yvonne slowed down to drop Denis at the bus shelter, they saw a man on a bicycle emerge from a gateway further along the road.

'That's one of them cons,' said Denis.

'Yes,' said Yvonne.

'They're working up at the church. I've seen them.'

'So I believe,' said Yvonne, who had heard talk in the shop.

'Must be a cushy number,' said Denis. 'Better than being in the nick.'

'I'm sure you're right,' said Yvonne drily. 'And it's supposed to prepare them for rejoining society.'

Denis always wanted to mimic her when she talked in that lah-di-dah way, but he knew better than to try when she was within earshot. To help himself resist the urge, he cupped his hands over his ears and writhed in his seat.

'We've arrived, Denis,' Yvonne pointed out, and added, 'I'm surprised you haven't got a Walkman; you're always pretending to be listening to one.'

'I did have,' said Denis. 'It got nicked.' His mother had popped it to buy drink. 'I'm getting another.'

'Well, watch out when you're wearing it,' Yvonne warned. 'They're dangerous things in traffic. You can't hear anyone coming up behind you.'

And you couldn't hear rows, either, or people cursing you, or not very plainly.

'Yeah, I know,' said Denis.

He got out of the car, banging the door, and watched her disappear round a bend in the road. He would not admit, even to himself, that he enjoyed the time spent at Ford House. For one thing, no one got at you, and she was all right, handing out food. The silence in the garden had got him down at first and it was a relief when he heard a car or lorry pass in the road, but once you started to listen there were other sounds – birds twittering and dogs barking.

They'd got no dogs at the house. You'd think they would, with all that space, and it would be nice for the kids. Anyone planning a heist would be glad to know about that.

Whistling, Denis stood inside the bus shelter waiting for someone to come along and give him a lift.

He'd get another Walkman that afternoon. He'd find one somewhere, just waiting to be tucked up inside his jacket.

2

Returning from the playgroup with Robin, Yvonne slowed as she passed the gates through which the man on the cycle had ridden. As she had thought, it was Ivy Lodge. That was where the old lady in the tweed hat lived. Yvonne had seen her walking around the district. She went for miles, always alone. Yvonne had met her in the shop and noticed her awkward, gruff manner. She did not know her name, but then she scarcely knew anyone yet, not even the other mothers at the playgroup. They all seemed very friendly amongst themselves, but she was always in too much of a hurry to stop and chat. When she got home, if it was not household tasks that must be done, there was her sewing.

She did not like the thought of those convicts roaming, apparently freely, round the village. It was no wonder Ford House had hung fire on the market so long. People wouldn't want such neighbours, any more than Charles did. He had wanted to withdraw from the purchase when they learned about the prison.

'They'll be escaping. We'll have murderers and rapists at large,' he said. 'And there will be times when I'll be late home from work, or even away. It won't be safe for you or the children.'

'Men like that aren't kept in open prisons,' said Yvonne, with the confidence of ignorance. 'They're all con men and embezzlers. Not violent men. And they don't escape much. It stands to reason, after all. These places wouldn't exist if they did.'

She knew Charles was in many ways reluctant to move to the country, and not just because of the added financial burden of buying Ford House. They would be living much further from his daughters, and visits would

16

not be so easy. Yvonne, however, had never been happy living in town, and now that there was their own small son, Robin, to consider, Charles had conceded that a freer way of life might be possible if they moved.

They soon discovered that some of the prisoners at Lockley had, indeed, committed major crimes, but were considered to have atoned for them and to be no danger to the public. Yvonne had never seen them cycling to or from the prison, which they did unattended. The lone man on his cycle today was the first she had observed actually in the street, where he might encounter Philip and Emily if they went into the village on their own. They had not done so yet; she took them to school every morning and collected them again each afternoon, but she had thought that before long they might at least come back by themselves.

She would never let them do that while the prisoners were working in the village.

That evening she told Charles about the one she had seen. When he came home, Robin and Emily were in bed and Philip was in his pyjamas in his room, learning the words he was supposed to be able to spell the next day. It had been a pleasant surprise to Yvonne to discover that spelling was considered important by the Coxton primary school headmaster, who set high standards for his pupils and achieved excellent results.

Charles had looked in on Robin, who lay on his back, petal mouth slightly open, breathing softly, a small Paddington Bear tucked in beside him. Emily was awake, listening to a story on the tape recorder beside her. Charles pretended not to notice, because it was against the rules; he knew that it meant Yvonne hadn't had time to read to her this evening. He tiptoed away, unseen. Philip began to tell him eagerly about the day at school and showed Charles a drawing he had done in class, but while he was doing this Charles's attention

17

began to wander in the direction of a new line in tooling machinery which his firm was about to produce.

'Off to bed now,' he said, before Philip had finished his story.

Philip did not protest. Charles wasn't his real father, so he couldn't be expected to show the same interest in him as in Robin, for instance. He was pretty good on the whole, however, and had brought them from the small house where they had lived all their lives to this enormous place, where you could do almost anything from climbing trees to riding your bike round and round at top speed and pretending to be in a Ferrari. In Philip's mind there lurked a fantasy figure of a big, tall man in Australia. He rode a chestnut horse with a flowing mane and wore a leather hat while he rounded up thousands of sheep which he proceeded to shear faster than anyone else in the outback. This man, his real father, would have liked to be with him and Emily, of course, but fate had decided that he must live at the far side of the world instead. Philip knew that in some way he had been mean, leaving them with no money and making Mum very sad, but it must all have been due to something he couldn't help. He wasn't really bad, and one day he would ask them out for a very long visit. Meanwhile, Charles was all right. Things were easier for Mum and they weren't so poor, though Charles was always saying they had no money. It couldn't be true, because they were living in a huge house and Charles drove a BMW. They were lucky. Even Rosalind and Celia, Charles's daughters, who had come to stay in the summer, were quite nice, for girls. Before that, they had only ever come for a day as there was so so little room in the old house. Emily, though only seven, liked playing with Celia, who was eleven, and who was always nice to Robin, though both she and Rosalind, who was nearly fourteen, were often rather snappy with Mum. Once, Philip, who would soon be ten, had seen his mother walking off down

18

the garden, very fast, her arms folded across her chest and her head down, and he knew that she was crying. He had gone after her and she'd pretended that she was going to look for late raspberries, a silly excuse because they'd been over even before the move and the canes were in an awful tangle needing sorting out. They had done that, he and Mum and Robin, cleared out the canes, cutting down the old ones and tying in the ones Mum thought would bear fruit next year, that very day while the three girls played some silly game.

He supposed Rosalind and Celia found him and Emily a pain. Why should they like them? They must mind that Charles preferred Mum to their mother.

That evening, when Charles and Yvonne were having dinner, Robin began to cry.

'I'll go,' said Charles.

He had been good at soothing Rosalind and Celia when they were small, reading to them and sitting with them until whatever trouble had woken them had been forgotten, and he had often been the one to get up in the night when Robin was teething. Since then, the little boy had been a good sleeper until the move. Now he had nightmares several times a week and though she ridiculed herself for thinking it, Yvonne had begun to wonder if the house could be haunted. Charles was certain, though, that it was simply the change of surroundings. He did not believe in ghosts. He was always patient with Robin, overjoyed and proud to have a son.

After he had gone upstairs, Yvonne sat for a while amid the remains of their dinner while Charles's blackcurrant sorbet slowly dissolved on his abandoned plate. A new resolution at Ford House had been to present a delicious meal every evening, with the dining room table properly laid and the children all quietly stowed away in their beds, but she had discovered years ago that being a wife was more difficult than being a mistress. Before the

19

move, she had attributed their worst problems to the cramped conditions in which they were living. Charles had come to live with her and the children after calling Olivia's bluff in one of the hysterical scenes she was always contriving during their marriage. She frequently said that she wanted to resume her career as an actress and that he got in her way. During this uneasy period he had met Yvonne and their affair began. Finally he decided that he had had enough; if Olivia did not need him, Yvonne certainly did, and he moved out.

Olivia had never done more than tiny parts in a few television series and one or two commercials. Now she performed strongly as the wronged wife, accusing Charles of being unfaithful throughout their marriage. This was untrue; Yvonne was Charles's first adventure of that sort. Ironically enough, he met her at a theatrical party; she had made the curtains for the new house into which the host had just moved. After Charles left home, a struggling actor ten years younger than Olivia had moved into the house in Gerrards Cross, but that had lasted little more than a year. Then Olivia had met Hugh, who owned three jewellery shops and was nearly old enough to be her father. Hugh was still married, and it took time for the legal niceties to be arranged, but at last, earlier this year, he and Olivia had married and Charles was freed from the financial burden of supporting her as well as the girls.

Now he had a son, who would draw them all together, but that did not compensate for the partial loss of his daughters, whom Charles saw only once a month. Before, they had come for the day on alternate Sundays. Now, they spent every fourth weekend at Ford House, where each had her own room for which Yvonne had made pretty curtains and bedspreads before she did any others, so that everything was ready when they stayed for a fortnight in August while Olivia and Hugh were touring in France.

After Charles had settled Robin, he went into the small room that had become his study. That meant he had brought work home and did not want to be disturbed.

Well, Yvonne could work, too. There was plenty to do in her attic room.

She went up there as soon as she had cleared away the dishes. Before the move Charles had always helped wash up and then they had spent the evening together. Here, there was a dishwasher.

Charles's mother had died a year ago, and his father had sold the family house. He had given Charles and Yvonne the surplus furniture and was now living in a bungalow near Sidmouth. He had not yet seen Ford House. After Yvonne's father had died, when she was still at school, her mother had opened a guest house in the Lake District. Before Charles had moved in with them, Yvonne and the children had gone there for frequent visits during off-season times, but this had lapsed. Yvonne's mother thought she was making a mistake in throwing her lot in with Charles, and did not disguise her reservations about the marriage.

'I'll look after Yvonne and the children,' Charles had told her. 'Things will be much easier for all of them now.'

Yvonne's mother thought that it would be her daughter looking after Charles. She was pleased, however, about the move to the country, and it was she who had given them the dishwasher as a house-warming present.

While Charles studied sales figures and graphs, Yvonne sat in her attic workroom with the door ajar in case a child cried out. She started drawing together pinch pleats on some gold brocade curtains promised for the following week.

Denis was still in the bus shelter when the prisoners who had been working in the churchyard, also defeated by

21

the weather, started back to Lockley. He had waited, thumb extended when any vehicle approached, for some time. Then he had felt hungry and had gone across to the shop for some crisps and a tin of Coke. While he was in the shop the bus went past, not that he'd intended to take it, but he might have this once, since people were so mean, driving by without even pausing. He returned to the shelter, where he threw down the empty crisp packet and the tin when he had finished their contents.

Four men on cycles rode up, propped their machines against the wall of the shelter, stepped inside and lit up cigarettes. It was raining hard now and they were in no hurry to get back to the prison.

'Hullo, kid,' said one. 'Like a smoke?'

'I don't mind,' said Denis. 'Ta.'

He didn't like smoking much, but this was not the time to say so. The man rolled him a cigarette, sealing it neatly, then handed it over. Denis puffed inexpertly at the result, affecting an air of nonchalance. Then one of the men asked him to go across to the shop, which had a licence, and buy them some beer.

'You got enough cash for that?' he asked, grinning. He knew they got very little in prison.

They had, but shopping by proxy was wiser than spending it themselves since they had been given it by a well-meaning parishioner who had not realized that they were allowed to handle very little cash.

Denis took the money and scampered off down the road again, one hand over an ear. Soon he returned with four small cans. One of the men offered him a swig, which, although he wanted to be friendly, he refused. He never drank. He had seen the effect of alcohol on his parents and was afraid of it.

He told them about Ford House, and what he had seen there, and about the keys that hung on the dresser, and one of them told him how he could make an impression on soap. They could easily cut a key in the prison workshop and it would be simple to enter the house.

'You don't want to bother with that, Len,' said another man, frowning. 'Don't give the kid ideas.'

But the man called Len, who was due out in two weeks' time, thought it sounded an excellent way to get back into business.

'I'll need a bit of this and that,' he said. 'You're on, kid. I'll cut you in.'

Denis was to hide his piece of soap under a loose stone in the wall just along the road from the bus shelter; Len chose a place in the exterior wall of a cottage whose owners both went out to work every day, as the prisoners already knew. A mark scratched on the side of the shelter would be a sign that the job was done.

Denis was delighted with this encounter. He stood looking after the men as they cycled away and almost missed signalling an approaching car. Its driver took pity on him and gave him a lift all the way back to Leckerton.

It was too wet to go looking for a Walkman but, as usual when his mother was out, the house was locked. He had no key, nor was one hidden so that he could get in when the place was empty. His mother thought he was at school, but that made no difference. She might not be home for hours. He could not remember when she had been waiting there, with his tea. He'd been locked out for years.

He had had enough of it. He walked down an alley that separated the rows of terraced houses and along the narrow path that divided it from another row at the back. Some of these places had been smartened up and turned into chic homes for first buyers, but Denis's parents' house remained dark and shabby, with grubby net curtains across the ground-floor windows.

Denis took off a trainer, put his hand inside it and used it to break the glass of the back door, which he then

23

unlocked. He went inside and used up all the hot water in a steaming bath.

He thought about leaving home. It wasn't a new idea, but where would he go? He didn't fancy sleeping rough in the park, or putting himself where the police might pick him up and take him into care. He'd have to wait a while, maybe until that man Len had done the job at Ford House. He'd have money, then.

He'd stick it out till that happened, even if his father beat him up for breaking the door down.

And his father did.

3

Jim Sawyer liked working for Mrs Bannerman. After planting the hedge he suggested re-laying the uneven flagstones on her patio.

'It's a terrace,' she told him sternly. 'Strictly speaking, a patio is a courtyard. It comes from the Spanish.'

'Oh.' It made no difference to Jim. He'd call it the terrace if that was what she wanted.

'People are careless about words,' she added.

'Sorry,' said Jim.

He got on with Mrs Bannerman. She didn't talk a lot, but she told you plainly what she wanted and she took him into the house to sit down in a comfortable chair while he drank his coffee.

'That's good, isn't it?' she said, her craggy face softening into what was almost a smile as he lowered himself into a deep armchair covered in flowered linen.

'Yes,' he agreed. 'I'd almost forgotten.'

'How much longer have you to do?' she asked.

'Eight months,' said Jim. 'If I get full remission.'

'Well, you'll have some home leave, won't you?' she asked.

He shrugged and his face closed up.

'You will, surely?' she said.

'Maybe,' said Jim.

She knew he had been convicted of embezzling funds at the building society where he had worked for nearly ten years.

'Where else have you been?' she asked him, and he told her about the other prisons where he had served the first part of his sentence.

'This place is like heaven after them,' he said.

25

'I'm sure it is,' she agreed. 'But the worst place of all must be Holloway.'

As she said this, she seemed to shiver. She couldn't have been inside herself, could she? Jim looked at her with renewed interest. She was about sixty, maybe more, and thin, with neatly styled grey hair and a very pale face. She always wore a tweed hat in the garden, but it wasn't an old, shapeless thing; it was made of checked fabric and looked expensive.

She might have done some shoplifting and been sent down for a bit. It wasn't the sort of thing you could ask about, however.

'They fill the women up with drugs when they should be in hospital, not in prison,' she was saying.

'That's true of some of the men, too,' he said. 'I mean, that they shouldn't be locked up. Not me,' he added. 'I deserve what I got. But there are blokes inside who don't really know the time of the day.'

'Why did you do it?' Audrey asked.

'I wanted nice things for my wife and daughter,' said Jim simply. 'More than I could afford.'

Audrey nodded.

'And my wife got into debt. She had a credit card, you see, and it was too easy for her to overspend.'

'Yes.' Audrey, too, had a credit card and constantly received mail shots suggesting she apply for large loans which would be instantly granted. 'How's your wife managing now?' she asked.

'She doesn't visit any more, or write,' said Jim, staring at his hands.

She's found someone else, thought Audrey. It was a familiar story.

Audrey had seen the young woman from Ford House driving through the village in her battered blue Mini and with her little boy in the shop, where one day Audrey had nodded and said 'Good morning'. Then the child had helped himself to a packet of sweets and had to be reproved, so no further conversation resulted.

It was difficult to meet new people. Audrey went to church, not from conviction but because it was part of the pattern and had always been expected of her; she had made some acquaintances in Coxton as a consequence and had even been invited out to coffee and to drinks. Each time she had dutifully asked her hosts back, but that was where it had stopped. Audrey had never been good at making conversation, and no mutual interests were discovered.

She decided to call on Mrs Davies one morning, when presumably, with the children at school, she would not be too busy.

Audrey drove up to Ford House a week after Denis's meeting with the prisoners, and he was the first person she saw as she negotiated the potholes in the drive. He was ambling across the lawn towards the house, his hands in his pockets, occasionally executing a small skip as he progressed.

Audrey parked outside the front door and got out of her Fiat.

'Good morning,' she called to the approaching youth, who did not answer. His gaze was rapt and far away, and she realized then that he had a headset clamped to his bristly skull. 'Is Mrs Davies in?' she asked loudly, in a curt tone.

The boy had seen the car and his attention was diverted from his tape. Taking his time, he freed one ear and said, 'Uh?'

'Is Mrs Davies in?' repeated Audrey. Who could he be? Certainly not one of the family.

'Yeah,' said Denis.

'I'll ring, then,' said Audrey, and stepped forward to the front door. She paused for a moment, staring at it. It was made of solid oak, and she touched it gently, then

27

turned to the bell pull, which she tugged. There was a jangle from within the house.

'She won't hear you,' Denis said. 'She'll be up in the attic at her sewing.'

'Oh.' Audrey wavered. What sewing?

'She'll be down. Comes to get me cocoa,' said Denis. 'Doesn't use this door a lot.'

He stumped off round the side of the house, his earphone back in place, an awkward, sturdy figure. Audrey hesitated, then rang the bell again. Mrs Davies would hear it from the kitchen.

A few moments later the door opened to reveal a woman of about thirty-six with dark hair reaching well below her shoulders and large blue eyes. She wore jeans and an over-washed yellow sweater.

Audrey's instinctive reaction was that her hair was a mess and she was too old to wear it so long; her next, that she looked tired and she had a small spot on her chin.

'Mrs Davies?' she asked.

'Yes.' Yvonne waited for Audrey to explain her presence. She held no collecting box but she must be wanting something.

Audrey was seeking appropriate words.

'I – er – I –' she began.

'Are you collecting for a jumble sale?' Yvonne asked abruptly.

'I – no. No, indeed,' said Audrey. 'I came to call. I used to live here,' she burst out.

'In this house, do you mean?' Yvonne asked, startled. She took a grip on herself. Though her time was precious and strictly rationed, she must not be inhospitable. This old woman, who looked stern, even hostile, could be given a cup of coffee while Denis drank his chocolate, and then swiftly coaxed upon her way. 'Come in,' she said, and smiled. 'I hope you don't mind the kitchen.'

Audrey hoped she often smiled; it transformed her face and made her almost pretty. She followed Yvonne

28

through the large square hall to the back of the house, casting curious glances to right and left. The place looked different: lighter, and more spacious.

'You lived in the house?' Yvonne prompted. 'When?'

'From the time I was thirteen until I married,' Audrey answered.

'Did you?' Now Yvonne sounded interested. They had reached the kitchen, and as they entered, Audrey saw Denis sitting at the table, quite at home.

'This is Denis, who helps in the garden,' said Yvonne.

'We met outside,' said Audrey.

'Do sit down,' said Yvonne, crossing to the old cream Aga. Could it be the original one that Audrey remembered being installed?

Yvonne moved a saucepan on to the hot plate.

'Coffee?' she asked briskly, crossing to the larder.

'Thank you.'

Audrey pulled up one of the chairs that were drawn up to the table and sat down facing Denis. The youth had not attempted to stand up when she entered. Young people were so mannerless these days.

'What did you say your name was?' Yvonne asked, returning with more milk which she poured into the pan. She took a mug from the dresser.

'Bannerman, Audrey Bannerman. I live at Ivy Lodge.'

Denis blinked. That was where the con had come from that he'd seen the week before. He'd checked it, later.

'And you used to live here?' Yvonne tipped coffee powder into two mugs and chocolate into another. The milk came up and she poured it into them, stirring.

'Yes.'

Their drinks made, Yvonne sat down herself, then rose again to fetch the cake. She offered Audrey a slice.

'No, thank you,' Audrey said. 'It looks delicious, though.'

Yvonne cut a wedge for Denis, giving it to him on a plate and waiting for his thanks, which came belatedly.

'Do you hate us for living in your former home?' she asked, astonishing Audrey.

'What a strange idea! Why should I?' Audrey answered. 'Of course not. I'm glad a family with children has come here.'

'We'll put it straight,' said Yvonne. 'But not immediately. We haven't got much money.'

In Audrey's youth it was bad form to discuss finances, but people did it all the time now.

'Employing builders is expensive,' she said.

'We're hard up because we've both been married before,' said Yvonne, who had discovered that it was wise to explain this early to a new acquaintance, before false assumptions were made. 'Now come along, Denis. It's time for you to go back to work.'

'Oh, all right.' Taking his time, Denis finished his chocolate and slouched from the room.

'Denis is doing wonders with the garden,' he heard Yvonne say as he resumed his boots. When the back door had closed behind him, she told Audrey, 'I wanted him to hear that I was pleased with him. He's a funny boy.'

'Is he local?'

'He lives in Leckerton with his grandmother,' said Yvonne.

'He's very young.'

'He says he's seventeen.'

'Hm.' Audrey raised an eyebrow as she drank her coffee.

'I couldn't get anyone else. There was just a very old man who applied when I put a card in the shop. I don't know his name.'

That was a pity. Audrey might have remembered him.

'Old men who have spent their lives digging can

30

'often carry on almost to the end,' she said, in her tart voice.

Yvonne prickled at the implied criticism.

'It's heavy work. It seemed best to have someone young and strong,' she retorted. 'Of course, if I'd known you were in the village, I could have asked for your advice.'

Audrey did not notice her intended sarcasm.

'I would have been very little use,' she answered. 'I've been back here only a year, myself. No one remembers me now.'

'I see.' What a scratchy old woman, thought Yvonne, wondering how to get rid of her since she wanted to get back to work.

'You do sewing, the boy said. What did he mean?' asked Audrey.

'I make soft furnishings,' said Yvonne. 'I've got a workroom on the top floor. Do you want to come and see it?'

It was not a graciously worded invitation, but Audrey, who would have expressed herself in just the same way, took it as kindly meant.

'I'd like to, very much,' she said, and rose. 'Thank you for the coffee.'

'We'll use the back staircase,' said Yvonne.

Audrey followed her up the steep stairs to the main landing, where they walked a little way and then climbed the narrow staircase that led to the top floor.

'I suppose maids slept here in your day,' said the younger woman.

'Yes.' Audrey remembered them all: Daisy and Maud, and the cook, Mrs Truman. 'Do you have any help?'

'No,' said Yvonne. 'Only Denis.'

'I think that's wonderful,' said Audrey. 'Running a big house and bringing up a family. How many children have you got?'

31

'Two of my own. Then we had Robin,' Yvonne said. 'Charles has two daughters who come sometimes.' She opened the door of what had been Mrs Truman's room. 'I often think I don't do any of it very well,' she confessed.

'It can't be easy,' Audrey said. 'Oh, what pretty chintz.'

She had followed Yvonne into her workroom and saw some finished curtains hanging on an old towel horse.

'Yes, I like it too,' said Yvonne. 'Those are for a merchant banker who lives in Islington.'

'Really?'

'Yes. I work for an interior decorator, but I'm planning to set up on my own.'

'Are you? I wish you luck,' said Audrey. She eyed the bales of fabric and trimmings stored on some old bookshelves along one wall. Then she sensed a restlessness in the younger woman. 'I must go. I expect you want to get on.'

'I'm working to a deadline,' said Yvonne flatly. 'And soon I'll have to fetch Robin from playgroup.'

'I'll be off, then. There's no need to show me out,' said Audrey. 'I know the way.' She moved to the door and stood there, hovering. 'I hope you'll be happy here,' she said.

'We must be,' said Yvonne. 'A lot's at stake.' She picked up a piece of material. 'You know all about us now,' she added.

'I'm sorry.' Audrey felt rebuffed and answered harshly. 'I didn't intend to pry. I meant my visit to be neighbourly.' She turned and started off along the passage to the stairs.

Yvonne flung down her work and hurried after her.

'Mrs Bannerman, please don't leave like that,' she said. 'I didn't mean to be rude. It was good of you to come.'

Audrey was hastening on, but Yvonne caught her by

the arm. 'Please come and talk to me while I stitch a hem. It's too noisy to talk when I'm using the machine.'

No one, apart from the dentist and the hairdresser, and sometimes a chiropodist, had physically touched Audrey for a very long time. She turned towards Yvonne, whose expression was contrite, and allowed herself to be led back to the workroom. Now it was her turn to apologize.

'I'm sorry,' she said. 'All my life I've offended people because I'm so abrupt.'

'I'm sure that isn't true,' said Yvonne. 'I was the graceless one. Please forgive me. I'm a bit touchy, I suppose, on the subject of our mixed household. Not everyone understands.'

'It's quite usual nowadays, I believe,' said Audrey. She looked squarely at the younger woman. 'You've both got a second chance, haven't you, and you want to make it work.'

'That's right,' said Yvonne. She still held Audrey's arm; it felt bony beneath her jacket. 'Come and sit down,' she said. 'Tell me about your life after you left here. Have you any family?'

'Not now,' said Audrey. 'I had a daughter, but she died, and then my husband left me.'

Denis, banished from the kitchen, had not hurried back to work. He had loitered near the house and, peering through the window, had seen the two women leave the kitchen.

In seconds he was back in the house, and had seized a piece of soap from the kitchen sink. It was reasonably pliable and he made a clear impression of the key that hung, with Yvonne's car keys, on the dresser. Returning to his digging, he nursed the soap and laid it under a shrub while he finished his morning stint.

Yvonne missed the soap, and, after searching for it for

a while, decided she must have thrown it out with the rubbish.

That evening she told Charles about Mrs Bannerman's visit.

'Fancy her having lived here,' she said. 'She seems a sad sort of person. I gather she and her husband stayed together because of the daughter, and when that reason had gone, bingo! It was over. She told me quite lot about it, once she got going. It was a bit as if a dam had been unstopped.'

'Oh.'

Charles was not interested in this old and cranky neighbour.

'Her husband took off with some woman she'd been at school with,' said Yvonne. 'It had been going on for years. I don't know why the daughter died. She didn't tell me that.'

'Watch out. She could become a nuisance,' Charles warned. 'You don't want that.'

Yvonne did not tell him that she had invited Audrey to tea the following week. She was already regretting the impulse.

4

Len hadn't been very serious when he spoke to the kid about making a key to that house on the edge of Coxton. He'd get into the place without one, if he'd a mind to do it. Even so, being able to open the door without effort would give it to him on a plate. He'd be needing some money when he got out. Len knew his chances of getting a job, even with the help of his probation officer, were non-existent, with his record. Besides, he didn't like regular work. You could pick up enough here and there if you kept your eyes open, and dodging the law was a challenge.

He didn't really believe that the kid would produce the mould, but soon after their conversation, stopping again for a smoke at the bus shelter before returning to Lockley, he saw the agreed signal and there, under the stone, was the cleanly marked soap.

Len pocketed it. He knew several men in the metal shop who would enjoy cutting a key under the noses of the screws.

Denis was delighted when he discovered that the soap had gone. Things were moving. He was in business. But how would he learn when the hit would be made? That man Len didn't know how to get hold of him to give him his cut. He'd hardly come looking for him at Ford House. Denis mulled away at the problem while he continued digging.

The little boy had not gone to his playgroup that day. When Denis went into the house for his chocolate, Robin was sitting at the table doing a simple jigsaw.

'I'll help you with that,' said Denis, sitting down and leaning over the large wooden pieces. 'See, that pig goes in there.' He picked up a section and slotted it in,

35

heedless of Robin's affronted expression. Half the child's pleasure in doing the puzzle was its familiar ease. 'Why ain't you at school today?'

'He had a bad night – bad dreams,' said Yvonne.

'You look pretty rough yourself,' said Denis.

Yvonne knew what he said was true. She had had little sleep for several nights because of Robin's nightmares, which ended with the child coming into bed with her and Charles.

'I sometimes wonder if the house is haunted,' she confessed.

'Course it is, an old place like this,' said Denis. 'Didn't you know?' Memories of something he had seen on television came to him. 'Some kid was murdered here, by its sister or some such,' he declared, biting into his slice of cake.

'That's not true,' said Yvonne, but her already pale face went even paler.

''Tis. Happened a hundred years ago, or so,' said Denis more confidently. 'Smothered with a pillow, he was. Happened in that room that looks out over the pond,' he added.

The story might have been better if he'd said the kid had drowned in the pond, but it was too late to change the script. The pond itself was covered with a strong wire frame clamped into place so that no child could drown there now.

The room Denis had mentioned was the one occupied by Robin. Denis knew that. He had scant opportunity for prowling round the house because Yvonne was always there but last week, after that old girl had come round, she was rattled and had gone to fetch Robin without locking up. Denis had knocked off work as soon as he saw her leave – there was no point in overdoing things – and had sauntered up to try the door.

He'd already made the key impression, so now was his chance for a quick look round. She'd be gone at least fifteen minutes. By the time she came back, he had seen the attic room where she worked, and the children's bedrooms. Each had one to him or herself, and they were huge, with everything clean and fresh, though rather bare. Denis had worked it all out. In a small room on the ground floor there was a photograph of a man with two girls. It stood on a desk with another of Mrs Davies and Robin. She'd said that morning that they had both been married before. Denis saw that these were the two families.

All information was useful. He might get a chance to use this some day. Now, he was pleased with the effect of his words on Mrs Davies.

'You want to watch it,' he suggested. 'Those other kids might have it in for this one.' He left it to her to decide if he meant her two, or the girls in the photograph.

'You're very silly, Denis,' said Yvonne.

But that night she persuaded Philip to let Robin sleep in his bed and the small boy never woke. Philip, however, in Robin's room, did. He did not cry out, simply turning on his light and reading for a while until in the end he fell asleep over his book.

Charles did not object when Yvonne proposed changing the children's rooms. Robin had been given the one nearest his parents because he was the youngest, but it was smaller than Rosalind's, which was across the passage. Would she feel put down if they exchanged?

'No,' said Charles. There was a washbasin in the room now proposed as hers, and Rosalind would like that as there was only one bathroom upstairs. There was another on the ground floor, once used by the staff, Yvonne supposed. She must ask Mrs Bannerman about it. The older children used it now. Eventually, when they could afford to put a second bathroom in upstairs, it would become a utility room.

Charles helped her move the things across. Rosalind

had seemed satisfied with her former room, which looked out over the front of the house, but she would like this one better. It had a much nicer view and when the leaves were off the trees you would be able to see right across to the river.

When he left Ford House that Friday, Denis was elated with a sense of power. All he'd had to do was to agree that the place was haunted, and Mrs Davies had lapped it up as the truth. Thinking of something to tell her that involved a kid was a stroke of genius. If he'd said the ghost was a knight in armour clanking chains, she'd have taken no notice. Now she'd be moving everything round just because of what he'd said. Mind you, the change might stop the kid dreaming. He was a nice little lad and he'd got everything given to him with a golden spoon. No drunk mother for him, just a re-modelled family. Probably the older kids spoiled him rotten as he was the baby.

He went down to the churchyard to look for Len, but the work there was finished. When was Len coming out? If that other man was still working at Ivy Lodge, he might take a message.

Denis wandered back until he came to the house. The gates were open but there was no one about. No cycle was parked in sight, but a con would probably put it round at the back in case someone nicked it. Whistling, Denis sauntered up the path. If the old girl was in, he'd think of some excuse for calling. He could always say he was looking for work.

If she wasn't in, he could have a look round.

Denis rang the bell, pressing it firmly. The sound echoed round the house – a sharp buzz: none of your melodic chimes here. Silence followed, apart from the sound of a car going past in the road. Denis rang again, and when no one answered he walked all round the house looking in through the windows, even trying one

38

at the back. All were secure. She'd got those special window locks recommended by the police. Well, it was useful to know that this wouldn't be an easy place to do over.

There was no sign of the prisoner.

Denis tried the garage. The doors were fastened but not locked, and the car was out. She had a Fiat, he remembered. There was nothing inside the garage that would be of use to him. It contained only a hosepipe coiled round a drum, a plastic pail and rubber sponge, and a long aluminium ladder slung on hooks against the wall. He'd seen a shed in the garden. That must be where she kept her tools, like Mrs Davies, whose garden shed was vast though it let in rain at one end and had a door that had to be tied with string to close it.

He didn't want to get caught nosing about. Denis left.

When he got back to Leckerton, there was nothing to do.

He spent some of his pay at the new Pizza Parlour on a good, filling meal. Then he went home and tried the doors. It was locked up, as usual. Even quite little kids at school had keys, or knew where one was kept so that they could let themselves in. He didn't feel like breaking in again and getting another beating.

The mood of what, in Denis, passed for happiness, which had filled him earlier, ebbed. What was he supposed to do while he waited for someone to come home? Get into trouble? It was a wonder he hadn't done anything seriously bad before now. The fact that he was supposed to be at school went for nothing. Kids got sent home when they felt ill. They could let themselves in, couldn't they?

There was nowhere to go, only the cinema which opened at four and which cost money. You could sometimes get in through the exit doors, though, once the paying customers had been admitted.

Denis tried it, and succeeded. He spent two hours

watching a pseudo-psychological thriller which he found difficult to follow. There were some powerful sex scenes which made him laugh. His sniggers provoked 'Sshing' sounds from the other people in the audience, which was sparse.

That gave him an idea.

When the showing was over, he went to a café nearby and had some beans on toast while the second house audience bought their tickets and filed in.

The nearest telephone box needed a phone card, but you could dial 999 from anywhere. Denis did so, and when a voice asked him which service he wanted, he just answered, 'There's a bomb at the cinema.'

The authorities had to take such calls seriously.

Denis had the satisfaction of seeing the cinema audience trooping from the building and milling about in the mizzling rain which had begun to fall. Police cars came, and sniffer dogs, and it was brilliant. He mingled with the cinema-goers as they were herded to a supposedly safe distance. Some of them decided not to wait until the scare was over, and when they drifted off, he went too.

When he got home, his father was waiting for him. Someone had been down from the school and had said Denis had been absent at least twice a week all term and was not there today.

His father took a belt to him. Denis managed not to make a sound while he was beaten, but, in his bedroom later, he could not suppress a whimper.

He didn't have to stay here. Maybe they wanted him to go and that was why they treated him so badly.

He didn't take a lot, just his new Walkman and his better clothes, in some plastic bags. He found some money, though, in the handbag which his mother had left in the kitchen when she went up to bed. Denis unlocked the back door and just walked away, leaving the place open, hoping someone else would come and take anything they fancied.

He did not think about the beating he had had; there would not be another. Instead, he remembered the commotion he had caused at the cinema, all those coppers out there telling people what to do, the blue lights flashing and the traffic cones and cordons, cars stopped from passing by, and people made to go another way.

That was power.

He spent what was left of the night in a bus shelter and, when first light came, he went round to his sister. Tracy would give him breakfast, let him keep his things there. And she did. When she and Alan had gone off to work – they both worked most Saturdays – Denis, trusted with her key, climbed into their bed. It smelled of various things, some nice and some faintly disturbing, but Denis did not wonder for long what they were. He slept for hours.

5

Jim Sawyer's work at Ivy Lodge was complete after only four visits and he wished it could have been prolonged. After he had finished the outdoor jobs, he painted the kitchen, and Mrs Bannerman had left him alone in the house while he did it. She'd gone off for a walk, and was away more than an hour.

When she came back, she admired what he had done and they had tea in her sitting room. She used real bone china cups and saucers and a small silver teapot.

She asked if his wife had written yet and he said that she hadn't. Prisoners in open prisons were allowed to make telephone calls and in desperation he had rung her several times without getting through. In the end, he had realized that she had changed the telephone number and gone ex-directory. Inquiries made through his probation officer had produced only the information that she was still living in the same house and had a job at a local factory, now that Nicola went to school.

'It's awful, not knowing what's happened,' he said. 'I suppose she hates me. But there's Nicola, too.'

'Shall I go and see her for you?'

Audrey heard herself utter the words and wished them unsaid as soon as they were spoken. She had no wish to travel to wherever he lived and put personal questions to an unknown woman, become involved in what was not her business.

Jim stared at her.

'Would you?'

She could not back off now.

'If you wish.' She spoke grimly, sitting in her wing armchair, knees together, thin legs in ribbed tights.

Jim glanced down at her feet. She wore wide, soft,

42

shabby brown shoes which had open toes and were loosely laced across feet distorted by enormous bunions. He hadn't noticed that before.

'Where do you live?' she asked.

'In Reading,' Jim replied.

'That's not so very far,' said Audrey, relieved. He might have said Birkenhead. 'Write down the address.' She pointed to a table where, beside the telephone, there was a notepad and ballpoint pen. While he obeyed, she found a street plan of Reading in a big road map and he showed her where it was, though the actual road was not marked on the plan.

'Thanks,' he muttered. 'It's very good of you.'

'I'll write to you at the prison,' she told him. 'I can't come and see you. I'm sorry.'

'I wouldn't expect you to,' said Jim. 'It isn't very nice. But it would be best if I phoned you. It's allowed.'

She understood. His letters would be read.

'Try not to brood about it,' she advised. 'That's difficult to do, but it's sense.'

'Yes.' Jim fidgeted, then said, awkwardly, 'I'll miss coming here.'

Audrey was going to miss him, too, but she would not say so.

'What will you be doing next?' she asked.

'I don't know. Farm work, perhaps.'

She couldn't give him anything. If she were to give him cash and it was found on him, he'd be in trouble. He was just the sort of man to get caught if he attempted some trivial contravention of the rules and it might cost him part of his remission.

Back in his room at the prison, Jim thought about Maureen. Dreaming about his release, and his return to her and Nicola, had kept him going through the first part of his sentence. The few visits she had made were painful, and she didn't bring Nicola. A prison, she said,

43

was no place for a child. How could you talk, sitting at a table watched by screws who had eyes in the backs of their heads as they looked this way and that, expecting to catch prisoners passing drugs across as they kissed, or touched hands under the table? You couldn't blame them, really. It was their job. Jim wouldn't have believed what went on right under their noses until he saw it for himself.

She had never been to Lockley, where his own life was undemanding and had become almost pleasant. He had privacy in his room, and he enjoyed working outside. He'd got to know other men and most of them were reasonable beings; even those who had a string of convictions behind them could be good company. One, Bob Waters, was dreading leaving the prison.

'I've got a nice room to myself, three meals a day, enough work to keep me busy,' he said. 'What have I to go out for? A high-rise flat with water dripping down the walls and piss on the stairs. Half the time the lift doesn't work and my old woman has to lug the shopping up eleven flights. That's no life. It's better here.'

Jim believed him, and he had seen the wife, too: a tough-looking woman with orange hair and purple lips, and an angry face. Perhaps Bob had taken to petty thieving to escape.

He and Bob had become quite friendly. They played cards together and had both worked in the carpenter's shop. Jim had tried various classes but he wasn't in for long enough to complete an open university course. He had settled for French, and had been getting on quite well until he started to worry about Maureen and Nicola.

When he came out, they would have to start all over again. He'd have no job, though he was determined to find one. In the past he had tried to give Maureen everything she wanted, and it was buying her goodwill, combined with her extravagance, that had led him into crime. In a fundamental way he knew that really she craved something other than the material goods she had bought on credit. She had an emotional need that he did not understand, although she must know that he had never looked at another woman and thought the sun rose and set with her. Without her and Nicola, there was nothing to live for.

He looked at their photographs, both out of date. Nicola was five now, not a toddler as she had been when he was sentenced. You'd think Maureen would send him some new ones. From thinking about his own daughter, he progressed to wondering about Mrs Bannerman's. He had seen her photograph on Mrs Bannerman's desk. She was a pretty girl with dark curly hair and a lovely smile. When asked, Mrs Bannerman had agreed that this was her daughter but had added no information about her, and some instinct stopped Jim from asking.

Where was she now? Married, with a family?

On Mondays Charles was always eager to go back to work. In theory he unwound at weekends, but in practice he worried about problems at the office, and he consciously missed his daughters. That seemed to get no better with time; it was a constant dull ache, and when he looked at Yvonne's small, dark-haired Emily, he wished she would turn into his blonde Celia.

Philip and Emily were nice children and Charles liked them, but he became impatient when Philip was late for meals because he had been out in the garden studying beetles and lost all sense of time. At the moment he thought he might become an entomologist, and he kept collections of various creatures in boxes in his room.

'Just as long as they stay there and don't escape,' Charles had said. So far, they had.

They were both good with Robin, and Emily, in particular enjoyed playing with him. He supposed she had a built-in maternal streak.

While Charles was eating his muesli and two slices of toast, he was planning the day ahead at the office. Meetings and consultations must be arranged. Much could be predicted, but unexpected developments would require him to show the initiative which the board had already commended more than once. Egos would be on parade and hobby horses would be ridden; surprise tactics would be used by some, including Charles, to influence thinking and move decisions in certain directions. There might be complaints from customers to be dealt with, or from personnel, but usually something similar would have happened before and there would be a precedent to follow. Secretaries sometimes left, and that could be devastating, but Charles had had the same one now for three years and she looked like staying, though nothing in this world was certain.

He liked the early drive through the lanes to the motorway, then the fast trip to the works. It was very different from the mornings in Shepherds Bush, when he had left home an hour later and still missed the rush-hour traffic. The seasons meant nothing, then; now, he was aware of the trees, their leaves lingering unusually late in this wet autumn, the colours varied, yellow and umber and russet, and the mixed greens of the grassland. Once he had decided what he would do after he had dealt with his mail at the office, he listened to tapes and at the moment was busy with Dickens. There were large gaps in his knowledge which Charles sought to fill, and this was a way of using time well. Yvonne read very little, but she liked music and could play the flute. Later on she might have time to take it up again and join an amateur orchestra. Leckerton was large enough to have something like that. He wanted her to use her talents and yet her independence, which seemed to grow daily, alarmed him. What if she no longer needed him?

When they met, Yvonne was feeling very low, her self-esteem at zero. She had had some minor romance

46

between her husband disappearing and their meeting, but the man, unable to handle a ready-made family, had ended their relationship. What put him off fired Charles with its challenge. He was drawn, at first, by her lost look, her somewhat forlorn air. She scraped along on a meagre income; he did not see how she managed to feed herself and the children on what she earned from her work. The house though, was hers: lawyers had managed to get her husband to pay off the mortgage and make it over to her and she was planning to move. She could get more for it than she would have to pay for a cottage somewhere in the country.

Meeting Charles had changed that. He found her company restful after squalls at home when Olivia threw tantrums. Yvonne seemed, by contrast, blessedly calm. Soon Charles convinced himself that she needed him and that he had a major role to play in her life. The physical attraction between them was strong, and a new joy for Yvonne. After Charles came to live with them, there was no more talk of moving until after Robin was born. Even then, it took years to happen, and meanwhile Yvonne had changed. Now she rarely asked his advice about anything, making decisions about her own children without consulting him, though she did refer to him before entering Robin for the playgroup. She was becoming forceful, and Charles saw himself being written out of the role he had thought was his. Work had always absorbed him; he had plenty of energy and enjoyed manipulating people. Often, these days, he stayed late at the works where it was quiet and peaceful, with only the cleaners moving around the offices; they left his till last.

If he were to be appointed to the board, financially things would be transformed and Robin would benefit. Yvonne had given him this wonderful stake in the future and nothing would be too good for his son, but he longed for his daughters' visits. When they were due, he collected them after work on the Friday, leaving earlier than usual, and he returned them to their mother on Sunday evening, driving back to his former home where Olivia now lived with Hugh. She had remained in their old social circle, and their friends frowned on him because he had walked out of the marriage.

Charles did not mind that. He had colleagues at work and Yvonne at home; he had no time for anyone else.

It was only a few days now until the weekend when the girls were coming. This happy thought deflected Charles's attention from *Bleak House* as he wondered what they would like to do on Saturday. It was difficult to find things that were suitable for all of them, from Rosalind down to Robin. He would go to the video shop and pick up some film for the older ones to watch, and perhaps they might all visit the Severn Wildfowl Trust if the weather was good.

With this thought he reached the works gates and there was his reserved parking slot. In the office, his secretary would bring him a cup of strong black coffee when she arrived, some time after him. A well-organized man, Charles complacently pitied those now enmeshed in traffic snarls on the road behind him as the rush hour got under way. Like a juggler, he had to maintain a number of balls in simultaneous motion, but he managed to keep an eye on them all. He was in control.

Audrey was annoyed with herself for offering to look into Jim Sawyer's problems. They were no concern of hers. Still, having volunteered, she must see it through, and without delay.

First, she attended to various things. She had booked a holiday in Florence for the following spring. Rupert had never wanted to travel, and since they had parted she was gradually visiting all the places she had once longed to see. Planning her trips gave her something to fix on in the future, and she read widely before each expedition. She was often the best-informed member of the exclusive tours she joined and tried to be helpful to the courier. She liked to think she was useful as she helped inexperienced tourists when they needed advice about traveller's cheques and where to meet the coach, though few seemed grateful and no one ever asked for her address at the end of the holiday.

She had finished her current piece of knitting, a soft sweater in shades of blue and purple. She wrapped it in tissue paper, then in a polythene bag, and put it away in a drawer upstairs. Next, she would make something in yellow; maybe a dress. Jenny would have grown out of the last one by now. She would get the wool and the pattern tomorrow; there was a good wool shop in Leckerton, new since her day, of course, but then Leckerton was totally changed. Once, it had been a busy market town, but in the sixties the centre had been razed and a vast shopping complex built. New factories and houses had sprung up on the outskirts and people had moved in from other areas, attracted by its possibilities. The town had lost its former community spirit and was now an agglomerate of different groups and areas, still expanding, with petty crime on the increase and even serious incidents now common. Drunken brawls in the old market square were a usual weekend occurrence, and in the last year two policemen had been attacked and badly hurt. To Audrey, everyone looked so young: youths in jeans strode about or loitered outside the fish and chip shops. Very young women pushed babies in stroller prams, the children always facing away from their mothers into the wind and the weather, and deprived of communication with their attendant.

Audrey had pushed Hesther in a big, deep pram, bought secondhand because such things were scarce after the war. There had been a large hood to protect her from the rain, and a mackintosh apron to hook over the blanket. When she was old enough to sit up, Hesther had peeped out across the bib of the apron which stretched across the lower part of the hood, attached by elastic loops. Inside, she was warm and snug and she could talk to her mother, and have things of interest pointed out. They would look at cows and sometimes go to the railway line to wave at the engine drivers who usually waved back. Later, Hesther had graduated from this fine carriage to a small folding one with an end that let down so that she could step in and out. She still faced her mother and they could talk. Modern children were swept along in an isolated capsule behind thick plastic sheeting, or else exposed to the tempest, their little faces blue. What must it be like to be propelled towards an advancing forest of knees? No wonder juvenile aggression was a current problem.

Audrey took out the street map of Reading and studied it again, then the route to the town. Once on the motorway, it wasn't far. She would be there in just an hour, say an hour and a half to be on the safe side.

Perhaps she would get the wool in Reading. It would make a change. In that case, she could go tomorrow.

6

Jim had given Audrey directions for finding his house but when she reached the outskirts of Reading she misread a sign, entered the wrong traffic stream and therefore missed a vital turning. Without intending to, she went through the centre of the town and became thoroughly confused by one-way systems, sunken roads and a heavy flow of traffic. She almost despaired of ever discovering the right area, but at last she found herself in a residential district where the traffic was less dense, able to ask advice, and in the end she reached the street.

It was part of a private estate of identical houses set in rows radiating from a main road. Doors were painted different colours; gardens varied; windows displayed pot plants or china figures, or were unadorned; others had net curtains stretched across. Number 15 looked in good order, its paintwork smart, a large pot of leafy plants standing on the window sill of the front room. Audrey could not identify them; she did not like foliage that reminded her of aquaria, preferring blooms. She sat in the car and checked her own appearance in her compact mirror, dabbing more powder on her long thin nose. Then she got out of the car and walked up to the front door.

A few people were about, mostly women pushing children in the strollers she abhorred, some with toddlers walking beside them. She rang the bell.

There was no response, and Audrey rang it again, pressing it for longer. Then she remembered that Jim had said his wife was working. How stupid to have forgotten that. Of course, she would be out until the child came back from school. She turned away, but as

51

she did so heard the sound of movement from the house, and the door was opened.

A burly man stood there. He was about twenty-eight, with a chin shadowed with stubble and dark untidy hair falling over his face. He wore a singlet and slacks, and Audrey formed the distinct impression that he had just got out of bed. Was he the reason for Maureen's silence?

'Good morning,' she said briskly. 'I've come to see Mrs Sawyer and Nicola.'

'Oh!' The man smothered a yawn and rubbed his eyes. 'They're out. I'm sorry. Can I help? You must be from the welfare.' They'd been before, checking on how Maureen was coping.

Audrey did not correct him.

'Mrs Sawyer's at work, I suppose,' she said. 'And Nicola's at school?'

'That's right,' agreed the man. 'Would you like to come in?'

Audrey decided that if she did, she could form an impression of how things were and also of this man. It would be a pity if Maureen had replaced Jim with an out-of-work slob. She stepped into the hall, which had a polished wood-laid floor covered with a good rug. The living room into which he led her was clean and bright, with gold and white striped wallpaper and a sofa covered in gold Dralon, with two matching chairs. A large rubber plant stood in a corner, and there was a television set with a video recorder underneath. A child's doll lay on the floor and some picture books were scattered about.

'I'm afraid you've caught me,' the young man said. 'I'm on nights.'

'You're not a lodger,' Audrey stated.

'No. And Maureen's not getting supplementary benefit. There's no fiddle,' said the man. 'I moved in a while ago – nearly three months, it must be now. Me and Maureen are thinking of getting married, as soon as she can sort things out with her husband.' He laughed. 'It's funny, really. I'm a policeman.'

'Oh!' That startled Audrey. 'He doesn't know about you,' she said.

'Well, how do you tell a guy that sort of thing when he's inside?' asked the man. 'It needs working out. How to do it, I mean. He's not a bad guy, Jim. Just a bit user-friendly with other people's money. Would you like some coffee? I can do with some.'

'That would be very nice,' said Audrey.

'Take a seat,' he said, and she sat down on the sofa while he went off to the kitchen.

Exactly what she suspected was what had happened. Well, it was better for Jim to know the truth than struggle on in doubt. He'd have time to face up to things and plan some sort of future before his release.

Her host returned, carrying a tray with two cups and saucers of steaming coffee and a plate of custard cream biscuits. He had slicked down his hair and washed his face, and she saw now that he was a good-looking man, if a trifle overweight. She was very ready for the coffee, and she ate a biscuit.

'I should have come in the evening,' she remarked.

'Yes – well, you've got other folk to see. More urgent cases,' said the man. She was older than the usual social worker. He rasped his hand across his chin. 'Sorry I haven't shaved,' he said.

Audrey waved a hand.

'I've disturbed your rest,' she said.

'Maureen had better write to Jim,' said the man. 'We've let things drift.' He drank some coffee. 'The marriage was on the rocks anyway, before he got nicked. He kept buying things for Maureen because he thought they'd keep her happy. Nice things for the house – smart clothes – jewellery. Everything she has is the best.'

'I can see that,' said Audrey. This wasn't quite Jim's

version of events. He had implied that Maureen had run up debts.

'He was great at do-it-yourself,' said the man. 'Laid the floor in the hall himself.'

'There's no hope then,' Audrey said. 'Of a reconciliation, I mean.'

'Not a one. Of course, he'll see Nicola when he comes out, if he keeps his nose clean. I suppose he may do that. He's not a hardened villain, after all.'

'What about Maureen's job?' asked Audrey. 'She likes it?'

'Oh yes. She's been promoted. She's in the sales office now.'

'Ah. So she does a full day?'

'Stops at four. The next-door neighbour takes care of Nicola after school until she gets back.'

'I see. Well, that seems satisfactory for the moment,' Audrey said, and stood up. 'I must be going now, Mr – Er –?'

'Trevor Black,' said the man. 'Traffic division.'

He watched her go down the short path to the road. She walked a little stiffly. She'd got terrible feet; he'd noticed them as she sat with them planted side by side on Maureen's yellow carpet. He saw her get into a small black Fiat parked outside. He did not wait to watch her drive away.

She would have to see Maureen. Audrey knew that she could not go home able only to tell Jim that he had been supplanted by a personable policeman; unshaven and half dressed though he had been, Trevor Black was in another category altogether than poor balding Jim.

She should see the child, too.

Audrey looked at her watch. It was nearly noon. She would go into the town as she had planned, and buy her wool and pattern, then return. The route might be a little easier tackled for a second time. She'd come back at four.

By three thirty she had parked the car across the road from Number 15. In the back was her package of wool and a new pair of shoes she had bought after seeing wide fittings displayed in a window. Her mother had had narrow, neat feet, and could not accept that Audrey had inherited her father's broad frame. Regularly, her feet had been crammed into shoes much too tight, and Audrey had continued to buy shoes too narrow for years until a trained fitter had given her better advice, but by then it was too late and her feet had been badly damaged. However, they were rarely painful if she wore loose, easy shoes; they were a fact of life, like requiring spectacles and the two teeth on a plate which she had had to accept as necessary. Audrey's mother had never become socially confident and had indoctrinated Audrey with the importance of maintaining appearances. She had clung to this training during her marriage, aware that to Rupert they mattered too, but in a different way. He and his sisters, and Felicity, now his wife, had known automatically what was appropriate and when it was acceptable to wear what looked like rags.

These things didn't matter so much nowadays. People were no longer docketed and labelled according to clothes and voice. In Coxton, Audrey had once had an assured position because she had lived in the big house. Her marriage to Rupert repeated the pattern, and she had thought by returning to Coxton, even after so many years, she would slot into her former place. It no longer existed. The village had grown and was full of hard-working couples with two cars and two salaries, living in new houses ten times more comfortable than Ford House had ever been, or was now. There were a few retired couples, and several widows. Audrey had not joined in any of the charitable activities they undertook in the village, and even the vicar had shown only fragmentary interest in hearing that her father had bought Ford House just before the war. He had risen from obscurity in the Midlands to run a factory making metal components and had made a great deal of money. He had moved to Ford House to become a country gentleman, but he did not hunt or shoot and had no wish to learn. He had married his secretary, who had always been shy and soon became physically frail. They had done the accepted things for Audrey: sent her away to school to acquire the right accent, and later to a gentle institution where she learned some cooking, how to arrange flowers, and a little shorthand and typing. It was here that she met Felicity Morton, who invited her home for a weekend. It was the first time she had ever stayed as a guest in a private house.

Rupert Bannerman's family lived nearby in a small manor house where they farmed several hundred acres. Mortons and Bannermans had always been friends, and when Audrey met Rupert he was on leave after being a prisoner of war for nearly four years. He had had a bad time in the weeks before the German surrender, being moved from camp to camp and threatened with death. Audrey asked him about his experiences in a forthright way, which he found refreshing after the velvet-glove approach of everyone else, and he found himself telling her the truth about his fears, his guilt at having survived when others died, his nightmares.

Later, he came down to the school and took the two girls out for the day in his battered MG. They took turns to sit in the tiny cramped rear space. Later still, Audrey was invited to stay at the Mortons to go to a charity ball. They went with a group of young people, but Rupert monopolized Audrey, who had expected to be a wallflower, which was her usual experience at the few such events she had attended.

Soon after the ball he came to Coxton to see her, arriving unexpectedly, his MG scattering the gravel as he turned with a flourish outside the front door. Her

56

mother was put into quite a flutter but the house was always clean and tidy, the flowers just so, and in the kitchen Mrs Truman was able to stretch lunch to include him. Excited and flattered, Audrey supposed this was love.

When he proposed, she instantly accepted, for her whole upbringing had been geared to this future. She had no need to make her way in the world; she had been trained for marriage, the aim of most upper- and middle-class girls at that time when only a few of them went to university.

Six months after her wedding her father had a stroke and died, and her mother, with no further reason for continuing her frail existence, faded away and followed him within a month.

That was long ago, and now Audrey was outside the home of a woman whose husband was serving a well-deserved prison sentence. Why was she meddling in their affairs? He had broken the law and merited no pity. Still, his wife should have kept in touch, written about the child and then, if she felt they could never be reconciled, have had the courage to tell him the truth.

As she watched, a woman propelling a small child in a pushchair came into view. Two small girls skipped along in front of them, one with tight red curls and the other with dark hair drawn into two bunches. The quartet turned into Number 14, the red-haired girl opening and closing the gate for them all. Half an hour later, during which several other people passed, a woman in a pink raincoat and high-heeled leather boots came hurrying along. Her hair was fashionably styled like the tangled mane of a lion and it bounced as she walked up to the door of Number 14, which opened at once. The long-haired little girl appeared and reached up to be kissed by her mother, then kissed the second woman, who now stood behind her. You did not have to be a trained social worker to conclude that there was nothing much wrong here.

Audrey got out of her car. She wondered if Trevor Black was still in the other house as she waylaid Maureen Sawyer beside her own gate.

'Mrs Sawyer,' she began.

'Yes?' Maureen, who was in a hurry to get home, paused and looked questioningly at the trim elderly woman in her tweed hat and expensive fawn quilted jacket.

This was no time for finesse, even if Audrey had been capable of it.

'You haven't written to Jim for months, and you've gone ex-directory,' she accused.

Maureen paled. It was as if someone had pulled a plug and drained all her blood away. She almost staggered on her spindly high heels.

'I've met your friend Mr Black,' Audrey pressed her. 'Don't you think Jim has a right to know the position?'

'What business is it of yours?' Maureen retorted.

'I'm concerned with his welfare,' said Audrey, taking her cue from Trevor Black's earlier assumption.

'Mum, I want to go home,' Nicola said, swinging on her mother's arm.

'Shush, Nicola. We won't be long. The lady has something to say to Mummy,' said Maureen giving the child a little push. 'You run ahead.'

'I've seen Jim recently,' Audrey told her as Nicola obeyed. 'He's worried and I promised to speak to you.'

Maureen had recovered her poise.

'Yes, well, I'm afraid you're wasting your time,' she said. 'How can he think – after what he did –' Her voice trailed off. 'I've got a good future now,' she said in a defiant tone. 'I'm happy.'

'Are you?' asked Audrey, who wondered if anyone ever was, for long.

'Certainly. I just want Jim to leave me alone and keep out of my life,' said Maureen.

'What about Nicola?' Audrey asked.

The child was by now standing on her own doorstep, vigorously pushing the bell. Since no one had opened the door, Trevor Black must be out.

'Her too,' Maureen said. 'I've been so ashamed.'

'He did it for you. You must know that,' said Audrey.

'Look, bits of jewellery and new clothes don't make up for other things – not getting along, not having what it takes,' said Maureen.

'What does it take?'

'Oh, surely I don't have to spell it out?' exclaimed the younger woman, exasperated now. 'Excuse me. I must get Nicola her tea.'

Audrey pictured the young policeman. She meant sex.

'I see,' she said slowly. The money was only a symptom.

'It's over. Finished,' said Maureen. 'If you want to help Jim, you'll get him to see that. Please make him understand.'

'You should do it yourself. You should visit and tell him.'

'I can't,' said Maureen.

'Well, write, then.'

'I've tried. I can't find the words,' said Maureen. 'I just don't want to have anything more to do with him and I've Trevor to think of now.'

No doubt the wife of a convict was not the most desirable companion for an ambitious constable. Audrey walked back to her car, defeated. If it hadn't been this man, it would have been someone else, some man met at work, perhaps. Sex would have been the alchemy that precipitated events.

Had that been what drew Rupert and Felicity together? They should have married when they were young. Rupert's pursuit of her had been some absurd

59

quixotic post-war folly, and when he realized his mistake he had stayed with her from convention or duty. Besides, Felicity had married a year after their wedding. Her husband was a naval officer, at that time stationed in Malta. They had three children, two boys and a girl, and Felicity now was a grandmother. Rupert and Felicity had been clandestinely meeting for years before the death of Felicity's husband, who by then was long retired and farming in Hampshire.

Such thoughts were painful. Driving home, Audrey sternly banished them. She would concentrate on something pleasant, like her next visit to Ford House. It was kind of Yvonne to have asked her. Perhaps the girl would like to make her some curtains. The blue velvet ones in the dining room, which she had bought with the house, were quite shabby and she had always intended to replace them, but had somehow never mustered enough interest and energy. A commission on the doorstep might help Yvonne.

She must take the children something when she went to tea. What would they like? A toy car, perhaps, for the small boy, but the bigger one would be more difficult to please, and there was the little girl, too.

She would go into Leckerton where there was a large toyshop and seek a helpful assistant, if such a person existed in a world where it had become difficult to pay for one's wants in such places as Boots with tills only sparsely distributed throughout the store. It would be quite a treat to think about something so far removed from today's expedition.

7

Denis was happy. He had money in his pocket, his personal Walkman and a place to live.

He was sleeping in Alan's van. Tracy had found him a sleeping bag and a blanket, and she gave him a thermos of cocoa to take out there each evening.

Alan wasn't too happy about the arrangement and stressed that it was temporary. He had a feeling that the law wouldn't like it, if a copper looked in the van one night. It had to be left in the street: the one parking space outside the house was used by Mrs Dove from the first floor, where she had a real flat, not a bedsitter. However, Alan was sympathetic, for hadn't he rescued Tracy from the very situation which Denis had left? She, though, was older and had a job at the check-out in one of Leckerton's supermarkets.

'You ought to go back to school, Denis,' he said.

'What for? It's boring,' said Denis. He wasn't going to admit that there were things he had enjoyed, like woodwork and football. 'Anyway, I'll be sixteen next month.'

He'd soon have the money from Len. Denis could even provide wheels for the job, if Len had none; they'd need a getaway car and he was king of Alan's blue van. Meanwhile, to keep in funds, he bought a brown plastic pail and a large rubber sponge and went round the better areas of Leckerton looking for cars to wash. He charged two pounds, the middle price at the automatic car-wash in Market Street, and it was surprising how many people were willing to pay for his services. He made a good job of what he did, getting satisfaction from seeing the paintwork come up and the chrome shine.

Denis could manage on very little money. He gave

some to Tracy, who included him in the evening meal, and he helped wash up. He could tell that Alan wished he wasn't there but didn't know how to get rid of him. Denis cleared off as soon as they had eaten and wandered round the town until he was too tired or bored to stay out any longer. There was little enough to do in the evenings, as he already knew. The youth club was all right if you liked playing snooker, and sometimes it ran a disco, but Denis felt silly prancing about under the strobe lights, though he was happy gyrating alone to the sound of his Walkman. He didn't go for girls, except Tracy, who was different. Most girls were silly and giggly and all they wanted to do was get married and have kids and expect to be kept for life, or that's what his father had said. Often enough, Denis had heard his father calling his mother names and saying she'd caught him, whatever that meant. He'd hit her, which made Denis feel sick. After that there would be scuffling and noises and it would all end upstairs in a lot of animal sounds which Denis found frightening. He'd gone in once, when he was about seven, thinking his father was still beating his mother, but they'd both yelled to him to go out and get lost and after that his father had given him a belting. It was a few years before he understood what had been going on and he didn't like the discovery.

Sometimes his mother was nice. She would buy him a new shirt or sweater and ask if he'd like to have another boy round to play, but how could Denis let that happen when he never knew what would be going on at home? How could he foretell if his mother would be in a good mood when the day came? It was better to keep to himself, and when he was able to get into the house after school he stayed in his room as quiet as a mouse, with his transistor, which he'd saved up for. Sometimes his mother gave him money to keep out of the way. He'd go down the town and spend it on something to eat or on tapes, and occasionally on comics. He liked the ones with pictures of scary monsters and spacemen; they were different from what really went on all around.

School began to go wrong when he grew big and started to make wise-cracking answers in class when he didn't know what else to say. The other pupils laughed, but it didn't go down well with the staff and he was often kept in and given extra work to do. Gradually he began staying away, at first missing the lessons he found difficult and avoiding the teachers he thought picked on him, then more frequently as he got older. Once he wrote a note making out that it came from his mother and saying he was ill. Another time he wrote in her name, alleging that she was ill herself and that he was looking after her. After these breaks, which ended when he ran out of things to do in town and couldn't think of how to pass the time, he'd give school another brief trial, maybe staying as long as a week, but it never lasted.

Unknown to Denis, staff had come round from the school to see his parents but had never found anyone in. Something must be done, people said, if this went on, and each time that decision was reached, Denis would thwart it by a new appearance in class.

The best time was when he had a key to the house, but that was two years ago. One Saturday, he took his mother's from her bag and had one cut in town. He returned hers without it being missed. He'd had one cut for Tracy, too. Though she was already working, she hadn't been allowed to have her own key. It was good after that. He could watch television and make himself things to eat after school. He always went out before they got home, and he cleaned up after himself, too. But one day he forgot the time and was watching television when his mother caught him. She found his key, took it away and had the lock changed in case he'd been sly enough to have another one hidden somewhere.

Tracy had given him a key to the bedsit. She was a good girl and he didn't want to make things hard for her and Alan. To him, they seemed rich, with Alan earning good money on the building site, and Tracy getting her regular wages from the supermarket, but they had to pay out forty pounds a week for just this one room with the use of the bathroom. All they'd got to cook on was a couple of gas rings.

He gave them a toaster, that took four slices of bread all at once. They both thought he'd bought it with his earnings, but he hadn't. He'd lifted it from a big electrical store and it was quite a challenge. It was a bit large to hide under his loose jacket and he'd taken a chance, sliding it in under his arm and clamping it to his side while looking at something else. He'd already bought a plug so as to seem like a genuine customer. He'd fitted the plug. As a gift, it was a huge success. They all enjoyed toast for breakfast.

He had to go out on Saturday because Tracy had the day off and Alan, who worked most Saturdays, had decided to skip this one although overtime was welcome. Denis had handed over his Ford House pay the previous day and he needed more money, but he couldn't go car-washing today for it was raining. No one would pay him to wash their cars in a downpour.

He hitched out to the prison, getting a lift in a lorry for most of the way and walking the last part along the lane to the former military camp which was now used to house several hundred men. He went up to the gate as bold as brass, and asked for Len.

'Which Len?' asked the gate officer.

'Well – er – he was working in Coxton,' Denis said.

'You want to keep away from here, son. You might find yourself on the wrong side of the fence,' warned the officer. 'The proper procedure for visiting is to apply – '

'Ta,' interrupted Denis, and was about to walk off when the man called him back.

'Len White worked in Coxton. He's out now,' he said. 'Left last week.'

He'd be getting in touch any day, then, thought Denis. Len knew that Denis worked at Ford House on Tuesdays and Fridays. He'd make contact there, or with a note under the stone they'd used before.

He walked away briskly, his Walkman in place.

Having committed herself to Audrey's visit, Yvonne wanted to make it a success. She must ensure that her guest felt really welcome. Audrey probably wouldn't stay long.

She arrived promptly at four and the small girl, Emily, appeared round the side of the house to lead her inside. It seemed that they never used the front door.

Emily was friendly. She showed Audrey a Plasticine model she had made at school.

'Very nice,' said Audrey. 'And how did you think of making a mouse?'

'It's not a mouse, it's a hedgehog,' said Emily. 'Can't you see the prickles?' And indeed, along the body of the creature were etched faint, spiky lines.

'Of course it's a hedgehog. I see that now,' said Audrey.

'They get run over,' said Emily.

'Yes.'

'It's sad.'

Audrey agreed.

Yvonne appeared then, coming to greet them still dressed in jeans and loose sweater, a bright smile in position.

Hesther had worn jeans and loose sweaters, too, but Hesther had bitten her nails to the quick and often her hair and her clothes were dirty. Sometimes, she even smelled.

Audrey pushed the image away. She gave the children the toys she had bought for them, a toy car to push for Robin, a vintage model for Philip to make, and a colouring book for Emily, with a huge box of crayons. All were received with evident approval and Audrey was flustered by their gratitude. She gave few gifts, these days.

She was unused to children, too, but she managed to sustain a conversation with these three until tea, set out on the kitchen table, was ready. There was an orange sponge cake, iced, and a plate of chocolate biscuits. The children all walked about as they ate and returned to the table merely to drink or pick up something else to eat. Emily had begun her colouring, her book spread out on the floor, and Philip was eager to start on his model. Robin had parked the car under the table and joined it there, in its garage, as he said. Audrey pursed her lips as she witnessed this conduct. Hesther had been made to sit at table with washed hands and face, and she had to eat a slice of bread and butter before she might have any cake.

Yes, and now she was dead.

The bleak recognition of what had happened chilled Audrey again, as it did every day of her life.

'I wondered if you'd make me some curtains,' she said abruptly. 'For the dining room. And perhaps some cushions as well.'

'Oh! Yes, I'd be glad to,' said Yvonne, surprised. 'Not at once, I'm afraid.' She had a new commission for bedspreads and curtains and would be pressed to finish it by the decreed date.

'Oh, there's no hurry,' said Audrey. 'Perhaps you could come and have a look when you're collecting the children one day.' She must repay this hospitality by inviting them round, although the children would be bored. She had a button box, though: a tin full of various buttons which Hesther, when she was small, had loved arranging on the floor.

'Yes, of course,' said Yvonne.

After tea she showed Audrey the rest of the house. She and Charles occupied the bedroom where Audrey's parents had slept. It was odd seeing the big, sagging double bed in the room where twin beds had stood, with a gap between, against a different wall. The carpet was worn and faded but there were fresh apricot curtains patterned with white which matched the duvet cover. Audrey felt that she was having a revelation of intimacy thrust upon her.

'We need a new carpet,' said Yvonne. 'This one came with the house and it's pretty grotty.'

Audrey could see that.

'The carpets were left in my house, too,' she said. She had changed them at once. 'I had mushroom broadloom fitted throughout,' she added. 'It goes with anything.'

'Very wise,' said Yvonne.

'I had it in my flat, too,' Audrey said, waxing loquacious. 'I had a flat in Sussex for several years before I decided to come back here.'

'Oh, did you? Are you glad you moved?' Yvonne paused with her hands on the doorknob of what had been Robin's room and was now ready for Rosalind.

'I think so,' she answered.

Yvonne had opened the bedroom door.

'Robin used to be in here, but he had nightmares,' said Yvonne. 'So I've moved him. This is for my elder stepdaughter.'

'Lucky girl,' said Audrey. 'It's delightful.'

'I hope she won't have bad dreams too,' said Yvonne.

'Why should she?'

'Well, there was a murder here, wasn't there? Long ago,' said Yvonne. She laughed nervously. 'I'm afraid the house may be haunted.'

'What nonsense,' said Audrey. 'There aren't any ghosts except those we make ourselves. And who's been talking about a murder?'

'Oh, just someone. A child was murdered, he said.'

'Well, I've never heard of it,' said Audrey robustly.

'It's an old house and must have seen births and deaths in its time.' She was about to say that her parents had died here, but decided against it; the girl seemed rather morbid. 'It all happens in the course of natural life.'

'Are you certain there was no murder?'

'Positive,' said Audrey.

'What was this room in your day?'

'A spare bedroom,' Audrey replied. 'I had the one at the end of the corridor.'

'That's Philip's,' said Yvonne. She showed Audrey the room, where Philip's precious possessions were arranged. There were several small labelled boxes on shelves. 'He collects beetles,' said Yvonne. 'Nasty!' She smiled.

'It's a good interest,' Audrey said. 'Children need interests.'

'What about your daughter?' asked Yvonne. 'What did she like doing.'

'Riding, when she was young. Then she went to university. I was proud.' Audrey picked up a beetle box, looked inside at a defunct earwig and closed it again.

'What happened?' asked Yvonne.

'I'll tell you,' Audrey said.

To her own amazement, she found herself talking freely, telling Yvonne about Hesther's gradual distancing of herself from her home and her parents, her baffling loss of self-esteem.

'She'd had a good home, we thought,' Audrey said. 'Everything she could want. An allowance, too, and a good job. Why did she need to steal?' She stared at Yvonne as she said that, hardly noticing the younger woman's startled expression. 'Oh yes, she stole,' Audrey said. 'She went to prison, but she was ill. It was hospital that she needed, not locking up.' She shuddered. 'It was dreadful. Body searches. Filth. She was sedated to keep her quiet. When she came out she went to a clinic as a voluntary patient but she ran away. She jumped in front of an Underground train in the rush hour one Wednesday evening.'

8

Charles was angry. At six o'clock, as arranged, he had arrived to collect his daughters for the weekend and found only Celia ready. Rosalind had been invited to a party that evening and did not want to miss it. The party was not due to end until eleven o'clock.

'How's she proposing to get home?' Charles asked, standing in the front hall of Olivia's house, which for so long had also been his home.

'I shall fetch her,' said Hugh, looming large and bearded behind Olivia. 'Come and have a drink, Charles.'

'Not when I'm driving,' said Charles.

'How prissy you've got,' Olivia mocked. 'There was a time –'

She was right, but he preferred to forget the early years of their marriage when they had both drunk enough to make them foolish and amorous. He looked at her now, this woman with her corn-coloured ringlets who had shared with him moments of rapture and moments of misery. She must remember them too, and this knowledge fuelled his wrath.

'The arrangement is – ' he began.

'But Daddy, I want to go to this party. It's important,' said Rosalind. 'I can see you another time.'

'Or you can fetch her tomorrow,' Olivia offered. She was not going to suggest that she or Hugh would drive Rosalind over to Coxton; that would be making things much too easy.

She seemed very calm, not like the woman who had flung things at Charles and made scenes.

It was pointless to antagonize Rosalind.

'I'll come back for you in the morning,' Charles told her. 'Come along, Celia.'

Celia was happy to go off alone with her father. She couldn't remember when it had last happened. It wouldn't be for long, because when they reached Ford House the other children would be there. She quite liked them, especially Robin who was a sweet little boy, small and cuddly; she enjoyed reading to him, curled up together in a big armchair, one of those which she remembered from her own babyhood and which Mummy hadn't wanted to keep when she married Hugh. Mummy's cuddles were all with Hugh now. Celia hadn't got used to seeing him tucked up in bed with Mummy; she didn't like going into their bedroom when he was there. She had never gone into the room Daddy shared with Yvonne. Of course, she understood all about it. People got tired of one another and preferred someone else, and Daddy had tired of Mummy. They'd had awful rows; she remembered that. Mum was better now, with Hugh, but it was sad, all the same. She would never get married in case it happened to her.

Philip and Emily were all right and they let her play with their toys and games, but they lived all the time with Daddy and it made her feel left out of things. Why should they go swimming with Daddy? He'd been teaching Philip to dive. They weren't his children. Celia was not proud of these feelings; they made her feel mean; but nevertheless, they were strong.

So now she sat in the back of the car as her father drove off and hugged to herself her moment of joy. She looked with love at the back of his head, the crisp, dark hair that curled at the nape of his neck, his ears, rather pink, slightly pointed. He looked much nicer than Hugh, who was a bit like a bear, though a kind one.

They hadn't gone far before he picked up the telephone to talk to Yvonne. Celia thought the car phone was brilliant and Daddy had said it was useful to let Yvonne know when he would be home and if he had got held up in the traffic. Now, he put on the special voice

71

he used to talk to her, the one he had used when Mum was in a rage and he'd tried to calm her down, sort of deep and coaxing. Calling her 'darling' with every other word, as it seemed to Celia, he was explaining about Rosalind and saying that he'd be collecting her the next day. Celia could imagine Yvonne's response. She'd speak quietly, in that clipped way she had, not letting you see if she really minded. Of course, she'd really be glad, though she'd have to pretend to Dad. She didn't want Celia and Rosalind there. She had to put up with them, just as they had to put up with Philip and Emily. She was always nice to them, and gave them lovely meals. She was a much better cook than Mummy, but Celia would never say so aloud; it would be too disloyal to Mummy. In a way it would be easier if she wasn't so kind, if she was mean and nasty and fed them on gruel and pinched them when Dad wasn't looking. Then Celia wouldn't feel so bad about everything.

They came to Coxton and drove slowly through the village, past the telephone box and the shop, and the school where Philip and Emily went, then along the lane that led to Ford House.

It was a lovely house. In spite of herself, Celia's spirits rose when the headlights picked out the trees that dotted the long grass at one side of the drive and then lit up the building. It was a good place for biking, and Dad had got them cycles which were kept here, although they had others at home. She liked the big front door with its heavy knocker and funny chain bellpull. The outside light was on, and there were lights showing at some of the upper windows. Yvonne, the perfect Yvonne who cooked and sewed and never got into rages, hadn't yet made curtains for the landing and stairs windows.

Celia ran into the house, willing and eager to say hullo to Philip and Emily. Robin had been allowed to stay up till they arrived and he welcomed her with flattering delight. She managed to dodge kissing Yvonne.

It was lasagne for supper, her favourite. Celia accepted a glass of Coca-Cola as a treat and began to eat her supper. Then she laid down her fork and stared at her plate. It would be hard to do it, but she would manage.

'I'm not hungry,' she said. 'I don't want any supper.'

She allowed herself to be coaxed and cajoled into eating the runner beans that Yvonne had cooked to go with the lasagne, and to toy with some apple crumble, and her self-martyrdom was worth enduring when Yvonne went all quiet and her nose turned pinched at the end. She'd got the message.

In the morning there was a discussion about what Charles called the logistics of fetching Rosalind. Who should go with him? Celia, obviously, because she would not want to forego two hours of his company.

'Can I come?' asked Philip, who liked going out in the BMW.

If he said no, the boy and his mother would be hurt. If he said yes, he would not have his girls to himself.

'I thought we might go swimming,' said Yvonne.

'But Rosalind will miss out. Couldn't we go this afternoon?' said Charles.

'I can't. I promised to go to a bring-and-buy sale in the village,' said Yvonne.

'Whatever made you let yourself in for that?' asked Charles.

'I was asked to go.' In fact, Audrey Bannerman had said that she meant to be there and suggested Yvonne should come too, as a way of meeting some people. Yvonne had seen it as a means of leaving Charles alone with his children, for she would take hers, and Robin, with her. 'I think we ought to take part in a few village events,' she said. 'I'm not helping. It just means putting in an appearance, and I might pick up a few useful things.' There would be a jumble stall and over the years she had found bargains for both herself and the children at such events, but it was better for Charles not to know that.

Charles would not take all four older children swimming without her; the morning expedition would stand, Yvonne knew, as she waited for Celia to decide what she meant to do.

Must she go with Daddy all the way back to Mum's again, or could she go swimming with the others? Celia thought Dad might be hurt if she chose that.

She did, and he was.

You managed to solve one set of problems only to find you had acquired others which were as difficult to handle. Charles acknowledged this as he drove to fetch Rosalind. He faced no dramatic scenes now, no storms of tears if he were late home. Olivia used to create a situation implying that she had seen herself as a widow if he were delayed, even though he always telephoned a warning. There would be high emotion over every decision, from whether Celia should learn the piano to the location of the holiday. All that had ended, replaced by regular demands for increasing sums to support the girls which Charles did his best to meet; why should they lose out?

If Yvonne had not owned her house and sold it well, so that she had been able to help buy Ford House, the move would have been more difficult. So much was down to money: what you ought to afford, what you could afford. The girls needed tennis rackets, and Rosalind wanted to go on a school trip to France. What about when Robin began to cost more? Philip and Emily would move on to Leckerton Comprehensive when they left the village school, but Charles wanted his son to go to his old public school. There was no end to it.

There would be more weekends like this one, when Rosalind's wishes conflicted with what had been arranged by her elders. Naturally she wanted the best of both worlds, and Celia too.

She was ready when he arrived, which was something, and came running out of the house with her belongings in a Laura Ashley carrier bag. She wore a pink padded jacket over a dark sweater and jeans, and had on shabby trainers. It was a relief to see her thus; Charles felt afraid when she was dressed up and looking older than her age; he was too aware of the threats that would soon surround her. Today, she had put on some eye make-up, or possibly, like the pink streak in her hair, it was left over from the previous evening. Her face was white. Perhaps she was tired after a late night.

She was pleased to see him, kissed him warmly and jumped into the car beside him. She was old enough now to sit in front.

'Sorry about last night,' she said.

'Never mind,' said Charles. 'Was it a good party?'

'I suppose so,' said Rosalind.

'Well, did you enjoy it?'

'Yes and no. You dance and drink – all that – but it doesn't lead anywhere much.'

What did she mean? Where should it lead?

'What sort of drink?' Charles asked suspiciously.

'Oh, Coke and stuff,' said Rosalind, deeming it wiser not to mention that there had been wine and beer. 'You can't talk much, it's too noisy,' she added. 'Saves trouble, really.' She saw her father's expression and laughed. 'Don't worry, Daddy. Nothing wild happened.'

'I hope not. You're only thirteen,' he reminded her. 'And Hugh brought you home?' He needed to hear it confirmed.

'Mm.'

But it was he, Charles, who should be collecting her from her hazardous social engagements, not this other man whom he scarcely knew. Charles put his foot down hard and drove the car on through the cold, damp morning. The road glistened and water was sprayed up by the wheels of other traffic. He wanted to talk to Rosalind, find out how she was coping with adolescence and the problems of her divided life, but he was afraid of the answers.

'Yvonne's changed your room,' he said. 'She's moved you to the one that was Robin's. I hope you won't mind.'

How weak of him to lay the blame on Yvonne, when he had been party to the decision.

'Oh, that's all right,' said Rosalind sunnily. 'I like his room. It's got a terrific view.'

'It's a bit smaller,' said Charles.

'I'm not there very often, am I?' Rosalind said carelessly. 'I expect Robin will have trains and stuff before long, all spread out on the floor.'

She thought Robin quite cute, though she didn't go overboard for him the way Celia did.

'The others have all gone swimming,' Charles said, as he turned in at the gate, driving carefully between the potholes on the neglected drive. The whole thing needed resurfacing but that was impossible. He'd get some ballast and fill up the worst of the holes before he injured the car by hitting a bump.

'Oh, why couldn't they wait for me?' wailed Rosalind.

'Yvonne has to go to some do in the village later,' said Charles, and could not resist adding, 'If you'd come last night, you'd have been able to go too.'

This time she let him off.

'Never mind,' she said. 'I've got you all to myself for a bit instead.'

Charles hugged the moment. It could be a long time before it happened again.

*

The mail had arrived after he left that morning.

Charles saw that there were three bills and some junk circulars. He took everything, unopened, into his study and clasped them together with a big clip marked PENDING and laid the bundle on top of the walnut desk that had belonged to his father.

Rosalind had dumped her carrier bag on the floor in the hall and run out to the kitchen to make some coffee.

'Like some, Daddy?' she called.

'Yes, please.'

Charles followed her along the passage.

'You had no breakfast, I suppose,' he said.

She shrugged.

'No time,' she answered, lifting the Aga lid and moving the kettle across. 'What a slow old thing this is,' she added. 'You should have one of those plastic jugs without a flex. Mum's got one.'

'Bully for her,' said Charles.

'Will Yvonne mind if I take some cake?' Rosalind asked.

'Of course not,' said Charles. 'It'll be in the larder.'

Rosalind found a tin and cut a big slice from the new cake destined for tea that afternoon. She came back into the kitchen holding it, and as she took a bite a shower of crumbs fell to the floor. Charles gazed fondly at his pretty daughter and took down two mugs from the dresser. He made the coffee while Rosalind strolled about eating her cake. Then he tidied everything neatly away.

'You're so fussy, Daddy. I'd have done that,' she said.

'Would you, Ros? You might have forgotten,' said Charles mildly.

'Hugh isn't fussy,' Rosalind remarked. 'But he can usually find things for Mum when she loses them.'

Olivia was very untidy. She left a trail of scarves shed, bracelets removed, even her rings, wherever she went.

At first Charles had been amused by this careless habit but later it wearied him. Luckily Yvonne was orderly in most respects, although she allowed the children to leave their toys about more than he thought they should.

He suddenly felt a desperate urge to hear details of Olivia's life with Hugh. Did they really get on? Did they argue and make it up in bed? Was Hugh generous with money? Did he succeed where Charles had failed? But he must not turn Rosalind into an informer.

'Things are all right, then?' he said.

'What's all right?' she asked. 'I suppose so. You know Mum.'

He did, and, after eleven years of marriage, probably better than Hugh, but she would be different with him, as Charles was with Yvonne.

Rosalind had got up to put her mug in the dishwasher. She glanced out of the window.

'Who's that?' she asked.

'Where?'

Charles came behind her and looked out. He saw a youth in jeans and a combat jacket dancing across the yard towards the back door.

'I've no idea,' he said, and went to discover.

Denis, leaving the prison, had decided to take a look at the target. He'd think of some excuse for his visit when the need arose. Yvonne's car was out, but he saw the BMW and supposed it belonged to Charles, whom he had never met.

'Hi,' he said, when the man came to the back door. He had pushed his earphones up but Charles could hear the tinny sound of his Walkman.

'Yes?' Charles frowned down at him, his eyebrows, which would be thick and bushy when he was old, raised above his grey eyes.

'I was just passing and remembered Mrs Davies had said the yard needed sweeping,' Denis invented. 'I told her I didn't mind.'

Light dawned. Yvonne had mentioned that the young gardener was addicted to his Walkman.

'You're Denis?'

'Who else?'

'Hmph.' Yvonne had said nothing about expecting him today, but it was true that the yard was a mess. Damp leaves had blown into the corners and were slimy after the rain.

'She'll be pleased to see it done,' Denis declared. 'I could clean out the garage, too. Maybe wash the cars now it's stopped raining.' There was no end to his willingness to help. 'Where's she gone, then?' he added, curious.

'She's taken the children swimming,' said Charles. 'Very well. You know where everything is, I suppose. The stiff broom – all that?'

'Too right,' said Denis, in Oz style. 'I'll need a bag for the rubbish.'

'Put it on the bonfire,' said Charles. 'I'll light it later, if the rain holds off.'

Denis set to work, aware that Charles might watch him start. He began industriously scraping leaves and sludge from under a water butt, and was sweeping them into a heap when Rosalind sauntered across, her hands in her pockets.

'Hullo,' she said. 'What are you listening to?'

Denis never knew what to say to girls. Sometimes he made defensively lewd remarks but that wouldn't do here.

'Michael Jackson,' he mumbled.

'I don't go for him,' said Rosalind. 'I like Madonna.'

'What? And you a girl?' Denis crowed with laughter.

Such a comment was too silly to answer.

'Do you work every Saturday?' she asked.

'No. Just thought I'd offer today, seeing your mum wanted the place done,' said Denis.

'She's not my mum,' said Rosalind coldly. 'She's my stepmother.'

'Well, she's all right, is Mrs Davies,' Denis pronounced, turning his back on the two thin, denim-clad legs which composed the only section of her he was able to look at without extreme discomfort. That hair with the funny pink streak and the bright eyes made him feel very uneasy.

There was no amusement to be had here. Rosalind turned back to the house wondering what to do now. Her father had gone off to his study. He'd be opening his mail. He had said he wanted her here but they soon ran out of things to talk about. This was called access: his to her, or hers to him? It was meant to be two-way, wasn't it? She sighed, weighed down by the problems that lay in a future peppered with these weekends when she didn't really know where she wanted to be .

Still, the house was great. It was a pity none of her friends could be brought round to see it; they'd be impressed. Rosalind went upstairs to her new bedroom and unpacked her belongings. She hadn't brought much.

Dad couldn't really be as hard up as he made out if he could buy this place. When Mum said she wanted to get a bit more out of him, Hugh told her he'd done it all on the bank, whatever that meant. A mortgage, she supposed. Hugh told Mum not to be greedy. Dad was pretty good; he paid up for extras and anything else they needed. She supposed he had to, really, or he'd feel very bad as he was the one who had walked out on the marriage. And he'd walked out on her and Celia, too. That was what hurt. He liked Yvonne best.

She was glad when the others returned from swimming and she successfully pretended she hadn't minded not going.

Yvonne was surprised to find Denis busy washing the BMW. She supposed Charles intended to pay him and would not leave it to her. He was allowing Robin to help him, giving the small boy a fragment of sponge and telling him to do the wheels, which Denis himself had already scrubbed. That endeared him to Yvonne. She'd find him some lunch, later on; there was quite enough for them all. His grandmother probably found coping with his large appetite demanding.

Yvonne never discovered that Denis had let Charles think she had asked him to come round.

Full of shepherd's pie and treacle tart, which he had eaten in the kitchen with all the family, and the richer by five pounds, Denis set off for Ivy Lodge. He had decided to offer his services to the old bat he had met at Ford House. He felt refreshed and benign. Those kids didn't know they were born, living in a great place like that with food better even than his gran's had been. Denis often thought wistfully of those long-ago visits when he and Tracy were fed on lamb with fresh vegetables out of the garden, and helped pick the fruit that was made into puddings and jam.

The old girl came to the door when he rang. She was blinking and rubbing her eyes. Getting past it, thought Denis, who had woken Audrey after her own humble meal of soup and a wholemeal roll. She often slept badly at night and would drop off in her chair after lunch if there was nothing she had to do.

'Can I do any jobs for you, Missis?' he asked.

Audrey frowned at him, trying to remember who he was. She had certainly seen him before.

'Mrs Davies thought you might need some help,' he declared. 'I've been up there this morning.'

'I see.' Now Audrey remembered him.

She pondered. A young person eager to work should, if possible, be encouraged.

'I could wash the car,' he suggested.

She'd had it done by the machine in Leckerton only

the other day, but in this weather it didn't stay clean for long.

'Very well,' she said. 'I'll just get it out of the garage for you.'

'I'll do that,' Denis volunteered.

'It's not insured for anyone else to drive,' said Audrey firmly.

He watched while she backed it out and pointed to the hose and pail which he had noticed before.

'The tap's on the side of the house,' she explained. 'Come and tell me when you've finished.'

He did it well, leathering the car off with a chamois he found hanging in the garage behind the door. He didn't mind this sort of work. One day he'd have someone doing it for him, when he had a big house like Mrs Davies, not that he'd want an old place full of draughts, oh no. Give him a nice pad on the Costa Brava: that would be a bit more like it, with a flash car and a speedboat. Oh, and a big pool. He liked swimming.

Mrs Bannerman gave him a cup of tea and a chocolate digestive biscuit, and three pounds, a pound more than she would have paid at the car-wash, because he had done it so well.

He got a lift back to Leckerton quite easily and took himself off to McDonald's for something to eat, beans and sausage and chips. The waitress was cheeky, asking him if he could pay before she served him. He knew her: she'd been at the same school. Afterwards, he went to the cinema, but on the way there he rang the emergency services and said there was a fire at McDonald's. He heard the fire engine coming as he went on his way. They'd lose trade while the place was emptied. That would show them.

Tracy had put his flask of cocoa in the van. After his busy day, and with his stomach full, Denis curled up in his sleeping bag, quite content. He'd still got some money and soon he'd have more, when Len got in touch.

9

The best way to break bad news was firmly, without equivocation, and when Jim telephoned Mrs Bannerman she told him bluntly that a man was living in the house with Maureen and there was no chance of a reconciliation. He heard her words but he couldn't accept their message and he decided that he must go home to sort things out, face to face. It must all be some dreadful mistake and if he could just kiss Maureen's soft lips and soothe her, she would change her mind. Besides, there was Nicola.

Jim had scarcely slept since he heard what Mrs Bannerman had to say. When he thought of Maureen in bed with that unknown man, rage overcame his despair and he was filled with jealous hatred of his usurper. What had happened to the promises he and Maureen had exchanged at their wedding, a church one with her in white satin and tulle and Jim in a hired morning coat? He had known himself to be the luckiest man in the world on that memorable day. He was ten years older than Maureen but he had been able to cut out younger rivals. She had wanted security and he could provide it, but she had expected too much from marriage. Maybe most people did. You were only two imperfect humans, after all.

He'd make up to her for the shame of his prison sentence if she backed him up now. Somehow he would find a job when he came out, even if it was nothing special, and in time things would improve. There was no other future for he could not face life without her.

Jim's desire to see Maureen became an obsession. Now he had something to plan for, though he would lose remission if he broke out. It might not be much if he gave himself up or came back as soon as he had got some sort of assurance about the future from Maureen. If he failed, what happened to him didn't matter. Tossing and turning in his prison bed, he rehearsed what he would say to her. He'd surprise her if he let himself into the house while she was out. He had no key but he had learned how to open windows. He'd make sure the man wasn't there, of course. Mrs Bannerman said he was on nights but his shift might have changed. She hadn't said what he did, and Jim had been too upset to ask.

It might be better not to catch her unawares. She'd be scared if she came home and found someone there; it might take her a minute to realize that it was him and she had nothing to fear.

With a head full of dreams, Jim never went back to the prison on Wednesday after leaving the farm where he had been working for the past week. Instead he cycled off in the other direction.

He wouldn't be missed at once, and when he was, there wouldn't be much of a fuss at first because he had no record of violence and offered no threat to the public. It was not unknown for men to stay out for a night or two and then return. Others absconded and were soon retrieved. Most didn't mind coming back after a taste of freedom, a booze-up somewhere, maybe a meet with a woman.

A drizzling rain was falling. Autumn this year was unusually wet but it was also extremely mild. Jim pedalled along unfamiliar lanes. He had never worked in this area and would have to travel in a wide arc to get round to the motorway, but he could not go all the way to Reading on his cycle. They were not allowed on motorways and anyway it was much too far.

The rain was cold on his face. He felt very conscious of his prison overalls but, in his navy donkey jacket, anyone noticing him would think he was some sort of labourer going home. His striped shirt would be more of a give-away, and that was well covered.

Most of the traffic was coming towards him; people returning from work, he supposed. He found the head-lights dazzling and was quite surprised when he saw that he was coming into a village. It was only a hamlet, a few dwellings strung out along a narrow road, too small and remote to have attracted the property developers.

There was no street lighting.

Jim soon saw several cars parked by the wide grass verge.

He knew that people were careless. He had heard often enough, inside, that it was easy to find unlocked cars with their keys in position. There was no need for clever stuff with wires. He dismounted and pushed his cycle towards a small Citroën.

It was locked, but the third vehicle he tried, a Honda pick-up, was unlocked and the key was there.

Jim put his bike in the back before driving away.

The pick-up was not missed until the next morning.

The Honda had enough petrol to get Jim to Reading and back. He settled down behind the wheel. Clothes were next. He needed some nondescript sort of coat instead of his jacket.

Suppose he went into a pub? Would anyone notice him, a stranger, in the general bustle? Maybe not, if the place was crowded, as pubs sometimes were soon after opening time. He had enough money to buy a half of mild, and maybe someone would have slung a coat over a chair or somewhere in such a way that he could snatch it without being seen.

At the next village he turned down a side road and soon came to the Coach and Horses. It had a big parking area at the back, and Jim stopped. He tried all the cars but though some were unlocked, he found no coat. He couldn't be that lucky twice.

But he was.

He walked up to the door and went in. To his left was the snug, to his right, the saloon, and on hooks in the lobby ahead hung several coats. There was a buzz of noise from the main bar and the publican was busy with orders. Most of his customers were regulars calling in on their way home. Men liked to unwind after leaving the office before going home to their wives, and women, too, often sought a break between work and home. He did not see Jim swiftly take down the nearest coat, a bulky beige anorak, rather worn, and scuttle out. No one else noticed, either. No outraged owner rushed in pursuit.

Some men in prison said all you needed was nerve. It seemed they were right.

Hopes high, he returned to the pick-up. Things were going his way. Such a good beginning was an omen for the success of his enterprise, and he resumed his journey weaving a scenario in which Maureen and her boyfriend would have quarrelled, and she would be overjoyed to see him. After a rapturous reunion, a further short separation would seem like no sentence at all.

Len had never liked the country. Some of the blokes in the nick thought it was wonderful, all that open space and air, but he liked to see buildings around him and to have a bit of noise about, people on the move, traffic passing, something happening. The only time he liked it quiet and peaceful was when he was on a job. In the country, you were always aware of the weather; the rain was wetter there than in the town, or so it seemed, and the wind blew harder. In town, one season was much like another and you had to go to the park to notice the difference because a few flowers might be out, or the trees in leaf.

He'd had a good welcome after his release. Bet had been working as a barmaid at the Grapes, and it hadn't been easy for her on her own, especially when Fingers,

86

who'd done that job with him, failed to come up with the money she should have received. Len would have to settle that with him, one day. But he had nothing either, only the small sum they gave you on your release, and what he got from social security. She'd soon start to moan if he didn't bring in a bit more.

He liked working in daylight. He was expert at walking along a residential street sussing out which houses were empty, sliding round to the back to discover a vulnerable window or door. It was best to go prepared in case you'd made a mistake and someone surprised you, and Len always had a neat little cosh tucked up his sleeve when he went to work. It was just a slim stick, but it had an effectively loaded head. He had used it only once when he'd done that warehouse job, joining up with Fingers Smith whom he'd met in the Scrubs. The nightwatchman had caught them while Fingers was fiddling the safe, and Len had given him one. He'd caught the wrong spot, it seemed, as the bloke, instead of just being out for the count, had died in hospital. Len's brief had made out he'd had a bad heart and all that, and he'd got away with manslaughter. After being sent down for seven years, he'd served less than three because of parole and the time he had spent on remand. Fingers had a shorter sentence and had promised to look after Bet, but his old woman had got hold of the money and taken off with some young bloke.

It proved he was better working alone. Forcing safes wasn't his line; his best field was the domestic scene.

He'd got that key, the one made from the soap mould the kid had provided. That house would have plenty worth taking. There would be a television, for sure, maybe two, and other things he and the family might enjoy using besides what he could sell. The kid said there was a fancy sewing machine upstairs, and there'd be one or two cars in the garage, probably something flashy like a Porsche or a Mercedes. He knew where to pass on a car.

It made sense to work away from his usual area: it would put the fuzz off; they wouldn't connect it with him. Anyway, he never left prints. He and Fingers had been caught through a car; a bright copper had stopped them in one they had lifted two days before.

Nothing like that would go wrong if he worked quietly on his own, like before. He might go down to Coxton and have a quick look around.

That afternoon, Yvonne's Mini had refused to start when it was time to collect Philip and Emily from school. It gave a few moans and then seemed to expire.

It took less than five minutes to nip down in the car but nearer fifteen to walk, even wheeling Robin in the pushchair, which would have to be used to save time.

She had better ring the headmaster and explain.

Yvonne had been cutting it fine, anyway, finishing a seam on a bedspread before setting off. She unfastened Robin's seat belt and tugged him out of the car, leaving him to follow her as she ran in through the fine rain to call the headmaster.

He accepted her explanation and said he would keep the children until she arrived. Yvonne hurriedly put on her wellingtons and picked up an umbrella. Robin's plastic cover-up had long since been discarded since the pushchair was so seldom used, and she set off with the umbrella held more over him than herself. They would all get horribly wet walking home.

Audrey, returning from Leckerton, saw the quartet trudging back towards Ford House. The pushchair was being propelled head-on into the rain, and the other two children, in wellington boots, were walking doggedly along, heads down, lunch boxes in their hands. In fact they were looking for puddles to jump in but to Audrey they seemed a desolate group. She stopped her car and offered to drive them home.

'Oh, you angel,' cried Yvonne. 'Thank you. My car's packed up.'

Gratefully, she bundled the three damp children into the back of the Fiat and folded the pushchair, stowing it in beside them. Then she got into the seat beside Audrey.

'Those pushchairs are terrible things,' said Audrey. 'They don't protect the child at all.'

'No, well, we hardly ever use it now, but this was an emergency,' said Yvonne.

'Are the fields flooded yet?' Audrey asked. 'They used to come out whenever it rained for more than a day or two.'

'I don't know,' Yvonne confessed. 'I've been sewing all day and I haven't looked out.'

'There's a ford across,' Audrey said. 'Near the house. That's where it got its name.'

'Oh, of course. I never thought. How stupid of me,' said Yvonne. 'You must show us where it is when the weather's better.'

'There's a swimming place, too,' said Audrey. 'I expect the village children still go there.'

Yvonne invited her in for tea but Audrey refused. She was very tired and wanted to go home.

'Telephone if the car won't start in the morning,' she said. 'I'll gladly run the children to school. I'm always up early.'

'Oh, thanks,' Yvonne said. 'I haven't got anything worked out with the other mothers, but no one else lives in this direction.'

Philip thought someone did: children came to the school from several villages around. He said so.

'Well, we'd better get together, then,' Yvonne said. 'You must point out the mothers.'

Audrey drove home. Her passengers had made the car very wet inside; small pools had dripped on the mat at the back. She put it away and went into the house.

That afternoon, she had gone to a charity shop in

Leckerton and offered her services. She knew she was leading too reclusive a life and thought it would be a way of changing things.

'I don't mind giving you a day or two each week,' was how she had phrased her offer.

Looking at her pale, unsmiling face, her severe hair under the tweed hat, her expensive padded coat, the woman in charge had felt instant antipathy.

'Thank you, but we're fully staffed at present,' she had replied austerely.

It wasn't true, but such a haughty recruit would not fit in with the other helpers. Audrey, snubbed, had inwardly shrivelled. She still felt battered by the rejection.

She took out her knitting. The yellow dress was coming on well. It would be perfect for Jenny.

Perhaps she should have accepted Yvonne's invitation after all. She never had tea herself until half past four; the day had to be divided into orderly sections with regular things at regular times, otherwise existence became chaotic.

She sat knitting, thinking about other charitable work she might undertake. There must be something needed. She could visit old people, perhaps, but the trouble was that she didn't enjoy their company. In fact, she had to admit, she was not much good with anyone.

Her mind flitted, as so often, to Rupert. He'd be at home by the fire now. She still thought of it as home; she had lived there for nearly thirty years. He might be reading *The Field*, or perhaps *The Times* if he hadn't done that earlier, and Felicity would be sitting in what had been her chair, or perhaps she would be in the kitchen preparing dinner.

Rupert had been a regular soldier and after their wedding he and Audrey went to Germany, where he was stationed. She did her best to fit in with the other wives, accepting the general pecking order and the duties that went with it. After all, it was not unlike school, with privileges allied to seniority. But at functions she was silent, looking bored when in fact she was paralytically shy. She took German lessons, which was thought eccentric, and went for long walks with a dog they had acquired. The enclosed society in which they were obliged to live, not mingling with the local population, irritated her, though she did her best to come to terms with it. When she became pregnant, however, everything changed. Now her life held purpose.

After the baby was born in the military hospital, Audrey was quite ill for a time. Then Rupert, who had lost seniority while a prisoner, being outpaced by his contemporaries, was posted to the War Office and the couple, with their baby daughter, lived in a rented house in Purley, from where he travelled up by train each day.

He hated working in London, especially being confined in the train and then in the office. The war had given him a legacy of mild claustrophobia. As he had little hope of reaching field rank, he sent in his papers. There was plenty for him to do at home, helping his father run the farm and put the estate in order. He went to an agricultural college while Audrey and Hesther lived in a cottage on the estate, and after that he lived a life of apparently busy contentment. By the time his father died, he was on the local council, and later he became a magistrate, thus fulfilling some of the traditional roles of a landowner.

Audrey and he had drifted apart, but not acrimoniously. Her gaucheness, which at first had attracted him, grew no less, and after a time began to irritate him. It hampered her socially, and the people on the estate interpreted it as conceit. Both of them, though, adored their daughter, Hesther Isabel, named after each of their mothers.

When she died, there was nothing to hold them together. A so-called friend told Audrey about Rupert's affair with Felicity. The fact that it had been common knowledge, or so it seemed to Audrey, for years, was humiliating.

She had her own income, left to her by her father in trust for her lifetime, and could be independent, so she packed her bags, told Rupert she was leaving, and went to stay in a Sussex hotel while she decided what to do next. Sussex was a long way from home.

Rupert had found her there. There had been a talk during which he showed extreme distress and she remained icily calm.

'You must try to be happy,' she said. 'You and Felicity. Let that, at least, be saved.'

He had stared at her, unable to reply. She could remember it all as if it was yesterday.

Audrey put down her knitting, made her tea, and laced it with a generous slug of whisky.

10

Len took the train to Leckerton. He'd find a car there to get him to Coxton. If he dumped it after the job and took one from the house, the police would think it was a local job.

It was raining, and the town looked bleak, everyone hurrying past with raincoats on and umbrellas up. He decided to find somewhere warm and dry while he thought things through. The job couldn't be done until after dark, and if it was still raining, he might have to put it off or look for some casual pickings.

He went into a café just off the market square and ordered tea and a cheese sandwich.

He couldn't believe it when the kid appeared. There he was, standing in the doorway in his combat jacket, jeans and trainers, his short hair on end, his eyes alert. Len had never expected to meet him again.

Denis had recognized him instantly. He came lumbering over, a grin of astonished delight on his rosy face, and sat down facing Len.

'You going to do it, then?' he asked. 'Is that why you're here?'

A great warm glow had flooded his body. Len hadn't forgotten that they were mates, and he'd come to look for him. Denis forgot that Len didn't know he lived in Leckerton.

'Shut your gob,' said Len, looking round in case anyone could overhear.

'You'll need help,' Denis said. 'I know where there's a van you could use.'

'We can't take it until they're asleep,' said Denis.

He had explained to Len about how he was sleeping in Alan's van.

'Can you drive it?' asked Len.

'Course I can,' boasted Denis. 'Only I haven't got a licence so it might be best if you took it out.'

'Hm.'

The idea of the van was tempting. It wouldn't be missed and the kid could bring it back after the job, when Len had got away in the car from the house. He could be paid off with something from the house – a radio, something he would find easy to sell if he didn't want to use it. Len was not very handy with cars, and although he knew how to start one without a key he had never done it. Stealing cars wasn't really his line, apart from taking a ride in one with the key already there. Whenever he'd done that, he'd kept the keys and he had quite a little collection which was a help when he needed a ride. Sometimes he'd find one that was a perfect fit.

'Could you get the van keys?' he asked.

'Easy,' said Denis confidently.

He blessed Tracy for giving him keys to the house and to their room. She had wanted him not to feel shut out and abandoned, as he had done at home.

'You've to go into their room?'

'Yeah.'

'Will you be able to do it without waking them?'

With his practice at burglary, Len might succeed in creeping more quietly into the place, but if he happened to wake them, there'd be an uproar, whereas if it was only the kid, they wouldn't be alarmed. Len, himself, could scarper and go it alone, and let the kid talk himself out of the mess he'd be in.

'Course,' said Denis confidently. 'Mind, we'll have to put the van back by morning.'

'We'll do that,' said Len. If the kid got into trouble driving home on his own, the whole thing could be put down to joy-riding.

Len told Denis that he must see where the van would be parked. Then they would split up until after midnight. He didn't query Denis's domestic arrangements. Plenty of kids left home; he'd done so himself. Denis was lucky to have a sister to turn to. He, Len, had slept rough before now, most recently just before he was nicked when Bet had locked him out because she said she was fed up with his life style, as she called it. Still, she was happy enough whenever he made a good haul. Once, they'd gone to Tenerife, to a self-catering apartment with a pool and shops nearby and she'd toasted herself golden brown and been very warm and loving. It would be nice to do that again.

After parting from Denis, Len wandered the streets of Leckerton. The rain had stopped and people were coming home from work as the shops shut. It wasn't a good time for a casual break-in: he must bide his time until later.

He went to a pub and made two halves last him all night while he read the paper and planned how to spend what he'd get from tonight's operation.

He liked padding about in a quiet house, knowing that those upstairs in bed were unaware of his presence. He preferred not to go into bedrooms unless it was a daytime job in an empty house. You could find quite a lot downstairs, like cheque books, and often women's handbags. Televisions and radios were downstairs, too, and drink. And silver, in the places that had it.

There'd be some at Ford House, for sure.

Denis lay in the van in his sleeping bag listening to his stereo, twitching his limbs and pounding his fists together in the darkness. Tomorrow he'd be in the money and could do anything he liked.

He dozed off by mistake and woke with a start, wondering what the time was. He had a torch, and shone it on his digital watch which his mother, in a rare moment of affection, had given him for his fourteenth birthday. It was only ten o'clock. He set the alarm for twelve, in case he fell asleep again.

After parting from Len, he had run into a boy from school who had told him questions were being asked about his absence. Masters had wanted to know if other boys had seen him.

'I've been ill,' said Denis. 'There were letters.' He'd sent another one last week.

'Yeah – wrote them yourself, didn't you?' guessed his informant.

What if they set the police or the social services on to searching for him? Would anyone come round to Tracy's? His parents didn't know he was there. Tracy had promised not to tell them, if she ran into their mother.

He decided to forget it. After tonight, he could run. They'd never find him in London.

The small piping notes of the alarm woke him, piercing the heavy sleep that had suddenly claimed him.

Now he had to get the keys.

Denis opened the door into the communal hall of the house and stood listening. The ground-floor front room was occupied by a man who worked in a Leckerton factory. He kept late hours, but Denis had seen his motor-bicycle in the tiny front garden, where he left it out of the way of Mrs Dove's car. So he was in, but he might not be asleep though there was no light in his room. At the back was old Mrs Crow, who seldom went out and had few visitors. Denis thought it was cruel, her living like that on her own, and that she should be put in a home, but Tracy admired her independence and said why shouldn't she keep her own place? She wasn't ill, only old. She had the use of an outside lavatory beyond her kitchenette. Alan's room was at the back, upstairs, and Mrs Dove had the rest of the space, quite a nice flat with her own bathroom. Tracy and Alan shared the other bathroom with Steve Fox from downstairs, and Mrs Crow when she felt bold enough to climb the stairs.

Denis could hear nothing. He had brought a torch, to avoid putting on the main light, which worked from a time switch. Softly, in his trainers, he went up the stairs. One creaked and he froze, but there was no other sound. He reached the door to Alan and Tracy's room, slipped the key in and turned it carefully. It made a small click and he paused again, but all was silent. He crept into the room, his hand over his torch, his fingers glowing red, and almost stumbled over one of Tracy's slippers which she had left carelessly in the middle of the floor. Where would Alan have put his keys?

Denis felt his way over to the chest of drawers where hairbrushes and cosmetics were jumbled together. Were they there? He couldn't see them.

A sigh came from the bed and he doused his light, freezing again, holding his own breath until he thought he would explode. If they woke, he would say he had a headache and was looking for an aspirin.

To the right of the bed was a sagging armchair and a small table. Alan had been living here for a year before Tracy moved in, and since then they had exchanged his single bed for a double divan. Apart from that, there was a beanbag to sit on, and Denis bumped into it now as he moved to the chair looking for Alan's jacket. The keys might be in his pocket.

The jacket wasn't on the chair. He shone his shrouded torch round again. If he failed to find them, the whole deal would be off, and he'd lose face with Len.

Then he caught sight of something on the back of the door. Of course! There were several hooks there, put up by Tracy in an effort to win more space. Alan's jacket hung on one and the keys were in the pocket.

Denis almost whooped for joy but he controlled himself, going quietly from the room and closing the door behind him. Again, it clicked as the lock engaged, but he was outside now and it wouldn't matter if they woke.

He hurried downstairs and out to the road. They would see nothing from their room. Only Mrs Dove or Steve Fox would be able to watch the van move off, if by chance they heard it start and were curious enough to look out.

As he reached the van, Len emerged from the shadows behind it. Denis's pounding heart seemed to fill his whole chest. He had never felt so excited in his life.

'I got them!' he said, waving them.

'Ssh,' said Len. 'Hand them over and get in.'

Denis obeyed. Len slid into the driver's seat and ran his eye over the controls. It was some time since he had driven a motor vehicle but he did not want Denis to realize this.

'Choke's there, and that's where the indicators are,' said Denis helpfully. 'You don't want to blow the horn by mistake,' he added.

Len silently agreed. He pulled out the choke and turned the key. The van fired at once, loudly and a little roughly, but soon settling down. Len did not adjust the throttle. He pulled out from the kerb and set off along the road in the yellow glow from the street lamps.

Denis leaned over and switched on the lights. This was the life! He might never see Leckerton again. He began to sing tunelessly as they went along, until Len told him to shut up.

'I can't concentrate with you making that row,' he said.

Denis sat back. His Walkman was in the rear with his sleeping bag and few belongings. Now he'd forgotten his plan to return the van for Alan to use the next day. He'd got all he needed for life in London. He and Len might stop for a meal at one of those big service stations on the motorway. It would be great. He'd been to London several times on school trips to museums, which he found boring, and once with two other boys. They'd ridden on the Underground for hours and only surfaced when they were hungry. It was a weird place, people playing guitars or violins with hats or bags on the ground for money and crowds on the pavements. Denis did not remember how glad he had been to get back to Leckerton, where if you were really determined you could walk from one side of the town to the other in a couple of hours, not that he'd ever done it.

'Which way?' asked Len at the roundabout outside Leckerton.

'Left. Then it's straight on for a bit,' said Denis. He was hungry again. He'd eaten his supper very quickly, hurrying out to the van as usual to leave Tracy and Alan alone, and it seemed a long time ago. Never mind. There would be plenty of food at Ford House. He and Len could have some of Mrs Davies's cake, even cook a meal on that old-fashioned range of hers.

As he reached this comforting reflection, they came to the turning for Coxton. Len's driving was rough when he had to change gear, but the van was in good order and once it had warmed up, ran well. He hadn't liked it when the kid leaned over to push in the choke. Interfering, that was.

'Give over,' Len had said.

Denis didn't mind. He knew Len saw himself as the boss but he, Denis, was the one with the local knowledge.

Len, however, also knew Coxton, although he had not approached it from the Leckerton side before. The first houses on the edge of the village came into sight, dark windows glinting in the headlights. He slowed down. There were a few street lights set widely apart along the narrow, twisting road. They passed the pub and the shop, and the lane that led down to the church and a small close of bungalows which Len had looked at with a professional eye during his stints in the graveyard. One often had a window open and the car gone from the garage; it had been hard to pass by without trying his luck. The van swerved as he glanced down the lane and Denis shrieked at him to mind where he was going.

Nearly a mile past the last building, a renovated Victorian chapel now occupied by an accountant and his wife, who was a nurse, they reached the entrance to Ford House. Len knew that further on a small humped bridge crossed the narrow river and the road eventually led to the prison. This was the way he had cycled so many times. He pulled the van on to the grass verge and turned off the lights.

'We'll go the rest of the way on foot,' he said. 'Is it a long drive?'

'Depends what you mean by long,' said Denis, still unnerved by Len's steering lapse. He'd thought they were going to hit a lamp post. 'Couple of hundred metres, maybe,' he added as they got out of the van.

Denis stepped forth boldly and led the way up the drive, trotting along in his trainers and carrying the torch he kept in the van. The heavy clouds which had brought the rain earlier in the day had parted, and a thin moon showed as the two padded along. Len stumbled once and cursed.

'Drive's full of holes,' Denis said cheerfully. 'I've offered to fill them in for the guy and he's thinking about it. Costs money to buy the ballast they'd need.' As he spoke, Denis really believed he had had this conversation.

Len was not interested. He was peering ahead to the dark shape of the house. A light showed at an upper uncurtained window and they both halted.

'It'll be for the kids, in case they wake,' said Denis.

'You never said there was kids,' said Len.

'You didn't ask,' answered Denis. 'There's three. One of them's pretty young, three or four.'

Len had imagined a prosperous middle-aged couple

100

living here in comfort, with their children off their hands and away from home.

'Where're the cars kept?' he muttered.

'Round the back.' Denis turned on his torch and brandished its beam in the direction of the yard.

'Turn that thing out,' hissed Len. He took the key from his pocket and went up to the front door, where he had to ask Denis to supply some light as he fitted it into the lock. He turned it and tried the latch, but the door held fast.

'Must be bolted,' said Denis, hiding his dismay. He had imagined them walking straight in through the front hall and helping themselves at their leisure.

Len was cursing.

'Not got a burglar alarm, have they?' he asked. He'd seen no sign, but then he hadn't really looked for one.

The idea had never occurred to Denis.

'Don't think so,' he said. 'We might get in at the back,' he added.

The pair went round to the yard and Len tried the back door. Naturally enough, it was locked. So much for making an easy entry: he was tempted to give Denis a piece of his mind but checked himself. That would have to wait.

'We'll try a window,' he said. He wouldn't give up now.

He moved towards the kitchen window and took out a knife. Just as he did so, they heard the sound of a car.

'Quick, hide somewhere,' Len snarled. What had he got himself into with this stupid kid?

Denis had already melted away into the space between the oil tank and the rear wall of the house. Len squeezed in beside him as a car turned the corner into the yard, its lights picking up the open doors of one of the garages. Charles Davies had been to a business function and had only now come home.

Len and Denis crouched where they were while he got

out of the car, locked it, then closed the garage. He walked right past them to the back door and Denis, who could see him clearly, watched him take a key from beneath a water butt and let himself in. He prayed that Len, crouched behind him, had not noticed.

Now lights began coming on in the house.

'We stay here till he's gone upstairs,' said Len, pulling Denis back as he started to move. The man had only to look out of the window to see them.

They waited for over half an hour, during which time they heard water gurgling down a nearby drainpipe and the sound of a lavatory flushing.

'There's a way out through the garden,' Denis said. 'We needn't go near the drive.'

It was implicit that the job was off. Both were impatient to escape undetected.

They got very wet about the feet on their journey down a rough grass path and across a patch of lawn. Len uttered some obscenities and he called Denis unflattering names for not finding out about the man Davies's movements.

'I didn't know you were coming today, did I?' Denis retorted. 'You didn't tell me.'

He marched on in silence and decided not to warn Len about two steps ahead of them in the darkness, with the result that Len lost his balance and fell, twisting his ankle painfully.

They got back into the van and after rubbing his ankle and swearing for several minutes, Len started the engine.

'We'll try somewhere else,' he said. He couldn't go home empty-handed after all this effort. 'There'll be another place hereabouts worth a try.'

'There's Ivy Lodge,' said Denis, ever helpful, mentioning the only other house in the village of which he had any knowledge. 'Belongs to a rich old lady. She's got lots of silver and stuff.' He wasn't sure about that, but he'd seen that it was full of that shiny dark old furniture people were so mad about. 'It's back in the village.'

Len turned the van round and they returned the way they had come, headlights dipped. Denis pointed out Ivy Lodge.

'But it's no size,' said Len, who had expected another mansion.

'Doesn't matter. She's got plenty,' said Denis. 'And a car, and money.' She'd had a wad of notes in her wallet when she paid him the other day. 'Course I haven't got a key.'

'No. Well, it wouldn't fit if you had, would it?' said Len nastily. His ankle was easing a little, still aching but he could operate the clutch with less effort. He parked beyond Ivy Lodge, two wheels up on the verge, leaving the driveway clear. Then the pair went through the gate.

'I can get in if she's asleep,' Len said. 'But you wait outside. Keep watch. I don't want you getting in my way.'

Denis followed him round as he looked at the windows, testing each in turn. All seemed to be held with security locks and were also double-glazed; then, round at the back, he saw one on the latch upstairs. Audrey always slept with her bedroom window open unless the weather was too bad.

Silently, Len pointed.

'It's upstairs,' Denis objected.

'What's wrong with that?' Len replied. It wasn't what he would have chosen but it proved his theory that you could get into most places without too much grief. 'I wonder if there's a ladder?'

'There's one in the garage,' said Denis.

Len made short work of undoing the padlock which fastened Audrey's garage doors together. He allowed Denis to help him carry the ladder to the rear of the house.

'What if she wakes up?' Denis asked, as Len tested the ladder, wincing a little as his ankle gave him a twinge.

'I'll deal with her,' Len said, and he let Denis see the cosh as he slid it down his sleeve and into his gloved hand.

11

Audrey had been dreaming about Hesther. In her dream, she was walking through the fields with a small girl in a print dress, holding a doll. Suddenly the dream changed and she was in a cold, stark room with barred windows, facing a haggard woman whom she scarcely recognized, with huge pouches below her eyes and a blank, sedated stare.

The nightmare made her start awake, and then she heard a sound. She sat up in bed. A cool draught blew in through the open window. The noise was probably the branch of a tree creaking outside, or the old wood of the house stretching. She lay down again, pulling the covers round her, closing her eyes, trying to think of something soothing, but it was useless. Her mind was full of the image of Hesther as she had been during those months in Holloway. Rupert had been stricken by Hesther's deterioration, and her failure to respond to subsequent medical treatment had been heartbreaking for them both. For the umpteenth time, Audrey embarked on the mental circle of self-examination and recrimination: what could she have done that would have made a difference? How could Hesther have been saved?

Certainly not by being sentenced to prison for minor theft.

'To teach you a lesson,' the judge had said. 'And to act as a warning to others.' No proper assessment of her mental state was ever made, though she had been held on remand for psychiatric investigation. There was a doctor who showed concern for her, but was powerless to get her proper treatment and she had seen him only twice.

Audrey knew she would not sleep now. She pulled on

her green woollen dressing gown and tied the sash round her thin waist. Often at night she would fall asleep easily, her eyes closing as she read some undemanding book, and then an hour or so later she would start awake after a troubled dream and find her mind churning out of control. Sometimes making a cup of tea and reading again, or listening to the BBC World Service, would settle her down eventually.

She crossed to the door and found it ajar. That was odd. She always shut it when she went to bed, and it fitted properly, never coming open once it was closed. Then she saw the window was wide open, not latched as she always left it. Audrey barely took these facts in as she switched on the landing light and descended the stairs; she certainly did not suspect that there was an intruder in the house. . .

Len heard her coming. He was in the sitting room, going through her desk looking for a cheque book and anything else of use. He had decided to leave the bedroom, where there would be jewellery and maybe furs, until last, in case he disturbed her.

Audrey put on the hall light on her way to the kitchen. She opened the door and stretched out her hand to turn on that light, too. It was then that Len struck her from behind with his cosh.

Denis, bored outside the house with no active role to play in the burglary, had seen the bedroom light come on several minutes after Len had disappeared through the upstairs window.

What should he do? How could he warn Len?

He dithered about on the damp lawn. A blind was drawn across the dark kitchen window but it was not a perfect fit, and Denis peered anxiously through the gap at one side. He was in time to see, illumined by the hall light from behind her, a figure in a green dressing gown, her grey hair in disorder, and the sudden O of her mouth

106

as Len delivered his blow. Audrey crumpled forward and Denis heard a curious muffled sound, part moan, part scream. Paralysed with horror, he saw Len advance, bend over the woman who now lay on the floor, and raise his arm to strike her again.

It was Denis's turn to utter a strangled groan. He clamped his hand to his mouth and ran back to the front of the house, where he crouched on the new patio, shaking with fear.

He must get away. Len had done murder, and he, Denis, had seen it and would be blamed when it was discovered. The exciting adventure had gone horribly wrong. There had been no talk of violence when all this was set up. Helping yourself to this and that was one thing; mugging folk was another, and Denis thought he was going to be sick. Gasping into his hands, which he clasped over his mouth, he ran out into the lane.

There was the van. He could escape.

He was trembling as he hurried towards it. He flung open the driver's door to see if the keys were there.

They were.

Denis got in and started the engine. Now he would have to prove he could drive.

Len made sure that the woman was out for the count. He administered a third blow to her head before he was satisfied that she was no further danger.

Funny that she went to the kitchen and not to the telephone. Maybe she hadn't heard him. Still, that was her hard luck; if she'd stayed quietly in bed no harm would have come to her. He was safe now, and could take his time.

He had already seen bottles in the dining room: whisky and sherry. The old cow liked her drop and so did he. Len pushed her with his foot before going off for a restorative nip. He drank from the bottle of Haig, wiping the rim with his leather-gloved hand before setting it down. That was better! No need to panic. He'd be well away before she came round. The kid needn't know there'd been a bit of rough stuff. Still, it meant he couldn't be let into the house to help carry things out to the van, as Len had intended; he was stupid enough to want to go looking for food and might see her lying there.

He'd stick to easily portable things.

Len found Audrey's jewellery – a pearl necklace, two rings, some brooches, and, beside the bed, a gold watch. He took her clock radio and a small colour television set she had in her bedroom, and a gold carriage-clock which he found on the sitting room mantelpiece. Her brown leather handbag was upstairs. He opened it and took her wallet which contained a bank card and about sixty pounds in cash. Her car keys were there, too, and a cheque book. He'd need a holdall to carry the stuff away.

He found several cases in a cupboard set into the wall on the landing, the zipped Antler bags Audrey used for her holiday trips. He packed up his haul, added the video recorder from beneath the larger television downstairs, which he left with regret; it was too heavy to manage alone. Then he opened the front door. He'd get rid of the kid now, tell him they'd best split.

But where was he? There was no sign of him. Len left the door ajar as he went searching for Denis. In the end he thought of going into the lane and he saw that the van had gone.

Bloody kid! What made him take off? He couldn't have seen anything of what had happened in the house. He'd just got bored, or was car crazy and wanted to get his hands on the van. What if there had been no car here for Len to use?

He'd got the keys, and the Fiat started at once. Len backed it out of the garage and loaded it up. He turned off the lights in the house and shut the door. Then he closed the garage and drove through the gates, turning away from Leckerton.

There wasn't a cat's eye in sight in the dark lane and the trees seemed to bend towards the twin beams of his headlights as he steered his way past Ford House again and over the bridge. It began to rain and he struggled to find the switch for the wipers. The damn kid would have known at once where it was.

He must get to a town. Not home: he didn't want to take the Fiat anywhere familiar, where he could be recognized by some nosy copper who knew his face, but in some other town, with people about, street lights, traffic, Len would feel safe, and he could lose himself and the car in the bustle. There were times when it seemed to Len that he was treading on top of the world, and this was one of them: he'd carried off a successful job, avoided being caught, and got quite a respectable haul. The cheque book and bank card would mean he could count on some money. He must simply decide where to go.

The lanes seemed to last for ever. He took an occasional turn one way or another; then he saw a sign indicating Swindon. That was a big place. He could go there.

He headed west.

Denis's departure from Coxton was shaky. He crashed the gears and scraped the side of the van against a wall as he turned into the village street. Still, there was no traffic about to get in his way and he moved jerkily onwards towards the Leckerton road. After a while he felt calmer and began to think about what he was doing. He had studied Alan and other drivers; he knew the procedure. His progress became steadier but then a car came towards him, its lights dazzling him, making him want to veer towards it. Concentrating hard, he managed to hold his course. It seemed easiest when he went slowly, but you shouldn't grind along in low gear. Now he realized that he had gained nothing at all from the night's expedition, not even as much as a pound coin, only the chance to drive the van.

Could he get it safely back so that Alan would never know he had borrowed it?

Approaching Leckerton, more cars came towards him and there was one on his tail, its lights reflected in the mirror on the door distracting him. Denis set his mind to keeping in to the kerb, and when the driver behind saw his chance, he passed. Denis went faster then, briefly reckless. He was getting the feel of it now. It wasn't so difficult.

The street lights in Leckerton made things easier. He drove slowly along, not impeded by other traffic as he made the various turns, but when he tried to put the van back in the space it had occupied outside the house he met trouble. Luckily Alan had left it next to the driveway, which had to be kept clear for Mrs Dove, so he had some room to manoeuvre, but as he went back and forth in first gear and reverse, he thought the noise would waken the whole of Birch Street. He stalled the engine twice and, lacking the skill to inch forwards, hit the car in front of him. He sat trembling, forcing himself to reverse away. When he finally stopped and turned off the engine he was shaking all over, crouching there in the driving seat, wet through with perspiration and weak with shock.

But he had done it.

Lights off, he sat gratefully in the darkness. Now he had somehow to return the key to Alan's jacket.

When he had calmed down, Denis got out of the van and looked at the car in front to see if he had done much damage. There were several dents and scrapes on the paintwork, and the bumper was bent. He couldn't have done all that. The car was an old Austin Maxi, long past its prime and regularly parked in the road. Even if some of the marks were new, the owner wouldn't be able to prove it. Denis looked at the van. It had a good strong front, and there was no obviously raw scratch. He glanced at the wing which he had scraped leaving Coxton. There was a slight scar. With luck Alan might not notice it for a few days and then he might blame a passing motorist for damaging it when it was parked.

It was getting on for four o'clock in the morning. Denis let himself into the house again and crept upstairs. He opened Alan and Tracy's door. This time he did not need to enter the room. A small moan came from within as he felt for the jacket on its hook, and dropped the key in the pocket.

He'd done it! He'd got away with it!

Denis went back downstairs as fast as he could, the tensions slackening. Suddenly, now, his bladder was bursting. He urinated into the bushes in the front garden, sighing with relief, then got into the back of the van. Climbing into his sleeping bag, zipping it up, fitting his earphones over his head to blot out the silence, Denis felt safe. Only then did he spare a thought for Mrs Bannerman, brutally struck down. She might not be dead after all. She could have come round by now and have called the police.

In the ground-floor room at the back of the house, old Mrs Crow awoke. She got up to make herself some tea. Steve Fox, in his room, slept until six when his alarm went and the radio began to play. Tracy and Alan woke up to make love before it was time to start their working day. Only Mrs Dove had heard the noise in the night as Denis struggled to park the van, and she pulled the duvet over her head to muffle the sound as she buried herself in sleep.

Next morning, Alan expected to find the keys in the right hand pocket of his jacket and was mildly surprised that they were in the left, but he gave that no special

111

thought as he departed in his usual early morning rush. Nor did he notice that the van was not parked as tight against the kerb as usual.

12

By the time Jim reached the outskirts of Reading people had settled down to their evening's occupation, whatever that might be, but though it would be some time before the pubs and cinemas emptied, there was enough traffic to worry him; he had not driven since his arrest. He kept well below the speed limit; Jim had always been a cautious motorist.

As he approached his own house a tight feeling came into his throat and his heart beat hard under his stolen anorak. It seemed to thunder in his chest as he stopped the car and looked at the chinks of light showing between the curtains. Maureen was in there, with their child.

What was he going to say to her? How could he win her round? What if he rang the bell and the man answered?

Jim's resolution faltered, now that fantasy must be replaced by fact. He sat staring at the house for over half an hour before he decided that he must wait till morning. Perhaps he could catch Maureen when she left for work, or to take Nicola to school. How did she organize her routine? He knew not the slightest thing about her present daily life.

To postpone action was a big relief, but he must avoid being picked up before he had accomplished his purpose. Surely Maureen would be moved by the fact that winning her back meant so much to him that he had absconded?

He had better dump the pick-up. It would be stupid to get caught with that and by now the police might be searching for it. He left it, with his prison jacket inside it, in the station car park where, at this hour, there was ample space. He shoved the key into the pocket of his anorak and his fingers met some objects – a few coins, a twist of paper. He pulled it out and saw that it was a five-pound note. What luck! Now he could get something to eat, but he did not dare risk the station buffet. Was it even open at this hour? He'd be conspicuous if he went to see.

Wearily, he lifted his bicycle out of the pick-up and rode away from the city centre, by now almost incapable of rational thought. So much positive action had exhausted him. He was unused to that sort of effort; rearranging figures to appropriate money was merely mental exercise, a cleaner crime than stealing something tangible. He felt no guilt about taking the pick-up or the anorak, or his intention of spending the five pounds if he found a suitable café.

Riding on, he reached a district of large houses, few of them now occupied. Most were offices and empty until work began next day. Jim felt cold and afraid. He was too tired to ride on any further, and making sure that no passing car could see him, he turned into the entrance of the next large house with unlit, uncurtained windows, and thrust his bicycle into the shelter of some shrubs in the front garden. Then he went round to the back of the building, where he might find shelter in a garden shed or summer house, or even in a porch. He would not try to break into the house itself as it was sure to be wired up to an alarm.

He stumbled around in the darkness. Without a torch, he could distinguish very little, but at the rear there was a row of outbuildings which had once been the coal shed and store space. Jim tried the doors. One was loosely secured by a padlock on a hasped hook and it would be very easy to unfasten. Surely this wouldn't be connected to the alarm? If it was, he'd soon hear it and could be away on his bike before the police arrived.

He took the key of the pick-up from his pocket and used it to prise off the loop through which the padlock was attached, pausing as he worked, ready for the wail to start, but all was silent. He opened the door and slipped inside, sensing a solid mass ahead of him, and his outstretched hand met metal, but it was cool. He had found the boiler room.

Jim sank down on the floor, drawing his knees up, shuddering with fatigue and fright. Now he was safe for a while. It was dry in his retreat, and after a time his shudders eased and he laid his head on his knees. He was too stressed to sleep properly, and his shelter grew cold for the boiler did not operate at night, but eventually he lapsed into a fitful doze.

He woke early in the morning, and soon his refuge got warmer as the boiler came on and the pipes leading from it to the house heated up. It made a great roaring noise, but it was comforting and he enjoyed it for a while. He must not linger, though, for cleaners might soon arrive, or a handyman whose job it was to maintain this monster.

Jim left his shelter. He could not refasten the lock and it would be obvious that someone had entered the place. His bicycle was still under the bush; he retrieved it and pedalled off into the early morning traffic. Now it would be safe to go to the station. He parked his cycle outside and went into the washroom. Without a razor, there were limits to what he could do about his appearance but he felt better after a wash. He hurried, keeping his anorak on, fearful of someone identifying his prison shirt and overalls. By now the call would have gone out for him all over the country.

After two cups of coffee and some sandwiches in the buffet, Jim felt better. Now for Maureen.

His cycle had gone.

He had had no padlock for it. He hadn't needed one, working from the prison. You'd think it would be safe for half an hour. What a world it was.

With a feeling of fatalism, he caught a bus out to the suburb where he had lived for the span of his marriage. He tendered a pound coin. But for the money in the stolen jacket, he couldn't have eaten or taken this ride.

The bus dropped him at the end of the road. This time there must be no turning back, and Jim's feet seemed made of lead as he walked past the neat houses with their white wood trim and bright tiled roofs towards his own. He supposed it was still his.

In daylight, he saw that the front door, formerly green, had been painted blue. It gave him a shock and made the place seem strangely alien. He looked up at the windows and imagined Maureen moving about inside, perhaps in her housecoat, preparing breakfast. Was that man sitting at the table in the kitchen, Nicola beside him, eating cornflakes from the bowls they'd bought at Habitat?

Jim walked straight up the path and pressed the bell. As the chimes echoed inside the house he realized that he had brought nothing for Nicola, no toy, not even any sweets; he could have bought something at the station but it was too late now.

The door opened and Maureen stood there. Her hair was done a new way which altered her appearance, but she was still beautiful.

Jim saw her expression change from puzzlement to a look of horror as she recognized the gaunt man with the grey-stubbled chin who stood before her. Shock stopped her from banging the door in his face, and before she could recover enough to do so, Jim had thrust his foot in the way. He elbowed past her into the hall.

'What do you want?' she ground out. 'What are you doing here? You haven't been let out.' It was a statement, not a question.

'I had to see you,' Jim replied. 'Is he here? Your – that man you're living with?'

Maureen shook her head.

'How do you know about him?' she asked, her voice faint.

'Never mind.' Jim felt a surge of adrenaline giving him energy. He had the initiative and was safe for the moment. 'You never write. You've had the telephone number changed. You don't visit. Why?' he accused.

Maureen was beginning to recover.

'I don't want anything more to do with you,' she said. 'I told that woman the other day. What do you mean by bursting in here?'

She had looked at him with scorn, even contempt, before; she had not, however, displayed the disgust and loathing he saw now on her face.

'I had to see you,' Jim repeated.

He moved towards her, his arms outstretched. Somehow he must wipe that look off her face.

'Don't touch me!' she cried, backing away.

'Can't we talk? Can't we plan for the future?' he begged her. 'And where's Nicola? I want to see her.'

'I won't let you. Do you know what you look like? You're dirty – dirty – dirty – dirty.' She almost sobbed, then took a breath and hissed at him. 'Get out of here.'

'Mummy, is that a bad man?' came a voice. 'It's a stranger,' and suddenly Nicola was there, in her pyjamas, clinging to Maureen's skirt and staring at him with an expression that mirrored her mother's.

Jim saw that the child he thought about daily was terrified of him. Moreover, she did not recognize her own father.

'It's all right, Nicky. I'm not a stranger,' Jim said, bending down. 'Don't you know me?' I'm your – '

'Don't worry, Nicola. He isn't going to hurt us and he's just going. Go upstairs and get dressed,' said Maureen.

She glared at Jim as she spoke, and he stood up slowly. She was lovely and desirable, and she hated him.

'Mummy?' Nicola's voice was questioning.

117

'It's all right, Nicola. Run along,' said Maureen.

Casting a backward glance, Nicola obeyed. They heard her plodding steps ascending.

'She's my daughter,' Jim said. 'I've got rights.'

'Not now, you haven't,' said Maureen. 'You gave those up when you did what you did.' She sensed the short battle was won and moved away from the wall that had been her support. 'I've got a chance of a future now, for her and for me, and if you care anything at all about either of us, you'll not mess that up. We've both had enough shame and disgrace.'

'You should have told me,' Jim said. 'You should have written.'

To her dismay, Maureen saw tears start in his red-rimmed eyes. He looked terrible, and years older.

'Well, what could I say?' she answered, truculently, because she knew she was in the wrong. Still, she'd see it through now. 'I'm getting a divorce,' she went on. 'It's been more than two years. It'll be easy.' And if he tried to oppose it, there was always unreasonable conduct: going to gaol was surely that.

'What about Nicola?' he asked.

'If you want what's best for her, you'll stay out of her life,' said Maureen. 'How's she going to like having a convict for a father, when she's old enough to understand? It's much better if she thinks you're dead.' She went on, in a gentler tone. 'She loves Trevor. He's wonderful with her.'

So that was his name: Trevor. Jim felt like spitting.

'And that's supposed to make me feel better?'

'Yes.'

She would have left him anyway. She was a proud and fiery woman, and he bored her. Some man would have lured her away, whatever happened; it was simply this Trevor who had come along. He sank down on the floor, drawing his knees to his chin and, bowing his head, he began to weep.

118

Maureen felt a kind of awkward pity. Now she could afford to be generous.

'They'll come looking for you here,' she said. 'That's certain. I won't say you've been. It'll give you time to get away.'

'Thank you.' Jim's voice was muffled.

'It's not for your sake. It's for ours,' said Maureen. 'I don't want any more trouble. I'll give you some money. The best thing you can do is give yourself up, and don't mention that you've been here.'

As he heard her footsteps move away, he raised his head and looked slowly round the small hall, with its gleaming floor, his handiwork. He stayed there, motionless, until Maureen came back.

'Get up. Go away,' she ordered.

Jim gazed up at her. She was standing above him, holding out two ten-pound notes. Slowly he got to his feet and took the money.

'Is that all?' he said.

She misunderstood.

'It's all I can spare,' she snapped. Then she opened the door. 'Now go.'

Moving like an automaton, Jim obeyed. He had not touched her, not even the hem of her garment.

There was no cover nearby from which he could watch her leave later, with Nicola. Jim could not stand outside the house until they emerged. He stumbled off down the road, not caring where he was going, occasionally taking a turning one way or the other. If a policeman had come along then, he might have surrendered, but some thread of sanity made him aware that if he was picked up so near the house, Maureen would not avoid involvement. Perhaps he could get himself all the way back to Lockley and make out that he had hidden locally, just for the hell of it. He could send her back her twenty pounds.

But why should he? She'd accepted what he gave her over the years, hadn't she? Her Habitat curtains and china, her pretty furniture, her holidays abroad. He'd spend her money and enjoy it. At least he'd have a good meal, and perhaps a shave. Not here though. He'd have to put miles between them.

Jim had been gone less than a quarter of an hour when Maureen's bell rang again.

This time it was a uniformed policewoman who stood outside. Because Trevor Black was in the traffic division, she knew nothing of him or of his connection with Maureen.

'I'd better come in, love,' she said, when Maureen opened the door, and added, 'You're going to have a bit of a shock when I tell you why I'm here.'

Oddly, Maureen was glad that she already knew the reason. She steeled herself to react with surprise when told that her husband, Jim Sawyer, had absconded.

'He's most likely holed up in the area near the prison,' said the policewoman. 'But sometimes they run because they want to come home.'

'I'll let you know if he turns up,' said Maureen calmly, hoping that Nicola, who was now eating her breakfast, would not suddenly appear and mention their earlier visitor. 'There's no place for him here now,' she added.

The policewoman thought that she looked somewhat strained but that was hardly surprising, and no doubt the news was a shock.

'Are you coping all right?' she asked.

'Oh yes. I've got a good job,' said Maureen. 'And I'm going to get a divorce and get married again.' She'd get on with it now and make Trevor come up to scratch. He'd be a protection when finally Jim was released. Who better than a policeman? 'My boyfriend's a copper,' she added.

'Is that right?' The officer grinned. 'Well, good for you.'

If Jim was picked up along the road, Maureen hoped he would keep his head and not mention that he had been to the house. In a weird way, she did not want him to be taken, though his recapture was inevitable. Sometimes men managed to escape and vanish, but he wouldn't; he wasn't a crook in that sense, with a network of crooked friends to help him, though he might have acquired some in prison.

She'd tell Trevor that Jim had broken out; that was all he needed to know.

13

Yvonne had heard Charles come home very late after his dinner, but she had pretended to be asleep and he crept quietly about, undressing in the bathroom and getting into bed carefully so as not to waken her. There had been a time when she would have been eager to greet him, no matter how late he was. In a way he was glad not to have to make any effort now; there was always Saturday night.

In the morning, when she asked how the evening had gone, he was non-committal. Still tired and mildly hung over, he did not want the bother of describing what had happened.

Yvonne remembered the many nights when, very late, he had left her to return to Olivia. What had he told Olivia then? Had he really been to a business dinner this time? What he had done once, he could repeat.

He left home so early that, now the mornings were dark, she had given up coming down to have coffee with him before he went. Instead, she snatched at the chance of an extra half hour in bed, often with Robin tucked up beside her. Today he had appeared while Charles was in the bathroom shaving. He had wandered about in his pyjamas with Thomas the Tank Engine displayed across his chest and Charles had ordered him quite crossly to go back to his own bed. Robin had uttered a few shrieks of protest for form's sake before obeying, but as soon as his father had gone downstairs he had reappeared, singing cheerfully.

After a while, Yvonne took a grip on herself, put on her dressing gown and went down to the kitchen where Charles was standing warming his back at the Aga and drinking his instant coffee, a report in his hand. His briefcase was open on the table. Perhaps it really had been a business dinner.

Yvonne wished she had stayed upstairs as he glanced up impatiently and then made an effort to smile.

'My car wouldn't start yesterday,' she said. 'I had to walk down to the school. It was tipping with rain. Mrs Bannerman brought us back.'

'I haven't time to look at it now,' said Charles. 'You'll have to cope.'

'I didn't mean you to,' said Yvonne.

'It's the damp, I expect,' said Charles. 'If you run a hair dryer on the plugs, it might do the trick.'

After offering her this counsel, he left.

He'd got jump leads. He could have started the car with those. It wouldn't have taken ten minutes. Yvonne sighed. A year ago, he'd have done it. But a year ago he was living near his work.

While the children were having their breakfast, she went out to try to start the car. There wasn't a sign of life in it, and the rain was pouring down.

Audrey Bannerman had offered to run the children to school. Faced with another wet walk with the three of them, Yvonne decided to take her at her word. She and Robin could stay at home so that she need not make a double trip. Audrey had said she always woke early. At eight fifteen Yvonne dialled her number.

There was no answer.

Fifteen minutes later, she tried again, then five minutes after that. Still no reply, and now they must leave or they would be late.

In boots and raincoats, with Robin strapped into his pushchair and holding an umbrella over his head, they set off. Philip and Emily had wanted to go alone, but Yvonne would not give Philip the responsibility of getting his small sister safely there.

Once they were outside it didn't seem so bad, and all

of them had glowing cheeks by the time they reached the school.

Passing Ivy Lodge on the way back, Yvonne paused. It was odd that Audrey hadn't answered the telephone. Perhaps it was out of order. Sometimes, when that happened, it sounded to the caller as though the number was ringing. But she might be ill. She was getting on, though she seemed quite fit; hard to tell how old she was, really. Yvonne hesitated at the gate, then saw that the curtains were drawn at every window facing the front. Audrey must have overslept. But wouldn't the telephone have woken her? Not if she had no extension in her bedroom.

Yvonne pushed Robin through the gates and up the short drive. There was a milk bottle on the step and a newspaper was thrust through the letter box. Lucky Audrey to have one delivered: the boys would not go as far as Ford House and Yvonne saw no paper except *The Times* when Charles brought it back. She never bothered to read it. She'd no time for a paper, really, but she sometimes thought it would be nice to see one occasionally.

She glanced at the garage. The doors were closed.

It was after nine o'clock. Yvonne rang the bell. It echoed through the house and after a pause she rang it again. Nothing happened.

Yvonne parked Robin in the front porch, took away the umbrella before he used it to damage himself or Audrey's property, put the brake on the pushchair and walked round to the back of the house.

She saw the ladder at once, and above it, the open window.

Yvonne tried the back door before she climbed the ladder, but it was securely bolted. The blind was down, and she tried to peer round it but could see very little.

She went back to Robin, who was now getting

impatient, demanding to be released. She wheeled him round to the back of the house and told him to watch her climb the ladder.

'I'll come too,' he offered.

'No, you won't,' she said. 'Be good and I'll let you out in a minute.'

At least she could see him while she made her ascent. Intending at first only to look through the window, Yvonne climbed up. She saw Audrey's empty, disturbed bed, and the dressing-table drawers left open. Audrey's handbag lay on the bed, her compact and comb beside it.

Yvonne, in her jeans and waxed jacket, climbed over the window sill and made her way through the dim house. She pulled back the landing curtain to let in some light and looked in every room, calling Audrey's name as she went.

Then she found her.

There was blood on the floor of the kitchen, and Yvonne thought that Audrey was dead. But although her face, which was turned to one side, felt chilled, it was not icy and she seemed to be faintly breathing.

Yvonne rushed to the telephone in the hall and dialled the emergency services. Then she ran upstairs and pulled blankets from Audrey's bed and brought them down to cover her. She heard Robin begin to wail in the garden and went out to bring him indoors after she had put the kettle on, closing the kitchen door so that he could not see Audrey's still, huddled shape. She put him in the sitting room and turned on the television, telling him to stay there. Then she hunted upstairs for a hot-water bottle, in vain until she thought of looking in Audrey's bed, where she found a blue one in a hand-knitted cover which she filled and laid against the unconscious woman's stomach. There was nothing else she could do.

Robin was thrilled when the ambulance and the police arrived, and he enjoyed being driven home with his mother in the police car, but that didn't happen for quite some time.

'What relatives has she?'

The uniformed constable who had arrived first at Ivy Lodge, just after the ambulance had rushed through the village with its siren wailing, turned to Yvonne as they stood together in the garden.

The rain had stopped but the air was heavy with damp which clung to every vestige of leaf and blade of grass. A few late chrysanthemums bowed sodden heads in a bed to the right of the house. Dead leaves lay on the grass under an apple tree, and it seemed to Yvonne that the whole place was shrouded in a miasma of mourning.

PC Lucking had explained that they must not add their own finger and footprints to those already in the house because the CID would be coming along to investigate. But of necessity, Yvonne's entrance and attempts at first aid, and the arrival of the ambulance men, had overlaid any clues there might have been. Robin was kicking about among the leaves. He said he was hunting hedgehogs.

'She's divorced,' Yvonne said. 'She had a daughter, who died. I haven't heard her mention anybody. Someone else might know – a neighbour – the vicar –' Her voice trailed off.

'We'll inquire,' said the constable. 'But she lived alone, and you know of no one who should be sent for at once?'

'No,' said Yvonne, shaking her head. It seemed so inexpressibly sad. 'Who could have done this? Some casual thief?'

'Probably,' said the constable. 'She must have heard something and surprised him.'

At this moment, the ambulance men came out of the house with their burden. One of them shook his head at the constable.

'Is she dead? She wasn't,' Yvonne said.

The constable went over to ask while Yvonne prevented Robin from going to inspect the patient. Audrey would want nightdresses, her washing things, she thought: but perhaps there was no urgency about any of that. She might not need them.

Lucking returned.

'She's not too good, but she's still alive,' he told Yvonne. 'A man escaped from Lockley Prison last night,' he added. 'He may have done this.' All patrols had been instructed to look out for Jim Sawyer.

'Some prisoners have been working in the village,' said Yvonne. 'They were tidying up the graveyard. I don't think there was any trouble, but I was a bit surprised at the freedom they had to move around.' Then she remembered. 'One of them worked for Mrs Bannerman. He did some painting and gardening, I think.'

'I wonder if that could have been Sawyer,' said Lucking.

Detective Inspector Wright wondered the same thing when he arrived later. It wouldn't take long to find out.

Len had decided that Swindon was too near Leckerton to start using the stolen card and cheque book, and to dump the car which now he dared not risk trying to sell. Besides, it was not yet morning when he got there.

He went on to Bristol, a city strange to him, but it was large and there would be anonymous areas where he could move unnoticed. He was still elated. When he had loaded up with more loot, he'd go home to a fine welcome from Bet and the kids.

He'd hit the woman hard, but if she'd stayed in her bed she'd have been unharmed, or so he told himself now. As for the kid, Denis, it was as well that he had scarpered. He hadn't the stomach for seeing a job through, that was obvious. Still, the van had been useful.

Len felt a moment's unease lest the kid shop him, but decided he'd be too keen on preserving his own skin. Besides, he didn't know what had happened in the kitchen. If he got picked up driving the van he'd be intent on saving himself and it was better to be charged with a driving offence than breaking and entering, not to mention assault. No, he was safe enough.

He whistled, spinning along in the Fiat. There was a big service area outside Bristol and he stopped there for breakfast, enjoying an excellent meal among representatives and businessmen on their way to work. Traffic was piling into the city when he entered it. He drove towards the centre, and when he saw a multi-storey car park, he turned into it. The car would be safe from observation there, if an alert was out for it, and he would merge with the ordinary folk on the street.

Before he got out of the car he did a little job on Audrey's bank card, rubbing her signature down with a fine piece of glass paper. He signed A. Bannerman over the top, in bold writing. It would stand up to a cursory examination; only someone inspecting it closely would notice what he had done. How lucky that her name was not printed in full on the card, showing that it belonged to a woman.

He did a great deal of shopping, charging things and signing the flimsy forms A. Bannerman, spending under fifty pounds in each shop so that no one would ring up for sanction. He bought spirits, radios, a telephone, and when he could carry no more, he took them back to the Fiat and stashed them away. They were all highly saleable and would bring in easy money.

Then he decided to cash some cheques and had such success at three different branches of Audrey's bank that he made up his mind to hire a car.

He paid cash, using his own driving licence, and acquired a handsome Sierra which he drove to the park where he had left the Fiat. He had to wait for a while before a space near the smaller car became vacant, but at last one was free, two slots away from the Fiat. How lucky could you be?

Len transferred his haul from one car to the other, both of them backed against the wall. Nobody passing took any notice.

Minutes later, he was driving the Sierra down the ramp and heading for home. The Fiat might not be found for days.

After his nocturnal adventures, Denis had decided to spend the next day safely at school.

He had been certain that Alan would notice the van was not parked as he had left it, even if he did not at first see the scrape it had received, but he didn't. He got straight in, started it up and drove off, with Tracy beside him. He took her to the bus stop every morning.

Denis went up to their room for his breakfast. Tracy always left the bread out, and a packet of cereal, and after the first few days he had begun to tidy up, washing his own mug and plate and anything she had left by the basin which did double duty as sink. This morning he felt hungry and after eating a large bowl of cornflakes, helped himself to two slices of toast and margarine thickly spread with jam. He didn't think about the old woman at first, but as he was drinking his tea he started to wonder what had happened after he left Ivy Lodge. If she had come round quite quickly and phoned the police, Len might have been caught already.

Had she got a good look at him? He'd hit her from behind, Denis had seen that, but she might have glimpsed his face. One thing was certain, and that was that she hadn't seen Denis.

If the police hadn't arrested Len, they'd be all over the place today, harassing everyone in sight. He'd better not hang about in town in case they fancied roughing him up. Denis couldn't risk questions about being a truant. It

129

should all have ended by now. He should have had money and been on his way to join a gang in the smoke.

The brave would-be gangster washed his face, found his school trousers and a once-white shirt, and knotted his tie round his neck. He passed Tracy's brush through his hair which was getting too long for his taste and set off for school, where his appearance was greeted with surprise and a good deal of sarcasm. He would have earned a reproof for his grubby appearance if the school had not formed the opinion that his home conditions were far from ideal. The various notes that had excused his absence were regarded as suspect, and only the fact that his birthday was so near and he was academically such an unpromising pupil had prevented a proper inquiry into the true position.

Now, when asked how he was, he remembered that allegedly he had been ill.

'Not too wonderful,' he said, putting on a brave look.

Various boys who had seen him about the town tittered, and made muffled comments. However, beneath his naturally ruddy complexion, he was pale, and there were dark smudges under his eyes. He bent earnestly over the text the rest of the class had studied during his absence but his boredom threshold had not altered, and soon he began to sigh and gaze out of the window.

Unable to concentrate, Denis left after the dinner break.

The cinema would soon be open, and he could spend the afternoon safely there, in the dark.

Later, he'd decide what to do next.

Jim had to see Nicola properly, just once. He had to wipe out the image of her frightened little face as she asked if he was a bad man. Children were warned against strangers.

He turned into a side road. Further on was a cluster of

shops which served the estate, and beyond them was the school.

If he waited nearby, he would see her arrive. Did Maureen bring her, or some friend? He had no notion of the child's routine.

It was really no wonder that Nicola had not recognized him, since clearly her mother was hoping he would soon be forgotten. There'd be no photographs around, no affectionate talk about him. He'd seen other cons receive warm greetings from their children, although visiting was always a strange, unnatural time. But he had been gone for over two years. How could a child her age remember?

He plodded on, an unremarkable man in his stolen anorak and dark trousers. The streets were busy now, with the rush hour under way. Children going to school walked past, older ones in groups together, smaller ones with mothers. Jim fell in behind a mother with a small boy beside her and two toddlers in a double pushchair. Soon they came to the school, a modern building with big windows and an asphalt playground.

A crossing patrol warden in her overall and cap held up the traffic to allow the children to cross the road by the school. Jim walked past and stood on the opposite corner. He'd see Maureen if she came along. If someone else brought Nicola, he might have trouble identifying his own child. She'd grown so much! In that fleeting moment he had seen such a change in her. You'd think Maureen could at least have sent him some photos. How cruel she was! He had never realized what a core of steel she possessed.

Then he saw them both, Maureen in her pink raincoat, her blonde curls standing out round her head, holding an umbrella in one hand and Nicola by the other. The little girl wore a green duffle coat; white socks twinkled below. There was another little girl with them, with red hair. Jim watched the trio cross the road under the benevolent gaze of the lollipop lady and disappear into the yard. So Maureen was careful; she took the child right into the building. He was glad of that. You never knew who was hanging about these days.

Nicola had been chatting eagerly to her mother as they came along the road. Neither of them had glanced his way.

Jim moved off before Maureen emerged from the school yard. If she saw him again, she might change her mind about turning him in.

14

Felicity Bannerman saw the police car coming up the drive.

She had been down the garden to pick parsley and dill to decorate the salmon mousse she had made for tonight's dinner party. She and Rupert occasionally entertained other couples of similar ages and tastes, most of whom they had known for years although Felicity had been absent from the area during her first marriage.

She had been happy then. She had enjoyed stations in Malta and Gibraltar, where Harry had had shore jobs, and she had settled easily into the house near Fareham which they later bought as a base and where she had spent long spells with the children while he was at sea. Harry was charming and handsome, and he had swept her off her feet when they met at a dance just after the war. Now, she understood that he had been ready to marry then and was looking for a suitable wife, programmed, as she was, to fall in love. It had worked out well enough; with three children born in quick succession, she had been too busy to question her own contentment, though she was often lonely. Their reunions had always been romantic, and Harry had always gone again before either could feel any strain. She became efficient at coping with things on her own and made friends with other wives similarly placed. Sometimes his return was almost a nuisance, interrupting the routine she had evolved.

When she met Rupert again, their easy friendship, long established in youth, was soon re-established, and when she learned about Hesther's problems Felicity felt infinite pity for the girl and her parents. Only gradually

133

did Rupert reveal that he and Audrey lived like amiable strangers.

'She can't face what's happened to Hesther,' he had told her when the trouble began. 'She has such rigid ideas – high standards, if you like – that she can't understand how Hesther fell into such a way of life. She won't talk about it.'

'You should make her,' said Felicity.

'I can't. I can't bear quarrels,' said Rupert.

'Must a discussion become a quarrel?'

'It can if the least comment is interpreted as criticism, which is what happens with Audrey. But you see, I understand her. She's so insecure, and I've never been able to make her feel otherwise. It's my failure,' said Rupert.

'She was an odd, touchy girl,' said Felicity. 'I liked her because she was so straightforward – there was no guile in her – and I was sorry for her because she was socially inept. She got a lot of teasing and she never lost her temper, just went quiet, and then would come out with some hopelessly inappropriate remark in an attempt to put things right. She had a genius for putting her foot in – asking about someone's mother, for instance, when everyone else knew she was terribly ill and likely to die.'

'But she asked,' Rupert said. 'She wanted to do the right thing.'

'Yes, but she couldn't find the proper response – the sympathetic touch that comes naturally to some people. I thought she'd learn in time, and that being friends with me would help.'

'It did, to some extent,' said Rupert.

'It brought her you,' said Felicity.

'Mm.' He had felt protective towards her, and that was a sort of love, Rupert supposed.

'If she'd had brothers and sisters, she'd have lost some of her prickles,' said Felicity. 'But she was the one ewe lamb of that elderly couple – the hardheaded businessman who'd come up from the bottom, and that sweet, timid wife. If they'd lived in some comfortable house in a town among other wealthy industrialists, it might have been easier for Audrey to learn to mix, but there she was, isolated in that huge place in the middle of nowhere, with no friends.'

'Ford House wasn't all that large,' Rupert demurred. 'Not as big as Tettlebury.'

'No, and you thought she'd slot easily from one to the other. In some ways, I suppose she did.'

'She slid from one form of isolation to another,' said Rupert. 'I can't bridge it.'

Their affair had been almost inevitable, but they had been discreet. Felicity did not want to hurt Harry, and she was sometimes astounded at her own duplicity, but like other lovers since time immemorial, she had decided that as long as he never found out, no harm would be done, and Rupert felt the same about Audrey.

He found it easier to be patient with Audrey and her brusque ways when he knew that he would soon be alone with Felicity. Even after years of marriage, Audrey would ask someone met at a party why she had chosen to wear that particular shade of yellow, implying that she thought the colour unbecoming, when all she had intended was to show interest in an unusual choice. As a dinner guest, she would refuse some dish she disliked, unable to toy with even a token fragment.

'Why should I?' she would retort, if Rupert suggested a little dissembling. 'It's so wasteful, leaving food on your plate.'

She would never compromise.

Hesther could dissemble only too well, as they discovered. She had her father's charm but no great self-confidence. By the time Audrey understood that the girl was more like her than her father though less resilient than either, it was too late to prevent her headlong descent into self-destruction.

Though Felicity often thought of Audrey, and with guilty remorse even now, she was not in Felicity's mind as she crossed the garden to greet the police officer getting out of his white Ford Escort. She saw that he was not the constable who lived in the village, and who, although he was attached to headquarters in Swalton, knew most of what happened in Tettlebury.

'Good morning,' Felicity said in a questioning tone as she approached the man.

'Mrs Bannerman?' he asked.

'Yes.'

'Is Mr Bannerman at home? Mr Rupert Bannerman?'

'He's over at the farm office with the VAT man,' said Felicity. 'Can I help?'

'Well, I don't know about that,' said PC Wilson. 'It's more a question of breaking some news to him.'

'News? What sort of news?'

Policemen didn't break good news. One had come in the night to tell Felicity that her son had had a car accident, fortunately not very serious, and Rupert had told her how another had woken him and Audrey one night to tell them that Hesther was dead.

'It's about Mrs Audrey Bannerman,' said Wilson.

'Audrey?'

'She's a relative? Mrs Bannerman of Coxton?'

'My husband's first wife,' said Felicity. 'What's happened? Is she ill?'

'You could say so,' said Wilson cautiously. He wetted his lips with his tongue. This was a tricky one.

'Well, either she is or she isn't,' said Felicity with a tartness worthy of Audrey herself.

'I'm sorry to say she's met with an accident,' said Wilson unhappily. 'She's in a critical condition in intensive care in Leckerton Hospital, and there seems to be no next of kin. Except possibly Mr Bannerman, that is. The local officers found his name and address at her house.

'Oh, poor Audrey! How dreadful,' Felicity exclaimed. 'I suppose it was a car accident. It's not likely to have been her fault. She's a very good driver.' Audrey was, in fact, efficient in a great many ways and intolerant of lesser capabilities in others.

'No. I'm afraid she was mugged,' said Wilson. 'Someone broke into her house during the night and she was attacked.'

'Oh no! That's awful!' Felicity was appalled. 'Come in while I ring through to my husband.'

She led the way into the mellow old house built of Cotswold stone, and she knew as she stepped over the threshold that she would never forget this moment. Life could be changed – even lost – all in seconds, and Rupert was going to experience terrible guilt.

Wires and tubes ran from Audrey's body to various pieces of equipment. A heart monitor ticked.

Rupert stood gazing down at her, and as a nurse moved the covering over her legs, he had a brief sight of her ugly, distorted feet. The glimpse made her real to him, for the deeply unconscious, grey-faced woman, her head bandaged, looked like no one he knew. Her hand lay exposed, the knuckles large, the metacarpal bones standing out against the pale transparent skin. They were capable hands; she was a good gardener, a good cook, and a skilful knitter.

A policewoman sat nearby in case she came round and could give a description of her attacker.

Rupert had seen a doctor who had said that her skull had been fractured. They had operated to relieve pressure but at this stage it was difficult to prognosticate. Her heart was not very good, he added.

To Rupert she looked as if she was dead already. Was she being kept alive solely by all this machinery? What could he do to help her? He put his hand over the thin little shell of bones that was hers. She felt cold. A sense of failure oppressed him as he turned to the policewoman, who told him that routine inquiries were under way and that it was thought the attacker might be an escaped convict who had once done some work for Audrey.

So she was still mixed up with prisons. Before she moved to Coxton, while she was living in that impersonal flat in Sussex to which she had gone after they parted, she had been involved with some form of after care. What had happened to Hesther had shown them both that terrible things could be done in the name of justice, and Audrey, aware that it was too late to help her own child, had tried to do something for others.

He never quite knew what had made her give up and move back to Coxton. Perhaps she had known that her heart had begun to fail and had sought comfort in familiar surroundings.

He went straight from the hospital to the local police headquarters to find out what was being done and why a dangerous man had been allowed to work for an elderly woman.

'Jim Sawyer was convicted for fraud. He wasn't a dangerous man,' said Detective Superintendent Hawkes.

'But under altered circumstances, he might become violent,' Rupert suggested. 'If she told him to give himself up, for instance.'

'Anything's possible,' said the superintendent.

'That's what she'd have done,' said Rupert. 'She wouldn't meekly hand over her cash and wave him goodbye.' He could imagine her rounding on the man, ticking him off severely.

'She was struck several blows on the back of the head,' said the superintendent.

'She might have turned away to pick up the telephone,' said Rupert. Audrey, he knew, would show no fear; indeed, she might have felt none.

Hawkes knew there was no telephone in the kitchen at Ivy Lodge.

'It wasn't quite like that,' he said. 'She must have heard a noise and come down to investigate. He heard her, hid, and surprised her. I doubt if she even saw him.'

'He didn't – there was no sort of attack?'

'No,' Hawkes reassured him. 'Nothing like that.'

'Thank God.' Monstrous assaults on elderly women seemed to be part of a great many robberies these days. 'Well, at least you know who to look for,' said Rupert. 'You'll find him in time, I suppose.'

'Oh, we'll do that all right,' said Hawkes. 'And he'll be facing a very serious charge.'

If she died, it would be murder.

Jim walked away from the school, more than twenty pounds in his pocket and without a plan but reluctant, now, to go back to prison before he had spent it.

Soon he came to a bus stop, and almost at once a bus came along. It was going to Oxford. He climbed aboard and paid to travel the whole way. He was used to being told what to do and where to go, and it was restful to sit there being borne onwards, regardless. Soon he began to relax, and after a while the long, wakeful hours of the night caught up with him, and he slept.

He woke to find himself wedged into his seat by a large woman with bulging thighs and two big shopping bags on her lap. She smiled when she saw him looking at her.

'You were dead to the world,' she said.

'I was,' Jim agreed.

That night, when his photograph appeared on television news programmes because he was wanted in connection with the attack on Audrey Bannerman, she was supremely confident that he was the man on the bus. She achieved instant local fame and was considered by her neighbours to have had a lucky escape herself.

'He seemed quite normal,' she said. 'But he needed a

shave. He was asleep when I got on the bus.' She'd been on her way to visit her married daughter, and the man had taken such an interest in what she told him about her three grandchildren. He had a daughter himself, he had said.

She discovered that that was true.

Jim had been to Oxford before, but he did not know it well. He felt lost and alone, wandering the busy streets in his stolen coat. The pavements were crowded, and although the centre of the city seemed to be a precinct of sorts, taxis and buses came wandering through. He walked down a road and, realizing that a sombre fortress to his left was the prison, turned quickly back and went to the library, which he had seen at the top of the hill, where he sat quietly reading the paper for quite some time. He couldn't stay there all day and at last he went out into the street again and wandered into Marks and Spencer's where he bought a pair of socks. He would have liked to buy a shirt too, but he could not afford one.

He wandered along another street and, at the end of it, saw a cinema.

Like Denis, he found it a haven for the afternoon.

When he came out, Jim walked up the road towards some traffic lights. On the corner there was a news vendor selling the *Oxford Mail*, and on the billboard beside him Jim saw the words: WOMAN ATTACKED. MAN SOUGHT.

He bought the paper, but not because of that message. He tucked it under his arm and saw a bus pass, heading north. It stopped, and he got on.

'All the way,' he said, and was charged so little that he couldn't be going far.

As his bus travelled up St Giles and the Woodstock Road, Jim read in the newspaper that Audrey Bannerman had been attacked. Someone had broken into her house during the night, stolen various things, and taken her Fiat car. The police wanted to interview Jim Sawyer, thirty-eight, who had absconded from Lockley prison that evening.

Jim's heart thudded as he read the text. He was described, but the paper had gone to press before a photograph was available. Nevertheless, he felt as if every eye in the bus must be noticing his balding head, grey eyes and pale complexion.

The bus went relentlessly on. It had stopped once, but now bore inexorably up the wide street with large houses on either side towards a roundabout at the top, which it crossed. Then at some lights, it made a right turn. Jim had mounted the Park and Ride bus and was now delivered to the parking lot where people were encouraged to leave their cars before entering the city. Everyone hastened off, many with larger carrier bags labelled Selfridges or Marks and Spencer. It was too early for office workers to be going home.

Jim too got off the bus, throwing his ticket in the bin provided, and walked away towards the road, feeling sick and giddy.

He knew that his fingerprints, and probably traces from his clothing, would be found in Mrs Bannerman's house because he had painted her kitchen and sat in her armchair. He could not prove that he had been in the boiler room in Reading when she was attacked. The police would say he had fled there later, if they found evidence of his presence in the place. In any case, he doubted if he could find it again, and even if the broken lock had been reported, the police wouldn't go chasing that up just to get him off the hook. It would be child's play to fix the blame on him, unless Mrs Bannerman had seen her attacker and recovered enough to describe him.

Who had done such a thing? Who would mug a decent old lady like Mrs Bannerman? Some thug without any mercy, obviously.

There was no question of giving himself up now. He

was not going to face such a serious charge if, by lying low, he could avoid it and wait for her to recover.

Jim had turned right at the entrance to the car park. A big roundabout lay ahead, with massive roadworks in progress beyond it, and, nearby, a motel and service station. The mass of traffic was daunting. It was no place for pedestrians and no one would stop here to give him a lift.

He still had the keys to the pick-up.

Jim returned to the big car park where the bus had stopped. It had gone now, with a fresh load of passengers, but another pulled in as he walked towards the furthest row of parked vehicles, where his efforts to snatch a car would be remote from observation. People were returning to their vehicles from the new bus, and others who had just arrived hastened to board it. Soon it moved off again and things became quieter, though another car drove in as Jim began trying doors. He looked for a Honda, hoping the key he had might fit, but though he found one, it didn't. He discovered an unlocked Vauxhall but the key had gone. Then he remembered something he had heard a con say. As another bus drew in, he sat in the Vauxhall and felt under the dash: no spare key. When the bus had gone and once again there was no one near him, he began feeling under the wings and rears of cars parked some distance from the entrance where his activities might not be noticed. He found a spare key securely taped under the wing of a VW Polo. A few seconds later he drove off in it, hurrying, lest its driver be on the next bus.

There were traffic lights outside the car park. Jim turned north towards the roundabout. He went three quarters of the way round it, heading for Bicester, then, at the next, bore left and found himself in Kidlington. He contemplated stopping to buy a razor and some hair dye, for he knew that he must disguise himself. Then he saw that he was passing the headquarters of the Thames Valley Police.

His heart raced as he accelerated onwards, but those inside had no presentiment of his passage and he went safely by, heading for Banbury.

He'd need more money, and he'd have to steal it.

15

Len parked the Sierra outside the high-rise block where Bet had her flat.

He'd moved in with Bet after her husband had disappeared leaving her alone with a small baby, and since then they'd had one of their own. Sharon was seven now, and Bruce five; Len had seen them regularly during his time in prison and hadn't lost touch. His relationship with Bet was stormy but self-renewing. He didn't believe she had lived like a nun while he was inside, that wouldn't be natural for someone like her, but she seemed pleased enough when he came out, and he'd seen no other bloke hanging about. If he went on a drinking bender, she was ready to join in, and if he occasionally cuffed her, she hit back. Her mother lived nearby, and when he was inside she stayed with the children while Bet worked at the Grapes. Len wouldn't like it at all if Bet slung him out, and he'd done last night's job to keep her happy.

She knew very well that he hadn't come honestly by the car, though he told her truthfully that he had hired it. He set to work fitting up the small television set and the video.

'I don't want to know where you got those,' Bet remarked. 'Then if someone comes asking, I won't give any wrong answers.'

'I had a win on the dogs,' said Len, grinning.

He was exciting, she had to grant that. Now that he was back, her life had taken on an extra dimension. They'd had good times in the past and they would again. Bruce was happy to have his dad home; she just hoped he'd keep out of trouble, by which she meant that she hoped he wouldn't get caught.

He'd disposed of some of the liquor on the way home, and he had cash in his pocket. It was a pity Bet had to go down to the Grapes that night. He'd get in a Chinese meal to enjoy when she returned, and on Saturday they'd take the kids out somewhere.

He had a few drinks while he waited for closing time. Bet's mum was quite glad to be freed from babysitting; she didn't like leaving her old man on his own. Quite like Darby and Joan, they were, those two; Bet's dad was a postman and her mum worked part time in a corner shop selling papers and sweets. They'd been married for over thirty years.

The Chinese meal had been delivered and was ready to heat up again. Pity that old cow down at Coxton hadn't had a microwave oven; one would be useful for Bet. He'd get one as soon as he could. It would mean calling at several banks, picking up fifty pounds at each one. The card and the cheque book might see them through for quite a while.

Bet was a good sort. Len sighed uxoriously, anticipating the night ahead. He'd missed it, inside. He turned on the television.

The news bulletin included a short clip about a robbery in Coxton during the previous night, when an elderly woman had been attacked and seriously injured. Pastoral shots of Coxton were shown, the twisting main street with its shop and the houses around, then Ivy Lodge, white tapes at the gate. A drab photograph of Audrey Bannerman, taken from her passport, appeared on the screen, followed by a mug shot of Jim Sawyer who was wanted by the police for questioning in connection with the assault.

'Phew!' whistled Len, who had watched the short sequence intently. He remembered Jim Sawyer at Lockley, a quiet, grey bloke who never said much. Now that he thought about it, Jim had worked somewhere in

Coxton but not at the churchyard. What a break! And fancy Jim blowing! Well, he was for it now.

There was no need for Len to worry. No one was going to think of questioning him.

Not unless the kid mentioned that Jim hadn't been there at all, and why should he do that?

By the time Jim reached Banbury he had calmed down enough to resume his normal careful driving style. It would be stupid to get stopped for speeding now. He looked about for a permitted parking slot while he went shopping, but when he left the Polo in a space between two other cars he did not realize it was a pay-and-display area and he went off towards the shops without buying a ticket.

He found a large chemist's shop and bought a toothbrush, razor, soap, shaving cream and some hair dye which you washed in – he read the instructions carefully – in a colour called Honeyglow. His beard was so grey that he would have to remain clean-shaven or look very odd, but he would let his moustache grow. Now he must find somewhere with a washbasin where he could carry out his transformation.

When he returned to the car, there was a parking ticket under the wiper. He threw it away.

The shops were closing now, and the traffic was heavy as Jim drove on northwards, skirting the Cross. He had never been here before. He came to some traffic lights, then, at the foot of a hill, some more, and as he was already in the left-hand stream, he turned that way. Crawling along, cars nose to tail, he saw to his right a large modern police station. Jim put up a hand to hide his face as he went past.

He needed money to rent a room where he could lie low until something happened to bring the true attacker of Mrs Bannerman to the notice of the police. Whoever it was might do something else, Jim reasoned, and be picked up for that.

Passing a filling station, he thought about trying to raid a till, but at this hour they were all much too busy. That was a crime for the dead hours. However, he might be able to deal with his hair at one; many had washrooms behind, and unlike public lavatories, they were small, often unisex, if he remembered correctly, and little used. There was still plenty of petrol in the car; he had no need to waste money buying more and he decided to park openly at the side of the forecourt, out of the way of other customers. and hurry round to the back of the place as if in some discomfort.

Jim stopped at the next one, tucking the car into a corner and slipping round behind the buildings to where there was a chilly little cubicle containing a basin and lavatory. He locked himself in and had a quick cold shave while the rinse was taking, not daring to wait for the recommended length of time, but no one came and rattled the door while he was inside; most customers were in a hurry to get home. He'd been lucky to find the place unlocked. He remembered Maureen having to ask for a key before now, when she and Nicola had wished to pay a visit.

No one questioned him. A damp honey blond, with a clean fresh chin, wearing new socks, Jim drove steadily on. He had shoved his old pair of socks into his pocket; he'd wash them when he got a chance. He hated wearing dirty socks.

He would have to dump the car. It would probably have been reported stolen by now and he could be stopped at any minute. Jim knew about the computer which verified registration numbers instantly.

He turned left at a junction, anxious to get away from the heaviest traffic. There was less chance of being stopped on a minor road, or so he hoped.

He had to concentrate, however: the road was twisty

and there were a lot of sharp bends. Some impatient people dashed past him when he thought it most unsafe to do so. Eventually he came to a very steep descent; he went down it behind a lorry, engaging low gear as advised by a notice beside the road. It was dark now, so Jim did not see spread before him the glorious plain beneath Edge Hill, site of a famous battle in the Civil War. He concentrated on keeping a safe distance from the lorry, which he passed later, and before long found himself entering Stratford-upon-Avon.

He had studied *Julius Caesar* at school and before his marriage had enjoyed the theatre but he had no time to think about Shakespeare now.

He decided to leave the car in a quiet road where it might not attract attention straight away. He turned off at a large roundabout, filtering into the traffic, then took a side turning which led him into a residential road. He parked the car there, between two others, and walked off with his carrier bag of toilet things and the two car keys. He might find them useful.

He knew he looked very different now from the man in the photograph. Colouring his hair had made him look younger, he had decided in the washroom. He would get something to eat – there would be plenty of places in such a popular tourist town – and they wouldn't all be expensive. He passed one big hotel before walking over Clopton Bridge and ahead was the mass of another. To his left, its lights glinting in the water of the river, was the theatre. A lot of traffic was crossing the bridge and there were a great many people on foot. Jim felt uncomfortable among them, but they offered protection, intent as they all were on going on their own way, some of them to the theatre. Jim did not know that there were now three in the town.

Very soon he saw several restaurants, and most displayed menus outside. Jim studied them and chose one that seemed among the least expensive. It was busy, and he thought he would not attract attention among so many other people. He ordered fish and chips, ate them as quickly as possible and then went back to the safety of the street. The food had done him good; he had eaten nothing since his meal at Reading station early that morning.

He walked past the Memorial Theatre and saw cars in the road beside some gardens. A few might be unlocked, but it was a busy, well-lit area and if he started trying doors looking for wallets or purses, he would soon be observed. He went on and turned right, passing an old timbered house, something to do with Shakespeare, he supposed. *Hall's Croft*, he read on a plaque.

He walked right through the town, which was easily done in quite a short time, and finally he went into an old, dark pub furnished with oak tables and benches, and, though his money had almost gone, he ordered a beer.

It gave him courage, and he got his chance as the place filled. One group of people left a corner by the fireplace under a low beam, and he took a vacant place on an oak settle. The woman who had already set her handbag down on the floor had no reason to suspect the quiet fair man in the anorak who sat beside her, staring into space. She talked animatedly with her three companions who faced away from Jim, and no one noticed him hook a foot round the bag and draw it towards him, then bend down and take out her purse. He manoeuvred the bag back to its original position before finishing his drink and leaving. She did not miss her purse until the next morning.

Once outside the pub, Jim walked rapidly up the road expecting to hear shouts of 'Stop, thief!' at any second, but there was no pursuit.

There was a lot of money in the purse, enough to pay for an overnight stay at a bed and breakfast place and have plenty over. There were credit cards, too. Jim was calmly proud: all he'd needed was nerve, and it had worked. He returned to a street where, earlier, he had noticed a number of houses displaying bed and breakfast signs and picked the most modest, putting on his best manner as he spoke to the landlady and quite impressing her by his pleasant approach. He looked vaguely familiar and she asked him if he had stayed there before, but he said no.

She had seen Jim's mug shot on the television news at six o'clock, but his blond hair dye had effectively changed his appearance, and she had other worries on her mind as she answered the door to this late caller.

In the morning, Jim thought of leaving without paying, but that would only arouse suspicion, and anyway the woman was entitled to her money. Instead, he enjoyed the excellent breakfast she provided, eggs and bacon, fried bread and sausage, and departed, bathed and with his singlet, socks and pants washed and dried over the heater in his room.

From the house, he walked straight to Marks and Spencer's, which he had seen the evening before. The purse he had taken contained a Marks and Spencer's charge card and Jim had studied it carefully. L. Wilson was the woman's name, and she had signed it Lesley. That was a unisex name, though men, he thought, spelled it with an *ie* at the end. He practised her signature on a corner of newspaper until he could do it easily; he was good at that sort of thing. He used the card to buy trousers, a shirt, a blue crew-neck sweater and a small holdall. No one challenged his signature and the card had not yet been reported lost.

He changed into his new clothes in a public lavatory, bundling up his prison garb into the carrier from the Banbury chemist and dumping it in a litter bin he saw in the street. Then he went to the railway station. He'd go to Birmingham, a huge city, where he might be able to survive.

There would be other chances to steal enough money to live on, or he might get a job and he could use Lesley Wilson's bank card to charge up small amounts.

On the way to the station, he bought a newspaper and looked in it for news of Mrs Bannerman. She had not made the front page of the national press, and he saw only a small paragraph inside, but there was a grainy photograph of him reproduced from the one taken when he was arrested. SAVAGE ATTACK. MAN WANTED, he read.

Jim had looked at himself in a plate-glass window as he walked along and was satisfied with his disguise. His moustache was meagre, but another couple of days would make a difference. He might get a jacket to match his new trousers, and then he would look like the white-collar worker he had been before his conviction.

By nightfall, he had acquired the jacket and had rented a room in a cheap lodging house in an area of dark rows of terraced houses some way from the centre of Birmingham. He went down the road to a pub for something to eat; it was noisy and crowded there, and he hid behind a newspaper, not wanting to talk. There was a television set in the bar, and he saw on the news that Audrey Bannerman had died that afternoon.

Jim was wanted for murder.

He fled from the pub before any of the drinkers present connected the well-dressed man with sparse blond hair and an infant moustache with the depressed image now flashed upon the screen.

Jim rushed back to his dingy room and locked himself in.

Now he was well and truly on the run.

16

After the police had driven her and Robin home, Yvonne found it hard to concentrate on any of the things she should be doing. They had taken a statement, which she had signed, and they had treated her with kindness, aware that she had undergone a shocking experience. Robin was the only one to have found the morning thoroughly satisfactory, with the comings and goings of the various vehicles and the final treat of the ride in the white car with its blue light on the roof, which the driver had operated for his entertainment as soon as they passed through the gates of Ford House.

She had just suggested that Robin should bring some toys upstairs to her workroom when she remembered that her car was still out of action.

If Charles had started it for her, she would have driven straight past Ivy Lodge without giving a thought to Audrey, who would still be lying on her kitchen floor. She could have lain there all day, even for several days, without being discovered. It was a terrible thought.

Yvonne telephoned a garage who sent out a man in a van. He was able to start her car and fitted a new battery.

'This'll last for years,' he told her. 'Modern ones do, but they run down if you leave the lights on and that sort of thing.'

'I know,' said Yvonne, who had not left the lights on but had never replaced the battery since she had had the Mini. This little incident was going to cost money and she would have to find it; why should Charles pay for her car?

That afternoon she rang up the hospital to ask about Audrey, wondering as she did so whether anyone else would bother to inquire. She learned that after an operation, Audrey was in a critical condition and in intensive care.

Charles arrived home at eight o'clock, earlier than usual. He had telephoned from the car to tell her when to expect him. Most evenings she got on with some work after Robin was tucked up. She had weakly lapsed into allowing the others to watch television if they had nothing else to do, though there had been a time when they played games or read together before bed. She comforted herself by reflecting that they were older now, and more independent, but she resolved that as the winter approached she would sit with them round the fire, even if she had to be sewing.

Over dinner, she told Charles about Audrey.

'I told you those convicts shouldn't be allowed out in the village,' he said.

'Charles, it was awful. She lay there on the kitchen floor with blood in her hair and I thought she was dead. She's very likely to die, in fact.'

'Poor darling, what a shock for you,' said Charles.

'Yes, it was,' Yvonne said. 'I climbed into the house through her bedroom window, the way the burglar went.'

'It might have been wiser to call the police and let them do the climbing,' Charles suggested.

'It would have taken longer. I'd got her covered up with blankets and a hot-water bottle by the time they arrived,' said Yvonne.

'Well done,' said Charles, spearing a piece of potato with his fork and hoovering it round his plate to absorb the sauce from the pork chops Yvonne had casseroled.

'Charles, this is Coxton, not some inner city. Audrey was mugged,' said Yvonne.

'Well, you were the one who wanted to live in the country,' said Charles.

Alan and Tracy had not heard about the crime in

Coxton. Alan's work that day had lain in the other direction, and the news had not been discussed in Tracy's supermarket. Unable to face them over the evening meal, Denis called on her at her check-out after the cinema to tell her that he would not be in to eat. He went to McDonald's and had a hamburger, then stood on a street corner talking to some boys from school. He told them he was leaving Leckerton and joining the Marines.

'Pull the other one,' said one boy.

'It's the truth,' Denis declared, and in that moment it became his intention.

'They won't take you,' jeered another boy.

'You'll see,' Denis told him.

Eventually the other boys drifted off to the snooker club and Denis decided to go back to the van. He would be safe there, in the darkness, curled up in his sleeping bag listening to his tapes. The old woman must be all right by now, and Len would have got clean away. He'd been wrong to hit her like that. She was only an old bag, true, but she'd done nothing to harm Len, and she'd let Denis wash her car and paid him a fair price. Len could have tied her up or something, stuffed a rag in her mouth to keep her quiet. Denis would have lent a hand with that. Or would he? Thinking about it, he wasn't sure. He wouldn't have liked touching her, feeling her flesh, knowing that she was a person, not a beetle to be treated like this.

He didn't like his uncomfortable thoughts and he turned his mind towards Ford House and the problem of whether or not he should go there the next day. Mrs Davies would be expecting him, and he'd quite like to complete turning over the vegetable bed. He'd quit when that was done, and he might help himself to a few things from the place before leaving, but then again, he might not. Mrs Davies was sharp and she'd miss even a quid from her purse. She'd know who had had the opportunity to lift it, and she wouldn't have any mercy.

If Len had got into Ford House the previous night, he might have mugged Mrs Davies.

That was a new and unwelcome thought, with those kids in the house and all. You couldn't just go about mugging anyone who got in your way. Lifting things was different, especially from a shop, when they didn't belong to anyone. Shops could afford it, even expected thieving, and a bloke had to look after himself. The main thing was not to get caught and that wasn't easy, with video cameras fitted all over the place and people disguised as ordinary shoppers who were really detectives.

Denis was up early on Friday morning and he told Tracy he would go to the launderette for her that afternoon, if she liked. She was grateful, and said she would leave out two bags of washing and some money.

She was worrying about having Denis there. The school authorities might catch up with him, and it was asking a lot of Alan to let him sleep in the van. Luckily Denis would always do as she said and he was a good kid in some ways, but it wasn't right for him to be hanging about with no proper work, though she knew he had washed a good few cars, and he had this gardening job over at Coxton. Alan had been amazed that he had stuck to it but Denis had always liked that sort of thing. Tracy could remember their visits to their grandparents years ago. They had lived in a village near the sea and Denis had liked helping their grandfather dig and feed the chickens and mend fences; he was good with his hands, and if he could take up some practical work he would be all right. She supposed he would have to survive in this hand-to-mouth way till his birthday but after that he would have to leave. He'd be able to sign on, if he couldn't find a job straight away, and he could get digs somewhere.

It was a pity their grandparents weren't still in that village; he could have gone to them. Their grandmother had died and their grandfather was in a home. Tracy meant to visit him, but it was a long way and she hadn't managed to do it yet.

Denis was really quite thoughtful. Many a kid wouldn't have bothered to mention that he wasn't coming in to eat, like he had the previous evening, and now he'd offered to do the washing. She was sure he'd remember: look how he kept giving her money for food. He was all right; once he got going in the adult world, he'd make out.

Denis was lucky in getting a lift to Coxton that morning but the motorist who stopped for him dropped him outside the village and he had to walk through it, past Ivy Lodge.

A policeman stood outside the house and part of the garden was marked off with white tapes. What did that mean? His scalp prickled as he continued on past the bus stop towards Ford House. He was nearly there when Mrs Davies stopped beside him, on her way back from dropping the children at school and playgroup.

'Hop in, Denis. Save yourself five minutes,' she said, as she leaned over to open the passenger door.

'Been keeping all right, then?' he asked brightly, getting in.

'Yes, thanks,' said Yvonne. 'You too, I hope. We're lucky not to be lying half dead in Leckerton Hospital.'

Denis blinked.

'Why?' he asked cautiously.

'Mrs Bannerman is. Haven't you heard?' said Yvonne. 'You've met her – she came to tea once when you were here. About two weeks ago it was, I think. She lives at Ivy Lodge. You must have seen the policeman outside.'

'Yeah. I wondered what was up,' said Denis.

'Someone broke into her house during Wednesday

night and attacked her. Left her for dead,' said Yvonne. 'But she wasn't, quite. I found her the next morning.'

'You did?' Denis stared at her in astonishment. 'How come?'

They had arrived outside the house now. Yvonne unfastened her seat belt and got out of the car, and Denis slowly did the same.

'I was passing and saw her curtains drawn and the milk on the step,' answered Yvonne. 'It was on the television news last night. Didn't you see it?'

'No. I don't see much telly,' said Denis.

'They think it was one of the men from the prison,' said Yvonne. 'Someone escaped that night and was on the run. A man called Sawyer. I think he was the man who did some work for Mrs Bannerman.'

'Never!' said Denis, truly amazed.

'That's what the police think,' Yvonne said. 'He took her car.'

'Bloody hell!' Denis could not believe it. Now the heat would be off and he could breathe freely. He beamed at her.

'It's nothing to grin about, Denis,' Yvonne rebuked him sharply. 'Mrs Bannerman may die.'

'Oh, I'm not laughing at that, Mrs Davies,' said Denis quickly, composing his features into a more solemn expression. 'I was just thinking it was smart to get on to the villains so fast.'

'Only one villain, Denis,' said Yvonne. 'As far as we know.'

Trevor was off nights now, and when he came back after his shift on Thursday, he already knew that Jim had escaped.

'I've got something to tell you, love,' he said to Maureen, just as she was about to utter the very same words.

'You first,' she said.

157

In the end, what he had to say made it easier for her.

'A policewoman came round this morning,' she said. 'She seemed to think he might come here.' How easy it was not to mention that that was exactly what had happened.

'There's a bit more to it now,' said Trevor. 'The WPC wouldn't have known, if she came so early.' Maureen had explained that the visit was before she went to work.

'Known what?' Had he been recaptured? Been hurt, perhaps, in some chase? Maureen wanted to think that it served him right, but she couldn't; it would be so typical of Jim to make a mess of things, even get in the way of a bullet.

'He's wanted for assaulting an elderly woman,' said Trevor. 'It seems he broke into a house in a village where he'd worked when he was out from the nick on one of those schemes. She was found there this morning, unconscious, and the place had been done over.'

'Oh no! Oh, I don't believe it!' Maureen stared at him. 'Jim wouldn't do a thing like that.'

'Wouldn't he? He'd need money, on the run. He took her car and everything of any use from her handbag.' Trevor, on patrol, had been looking out for the Fiat.

'But then – ' Maureen began. She had been about to say that Jim had been glad to have the twenty pounds she had given him. He wouldn't have needed that, if he'd robbed someone. 'That's not like Jim,' she said instead. 'He was never violent.' She pictured him crouched on the floor in the hall. That weeping man couldn't hurt a mouse, much less an old woman.

'Well, it seems that he did,' said Trevor. 'She's pretty bad. You must face it, love. The local lads have found his dabs eveywhere. There's quite enough evidence to get a conviction. If she dies he'll be down for murder, though a sharp brief might get a manslaughter verdict.'

'But he hasn't been caught?'

'Not yet. It's only a matter of time.'

'People seem to escape and not get caught,' Maureen pointed out.

'Hardly ever,' said Trevor. 'In the end they give themselves away. They need cash and food. They can't stay in hiding unless they've got pals to help them, and I doubt if Jim has those sort of friends. I suppose he went stir-crazy and just had to get out. It's easy enough at these open places.'

Someone might have seen him in this neighbourhood that morning. Well, she would deny that she had done so, whatever happened and however many times she was asked. She wanted no more trouble. All the same, it was hard to believe that Jim could have resorted to violence and she said so again.

'He just isn't like that,' she repeated.

'The woman probably disturbed him and he got scared,' said Trevor. 'That's how it happens. That's why he might get manslaughter.'

'Has anyone thought that somebody else could have done it?' Maureen demanded. 'Why are they so sure it was Jim?'

'Well, his prints were there and he broke out that night,' said Trevor. 'Who else could it have been?'

'You said he'd worked for the woman. That could explain the prints.'

'Sorry, love. It looks like an open and shut case,' said Trevor. 'He'll be running now.'

Maureen shivered and clasped her hands over her chest.

'I'm going to get a divorce, Trev,' she said. 'I'm not taking any more of this. I want out.'

'That's my girl,' said Trevor. They'd discussed it often enough. He'd have to face up to it now, taking her and the kiddie on properly, doing it right. Once the bloke was locked up for a good spell, it wouldn't be difficult; no chance of him suddenly turning up and making a scene.

'Don't let him in, if he comes here,' he warned. 'He might think you would help him.'

'No chance,' said Maureen. 'I'd turn him right in.'

17

After all the rain, the soil was heavy and clogged Denis's fork as he dug. He felt quite sorry that he would not see what grew here in the spring. He should finish his task today, which was just as well because the ground was almost too wet to work. There wasn't much to do in a garden in the winter, and he didn't think Mrs Davies would have other jobs lined up for him. It might be safer to stay away from Coxton for a while; he hadn't liked seeing that policeman outside Mrs Bannerman's house. Coppers were apt to ask you what you were doing when you were simply minding your own business, and they could soon fit you up with a charge when they wanted to score a few arrests.

'You'll not be needing me any more,' he told Yvonne after she had inspected his completed work.

'Well, you'll soon be starting your YTS programme, won't you?' she said.

'I'm going into the Marines instead,' Denis announced.

'Are you? What a good idea. You'll see the world,' said Yvonne. 'Your parents don't object, then?'

'Why should they?'

'Well, you said you live with your grandmother because you can't get along with them,' she reminded him.

'They'll be glad to get rid of me,' said Denis with conviction.

He didn't seem to feel sorry for himself; Yvonne studied his round face with its tough expression. He'd had rebuffs enough in his life, she thought.

'Where does your grandmother live?' she asked. 'In what part of Leckerton?'

'Why do you want to know?' Denis asked warily.

'I'd like to know where to find you, in case I have some odd jobs to be done before you go,' she replied. 'You'd think about doing some painting, wouldn't you?' She and Charles were going to take months to get through what had to be done.

'I might,' he allowed. 'It's Seven Birch Street, near the old asylum. But you'd better write, not call. My gran's a bit forgetful and she might not pass on the message if I was out.'

'Very well,' said Yvonne. 'What's your last name, Denis?'

He would not tell her the truth.

'Crow,' he said, at random, not consciously thinking of the old woman who lived at the back of the house.

'Right,' said Yvonne. 'I'll give you some lunch today, Denis, and run you back into town. I'm going to see Mrs Bannerman this afternoon.'

The thought that Audrey might lie there without any visitors had distressed her. What matter if she seemed to be in a coma? She might drift in and out of consciousness and be vaguely aware of a friendly presence. Yvonne had arranged to take Robin round to the vicarage, where Amy Parker would look after him for a couple of hours. It was the first time she had asked such a favour from anyone in the village. She must do it again and show herself willing to have other children round to play. They all needed a social circle.

Yvonne had asked whether the vicar was going to see how Audrey was, and learned he had been to the hospital the previous evening. At the moment there was nothing he could usefully do, he had said. Audrey was deeply unconscious. The hospital had its own chaplain who would see her on his regular rounds. The vicar would keep in touch and would pray for Audrey, but he had other claims on his time.

Fat lot of good that would do, thought Yvonne,

offended by such logic. Audrey should not be left to the total care of strangers.

She asked Denis to tidy up the garden shed while she went to fetch Robin from playgroup. Then the three of them sat round the kitchen table eating mashed potato with mince and carrots. The amount Yvonne had prepared would have fed her and Robin several times but there was none left after Denis had had two big helpings. They had stewed apples and custard for pudding.

'You'll get well fed in the Marines, Denis,' said Yvonne.

'I've not applied yet,' he said cautiously. 'I haven't found out how to do it.'

'The library would know,' said Yvonne. 'That's the place to go for that sort of information. I expect there's somewhere you can write to for forms and things.'

She made it sound simple, and she dropped him outside the library on her way to the hospital.

'Let me know how you get on, Denis,' she said.

He gave her a casual, embarrassed wave as he sauntered towards the swing doors of the library, his Walkman in place. That would have to go, for a start, she thought, if the Marines took him. Was he old enough to join? He was an odd, tiresome boy, and yet there was good in him, waiting to be drawn out. He worked hard and he'd been nice to Robin. The Marines could be the making of him.

Yvonne was told at the hospital that Audrey was too ill for visitors, except relatives, but when she explained that it was she who had found her, Yvonne was allowed to go into the ward.

An elderly man was sitting beside Audrey's bed. He had thick silver hair and, as he rose to his feet at Yvonne's approach, she saw that he had piercing blue eyes under strong, bushy brows.

Rupert Bannerman introduced himself.

How weird, thought Yvonne. Here was Audrey's ex-husband. What a marvellous looking old boy!

'I was afraid no one would come,' she said aloud.

'That's why I'm here,' he replied.

Yvonne couldn't imagine her ex-husband feeling the slightest pang if she ended up in such a state.

'Tell me how you came to find her,' said Rupert, who had heard only a bare account from Detective Superintendent Hawkes.

In a quiet voice Yvonne explained, glancing now and then at the unconscious woman as she spoke.

'I was too late, though,' she said. 'If she'd been found sooner —'

'I don't know,' said Rupert. 'Maybe. I doubt if anyone can tell. Her heart's none too good, it seems. She had a slight heart attack some time ago, but I didn't know that.'

'Fancy leaving her in that state, though. I mean, whoever did it — fancy going off,' said Yvonne.

'Well, whoever was responsible was hardly likely to ring for an ambulance before making his getaway,' said Rupert with a smile for this rather solemn young woman. Finding Audrey unconscious must have been a shocking experience. He said so.

'It was, and I so nearly didn't go in,' said Yvonne. 'Only the day before she'd given me and my children a lift because my car wouldn't start.'

'Did — do you know her well?'

'No. I don't think anyone did, in the village,' said Yvonne, unconsciously using the past tense.

Yvonne had heard the other play group mothers discussing the attack. Few had spoken to Audrey though most had seen her about the village and one had wondered why she didn't have a dog, as she seemed to like walking.

'She was very shy,' said Rupert. 'Most people manage to cope with that as they grow older, but she never did.'

164

He frowned. 'My fault, perhaps.' He smiled again, turning his sharp gaze towards Yvonne. 'So you live at Ford House. It's a nice old place. I think Audrey hoped to put the clock back in some way by returning to Coxton, looking for some sort of security she had in her childhood, but one can never do that.'

'It's changed,' said Yvonne, 'It's bigger. There are quite a few new houses, and it's deserted by day except for mothers with young children and a few retired couples. Everyone else goes to work. There are plenty of jobs in Leckerton.'

Rupert nodded. He had driven through the town's expanding industrial area.

'Does your husband work here?' he asked.

'No.' Yvonne explained about Charles's job.

'A lot of travelling,' was Rupert's comment.

'Yes, but it's worth it to live in the country.' To Rupert, Yvonne suddenly sounded defensive. 'I'll have to go,' she said. 'I've got to pick up my children from school.'

'Give me your telephone number,' said Rupert. 'I'll let you know if there's any news.'

'You're staying?'

He nodded.

'Someone must hold her hand if she's dying,' he said.

Yvonne had been home for only half an hour when he telephoned to tell her that Audrey had died.

In Detective Superintendent Hawkes's opinion, there was no mystery about how Audrey Bannerman had met her death. She was the victim of a savage assault made by Jim Sawyer after he absconded from Lockley Prison, and he had to be found and arrested without delay. There was plenty of evidence with which to convict him: his prints were in the house and especially in the kitchen, where she had been attacked, though he had left none on a glass from which he had drunk some whisky. It could

165

not have been Audrey who used the glass or hers would have been found. There were other prints about, of course, some of them the dead woman's, and naturally she would have had visitors. There was no sign of the weapon, something thin but heavy, the surgeon who had operated on Audrey had said. A poker from the house had been inspected, but bore no traces of such misuse and Audrey's own fingerprints were on the handle.

House-to-house inquiries in Coxton had not been productive. Audrey's immediate neighbours, a young couple on one side and a middle-aged woman on the other, all said that they barely knew her. She seemed to want to keep herself to herself. The young couple had asked her round for coffee after dinner one evening but she had refused. The middle-aged woman, an account-ant working in Leckerton, had exchanged a few words with her when they met in the road, but, she said, to be frank, Mrs Bannerman had not seemed very friendly and so she had not asked her round. Of course she regretted that now.

On the night in question, the middle-aged woman had been woken by the sound of a car starting up nearby, but she had gone straight back to sleep and had not noticed the time. The couple had heard nothing.

The detective constable who had visited these neigh-bours had noticed some tyre marks on the grass verge just past Ivy Lodge, but as the man they were seeking had taken Mrs Bannerman's car, they seemed irrelevant and he did not mention them in his report.

No one else in the village had noticed anything unusual. Percy Bates, who lived with his widowed mother near the church, had been coming home from Leckerton some time after three o'clock in the morning and had met a blue van which was wandering about all over the road, but as he had had a heavy night out himself, which had ended up in an illicit amorous adventure, he kept quiet, too. It was, anyway, nothing to do with what had happened; the police were not asking about sightings of vehicles other than Mrs Bannerman's Fiat.

Jim Sawyer had taken a prison cycle, and that hadn't been found. He must have abandoned it, as it would not have fitted into the Fiat. A search for it in the neighbourhood had so far been unsuccessful. Some boys might have found it and put it to use. It had to be traced.

In a village eight miles from Lockley Prison, and twelve miles from Coxton, a Honda pick-up had been stolen from outside a house. Some miles further on a man's anorak had disappeared from a pub. Had it not been for the crime in Coxton, these episodes might have been linked with the prison escape, but because of the attack, they were thought to be separate incidents. So far, the pick-up had not been found.

Hawkes looked at the other reports. A woman travelling by bus from Reading to Oxford had sat next to Jim Sawyer on Thursday morning. Well, he would have had plenty of time to get there after committing the crime, though he would surely realize that the police would look for him there. The Fiat might turn up in Reading, since clearly he had dumped it. A car had been stolen from a Park and Ride car park in Oxford later that day. That could have been Sawyer.

It seemed, for the moment, as if he had got clean away, but he'd show up soon. He would start passing Audrey's cheques or using her bank card.

The police had found her bank statements, neatly filed away in a drawer, and they had been able to put a stop on her account.

No one who lived in the quiet road where Jim had left his stolen car had thought of mentioning its arrival to the police. It was in no one's way, and for all anyone knew had been acquired by a resident.

18

Rupert told Felicity that the inquest would be opened on
Monday so that funeral arrangements could be made for
Audrey.

His face was grey. The last time Felicity had seen him
looking like this was after Hesther had died.

'She was really being kept alive by technology,' he
said. 'In the end her heart beat even that.'

'From what you've said, she can't have known a lot
about what happened,' suggested Felicity.

'No, I don't suppose she did.' And she wouldn't have
known that he was there at the end, not that such
knowledge would have been any comfort to her.

'It's no good making yourself wretched by feeling
responsible for what's happened,' said Felicity gently.
'It's like a road accident. She just got in the way of that
man.'

'You're right, of course.' But if she had still been living
at Tettlebury, she wouldn't have been in Coxton that
night.

'You said there'd been no struggle.'

'No. She was knocked out cold from behind with some
sort of heavy rod or bar,' said Rupert. 'I've spoken to her
solicitor – a man in Sussex. She wants – wanted to be
buried in Coxton near her parents. I've agreed to meet
him at her house to discuss things. There isn't anyone
else. I'm sorry, darling, but I'll have to do it.'

'Of course you must see to things, Rupert,' said
Felicity. 'She's always been your responsibility.'

'Friday, we thought,' Rupert said. 'For the funeral I
mean. The vicar's got to go to some meeting or other on
Thursday and said that would be difficult. Wednesday
seemed a bit soon after the inquest, somehow.'

'Friday seems a good choice,' said Felicity, thinking drat the vicar and his previous engagement, though it would make no difference to poor Audrey.

'We'll be in for a battering, I'm afraid,' said Rupert. 'The press will probably drag all that up about Hesther again. It's too much to hope that no one will remember and make the connection.'

If they missed it now, they wouldn't when the man Sawyer was caught and brought up for trial.

'It can't hurt her now, or her mother,' said Felicity. 'It can only hurt you, my dear, and by extension, me. It will pass,' she added. 'Things do.'

At the Bell in Coxton the talk was all of their local murder. Television and newspaper reporters flocked to the village seeking people to provide human interest stories about the dead woman, and they soon discovered that she had been found by someone who lived in Audrey Bannerman's former home. That could be turned into a real tear-jerker.

No one had much to say about the dead woman herself. She had never been into the Bell, though she walked about the village and used the shop. One woman said she often took the field path to the river, when it wasn't too wet. She had no dog, so there was no moping pet needing a home.

'A cat?' someone asked, but no: she had not had even a canary.

'A recluse,' one reporter suggested, and it seemed that to some extent she was, though it was known that she had been to France the summer before. She drove into Leckerton two or three times a week, presumably to shop. She did not employ a cleaning woman, though she had made inquiries about finding someone. Such help was difficult to get in the village; people preferred to work in Leckerton factories and several firms arranged transport for their employees.

Old Mrs Feathers, who always went into the snug for a stout at six o'clock sharp, remembered the family at Ford House before Audrey married. The father had been respected, even liked; he did all the right things, subscribing to village appeals and allowing the garden to be used for fêtes, though it was too far out to be much requested. The mother was frail, almost an invalid. Audrey had been a quiet girl and Mrs Feathers remembered nothing remarkable about her except her wedding in the church, an affair of white satin and tulle. She'd looked nice enough; most girls did on their wedding day, Mrs Feathers opined, but she was never a beauty. The family had not lived in the village through generations, as their predecessors at Ford House had done; they had made little impact.

The reporters departed to go to Ford House. They'd get some reactions from Mrs Davies.

As they left, Mrs Feathers spoke to the landlord.

'Ring Ford House, Albert,' she said. 'It's a shame what these people do and she's got those three kiddies to get to bed. Tell her to lock herself in and keep those reporters outside.'

The other regulars thought this was a good idea, and Albert managed to get through just in time. Yvonne was battened down, not responding, by the time the press came battering at her door. She rang the police and asked them to come and send the reporters away.

When Charles arrived back on Friday night he found a small group of them in the road. As the gates were closed he had to get out of the car to open them. The journalists converged round him like bees round their hive.

'How do you feel about your wife finding the body?' called one.

'How well did you know the dead woman?' asked another.

Until now, Charles had not known that Audrey had

died. Yvonne had not told him when he telephoned to announce his time of arrival. In silence, he pushed through the mob to get into the car again and edged forwards as if he were driving through a flock of sheep.

Grim-faced Charles Davies returns to fatal mansion, said one paper less than accurately the next morning, and showed a blurred photograph of a scowling Charles.

He was furious. The weekend would be ruined if the house were under siege from the press. If only Yvonne had minded her own business, they would not have been involved.

He knew he was being unreasonable. Her warm heart was one of her charms. He had bought her some flowers because he knew he had been short-tempered lately, but things seemed to be slipping from his control. Charles liked to feel that he was in charge.

'He can't go on living in the van,' said Alan.

'I know.'

Denis had taken the washing to the launderette, as he promised, and brought it back all nicely tumble-dried. Now Tracy was folding what could be worn unpressed, and making a pile of things to be ironed. She liked ironing.

'What's he going to do?' Alan asked. 'It'll be too cold out there soon.'

'He wants to join the Marines,' said Tracy. 'He went to the library today and found out how to apply. He's got an address to write to.'

'What a good idea!'

'Yes. If he gets in, they'll look after him – give him somewhere to live, and a training,' said Tracy. 'They'll take you at sixteen.'

'He'd see the world,' said Alan enthusiastically.

'Yes,' said Tracy. 'He's a funny one, sort of a loner. He's never been one to run with the other kids and he doesn't seem interested in girls.'

'Late developer,' Alan pronounced.

'Maybe. Anyway, it's his birthday soon and after that he'll be able to sign on and go to the Job Centre in the proper way, if the Marines don't take him straight off. I expect there are things you have to do first, like pass the doctor.'

'Well, he seems fit enough,' said Alan.

'Yes. He likes all that outdoor stuff. The Marines would suit him. Or the army. Anything like that,' Tracy said. 'You didn't know you were taking him on too, when you rescued me,' she added, getting out the iron and plugging it in.

'I needed a woman,' said Alan. 'Otherwise I'd got to do my own ironing, hadn't I?'

She threw a towel at him and he caught her wrists and pulled her down to him, both of them laughing, Tracy pretending reluctance to turn her face to his. She had to break free to unplug the iron and as she turned eagerly back to him, the fleeting question went through her head as to whether her parents had ever felt like this: had she been conceived in such a moment of joy? If so, how had things managed to go so terribly wrong?

She knew that her parents still came together, but it was in a fierce act of hate; never love.

Later, watching television, they learned for the first time of the attack in Coxton and that the victim had died. There were shots of the village and of Detective Superintendent Hawkes referring to 'this heartless assault on an elderly woman.'

'Poor old soul,' said Tracy. 'I wonder if Denis met her when he was working over there. I must ask him.'

But Denis did not come in for breakfast until they were leaving for work, and by then she had forgotten.

He spent most of Saturday washing cars, and as the recent weather had made them extremely dirty, he had plenty of customers. The rain held off, and on Sunday he was washing the van when Tracy and Alan surfaced. He had got water from Mrs Crow, who had let him use her Fairy Liquid, and he scrubbed away, wiping off what he could of the scrape he had caused and cleaning the wheels.

Tracy and Alan were going to spend the day in the country. He pretended that he had arranged to meet a friend, and when they had gone he locked himself in their room where he spent the day.

Len and his family had a lovely day out on Saturday. The rain held off and they went to Alton Towers, where the children had a high old time, or Len decided they did, ignoring Bruce's near hysteria on the roller-coaster.

Complacent because Jim Sawyer was being blamed for what he had done, Len had not given a thought to his victim, and he did not learn she had died until the next morning, when he went down to the corner shop to buy the paper. The attack was written up in sensational terms and Jim's photograph, enlarged and grainy, was published again. It did not look very like him, Len decided, squinting at it critically.

He had better return the hired car. It was a shame to give it up so soon, but when the police discovered that the stolen bank card had been used in Bristol, which they would soon enough, they'd be nosing about down there looking for more clues and they might find the Fiat. He'd better sever his connections with the place.

He told Bet he'd be gone for most of the day. She was quite upset; she'd made up her mind that they'd have another day out, maybe go to the coast.

'Sorry,' he said. 'Some other time.'

After he had gone, she pottered about doing a bit of dusting. It was nice having him at home and in funds. Her philosophy was to enjoy this good spell while she could. He'd get done again one day, that was certain, and in time she would have to find someone else; this was an insecure way of life but it was great while it lasted.

173

He'd given her quite a flash ring, rubies and diamonds. It was old-fashioned, not really her style, but it fitted and she'd worn it all day yesterday.

It might be worth a bit, if he went down again. She decided to hide it away so that he couldn't get hold of it and sell it himself, if the money ran out. The children were watching cartoons on television, not interested in what she was doing. Bet buried it in a bag of flour in the store cupboard.

After taking this precaution, she sat down at the kitchen table to have a smoke and a cup of coffee. She was still in her dressing gown, a pink quilted one she'd treated herself to before Len came out. She hadn't let herself go while he was inside; her looks and her bright manner had got her the job in the bar and these were assets she took care of, for they were all she had. You had only yourself to depend on, when it came to the crunch; the odd bit of luck on the way was just that: a bonus. Len would never be in the league who set up major heists and ended up living in Spain. Sooner or later he made a mistake, or got rough, or both.

He had left the paper behind. She turned the pages, reading the latest speculation about one royal marriage and a rumoured pregnancy in another. There had been a drugs scandal in the world of show business.

Her attention was drawn to the piece about the events in Coxton rather by chance, when her eye caught the name of Lockley Prison from which the wanted man had escaped. That was where Len had been for the last part of his sentence. She'd visited him with the kids, and each time Bruce had screamed fit to bust, though it was nice there compared with other places he'd been in. He'd worked outside, from Lockley; hadn't he mentioned Coxton?

Bet read the piece carefully. An elderly woman, Mrs Audrey Bannerman, had been attacked by an intruder

174

on Wednesday night and had not been found until Thursday morning.

Len had gone away on Wednesday and had not returned until late on Thursday, with the hired car and the loot. If the paper had not stated, in black and white, that the police wanted to question Jim Sawyer about the crime, she would be wondering where Len had been at the time. The job had just his touch. He took that small cosh whenever he went thieving and look what happened on that last warehouse job. It was a neat little weapon he'd picked up somewhere, a slim leaded club with a narrow, leather-bound handle. He'd shown her how easy it was to tuck it up his sleeve or into his sock.

Bruce had been quite tiny when his father went down for using it on the night watchman. Len was only on parole now, after serving just a third of his sentence; he'd go back fast enough if he offended again.

She would ask him about this Jim Sawyer when he came home from wherever he'd gone, and about Coxton. Or maybe she wouldn't. There were some things it was best not to know.

After seeing the television news on Friday night, Jim slept only fitfully. He kept waking up imagining that any moment he would be arrested and put into a cell. Outside in the street cars passed, and he heard the wail of a police siren which grew louder and louder. He held his breath until it faded away. Towards dawn he gave up and lay on his back with his hands clasped under his head, staring at the ceiling. The immense problem of evading capture was almost too much to contemplate at this chill, dead hour and he longed for his safe room at Lockley. That would be denied him now. There would be no more open prison if he went down for murder, or not for years, and no parole unless he were to admit the offence. He couldn't do that. He hadn't killed that woman.

However little she cared for him, surely Maureen would never believe him capable of such a terrible crime?

His room was damp and cold. There was a gas fire with a meter but he had no matches. He would have to go out and buy a few things to enable him to survive the weekend. If he stayed here for a few days the police would accept that the trail had grown cold and their search would become nationwide. Birmingham was a large city and unless, by ill luck, someone recognized him, he would be relatively safe. In cities there were plenty of people with things to hide and no curiosity about others. It wasn't as if he had a circle of criminal friends whom the police would watch.

Against the increasing traffic noise from the street, a radio suddenly blared in the room below. The fact that there were other people in the building was both a reassurance and disturbing. For so long Jim had been used to institutional life, where his days were ordered, that the effect of locking the door of this shabby room and closing himself in alien isolation had been eerie. All the self-congratulation that had sustained him earlier had evaporated.

The blankets on his bed were frayed and thin and the sheets were rough and scratchy. Lockley Prison seemed like the Ritz by comparison. He almost laughed at the thought. Then the knowledge that no one was looking for the real killer of Mrs Bannerman made him start shaking with fear. That man might be caught only if he attacked someone else, and even then, unless he confessed, who would link him with events in Coxton? For the first time, Jim began to wonder who had been responsible. Was it just chance? Had some passing villain simply had a go? Some lad from the area, perhaps, who knew she lived alone and thought he'd get easy pickings, then panicked when she came downstairs? Mrs Bannerman wouldn't be one to shrink from confronting an intruder; he could imagine her being foolhardy enough to challenge the man.

At last the appalling nature of what had happened to her penetrated through his absorption with his own fate and he felt reluctant anger on her behalf. The real killer must be found, not only to save his own neck but in the name of justice.

The house was stirring. Jim got up and went down to the bathroom on the floor below. It was occupied. He would not risk waiting outside but left his door ajar, hoping to hear when whoever was in there emerged, and as a youth in jeans went pattering down the bare stairs, Jim took his place and locked himself in. He did not want to meet any of the other residents.

He had breakfast at a snack bar among a row of shops some half a mile away. While he ate, he read the paper, which he had bought on the way. The crime was thoroughly reported. Much had been made of Mrs Bannerman's isolation. *Lonely recluse*, declared the tabloid paper he had chosen because the story was on the front page. Inside, there was his photograph again. Did he really look like that?

Jim had scrutinized himself that morning in the small mirror in the bathroom. The pale face that looked back at him as he shaved, carefully missing out his tiny moustache, had not seemed at all familiar, surmounted as it was by its honey hair, but the features were still his, the thin lips not yet shadowed by the growth above them, and the hunted eyes. Perhaps he should get some dark glasses, but wouldn't they draw attention to him?

He looked smart, though, in his suit, almost too smart for this run-down area. He must behave normally, not skulk about in places where the police would be looking for anyone acting suspiciously, not because they expected to find him but because that was their way.

Bracing himself, he left the snack bar and went shopping. He bought a cheap electric kettle, some packets of soup, a loaf of bread, cheese and half a dozen eggs, which he could boil in the kettle. He found some ham sealed in a package. That would do over the weekend. Finally he bought a small radio, because he must somehow survive the time he would spend in hiding.

He'd read a lot in prison. Passing a junk shop with a row of shabby paperbacks displayed outside, Jim picked up the fattest and looked at the first page. *I am born*, he read. He bought *David Copperfield* for twenty pence, and he also bought, for the same price, a bundle of steel cutlery which would provide a spoon, knife and fork, not that he could be fussy about how he ate. On the way back to his room, he thought about milk and instant coffee. Funny how you got out of the way of housekeeping: he'd always enjoyed going shopping with Maureen at weekends.

He had spent a fair bit of money and he would have to get hold of some more. Returning to the house, he saw some letters on a shelf in the hall. One was from the DHSS and he knew what it was, a cheque. He saw another letter addressed to the same name, and he took them both. One would provide proof of his identity when he cashed the cheque contained in the other.

You learned some useful tricks in prison.

19

A red Citroën drew up outside Ford House on Sunday morning.

The three children were in the garden riding their bicycles. Even Robin had a two-wheeler, though with stabilizers attached. He wore a policeman's helmet which had once belonged to Philip and was uttering shrill siren sounds. Emily was pretending to be on a pony and Philip was circling aloofly further afield, as befitted the eldest. He was on his way in a large jet to Australia, and had just reached Singapore. When he arrived in Sydney or Melbourne, or maybe in Perth, he hadn't decided which, his father would meet him and take him out to a farm with a thousand sheep.

When a police officer in uniform got out of the car, the children came towards him. He asked to see their mother, and Philip cycled round to the rear of the house calling out, 'Mum, a policeman wants to see you.'

It was Charles who came to the front door. He wore stained overalls and had a smudge of pale green emulsion on one cheek.

'Can I help you?' he said. 'I'm Charles Davies.'

'It's Mrs Davies I want to see, sir,' said the policeman. 'Constable Moody from the Coroner's office.'

'You'd better come in,' said Charles. 'Carry on playing,' he called to the children. 'And keep well away from the policeman's car. That means you, too, Robin.'

'Fine family you've got there, sir,' said the constable, following Charles into the house.

'Yes,' said Charles. 'The two older ones belong to my wife. The other one's ours.' Sometimes he felt obliged to make this distinction.

'I see, sir,' said Moody calmly.

'I suppose it's about Mrs Bannerman's death,' Charles said. 'I'm sure my wife's told you all she can.'

'I'm sure she has, sir, but she'll be needed at the inquest. That's why I'm here.' As Coroner's officer, PC Moody always tried to deal personally with witnesses.

'Oh, surely that won't be necessary? She only found the body,' said Charles.

'Mrs Bannerman wasn't dead then, Mr Davies,' said Moody. 'I'm afraid she will have to appear.'

Yvonne had been up in her workroom when Philip called. Receiving no answer, he had entered the house by the back door and rushed upstairs to tell her about the visitor. Now she appeared, descending the staircase into the hall, a pale young woman with her long dark hair tied into a pony tail. Moody thought she looked exhausted.

'I must insist that she be excused,' said Charles. 'The whole thing was a most unpleasant experience for her.'

'Charles, please let me speak for myself,' said Yvonne. 'Of course I must go if I'm needed.' She spoke from the half landing and continued on down the stairs, moving in what was almost a glide. She should be wearing a crinoline gown with some of her hair swept up on to the top of her head and ringlets round her ears, thought Moody fancifully. She would look the part of the chatelaine of this sort of house, dressed like that.

'It's only red tape,' said Charles.

'I found poor Audrey. I rang for the police and the ambulance. By climbing through the window I obscured evidence that might have helped the police,' Yvonne recited.

Charles stared at her. He was only trying to help her, have her spared further distress. Why oppose him?

'It's tomorrow at eleven, at the hospital, Mrs Davies,' said PC Moody. 'There's no coroner's court in Leckerton, so inquests have to be held wherever's most convenient and there's a room at the hospital we often use. It's quite handy – no problem over parking and so on.'

'I'll be there,' said Yvonne.

'Can you get there? We can arrange transport, if not,' offered Moody.

'No, that's all right,' said Yvonne. 'I'll have to make some arrangements for Robin. The other children will be at school.'

'If you have to bring him, a police officer will look after him for however long it takes,' said Moody. 'It won't be a long business, it's just to identify the deceased and enable funeral arrangements to be made. It will be adjourned and re-opened at a later date when there's been time to go into all the circumstances.'

'But you know who did it, officer,' said Charles testily. 'This convict. He must have had his eye on the place after working there. They should never be let out to roam around among law-abiding citizens.'

'The man we want to interview was in for fraud, Mr Davies,' said Moody. 'He had no history of violence. And sooner or later most prisoners are returned to society. Best they get gradually acclimatized.' He smiled at Yvonne. 'Thank you, Mrs Davies. I'll see you tomorrow, then.'

'Yes.' She would ask Amy Parker to take Robin for an extra morning and keep him until she collected him.

'If you'd just left that to me, Yvonne, and not interrupted, the constable would soon have seen that your presence at the inquest isn't essential.' Charles spoke brusquely after PC Moody had gone.

'He wouldn't have, Charles. It's legal procedure,' said Yvonne. 'And it's no good you planning to telephone the Chief Constable or our MP to get me let off, because I intend to be there.' She turned away from him and stalked off upstairs.

How had she had known that he was thinking of

ringing the Chief Constable? What had got into her since they came to this house?

He went crossly away, unaware that Yvonne was crying in her workroom. She was afraid. She had pinned all her hopes on the move to this spacious house where they would no longer all be on top of one another but the result was a new isolation.

Charles returned to his painting, viciously daubing great swathes of pale green on the yellowed cream that had previously covered the drawing room walls. He worked thoroughly over the plastered expanse which he had previously washed and rubbed down. He cut no corners with this type of undertaking.

He had painted the house where Olivia and he had lived after their marriage, then he had papered the walls when she tired of their first choice. He had stuck a frieze of animals around Rosalind's room before she was born. He had fetched and carried, dried Olivia's hysterical tears when they fell, worked long hours at the office in order to advance his career and had gradually dropped his own former pursuits, his tennis and squash, his occasional round of golf. Olivia was uninterested in any sport and had begrudged him time thus spent. It wasn't enough, though. She had not been content and in time he had become less ready to placate her; then he had met Yvonne, who seemed to him to need help. Her brave insouciance had been appealing because he had read into it a longing to offload some of her cares. He had been wrong. She was self-reliant and he found that a threat.

He supposed you could live with someone for twenty years and still be surprised by something they said or did.

Playing father to another man's children was not easy; Charles was serious about his role and anxious to provide a strong male influence for Philip. Emily was a pretty little girl, and both children were polite and biddable, but as time passed he began to wonder about their own father, to resent the years he had spent with Yvonne and to wonder what characteristics they had inherited.

You could only do your best, he supposed, and no one could say he had not done that. There were families like his all over the globe, reshuffled like packs of cards.

Now this business in the village – this murder – had come to upset things further. If only Yvonne had not got involved, had left the old woman to be found by somebody else, it need not have affected them and would have made no difference to Mrs Bannerman in the long run. Now they had reporters at their gate and had been obliged to leave the telephone off the hook, since they had had several calls asking for comment. Such notoriety was unfortunate, to say the least.

He painted on. At least the children were playing in the garden, and so far in peaceful concord. Emily was good at watching out for Robin, and Philip, though he sometimes distanced himself from the others, kept an eye on them. It was right for the older ones to have a care for younger children.

Things would improve. Yvonne was over-reacting to the tragedy in the village. He had only wanted to spare her more distress and she would recognize, in time, that he was right.

Jim spent Sunday in his room. It was quieter outside in the street than it had been the day before, and he felt it would be very risky to go out and buy a paper. Suppose his face stared back at him from the front page? It would stare back at every other reader, too.

He had a bath and rinsed his hair again, to make his blondness more secure. It was a pity it was sparse; his disguise would be more effective if he had a thicker crop. His moustache was becoming quite presentable, however; it was neat and dark, with, when you looked at it more closely, some grey hairs among the brown. Perhaps he'd better dye it, too.

There was nothing else to do.

He had bread and cheese for his lunch, and boiled eggs for supper, thinking wistfully of the substantial meal his former companions would be eating in the prison.

That night he slept badly again, missing the fresh air and exercise to which he had become accustomed. Images of Maureen curled up with her lover made him writhe with jealousy, tormenting himself in the darkness. A quarrel broke out somewhere nearby and disturbed the night. He heard insults hurled back and forth between a man and a woman. That was marriage, he thought.

He had spent some of the day listening to the radio, and he had read a great deal of *David Copperfield*, who, despite misfortune, seemed certain to win through. He'd had friends. People didn't have time for friendship these days; all they thought about was sex and money.

On Monday morning he packed up his few belongings, put on his suit and caught a bus into town. It would be foolish to try to cash the DHSS cheque in an area where the genuine recipient was known. He had a good breakfast with eggs and bacon and felt better after that. No one paid him any attention in the café, which was full of men eating before they went to work. Did they all live in lodgings?

He successfully cashed the cheque at a busy post office and was not asked for any identification. Outside, he dropped the second letter he had taken into the mail box. It might as well go to its true destination now. After this, he had gained enough courage to buy a newspaper. It contained no reference to Audrey Bannerman. Perhaps public interest was already dying down. It was the police whom he must fear; his photograph would be displayed in every police station in the country.

Made bold now, Jim booked a room at a four-star hotel in the name of Lesley Wilson. He said that he was in Birmingham on company business and would be staying for the week, mentioning the name of a well-known frozen food firm whom he said would pay the account. Wearing his sharp suit, his anorak over one arm, he was every inch the executive and was given a room with bath, television, tea-making equipment and a trouser press without demur.

This was better. He could stay here in comfort watching house movies on the video, and leave before the week was up and the bill presented. He might eat in the restaurant, if his nerve held, but otherwise there was always room service.

Yvonne sat at the back of the room where the inquest was to be held. PC Moody had greeted her when she arrived and, remembering that she had a small boy to park, had asked what she had done with him. Yvonne immediately felt calmer as she replied that he was being looked after in the village.

Moody cared deeply about his job. Sudden deaths needing investigation were often tragedies – road accidents, suicides, even murder. There were always shocked relatives and friends who, while grieving, still had to comply with bureaucratic demands. To each, their own disaster was the worst in the world; it was only to outsiders that some seemed more dreadful than others, but by any standards the death of Audrey Bannerman was appalling.

Moody left Yvonne to speak to some new arrivals and Yvonne recognized Rupert Bannerman. With him was a small, plump woman with smooth white hair. She wore a navy coat. Yvonne realized that this was Audrey's supplanter, as she was Olivia's: an uncomfortable thought. When they came across and Rupert introduced his wife, Yvonne saw that her fresh colour came from a

185

threadwork of broken veins, apparently innocent of make-up, and she had a sudden fleeting vision of Audrey's careful matt complexion. A surge of loyalty towards the dead woman swept over her, and Felicity noticed her expression suddenly hardening. Not understanding why, she supposed it was because Yvonne resented being dragged into a distressing experience which was not her affair.

'This won't take long, I believe,' she said.

'No.' Yvonne was curt. She turned to Rupert. 'Is there any more news? Have they found Sawyer yet?'

'No,' said Rupert. 'I don't think they've got the faintest notion where he is.'

The three sat together. Rupert gave evidence of identification and the coroner asked Yvonne to describe how she found the injured woman. He thanked her for her public spirit in acting as she had, gave permission for the funeral to go ahead, and arranged a date for re-opening proceedings two months hence.

'We're going out to Coxton now,' said Rupert as they filed from the room. 'Audrey's solicitor is meeting us at the house. There are things to see to, and we're going to talk to the vicar about the funeral.'

'I see,' said Yvonne.

'It's all a little unusual,' said Rupert. He sounded embarrassed. 'Audrey had no one else, you see.'

'I know.'

'Can we give you a lift home?'

'Thank you, no. I've got my car here,' Yvonne answered. Equipped with its new battery, it had started instantly that morning.

'Lunch, then? We thought we'd try the village pub. Is it all right? Would you join us? Perhaps you could tell us about Audrey's life there.'

'I can't,' said Yvonne. 'I'd only just met her. She seemed to be a rather private person.'

Rupert nodded.

'It's kind of you to suggest lunch,' Yvonne added. 'I don't think the pub does more than toasted sandwiches, but in any case I'm afraid I must get on with my work.'

'What do you do?' asked Felicity.

The gaze that Yvonne turned towards her was so frosty that Felicity could almost feel a physical chill.

'I make soft furnishings for an interior decorator,' said Yvonne.

'And you've lost several precious hours already. We mustn't keep you, then,' said Felicity.

'No. I'll get off, if you'll excuse me,' said Yvonne.

To avoid the traffic in the town centre, she took a route round the outskirts. Her way led through streets of houses and, pausing at a junction, she noticed the sign *Birch Street* on a wall. Surely that was where Denis lived? She had missed him on Friday. He had been coming to Ford House for only a few weeks but she had grown used to his difficult, ungracious company over their morning break. Last night Charles had said it was a pity she had let him go; the boy could have begun clearing the weeds from the former tennis lawn which Charles meant to restore, chiefly to attract his daughters. Denis, employed casually, would be cheaper than getting a firm in to raze the lot and re-sow it, and he might be just as competent in the long run.

Yvonne had not felt cooperative. She had muttered that she would try to find him when she had the time. Now was her chance. If he was out, his grandmother could give him a message. She turned into Birch Street and began looking for Number 7.

She soon found the house, one in a semi-detached row dating from the thirties and now mostly turned into flats or bedsitters, though a few were still occupied by families. Some had been renovated; this district would soon be on the way up.

There were various bells by the door.

Yvonne rang one marked *Crow* and after a long delay a

187

very old woman wearing a pinafore appeared. She smelled of stew and tobacco, and other things Yvonne preferred not to identify. Rather dismayed, Yvonne put on her best smile.

'Good morning, Mrs Crow. I wonder if you would give a message to Denis?' she said. 'I don't suppose he's in now.'

'Denis? Denis who?' asked Mrs Crow irritably. She had been watching television. Those educational programmes in the mornings were very interesting and she did not care for interruptions.

'Denis Crow, of course. Your grandson,' Yvonne answered, startled.

'I don't know no Denis,' said Mrs Crow. 'My grandson's in America with his dad and I haven't seen none of them for twenty years, nor will now, likely enough.'

Yvonne stared.

'Are you sure?' she asked.

'Course I'm sure. I know about my own family, don't I?'

'But he's been working for me. He said he lived with his grandmother at this address and his name's Denis Crow.' Yvonne knew she had the right number because it was the same as Emily's age.

'He was having you on,' said Mrs Crow, sucking at her dentures.

'Well, who is he, then?' Yvonne demanded. 'Does a boy live here – about seventeen? Round red face and short brown hair. He has a Walkman.' She put her hands to her ears to demonstrate.

'Oh, that's the young lad as sleeps in the van,' Mrs Crow said. 'Brother of the girl upstairs at the back. And they're not married, neither.'

'Who aren't?' Yvonne's head was spinning.

'The girl upstairs and the young fellow, Alan. Some sort of builder, he is. Has his own van – a blue one –

keeps it outside in the road. This lad's been sleeping in it.'

'Well!' Yvonne didn't know what to make of this information. Why had Denis lied to her about his name? Was he just teasing, as Mrs Crow implied? If so, he had an odd sense of humour. 'If you see him, perhaps you'd tell him that Mrs Davies came round and there's more work for him, if he wants it.'

'I'll make a point of it, dear,' said Mrs Crow, who had mellowed enough to start enjoying this encounter.

Yvonne drove home feeling cross and bewildered. Denis had told her a pack of lies about his circumstances, but she would hardly have engaged him if she had known he was living rough. Or would she? Perhaps all he needed was a chance to get on. He had worked well and he was healthy and strong. He wouldn't get into the Marines if he tried to deceive them, that was certain. Perhaps that had all been a fairytale, too.

She did not expect to see him again.

20

After the inquest, Detective Superintendent Hawkes
sent a sergeant to Ivy Lodge with Rupert. The police had
finished in the house and were going to hand the keys to
the solicitor, who had been unable to get over to
Leckerton in time for the brief inquiry.

He had not arrived when they reached the house. He
had to travel from Sussex, where Audrey had lived
before.

Detective Sergeant Dale unlocked the door and led the
way inside. Treading reluctantly, Rupert and Felicity
felt they were intruding on the dead woman's privacy as
they entered her home. The police had been through
some of her papers but they had no need to inspect
everything; they had wanted to look at her insurance
policy in case specific items of value were mentioned, but
little was separately listed and Rupert had already
supplied a description of what might have been stolen.

When Mr Gray, the solicitor, arrived, Dale handed
him the keys and said that before he left there was a
matter on which he wanted advice. The two went
upstairs leaving Rupert and Felicity looking uncomfortably round the room, where they recognized pieces of
furniture Audrey had brought to Tettlebury after Ford
House was sold. Felicity pulled her coat collar closer,
shivering slightly although the house was warm; the
police had left the heating on low to prevent things
getting damp. Rupert fretted about leaving the house
empty; would Gray ask someone local to look after it?
Not that it mattered now Audrey would not be
returning.

Mr Gray and Detective Sergeant Dale came back, and
Gray spoke to Rupert.

'Could I ask you to come and see what the police have found? You may know something about Mrs Bannerman's interests,' he said. 'You too, Mrs Bannerman, if you wouldn't mind. We men are at sea over this.'

A tall, thin man with fair greying hair, he led the way to a bedroom. There was a patchwork quilt on the bed, and the room was painted white with flowered curtains on a yellow ground at the window. There were china ornaments displayed on shelves, and a number of books. It was Hesther's girlhood room re-created in miniature.

Rupert had scarcely taken this in before Dale was showing him the contents of a drawer in a mahogany chest which had come originally from Ford House. It was full of knitted garments carefully sealed in plastic bags. A second drawer, then a third, was opened, similarly filled.

It was Felicity who examined them more closely and saw that the garments ranged from baby jackets to sweaters and dresses for first a toddler, then a larger girl, right up to teenage size. In the end they opened some of the bags to make certain of their contents.

'They were for Jenny,' said Rupert, and he felt as if a bar of ice had entered his soul. He turned to the two men. 'We had a daughter who died. You both know that. She became very depressed after a miscarriage. The child was a girl and she – my daughter – spoke of her as Jenny. It seems she didn't die for her grandmother either.'

'Oh!' Felicity turned away, her hand to her mouth.

'She'd have been fourteen by now,' Rupert said.

Felicity wondered why Rupert had not guessed what Audrey was knitting before they parted, for many of these things went back that far. Had they discussed nothing? She kept silent, waiting for someone else to speak.

Dale had seen plenty of strange things in his time and so had the solicitor, but this was a new experience for them both. Macabre, thought Gray, but she had been a strange woman.

'I'm the sole executor,' he told Rupert. 'But I'd like your advice about disposing of these.'

'Some charity for children?' suggested Rupert, surprised that he could utter at all.

Gray nodded.

'She left everything to an organization for the rehabilitation of prisoners, specifically for women. The house is to be offered to them as a hostel, for women who need care rather than incarceration, with the freedom to sell it and use the money to buy a property elsewhere if that seems more appropriate.'

Coxton would be glad to know that, thought Felicity. The village had had enough contacts with convicts already, from what she had heard lately.

'I see,' Rupert said.

'Before she came down here, she worked among women offenders,' said Gray. 'Maybe you didn't know that. She travelled to London, but in the end it became too much for her. Her heart wasn't too good latterly, though she ignored it.'

Dale, listening to this exchange, chose not to mention some other knitting, pale yellow wool, work in progress, found in a workbag in the dead woman's desk. Gray would come to it in time.

It was decided to ask the vicar to hold the key for the present, in case it was necessary to enter the house. Dale had found it hanging on the back of the door. The heating oil tank was full; Audrey would, Rupert knew, be too well organized to let it run low. He could not bear to think of the place getting damp and musty and was relieved when Mr Gray decreed that the heating should be kept on at a low temperature. The legatees would not want a sodden house and possibly, later, frozen and burst pipes.

'I hope you won't give Audrey's clothes to a jumble sale,' he told Mr Gray as they went out to the cars which were in the road.

'Oxfam, I thought, or the WRVS,' said Gray.

Rupert nodded. He did not want the inhabitants of Coxton fingering Audrey's skirts and sweaters in the village hall.

Detective Sergeant Dale drove back to Leckerton, and the others went to the vicarage.

Felicity thought she had never spent a more harrowing day in her life.

Back at headquarters, Dale told Detective Inspector Wright who, under Detective Superintendent Hawkes, was heading the inquiry, about the collection of knitted garments, and Wright decided that they had better learn the facts concerning the daughter's death, though it was not relevant to the case. He ordered a report to be made.

The police were not the only ones to express interest in the past. A reporter of the *Swalton Weekly Herald* had suspected that the victim was the former wife of one of the town's retired magistrates. When Rupert and Felicity arrived back at Tettlebury Manor, he was waiting for them.

Apart from saying that he was shocked and saddened by the tragedy, Rupert refused to comment, but this did not deter the reporter. On his way back to the office, he stopped off in the village and asked about the family. Soon he learned about the daughter, and when he checked the files he found the report on Hesther Bannerman's death. Because she had died in London, the inquest was held there, but the *Herald* had recorded the verdict and much of her story.

When he could, the reporter acted as stringer for a London daily. Soon the news was on its way.

*

193

Denis thought about trying school again on Monday morning, but instead he wrote his letter to the Marines. Tracy had got him an envelope and a sheet of paper; letter-writing did not feature in her life or Alan's, but she had begged them from Mrs Dove in the front flat.

Denis gave the Birch Street address and wrote the letter out in rough first, on the back of a bill. Then he went into town to buy a first-class stamp and post it. After that he went to the Pizza Parlour, where some youths he knew ribbed him, saying that they had heard his father had been to the school to answer questions about his absence.

'That's a lie,' Denis said. 'My mum's very ill and I'm looking after her. She'll probably die.'

The boys, who had made their assertion in order to bait him, were not sure if he was telling the truth. He had a reputation for invention, but he had been seen at school with a bruise on his face which he alleged had been caused by walking into a door, and one or two of them felt awkward about adding to his possible problems. After a few more taunts they grew bored with goading him, but when Denis left the Pizza Parlour he telephoned the emergency services and said that the school was on fire. Then he went back to Birch Street where he could lie on the bed watching television until Tracy came home.

He was just going upstairs when Mrs Crow came out of her ground-floor room and called him.

'You come here, young man,' she ordered. 'I want a word with you.'

Denis hesitated. He could ignore her; the old bag wouldn't come upstairs after him. He knew she rarely made it to the bathroom and had her own place at the back.

'Come on down,' she repeated.

Denis found himself turning to face her, staying half-way up the stairs where he could look down at her. She was such a little person. One good shove and she'd topple over.

'What did you mean by telling that Mrs Davies that I'm your grandmother?' Mrs Crow demanded.

Denis gaped at her.

'Yes, you may well look like that,' said Mrs Crow. 'She came round, Mrs Davies did. Thought you lived with me and that I'm your gran.' The old woman gave a sudden cackle. 'I can tell you, if I was, I'd send you about your business fast enough. Idle, you are.'

'I've done good work for Mrs Davies,' said Denis.

'Hm. So you say. Well, she's got more for you to do, if you're interested,' said Mrs Crow. 'That's why she came round. You're to go over there.'

'Did you tell her you're not my gran?' Denis came down a step.

'Course I did.'

'What did she say?'

'Bit surprised,' said Mrs Crow.

'She'd still give me work?'

'Seems so. I hope you behave yourself round there,' said the old woman.

'I must do, mustn't I, or she wouldn't be so keen to get me,' Denis retorted.

'What's to become of you?' asked Mrs Crow, shaking her head. 'Sleeping in that van's not right.'

'I'm joining the Marines,' Denis declared.

'Think they'll have you, do you?'

'Why shouldn't they?'

'You been in trouble with the law?'

'No.'

'Then why're you hiding out here?'

'I'm not hiding. I left home, that's all,' said Denis. 'Tracy did, too, but she was going with Alan anyway.'

'Hm. Well, if I was you, I'd go round to Mrs Davies and get myself fixed up, before she changes her mind,' said Mrs Crow, tiring now and ready to conclude the interview.

'I'll think about it,' Denis said.

He slept a while on Tracy's bed. It was so warm and soft, and there was that smell. He was still there when she came home and she was none too pleased to find him lying on the duvet in his jeans.

He went out then and stole a bicycle, cutting the chain that secured it to a railing with some pliers he'd taken from the shed at Ford House. He put them in the bike's saddlebag and rode off. It was a good bike, with seven gears. As he went through the town he passed a gang of youths who had been drinking; they were scuffling together on the pavement, spoiling for a fight. Denis swerved away from them, pedalling past so that none was tempted to pick on him and pull him from the bike. Drink did bad things to you. He meant to keep away from it.

He put the bike round at the back of the house, beside Mrs Crow's private washroom. He'd tell her that he'd bought it from his wages.

He'd sell it when he went off to the Marines, and give the money to Tracy.

21

It was a long time since Jim had been so comfortable.

He had a deep, steaming bath and strolled round his hotel room examining the various refinements. There was a leather folder containing leaflets about various local attractions and instructions on how to view the house video, obtain laundry service, dial overseas calls, summon room service and even a doctor. There was also writing paper. The sheets were large and white. He fingered one, making up his mind. Then, with a razor blade, he cut the headed address from two of the sheets. On one blank page he printed his name and the words ALIBI. WHITE HONDA PICK-UP TAKEN WEST OF LOCKLEY PRISON WEDNESDAY EVENING. BEIGE ANORAK TAKEN FROM THE COACH AND HORSES. VAN LEFT IN READING STATION CAR PARK.

He folded the paper in three sections, like a circular, tucking one fold into another, and addressed it in capital letters to POLICE HQ, LECKERTON. They would check it for prints and find that it was genuine, but if he posted it in Birmingham, they would know where to look for him. Now came the gamble of the second letter.

Dear Maureen, he wrote. *I didn't kill Mrs Bannerman. She's the one who came to see you. Someone else did it but they will pin it on me unless he's found. Please post the enclosed and don't tell anyone. DESTROY THIS. Am OK. Jim.*

She'd know that the letter genuinely came from him, but if it were to be found by the police it said nothing to indicate that he had seen her. He put the message and the note to the police in an envelope, addressed it to her in capitals and went down to the foyer where he bought a first-class stamp from the hall porter, who barely glanced at him. He dropped it in the box provided for guests. He had probably missed the evening clearance but that didn't matter. Now he must will Maureen to do as he had asked. The name of the hotel was printed on the envelope and he must trust her not to make use of that information to betray him.

He hoped the man, her lover, would not see the letter and ask questions.

Jim ordered a meal from room service, soup, then steak with chips and vegetables. He ordered some wine, too. Why not? He would not be paying. When the meal arrived, he made himself busy in the bathroom, calling out to the waiter to leave it. He didn't want too many people looking at his face.

There was nothing on the television that night about the crime. Audrey Bannerman was not a missing child or pretty girl, nor even a brave inner-city ancient sending off a mugger. She was not the stuff, for long, of headlines.

Maureen did not receive the letter until Wednesday. The post came before she left for work and she opened it at once, puzzled by the address on the envelope and not recognizing Jim's writing from the capitals. As soon as she read the contents, her heart seemed to plummet. Then she rallied. So he was in Birmingham. Well, that, at least was a long way from Reading. She had seen a television interview with the stout woman who had sat next to him on the bus to Oxford, and had breathed more freely knowing he had left the area.

She hadn't recognized the dead woman as her visitor. The press had only a passport photograph of Audrey to use and it was not a good likeness. Fancy thinking she was from the welfare! What was she doing, interfering in things that were not her business?

Jim hadn't put a stamp on his weird message addressed to the police. She read it and believed what was written, so she stamped it and posted it on the way to work. She tore up his note to her, and the envelope, and burned the pieces in a saucer, much to the amazement of Nicola. Then she flushed the ashes down the lavatory. They failed to disappear at first, and she waited for the cistern to re-fill. This time, helped by a shove from the brush, they were swirled away.

Wednesday morning's tabloids told Hesther's story and brought Audrey's murder back to the front pages.

CONVICT DAUGHTER'S SUICIDE read one headline, and there was a picture of Hesther, her hair cropped short, face gaunt and lined. The paragraph below revealed that she had been sent to prison for stealing three items worth less than ten pounds. The act had been a cry for help, said the piece, but instead of giving it to her, by means of hospital treatment, she had been sentenced to eighteen months detention from which she had emerged so depressed that eventually she had killed herself.

Rupert read only a small paragraph in *The Times*; it was Felicity who was curious enough to see what the popular press had to say. One paper went far enough back to recount that before her lapse Hesther had lived in a flat in Pimlico and worked for a wine merchant. Felicity remembered how interested she had become in viniculture after a trip to France, and how pleased and amused Rupert had been as he discussed vintages with her and asked her advice about what to buy. Then her visits home had become less frequent. Her parents supposed she was involved in a romance and because she brought no man home, Rupert feared that she might be mixed up with someone who was married. He had tried, on one of her rare visits, when she was obviously unhappy and looked ill, to get her to confide in him, but she had closed up into mulish silence. After that she did not come for six months, always making excuses when they tried to press her. Then she arrived one day without warning and was clearly unwell. Audrey realized what was wrong at once: she had had an abortion, a late one, as they discovered afterwards, but since Hesther refused to discuss it with her, it was only much later, when she was in prison, that the full truth was acknowledged. Long before her arrest, Hesther had given up her job and was drifting along, eating little and smoking too much – not drugs, just tobacco – unable to sleep. She had money enough to live on, had she chosen to use it, for her father gave her an allowance and her parents, between them, had bought her the flat.

After she was released from Holloway, she was like a stranger, refusing to talk either to Rupert or Audrey who had both visited her regularly, sitting in silence with her because she could find nothing to say and was patently uninterested in the small stories they dredged up in attempts to amuse her. She spent a short time at home before going as a voluntary patient to a psychiatric hospital. One day she disappeared and went to London, where she took her own life.

Even now, Rupert liked to think that the loss of her baby had been a natural event. Neither he nor Audrey could accept the truth, and now Audrey, knitting for the infant that never was, working with other offenders, had met her own death at the hands of a convict she had employed. It would never end, thought Felicity sadly.

Hesther's crime was so trivial. She had taken a few items from, of all places, a cosmetic counter in a big store, she who by now was plain and unattractive and used no make-up. She was twenty-eight years old when she died. There was something very wrong about a society which incarcerated among hardened criminals a sick woman who had stolen goods worth only a trifling sum and which allowed drunken motorists who killed people to go free.

Hesther had needed love and had not allowed those who wanted to cherish her the chance to do so. Now the past had been resurrected to haunt her father.

Leckerton police's current preoccupation was their murder, but other crimes continued to be committed. There were stolen cars, drunken brawls, burglaries, motoring offences, failures to pay fines and taxes, neighbours' disputes and accidents, plenty to keep them busy.

Audrey's nightdress and dressing gown had been sent for analysis. The discovery of traces from the killer's person or clothing would be useful when Jim Sawyer came to court, as he would in time. Because the victim had had a minor heart condition, the defence might go for manslaughter; indeed, Sawyer would be wise to admit to that as such a plea might be accepted, but nevertheless the prosecution must mount a case.

An irritation for the police was the number of hoax emergency calls there had been in recent weeks, one naming the cinema, one McDonald's, and one the comprehensive school. The last one indicated a disaffected pupil and perhaps they were all linked. The matter must be investigated; public time could not be wasted in this way and one day there might be a genuine alarm which could not be answered because of another false call.

Jim Sawyer's letter arrived on Thursday. Checks on it for fingerprints proved that it genuinely came from him.

'So he went to Reading after all,' said Detective Inspector Wright, examining the good quality paper, cut along one edge. 'He's removed the heading. He's holed up in a hotel spending Mrs Bannerman's money.'

The only flaw in this theory was that they now knew that her credit card had been used in Bristol. A great many things had been bought, ranging from alcohol to telephones.

'He's stocked up to make a sale,' said Detective Sergeant Dale. 'He'd have learned about that in the nick.'

They found the Fiat in Bristol, in a multi-storey car

park, with several sets of fingerprints inside, none of them Sawyer's.

He had never touched Audrey's car. He had not even washed it when he worked for her.

The stolen Honda pick-up had not been recovered. In fact it had been stolen by someone else, repainted and sold. Its owner never got it back.

Hotels in Reading and around the area had to be checked out.

'He may be hanging about hoping to see his wife and the kiddie,' Wright declared. The wife had denied seeing him but she could be helping him secretly. She would have to be watched.

The small church in Coxton was well filled for Audrey's funeral. Julian Parker, the vicar, was agreeably surprised to see faces familiar and unfamiliar ranged before him as he read the lesson, Revelations XXI, always appropriate. People had been so shocked by the violence in their midst that those who could make the gesture of attending had done so.

Rupert and Felicity sat near the back of the church, and as they moved out to the graveyard, rain started to fall from the leaden sky. To Felicity, it seemed as though every day, this autumn, had been wet.

A large spray of white flowers had rested on the coffin throughout the service. They bore no card, for Rupert had not known what to write. Several bunches of chrysanthemums and a few late dahlias had been left at the church, and Yvonne had brought a small posy of anemones. On her way to buy them, she had had her hair cut in a bob to just beneath her ears. Felicity, sitting in the pew behind her, thought it a big improvement.

Yvonne did not stay for the interment, but Detective Inspector Wright and Detective Sergeant Dale were there to observe who remained. It had been known before for killers to attend their victims' funerals.

This one did not.

'Didn't you see anything that night, Charles?' Yvonne asked over dinner.

'What night?' Charles had been enjoying the chicken casserole which Yvonne had taken from the freezer for their meal. Lately, they had had a lot of casseroles. Not so long ago she had taken much more trouble over meals.

Now she'd had all that hair, which had reached to between her shoulder blades, lopped off. It made her look different: older, assured. He wasn't sure that he liked it.

'Wednesday night, last week. The night poor Audrey was attacked,' said Yvonne impatiently. 'You were very late home. I hadn't thought about it before but you could have seen something as you came through the village. Did you?'

'No, not a thing,' said Charles. He ate two more mouthfuls. She'd put almonds in the sauce, which was a nice touch. Then he remembered. 'There was a van parked across the road from our gate,' he said. 'Some couple necking, I suppose.'

'What sort of van?'

'A blue one. A Bedford or Ford, I think it was. I didn't take a lot of notice.'

'That might be important, Charles,' said Yvonne.

'Why? It was nowhere near Ivy Lodge, and he took her car, didn't he? The convict?'

'I know, but you don't usually see blue vans outside our gate when you come back late, do you? Have you ever before?'

'No.'

'You should tell the police,' said Yvonne.

'Why? They know who did it. It's just a matter of picking him up.'

'Yes, but suppose the van was involved. They could look for it. It could be important. Where is it now?

Maybe he had an accomplice who met him outside the prison.'

It was this last theory that swayed Charles. Tiresome though it would be, he must do his duty.

Detective Sergeant Dale came out straight after he had telephoned, though it was after nine o'clock. He listened to what Charles had to say and then they both went to examine the spot where the van had been pulled off the road on to the grass verge.

More than a week later there were still faint tyre marks visible, but they were too indistinct to yield useful impressions.

A Bedford or Ford van was not what Jim Sawyer had mentioned in his note, and the Honda pick-up stolen that night had been white. The blue one was nothing to do with the case and could be discounted.

No one was looking for Jim Sawyer in Birmingham. He had moved from the first hotel to another on Thursday, walking quietly out through the rear entrance, leaving his bill unpaid. The new one was just as comfortable. He'd go on to Coventry next, then, perhaps, Leeds. He could keep this up indefinitely, he had decided, as he passed the quiet days. He had been on the run for more than a week, and his moustache was a definite structure on his short upper lip. He could see it from the corner of his eye when he peered downwards. He touched it up with dye every day.

He was more confident now, walking round in his smart suit, but the days were long. He still read a great deal. David Copperfield had married his Agnes, and because the book had been so solid, Jim had bought *Great Expectations*. He wandered round busy stores playing the game of Let's Pretend by picking out things Maureen would like. He chose a doll for Nicola, and almost bought it, but then realized that her mother would not allow her to keep it if it had come from him.

Most evenings he ate in his room, watching television. Room service was efficient and it was wiser to charge up his meals to his bill than go outside to a restaurant where he would have to use Lesley Wilson's card. He always ordered half a bottle of wine with his dinner, and he had put on weight.

On Saturday afternoon he went to the cinema. He had visited several during the week. It made a change from television and he had to get out of the hotel to allow his room to be cleaned. Fresh sheets every day were a treat, and the towels were large and soft.

When he came out of the cinema it was raining hard. His anorak covered only his upper half and, by comparison with his suit, it was very shabby. He needed a proper raincoat.

The shops were still open and, on impulse, Jim decided to buy one. Making his choice, he presented the bank card which he had used before for minor purchases. He forgot that a sanction was required for more than a certain sum.

He was arrested there in the shop. The assistant, going away on the pretext of folding the coat before packing it into a bag, asked someone else to call the police and delayed the unsuspecting Jim long enough for them to arrive.

They did not realize who he was for some time, since at first Jim would not utter a word.

22

Bet learned about Jim's arrest on the radio on Sunday morning.

'Got that bloke,' she told Len, relieved. Len was still in bed while she had been giving Bruce and Sharon their breakfast. She took Len a cup of tea and told him what she had heard. Now she could stop wondering where Len had been at the time of the crime.

'How? Where?' Len sat up in bed, alert.

'In Birmingham, it seems,' Bet replied. 'They didn't give any details.'

'Hmph.' Len lay back against the pillows. 'He'll be for it now,' he said.

He would lose no sleep over Jim. It was his bad luck, picking the same night to break out. Now he, Len, was safe. The police wouldn't go looking for evidence for the defence.

Bet was going to say that Sawyer deserved all he got for doing in a defenceless old woman, but decided to keep her opinion to herself. Len could be violent; he had just served a sentence for manslaughter and he had struck her before now, though never the kids. He knew that would mean curtains. Since he'd been home this time he'd been soft with them all, which was nice, but it might not last.

He'd be inside again before long. She knew that. He couldn't resist easy money.

As soon as he had finished his tea, Len got up and dressed and went down to the shop to buy a paper.

The arrest made headline news in the tabloids and he read how Jim had been caught using a stolen bank card. The silly sod; you needed to be careful with those, keep the purchases small, not be greedy.

206

Now he dared not risk using Audrey Bannerman's card again because to do so would show that whoever had taken it was still at large and was therefore not Jim Sawyer. When Bet was busy, he cut it and her cheque book into small pieces and dropped them in the litter bin. Then he took the bag down to the large bins in the basement, a task he rarely undertook. Bet noticed that their own bin had been emptied and a new plastic liner fitted. It had not been full and she thought it wasteful; however, as Len had been so helpful she made no complaint, but thanked him and asked him to peel the potatoes for the roast they were going to have at midday. Len was good about the place when he was at home; he did not find household tasks demeaning.

Peeling away, Len thought about the kid who had been with him on the job. He didn't even know his name. Perhaps it was just as well, though the kid knew him as Len. The blinds had been down in the kitchen and the kid wouldn't have seen a thing, but he knew Len had been there. Suppose he grassed? He was a wild kid and might get into trouble on his own account. Then he'd split on Len and get himself off the hook.

Len decided that something would have to be done about him.

Jim admitted who he was as soon as a constable looked from him to a poster on the wall in the police station to which he was taken after his arrest.

'Changed yourself quite a bit, haven't you?' said the arresting officer, and his manner hardened. Until then, he had thought that the prisoner was merely a thief; now he knew that he was a killer, one who mugged old women.

He didn't look much of a menace, standing there in his smart suit, but some of the most merciless murderers in history had been mild-looking men.

Jim was charged with using a stolen bank card. That

would do for the moment, while the police team investigating the crime in Coxton were told that their hunt was over and took charge of the prisoner.

He was driven to Leckerton that night.

Jim was left alone in a cell for a long time before anyone spoke to him. He was given no cup of tea, nor any food.

At some stage it was his right to be fed; it was also his right not to talk, and to be represented by a solicitor. All this was very different from his first arrest, but even then he had not been allowed bail, although the prisons were bursting at the seams and he was no threat to public safety. In the end, he had decided it was just as well, because Maureen was so bitter and unforgiving. She could not understand why he had done what he had; all she could think of was the disgrace.

He should have realized that an appeal to her would be useless. Mrs Bannerman had said that her mind was made up and she had been right. Now she – his one friend, as it seemed to Jim – was dead, and he was banged up again. At least he wasn't responsible for what had happened to her; that was a separate matter, whatever the law might decide. If he went down for her murder, it wouldn't be like his last conviction, when he was a category C offender. This time he would be sent to a maximum security prison where there would be hard men, terrorists and multiple murderers, real villains who should be locked away for the rest of their lives. Jim might be sentenced to twenty years, and unless he admitted his guilt he would never be considered for parole. Sitting there, chilled and hungry, Jim's not very vivid imagination delivered up to him dire scripts of the future.

He was too tired and depressed to consider how to establish his innocence, but he remembered advice from old lags in Lockley. Say as little as possible and press for your right to a brief.

At last he was taken to an interview room, where Detective Superintendent Hawkes and Detective Inspector Wright came to see him. They asked him what he had done after leaving the prison, and he told them the truth. When he said he had gone straight to Reading, they suggested that, on the contrary he had gone out to Coxton after taking the pick-up.

'Why would I do that? It was near the prison and I had my bike, if that was what I meant to do. I could have hidden up somewhere till it was dark,' Jim dredged up some defiance.

'You only thought of it after you'd got the pick-up,' said Wright.

'Haven't you found it? The pick-up?' Jim asked. 'I left it in the station car park in Reading.'

'So you said in your note, but it wasn't there when we looked, and it's still missing,' said Wright.

'I'd still got the key,' Jim said. 'You've got it now, with my things.' All his possessions had been surrendered, put in bags and listed.

'That proves nothing. You could have left it in Coxton, preferring the Fiat, and some kid could have taken it to get home,' said Wright.

'Where's the Fiat key, then, or Mrs Bannerman's cheque book and such?' Jim asked.

It was true that although the Fiat had been found its key was missing.

'You got rid of them,' Wright suggested.

'It's not true,' said Jim. 'None of it's true. You should be looking for somebody else.'

Naturally enough, they didn't believe him and they kept him there for most of the night, going over and over the ground and asking him what he had done with the stolen jewellery.

Jim stuck to his story.

'I've told you what happened. I went to Reading to see my wife. I left the pick-up and cycled out towards

Calcot. I found a boiler room behind some offices and spent the night there. Then I went home the next day but Maureen – ' he choked, mentioning her name – 'was out and I had to give up.'

'You took the Fiat and drove to Bristol, where you did a good bit of shopping,' said Hawkes. 'Then you spent time in Reading before moving on to Birmingham.'

'Bristol? I've never been there in my life,' said Jim.

At some stage in the proceedings he was given sandwiches and tea, and after that he simply repeated that he had told them the truth and had nothing more to say. He was reeling with fatigue, and eventually he was sent back to his cell for what was left of the night.

'It's all down to forensic, now,' said Hawkes. 'Let's hope the lab comes up with something good.' He'd have probably worn the anorak at Ivy Lodge, though he wouldn't have had the suit by then. 'He can't prove he was anywhere else.'

'I suppose he wasn't?' remarked Wright.

Hawkes gave him a look.

'He couldn't have been driving to Bristol in that Fiat while he was on a bus going to Oxford,' Wright stated.

'A wrong identification,' said Hawkes. 'That's the explanation. The woman made a mistake.'

Witnesses had made such mistakes before. Identification was not always easy.

A solicitor came in the morning. He spent a long time with Jim, who had been given a good hot breakfast. He was safely locked up now and could murder no more old ladies; correct procedures must be followed; no one wanted complaints about the prisoner's treatment. The solicitor, Gordon Stone, a young man who had not minded losing his Sunday's golf because he was interested in criminal law, spent a long time with Jim.

'What time did you break into the house in Coxton?' he asked, and 'Where did you leave Mrs Bannerman's car?' He tried plenty of trick questions and was not satisfied with all that Jim told him, but he was also not convinced that he had committed the offence for which he was being held.

When Jim was originally arrested for fraud, he had soon seen that the game was up and had been frank in admitting what he had done. This time, he declared that he was innocent of murder although he had stolen a purse and used the Marks and Spencer's charge card and the bank card as well as the cash it contained. He also revealed where he had stayed in Birmingham and that he had left the first hotel without paying, and the second, though not voluntarily. The police had checked this and had collected his things from the second hotel. He was hardly a skilful criminal, the solicitor decided, surveying his blond client who now had the grizzled stubble of overnight beard on his chin.

'I dyed my hair,' Jim said sadly.

'Yes.' Gordon Stone saw a broken man who must always have been weak, like so many whom he found himself attempting to defend. 'Why did you abscond?' he prompted.

'I wanted to see my wife. I wanted to sort things out with her. I knew she'd found someone else.' Now the words poured from him. He had been alone for over a week, a period in which he had spoken only minimal sentences to do with obtaining food or the few other things he had needed. He had fought against being loquacious with the police, aware of the danger, but this man was on his side. 'There's not much to think about in prison,' he explained. 'I knew it was all up, really – she didn't visit or write – but I couldn't accept it.' He sighed heavily.

'Go on,' Stone urged.

'When I went to work for Mrs Bannerman, she was nice,' said Jim. 'She treated me very well and she knew about prison. I wondered if she'd been inside herself, as a matter of fact. Of course, I know now that it was all on account of her daughter.' He had read every report. 'I asked her to find out how Maureen was, and Nicola, my daughter.'

'Did Mrs Bannerman visit you at the prison?'

'No. We spoke on the telephone.'

That was a pity. A visit would have been recorded, but though a telephone call would have been noted, if Sawyer paid for it, the number might not have been registered. He would check it. The man's wife would have to admit meeting Mrs Bannerman, if challenged. Still, proving this part of his story to be true did not disqualify him from having carried out the robbery.

'I'd stopped working for her by then, you see,' Jim went on. 'I wouldn't have hurt her, Mr Stone. Whoever did it should be strung up.' He looked fierce as he said this.

'Who do you think it was?'

'How should I know? Anyone passing. But why her? Her place isn't all that big.'

'Because they knew an old lady lived there?' suggested Stone.

'She wasn't that old,' said Jim. 'Just getting on a bit. She kept the place herself and did the garden, except the heavy stuff. That's why she needed me, to plant a hedge and then lay some stones on the pat – on the terrace. And I painted the kitchen.'

'And you left your fingerprints there.'

'I suppose so,' said Jim.

'There's a lot of circumstantial evidence against you,' said Stone.

'I can see that.'

And there was no obligation on the police to look for evidence against Jim's complicity: none at all.

'You stole the pick-up and coat,' Stone confirmed. Jim had described his night on the run and his misery as he huddled in the boiler room. Such a tale had to be true.

212

Most men on the run would have hung on to the stolen vehicle, parked it in a field or copse somewhere out of the way and spent the night in it, but not this ineffectual muddler.

'You never saw your wife?'

Jim did not hesitate.

'No,' he said. 'She was out. Must have gone to work.'

'You didn't wait till she got back?'

'No. I thought her bloke might turn up. Mrs Bannerman said he was on nights.'

'You could have gone to her work place.'

'Too risky.'

'You gave up very easily.'

'Yes.' Jim could not let Maureen down by telling Stone what had really happened.

Stone knew that it made no difference whether he was speaking the truth or not: he could have committed the crime in question and gone to Reading afterwards.

'So you caught a bus to Oxford and sat next to a woman who later reported seeing you?'

Jim nodded.

'Then what did you do?'

'I was thinking of going back to Lockley or giving myself up at a police station, but then I read about what had happened to Mrs Bannerman and that I was being blamed, so I decided to run for it,' said Jim.

He described his theft of the car in Oxford and his journey to Banbury where he had bought the hair dye and a razor.

'What about the car?' asked Stone.

'I left it in a street in Stratford-on-Avon,' said Jim.

'Have you told the police that?'

'I'm not sure – I don't think so. What difference will it make?'

'Not a lot, but they might make sure its owner gets it back, if he hasn't already,' said Stone mildly.

'I stole a purse in Stratford,' said Jim. 'At a pub. I was

213

using the card from it when they took me. There was a Marks and Spencer's card, too. I bought this suit with it.' For the first time a faint smile appeared on his face. 'I felt good, doing that.' He said this with some complacence.

'I can imagine,' said Stone drily. 'I expect you practised the signature first.'

'Yes,' said Jim, looking surprised at this perspicacity.

'You dumped your prison gear?'

'Yes. In a litter bin. I left my jacket in the Honda.'

There was no point in trying to locate the clothing. It could be proved that Sawyer was where he said he was after the crime was committed. If the real perpetrator had been using Audrey Bannerman's bank card, and maybe passing her cheques elsewhere while Jim was known to be in Birmingham, it might help his case. In France, such a line of investigation would be followed as a matter of course; in Britain, no such duty rested with the police but he, Stone, could set inquiries in train.

They would not necessarily prove that his client had not killed Audrey Bannerman. The prosecution would argue that he had panicked and dumped the car, cheque book and bank card and someone else had found them and used them.

It was going to be very difficult indeed to prove that Jim Sawyer had not been in Coxton on Wednesday night.

Len thought about that odd kid while his family enjoyed their roast pork and crackling. To follow, there was apple tart and custard. Bet was a really good cook when she put her mind to it.

'When I retire, we might run a pub, with you doing the grub,' he said, spiking a crisp roast potato on his fork and running it round his plate to mop up the gravy.

'When you retire? Don't make me laugh,' said Bet.

He shrugged.

'One bit of luck and we'd be set up for life,' he told her. He went into a dream of robbing a bank and gaining half a million pounds.

'Like winning the pools?' mocked Bet.

'Right.'

He was planning something now, she could tell. He'd never go straight, whatever he said, but the trouble was that he was too ambitious. He'd done loads of small jobs and never got caught, but as soon as he had tried something big, it had gone wrong.

They went to the park in the afternoon, so that Bruce and Sharon could play on the slide and the swings. It was pleasant there, a mild late autumn day, but after a time it began to rain and they hurried home.

Bet put on the kettle to make some tea. Len drank his quickly and then he went out.

'I may be late back,' he said. 'Don't you worry, love, if I am.'

It wasn't another woman. She knew that. It was a stronger attraction, the lure of getting something for nothing, and perhaps the spice of danger attached to the way it was done.

Len needed a car.

He walked round the town looking for one that had been left unlocked or that one of the keys in his collection would fit, and he still had the key of Mrs Bannerman's Fiat. He looked out for another Fiat: it stood to reason a car of the same make was the most likely one to suit.

It took him nearly an hour to find one, but he succeeded. The key needed a bit of jockeying before the engine would start, but it worked. He found he couldn't withdraw it again, or not without using a lot of force, but that didn't matter. He'd go and attend to the boy, then put the car back somewhere near the place where he had found it.

He took his cosh.

Denis knew that Jim Sawyer had been arrested.

He lay in the van, zipped into his sleeping bag, his earphones silent so that he could think.

The guy hadn't done it, so he'd get off, wouldn't he? Be able to prove he was somewhere else? But people did get nicked for things they hadn't done. Everyone knew that. Even for murder.

He could go out and make a phone call, tell the police they were wrong. He could say that the real killer was a man called Len who had been in Lockley Prison up to a few weeks ago. They'd be able to trace him, then. But if Len was caught, he'd split on Denis, because he'd know who had tipped off the cops, and if that happened, he wouldn't get into the Marines. The papers had come already and needed a lot of studying, but you'd no chance if you'd got a record, or not until years afterwards. He'd understood that much. He and Tracy had looked at them together.

She and Alan had been good to him this weekend. The night before, Saturday, they'd taken him to the cinema and then a meal, paying for him, and today he'd had the use of their room while they were out. He knew they felt bad because Alan had said he couldn't go on sleeping in the van after the end of next week. He must look for a place of his own, like a bed in a hostel for homeless people, and try for a regular job.

'I can go back to Mrs Davies,' Denis told him. 'She sent a message. Can't do without me.' He grinned defiantly. 'Trust me, Alan. It'll work out.'

He could ride to Coxton on his new bike. He'd been out for a spin that afternoon. Mrs Crow had seen it and said it was all right to keep it round the back. She wasn't so bad, after all.

He didn't want Tracy or Alan to find out he'd got it. They'd know he wouldn't have had enough money to buy it.

He'd ride out to Ford House in the morning and see what Mrs Davies wanted. Then he'd find digs.

Falling asleep, Denis wove a fantasy in which Mrs Davies offered to take him in as a lodger, in one of those fancy rooms upstairs in the big, comfortable house.

Len opened the door of the van and shone his torch full on Denis's face.

'Come on, lad, we've work to do,' he said, catching hold of the end of the sleeping bag and giving Denis's foot a hard tweak.

'What –?' Terrified, Denis sat up. When he realized who had woken him, he was still more afraid.

'Ran out on me, didn't you?' Len said. He spoke pleasantly. No sense in getting the kid's back up. He was a strong young chap and Len didn't want to cosh him here, where he'd have to get rid of the body. He wanted the kid's cooperation in his own destruction, for destroyed he must be. Len had decided that he had no choice in the matter.

'I – I –' Denis did not know what to say.

'I expect you wanted to get your hands on the van, try a bit of driving yourself,' Len suggested.

'Yes, that was it,' gasped Denis.

'Well, get up kid. Get your clothes on,' said Len. 'We're going out.'

'I – I don't want to,' said Denis feebly.

'You don't want to, eh? Too bad. I'm afraid you've got to come,' said Len. He slid the cosh down his sleeve and into his hand. The kid might try yelling, but not if he was sufficiently afraid. Folk never realized how a good yell might save them. Women faced by rapists were too polite; a good scream might make the man run off, but they didn't like raising their voices. 'We're going out to the place you got the key for,' he said. 'It's a pity to waste it.'

'But – but –' Denis spluttered.

Len let him see the cosh.

'If I hit your hand with this, you won't like it,' he said conversationally. 'It'll break your bones. Them bones in your hand aren't strong, you know, and they don't mend easy. You and me are in this together, my lad. We're mates, remember? If I go down, so do you. A lad like you was hanged years ago when he was out on a job with another fellow who killed a guy. He didn't do it, mind, the one that was hanged. His mate did, but he swung for it.'

'They don't hang no one now,' said Denis. He trembled as he began climbing slowly out of his sleeping bag. He slept in his sweater; it got cold in the van.

'No, they get sent down for life instead,' said Len. 'Sometimes they get out quite quick. Sometimes they're in for twenty years. It depends. Now, hurry.'

Denis slowly pulled on his jeans, then reached for his trainers. He felt sick with fright as he got out of the van, pulling his anorak on. Perhaps he could run away once he got into the road.

But Len had thought of that. He took hold of the boy's arm and twisted it up behind his back, forcing Denis to go where he was bidden.

He thought that perhaps Len wanted to use the van again. If so, and Denis had to get the keys, he'd wake Alan and Tracy no matter how much trouble he got into afterwards.

But this wasn't what Len had planned.

'I've got wheels,' he said, pushing Denis along the road to where a yellow Fiat was parked. Denis noticed that it was the same model as Mrs Bannerman's. For a wild moment he thought that it might be her car, resprayed, but as soon as he was bundled inside, he saw that the upholstery was a different colour.

'Now, don't get any fancy ideas about running away again,' said Len. 'You got nothing out of that other job. That was stupid of you, wasn't it? If you'd stayed, you'd have had some loot.'

'You – you killed Mrs Bannerman,' whispered Denis.

'No, I didn't. She slept sweetly all the time I was there,' said Len. 'Jim Sawyer came along later and did for her. Funny, that, wasn't it? Him breaking out the same night.'

If Denis hadn't seen for himself what had really happened, he might have believed Len.

Len bundled him into the back of the car and gave him a hard rap over the knuckles as he did so. The heavy cosh hurt and Denis smothered a whimper of pain.

What if he yelled for help?

Len seemed to read his thoughts as he got into the driver's seat.

'No good shouting,' he said. 'You'd be in just as much trouble as me. You took the van that night, after all. I can say I wasn't there. It'd be your word against mine. I didn't leave any prints.'

He was wearing gloves now. Denis saw the cosh held in one stubby hand. Perhaps it was the very weapon that had killed Mrs Bannerman. He shuddered.

'What you need's a drink,' Len said kindly. He put the cosh down.

Denis was wondering if he could somehow get out of the car and run, but if he tried to tip the front passenger seat forward to open the door, Len would have time to pick up the cosh and hit him.

Len had picked up a bottle from somewhere in the car. He undid it and passed it to Denis.

'Have some of this,' he said. 'It will make you feel better.'

'I don't drink,' muttered Denis.

'Don't know what you're missing, then,' said Len. 'Go on. Drink it down.' He lifted the cosh threateningly. Denis raised the bottle to his lips and Len tilted it so that he was forced to swallow some of the whisky it contained. It took his breath away but almost at once a warm glow seemed to spring up inside him. Len made him swallow some more, and this time Denis was less reluctant.

'There,' said Len, when he was satisfied. 'That wasn't so bad, was it?' He hadn't reckoned on the kid not drinking. The scotch would have quite an effect on him, more than he'd expected when he thought of giving him alcohol. The right amount would make him easier to handle; too much might make him aggressive.

He started the car and drove off down the road.

Denis sat in the back, hugging his arms across his body. What was going to happen now? Were they really going to Coxton? Len was driving through the town, heading towards the country. If only a police car would come along and stop them! Denis would say he had been abducted. When the police saw the cosh, they'd believe him.

After a few more miles, Len stopped the car again and made Denis swallow some more whisky. He had none himself; that was for later.

Denis felt rather swimmy now but much less afraid. Something would happen to save him. He peered out of the window, recognizing various landmarks as they drove through the countryside. The night was dry, with fitful interludes when clouds blew past the moon and a pale silver light shone down. Soon they reached Coxton, passing the shop and Ivy Lodge.

Len had had a look round earlier, before darkness fell. He remembered cycling over a narrow bridge crossing a small river when he came from the prison. It was near the big house, and he'd seen, today, that after so much rain the river was in spate, its dark water rushing towards the bigger river which it joined further on. He'd decided to tip the kid in, then go on to Ford House and do the job that had failed before.

They met no other traffic. Len stopped in a small parking bay by the river, where fishermen and picnickers left their cars. Then he turned off the lights and got out.

'Want to do a bit of driving, kid?' he asked.

Denis had been very relieved when they drove past the gates to Ford House. Perhaps Len was only having him on. What now, though?

'Get into the front and have a feel of the wheel,' Len urged. That would get the kid's prints all over it. The fact that he could not have stolen the car locally, since Len had travelled sixty miles in it, was not important. If he managed to take the BMW, he would abandon the Fiat and the police would think the kid had been joy-riding.

Denis blundered out of the car, the world swaying around him, and Len pushed him towards the driver's seat. Denis's legs stuck out of the car but his hands gripped the wheel as he tried to keep his balance. Then he struggled out to stand beside Len, holding on to the car to stop himself falling over.

Len twisted Denis's arm up behind his back again and pushed him towards the river bank, meeting little resistance because the boy's head was spinning.

As they reached the water's edge, Len let Denis go and gave him a push, but, fuddled though the boy was, he realized what was happening and thrust himself back against Len, who raised the cosh to strike him. They grappled in the darkness, two blurred shapes who could barely distinguish each other. Denis sensed the man's movement and lifted an arm to ward off the blow that was aimed at his head. The cosh struck his forearm hard and knocked him off balance into the water. There was a loud splash, then silence.

Len leaned over to discover the fate of his victim but

221

could make out nothing. The water was swirling by. He went to the car and got his torch, which he shone at the point where Denis had fallen in and towards the small bridge, but the boy had vanished. He crossed the bridge and looked in the water there, the cosh ready to use, but he saw nothing, and all he could hear was the sigh of the water rushing past.

It was time for him to hurry, too. Len turned back to walk the short distance to Ford House, the key for which Denis had provided the mould in his pocket.

The door might not be bolted tonight.

Earlier that night, Philip lay in bed thinking about the day that had ended. On the whole it had been a good one. Charles had finished painting the drawing room and had allowed Philip to help, giving him a small brush and telling him to crawl round and do the skirting boards. Philip had concentrated on the task, doing his very best and not making a single smudge on the pale walls. Charles encouraged silent working, saying Philip must pay attention to what he was doing, but at the end he praised what had been done.

'It's nice to have help,' he said. 'You did a good job.'

Philip understood Charles's problem. They were not father and son, and it was rough on Charles to have to put up with him and Emily when he would much rather be living with Rosalind and Celia. When they came, the whole family tended to have treats, go on an excursion somewhere, maybe the cinema or swimming in Swindon, things there wasn't time for in the ordinary way because Mum had to work so hard to pay their share.

Now, in the darkness, he wondered if his own father, out in Australia, had married again and had more children. If so, they'd be half related, like Robin. The thought had never occurred to him before but he supposed it was highly likely. It was tough, living alone.

Mum had said so when Charles moved in and had explained that he would help her look after them. It was only much later, because of something Celia had said, that he realized Charles had left that other family because of Mum.

If he'd done that once, he could do it again. Suppose he met someone else in London? Philip couldn't imagine Charles finding anyone nicer than Mum, but it might happen. In a way, he almost hoped it would. Then they'd be on their own again, though this time with Robin, too. Perhaps it would be rather hard on Robin. He was too little to understand these things.

Philip wasn't sure that he understood them, either. Puzzling about it, eventually he fell asleep.

They had all tried hard that Sunday. Yvonne had kept the children out of Charles's way while he got on with the painting, and she had appreciated the gesture he made in requesting Philip's help. During a fine spell in the afternoon, they had all gone for a walk over the fields to the river, squelching in their boots because the ground, after so much rain, was waterlogged. If it went on, the river would burst its banks and the fields would flood. Audrey Bannerman had told her that she had skated on the frozen flood water during the war.

They might have become friends, if she had not died. They had got past the first hurdle of Audrey's defensive shyness and her own reluctance to spread her energy beyond the family. Yvonne knew that friendship across the generations could be very rewarding. What a waste it all was.

After tea, with the painting done, they had played Racing Demon with Robin and Charles as invincible partners. Emily had cried because she had not managed to win a single game, but she stopped quickly when Charles told her that you had to take the rough with the smooth. She didn't like making him angry and, indeed, rarely did so; she was a child who had learned early in life how to stay out of trouble.

It had all been rather a strain, thought Yvonne, gazing into the darkness after Charles had fallen asleep. Even making love had become an effort. Where was the fun and laughter? Surely there had been plenty of both in those first years?

Things would improve in the summer, when the children could play outside in the sun, if there was any. After all, they had come here to enjoy the peace of country life.

It hadn't been very peaceful in recent days, since the attack on Audrey. Yvonne's thoughts kept returning to that. Still, the man Sawyer had been arrested so he wouldn't be hurting anyone else.

It was odd about the blue van that Charles had seen in the road on the fatal night. She would like to know what it had been doing there.

Someone else had mentioned a blue van to her lately. Who was it?

The water was bitterly cold, and the shock of it, when his head went under, jerked Denis out of his immediate torpor. Automatically, he thrashed out with his arms and kicked with his legs, and while he struggled to gather his fuddled wits, the thick padded anorak spread out on the water and kept him afloat as the fast-running river carried him under the bridge and out of Len's sight.

Len could not have known that when Denis and Tracy had stayed with their grandparents they had both learned to swim. Denis had loved it and lamented that there was no public pool in Leckerton. Discussions about building one had been going on for years but each new scheme came to nothing.

He bumped into the stonework under the bridge and, still spluttering, clutched at it, shaking his head, trying to clear it, taking in the fact that Len had tried to kill him. Still affected by the whisky, it was instinct rather than reason which told him to stay still and make no noise. Len might come after him. He saw the torch beam flashing beyond the bridge as Len crossed it to look over the far side, then it disappeared.

Denis waited under the bridge for several minutes. He did not hear the car start up, nor any other sounds. After a while he struggled on and worked his way towards the bank. When he got there, groping among the reeds, it was an effort to pull himself up, but he managed it and staggered to his feet. He was promptly very sick, shuddering and spluttering, vomiting river water and whisky. The taste in his mouth was vile and he thought he was going to die, but at last the retching was over.

He turned and trudged wearily back over the bridge, his one thought to find help. He was cold and felt ill and more frightened than he had ever been in his life. He'd go to Mrs Davies. She would look after him.

He had forgotten that Len had said they were going to finish the job abandoned before.

Then he saw the Fiat, parked by the river.

Denis was past using caution. He did not look to see if Len was hanging about but tottered towards the car, opened the door and slid into the driver's seat. It was a little while before he had recovered enough to try to start it, and then the key didn't seem to connect very well and he had to twiddle it to get it to work. After that he had to find the light switch. His teeth were chattering and he was sobbing as he managed to swing the car round without driving it into the river. He headed back the way they had come.

Somehow he turned between the gates of Ford House, gripping the wheel, peering ahead and bouncing from pothole to pothole along the drive, travelling fast in second gear.

Then he saw a man on the gravel sweep in front of the house.

Len turned and began to run when he saw the lights. The front door key he'd had made hadn't worked before and it didn't work now, and he was looking for a window by which to enter. He was caught like a dazzled rabbit in the headlights of the approaching car, and he froze for several seconds before dashing round to the yard where he and the boy had hidden before.

The car came after him.

Afterwards, Denis said he hadn't known what he was doing when he drove straight at Len, who had been caught by the car's wing as he tried to leap to one side, and in a way it was true. It had all seemed to happen in slow motion. Had he reached for the brake with his foot, or had he stepped more firmly on the accelerator? All that was certain was that Len was pinned against the wall of the house as the car struck it, and Denis collapsed over the wheel in a shower of shattered glass as the windscreen splintered. The headlights went out and in the sudden darkness his bulk caused the horn to sound, and it went on echoing into the night until Mrs Davies arrived in a blaze of light from the rear of the building.

She opened the driver's door, leaned in and pulled Denis back from the wheel, then switched off the ignition because although the engine had stalled, there could be a risk of fire. Later, she was surprised that she had done this automatically before she helped Denis clamber out of the car. There was blood on his face and he held an arm to his side.

Somehow it was no great shock to discover his identity.

'What have you been up to, Denis?' she asked him calmly. Nothing good, that was certain, at this time of night, and where had he found the car? Had he been joy-riding round the district? Was this how he spent his spare time? The answer to something that had been puzzling her came into her mind like a revelation and she said, 'It was your van that night. You sleep in a blue van.'

Denis wasn't listening.

'There's someone – ' he gasped. 'A man – Len – '

'Don't try to talk,' Yvonne instructed. 'It'll keep. Let's get you indoors and look at the damage.'

Denis was shivering, and as Yvonne pu' her arm round him, she realized that his clothes were sodden. He groaned as she led him into the house, limping along, a hand to his chest.

'You're soaking wet,' she said.

'I've been in the river,' said Denis. 'He – ' and he tried to point back towards the car but the effort made him groan again.

'Well, never mind now,' said Yvonne, coaxing him into a chair. He was not complaining of being unable to see, so the cuts on his face and head might be superficial; head wounds bled freely, she knew. He had not been wearing a seat belt so he had been lucky not to be catapulted through the windscreen, but only the side of the car had struck the house; it had not been a head-on collision.

She had poured warm water into a bowl and was beginning to dab the boy's forehead below his bristle of brown hair when Charles appeared in his blue towelling robe.

'What on earth's going on?' he exclaimed.

'It's Denis,' said Yvonne. 'He's smashed up some car outside, and himself, too, but I don't think he's too bad.'

'Oh Christ,' said Charles. He had taken only vague notice of Yvonne's sudden departure from their bed, thinking she was going to one of the children, although she had shaken him awake and muttered some urgent words. It was sounds from downstairs that had roused him properly and brought him to investigate.

'There's someone out there,' Denis managed to say at last. 'A man.'

'What? You weren't alone?' Charles snapped the words.

'He pushed me into the river – Len did. He tried to kill me,' said Denis, and added, 'He killed Mrs Bannerman.'

'Do you mean there's some murderer prowling about outside? Charles demanded.

'I don't think he's prowling now,' said Denis, and uttered a curious croak that was almost a laugh. 'He got in the way of the car.'

'I'll take a look round,' said Charles. 'Can you cope here?' he asked Yvonne.

'Of course,' she replied. 'But be careful. Hadn't you better take something with you, just in case? A stick or something?'

Charles picked up a heavy torch that was kept on the dresser and Yvonne continued dabbing at Denis's face. She had just decided that it was more important to get him out of his wet clothes than to deal with his injuries when Philip came into the room carrying a small cricket bat upraised like a weapon.

'I heard noises,' he said. 'But it isn't burglars, is it?' He had armed himself when he found Yvonne and Charles were not in their room.

'It's only Denis,' said his mother, as if such nocturnal visits were nothing out of the ordinary. 'He's had an accident and got very wet. It's a good thing you've come – you can be a help. Could you pop back upstairs and get a blanket from the spare room?'

'Right, Mum.' Philip, trailing the bat, went away and Yvonne started to help Denis out of his clothes. Blood was still oozing from several of the cuts on his head but it was starting to clot and she thought the wounds were best left until a doctor could see them. She was afraid some of them contained fragments of glass.

'So you ran into this man, did you?' she asked.

'He was in the way, wasn't he?' Denis repeated. 'He

228

was going to break in,' he added, remembering, and uttered a wail of protest as she drew off his jacket.

'Your chest hurts, does it?'

'Just here.' Denis clutched his side again.

'I expect you've cracked a few ribs,' said Yvonne. 'They'll mend. You've been lucky.'

Somehow, between them, they got his sweater off, Denis reluctant to lift his arm. Perhaps he'd broken his collar-bone, she thought. Then Philip appeared with the blanket.

'Oh thanks, Philip,' said his mother. 'Now, could you make Denis some cocoa? I think he'd like a hot drink before we get him off to hospital. You might like one, too.' She began extracting Denis from his heavy sweater.

'We must get the police,' said Charles, coming back into the room clearly in a highly charged condition. 'There's a dead man out there, pinned under a car.'

Philip, already carefully pouring milk into a saucepan, almost dropped it at these words.

'You're sure he's dead?' Yvonne shot Charles a sharp look.

'Certain,' said Charles grimly.

Yvonne was unlacing Denis's trainers. She felt the smooth soles at the same time as she felt Denis himself become less tense.

She was silent for a moment. Then she said, 'I expect Denis's foot slipped on the brake. Is that what happened, Denis? It can, with wet shoes.'

Denis stared at her, still shivering.

'Stand up and take off your jeans. We've got to get you warm and dry,' Yvonne ordered. 'It did slip, didn't it? Your foot?' she repeated as he obeyed.

'Yes. Yes, it did. It must have,' said Denis.

'Don't forget that, Denis,' Yvonne said. 'When you're telling the police what happened. We must telephone them now. You understand that, don't you?'

she added, as she wrapped the blanket round the boy's sturdy naked form.

Charles had gone out of the room and now he returned with a bottle of brandy.

'The boy needs picking up,' he said. 'Give him a tot.'

'No,' said Yvonne sharply. 'Not with the police coming. They'll breath-test him.'

'Have you been drinking?' Charles asked Denis.

'He made me. Len did. I've puked up most of it,' Denis muttered.

Husband and wife exchanged glances. Then Charles astonished Yvonne.

'Best if he has some brandy now. Then we can tell the police we gave him some to pull him round and the test will be invalid,' he said. 'Pour it into his cocoa or whatever you're giving him.'

By this time Philip had regained his calm and was solemnly watching the pan of milk which he had put on the stove. A mug stood nearby. Yvonne silently held it out towards Charles who slopped in some brandy.

'I won't be able to join the Marines now, will I?' Denis asked mournfully as he sipped his drink. A warm glow began to spread from the centre of his body to his extremities and his shivering eased.

'I don't suppose you will,' Yvonne agreed.

What would happen to him? He'd be up for careless driving, maybe manslaughter. Where had he got the car? And what did he know about Audrey's death? He'd said the man Len lying dead outside had killed her. Denis must have been there with the blue van, an accessory. Surely he couldn't have had anything to do with the actual murder?

'How old are you, Denis?' she asked. 'Are you really seventeen?'

'I'm almost sixteen,' he mumbled.

A liar, too. She sighed. Would he be treated as a juvenile offender and get off more lightly than someone older? Yvonne didn't know, but it was a fact that if he hadn't knocked Len down with the car that had crashed outside, the man might have broken into the house and attacked them, and that was a terrifying thought.

'What about your parents?' she said. 'You told me that old woman, Mrs Crow, was your grandmother, but that was another of your lies, wasn't it?'

'I've left home,' Denis said. 'My dad beat me up once too often so I walked out. They didn't bother. Glad to get rid of me.'

That sounded much more like the truth, and if it was, what sort of future waited for him after he served the punishment he was sure to receive for this night's work?

Yvonne became aware of Philip listening in fascination to all this.

'Off to bed,' she told him. 'I'll come up as soon as Denis has gone.' For the moment it seemed very important not to abandon Denis. 'Take your cocoa with you.'

'I'll tuck you up, old man,' said Charles, putting a hand on Philip's shoulder and propelling him away.

'Your sister.' Yvonne spoke to Denis. 'She'll stick by you.'

He shrugged.

'Maybe,' he said.

'I'm sure she will,' Yvonne declared. 'I'll go and see her. I'll explain.'

'Will you?'

She nodded.

'You can trust me, Denis,' she said. 'Just tell me what really happened when Mrs Bannerman died.'

Somehow he managed to do so, leaving out only the part about the key to Ford House whose impression he had obtained. Most of the rest was the truth, though he said that Len had insisted on taking the van, not that he had offered it.

Charles met the two constables whose patrol car had

been the nearest to Coxton when the call was received. He led them to where Len's body lay dark and unmoving beneath the car.

'We have a young lad in the house who was driving the Fiat,' said Charles. 'He told us this man – Len, he called him – killed Mrs Bannerman.' Charles had mentioned this on the telephone.

'We're holding someone for that. An escaped con,' said one of the officers.

'Seems you've got the wrong man, then, doesn't it?' Charles remarked.

The men soon radioed in for help, and it was a long time before they all left Ford House. A doctor had to be summoned to pronounce Len definitely dead, and Denis described how Len had taken Alan's van on the night of the original crime.

'Keys in it, were they?' asked one of the officers.

'He'd got one that fitted. Had a whole bunch,' said Denis, inspired.

Later, the police found signs of a scuffle on the river bank and marks further along showing where Denis had climbed out of the water. His sodden clothes, which could be tested for corroborative evidence that they were drenched with river water, were borne away in polythene bags.

Denis was also removed.

Len was identified when the police learned that he had recently been a prisoner in Lockley who worked in the village. They found the key to Ford House in his pocket among various other keys and paid no particular attention to it, deciding that it was simply part of his burglar's collection of useful accessories. They did, however, connect the key in the crashed Fiat with Audrey, and found her door key with it, linked together on a ring with a worn leather fob stamped with her initials.

Charles and Yvonne, curled up warmly together in

bed for what little was left of the night, were unable to sleep.

'Denis never meant to kill that man,' Yvonne reassured them both. 'He just meant to stop him breaking into the house. That's why he came here when he got into the car after climbing out of the river. Otherwise he'd have driven back to Leckerton. The man must have told him he was going to rob us.'

'Mm. Maybe.' Charles felt sure of nothing now. 'How did he ever get mixed up with such a villain?'

'He didn't say,' answered Yvonne. 'I suppose the man saw him about the village and got talking, and then it was chance when they met in Leckerton the night Audrey died and he needed transport.'

'I wonder why they parked outside here?' Charles remarked. 'We never asked Denis that.'

'They were probably waiting until Audrey was asleep,' Yvonne said. 'They must have been in the van when you came back that night.'

'I didn't notice if anyone was in it,' Charles said, and yawned. 'I never liked being so near that prison,' he added.

'They'll let Sawyer go now, anyway,' Yvonne said, not sure herself how she felt about it now.

'They won't. He stole bank cards and walked out of hotels without paying, and he broke out of gaol. Stole cars, too, didn't he?' Charles reminded her.

'Well, at least he won't be charged with killing Audrey when he didn't,' said Yvonne. 'That's something.'

'I suppose so.'

'I wonder how Denis really feels,' said Yvonne. 'After all, he has killed a man, even if it was an accident.'

'Shouldn't think he's really taken it in,' said Charles, who was at last beginning to feel sleepy though it would soon be time to get up. 'Too busy with his bad ankle and his ribs and his cuts and bruises.'

233

'Too shocked,' said Yvonne. 'I'll go and see his sister tomorrow.'

Charles wished she wouldn't, wished she would walk away from it all, avoid further involvement, but he was beginning to learn not to expect indifference from his wife. 'Try not to promise to visit him in gaol,' he urged, and she laughed.

The police, having made a full identification of Len, went to see Bet, taking a search warrant. They found Audrey's jewellery stashed under a floorboard but they did not discover the ring Bet had hidden in the flour. She would sell it later when all the fuss had died down; it was her only insurance. The television set and radio were removed; Audrey had marked them, as advised by the police, with an invisible pen.

When Mrs Crow heard what had happened to Denis, she waited until it was dark, then wheeled out his splendid new bike. Of course the boy had stolen it; she should have known as much. She pushed it down to the end of the road where she propped it against a wall.

Someone else would soon ride it away. Denis had trouble enough.

LONG WALK
TO FREEDOM

THE AUTOBIOGRAPHY OF
NELSON MANDELA

Macdonald Purnell

A *Macdonald Purnell* Book

First published in South Africa in 1994
by Macdonald Purnell (PTY) Ltd.

Reprinted 1994, 1995

Copyright © 1994 by Nelson Rolihlahla Mandela

The moral right of the author has been asserted.

All rights reserved.
No part of this publication may be reproduced,
stored in a retrieval system, or transmitted, in any
form or by any means, without the prior
permission in writing of the publisher, nor be
otherwise circulated in any form of binding or
cover other than that in which it is published and
without a similar condition including this
condition being imposed on the subsequent purchaser.

ISBN 0 316 87496 5

Typeset by Hewer Text Composition Services, Edinburgh
Printed and bound in Great Britain by
Clays Ltd, St Ives plc.

Macdonal Purnell (PTY) Ltd.
10 Burke Street
Randburg 2194
South Africa

CONTENTS

I dedicate this book to my six children, Madiba and Makaziwe (my first daughter), who are now deceased, and to Makgatho, Makaziwe, Zenani and Zindzi, whose support and love I treasure; to my twenty-one grandchildren and three great-grandchildren, who give me great pleasure; and to all my comrades, friends and fellow South Africans whom I serve and whose courage, determination and patriotism remain my source of inspiration.

ACKNOWLEDGEMENTS

As readers will discover, this book has a long history. I began writing it clandestinely in 1974 during my imprisonment on Robben Island. Without the tireless labour of my old comrades Walter Sisulu and Ahmed Kathrada for reviving my memories, it is doubtful the manuscript would have been completed. The copy of the manuscript which I kept with me was discovered by the authorities and confiscated. However, in addition to their unique calligraphic skills, my co-prisoners Mac Maharaj and Isu Chiba had ensured that the original manuscript safely reached its destination. I resumed work on it after my release from prison in 1990.

Since my release, my schedule has been crowded with numerous duties and responsibilities, which have left me little free time for writing. Fortunately, I have had the assistance of dedicated colleagues, friends and professionals who have helped me complete my work at last, and to whom I would like to express my appreciation. Thanks again to my comrade Ahmed Kathrada for the long hours spent revising, correcting and giving accuracy to the story.

I am deeply grateful to Richard Stengel who collaborated with me in the creation of this book, providing invaluable assistance in editing and revising the first parts and in the writing of the latter parts. I recall with fondness our early morning walks in the Transkei and the many hours of interviews at Shell House in Johannesburg and my home in Houghton. A special tribute is owed to Mary Pfaff who assisted Richard in his work. I have also benefited from the advice and support of Fatima Meer, Peter Magubane, Nadine Gordimer and Ezekiel Mphahlele.

Many thanks to my ANC office staff who patiently dealt with the logistics of the making of this book, but in particular to Barbara Masekela for her efficient co-ordination. Likewise, Iqbal Meer has devoted many hours to watching over the business aspects of the book. I am grateful to my editor, William Phillips of Little, Brown, who has guided this project from early 1990 on, and edited the text. He was ably assisted by Jordan Pavlin and Steve Schneider. I would also like to thank Professor Gail Gerhart for her factual review of the manuscript.

PART ONE

———

A Country Childhood

1

Apart from life, a strong constitution and an abiding connection to the Thembu royal house, the only thing my father bestowed upon me at birth was a name, Rolihlahla. In Xhosa, Rolihlahla literally means 'pulling the branch of a tree', but its colloquial meaning more accurately would be 'troublemaker'. I do not believe that names are destiny or that my father somehow divined my future, but in later years, friends and relatives would ascribe to my birth name the many storms I have both caused and weathered. My more familiar English or Christian name was not given to me until my first day of school. But I am getting ahead of myself.

I was born on 18 July 1918 at Mvezo, a tiny village on the banks of the Mbashe River in the district of Umtata, the capital of the Transkei. The year of my birth marked the end of the Great War; the outbreak of an influenza epidemic that killed millions throughout the world; and the visit of a delegation of the African National Congress to the Versailles peace conference to voice the grievances of the African people of South Africa. Mvezo, however, was a place apart, a tiny precinct removed from the world of great events, where life was lived much as it had been for hundreds of years.

The Transkei is 800 miles east of Cape Town, 550 miles south of Johannesburg, and lies between the Kei River and the Natal border, between the rugged Drakensberg mountains to the north and the blue waters of the Indian Ocean to the east. It is a beautiful country of rolling hills, fertile valleys, and a thousand rivers and streams which keep the landscape green even in winter. The Transkei used to be one of the largest territorial divisions within South Africa, covering an area the size of Switzerland, with a population of about three and a half million Xhosas and a tiny minority of Basothos and whites. It is home to the Thembu people, who are part of the Xhosa nation, of which I am a member.

My father, Gadla Henry Mphakanyiswa, was a chief by both blood and custom. He was confirmed as chief of Mvezo by the king of the Thembu tribe but, under British rule, his selection had to be ratified by the government, which in Mvezo took the form of the local magistrate. As a government-appointed chief, he was eligible for a stipend as well as a portion of the fees the government levied on the community for vaccination of livestock and communal grazing land. Although the role of chief was a venerable and esteemed one, it had, even seventy-five years ago, become debased by the control of an unsympathetic white government.

The Thembu tribe reaches back for twenty generations to King Zwide. According to tradition, the Thembu people lived in the foothills of the Drakensberg mountains and migrated towards the coast in the sixteenth century, where they were incorporated into the Xhosa nation. The Xhosa are part of the Nguni people who have lived, hunted and fished in the rich and temperate southeastern region of South Africa, between the great interior plateau to the north and the Indian Ocean to the south, since at least the eleventh century. The Nguni can be divided into a northern group – the Zulu and the Swazi people – and a southern group, which is made up of amaBaca, amaBomvana, amaGcaleka, amaMfengu, amaMpodomise, amaMpondo, abeSotho and abeThembu, and together they comprise the Xhosa nation.

The Xhosa are a proud and patrilineal people with an expressive and euphonious language and an abiding belief in the importance of laws, education and courtesy. Xhosa society was a balanced and harmonious social order in which every individual knew his or her place. Each Xhosa belongs to a clan that traces its descent back to a specific forefather. I am a member of the Madiba clan, named after a Thembu chief who ruled in the Transkei in the eighteenth century. I am often addressed as Madiba, my clan name, as a sign of respect.

Ngubengcuka, one of the greatest monarchs, who united the Thembu tribe, died in 1832. As was the custom, he had wives from the principal royal houses: the Great House, from which the heir is selected, the Right Hand House, and the Ixhiba, a minor house that is referred to by some as the Left Hand House. It was the task of the sons of the Ixhiba or Left Hand House to settle royal disputes. Mthikrakra, the eldest son of the Great House, succeeded Ngubengcuka and among his sons were Ngangelizwe and Matanzima. Sabata, who ruled the Thembu from 1954, was the grandson of Ngangelizwe a senior to Kalzer Daliwonga, better known as K.D. Matanzima, the former chief minister of the Transkei – my nephew, by law and custom – who was a descendant of Matanzima. The eldest son of the Ixhiba house was Simakade, whose younger brother was Mandela, my grandfather.

Although over the decades there have been many stories that I was in the line of succession to the Thembu throne, the simple genealogy I have just outlined exposes those tales as a myth. Although I was a member of the royal household, I was not among the privileged few who were trained for rule. Instead, as a descendant of the Ixhiba house, I was groomed, like my father before me, to counsel the rulers of the tribe.

My father was a tall, dark-skinned man with a straight and stately posture, which I like to think I inherited. He had a tuft of white hair just above his forehead and, as a boy, I would take white ash and rub it into my hair in imitation of him. My father had a stern manner and did not spare the rod when disciplining his children. He could be exceedingly stubborn, another trait that may unfortunately have been passed down from father to son.

My father has sometimes been referred to as the prime minister of Thembuland during the reigns of Dalindyebo, the father of Sabata, who ruled in the early 1900s, and that of his son, Jongintaba, who succeeded him. That is a misnomer in that no such title existed, but the role he played was not so different from what the designation implies. As a respected and valued counsellor to both kings, he accompanied them on their travels and was usually to be found by their sides during important meetings with government officials. He was an acknowledged custodian of Xhosa history, and it was partly for that reason that he was valued as an adviser. My own interest in history had early roots and was encouraged by my father. Although my father could neither read nor write, he was reputed to be an excellent orator who captivated his audiences by entertaining them as well as teaching them.

In later years, I discovered that my father was not only an adviser to kings but a kingmaker. After the untimely death of Jongilizwe in the 1920s, his son Sabata, the infant of the Great Wife, was too young to ascend to the throne. A dispute arose as to which of Dalindyebo's three most senior sons from other mothers – Jongintaba, Dabulamanzi and Melithafa – should be selected to succeed him. My father was consulted and recommended Jongintaba on the ground that he was the best educated. Jongintaba, he argued, would not only be a fine custodian of the crown but an excellent mentor to the young prince. My father, and a few other influential chiefs, had the great respect for education that is often present in those who are uneducated. The recommendation was controversial, for Jongintaba's mother was from a lesser house, but my father's choice was ultimately accepted by both the Thembus and the British government. In time, Jongintaba would return the favour in a way that my father could not then imagine.

All told, my father had four wives, the third of whom, my mother, Nosekeni Fanny, the daughter of Nkedama from the amaMpemvu clan of the Xhosa, belonged to the Right Hand House. Each of these wives –

the Great Wife, the Right Hand wife (my mother), the Left Hand wife and the wife of the Iqadi or support house – had her own kraal. A kraal was a homestead and usually included a simple fenced-in enclosure for animals, fields for growing crops, and one or more thatched huts. The kraals of my father's wives were separated by many miles and he commuted among them. In these travels, my father sired thirteen children in all, four boys and nine girls. I am the eldest child of the Right Hand House, and the youngest of my father's four sons. I have three sisters, Baliwe, who was the oldest girl, Notancu, and Makhutswana. Although the eldest of my father's sons was Mlahlwa, my father's heir as chief was Daligqili, the son of the Great House, who died in the early 1930s. All of his sons, with the exception of myself, are now deceased, and each was my senior not only in age but in status.

When I was not much more than a newborn child, my father was involved in a dispute that deprived him of his chieftainship at Mvezo and revealed a strain in his character I believe he passed on to his son. I maintain that nurture, rather than nature, is the primary moulder of personality, but my father possessed a proud rebelliousness, a stubborn sense of fairness, that I recognize in myself. As a chief – or headman, as it was often known among the whites – my father was compelled to account for his stewardship not only to the Thembu king but to the local magistrate. One day one of my father's subjects lodged a complaint against him involving an ox that had strayed from its owner. The magistrate accordingly sent a message ordering my father to appear before him. When my father received the summons, he sent back the following reply: '*Andizi, ndisaqula*' ('I will not come, I am still girding for battle'). One did not defy magistrates in those days. Such behaviour would be regarded as the height of insolence – and in this case it was.

My father's response bespoke his belief that the magistrate had no legitimate power over him. When it came to tribal matters, he was guided not by the laws of the king of England, but by Thembu custom. This defiance was not a fit of pique, but a matter of principle. He was asserting his traditional prerogative as a chief and was challenging the authority of the magistrate.

When the magistrate received my father's response, he promptly charged him with insubordination. There was no inquiry or investigation; that was reserved for white civil servants. The magistrate simply deposed my father, thus ending the Mandela family chieftainship.

I was unaware of these events at the time, but I was not unaffected. My father, who was a wealthy nobleman by the standards of his time, lost both his fortune and his title. He was deprived of most of his herd and land, and the revenue that came with them. Because of our straitened circumstances, my mother moved to Qunu, a slightly larger village north of Mvezo, where she would have the support of friends and relations. We lived in a less grand style in Qunu, but it was in that village near Umtata that I spent some of the happiest years of my boyhood and whence I trace my earliest memories.

2

The village of Qunu was situated in a narrow, grassy valley crisscrossed by clear streams, and overlooked by green hills. It consisted of no more than a few hundred people who lived in huts, which were beehive-shaped structures of mud walls, with a wooden pole in the centre holding up a peaked grass roof. The floor was made of crushed ant-heap, the hard dome of excavated earth above an ant colony, and was kept smooth by smearing it regularly with fresh cow dung. The smoke from the hearth escaped through the roof, and the only opening was a low doorway one had to stoop to walk through. The huts were generally grouped in a residential area that was some distance away from the maize fields. There were no roads, only paths through the grass worn away by barefooted boys and women. The women and children of the village wore blankets dyed in ochre; only the few Christians in the village wore Western-style clothing. Cattle, sheep, goats and horses grazed together in common pastures. The land around Qunu was mostly treeless except for a cluster of poplars on a hill overlooking the village. The land itself was owned by the state. With very few exceptions, Africans at that time did not enjoy private title to land in South Africa but were tenants paying rent annually to the government. In the area, there were two small primary schools, a general store, and a dipping tank to rid the cattle of ticks and diseases.

Maize (what we called mealies and people in the West call corn), sorghum, beans and pumpkins formed the largest portion of our diet, not because of any inherent preference for these foods, but because the people could not afford anything richer. The wealthier families in our village supplemented their diets with tea, coffee and sugar, but for most people in Qunu these were exotic luxuries far beyond their means. The water used for farming, cooking and washing had to be fetched in buckets from streams and springs. This was women's work and, indeed, Qunu was a village of women and children: most of the men spent the greater part of the year working on remote farms or in the mines along the Reef, the great ridge of gold-bearing rock and shale that forms the southern boundary of

Johannesburg. They returned perhaps twice a year, mainly to plough their fields. The hoeing, weeding and harvesting were left to the women and children. Few if any of the people in the village knew how to read or write, and the concept of education was still a foreign one to many.

My mother presided over three huts at Qunu which, as I remember, were always filled with the babies and children of my relations. In fact, I hardly recall any occasion as a child when I was alone. In African culture, the sons and daughters of one's aunts or uncles are considered brothers and sisters, not cousins. We do not make the same distinctions among relations practised by whites. We have no half-brothers or half-sisters. My mother's sister is my mother; my uncle's son is my brother; my brother's child is my son, my daughter.

Of my mother's three huts, one was used for cooking, one for sleeping and one for storage. In the hut in which we slept, there was no furniture in the Western sense. We slept on mats and sat on the ground. I did not discover pillows until I went to Mqhekezweni. My mother cooked food in a three-legged iron pot over an open fire in the centre of the hut or outside. Everything we ate we grew and made ourselves. My mother planted and harvested her own mealies. Mealies were harvested from the field when they were hard and dry. They were stored in sacks or pits dug in the ground. When preparing the mealies, the women used different methods. They could ground the kernels between two stones to make bread, or boil the mealies first, producing *umphothulo* (mealie flour eaten with sour milk) or *umngqusho* (samp, sometimes plain or mixed with beans). Unlike mealies, which were sometimes in short supply, milk from our cows and goats was always plentiful.

From an early age, I spent most of my free time in the veld playing and fighting with the other boys of the village. A boy who remained at home tied to his mother's apron strings was regarded as a sissy. At night, I shared my food and blanket with these same boys. I was no more than five when I became a herd-boy looking after sheep and calves in the fields. I discovered the almost mystical attachment that the Xhosa have for cattle, not only as a source of food and wealth, but as a blessing from God and a source of happiness. It was in the fields that I learned how to knock birds out of the sky with a slingshot, to gather wild honey and fruits and edible roots, to drink warm, sweet milk straight from the udder of a cow, to swim in the clear, cold streams, and to catch fish with twine and sharpened bits of wire. I learned to stick-fight – essential knowledge to any rural African boy – and became adept at its various techniques, parrying blows, feinting in one direction and striking in another, breaking away from an opponent with quick footwork. From these days I date my love of the veld, of open spaces, the simple beauties of nature, the clean line of the horizon.

As boys, we were mostly left to our own devices. We played with toys we made ourselves. We moulded animals and birds out of clay. We made ox-drawn sledges out of tree branches. Nature was our playground. The hills above Qunu were dotted with large smooth rocks which we transformed into our own roller-coaster. We sat on flat stones and slid down the face of the large rocks. We did this until our backsides were so sore we could hardly sit down. I learned to ride by sitting atop weaned calves – after being thrown to the ground several times, one got the hang of it.

I learned my lesson one day from an unruly donkey. We had been taking turns climbing up and down its back and when my chance came I jumped on and the donkey bolted into a nearby thornbush. It bent its head, trying to unseat me, which it did, but not before the thorns had pricked and scratched my face, embarrassing me in front of my friends. Like the people of the East, Africans have a highly developed sense of dignity, or what the Chinese call 'face'. I had lost face among my friends. Even though it was a donkey that unseated me, I learned that to humiliate another person is to make him suffer an unnecessarily cruel fate. Even as a boy, I defeated my opponents without dishonouring them.

Usually the boys played among themselves, but we sometimes allowed our sisters to join us. Boys and girls would play games like *ndize* (hide and seek) and *icekwa* (tag). But the game I most enjoyed playing with the girls was what we called *khetha*, or choose-the-one-you-like. This was not so much an organized game, but a spur-of-the-moment sport that took place when we accosted a group of girls our own age and demanded that each select the boy she loved. Our rules dictated that the girl's choice be respected and once she had chosen her favourite, she was free to continue on her journey escorted by the lucky boy she loved. But the girls were nimble-witted – far cleverer than we doltish lads – and would often confer among themselves and choose one boy, usually the plainest fellow, and then tease him all the way home.

The most popular game for boys was *thinti*, and like most boys' games it was a youthful approximation of war. Two sticks, used as targets, would be driven firmly into the ground in an upright position about a hundred feet apart. The goal of the game was for each team to hurl sticks at the opposing target and knock it down. We each defended our own target and attempted to prevent the other side from retrieving the sticks that had been thrown over. As we grew older, we organized matches against boys from neighbouring villages and those who distinguished themselves in these fraternal battles were greatly admired, as generals who achieve great victories in war are justly celebrated.

After games such as these, I would return to my mother's kraal where she was preparing supper. Whereas my father once told stories of historic battles and heroic Xhosa warriors, my mother would enchant us with Xhosa legends and fables that had come down from numberless generations. These tales stimulated my childish imagination, and usually contained some moral lesson. I recall one my mother told us about a traveller who was approached by an old woman with terrible cataracts on her eyes. The woman asked the traveller for help, and the man averted his eyes. Then another man came along and was approached by the old woman. She asked him to clean her eyes, and even though he found the task unpleasant, he did as she asked. Then, miraculously, the scales fell from the old woman's eyes and she became young and beautiful. The man married her and became wealthy and prosperous. It is a simple tale, but its message is an enduring one: virtue and generosity will be rewarded in ways that one cannot know.

Like all Xhosa children, I acquired knowledge mainly through observation. We were meant to learn through imitation and emulation, not through questions. When I first visited the homes of whites, I was often dumbfounded by the number and nature of questions that children asked their parents – and their parents' unfailing willingness to answer them. In my household, questions were considered a nuisance; adults imparted such information as they considered necessary.

My life, and that of most Xhosas at the time, was shaped by custom, ritual and taboo. This was the alpha and omega of our existence, and went unquestioned. Men followed the path laid out for them by their fathers; women led the same lives as their mothers had before them. Without being told, I soon assimilated the elaborate rules that governed the relations between men and women. I discovered that a man may not enter a house where a woman has recently given birth, and that a newly married woman would not enter the kraal of her new home without elaborate ceremony. I also learned that to neglect one's ancestors would bring ill-fortune and failure in life. If you dishonoured your ancestors in some way, the only way to atone for that lapse was to consult a traditional healer or tribal elder, who communicated with the ancestors and conveyed profound apologies. All of these beliefs were perfectly natural to me.

I came across few whites as a boy at Qunu. The local magistrate, of course, was white, as was the nearest shopkeeper. Occasionally white travellers or policemen passed through our area. These whites appeared as grand as gods to me, and I was aware that they were to be treated with a mixture of fear and respect. But their role in my life was a distant one, and I thought little if at all about the white man in general or relations between my own people and these curious and remote figures.

The only rivalry between different clans or tribes in our small world at Qunu was that between the Xhosas and the amaMfengu, a small number of whom lived in our village. AmaMfengu arrived on the eastern Cape after fleeing from Shaka Zulu's armies in a period known as the iMfecane, the great wave of battles and migrations between 1820 and 1840 set in motion by the rise of Shaka and the Zulu state, during which the Zulu warrior sought to conquer and then unite all the tribes under military rule. The amaMfengu, who were not originally Xhosa-speakers, were refugees from the iMfecane and were forced to do jobs that no other African would do. They worked on white farms and in white businesses, something that was looked down upon by the more established Xhosa tribes. But the amaMfengu were an industrious people, and because of their contact with Europeans, they were often more educated and 'Western' than other Africans.

When I was a boy, the amaMfengu were the most advanced section of the community and furnished our clergymen, policemen, teachers, clerks and interpreters. They were also among the first to become Christians, to build better houses and to use scientific methods of agriculture, and they were wealthier than their Xhosa compatriots. They confirmed the missionaries' axiom, that to be Christian was to be civilized, and to be civilized was to be Christian. There still existed some hostility towards the amaMfengu, but in retrospect I would attribute this more to jealousy than tribal animosity. This local form of tribalism that I observed as a boy was relatively harmless. At that stage, I did not witness nor even suspect the violent tribal rivalries that would subsequently be promoted by the white rulers of South Africa.

My father did not subscribe to the local prejudice towards the amaMfengu and befriended two amaMfengu brothers, George and Ben Mbekela. The brothers were an exception in Qunu: they were educated and Christian. George, the elder, was a retired teacher and Ben was a police sergeant. Despite the proselytizing of the Mbekela brothers, my father remained aloof from Christianity and instead reserved his own faith for the great spirit of the Xhosas, Qamata, the God of his fathers. My father was an unofficial priest and presided over ritual slaughtering of goats and calves and officiated at local traditional rites concerning planting, harvest, birth, marriage, initiation ceremonies and funerals. He did not need to be ordained, for the traditional religion of the Xhosas is characterized by a cosmic wholeness, so that there is little distinction between the sacred and the secular, between the natural and the supernatural.

While the faith of the Mbekela brothers did not rub off on my father, it did inspire my mother, who became a Christian. In fact, Fanny was literally her Christian name, for she had been given it in church. It was due to the influence of the Mbekela brothers that I myself was baptized into the Methodist, or Wesleyan Church as it was then known, and sent to school.

The brothers would often see me playing or minding sheep and come over to talk to me. One day, George Mbekela paid a visit to my mother. 'Your son is a clever young fellow,' he said. 'He should go to school.' My mother remained silent. No one in my family had ever attended school and my mother was unprepared for Mbekela's suggestion. But she did relay it to my father who, despite – or perhaps because of – his own lack of education, immediately decided that his youngest son should go to school.

The schoolhouse consisted of a single room, with a Western-style roof, on the other side of the hill from Qunu. I was seven years old, and on the day before I was to begin, my father took me aside and told me that I must be dressed properly for school. Until that time, I, like all the other boys in Qunu, had worn only a blanket, which was wrapped round one shoulder and pinned at the waist. My father took a pair of his trousers and cut them at the knee. He told me to put them on, which I did, and they were roughly the correct length, although the waist was far too large. My father then took a piece of string and drew the trousers in at the waist. I must have been a comical sight, but I have never owned a suit I was prouder to wear than my father's cut-off trousers.

On the first day of school my teacher, Miss Mdingane, gave each of us an English name and said that thenceforth that was the name we would answer to in school. This was the custom among Africans in those days and was undoubtedly due to the British bias of our education. The education I received was a British education, in which British ideas, British culture and British institutions were automatically assumed to be superior. There was no such thing as African culture.

Africans of my generation – and even today – generally have both a Western and an African name. Whites were either unable or unwilling to pronounce an African name, and considered it uncivilized to have one. That day, Miss Mdingane told me that my new name was Nelson. Why she bestowed this particular name upon me I have no idea. Perhaps it had something to do with the great British sea captain Lord Nelson, but that would be only a guess.

3

One night, when I was nine years old, I was aware of a commotion in the household. My father, who took turns visiting his wives and usually came to us for perhaps one week a month, had arrived. But it was not at his accustomed time, for he was not scheduled to be with us for another few days. I found him in my mother's hut, lying on his back on the floor, in the midst of what seemed like an endless fit of coughing. Even to my young eyes, it was clear that my father was not long for this world. He was ill with some type of lung disease, but it was not diagnosed, as my father had never visited a doctor. He remained in the hut for several days without moving or speaking, and then one night he took a turn for the worse. My mother and my father's youngest wife, Nodayimani, who had come to stay with us, were looking after him, and late that night he called for Nodayimani. 'Bring me my tobacco,' he told her. My mother and Nodayimani conferred, and decided that it was unwise that he have tobacco in his current state. But he persisted in calling for it, and eventually Nodayimani filled his pipe, lit it, and then handed it to him. My father smoked and became calm. He continued smoking for perhaps an hour, and then, his pipe still lit, he died.

I do not remember experiencing great grief so much as feeling cut adrift. Although my mother was the centre of my existence, I defined myself through my father. My father's passing changed my whole life in a way that I did not suspect at the time. After a brief period of mourning, my mother informed me that I would be leaving Qunu. I did not ask her why, or where I was going.

I packed the few things that I possessed and early one morning we set out on a journey westward to my new residence. I mourned less for my father than for the world I was leaving behind. Qunu was all that I knew, and I loved it in the unconditional way that a child loves his first home. Before we disappeared behind the hills, I turned and looked for what I imagined was the last time at my village. I could see the simple huts and the people going about their chores; the stream where I had splashed and played with the other boys; the maize fields and green pastures where the herds and flocks were lazily grazing. I imagined my friends out hunting for small birds, drinking the sweet milk from the cow's udder, cavorting in the pond at the end of the stream. Above all else, my eyes rested on the three simple huts where I had enjoyed my mother's love and protection. It was these three huts that I associated with all my happiness, with life itself, and I rued the fact that I had not kissed each of them before I left. I could not imagine that the future I was walking towards could compare in any way with the past that I was leaving behind.

We travelled by foot and in silence until the sun was sinking slowly towards the horizon. But the silence of the heart between mother and child is not a lonely one. My mother and I never talked very much, but we did not need to. I never doubted her love or questioned her support. It was an exhausting journey, along rocky dirt roads, up and down hills, past numerous villages, but we did not pause. Late in the afternoon, at the bottom of a shallow valley surrounded by trees, we came upon a village at the centre of which was a large and gracious home that so far exceeded anything that I had ever seen that all I could do was marvel at it. The buildings consisted of two *iingxande* (or rectangular houses) and seven stately rondavels (superior huts), all washed in white lime, dazzling even in the light of the setting sun. There was a large front garden and a maize field bordered by rounded peach trees. An even more spacious garden spread out behind it, which boasted apple trees, a vegetable garden, a strip of flowers and a patch of wattles. Nearby was a white stucco church.

In the shade of two gum trees that graced the doorway of the front of the main house sat a group of about twenty tribal elders. Encircling the property, contentedly grazing on the rich land, was a herd of at least fifty cattle and perhaps five hundred sheep. Everything was beautifully tended, and it was a vision of wealth and order beyond my imagination. This was the Great Place, Mqhekezweni, the provisional capital of Thembuland, the royal residence of Chief Jongintaba Dalindyebo, acting regent of the Thembu people.

As I contemplated all this grandeur an enormous motor car rumbled through the western gate and the men sitting in the shade immediately doffed their hats and then jumped to their feet shouting, '*Bayete a-a-a, Jongintaba!*' ('Hail, Jongintaba!'), the traditional salute of the Xhosas for their chief. Out of the motor car (I learned later that this majestic vehicle was a Ford V8) stepped a short, thickset man wearing a smart suit. I could see that he had the confidence and bearing of a man who was used to the exercise of authority. His name suited him, for Jongintaba literally means 'One who looks at the mountains', and he was a man with a sturdy presence upon whom all eyes gazed. He had a dark complexion and an intelligent face, and he casually shook hands with each of the men beneath the tree, men who as I later discovered comprised the highest Thembu Court of Justice. This was the regent who was to become my guardian and benefactor for the next decade.

In that moment of beholding Jongintaba and his court I felt like a sapling pulled root and branch from the earth and flung into the centre of a stream whose strong current I could not resist. I felt a sense of awe mixed with bewilderment. Until then I had had no thoughts of anything but my own pleasures, no higher ambition than to eat well and become a champion stick-fighter. I had no thought of money, or class, or fame, or power. Suddenly a new world opened before me. Children from poor homes often find themselves beguiled by a host of new temptations when suddenly confronted by great wealth. I was no exception. I felt many of my established beliefs and loyalties begin to ebb away. The slender foundation built by my parents began to shake. In that instant, I saw that life might hold more for me than being a champion stick-fighter.

I learned later that, in the wake of my father's death, Jongintaba had offered to become my guardian. He would treat me as he treated his other children, and I would have the same advantages as they. My mother had no choice; one did not turn down such an overture from the regent. She was satisfied that, although she would miss me, I would have a more advantageous upbringing in the regent's care than in her own. The regent had not forgotten that it was due to my father's intervention that he had become acting paramount chief.

My mother remained in Mqhekezweni for a day or two before returning to Qunu. Our parting was without fuss. She offered no sermons, no words of wisdom, no kisses. I suspect she did not want me to feel bereft at her departure and so was matter-of-fact. I knew that my father had wanted me to be educated and prepared for a wide world, and I could not do that in Qunu. Her tender look was all the affection and support I needed, and as she departed she turned to me and said, '*Uqinisufokotho, Kwedini!*' ('Brace yourself, my boy!'). Children are often the least sentimental of creatures, especially if they are absorbed in some new pleasure. Even as my dear mother and first friend was leaving, my head was swimming with the delights of my new home. How could I not be braced up? I was already wearing the handsome new outfit purchased for me by my guardian.

I was quickly caught up in the daily life of Mqhekezweni. A child adapts rapidly, or not at all – and I had taken to the Great Place as though I had been raised there. To me, it was a magical kingdom; everything was delightful; the chores that were tedious in Qunu became an adventure in Mqhekezweni. When I was not in school, I was a ploughboy, a waggon guide, a shepherd. I rode horses and shot birds with slingshots and found boys to joust with, and some nights I danced the evening away to the beautiful singing and clapping of Thembu maidens. Although I missed Qunu and my mother, I was completely absorbed in my new world.

I attended a one-room school next door to the palace and studied English, Xhosa, history and geography. We read *Chambers English Reader* and did our lessons on black slates. Our teachers, Mr Fadana and, later, Mr Giqwa, took a special interest in me. I did well in school not so much through cleverness as through doggedness. My own self-discipline was reinforced by my aunt Phathiwe, who lived in the Great Place and scrutinized my homework every night.

Mqhekezweni was a mission station of the Methodist Church and far more up-to-date and Westernised than Qunu. People dressed in modern clothes. The men wore suits and the women affected the severe Protestant style of the missionaries: thick long skirts and high-necked blouses, with a blanket draped over the shoulder and a scarf wound elegantly around the head.

If the world of Mqhekezweni revolved around the regent, my smaller world revolved around his two children. Justice, the elder, was his only son and heir to the Great Place, and Nomafu was the regent's daughter. I lived with them and was treated exactly as they were. We ate the same food, wore the same clothes, performed the same chores. We were later joined by Nxeko, the older brother to Sabata, the heir to the throne. The four of us formed a royal quartet. The regent and his wife No-England brought me up as if I were their own child. They worried about me, guided me and punished me, all in a spirit of loving fairness. Jongintaba was stern, but I never doubted his love. They called me by the pet name of Tatomkhulu, which means 'Grandpa', because they said when I was very serious, I looked like an old man.

Justice was four years older than me and became my first hero after my father. I looked up to him in every way. He was already at Clarkebury, a boarding school about sixty miles away. Tall, handsome and muscular, he was a fine sportsman, excelling in track and field events, cricket, rugby and soccer. Cheerful and outgoing, he was a natural performer who enchanted audiences with his singing and transfixed them with his ballroom dancing. He had a bevy of female admirers – but also a coterie of critics, who considered him a dandy and a playboy. Justice and I became the best of friends, though we were opposites in many ways: he was extroverted, I was introverted; he was lighthearted, I was serious. Things came easily to him; I had to drill myself. To me, he was everything a young man should be and everything I longed to be. Though treated alike, our destinies were different: Justice would inherit one of the most powerful chieftainships of the Thembu tribe, while I would inherit whatever the regent, in his generosity, decided to give me.

Every day I was in and out of the regent's house doing errands. Of those I did for the regent, the one I enjoyed most was pressing his suits, a job in which I took great pride. He owned half a dozen Western suits, and I spent many an hour carefully making the creases in his trousers. His palace, as it were, consisted of two large Western-style houses with tin roofs. In those days, very few Africans had Western houses and they were considered a mark of great wealth. Six rondavels stood in a semicircle around the main house. They had wooden floorboards, something I had never seen before. The regent and the queen slept in the right-hand rondavel, the queen's sister in the centre one, and the left-hand hut served as a pantry. Under the floor of the queen's sister's hut was a beehive, and we would sometimes take up a floorboard or two and feast on its honey. Shortly after I moved to Mqhekezweni, the regent and his wife moved to the *uxande* (middle house), which automatically became the Great House. There were three small rondavels near it; one for the regent's mother, one for visitors and one shared by Justice and myself.

The two principles that governed my life at Mqhekezweni were chieftaincy and the Church. These two doctrines existed in uneasy harmony, although I did not then see them as antagonistic. For me, Christianity was not so much a system of beliefs as it was the powerful creed of a single man: Reverend Matyolo. For me, his powerful presence embodied all that was alluring in Christianity. He was as popular and beloved as the regent, and the fact that he was the regent's superior in spiritual matters made a strong impression on me. But the Church was as concerned with this world as the next: I saw that virtually all of the achievements of Africans seemed to have come about through the missionary work of the Church. The mission schools trained the clerks, the interpreters and the policemen, who at the time represented the height of African aspirations.

Reverend Matyolo was a stout man in his mid-fifties, with a deep and potent voice that lent itself to both preaching and singing. When he preached at the simple church at the western end of Mqhekezweni, the hall was always brimming with people. The hall rang with the hosannas of the faithful, while the women knelt at his feet to beg for salvation. The first tale I heard about him when I arrived at the Great Place was that he had chased away a dangerous ghost with only a Bible and a lantern as weapons. I saw neither implausibility nor contradiction in this story. The Methodism preached by Reverend Matyolo was of the fire-and-brimstone variety, seasoned with a bit of African animism. The Lord was wise and omnipotent, but He was also a vengeful God who let no bad deed go unpunished.

At Qunu, the only time I had ever attended church was on the day that I was baptized. Religion was a ritual that I indulged in for my mother's sake and to which I attached no meaning. But at Mqhekezweni, religion was a part of the fabric of life and I attended church each Sunday along with the regent and his wife. The regent took his religion very seriously. In fact the only time that I was ever given a hiding by him was when I dodged a Sunday service to take part in a fight against boys from another village, a transgression I never committed again.

That was not the only rebuke I received on account of my trespasses against the reverend. One afternoon, I crept into Reverend Matyolo's garden and stole some maize, which I roasted and ate on the spot. A young girl saw me eating the corn in the garden and immediately reported my presence to the priest. The news quickly made the rounds and reached the regent's wife. That evening, she waited until prayer time – which was a daily ritual in the house – and confronted me with my misdeed, reproaching me for taking the bread from a poor servant of God and disgracing the family. She said the devil would certainly take me to task for my sin. I felt an unpleasant mixture of fear and shame – fear that I would get some cosmic comeuppance and shame that I had abused the trust of my adopted family.

Because of the universal respect the regent enjoyed – from both black and white – and the seemingly untempered power that he wielded, I saw chieftaincy as being the very centre around which life revolved. The power and influence of chieftaincy pervaded every aspect of our lives in Mqhekezweni and was the pre-eminent means through which one could achieve influence and status.

My later notions of leadership were profoundly influenced by observing the regent and his court. I watched and learned from the tribal meetings that were regularly held at the Great Place. These were not scheduled, but were called as needed, and were held to discuss national matters such as a drought, the culling of cattle, policies ordered by the magistrate, or new laws decreed by the government. All Thembus were free to come – and a great many did, on horseback or by foot.

On these occasions, the regent was surrounded by his *amaphakathi*, a group of councillors of high rank who functioned as the regent's parliament and judiciary. They were wise men who retained the knowledge of tribal history and custom in their heads and whose opinions carried great weight.

Letters advising these chiefs and headmen of a meeting were dispatched from the regent, and soon the Great Place became alive with important visitors and travellers from all over Thembuland. The guests would gather in the courtyard in front of the regent's house and he would open the meeting by thanking everyone for coming and explaining why he had summoned them. From that point on, he would not utter another word until the meeting was nearing its end.

Everyone who wanted to speak did so. It was democracy in its purest form. There may have been a hierarchy of importance among the speakers, but everyone was heard: chief and subject, warrior and medicine man, shopkeeper and farmer, landowner and labourer. People spoke without interruption and the meetings lasted for many hours. The foundation of self-government was that all men were free to voice their opinions and were equal in their value as citizens. (Women, I am afraid, were deemed second-class citizens.)

A great banquet was served during the day, and I often gave myself a bellyache by eating too much while listening to speaker after speaker. I noticed how some speakers rambled and never seemed to get to the point. I grasped how others came to the matter at hand directly, and who made a set of arguments succinctly and cogently. I observed how some speakers used emotion and dramatic language, and tried to move the audience with such techniques, while others were sober and even, and shunned emotion.

At first, I was astonished by the vehemence – and candour – with which people criticized the regent. He was not above criticism – in fact, he was often the principal target of it. But no matter how serious the charge, the regent simply listened, not defending himself, showing no emotion at all.

The meetings would continue until some kind of consensus was reached. They ended in unanimity or not at all. Unanimity, however, might be an agreement to disagree, to wait for a more propitious time to propose a solution. Democracy meant all men were to be heard, and a decision was taken together as a people. Majority rule was a foreign notion. A minority was not to be crushed by a majority.

Only at the end of the meeting, as the sun was setting, would the regent speak. His purpose was to sum up what had been said and form some consensus among the diverse opinions. But no conclusion was forced on people who disagreed. If no agreement could be reached, another meeting would be held. At the very end of the council, a praise-singer or poet would deliver a panegyric to the ancient kings, and a mixture of compliments to and satire on the present chiefs; the audience, led by the regent, would roar with laughter.

As a leader, I have always followed the principles I first saw demonstrated by the regent at the Great Place. I have always endeavoured to listen to what each and every person in a discussion had to say before venturing my own opinion. Oftentimes, my own opinion will simply represent a consensus of what I heard in the discussion. I always remember the regent's axiom: a leader, he said, is like a shepherd. He stays behind the flock, letting the most nimble go on ahead, whereupon the others follow, not realizing that all along they are being directed from behind.

It was at Mqhekezweni that I developed my interest in African history. Until then I had heard only of Xhosa heroes, but at the Great Place I learned of other African heroes like Sekhukhune, king of the Bapedi, the Basotho king, Moshoeshoe, and Dingane, king of the Zulus, and others such as Bambatha, Hintsa and Makana, Montshiwa and Kgama. I learned of these men from the chiefs and headmen who came to the Great Place to settle disputes and try cases. Though not lawyers, these men presented cases and then adjudicated them. Some days, they would finish early and sit around telling stories. I hovered silently and listened. They spoke in an idiom that I'd never heard before. Their speech was formal and lofty, their manner slow and unhurried, and the traditional clicks of our language were long and dramatic.

At first, they shooed me away and told me I was too young to listen. Later they would beckon me to fetch fire or water for them, or to tell the women they wanted tea, and in those early months I was too busy running errands to follow their conversation. But, eventually, they permitted me to stay, and I discovered the great African patriots who fought against Western domination. My imagination was fired by the glory of these African warriors.

The most ancient of the chiefs who regaled the gathered elders with ancient tales was Zwelibhangile Joyi, a son from the Great House of King Ngubengcuka. Chief Joyi was so old that his wrinkled skin hung on him like a loose-fitting coat. His stories unfolded slowly and were often punctuated by a great wheezing cough, which would force him to stop for minutes at a time. Chief Joyi was the great authority on the history of the Thembus in large part because he had lived through so much of it.

But as grizzled as Chief Joyi often seemed, the decades fell off him when he spoke of the *impis*, or warriors, in the army of King Ngangelizwe. In pantomime, Chief Joyi would fling his spear and creep along the veld as he narrated the victories and defeats. He spoke of Ngangelizwe's heroism, generosity and humility.

Not all of Chief Joyi's stories revolved around the Thembus. When he first spoke of non-Xhosa warriors, I wondered why. I was like a boy who worships a local soccer hero and is not interested in a national soccer star with whom he has no connection. Only later was I moved by the broad sweep of African history, and the deeds of all African heroes regardless of tribe.

Chief Joyi railed against the white man, whom he believed had deliberately sundered the Xhosa tribe, dividing brother from brother. The white man had told the Thembus that their true chief was the great white queen across the ocean and that they were her subjects. But the white queen brought nothing but misery and perfidy to the black people; if she was a chief, she was an evil chief. Chief Joyi's war stories and his indictment of the British made me feel angry and cheated, as though I had already been robbed of my own birthright.

Chief Joyi said that the African people lived in relative peace until the coming of the *abelungu*, the white people, who arrived from across the sea with fire-breathing weapons. Once, he said, the Thembu, the Pondo, the Xhosa, and the Zulu were all children of one father, and lived as brothers. The white man shattered the *abantu*, the fellowship, of the various tribes. The white man was hungry and greedy for land, and the black man shared the land with him as they shared the air and water; land was not for man to possess. But the white man took the land as you might seize another man's horse.

I did not yet know that the real history of our country was not to be found in standard British textbooks, which claimed South Africa began with the landing of Jan van Riebeeck at the Cape of Good Hope in 1652. It was from Chief Joyi that I began to discover that the history of the Bantu-speaking peoples began far to the north, in a country of lakes and green plains and valleys, and that slowly over the millennia we made our way down to the very tip of this great continent. However, I later discovered that Chief Joyi's account of African history, particularly after 1652, was not always so accurate.

In Mqhekezweni, I felt not unlike the proverbial country boy who comes to the big city. Mqhekezweni was far more sophisticated than Qunu, whose residents were regarded as backward by the people of Mqhekezweni. The regent was loath for me to visit Qunu, thinking I would regress and fall into bad company back in my old village. When I did visit, I sensed that my mother had been briefed by the regent, for she would question me closely as to whom I was playing with. On many occasions, however, the regent would arrange for my mother and sisters to be brought to the Great Place.

When I first arrived in Mqhekezweni, I was regarded by some of my peers as a yokel who was hopelessly unequipped to exist in the rarefied atmosphere of the Great Place. As young men will, I did my best to appear suave and sophisticated. In church one day, I had noticed a lovely young woman who was one of the daughters of the Reverend Matyolo. Her name was Winnie and I asked her out and she accepted. She was keen on me, but her eldest sister, nomaMpondo, regarded me as hopelessly backward. She told her sister that I was a barbarian who was not good enough for the daughter of Reverend Matyolo. To prove to her younger sister how uncivilized I was, she invited me to the rectory for lunch. I was still used to eating at home, where we did not use a knife and fork. At the family table, this mischievous older sister handed me a plate that contained a single chicken wing. But the wing, instead of being soft and tender, was a bit tough, so the meat did not fall easily off the bone.

I watched the others using their knives and forks with ease and slowly picked up mine. I observed the others for a few moments, and then attempted to carve my little wing. At first I just moved it around the plate, hoping that the flesh would fall from the bone. Then I tried in vain to pin the thing down and cut it, but it eluded me, and in my frustration I was clanking my knife on the plate. I tried this repeatedly and then noticed that the older sister was smiling at me and looking knowingly at the younger sister as if to say, 'I told you so.' I struggled and struggled and became wet with perspiration, but I did not want to admit defeat and pick the infernal thing up with my hands. I did not eat much chicken that day at luncheon.

Afterwards the older sister told the younger, 'You will waste your whole life if you fall in love with such a backward boy,' but I am happy to say the young lady did not listen – she loved me, backward as I was. Eventually, of course, we went different ways and drifted apart. She attended a different school, and qualified as a teacher. We corresponded for a few years and then I lost track of her, but by that time I had considerably improved my table etiquette.

4

When I was sixteen, the regent decided that it was time that I became a man. In Xhosa tradition, this is achieved through one means only: circumcision. In my tradition, an uncircumcised male cannot be heir to his father's wealth, cannot marry or officiate in tribal rituals. An uncircumcised Xhosa man is a contradiction in terms, for he is not considered a man at all, but a boy. For the Xhosa people, circumcision represents the formal incorporation of males into society. It is not just a surgical procedure, but a lengthy and elaborate ritual in preparation for manhood. As a Xhosa, I count my years as a man from the date of my circumcision.

The traditional ceremony of the circumcision school was arranged principally for Justice. The rest of us, twenty-six in all, were there mainly to keep him company. Early in the new year, we journeyed to two grass huts in a secluded valley on the banks of the Mbashe River, known as Tyhalarha, the traditional place of circumcision for Thembu kings. The huts were seclusion lodges, where we were to live isolated from society. It was a sacred time; I felt happy and fulfilled taking part in my people's customs and ready to make the transition from boyhood to manhood.

We had moved to Tyhalarha by the river a few days before the actual circumcision ceremony. These last few days of boyhood were spent with the other initiates, and I found the camaraderie enjoyable. The lodge was near the home of Banabakhe Blayi, the wealthiest and most popular boy at the circumcision school. He was an engaging fellow, a champion stick-fighter and a glamour boy, whose many girlfriends kept us all supplied with delicacies. Although he could neither read nor write, he was one of the most intelligent among us. He regaled us with stories of his trips to Johannesburg, a place that none of us had ever been to. He so thrilled us with tales of the mines that he almost persuaded me that to be a miner was more alluring than to be a monarch. Miners had a mystique; to be a miner meant to be strong and daring: the ideal of manhood. Much later, I realized that it was the exaggerated tales of boys like Banabakhe that caused so many young men to run away to work in the mines of Johannesburg, where they often lost their health and their lives. In those days, working in the mines was almost as much of a rite of passage as circumcision school, a myth that helped the mine-owners more than it helped my people.

A custom of circumcision school is that one must perform a daring exploit before the ceremony. In days of old, this might have involved a cattle raid or even a battle, but in our time the deeds were more mischievous than martial. Two nights before we moved to Tyhalarha, we decided to steal a pig. In Mkhekezweni, there was a tribesman with a typical old pig. To avoid making a noise and alarming the farmer, we arranged for the pig to do our work for us. We took handfuls of sediment from homemade African beer, which has a strong scent much favoured by pigs, and placed it upwind of the animal. It was so aroused by the scent that he came out of the kraal, following a trail we had laid and gradually made his way to us, wheezing and snorting, and eating the sediment. When he got near us, we captured the poor pig, slaughtered it, and then built a fire and ate roast pork underneath the stars. No piece of pork has ever tasted as good before or since.

The night before the circumcision, there was a ceremony near our huts with singing and dancing. Women came from the nearby villages and we danced to their singing and clapping. As the music became faster and louder, our dance turned more frenzied and we forgot for a moment what lay ahead.

At dawn, when the stars were still in the sky, we began our preparations. We were escorted to the river to bathe in its cold waters, a ritual that signified our purification before the ceremony. The ceremony was at midday, and we were commanded to stand in a row in a clearing some distance from the river where a crowd of parents and relatives, including the regent, as well as a handful of chiefs and counsellors, had gathered. We were clad only in our blankets and as the ceremony began, with drums pounding, we were ordered to sit on a blanket on the ground with our legs spread out in front of us. I was tense and anxious, uncertain of how I would react when the critical moment came. Flinching or crying out was a sign of weakness and stigmatized one's manhood. I was determined not to disgrace myself, the group or my guardian. Circumcision is a trial of bravery and stoicism; no anaesthetic is used; a man must suffer in silence.

To the right, out of the corner of my eye, I could see a thin, elderly man emerge from a tent and kneel in front of the first boy. There was excitement in the crowd, and I shuddered slightly, knowing that the ritual was about to begin. The old man was a famous *ingcibi*, a circumcision expert, from Gcalekaland, who would use his assegai to change us from boys to men with a single blow.

Suddenly I heard the first boy cry out, '*Ndiyindoda!*' ('I am a man!'), which we had been trained to say at the moment of circumcision. Seconds later, I heard Justice's strangled voice pronounce the same phrase. There were now two boys before the *ingcibi* reached me, and my mind must have gone blank because, before I knew it, the old man was kneeling in front of me. I looked directly into his eyes. He was pale, and though the day was cold, his face was shining with perspiration. His hands moved so fast they seemed to be controlled by an otherworldly force. Without a word, he took my foreskin, pulled it forward, and then, in a single motion, brought down his assegai. I felt as if fire was shooting through my veins; the pain was so intense that I buried my chin in my chest. Many seconds seemed to pass before I remembered the cry, and then I recovered and called out, '*Ndiyindoda!*'

I looked down and saw a perfect cut, clean and round like a ring. But I felt ashamed because the other boys seemed much stronger and firmer than I had been; they had called out more promptly than I had. I was distressed that I had been disabled, however briefly, by the pain, and I did my best to hide my agony. A boy may cry; a man conceals his pain.

I had now taken the essential step in the life of every Xhosa man. Now I might marry, set up my own home and plough my own field. I could now be admitted to the councils of the community; my words would be taken seriously. At the ceremony, I was given my circumcision name, Dalibhunga, meaning 'Founder of the Bungha', the traditional ruling body of the Transkei. To Xhosa traditionalists, this name is more acceptable than either of my two previous given names, Rolihlahla or Nelson, and I was proud to hear my new name pronounced: Dalibhunga.

Immediately after the blow had been delivered, an assistant who followed the circumcision master took the foreskin that was on the ground and tied it to a corner of our blankets. Our wounds were then dressed with a healing plant, the leaves of which were thorny on the outside but smooth on the inside, which absorbed the blood and other secretions.

At the conclusion of the ceremony, we returned to our huts, where a fire was burning with wet wood that cast off clouds of smoke, which was thought to promote healing. We were ordered to lie on our backs in the smoky huts, with one leg flat, and one leg bent. We were now *abakwetha*, initiates into the world of manhood. We were looked after by an *amakhankatha*, or guardian, who explained the rules we had to follow if we were to enter manhood properly. The first chore of the *amakhankatha* was to paint our naked and shaved bodies from head to foot in white ochre, turning us into ghosts. The white chalk symbolized our purity, and I still recall how stiff the dried clay felt on my body.

That first night, at midnight, an attendant, or *ikhankatha*, crept around the hut, gently waking each of us. We were then instructed to leave the hut and go tramping through the night to bury our foreskins. The traditional reason for this practice was so that our foreskins would be hidden before wizards could use them for evil purposes, but, symbolically, we were also burying our youth. I did not want to leave the warm hut and wander through the bush in the darkness, but I walked into the trees and, after a few minutes, untied my foreskin and buried it in the earth. I felt as though I had now discarded the last remnant of my childhood.

We lived in our two huts – thirteen in each – while our wounds healed. When outside the huts, we were covered in blankets, for we were not allowed to be seen by women. It was a period of quietude, a kind of spiritual preparation for the trials of manhood that lay ahead. On the day of our re-emergence, we went down to the river early in the morning to wash away the white ochre in the waters of the Mbashe. Once we were clean and dry, we were coated in red ochre. The tradition was that one should sleep with a woman, who later might become one's wife, and she rubs off the pigment with her body. In my case, however, the ochre was removed with a mixture of fat and lard.

At the end of our seclusion, the lodges and all their contents were burned, destroying our last links to childhood, and a great ceremony was held to welcome us as men to society. Our families, friends and local chiefs gathered for speeches, songs and gift-giving. I was given two heifers and four sheep, and felt far richer than I ever had before. I, who had never owned anything, suddenly possessed property. It was a heady feeling, even though my gifts were paltry next to those of Justice, who inherited an entire herd. I was not jealous of Justice's gifts. He was the son of a king; I was merely destined to be a counsellor to a king. I felt strong and proud that day. I remember walking differently on that day, straighter, taller, firmer. I was hopeful, and thinking that I might some day have wealth, property and status.

The main speaker of the day was Chief Meligqili, the son of Dalindyebo, and after listening to him, my gaily coloured dreams suddenly darkened. He began conventionally, remarking how fine it was that we were continuing a tradition that had been going on for as long as anyone could remember. Then he turned to us and his tone suddenly changed. 'There sit our sons,' he said, 'young, healthy and handsome, the flower of the Xhosa tribe, the pride of our nation. We have just circumcised them in a ritual that promises them manhood, but I am here to tell you that it is an empty, illusory promise, a promise than can never be fulfilled. For we Xhosas, and all black South Africans, are a conquered people. We are slaves in our own country. We are tenants on our own soil. We have no strength, no power, no control over our own destiny in the land of our birth. They will go to cities where they will live in shacks and drink cheap alcohol, all because we have no land to give them where they could prosper and multiply. They will cough their lungs out deep in the bowels of the white man's mines, destroying their health, never seeing the sun, so that the white man can live a life of unequalled prosperity. Among these young men are chiefs who will never rule because we have no power to govern ourselves; soldiers who will never fight for we have no weapons to fight with; scholars who will never teach because we have no place for them to study. The abilities, the intelligence, the promise of these young men will be squandered in their attempt to eke out a living doing the simplest, most mindless chores for the white man. These gifts today are naught, for we cannot give them the greatest gift of all, which is freedom and independence. I well know that Qamata [God] is all-seeing and never sleeps, but I have a suspicion that Qamata may in fact be dozing. If this is the case, the sooner I die the better, because then I can meet him and shake him awake and tell him that the children of Ngubengcuka, the flower of the Xhosa nation, are dying.'

The audience had become more and more quiet as Chief Meligqili spoke and, I think, more and more angry. No one wanted to hear the words that he spoke that day. I know that I myself did not want to hear them. I was cross rather than aroused by the chief's remarks, dismissing his words as the abusive comments of an ignorant man who was unable to appreciate the value of the education and benefits that the white man had brought to our country. At the time, I looked on the white man not as an oppressor but as a benefactor, and I thought the chief was enormously ungrateful. This upstart chief was ruining my day, spoiling the proud feeling with wrong-headed remarks.

But without exactly understanding why, his words soon began to work on me. He had sown a seed, and though I let that seed lie dormant for a long season, it eventually began to grow. Later I realized that the ignorant man that day was not the chief but myself.

After the ceremony, I walked back to the river and watched it meander on its way to where, many miles distant, it emptied into the Indian Ocean. I had never crossed that river, and I knew little or nothing of the world beyond it, a world that beckoned me that day. It was almost sunset and I hurried on to where our seclusion lodges had been. Though it was forbidden to look back while the lodges were burning, I could not resist. When I reached the area, all that remained were two pyramids of ashes by a large mimosa tree. In these ash heaps lay a lost and delightful world, the world of my childhood, the world of sweet and irresponsible days at Qunu and Mqhekezweni. Now I was a man, and I would never again play *thinti*, or steal maize, or drink milk from a cow's udder. I was already in mourning for my own youth. Looking back, I know that I was not a man that day and would not truly become one for many years.

5

Unlike most of the others with whom I had been at circumcision school, I was not destined to work in the gold mines on the Reef. The regent had often told me, 'It is not for you to spend your life mining the white man's gold, never knowing how to write your name.' My destiny was to become a counsellor to Sabata, and for that I had to be educated. I returned to Mqhekezweni after the ceremony, but not for very long, for I was about to cross the Mbashe River for the first time on my way to Clarkebury Boarding Institute in the district of Engcobo.

I was again leaving home, but I was eager to see how I would fare in the wider world. The regent himself drove me to Engcobo in his majestic Ford V8. Before leaving, he had organized a celebration for my having passed Standard V and being admitted to Clarkebury. A sheep was slaughtered and there was dancing and singing – it was the first celebration that I had ever had in my own honour, and I greatly enjoyed it. The regent gave me my first pair of boots, a sign of manhood, and that night I polished them anew, even though they were already shiny.

Founded in 1825, the Clarkebury Institute was located on the site of one of the oldest Wesleyan missions in the Transkei. At the time, Clarkebury was the highest institution of learning for Africans in Thembuland. The regent himself had attended Clarkebury, and Justice had followed him there. It was both a secondary school and a teacher-training college, but it also offered courses in more practical disciplines such as carpentry, tailoring and tin-smithing.

During the trip, the regent advised me on my behaviour and my future. He urged me to behave in a way that brought only respect to Sabata and to himself, and I assured him that I would. He then briefed me on the Reverend C. Harris, the governor of the school. Reverend Harris, he explained, was unique: he was a white Thembu, a white man who in his heart loved and understood the Thembu people. The regent said when Sabata was older, he would entrust the future king to Reverend Harris, who would train him as both a Christian and a traditional ruler. He said that I must learn from Reverend Harris because I was destined to guide the leader that Reverend Harris was to mould.

At Mqhekezweni I had met many white traders and government officials, including magistrates and police officers. These were men of high standing, and the regent received them courteously, but not obsequiously; he treated them on equal terms as they did him. At times, I even saw him upbraid them, though this was extremely rare. I had very little experience in dealing directly with whites. The regent never told me how to behave, and I observed him and followed his example. In talking about Reverend Harris, however, the regent, for the first time, gave me a lecture on how I was to conduct myself. He said I must afford the reverend the same respect and obedience that I gave to him.

Clarkebury was far grander even than Mqhekezweni. The school itself consisted of a cluster of two dozen or so graceful, colonial-style buildings, which included individual homes as well as dormitories, the library and various instructional halls. It was the first place I'd lived that was Western, not African, and I felt I was entering a new world whose rules were not yet clear to me.

We were taken in to Reverend Harris's study, where the regent introduced me and I stood to shake his hand, the first time I had ever shaken hands with a white man. Reverend Harris was warm and friendly, and treated the regent with great deference. The regent explained that I was being groomed to be a counsellor to the king and that he hoped the reverend would take a special interest in me. The reverend nodded, adding that Clarkebury students were required to do manual labour after school hours, and he would arrange for me to work in his garden.

At the end of the interview, the regent bade me good-bye and handed me a pound note for pocket money, the largest amount of money I had ever possessed. I bade him farewell and promised that I would not disappoint him.

Clarkebury was a Thembu college, founded on land given by the great Thembu king Ngubengcuka; as a descendant of Ngubengcuka I presumed that I would be accorded the same deference at Clarkebury that I had come to expect in Mqhekezweni. But I was painfully mistaken, for I was treated no differently from everyone else. No one knew or even cared that I was a descendant of the illustrious Ngubengcuka. The house- master received me without a blowing of trumpets and my fellow students did not bow and scrape before me. At Clarkebury, plenty of the boys had distinguished lineages, and I was no longer unique. This was an important lesson, for I suspect I was a bit stuck-up in those days. I quickly realized that I had to make my way on the basis of my ability, not my heritage. Most of my classmates could outrun me on the playing field and outthink me in the classroom, and I had a good deal of catching up to do.

Classes commenced the following morning, and along with my fellow students I climbed the steps to the first floor where the classrooms were located. The room itself had a beautifully polished wooden floor. On this first day of classes I sported my new boots. I had never worn boots before of any kind, and that first day I walked like a newly shod horse. I made a terrible racket walking up the steps and almost slipped several times. As I clomped into the classroom, my boots crashing on that shiny wood floor, I noticed two female students in the first row were watching my lame performance with great amusement. The prettier of the two leaned over to her friend and said loud enough for all to hear: 'The country boy is not used to wearing shoes,' at which her friend laughed. I was blind with fury and embarrassment.

Her name was Mathona, and she was a bit of a smart Aleck. That day I vowed never to talk to her. But as my mortification wore off (and I became more adept at walking with boots) I also got to know her, and she was to become my greatest friend at Clarkebury. She was my first true female friend, a woman I met on equal terms with whom I could confide and share secrets. In many ways, she was the model for all my subsequent friendships with women, for with women I found I could let my hair down and confess to weaknesses and fears I would never reveal to another man.

I soon adapted to life at Clarkebury. I participated in sports and games as often as I could, but my performances were no more than mediocre. I played for the love of sport, not the glory, for I received none. We played lawn tennis with home-made wooden rackets and soccer with bare feet on a field of dust.

For the first time, I was taught by teachers who had themselves been properly educated. Several of them held university degrees, which was extremely rare. One day, I was studying with Mathona, and I confided to her my fear that I might not pass my exams in English and history at the end of the year. She told me not to worry because our teacher, Gertrude Ntlabathi, was the first African woman to obtain a BA. 'She is too clever to let us fail,' Mathona said. I had not yet learned to feign knowledge that I did not possess, and as I had only a vague idea what a BA was, I questioned Mathona. 'Oh, yes, of course,' she answered. 'A BA is a very long and difficult book.' I did not doubt her.

Another African teacher with a bachelor of arts degree was Ben

Mahlasela. We admired him not only because of his academic achievement, but because he was not intimidated by Reverend Harris. Even
the white faculty behaved in a servile manner to Reverend Harris, but
Mr Mahlasela would walk into the reverend's office without fear, and
sometimes would even fail to remove his hat! He met the reverend on
equal terms, disagreeing with him where others simply assented. Though
I respected Reverend Harris, I admired the fact that Mr Mahlasela would
not be cowed by him. In those days, a black man with a BA was expected
to scrape before a white man with a primary school education. No matter
how high a black man advanced, he was still considered inferior to the
lowest white man.

Reverend Harris ran Clarkebury with an iron hand and an abiding sense
of fairness. Clarkebury functioned more like a military school than a
teacher-training college. The slightest infractions were swiftly punished.
In assemblies, Reverend Harris always wore a forbidding expression, and
was not given to levity of any kind. When he walked into a room, members
of the staff, including white principals of the training and secondary schools,
together with the black principal of the industrial school, rose to their feet.

    Among students, he was feared more than loved. But in the garden,
I saw a different Reverend Harris. Working in his garden had a double
benefit: it planted in me a lifelong love of gardening and growing
vegetables, and it helped me get to know the reverend and his family
– the first white family with whom I had ever been on intimate terms.
In that way, I saw that Reverend Harris had a public face and a private
manner that were quite different from one another.

    Behind the reverend's mask of severity was a gentle, broad-minded
individual who believed fervently in the importance of educating young
Africans. Often, I found him lost in thought in his garden. I did not
disturb him and rarely talked to him, but as an example of a man
unselfishly devoted to a good cause, Reverend Harris was an important
model for me.

    His wife was as talkative as he was taciturn. She was a lovely woman
and she would often come into the garden to chat with me. I cannot for
the life of me remember what we talked about, but I can still taste the
delicious warm scones that she brought out to me in the afternoons.

After my slow and undistinguished start, I managed to get the hang of
things, and accelerated my programme, completing the junior certificate
in two years instead of the usual three. I developed the reputation of
having a fine memory, but in fact I was simply a diligent worker. When
I left Clarkebury, I lost track of Mathona. She was a day scholar, and

her parents did not have the means to send her for further education. She was an extraordinarily clever and gifted person, whose potential was limited because of her family's meagre resources. This was an all too typical South African story. It was not lack of ability that limited my people, but lack of opportunity.

My time at Clarkebury broadened my horizons, yet I would not say that I was an entirely open-minded, unprejudiced young man when I left. I had met students from all over the Transkei, as well as a few from Johannesburg and Basutoland, as Lesotho was then known, some of whom were sophisticated and cosmopolitan in ways that made me feel provincial. Though I emulated them, I never thought it possible for a boy from the countryside to rival them in their worldliness. Yet I did not envy them. Even as I left Clarkebury, I was still, at heart, a Thembu, and I was proud to think and act like one. My roots were my destiny, and I believed that I would become a counsellor to the Thembu king, as my guardian wanted. My horizons did not extend beyond Thembuland and I believed that to be a Thembu was the most enviable thing in the world.

6

In 1937, when I was nineteen, I joined Justice at Healdtown, the Wesleyan College in Fort Beaufort, about 175 miles southwest of Umtata. In the nineteenth century, Fort Beaufort was one of a number of British outposts during the so-called Frontier Wars, in which a steady encroachment of white settlers systematically dispossessed the various Xhosa tribes of their land. Over a century of conflict, many Xhosa warriors achieved fame for their bravery, men like Sandile, Makhanda and Moqoma, the last two of whom were imprisoned on Robben Island by the British authorities, where they died. By the time of my arrival at Healdtown there were few signs of the battles of the previous century, except the main one: Fort Beaufort was a white town where once only the Xhosa lived and farmed.

Located at the end of a winding road overlooking a verdant valley, Healdtown was far more beautiful and impressive than Clarkebury. It was, at the time, the largest African school south of the equator, with more than a thousand students, both male and female. Its graceful ivy-covered colonial buildings and tree-shaded courtyards gave it the feeling of a privileged academic oasis, which is precisely what it was. Like Clarkebury, Healdtown was a mission school of the Methodist Church, and provided a Christian and liberal arts education based on an English model.

The principal of Healdtown was Dr Arthur Wellington, a stout and stuffy Englishman who boasted of his connection to the Duke of Wellington. At the outset of assemblies, Dr Wellington would walk on stage and say, in his deep bass voice, 'I am the descendant of the great Duke of Wellington, aristocrat, statesman, and general, who crushed the Frenchman Napoleon at Waterloo and thereby saved civilization for Europe – and for you, the natives.' At this, we would all enthusiastically applaud, each of us profoundly grateful that a descendant of the great Duke of Wellington would take the trouble to educate natives such as ourselves. The educated Englishman was our model; what we aspired to be were 'black Englishmen', as we were sometimes derisively called. We were taught – and believed – that the best ideas were English ideas, the best government was English government and the best men were Englishmen.

Healdtown life was rigorous. First bell was at 6 a.m. We were in the dining hall by 6.40 for a breakfast of dry bread and hot sugar water, watched over by a sombre portrait of George VI, the king of England. Those who could afford butter on their bread bought it and stored it in the kitchen. I ate dry toast. At eight we assembled in the courtyard outside our dormitory for 'observation', standing to attention as the girls arrived from separate dormitories. We remained in class until 12.45, and then had a lunch of samp, sour milk and beans, seldom meat. We then studied until 5 p.m., followed by an hour's break for exercise and dinner, and then studied again from seven until nine. Lights went out at 9.30.

Healdtown attracted students from all over the country, as well as from the protectorates of Basutoland, Swaziland and Bechuanaland. Though it was a mostly Xhosa institution, there were also students from different tribes. After school and at weekends, students from the same tribe kept together. Even the members of various Xhosa tribes would gravitate together, such as the amaMpondo with the amaMpondo, and so on. I adhered to this same pattern, but it was at Healdtown that I made my first Sotho-speaking friend, Zachariah Molete. I remember feeling quite bold at having a friend who was not a Xhosa.

Our zoology teacher, Frank Lebentlele, was also Sotho-speaking and was very popular among the students. Personable and approachable, Frank was not much older than us and mixed freely with students. He even played in the college's first soccer team, where he was a star performer. But what most amazed us about him was his marriage to a Xhosa girl from Umtata. Marriages between tribes were then extremely unusual. Until then, I had never known of anyone who had married outside his tribe. We had been taught that such unions were taboo. But seeing Frank and his wife began to undermine my parochialism and loosen the hold of the tribalism that still imprisoned me. I began to sense my identity as an African, not just a Thembu or even a Xhosa. But this was still a nascent feeling.

Our dormitory had forty beds in it, twenty on either side of a central passageway. The housemaster was the delightful Reverend S. S. Mokitimi, who later became the first African president of the Methodist Church of South Africa. Reverend Mokitimi, who was also Sotho-speaking, was much admired among students as a modern and enlightened fellow who understood our complaints.

Reverend Mokitimi impressed us for another reason: he stood up to

Dr Wellington. One evening, a quarrel broke out between two prefects on the main thoroughfare of the college. Prefects were responsible for preventing disputes, not provoking them. Reverend Mokitimi was called in to make peace. Dr Wellington, returning from town, suddenly appeared in the midst of this commotion, and his arrival shook us considerably. It was as if a god had descended to solve some humble problem.

Dr Wellington pulled himself to a great height and demanded to know what was going on. Reverend Mokitimi, the top of whose head did not even reach Dr Wellington's shoulders, said very respectfully, 'Dr Wellington, everything is under control and I will report to you tomorrow.' Undeterred, Dr Wellington said with some irritation, 'No, I want to know what the matter is right now.' Reverend Mokitimi stood his ground: 'Dr Wellington, I am the housemaster and I have told you that I will report to you tomorrow, and that is what I will do.' We were stunned. We had never seen anyone, much less a black man, stand up to Dr Wellington, and we waited for an explosion. But Dr Wellington simply said, 'Very well', and left. I realized then that Dr Wellington was less than a god and Reverend Mokitimi more than a lackey, and that a black man did not have to defer automatically to a white, however senior he was.

Reverend Mokitimi sought to introduce reforms to the college. We all supported his efforts to improve the diet and the treatment of students, including his suggestion that students be responsible for disciplining themselves. But one change worried us, especially students from the countryside. This was Reverend Mokitimi's innovation of having male and female students dine together in hall at Sunday lunch. I was very much against this for the simple reason that I was still inept with a knife and fork, and I did not want to embarrass myself in front of these sharp-eyed girls. But Reverend Mokitimi went ahead and organized the meals, and every Sunday I left the hall hungry and depressed.

I did, however, enjoy myself on the playing fields. The quality of sports at Healdtown was far superior to that of Clarkebury. In my first year I was not skilled enough to make any of the teams. But during my second year my friend Locke Ndzamela, Healdtown's champion hurdler, encouraged me to take up a new sport: long-distance running. I was tall and lanky, which Locke said was the ideal build for a long-distance runner. With a few hints from him, I began training. I enjoyed the discipline and solitariness of long-distance running, which allowed me to escape from the hurly-burly of school life. At the same time, I also took up a sport that I seemed less suited for, and that was boxing. I trained in a desultory way, and only years later, when I had put on a few more pounds, did I begin to box in earnest.

*   *   *

During my second year at Healdtown, I was appointed a prefect by Reverend Mokitimi and Dr Wellington. Prefects had different responsibilities, and the newest prefects had the least desirable duties. In the beginning, I supervised a group of students who worked as window cleaners during our manual work time in the afternoon, and led them to different buildings each day.

I soon graduated to the next level of responsibility, which was night duty. I have never had a problem in staying up all night, but during one such night I was put in a moral quandary that has remained in my memory. We did not have toilets in the dormitory, but there was an outhouse about a hundred feet behind the residence. On rainy evenings, when students woke up in the middle of the night, they wouldn't want to trudge through the grass and mud to the outhouse. Instead, students would stand on the veranda and urinate into the bushes. This practice, however, was strictly against regulations and one job of the prefect was to take down the names of students who indulged in it.

One night, I was on duty when it was pouring with rain, and I caught quite a few students – perhaps fifteen or so – relieving themselves from the veranda. Towards dawn, I saw a chap come out, look both ways, and stand at one end of the veranda to urinate. I made my way over to him and announced that he had been caught, whereupon he turned round and I realized that he was a prefect. I was in a predicament. In law and philosophy, one asks, '*Quis custodiet ipsos custodes?*' ('Who will guard the guardians themselves?'). If the prefect does not obey the rules, how can the students be expected to obey? In effect, the prefect was above the law because he *was* the law, and one prefect was not supposed to report another. But I did not think it fair to avoid reporting the prefect and mark down the fifteen others, so I simply tore up my list and charged no one.

In my final year at Healdtown, an event occurred that for me was like a comet streaking across the night sky. Towards the end of the year, we were informed that the great Xhosa poet, Krune Mqhayi, was going to visit the school. Mqhayi was actually an *imbongi*, a praise singer, a kind of oral historian who marks contemporary events and history with poetry that is of special meaning to his people.

The day of his visit was declared a holiday by the school authorities. On the appointed morning, the entire school, including staff members both black and white, gathered in the dining hall, which was where we held school assemblies. There was a stage at one end of the hall and from it a door led to Dr Wellington's house. The door itself was nothing special, but we thought of it as Dr Wellington's

door, for no one ever walked through it except Dr Wellington himself.

Suddenly, the door opened and out walked not Dr Wellington, but a
black man dressed in a leopard-skin kaross and matching hat, who was
carrying a spear in either hand. Dr Wellington followed a moment later,
but the sight of a black man in tribal dress coming through that door
was electrifying. It is hard to explain the impact it had on us. It seemed
to turn the universe upside down. As Mqhayi sat on the stage next to
Dr Wellington, we were barely able to contain our excitement.

But when Mqhayi rose to speak, I confess to being disappointed.
I had formed a picture of him in my mind, and in my youthful
imagination I expected a Xhosa hero like Mqhayi to be tall, fierce and
intelligent-looking. But he was not terribly distinguished and, except for
his clothing, seemed entirely ordinary. When he spoke in Xhosa, he did
so slowly and haltingly, frequently pausing to search for the right word
and then stumbling over it when he found it.

At one point, he raised his assegai into the air for emphasis, and
accidentally hit the curtain wire above him, which made a sharp noise
and caused the curtain to sway. The poet looked at the point of his spear
and then the curtain wire and, deep in thought, walked back and forth
across the stage. After a minute, he stopped walking, faced us, and newly
energized, exclaimed that this incident – the assegai striking the wire –
symbolized the clash between the culture of Africa and that of Europe. His
voice rose and he said, 'The assegai stands for what is glorious and true in
African history; it is a symbol of the African as warrior and the African
as artist. This metal wire,' he said, pointing above, 'is an example of
Western manufacturing, which is skilful but cold, clever but soulless.'

'What I am talking about,' he continued, 'is not a piece of bone touching
a piece of metal, or even the overlapping of one culture and another, what
I am talking to you about is the brutal clash between what is indigenous
and good, and what is foreign and bad. We cannot allow these foreigners
who do not care for our culture to take over our nation. I predict that,
one day, the forces of African society will achieve a momentous victory
over the interloper. For too long we have succumbed to the false gods of
the white man. But we shall emerge and cast off these foreign notions.'

I could hardly believe my ears. His boldness in speaking of such delicate
matters in the presence of Dr Wellington and other whites seemed utterly
astonishing to us. Yet at the same time it aroused and motivated us, and
began to alter my perception of men like Dr Wellington, whom I had
automatically considered my benefactor.

Mqhayi then began to recite his well-known poem in which he
apportions the stars in the heavens to the various nations of the

world. I had never before heard it. Roving the stage and gesturing with his assegai towards the sky, he said that to the people of Europe – the French, the Germans, the English – 'I give you the Milky Way, the largest constellation, for you are a strange people, full of greed and envy, who quarrel over plenty.' He allocated certain stars to the Asian nations, and to North and South America. He then discussed Africa and separated the continent into different nations, giving specific constellations to different tribes. He had been dancing about the stage, waving his spear, modulating his voice, and now, suddenly, he became still, and lowered his voice.

'Now, come you, O House of Xhosa,' he said, and slowly began to lower himself so that he was on one knee. 'I give unto you the most important and transcendent star, the Morning Star, for you are a proud and powerful people. It is the star for counting the years – the years of manhood.' When he spoke this last word, he dropped his head to his chest. We rose to our feet, clapping and cheering. I did not want ever to stop applauding. I felt such intense pride at that point, not as an African, but as a Xhosa; I felt like one of the chosen people.

I was galvanized, but also confused by Mqhayi's performance. He had moved from a more nationalistic, all-encompassing theme of African unity to a more parochial one addressed to the Xhosa people, of whom he was one. As my time at Healdtown was coming to an end, I had many new and sometimes conflicting ideas floating in my head. I was beginning to see that Africans of all tribes had much in common, yet here was the great Mqhayi praising the Xhosa above all; I saw that an African might stand his ground with a white man, yet I was still eagerly seeking benefits from whites, which often required subservience. In a sense, Mqhayi's shift in focus was a mirror of my own mind because I went back and forth between pride in myself as a Xhosa and a feeling of kinship with other Africans. But as I left Healdtown at the end of the year, I saw myself as a Xhosa first and an African second.

7

Until 1960, the University College of Fort Hare in the municipality of Alice, about twenty miles due east from Healdtown, was the only residential centre of higher education for blacks in South Africa. Fort Hare was more than that: it was a beacon for African scholars from all over Southern, Central and Eastern Africa. For young black South Africans like myself, it was Oxford and Cambridge, Harvard and Yale, all rolled into one.

The regent was anxious for me to attend Fort Hare and I was pleased to be accepted there. Before I went up to the university, the regent bought me my first suit. Double-breasted and grey, the suit made me feel grown-up and sophisticated; I was twenty-one years old and could not imagine anyone at Fort Hare smarter than I.

I felt that I was being groomed for success in the world. I was pleased that the regent would now have a member of his clan with a university degree. Justice had remained at Healdtown to work for his junior certificate. He enjoyed playing more than studying, and was an indifferent scholar.

Fort Hare had been founded in 1916 by Scottish missionaries on the site of what was the largest nineteenth-century frontier fort in the eastern Cape. Built on a rocky platform and moated by the winding arc of the Tyume River, Fort Hare was perfectly situated to enable the British to fight the gallant Xhosa warrior Sandile, the last Rharhabe king, who was defeated by the British in one of the final frontier battles in the 1800s.

Fort Hare had only 150 students, and I already knew a dozen or so of them from Clarkebury and Healdtown. One of them, who I was meeting for the first time, was K.D. Matanzima. Though K.D. was my nephew according to tribal hierarchy, I was younger and far less senior to him. Tall and slender and extremely confident, K.D. was a third-year student and he took me under his wing. I looked up to him as I had to Justice.

We were both Methodists, and I was assigned to his hostel, known as Wesley House, a pleasant two-storey building on the edge of the campus. Under his tutelage, I attended church services with him at nearby Loveday, took up soccer (in which he excelled), and generally followed his advice. The regent did not believe in sending money to his children at school, and I would have had empty pockets had not K.D. shared his allowance with me. Like the regent, he saw my future role as counsellor to Sabata, and he encouraged me to study law.

Fort Hare, like Clarkebury and Healdtown, was a missionary college. We were exhorted to obey God, respect the political authorities and be grateful for the educational opportunities afforded to us by the Church and the government. These schools have often been criticized for being colonialist in their attitudes and practices. Yet, even with such attitudes, I believe their benefits outweighed their disadvantages. The missionaries built and ran schools when the government was unwilling or unable to do so. The learning environment of the missionary schools, while often morally rigid, was far more open than the racist principles underlying government schools.

Fort Hare was both home and incubator of some of the greatest African scholars the continent has ever known. Professor Z.K. Matthews was the very model of the intellectual. A child of a miner, Z.K. had been influenced by Booker Washington's autobiography, *Up from Slavery*, which preached success through hard work and moderation. He taught social anthropology and African law and spoke out bluntly against the government's social policies.

Fort Hare and Professor D.D.T. Jabavu are virtually synonymous. He was the first member of staff when the university opened in 1916. Professor Jabavu had been awarded a degree in English from the University of London, which seemed an impossibly rare feat. Professor Jabavu taught Xhosa, as well as Latin, history and anthropology. He was an encyclopedia when it came to Xhosa genealogy and told me facts about my father that I had never known. He was also a persuasive spokesman for African rights, becoming the founding president of the All-African Convention in 1936, which opposed legislation in Parliament designed to end the common voters' roll in the Cape.

I recall once travelling from Fort Hare to Umtata by train, riding in the African compartment, in which were the only seats open to blacks. The white train inspector came to check our tickets. When he saw that I had got on at Alice, he said, 'Are you from Jabavu's school?' I nodded yes, whereupon the conductor cheerfully punched my ticket and mumbled something about Jabavu being a fine man.

*   *   *

In my first year, I studied English, anthropology, politics, native administration and Roman Dutch law. Native administration dealt with the laws relating to Africans and was advisable for anyone who wanted to work in the Native Affairs Department. Although K.D. was counselling me to study law, I had my heart set on being an interpreter or a clerk in the Native Affairs Department. At that time, a career as a civil servant was a glittering prize for an African, the highest that a black man could aspire to. In the rural areas, an interpreter in the magistrate's office was considered second only in importance to the magistrate himself. When, in my second year, Fort Hare introduced an interpreting course taught by a distinguished retired court interpreter, Tyamzashe, I was one of the first students to sign up.

Fort Hare could be a rather elitist place, and was not without the problems common to many institutions of higher learning. Seniors treated the juniors with haughtiness and disdain. When I first arrived on campus, I spotted Gamaliel Vabaza across the central courtyard. He was several years older and I had been with him at Clarkebury. I greeted him warmly, but his response was exceedingly cool and superior, and he made a disparaging remark about the fact that I would be staying in the freshman dormitory. Vabaza then informed me that he was on the House Committee of my dormitory even though, as a senior, he no longer shared the dormitory. I found this odd and undemocratic, but it was the accepted practice.

One night, not long after that, a group of us discussed the fact that no residents or freshmen were represented on the House Committee. We decided that we should depart from tradition and elect a House Committee made up of these two groups. We held discussions and lobbied all the residents of the house, and within weeks elected our own House Committee, defeating the seniors. I myself was one of the organizers and was elected to this newly constituted committee.

But the seniors were not so easily subdued. They held a meeting at which one of them, Rex Tatane, an eloquent English-speaker, said, 'This behaviour on the part of freshers is unacceptable. How can we seniors be overthrown by a backward fellow from the countryside like Mandela, a fellow who cannot even speak English properly!' Then he proceeded to mimic the way I spoke, giving me what he perceived to be a Gcaleka accent, at which his own claque laughed heartily. Tatane's sneering speech made us all more resolute. We freshers now constituted the official House Committee and we assigned the seniors the most unpleasant tasks, which was a great indignity for them.

The warden of the college, Reverend A. J. Cook, learned of this dispute and called us into his office. We felt we had right on our side and were not prepared to yield. Tatane appealed to the warden to overrule us, and in the midst of his speech, broke down and wept. The warden asked us to modify our stand, but we would not bend. Like most bullies, Tatane had a brittle but fragile exterior. We informed the warden that if he overruled us we would all resign from the House Committee, depriving the committee itself of any integrity or authority. In the end, the warden decided not to intervene. We had remained firm, and we had won. This was one of my first battles with authority, and I felt the sense of power that comes from having right and justice on one's side. I would not be so lucky in the future in my fight against the authorities at the college.

My education at Fort Hare was as much outside as inside the classroom. I was a more active sportsman than I had been at Healdtown. This was due to two factors: I had grown taller and stronger but, more important, Fort Hare was so much smaller than Healdtown that I had less competition. I was able to compete in both soccer and cross-country running. Running taught me valuable lessons. In cross-country competition, training counted more than intrinsic ability, and I could compensate for a lack of natural aptitude with diligence and discipline. I applied this in everything I did. Even as a student, I saw many young men who had great natural ability, but who did not have the self-discipline and patience to build on their endowment.

I also joined the drama society and acted in a play about Abraham Lincoln that was adapted by my classmate Lincoln Mkentane. Mkentane came from a distinguished Transkeian family, and was another fellow whom I looked up to. This was literally true, as he was the only student at Fort Hare taller than I was. Mkentane portrayed his namesake, while I played John Wilkes Booth, Lincoln's assassin. Mkentane's depiction of Lincoln was stately and formal, and his recitation of one of the greatest of all speeches, the Gettysburg Address, won a standing ovation. My part was the smaller one, though I was the engine of the play's moral, which was that men who take great risks often suffer great consequences.

I became a member of the Students Christian Association and taught Bible classes on Sundays in neighbouring villages. One of my comrades on these expeditions was a serious young science scholar whom I had met on the soccer field. He came from Pondoland, in the Transkei, and his name was Oliver Tambo. From the start, I saw that Oliver's intelligence was diamond-edged; he was a keen debater and did not accept the platitudes that so many of us automatically subscribed to. Oliver lived in Beda Hall, the Anglican hostel, and though I did not have much contact with him at Fort Hare, it was easy to see that he was destined for great things.

On Sundays a group of us would sometimes walk into Alice, to have a meal at one of the restaurants in town. The restaurant was run by whites, and in those days it was inconceivable for a black man to walk in at the front door, much less take a meal in the dining room. Instead, we would pool our resources, go round to the kitchen, and order what we wanted.

I learned not only about physics at Fort Hare, but another precise physical science: ballroom dancing. To a crackly old phonograph in the dining hall, we spent hours practising fox-trots and waltzes, each of us taking turns leading and following. Our idol was Victor Sylvester, the world champion of ballroom dancing, and our tutor was a fellow student, Smallie Siwundla, who seemed a younger version of the master.

In a neighbouring village, there was an African dance-hall known as Ntselamanzi, which catered to the cream of local black society and was off-limits to undergraduates. But one night, desperate to practise our steps with the gentler sex, we put on our suits, stole out of our dormitory, and made it to the dance-hall. It was a sumptuous place, and we felt very daring. I noticed a lovely young woman across the floor and politely asked her to dance. A moment later, she was in my arms. We moved well together and I imagined what a striking figure I was cutting on the floor. After a few minutes, I asked her her name. 'Mrs Bokwe,' she said softly. I almost dropped her on the spot and scampered off the floor. I glanced across the floor and saw Dr Roseberry Bokwe, one of the most respected African leaders and scholars of the time, chatting with his brother-in-law and my professor Z.K. Matthews. I apologized to Mrs Bokwe and then sheepishly escorted her to the side under the curious eyes of Dr Bokwe and Professor Matthews. I wanted to sink beneath the floorboards. I had violated any number of university regulations. But Professor Matthews, who was in charge of discipline at Fort Hare, never said a word to me. He was willing to tolerate what he considered high spirits as long as it was balanced by hard work. I don't think I ever studied more diligently than in the weeks after our evening at Ntselamanzi.

Fort Hare was characterized by a level of sophistication, both intellectual and social, that was new and strange to me. By Western standards, Fort Hare's worldliness may not seem much, but to a country boy like myself, it was a revelation. I wore pyjamas for the first time, finding them uncomfortable in the beginning, but gradually growing used to them. I had never used a toothbrush and toothpaste before; at home, we used ash to whiten our teeth and toothpicks to clean them. The water-flush toilets and hot-water showers were also a novelty to me. I used toilet soap for the first time, not the blue detergent that I had washed with for so many years at home.

Perhaps as a result of all this unfamiliarity, I yearned for some of the simple pleasures that I had known as a boy. I was not alone in this feeling, and I joined a group of young men who engaged in secret evening expeditions to the university's farmland, where we built a fire and roasted mealies. We would then sit around, eating the ears of corn and telling tall tales. We did not do this because we were hungry, but out of a need to recapture what was most homelike to us. We boasted about our conquests, our athletic prowess and how much money we were going to make once we had graduated. Although I felt myself to be a sophisticated young fellow, I was still a country boy who missed country pleasures.

While Fort Hare was a sanctuary removed from the world, we were keenly interested in the progress of the Second World War. Like my classmates, I was an ardent supporter of Great Britain, and I was enormously excited to learn that the speaker at the university's graduation ceremony at the end of my first year would be England's great advocate in South Africa, the former prime minister Jan Smuts. It was a great honour for Fort Hare to play host to a man acclaimed as a world statesman. Smuts, then deputy prime minister, was campaigning around the country for South Africa to declare war on Germany while the prime minister, J. B. Hertzog, advocated neutrality. I was extremely curious to see a world leader like Smuts up close.

While Hertzog had, three years earlier, led the drive to remove the last African voters from the common voters' roll in the Cape, I found Smuts a sympathetic figure. I cared more that he had helped to found the League of Nations, promoting freedom around the world, than the fact that he had repressed freedom at home.

Smuts spoke about the importance of supporting Great Britain against the Germans and the idea that England stood for the same Western values that we, as South Africans, stood for. I remember thinking that his accent in English was almost as poor as mine! Along with my fellow classmates, I heartily applauded him, cheering Smuts's call to do battle for the freedom of Europe, forgetting that we did not have that freedom here in our own land.

Smuts was preaching to the converted at Fort Hare. Each evening the warden of Wesley House used to review the military situation in Europe, and late at night we would huddle around an old radio and listen to BBC broadcasts of Winston Churchill's stirring speeches. But even though we supported Smuts's position, his visit provoked much discussion. During one session, a contemporary of mine, Nyathi Khongisa, who was considered an extremely clever fellow, condemned Smuts as a racist. He said that we might consider ourselves 'black Englishmen', but the English had oppressed us at the same time that they tried to 'civilize' us. Whatever the mutual antagonism between Boer and British, he said, the two white groups would unite to confront the black threat. Khongisa's views stunned us and seemed dangerously radical. A fellow student whispered to me that Nyathi was a member of the African National Congress, an organization that I had vaguely heard of but knew very little about. Following South Africa's declaration of war against Germany, Hertzog resigned and Smuts became prime minister.

During my second year at Fort Hare, I invited my friend Paul Mahabane to spend the winter holidays with me in the Transkei. Paul was from Bloemfontein and was well known on campus because his father, the Reverend Zaccheus Mahabane, had twice been president-general of the African National Congress. His connection with this organization, about which I still knew very little, gave him the reputation of a rebel.

One day during the holiday, Paul and I went to Umtata, the capital of the Transkei, which then consisted of a few paved streets and some government buildings. We were standing outside the post office when the local magistrate, a white man in his sixties, approached Paul and asked him to go inside to buy him some postage stamps. It was quite common for any white person to call on any black person to perform a chore. The magistrate attempted to hand Paul some change, but Paul would not take it. The magistrate was offended. 'Do you know who I am?' he said, his face turning red with irritation. 'It is not necessary to know who you are,' Mahabane said. 'I know what you are.' The magistrate asked him exactly what he meant by that. 'I mean that you are a rogue!' Paul said heatedly. The magistrate boiled over and exclaimed, 'You'll pay dearly for this!' and then walked away.

I was extremely uncomfortable with Paul's behaviour. While I respected his courage, I also found it disturbing. The magistrate knew precisely who I was and I knew that if he had asked me rather than Paul, I would have simply performed the errand and forgotten about it. But I admired Paul for what he had done, even though I was not yet ready to do the same myself. I was beginning to realize that a black man did not have to accept the dozens of petty indignities directed at him each day.

After my holiday, I returned to school early in the new year feeling strong and renewed. I concentrated on my studies, leading to examinations in October. In a year's time, I imagined that I would have a BA, just like clever Gertrude Ntlabathi. A university degree, I believed, was a passport not only to community leadership but to financial success. We had been told over and over again by the principal, Dr Alexander Kerr, and Professors Jabavu and Matthews how, as graduates of Fort Hare, we were the African elite. I believed that the world would be at my feet.

As a BA, I would finally be able to restore to my mother the wealth and prestige that she had lost after my father's death. I would build her a proper home in Qunu, with a garden and modern furniture and fittings. I would support her and my sisters so that they could afford the things that they had so long been denied. This was my dream and it seemed within reach.

During that year, I was nominated to stand for the Student Representative Council, which was the highest student organization at Fort Hare. I did not know at the time that the events surrounding a student election would create difficulties that would change the course of my life. The SRC elections were held in the final term of the year, while we were in the midst of examination preparations. According to the Fort Hare constitution, the entire student body elected the six members of the SRC. Shortly before the election, a meeting of all students was held to discuss problems and voice our grievances. The students unanimously felt that the diet at Fort Hare was unsatisfactory and that the powers of the SRC needed to be increased so that it would be more than a rubber stamp for the administration. I agreed with both motions, and when a majority of students voted to boycott the elections unless the authorities accepted our demands, I voted with them.

Shortly after this meeting, the scheduled voting took place. The majority of the students boycotted the election, but twenty-five, about one-sixth of the student body, showed up and elected six representatives, one of whom was myself. That same day, the six elected *in absentia* met to discuss these events. We unanimously decided to tender our resignations on the ground that we supported the boycott and did not enjoy the support of the majority of the students. We then drafted a letter, which we handed to Dr Kerr.

But Dr Kerr was clever. He accepted our resignations and then announced that new elections were to be held the next day in the dining hall at suppertime. This would ensure that all the students would be present and that there would be no excuse that the SRC did not have the support of the entire student body. That evening the election was held, as the principal ordered, but only the same twenty-five voted, returning the same six SRC members. It would seem that we were back where we started.

Only this time, when the six of us met to consider our position, the voting was very different. My five colleagues held to the technical view that we had been elected at a meeting at which all the students were present and therefore we could no longer argue that we did not represent the student body. The five believed we should now accept office. I countered that nothing in fact had changed; while all the students had been there, a majority of them had not voted, and it would be morally incorrect to say that we enjoyed their confidence. Since our initial goal was to boycott the election, an action that had the confidence of the student body, our duty was still to abide by that resolution, and not be deterred by some trickery on the part of the principal. Unable to persuade my colleagues, I resigned for the second time, the only one of the six to do so.

The following day I was called in to see the principal. Dr Kerr, a graduate of Edinburgh University, was virtually the founder of Fort Hare and was a greatly respected man. He calmly reviewed the events of the past few days and then asked me to reconsider my decision to resign. I told him I could not. He told me to sleep on it and give him my final decision the following day. He did warn me, however, that he could not allow his students to act irresponsibly, and he said that if I insisted on resigning, he would be compelled to expel me from Fort Hare.

I was shaken by what he had said and spent a restless night. I had never had to make such a weighty decision before. That evening I consulted with my friend and mentor, K.D., who felt that as a matter of principle I was correct to resign, and should not capitulate. I think at the time I feared K.D. even more than I did Dr Kerr. I thanked K.D. and returned to my room.

Even though I thought what I was doing was morally right, I was still uncertain as to whether it was the correct course. Was I sabotaging my academic career over an abstract moral principle that mattered very little? I found it difficult to swallow the idea that I would sacrifice what I regarded as my obligation to the students for my own selfish interests. I had taken a stand, and I did not want to appear to be a fraud in the eyes of my fellow students. At the same time, I did not want to throw away my career at Fort Hare.

I was in a state of indecision when I reached Dr Kerr's office the next morning. It was only when he asked me if I had reached a decision that I actually made up my mind. I told him that I had and that I could not in good conscience serve on the SRC. Dr Kerr seemed a bit taken aback by my response. He thought for a moment or two before speaking. 'Very well,' he said. 'It is your decision, of course. But I have also given the matter some thought, and I propose to you the following: you may return to Fort Hare next year provided you join the SRC. You have all summer to consider it, Mr Mandela.'

I was, in a way, as surprised by my response as Dr Kerr. I knew it was foolhardy for me to leave Fort Hare, but at the moment when I needed to compromise, I simply could not do so. Something inside me would not let me. While I appreciated Dr Kerr's position and his willingness to give me another chance, I resented his absolute power over my fate. I should have had every right to resign from the SRC if I wished. This injustice rankled, and at that moment I saw Dr Kerr less as a benefactor than as a not-altogether-benign dictator. When I left Fort Hare at the end of the year, I was in an unpleasant state of limbo.

8

Usually when I returned to Mqhekezweni I did so with a sense of ease and completion. But not this time. After passing my exams and returning home, I told the regent what had transpired. He was furious, and could not comprehend the reasons for my actions. He thought it utterly senseless. Without even hearing my full explanation, he bluntly informed me that I would obey the principal's instructions and return to Fort Hare in the autumn. His tone invited no discussion. It would have been pointless as well as disrespectful for me to argue with my benefactor. I resolved to let the matter rest awhile.

Justice had also returned to Mqhekezweni and we were mightily glad to see one another. No matter how long Justice and I were apart, the brotherly bonds that united us were instantly renewed. Justice had left school the year before and was living in Cape Town.

Within a few days, I resumed my old life at home. I looked after matters for the regent, including his herd and his relations with other chiefs. I did not dwell on the situation at Fort Hare, but life has a way of forcing decisions on those who vacillate. It was an entirely different matter unrelated to my studies that forced my hand.

A few weeks after my homecoming, the regent summoned Justice and me to a meeting. 'My children,' he said in a very sombre tone, 'I fear that I am not much longer for this world, and before I journey to the land of the ancestors, it is my duty to see my two sons properly married. I have, accordingly, arranged unions for both of you.'

This announcement took us both by surprise, and Justice and I looked at each other with a mixture of shock and helplessness. The two girls came from very good families, the regent said. Justice was to marry the daughter of Khalipa, a prominent Thembu nobleman, and Rolihlahla, as the regent always called me, was to marry the daughter of the local Thembu priest. The marriages, he said, were to take place immediately. *Lobola*, the brideprice or dowry, is normally paid in the form of cattle by the groom's father, and would be paid by the community in Justice's case and in my own by the regent himself.

Justice and I said little. It was not our place to question the regent, and as far as he was concerned, the matter was settled. The regent brooked no discussion: the bride had already been selected and *lobola* paid. It was final.

Justice and I walked out of our interview with our heads down, dazed and dejected. The regent was acting in accordance with Thembu law and custom, and his own motives could not be impugned: he wanted us to be settled during his lifetime. We had always known that the regent had the right to arrange marriages for us, but now it was no longer an abstract possibility. The brides were not fantasies, but flesh-and-blood women whom we actually knew.

With all due respect to the young woman's family, I would be dishonest if I said that the girl the regent had selected for me was my dream bride. Her family was prominent and respected and she was attractive in a rather dignified way, but this young lady, I am afraid, had long been in love with Justice. The regent would not have known this, as parents rarely know the romantic side of their children's lives. My intended partner was undoubtedly no more eager to be burdened with me than I was with her.

At that time, I was more advanced socially than politically. While I would not have considered fighting the political system of the white man, I was quite prepared to rebel against the social system of my own people. Ironically, it was the regent himself who was indirectly to blame for this, for it was the education he had afforded me that had caused me to reject such traditional customs. I had attended college and university with women for years, and had had a small handful of love affairs. I was a romantic, and I was not prepared to have anyone, even the regent, select a bride for me.

I made an appointment with the queen, the regent's wife, and put my case to her. I could not tell her that I did not want the regent to arrange a bride for me under any circumstances, as she would naturally have been unsympathetic. Instead, I devised an alternative plan, and told her that I preferred to marry a girl who was a relative of the queen's, whom I found desirable as a prospective partner. This young lady was in fact very attractive, but I had no idea as to what she thought of me. I said I would marry her as soon as I completed my studies. This was half a ruse, but it was a better option than the regent's plan. The queen took my side in the matter, but the regent could not be dissuaded. He had made his decision and he was not going to alter it.

I felt as though he had left me no choice. I could not go through with this marriage, which I considered unfair and ill-advised. At the same time, I believed that I could no longer remain under the regent's guidance if I rejected his plan for me. Justice agreed, and the two of us decided that the only choice remaining was to run away, and the only place to run to was Johannesburg.

In retrospect, I realize that we did not exhaust all the options available to us. I could have attempted to discuss the matter with the regent through intermediaries and perhaps come to some settlement within the framework of our tribe and family. I could have appealed to the regent's cousin, Chief Zilindlovu, one of the most enlightened and influential chiefs at the court of Mqhekezweni. But I was young and impatient, and did not see any virtue in waiting. Escape seemed the only course.

We kept our plot secret while we worked out its details. First, we needed an opportunity. The regent believed Justice and I brought out the worst in each other, or at least Justice's penchant for adventures and high-jinks influenced my more conservative disposition. As a result, he took pains to keep us separate as much as possible. When the regent was travelling, he generally asked one of us to accompany him so that we would not be alone together in his absence. More often than not, he took Justice with him, as he liked me to remain in Mqhekezweni to look after his affairs. But we learned that the regent was preparing to leave for a full week to attend a session of the Bungha, the Transkeian legislative assembly, without either of us, and we decided this was the ideal time to steal away. We resolved that we would depart for Johannesburg shortly after the regent left for the Bungha.

I had few clothes, and we managed to fit whatever we had into a single suitcase. The regent left early on Monday, and by late morning we were ready to go. But just as we were preparing to leave, he unexpectedly returned. We saw his car drive in and we ran into the garden and hid among the mealie stalks. The regent came into the house and his first question was 'Where are those boys?' Someone replied, 'Oh, they are around.' But the regent was suspicious, and was not content with that reply. He had returned, he said, because he had forgotten to take his Epsom salts. He looked around a bit, and then seemed satisfied. I realized that he must have had some kind of premonition because he could easily buy Epsom salts in town. When his car disappeared behind the hills, we were on our way.

We had almost no money between us, but that morning we went to see a local trader and made a deal to sell him two of the regent's prize oxen. The trader assumed that we were selling the animals at the regent's behest, and we did not correct him. He paid us a very good price, and with that money we hired a car to take us to the local station where we would catch a train to Johannesburg.

All seemed to be going smoothly, but unbeknown to us, the regent had driven to the station and instructed the manager that if two boys fitting our description came to buy tickets for Johannesburg, the manager must turn them away because they were not to leave the Transkei. We arrived at the station only to find that the manager would not sell us tickets. We asked him why, and he said, 'Your father has been here and says you are trying to run away.' We were stunned by this, and dashed back to our hired car and told the driver to go to the next station. It was nearly fifty miles away, and it took us more than an hour to get there.

We managed to get a train, but it went only as far as Queenstown. In the 1940s, travelling for an African was a complicated process. All Africans over the age of sixteen were compelled to carry 'Native passes' issued by the Native Affairs Department, and were required to show that pass to any white policeman, civil servant or employer. Failure to do so could mean arrest, trial, a jail sentence or fine. The pass stated where the bearer lived, who his chief was, and whether he had paid the annual poll tax, which was a tax levied only on Africans. Later, the pass took the form of a booklet or 'Reference Book', as it was known, containing detailed information that had to be signed by one's employer every month.

Justice and I had our passes in order, but for an African to leave his magisterial district and enter that of another for the purpose of working or living, he needed travel documents, a permit and a letter from his employer or, as in our case, his guardian – none of which we had. Even at the best of times, when one had all these documents, a police officer might harass you because one of them was missing a signature or had an incorrect date. Not having any was extremely risky. Our plan was to disembark in Queenstown, make our way to the house of a relative, and then arrange the necessary documents. This was also an ill-considered plan, but we came in for a bit of luck because at the house in Queenstown we accidentally met Chief Mpondombini, a brother of the regent, who was fond of Justice and myself.

Chief Mpondombini greeted us warmly, and we explained that we needed the requisite travel documents from the local magistrate. We lied about why we required them, claiming that we were on an errand for the regent. Chief Mpondombini was a retired interpreter from the Native Affairs Department and knew the chief magistrate well. He had no reason to doubt our story and not only escorted us to the magistrate, but vouched for us and explained our predicament. After listening to the chief, the magistrate rapidly made out the necessary travel documents and affixed the official stamp. Justice and I looked at each other and smiled in complicity. But just as the magistrate was handing over the documents to us, he recalled something and said that, as a matter of courtesy, he ought to inform the chief magistrate of Umtata, in whose jurisdiction we fell. This made us uneasy, but we stayed seated in his office. The magistrate used his telephone to reach his colleague in Umtata. As luck would have it, the regent was just then paying a call on the chief magistrate of Umtata and was in his very office.

As our magistrate was explaining our situation to the chief magistrate of Umtata, the latter gentleman said something like, 'Oh, their father just happens to be right here,' and then put the regent on the line. When the magistrate informed the regent what we were requesting, the regent exploded. 'Arrest those boys!' he shouted, loud enough for us to hear his voice through the receiver. 'Arrest them and bring them back here immediately!' The chief magistrate put down the phone. He regarded us angrily. 'You boys are thieves and liars,' he told us. 'You have presumed upon my good offices and then deceived me. Now I am going to have you arrested.'

I immediately rose to our defence. From my studies at Fort Hare I had a little knowledge of law, and I put it to use. I said that we had told him lies, that was true. But we had committed no offence and violated no laws, and we could not be arrested simply on the recommendation of a chief, even if he happened to be our father. The magistrate backed down and did not arrest us, but told us to leave his office and never to darken his door again.

Chief Mpondombini was also annoyed, and left us to our own devices. Justice remembered that he had a friend in Queenstown named Sidney Nxu who was working in the office of a white attorney. We went to see this man and explained our situation; he told us that the mother of the attorney he worked for was driving into Johannesburg and he would see if she would offer us a lift. He told us that his mother would give us a ride if we paid a fee of £15 sterling. This was a vast sum, far more than the cost of a train ticket. The fee virtually depleted our savings, but we had no choice. We decided to risk getting our passes stamped and to obtain the correct travel documents once we were in Johannesburg.

We left early the following morning. In those days, it was customary for blacks to ride in the back seat of the car if a white was driving. The two of us sat in that fashion, with Justice directly behind the woman. Justice was a friendly, exuberant person and immediately began chatting to me. This made the old woman extremely uncomfortable. She had obviously never been in the company of a black who had no inhibitions about whites. After only a few miles, she told Justice that she wanted him to switch seats with me, so that she could keep an eye on him, and for the rest of the journey she watched him like a hawk. But, after a while, Justice's charm worked on her and she would occasionally laugh at something he said.

At about ten o'clock that evening, we saw before us, glinting in the distance, a maze of lights that seemed to stretch in all directions. Electricity, to me, had always been a novelty and a luxury, and here was a vast landscape of electricity, a city of light. I was terribly excited to see the city I had been hearing about since I was a child. Johannesburg had always been depicted as a city of dreams, a place where one could transform oneself from a poor peasant into a wealthy sophisticate, a city of danger and of opportunity. I remembered the stories that Banabakhe had told us at circumcision school, of buildings so tall you could not see the tops, of crowds of people speaking languages you had never heard of, of sleek motor cars and beautiful women and dashing gangsters. It was eGoli, the city of gold, where I would soon be making my home.

On the outskirts of the city the traffic became denser. I had never seen so many cars on the road at one time – even in Umtata, there were never more than a handful of cars and here there were thousands. We drove around the city, rather than through it, but I could see the silhouette of the tall blocks of buildings, even darker against the dark night sky. I looked at great billboards by the side of the road advertising cigarettes and candy and beer. It all seemed tremendously glamorous.

Soon we were in an area of stately mansions, even the smallest of which was bigger than the regent's palace, with grand front lawns and tall iron gates. This was the suburb where the old lady's daughter lived, and we pulled into the long driveway of one of these beautiful homes. Justice and I were dispatched to the servants' wing, where we were to spend the night. We thanked the old lady, and then crawled off to sleep on the floor. But the prospect of Johannesburg was so exciting to me that I felt as though I slept on a beautiful feather bed that night. The possibilities seemed infinite. I had reached the end of what seemed like a long journey, but it was actually the very beginning of a much longer and more trying journey that would test me in ways that I could not then have imagined.

PART TWO

———

Johannesburg

9

It was dawn when we reached the offices of Crown Mines, which were located on the plateau of a great hill overlooking the still, dark metropolis. Johannesburg had been built up around the discovery of gold on the Witwatersrand in 1886, and Crown Mines was the largest gold mine in the city of gold. I expected to see a grand building like the government offices in Umtata, but the Crown Mine offices were rusted tin shanties on the face of the mine.

There is nothing magical about a gold mine. Barren and pockmarked, all dirt and no trees, fenced in on all sides, a gold mine resembles a war-torn battlefield. The noise was harsh and ubiquitous: the rasp of shaft-lifts, the jangling power drills, the distant rumble of dynamite, the barked orders. Everywhere I looked I saw black men in dusty overalls looking tired and bent. They lived on the grounds in bleak, single-sex barracks that contained hundreds of concrete bunks separated from each other by only a few inches.

Gold-mining on the Witwatersrand was costly because the ore was low grade and deep under the earth. Only the presence of cheap labour in the form of thousands of Africans working long hours for little pay with no rights made gold-mining profitable for the mining houses – white-owned companies that became wealthy beyond the dreams of Croesus on the backs of the African people. I had never seen such enterprise before, such great machines, such methodical organization and such backbreaking work. It was my first sight of South African capitalism at work, and I knew I was in for a new kind of education.

We went straight to the chief *induna*, or headman. Piliso was a tough old fellow who had seen life at its most pitiless. He knew about Justice, as the regent had sent a letter months before making arrangements for him to get a clerical job, the most coveted and respected job in the mine compound. I, however, was unknown to him. Justice explained that I was his brother.

'I was expecting only Justice,' Piliso responded. 'Your father's letter mentions nothing about a brother.' He looked me over rather sceptically. But Justice pleaded with him, saying it had simply been an oversight, and that the regent had already posted a letter about me. Piliso's crusty exterior hid a sympathetic side, and he took me on as a mine policeman, saying that if I worked well, he would give me a clerical post in three months' time.

The regent's word carried weight at Crown Mines. This was true of all chiefs in South Africa. Mining officials were eager to recruit labour in the countryside, and the chiefs had authority over the men they needed. They wanted the chiefs to encourage their subjects to come to the Reef. The chiefs were treated with great deference; the mining houses provided special lodgings for them whenever they came to visit. One letter from the regent was enough to secure a man a good job, and Justice and I were treated with extra care because of our connection. We were to be given free rations, sleeping quarters and a small salary. We did not stay in the barracks that first night. For our first few days, Piliso, out of courtesy to the regent, invited Justice and me to stay with him.

Many of the miners, especially those from Thembuland, treated Justice as a chief and greeted him with gifts of cash, the custom when a chief visited a mine. Most of these men were in the same hostel; miners were normally housed according to tribe. The mining companies preferred such segregation because it prevented different ethnic groups from uniting around a common grievance and it reinforced the power of the chiefs. The separation often resulted in factional fights between different ethnic groups and clans, which the companies did not effectively discourage.

Justice shared some of his booty with me and gave me a few extra pounds as a bonus. For those first few days, my pockets jingling with newfound riches, I felt like a millionaire. I was beginning to think I was a child of fortune, that luck was shining on me, and that if I had not wasted precious time studying at college I could have been a wealthy man by then. Once again, I did not see that fate was busy setting snares around me.

I started work immediately as a night watchman. I was given a uniform, a new pair of boots, a helmet, a flashlight, a whistle and a knobkerrie, which is a long wooden stick with a heavy ball of wood at one end. The job was a simple one: I waited at the compound entrance next to the sign that read, 'BEWARE: NATIVES CROSSING HERE', and checked the credentials of all those entering and leaving. For the first few nights, I patrolled the grounds of the compound without incident. I did challenge a rather drunken miner late one evening, but he meekly showed his pass and retired to his hostel.

Flushed with our success, Justice and I boasted of our cleverness to a friend of ours whom we knew from home, who was also working at the mines. We explained how we had run away and tricked the regent into the bargain. Although we swore this fellow to secrecy, he went straight away to the *induna* and revealed our secret. A day later, Piliso called us in and the first question he asked Justice was, 'Where is the permission from the regent for your brother?' Justice said that he had already explained that the regent had posted it. Piliso was not mollified by this, and we sensed that something was wrong. He then reached inside his desk and produced a telegram. 'I have had a communication from the regent,' he said in a serious tone of voice, and handed it to us. It contained a single sentence: 'SEND BOYS HOME AT ONCE.'

Piliso then vented his anger on us, accusing us of lying to him. He said we had presumed on his hospitality and the good name of the regent. He told us that he was taking up a collection among the miners to put us on a train back to the Transkei. Justice protested against going home, saying that we simply wanted to work at the mine, and that we could make decisions for ourselves. But Piliso turned a deaf ear. We felt ashamed and humiliated, but we left his office determined not to return to the Transkei.

We rapidly hatched another plan. We went to see Dr A.B. Xuma, an old friend of the regent's who was the president-general of the African National Congress. Dr Xuma was from the Transkei, and was an extremely well-respected physician.

Dr Xuma was pleased to see us, and politely questioned us about family matters in Mqhekezweni. We told him a series of half-truths about why we were in Johannesburg, and that we greatly desired jobs in the mines. Dr Xuma said he would be glad to assist us, and immediately telephoned a Mr Wellbeloved at the Chamber of Mines, a powerful organization representing the mining houses and exerting monopoly control over the hiring of mine labour. Dr Xuma told Mr Wellbeloved what splendid fellows we were and that he should find places for us. We thanked Dr Xuma and went off to see Mr Wellbeloved.

Mr Wellbeloved was a white man whose office was grander than any I had ever seen; his desk seemed as wide as a football field. We met him in the company of a mine boss named Festile, and we told him the same fabrications that we had told Dr Xuma. Mr Wellbeloved was impressed with my not-entirely-truthful explanation that I had come to Johannesburg to continue my studies at the University of the Witwatersrand. 'Well, boys,' he said, 'I will put you in touch with the manager of Crown Mines, a Mr Piliso, and I will tell him to give you jobs as clerks.' He said he had worked with Mr Piliso for thirty years and in all that time Piliso had never lied to him. Justice and I squirmed at this but said nothing. Despite some misgivings, we naively felt we had the upper hand with Mr Piliso now that we had his boss, Mr Wellbeloved, on our side.

We returned to the Crown Mine offices, where the white compound manager was considerate to us because of the letter we presented from Mr Wellbeloved. Just then, Mr Piliso passed by the office, saw us, and then stormed in. 'You boys! You've come back!' he said with irritation. 'What are you doing here?'

Justice was calm. 'We've been sent by Mr Wellbeloved,' he replied, his tone bordering on defiance. Mr Piliso considered this for a moment. 'Did you tell him that you ran away from your father?' Piliso then countered. Justice was silent.

'You'll never be employed in any mine that I run!' he yelled. 'Now get out of my sight!' Justice waved Wellbeloved's letter. 'I don't give a damn about a letter!' Piliso said. I looked to the white manager, hoping that he might overrule Piliso, but he was as still as a statue and seemed as intimidated as we were. We had no rejoinder for Piliso, and we sheepishly walked out of the office, feeling even more humbled than we had on the first occasion.

Our fortunes were now reversed. We were without jobs, without prospects and without a place to stay. Justice knew various people in Johannesburg, and he went into town to investigate a place for us to stay. In the meantime, I was to fetch our suitcase, which was still at Piliso's, and then meet Justice at George Goch, a small township in southern Johannesburg, later that day.

I prevailed upon a fellow named Bikitsha, whom I knew from home, to help me carry the suitcase to the front gate. A watchman at the gate stopped us both and said he needed to search the bag. Bikitsha protested, asserting there was no contraband in the suitcase. The watchman replied that a search was routine, and he looked through the bag in a cursory way, not even disturbing the clothing. As the watchman was closing it, Bikitsha, who was a cocky fellow, said, 'Why do you make trouble? I told you there was nothing there.' These words irked the watchman, who then decided to search the case with a fine-toothed comb. I became increasingly nervous as he opened every compartment and probed every pocket. He then reached all the way to the bottom of the case and found the very thing I prayed he would not: a loaded revolver wrapped inside some of my clothing.

He turned to my friend and said, 'You are under arrest.' He then blew his whistle, which brought a team of guards over to us. My friend looked at me with a mixture of consternation and confusion as they led him away to the local police station. I followed them at a distance, considering my

options. The gun, an old revolver, had been my father's and he had left
it to me when he died. I had never used it, but as a precaution, I had
brought it with me to the city.

I could not let my friend take the blame in my stead. Not long after he
had entered the police station, I went inside and asked to see the officer
in charge. I was taken to him and spoke as directly and forthrightly as
I could: 'Sir, that is my gun that was found in my friend's suitcase. I
inherited it from my father in the Transkei and I brought it here because
I was afraid of gangsters.' I explained that I was a student from Fort
Hare, and that I was only in Johannesburg temporarily. The officer in
charge softened a bit as I spoke, and said that he would release my friend
at once. He said he would have to charge me for possession of the gun,
though he would not arrest me, and that I should appear in court first
thing on Monday morning to answer the charge. I was grateful, and told
him that I would certainly appear in court on Monday. I did go to court
that Monday, and received only a nominal fine.

In the meantime I had arranged to stay with one of my cousins, Garlick
Mbekeni, in George Goch township. Garlick was a hawker who sold
clothing, and had a small box-like house. He was a friendly, solicitous
man, and after I had been there a short while, I told him that my real
aspiration was to be a lawyer. He commended me for my ambition and
said he would think about what I had said.

A few days later, Garlick told me that he was taking me to see 'one of
our best people in Johannesburg'. We took the train to the office of an
estate agent in Market Street, a dense and rollicking thoroughfare with
trams groaning with passengers, pavement vendors on every street, and
a sense that wealth and riches were just around the next corner.

Johannesburg in those days was a combination frontier town and
modern city. Butchers cut meat on the street next to office buildings.
Tents were pitched beside bustling shops, and women hung out their
washing next door to high-rise buildings. Industry was energized due
to the war effort. In 1939 South Africa, a member of the British
Commonwealth, had declared war on Nazi Germany. The country was
supplying men and goods to the war effort. Demand for labour was high,
and Johannesburg became a magnet for Africans from the countryside
seeking work. Between 1941, when I arrived, and 1946, the number of
Africans in the city would double. Every morning, the township felt larger
than it had the day before. Men found jobs in factories and housing in
the 'non-European townships' of Newclare, Martindale, George Goch,
Alexandra, Sophiatown and the Western Native Township, a prison-like
compound of a few thousand matchbox houses on treeless ground.

Garlick and I sat in the estate agent's waiting room while a pretty

African receptionist announced our presence to her boss in the inner office. After she relayed the message, her nimble fingers danced across the keyboard as she typed a letter. I had never in my life seen an African typist before, much less a female one. In the few public and business offices that I had visited in Umtata and Fort Hare, the typists had always been white and male. I was particularly impressed with this young woman because those white male typists had only used two slow-moving fingers to peck out their letters.

She soon ushered us into the inner office, where I was introduced to a man who looked to be in his late twenties, with an intelligent and kindly face, light in complexion, and dressed in a double-breasted suit. Despite his youth, he seemed to me an experienced man of the world. He was from the Transkei, but spoke English with a rapid urban fluency. To judge from his well-populated waiting room and his desk piled high with papers, he was a busy and successful man. But he did not rush us and seemed genuinely interested in our errand. His name was Walter Sisulu.

Sisulu's office specialized in properties for Africans. In the 1940s, there were still quite a few areas where freehold properties could be purchased by Africans, smallholdings located in such places as Alexandra and Sophiatown. In some of these areas, Africans had owned their own homes for several generations. The rest of the African areas were municipal townships containing matchbox houses for which the residents paid rent to the Johannesburg City Council.

Sisulu's name was becoming prominent as both a businessman and a local leader. He was already a force in the community. He paid close attention as I explained my difficulties at Fort Hare, my ambition to be a lawyer, and how I intended to register at the University of South Africa to finish my degree by correspondence course. I neglected to tell him the circumstances of my arrival in Johannesburg. When I had finished, he leaned back in his chair and pondered what I had said. Then he looked me over one more time, and said that there was a white lawyer with whom he worked named Lazar Sidelsky, whom he believed to be a decent and progressive fellow. Sidelsky, he said, was interested in African education. He would talk to him about taking me on as an articled clerk.

In those days, I believed that proficiency in English and success in business were the direct result of high academic achievements and I assumed as a matter of course that Sisulu was a university graduate. I was greatly surprised to learn from my cousin after I left the office that Walter Sisulu had never gone beyond Standard VI. It was another lesson from Fort Hare that I had to unlearn in Johannesburg. I had been taught that to have a BA meant to be a leader, and to be a leader one needed a BA. But in Johannesburg I found that many of the most outstanding leaders had never been to university at all. Even though I had done all the courses in English that were required for a BA, my English was neither as fluent nor as eloquent as that of many of the men I met in Johannesburg who had not even received a school certificate.

After a brief time staying with my cousin, I arranged to move in with the Reverend J. Mabutho of the Anglican Church at his home in Eighth Avenue in Alexandra township. Reverend Mabutho was a fellow Thembu, a friend of my family, and a generous, God-fearing man. His wife, whom we called Gogo, was warm, affectionate, and a splendid cook who was liberal with her helpings. As a Thembu who knew my family, Reverend Mabutho felt responsible for me. 'Our ancestors have taught us to share,' he once told me.

But I had not learned from my experience at Crown Mines, for I did not tell Reverend Mabutho about the circumstances of my leaving the Transkei. My omission had unhappy consequences. A few days after I had moved in with the Mabuthos, I was having tea with them when a visitor arrived. Unfortunately their friend was Mr Festile, the *induna* at the Chamber of Mines who had been present when Justice and I met Mr Wellbeloved. Mr Festile and I greeted each other in a way that suggested we knew one another, and though nothing was said of our previous meeting, the next day Reverend Mabutho took me aside and made it clear that I could no longer remain under their roof.

I cursed myself for not having told the whole truth. I had become so used to my deceptions that I lied even when I did not have to. I am sure that Reverend Mabutho would not have minded, but when he learned of my circumstances from Festile, he felt deceived. In my brief stay in Johannesburg, I had left a trail of mistruths and, in each case, the falsehood had come back to haunt me. At the time, I felt that I had no alternative. I was frightened and inexperienced, and I knew that I had not got off on the right foot in my new life. In this instance, Reverend Mabutho took pity on me and found me accommodation with his next-door neighbours, the Xhoma family.

Mr Xhoma was one of an elite handful of African landowners in Alexandra. His house – 46, Seventh Avenue – was small, particularly as he had six children, but it was pleasant, with a veranda and a tiny garden. In order to make ends meet, Mr Xhoma, like so many other residents of Alexandra, rented rooms to boarders. He had built a tin-roofed room at the back of his property, no more than a shack, with a dirt floor, no heat, no electricity, no running water. But it was a place of my own and I was happy to have it.

In the meantime, on Walter's recommendation, Lazar Sidelsky had agreed to take me on as a clerk while I completed my BA degree. The firm of Witkin, Sidelsky and Eidelman, one of the largest law firms in the city, handled business from blacks as well as whites. In addition to studying law and passing certain exams, in order to qualify as an attorney in South Africa one had to undergo several years of apprenticeship to a practising lawyer, which is known as serving articles. But in order for me to become articled, I first had to complete my BA degree. To that end, I was studying at night with UNISA, short for the University of South Africa, a respected educational institution that offered credits and degrees by correspondence.

In addition to trying conventional law cases, Witkin, Sidelsky and Eidelman oversaw property transactions for African customers. Walter brought the firm clients who needed a mortgage. The firm would handle their loan applications, and then take a commission, which it would split with the estate agent. In fact, the law firm would take the lion's share of the money, leaving only a pittance for the African estate agent. Blacks were given the crumbs from the table, and had no option but to accept them.

Even so, the law firm was far more liberal than most. It was a Jewish firm, and in my experience I have found Jews to be more broad-minded than most whites on issues of race and politics, perhaps because they themselves have historically been victims of prejudice. The fact that Lazar Sidelsky, one of the firm's partners, would take on a young African as an articled clerk – something almost unheard-of in those days – was evidence of that liberalism.

Mr Sidelsky, whom I came to respect greatly and who treated me with enormous kindness, was a graduate of the University of the Witwatersrand and was in his mid-thirties when I joined the firm. He was involved in African education, donating money and time to African schools. A slender, courtly man, with a pencil moustache, he took a genuine interest in my welfare and future, preaching the value and importance of education – for me individually and for Africans in general. Only mass education, he used to say, would free my people, arguing that an educated man could not be oppressed because he could think for himself. He told me over and over again that becoming a successful attorney and thereby a model of achievement for my people was the most worthwhile path I could follow.

I met most of the firm's staff on my first day in the office, including the one other African employee, Gaur Radebe, with whom I shared an office. Ten years my senior, Gaur was a clerk, interpreter and messenger. He was a short, stocky, muscular man, fluent in English, Sotho and Zulu, and expressing himself in all of them with precision, humour and confidence.

He had strong opinions and even stronger arguments to back them up and was a well-known figure in black Johannesburg.

That first morning at the firm, a pleasant young white secretary, Miss Lieberman, took me aside and said, 'Nelson, we have no colour bar here at the law firm.' She explained that at midmorning, the tea-man arrived in the front parlour with tea on a tray and a number of cups. 'In honour of your arrival, we have purchased two new cups for you and Gaur,' she said. 'The secretaries take cups of tea to the principals but you and Gaur will take your own tea, just as we do. I will call you when the tea comes, and then you can take your tea in the new cups.' She added that I should convey this message to Gaur. I was grateful for her ministrations, but I knew that the 'two new cups' she was so careful to mention were evidence of the colour bar that she said did not exist. The secretaries might share tea with two Africans, but not the cups with which to drink it.

When I told Gaur what Miss Lieberman had said, I noticed his expression change as he listened, just as you can see a mischievous idea enter the head of a child. 'Nelson,' he said, 'at teatime, don't worry about anything. Just do as I do.' At 11 o'clock, Miss Lieberman informed us that tea had arrived. In front of the secretaries and some of the other members of the firm, Gaur went over to the tea tray and ostentatiously ignored the two new cups, selecting instead one of the old ones, and proceeded to put in generous portions of sugar, milk and then tea. He stirred his cup slowly, and then stood there drinking it in a very self-satisfied way. The secretaries stared at Gaur and then Gaur nodded to me, as if to say, 'It is your turn, Nelson.'

For a moment I was in a quandary. I neither wanted to offend the secretaries nor alienate my new colleague, so I settled on what seemed to me the most prudent course of action: I declined to have any tea at all. I said I was not thirsty. I was then just twenty-three years old, and just finding my feet as a man, as a resident of Johannesburg and as an employee of a white firm, and I saw the middle path as the best and most reasonable one. Thereafter, at teatime, I would go to the small kitchen in the office and take my tea there in solitude.

The secretaries were not always so thoughtful. Some time later, when I was more experienced at the firm, I was dictating some information to a white secretary when a white client whom she knew came into the office. She was embarrassed, and to demonstrate that she was not taking dictation from an African, she took a sixpence from her purse and said stiffly, 'Nelson, please go out and get me some shampoo from the chemist.' I left the room and got her shampoo.

In the beginning, my work at the firm was quite rudimentary. As a combination of a clerk and a messenger, I would find, arrange and file documents and serve or deliver papers around Johannesburg. Later, I would draw up contracts for some of the firm's African clients. Yet, no matter how small the job, Mr Sidelsky would explain to me what it was for and why I was doing it. He was a patient and generous teacher, and sought to impart not only the details of the law but the philosophy behind it. His view of the law was broad rather than narrow, for he believed that it was a tool that could be used to change society.

While Mr Sidelsky imparted his views of the law, he warned me against politics. Politics, he said, brings out the worst in men. It was the source of trouble and corruption, and should be avoided at all costs. He painted a frightening picture of what would happen to me if I drifted into politics, and counselled me to avoid the company of men he regarded as troublemakers and rabble-rousers, specifically Gaur Radebe and Walter Sisulu. While Mr Sidelsky respected their abilities, he abhorred their politics.

Gaur was indeed a 'troublemaker', in the best sense of that term, and was an influential man in the African community in ways that Mr Sidelsky did not know or suspect. He was a member of the Advisory Board in the Western Native Township, an elected body of four local people who dealt with the authorities on matters relating to the townships. While it had little power, the board had great prestige among the people. Gaur was also, as I soon discovered, a prominent member of both the ANC and the Communist Party.

Gaur was his own man. He did not treat our employers with exaggerated courtesy, and often chided them for their treatment of Africans. 'You people stole our land from us,' he would say, 'and enslaved us. Now you are making us pay through the nose to get the worst pieces of it back.' One day, after I returned from doing an errand and entered Mr Sidelsky's office, Gaur turned to him and said, 'Look, you sit there like a lord whilst my chief runs around doing errands for you. The situation should be reversed, and one day it will, and we will dump all of you into the sea.' Gaur then left the room, and Mr Sidelsky just shook his head ruefully.

Gaur was an example of a man without a BA who seemed infinitely better educated than the fellows who left Fort Hare with glittering degrees. Not only was he more knowledgeable, he was bolder and more confident. Although I intended to finish my degree and enter law school, I learned from Gaur that a degree was not in itself a guarantee of leadership and that it meant nothing unless one went out into the community to prove oneself.

I was not the only articled clerk at Witkin, Sidelsky and Eidelman. A fellow about my age named Nat Bregman had started work shortly before I had. Nat was bright, pleasant, and thoughtful. He seemed entirely colour-blind and became my first white friend. He was a deft mimic, and could do fine imitations of the voices of Jan Smuts, Franklin Roosevelt and Winston Churchill. I often sought his counsel on matters of law and office procedure, and he was unfailingly helpful.

One day, at lunchtime, we were sitting in the office and Nat took out a packet of sandwiches. He removed one sandwich and said, 'Nelson, take hold of the other side of the sandwich.' I was not sure why he asked me to do this, but as I was hungry, I decided to oblige. 'Now, pull,' he said. I did so, and the sandwich split roughly in two.

'Now, eat,' he said. As I was chewing, Nat said, 'Nelson, what we have just done symbolizes the philosophy of the Communist Party: to share everything we have.' He told me he was a member of the party and explained the rudiments of what it stood for. I knew that Gaur was a member of the party, but he had never canvassed for it. I listened to Nat that day, and on many subsequent occasions when he preached the virtues of communism and tried to persuade me to join the party. I heard him out, asked questions, but did not join. I was not inclined to join any political organization, and the advice of Mr Sidelsky was still ringing in my ears. I was also quite religious, and the party's antipathy to religion put me off. But I appreciated half that sandwich.

I enjoyed Nat's company and we often went about together, including to a number of lectures and CP meetings. I went primarily out of intellectual curiosity. I was just becoming aware of the history of racial oppression in my own country, and saw the struggle in South Africa as purely racial. But the party saw South Africa's problems through the lens of the class struggle. To them, it was a matter of the Haves oppressing the Have-nots. This was intriguing to me, but did not seem particularly relevant to present-day South Africa. It might have been applicable to Germany or England, or Russia, but it did not seem appropriate for the country that I knew. Even so, I listened and learned.

Nat invited me to a number of parties where there was a mixture of whites, Africans, Indians and Coloureds. The get-togethers were arranged by the party and most of the guests were party members. I remember being anxious the first time I went, mainly because I did not think I had the proper attire. At Fort Hare, we were taught to wear a tie and jacket to a social function of any kind. Though my wardrobe was severely limited, I managed to find a tie to wear to the party.

I discovered a lively and gregarious group of people who did not seem to pay attention to colour at all. It was one of the first mixed gatherings I had ever attended, and I was far more of an observer than a participant. I felt extremely shy, wary of committing a *faux pas*, and unequipped to participate in the high-flown and rapid-fire conversations. My thoughts seemed undeveloped by comparison to the sophisticated dialogue around me.

At one point in the evening I was introduced to Michael Harmel, whom I was told had a master's degree in English from Rhodes University. I was impressed with his degree, but when I met him, I thought to myself, 'This chap has an MA, and he is not even wearing a tie!' I just could not reconcile this discrepancy. Later, Michael and I became friends, and I came to admire him greatly, in no small measure because he rejected so many of the rather foolish conventions I once embraced. He was not only a brilliant writer, but was so committed to communism that he lived in the same manner as an African, though he could have lived on a grander scale.

10

Life in Alexandra was exhilarating and precarious. Its atmosphere was alive, its spirit adventurous, its people resourceful. Although the township did boast some handsome buildings, it could fairly be described as a slum, living testimony to the neglect of the authorities. The roads were unpaved and dirty, and filled with hungry, undernourished children scampering around half-naked. The air was thick with the smoke from coal fires in tin braziers and stoves. A single water tap served several houses. Pools of stinking, stagnant water full of maggots collected by the side of the road. Alexandra was known as 'Dark City' for its complete absence of electricity. Walking home at night was perilous, for there were no lights, the silence pierced by yells, laughter and occasional gunfire. So different from the darkness of the Transkei, which seemed to envelop one in a welcome embrace.

The township was desperately overcrowded; every square foot was occupied by either a ramshackle house or a tin-roofed shack. As so often happens in desperately poor places, the worst elements came to the fore. Life was cheap; the gun and the knife ruled at night. Gangsters – known as *tsotsis* – carrying flick-knives or switchblades were plentiful and prominent; in those days they emulated American movie stars and wore fedoras and double-breasted suits and wide, colourful ties. Police raids were a regular feature of life in Alexandra. The police routinely arrested masses of people for pass violations, possession of liquor and failure to pay the poll tax. On almost every corner there were shebeens, illegal saloons that were shacks where home-brewed beer was served.

In spite of the hellish aspects of life in Alexandra, the township was also a kind of heaven. As one of the few areas of the country where Africans could acquire freehold property and run their own affairs, where people did not have to kowtow to the tyranny of white municipal authorities, Alexandra was an urban Promised Land, evidence that a section of our people had broken their ties with the rural areas and become permanent city-dwellers. The government, in order to keep Africans in the countryside or working in the mines, maintained that Africans were by nature a rural people, ill suited to city life. Alexandra, despite its problems and flaws, gave the lie to that argument. Its population, drawn from all African language groups, was well adapted to city life and politically conscious. Urban life tended to abrade tribal and ethnic distinctions, and instead of being Xhosas, or Sothos, or Zulus or Shangaans, we were Alexandrans. This created a sense of solidarity, which caused great concern among the white authorities. The government had always utilized divide-and-rule tactics when dealing with Africans and depended on the strength of ethnic divisions between the people. But in places like Alexandra, these differences were being erased.

Alexandra occupies a treasured place in my heart. It was the first place I ever lived away from home. Even though I was later to live in Orlando, a small section of Soweto, for a far longer period than I did in Alexandra, I always regarded Alexandra Township as a home where I had no specific house, and Orlando as a place where I had a house but no home.

In that first year, I learned more about poverty than I did in all my childhood days in Qunu. I never seemed to have money and I managed to survive on the meagrest of resources. The law firm paid me a salary of £2 per week, having generously waived the premium the articled clerks normally paid the firm. Out of that £2, I paid 13s. 4d. a month for my room at the Xhomas'. The cheapest means of transport to and from Alexandra was the 'Native' bus – for Africans only – which at £1 10s. a month made a considerable dent in my income. I was also paying fees to the University of South Africa in order to complete my degree by correspondence. I spent another pound or so on food. Part of my salary was spent on an even more vital item – candles – for without them I could not study. I could not afford a paraffin lamp; candles allowed me to read late into the night.

I was inevitably short of more than a few pence each month. On many days I walked the six miles to town in the morning and the six back in the evening in order to save the bus fare. I often went days without more than a mouthful of food and without a change of clothing. Mr Sidelsky, who was my height, once gave me an old suit of his and, assisted by considerable stitching and patching, I wore that suit every day for almost five years. In the end, there were more patches than suit.

One afternoon I was returning to Alexandra by bus and took a seat next to another fellow about my age. He was one of those young men who affected a style of dress that mimicked the well-tailored gangsters in American movies. I realized that my suit was just touching the hem of his jacket. He noticed it also and very carefully moved away so that my jacket would not sully his. It was a tiny gesture, comical in retrospect, but painful at the time.

There is little to be said in favour of poverty, but it was often an incubator of true friendship. Many people will appear to befriend you when you are wealthy, but precious few will do the same when you are poor. If wealth is a magnet, poverty is a kind of repellent. Yet poverty often brings out the true generosity in others. One morning I decided to walk to town to save money and spotted a young lady who had been with me at Fort Hare. Her name was Phyllis Maseko and she was walking towards me on the same side of the street. I was embarrassed by my threadbare clothing and crossed to the other side, hoping she would not recognize me. But I heard her call out, 'Nelson . . . Nelson!' I stopped and crossed over, pretending that I had not noticed her until that moment. She was pleased to see me, but I could tell that she observed how shabby I looked. 'Nelson,' she said, 'here is my address, 234 Orlando East. Come and visit me.' I resolved not to humiliate myself again, but one day I was in need of a proper meal and dropped in. She fed me without alluding to my poverty, and from then on I continued to visit her.

My landlord, Mr Xhoma, was not wealthy, but he was a kind of philanthropist. Every Sunday, for all the time I lived on his property, he and his wife gave me lunch, and those steaming plates of pork and vegetables were often my only hot meal of the week. No matter where I was or what I was doing, I would never fail to be at the Xhomas' on Sunday. For the rest of the week I would sustain myself on bread, and sometimes the secretaries at the firm would bring me some food.

I was very backward in those days and the combination of poverty and provincialism made for some amusing incidents. One day, not long after I had moved in with the Xhomas, I was on my way home from Johannesburg and very hungry. I had some money that I had saved and decided to splurge on some fresh meat, which I had not had in a long time. I did not see a proper butcher around, so I went into a delicatessen, a type of shop I had never encountered until I came to Johannesburg. Through the glass I saw a large and appetizing piece of meat and asked the man behind the counter to carve off a piece. He wrapped it up, and I put it under my arm and headed home, dreaming of the dinner that awaited me.

When I returned to my room in Alexandra, I called to one of the young daughters in the main house. She was only seven, but a clever girl. I said to her, 'Would you take this piece of meat to one of your older sisters and ask her to cook it for me?' I could see her trying to suppress a smile, but she was too respectful of her elders to laugh. With some irritation, I asked her whether something was wrong. Very softly she said, 'This meat is cooked.' I asked her what she was talking about. She explained that I had bought a piece of smoked ham, and that it was meant to be eaten just as it was. This was entirely new to me, and rather than confess complete ignorance, I told her that I knew it was smoked ham but that I wanted it warmed up. She knew I was bluffing, but ran off anyway. The meat was very tasty.

In Alexandra I rekindled a friendship with the lively, ever-cheerful Ellen Nkabinde, whom I knew from Healdtown, and who was then teaching at one of the township schools. In fact, Ellen and I fell in love. I had known her only slightly at Healdtown, and it was not until I saw her again in Alexandra that our relationship blossomed. What little spare time I had in those months I spent with her. Courtship was difficult: we were always surrounded by people, and there were few places to go. The only place we could be alone was outside under the sun or the stars. So Ellen and I wandered together in the veld and hills surrounding the township. Mostly, we would just walk, and when we both had the time, we might have a picnic.

Ellen was a Swazi, and though tribalism was fading in the township, a close friend of mine condemned our relationship on purely tribal grounds. I categorically rejected this. But our different backgrounds posed certain problems. Mrs Mabutho, the minister's wife, did not care for Ellen, largely because she was a Swazi. One day, while I was at the Mabuthos', Mrs Mabutho answered a knock at the door. It was Ellen, who was looking for me, and Mrs Mabutho told her I was not inside. Only later did she say to me, 'Oh, Nelson, some girl was here looking for you.' Mrs Mabutho then said to me, 'Is that girl a Shangaan?' Although the Shangaans are a proud and noble tribe, at the time Shangaan was considered a derogatory term. I took offence at this and said, 'No, she is not a Shangaan, she is a Swazi.' Mrs Mabutho felt strongly that I should take out only Xhosa girls.

Such advice did not deter me. I loved and respected Ellen, and felt not a little bit noble in discarding the counsel of those who disapproved. The relationship was to me a novelty, and I felt daring in having a friendship with a woman who was not a Xhosa. I was young and rather lost in the city, and Ellen played the role not only of romantic partner but of a mother, supporting me, giving me confidence and endowing me with strength and hope. But within a few months Ellen moved away and, sadly, we lost touch with one another.

The Xhoma family had five daughters, each of them lovely, but the loveliest of all was named Didi. Didi, about my age, spent most of the week working as a domestic worker in a white suburb of Johannesburg. When I first moved to the house, I saw her only seldom and fleetingly. But later, when I made her acquaintance properly, I also fell in love with her. But Didi barely took any notice of me, and what she did notice was the fact that I owned only one patched-up suit and a single shirt, and that I did not present a figure much different from a tramp.

Every weekend Didi returned to Alexandra. She was brought home by a young man whom I assumed was her boyfriend, a flashy, well-to-do fellow who had a car, something that was most unusual. He wore expensive double-breasted American suits and wide-brimmed hats, and paid a great deal of attention to his appearance. He must have been a gangster of some sort, but I cannot be sure. He would stand outside in the yard and put his hands in his waistcoat and look altogether superior. He greeted me politely, but I could see that he did not regard me as much competition.

I yearned to tell Didi I loved her, but I was afraid that my advances would be unwanted. I was hardly a Don Juan. Awkward and hesitant around girls, I did not know or understand the romantic games that others seemed to play effortlessly. At weekends, Didi's mother would sometimes ask her to bring out a plate of food to me. Didi would arrive on my doorstep with the plate and I could tell that she simply wanted to perform her errand as quickly as possible, but I would do my best to delay her. I would ask her opinion on things, all sorts of questions. 'Now, what standard did you attain in school?' I would say. 'Standard V,' she replied. 'Why did you leave?' I asked. She was bored, she replied. 'Ah, well, you must go back to school,' I said. 'You are about the same age as I am,' I continued, 'and there is nothing wrong with returning to school at this age. Otherwise you will regret it when you are old. You must think seriously about your future. It is nice for you now because you are young and beautiful and have many admirers, but you need to have an independent profession.'

I realize that these are not the most romantic words that have ever been uttered by a young man to a young woman with whom he was in love, but I did not know what else to talk to her about. She listened seriously, but I could tell that she was not interested, that in fact she felt a bit superior to me.

I wanted to propose to her but I was unwilling to do so unless I was certain she would say yes. Although I loved her, I did not want to give her the satisfaction of rejecting me. I kept up my pursuit, but I was timid and hesitant. In love, unlike politics, caution is not usually a virtue. I was neither confident enough to think that I might succeed nor secure enough to bear the sense of failure if I did not.

I stayed at that house for about a year and, in the end, I uttered nothing about my feelings. Didi did not show any less interest in her boyfriend or any more interest in me. I bade my good-bye with expressions of gratitude for her friendliness and the hospitality of the family. I did not see Didi again for many years. One day, much later, when I was practising law in Johannesburg, a young woman and her mother walked into my office. The woman had had a child, and her boyfriend did not want to marry her; she was seeking to institute an action against him. That young woman was Didi, only now she looked haggard and wore a faded dress. I was distressed to see her, and thought how things might have turned out differently. In the end, she did not bring a suit against her boyfriend, and I never saw her again.

Despite my romantic deficiencies, I gradually adjusted to township life and began to develop a sense of inner strength, a belief that I could do well outside the world in which I had grown up. I slowly discovered that I did not have to depend on my royal connections or the support of family in order to advance, and I forged relationships with people who did not know or care about my link to the Thembu royal house. I had my own home, humble though it was, and I was developing the confidence and self-reliance necessary to stand on my own two feet.

At the end of 1941 I received word that the regent was visiting Johannesburg and wanted to see me. I was nervous, but knew that I was obliged to see him, and indeed wanted to do so. He was staying at the WNLA compound, the headquarters of the Witwatersrand Native Labour Association, the recruiting agency for mine workers along the Reef.

The regent seemed greatly changed, or perhaps it was I who had changed. He never once mentioned the fact that I had run away, Fort Hare, or the arranged marriage that was not to be. He was courteous and solicitous, questioning me in a fatherly way about my studies and future plans. He recognized that my life was starting in earnest and would take a different course from the one he had envisaged and planned for me. He did not try to dissuade me from my course, and I was grateful for this implicit acknowledgment that I was no longer his charge.

My meeting with the regent had a double effect. I had rehabilitated myself and at the same time restored my own regard for him and the Thembu royal house. I had become indifferent to my old connections, an attitude I had adopted in part to justify my flight and somehow alleviate the pain of my separation from a world I loved and valued. It was reassuring to be back in the regent's warm embrace.

While the regent seemed satisfied with me, he was vexed with Justice, who he said must return to Mqhekezweni. Justice had formed a liaison with a young woman, and I knew he had no intention of going home. After the regent departed, Bangindawo, one of his headmen, instituted proceedings against Justice, and I agreed to help Justice when he was

called before the native commissioner. At the hearing, I pointed out that
Justice was an adult, and he did not have to return to Mqhekezweni
merely because his father ordered it. When Bangindawo spoke, he did
not reply to my argument but played on my own loyalties. He addressed
me as Madiba, my clan name, something that was well calculated to
remind me of my Thembu heritage. 'Madiba,' he said, 'the regent has
cared for you, educated you, and treated you like his own son. Now you
want to keep his true son from him. This is contrary to the wishes of the
man who has been your faithful guardian, and contrary to the path that
has been laid out for Justice.'

Bangindawo's speech hit me hard. Justice did have a different destiny
from that of myself. He was the son of a chief, and a future chief in his
own right. After the hearing, I told Justice that I had changed my mind,
and I thought he should return. He was mystified by my reaction and
refused to listen to me. He resolved to stay, and must have informed his
girlfriend of my advice, for she never thereafter spoke to me.

At the beginning of 1942, in order to save money and be closer to
downtown Johannesburg, I moved from the room at the back of the
Xhomas' to the WNLA compound. I was assisted by Mr Festile, the
induna at the Chamber of Mines, who was once again playing a fateful
role in my life. On his own initiative he had decided to offer me free
accommodation in the mining compound.

The WNLA compound was a multi-ethnic, polyglot community of
modern, urban South Africa. There were Sothos, Tswanas, Vendas,
Zulus, Pedis, Shangaans, Namibians, Mozambicans, Swazis and Xhosas.
Few spoke English, and the lingua franca was an amalgam of many
tongues known as Fanagalo. There, I saw not only flare-ups of ethnic
animosity, but the comity that was also possible among men of different
backgrounds. Yet I was a fish out of water. Instead of spending my days
underground, I was studying or working in a law office where the only
physical activity was running errands or putting files in a cabinet.

Because the WNLA was a way-station for visiting chiefs, I had the
privilege of meeting tribal leaders from all over southern Africa. I recall
on one occasion meeting the queen regent of Basutoland, or what is now
Lesotho, Mantsebo Moshweshwe. She was accompanied by two chiefs,
both of whom knew Sabata's father, Jongilizwe. I asked them about
Jongilizwe, and for an hour I seemed to be back in Thembuland as they
told colourful tales about his early years.

The queen took special notice of me and at one point addressed me
directly, but she spoke in Sesotho, a language in which I knew few words.
Sesotho is the language of the Sotho people as well as the Tswana, a large

number of whom live in the Transvaal and the Orange Free State. She looked at me with incredulity, and then said in English, 'What kind of lawyer and leader will you be who cannot speak the language of your own people?' I had no response. The question embarrassed and sobered me; it made me realize my parochialism and just how unprepared I was for the task of serving my people. I had unconsciously succumbed to the ethnic divisions fostered by the white government and I did not know how to speak to my own kith and kin. Without language, one cannot talk to people and understand them; one cannot share their hopes and aspirations, grasp their history, appreciate their poetry or savour their songs. I again realized that we were not different people with separate languages; we were one people, with different tongues.

Less than six months after the regent's visit, Justice and I learned of his father's death in the winter of 1942. He had seemed weary when last I saw him and his death did not come as a great surprise. We read of the death in the newspaper because the telegram that had been sent to Justice had gone astray. We hastened down to the Transkei, arriving the day after the regent's funeral.

Though I was disappointed to miss the burial, I was inwardly glad that I had become reconciled with him before his death. But I was not without stabs of guilt. I always knew, even when I was estranged from the regent, that all my friends might desert me, all my plans might founder, all my hopes be dashed, but the regent would never abandon me. Yet I had spurned him, and I wondered whether my desertion might have hastened his death.

The passing of the regent removed from the scene an enlightened and tolerant man who achieved the goal that marks the reign of all great leaders: he kept his people united. Liberals and conservatives, traditionalists and reformers, white-collar officials and blue-collar miners, all remained loyal to him, not because they always agreed with him, but because the regent listened to and respected different opinions.

I spent nearly a week in Mqhekezweni after the funeral and it was a time of retrospection and rediscovery. There is nothing like returning to a place that remains unchanged to find the ways in which you yourself have altered. The Great Place went on as before, no different from when I had grown up there. But I realized that my own outlook and world views had evolved. I was no longer attracted by a career in the civil service, or being an interpreter in the Native Affairs Department. I no longer saw my future bound up with Thembuland and the Transkei. I was even informed that my Xhosa was no longer pure and was now influenced by Zulu, one of the dominant languages in the Reef. My life in Johannesburg, my exposure to men like Gaur Radebe, my experiences at the law firm had radically altered my beliefs. I looked back on that young man who had left Mqhekezweni as a naive and countrified fellow who had seen very little of the world. I now believed I was seeing things as they were. That too, of course, was an illusion.

I still felt an inner conflict between my head and my heart. My heart told me that I was a Thembu, that I had been raised and sent to school so that I could play a special role in perpetuating the kingship. Had I no obligations to the dead? To my father, who had put me in the care of the regent? To the regent himself, who had cared for me like a father? But my head told me that it was the right of every man to plan his own future as he pleased and choose his role in life. Was I not permitted to make my own choices?

Justice's circumstances were different from my own, and after the regent's death he had important new responsibilities thrust upon him. He was to succeed the regent as chief and had decided to remain in Mqhekezweni and take up his birthright. I had to return to Johannesburg, and could not even stay to attend his installation. In my language there is a saying: 'Ndiwelimilambo enamagama' ('I have crossed famous rivers'). It means that one has travelled a great distance, that one has had wide experience and gained some wisdom from it. I thought of this as I returned to Johannesburg alone. I had, since 1934, crossed many important rivers in my own land: the Mbashe and the Great Kei, on my way to Healdtown; and the Orange and the Vaal, on my way to Johannesburg. But I had many rivers yet to cross.

At the end of 1942 I passed the final examination for my BA degree. I had now achieved the rank I once considered so exalted. I was proud to have achieved my BA, but I also knew that the degree itself was neither a talisman nor a passport to easy success.

At the firm, I had become closer to Gaur, much to Mr Sidelsky's exasperation. Education, Gaur argued, was essential to our advancement, but he pointed out that no people or nation had ever freed itself through education alone. 'Education is all well and good,' Gaur said, 'but if we are to depend on education, we will wait a thousand years for our freedom. We are poor, we have few teachers and even fewer schools. We do not even have the power to educate ourselves.'

Gaur believed in finding solutions rather than in spouting theory. For Africans, he asserted, the engine of change was the African National Congress; its policies were the best way to pursue power in South Africa. He stressed the ANC's long history of advocating change, noting that the ANC was the oldest national African organization in the country, having been founded in 1912. Its constitution denounced racialism, its presidents had been from different tribal groups, and it preached the goal of Africans as full citizens of South Africa.

Despite Gaur's lack of formal education, he was my superior in virtually every sphere of knowledge. During lunch breaks he would often give impromptu lectures; he lent me books to read, recommended people for me to talk to, meetings for me to attend. I had taken two courses in modern history at Fort Hare, and while I knew many facts, Gaur was able to explain the causes for particular actions, the reasons that men and nations had acted as they did. I felt as though I was learning history afresh.

What made the deepest impression on me was Gaur's total commitment to the freedom struggle. He lived and breathed the quest for liberation. Gaur sometimes attended several meetings a day where he featured prominently as a speaker. He seemed to think of nothing but revolution.

I went along with Gaur to meetings of both the Township Advisory Board and the ANC. I went as an observer, not a participant, for I do not think I ever spoke. I wanted to understand the issues under discussion, evaluate the arguments, see the calibre of the men involved. The Advisory Board meetings were perfunctory and bureaucratic, but the ANC meetings were lively with debate and discussion about Parliament, the pass laws, rents, bus fares – any subject under the sun that affected Africans.

In August 1943 I marched with Gaur and ten thousand others in support of the Alexandra bus boycott, a protest against the raising of fares from four pence to five. Gaur was one of the leaders, and I watched him in action. This campaign had a great effect on me. In a small way, I had departed from my role as an observer and become a participant. I found that to march with one's people was exhilarating and inspiring. But I was also impressed by the boycott's effectiveness: after nine days, during which the buses ran empty, the company reinstated the fare to four pence.

Gaur's views were not the only ones I paid attention to at the firm. Hans Muller, a white estate agent who did business with Mr Sidelsky, would engage me in discussion. He was the prototypical businessman who saw the world through the prism of supply and demand. One day, Mr Muller pointed out of the window. 'Look out there, Nelson,' he said. 'Do you see those men and women scurrying up and down the street? What is it that they are pursuing? What is it they are working for so feverishly? I'll tell you: all of them, without exception, are after wealth and money. Because wealth and money equal happiness. That is what you must struggle for: money, and nothing but money. Once you have enough cash, there is nothing else you will want in life.'

William Smith was a Coloured man involved in the African property business who was often around the office. Smith was a veteran of the ICU (the Industrial and Commercial Workers Union), South Africa's first black trade union founded by Clements Kadalie, but his views had shifted dramatically since those days. 'Nelson,' he said, 'I have been involved in politics for a long time, and I regret every minute of it. I wasted the best years of my life in futile efforts serving vain and selfish men who placed their interests above those of the people they pretended to serve. Politics, in my experience, is nothing but a racket to steal money from the poor.'

Mr Sidelsky did not join these discussions. He seemed to regard discussing politics as almost as much of a waste of time as participating in it. Again and again he would counsel me to avoid politics. He warned me about Gaur and Walter Sisulu. 'These men will poison your mind,' he said. 'Nelson,' he asked, 'you want to be a lawyer, don't you?' I said yes. 'And if you are a lawyer, you want to be a successful lawyer, do you not?' Again, I said yes. 'Well, if you get into politics,' he said, 'your practice will suffer. You will get into trouble with the authorities who are often your allies in your work. You will lose all your clients, you will go bankrupt, you will break up your family and you will end up in jail. That is what will happen if you go into politics.'

I listened to these men and weighed their views carefully. All of the arguments had some merit. I was already leaning towards some type of political involvement, but I did not know what or how, and I lingered on the sidelines, uncertain what to do.

As far as my profession was concerned, it was Gaur who did more than offer advice. One day in early 1943, when I had been at the firm for less than two years, he took me aside and said, 'My boy, as long as I am here at the firm, they will never article you, whether or not you have a degree.' I was startled, and told Gaur that it could not be true, as he was not even in training to be a lawyer. 'That does not make a difference, Nelson,' he continued. 'They will say, "We have Gaur, he can speak law to our people, why do we need someone else? Gaur is already bringing in clients to the firm." But they will not tell you this to your face; they will just postpone and delay. It is important to the future of our struggle in this country for you to become a lawyer, and so I am going to leave the firm and start my own estate agency. When I am gone, they will have no choice but to article you.'

I pleaded with him not to resign, but he was immovable. Within a few days, he handed Mr Sidelsky his resignation, and Mr Sidelsky eventually articled me as promised. I cannot say whether Gaur's absence had anything to do with it, but his resignation was another example of his generosity.

Early in 1943, after passing my examination through UNISA, I returned to Fort Hare for my graduation. Before leaving for the university, I decided to treat myself to a proper suit. In order to do so, I had to borrow the money from Walter Sisulu. I had had a new suit when I went up to Fort Hare, purchased for me by the regent, and now I would have a new suit when I went down. I borrowed academic dress from Randall Peteni, a friend and fellow alumnus.

My nephew, K.D. Matanzima, who had graduated several years before, drove my mother and No-England, the regent's widow, to the ceremony. I was gratified to have my mother there, but the fact that No-England came made it seem as though the regent himself had blessed the event.

After the graduation I spent a few days with Daliwonga (K. D.'s clan name, which is what I called him), at his home in Qamata. Daliwonga had already chosen the path of traditional leadership. He was in the line of succession to become the head of Emigrant Thembuland, which lies in the westernmost part of the Transkei, and while I was staying with him he pressed me to return to Umtata after qualifying as an attorney. 'Why do you stay in Johannesburg?' he said. 'You are needed more here.'

It was a fair point: there were certainly more professional Africans in the Transvaal than in the Transkei. I told Daliwonga that his suggestion was premature. But in my heart I knew I was moving towards a different commitment. Through my friendship with Gaur and Walter, I was beginning to see that my duty was to my people as a whole, not just to a particular section or branch. I felt that all the currents in my life were taking me away from the Transkei and towards what seemed like the centre, a place where regional and ethnic loyalties gave way to a common purpose.

The graduation at Fort Hare offered a moment of introspection and reflection. I was struck most forcefully by the discrepancy between my old assumptions and my actual experience. I had discarded my presumptions that graduates automatically became leaders and that my connection to the Thembu royal house guaranteed me respect. Having a successful career and a comfortable salary were no longer my ultimate goals. I found myself being drawn into the world of politics because I was not content with my old beliefs.

In Johannesburg, I moved in circles where common sense and practical experience were more important than high academic qualifications. Even as I was receiving my degree, I realized that hardly anything I had learned at university seemed relevant in my new environment. At the university, teachers had shied away from topics like racial oppression, lack of opportunities for Africans and the nest of laws and regulations that subjugate the black man. But in my life in Johannesburg, I confronted these things every day. No one had ever suggested to me how to go about removing the evils of racial prejudice, and I had to learn by trial and error.

When I returned to Johannesburg at the beginning of 1943 I enrolled at the University of the Witwatersrand for a bachelor of law degree, the preparatory academic training for a lawyer. The University of the Witwatersrand, known to all as 'Wits', is located in Braamfontein in north-central Johannesburg, and is considered by many to be the premier English-speaking university in South Africa.

While working at the law firm brought me into regular contact with whites for the first time, the university introduced me to a group of whites of my own age. At Fort Hare we had occasional contacts with white students from Rhodes University in Grahamstown, but at Wits I was attending classes with white students. This was as new to them as it was to me, for I was the only African student in the law faculty.

The English-speaking universities of South Africa were great incubators of liberal values. It was a tribute to these institutions that they allowed black students. For the Afrikaans universities, such a thing was unthinkable.

Despite the university's liberal values, I never felt entirely comfortable there. Always to be the only African, except for menial workers, to be regarded at best as a curiosity and at worst as an interloper, is not a congenial experience. My manner was always guarded, and I met both generosity and animosity. Although I was to discover a core of sympathetic whites who became friends and later colleagues, most of the whites at Wits were not liberal or colour-blind. I recall getting to a lecture a few minutes late one day and taking a seat next to Sarel Tighy, a classmate who later became a Member of Parliament for the United Party. Though the lecture had already started and there were only a few empty seats, he ostentatiously collected his things and moved to a seat away from me. This type of behaviour was the rule rather than the exception. No one uttered the word 'kaffir'; their hostility was more muted, but I felt it just the same.

Our law professor, Mr Hahlo, was a strict, cerebral sort, who did not tolerate much independence on the part of his students. He held a curious view of the law when it came to women and Africans: neither group, he said, was meant to be lawyers. His view was that law was a social science and that women and Africans were not disciplined enough to master its intricacies. He once told me that I should not be at Wits but studying for my degree through UNISA. Although I disagreed with his views, I did little to disprove them. My performance as a law student was dismal.

At Wits, I met many people who were to share with me the ups and downs of the liberation struggle, and without whom I would have accomplished very little. Many white students went out of their way to make me feel welcome. During my first term at Wits I met Joe Slovo and his future wife, Ruth First. Then as now, Joe had one of the sharpest, most incisive minds I have ever encountered. He was an ardent communist, and was known for his high-spirited parties. Ruth had an outgoing personality and was a gifted writer. Both were the children of Jewish immigrants to South Africa. I began lifelong friendships with George Bizos and Bram Fischer. George, the child of Greek immigrants, was a man who combined a sympathetic nature with an incisive mind. Bram Fischer, a part-time lecturer, was the scion of a distinguished Afrikaner family: his grandfather had been prime minister of the Orange River Colony and his father was judge-president of the Orange Free State. Although he could have been prime minister of South Africa, he became one of the bravest and staunchest friends of the freedom struggle that I have ever known. I befriended Tony O'Dowd, Harold Wolpe, Jules Brawde and his wife Slema, all of whom were political radicals and members of the Communist Party.

I also formed close friendships with a number of Indian students. Although there had been a handful of Indian students at Fort Hare, they stayed in a separate hostel and I seldom had contact with them. At Wits I met and became friends with Ismail Meer, J.N. Singh, Ahmed Bhoola and Ramlal Bhoolia. The centre of this tight-knit community was Ismail's apartment, Flat 13, Kholvad House, four rooms in a residential building in the centre of the city. There we studied, talked and even danced until the early hours of the morning, and it became a kind of headquarters for young freedom fighters. I sometimes slept there when it was too late to catch the last train back to Orlando.

Bright and serious, Ismail Meer was born in Natal, and while at law school at Wits he became a key member of the Transvaal Indian Congress. J.N. Singh was a popular, handsome fellow, who was at ease with all colours and also a member of the Communist Party. One day, Ismail, J.N. and myself were in a rush to get to Kholvad House, and we boarded the tram despite the fact that while Indians could use them, Africans could not. We had not been travelling long when the conductor turned to Ismail and J.N. and said in Afrikaans that their 'kaffir friend' was not allowed on. Ismail and J.N. exploded at the conductor, telling him that he did not even understand the word 'kaffir' and that it was offensive to call me that name. The conductor promptly stopped the tram and hailed a policeman, who arrested us, took us down to the station and charged us. We were ordered to appear in court the following day. That night, Ismail and J.N. arranged for Bram Fischer to defend us. The next day, the magistrate seemed in awe of Bram's family connections. We were promptly acquitted, and I saw at first hand that justice was not at all blind.

Wits opened a new world to me, a world of ideas and political beliefs and debates, a world where people were passionate about politics. I was among white and Indian intellectuals of my own generation, young men who would form the vanguard of the most important political movements of the next few years. I discovered for the first time people of my own age firmly aligned with the liberation struggle, who were prepared, despite their relative privilege, to sacrifice themselves for the cause of the oppressed.

PART THREE

Birth of a Freedom Fighter

11

I cannot pinpoint a moment when I became politicized, when I knew that I would spend my life in the liberation struggle. To be an African in South Africa means that one is politicized from the moment of one's birth, whether one acknowledges it or not. An African child is born in an Africans Only hospital, taken home in an Africans Only bus, lives in an Africans Only area and attends Africans Only schools, if he attends school at all.

When he grows up, he can hold Africans Only jobs, rent a house in Africans Only townships, ride Africans Only trains and be stopped at any time of the day or night and be ordered to produce a pass, without which he can be arrested and thrown in jail. His life is circumscribed by racist laws and regulations that cripple his growth, dim his potential and stunt his life. This was the reality, and one could deal with it in a myriad of ways.

I had no epiphany, no singular revelation, no moment of truth, but a steady accumulation of a thousand slights, a thousand indignities and a thousand unremembered moments produced in me an anger, a rebelliousness, a desire to fight the system that imprisoned my people. There was no particular day on which I said, Henceforth I will devote myself to the liberation of my people; instead, I simply found myself doing so, and could not do otherwise.

I have mentioned many of the people who influenced me, but more and more I had come under the wise tutelage of Walter Sisulu. Walter was strong, reasonable, practical and dedicated. He never lost his head in a crisis; he was often silent when others were shouting. He believed that the African National Congress was the means to effect change in South Africa, the repository of black hopes and aspirations. Sometimes one can judge an organization by the people who belong to it, and I knew that I would be proud to belong to any organization of which Walter was a member. At the time, there were few options. The ANC was the one organization that welcomed everyone, that

saw itself as a great umbrella under which all Africans could find
shelter.

Change was in the air in the 1940s. The Atlantic Charter of 1941,
signed by Roosevelt and Churchill, reaffirmed faith in the dignity of
each human being and propagated a host of democratic principles.
Some in the West saw the charter as empty promises, but not those
of us in Africa. Inspired by the Atlantic Charter and the fight of the
Allies against tyranny and oppression, the ANC created its own charter,
called African Claims, which called for full citizenship for all Africans,
the right to buy land and the repeal of all discriminatory legislation. We
hoped that the government and ordinary South Africans would see that
the principles they were fighting for in Europe were the same ones we
were advocating at home.

Walter's house in Orlando was a mecca for activists and ANC members.
It was a warm, welcoming place and I was often there to sample either
a political discussion or Ma Sisulu's cooking. One night in 1943 I met
Anton Lembede, who held Master of Arts and Bachelor of Law degrees,
and A.P. Mda. From the moment I heard Lembede speak, I knew I was
seeing a magnetic personality who thought in original and often startling
ways. He was then one of a handful of African lawyers in the whole of
South Africa and was the legal partner of the venerable Dr Pixley ka
Seme, one of the founders of the ANC.

Lembede said that Africa was a black man's continent, and it was up
to Africans to reassert themselves and reclaim what was rightfully theirs.
He hated the idea of the black inferiority complex and castigated what he
called the worship and idolization of the West and its ideas. The inferiority
complex, he affirmed, was the greatest barrier to liberation. He noted that
wherever the African had been given the opportunity, he was capable of
developing to the same extent as the white man, citing such African
heroes as Marcus Garvey, W.E.B. Du Bois and Haile Selassie. 'The
colour of my skin is beautiful,' he said, 'like the black soil of Mother
Africa.' He believed blacks had to improve their own self-image before
they could initiate successful mass action. He preached self-reliance and
self-determination, and called his philosophy Africanism. We took it for
granted that one day he would lead the ANC.

Lembede declared that a new spirit was stirring among the people, that
ethnic differences were melting away, that young men and women thought
of themselves as Africans first and foremost, not as Xhosas or Ndebeles
or Tswanas. Lembede, whose father was an illiterate Zulu peasant from
Natal, had trained as a teacher at Adam's College, an American Board
of Missions institution. He had taught for years in the Orange Free

State, learned Afrikaans, and had come to see Afrikaner nationalism as a prototype of African nationalism.

As Lembede later wrote in the newspaper *Inkundla ya Bantu*, an African newspaper in Natal:

> The history of modern times is the history of nationalism. Nationalism has been tested in the people's struggles and the fires of battle and found to be the only antidote against foreign rule and modern imperialism. It is for that reason that the great imperialistic powers feverishly endeavour with all their might to discourage and eradicate all nationalistic tendencies among their alien subjects; for that purpose huge and enormous sums of money are lavishly expended on propaganda against nationalism which is dismissed as 'narrow', 'barbarous', 'uncultured', 'devilish', etc. Some alien subjects become dupes of this sinister propaganda and consequently become tools or instruments of imperialism, for which great service they are highly praised by the imperialistic power and showered with such epithets as 'culture', 'liberal', 'progressive', 'broadminded', etc.

Lembede's views struck a chord in me. I, too, had been susceptible to paternalistic British colonialism and the appeal of being perceived by whites as 'cultured' and 'progressive' and 'civilized'. I was already on my way to being drawn into the black elite that Britain sought to create in Africa. That is what everyone from the regent to Mr Sidelsky had wanted for me. But it was an illusion. Like Lembede, I came to see the antidote as militant African nationalism.

Lembede's friend and partner was Peter Mda, better known as A.P. While Lembede tended to imprecision and was inclined to be verbose, Mda was controlled and exact. Lembede could be vague and mystical; Mda was specific and scientific. Mda's practicality was a perfect foil for Lembede's idealism.

Other young men were thinking along the same lines and we would all meet to discuss these ideas. In addition to Lembede and Mda, these men included Walter Sisulu; Oliver Tambo; Dr Lionel Majombozi; Victor Mbobo, my former teacher at Healdtown; William Nkomo, a medical student who was a member of the CP; Jordan Ngubane, a journalist from Natal who worked for *Inkundla* as well as *Bantu World*, the largest selling African newspaper, David Bopape, secretary of the ANC in the Transvaal and a member of the Communist Party and many others. Many felt, perhaps unfairly, that the ANC as a whole had become the preserve of a tired, unmilitant, privileged African elite more concerned with protecting their own rights than those of the masses. The general consensus was that some action must be taken, and Dr Majombozi proposed forming a Youth League as a way of lighting a fire under the leadership of the ANC.

In 1943 a delegation including Lembede, Mda, Sisulu, Tambo, Nkomo and I went to see Dr Xuma, who was head of the ANC, at his rather grand house in Sophiatown. Dr Xuma had a surgery at his home in addition to a small farm. He had performed a great service to the ANC. He had roused it from its slumbering state under Dr Seme, when the organization had shrunk in size and importance. When he assumed the presidency, the ANC had 17s. 6d. in its treasury, and he had boosted the amount to £4,000. He was admired by traditional leaders, had relationships with cabinet ministers and exuded a sense of security and confidence. But he also carried himself with an air of superciliousness that did not befit the leader of a mass organization. Devoted as he was to the ANC, his medical practice took precedence. Xuma presided over the era of delegations, deputations, letters and telegrams. Everything was done in the English manner, the idea being that despite our disagreements we were all gentlemen. He enjoyed the relationships he had formed with the white establishment and did not want to jeopardize them with political action.

At our meeting, we told him that we intended to organize a Youth League and a campaign of action designed to mobilize mass support. We had brought a copy of the draft constitution and manifesto with us. We told Dr Xuma that the ANC was in danger of becoming marginalized unless it stirred itself and took up new methods. Dr Xuma felt threatened by our delegation and strongly objected to a Youth League constitution. He thought the league should be a more loosely organized group and act mainly as a recruiting committee for the ANC. In a paternalistic way, Dr Xuma went on to tell us that Africans as a group were too unorganized and undisciplined to participate in a mass campaign and that such a campaign would be rash and dangerous.

Shortly after the meeting with Dr Xuma, a provisional committee of the Youth League was formed under the leadership of William Nkomo. The members of the committee journeyed to the ANC annual conference in Bloemfontein in December 1943, where they proposed the formation of a Youth League to help recruit new members to the organization. The proposal was accepted.

The actual formation of the Youth League took place on Easter Sunday 1944 at the Bantu Men's Social Centre in Eloff Street. There were about a hundred men there, some coming from as far away as Pretoria. It was a select group, an elite group, a great number of us being Fort Hare graduates; we were far from a mass movement. Lembede gave a lecture on the history of nations, a tour of the horizon from ancient Greece to medieval Europe to the age of colonization. He emphasized the historical achievements of Africa and Africans, and noted how foolish it was for whites to see themselves as a chosen people and an intrinsically superior race.

Jordan Ngubane, A.P. Mda and William Nkomo all spoke, and emphasized the emerging spirit of African nationalism. Lembede was elected president, Oliver Tambo secretary, and Walter Sisulu became treasurer. A.P. Mda, Jordan Ngubane, Lionel Majombozi, Congress Mbata, David Bopape and I were elected to the Executive Committee. We were later joined by prominent young men such as Godfrey Pitje, a student (later teacher then lawyer); Arthur Letele, Wilson Conco, Diliza Mji and Nthatho Motlana, all medical doctors; Dan Tloome, a trade unionist; and Joe Matthews, Duma Nokwe and Robert Sobukwe, all students. Branches were soon established in all the provinces.

The basic policy of the league did not differ from the ANC's first constitution in 1912. But we were reaffirming and underscoring those original concerns, many of which had gone by the wayside. African nationalism was our battle cry, and our creed was the creation of one nation out of many tribes, the overthrow of white supremacy, and the establishment of a truly democratic form of government. Our manifesto stated: 'We believe that the national liberation of Africans will be achieved by Africans themselves. . . . The Congress Youth League must be the brains-trust and power-station of the spirit of African nationalism.'

The manifesto utterly rejected the notion of trusteeship, the idea that the white government somehow had African interests at heart. We cited the crippling anti-African legislation of the past forty years, beginning with the 1913 Land Act, which ultimately deprived blacks of 87 per cent of the territory in the land of their birth; the Urban Areas Act of 1923, which created teeming African slums, politely called 'native locations', in order to supply cheap labour to white industry; the Colour Bar Act of 1926, which banned Africans from practising skilled trades; the Native Administration Act of 1927, which made the British Crown, rather than the Paramount Chiefs, the supreme chief over all African areas; and finally, in 1936, the Representation of Natives Act, which removed Africans from the common voters' roll in the Cape, thereby shattering any illusion that whites would allow Africans to have control over their own destiny.

We were extremely wary of communism. The document stated: 'We may borrow . . . from foreign ideologies, but we reject the wholesale importation of foreign ideologies into Africa.' This was an implicit rebuke to the Communist Party, which Lembede and many others, including myself, considered a 'foreign' ideology unsuited to the African situation. Lembede felt that the Communist Party was dominated by whites, which undermined African self-confidence and initiative.

A number of committees were formed that day, but the primary purpose of the Youth League was to give direction to the ANC in its quest for political freedom. Although I agreed with this, I was nervous about joining the league and still had doubts about the extent of my political commitment. I was then working full-time and studying part-time, and had little time outside those two activities. I also possessed a certain insecurity, feeling politically backward compared to Walter, Lembede and Mda. They were men who knew their minds, and I was, as yet, unformed. I still lacked confidence as a speaker, and was intimidated by the eloquence of so many of those in the league.

Lembede's Africanism was not universally supported because his ideas were characterized by a racial exclusivity that disturbed some of the other Youth Leaguers. Some of the members felt that a nationalism that would include sympathetic whites was a more desirable course. Others, including myself, countered that if blacks were offered a multiracial form of struggle, they would remain enamoured of white culture and prey to a continuing sense of inferiority. At the time, I was firmly opposed to allowing communists or whites to join the league.

Walter's house was my home from home. For several months in the early 1940s, it actually was my home when I had no other place to stay. The house was always full, and it seemed there was a perpetual discussion going on about politics. Albertina, Walter's wife, was a wise and wonderful presence, and a strong supporter of Walter's political work. (At their wedding, Anton Lembede said: 'Albertina, you have married a married man: Walter married politics long before he met you.')

It was in the lounge of the Sisulus' home that I met Evelyn Mase, my first wife. She was a quiet, pretty girl from the countryside who did not seem overawed by the coming and goings at the Sisulus'. She was then training as a nurse with Albertina and Peter Mda's wife, Rose, at the Johannesburg non-European General Hospital.

Evelyn was from Engcobo, in the Transkei, some distance west of Umtata. Her father, a mineworker, had died when she was an infant, and her mother when she was twelve. After completing primary school, Evelyn was sent to Johannesburg to attend high school.

She stayed with her brother, Sam Mase, who was then living at the Sisulus' house. Ma Sisulu, Walter's mother, was the sister of Evelyn's mother. The Sisulus treated Evelyn as if she was a favourite daughter, and was much loved by them.

I asked Evelyn out very soon after our first meeting. Almost as quickly, we fell in love. Within a few months I had asked her to marry me, and she accepted. We were married in a civil ceremony requiring only signatures and a witness at the Native Commissioner's Court in Johannesburg, for we could not afford a traditional wedding or feast. Our most immediate problem was finding a place to live. We first went to stay with her brother in Orlando East and later with Evelyn's sister at City Deep Mines, where her sister's husband, Msunguli Mgudlwa, worked as a clerk.

12

In 1946 a number of critical events occurred that shaped my political development and the directions of the struggle. The mineworkers' strike, in which 70,000 African miners along the Reef went on strike, affected me greatly. At the initiative of J.B. Marks, Dan Tloome, Gaur Radebe and a number of ANC labour activists, the African Mine Workers' Union (AMWU) had been created in the early 1940s. There were as many as 400,000 African miners working on the Reef, most of them making no more than two shillings a day. The union leadership had repeatedly pressed the Chamber of Mines for a minimum wage of ten shillings a day, as well as family housing and two weeks' paid leave. The chamber ignored the union's demands.

In one of the largest such actions in South African history, the miners went on strike for a week and maintained their solidarity. The state's retaliation was ruthless. The leaders were arrested, the compounds surrounded by police, and the AMWU offices ransacked. A march was brutally repulsed by police; twelve miners died. The Natives' Representative Council adjourned in protest. I had a number of relations who were mineworkers, and during the week of the strike I visited them, discussed the issues and expressed my support.

J.B. Marks, a longtime member of the ANC and the Communist Party, was then president of the African Mine Workers' Union. Born in the Transvaal of mixed parentage, Marks was a charismatic figure with a distinctive sense of humour. He was a tall man with a light complexion. During the strike I sometimes went with him from mine to mine, talking to workers and planning strategy. From morning to night, he displayed cool and reasoned leadership, with his humour leavening even the most difficult crisis. I was impressed by the organization of the union and its ability to control its membership, even in the face of such savage opposition.

In the end, the state prevailed: the strike was suppressed and the union crushed. The strike was the beginning of my close relationship with

Marks. I visited him often at his house, and we discussed my opposition to communism at great length. Marks was a stalwart member of the party, but he never took my objections personally, and felt that it was natural for a young man to embrace nationalism, but that as I grew older and more experienced, my views would broaden. I had these same discussions with Moses Kotane and Yusuf Dadoo, both of whom believed, like Marks, that communism had to be adapted to the African situation. Other communist members of the ANC condemned me and the other Youth Leaguers, but Marks, Kotane and Dadoo never did.

After the strike, fifty-two men, including Kotane and Marks, and many other communists, were arrested and prosecuted, first for incitement, then for sedition. It was a political trial, an effort by the state to show that it was not soft on the Red Menace.

That same year, another event forced me to recast my whole approach to political work. In 1946 the Smuts government passed the Asiatic Land Tenure Act, which curtailed the free movement of Indians, circumscribed the areas where Indians could reside and trade, and severely restricted their right to buy property. In return, they were provided with representation in Parliament by token white surrogates. Dr Dadoo, president of the Transvaal Indian Congress, castigated the restrictions and dismissed the offer of parliamentary representation as 'a spurious offer of a sham franchise'. This law – known as the Ghetto Act – was a grave insult to the Indian community and anticipated the Group Areas Act, which would eventually circumscribe the freedom of all South Africans of colour.

The Indian community was outraged and launched a concerted two-year campaign of passive resistance to oppose the measures. Led by Dr Dadoo and Dr G.M. Naicker, president of the Natal Indian Congress (NIC), the Indian community conducted a mass campaign that impressed us with its organization and dedication. Housewives, priests, doctors, lawyers, traders, students and workers took their place in the front lines of the protest. For two years, people suspended their lives to take up the battle. Mass rallies were held; land reserved for whites was occupied and picketed. No fewer than 2,000 volunteers went to jail, and Dr Dadoo and Dr Naicker were sentenced to six months' hard labour.

The campaign was confined to the Indian community, and the participation of other groups was not encouraged. Even so, Dr Xuma and other African leaders spoke at several meetings, and along with the Youth League gave full moral support to the struggle of the Indian people. The government crippled the rebellion with harsh laws and intimidation, but we in the Youth League and the ANC had witnessed the Indian people

register an extraordinary protest against colour oppression in a way that
Africans and the ANC had not.

Ismail Meer and J.N. Singh suspended their studies, said good-bye
to their families and went to prison. Ahmed Kathrada, who was still
a high-school student, did the same thing. I often visited the home of
Amina Pahad for lunch, and then, suddenly, this charming woman put
aside her apron and went to jail for her beliefs. If I had once questioned
the willingness of the Indian community to protest against oppression, I
no longer could.

The Indian campaign became a model for the type of protest that we
in the Youth League were calling for. It instilled a spirit of defiance and
radicalism among the people, broke the fear of prison, and boosted the
popularity and influence of the NIC and TIC. They reminded us that the
freedom struggle was not merely a question of making speeches, holding
meetings, passing resolutions and sending deputations, but of meticulous
organization, militant mass action and, above all, the willingness to suffer
and sacrifice. The Indians' campaign harkened back to the 1913 passive
resistance campaign in which Mahatma Gandhi led a tumultuous procession
of Indians crossing illegally from Natal to the Transvaal. That was history;
this campaign was taking place before my own eyes.

Early in 1946, Evelyn and I moved to a two-room municipal house of
our own in Orlando East and thereafter to a slightly larger house at
No. 8115 Orlando West. Orlando West was a dusty, spartan area of
boxy municipal houses that would later became part of Greater Soweto,
Soweto being an acronym for South-Western Townships. Our house was
situated in an area nicknamed Westcliff by its residents after the fancy
white suburb to the north.

The rent of our new home was 17s. 6d. per month. The house itself
was identical to hundreds of others built on postage-stamp-size plots on
dirt roads. It had the same standard tin roof, the same cement floor, a
narrow kitchen, and a bucket toilet at the back. Although there were
streetlamps outside, we used paraffin lamps inside as the homes were
not yet electrified. The bedroom was so small that a double bed took up
almost the entire floor space. These houses were built by the municipal
authorities for workers who needed to be near town. To relieve the
monotony, some people planted small gardens or painted their doors
in bright colours. It was the very opposite of grand, but it was my first
true home of my own and I was mightily proud. A man is not a man
until he has a house of his own. I did not know then that it would be
the only residence that would be entirely mine for many, many years.

The state had allocated the house to Evelyn and me because we were no longer just two, but three. That year our first son, Madiba Thembekile, was born. He was given my clan name of Madiba, but was known by the nickname Thembi. He was a solid, happy little boy who most people said resembled his mother more than his father. I had now produced an heir, though I had little as yet to bequeath to him. But I had perpetuated the Mandela name and the Madiba clan, which is one of the basic responsibilities of a Xhosa male.

I finally had a stable base, and I went from being a guest in other people's homes to having guests in my own. My sister Leabie joined us and I took her across the railway line to enrol her at Orlando High School. In my culture, all the members of one's family have a claim to the hospitality of any other member of the family; the combination of my large extended family and my new house meant a great number of guests.

I enjoyed domesticity, even though I had little time for it. I delighted in playing with Thembi, bathing him and feeding him, and putting him to bed with a little story. In fact, I love playing with children and chatting with them; it has always been one of the things that makes me feel most at peace. I enjoyed relaxing at home, reading quietly, taking in the sweet and savoury smells emanating from pots boiling in the kitchen. But I was rarely at home to enjoy these things.

During the latter part of that year, the Reverend Michael Scott came to stay with us. Scott was an Anglican clergyman and a great fighter for African rights. He had been approached by a man named Komo, who was representing a squatter camp outside Johannesburg that the government was seeking to relocate. Komo wanted Scott to protest against the removal. Scott said, 'If I am going to help you I must be one of you,' and he proceeded to move to the squatter camp and start a congregation there. Scott's shanty-town for the homeless was built near a rocky knoll, and the residents christened it Tobruk, after the battle in the North Africa campaign of the war. It was a place I sometimes took Thembi on Sunday morning, as he liked to play hide-and-seek among the rocks. After Scott had set up his congregation, he found that Komo was embezzling money from people who were contributing to the fight against the removal. When Scott confronted Komo, Komo drove Scott out of the camp and threatened his life.

Scott took refuge with us in Orlando and brought along an African priest named Dlamini, who also had a wife and children. Our house was tiny, and Scott slept in the sitting-room, Dlamini and his wife slept in another room, and we put all the children in the kitchen. Michael Scott was a modest, unassuming man, but Dlamini was a bit hard to take. At mealtimes, he would complain about the food. 'Look here,' he would say, 'this meat of yours, it's very lean and hard, not properly cooked at all. I'm not used to meals like this.' Scott was appalled by this, and admonished Dlamini, but Dlamini took no heed. The next night he might say, 'Well, this is a bit better than yesterday, but far from well prepared. Mandela, you know your wife just cannot cook.'

Dlamini indirectly caused the situation to be resolved because I was so eager to have him out of the house that I went to the squatter camp myself and explained that Scott was a true friend of theirs, unlike Komo, and that they had to choose between the two. They then organized an election in which Scott triumphed, and he moved back to the squatter camp, taking Father Dlamini with him.

Early in 1947 I completed the requisite period of three years for articles and my time at Witkin, Sidelsky and Eidelman came to an end. I resolved to become a full-time student in order to gain my LLB so that I could go out on my own and practise as an attorney. The loss of the £8 10s. 1d. per month that I earned at Sidelsky was devastating. I applied to the Bantu Welfare Trust at the South African Institute of Race Relations in Johannesburg for a loan of £250 sterling to help finance my law studies, which included university fees, textbooks and a monthly allowance. I was given a loan of £150.

Three months later, I wrote to them again, noting that my wife was about to take maternity leave, and we would lose her salary of £17 per month, which was absolutely necessary to our survival. I did receive the additional money, for which I was grateful, but the circumstances which warranted it were unfortunate. Our daughter Makaziwe's birth was not difficult, yet she was frail and sickly. From the start, we feared the worst. Many nights, Evelyn and I took turns looking after her. We did not know the name of whatever was consuming this tiny girl and the doctors could not explain the nature of the problem. Evelyn monitored the baby with the combination of a mother's tirelessness and a nurse's professional efficiency. When she was nine months old, Makaziwe passed away. Evelyn was distraught, and the only thing that helped to temper my own grief was trying to alleviate hers.

In politics, no matter how much one plans, circumstances often dictate events. In July 1947, during an informal discussion with Lembede about Youth League business, he complained to me of a sudden pain in his stomach and an accompanying chill. When the pain worsened we drove him to Coronation Hospital, and that same night he was dead at the age of thirty-three. Many were deeply affected by his death. Walter Sisulu seemed almost prostrate with grief. His passing was a setback to the movement, for Lembede was a fount of ideas and attracted others to the organization.

Lembede was succeeded by Peter Mda, whose analytical approach, ability to express himself clearly and simply and tactical experience made him an excellent politician and an outstanding leader of the Youth League. Mda was a lean fellow with no excess weight, just as he used no excess words. In his broad-minded tolerance of different views, his own thinking was more mature and advanced than that of Lembede. It took Mda's leadership to advance Lembede's cause.

Mda believed the Youth League should function as an internal pressure group, a militant nationalistic wing within the ANC as a whole that would propel the organization into a new era. At the time, the ANC did not have a single full-time employee, and was generally poorly organized, operating in a haphazard way. (Later, Walter became the first and only full-time ANC staff member at an extremely meagre salary.)

Mda quickly established a branch of the Youth League at Fort Hare under the guidance of Z.K. Matthews and Godfrey Pitje, a lecturer in anthropology. They recruited outstanding students, bringing in fresh blood and new ideas. Among the most outstanding were Professor Matthews's brilliant son Joe, and Robert Sobukwe, a dazzling orator and incisive thinker.

Mda was more moderate in his nationalism than Lembede, and his thinking was without the racial tinge that characterized Lembede's. He hated white oppression and white domination, not white people themselves. He was also less extreme in his opposition to the Communist Party than Lembede – or myself. I was among the Youth Leaguers who were suspicious of the white left. Even though I had befriended many white communists, I was wary of white influence in the ANC, and I opposed joint campaigns with the party. I was concerned that the communists were intent on taking over our movement under the guise of joint action. I believed that it was an undiluted African nationalism, not Marxism or multi-racialism, that would liberate us. With a few of my colleagues in the league, I even went so far as breaking up CP meetings by storming the stage, tearing up signs and capturing the microphone. At the national conference of the ANC in December, the Youth League introduced a motion demanding the expulsion of all members of the Communist Party, but we were soundly defeated. Despite the influence the Indian passive resistance campaign of 1946 had on me, I felt about the Indians the same way I did about the communists: that they would tend to dominate the ANC, in part because of their superior education, experience and training.

*   *   *

In 1947 I was elected to the Executive Committee of the Transvaal ANC and served under C.S. Ramohanoe, president of the Transvaal region. This was my first position in the ANC proper, and it represented a milestone in my commitment to the organization. Until that time, the sacrifices I had made had not gone much further than being absent from my wife and family during weekends and returning home late in the evening. I had not been directly involved in any major campaign, and I did not yet understand the hazards and unending difficulties of the life of a freedom fighter. I had coasted along without having to pay a price for my commitment. From the time I was elected to the Executive Committee of the Transvaal region, I came to identify myself with the Congress as a whole, with its hopes and despairs, its success and failures; I was now bound heart and soul.

Ramohanoe was another one of those from whom I learned. He was a staunch nationalist and a skilful organizer who was able to balance divergent views and come forward with a suitable compromise. While Ramohanoe was unsympathetic to the communists, he worked well with them. He believed that the ANC was a national organization that should welcome all those who supported our cause.

In 1947, in the wake of the Indian passive resistance campaign, Dr Xuma, Dr Dadoo and Dr Naicker, presidents respectively of the ANC, the Transvaal Indian Congress and the Natal Indian Congress, signed the Doctors' Pact agreeing to join forces against a common enemy. This was a significant step towards the unity of the African and Indian movements. Rather than creating a central political body to direct all the various movements, they agreed to cooperate on matters of common interest. Later, they were joined by the African People's Organization (APO), a Coloured organization.

But such an agreement was at best tentative, for each national group faced problems peculiar to itself. The pass system, for example, barely affected Indians or Coloureds. The Ghetto Act, which had prompted the Indian protests, barely affected Africans. Coloured groups at the time were more concerned about the race classification and job reservation, issues that did not affect Africans and Indians to the same degree.

The Doctors' Pact laid a foundation for the future cooperation of Africans, Indians and Coloureds, since it respected the independence of each individual group, but acknowledged the achievements that could be realized from acting in concert. The Doctors' Pact precipitated a series of nonracial, antigovernment campaigns around the country, which sought to bring together Africans and Indians in the freedom struggle. The first of these campaigns was the First Transvaal and Orange Free State People's

Assembly for Votes for All, a campaign for the extension of the franchise to all black South Africans. Dr Xuma announced ANC participation at a press conference over which I presided. At the time, we believed the campaign would be run by the ANC, but when we learned that the ANC would not be leading the campaign, the Transvaal Executive Committee decided that the ANC should withdraw. My idea at the time was that the ANC should be involved only in campaigns that the ANC itself led. I was more concerned with who got the credit than whether the campaign would be successful.

Even after the withdrawal, Ramohanoe, president of the Transvaal region of the ANC, issued a press statement calling on Africans in the province to take part in the Votes for All campaign in clear contravention of the decision of the Transvaal Executive Committee. This was an act of disobedience the Executive could not tolerate. At a conference called to resolve this dispute, I was asked to move a no-confidence motion against Ramohanoe for his disobedience. I felt an acute conflict between duty and personal loyalty, between my obligations to my organization and to my friend. I well knew that I would be condemning the action of a man whose integrity and devotion I never questioned, a man whose sacrifice in the liberation struggle was far greater than my own. I knew that the action that he had called for was in fact a noble one; he believed that Africans should help their Indian brothers.

But the seriousness of Ramohanoe's disobedience was too strong. While an organization like the ANC is made up of individuals, it is greater than any of its individual parts, and loyalty to the organization takes precedence over loyalty to an individual. I agreed to lead the attack and proposed the motion condemning him, which was seconded by Oliver Tambo. This caused an uproar in the house, with verbal battles between those in the region who supported their president and those who were on the side of the Executive. The meeting broke up in disorder.

13

Africans could not vote, but that did not mean that we did not care who won elections. In the white general election of 1948, the ruling United Party, led by General Smuts, then at the height of his international regard, opposed the revived National Party. While Smuts had enlisted South Africa on the side of the Allies in the Second World War, the National Party refused to support Great Britain and publicly sympathized with Nazi Germany. The National Party's campaign centred on the '*swart gevaar*' (the 'black danger'), and they fought the election on the twin slogans of '*Die kaffer op sy plek*' ('the nigger in his place') and '*Die koelies uit die land*' ('the coolies out of the country') – coolies being the Afrikaner's derogatory term for Indians.

The Nationalists, led by Dr Daniel Malan, a former minister of the Dutch Reformed Church and a newspaper editor, were a party animated by bitterness – bitterness towards the English, who had treated them as inferiors for decades, and bitterness towards the African, who the Nationalists believed was threatening the prosperity and purity of Afrikaner culture. Africans had no loyalty to General Smuts, but we had even less for the National Party.

Malan's platform was known as apartheid. *Apartheid* was a new term but an old idea. It literally means 'apartness', and it represented the codification in one oppressive system of all the laws and regulations that had kept Africans in an inferior position to whites for centuries. What had been more or less *de facto* was to become relentlessly *de jure*. The often haphazard segregation of the past three hundred years was to be consolidated into a monolithic system that was diabolical in its detail, inescapable in its reach and overwhelming in its power. The premise of apartheid was that whites were superior to Africans, Coloureds and Indians, and the function of it was to entrench white supremacy for ever. As the Nationalists put it, '*Die wit man moet altyd baas wees*' ('The white man must always remain boss'). Their platform rested on the term: *baasskap*, literally 'boss-ship', a loaded word that stood for white supremacy in all its harshness. The policy was supported by the Dutch Reformed Church, which furnished apartheid with its religious underpinnings by suggesting that Afrikaners were God's chosen people and that blacks were a subservient species. In the Afrikaner's world view, apartheid and the church went hand in hand.

The Nationalists' victory in the Anglo-Boer War was the beginning of the end of the domination of the Afrikaner by the Englishman. English would now take second place to Afrikaans as an official language. The Nationalists' slogan encapsulated their mission: '*Eie volk, eie taal, eie land*' – 'Our own people, our own language, our own land'. In the distorted cosmology of the Afrikaner, the Nationalist victory was like the Israelites' journey to the Promised Land. This was the fulfilment of God's promise, and the justification for their view that South Africa should be a white man's country for ever.

The victory was a shock. The United Party and General Smuts had beaten the Nazis, and surely they would defeat the National Party. On election day, I attended a meeting in Johannesburg with Oliver Tambo and several others. We barely discussed the question of a Nationalist government because we did not expect one. The meeting went on all night, and we emerged at dawn and found a newspaper stall selling the *Rand Daily Mail*: the Nationalists had triumphed. I was stunned and dismayed, but Oliver took a more considered line. 'I like this,' he said. 'I like this.' I could not imagine why. He explained, 'Now we will know exactly who our enemies are and where we stand.'

Even General Smuts realized the dangers of this harsh ideology, decrying apartheid as 'a crazy concept, born of prejudice and fear'. From the moment of the Nationalists' election, we knew that our land would henceforth be a place of tension and strife. For the first time in South African history, an exclusively Afrikaner party led the government. 'South Africa belongs to us once more,' Malan proclaimed in his victory speech.

That same year, the Youth League outlined its policy in a document written by Mda and issued by the league's Executive Committee. It was a rallying cry to all patriotic youth to overthrow white domination. We rejected the communist notion that Africans were oppressed primarily as an economic class rather than as a race, adding that we needed to create a powerful national liberation movement under the banner of African nationalism and 'led by Africans themselves'.

We advocated the redivision of land on an equitable basis, the abolition of colour bars prohibiting Africans from doing skilled work and the need for free and compulsory education. The document also spotlighted the push-and-pull between two rival theories of African nationalism, between the more extreme, Marcus Garvey-inspired, 'Africa for the Africans' nationalism and the Africanism of the Youth League, which recognized that South Africa was a multiracial country.

I was sympathetic to the ultra-revolutionary stream of African nationalism. I was angry at the white man, not at racism. While I was not prepared to hurl the white man into the sea, I would have been perfectly happy if he had climbed aboard his steamships and left the continent of his own volition.

The Youth League was marginally more friendly to the Indians and the Coloureds, stating that Indians, like Africans, were oppressed, but that Indians had India, a mother country that they could look to. The Coloureds, too, were oppressed, but unlike the Indians had no mother country except Africa. I was prepared to accept Indians and Coloureds provided they accepted our policies; but their interests were not identical with ours, and I doubted whether or not they could truly embrace our cause.

In short order, Malan began to implement his pernicious programme. Within weeks of coming to power, the Nationalist government pardoned Robey Leibbrandt, the wartime traitor who had organized uprisings in support of Nazi Germany. The government announced their intention to curb the trade union movement and do away with the limited franchises of the Indian, Coloured and African peoples. The Separate Representation of Voters Bill eventually robbed the Coloureds of their representation in Parliament. The Prohibition of Mixed Marriages Act was introduced in 1949 and was followed in rapid succession by the Immorality Act, making sexual relations between white and nonwhite illegal. The Population and Registration Act labelled all South Africans by race, making colour the single most important arbiter of an individual. Malan introduced the Group Areas Act – which he described as 'the very essence of apartheid' – requiring separate urban areas for each racial group. In the past, whites took land by force; now they secured it by legislation.

In response to this new and much more powerful threat from the state, the ANC embarked on an unaccustomed and historic path. In 1949, it launched a landmark effort to turn itself into a truly mass organization. The Youth League drafted a Programme of Action, the cornerstone of which was a campaign of mass mobilization.

At the ANC annual conference in Bloemfontein, the organization adopted the league's Programme of Action, which called for boycotts, strikes, stay-at-homes, passive resistance, protest demonstrations and other forms of mass action. This was a radical change: the ANC's policy had always been to keep its activities within the law. We in the Youth League had seen the failure of legal and constitutional means to strike at racial oppression; now the entire organization was set to enter a more activist stage.

These changes did not come without internal upheaval. A few weeks before the conference, Walter Sisulu, Oliver Tambo, A.P. Mda and I met Dr Xuma privately at his home in Sophiatown. We explained that we thought the time had come for mass action along the lines of Gandhi's non-violent protests in India and the 1946 passive resistance campaign, asserting that the ANC had become too docile in the face of oppression. The ANC's leaders, we said, had to be willing to violate the law and if necessary go to prison for their beliefs as Gandhi had.

Dr Xuma was adamantly opposed, claiming that such strategies were premature and would merely give the government an excuse to crush the ANC. Such forms of protest, he said, would eventually take place in South Africa, but at the moment such a step would be fatal. He made it clear that he was a doctor with a wide and prosperous practice that he would not jeopardize by going to prison.

We gave Dr Xuma an ultimatum: we would support him for re-election to the presidency of the ANC provided he supported our proposed Programme of Action. If he would not support our programme, we would not support him. Dr Xuma became heated, accusing us of blackmail and laying down the conditions on which we would vote for him. He told us that we were young and arrogant, and treating him without respect. We remonstrated with him, but to no avail. He would not go along with our proposal.

He unceremoniously showed us out of his house at 11 p.m., and closed the gate behind him. There were no streetlights in Sophiatown and it was a moonless night. All forms of public transport had long since ceased and we lived miles away in Orlando. Oliver remarked that Xuma could at the very least have offered us some transport. Walter was friendly with a family that lived nearby, and we prevailed upon them to take us in for the night.

At the conference that December, we in the Youth League knew we had the votes to depose Dr Xuma. As an alternative candidate, we sponsored Dr J.S. Moroka for the presidency. He was not our first choice. Professor Z.K. Matthews was the man we wanted to lead us, but Z.K. considered us too radical and our plan of action too impractical. He called us naive firebrands, adding that we would mellow with age.

Dr Moroka was an unlikely choice. He was a member of the All-African Convention (AAC) which was dominated by Trotskyite elements at that time. When he agreed to stand against Dr Xuma, the Youth League then enrolled him as a member of the ANC. When first approached, he consistently referred to the ANC as the African National 'Council'. He was not very knowledgeable about the ANC, neither was he an experienced activist, but he was respectable, and amenable to our programme. Like Dr Xuma he was a doctor, and one of the wealthiest black men in South Africa. He had studied at Edinburgh and Vienna. His great-grandfather had been a chief in the Orange Free State, and had greeted the Afrikaner *voortrekkers* of the nineteenth century with open arms and gifts of land, and then been betrayed. Dr Xuma was defeated and Dr Moroka became president-general of the ANC. Walter Sisulu was elected the new secretary-general, and Oliver Tambo was elected to the National Executive.

The Programme of Action approved at the annual conference called for the pursuit of political rights through the use of boycotts, strikes, civil disobedience and non-cooperation. In addition, it called for a national day of work stoppage in protest against the racist and reactionary policies of the government. This was a departure from the days of decorous protest, and many of the old stalwarts of the ANC were to fade away in this new era of greater militancy. Youth League members had now graduated to the senior organization. We had now guided the ANC to a more radical and revolutionary path.

I could only celebrate the Youth League's triumph from a distance, for I was unable to attend the conference. I was then working for a new law firm, and they did not give me permission to take two days off to attend the conference in Bloemfontein. The firm was a liberal one, but wanted me to concentrate on my work and forget politics. I would have lost my job if I had attended the conference, and I could not afford to do that.

The spirit of mass action surged, but I remained sceptical of any action undertaken with the communists and Indians. The 'Defend Free Speech Convention' in March 1950 organized by the Transvaal ANC, the Transvaal Indian Congress, the African People's Organization and the District Committee of the Communist Party drew ten thousand people to Johannesburg's Market Square. Dr Moroka, without consulting the Executive, agreed to preside over the convention. The convention was a success, yet I remained wary, as the prime mover behind it was the party.

At the instigation of the Communist Party and the Indian Congress, the convention passed a resolution for a one-day general strike, known as Freedom Day, on 1 May, calling for the abolition of the pass laws and all discriminatory legislation. Although I supported these objectives,

I believed that the communists were trying to steal the thunder from the ANC's National Day of Protest. I opposed the May Day strike on the grounds that the ANC had not originated the campaign, believing that we should concentrate on our own campaign.

Ahmed Kathrada was then barely twenty-one and, like all youths, eager to flex his muscles. He was a key member of the Transvaal Indian Youth Congress and had heard I was opposed to the May Day strike. One day, while walking along Commissioner Street, I met Kathrada and he heatedly confronted me, charging that I and the Youth League did not want to work with Indians or Coloureds. In a challenging tone, he said, 'You are an African leader and I am an Indian youth. But I am convinced of the support of the African masses for the strike and I challenge you to nominate any African township for a meeting and I guarantee the people will support me.' It was a hollow threat, but it angered me all the same. I even complained to a joint meeting of the Executive Committees of the ANC, the South African Indian Congress and the Communist Party, but Ismail Meer calmed me down, saying, 'Nelson, he is young and hotheaded. Don't you be the same.' I consequently felt a bit sheepish about my actions and I withdrew the complaint. Although I disagreed with Kathrada, I admired his fire, and it was an incident we came to laugh about.

The Freedom Day strike went ahead without official ANC support. In anticipation, the government banned all meetings and gatherings on 1 May. More than two-thirds of African workers stayed at home during the one-day strike. That night, Walter and I were in Orlando West on the fringes of a Freedom Day crowd that had gathered despite the government's restrictions. The moon was bright, and as we watched the orderly march of protesters, we could see a group of policemen camped across a stream about five hundred yards away. They must have seen us as well, because all of a sudden they started firing in our direction. We dived to the ground, and remained there as mounted police galloped into the crowd, smashing people with batons. We took refuge in a nearby nurses' dormitory, where we heard bullets smashing into the wall of the building. Eighteen Africans died and many others were wounded in this indiscriminate and unprovoked attack.

Despite protest and criticism, the Nationalist response was to tighten the screws of repression. A few weeks later the government introduced the notorious Suppression of Communism Act, and the ANC called an emergency conference in Johannesburg. The act outlawed the Communist Party of South Africa and made it a crime, punishable by a maximum of ten years' imprisonment, to be a member of the party or to further the aims of communism. But the bill was drafted in such a broad way that it outlawed all but the mildest protest against the state, deeming it a crime to advocate any doctrine that promoted 'political, industrial, social or economic change within the Union by the promotion of disturbance or disorder'. Essentially, the bill permitted the government to outlaw any organization and to restrict any individual opposed to its policies.

The ANC, the SAIC and the APO again met to discuss these new measures, and Dr Dadoo, among others, said that it would be foolish to allow past differences to thwart a united front against the government. I spoke and echoed his sentiments: clearly, the repression of any one liberation group was repression of all liberation groups. It was at that meeting that Oliver uttered prophetic words: 'Today it is the Communist Party. Tomorrow it will be our trade unions, our Indian Congress, our APO, our African National Congress.'

Supported by the SAIC and the APO, the ANC resolved to stage a National Day of Protest on 26 June 1950 against the government's murder of eighteen Africans on 1 May and the passage of the Suppression of Communism Act. The proposal was ratified, and in preparation for the Day of Protest, we closed ranks with the SAIC, the APO and the Communist Party. Here, I believed, was a sufficient threat that compelled us to join hands with our Indian and communist colleagues.

Earlier that year I had been co-opted onto the National Executive Committee of the ANC, taking the place of Dr Xuma, who had resigned after his failure to be re-elected president-general. I was not unmindful of the fact that it had been Dr Xuma who had tried to help me get my first job when I came to Johannesburg ten years before, when I had no thought of entering politics. Now, as a member of the National Executive, I was playing in the first team with the most senior people in the ANC. I had moved from the role of a gadfly within the organization to one of the powers that I had been rebelling against. It was a heady feeling, and not without mixed emotions. In some ways, it is easier to be a dissident, for then one is without responsibility. As a member of the Executive, I had to weigh arguments and make decisions, and expect to be criticized by rebels like myself.

Mass action was perilous in South Africa, where it was a criminal offence for an African to strike, and where the rights of free speech and movement were unmercifully curtailed. By striking, an African worker stood to lose not only his job but his entire livelihood and his right to stay in the area in which he was living. In my experience, a political strike is always riskier than an economic one. A strike based on a political grievance rather than on clear-cut issues such as higher wages or shorter hours is a more precarious form of protest and demands particularly efficient organization. The Day of Protest was a political rather than an economic strike.

In preparation for 26 June, Walter travelled around the country consulting local leaders. In his absence, I took charge of the bustling ANC office, the hub of a complicated national action. Every day, various leaders looked in to see that matters were going according to plan: Moses Kotane, Dr Dadoo, Diliza Mji, J.B. Marks, president of the Transvaal ANC, Yusuf Cachalia and his brother Maulvi, Gaur Radebe, secretary of the Council of Action, Michael Harmel, Peter Raboroko, Nthatho Motlana. I was coordinating the actions in different parts of the country, and talking by phone with regional leaders. We had left ourselves little time, and the planning was hastily done.

The Day of Protest was the ANC's first attempt to hold a political strike on a national scale, and it was a moderate success. In the cities, the majority of workers stayed at home and black businesses did not open. In Bethal, Gert Sibande, who later became president of the Transvaal ANC, led a demonstration of five thousand people, which received headlines in the major papers across the country. The Day of Protest boosted our morale, made us realize our strength and sent a warning to the Malan government that we would not remain passive in the face of apartheid. 26 June has since become a landmark day in the freedom struggle, and within the liberation movement it is observed as Freedom Day.

It was the first time I had taken a significant part in a national campaign, and I felt the exhilaration that springs from the success of a well-planned battle against the enemy and the sense of comradeship that is born of fighting against formidable odds.

The struggle, I was learning, was all-consuming. A man involved in the struggle was a man without a home life. It was in the midst of the Day of Protest that my second son, Makgatho Lewanika, was born. I was with Evelyn at the hospital when he came into the world, but it was only a brief respite from my activities. He was named for Sefako Mapogo Makgatho, the second president of the ANC from 1917 until 1924, and Lewanika, a leading chief in Zambia. Makgatho, the son of a Pedi chief, had led volunteers to defy the colour bar that did not permit Africans to walk on the pavements of Pretoria, and his name for me was an emblem of indominability and courage.

One day, during this same time, my wife informed me that my elder son, Thembi, then five, had asked her, 'Where does Daddy live?' I had been returning home late at night, long after he had gone to sleep, and departing early in the morning before he woke. I did not relish being deprived of the company of my children. I missed them a great deal during those days, long before I had any inkling that I would spend decades apart from them.

I was far more certain in those days of what I was against than what I was for. My long-standing opposition to communism was breaking down. Moses Kotane, the general secretary of the party and a member of the Executive of the ANC, often came to my house late at night and we would debate until morning. Clear-thinking and self-taught, Kotane was the son of peasant farmers in the Transvaal. 'Nelson,' he would say, 'what do you have against us? We are all fighting the same enemy. We do not seek to dominate the ANC; we are working within the context of African nationalism.' In the end, I had no good response to his arguments.

Because of my friendships with Kotane, Ismail Meer and Ruth First, and my observation of their own sacrifices, I was finding it more and more difficult to justify my prejudice against the party. Within the ANC, party members such as J.B. Marks, Edwin Mofutsanyana, Dan Tloome and David Bopape among others were devoted and hard-working, and could not be faulted as freedom fighters. Dr Dadoo, one of the leaders of the 1946 resistance, was a well-known Marxist whose role as a fighter for human rights had made him a hero to all groups. I could not, and no longer did, question the bona fides of such men and women.

If I could not challenge their dedication, I could still question the philosophical and practical underpinnings of Marxism. But I had little knowledge of Marxism, and in political discussions with my communist friends I found myself handicapped by my ignorance of their philosophy. I decided to remedy this.

I acquired the complete works of Marx and Engels, Lenin, Stalin, Mao Tse-tung and others, and probed the philosophy of dialectical and historical materialism. I had little time to study these works properly. While I was stimulated by the *Communist Manifesto*, I was exhausted by *Das Kapital*. But I found myself strongly drawn to the idea of a classless society which, to my mind, was similar to traditional African culture where life was shared and communal. I subscribed to Marx's basic dictum, which has the simplicity and generosity of the Golden Rule: 'From each according to his ability; to each according to his needs.'

Dialectical materialism seemed to offer both a searchlight illuminating the dark night of racial oppression and a tool that could be used to end it. It helped me to see the situation other than through the prism of black and white relations, for if our struggle was to succeed, we had to transcend black and white. I was attracted to the scientific underpinnings of dialectical materialism, for I am always inclined to trust what I can verify. Its materialistic analysis of economics rang true to me. The idea that the value of goods was based on the amount of labour that went into them seemed particularly appropriate for South Africa. The ruling class paid African labour a subsistence wage and then added value to the cost of the goods, which they retained for themselves.

Marxism's call to revolutionary action was music to the ears of a freedom fighter. The idea that history progresses through struggle and that change occurs in revolutionary jumps was similarly appealing. In my reading of Marxist works, I found a great deal of information that bore on the types of problems that face a practical politician. Marxists gave serious attention to national liberation movements, and the Soviet Union in particular supported the national struggles of many colonial peoples. This was another reason why I amended my view of communists and accepted the ANC position of welcoming Marxists into its ranks.

A friend once asked me how I could reconcile my creed of African nationalism with a belief in dialectical materialism. For me, there was no contradiction. I was first and foremost an African nationalist fighting for our emancipation from minority rule and the right to control our own destiny. But, at the same time, South Africa and the African continent were part of the larger world. Our problems, while distinctive and special, were not unique, and a philosophy that placed those problems in an international and historical context of the greater world and the course of history was valuable. I was prepared to use whatever means necessary to speed up the erasure of human prejudice and the end of chauvinistic and violent nationalism. I did not need to become a communist in order to work with them. I found that African nationalists and African communists generally had far more to unite them than to divide them. The cynical have always suggested that the communists were using us. But who is to say that we were not using them?

14

If we had any hopes or illusions about the National Party before they came into office, we were disabused of them quickly. Their threat to put the kaffir in his place was not an idle one. Apart from the Suppression of Communism Act, two laws passed in 1950 formed the cornerstones of apartheid: the Population and Registration Act and the Group Areas Act. As I have mentioned, the Population and Registration Act authorized the government officially to classify all South Africans according to race. If it had not already been so, race became the *sine qua non* of South African society. The arbitrary and meaningless tests to decide black from Coloured or Coloured from white often resulted in tragic cases where members of the same family were classified differently, all depending on whether one child had a lighter or darker complexion. Where one was allowed to live and work could rest on such absurd distinctions as the curl of one's hair or the size of one's lips.

The Group Areas Act was the foundation of residential apartheid. Under its regulations, each racial group could own land, occupy premises and trade only in its own separate area. Indians could henceforth only live in Indian areas, Africans in African, Coloureds in Coloured. If whites wanted the land or houses of another group, they could simply declare the land a white area and take it. The Group Areas Act initiated the era of forced removals, when African communities, towns and villages in newly designated 'white' urban areas were violently relocated because the nearby white landowners did not want Africans living near them or simply wanted their land.

At the top of the list for removal was Sophiatown, a vibrant community of more than fifty thousand people, which was one of the oldest black settlements in Johannesburg. Despite its poverty, Sophiatown brimmed with a rich life and was an incubator of so much that was new and valuable in African life and culture. Even before the government's efforts to remove it, Sophiatown held a symbolic importance for Africans disproportionate to its small population.

The following year, the government passed two more laws that directly attacked the rights of Coloureds and Africans. The Separate Representation of Voters Act aimed to transfer Coloureds to a separate voters' roll in the Cape, thereby diluting the franchise rights that they had enjoyed for more than a century. The Bantu Authorities Act abolished the Natives' Representative Council, the one indirect forum of national representation for Africans, and replaced it with a hierarchical system of tribal chiefs appointed by the government. The idea was to restore power to traditional and mainly conservative ethnic leaders in order to perpetuate ethnic differences that were beginning to erode. Both laws epitomized the ethos of the Nationalist government, which pretended to preserve what they were attempting to destroy. Laws stripping people of their rights were inevitably described as laws restoring those rights.

The Coloured people rallied against the Separate Representation of Voters Act, organizing a tremendous demonstration in Cape Town in March 1951 and a strike in April that kept shops closed and schoolchildren at home. It was in the context of this spirit of activism by Indians, Coloureds and Africans that Walter Sisulu first broached the idea to a small group of us of a national civil disobedience campaign. He outlined a plan under which selected volunteers from all groups would deliberately invite imprisonment by defying certain laws.

The idea immediately appealed to me, as it did to the others, but I differed from Walter on the question of who should take part. I had recently become national president of the Youth League, and in my new role I urged that the campaign should be exclusively African. The average African, I said, was still cautious about joint action with Indians and Coloureds. While I had made progress in terms of my opposition to communism, I still feared the influence of Indians. In addition, many of our grassroots African supporters saw Indians as exploiters of black labour in their role as shopkeepers and merchants.

Walter vehemently disagreed, suggesting that the Indians, Coloureds and Africans were inextricably bound together. The issue was taken up at a meeting of the National Executive Committee and my view was voted down, even by those who were considered staunch African nationalists. But I was nevertheless persistent and I raised the matter once more at the national conference in December 1951, where the delegates dismissed my view as emphatically as the National Executive had done. Now that my view had been rejected by the highest levels of the ANC, I fully accepted the agreed-upon position. While my speech advocating a go-it-alone strategy was met with a lukewarm reception, the speech I gave as president of the Youth League after the league pledged its support for the new policy of cooperation was given a resounding ovation.

At the behest of a joint planning council consisting of Dr Moroka, Walter, J.B. Marks, Yusuf Dadoo and Yusuf Cachalia, the ANC conference endorsed a resolution calling upon the government to repeal the Suppression of Communism Act, the Group Areas Act, the Separate Representation of Voters Act, the Bantu Authorities Act, the pass laws and stock limitation laws by 29 February 1952. The law was intended to reduce overgrazing by cattle, but its impact would be to further curtail land for Africans. The council resolved that the ANC would hold demonstrations on 6 April 1952 as a prelude to the launching of the Campaign for the Defiance of Unjust Laws. That same day white South Africans would be celebrating the three-hundredth anniversary of Jan van Riebeeck's arrival at the Cape in 1652. 6 April is the day white South Africans annually commemorate as the founding of their country – and Africans revile as the beginning of three hundred years of enslavement.

The ANC drafted a letter to the prime minister advising him of these resolutions and the deadline for repealing the laws. Because the letter was to go out under the name of Dr Moroka, and Dr Moroka had not participated in the writing of it, I was instructed to take him the letter by driving to his home in Thaba 'Nchu, a town near Bloemfontein in the Orange Free State, a very conservative area of the country. I almost did not make it there to see him.

Only a few weeks before, I had taken my driving test. In those days, a driver's licence was an unusual thing for an African, for very few blacks had cars. On the appointed day, I borrowed a car to use for the test. I was a bit cocky, and decided to drive the car there myself. I was running late and was driving faster than I should, and as I manoeuvred the car along a side street that met a main road, I failed to look both ways and collided with a car coming in another direction. The damage was minimal, but now I would certainly be late. The other driver was a reasonable fellow and we simply agreed to pay our own expenses.

When I reached the testing station, I observed a white woman ahead of me in the middle of her test. She was driving properly and cautiously. When the test was finished, the driving inspector said, 'Thank you. Would you please park the car over there', gesturing to a space nearby. She had performed the test well enough to pass, but as the woman drove over to the parking place, she did not negotiate a corner properly and the back wheel jumped the kerb. The inspector hurried over and said, 'I'm sorry, madam, you've failed the test, please make another appointment.' I felt my confidence ebbing. If this fellow tricks a white woman into failing her test, what hope would I have? But I performed well on the test, and when the inspector told me to park the car at the end of the exam, I drove so carefully that I thought he might penalize me for going too slowly.

Once I could legally drive, I became a one-man taxi service. It was one's obligation to give rides to comrades and friends. I was thus deputized to take the letter to Dr Moroka. This was no hardship to me as I have always found it enjoyable to gaze out of the window while driving. I seemed to have my best ideas while driving through the countryside with the wind whipping through the window.

On my way down to Thaba 'Nchu I passed through Kroonstad, a conservative Free State town about 120 miles south of Johannesburg. I was driving up a hill and saw two white boys ahead of me on bicycles. My driving was still a bit unsteady, and I came too close to them, one of whom suddenly made a turn without signalling, and we collided. He was knocked off his bicycle and was groaning when I got out of the car to help him. He had his arms out, indicating that I should pick him up, but just as I was about to do so, a white truck-driver yelled for me not to touch the boy. The truck-driver scared the child, who then dropped his arms as though he did not want me to pick him up. The boy was not badly hurt, and the truck-driver took him to the police station, which was close by.

The local police arrived a short time later, and the white sergeant took one look at me and said, '*Kaffer, jy sal kak vandag!*' ('Kaffir, you will shit today!') I was shaken by the accident and the violence of his words, but I told him in no uncertain terms that I would shit when I pleased, not when a policemen told me to. At this, the sergeant took out his notebook to record my particulars. Afrikaans policemen were surprised if a black man could speak English, much less answer back.

After I identified myself, he turned to the car, which he proceeded to ransack. From under the floor mat he pulled out a copy of the left-wing weekly, *The Guardian*, which I had hidden immediately after the accident. (I had slipped the letter to Dr Moroka inside my shirt.) He looked at the title and then held it up in the air like a pirate with his booty: '*Wragtig ons het 'n Kommunis gevang!*' he cried. ('My word, we've caught a communist!') Brandishing the newspaper, he hurried off.

The sergeant returned after about four hours, accompanied by another officer. This sergeant, also an Afrikaner, was intent on doing his duty correctly. He said he would need to take measurements at the site of the accident for police records. I told the sergeant that it was not proper to take measurements at night when the accident had occurred in daylight. I added that I intended to spend the night in Thaba 'Nchu, and that I could not afford to stay in Kroonstad. The sergeant eyed me impatiently and said, 'What is your name?'

'Mandela,' I said.

'No, the first one,' he said. I told him.

'Nelson,' the sergeant said, as if he were talking to a boy, 'I want to help you resume your journey. But if you are going to be difficult with me I will have no alternative but to be difficult with you and lock you up for the night.' That brought me down to earth and I consented to the measurements.

I resumed my journey late that night, and the next morning I was travelling through the district of Excelsior when my car ground to a halt. I had run out of petrol. I walked to a nearby farmhouse and explained in English to an elderly white lady that I would like to buy some petrol. As she was closing the door, she said, 'I don't have any petrol for you.' I tramped two miles to the next farm and, chastened by my unsuccessful first effort, tried a different approach. I asked to see the farmer, and when he appeared I assumed a humble demeanour. 'My *baas* has run out of petrol,' I said. (*Baas*, the Afrikaans word for boss or master, signifies subservience.) Friendly and helpful, the farmer was a relation of Prime Minister Strydom. Yet I believe he would have given me the petrol had I told him the truth and not used the hated word *baas*.

The meeting with Dr Moroka proved far less eventful than my journey there. He approved of the letter and I made my way back to Johannesburg without incident. The letter to the prime minister noted that the ANC had exhausted every constitutional means at our disposal to achieve our legitimate rights, and that we demanded the repeal of the six 'unjust laws' by 29 February 1952, or else we would take extra-constitutional action. Malan's reply, signed by his private secretary, asserted that whites had an inherent right to take measures to preserve their own identity as a separate community, and ended with the threat that if we pursued our actions the government would not hesitate to make full use of its machinery to quell any disturbances.

We regarded Malan's curt dismissal of our demands as a declaration of war. We now had no alternative but to resort to civil disobedience, and we embarked in earnest on preparations for mass action. The recruitment and training of volunteers was one of the essential tasks of the campaign and would in large part be responsible for its success or failure. On 6 April preliminary demonstrations took place in Johannesburg, Pretoria, Port Elizabeth, Durban and Cape Town. While Dr Moroka addressed a crowd at Freedom Square in Johannesburg, I spoke to a group of potential volunteers at the Garment Workers' Union. I explained to a group of several hundred Africans, Indians and Coloureds that volunteering was a difficult and even dangerous duty as the authorities would seek to intimidate, imprison and perhaps attack the volunteers. No matter what the authorities did, the volunteers could not retaliate, otherwise they would undermine the value of the entire enterprise. They must respond to violence with non-violence; discipline must be maintained at all costs.

On 31 May the Executives of the ANC and the SAIC met in Port Elizabeth and announced that the Defiance Campaign would begin on 26 June, the anniversary of the first National Day of Protest. They also created a National Action Committee to direct the campaign and a National Volunteer Board to recruit and train volunteers. I was appointed national volunteer-in-chief of the campaign and chairman of both the Action Committee and the Volunteer Board. My responsibilities were to organize the campaign, coordinate the regional branches, canvass for volunteers and raise funds.

We also discussed whether the campaign should follow the Gandhian principles of non-violence or what the Mahatma called *satyagraha*, a non-violence that seeks to conquer through conversion. Some argued for non-violence on purely ethical grounds, saying it was morally superior to any other method. This idea was strongly affirmed by Manilal Gandhi, the Mahatma's son and the editor of the newspaper *Indian Opinion*, who was a prominent member of the SAIC. With his gentle demeanour, Gandhi seemed the very personification of non-violence, and he insisted that the campaign be run along identical lines to that of his father's in India.

Others said that we should approach this issue not from the point of view of principles but of tactics, and that we should employ the method demanded by the conditions. If a particular method or tactic enabled us to defeat the enemy, then it should be used. In this case, the state was far more powerful than we, and any attempts at violence by us would be devastatingly crushed. This made non-violence a practical necessity rather than an option. This was my view, and I saw non-violence on the Gandhian model not as an inviolable principle but as a tactic to be used as the situation demanded. The principle was not so important that the strategy should be used even when it was self-defeating, as Gandhi himself believed. I called for non-violent protest for as long as it was effective. This view prevailed, despite Manilal Gandhi's strong objections.

The joint planning council agreed upon an open-ended programme of non-cooperation and non-violence. Two stages of defiance were proposed. In the first stage, a small number of well-trained volunteers would break selected laws in a handful of urban areas. They would enter proscribed areas without permits, use Whites Only facilities such as toilets, Whites Only railway compartments, waiting rooms and post office entrances. They would deliberately remain in town after curfew. Each batch of defiers would have a leader who would inform the police in advance of the act of disobedience so that the arrests could take place with a minimum of disturbance. The second stage was envisioned as mass defiance, accompanied by strikes and industrial actions across the country.

Prior to the inauguration of the Defiance Campaign, a rally, called the Day of the Volunteers, was held in Durban on 22 June. Chief Luthuli, president of the Natal ANC, and Dr Naicker, president of the Natal Indian Congress, both spoke and committed themselves to the campaign. I had driven down the day before and was the main speaker. About ten thousand people were in attendance, and I told the crowd that the Defiance Campaign would be the most powerful action ever undertaken by the oppressed masses in South Africa. I had never addressed such a great crowd before, and it was an exhilarating experience. One cannot speak to a mass of people as one addresses an audience of two dozen. Yet I have always tried to take the same care to explain matters to great audiences as to small ones. I told the people that they would make history and focus the attention of the world on the racist policies of South Africa. I emphasized that unity among the black people – Africans, Coloureds and Indians – in South Africa had at last become a reality.

All across the country, those who defied on 26 June did so with courage, enthusiam and a sense of history. The campaign began in the early morning hours in Port Elizabeth, where thirty-three defiers, under the leadership of Raymond Mhlaba, entered a railway station through a Whites Only entrance and were arrested. They marched in singing freedom songs, to the accompanying cheers of friends and family. In a call and response, the defiers and the crowd yelled, '*Mayibuye! Afrika!* ('Let Africa come back!')

On the morning of the twenty-sixth, I was in the ANC office overseeing the day's demonstrations. The Transvaal batch of volunteers was scheduled to go into action at midday at an African township near Boksburg, east of Johannesburg. Led by the Reverend N.B. Tantsi, they were to court arrest by entering the township without permission. Reverend Tantsi was an elderly fellow, a minister in the African Methodist Episcopal Church, and the acting president of the Transvaal ANC.

It was late morning, and as I was waiting for Reverend Tantsi to arrive from Pretoria he telephoned me at the office. With regret in his voice, he told me that his doctor advised him against defying and going to prison. I assured him that we would provide him with warm clothing and that he would spend only a night in jail, but to no avail. This was a grave disappointment, for Reverend Tantsi was a distinguished figure and had been selected in order to show the authorities that we were not just a group of young rabble-rousers.

In place of Reverend Tantsi, we quickly found someone equally venerable: Nana Sita, the president of the Transvaal Indian Congress, who had served a month in jail for his passive resistance during the 1946 protest campaign. Despite his advanced age and acute arthritis, Sita was a fighter and agreed to lead our defiers.

In the afternoon, as we were preparing to go to Boksburg, I realized that the secretary of the Transvaal branch of the ANC was nowhere to be found. He was meant to accompany Nana Sita to Boksburg. This was another crisis, and I turned to Walter and said, 'You must go.' This was our first event in the Transvaal, and it was necessary to have prominent figures to lead the defiers, otherwise the leaders would appear to be hanging back while the masses took the punishment. Even though Walter was one of the organizers and was scheduled to defy later, he readily agreed. My main concern was that he was wearing a suit, impractical dress for prison, but we managed to find him some old clothes instead.

We then left for Boksburg, where Yusuf Cachalia and I planned to deliver a letter to the Boksburg magistrate, advising him that fifty of our volunteers would enter the African township in his area that day without permits. When we arrived at the magistrate's office, we found a large contingent of pressmen and photographers. As I handed the envelope to the magistrate, the photographers went into action. The magistrate shielded himself from the camera flashes and then invited Yusuf and me into his chambers to discuss the matter privately. He was a reasonable man, and said his office was always open to us, but that excessive publicity would only worsen matters.

From the magistrate's office we went straight to the township where the demonstration was taking place, and even from half a mile away we heard the robust singing of our volunteers and the great crowd of supporters who had come to encourage them. At the scene, we found the high metal gates to the township locked and our volunteers waiting patiently outside, demanding entrance. There were fifty-two volunteers in all, both Africans and Indians, and a crowd of several hundred enthusiastic spectators and journalists. Walter was at the head of the defiers; his presence was evidence that we meant business. But the guiding spirit of the demonstrators was Nana Sita who, despite his arthritis, was moving among the demonstrators in high spirits, slapping them on the back and bolstering their confidence with his own.

For the first hour there was a standoff. The police were uncharacter-istically restrained and their behaviour baffled us. Was their restraint a strategy to exhaust the volunteers? Were they waiting for the journalists to depart and then planning to stage a massacre under the cover of darkness? Or were they faced with the dilemma that by arresting us – which is what they would have normally done – they would be doing the very thing we wanted? But even while we were wondering, the situation suddenly changed. The police ordered the gates opened. Immediately the volunteers surged through the gate, thus breaking the law. A police lieutenant blew a whistle and seconds later the police had surrounded the volunteers and began arresting them. The campaign was under way. The demonstrators were carted off to the local police station and charged.

That same evening, the leaders of the Action Committee, which included Oliver Tambo, Yusuf Cachalia and myself, attended a meeting in the city to discuss the day's events and to plan for the week ahead. It was near the area where the second batch of defiers, led by Flag Boshielo, chairman of the central branch of the ANC, were courting arrest. Shortly after eleven o'clock, we found them marching in unison in the street; at eleven, curfew regulations went into effect and Africans needed a permit to be outside.

We emerged from our meeting at midnight. I felt exhausted, and was thinking not of defiance but of a hot meal and a night's sleep. At that moment, a policeman approached Yusuf and me. It was obvious that we were going home, not protesting. 'No, Mandela,' the policeman called out. 'You can't escape.' He pointed with his nightstick to the police waggon parked nearby and said, 'Into the van.' I felt like explaining to him that I was in charge of running the campaign on a day-to-day basis and was not scheduled to defy and be arrested until much later, but of course that would have been ridiculous. I watched as he arrested Yusuf, who burst out laughing at the irony of it all. It was a lovely sight to see him smiling as he was led away by the police.

Moments later, Yusuf and I found ourselves among the more than fifty of our volunteers led by Flag Boshielo who were being taken in trucks to the red-brick police station known as Marshall Square. As the leaders of the Action Committee, we were worried that the others would wonder at our absence and I was concerned about who would be running the campaign. But spirits were high. Even on the way to prison, the vans swayed to the rich voices of the defiers singing 'Nkosi Sikelel' iAfrika' ('God Bless Africa'), the hauntingly beautiful African national anthem.

That first night, in the drill yard, one of us was pushed so violently by a white warder that he fell down some steps and broke his ankle. I protested to the warder about his behaviour, and he lashed out by kicking me in the shin. I demanded that the injured man receive medical attention and we initiated a small but vocal demonstration. We were curtly informed that the injured man could make a request for a doctor the next day if he so wished. We were aware throughout the night of his acute pain.

Until then I had spent bits and pieces of time in prison, but this was my first concentrated experience. Marshall Square was squalid, dark and dingy, but we were all together and so impassioned and spirited that I barely noticed my surroundings. The camaraderie of our fellow defiers made the two days pass very quickly.

On that first day of the Defiance Campaign more than 250 volunteers around the country violated various unjust laws and were imprisoned. It was an auspicious beginning. Our troops were orderly, disciplined, and confident.

Over the next five months, 8,500 people took part in the campaign. Doctors, factory workers, lawyers, teachers, students, ministers, defied and went to jail. They sang, 'Hey, Malan! Open the jail doors. We want to enter.' The campaign spread throughout the Witswatersrand, to Durban and to Port Elizabeth, East London and Cape Town, and smaller towns in the eastern and western Cape. Resistance was beginning to percolate even in the rural areas. For the most part, the offences were minor, and the penalties ranged from no more than a few nights in jail to a few weeks, with the option of a fine which rarely exceeded £10. The campaign received an enormous amount of publicity and the membership of the ANC shot up from some 20,000 to 100,000, with the most spectacular increase occurring in the eastern Cape, which contributed half of all new members.

During the six months of the campaign I travelled a great deal throughout the country. I generally went by car, leaving at night or very early in the morning. I toured the Cape, Natal and the Transvaal, explaining the campaign to small groups, sometimes going from house to house in the townships. Often, my task was to iron out differences in areas that were about to launch actions or had recently done so. In those days, when mass communication for Africans was primitive or non-existent, politics were parochial. We had to win people over one by one.

On one occasion I drove to the eastern Cape to resolve a dispute involving Alcott Gwentshe, who was running the campaign in East London. Gwentshe, a successful shopkeeper, had played an important role in organizing East London for the stay-at-home of 26 June two years before. He had briefly gone to jail at the beginning of the Defiance Campaign. He was a strong and able man, but he was an individualist who ignored the advice of the Executive and took decisions unilaterally.

He was now at odds with his own executive, which was mainly populated with intellectuals.

Gwentshe knew how to exploit certain issues in order to discredit his opponents. He would speak before local members who were workers, not intellectuals, and say – in Xhosa, never English, for English was the language of the intellectuals – 'Comrades, I think you know that I have suffered for the struggle. I had a good job and then went to jail at the beginning of the Defiance Campaign and I lost that job. Now that I am out of prison, these intellectuals have come along and said, "Gwentshe, we are better educated than you, we are more capable than you, let us run this campaign."'

When I investigated the situation I found that Gwentshe had indeed ignored the advice of the Executive. But the people were behind him, and he had created a disciplined and well-organized group of volunteers who had defied in an orderly fashion even while Gwentshe was in prison. Even though I thought Gwentshe was wrong for disregarding the Executive, he was doing a good job and was so firmly entrenched that he could not easily be dislodged. When I saw the members of the Executive, I explained that it was impractical to do anything about the situation now, but if they wanted to remedy it, they must defeat him at the next election. It was one of the first times that I saw that it was foolhardy to go against the people. It is no use to take an action to which the masses are opposed, for it will then be impossible to enforce.

The government saw the campaign as a threat to its security and its policy of apartheid. They regarded civil disobedience not as a form of protest but as a crime, and were perturbed by the growing partnership between Africans and Indians. Apartheid was designed to divide racial groups, and we showed that different groups could work together. The prospect of a united front between Africans and Indians, between moderates and radicals, greatly worried them. The Nationalists insisted that the campaign was instigated and led by communist agitators. The minister of justice announced that he would soon pass legislation to deal with our defiance, a threat he implemented during the 1953 parliamentary session with the passage of the Public Safety Act, which empowered the government to declare martial law and to detain people without trial, and the Criminal Laws Amendment Act, which authorized corporal punishment for defiers.

The government tried a number of underhanded means to interrupt the campaign. Government propagandists repeatedly claimed that the leaders of the campaign were living it up in comfort while the masses were languishing in jail. This allegation was far from the truth, but it achieved a certain currency. The government also infiltrated spies and *agents provocateurs* into the organization. The ANC welcomed virtually anyone who wanted to join. Although our volunteers were carefully screened before they were selected to defy, the police managed to penetrate not only our local branches but some of the batches of defiers. When I was arrested and sent to Marshall Square, I noticed two fellows among the defiers, one of whom I had never seen before. He wore unusual prison garb: a suit and tie with an overcoat and a silk scarf. What kind of person goes to jail dressed like that? His name was Ramaila, and on the third day when we were due to be released, he simply vanished.

The second man, whose name was Makhanda, stood out because of his military demeanour. We were out in the courtyard and all in high spirits. The defiers would march in front of Yusuf and me and salute us. Makhanda, who was tall and slender, marched in a soldierly manner and then gave a crisp, graceful salute. A number of the fellows teased him that he must be a policeman to salute so well.

Makhanda had previously worked as a janitor at ANC headquarters. He was very industrious and was popular because he would run out and get fish and chips whenever anyone was hungry. But at a later trial we discovered that both Makhanda and Ramaila were police spies. Ramaila testified that he had infiltrated the ranks of the defiers; the trusty Makhanda was actually Detective Sergeant Motloung.

Africans who worked as spies against their own brothers generally did so for money. Many blacks in South Africa believed that any effort by the black man to challenge the white man was foolhardy and doomed to failure; the white man was too smart and too strong. These spies saw us not as a threat to the white power structure but to black interests, for whites would mistreat all blacks based on the conduct of a few agitators.

Yet there were many black policemen who secretly aided us. They were decent fellows and found themselves in a moral quandary. They were loyal to their employer and needed to keep their jobs to support their families, but they were sympathetic to our cause. We had an understanding with a handful of African officers who were members of the security police that they would inform us when there was going to be a police raid. These men were patriots who risked their lives to help the struggle.

The government was not our only impediment. Others who might have helped us hindered us instead. At the height of the Defiance Campaign, the United Party sent two of its MPs to urge us to halt the campaign. They said that if we abandoned our campaign in response to a call made by J.G.N. Strauss, the United Party leader, it would help the party defeat the

Nationalists in the next election. We rejected this and Strauss proceeded to attack us with the same scorn used by the Nationalists.

We also came under attack from a breakaway ANC group called the National Minded Bloc. Led by Selope Thema, a former member of the National Executive, the group split from the ANC when J.B. Marks was elected president of the Transvaal ANC. Thema, who was editor of the newspaper *Bantu World*, fiercely criticized the campaign in his paper, claiming that communists had taken over the ANC and that Indians were exploiting the Africans. He asserted that the communists were more dangerous now that they were working underground, and that Indian economic interests were in conflict with those of Africans. Although he was in a minority in the ANC, his views got a sympathetic hearing among certain radical Youth Leaguers.

In May, during the middle of the Defiance Campaign, J. B. Marks was banned under the 1950 Suppression of Communism Act for 'furthering the aims of communism'. Banning was a legal order by the government, and generally entailed forced resignation from indicated organizations, and restriction from attending gatherings of any kind. It was a kind of walking imprisonment. To ban a person, the government required no proof, offered no charges; the minister of justice simply declared it so. It was a strategy designed to remove the individual from the struggle, allowing him to live a narrowly defined life outside politics. To violate or ignore a banning order was to invite imprisonment.

At the Transvaal conference that year in October, my name was proposed to replace the banned J. B. Marks, who had recommended that I succeed him. I was the national president of the Youth League, and the favourite for Marks's position, but my candidacy was opposed by a group from within the Transvaal ANC that called itself 'Bafabegiya' ('Those Who Die Dancing'). The group consisted mainly of ex-communists turned extreme African nationalists. They sought to cut all links with Indian activists and to move the ANC in the direction of a more confrontational strategy. They were led by MacDonald Maseko, a former communist who had been chairman of the Orlando branch of the ANC during the Defiance Campaign, and Seperepere Marupeng, who had been the chief volunteer for the Defiance Campaign in the Witwatersrand. Both Maseko and Marupeng intended to stand for the presidency of the Transvaal.

Marupeng was considered something of a demagogue. He used to wear a military-style khaki suit adorned with epaulets and gold buttons, and carried a baton like that made famous by Field Marshal Montgomery. He would stand up in front of meetings, his baton clutched underneath his arm, and say: 'I am tired of waiting for freedom. I want freedom now! I will meet Malan at the crossroads and I will show him what I want.' Then, banging his baton on the podium, he would cry, 'I want freedom now!'

Because of speeches like these, Marupeng became extremely popular during the Defiance Campaign, but popularity is only one factor in an election. He thought that because of his newfound prominence he would be a certainty for the presidency. Before the election, when it was known that I would be a candidate, I approached him and said, 'I would like you to stand for election to the Executive so that you can serve with me when I am president.' He regarded this as a slight, that I was in effect demoting him, and he refused, choosing instead to run for the presidency himself. But he had miscalculated, for I won the election with an overwhelming majority.

On 30 July 1952, at the height of the Defiance Campaign, I was at work at my then law firm of H.M. Basner when the police arrived with a warrant for my arrest. The charge was violation of the Suppression of Communism Act. The state made a series of simultaneous arrests of campaign leaders in Johannesburg, Port Elizabeth and Kimberley. Earlier in the month, the police had raided homes and offices of ANC and SAIC officials all over the country and confiscated papers and documents. This type of raid was something new and set a pattern for the pervasive and illegal searches that subsequently became a regular feature of the government's behaviour.

My arrest and those of the others culminated in a trial in September in Johannesburg of twenty-one accused, including the presidents and general secretaries of the ANC, the SAIC, the ANC Youth League and the Transvaal Indian Congress. Among the twenty-one on trial in Johannesburg were Dr Moroka, Walter Sisulu and J.B. Marks. A number of Indian leaders were arrested, including Dr Dadoo, Yusuf Cachalia and Ahmed Kathrada.

Our appearances in court became the occasion for exuberant political rallies. Massive crowds of demonstrators marched through the streets of Johannesburg and converged on the city's magistrates' court. There were white students from the University of the Witswatersrand, old ANC campaigners from Alexandra, Indian schoolchildren from primary and secondary schools, people of all ages and colours. The court had never been deluged with such crowds before. The courtroom itself was packed with people, and shouts of '*Mayibuye Afrika!*' punctuated the proceedings.

The trial should have been an occasion of resolve and solidarity, but it was sullied by a breach of faith by Dr Moroka. Moroka, the president-general of the ANC and the figurehead of the campaign, shocked us all by employing his own attorney. The plan was for all of us to be tried together. My fellow accused appointed me to discuss the matter with Dr Moroka and attempt to persuade him not to separate himself. The day before the trial I went to see Dr Moroka at Village Deep, Johannesburg.

At the outset of our meeting, I suggested alternatives to him, but he was not interested and instead aired a number of grievances. He felt that he had been excluded from the planning of the campaign. Yet Moroka was often quite uninterested in ANC affairs and content to be so. But he said the matter that disturbed him more than any other was that by being defended with the rest of us, he would be associated with men who were communists. Dr Moroka shared the government's animosity to communism. I remonstrated with him and said that it was the tradition of the ANC to work with anyone who was against racial oppression. But Moroka was unmoved.

The greatest jolt came when Moroka tendered a humiliating plea in mitigation to Judge Rumpff and took the witness stand to renounce the very principles on which the ANC had been founded. Asked whether he thought there should be equality between black and white in South Africa, Moroka replied that there would never be such a thing. We felt like slumping in despair in our seats. When his own lawyer asked him whether there were some among the defendants who were communists, Moroka actually began to point his finger at various people, including Dr Dadoo and Walter Sisulu. The judge informed him that that was not necessary.

His performance was a severe blow to the organization, and we all immediately realized that Dr Moroka's days as ANC president were numbered. He had committed the cardinal sin of putting his own interests ahead of those of the organization and the people. He was unwilling to jeopardize his medical career and fortune for his political beliefs, and thereby he had destroyed the image he had built during three years of courageous work on behalf of the ANC and the Defiance Campaign. I regarded this as a tragedy, for Dr Moroka's faintheartedness in court took away some of the glow from the campaign. The man who had gone round the country preaching the importance of the campaign had now forsaken it.

On 2 December we were all found guilty of what Judge Rumpff defined as 'statutory communism' – as opposed to what he said 'is commonly known as communism'. According to the statutes of the Suppression of Communism Act, virtually anyone who opposed the government in any way could be defined as – and therefore convicted of being – a 'statutory communist', even without ever having been a member of the party. The judge, who was fair-minded and reasonable, said that although we had planned acts that ranged from 'open non-compliance of laws to something that equals high treason', he accepted that we had consistently advised our members 'to follow a peaceful course of action and to avoid violence in any shape or form'. We were sentenced to nine months' imprisonment with hard labour, but the sentence was suspended for two years.

We made many mistakes, but the Defiance Campaign marked a new chapter in the struggle. The six laws we singled out were not overturned; but we never had any illusion that they would be. We selected them as the most immediate burden pressing on the lives of the people, and the best way to engage the greatest number of people in the struggle.

Prior to the campaign, the ANC was more talk than action. We had no paid organizers, no staff and a membership that did little more than pay lip-service to our cause. As a result of the campaign, our membership swelled to 100,000. The ANC emerged as a truly mass-based organization with an impressive corps of experienced activists who had braved the police, the courts and the jails. The stigma usually associated with imprisonment had been removed. This was a significant achievement, for fear of prison is a tremendous hindrance to a liberation struggle. From the Defiance Campaign onward, going to prison became a badge of honour among Africans.

We were extremely proud of the fact that during the six months of the campaign, there was not a single act of violence on our side. The discipline of our resisters was exemplary. During the later part of the campaign, riots broke out in Port Elizabeth and East London in which more than forty people were killed. Though these outbreaks had nothing whatsoever to do with the campaign, the government attempted to link us with them. In this, the government was successful, for the riots poisoned the views of some whites who might otherwise have been sympathetic.

Some within the ANC had unrealistic expectations and were convinced that the campaign could topple the government. We reminded them that the idea of the campaign was to focus attention on our grievances, not eradicate them. They argued that we had the government where we wanted it, and that we should continue the campaign indefinitely. I stepped in and said that this government was too strong and too ruthless to be brought down in such a manner. We could embarrass it, but overthrowing it as a result of the Defiance Campaign was impossible.

As it was, we continued the campaign for too long. We should have listened to Dr Xuma. When the planning committee met Dr Xuma during the tail-end of the campaign, he told us that it would soon lose momentum and it would be wise to call it off before it fizzled out altogether. To halt the campaign while it was still on the offensive would be a shrewd move that would capture the headlines. Dr Xuma was right: the campaign soon slackened, but in our enthusiasm and even arrogance, we brushed aside his advice. My heart wanted to keep it going but my head told me that it should stop. I argued for closure but went along with the majority. By the end of the year, the campaign foundered.

The Defiance Campaign never expanded beyond the initial stage of small batches of mostly urban defiers. Mass defiance, especially in the rural areas, was never achieved. The eastern Cape was the only region where we succeeded in reaching the second stage and where a strong resistance movement emerged in the countryside. In general, we did not penetrate the countryside, a historical weakness of the ANC. The campaign was hampered by the fact that we did not have any full-time organizers. I was attempting to organize it and practise as a lawyer at the same time, and that is no way to wage a mass campaign. We were still amateurs.

I nevertheless felt a great sense of accomplishment and satisfaction: I had been engaged in a just cause and had the strength to fight for it and win. The campaign freed me from any lingering sense of doubt or inferiority I might still have felt; it liberated me from the feeling of being overwhelmed by the power and seeming invincibility of the white man and his institutions. But now the white man had felt the power of my punches and I could walk upright like a man, and look everyone in the eye with the dignity that comes from not having succumbed to oppression and fear. I had come of age as a freedom fighter.

PART FOUR

The Struggle Is My Life

15

At the ANC annual conference at the end of 1952, there was a changing of the guard. The ANC designated a new, more vigorous, president for a new, more activist, era: Chief Albert Luthuli. In accordance with the ANC constitution, as provincial president of the Transvaal, I became one of the four deputy presidents. Furthermore, the National Executive Committee appointed me as First Deputy President. Luthuli was one of a handful of ruling chiefs who were active in the ANC and had staunchly resisted the policies of the government.

The son of a Seventh Day Adventist missionary, Luthuli was born in what was then Southern Rhodesia and educated in Natal. He had trained as a teacher at Adam's College near Durban. A fairly tall, heavy-set, dark-skinned man with a great broad smile, he combined an air of humility with deep-seated confidence. He was a man of patience and fortitude, who spoke slowly and clearly as though every word was of equal importance.

I had first met him in the late 1940s when he was a member of the Natives' Representative Council. In September 1952, only a few months before the annual conference, Luthuli had been summoned to Pretoria and given an ultimatum: he must either renounce his membership of the ANC and his support of the Defiance Campaign, or he would be dismissed from his position as an elected and government-paid tribal chief. Luthuli was a teacher, a devout Christian and a proud Zulu chief, but he was even more firmly committed to the struggle against apartheid. Luthuli refused to resign from the ANC and the government dismissed him from his post. In response, he issued a statement of principles called 'The Road to Freedom is via the Cross', in which he reaffirmed his support for non-violent passive resistance and justified his choice with words that still echo plaintively today: 'Who will deny that thirty years of my life have been spent knocking in vain, patiently, moderately and modestly at a closed and barred door?'

I supported Chief Luthuli, but I was unable to attend the national conference. A few days before the conference was to begin, fifty-two leaders around the country were banned from attending any meetings or gatherings for six months. I was among those leaders, and my movements were restricted to the district of Johannesburg for that same period.

My bans extended to meetings of all kinds, not only political ones. I could not, for example, attend my son's birthday party. I was prohibited from talking to more than one person at a time. This was part of a systematic effort by the government to silence, persecute and immobilize the leaders of those fighting apartheid and was the first of a series of bans on me that continued with brief intervals of freedom until the time I was deprived of all freedom some years later.

Banning not only confines one physically, it imprisons one's spirit. It induces a kind of psychological claustrophobia that makes one yearn for not only freedom of movement but spiritual escape. Banning was a dangerous game, for one was not shackled or chained behind bars; the bars were laws and regulations that could easily be violated and often were. One could slip away unseen for short periods of time and have the temporary illusion of freedom. The insidious effect of bans was that at a certain point one began to think that the oppressor was not without but within.

Although I was prevented from attending the 1952 annual conference, I was immediately informed as to what had transpired. One of the most significant decisions was one taken in secret and not publicized at the time.

Along with many others, I had become convinced that the government intended to declare the ANC and the SAIC illegal organizations, just as it had done with the Communist Party. It seemed inevitable that the state would attempt to put us out of business as a legal organization as soon as it could. With this in mind, I approached the National Executive with the idea that we must come up with a contingency plan for just such an eventuality. I said it would be an abdication of our responsibility as leaders of the people if we did not do so. They instructed me to draw up a plan that would enable the organization to operate from underground. This strategy came to be known as the Mandela-Plan or, simply, M-Plan.

The idea was to set up organizational machinery that would allow the ANC to take decisions at the highest level, which could then be swiftly transmitted to the organization as a whole without calling a meeting. In other words, it would allow an illegal organization to continue to function and enable leaders who were banned to continue to lead. The M-Plan was designed to allow the organization to recruit new members, respond to local and national problems and maintain regular contact between the membership and the underground leadership.

I held a number of secret meetings among ANC and SAIC leaders, both banned and not banned, to discuss the parameters of the plan. I worked on it for a number of months and came up with a system that was broad enough to adapt itself to local conditions and not fetter individual initiative, but detailed enough to facilitate order. The smallest unit was the cell, which in urban townships consisted of roughly ten houses on a street. A cell steward would be in charge of each of these units. If a street had more than ten houses, a street steward would take charge and the cell stewards would report to him. A group of streets formed a zone directed by a chief steward, who was in turn responsible to the secretariat of the local branch of the ANC. The secretariat was a subcommittee of the branch executive, which reported to the provincial secretary. My notion was that every cell and street steward should know every person and family in his area, so that he would be trusted by the people and would know whom to trust. The cell steward arranged meetings, organized political classes and collected dues. He was the linchpin of the plan. Although the strategy was primarily created for predominantly urban areas, it could be adapted to rural ones.

The plan was accepted, and was to be implemented immediately. Word went out to the branches to begin to prepare for this covert restructuring. Although it was accepted at most branches, some of the more far-flung outposts felt that the plan was an effort by Johannesburg to centralize control over the regions.

As part of the M-Plan, the ANC introduced an elementary course of political lectures for its members throughout the country. These lectures were meant not only to educate but to hold the organization together. They were given in secret by branch leaders. Those members in attendance would in turn give the same lectures to others in their homes and communities. In the beginning, the lectures were not systematized, but within a number of months there was a set curriculum.

There were three courses, 'The World We Live In', 'How We Are Governed' and 'The Need for Change'. In the first course, we discussed the different types of political and economic systems around the world as well as in South Africa. It was an overview of the growth of capitalism as well as socialism. We discussed, for example, how blacks in South Africa were oppressed both as a race and an economic class. The lecturers were mostly banned members, and I myself frequently gave lectures in the evening. This arrangement had the virtue of keeping banned individuals active as well as keeping the membership in touch with these leaders.

During this time, the banned leadership would often meet secretly and alone, and then arrange to meet the present leaders. The old and the new leadership meshed very well, and the decision-making process was collective as it had been before. Sometimes it felt as if nothing had changed except that we had to meet in secret.

The M-Plan was conceived with the best intentions, but it was instituted with only modest success and its adoption was never widespread. The most impressive results were once again in the eastern Cape and Port Elizabeth. The spirit of the Defiance Campaign continued in the eastern Cape long after it vanished elsewhere, and ANC members there seized on the M-Plan as a way of continuing to defy the government.

The plan faced many problems: it was not always adequately explained to the membership, there were no paid organizers to help implement or administer it and there was often dissension within branches that prevented agreement on imposing the plan. Some provincial leaders resisted it because they believed it undermined their power. To some, the government's crackdown did not seem imminent so they did not take the precautions necessary to lessen its effect. When the government's iron fist did descend, they were not prepared.

16

My life, during the Defiance Campaign, ran on two separate tracks: my work in the struggle and my livelihood as an attorney. I was never a full-time organizer for the ANC; the organization had only one, and that was Thomas Titus Nkobi. The work I did had to be arranged around my schedule as an attorney. In 1951, after I had completed my articles at Witkin, Sidelsky and Eidelman, I went to work for the law firm of Terblanche & Briggish. When I completed my articles, I was not yet a fully-fledged attorney, but I was in a position to draw court pleadings, send out summonses and interview witnesses – all of which an attorney must do before a case goes to court.

After leaving Sidelsky, I had investigated a number of white firms – there were, of course, no African law firms. I was particularly interested in the scale of fees charged by these firms and was outraged to discover that many of the most blue-chip law firms charged Africans even higher fees for criminal and civil cases than they did their far wealthier white clients.

After working for Terblanche & Briggish for about one year, I joined the firm of Helman and Michel. It was a liberal firm, and one of the few that charged Africans on a reasonable scale. In addition, it prided itself on its devotion to African education, towards which it donated handsomely. Mr Helman, the firm's senior partner, was involved with African causes long before they became popular or fashionable. The firm's other partner, Rodney Michel, a veteran of the Second World War, was also extremely liberal. He was a pilot, and years later helped fly ANC people out of South Africa during the worst periods of repression. Michel's only discernible vice was that he was a heavy smoker who puffed on one cigarette after another all day long at the office.

I stayed at Helman and Michel for a number of months while I was studying for my qualification exam, which would establish me as a fully-fledged attorney. I had given up studying for an LLB degree at the University of the Witwatersrand after failing my exams several times. I opted to take the qualifying exam so that I could practise and begin to earn enough money to support my family. At the time, my sister was living with us and my mother had come to visit, and Evelyn's wages as a trainee nurse plus my own paltry income were not enough to keep everyone warm and fed.

When I passed the qualification exam, I went to work as a fully-fledged attorney at the firm of H.M. Basner. Basner had been an Africans' representative in the Senate, an early member of the Communist Party, and a passionate supporter of African rights. As a lawyer, he was a defender of African leaders and trade unionists. For the months that I worked there, I was often in court representing the firm's many African clients. Mr Basner was an excellent boss and as long as I got my work done at the firm he encouraged my political activities. After the experience I gained there, I felt ready to go off on my own.

In August 1952 I opened my own law office. What early success I enjoyed I owed to Zubeida Patel, my secretary. I had met her when she had gone to work at H.M. Basner as a replacement for an Afrikaans-speaking secretary, Miss Koch, who had refused to take my dictation. Zubeida was the wife of my friend Cassim Patel, a member of the Indian Congress, and she was without any sense of colour bar whatsoever. She had a wide circle of friends, knew many people in the legal world, and when I went out on my own, she agreed to work for me. She brought a great deal of business through the door.

Oliver Tambo was then working for a firm called Kovalsky and Tuch. I often visited him there during his lunch hour, and made a point of sitting in a Whites Only chair in the Whites Only waiting room. Oliver and I were very good friends, and we mainly discussed ANC business during those lunch hours. He had first impressed me at Fort Hare where I noticed his thoughtful intelligence and sharp debating skills. With his cool, logical style he could demolish an opponent's argument – precisely the sort of intelligence that is useful in a courtroom. Before Fort Hare, he had been a brilliant student at St Peter's in Johannesburg. His even-tempered objectivity was an antidote to my more emotional reactions to issues. Oliver was deeply religious and had for a long time considered the ministry to be his calling. He was also a neighbour: he came from Bizana in Pondoland, part of the Transkei, and his face bore the distinctive scars of his tribe. It seemed natural for us to practise together and I asked him to join me. A few months later, when Oliver was able to extricate himself from his firm, we opened our own office in downtown Johannesburg.

'Mandela and Tambo' read the brass plate on our office door in

Chancellor House, a small building just across the street from the marble statues of justice standing in front of the magistrates' court in central Johannesburg. Our building, owned by Indians, was one of the few places where Africans could rent offices in the city. From the beginning, Mandela and Tambo was besieged with clients. We were not the only African lawyers in South Africa, but we were the only firm of African lawyers. For Africans, we were the firm of first choice and last resort. To reach our offices each morning, we had to move through a crowd of people in the corridors, on the stairs and in our small waiting room.

Africans were desperate for legal help in government buildings: it was a crime to walk through a Whites Only door, a crime to ride a Whites Only bus, a crime to use a Whites Only drinking fountain, a crime to walk on a Whites Only beach, a crime to be on the streets after 11 p.m., a crime not to have a pass book and a crime to have the wrong signature in that book, a crime to be unemployed and a crime to be employed in the wrong place, a crime to live in certain places and a crime to have no place to live.

Every week we interviewed old men from the countryside who told us that generation after generation of their family had worked a bleak piece of land from which they were now being evicted. Every week we interviewed old women who brewed African beer as a way to supplement their tiny incomes, who now faced jail terms and fines they could not afford to pay. Every week we interviewed people who had lived in the same house for decades only to find that it was now in what was declared a white area and they had to leave without any recompense. Every day we heard and saw the thousands of humiliations that ordinary Africans confronted every day of their lives.

Oliver had a prodigious capacity for work. He spent a great deal of time with each client, not so much for professional reasons but because he was a man of limitless compassion and patience. He became involved in his clients' cases and in their lives. He was touched by the plight of the masses as a whole and by each and every individual.

I realized quickly what Mandela and Tambo meant to ordinary Africans. It was a place where they could come and find a sympathetic ear and a competent ally, a place where they would not be either turned away or cheated, a place where they might actually feel proud to be represented by men of their own skin colour. This was the reason I had become a lawyer in the first place, and my work often made me feel I had made the right decision.

We often dealt with half a dozen cases in a morning, and were in and out of court all day long. In some courts we were treated with courtesy, in others with contempt. But even as we practised and fought and won cases, we always knew that no matter how well we pursued our careers as attorneys, we could never become a prosecutor, a magistrate, a judge. Although we were dealing with officials whose competence was no greater than our own, their authority was founded on and protected by the colour of their skin.

We frequently encountered prejudice in the court itself. White witnesses often refused to answer questions from a black attorney. Instead of citing them for contempt of court, the magistrate would then pose the questions they would not answer from me. I routinely put policemen on the stand and interrogated them; though I would catch them in discrepancies and lies, they never considered me anything but a 'kaffir lawyer'.

I recall once being asked at the outset of a trial to identify myself. This was customary. I said, 'I am Nelson Mandela and I appear for the accused.' The magistrate said, 'I don't know you. Where is your certificate?' A certificate is the fancy diploma that one frames and hangs on the wall; it is not something that an attorney ever carries with him. It would be like asking a man for his university degree. I requested that the magistrate begin the case, and I would bring in my certificate in due course. But the magistrate refused to hear the case, even going so far as to ask a court officer to evict me.

This was a clear violation of court practice. The matter eventually came before the Supreme Court and my friend, George Bizos, an advocate, appeared on my behalf. At the hearing, the presiding judge criticized the conduct of the magistrate and ordered that a different magistrate must hear the case.

Being a lawyer did not guarantee respect out of court either. One day, near our office, I saw an elderly white woman whose motorcar was sandwiched between two cars. I immediately went over and pushed the car, which helped free it. The English-speaking woman turned to me and said, 'Thank you, John' – John being the name whites used to address any African whose name they did not know. She then handed me a sixpence coin, which I politely refused. She pushed it towards me, and again I said no, thank you. She then exclaimed, 'You refuse a sixpence. You must want a shilling, but you shall not have it!' and then threw the coin at me, and drove off.

Within a year, Oliver and I discovered that under the Urban Areas Act we were not permitted to occupy business premises in the city without ministerial consent. Our request was denied, and we received instead a temporary permit under the Group Areas Act, which soon expired. The authorities refused to renew it, insisting that we move our offices to an

African location many miles away and virtually unreachable for our clients. We interpreted this as an effort by the authorities to put us out of business, and occupied our premises illegally, with threats of eviction constantly hanging over our heads. Working as a lawyer in South Africa meant operating under a debased system of justice, a code of law that did not enshrine equality but its opposite. One of the most pernicious examples of this was the Population Registration Act, which defined that inequality. I once handled the case of a Coloured man who was inadvertently classified as an African. He had fought for South Africa during the Second World War in North Africa and Italy, but after his return, a white bureaucrat had reclassified him as African. This was the type of case, not at all untypical in South Africa, that offered a moral jigsaw puzzle. I did not support or recognize the principles in the Population Registration Act, but my client needed representation, and he had been classified as something he was not. There were many practical advantages to being classified as Coloured rather than African, such as the fact that Coloured men were not required to carry passes.

On his behalf, I appealed to the Classification Board, which adjudicated cases falling under the Population Registration Act. The board consisted of a magistrate and two other officials, all white. I had formidable documentary evidence to establish my client's case, and the prosecutor formally indicated that he would not oppose our appeal. But the magistrate seemed uninterested in both my evidence and the prosecutor's demurral. He stared at my client and gruffly asked him to turn round so that his back faced the bench. After scrutinizing my client's shoulders, which sloped down sharply, he nodded to the other officials and upheld the appeal. In the view of the white authorities in those days, sloping shoulders were one stereotype of the Coloured physique. And so it came about that the course of this man's life was decided purely on a magistrate's opinion about the structure of his shoulders.

We tried many cases involving police brutality, though our success rate was quite low. Police assaults were always difficult to prove. The police were clever enough to detain a prisoner long enough for the wounds and bruises to heal, and often it was simply the word of a policeman against our client. The magistrates naturally sided with the police. The coroner's verdict on a death in police custody would often read 'Death due to multiple causes' or some vague explanation that let the police off the hook.

Whenever I had a case outside Johannesburg, I applied to have my bans temporarily lifted, and this was often granted. For example, I travelled to the eastern Transvaal, and defended a client in the town of Carolina. My arrival caused quite a sensation, as many of the people had never before seen an African lawyer. I was received warmly by the magistrate and prosecutor, and the case did not begin for quite a while as they asked me numerous questions about my career and how I became a lawyer. The court was similarly crowded with curious townspeople.

In a nearby village I appeared for a local medicine man charged with witchcraft. This case also attracted a large crowd – not to see me, but to find out whether the white man's laws could be applied to a *sangoma*. The medicine man exerted tremendous power in the area, and many people both worshipped and feared him. At one point, my client sneezed violently, causing a virtual stampede in the courtroom; most observers believed he was casting a spell. He was found not guilty, but I suspect that the local people attributed this not to my skill as a lawyer, but to the power of the medicine man's herbs.

As an attorney, I could be rather flamboyant in court. I did not act as though I were a black man in a white man's court, but as if everyone else – white and black – was a guest in my court. When presenting a case, I often made sweeping gestures and used high-flown language. I was punctilious about all court regulations, but I sometimes used unorthodox tactics with witnesses. I enjoyed cross-examinations, and often played on racial tension. The spectators' gallery was usually crowded, because people from the township attended court as a form of entertainment.

I recall once defending an African woman who worked as a domestic worker in town. She was accused of stealing her 'madam's' clothes. The clothing that was allegedly stolen was displayed on a table in court. After the 'madam' had testified, I began my cross-examination by walking over to the table of evidence. I studied the clothing and then, with the tip of my pencil, I picked up an item of ladies' underwear. I slowly turned to the witness box brandishing the panties and simply asked, 'Madam, are these . . . yours?' 'No,' she replied quickly, too embarrassed to admit that they were. Because of this response, and other discrepancies in her evidence, the magistrate dismissed the case.

17

Situated four miles west of Johannesburg's centre, on the face of a rocky outcrop overlooking the city, was the African township of Sophiatown. Father Trevor Huddleston, one of the township's greatest friends, once compared Sophiatown to an Italian hill town, and from a distance the place did indeed have a good deal of charm: the closely packed, red-roofed houses; the smoke curling up into a pink sky; the tall and slender gum trees that hugged the township. Up close one saw the poverty and squalor in which too many of Sophiatown's people lived. The streets were narrow and unpaved, and every plot was filled with dozens of shanties huddled close together.

Sophiatown was part of what was known as the Western Areas townships, along with Martindale and Newclare. The area was originally intended for whites, and a property developer actually built a number of houses there for white buyers. But because of a municipal refuse dump in the area, whites chose to live elsewhere. Reluctantly, the developer sold his houses to Africans. Sophiatown was one of the few places in the Transvaal where Africans had been able to buy stands, or plots, prior to the 1923 Urban Areas Act. Many of these old brick and stone houses, with their tin-roofed verandas, still stood in Sophiatown, giving the township an air of Old World graciousness. As industry in Johannesburg grew, Sophiatown became the home of a rapidly expanding African workforce. It was convenient and close to town. Workers lived in shanties that were erected in the back and front yards of older residences. Several families might all be crowded into a single shanty. Up to forty people could share a single water tap. Despite the poverty, Sophiatown had a special character; for Africans, it was the Left Bank in Paris, Greenwich Village in New York, the home of writers, artists, doctors and lawyers. It was both bohemian and conventional, lively and sedate. It was home to both Dr Xuma, where he had his practice, and assorted *tsotsis* (gangsters) like the Berliners and the Americans who adopted the names of American movie stars like John Wayne and Humphrey Bogart.

Sophiatown boasted the only swimming pool for African children in Johannesburg.

In Johannesburg, the Western Areas Removal scheme meant the evacuation of Sophiatown, Martindale and Newclare, with a collective population that was somewhere between 60,000 and 100,000. In 1953, the Nationalist government had purchased a tract of land called Meadowlands, thirteen miles from the city. People were to be resettled there in seven different 'ethnic groups'. The excuse given by the government was slum clearance, a smokescreen for the government policy that regarded all urban areas as white areas where Africans were temporary residents.

The government was under pressure from its supporters in the surrounding areas of Westdene and Newlands, which were comparatively poor white areas. These working-class whites were envious of some of the fine houses owned by blacks in Sophiatown. The government wanted to control the movements of all Africans, and such control was far more difficult in freehold urban townships, where blacks could own property, and people came and went as they pleased. Though the pass system was still in effect, one did not need a special permit to enter a freehold township, as was the case with municipal locations. Africans had lived and owned property in Sophiatown for over fifty years; now the government was callously planning on relocating all Sophiatown's African residents to another black township. So cynical was the government's plan that the removal was to take place even before the houses were built to accommodate the evacuated people. The removal of Sophiatown was the first major test of strength for the ANC and its allies after the Defiance Campaign.

Although the government's removal campaign for Sophiatown had started in 1950, efforts by the ANC to combat it did not begin in earnest until 1953. By the middle of the year, the local branches of the ANC and the TIC and the local Ratepayers Association were mobilizing people to resist. In June 1953 a public meeting was called by the provincial executive of the ANC and the TIC at Sophiatown's Odin cinema to discuss opposition to the removal. It was a lively, exuberant meeting attended by more than twelve hundred people, none of whom seemed intimidated by the presence of dozens of heavily armed policemen.

Only a few days before the meeting, my banning orders, as well as Walter's, had expired. This meant that we were no longer prevented from attending or speaking at gatherings, and arrangements were quickly made for me to speak at the cinema.

Shortly before the meeting was to begin, a police officer saw Walter and me outside the cinema talking with Father Huddleston, one of the leaders of the opposition to the removal. The officer informed the two of us that as banned individuals we had no right to be there, and he then ordered his officers to arrest us. Father Huddleston shouted to the policemen coming towards us, 'No, you must arrest me instead, my dears.' The officer ordered Father Huddleston to stand aside, but he refused. As the policemen moved Father Huddleston out of the way, I said to the officer, 'You must make sure whether we are under a ban or not. Be careful, because it would be a wrongful arrest to take us in if our bans have expired. Now, do you think we would be here tonight talking to you if our bans had not expired?'

The police were notorious for keeping very poor records and were often unaware when bans ended. The officer knew this as well as I did. He pondered what I had said, then told his men to pull back. They stood aside as we entered the hall.

Inside, the police were provocative and contemptuous. Equipped with pistols and rifles, they strutted around the hall pushing people around, making insulting remarks. I was sitting on stage with a number of other leaders and, as the meeting was about to begin, I saw Major Prinsloo come swaggering in through the stage door, accompanied by a number of armed officers. I caught his eye and made a gesture as if to say, 'Me?' and he shook his head. He then walked over to the podium, where Yusuf Cachalia had already begun to speak, and ordered the other officers to arrest him, whereupon they took him by the arms and started to drag him off. Outside, the police had already arrested Robert Resha and Ahmed Kathrada.

The crowd began yelling and booing, and I saw that matters could turn extremely ugly if the crowd did not control itself. I jumped to the podium and started singing a well-known protest song, and as soon as I pronounced the first few words the crowd joined in. I feared that the police might have opened fire if the crowd had become too unruly.

The ANC was then holding meetings every Sunday evening in Freedom Square, in the centre of Sophiatown, to mobilise opposition to the removal. These were vibrant sessions, punctuated by repeated cries of '*Asihambi!*' ('We are not moving!') and the singing of '*Sophiatown likhaya lam asihambi*' ('Sophiatown is my home; we are not moving'). The meetings were addressed by leading ANC members, standholders, tenants, city councillors, and often by Father Huddleston, who ignored police warnings to confine himself to church affairs.

One Sunday evening, not long after the incident at the Odin cinema, I was scheduled to speak in Freedom Square. The crowd that night was passionate, and their emotion undoubtedly influenced mine. There were a great many young people present, and they were angry and eager for action. As usual, policemen were clustered around the perimeter, armed with both guns and pencils, the latter to take notes of who was speaking and what the speaker was saying. We tried to make this into a virtue by being as open with the police as possible to show them that in fact we had nothing to hide, not even our distaste for them.

I began by speaking about the increasing repressiveness of the government in the wake of the Defiance Campaign. I said the government was now scared of the might of the African people. As I spoke, I grew more and more indignant. In those days, I was something of a rabble-rousing speaker. I liked to incite an audience, and I was doing so that evening.

As I condemned the government for its ruthlessness and lawlessness, I overstepped the line: I said that the time for passive resistance had ended, that non-violence was a useless strategy and could never overturn a white minority regime bent on retaining its power at any cost. At the end of the day, I said, violence was the only weapon that would destroy apartheid and we must be prepared, in the near future, to use that weapon.

The crowd was excited; the youth in particular were clapping and cheering. They were ready to act on what I said right then and there. At that point I began to sing a freedom song, the lyrics of which say, 'There are the enemies, let us take our weapons and attack them.' I sang and the crowd joined in, and when it was finished, I pointed to the police and said, 'There, there are our enemies!' The crowd again started cheering and made aggressive gestures in the direction of the police. The police looked nervous, and a number of them pointed back at me as if to say, 'Mandela, we will get you for this.' I did not mind. In the heat of the moment I did not think of the consequences.

But my words that night did not come out of nowhere. I had been thinking of the future. The government was busily taking measures to prevent anything like the Defiance Campaign from recurring. I had begun to analyse the struggle in different terms. The ambition of the ANC was to wage a mass struggle, to engage the workers and peasants of South Africa in a campaign so large and powerful that it might overcome the *status quo* of white oppression. But the Nationalist government was making any legal expression of dissent or protest impossible. I saw that it would ruthlessly suppress any legitimate protest on the part of the African majority. A police state did not seem far off.

I began to suspect that both legal and extra-constitutional protests would soon be impossible. In India, Gandhi had been dealing with a foreign power that ultimately was more realistic and far-sighted. That was not the case with the Afrikaners in South Africa. Non-violent passive resistance is effective as long as your opposition adheres to the same rules as you do. But if peaceful protest is met with violence, its efficacy is at an end. For me, non-violence was not a moral principle but a strategy; there is no moral goodness in using an ineffective weapon. But my thoughts on this matter were not yet formed, and I had spoken too soon.

That was certainly the view of the National Executive. When they learned of my speech, I was severely reprimanded for advocating such a radical departure from accepted policy. Although some on the Executive sympathized with my remarks, no one could support the intemperate way that I had made them. They admonished me, noting that the impulsive policy I had called for was not only premature but dangerous. Such speeches could provoke the enemy to crush the organization entirely while the enemy was strong and we were as yet still weak. I accepted the censure, and thereafter faithfully defended the policy of non-violence in public. But, in my heart, I knew that non-violence was not the answer.

In those days I was often in hot water with the Executive. In early 1953, Chief Luthuli, Z. K. Matthews and a handful of other high-ranking ANC leaders were invited to a meeting with a group of whites who were in the process of forming the Liberal Party. A meeting of the ANC Executive took place afterwards at which a few of us asked for a report of the earlier meeting with the white liberals. The participants refused, saying that they had been invited in their private capacity, not as members of the ANC. We continued to pester them, and finally Professor Matthews, who was a lawyer, said that it had been a privileged conversation. In a fit of indignation, I said, 'What kind of leaders are you who can discuss matters with a group of white liberals and then not share that information with your colleagues at the ANC? That's the trouble with you, you are scared and overawed of the white man. You value his company more than that of your African comrades.'

This outburst provoked the wrath of both Professor Matthews and Chief Luthuli. First, Professor Matthews responded: 'Mandela, what do you know about whites? I taught you whatever you know about whites and you are still ignorant. Even now, you are barely out of your student uniform.' Luthuli was burning with a cold fire and said, 'All right, if you are accusing me of being afraid of the white man, I have no other recourse but to resign. If that is what you say, then that is what I intend to do.' I did not know whether Luthuli was bluffing, but his threat frightened me. I had spoken hastily, without thinking, without a sense of responsibility, and I now greatly regretted it. I immediately withdrew my charge and apologized. I was a young man who attempted to make up for his ignorance with militancy.

*   *   *

At the same time as my speech in Sophiatown, Walter Sisulu informed me that he had been invited to attend the World Festival of Youth and Students for Peace and Friendship in Bucharest as a guest of honour. The timing of the invitation gave him virtually no opportunity to consult with the National Executive. I was keen that he should go and encouraged him to do so, whether or not he conferred with the Executive. Walter resolved to go, and I helped him to arrange for a substitute passport, an affidavit stating his identity and citizenship. (The government would never have issued him with a proper passport.) The group, which was headed by Walter Sisulu and Duma Nokwe, travelled on the only airline that would accept such an affidavit: El Al.

I was convinced, despite my reprimand from the Executive, that the policies of the Nationalists would soon make non-violence an even more limited and ineffective policy. Walter was privy to my thoughts and, before he left, I made a suggestion: he should arrange to visit the People's Republic of China and discuss with them the possibility of supplying us with weapons for an armed struggle. Walter liked the idea, and promised to make the attempt.

This action was taken purely on my own and my methods were highly unorthodox. To some extent, they were the actions of a hotheaded revolutionary who had not thought things through and who acted without discipline. They were the actions of a man frustrated with the immorality of apartheid and the ruthlessness of the state in protecting it.

Walter's visit caused a storm within the Executive. I undertook the task of personally conveying his apologies, without mentioning my secret request. Luthuli objected to the flouting of the ANC's code of conduct, and Professor Matthews expressed dismay about Walter visiting socialist countries. The Executive was sceptical about Walter's motives, and questioned my explanation of the circumstances. A few wanted to censure Walter and me formally, but in the end did not.

Walter managed to reach China, where the leadership received him warmly. They conveyed their support of our struggle, but they were wary and cautious when he broached the idea of an armed struggle. They warned him that this was an extremely grave undertaking, and they questioned whether the liberation movement had matured sufficiently to justify such an endeavour. Walter came back with encouragement but no guns.

18

In Johannesburg, I had become a man of the city. I wore smart suits, I drove a colossal Oldsmobile and I knew my way around the back alleys of the city. I commuted daily to a downtown office. But in fact I remained a country boy at heart, and there was nothing that lifted my spirits as much as blue skies, the open veld and green grass. In September, as my banning orders had ended, I decided to take advantage of my freedom and get some respite from the city. I took on a case in the little dorp of Villiers in the Orange Free State.

The drive to the Orange Free State from Johannesburg used to take several hours, and I set out from Orlando at 3 a.m, which has always been my favourite hour for departure. I am an early riser anyway, and at 3 a.m. the roads are empty and quiet, and one can be alone with one's thoughts. I like to see the coming of dawn, the change between day and night, which is always majestic. It was also a convenient hour for departure because the police were usually nowhere to be found.

The province of the Orange Free State has always had a magical effect on me, though some of the most racist elements of the white population call the Free State their home. With its flat dusty landscape as far as the eye can see, the great blue ceiling above, the endless stretches of yellow mealie fields, scrub and bushes, the Free State's landscape gladdens my heart no matter what my mood. When I am there I feel that nothing can shut me in, that my thoughts can roam as far and wide as the horizons.

The landscape bore the imprint of General Charles R. de Wet, the gifted Boer commander who outclassed the British in dozens of engagements during the final months of the Anglo-Boer war; fearless, proud and shrewd, he would have been one of my heroes had he been fighting for the rights of all South Africans, not just Afrikaners. He demonstrated the courage and resourcefulness of the underdog, and the power of a less sophisticated but patriotic army against a tested war machine. As I drove, I imagined the hiding places of General de Wet's army and wondered whether they would some day shelter African rebels.

The drive to Villiers cheered me considerably, and I was labouring under a false sense of security when I entered the small courthouse on the morning of 3 September. I found a group of policemen waiting for me. With nary a word, they served me with an order under the Suppression of Communism Act requiring me to resign from the ANC, restricting me to the Johannesburg district and prohibiting me from attending any meetings or gatherings for two years. I knew such measures would come, but I had not expected to receive my bans in the remote village of Villiers.

I was thirty-five, and these new and more severe bans ended a period of nearly a decade of involvement with the ANC, years that had been the time of my political awakening and growth, and my gradual commitment to the struggle that had become my life. Henceforth, all my actions and plans on behalf of the ANC and the liberation struggle would become secret and illegal. Once served, I had to return to Johannesburg immediately.

My bans drove me from the centre of the struggle to the sidelines, from a role that was primary to one that was peripheral. Though I was often consulted and was able to influence the direction of events, I did so at a distance and only when expressly asked. I no longer felt like a vital organ of the body – the heart, lung or backbone – but a severed limb. Even freedom fighters, at least then, had to obey the laws and, at that point, imprisonment for violating my bans would have been useless to the ANC and to myself. We were not yet at the point where we were open revolutionaries, overtly fighting the system no matter what the cost. We believed then that it was better to organize underground than to go to prison. When I was forced to resign from the ANC, the organization had to replace me, and no matter what I might have liked, I could no longer wield the authority I once possessed. While driving back to Johannesburg, the Free State scenery did not have quite the same elevating effect on me as before.

At the age of
nineteen, in Umtata,
Transkei. *(P. K. A.
Gaeshwe/Black Star)*

Oliver and I opened
the doors to our
office on Fox Street
in 1952; it was the
first black law
practice in
Johannesburg.
(Jurgen Schadeberg)

Opposite:
Under the
Suppression of
Communism Act,
bans became a
routine part of the
life of a freedom
fighter. *(Bailey's)*

Outside the
courtroom with Dr
James Moroka and
Yusuf Dadoo during
the Defiance
Campaign.
*(Jurgen Schadeberg/
Associated Press)*

With Patrick Moloa
and Robert Resha at
the Transvaal
Supreme Court after
receiving a nine-
month suspended
sentence. *(Jurgen
Schadeberg)*

Yusuf Dadoo, ex-president, SAIC.

Nelson Mandela, ex-president, Tvl. ANC.

James Phillips, ex-chairman, Tvl. CPAC.

Duma Nokwe, secretary, ANC Y.L.

Walter Sisulu, ex-secretary, ANC.

Albert Luthuli, president, ANC.

Yusuf Cachalia, secretary, SAIC.

John B. Marks, ex-president, Tvl. ANC.

Stephen Sello, ex-Tvl. acting secretary.

David Bopape, ex-secretary, Tvl. ANC.

Moses Kotane, ex-leader, ANC.

Dr. Z. Njongwe, ex-chairman, ANC.

Cassim Amra, ex-leader, Indian C.

Dr. Diliza Mji, ex-secretary, ANC.

Dr. Silas M. Molema, ex-treasurer, ANC.

Maulvi Cachalia, ex-secretary, Tvl. I.C.

The Effects of New Laws: 2

BANNED MEN

DURING the last few months, nearly all the non-White leaders in South Africa have been restricted in their movements and activities. Most of them have been called upon to resign their positions in the African National Congress or the South African Indian Congress. Many of them have been forbidden to attend any gatherings, or to enter certain magisterial districts in the Union.

Albert Luthuli, for instance,

president of the African National Congress, is forbidden to move away from his own district at Groutville, Natal. He cannot visit the shops in Durban, thirty miles away, or attend the cathedral there.

Most of the bans are in force for two years, after which time they may be renewed; some have already been renewed.

The bans take effect under the Suppression of Communism Act of 1950. This allows the Minister of Justice to pro-

hibit from gatherings or organisations anyone suspected of furthering the aims of Communism. 'Communism' is defined under the act as aiming to bring about social economic or political changes in the country.

Many of those convicted or 'named' under the Suppression of Communism Act are not 'Communists' in the usual sense of the term, but 'Statutory Communists' who come within the definition of the act.

J. Mavuso, ex-Transvaal ANC leader.

Nana Sitha, ex-president, Transvaal I.C.

Dan Tloome, ex-leader, ANC.

Flag Boshielo, ex-leader, Transvaal ANC.

N. Thandray, ex-Tvl. secretary, I.C.

Hosia Seperepere, ex-leader, ANC.

Frank Marquard, ex-president, Cape F.W.U.

Joseph Matthews, ex-president, ANC Y.L.

Robert Matji, ex-secretary, Cape ANC.

MacDon. Maseko, ex-leader, ANC.

Ismail Bhoola, ex-sec., Tvl. Indian YC.

Harrison Motlana, ex-secretary, Tvl. Y.L.

Dr Moroka, after handing over the presidency of the ANC to Chief Albert Luthuli. *(G. R. Naidoo/Bailey's)*

Chief Luthuli giving the "*Afrika*" salute to ANC delegates at the forty-first annual congress in Queenstown. *(Bob Gosani/Bailey's)*

With youth leader
Peter Nthite in 1955.
(Peter Magubane)

Under the Group
Areas Act, the vital
township of
Sophiatown was
declared a "black
spot"; removals to
Meadowlands were
scheduled to begin in
1955. *(Jurgen
Schadeberg)*

One of the lessons I took away from the failed Western Areas anti-removal campaign was that it is the oppressor who defines the nature of the struggle; in the end, we would have no alternative but to resort to an armed resistance. *(Jurgen Schadeberg)*

Speaking to a group of women during their march to Pretoria Union Buildings to protest the pass laws. *(Peter Magubane/Associated Press)*

Tense times. 1956
(Ian Berry/Magnum)

The Treason Trial,
1956. The accused
were bussed every day
from Johannesburg
to Pretoria. *(Peter
Magubane)*

We were forbidden from attending political gatherings of any kind, but so many leaders had been brought together for the Treason Trial that our afternoon breaks often felt like meetings of the National Executive Committee. *(Ian Berry/Magnum)*

Our supporters joined us in song outside the court in Pretoria, 1958. *(Peter Magubane)*

19

When I received my banning, the Transvaal conference of the ANC was due to be held the following month, and I had already completed the draft of my presidential address. It was read to the conference by Andrew Kunene, a member of the Executive. In that speech, which subsequently became known as 'The No Easy Walk to Freedom' speech, a line taken from Jawaharlal Nehru, I said that the masses now had to be prepared for new forms of political struggle. The new laws and tactics of the government had made the old forms of mass protest – public meetings, press statements, stay-aways – extremely dangerous and self-destructive. Newspapers would not publish our statements and printing presses refused to print our leaflets, all for fear of prosecution under the Suppression of Communism Act. 'These developments require the evolution of new forms of political struggle. The old methods,' I said, were now 'suicidal'.

'The oppressed people and the oppressors are at loggerheads. The day of reckoning between the forces of freedom and those of reaction is not very far off. I have not the slightest doubt that when that day comes truth and justice will prevail . . . The feelings of the oppressed people have never been more bitter. The grave plight of the people compels them to resist to the death the stinking policies of the gangsters that rule our country . . . To overthrow oppression has been sanctioned by humanity and is the highest aspiration of every free man.'

In April 1954 the Law Society of the Transvaal applied to the Supreme Court for my name to be struck off the roll of accredited attorneys on the ground that the political activities for which I was convicted in the Defiance case amounted to unprofessional and dishonourable conduct. This occurred at a time when the firm of Mandela and Tambo was flourishing and I was in court dozens of times a week.

The documents were served at my office, and as soon as the application against me had been made and publicized, I began to receive offers of support and help. I received offers of help even from a number of well-known Afrikaner lawyers. Many of these men were supporters of the Nationalist Party, but they believed that the application was biased and unfair. Their response suggested to me that even in racist South Africa professional solidarity can sometimes transcend colour, and that there were still attorneys and judges who refused to be the rubber stamps of an immoral regime.

My case was ably defended by advocate Walter Pollack, Q.C., chairman of the Johannesburg Bar Council. At the time that I retained Walter Pollack, I was advised that I should also retain someone who was not connected with the struggle, as that would positively influence the Transvaal Bar. To that end, we retained William Aaronsohn, as instructing attorney, who was head of one of the oldest law firms in Johannesburg. Both men acted for me without charge. We argued that the application was an affront to the idea of justice and that I had an inherent right to fight for my political beliefs, which was the right of all men in a state where the rule of law applied.

But the argument that had great weight was Pollack's use of the case of a man called Strijdorn, who was detained during the Second World War together with B.J. Vorster (who later became Prime Minister). Both were interned for their pro-Nazi stance. Following a failed escape attempt, Strijdorn had been found guilty of car theft. Later, after he was released, he applied to the Bar for admittance as an advocate. Despite his crimes, Pollack said, 'There are of course differences between Strijdom and Mandela. Mandela is not a Nationalist and Mandela is not a white.'

Judge Ramsbottom, who heard the case, was an example of a judge who refused to be a mouthpiece for the Nationalists and upheld the independence of the judiciary. His judgment in the case completely upheld our claim that I had a right to campaign for my political beliefs even though they were opposed to the government, and he dismissed the Law Society's application, and, in an unusual move, ordered the Law Society to pay its own costs.

20

The anti-removal campaign in Sophiatown was a long-running battle. We held our ground, as did the state. Throughout 1954 and into 1955, rallies were held twice a week, on Wednesday and Sunday evenings. Speaker after speaker continued to decry the government's plans. The ANC and the Ratepayers Association, under the direction of Dr Xuma, protested to the government in letters and petitions. We ran the anti-removal campaign on the slogan 'Over Our Dead Bodies', a motto often shouted from the platforms and echoed by the audience. One night it even roused the otherwise cautious Dr Xuma to utter the electrifying slogan used to rally African warriors to battle in the previous century: *'Zemk' inkomo magwalandini!'* ('The enemy has captured the cattle, you cowards!')

The government had scheduled the removal for 9 February 1955. As the day approached, Oliver Tambo and I were in the township daily, meeting local leaders, discussing plans and acting in our professional capacity for those being forced out of the area or prosecuted. We sought to prove to the court that the government's documentation was often incorrect and that many orders to leave were therefore illegal. But this was only a temporary measure; the government would not let a few illegalities stand in its way.

Shortly before the scheduled removal, a special mass meeting was planned for Freedom Square. Ten thousand people gathered to hear Chief Luthuli speak. But upon his arrival in Johannesburg he was served with a banning order that forced him to return to Natal.

The night before the removal, Joe Modise, one of the most dedicated of the local ANC leaders, addressed a tense meeting of more than five hundred youthful activists. They expected the ANC to give them an order to defy the police and the army. They were prepared to erect barricades overnight and engage the police with weapons and whatever came to hand the next day. They assumed our slogan meant what it said: that Sophiatown would be removed only over our dead bodies.

But after discussions with the ANC leadership, including myself, Joe told the youth to stand down. They were angry and felt betrayed. But we believed that violence would have been a disaster. We pointed out that an insurrection required careful planning or it would become an act of suicide. We were not yet ready to engage the enemy on its own terms.

In the hazy dawn hours of 9 February, four thousand police and army troops cordoned off the township while workers razed empty houses, and government trucks began moving families from Sophiatown to Meadowlands. The night before, the ANC had evacuated several families to prearranged accommodation with pro-ANC families in the interior of Sophiatown. But our efforts were too little and too late, and could be only a stopgap measure. The army and the police were relentlessly efficient. After a few weeks, our resistance collapsed. Most of our local leaders had been banned or arrested and, in the end, Sophiatown died not to the sound of gunfire but to the sound of rumbling trucks and sledgehammers.

One can always be correct about a political action one is reading about in the next day's newspaper, but when you are in the centre of a heated political fight, you are given little time for reflection. We made a variety of mistakes in the Western Areas anti-removal campaign and learned a number of lessons. 'Over Our Dead Bodies' was a dynamic slogan, but it proved as much a hindrance as a help. A slogan is a vital link between the organization and the masses it seeks to lead. It should synthesize a particular grievance into a succinct and pithy phrase, while mobilizing the people to combat it. Our slogan caught the imagination of the people, but it led them to believe that we would fight to the death to resist the removal. In fact, the ANC was not prepared to do that at all.

We never provided the people with an alternative to moving to Meadowlands. When the people in Sophiatown realized we could neither stop the government nor provide the tenants with housing elsewhere, their own resistance waned and the flow of people to Meadowlands increased. Many tenants moved willingly, for they found they would have more space and cleaner housing in Meadowlands. We did not take into account the different situations of landlords and tenants. While the landlords had reasons to stay, many tenants had an incentive to leave. The ANC was criticized by a number of Africanist members who accused the leadership of protecting the interests of the landlords at the expense of the tenants.

The lesson I took away from the campaign was that, in the end, we had no alternative to armed and violent resistance. Over and over again, we had used all the non-violent weapons in our arsenal – speeches, deputations, threats, marches, strikes, stay-aways, voluntary imprisonment – all to no avail, for whatever we did was met by an iron hand. A freedom fighter learns the hard way that it is the oppressor who defines the nature of the struggle, and the oppressed is often left no recourse but to use methods that mirror those of the oppressor. At a certain point, one can only fight fire with fire.

Education is the great engine of personal development. It is through education that the daughter of a peasant can become a doctor, that the son of a mineworker can become the head of the mine, that a child of farmworkers can become the president of a great nation. It is what we make out of what we have, not what we are given, that separates one person from another.

Since the turn of the century, Africans owed their educational opportunities primarily to the foreign churches and missions that created and sponsored schools. Under the United Party, the syllabus for African secondary schools and white secondary schools was essentially the same. The mission schools provided Africans with Western-style English-language education, which I myself received. We were limited by lesser facilities, but not by what we could read or think or dream.

Yet even before the Nationalists came to power, the disparities in funding tell a story of racist education. The government spent about six times as much per white student as per African student. Education was not compulsory for Africans and was free only in the primary grades. Fewer than half of all African children of school age attended any school at all, and only a tiny number of Africans received high school certificates.

Even this amount of education proved distasteful to the Nationalists. The Afrikaner has always been unenthusiastic about education for Africans. To him it was simply a waste, for the African was inherently ignorant and lazy and no amount of education could remedy that. The Afrikaner was traditionally hostile to Africans learning English, for English was a foreign tongue to the Afrikaner and the language of emancipation to us.

In 1953 the Nationalist-dominated Parliament passed the Bantu Education Act, which sought to put apartheid's stamp on African education. The act transferred control of African education from the Department of Education to the much loathed Native Affairs Department. Under the act, African primary and secondary schools operated by Church and mission bodies were given the choice of turning over their schools to the government or receiving gradually diminished subsidies; either the government took over education for Africans or there would be no education for Africans. African teachers were not permitted to criticize the government or any school authority. It was intellectual *baasskap*, a way of institutionalizing inferiority.

Dr Hendrik Verwoerd, the minister of Bantu Education, explained that education 'must train and teach people in accordance with their opportunities in life.' His meaning was that Africans did not and would not have any opportunities; therefore, why educate them? 'There is no place for the Bantu in the European community above the level of certain forms of labour,' he said. In short, Africans should be trained to be menial workers, to be in a position of perpetual subordination to the white man.

To the ANC, the act was a deeply sinister measure designed to retard the progress of African culture as a whole and, if enacted, permanently set back the freedom struggle of the African people. The mental outlook of all future generations of Africans was at stake. As Professor Matthews wrote at the time, 'Education for ignorance and for inferiority in Verwoerd's schools is worse than no education at all.'

The act and Verwoerd's crude exposition of it aroused widespread indignation from both black and white. With the exception of the Dutch Reformed Church, which supported apartheid, and the Lutheran mission, all Christian churches opposed the new measure. But the unity of the opposition extended only to condemning the policy, not resisting it. The Anglicans, the most fearless and consistent critics of the new policy, were divided. Bishop Ambrose Reeves of Johannesburg took the extreme step of closing his schools, which had a total enrolment of ten thousand children. But the archbishop of the church in South Africa, anxious to keep children off the streets, handed over the rest of the schools to the government. Despite their protests, all the other churches did the same with the exception of the Roman Catholics, the Seventh Day Adventists, and the United Jewish Reformed Congregation – who soldiered on without state aid. Even my own Church, the Wesleyan, handed over their two hundred thousand African students to the government. If all the other Churches had followed the example of those who resisted, the government would have been confronted with a stalemate that might have forced a compromise. Instead, the state marched over us.

The transfer of control to the Native Affairs Department was set to take place on 1 April 1955, and the ANC began to discuss plans for a school boycott that would begin on that date. Our secret discussions in the Executive turned on whether we should call on the people to stage a protest for a limited period or whether we should proclaim a permanent school boycott to destroy the Bantu Education Act before it could take root. The discussions were fierce, and both sides had forceful advocates. The argument for an indefinite boycott was that Bantu Education was a poison one could not drink even at the point of death from thirst. To accept it in any form would cause irreparable damage. They argued that the country was in an explosive mood and the people were hungry for something more spectacular than a mere protest.

Although I had the reputation of being a firebrand, I always felt that the organization should never promise to do more than it was able, for the people would then lose confidence in it. I took the stance that our actions should be based not on idealistic considerations but on practical ones. An indefinite boycott would require massive machinery and vast resources that we did not possess, and our past campaigns showed no indication that we were capable of such an undertaking. It was simply impossible for us to create our own schools fast enough to accommodate hundreds of thousands of pupils, and if we did not offer our people an alternative, we were offering next to nothing. Along with others, I urged a week's boycott.

The National Executive resolved that a week-long school boycott should begin on 1 April. This was recommended at the annual conference in Durban in December 1954, but the delegates rejected the recommendation and voted for an indefinite boycott. The conference was the supreme authority, even greater than the Executive, and we found ourselves saddled with a boycott that would be almost impossible to effect. Dr Verwoerd announced that the government would permanently close all schools that were boycotted and that children who stayed away would not be readmitted.

For this boycott to work, the parents and the community would have to step in and take the place of the schools. I spoke to parents and ANC members and told them that every home, every shack, every community structure, must become a centre of learning for our children.

The boycott began on 1 April and had mixed results. It was often sporadic, disorganized and ineffectual. On the east Rand it affected some seven thousand schoolchildren. Pre-dawn marches called on parents to keep their children at home. Women picketed the schools and plucked out children who had wandered into them.

In Germiston, a township southeast of the city, Joshua Makue, chairman of our local branch, ran a school for eight hundred boycotting children that lasted for three years. In Port Elizabeth, Barrett Tyesi gave up a government teaching post and ran a school for boycotting children. In 1956, he presented seventy of these children for the Standard VI exams; all but three passed. In many places, improvised schools (described as 'cultural clubs' in order not to attract the attention of the authorities) taught boycotting students. The government subsequently passed a law that made it an offence punishable by fine or imprisonment to offer unauthorized education. Police harassed these clubs, but many continued to exist underground. In the end, the community schools withered away and parents, faced with a choice between inferior education and no education at all, chose the former. My own children were at the Seventh Day Adventist school, which was private and did not depend on government subsidies.

The campaign should be judged on two levels: whether the immediate objective was achieved, and whether it politicized more people and drew them into the struggle. On the first level, the campaign clearly failed. We did not close down African schools throughout the country, neither did we rid ourselves of the Bantu Education Act. But the government was sufficiently rattled by our protest to modify the act, and at one point Verwoerd was compelled to declare that education should be the same for all. The government's November 1954 draft syllabus was a retreat from the original notion of modelling the school system on tribal foundations. In the end we had no option but to choose between the lesser of two evils, and agree to a diminished education. But the consequences of Bantu Education came back to haunt the government in unforeseen ways. For it was Bantu Education that produced in the 1970s the angriest, most rebellious generation of black youth the country had ever seen. When these children of Bantu Education entered their late teens and early twenties, they rose with a vehemence.

Several months after Chief Luthuli was elected president of the ANC, Professor Z. K. Matthews returned to South Africa after a year as a visiting professor in the US, armed with an idea that would reshape the liberation struggle. In a speech at the ANC annual conference in the Cape, he said: 'I wonder whether the time has not come for the African National Congress to consider the question of convening a national convention, a congress of the people, representing all the people of this country irrespective of race or colour, to draw up a Freedom Charter for the democratic South Africa of the future.'

Within months the ANC national conference accepted the proposal, and a Council of the Congress of the People was created, with Chief Luthuli as chairman and Walter Sisulu and Yusuf Cachalia as joint secretaries. The Congress of the People was to create a set of principles for the foundation of a new South Africa. Suggestions for a new constitution were to come from the people themselves, and ANC leaders all across the country were authorized to seek ideas in writing from everyone in their area. The charter would be a document born of the people.

The Congress of the People represented one of the two main currents of thought operating within the organization. It seemed inevitable that the government would ban the ANC, and many argued that the organization must be prepared to operate underground and illegally. At the same time, we did not want to give up the important public policies and activities that brought the ANC attention and mass support. The Congress of the People would be a public display of strength.

Our dream for the Congress of the People was that it would be a landmark event in the history of the freedom struggle – a convention uniting all the oppressed and all the progressive forces of South Africa to create a clarion call for change. Our hope was that it would one day be looked upon with the same reverence as the founding convention of the ANC in 1912.

We sought to attract the widest possible sponsorship and invited some two hundred organizations – white, black, Indian and Coloured – to send representatives to a planning conference at Tongaat, near Durban, in March 1954. The National Action Council created there was composed of eight members from each of the four sponsoring organizations. The chairman was Chief Luthuli, and the secretariat consisted of Walter Sisulu (later replaced by Oliver after Walter's banning forced him to resign), Yusuf Cachalia of the SAIC, Stanley Lollan of the South African Coloured People's Organization (SACPO) and Lionel Bernstein of the Congress of Democrats (COD).

Formed in Cape Town in September 1953 by Coloured leaders and trade unionists, SACPO was the belated offspring of the struggle to preserve the Coloured vote in the Cape and it sought to represent Coloured interests. SACPO's founding conference was addressed by Oliver Tambo and Yusuf Cachalia. Inspired by the Defiance Campaign, the COD was formed in late 1952 as a party for radical, left-wing, anti-government whites. The COD, though small and limited mainly to Johannesburg and Cape Town, had an influence disproportionate to its numbers. Its members, such as Michael Harmel, Bram Fischer and Rusty Bernstein, were eloquent advocates of our cause. The COD closely identified itself with the ANC and the SAIC and advocated a universal franchise and full equality between black and white. We saw the COD as a means whereby our views could be put directly to the white public. The COD served an important symbolic function for Africans; blacks who had come into the struggle because they were anti-white discovered that there were indeed whites of goodwill who treated Africans as equals.

The National Action Council invited all participating organizations and their followers to send suggestions for a freedom charter. Circulars were sent out to townships and villages all across the country. 'IF YOU COULD MAKE THE LAWS . . . WHAT WOULD YOU DO?' they said. 'HOW WOULD YOU SET ABOUT MAKING SOUTH AFRICA A HAPPY PLACE FOR ALL THE PEOPLE WHO LIVE

IN IT?' Some of the flyers and leaflets were filled with the poetic idealism that characterized the planning:

WE CALL THE PEOPLE OF SOUTH AFRICA BLACK AND WHITE – LET US SPEAK TOGETHER OF FREEDOM! – LET THE VOICES OF ALL THE PEOPLE BE HEARD. AND LET THE DEMANDS OF ALL THE PEOPLE FOR THE THINGS THAT WILL MAKE US FREE BE RECORDED. LET THE DEMANDS BE GATHERED TOGETHER IN A GREAT CHARTER OF FREEDOM.

The call caught the imagination of the people. Suggestions came in from sports and cultural clubs, church groups, ratepayers' associations, women's organizations, schools, trade union branches. They came on serviettes, on paper torn from exercise books, on scraps of foolscap, on the backs of our own leaflets. It was humbling to see how the suggestions of ordinary people were often far ahead of those of the leaders. The most commonly cited demand was for one-man-one-vote. There was a recognition that the country belongs to all those who have made it their home.

The ANC branches contributed a great deal to the process of writing the charter and in fact the two best drafts came from Durban and Pietermaritzburg. A combination of these drafts was then circulated to different regions and committees for comments and questions. The charter itself was drafted by a small committee of the National Action Council and reviewed by the ANC's National Executive.

The charter would be presented at the Congress of the People and each of its elements submitted to the delegates for approval. In June, a few days before the Congress was scheduled, a small group of us reviewed the draft. We made few changes, as there was little time and the document was already in good shape.

The Congress of the People took place at Kliptown, a multiracial village on a scrap of veld a few miles southwest of Johannesburg, on two clear, sunny days, 25 and 26 June 1955. More than three thousand delegates braved police intimidation to assemble and approve the final document. They came by car, bus, truck and foot. Although the overwhelming number of delegates were black, there were more than three hundred Indians, two hundred Coloureds and one hundred whites.

I drove to Kliptown with Walter. We were both under banning orders, so we found a place at the edge of the crowd where we could observe without mixing in or being seen. The crowd was impressive both in size and in its discipline. 'Freedom volunteers' wearing black, green and yellow armbands met the delegates and arranged for their seating. There were old women and young wearing Congress skirts, Congress blouses, Congress *doekies* (scarves); old men and young wearing Congress armbands and Congress hats. Signs everywhere said, 'FREEDOM IN OUR LIFETIME, LONG LIVE THE STRUGGLE'. The platform was a rainbow of colours: white delegates from the COD, Indians from the SAIC, Coloured representatives from SACPO all sat in front of a replica of a four-spoked wheel representing the four organizations in the Congress Alliance. White and African police and members of the Special Branch milled around, taking photographs, writing in notebooks and trying unsuccessfully to intimidate the delegates.

There were dozens of songs and speeches. Meals were served. The atmosphere was both serious and festive. On the afternoon of the first day, the charter was read aloud, section by section, to the people in English, Sesotho and Xhosa. After each section, the crowd shouted its approval with cries of '*Afrika!*' and '*Mayibuye!*' The first day of the Congress was a success.

The second day was much like the first. Each section of the charter had been adopted by acclamation, and at 3.30 the final approval was to be voted when a brigade of police and Special Branch detectives brandishing sten guns swarmed on to the platform. In a gruff Afrikaans-accented voice, one of the police took the microphone and announced that treason was suspected and that no one was to leave the gathering without police permission. The police began pushing people off the platform and confiscating documents and photographs, even signs such as 'SOUP WITH MEAT' and 'SOUP WITHOUT MEAT'. Another group of constables armed with rifles formed a cordon round the crowd. The people responded magnificently by loudly singing '*Nkosi Sikelel' iAfrika*'. The delegates were then allowed to leave one by one, each person interviewed by the police and his or her name taken down. I had been on the outskirts of the crowd when the police raid began, and while my instinct was to stay and help, discretion seemed the wiser course, because I would have immediately been arrested and tossed into jail. An emergency meeting had been called in Johannesburg, and I made my way back there. As I returned to Johannesburg, I knew that this raid signalled a harsh new turn on the part of the government.

Though the Congress of the People had been broken up, the charter itself became a great beacon for the liberation struggle. Like other enduring political documents, such as the American Declaration of Independence, the French Declaration of the Rights of Man and the

Communist Manifesto, the Freedom Charter is a mixture of practical goals and poetic language. It extols the abolition of racial discrimination and the achievement of equal rights for all. It welcomes all who embrace freedom to participate in the making of a democratic, non-racial South Africa. It captured the hopes and dreams of the people and acted as a blueprint for the liberation struggle and the future of the nation. The preamble reads:

> We, the people of South Africa, declare for all our country and the world to know: —
>
> That South Africa belongs to all who live in it, black and white, and that no government can justly claim authority unless it is based on the will of the people;
>
> That our people have been robbed of their birthright to land, liberty and peace by a form of government founded on injustice and inequality;
>
> That our country will never be prosperous or free until all our people live in brotherhood, enjoying equal rights and opportunities;
>
> That only a democratic state, based on the will of the people, can secure to all their birthright without distinction of colour, race, sex or belief;
>
> And therefore, we, the people of South Africa, black and white, together – equals, countrymen and brothers – adopt this FREEDOM CHARTER. And we pledge ourselves to strive together, sparing nothing of our strength and courage, until the democratic changes here set out have been won.

The charter then lays out the requirements for a free and democratic South Africa.

THE PEOPLE SHALL GOVERN!

> Every man and woman shall have the right to vote for and stand as a candidate for all bodies which make laws;
>
> All the people shall be entitled to take part in the administration of the country;
>
> The rights of the people shall be the same regardless of race, colour or sex;
>
> All bodies of minority rule, advisory boards, councils and authorities shall be replaced by democratic organs of self-government.

ALL NATIONAL GROUPS SHALL HAVE EQUAL RIGHTS!

There shall be equal status in the bodies of state, in the courts and in the schools for all national groups and races;

All national groups shall be protected by law against insults to their race and national pride;

All people shall have equal rights to use their own language and to develop their own folk culture and customs;

The preaching and practice of national, race or colour discrimination and contempt shall be a punishable crime;

All apartheid laws and practices shall be set aside.

THE PEOPLE SHALL SHARE IN THE COUNTRY'S WEALTH!

The national wealth of our country, the heritage of all South Africans, shall be restored to the people;

The mineral wealth beneath the soil, the banks and monopoly industry shall be transferred to the ownership of the people as a whole;

All other industries and trade shall be controlled to assist the well-being of the people;

All people shall have equal rights to trade where they choose, to manufacture and to enter all trades, crafts and professions.

THE LAND SHALL BE SHARED AMONG THOSE WHO WORK IT!

Restriction of land ownership on racial basis shall be ended, and all the land re-divided amongst those who work it, to banish famine and land hunger . . .

Some in the ANC, particularly the Africanist contingent who were anti-communist and anti-white, objected to the charter as being a design for a radically different South Africa from the one the ANC had called for throughout its history. They claimed the charter favoured a socialist order and believed the COD and white communists had had a disproportionate influence on its ideology. In June 1956, in the monthly journal *Liberation*, I pointed out that the charter endorsed private enterprise and would allow capitalism to flourish among Africans for the first time. The charter guaranteed that when freedom came, Africans would have the opportunity to own their own businesses in their own names, to own their own houses and property; in short, to prosper as capitalists and entrepreneurs. The charter does not speak about the eradication of classes and private property, or public ownership of the means of production, or promulgate any of the tenets of scientific socialism. The clause discussing the possible nationalization of the mines, the banks and monopoly industries was an action that needed to be taken if the economy was not to be solely owned and operated by white businessmen.

The charter was in fact a revolutionary document precisely because the changes it envisioned could not be achieved without radically altering the economic and political structure of South Africa. It was not meant to be capitalist or socialist but a melding together of the people's demands to end the oppression. In South Africa, merely to achieve fairness, one had to destroy apartheid itself, for it was the very embodiment of injustice.

21

In early September 1955, my bans expired. I had last had a holiday in 1948 when I was an untested lightweight in the ANC with few responsibilities beyond attending meetings of the Transvaal executive and addressing the odd public gathering. Now, at the age of thirty-eight, I had reached the light heavyweight division and carried more pounds and more responsibility. I had been confined to Johannesburg for two years, chained to my legal and political work, and had neglected Mandela family affairs in the Transkei. I was keen to visit the countryside again, to be in the open veld and rolling valleys of my childhood. I was anxious to see my family and confer with Sabata and Daliwonga on certain problems involving the Transkei, while the ANC was eager that I confer with them on political matters. I was to have a working holiday, the only kind of holiday I knew how to take.

The night before I left, a number of friends gathered at my home to see me off. Duma Nokwe, the young and good-natured barrister who was then national secretary of the Youth League, was among them. Duma had accompanied Walter on his trip to the Youth Festival in Bucharest, and that night he entertained us with the Russian and Chinese songs he had learned on his trip. At midnight, as my guests were getting ready to leave, my daughter Makaziwe, then two, woke up and asked if she could come along with me. I had been spending insufficient time with my family, and Makaziwe's request provoked pangs of guilt. Suddenly my enthusiasm for my trip vanished. But I carried her back to bed and kissed her good night and, as she dropped off to sleep, I made my final preparations for my journey.

I was embarking on a fact-finding mission, which I would combine with the pleasures of seeing the countryside and old friends and comrades. I had been isolated from developments in other parts of the country and was eager to see for myself what was transpiring in the hinterlands. Although I read a variety of newspapers from around the country, newspapers are only a poor shadow of reality; their information is important to a freedom fighter not because it reveals the truth, but because it discloses the biases and perceptions of both those who produce the paper and those who read it. On this trip I wanted to talk first hand with our people in the field.

I left shortly after midnight and within an hour I was on the highway to Durban. The roads were empty and I was accompanied only by the stars and gentle Transvaal breezes. Though I had not slept, I felt lighthearted and fresh. At daybreak I crossed from Volksrust to Natal, the country of Cetywayo, the last independent king of the Zulus, whose troops had defeated a British column at Isandhlwana in 1879. But the king was unable to withstand the firepower of the British and eventually surrendered his kingdom. Shortly after crossing the river on the Natal border I saw the Majuba Hills, the steep escarpment where a small Boer commando ambushed and defeated a garrison of British redcoats less than two years after the defeat of Cetywayo. At Majuba Hill the Afrikaner had stoutly defended his independence against British imperialism and struck a blow for nationalism. Now the descendants of those same freedom fighters were persecuting my people who were struggling for precisely the same thing the Afrikaners had once fought and died for. I drove through those historic hills, thinking less of the ironies of history by which the oppressed becomes the oppressor than of how the ruthless Afrikaners deserved their own Majuba Hill at the hands of my people.

This harsh reverie was interrupted by the happy music of Radio Bantu on my car radio. While I despised the conservative politics of Radio Bantu served up by the government-run South African Broadcasting Corporation, I revelled in its music. (In South Africa, African artists made the music, but white record companies made the money.) I was listening to a popular programme called 'Rediffusion Service', which featured most of the country's leading African singers: Miriam Makeba, Dolly Rathebe, Dorothy Masuku, Thoko Shukuma and the smooth sound of the Manhattan Brothers. I enjoy all types of music, but the music of my own flesh and blood goes right to my heart. The curious beauty of African music is that it uplifts even as it tells a sad tale. You may be poor, you may have only a ramshackle house, you may have lost your job, but that song gives you hope. African music is often about the aspirations of the African people, and it can ignite the political resolve of those who might otherwise be indifferent to politics. One merely has to witness the infectious singing at African rallies. Politics can be strengthened by music, but music has a potency that defies politics.

I made a number of stops in Natal, secretly meeting ANC leaders. Nearing Durban, I took the opportunity of stopping in Pietermaritzburg, where I spent the entire night with Dr Chota Motala, Moses Mabhida and others, reviewing the political situation in the country. I then travelled on to Groutville, spending the day with Chief Luthuli. Although he had been confined by banning orders for more than a year, the chief was well informed about ANC activities. He was uneasy about what he saw as the increasing centralization of the ANC in Johannesburg and the declining power of the regions. I reassured him that we wanted the regions to remain strong.

My next stop was a meeting in Durban with Dr Naicker and the Executive Committee of the Natal Indian Congress, where I raised a sensitive issue: the National Executive believed that the Indian Congress had become inactive of late. I was reluctant to do this as Dr Naicker was my senior and a man who had suffered far more than I, but we discussed ways to overcome government restrictions.

From Durban I drove south along the coast past Port Shepstone and Port St Johns, small and lovely colonial towns that dotted the shimmering beaches fronting the Indian Ocean. While mesmerized by the beauty of the area, I was constantly rebuked by the buildings and streets that bear the names of white imperialists who suppressed the very people whose names belonged there. At this point, I turned inland and drove to Umzumkulu to meet with Dr Conco, the treasurer-general of the ANC, for further discussions and consultations.

With excitement mounting, I then set off for Umtata. When I turned into York Road, the main street of Umtata, I felt the rush of familiarity and fond memories one gets from coming home after a long exile. I had been away for thirteen years, and while there were no banners and fatted calves to greet this prodigal son upon his return, I was tremendously excited to see my mother, my humble home and the friends of my youth. But my trip to the Transkei had a second motive: my arrival coincided with the meeting of a special committee appointed to oversee the transition of the Transkeian Bungha system to that of the Bantu Authorities.

The role of the Bungha, which consisted of 108 members, one-quarter of whom were white and three-quarters African, was to advise the government on legislation affecting Africans in the area and to regulate local matters like taxes and roads. While the Bungha was the most influential political body in the Transkei, its resolutions were advisory and its decisions subject to review by white magistrates. The Bungha was only as powerful as whites permitted it to be. Yet the Bantu Authorities Act would replace it with an even more repressive system: a feudalistic order resting on hereditary and tribal distinctions as decided by the state. The government suggested that Bantu Authorities would free the people from the control of white magistrates, but this was a smokescreen for the state's undermining of democracy and promotion of tribal rivalries. The

ANC regarded any acceptance of Bantu Authorities as a capitulation to the government.

On the night of my arrival, I briefly met a number of Transkeian councillors and my nephew, K. D. Matanzima, whom I called Daliwonga. Daliwonga was playing a leading part in persuading the Bungha to accept Bantu Authorities, for the new order would reinforce and even increase his power as the chief of Emigrant Thembuland. Daliwonga and I were on separate sides of this difficult issue. We had grown apart: he had opted for a traditional leadership role and was cooperating with the system. But it was late and, rather than begin a lengthy discussion, we resolved to meet the following day.

I spent that night in a boarding-house in town, rose early, and was joined for coffee in my room by two local chiefs to discuss their role in the new Bantu Authorities. In the middle of our conversation the owner of the boarding-house nervously ushered a white man into my room. 'Are you Nelson Mandela?' he demanded.

'And who is asking?' I said.

He gave his name and rank as a detective sergeant in the security police.

'May I see your warrant, please?' I asked. It was obvious that the sergeant resented my audacity, but he grudgingly produced an official document. Yes, I was Nelson Mandela, I told him. He informed me that the commanding officer wanted to see me. I replied that if he wanted to see me, he knew where I was. He then ordered me to accompany him to the police station. I asked him whether I was under arrest, and he replied that I was not.

'In that case,' I said, 'I am not going.' He was taken aback by my refusal but knew I was on firm legal ground. He proceeded to fire a succession of questions at me: when had I left Johannesburg? Where had I visited? Whom had I spoken with? Did I have a permit to enter the Transkei and how long would I be staying? I informed him that the Transkei was my home and that I did not need a permit to enter it. The sergeant stomped out of the room.

The chiefs were taken aback by my behaviour and upbraided me for my rudeness. I explained that I had merely treated him in the manner that he had treated me. The chiefs were unconvinced, and clearly thought I was a hotheaded young man who would get himself into trouble. These were men I was trying to persuade to reject Bantu Authorities, and it was apparent that I had not made a very good impression. The incident reminded me that I had returned to my homeland a different man from the one who had left thirteen years before.

The police were unsophisticated in the Transkei, and from the moment

I left the boarding-house, they followed me everywhere I went. After I talked to anyone, the police would confront the person and say, 'If you talk with Mandela, we will come and arrest you.'

I met briefly with a local ANC leader and was dismayed to learn of the organization's lack of funds, but at that moment I was thinking less about the organization than my next stop: Qunu, the village where I was brought up and where my mother still lived.

I roused my mother, who at first looked as though she was seeing a ghost. But she was overjoyed. I had brought some food – fruit, meat, sugar, salt and a chicken – and my mother lit the stove to make tea. We did not hug or kiss; that was not our custom. Although I was happy to be back, I felt a sense of guilt at the sight of her living all alone in such poor circumstances. I tried to persuade her to come to live with me in Johannesburg, but she swore that she would not leave the countryside she loved. I wondered – not for the first time – whether one was ever justified in neglecting the welfare of one's own family in order to fight for the welfare of others. Can there be anything more important than looking after one's ageing mother? Is politics merely a pretext for shirking one's responsibilities, an excuse for not being able to provide in the way one wanted?

After an hour or so with my mother, I left to spend the night at Mqhekezweni. It was night when I arrived, and in my enthusiasm I started to blow the horn of my car. I had not considered how this noise might be interpreted, and people emerged fearfully from their huts, thinking it might be the police. But when I was recognized, I was met with surprise and joy by a number of villagers.

But instead of sleeping like a child in my old bed, I tossed and turned that night, again wondering whether or not I had taken the right path. I did not doubt that I had chosen correctly. I do not mean to suggest that the freedom struggle is of a higher moral order than taking care of one's family. It is not; they are merely different.

Returning to Qunu the next morning, I spent the day reminiscing with people, and walking in the fields around the village. I also visited my sister Mabel, the most practical and easygoing of my sisters and of whom I was very fond. Mabel was married, but her union involved an interesting tale. My sister Baliwe, who was older than Mabel, had been engaged to be married, and *lobola* had already been paid. But two weeks before the wedding, Baliwa, who was a spirited girl, ran away. We could not return the cattle as they had already been accepted, so the family decided that Mabel would take Baliwe's place, and she did so.

I left late that afternoon to drive to Mqhekezweni. Again I arrived at night and announced my presence with loud hooting, only this time people emerged from their homes with the idea that Justice, their chief, had returned. Justice had been deposed from his chieftancy by the government and was then living in Durban. Though the government had appointed someone in his stead, a chief is a chief by virtue of his birth and wields authority because of his blood. They were happy to see me, but they would have been happier still to welcome Justice home.

My second mother, No-England, the widow of the regent, had been fast asleep when I arrived, but when she appeared in her nightdress and saw me, she became so excited that she insisted I drive her immediately to a nearby relative to celebrate. She hopped into my car and we set off on a wild ride through the untamed veld to get to the remote rondavel of her relative. There we woke up another family, and I finally went to sleep, tired and happy, just before dawn.

Over the next fortnight I moved back and forth between Qunu and Mqhekezweni, staying by turns with my mother and No-England, visiting and receiving friends and relatives. I ate the same foods I had eaten as a boy, I walked the same fields and gazed at the same sky during the day, the same stars at night. It is important for a freedom fighter to remain in touch with his own roots, and the hurly-burly of city life has a way of erasing the past. The visit restored me and revived my feelings for the place in which I grew up. I was once again my mother's son in her house; I was once again the regent's charge in the Great Place.

The visit was also a way of measuring the distance I had come. I saw how my own people had remained in one place, while I had moved on and seen new worlds and gained new ideas. If I had not realized it before, I knew that I was right not to have returned to the Transkei after Fort Hare. If I had returned, my political evolution would have been stunted.

When the Special Committee considering the introduction of the Bantu Authorities had adjourned, Daliwonga and I went to visit Sabata in hospital in Umtata. I had hoped to talk with Sabata about the Bantu Authorities, but his health made it impossible. I wanted Sabata and his brother, Daliwonga, to begin talks on this issue as soon as Sabata was well enough, and made this clear. I felt proud to be organizing a meeting between the descendants of Ngubengcuka, and mused for a moment on the irony that I was finally fulfilling the role of counsellor to Sabata for which I'd been groomed so many years before.

From Umtata, Daliwonga and I drove to Qamata, where we met his younger brother George, who was then a practising attorney. His two articled clerks were well known to me and I was pleased to see them both: A. P. Mda and Tsepo Letlaka. Both were still firm supporters of the organization who had given up teaching and decided to become lawyers.

In Qamata, we all sat down to examine the issue of the proposed Bantu Authorities.

My mission was to persuade Daliwonga – a man destined to play a leading role in the politics of the Transkei – to oppose the imposition of the Bantu Authorities. I did not want our meeting to be a showdown, or even a debate; I did not want any grandstanding or fault-finding, but a serious discussion among men who all had the best interests of their people and their nation at heart.

In many ways, Daliwonga still regarded me as his junior, both in terms of my rank in the Thembu hierarchy and in my own political development. While I was his junior in the former realm, I believed I had advanced beyond my one-time mentor in my political views. Whereas his concerns focused on his own tribe, I had become involved with those who thought in terms of the entire nation. I did not want to complicate the discussion by introducing grand political theories; I would rely on common sense and the facts of our history. Before we began, Daliwonga invited Mda, Letlaka and his brother George, to participate, but they demurred, preferring to listen to the two of us. 'Let the nephew and the uncle conduct the debate,' Mda said as a sign of respect. Etiquette dictated that I would make my case first and Daliwonga would not interrupt; then he would answer while I listened.

In the first place, I said, the Bantu Authorities were impractical because more and more Africans were moving out of the rural homelands to the cities. The government's policy was to try to put Africans into ethnic enclaves because they feared the power of African unity. The people, I said, wanted democracy, and political leadership based on merit not birth. The Bantu Authorities was a retreat from democracy.

Daliwonga's response was that he was trying to restore the status of his royal house that had been crushed by the British. He stressed the importance and vitality of the tribal system and traditional leadership, and did not want to reject a system that enshrined those things. He, too, wanted a free South Africa but he thought that goal could be achieved faster and more peacefully through the government's policy of separate development. The ANC, he said, would bring about bloodshed and bitterness. He ended by saying that he was startled and disturbed to learn that in spite of my own position in the Thembu royal house I did not support the principle of traditional leadership.

When Daliwonga finished, I replied that while I understood his personal position as a chief quite well, I believed that his own interests were in conflict with those of the community. I said that if I were in a similar position to his, I would try to subordinate my own interests to those of the people. I immediately regretted that last point because I have discovered that in discussions it never helps to take a morally superior tone to one's opponent. I noticed that Daliwonga stiffened when I made this remark and I quickly shifted the discussion to more general issues.

We talked the whole night, but came no closer to each other's position. As the sun was rising, we parted. We had embarked on different roads that put us in conflict with one another. This grieved me, because few men had inspired me as Daliwonga had, and nothing would have given me greater joy than to fight beside him. But it was not to be. On family issues, we remained friends; politically, we were in opposite and antagonistic camps.

I returned to Qunu that morning and spent another few days there. I tramped across the veld to visit friends and relatives, but the magic world of my childhood had fled. One evening I bade my mother and sister farewell. I visited Sabata in hospital to wish him a speedy recovery, and by 3 a.m. I was on my way to Cape Town. The bright moonlight and crisp breeze kept me fresh all the way across the Kei River. The road winds up the rugged mountains and as the sun rose my mood lifted. I had last been on that road eighteen years before, when Jongintaba had driven me to Healdtown.

I was driving slowly when I noticed a limping man at the side of the road raising his hand to me. I instinctively pulled over and offered him a ride. He was about my own age, of small stature and rather unkempt; he had not bathed in quite a while. He told me that his car had broken down on the other side of Umtata and he had been walking for several days towards Port Elizabeth. I noticed a number of inconsistencies in his story, and I asked him the make of his car. A Buick, he replied. And the registration? I said. He told me a number. A few minutes later, I said, 'What did you say that registration number was?' He told me a slightly different figure. I suspected he was a policeman, and decided to say very little.

My reserve went unnoticed by my companion as he talked the entire way to Port Elizabeth. He pointed out various curiosities and was well versed in the history of the region. He never asked who I was and I did not tell him. But he was entertaining, and I found his conversation useful and interesting.

I made a stop in East London and spoke to a few ANC people. Before leaving I had a conversation with some other people, in the township, one of whom struck me as a possible undercover policeman. My companion had learned my identity, and a few minutes after we were back in the car, he said to me, 'You know, Mandela, I suspected that one chap at the end was a policeman.' This raised my own suspicions, and I said to my companion, 'Look here, how do I know you're not a policeman yourself?

You must tell me who you are – otherwise I will dump you back on the road again.'

He protested and said, 'No, I will introduce myself properly.' He confessed that he was a smuggler and had been carrying *dagga* (marijuana) from the Pondoland coast when he ran into a police roadblock. When he saw it, he jumped out of the car and tried to make a run for it. The police fired, wounding him in the leg. That explained his limp and his lack of transportation. He waved me down because he assumed the police were hunting him.

I asked him why he had chosen such a dangerous livelihood. He had originally wanted to be a teacher, he told me, but his parents were too poor to send him to college. After school he had worked in a factory, but the wages were too meagre for him to live on his own. He started to supplement them by smuggling *dagga*, and soon found it so profitable that he left the factory altogether. He said that in any other country in the world he would have found an opportunity for his talents. 'I saw white men who were my inferiors in ability and brains earning fifty times what I was.' After a long pause, he announced in a solemn tone, 'I am also a member of the ANC.' He told me that he had defied during the 1952 Defiance Campaign and had served on various local committees in Port Elizabeth. I quizzed him on various personalities, all of whom he seemed to know, and later in Port Elizabeth I confirmed that he had told me the truth. In fact, he had been one of the most reliable of those who went to jail during the Defiance Campaign. The doors of the liberation struggle are open to all who choose to walk through them.

As an attorney with a fairly large criminal practice, I was conversant with such tales. Over and over again, I saw men as bright and talented as my companion resort to crime in order to make ends meet. While I do think certain individuals are disposed to crime because of their genetic inheritance or an abusive upbringing, I am convinced that apartheid turned many otherwise law-abiding citizens into criminals. It stands to reason that an immoral and unjust legal system would breed contempt for its laws and regulations.

We reached Port Elizabeth at sunset, and Joe Matthews, Z.K. Matthews's son, arranged accommodation. The next morning I met Raymond Mhlaba, Frances Baard, and Govan Mbeki, whom I was encountering for the first time. I knew his work, for as a student I had read his booklet *The Transkei in the Making*. He had been running a cooperative store in the Transkei which he was soon to give up to become an editor of the weekly *New Age*. Govan was serious, thoughtful and soft-spoken, equally at home in the world of scholarship and the world of political activism. He had been deeply involved in the planning of the Congress of the People and was destined for the highest levels of leadership in the organization.

I departed in the late morning for Cape Town, with only my radio for company. I had never before driven on roads between Port Elizabeth and Cape Town, and I was looking forward to many miles of entrancing scenery. It was hot, and the road was bordered by dense vegetation on either side. I had hardly left the city when I ran over a large snake slithering across the road. I am not superstitious and do not believe in omens, but the death of the snake did not please me. I do not like killing any living thing, even those creatures that fill some people with dread.

Once I had passed Humansdorp, the forests became denser and for the first time in my life I saw wild elephants and baboons. A large baboon crossed the road in front of me, and I stopped the car. He stood and stared at me as intently as if he were a Special Branch detective. It was ironic that I, an African, was seeing the Africa of storybooks and legend for the first time. Such a beautiful land, I thought, and all of it out of reach, owned by whites and untouchable for a black man. I could no more choose to live in such beauty than run for Parliament.

Seditious thoughts accompany a freedom fighter wherever he goes. At the town of Knysna, more than a hundred miles west of Port Elizabeth, I stopped to survey the surroundings. The road above the town affords a panoramic view as far as the eye can see. In every direction, I saw sprawling, dense forests and I dwelt not on the greenery but the fact that there were many places a guerrilla army could live and train undetected.

I arrived in Cape Town at midnight for what turned out to be a two-week stay. I stayed at the home of the Reverend Walter Teka, a leader in the Methodist Church, but I spent most of my days with Johnson Ngwevela and Greenwood Ngotyana. Ngwevela was chairman of the western Cape region of the ANC and Ngotyana a member of its executive. Both were communists as well as leading members of the Wesleyan Church. I travelled every day to meet ANC officials in places like Worcester, Paarl, Stellenbosch, Simonstown and Hermanus. I planned to work each day of my stay, and when I asked what had been arranged for Sunday – a working day for me in the Transvaal – they informed me that the sabbath was reserved for churchgoing. I protested, but to no avail. Communism and Christianity, at least in Africa, were not mutually exclusive.

While I was walking in the city one day, I noticed a white woman in the gutter gnawing on some fish bones. She was poor and apparently homeless, but she was young and not unattractive. I knew of course that there were poor whites, whites who were every bit as poor as Africans, but one rarely saw them. I was used to seeing black beggars on the street, and it startled me to see a white one. While I normally did not give to African beggars, I felt the urge to give this woman money. In that moment I realized the tricks that apartheid plays on one, for the everyday travails that afflict Africans are accepted as a matter of course, while my heart immediately went out to this bedraggled white woman. In South Africa, to be poor and black was normal, to be poor and white was a tragedy.

As I was preparing to leave Cape Town, I went to the offices of *New Age* to see some old friends and discuss their editorial policy. *New Age*, the successor to earlier banned left-wing publications, was a friend of the ANC. It was early in the morning of 27 September, and as I walked up the steps I could hear angry voices inside the office and furniture being moved. I recognized the voice of Fred Carneson, the manager of the newspaper and its guiding spirit. I also heard the gruff voices of the security police, who were in the process of searching the offices. I quietly left, and later discovered that this had not been an isolated incident but part of the largest nationwide raid undertaken in South African history. Armed with warrants authorizing the seizure of anything regarded as evidence of high treason, sedition or violations of the Suppression of Communism Act, the police searched more than five hundred people in their homes and offices around the country. My office in Johannesburg was searched, as well as the homes of Dr Moroka, Father Huddleston and Professor Matthews.

The raid cast a shadow over my last day in Cape Town, for it signalled the first move in the state's new and even more repressive strategy. At the very least, a new round of bannings would take place, and I was certain to be among them. That evening, Reverend Teka and his wife asked a number of people over to bid me farewell, and led by him, we knelt in prayer for the well-being of those whose homes had been raided. I left the house at my favoured departure time of 3 a.m., and within half an hour I was on the road to Kimberley, the rough-and-ready mining town where the South African diamond business had begun in the last century.

I was to stay at the home of Dr Arthur Letele for one night. Later to become the treasurer-general of the ANC, Arthur was a scrupulous medical practitioner. I had a cold, and when he greeted me on my arrival, he confined me to bed. He was a brave and dedicated man, and had led a small group of defiers to jail during the Defiance Campaign. This was a risky action for a doctor in a town where political action by blacks was rare. In Johannesburg, one has the support of hundreds and even thousands of others who are engaging in the same dangerous activities, but in a conservative place like Kimberley, with no liberal press or judiciary to oversee the police, such an action requires true valour. It was in Kimberley during the Defiance Campaign that one of the ANC's leading members was sentenced to lashes by the local magistrate.

Despite my cold, Arthur allowed me to address an ANC meeting in his house the following evening. I was preparing to leave the next morning at three, but Arthur and his wife insisted I remain for breakfast, which I did. I made good time on the way back to Johannesburg and arrived home just before supper, where I was met with excited cries from my children, who well knew that I was a father bearing gifts. One by one, I handed out the presents I had purchased in Cape Town and patiently answered the questions my children had for me about the trip. Though not a true holiday, it had the same effect: I felt rejuvenated and ready to take up the fight once more.

22

Immediately upon my return I reported on my trip to the Working Committee of the ANC. Their principal concern was whether or not the Congress Alliance was strong enough to halt the government's plans. I did not give them good news. I said the Transkei was not a well-organized ANC area and the power of the security police would soon immobilize what little influence the ANC had.

I put forth an alternative that I knew would be unpopular. Why shouldn't the ANC participate in the new Bantu Authority structures as a means of remaining in touch with the masses of the people? In time, such participation would become a platform for our own ideas and policies.

Any suggestion of participating in apartheid structures in any way was automatically met with angry opposition. In my early days, I, too, would have strenuously objected. But my sense of the country was that relatively few people were ready to make sacrifices to join the struggle. We should meet the people on their own terms, even if that meant appearing to collaborate. My idea was that our movement should be a great tent that included as many people as possible.

At the time, however, my report was given short shrift because of another related report with greater ramifications. The publication of the report of the Tomlinson Commission for the Socio-Economic Development of the Bantu Areas had set off a nationwide debate. The government-created commission proposed a plan for the development of the so-called Bantu Areas or Bantustans. The result was in fact a blueprint for 'separate development' or Grand Apartheid.

The Bantustan system had been conceived by Dr H.F.Verwoerd, the minister of native affairs, as a way of muting international criticism of South African racial policies but at the same time institutionalizing apartheid. The Bantustans, or reserves as they were also known, would be separate ethnic enclaves or homelands for all African citizens. Africans,

Verwoerd said, 'should stand with both feet in the reserves' where they were to 'develop along their own lines'. The idea was to preserve the *status quo* where three million whites owned 87 per cent of the land, and relegate the eight million Africans to the remaining 13 per cent.

The central theme of the report was the rejection of the idea of integration between the races in favour of a policy of separate development of black and white. To that end, the report recommended the industrialization of the African areas, noting that any programme of development that did not aim to provide opportunities for Africans in their own regions was doomed to failure. The commission pointed out that the present geographical configuration of the African areas was too fragmentary, and recommended instead a consolidation of African areas into what it termed seven 'historical-logical' homelands of the principal ethnic groups.

But the creation of individual, self-contained Bantustans, as proposed by the commission, was farcical. Transkei, the showpiece of the proposed homeland system, would be broken into three geographically separate blocks. The Swazi Bantustan, Lebowa and Venda were composed of three pieces each; Gazankule, four; the Ciskei, seventeen; Bophuthatswana, nineteen; and KwaZulu, twenty-nine. The Nationalists were creating a cruel jigsaw puzzle out of people's lives.

The government's intention in creating the homeland system was to keep the Transkei – and other African areas – as reservoirs of cheap labour for white industry. At the same time, the covert goal of the government was to create an African middle class to blunt the appeal of the ANC and the liberation struggle.

The ANC denounced the report of the Tomlinson Commission, despite some of its more liberal recommendations. As I told Daliwonga, separate development was a spurious solution to a problem that whites had no idea how to control. In the end, the government approved the report, but rejected a number of its recommendations as being too progressive.

Despite the encroaching darkness and my pessimism about the government's policies, I was thinking about the future. In February 1956 I returned to the Transkei to purchase a plot of land in Umtata. I have always thought a man should own a house near the place he was born, where he might find a restfulness that eludes him elsewhere.

With Walter, I journeyed down to the Transkei. He and I met various ANC people in both Umtata and Durban, where we went first. Once again, we were clumsily shadowed by Special Branch police. In Durban, we paid a call on our colleagues at the Natal Indian Congress in an effort to boost activism in the area.

In Umtata, with Walter's help, I made a down payment to C. K. Sakwe for a plot of land he owned in town. Sakwe was a member of the Bungha and had served on the Natives' Representative Council. While we were there he told us of an incident that had occurred the previous Saturday at Bumbhane, the Great Place of Sabata, at a meeting of government officials and chiefs about the introduction of the Bantustans. A number of the chiefs objected to the government's policy and verbally attacked the magistrate. The meeting broke up in anger; this gave us some sense of the grassroots objections to the Bantu Authorities Act.

In March 1956, after several months of relative freedom, I received my third ban, which restricted me to Johannesburg for five years and prohibited me from attending meetings for that same period. For the next sixty months I would be quarantined in the same district, seeing the same streets, the same mine dumps on the horizon, the same sky. I would have to depend on newspapers and other people for reports on what was occurring outside Johannesburg, another prospect I did not relish.

But this time my attitude towards my bans had changed radically. When I was first banned, I abided by the rules and regulations of my persecutors. I had now developed contempt for these restrictions. I was not going to let my involvement in the struggle and the scope of my political activities be determined by the enemy I was fighting against. To allow my activities to be circumscribed by my opponent was a form of defeat, and I resolved not to become my own jailer.

I soon became involved in mediating a bitter political dispute right in Johannesburg. It pitted two sides against each other, both of which were seeking my support. Each side within this particular organization had legitimate grievances and each was implacably opposed to the other. The altercation threatened to descend into an acrimonious civil war, and I did my best to prevent a rupture. I am speaking, of course, of the struggle at the boxing and weight-lifting club at the Donaldson Orlando Community Centre where I trained almost every evening.

I had joined the club in 1950, and on almost every free night I worked out at the Community Centre. For the previous few years I had taken my son Thembi with me, and by 1956, when he was ten years old, he was a keen if spindly paperweight boxer. The club was managed by Johannes (Skipper Adonis) Molotsi, and its membership consisted of both professional and amateur boxers, as well as a variety of dedicated weight-lifters. Our star boxer, Jerry (Uyinja) Moloi, later became the Transvaal lightweight champion and number one contender for the national title.

The gym was poorly equipped. We could not afford a ring and trained on a cement floor, which was particularly dangerous when a boxer was knocked down. We boasted a single punch-bag and a few pairs of boxing gloves. We had no medicine or speed balls, no proper boxing trunks or shoes, and no mouth guards. Almost no one owned head guards. Despite the lack of equipment, the gym produced such champions as Eric (Black Material) Ntsele, bantamweight champion of South Africa, and Freddie (Tomahawk) Ngidi, the Transvaal flyweight champion, who spent his days working for me as an assistant at Mandela and Tambo. Altogether, we had perhaps twenty or thirty members.

Although I had boxed a bit at Fort Hare, it was not until I lived in Johannesburg that I took up the sport in earnest. I was never an outstanding boxer. I was in the heavyweight division, and I had neither enough power to compensate for my lack of speed nor enough speed to make up for my lack of power. I did not enjoy the violence of boxing so much as the science of it. I was intrigued by how one moved one's body to protect oneself, how one used a strategy both to attack and retreat, how one paced oneself over a match. Boxing is egalitarian. In the ring, rank, age, colour and wealth are irrelevant. When you are circling your opponent, probing his strengths and weaknesses, you are not thinking about his colour or social status. I never did any real fighting after I entered politics. My main interest was in training; I found the rigorous exercise to be an excellent outlet for tension and stress. After a strenuous workout, I felt both mentally and physically lighter. It was a way of losing myself in something that was not the struggle. After an evening's workout I would wake up the next morning feeling strong and refreshed, ready to take up the fight again.

I attended the gym for one and a half hours each evening from Monday to Thursday. I would go home directly after work, pick up Thembi, then drive to the Community Centre. We did an hour of exercise, some combination of roadwork, skipping rope, calisthenics or shadow boxing, followed by fifteen minutes of bodywork, some weight-lifting and then sparring. If we were training for a fight or a tournament, we would extend the training time to two and a half hours.

We each took turns leading the training sessions in order to develop leadership, initiative and self-confidence. Thembi particularly enjoyed leading these sessions. Things would get a bit rough for me on the nights that my son was in charge, for he would single me out for criticism. He was quick to chastise me whenever I got lazy. Everybody in the gym called me 'Chief', an honorific he avoided, calling me 'Mr Mandela', and occasionally, when he felt sympathy for his old man, 'My bra', township slang meaning 'My brother'. When he saw me loafing, he would say in a stern voice, 'Mr Mandela, you are wasting our time this evening. If you cannot keep up, why not go home and sit with the old women?' Everyone enjoyed these jibes immensely, and it gave me pleasure to see my son so happy and confident.

The camaraderie of the club was shattered that year because of a spat between Skipper Molotsi and Jerry Moloi. Jerry and the other boxers felt that Skipper was not paying enough attention to the club. Skipper was a skilful coach, but was rarely present to impart his knowledge. He was a historian of boxing lore and could narrate all twenty-six rounds of Jack Johnson's famous bout in Havana in 1915 when the first black heavyweight champion of the world lost his title. But Skipper tended to appear only before a match or a tournament to collect the small fee that was his due. I myself was sympathetic to Jerry's point of view but did my best to patch up the quarrel in the interests of keeping harmony. In the end, even my son agreed with Jerry's criticism of Skipper and there was nothing I could do to prevent a rupture.

The boxers, under Jerry's leadership, threatened to secede from the club and start their own. I called a meeting for all the members and it was a lively session – conducted in Sesotho, Zulu, Xhosa and English. Shakespeare was even cited by Skipper in his attack against the rebellious boxers, accusing Jerry of double-crossing him as Brutus had betrayed Caesar. 'Who are Caesar and Brutus?' my son asked. Before I could answer, someone said, 'Aren't they dead?' To which Skipper replied, 'Yes, but the truth about the betrayal is very much alive!'

The meeting resolved nothing and the boxers left for another venue while the weight-lifters remained at the Community Centre. I joined the boxers and for the first few weeks of the separation we trained at an uncomfortable place for a freedom-fighter, the police gymnasium. Thereafter, the Anglican Church gave us premises at a reasonable rental in Orlando East, and we trained under Simon (Mshengu) Tshabalala, who later became one of the ANC's leading underground freedom fighters.

Our new facilities were no better than the old, and the club was never reconstituted. African boxers, like all black athletes and artists, were shackled by the twin handicaps of poverty and racism. What money an African boxer earned was typically used on food, rent, clothing, and whatever was left went to boxing equipment and training. He was denied the opportunity of belonging to the white boxing clubs that had the equipment and trainers necessary to produce a first-rate, world-class boxer. Unlike white professional boxers, African professional boxers had full-time day jobs. Sparring partners were few and poorly paid; without proper drilling and practice, the performance greatly suffered. Yet a number of African fighters were able to triumph over these difficulties, and achieve great success. Boxers like Elijah (Maestro) Mokone, Enoch

(Schoolboy) Nhlapo, Kangeroo Maoto, one of the greatest stylists of the ring, Levi (Golden Boy) Madi, Nkosana Mgxaji, Mackeed Mofokeng and Norman Sekgapane all won great victories, while Jake Tuli, our greatest hero, won the British and Empire flyweight title. He was the most eloquent example of what African boxers could achieve if given the opportunity.

PART FIVE

———

Treason

23

Just after dawn on the morning of 5 December 1956, I was woken by a loud knocking on my door. No neighbour or friend ever knocks in such a peremptory way, and I knew immediately that it was the security police. I dressed quickly and found Head Constable Rousseau, a security officer who was a familiar figure in our area, and two policemen. He produced a search warrant, at which point the three of them immediately began to comb through the entire house looking for incriminating papers or documents. By this time the children were awake, and with a stern look I bade them to be calm. The children looked to me for reassurance. The police searched drawers and cabinets and cupboards, any place where contraband might have been hidden. After forty-five minutes, Rousseau matter-of-factly said, 'Mandela, we have a warrant for your arrest. Come with me.' I looked at the warrant, and the words leapt out at me: 'HOOGVERRAAD – HIGH TREASON'.

I walked with them to the car. It is not pleasant to be arrested in front of one's children, even though one knows that what one is doing is right. But children do not comprehend the complexity of the situation; they simply see their father being taken away by the white authorities without an explanation.

Rousseau drove and I sat next to him, without handcuffs, in the front seat. He had a search warrant for my office in town, where we were now headed after dropping off the two other policemen in a nearby area. To get to downtown Johannesburg, one had to travel along a desolate highway that cut through an unpopulated area. While we were motoring along this stretch, I remarked to Rousseau that he must be very confident to drive with me alone and unhandcuffed. He was silent.

'What would happen if I seized you and overpowered you?' I said.

Rousseau shifted uncomfortably. 'You are playing with fire, Mandela,' he said.

'Playing with fire is my game,' I replied.

'If you continue speaking like this I will have to handcuff you,'
Rousseau said threateningly.

'And if I refuse?'

We continued this tense debate for a few more minutes, but as we
passed into a populated area near the Langlaagte police station, Rousseau
said to me: 'Mandela, I have treated you well and I expect you to do the
same to me. I don't like your jokes at all.'

After a brief stop at the police station, we were joined by another
officer and went to my office, which they searched for another forty-five
minutes. From there, I was taken to Marshall Square, the rambling
red-brick Johannesburg prison where I had spent a few nights in 1952
during the Defiance Campaign. A number of my colleagues were already
there, having been arrested and booked earlier that morning. Over the
next few hours, more friends and comrades began to trickle in. This was
the swoop the government had long been planning. Someone smuggled in
a copy of the afternoon edition of *The Star*, and we learned from its banner
headlines that the raid had been countrywide and that the premier leaders
of the Congress Alliance were all being arrested on charges of high treason
and an alleged conspiracy to overthrow the state. Those who had been
arrested in different parts of the country – Chief Luthuli, Monty Naicker,
Reggie September, Lilian Ngoyi, Piet Beyleveld – were flown by military
planes to Johannesburg, where they were to be arraigned. One hundred
and forty-four people had been arrested. The next day we appeared in
court and were formally charged. A week later, Walter Sisulu and eleven
others were arrested, bringing the total to one hundred and fifty-six. All
told, there were one hundred and five Africans, twenty-one Indians,
twenty-three whites and seven Coloureds. Almost the entire executive
leadership of the ANC, both banned and unbanned, had been arrested.
The government, at long last, had made its move.

We were soon moved to the Johannesburg Prison, popularly known as the
Fort, a bleak, castle-like structure located on a hill in the heart of the city.
Upon admission, we were taken to an outdoor quadrangle and ordered
to strip completely and line up against the wall. We were forced to stand
there for more than an hour, shivering in the breeze and feeling awkward
– priests, professors, doctors, lawyers, businessmen, men of middle or old
age, who were normally treated with deference and respect. Despite my
anger, I could not suppress a laugh as I scrutinized the men around me.
For the first time, the truth of the aphorism 'clothes make the man' came
home to me. If fine bodies and impressive physiques were essential to
being a leader, I saw that few among us would have qualified.

A white doctor finally appeared and asked whether any of us was ill.

No one complained of any ailment. We were ordered to dress, and then escorted to two large cells with cement floors and no furniture. The cells had recently been painted and reeked of paint fumes. We were each given three thin blankets plus a sisal mat. Each cell had only one floor-level latrine, which was completely exposed. It is said that no one truly knows a nation until one has been inside its jails. A nation should not be judged by how it treats its highest citizens, but its lowest ones – and South Africa treated its imprisoned African citizens like animals.

We stayed in the Fort for two weeks, and despite the hardships, our spirits remained extremely high. We were permitted newspapers and read with gratification of the waves of indignation aroused by our arrests. Protest meetings and demonstrations were being held throughout South Africa; people carried signs declaring 'We Stand by Our Leaders'. We read of protests around the world over our incarceration.

Our communal cell became a kind of convention for far-flung freedom fighters. Many of us had been living under severe restrictions, making it illegal for us to meet and talk. Now, our enemy had gathered us all under one roof for what became the largest and longest unbanned meeting of the Congress Alliance in years. Younger leaders met older leaders they had only read about. Men from Natal mingled with leaders from the Transvaal. We revelled in the opportunity to exchange ideas and experiences for two weeks while we awaited trial.

Each day, we put together a programme of activities. Patrick Molaoa and Peter Nthite, both prominent Youth Leaguers, organized physical training. Talks on a variety of subjects were scheduled, and we heard Professor Matthews discourse on both the history of the ANC and the American Negro. Debi Singh lectured on the history of the SAIC, Arthur Letele discussed the African medicine man, while the Reverend James Calata spoke on African music – and sang in his beautiful tenor voice. Every day Vuyisile Mini, who years later was hanged by the government for political crimes, led the group in singing freedom songs. One of the most popular was: *'Nans' indod' emnyama Strijdom, Bhasobha nans' indodemnyama Strijdom'* ('Here's the black man, Strijdom, beware the black man, Strijdom'). We sang at the top of our lungs, and it kept our spirits high.

One time, Masabalala Yengwa (better known as M.B. Yengwa), the son of a Zulu labourer and the provincial secretary of the Natal ANC, contributed to a lecture on music by reciting a praise song in honour of Shaka, the legendary Zulu warrior and king. Yengwa draped himself with a blanket, rolled up a newspaper to imitate a sword, and began to stride back and forth reciting the lines from the praise song. All of us, even those who did not understand Zulu, were entranced. Then he paused dramatically and called out the lines '*Inyoni edlezinya! Yathi isadlezinye, yadlezinya!*' The lines liken Shaka to a great bird of prey that relentlessly slays its enemies. At the conclusion of these words, pandemonium broke out. Chief Luthuli, who until then had remained quiet, sprang to his feet, and bellowed '*Ngu Shaka lowo!*' ('That is Shaka!'), and then began to dance and chant. His movements electrified us, and we all took to our feet. Accomplished ballroom dancers, sluggards who knew neither traditional nor Western dancing, all joined in the *indlamu*, the traditional Zulu war dance. Some moved gracefully, others resembled frozen mountaineers trying to shake off the cold, but all danced with enthusiasm and emotion. Suddenly there were no Xhosas or Zulus, no Indians or Africans, no rightists or leftists, no religious or political leaders; we were all nationalists and patriots bound together by a love of our common history, our culture, our country and our people. In that moment, something stirred deep inside all of us, something strong and intimate, that bound us to one another. In that moment we felt the hand of the great past that made us what we were and the power of the great cause that linked us all together.

After the two weeks, we appeared for our preparatory examination on 19 December at the Drill Hall in Johannesburg, a military structure not normally used as a court of justice. It was a great bare barn of a building with a corrugated iron roof, and considered the only public building large enough to support a trial of so many accused.

We were taken in sealed police vans escorted by half a dozen troop carriers filled with armed soldiers. One would have thought a full-scale civil war was under way from the precautions the state was taking with us. A massive crowd of our supporters was blocking traffic in Twist Street; we could hear them cheering and singing, and they could hear us answering from inside the van. The trip became like a triumphal procession as the slow-moving van was rocked by the crowd. The entire perimeter of the hall was surrounded by gun-toting policemen and soldiers. The vans were brought to an area behind the hall and parked so that we alighted straight from the van into the courtroom.

Inside, we were met by another crowd of supporters, so that the hall seemed more like a raucous protest meeting than a staid court of law. We walked in with our thumbs raised in the ANC salute and nodded to our supporters sitting in the Non-Whites Only section. The mood inside was more celebratory than punitive, as the accused mingled with reporters and friends.

The government was charging all 156 of us with high treason and a countrywide conspiracy to use violence to overthrow the present government and replace it with a communist state. The period covered by the indictment was 1 October 1952 to 13 December 1956: it included the Defiance Campaign, the Sophiatown removal and the Congress of the People. The South African law of high treason was based not on English law but on Roman Dutch antecedents, and defined high treason as a hostile intention to disturb, impair or endanger the independence or safety of the state. The punishment was death.

The purpose of a preparatory examination was to determine whether the government's charges were sufficient to put us on trial in the Supreme Court. There were two stages of giving evidence. The first stage was in a magistrates' court. If the magistrate determined that there was sufficient evidence against the accused, the case would move to the Supreme Court and be tried before a judge. If the magistrate decided there was insufficient evidence, the defendants were discharged.

The magistrate was Mr F.C.A. Wessel, the chief magistrate from Bloemfontein. That first day, when Wessel began to speak in his quiet voice, it was impossible to hear him. The state had neglected to provide microphones and loudspeakers, and the court was adjourned for two hours while amplification was sought. We assembled in a courtyard and had what was very much like a picnic, with food sent in from outside. The atmosphere was almost festive. Two hours later, court was recessed for the day because proper loudspeakers had not been found. To the cheers of the crowd, we were once again escorted back to the Fort.

The next day, the crowds outside were even larger; the police more tense. Five hundred armed police surrounded the Drill Hall. When we arrived, we discovered that the state had erected an enormous wire cage for us to sit in. It was made of diamond-mesh wire, attached to poles and scaffolding with a grille at the front and top. We were led inside and sat on benches, surrounded by sixteen armed guards.

In addition to its symbolic effect, the cage cut us off from communication with our lawyers, who were not permitted to enter. One of my colleagues scribbled on a piece of paper, which he then posted on the side of the cage: 'Dangerous. Please Do Not Feed'.

Our supporters and organization had assembled a formidable defence team, including Bram Fischer, Norman Rosenberg, Israel Maisels, Maurice Franks and Vernon Berrangé. None of them had ever seen such a structure in court before. Franks lodged a powerful protest in open court against the state's humiliating his clients in such a 'fantastic' fashion and treating them, he said, 'like wild beasts'. Unless the cage was removed forthwith, he announced, the entire defence team would walk out of court. After a brief adjournment, the magistrate decided that the cage would be pulled down; in the meantime, the front of it was removed.

Only then did the state begin its case. The chief prosecutor, Mr van Niekerk, began reading part of an 18,000-word address outlining the Crown case against us. Even with amplification he was barely audible against the shouting and singing outside, and at one point a group of policemen rushed out. We heard a revolver shot, followed by shouts and more gunfire. The court was adjourned while the magistrate held a meeting with counsel. Twenty people had been injured.

The reading of the charges continued for the next two days. Van Niekerk said that he would prove to the court that the accused, with help from other countries, were plotting to overthrow the existing government by violence and impose a communist government on South Africa. This was the charge of high treason. The state cited the Freedom Charter as both proof of our communist intentions and evidence of our plot to overthrow the existing authorities. By the third day, much of the cage had been dismantled. Finally, on the fourth day, we were released on bail. Bail was another example of the sliding scale of apartheid: £250 for whites, £100 for Indians and £25 for Africans and Coloureds. Even treason was not colour-blind. Well-wishers from diverse walks of life came forward to guarantee bail for each of the accused, gestures of support that later became the foundation for the Treason Trial Defence Fund started by Bishop Reeves, Alan Paton and Alex Hepple. The fund was ably administered during the trial by Mary Benson and then Freda Levson. We were released provided we reported once a week to the police, and were forbidden to attend public gatherings. Court was to resume in early January.

The following day I was at my office bright and early. Oliver and I had both been in prison, and our case-load had mounted in the meantime. While trying to work that morning, I was visited by an old friend named Jabavu, a professional interpreter whom I had not seen for several months. Before the arrests I had deliberately cut down my weight, in anticipation of prison, where one should be lean and able to survive on little. In jail, I had continued my exercises and was pleased to be so trim. But Jabavu eyed me suspiciously. 'Madiba,' he said, 'why must you look so thin?' In African cultures, portliness is often associated with wealth and well-being. He burst out: 'Man, you were scared of jail, that is all. You have disgraced us, we Xhosas!'

24

Even before the trial, my marriage to Evelyn had begun to unravel. In 1953, Evelyn had become set on upgrading her four-year certificate in general nursing. She enrolled in a midwifery course at King Edward VII Hospital in Durban that would keep her away from home for several months. This was possible because my mother and sister were staying with us and could look after the children. During her stay in Durban, I visited her on at least one occasion.

Evelyn returned, having passed her examinations. She was pregnant again, and later that year gave birth to Makaziwe, named after the daughter we had lost six years before. In our culture, to give a new child the name of a deceased child is considered a way of honouring the earlier child's memory and retaining a mystical attachment to the child who left too soon.

Over the course of the next year Evelyn became involved with the Watch Tower organization, part of the church of Jehovah's Witnesses. Whether this was due to some dissatisfaction with her life at the time, I do not know. The Jehovah's Witnesses took the Bible as the sole rule of faith and believed in a coming Armageddon between good and evil. Evelyn zealously began distributing their publication *The Watchtower*, and began to work on me as well, urging me to convert my commitment to the struggle to a commitment to God. Although I found some aspects of the Watch Tower's system to be interesting and worthwhile, I could not and did not share her devotion. There was an obsessional element to it that put me off. From what I could discern, her faith taught passivity and submissiveness in the face of oppression, something I could not accept.

My devotion to the ANC and the struggle was unremitting. This disturbed Evelyn. She had always assumed that politics was a youthful diversion, that I would someday return to the Transkei and practise there as a lawyer. Even as that possibility became remote, she never resigned herself to the fact that Johannesburg would be our home, or let go of the idea that we might move back to Umtata. She believed that once I was back in the Transkei, in the bosom of my family, acting as counsellor to Sabata, I would no longer miss politics. She encouraged Daliwonga's efforts to persuade me to come back to Umtata. We had many arguments about this, and I patiently explained to her that politics was not a distraction but my lifework, that it was an essential and fundamental part of my being. She could not accept this. A man and a woman who hold such different views of their respective roles in life cannot remain close.

I tried to persuade her of the necessity of the struggle, while she attempted to persuade me of the value of religious faith. When I would tell her that I was serving the nation, she would reply that serving God was above serving the nation. We were finding no common ground, and I was becoming convinced that the marriage was no longer tenable.

We also waged a battle for the minds and hearts of the children. She wanted them to be religious, and I thought they should be political. She would take them to church at every opportunity and read them Watch Tower literature. She even gave the boys *Watchtower* pamphlets to distribute in the township. I used to talk politics to the boys. Thembi was a member of the Pioneers, the juvenile section of the ANC, so he was already politically cognizant. I would explain to Makgatho in the simplest terms how the black man was persecuted by the white man.

Hanging on the walls of the house I had pictures of Roosevelt, Churchill, Stalin, Gandhi and the storming of the Winter Palace in St Petersburg in 1917. I explained to the boys who each of the men was, and what he stood for. They knew that the white leaders of South Africa stood for something very different. One day, Makgatho came running into the house, and said, 'Daddy, Daddy, there is Malan on the hill!' Malan had been the first Nationalist prime minister and the boy had confused him with a Bantu Education official, Willie Maree, who had announced that he would that day address a public meeting in the township. I went outside to see what Makgatho was talking about, for the ANC had organized a demonstration to ensure that the meeting did not succeed. As I went out, I saw a couple of police vans escorting Maree to the place he was meant to speak, but there was trouble from the start and Maree had fled without delivering his speech. I told Makgatho that it was not Malan but might as well have been.

My schedule in those days was relentless. I would leave the house very early in the morning and return late at night. After a day at the office, I would usually have meetings of one kind or another. Evelyn could not understand my meetings in the evening, and when I returned home late suspected that I was seeing other women. Time after time, I would explain what meeting I was at, why I was there and what was discussed. But she was not convinced. In 1955, she gave me an ultimatum: I had to choose between her and the ANC.

Walter and Albertina Sisulu were very close to Evelyn, and their fondest wish was for us to stay together. Evelyn confided in Albertina. At one point, Walter intervened in the matter and I was very short with him, telling him it was none of his business. I regretted the tone I took, because Walter had always been a brother to me and his friendship and support had never faltered.

One day, Walter told me he wanted to bring someone over to the office for me to meet. He did not tell me that it was my brother-in-law, and I was surprised but not displeased to see him. I was pessimistic about the marriage and I thought it only fair to inform him of my feelings.

We were discussing this issue cordially among the three of us, when either Walter or I used a phrase like 'Men such as ourselves', or something of that sort. Evelyn's brother-in-law was a businessman, opposed to politics and politicians. He became very huffy and said, 'If you chaps think you are in the same position as myself, that is ridiculous. Do not compare yourselves to me.' When he left, Walter and I looked at each other and started laughing.

After we were arrested in December and kept in prison for two weeks, I had one visit from Evelyn. But when I left on bail, I found that she had moved out and taken the children. I returned to an empty, silent house. She had even removed the curtains, and for some reason I found this small detail shattering. She had moved in with her brother, who told me, 'Perhaps it is for the best; maybe when things will have cooled down you will come back together.' It was reasonable advice, but it was not to be.

Evelyn and I had irreconcilable differences. I could not give up my life in the struggle, and she could not live with my devotion to something other than herself and the family. She was a very good woman, charming, strong and faithful, and a fine mother. I never lost my respect and admiration for her, but in the end we could not make our marriage work.

The breakup of any marriage is traumatic, especially for the children. Our family was no exception, and all the children were wounded by our separation. Makgatho took to sleeping in my bed. He was a gentle child, a natural peacemaker, and he tried to bring about some sort of reconciliation between me and his mother. Makaziwe was still very small, and I remember one day, when I was not in prison or in court, I visited her crèche unannounced. She had always been a very affectionate child, but that day when she saw me, she froze. She did not know whether to run to me or retreat, to smile or frown. She had some conflict in her small heart, which she did not know how to resolve. It was very painful.

Thembi, who was ten at the time, was the most deeply affected. He stopped studying and became withdrawn. He had once been keen on English and Shakespeare, but after the separation he seemed to become apathetic about learning. The principal of his school spoke to me on one occasion, but there was little that I was able to do. I would take him to the gym whenever I could, and occasionally he would brighten a bit. There were many times when I could not be there and later, when I was underground, Walter would take Thembi with him along with his own son. Once he took him to an event, and afterwards Walter said to me, 'Man, that chap is quiet.' Following the breakup, Thembi would frequently wear my clothes, even though they were far too large for him; they gave him some kind of attachment to his too often distant father.

25

On 9 January 1957 we once again assembled in the Drill Hall. It was the defence's turn to refute the state's charges. After summarizing the Crown's case against us, Vernon Berrangé, our lead counsel, announced our argument. 'The defence,' he said, 'will strenuously repudiate that the terms of the Freedom Charter are treasonable or criminal. On the contrary, the defence will contend that the ideas and beliefs which are expressed in this charter, although repugnant to the policy of the present government, are such as are shared by the overwhelming majority of mankind of all races and colours, and also by the overwhelming majority of the citizens of this country.' In consultation with our attorneys, we had decided that we were not merely going to prove that we were innocent of treason, but that this was a political trial in which the government was persecuting us for taking actions that were morally justified.

But the drama of the opening arguments was succeeded by the tedium of court logistics. The first month of the trial was taken up by the state's submission of evidence. One by one, every paper, pamphlet, document, book, notebook, letter, magazine and clipping that the police had accumulated in the last three years of searches was produced and numbered; 12,000 in all. The submissions ranged from the United Nations Declaration of Human Rights to a Russian cookery book. They even submitted the two signs from the Congress of the People: 'SOUP WITH MEAT', and 'SOUP WITHOUT MEAT'.

During the preparatory examination, which was to last for months, we listened day after day as African and Afrikaner detectives read out their notes of ANC meetings, or transcripts of speeches. These accounts were always garbled, and often either nonsensical or downright false. Berrangé later revealed in his deft cross-examination that many of the African detectives were unable to understand or write English, the language in which the speeches were made.

To support the state's extraordinary allegation that we intended to replace

the existing government with a Soviet-style state, the Crown relied on
the evidence of Professor Andrew Murray, head of the Department of
Political Science at the University of Cape Town. Murray labelled many
of the documents seized from us, including the Freedom Charter itself, as
communistic.

Professor Murray seemed, at the outset, relatively knowledgeable, but
that was until Berrangé began his cross-examination. Berrangé said that
he wanted to read Murray a number of passages from various documents
and then ask Murray to label them as communistic or not. Berrangé read
him the first passage, which concerned the need for ordinary workers to
cooperate with each other and not exploit one another. Communistic,
Murray said. Berrangé then noted that the statement had been made by
the former premier of South Africa, Dr Malan. Berrangé proceeded to
read him two other statements, both of which Professor Murray described
as communistic. These passages had in fact been uttered by the American
presidents Abraham Lincoln and Woodrow Wilson. The highlight came
when Berrangé read Murray a passage that the professor unhesitatingly
described as 'communism straight from the shoulder'. Berrangé then
revealed that it was a statement that Professor Murray himself had
written in the 1930s.

In the seventh month of the trial, the state said it would produce evidence of planned violence that occurred during the Defiance Campaign.
The state called the first of their star witnesses, Solomon Ngubase, who
offered sensational evidence that seemed to implicate the ANC. Ngubase
was a soft-spoken fellow in his late thirties, with a shaky command of
English, who was currently serving a sentence for fraud. In his opening
testimony, Ngubase told the court he had obtained a BA degree from
Fort Hare, and that he was a practising attorney. He said he became
secretary of the Port Elizabeth branch of the ANC as well as a member
of the National Executive. He claimed to have been present at a meeting
of the National Executive when a decision was made to send Walter
Sisulu and David Bopape to the Soviet Union to procure arms for a
violent revolution in South Africa. He said he was present at a meeting
that planned the 1952 Port Elizabeth riot and that he had witnessed an
ANC decision to murder all whites in the Transkei in the same manner
as the Mau Mau in Kenya. Ngubase's dramatic testimony caused a stir
in and out of court. Here at long last was evidence of a conspiracy.

But when Ngubase was cross-examined by Vernon Berrangé, it was
revealed that he was equal parts madman and liar. Berrangé, whose
cross-examining skills earned him the nickname of 'Isangoma' (a diviner
or healer who exorcises an illness) among the accused, quickly established
that Ngubase was neither a university graduate nor a member of the

ANC, much less a member of the National Executive. Berrangé produced evidence that Ngubase had forged certificates for a university degree, had practised law illegally for several years and had a further case of fraud pending against him. At the time of the meeting he claimed to have attended to plan the Port Elizabeth riot, he was serving a sentence for fraud in a Durban jail. Almost none of Ngubase's testimony bore even a remote resemblance to the truth. At the end of his cross-examination, Berrangé asked the witness, 'Do you know what a rogue is?' Ngubase said he did not. 'You, sir, are a rogue!' Berrangé exclaimed.

Joe Slovo, one of the accused and a superb advocate, conducted his own defence. He was an irritant to the state because of his sharp questions and attempts to show that the state was the violator of laws, not the Congress. Slovo's cross-examination was often as devastating as Berrangé's. Detective Jeremiah Mollson, one of the few African members of the Special Branch, claimed to recall lines verbatim from ANC speeches that he had heard. But what he reported was usually gibberish or outright fabrication.

Slovo: 'Do you understand English?'

Mollson: 'Not so well.'

Slovo: 'Do you mean to say that you reported these speeches in English but you don't understand English well?'

Mollson: 'Yes, Your Worship.'

Slovo: 'Do you agree that your notes are a lot of rubbish?'

Mollson: 'I don't know.'

This last response caused an outbreak of laughter from the defendants. The magistrate scolded us for laughing, and said, 'The proceedings are not as funny as they may seem.'

At one point, Wessel told Slovo that he was impugning the integrity of the court and fined him for contempt. This provoked the fury of most of the accused, and it was only Chief Luthuli's restraining hand that kept a number of the defendants from being cited for contempt as well.

As the testimony continued, much of it tedious legal manoeuvring, we began to occupy ourselves with other matters. I often brought a book to read or a legal brief to work on. Others read newspapers, did crossword puzzles or played chess or Scrabble. Occasionally the bench would reprimand us for not paying attention, and the books and puzzles would disappear. But, slowly, as the testimony resumed its snail's pace, the games and reading material re-emerged.

As the preparatory examination continued the state became increasingly desperate. It became more and more apparent that the state was gathering – often fabricating – evidence as it went along, to help in what seemed to be a lost cause.

Finally, on 11 September, ten months after we had first assembled in the Drill Hall, the prosecutor announced that the state's case in the preparatory examination was completed. The magistrate gave the defence four months to sift through the 8,000 pages of typed evidence and 12,000 documents to prepare its case.

The preparatory examination had lasted for the whole of 1957. Court adjourned in September, and the defence began reviewing the evidence. Three months later, without warning and without explanation, the Crown announced that charges against sixty-one of the accused were to be dropped. Most of these defendants were relatively minor figures in the ANC, but also among them were Chief Luthuli and Oliver Tambo. The Crown's release of Luthuli and Tambo pleased but bewildered us.

In January, when the government was scheduled to sum up its charges, the Crown brought in a new prosecutor, the formidable Oswald Pirow Q.C. Pirow was a former minister of justice and of defence and a pillar of National Party politics. He was a longtime Afrikaner nationalist, and an outspoken supporter of the Nazi cause; he once described Hitler as the 'greatest man of his age'. He was a virulent anti-communist. The appointment of Pirow was new evidence that the state was worried about the outcome and attached tremendous importance to a victory.

Before Pirow's summing-up, Berrangé announced that he would apply for our discharge on the ground that the state had not offered sufficient evidence against us. Pirow opposed this application for dismissal, and quoted from several inflammatory speeches by the accused, informing the court that the police had unearthed more evidence of a highly dangerous conspiracy. The country, he said portentously, was sitting on top of a volcano. It was an effective and highly dramatic performance. Pirow changed the atmosphere of the trial. We had become over-confident, and were reminded that we were facing a serious charge. Don't fool yourselves, counsel told us, you people might go to jail. Their warnings sobered us.

After thirteen months of the preparatory examination, the magistrate ruled that he had found 'sufficient reason' for putting us on trial in the Transvaal Supreme Court for high treason. Court adjourned in January with ninety-five remaining defendants committed to stand trial. When the actual trial would begin, we did not know.

26

One afternoon, during a recess in the preparatory examination, I drove a friend from Orlando to the medical school at the University of the Witwatersrand and went past Baragwanath Hospital, the leading black hospital in Johannesburg. As I passed a nearby bus stop, I noticed out of the corner of my eye a lovely young woman waiting for the bus. I was struck by her beauty, and I turned my head to get a better look at her, but my car had gone by too fast. This woman's face stayed with me – I even considered turning round to drive by her in the other direction – but I went on.

Some weeks thereafter, a curious coincidence occurred. I was at the office, and when I popped in to see Oliver, there was this same young woman with her brother, sitting in front of Oliver's desk. I was taken aback, and did my best not to show my surprise – or my delight – at this. Oliver introduced me to them and explained that they were visiting him on a legal matter.

Her name was Nomzamo Winnifred Madikizela, but she was known as Winnie. She had recently completed her studies at the Jan Hofmeyr School of Social Work in Johannesburg and was working as the first black female social worker at Baragwanath Hospital. At the time I paid little attention to her background or legal problem, for something in me was deeply stirred by her presence. I was thinking more of how I could ask her out than how our firm would handle her case. I cannot say for certain if there is such a thing as love at first sight, but I do know that the moment I first glimpsed Winnie Nomzamo, I knew that I wanted to have her as my wife.

Winnie was the sixth of eleven children of C. K. Madikizela, a school principal turned businessman. Her given name was Nomzamo, which means one who strives or undergoes trials, a name as prophetic as my own. She came from Bizana in Pondoland, an area adjacent to the part of the Transkei where I grew up. She is from the Phondo clan of amaNgutyana, and her great-grandfather was Madikizela, a powerful chief in nineteenth-century Natal who had settled in the Transkei at the time of the iMfecane.

I telephoned Winnie the next day at the hospital and asked her for help in raising money for the Treason Trial Defence Fund from the Jan Hofmeyr School. It was merely a pretext to invite her to lunch, which I did. I picked her up where she was staying in town, and took her to an Indian restaurant near my office, one of the few places that served Africans and where I frequently ate. Winnie was dazzling, and even the fact that she had never before tasted curry and drank glass after glass of water to cool her palate only added to her charm.

After lunch I took her for a drive to an area between Johannesburg and Evaton, an open veld just past Eldorado Park. We walked on the long grass, grass so similar to that of the Transkei where we had both been raised. I told her of my hopes and of the difficulties of the Treason Trial. I knew at once that I wanted to marry her – and I told her so. Her spirit, her passion, her youth, her courage, her wilfulness – I felt all of these things the moment I first saw her.

Over the next weeks and months we saw each other whenever we could. She visited me at the Drill Hall and at my office. She came to see me work out in the gym; she met Thembi, Makgatho and Makaziwe. She came to meetings and political discussions; I was both courting her and politicizing her. As a student, Winnie had been attracted to the Non-European Unity Movement, for she had a brother who was involved with that party. In later years, I would tease her about this early allegiance, telling her that had she not met me, she would have married a leader of the NEUM.

Shortly after I filed for divorce from Evelyn, I told Winnie she should visit Ray Harmel, the wife of Michael Harmel, for a fitting for a wedding dress. In addition to being an activist, Ray was an excellent dressmaker. I asked Winnie how many bridesmaids she intended to have, and suggested she go to Bizana to inform her parents that we were to be married. Winnie has laughingly told people that I never proposed to her, but I always told her that I asked her on our very first date and that I simply took it for granted from that day forward.

The Treason Trial was in its second year and it put a suffocating weight on our law practice. The Mandela and Tambo firm was falling apart as we could not be there, and both Oliver and I were experiencing grave financial difficulties. Since the charges against Oliver had been dropped, he was able to do some remedial work, but the damage had already been done. We had gone from a bustling practice that turned people away to one that was practically begging for clients. I could not even afford to pay the balance of £50 still owing on the plot of land that I had purchased in Umtata, and had to give it up.

I explained all this to Winnie. I told her it was more than likely that we would have to live on her small salary as a social worker. Winnie understood, and said she was prepared to take the risk and throw in her lot with me. I never promised her gold and diamonds, and I was never able to give them to her.

The wedding took place on 14 June 1958. I applied for a relaxation of my banning orders and was given six days' leave of absence from Johannesburg. I also arranged for *lobola*, the traditional brideprice, to be paid to Winnie's father.

The wedding party left Johannesburg very early on the morning of 12 June, and we arrived in Bizana late that afternoon. My first stop, as always when one was banned, was the police station to report that I had arrived. At dusk, we then went to the bride's place, Mbongweni, as was customary. We were met by a great chorus of local women ululating with happiness, and Winnie and I were separated; she went to the bride's house, while I went with the groom's party to the house of one of Winnie's relations.

The ceremony itself was at a local church, after which we celebrated at the home of Winnie's eldest brother, which was the ancestral home of the Madikizela clan. The bridal car was swathed in ANC colours. There was dancing and singing, and Winnie's exuberant grandmother did a special dance for all of us. The entire executive of the ANC had been invited, but bans limited their attendance. Among those who came were Duma Nokwe, Lilian Ngoyi, Dr James Njongwe, Dr Wilson Conco and Victor Tyamzashe.

The final reception was at the Bizana Town Hall. The speech I recall best was given by Winnie's father. He took note, as did everyone, that among the uninvited guests at the wedding were a number of security Police. He spoke of his love for his daughter, my commitment to the country and my dangerous career as a politician. When Winnie had first told him of the marriage, he had exclaimed, 'But you are marrying a jailbird!' At the wedding, he said he was not optimistic about the future, and that such a marriage, in such difficult times, would be unremittingly tested. He told Winnie she was marrying a man who was already married to the struggle. He bade his daughter good luck, and ended his speech by saying, 'If your man is a wizard, you must become a witch!' It was a way of saying that you must follow your man on whatever path he takes. Then, Constance Mbekeni, my sister, spoke on my behalf at the ceremony.

After the ceremony, a piece of the wedding cake was wrapped up for the bride to bring to the groom's ancestral home for the second part of the wedding. But it was never to be, for my leave of absence was up and we had to return to Johannesburg. Winnie carefully stored the cake in anticipation of that day. At our house, No. 8115 Orlando West, a large party of friends and family were there to welcome us back. A sheep had been slaughtered and there was a feast in our honour.

There was no time or money for a honeymoon, and life quickly settled into a routine dominated by the trial. We woke very early in the morning, usually at about four. Winnie prepared breakfast before I left. I would then take the bus to the trial or make an early morning visit to my office. As much as possible, afternoons and evenings were spent at my office attempting to keep our practice going and to earn some money. Evenings were often taken up with political work and meetings. The wife of a freedom fighter is often like a widow, even when her husband is not in prison. Though I was on trial for treason, Winnie gave me cause for hope. I felt as though I had a new and second chance at life. My love for her gave me added strength for the struggles that lay ahead.

27

The major event facing the country in 1958 was the general election – 'general' only in the sense that three million whites could participate, but none of the thirteen million Africans. We debated whether or not to stage a protest. The central issue was: did an election in which only whites could participate make any difference to Africans? The answer, as far as the ANC was concerned, was that we could not remain indifferent even when we were shut out of the process. We were excluded, but not unaffected: the defeat of the Nationalist Party would be in our interest and that of all Africans.

The ANC joined with the other congresses and SACTU, the South African Congress of Trade Unions, to call a three-day strike during the elections in April. Leaflets were distributed in factories and shops, at railway stations and bus stops, in beer halls and hospitals, and from house to house. 'THE NATS MUST GO!' was the main slogan of this campaign. Our preparations worried the government; four days before the election, the state ruled that a gathering of more than ten Africans in any urban area was illegal.

The night before a planned protest, boycott or stay-away, the leaders of the event would go underground in order to foil the police swoop that inevitably took place. The police were not yet monitoring us around the clock and it was easy to disappear for a day or two. The night before the strike, Walter, Oliver, Moses Kotane, J. B. Marks, Dan Tloome, Duma Nokwe and I stayed in the house of my physician, Dr Nthatho Motlana, in Orlando. Very early the next morning, we moved to another house in the same neighbourhood where we were able to keep in touch by telephone with other leaders around the city. Communications were not very efficient in those days, particularly in the townships where few people owned telephones, and it was a frustrating task to oversee a strike. Early the next morning, we dispatched men to strategic places around the townships to watch the trains, buses and taxis in order to determine whether people were going to work. They returned with bad news: the buses and trains were filled; people were ignoring the strike. Only then did we notice that the gentleman in whose house we were staying was nowhere to be found – he had slipped out and gone to work. The strike was shaping up as a failure.

We resolved to call off the strike. A three-day strike that is cancelled on the first day is only a one-day failure; a strike that fails three days running is a fiasco. It was humiliating to have to retreat, but we felt that it would have been more humiliating not to. Less than an hour after we had released a statement calling off the strike, the government-run South African Broadcasting Corporation read our announcement in full. Normally, the SABC ignored the ANC altogether; only in defeat did we make their broadcasts. This time, they even complimented us on our decision. This greatly annoyed Moses Kotane. 'To be praised by the SABC, that is too much,' he said, shaking his head. Kotane questioned whether we had acted too hastily and played into the state's hands. It was a legitimate concern, but decisions should not be taken out of pride or embarrassment, but out of pure strategy – and strategy here suggested we call off the strike. The fact that the enemy had exploited our surrender didn't mean we were wrong to surrender.

But some areas did not hear that the strike was called off, while others spurned our call. In Port Elizabeth, an ANC stronghold, the response was better on the second and third days than the first. In general, however, we could not hide the fact that the strike was a failure. As if that were not enough, the Nationalists increased their popular vote in the election by more than 10 per cent.

We had heated discussions about whether we ought to have relied on coercive measures. Should we have used pickets, which generally prevent people from entering their place of work? The hard-liners suggested that if we had deployed pickets, the strike would have been a success. But I have always resisted such methods. It is best to rely on the freely given support of the people; otherwise that support is weak and fleeting. The organization should be a haven, not a prison. However, if the majority of the organization or the people support a decision, coercion can be used in certain cases against the dissident minority in the interests of the majority. A minority, however vocal it might be, should not be able to frustrate the will of the majority.

In my own house, I attempted to use a different sort of coercion, but without success. Ida Mthimkhulu, a Sotho-speaking woman of my own age, was then our house assistant. Ida was more a member of the family than an employee, and I called her Kgaitsedi, which means 'Sister' and is a term of endearment. Ida ran the house with military efficiency, and

Winnie and I took our orders willingly; I often ran out to do errands at her command.

The day before the strike, I was driving Ida and her twelve-year-old son home, and I mentioned that I needed her to wash and press some shirts for me the following day. A long and uncharacteristic silence followed. Ida then turned to me and said with barely concealed disdain, 'You know very well that I can't do that.'

'Why not?' I replied, surprised by the vehemence of her reaction.

'Have you forgotten that I, too, am a worker?' she said with some satisfaction. 'I will be on strike tomorrow with my people and fellow workers!'

Her son saw my embarrassment and in his boyish way tried to ease the tension by saying that 'Uncle Nelson' had always treated her as a sister, not a worker. In irritation, she turned on her well-meaning son and said, 'Boy, where were you when I was struggling for my rights in that house? If I had not fought hard against your "Uncle Nelson" I would not today be treated like a sister!' Ida did not come to work the next day, and my shirts went unpressed.

28

Few issues touched a nerve as much as that of passes for women. The state had not weakened in its resolve to impose passes on women, and women had not weakened in their resolve to resist. Although the government now called passes 'reference books', women weren't fooled: they could still be fined £10 or imprisoned for a month for failing to produce their 'reference book'.

In 1957, spurred by the efforts of the ANC Women's League, women all across the country, in rural areas and in cities, reacted with fury to the state's insistence that they carry passes. The women were courageous, persistent, enthusiastic, indefatigable, and their protest against passes set a standard for anti-government protest that was never equalled. As Chief Luthuli said, 'When the women begin to take an active part in the struggle, no power on earth can stop us from achieving freedom in our lifetime.'

All across the southeastern Transvaal, in Standerton, Heidelberg, Balfour and other dorps, thousands of women protested. On recess from the Treason Trial, Frances Baard and Florence Matomela organized women to refuse passes in Port Elizabeth, their home town. In Johannesburg in October a large group of women gathered at the central pass office, and chased away women who had come to collect passes and clerks who worked in the office, bringing the office to a standstill. Police arrested hundreds of the women.

Not long after these arrests, Winnie and I were relaxing after supper when she quietly informed me that she intended to join the group of Orlando women who would be protesting the following day at the pass office. I was a bit taken aback, and while I was pleased at her sense of commitment and admired her courage, I was also wary. Winnie had become increasingly politicized since our marriage, and had joined the Orlando West branch of the ANC's Women's League, all of which I encouraged.

I told her I welcomed her decision, but that I had to warn her about the seriousness of her action. It would, I said, in a single act, radically change her life. By African standards, Winnie was from a well-to-do family and had been shielded from some of the more unpleasant realities of life in South Africa. At the very least, she never had had to worry about where her next meal was coming from. Before our marriage, she had moved in circles of relative wealth and comfort, a life very different from the often hand-to-mouth existence of the freedom fighter.

I told her that if she was arrested she would be certain to be sacked by her employer, the provincial administration – we both knew it was her small income that was supporting the household – and that she could probably never work again as a social worker, since the stigma of imprisonment would make public agencies reluctant to hire her. Finally, she was pregnant, and I warned her of the physical hardship and humiliations of jail. My response may sound harsh, but I felt responsibility, both as a husband and as a leader of the struggle, to be as clear as possible about the ramifications of her action. I myself had mixed emotions, for the concerns of a husband and a leader do not always coincide.

But Winnie is a determined person, and I suspect my pessimistic reaction only strengthened her resolve. She listened to all I said and informed me that her mind was made up. The next morning I rose early to make her breakfast, and we drove over to the Sisulus' house to meet Walter's wife, Albertina, one of the leaders of the protest. We then drove to the Phefeni station in Orlando, where the women would get the train into town. I embraced her before she boarded the train. Winnie was nervous yet resolute as she waved to me from the window, and I felt as though she were setting out on a long and perilous journey, the end of which neither of us could know.

Hundreds of women converged on the Central Pass Office in downtown Johannesburg. They were old and young; some carried babies on their backs, some wore tribal blankets while others dressed in smart suits. They sang, marched and chanted. Within minutes they were surrounded by dozens of armed police, who arrested all of them, packed them into vans and drove them to Marshall Square police station. The women were cheerful throughout; as they were being driven away, some called out to reporters, 'Tell our madams we won't be at work tomorrow!' All told, more than a thousand women were arrested.

I knew this not because I was the husband of one of the detainees but because Mandela and Tambo were called on to represent most of the women who had been arrested. I quickly made my way to Marshall Square to visit the prisoners and arrange bail. I managed to see Winnie, who beamed when she saw me and seemed as happy as one could be in a bare police cell. It was as though she had given me a great gift that she knew would please me. I told her I was proud of her, but I could not stay and talk as I had quite a lot of legal work to do.

By the end of the second day, the number of arrests had increased and nearly two thousand women were incarcerated, many of them remanded to the Fort to await trial. This created formidable problems not only for Oliver and me, but for the police and the prison authorities. There was simply not enough space to hold them all. There were too few blankets, too few mats and toilets, and too little food. Conditions at the Fort were cramped and dirty. While many in the ANC, including myself, were eager to bail out the women, Lilian Ngoyi, the national president of the Women's League, and Helen Joseph, secretary of the South African Women's Federation, believed that for the protest to be genuine and effective, the women should serve whatever time the magistrate ordered. I remonstrated with them but was told in no uncertain terms that the matter was the women's affair and that the ANC – as well as anxious husbands – should not meddle. I did tell Lilian that I thought she should discuss the issue with the women themselves before making a decision, and escorted her down to the cells where she could take a poll of the prisoners. Many were desperate to be bailed out and had not been adequately prepared for what would await them in prison. As a compromise, I suggested to Lilian that the women spend a fortnight in prison, after which we would bail them out. Lilian accepted.

Over the next two weeks I spent many hours in court arranging bail for the women. A few were frustrated and took their anger out on me. 'Mandela, I am tired of this case of yours,' one woman said to me. 'If this does not end today I will not ever reappear in court.' With the help of relatives and fund-raising organizations, we managed to bail them all out within two weeks.

Winnie did not seem the worse for wear from her prison experience. If she had suffered, she would not have told me anyway. While she was in prison she became friendly with two teenage Afrikaner wardresses. They were sympathetic and curious, and after Winnie was released on bail, we invited them to visit us. They accepted and travelled by train to Orlando. We gave them lunch at the house and afterwards Winnie took them for a tour of the township. Winnie and the two wardresses were about the same age and got on well. They laughed together as though they were all sisters. The two girls had an enjoyable day and thanked Winnie, saying that they would like to return. As it turned out, this was not to be, for in travelling to Orlando they had, of necessity, sat in a Non-European carriage. (There were no white trains to Orlando for the simple reason that no whites went to Orlando.) As a result, they attracted a great deal of attention and it was soon widely known that two Afrikaner wardresses from the Fort had visited Winnie and me. This was not a problem for us, but it proved to be one for them, because the prison authorities dismissed them. We never saw or heard from them again.

29

For six months – ever since the end of the preparatory hearings in January – we had been awaiting and preparing for our formal trial, which was to start in August 1958. The government set up a special high court – Mr Justice F.L. Rumpff, president of the three-man court, Mr Justice Kennedy and Mr Justice Ludorf. The panel was not promising: it consisted of three white men, all with ties to the ruling party. While Judge Rumpff was an able man and better informed than the average white South African, he was rumoured to be a member of the Broederbond, a secret Afrikaner organization whose aim was to solidify Afrikaner power. Judge Ludorf was a well-known member of the National Party, as was Judge Kennedy. Kennedy had a reputation as a hanging judge, having sent a group of twenty-three Africans to the gallows for the murder of two white policemen.

Shortly before the case resumed, the state played another unpleasant trick on us. They announced that the venue of the trial was to be shifted from Johannesburg to Pretoria, thirty-six miles away. The trial would be conducted in an ornate former synagogue that had been converted into a court of law. All of the accused as well as our defence team resided in Johannesburg, so we would be forced to travel each day to Pretoria. The trial would now take up even more of our time and money – neither of which we had in abundance. Those who had managed to keep their jobs had been able to do so because the court had been near their work. Changing the venue was also an attempt to crush our spirits by separating us from our natural supporters. Pretoria was the home of the National Party, and the ANC barely had a presence there.

Nearly all the ninety-two accused commuted to Pretoria in a lumbering, uncomfortable bus, with stiff wooden slats for seats, which left every day at six in the morning and took two hours to reach the Old Synagogue. The round-trip took us nearly five hours – time far better spent earning money to pay for food, rent and clothes for the children.

Once more we were privileged to have a brilliant and aggressive defence team, ably led by advocate Israel Maisels, and assisted by Bram Fischer, Rex Welsh, Vernon Berrangé, Sydney Kentridge, Tony O'Dowd and G. Nicholas. On the opening day of the trial, they displayed their combativeness with a risky legal manoeuvre that a number of us had decided on in consultation with the lawyers. Issy Maisels rose dramatically and applied for the recusal of Judges Ludorf and Rumpff on the grounds that both had conflicts of interest that prevented them from being fair arbiters of our case. There was an audible murmur in the courtroom. The defence contended that Rumpff, as the judge at the 1952 Defiance Trial, had already adjudicated on certain aspects of the present indictment and therefore it was not in the interest of justice that he try this case. We argued that Ludorf was prejudiced, because he had represented the government in 1954 as a lawyer for the police when Harold Wolpe had sought a court interdict to eject the police from a meeting of the Congress of the People.

This was a dangerous strategy, for we could easily win this legal battle but lose the war. Although we regarded both Ludorf and Rumpff as strong supporters of the National Party, there were far worse judges in the country who could replace them. In fact, while we were keen to have Ludorf step down, we secretly hoped that Rumpff, whom we respected as an honest broker, would decide not to recuse himself. Rumpff always stood for law, no matter what his own political opinions might be, and we were convinced that when it came to law, we could only be found innocent.

That Monday, the atmosphere was expectant when the three red-robed judges marched into the courtroom. Judge Ludorf announced that he would withdraw, adding that he had completely forgotten about the previous case. But Rumpff refused to recuse himself and instead offered the assurance that his judgment in the Defiance case would have no influence on him in this one. We were happy with his decision. To replace Ludorf, the state appointed Mr Justice Bekker, a man we liked right from the start and who was not linked to the National Party.

After the success of this first manoeuvre, we tried a second, nearly as risky. We began a long and detailed argument contesting the indictment itself. We claimed, among other things, that the indictment was vague and lacked particularity. We also argued that the planning of violence was necessary to prove high treason, and the prosecution needed to provide examples of its claim that we intended to act violently. It became apparent by the end of our argument that the three judges agreed. In August, the court quashed one of the two charges under the Suppression of Communism Act. On 13 October, after two more months of legal wrangling, the Crown suddenly announced the withdrawal of the indictment altogether. This was extraordinary, but we were too well versed in the devious ways of the state to celebrate. A month later the prosecution issued a new, more carefully worded, indictment and announced that the trial would proceed against only thirty of the accused; the others would be tried later. I was among the first thirty, all of whom were members of the ANC.

Under the new indictment, the prosecution was now required to prove the intention to act violently. As Pirow put it, the accused knew that the achievement of the goals of the Freedom Charter would 'necessarily involve the overthrow of the State by violence'. The legal sparring continued until the middle of 1959, when the court dismissed the Crown's indictment against the remaining sixty-one accused. For months on end, the activity in the courtroom consisted of the driest legal manoeuvring imaginable. Despite the defence's successes in showing the shoddiness of the government's case, the state was obdurately persistent. As the minister of justice said, 'This trial will be proceeded with, no matter how many millions of pounds it costs. What does it matter how long it takes?'

Just after midnight on 4 February 1958, I returned home after a meeting to find Winnie alone and in pain, about to go into labour. I rushed her to Baragwanath Hospital, but was told that it would be many hours before her time. I stayed until I had to leave for the trial in Pretoria. Immediately after the session ended, I sped back with Duma Nokwe to find mother and daughter doing extremely well. I held my newborn daughter in my arms and pronounced her a true Mandela. My relative, Chief Mdingi, suggested the name Zenani, which means 'What have you brought to the world?' – a poetic name that embodies a challenge, suggesting that one must contribute something to society. It is a name one does not simply possess, but has to live up to.

My mother came from the Transkei to help Winnie, and planned to give Zenani a Xhosa baptism by calling in an *inyanga*, a tribal healer, to give the baby a traditional herbal bath. But Winnie was adamantly opposed, thinking it unhealthy and outdated, and instead smeared Zenani with olive oil, plastered her little body with Johnson's Baby Powder, and filled her stomach with shark oil.

As soon as Winnie was up and about, I undertook the task of teaching the new mother of the household how to drive. Driving, in those days, was a man's business; very few women, especially African women, were to be seen in the driver's seat. But Winnie was independent-minded and intent on learning, and it would be useful because I was away so much of the time and could not act as her chauffeur. Perhaps I am an impatient teacher or perhaps I had a headstrong pupil, but when I attempted to give Winnie lessons along a relatively flat and quiet Orlando road, we could not seem to shift gears without quarrelling. Finally, after she had ignored one too many of my suggestions, I stormed out of the car and walked home. Winnie seemed to do better without my tutelage than with it, for she proceeded to drive around the township on her own for the next hour. By that time we were ready to make up, and it is a story we subsequently laughed about.

Married life and motherhood was an adjustment for Winnie. She was then a young woman of twenty-five who had yet to form her own character completely. I was already formed and rather stubborn. I knew that others often saw her as 'Mandela's wife'. It was undoubtedly difficult for her to form her own identity in my shadow. I did my best to let her bloom in her own right, and she soon did so without any help from me.

30

On 6 April 1959, the anniversary of Jan van Riebeeck's landing at the Cape, a new organization was born that sought to rival the ANC as the country's premier African political organization and repudiate the white domination that began three centuries before. With a few hundred delegates from around the country at the Orlando Communal Hall, the Pan-Africanist Congress launched itself as an Africanist organization that expressly rejected the multiracialism of the ANC. Like those of us who had formed the Youth League fifteen years before, the founders of the new organization thought the ANC was insufficiently militant, out of touch with the masses and dominated by non-Africans.

Robert Sobukwe was elected president and Potlako Leballo became national secretary, both of them former ANC Youth Leaguers. The PAC presented a manifesto and a constitution, along with Sobukwe's opening address, in which he called for a 'government of the Africans by the Africans and for the Africans'. The PAC declared that it intended to overthrow white supremacy and establish a government Africanist in origin, socialist in content and democratic in form. They disavowed communism in all its forms and considered whites and Indians 'foreign minority groups' or 'aliens' who had no natural place in South Africa. South Africa was for Africans, and no one else.

The birth of the PAC did not come as a surprise to us. The Africanists within the ANC had been loudly voicing their grievances for more than three years. In 1957 the Africanists had called for a vote of no confidence in the Transvaal Executive at the national conference, but had been defeated. They had opposed the election-day stay-at-home of 1958, and their leader, Potlako Leballo, had been expelled from the ANC. At the November 1958 ANC conference, a group of Africanists had declared their opposition to the Freedom Charter, claiming it violated the principles of African nationalism.

The PAC claimed that it drew its inspiration from the principles surrounding the ANC's founding in 1912, but its views derived principally

from the emotional African nationalism put forth by Anton Lembede and
A. P. Mda during the founding of the Youth League in 1944. The PAC
echoed the axioms and slogans of that time: Africa for the Africans and
a United States of Africa. But the immediate cause for the breakaway
was its objection to the Freedom Charter and the presence of whites and
Indians in the Congress Alliance leadership. It was opposed to interracial
cooperation, in large part because it believed that white communists and
Indians had come to dominate the ANC.

The founders of the PAC were all well known to me. Robert Sobukwe
was an old friend. He was the proverbial gentleman and scholar
(his colleagues called him 'Prof'). His consistent willingness to pay
the penalty for his principles earned my enduring respect. Potlako
Leballo, Peter Raboroko and Zephania Mothopeng were all friends
and colleagues. I was astonished and indeed somewhat dismayed to
learn that my political mentor Gaur Radebe had joined the PAC. I
found it curious that a former member of the Communist Party's Central
Committee had decided to align himself with an organization that then
explicitly rejected Marxism.

Many of those who cast their lot with the PAC did so out of personal
grudges or disappointments, and were thinking not of the advancement
of the struggle, but of their own feelings of jealousy or revenge. I have
always believed that to be a freedom fighter one must suppress many of
the personal feelings that make one feel like a separate individual rather
than part of a mass movement. One is fighting for the liberation of millions
of people, not the glory of one individual. I am not suggesting that a man
become a robot and rid himself of all personal feelings and motivations.
But in the same way that a freedom fighter subordinates his own family to
the family of the people, he must subordinate his own individual feelings
to the movement.

I found the views and the behaviour of the PAC immature. A philosopher once noted that something is odd if a person is not liberal when he is
young and conservative when he is old. I am not a conservative, but one
matures and regards some of the views of one's youth as undeveloped and
callow. While I sympathized with the views of the Africanists and once
shared many of them, I believed that the freedom struggle required one
to make compromises and accept the kind of discipline that one resisted
as a younger, more impulsive man.

The PAC put forward a dramatic and over-ambitious programme that
promised quick solutions. Its most dramatic – and naive – promise was
that liberation would be achieved by the end of 1963, and it urged
Africans to ready themselves for that historic hour. 'In 1960 we take
our first step,' it promised, 'in 1963, our last towards freedom and

independence.' Although this prediction inspired hope and enthusiasm among people who were tired of waiting, it is always dangerous for an organization to make promises it cannot keep.

Because of the PAC's anti-communism, it became the darling of the Western press and the American State Department, which hailed its birth as a dagger in the heart of the African left. Even the National Party saw a potential ally in the PAC: they viewed the PAC as mirroring their anti-communism and supporting their views on separate development. The Nationalists also rejected interracial cooperation, and both the National Party and the American State Department saw fit to exaggerate the size and importance of the new organization for their own ends.

While we welcomed anyone brought into the struggle by the PAC, the role of the organization was almost always that of a spoiler. They divided the people at a critical moment, and that was hard to forget. They would ask the people to go to work when we called a general strike, and make misleading statements to counter any pronouncement we would make. Yet the PAC aroused in me the hope that even though the founders were breakaway ANC men, unity between our two groups was possible. I thought that once the heated polemics had cooled, the essential commonality of the struggle would bring us together. Animated by this belief, I paid particular attention to their policy statement and activities, with the idea of finding affinities rather than differences.

The day after the PAC's inaugural conference I approached Sobukwe for a copy of his presidential address, as well as the constitution and other policy material. Sobukwe, I thought, seemed pleased by my interest, and said he would make sure I received the requested material. I saw him again not long afterwards and reminded him of my request and he said the material was on its way. I subsequently met Potlako Leballo and said, 'Man, you chaps keep promising me your material, but no one has given it to me.' He said, 'Nelson, we have decided not to give it to you because we know you only want to use it to attack us.' I disabused him of this notion, and he relented, giving me all that I had sought.

31

In 1959, Parliament passed the Promotion of Bantu Self Government Act, which created eight separate ethnic Bantustans. This was the foundation of what the state called *groot* or grand apartheid. At roughly the same time, the government introduced the deceptively named Extension of University Education Act, another leg of grand apartheid, which barred nonwhites from racially 'open' universities. In introducing the Bantu Self Government Act, de Wet Nel, the minister of Bantu administration and development, said that the welfare of every individual and population group could best be developed within its own national community. Africans, he said, could never be integrated into the white community.

The immorality of the Bantustan policy, whereby 70 per cent of the people would be apportioned only 13 per cent of the land, was obvious. Under the new policy, even though two-thirds of Africans lived in so-called white areas, they could have citizenship only in their own 'tribal homelands'. The scheme gave us neither freedom in white areas nor independence in what they deemed 'our' areas. Verwoerd said the creation of the Bantustans would engender so much goodwill that they would never become the breeding grounds for rebellion.

In reality, it was quite the opposite. The rural areas were in turmoil. Few areas fought so stubbornly as Zeerust, where Chief Abram Moilaw (with the able assistance of advocate George Bizos), led his people to resist the so-called Bantu Authorities. Such areas are usually invisible to the press, and the government uses their inaccessibility to veil the cruelty of the state's actions. Scores of innocent people were arrested, prosecuted, jailed, banished, beaten, tortured and murdered. The people of Sekhukhuneland also revolted, and the paramount chief, Moroamotshe Sekhukhune, Godfrey Sekhukhune, and other counsellors were arrested and banished. A Sekhukhune chief, Kolane Kgoloko, who was perceived as a government lackey was assassinated. By 1960, resistance in Sekhukhuneland had reached open defiance and people were refusing to pay taxes.

In Zeerust and Sekhukhuneland, ANC branches played a prominent part in the protests. In spite of the severe repression, a number of new ANC branches sprang up in the Zeerust area, one of them having recruited about two thousand members. Sekhukhuneland and Zeerust were the first areas in South Africa where the ANC was banned by the government, evidence of our power in these remote areas.

Protest erupted in eastern Pondoland, where government henchman were assaulted and killed. Thembuland and Zululand fiercely resisted, and were among the last areas to yield. People were beaten, arrested, deported and imprisoned. In Thembuland, resistance had been going on since 1955, with Sabata part of the forces of protest.

It was especially painful to me that in the Transkei, the wrath of the people was directed against my nephew and one-time mentor K.D. Matanzima. There was no doubt that Daliwonga was collaborating with the government. All the appeals I had made to him over the years had come to naught. There were reports that *impis* (traditional warriors) from Matanzima's headquarters had burned down villages that opposed him. There were several assassination attempts against him. Equally painful was the fact that Winnie's father was serving on Matanzima's council and was an unwavering supporter. This was terribly difficult for Winnie: her father and her husband were on opposite sides of the same issue. She loved her father, but she rejected his politics.

On a number of occasions, tribesmen and kinsmen from the Transkei visited me in Orlando to complain about chiefs collaborating with the government. Sabata was opposed to the Bantu Authorities and would not capitulate, but my visitors were afraid that Matanzima would depose him, which is eventually what happened. At one time, Daliwonga himself came to visit during the Treason Trial and I brought him with me to Pretoria. In the courtroom, Issy Maisels introduced him to the judges and they accorded him a seat of honour. But outside – among the accused – he was not treated so deferentially. He began aggressively to ask the various defendants, who regarded him as a turncoat, why they objected to separate development. Lilian Ngoyi remarked: '*Tyhini, uyadelela lo mntu*' ('Gracious, this man is provocative').

32

It is said that the mills of God grind exceedingly slowly, but even the Lord's machinations cannot compete with those of the South African judicial system. On 3 August 1959, two years and eight months after our arrests, and after a full year of legal manoeuvring, the actual trial commenced at the Old Synagogue in Pretoria. We were finally formally arraigned and all thirty of us pleaded not guilty.

Our defence team was once again led by Issy Maisels, and he was assisted by Sydney Kentridge, Bram Fischer and Vernon Berrangé. This time, at long last, the trial was in earnest. During the first two months of the case, the Crown entered some two thousand documents into the record and called 210 witnesses, 200 of whom were members of the Special Branch. These detectives admitted to hiding in wardrobes and under beds, posing as ANC members, perpetrating virtually any deception that would enable them to get information about our organization. Yet many of the documents the state submitted and the speeches they transcribed were public documents, public speeches, information available to all. As before, much of the Crown's evidence consisted of books, papers and documents seized from the accused during numerous raids that took place between 1952 and 1956, as well as notes taken by the police at Congress meetings during this same period. As before, the reports of our speeches by the Special Branch officers were generally muddled. We used to joke that between the poor acoustics of the hall and the confused and inaccurate reports of the Special Branch detectives, we could be fined for what we did not say, imprisoned for what we could not hear and hanged for what we did not do.

At lunchtime we were permitted to sit outside in the spacious garden of a neighbouring vicarage where we were supplied with a meal cooked by the redoubtable Mrs Thayanagee Pillay and her friends. They prepared a spicy Indian lunch for us almost every day, and also tea, coffee and sandwiches during the morning and afternoon breaks. These respites were like tiny vacations from court, and were a chance for us to

discuss politics with each other. Those moments under the shade of
the jacaranda trees on the vicarage lawn were the most pleasant of the
trial, for in many ways the case was more a test of our endurance than
a trial of justice.

On the morning of 11 October, as we were preparing to go to court,
we heard an announcement on the radio that the prosecutor, Oswald
Pirow, had died suddenly from a stroke. His death was a severe setback
to the government, and the effectiveness and aggressiveness of the Crown
team diminished from that point on. In court that day, Judge Rumpff
paid an emotional eulogy to Pirow, and praised his legal acumen and
thoroughness. Although we would benefit from his absence, we did
not rejoice at his death. We had developed a certain affection for
our opponent, for despite Pirow's noxious political views, he was a
humane man without the virulent personal racism of the government
he was acting for. His habitual polite reference to us as 'Africans'
(even one of our own attorneys occasionally slipped and referred to
us as 'natives') contrasted with his supremacist political leanings. In a
curious way, our small world inside the Old Synagogue seemed balanced
when, each morning, we observed Pirow reading the right-wing *Nuwe
Order* at his table and Bram Fischer reading the left-wing *New Age* at
ours. His donation to us of the more than a hundred volumes of the
preparatory examination free of charge was a generous gesture that
saved the defence a great deal of money. Advocate de Vos became the
new leader of the Crown's team, but could not match the eloquence
or acuity of his predecessor.

Shortly after Pirow's death, the prosecution concluded its submission
of evidence. It was then that the prosecution began its examination of
expert witnesses commencing with the long-suffering Professor Murray,
its supposed expert in communism who had proved so inept in his subject
during the preparatory examination. In a relentless cross-examination by
Maisels, Murray admitted that the charter was in fact a humanitarian
document that might well represent the natural reaction and aspirations
of non-whites to the harsh conditions in South Africa.

Murray was not the only Crown witness who did little to advance the
state's case. Despite the voluminous amount of Crown evidence and the
pages and pages of testimony from their expert witnesses, the prosecution
had not managed to produce any valid evidence that the ANC plotted
violence, and they knew it. Then, in March, the prosecution displayed a
new burst of confidence. They were about to release their most damning
evidence. With great fanfare and a long drumroll in the press, the state
played for the court a secretly recorded speech of Robert Resha's. This
had been given in his capacity as Transvaal Volunteer-in-Chief to a

roomful of Freedom Volunteers in 1956, a few weeks before we were all to be arrested. The courtroom was very quiet, and despite the static of the recording and the background din, one could make out Robert's words very clearly.

> When you are disciplined and you are told by the organization not to be violent, you must not be violent ... but if you are a true volunteer and you are called upon to be violent, you must be absolutely violent, you must murder! Murder! That is all.

The prosecution believed it had sealed its case. Newspapers prominently featured Resha's words and echoed the sensibilities of the state. To the Crown, the speech revealed the ANC's true and secret intent, unmasking the ANC's public pretence of non-violence. But in fact, Resha's words were an anomaly. Robert was an excellent if rather excitable platform speaker, and his choice of analogy was unfortunate. But as the defence would show, he was merely emphasizing the importance of discipline and that the volunteer must do whatever he is ordered, however unsavoury. Over and over, our witnesses would show that Resha's speech was not only taken out of context but did not represent ANC policy.

The prosecution concluded its case on 10 March 1960 and we were to call our first witness for the defence four days later. We had been in the doldrums for months, but as we started to prepare ourselves for our testimony, we were eager to go on the offensive. We had been parrying the enemy's attacks for too long.

There had been much speculation in the press that our first witness would be Chief Luthuli. The Crown apparently believed that as well, for there was great consternation among the prosecution when, on 14 March, our first witness was not Luthuli but Dr Wilson Conco.

Conco was the son of a Zulu cattle farmer from the beautiful Ixopo district of Natal. In addition to being a practising physician, he had been one of the founders of the Youth League, an active participant in the Defiance Campaign and the treasurer of the ANC. As a preparation for his testimony, he was asked about his brilliant academic record at the University of the Witwatersrand, where he graduated top of his medical school class, ahead of all the sons and daughters of white privilege. As Conco's credentials were cited, I got the distinct impression that Justice Kennedy, who was also from Natal, seemed proud. Natalians are noted for their loyalty to their region, and these peculiar bonds of attachment can sometimes even transcend colour. Indeed, many Natalians thought of themselves as white Zulus. Justice Kennedy had always seemed to be a fair-minded man and I sensed that, through Wilson Conco's example, he began to see us not as heedless rabble-rousers but men of worthy ambitions who could help their country if their country would only help them. At the end of Conco's testimony, when Conco was quoted for some medical achievement, Kennedy said in Zulu, a language in which he was fluent, 'Sinjalo thina maZulu', which means, 'We Zulus are like that.' Dr Conco proved a calm and articulate witness who reaffirmed the ANC's commitment to non-violence.

Chief Luthuli was next. With his dignity and sincerity, he made a deep impression on the court. He was suffering from high blood pressure, and the court agreed to sit only in the mornings while he gave evidence. His evidence-in-chief lasted several days and he was cross-examined for nearly three weeks. He carefully outlined the evolution of the ANC's policy, putting things simply and clearly, and his former positions as teacher and chief imparted an added gravity and authority to his words. As a devout Christian, he was the perfect person to discuss how the ANC had sincerely strived for racial harmony.

The chief testified to his belief in the innate goodness of man and how moral persuasion plus economic pressure could well lead to a change of heart on the part of white South Africans. In discussing the ANC's policy of non-violence, he emphasized that there was a difference between non-violence and pacifism. Pacifists refused to defend themselves even when violently attacked, but that was not necessarily the case with those who espoused non-violence. Sometimes men and nations, even when non-violent, had to defend themselves when they were attacked.

As I listened to Conco and Luthuli, I thought that here, probably for the first time in their lives, the judges were listening not to their domestic servants who said only what they knew their masters would like to hear, but to independent and articulate Africans spelling out their political beliefs and how they hoped to realize them.

The chief was cross-examined by Advocate Trengrove, who doggedly attempted to get him to say the ANC was dominated by communists and had a dual policy of non-violence intended for the public and a secret plan of waging violent revolution. The chief steadfastly refuted the implications of what Trengrove was suggesting. He himself was the soul of moderation, particularly as Trengrove seemed to lose control. At one point, Trengrove accused the chief of hypocrisy. The chief ignored Trengrove's aspersion and calmly remarked to the bench, 'My Lord, I think the Crown is running wild.'

But on 21 March the chief's testimony was interrupted by a shattering event outside the courtroom. On that day, the country was rocked by an occurrence of such magnitude that when Chief Luthuli returned to testify a month later, the courtroom – and all of South Africa – was a different place.

33

The December 1959 ANC annual conference was held in Durban during that city's dynamic anti-pass demonstrations. The conference unanimously voted to initiate a massive countrywide anti-pass campaign beginning on 31 March and climaxing on 26 June with a great bonfire of passes.

The planning began immediately. On 31 March, deputations were sent to local authorities. ANC officials toured the country, talking to the branches about the campaign. ANC field-workers spread the word in townships and factories. Leaflets, stickers and posters were printed and circulated and posted in trains and buses.

The mood of the country was grim. The state was threatening to ban the organization, with cabinet ministers warning the ANC that it would soon be battered with 'an ungloved fist'. Elsewhere in Africa the freedom struggle was marching on: the emergence of the independent republic of Ghana in 1957 and its pan-Africanist, anti-apartheid leader, Kwame Nkrumah, had alarmed the Nationalists and made them even more intent on clamping down on dissent at home. In 1960 seventeen former colonies in Africa were scheduled to become independent states. In February, the British prime minister Harold Macmillan visited South Africa and gave a speech before Parliament in which he talked of 'winds of change' sweeping Africa.

The PAC at the time appeared lost; they were a leadership in search of followers, and they had yet to initiate any action that put them on the political map. They knew of the ANC's antipass campaign and had been invited to join, but instead of linking arms with the Congress movement, they sought to sabotage us. The PAC announced that it was launching its own anti-pass campaign on 21 March, ten days before ours was to begin. No conference had been held by them to discuss the date, no organizational work of any significance had been undertaken. It was a blatant case of opportunism. Their actions were motivated more by a desire to eclipse the ANC than to defeat the enemy.

Four days before the scheduled demonstration, Sobukwe invited us to join with the PAC. Sobukwe's offer was not a gesture of unity but a tactical move to prevent the PAC from being criticized for not including us. He made the offer at the eleventh hour, and we declined to participate. On the morning of 21 March Sobukwe and his executive walked to the Orlando police station to turn themselves in for arrest. The tens of thousands of people going to work ignored the PAC men. In the magistrate's court, Sobukwe announced that the PAC would not attempt to defend itself, in accordance with its slogan: 'No bail, no defence, no fine'. They believed the defiers would receive sentences of a few weeks. But Sobukwe was sentenced not to three weeks but three years' imprisonment without the option of a fine.

The response to the PAC's call in Johannesburg was minimal. No demonstrations at all took place in Durban, Port Elizabeth or East London. But in Evaton Z.B. Molete, ably assisted by Joe Molefi, and Vusumuzi Make, mustered the support of the entire township as several hundred men presented themselves for arrest without passes. Cape Town saw one of the biggest anti-pass demonstrations in the history of the city. In Langa township, outside Cape Town, some thirty thousand people, led by the young student, Philip Kgosana, gathered and were spurred to rioting by a police baton-charge. Two people were killed. But the last of the areas where demonstrations took place was the most calamitous and the one whose name still echoes with tragedy: Sharpeville.

Sharpeville was a small township about thirty-five miles south of Johannesburg in the grim industrial complex around Vereeniging. PAC activists had done an excellent job of organizing the area. In the early afternoon, a crowd of several thousand surrounded the police station. The demonstrators were controlled and unarmed. The police force of seventy-five was greatly outnumbered and panicky. No one heard warning shots or an order to shoot, but suddenly the police opened fire on the crowd and continued to shoot as the demonstrators turned and ran in fear. When the area had cleared, sixty-nine Africans lay dead, most of them shot in the back as they were fleeing. All told, more than seven hundred shots had been fired into the crowd, wounding more than four hundred people, including dozens of women and children. It was a massacre, and the next day press photos displayed the savagery on front pages around the world.

The shootings at Sharpeville provoked national turmoil and a government crisis. Outraged protests came in from across the globe, including one from the American State Department. For the first time, the UN Security Council intervened in South African affairs, blaming the government for the shootings and urging it to initiate measures to bring about racial equality. The Johannesburg stock exchange plunged, and capital started to flow out of the country. South African whites began making plans to emigrate. Liberals urged Verwoerd to offer concessions to Africans. The government insisted that Sharpeville was the result of a communist conspiracy.

The massacre at Sharpeville created a new situation in the country. In spite of the amateurishness and opportunism of their leaders, the PAC rank and file displayed great courage and fortitude in their demonstrations at Sharpeville and Langa. In just one day, they had moved to the front lines of the struggle, and Robert Sobukwe was being hailed inside and outside the country as the saviour of the liberation movement. We in the ANC had to make rapid adjustments to this new situation, and we did so.

A small group of us – Walter, Duma Nokwe, Joe Slovo and I – held an all-night meeting in Johannesburg to plan a response. We knew we had to acknowledge the events in some way and give the people an outlet for their anger and grief. We conveyed our plans to Chief Luthuli, and he readily accepted them. On 26 March, in Pretoria, the chief publicly burned his pass, calling on others to do the same. He announced a nationwide stay-at-home for 28 March, a national Day of Mourning and protest for the atrocities at Sharpeville. In Orlando, Duma Nokwe and I then burned our passes before hundreds of people and dozens of press photographers.

Two days later, on the 28th, the country responded magnificently as several hundred thousand Africans observed the chief's call. Only a truly mass organization could coordinate such activities, and the ANC did so. In Cape Town a crowd of fifty thousand met in Langa township to protest against the shootings. Rioting broke out in many areas. The government declared a State of Emergency, suspending habeas corpus and assuming sweeping powers to act against all forms of subversion. South Africa was now under martial law.

34

At 1.30 in the morning on 30 March I was awakened by sharp, unfriendly knocks at my door, the unmistakable signature of the police. 'The time has come,' I said to myself as I opened the door to find half-a-dozen armed security policemen. They turned the house upside down, taking virtually every piece of paper they could find, including the transcripts I had recently been making of my mother's recollections of family history and tribal fables. I was never to see them again. I was then arrested without a warrant, and given no opportunity to call my lawyer. They refused to inform my wife as to where I was to be taken. I simply nodded at Winnie; it was no time for words of comfort.

Thirty minutes later we arrived at Newlands police station, which was familiar to me from the many occasions when I had visited clients there. The station was located in Sophiatown, or rather what was left of it, for the once bustling township was now a ruin of bulldozed buildings and vacant plots. Inside I found a number of my colleagues who had been similarly roused out of bed, and over the course of the night, more arrived; by morning we totalled forty in all. We were put in a cramped yard with only the sky as a roof and a dim bulb for light, a space so small and dank that we remained standing all night.

At 7.15 we were taken into a tiny cell with a single drainage hole in the floor which could be flushed only from the outside. We were given no blankets, no food, no mats and no toilet paper. The hole regularly became blocked and the stench in the room was insufferable. We issued numerous protests, among them the demand to be fed. These were met with surly rejoinders, and we resolved that the next time the door opened, we would surge out into the adjacent courtyard and refuse to return to the cell until we had been fed. The young policeman on duty took fright and left as we stampeded through the door. A few minutes later, a burly no-nonsense sergeant entered the courtyard and ordered us to return to the cell. 'Go inside!' he yelled. 'If you don't, I'll bring in fifty men with batons and we'll break your skulls!' After the horrors of Sharpeville, the threat did not seem empty.

The station commander approached the gate of the courtyard to observe us, and then came over and berated me for standing with my hands in my pockets. 'Is that the way you act around an officer?' he yelled. 'Take your bloody hands out of your pockets!' I kept my hands firmly rooted in my pockets as though I were taking a walk on a chilly day. I told him that I might condescend to remove my hands if we were fed.

At 3 p.m., more than twelve hours after most of us had arrived, we were delivered a container of thin mealie pap and no utensils. Normally I would have considered this unfit for consumption, but we reached in with our unwashed hands and ate as though we had been provided with the most delicious delicacies under the sun. After our meal, we elected a committee to represent us, which included Duma Nokwe and Z. B. Molete, the publicity secretary of the Pan-Africanist Congress, and me. I was elected spokesman. We immediately drew up a petition protesting at the unfit conditions and demanding our immediate release on the ground that our detention was illegal.

At 6 p.m. we received sleeping-mats and blankets. I do not think words can do justice to a description of the foulness and filthiness of this bedding. The blankets were encrusted with dried blood and vomit, ridden with lice, vermin and cockroaches, and reeked with a stench that actually competed with the stink of the drain.

Near midnight, we were told we were to be called out, but for what we did not know. Some of the men smiled at the expectation of release. Others knew better. I was the first to be called, and I was ushered over to the front gate of the prison where I was briefly released in front of a group of police officers. But before I could move, an officer shouted: 'Name!'

'Mandela,' I said.

'Nelson Mandela,' the officer said, 'I arrest you under the powers vested in me by the Emergency Regulations.' We were not to be released at all, but rearrested under the terms of what we only then discovered was a State of Emergency. Each of us in turn was released for mere seconds and then rearrested. We had been arrested illegally before the State of Emergency; now we were being properly arrested under the State of Emergency that had come into force at midnight. We drafted a memorandum to the commander asking to know our rights.

The next morning I was called to the commander's office, where I found my colleague Robert Resha, who had been arrested and was being interrogated by the station commander. When I walked into the room, Resha asked the commander why he had erupted at me the previous night.

His answer was that of the typical white *baas*: 'Mandela was cheeky.' I responded, 'I'm not bound to take my hands out of my pockets for the likes of you, then or now.' The commander jumped out of his chair, but was restrained by other officers. At this moment, Special Branch Detective Sergeant Helberg entered the office and said, 'Hello, Nelson!' in a pleasant way. To which I shot back, 'I am not Nelson to you, I am Mr Mandela.' The room was on the brink of becoming a full-scale battle when we were informed that we had to leave to attend the Treason Trial in Pretoria. I did not know whether to laugh or despair, but in the midst of this thirty-six hours of mistreatment and the declaration of a State of Emergency, the government still saw fit to take us back to Pretoria to continue their desperate and now seemingly outdated case against us. We were taken straight to Pretoria Local Prison and detained.

35

In the meantime, court resumed in our absence, on 31 March, but the witness box was conspicuously empty. Those who did attend, were the accused whom the police had failed to pick up under the State of Emergency. Chief Luthuli had been in the middle of his evidence, and Judge Rumpff asked for an explanation for his absence. He was informed that the chief had been taken into custody the night before. Judge Rumpff expressed irritation with the explanation and said he did not see why the State of Emergency should stand in the way of his trial. He demanded that the police bring the chief to court so that he could resume his testimony, and court was adjourned.

Later we discovered that after the chief's arrest, he had been assaulted. He had been walking up some stairs when he was jostled by a warder, causing his hat to fall to the floor. As he bent to pick it up, he was smacked across the head and face. This was hard for us to take. A man of immense dignity and achievement, a lifelong devout Christian and a man with a dangerous heart condition was treated like a barnyard animal by men who were not fit to tie his shoes.

When we were called back into session that morning, Judge Rumpff was informed that the police refused to bring the chief to court. The judge then adjourned court for the day, and we expected to go home. But as they were leaving the court grounds to find transport, we were all once again arrested.

But the police, with their usual disorganized overzealousness, made a comical mistake. Wilton Mkwayi, one of the accused and a longtime union leader and ANC man, had travelled to Pretoria for the trial from Port Elizabeth. Somehow he had become separated from his colleagues, and when he approached the gate and saw the commotion of his fellow accused being rearrested, he asked a policeman what was going on. The policeman ordered him to leave. Wilton stood there. The policeman again ordered him to leave, whereupon Wilton informed the officer he was one of the accused. The officer called him a liar, and threatened to arrest him for obstruction of justice. The officer then angrily ordered him to leave the area. Wilton shrugged his shoulders and walked out of the gate; that was the last anyone saw of him in court. He went underground for the next two months, successfully evading arrest, and then was smuggled out of the country, soon emerging as a foreign representative for the Congress of Trade Unions and later going for military training in China.

That night, we were joined by detainees from other parts of the Transvaal. The countrywide police raid had led to the detention without trial of more than two thousand people. These men and women belonged to all races and all anti-apartheid parties. A call-up of soldiers had been announced, and units of the army had been mobilized and stationed in strategic areas around the country. On 8 April both the ANC and the PAC were declared illegal organizations under the Suppression of Communism Act. Overnight, being a member of the ANC had become a felony punishable by a term in jail and a fine. The penalty for furthering the aims of the ANC was imprisonment for up to ten years. Now even non-violent law-abiding protests under the auspices of the ANC were illegal. The struggle had entered a new phase. We were now, all of us, outlaws.

For the duration of the State of Emergency we stayed at Pretoria Local, where the conditions were as bad as those at Newlands. Groups of five prisoners were pressed into cells measuring nine by seven feet; the cells were filthy, with poor lighting and worse ventilation. We had a single sanitary pail with a loose lid, and vermin-infested blankets. We were allowed outside for an hour a day.

On our second day in Pretoria, we sent a deputation to complain about the conditions to the prison's commanding officer, Colonel Snyman. The colonel's response was rude and abrupt. He demanded that we produce evidence, calling our complaints lies. 'You have brought the vermin into my prison from your filthy homes,' he sneered.

I said we also required a room that was quiet and well lit so that we could prepare our case. The colonel was again contemptuous: 'Government regulations do not require prisoners to read books, if you can read at all.' Despite the colonel's disdainful attitude, the cells were soon painted and fumigated and we were supplied with fresh blankets and sanitary pails. We were permitted to stay out in the yard for much of the day, while those of us involved in the Treason Trial were provided with a large cell for consultations, in which we were also permitted to keep legal books.

Pretoria Local would be our home for the foreseeable future. We would leave for the trial in the morning and return to the prison in the afternoon. The prison, according to apartheid dictates, separated detainees by colour. We were of course already separated from our white colleagues, but the separation from our Indian and Coloured comrades within the same non-white facility seemed like madness. We demanded to be accommodated together, and were given all sorts of absurd explanations why this was impossible. When the proverbial inflexibility of red tape is combined with the petty small-mindedness of racism, the result can be mind-boggling. But the authorities eventually yielded, allowing the Treason Trialists to be kept together.

Although we were kept together, our diet was fixed according to race. For breakfast, Africans, Indians and Coloureds received the same quantities, except that Indians and Coloureds received a half-teaspoonful of sugar, which we did not. For supper, the diets were the same, except that Indians and Coloureds received four ounces of bread while we received none. This latter distinction was made on the curious premise that Africans did not naturally like bread, which was a more sophisticated or 'Western' taste. The diet for white detainees was far superior to that for Africans. So colour-conscious were the authorities that even the type of sugar and bread supplied to blacks and whites differed: white prisoners received white sugar and white bread, while Coloured and Indian prisoners were given brown sugar and brown bread.

We complained vociferously about the inferior quality of the food and, as a result, our advocate Sydney Kentridge made a formal complaint in court. I stated that the food was unfit for human consumption. Judge Rumpff agreed to sample the food himself that day. Samp and beans was the best meal that the prison prepared, and in this case the authorities put in more beans and gravy than usual. Judge Rumpff ate a few spoonfuls and pronounced the food well cooked and tasty. He did allow that it should be served warm. We laughed among ourselves at the idea of 'warm' jail food; it was a contradiction in terms. Eventually the authorities supplied the detainees with what they called an Improved Diet: Africans received bread, while Indians and Coloureds received the same food as that provided for white prisoners.

I enjoyed one extraordinary privilege during our detention: weekend trips to Johannesburg. These were not a vacation from prison but a busman's holiday. Shortly before the State of Emergency, Oliver left South Africa on the instructions of the ANC. We had long suspected a clamp-down was coming, and Congress decided that certain members needed to leave the country to strengthen the organization abroad in anticipation of the time when it would be banned entirely.

Oliver's departure was one of the best-planned and fortunate actions ever taken by the movement. At the time we hardly suspected how absolutely vital the external wing would become. With his wisdom and calmness, his patience and organizational skills, his ability to lead and inspire without stepping on toes, Oliver was the perfect choice for this assignment.

Before leaving, Oliver had retained a mutual friend of ours, Hymie Davidoff, a local attorney, to close our office and wind up our practice. Davidoff made a special request to Colonel Prinsloo to permit me to come to Johannesburg at weekends to help him put things in order. In a fit of generosity, the colonel agreed, allowing me to be driven to Johannesburg on Friday afternoons to work in the office all weekend and then be driven back to the trial on Monday morning. Sergeant Kruger and I would leave after court adjourned at one o'clock on Friday, and after arriving at my office I would work with Davidoff and our accountant Nathan Marcus. I would spend the nights in Marshall Square prison and the days at the office.

Sergeant Kruger was a tall and imposing fellow who treated us with fairness. On the way from Pretoria to Johannesburg he would often stop the car and leave me inside while he went into a shop to buy biltong, oranges and chocolate for both of us. I thought about jumping out of the car, especially on Fridays, when the pavements and streets were busy and one could get lost in a crowd.

While at the office, I could walk downstairs to the ground-floor café to buy incidentals, and he turned his head aside on one or two occasions when Winnie came to visit me. We had a kind of gentleman's code between us: I would not escape and thereby get him into trouble, while he permitted me a degree of freedom.

36

On 25 April, the day before the trial was to resume, Issy Maisels called us together to discuss the grave effect the State of Emergency was having on the conduct of the trial. Because of the Emergency Regulations, consultations between the accused and our lawyers had become virtually impossible. Our lawyers, who were based in Johannesburg, had trouble seeing us in prison and were unable to prepare our case. They would often drive up and be informed that we were not available. Even when we were able to see them, consultations were harassed and cut short. More important, Maisels explained that under the Emergency Regulations, those already in detention would be exposing themselves to further detention merely by testifying, for they would inevitably make statements regarded as 'subversive', thereby subjecting themselves to greater penalties. Defence witnesses who were not imprisoned now risked detainment if they testified.

The defence team proposed that they withdraw from the case in protest. Maisels explained the serious implications of such a withdrawal and the consequences of our conducting our own defence in a capital case. Under the hostile atmosphere at the time, he said, the judges might see fit to give us longer terms of imprisonment. We discussed the proposal among ourselves, and each of the twenty-nine accused – we were now minus Wilton Mkwayi – was able to express his opinion. The resolution was unanimously endorsed, and it was agreed that Duma Nokwe and I would help in preparing the case in the absence of our lawyers. I was in favour of this dramatic gesture, for it highlighted the iniquities of the State of Emergency.

On 26 April Duma Nokwe, the first African advocate in the Transvaal, rose in court and made the sensational announcement that the accused were instructing defence counsel to withdraw from the case. Maisels then said simply, 'We have no further mandate and we will consequently not trouble Your Lordships any further,' after which the defence team silently filed out of the synagogue. This shocked the three-judge panel,

who warned us in direst terms about the dangers of conducting our own
defence. But we were angry and eager to take on the state. For the next
five months, until the virtual end of the Emergency, we conducted our
own defence.

Our strategy was simple and defensive in nature: to drag out the case
until the State of Emergency was lifted and our lawyers could return.
The case had gone on so long already that it did not seem to matter
if we stretched it out even further. In practice, this strategy became
rather comical. Under the law, each one of us was now entitled to
conduct his own defence and was able to call as a witness each of the
other accused; and each of the accused was entitled to cross-examine
each witness. We were arranged in alphabetical order according to the
docket and accused No. 1 was Farid Adams, of the Transvaal Indian
Youth Congress. Farid would open his case by calling accused No. 2,
Helen Joseph, as his first witness. After being examined by Farid, Helen
would then be cross-examined by the other twenty-seven co-accused. She
would then be cross-examined by the Crown and re-examined by accused
No. 1. Adams would then proceed to call accused No. 3 and so on, and the
whole procedure would duplicate itself until every accused was called in
this fashion. At that rate, we would be at trial until the millennium.

It is never easy to prepare a case from prison, and in this instance we
were hampered by the customary apartheid barriers. All of the accused
needed to be able to meet together, but prison regulations prohibited
meetings between male and female prisoners, and between black and
white, so we were not permitted to consult with Helen Joseph, Leon
Levy, Lilian Ngoyi and Bertha Mashaba.

Helen, as the first witness to be called, needed to prepare her
evidence in the presence of Duma, myself and Farid Adams, who
would be examining her. After protracted negotiations with the prison
authorities, we were permitted to have consultations under very strict
conditions. Helen Joseph, Lilian, Leon, and Bertha were to be brought
from their various prisons and sections (separated by race and gender)
to the African men's prison. The first stipulation was that there
could be no physical contact between white and black prisoners,
and between male and female prisoners. The authorities erected an
iron grille to separate Helen and Leon (as whites) from us and a
second partition to separate them from Lilian and Bertha (as African women), who were also participating in the preparations. Helen
needed to be separated from Lilian because of colour, and from us
because of sex and colour. Even a master architect would have had
trouble designing such a structure. In prison we were separated from

each other by this elaborate metal contraption, while in court we all mingled freely.

We first needed to coach Farid in the art of courtroom etiquette, and rehearse Helen's testimony. To help Helen, I was playing the role that Farid would play in court. I assumed the proper courtroom manner and began the examination.

'Name?' I said.

'Helen Joseph,' she replied.

'Age?'

Silence. I repeated, 'Age?'

Helen pursed her lips and waited. Then, after some moments, she scowled at me and said sharply, 'What has my age to do with this case, Nelson?'

Helen was as charming as she was courageous, but she also had an imperious side. She was a woman of a certain age, and sensitive about it. I explained that it was customary to note down the witness's particulars, such as name, age, address and place of birth. A witness's age helps the court to weigh her testimony and influences the sentencing.

I continued: 'Age?'

Helen stiffened. 'Nelson,' she said, 'I will cross that bridge when I come to it in court, but not until then. Let us move on.'

I then asked her a series of questions that she might expect from the Crown in a manner perhaps too realistic for her, because at one point Helen turned to me and said, 'Are you Mandela or are you the prosecutor?'

There were other light moments, some of which were quite encouraging. I was permitted to visit Helen Joseph at weekends and bring her records of the proceedings. On these occasions I met other women detainees and consulted with them as possible witnesses. I was always very cordial with the white wardresses, and I noticed that my visits caused considerable interest. The wardresses had never known there *was* such a species as an African lawyer or doctor, and regarded me as an exotic creature. But as I became more familiar they became more friendly and at ease, and I joked with them that I would handle any of their legal problems. Seeing prominent and educated white women discussing serious matters with a black man on the basis of perfect equality could only lead to the weakening of the wardresses' apartheid assumptions.

Once during a long interview with Helen, I turned to the wardress who was required to sit in on our conversation and said, 'I'm sorry to bore you with this endless consultation.' 'No,' she said, 'you are not boring me at all, I am enjoying it.' I could see she was following our conversation, and once or twice she even offered small suggestions. I saw this as one of the side benefits of the trial. Most of these wardresses had no idea why we were in prison, and gradually began to discover what we were fighting for and why we were willing to risk jail in the first place.

This is precisely why the National Party was violently opposed to all forms of integration. Only a white electorate indoctrinated with the idea of the black threat, ignorant of African ideas and policies, could support the monstrous racist philosophy of the National Party. Familiarity, in this case, would breed not contempt but understanding, and even, eventually, harmony.

The light moments in prison could not make up for the low ones. Winnie was allowed to visit on a number of occasions while I was in Pretoria, and each time she brought Zenani, who was then beginning to walk and talk. I would hold her and kiss her if the guards permitted, and towards the end of the interview, hand her back to Winnie. As Winnie was saying good-bye, and the guards were ushering them out, Zeni would often motion for me to come with them, and I could see from her small puzzled face that she did not understand why I could not.

In court, Farid Adams deftly led Helen through her evidence-in-chief. He argued frequently and fairly competently with the judges and sometimes outpointed them. We were now energized: no longer was anyone doing crossword puzzles to pass the time. As the accused took turns cross-examining the witnesses, the Crown and the prosecution began to get a sense for the first time of the true calibre of the men and women on trial.

According to South African law, since we were in the Supreme Court, Duma, as an advocate, was the only one permitted to address the judges direct. I, as an attorney, could instruct him, but I was not technically permitted to address the court, and neither were any of the other defendants. We dismissed our advocates under the correct assumption that an accused, in the absence of representation, would be permitted to address the court. I addressed the court and Justice Rumpff trying to frustrate us, interrupted me. 'You appreciate the fact, Mr Mandela,' he said, 'that Mr Nokwe, as an advocate, is the only lawyer who is permitted to address the court.' To which I replied, 'Very well, My Lord, I believe we are all prepared to abide by that as long as you are prepared to pay Mr Nokwe his fees.' From then on no one objected to any of the accused addressing the court.

While Farid was questioning Helen and the subsequent witnesses, Duma and I sat on either side of him, supplying him with questions, helping him to deal with legal issues as they arose. In general, he did not need much prompting. But one day, when we were under constant pressure, we were whispering suggestions to him every few seconds. Farid seemed weary, and Duma and I were running out of material. Then, without consulting us, Farid suddenly asked the judges for a postponement, saying he was fatigued. The judges refused his application, saying it was not sufficient reason for a postponement and reiterating the warning they gave us the day our lawyers withdrew.

That afternoon there was no singing as we returned to prison, and everyone sat with sullen faces. A crisis was brewing among the accused. Upon our arrival in prison, a handful of them demanded a meeting. I called all the men together, and J. Nkampeni, a businessman from Port Elizabeth who had helped out the families of defiers during the Defiance Campaign, led what turned out to be an attack.

'Madiba,' he said, using my clan name as a sign of respect, 'I want you to tell us why you drove away our lawyers.' I reminded him that the lawyers were not released by any one individual; their withdrawal had been approved by all, including himself. 'But what did we know about court procedure, Madiba?' he said. 'We relied on you lawyers.'

A substantial number of men shared Nkampeni's misgivings. I warned them against the dangers of being disheartened and insisted that we were doing quite well. I said that today was a minor setback, and that we would face worse difficulties. Our case was far more than a trial of legal issues between the Crown and a group of people charged with breaking the law. It was a trial of strength, a test of the power of a moral idea versus an immoral one, and I said we needed to worry about more than the legal technique of our advocates. The protest abated.

After Helen Joseph had been cross-examined and re-examined, accused No. 3, Ahmed Kathrada, opened his case. It was during the testimony of Kathy's second witness, accused No. 4, Stanley Lollan, a member of the executive of the Coloured People's Congress, that Prime Minister Verwoerd announced that the State of Emergency would soon be lifted. The Emergency had never been intended to be permanent, and the government believed that it had successfully stifled the liberation struggle. At this point our defence lawyers returned, to the general relief of all of us, though we remained in prison for another few weeks. We had been kept in detention and had functioned without our lawyers for more than five months.

My own testimony began on 3 August. I felt well prepared through my preparation of the others. After three years of silence, banning and internal exile, I looked forward to the chance to speak out before the people attempting to judge me. During my evidence-in-chief I preached moderation and reaffirmed the ANC's commitment to non-violent struggle. In answer to a question as to whether democracy could be achieved through gradual reforms, I suggested that it could.

> We demand universal adult franchise and we are prepared to exert economic pressure to attain our demands. We will launch defiance campaigns, stay-at-homes, either singly or together, until the Government should say, 'Gentlemen, we cannot have this state of affairs, laws being defied, and this whole situation created by stay-at-homes. Let's talk.' In my own view I would say, 'Yes, let us talk,' and the Government would say, 'We think that the Europeans at present are not ready for a type of government where they might be dominated by non-Europeans. We think we should give you 60 seats. The African population to elect 60 Africans to represent them in Parliament. We will leave the matter over for five years and we will review it at the end of five years.' In my view, that would be a victory, My Lords; we would have taken a significant step towards the attainment of universal adult suffrage for Africans, and we would then for the five years say that we will suspend civil disobedience.

The state was determined to prove that I was a dangerous, violence-spouting communist. While I was not a communist or a member of the party, I did not want to be seen as distancing myself from my communist allies. Although I could have been sent back to jail for voicing such views, I did not hesitate to reaffirm the tremendous support the communists had given us. At one point, the bench posed the question as to whether or not I thought a one-party state was a viable option for South Africa.

> NM: My Lord, it is not a question of form, it is a question of democracy. If democracy would be best expressed by a one-party system then I would examine the proposition very carefully. But if a democracy could best be expressed by a multiparty system, then I would examine that carefully. In this country, for example, we have a multiparty system at present, but so far as the non-Europeans are concerned, this is the most vicious despotism that you could think of.

I became testy with Judge Rumpff when he fell into the mistake made by so many white South Africans about the idea of a universal franchise. Their notion was that to exercise this responsibility, voters must be 'educated'. To a narrow-thinking person, it is hard to explain that to be 'educated' does not only mean being literate and having a

BA, and that an illiterate man can be a far more 'educated' voter than someone with an advanced degree.

> JUSTICE RUMPFF: What is the value of participation in the Government of a state of people who know nothing?
> NM: My Lord, what happens when illiterate whites vote . . .
> JUSTICE RUMPFF: Are they not subject as much to the influence of election leaders as children would be?
> NM: No, My Lord, this is what happens in practice. A man stands up to contest a seat in a particular area; he draws up a manifesto, and he says, 'These are the ideas for which I stand'; it is a rural area and he says, 'I am against stock limitation'; then, listening to the policy of this person, you decide whether this man will advance your interests if you return him to Parliament, and on that basis you vote for a candidate. It has nothing to do with education.
> JUSTICE RUMPFF: He only looks to his own interests?
> NM: No, a man looks at a man who will be able to best present his point of view and votes for that man.

I told the court that we believed we could achieve our demands without violence, through our numerical superiority.

> We had in mind that in the foreseeable future it will be possible for us to achieve these demands, and we worked on the basis that Europeans themselves, in spite of the wall of prejudice and hostility which we encountered, that they can never remain indifferent indefinitely to our demands, because we are hitting them in the stomach with our policy of economic pressure. The Europeans dare not look at it with indifference. They would have to respond to it and indeed, My Lord, they are responding to it.

The Emergency was lifted on the last day of August. We would be going home for the first time in five months. When people in Johannesburg heard about the end of the Emergency, they drove up on the chance that we might be released; when we were let go, we were met with a jubilant reception from friends and family. Winnie had got a ride to Pretoria and our reunion was joyous. I had not held my wife in five months or seen her smile with joy. For the first time in five months, I slept in my own bed that night.

After one has been in prison, it is the small things that one appreciates: being able to take a walk whenever one wants, going into a shop and buying a newspaper, speaking or choosing to remain silent. The simple act of being able to control one's person.

Even after the end of the Emergency, the trial continued for another nine months until 29 March 1961. In many ways, these were the glory days for the accused, for our own people were on the stand fearlessly enunciating ANC policy. Robert Resha forcefully disputed the government's absurd contention that the ANC wanted to induce the government to use violence so that we could use violence in return. Gert Sibande eloquently told the court of the miseries of African farmworkers. The venerable Isaac Behndy of Ladysmith, eighty-one years old, a lay preacher of the African Native Mission Church, explained why we opted for stay-at-homes instead of strikes.

In October the redoubtable Professor Matthews was called as our final witness. He was imperturbable on the witness stand and treated the prosecutors as though they were errant students who needed stern admonishment. Often he would reply to the arrogant prosecutor with some version of the following: 'What you really want me to say is that the speech which you allege is violent represents the policy of my organization. First, your contention is incorrect and second, I am not going to say that.'

He explained in beautiful language that the African people knew that a non-violent struggle would entail suffering but had chosen it because they prized freedom above all else. People, he said, will willingly undergo the severest suffering in order to free themselves from oppression. With Professor Matthews in the dock, the defence ended on a high note. After he finished testifying, Justice Kennedy shook his hand and expressed the hope that they would meet again under better circumstances.

37

After the lifting of the Emergency, the National Executive met secretly in September to discuss the future. We had had discussions in jail during the trial, but this was our first formal session. The state was arming itself not for an external threat but an internal one. We would not disband but carry on from underground. We would have to depart from the democratic procedures outlined in the ANC's constitution of holding conferences, branch meetings and public gatherings. New structures had to be created for communication with unbanned Congress organizations. But all of these new structures were illegal and would subject the participants to arrest and imprisonment. The Executive Committee and its subordinate structures would have to be severely streamlined to adapt to illegal conditions. Of necessity, we dissolved the ANC Youth League and Women's League. Some fiercely resisted these changes; but the fact was that we were now an illegal organization. For those who would continue to participate, politics went from being a risky occupation to a truly perilous one.

Though Mandela and Tambo had closed its doors and settled its remaining accounts, I continued to do whatever legal work I could. Numerous colleagues readily made their offices, staff and phone facilities available to me, but most of the time I preferred to work from Ahmed Kathrada's flat, No. 13 Kholvad House. Although my practice had dissolved, my reputation as a lawyer was undimmed. Soon, the lounge of No. 13 and the passage outside were crammed with clients. Kathy would return home and discover that the only room in which he could be alone was his kitchen.

During this period, I hardly had time for meals and saw very little of my family. I would stay late in Pretoria preparing for our case, or rush back to handle another case. When I could actually sit down to supper with my family, the telephone would ring and I would be called away. Winnie was pregnant again and infinitely patient. She was hoping her husband might actually be at the hospital when she gave birth. But it was not to be.

During the Christmas adjournment in 1960, I learned that Makgatho was ill in the Transkei where he was at school, and I violated my banning orders and went down to see him. I drove the entire night, stopping only for petrol. Makgatho required surgery, and I decided to bring him back with me to Johannesburg. I again drove all night, and took him to his mother's place while I went to arrange for his surgery. When I returned, I learned that Winnie had already gone into labour. I rushed to the non-European wing of Bridgman Memorial Hospital to find that mother and daughter were already in residence. The newborn girl was fine, but Winnie was very weak.

We named our new daughter Zindziswa, after the daughter of the poet laureate of the Xhosa people, Samuel Mqhayi, who had inspired me so many years before at Healdtown. The poet returned home after a very long trip to find that his wife had given birth to a daughter. He had not known that she was pregnant and assumed that the child had been fathered by another man. In our culture, when a woman gives birth, for ten days the husband does not enter the house where she is confined. In this case, the poet was too enraged to observe this custom, and he stormed into the house with an assegai, ready to stab both mother and daughter. But when he looked at the baby girl and saw that she was the image of himself, he stepped back, and said, 'u Zindzile,' which means, 'You are well established.' He named her Zindziswa, the feminine version of what he had said.

38

The Crown took over a month to do its summing up, which was often interrupted by interjections from the bench pointing out lapses in the argument. In March it was our turn. Issy Maisels categorically refuted the charges of violence. 'We admit that there is a question of non-cooperation and passive resistance,' he said. 'We shall say quite frankly that if non-cooperation and passive resistance constitute high treason, then we are guilty. But these are plainly not encompassed in the law of treason.'

Maisels's argument was continued by Bram Fischer, but on 23 March the bench cut short Bram's concluding argument. We still had weeks of argument ahead, but the judges asked for a week's adjournment. This was irregular, but we regarded it as a hopeful sign, for it suggested that they had already formed their opinion. We were to return to court six days later for what we presumed would be the verdict. In the meantime, I had work to do.

My bans were due to expire two days after the adjournment. I was almost certain that the police would not be aware of this, as they rarely kept track of when bans ended. It would be the first time in nearly five years that I would be free to leave Johannesburg, free to attend a meeting. That weekend was the long-planned All-in Conference in Pietermaritzburg. Its aim was to agitate for a national constitutional convention for all South Africans. I was secretly scheduled to be the main speaker at the conference. I would make the 300-mile drive down to Pietermaritzburg the night before I was down to speak.

The day before I was to leave, the National Working Committee met secretly to discuss strategy. After many meetings in prison and outside, we had decided that we would work from underground, adopting a strategy along the lines of the M-Plan. The organization would survive clandestinely. It was decided that if we were not convicted, I would go underground to travel about the country organizing the proposed national convention. Only someone operating full-time from underground would be free from the paralysing restrictions imposed by the enemy. It was decided that I would surface at certain events, hoping for a maximum of publicity, to show that the ANC was still fighting. It was not a proposal that came as a surprise to me, nor was it one I particularly relished, but it was something I knew I had to do. This would be a hazardous life, and I would be apart from my family, but when a man is denied the right to live the life he believes in, he has no choice but to become an outlaw.

When I returned home from the meeting it was as though Winnie could read my thoughts. Seeing my face, she knew that I was about to embark on a life that neither of us wanted. I explained what had transpired and that I would be leaving the next day. She took this stoically, as though she had expected it all along. She understood what I had to do, but that did not make it any easier for her. I asked her to pack a small suitcase for me. I told her that friends and relatives would look after her while I was gone. I did not tell her how long I would be away, and she did not ask. It was just as well, because I did not know the answer. I would return to Pretoria for what would probably be the verdict on Monday. No matter what the result, I would not be returning home: if we were convicted, I would go directly to prison; if we were discharged, I would immediately go underground.

My eldest son Thembi was in school in the Transkei, so I could not say good-bye to him, but that afternoon I fetched Makgatho and my daughter Makaziwe from their mother in Orlando East. We spent some hours together, walking on the veld outside town, talking and playing. I said good-bye to them, not knowing when I would see them again. The children of a freedom fighter also learn not to ask their father too many questions, and I could see in their eyes that they understood that something serious was occurring.

At home, I kissed the two girls good-bye and they waved as I got in the car with Wilson Conco and began the long drive to Natal.

Fourteen hundred delegates from all over the country representing 150 different religious, social, cultural and political bodies converged on Pietermaritzburg for the All-in Conference. When I walked out on stage on Saturday evening, 25 March, in front of this loyal and enthusiastic audience, it had been nearly five years since I had been free to give a speech on a public platform. I was met with a joyous reaction. I had almost forgotten the intensity of the experience of addressing a crowd.

In my speech I called for a national convention in which all South Africans, black and white, Indian and Coloured, would sit down in brotherhood and create a constitution that mirrored the aspirations of the country as a whole. I called for unity, and said we would be invincible if we spoke with one voice.

The All-in Conference called for a national convention of elected representatives of all adult men and women on an equal basis to determine a new non-racial democratic constitution for South Africa. A National Action Council was elected, with myself as honorary secretary, to communicate this demand to the government. If the government failed to call such a convention, we would call a countrywide three-day stay-away beginning on 29 May to coincide with the declaration of South Africa as a republic. I had no illusions that the state would agree to our proposal.

In October 1960 the government had held an all-white referendum on whether South Africa should become a republic. This was one of the long-cherished dreams of Afrikaner nationalism, to cast off ties with the country they had fought against in the Anglo-Boer war. The pro-republic sentiment won with 52 per cent of the vote, and the proclamation of the republic was set for 31 May 1961. We set our stay-at-home on the date of the proclamation to indicate that, for us, such a change was merely cosmetic.

Directly after the conference I sent Prime Minister Verwoerd a letter in which I formally enjoined him to call a national constitutional convention. I warned him that if he failed to call it we would stage the country's most massive three-day strike ever, beginning on 29 May. 'We have no illusions about the counter-measures your government might take,' I wrote. 'During the last twelve months we have gone through a period of grim dictatorship.' I also issued press statements affirming that the strike was a peaceful and non-violent stay-at-home. Verwoerd did not reply, except to describe my letter in Parliament as 'arrogant'. The government instead began to mount one of the most intimidating displays of force ever assembled in the country's history.

39

Even before the doors of the Old Synagogue opened on the morning of 29 March 1961, the day of the long-anticipated verdict in the Treason Trial, a crowd of supporters and press people jostled to get inside. Hundreds were turned away. When the judges brought the court to order, the visitors' gallery and the press bench were packed. Moments after Justice Rumpff pounded his gavel, the Crown made an extraordinary application to change the indictment. This was the fifty-ninth minute of the eleventh hour, and it was two years too late. The court rebuffed the prosecution and the gallery murmured its approval.

'Silence in court!' the orderly yelled, and Judge Rumpff announced that the three-judge panel had reached a verdict. Silence now reigned. In his deep, even voice, Judge Rumpff reviewed the court's conclusions. Yes, the African National Congress had been working to replace the government with a 'radically and fundamentally different form of state'; yes, the African National Congress had used illegal means of protest during the Defiance Campaign; yes, certain ANC leaders had made speeches advocating violence; and yes, there was a strong left-wing tendency in the ANC that was revealed in its anti-imperialist, anti-West, pro-Soviet attitudes, but:

> On all the evidence presented to this court and on our finding of fact it is impossible for this court to come to the conclusion that the African National Congress had acquired or adopted a policy to overthrow the state by violence, that is, in the sense that the masses had to be prepared or conditioned to commit direct acts of violence against the state.

The court said the prosecution had failed to prove that the ANC was a communist organization or that the Freedom Charter envisioned a communist state. After speaking for forty minutes, Justice Rumpff said, 'The accused are accordingly found not guilty and are discharged.'

The spectators' gallery erupted in cheers. We stood and hugged one another, and waved to the happy courtroom. All of us then paraded into the courtyard, smiling, laughing, crying. The crowd yelled and chanted as we emerged. A number of us hoisted our defence counsels on our shoulders, which was no easy task in the case of Issy Maisels, for he was such a large man. Flash-bulbs were popping all around us. We looked around for friends, wives, relatives. Winnie had come up, and I hugged her in joy, though I knew that while I might be free for this moment, I would not be able to savour that freedom. When we were all outside together, the Treason Trialists and the crowd all began to sing 'Nkosi Sikelel' iAfrika'.

After more than four years in court and dozens of prosecutors, thousands of documents and tens of thousands of pages of testimony, the state had failed in its mission. The verdict was an embarrassment to the government, both at home and abroad. Yet the result only made the state more bitter towards us. The lesson they took away was not that we had legitimate grievances but that they needed to be far more ruthless.

I did not regard the verdict as a vindication of the legal system or evidence that a black man could get a fair trial in a white man's court. It was the right verdict and a just one, but it was largely as a result of a superior defence team and the fair-mindedness of the panel of these particular judges.

The court system, however, was perhaps the only place in South Africa where an African could possibly receive a fair hearing and where the rule of law might still apply. This was particularly true in courts presided over by enlightened judges who had been appointed by the United Party. Many of these men still stood by the rule of law.

As a student, I had been taught that South Africa was a place where the rule of law was paramount and applied to all persons, regardless of their social status or official position. I sincerely believed this and planned my life based on that assumption. But my career as a lawyer and activist removed the scales from my eyes. I saw that there was a wide difference between what I had been taught in the lecture room and what I learned in the courtroom. I went from having an idealistic view of the law as a sword of justice to a perception of the law as a tool used by the ruling class to shape society in a way favourable to itself. I never expected justice in court, however much I fought for it, and though I sometimes received it.

In the case of the Treason Trial, the three judges rose above their prejudices, their education and their background. There is a streak of goodness in men that can be buried or hidden and then emerge unexpectedly. Justice Rumpff, with his aloof manner, gave the impression throughout the proceedings that he shared the point of view of the ruling white minority. Yet, in the end, an essential fairness dominated his judgment. Kennedy was less conservative than his colleagues and seemed attracted by the idea of equality. Once, for example, he and Duma Nokwe flew on the same plane from Durban to Johannesburg, and when the airline bus to town refused to take Duma, Kennedy also refused to ride in it. Judge Bekker always struck me as open-minded and seemed aware that the accused before him had suffered a great deal at the hands of the state. I commended these three men as individuals, not as representatives of the court or of the state or even of their race, but as exemplars of human decency under adversity.

Judge Bekker's wife was a person sensitive to the needs of others. During the State of Emergency, she collected goods which she brought to the accused.

But the consequence of the government's humiliating defeat was that the state decided never to let it happen again. From that day forth they were not going to rely on judges whom they had not themselves appointed. They were not going to observe what they considered the legal niceties that protected terrorists or permitted convicted prisoners certain rights in jail. During the Treason Trial, there were no examples of individuals being isolated, beaten and tortured in order to elicit information. All of those things became commonplace shortly thereafter.

PART SIX

———

The Black Pimpernel

40

I did not return home after the verdict. Although others were in a festive mood and eager to celebrate, I knew the authorities could strike at any moment, and I did not want to give them the opportunity. I was anxious to be off before I was banned or arrested, and I spent the night in a safe house in Johannesburg. It was a restless night in a strange bed, and I started at the sound of every car, thinking it might be the police.

Walter and Duma saw me off on the first leg of my journey, which was to take me to Port Elizabeth. There I met Govan Mbeki and Raymond Mhlaba to discuss the new underground structures of the organization. We met at the house of Dr Masla Pather, who would later be sentenced to two years in prison for allowing us to meet at his home. At safe houses arranged by the organization, I met the editor of the liberal *Port Elizabeth Morning Post* to discuss the campaign for a national convention, a goal several newspapers subsequently endorsed. I later visited Patrick Duncan, the editor and publisher of the liberal weekly *Contact*, a founding member of the Liberal Party, and one of the first white defiers during the Defiance Campaign. His newspaper had repeatedly been decrying ANC policy as being dictated by communists but, when he saw me, the first thing he said was that a close reading of the Treason Trial record had disabused him of that notion and he would correct it in his paper.

That night I addressed a meeting of African township ministers in Cape Town. I mention this because the opening prayer of one of the ministers has stayed with me over these many years and was a source of strength at a difficult time. He thanked the Lord for His bounty and goodnesss, for His mercy and His concern for all men. But then he took the liberty of reminding the Lord that some of His subjects were more downtrodden than others, and that it sometimes seemed as though He was not paying attention. The minister then said that if the Lord did not show a little more initiative in leading the black man to salvation, the black man would have to take matters into his own two hands. Amen.

On my last morning in Cape Town, I was leaving my hotel in the company of George Peake, a founding member of the South African Coloured People's Organization, and stopped to thank the Coloured manager of the hotel for looking after me so well. He was grateful, but also curious. He had discovered my identity and told me that the Coloured community feared that under an African government they would be just as oppressed as under the present white government. He was a middle-class businessman who probably had little contact with Africans, and feared them in the same way as whites did. This was a frequent anxiety on the part of the Coloured community, especially in the Cape, and though I was running late, I explained the Freedom Charter to this man and stressed our commitment to non-racialism. A freedom fighter must take every opportunity to make his case to the people.

The following day I joined a secret meeting of the ANC National Executive and the joint executives of the Congress movement in Durban to discuss whether the planned action should take the form of a stay-at-home or a fully-fledged strike with organized pickets and demonstrations. Those who argued for the strike said that the stay-at-home strategy we had used since 1950 had outlasted its usefulness, that at a time when the PAC was appealing to the masses, more militant forms of the struggle were necessary. The alternative view, which I advocated, was that stay-at-homes allowed us to strike at the enemy while preventing him from striking back. I argued that the confidence of the people in our campaigns had grown precisely because they realized that we were not reckless with their lives. Sharpeville, I said, for all the heroism of the demonstrators, had allowed the enemy to shoot down our people. I argued for stay-at-homes even though I was aware that our people around the country were becoming impatient with passive forms of struggle, but I did not think we should depart from our proven tactics without comprehensive planning, and we had neither the time nor the resources to do so. The decision was for a stay-at-home.

Living underground requires a seismic psychological shift. One has to plan every action, however small and seemingly insignificant. Nothing is innocent. Everything is questioned. You cannot be yourself; you must fully inhabit whatever role you have assumed. In some ways, this was not much of an adaptation for a black man in South Africa. Under apartheid, a black man lived a shadowy life between legality and illegality, between openness and concealment. To be a black man in South Africa meant not to trust anything, which was not unlike living underground for one's entire life.

I became a creature of the night. I would keep to my hideout during the day, and emerge to do my work when it became dark. I operated mainly from Johannesburg, but I would travel as necessary. I stayed in empty flats, in people's houses, wherever I could be alone and inconspicuous. Although I am a gregarious person, I love solitude even more. I welcomed the opportunity to be by myself, to plan, to think, to plot. But one can have too much solitude. I was terribly lonesome for my wife and family.

The key to being underground is to be invisible. Just as there is a way to walk into a room in order to make yourself stand out, there is a way of walking and behaving that makes you inconspicuous. As a leader, one often seeks prominence; as an outlaw, the opposite is true. When underground I did not walk as tall or stand as straight. I spoke more softly, with less clarity and distinction. I was more passive, more unobtrusive; I did not ask for things but let people tell me what to do. I did not shave or cut my hair. My most frequent disguise was as a chauffeur, chef or a 'garden boy'. I would wear the blue overalls of the field-worker and often wore round, rimless glasses known as Mazzawatee tea-glasses. I had a car and I wore a chauffeur's cap with my overalls. The pose of chauffeur was convenient because I could travel under the pretext of driving my master's car.

During those early months, when there was a warrant for my arrest and I was being pursued by the police, my outlaw existence caught the imagination of the press. Articles claiming that I had been here and there were on the front pages. Roadblocks were instituted all over the country, but the police repeatedly came up empty-handed. I was dubbed the Black Pimpernel, a somewhat derogatory adaptation of Baroness Orczy's fictional character the Scarlet Pimpernel, who daringly evaded capture during the French Revolution.

I travelled secretly about the country: I was with Muslims in the Cape, with sugar-workers in Natal, with factory workers in Port Elizabeth. I moved through townships in different parts of the country attending secret meetings at night. I would even feed the mythology of the Black Pimpernel by taking a pocketful of 'tickeys' (threepenny bits) and phoning individual newspaper reporters from telephone boxes and relaying stories of what we were planning or of the ineptitude of the police. I would pop up here and there to the annoyance of the police and to the delight of the people.

There were many wild and inaccurate stories about my experiences underground. People love to embellish tales of daring. I did have a number of narrow escapes, however, which no one knew about. On one occasion, I was driving in town and stopped at a traffic light. I looked to my left and in an adjacent car saw Colonel Spengler, the chief of the Witwatersrand Security Branch. It would have been a great plum for him to catch the Black Pimpernel. I was wearing a workman's cap, my blue overalls, and my glasses. He never looked my way, but even so the seconds I spent waiting for the light to change seemed like hours.

One afternoon, when I was in Johannesburg posing as a chauffeur and wearing my long dust-coat and cap, I was waiting on a corner to be picked up and I saw an African policeman striding deliberately towards me. I looked around to see if I had a place to run, but before I did, he smiled at me and surreptitiously gave me the thumbs-up ANC salute and was gone. Incidents like this happened many times, and I was reassured when I saw that we had the loyalty of many African policemen. There was a black sergeant who used to tip off Winnie as to what the police were doing. He would whisper to her, 'Make sure Madiba is not in Alexandra on Wednesday night because there is going to be a raid.' Black policemen have often been severely criticized during the struggle, but many have played covert roles that have been extremely valuable.

When I was underground, I remained as unkempt as possible. My overalls looked as though they had been through a lifetime of hard toil. The police had one picture of me with a beard, which they widely distributed, and my colleagues urged me to shave it off. But I had become attached to my beard, and I resisted all their efforts.

Not only was I not recognized, I was sometimes snubbed. Once, I was planning to attend a meeting in a distant area of Johannesburg and a well-known priest arranged with friends of his to put me up for the night. I arrived at the door, and before I could announce who I was, the elderly lady who answered exclaimed, 'No, we don't want such a man as you here!' and shut the door.

41

My time underground was mainly taken up in planning the 29 May stay-at-home. It was shaping up to be a virtual war between the state and the liberation movement. Late in May, the government staged countrywide raids on opposition leaders. Meetings were banned, printing presses were seized and legislation was rushed through Parliament permitting the police to detain charged prisoners for twelve days without bail.

Verwoerd declared that those supporting the strike, including sympathetic newspapers, were 'playing with fire', an ominous declaration, given the ruthlessness of the state. The government urged industries to provide sleeping accommodation for workers so that they would not have to return home during the strike. Two days before the stay-at-home, the government staged the greatest peacetime show of force in South African history. The military exercised its largest call-up since the war. Police holidays were cancelled. Military units were stationed at the entrances and exits of townships. While Saracen tanks rumbled through the dirt streets of the townships, helicopters hovered above, swooping down to break up any gathering. At night, the helicopters trained searchlights on houses.

The English-language press had widely publicized the campaign until a few days before it was to begin. But on the eve of the stay-at-home the entire English-language press crumbled and urged people to go to work. The PAC played the role of saboteur and released thousands of leaflets telling people to oppose the stay-at-home, and denouncing the ANC leaders as cowards. The PAC's actions shocked us. It is one thing to criticize, and that we can accept, but to attempt to break a strike by calling upon the people to go to work directly serves the interests of the enemy.

The night before the stay-at-home, I was scheduled to meet the Johannesburg leadership of the ANC at a safe house in Soweto. To avoid police roadblocks, I entered Soweto through Kliptown, which was normally not patrolled. But as I went around a blind corner I drove straight into what I had been trying to avoid: a roadblock. A white policeman indicated I should stop. I was dressed in my usual costume of overalls and chauffeur's cap. He squinted through the window at me and then stepped forward and searched the car on his own. Normally, this was the duty of the African police. After he had found nothing, he demanded my pass. I told him that I had left it at home by mistake, and casually recited a fictitious pass number. This seemed to satisfy him and he motioned me through.

On Monday 29 May, the first day of the stay-at-home, hundreds of thousands of people risked their jobs and livelihoods by not going to work. In Durban, Indian workers walked out of factories, while in the Cape thousands of Coloured workers stayed home. In Johannesburg, more than half of all employees stayed at home and in Port Elizabeth the rate was even higher. I praised the response as 'magnificent' to the press, lauding our people for 'defying unprecedented intimidation by the state'. The white celebration of Republic Day was drowned out by our protest.

Although reports on the first day of the stay-at-home suggested strong reactions in various parts of the country, the response as a whole appeared less than we had hoped. Communication was difficult, and bad news always seems to travel more efficiently than good. As more reports came in, I felt let down and disappointed by the reaction. That evening, feeling demoralized and rather angry, I had a conversation with Benjamin Pogrund of the *Rand Daily Mail* in which I suggested that the days of non-violent struggle were over.

On the second day of the stay-at-home, after consultations with my colleagues, I called it off. That morning in a safe flat in a white suburb I met various members of the local and foreign press, and I once again called the stay-at-home 'a tremendous success'. But I did not mask the fact that I believed a new day was dawning. I said, 'If the government reaction is to crush by naked force our non-violent struggle, we will have to reconsider our tactics. In my mind we are closing a chapter on this question of a non-violent policy.' It was a grave declaration, and I knew it. I was criticized by our Executive for making that remark before it was discussed by the organization, but sometimes one must go public with an idea to push a reluctant organization in the direction you want it to go.

The debate on the use of violence had been going on among us since early 1960. I had first discussed the armed struggle as far back as 1952 with Walter Sisulu. Now, I again conferred with him and we agreed that the organization had to set out on a new course. The Communist Party had secretly reconstituted itself underground and was now considering forming its own military wing. We decided that I should raise the issue of the armed struggle within the Working Committee, and I did so in a meeting in June of 1961.

I had barely commenced my proposal when Moses Kotane, the secretary of the Communist Party and one of the most powerful figures in the ANC Executive, staged a counter-assault, accusing me of not having thought out the proposal carefully enough. He said that I had been outmanoeuvred and paralysed by the government's actions, and now in desperation I was resorting to revolutionary language. 'There is still room,' he stressed, 'for the old methods if we are imaginative and determined enough. If we embark on the course Mandela is suggesting, we will be exposing innocent people to massacres by the enemy.'

Moses spoke persuasively and I could see that he had defeated my proposal. Even Walter did not speak on my behalf, and I backed down. Afterwards I spoke with Walter and voiced my frustration, chiding him for not coming to my aid. He laughed and said it would have been as foolish as attempting to fight a pride of angry lions. Walter is a diplomat and extremely resourceful. 'Let me arrange for Moses to come and see you privately,' he said, 'and you can make your case that way.' I was underground, but Walter managed to put the two of us together in a house in the township and we spent the whole day talking.

I was candid and explained why I believed we had no choice but to turn to violence. I used an old African expression: '*Sebatana ha se bokwe ka diatla*' ('The attacks of the wild beast cannot be averted with only bare hands'). Moses was a long-time communist, and I told him that his opposition was like the Communist Party in Cuba under Batista. The party had insisted that the appropriate conditions had not yet arrived, and waited because they were simply following the textbook definitions of Lenin and Stalin. Castro did not wait, he acted – and he triumphed. If you wait for textbook conditions, they will never occur. I told Moses point blank that his mind was stuck in the old mould of the ANC's being a legal organization. People were already forming military units on their own, and the only organization that had the muscle to lead them was the ANC. We had always maintained that the people were ahead of us, and now they were.

We talked the entire day, and at the end, Moses said to me, 'Nelson, I will not promise you anything, but raise the issue again in committee, and we will see what happens.' A meeting was scheduled in a week's time, and once again I raised the issue. This time, Moses was silent, and the general consensus of the meeting was that I should make the proposal to the National Executive in Durban. Walter simply smiled.

The Executive meeting in Durban, like all ANC meetings at the time, was held in secret and at night in order to avoid the police. I suspected I would encounter difficulties because Chief Luthuli was to be in attendance and I knew of his moral commitment to non-violence. I was also wary because of the timing: I was raising the issue of violence so soon after the Treason Trial, where we had contended that for the ANC non-violence was an inviolate principle, not a tactic to be changed as conditions warranted. I myself believed precisely the opposite; that non-violence was a tactic that should be abandoned when it no longer worked.

At the meeting I argued that the state had given us no alternative to violence. I said it was wrong and immoral to subject our people to armed attacks by the state without offering them some kind of alternative. I mentioned again that people on their own had taken up arms. Violence would begin whether we initiated it or not. Would it not be better to guide this violence ourselves, according to principles where we saved lives by attacking symbols of oppression, and not people? If we did not take the lead now, I said, we would soon be latecomers and followers to a movement we did not control.

The chief initially resisted my arguments. For him, non-violence was not simply a tactic. But we worked on him the whole night; and I think that in his heart he realized we were right. He ultimately agreed that a military campaign was inevitable. When someone later insinuated that perhaps the chief was not prepared for such a course, he retorted, 'If anyone thinks I'm a pacifist, let him try to take my chickens, and he will know how wrong he is!'

The National Executive formally endorsed the preliminary decision of the Working Committee. The chief and others suggested that we should treat this new resolution as if the ANC had not discussed it. He did not want to jeopardize the legality of our unbanned allies. His idea was that a military movement should be a separate and independent organ, linked to the ANC and under the overall control of the ANC, but fundamentally autonomous. There would be two separate streams of the struggle. We readily accepted the chief's suggestion. The chief and others warned against this new phase becoming an excuse for neglecting the essential tasks of organization and the traditional methods of struggle. That, too, would be self-defeating because the armed struggle, at least in the beginning, would not be the centrepiece of the movement.

The following night a meeting of the joint Executive was scheduled in Durban. This would include the Indian Congress, the Coloured People's Congress, the South African Congress of Trade Unions and the Congress of Democrats. Although these other groups customarily accepted ANC decisions, I knew that some of my Indian colleagues would strenuously oppose the move towards violence.

The meeting had an inauspicious beginning. Chief Luthuli, who was presiding, announced that even though the ANC had endorsed a decision on violence, 'it is a matter of such gravity, I would like my colleagues here tonight to consider the issue afresh.' It was apparent that the chief was not fully reconciled to our new course.

We began our session at 8 p.m., and it was tumultuous. I made the identical arguments that I had been making all along, but many people expressed reservations. Yusuf Cachalia and Dr Naicker pleaded with us not to embark on this course, arguing that the state would slaughter the whole liberation movement. J.N. Singh, an effective debater, uttered words that night which still echo in my head. 'Non-violence has not failed us,' he said, 'we have failed non-violence.' I countered by saying that in fact non-violence had failed us, for it had done nothing to stem the violence of the state or change the heart of our oppressors.

We argued the entire night, and in the early hours of the morning I began to feel we were making progress. Many of the Indian leaders were now speaking in a sorrowful tone about the end of non-violence. But then suddenly M.D. Naidoo, a member of the South African Indian Congress, burst forth and said to his Indian colleagues, 'Ah, you are afraid of going to jail, that is all!' His comment caused pandemonium in the meeting. When you question a man's integrity, you can expect a fight. The entire debate went back to square one. But towards dawn, there was a resolution. The Congresses authorized me to go ahead and form a new military organization, separate from the ANC. The policy of the ANC would still be that of non-violence. I was authorized to join with whomever I wanted or needed to create this organization and would not be subject to the direct control of the mother organization.

This was a fateful step. For fifty years, the ANC had treated non-violence as a core principle, beyond question or debate. Henceforth, the ANC would be a different kind of organization. We were embarking on a new and more dangerous path, a path of organized violence, the results of which we did not and could not know.

42

I, who had never been a soldier, who had never fought in battle, who had never fired a gun at an enemy, had been given the task of starting an army. It would be a daunting task for a veteran general, much less a military novice. The name of this new organization was Umkhonto we Sizwe (The Spear of the Nation) – or MK for short. The symbol of the spear was chosen because with this simple weapon Africans had resisted the incursions of whites for centuries.

Although the Executive of the ANC did not allow white members, MK was not thus constrained. I immediately recruited Joe Slovo and along with Walter Sisulu we formed the High Command with myself as chairman. Through Joe, I enlisted the efforts of white Communist Party members who had resolved on a course of violence and had already executed acts of sabotage such as cutting government telephone and communication lines. We recruited Jack Hodgson, who had fought in the Second World War with the Springbok Legion, and Rusty Bernstein, both party members. Jack became our first demolition expert. Our mandate was to wage acts of violence against the state – precisely what form those acts would take was yet to be decided. Our intention was to begin with what was least violent to individuals but most damaging to the state.

I began in the only way I knew how, by reading and talking to experts. What I wanted to find out were the fundamental principles for starting a revolution. I discovered that there was a great deal of writing on this very subject, and I made my way through the available literature on armed warfare and in particular guerrilla warfare. I wanted to know what circumstances were appropriate for a guerrilla war; how one created, trained and maintained a guerrilla force; how it should be armed; where it gets its supplies – all basic and fundamental questions.

Any and every source was of interest to me. I read the report of Blas Roca, the general secretary of the Communist Party of Cuba, about their years as an illegal organization during the Batista regime.

In *Commando* by Deneys Reitz, I read of the unconventional guerrilla tactics of the Boer generals during the Anglo-Boer War. I read works by and about Che Guevara, Mao Tse-tung, Fidel Castro. In Edgar Snow's brilliant *Red Star Over China* I saw that it was Mao's determination and non-traditional thinking that had led him to victory. I read *The Revolt* by Menachem Begin and was encouraged by the fact that the Israeli leader had led a guerrilla force in a country with neither mountains nor forests, a situation similar to our own. I was eager to know more about the armed struggle of the people of Ethiopia against Mussolini, and of the guerrilla armies of Kenya, Algeria and the Cameroons.

I went into the South African past. I studied our history both before and after the white man. I probed the wars of African against African, of African against white, of white against white. I made a survey of the country's chief industrial areas, the nation's transportation system, its communication network. I accumulated detailed maps and systematically analysed the terrain of different regions of the country.

On 26 June 1961, our Freedom Day, I released a letter to South African newspapers from underground, which commended the people for their courage during the recent stay-at-home, once more calling for a national constitutional convention. I again proclaimed that a countrywide campaign of non-co-operation would be launched if the state failed to hold such a convention. My letter read in part:

I am informed that a warrant for my arrest has been issued, and that the police are looking for me. The National Action Council has given full and serious consideration to this question . . . and has advised me not to surrender myself. I have accepted this advice, and will not give myself up to a Government I do not recognize. Any serious politician will realize that under present day conditions in the country, to seek for cheap martyrdom by handing myself to the police is naive and criminal . . .

I have chosen this course which is more difficult and which entails more risk and hardship than sitting in gaol. I have had to separate myself from my dear wife and children, from my mother and sisters, to live as an outlaw in my own land. I have had to close my business, to abandon my profession and live in poverty, as many of my people are doing. . . . I shall fight the Government side by side with you, inch by inch, and mile by mile, until victory is won. What are you going to do? Will you come along with us, or are you going to co-operate with the Government in its efforts to suppress the claims and aspirations of your own people? Are you going to remain silent and neutral in a matter of life and death to my people, to our people? For my own part I have made my choice. I will not leave South Africa, nor will I surrender. Only through hardship, sacrifice and militant action can freedom be won. The struggle is my life. I will continue fighting for freedom until the end of my days.

43

During those first few months underground I lived for a few weeks with a family in Market Street, after which I shared a one-room ground-floor bachelor flat with Wolfie Kodesh in Berea, a quiet white suburb a short distance north of downtown. Wolfie was a member of the Congress of Democrats, a reporter for *New Age*, and had fought in North Africa and Italy during the Second World War. His knowledge of warfare and his firsthand battle experience were extremely helpful to me. At his suggestion I read the Prussian general Karl von Clausewitz's classic work *On War*. Clausewitz's central thesis, that war was a continuation of diplomacy by other means, dovetailed with my own instincts. I relied on Wolfie to procure reading material for me and I fear that I took over his life, infringing on both his work and pleasure. But he was such an amiable, modest fellow that he never complained.

I spent nearly two months in his flat, sleeping on a camp bed, staying inside during the day with the blinds drawn reading and planning, leaving only for meetings or organizing sessions at night. I annoyed Wolfie every morning, for I would wake up at five, change into my running clothes and run on the spot for more than an hour. Wolfie eventually surrendered to my regimen and began working out with me in the morning before he left for town.

MK was then practising setting off explosions. One night I accompanied Wolfie to an old brickworks on the outskirts of town for a demonstration. It was a security risk, but I wanted to attend MK's first test of an explosive device. Explosions were common at the brickworks, for companies would use dynamite to loosen the clay before the great machines scooped it up to make bricks. Jack Hodgson had brought along a paraffin tin filled with nitroglycerine; he had created a timing device that used the inside of a ball-point pen. It was dark and we had only a small light, and we stood to the side as Jack worked. When it was ready, we stood back and counted down to thirty seconds; there was a great roar and much displaced earth. The explosion had been a success, and we all quickly returned to our cars and went off in different directions.

I felt safe in Berea. I did not go outside, and because it was a white area, the police would probably not think to look for me there. While I was reading in the flat during the day, I would often place a pint of milk on the windowsill to allow it to ferment. I am very fond of this sour milk, which is known as *amasi* among the Xhosa people and is greatly prized as a healthy and nourishing food. It is very simple to make and merely involves letting the milk stand in the open air and curdle. It then becomes thick and sour, rather like yogurt. I even prevailed upon Wolfie to try it, but he grimaced when he tasted it.

One evening, after Wolfie had returned, we were chatting in the flat when I overheard a conversation going on near the window. I could hear two young black men speaking in Zulu, but I could not see them, as the curtains were drawn. I motioned Wolfie to be quiet.

'What is "our milk" doing on that window ledge?' one of the fellows said.

'What are you talking about?' replied the other fellow.

'The sour milk – *amasi* – on the window ledge,' he said. 'What is it doing there?' Then there was silence. The sharp-eyed fellow was suggesting that only a black man would place milk on the ledge like that and what was a black man doing living in a white area? I realized then that I needed to move on. I left for a different hideout the next night.

I stayed at a doctor's house in Johannesburg, sleeping in the servants' quarters at night, and working in the doctor's study during the day. Whenever anyone came to the house during the day, I would dash out to the backyard and pretend to be the gardener. I then spent about a fortnight on a sugar plantation in Natal, living with a group of African labourers and their families in a small community called Tongaat, just up the coast from Durban. I lived in a hostel and posed as an agricultural demonstrator who had come at the behest of the government to evaluate the land.

I had been equipped by the organization with a demonstrator's tools and I spent part of each day testing the soil and performing experiments. I little understood what I was doing and I do not think I fooled the people of Tongaat. But these men and women, who were mostly farmworkers, had a natural kind of discretion and did not question my identity, even when they began seeing people arriving at night in cars, some of them well-known local politicians. Often I was at meetings all night and would sleep all day – not the normal schedule of an agricultural demonstrator. But even though I was involved in other matters I felt a closeness with the community. I would attend services on Sunday, and I enjoyed the old-fashioned Bible-thumping style of these Zionist Christian ministers. Shortly before I was planning to leave, I thanked one elderly fellow for having looked after me. He said, 'You are of course welcome, but, Kwedeni [young man], please tell us, what does Chief Luthuli want?' I was taken aback but quickly responded, 'Well, it would be better to ask him yourself and I cannot speak for him, but as I understand it, he wants our land returned, he wants our kings to have their power back, and he wants us to be able to determine our own future and run our own lives as we see fit.'

'And how is he going to do that if he does not have an army?' the old man said.

I wanted very much to tell the old man that I was busy attempting to form that army, but I could not. While I was encouraged by the old man's sentiments, I was nervous that others had discovered my mission as well. Again I had stayed too long in one place, and the following night I left as quietly as I had arrived.

44

My next address was more of a sanctuary than a hideout: Liliesleaf Farm, located in Rivonia, a bucolic northern suburb of Johannesburg, and I moved there in October. In those days Rivonia consisted mainly of farms and smallholdings. The farmhouse and property had been purchased by the movement for the purpose of having a safe house for those underground. It was an old house that needed work and no one lived there.

I moved in under the pretext that I was the houseboy or caretaker who would look after the place until my master took possession. I had taken the alias David Motsamayi, the name of one of my former clients. At the farm, I wore the simple blue overalls that were the uniform of the black male servant. During the day, the place was busy with workers, builders and painters who were repairing the main house and extending the outbuildings. We wanted to have a number of small rooms added to the house so that more people could stay. The workers were all Africans from Alexandra township and they called me 'waiter' or 'boy' (they never bothered to ask my name). I prepared breakfast for them and made them tea in the late morning and afternoon. They also sent me on errands about the farm, or ordered me to sweep the floor or pick up rubbish.

One afternoon, I informed them that I had prepared tea in the kitchen. They came in and I passed around a tray with cups, tea, milk and sugar. Each man took a cup, and helped himself. As I was carrying the tray, I came to one fellow who was in the middle of telling a story. He took a cup of tea, but he was concentrating more on his story than on me, and he simply held his teaspoon in the air while he was talking, using it to gesture and tell his tale rather than help himself to some sugar. I stood there for what seemed like several minutes and finally, in mild exasperation, I started to move away. At that point he noticed me, and said sharply, 'Waiter, come back here, I didn't say you could leave.'

Many people have painted an idealistic picture of the egalitarian nature of African society, and while in general I agree with this portrait, the fact is that Africans do not always treat each other as equals. Industrialization has played a large role in introducing the urban African to the perceptions of status common to white society. To those men, I was an inferior, a servant, a person without a trade, and therefore to be treated with disdain. I played the role so well that none of them suspected I was anything other than what I seemed.

Every day at sunset the workers would return to their homes and I would be alone until the next morning. I relished these hours of quiet, but on most evenings I would leave the property to attend meetings, returning in the middle of the night. I often felt uneasy coming back at such hours to a place I did not know well and where I was living illegally under an assumed name. I recall being frightened one night when I thought I saw someone lurking in the bushes; although I investigated, I found nothing. An underground freedom fighter sleeps very lightly.

After a number of weeks I was joined at the farm by Raymond Mhlaba, who had journeyed up from Port Elizabeth. Ray was a staunch trade unionist, a member of the Cape Executive and the Communist Party, and the first ANC leader to be arrested in the Defiance Campaign. He had been chosen by the ANC to be one of the first recruits for Umkhonto we Sizwe. He had come to prepare for his departure, with three others, for military training in the People's Republic of China; we had renewed the contacts that Walter had made back in 1952. Ray stayed with me for a fortnight and provided me with a clearer picture of the problems the ANC was having in the eastern Cape. I also enlisted his assistance in writing the MK constitution. We were joined by Joe Slovo as well as Rusty Bernstein, who both had hands in drafting it.

After Raymond left, I was joined for a brief time by Michael Harmel, a key figure in the underground Communist Party, a founding member of the Congress of Democrats, and an editor of the magazine *Liberation*. Michael, a brilliant theorist, was working on policy matters for the Communist Party and needed a quiet and safe place to work on this full time.

During the day, I kept my distance from Michael as it would have seemed exceedingly curious if a white professional man and an African houseboy were having regular conversations. But at night, after the workers left, we had long conversations about the relationship between the Communist Party and the ANC. One night I returned to the farm late after a meeting. When I was there alone, I made sure that all the gates were locked and the lights were out. I took quite a few precautions because a black man driving a car into a smallholding in Rivonia in the middle of the night would attract unwanted questions. But I saw that the house lights were on, and as I approached the house I heard a radio blaring. The front door was open and I walked in and found Michael in bed fast asleep. I was furious at this breach of security, and I woke him up and said, 'Man, how can you leave the lights on and the radio playing!' He was groggy but angry. 'Nel, must you disturb my sleep? Can't this wait until tomorrow?' I said it couldn't, it was a matter of security, and I reprimanded him for his lax conduct.

Soon after this Arthur Goldreich and his family moved into the main house as official tenants and I took over the newly built domestic worker's cottage. Arthur's presence provided a safe cover for our activities. He was an artist and designer by profession, a member of the Congress of Democrats and one of the first members of MK. His politics were unknown to the police and he had never been questioned or raided. In the 1940s, Arthur had fought with the Palmach, the military wing of the Jewish National Movement in Palestine. He was knowledgeable about guerrilla warfare and helped fill many gaps in my understanding. A flamboyant person, he gave the farm a buoyant atmosphere.

The final addition to the regular group at the farm was Mr Jelliman, an amiable white pensioner and old friend of the movement who became the farm foreman. Jelliman brought in several young workers from Sekhukhuneland, and the place soon appeared to be like any other smallholding in the country. He was not a member of the ANC, but he was loyal, discreet, and hard working. I used to prepare breakfast for him as well as supper, and he was unfailingly gracious. Much later, Jelliman risked his own life and livelihood in a courageous attempt to help me.

The loveliest times at the farm were when I was visited by my wife and family. Once the Goldreichs were in residence, Winnie would visit me at weekends. We were careful about her movements, and she would be picked up by one driver, dropped off at another place, and then picked up by a second driver before finally being delivered to the farm. Later, she would drive herself and the children, taking the most circuitous route possible. The police were not yet following her every move.

At these weekends time would sometimes seem to stop as we pretended that these stolen moments together were the rule not the exception of our lives. Ironically, we had more privacy at Liliesleaf than we ever had at home. The children could run about and play, and we were secure, however briefly, in this idyllic bubble.

Winnie brought me an old air rifle that I had in Orlando and Arthur and I would use it for target practice or hunting doves on the farm. One day, I was on the front lawn of the property and aimed the gun at a sparrow perched high in a tree. Hazel Goldreich, Arthur's wife, was watching me and jokingly remarked that I would never hit my target. But she had hardly finished the sentence when the sparrow fell to the ground. I turned to her and was about to boast, when the Goldreichs' son Paul, then about five years old, turned to me with tears in his eyes and said, 'David, why did you kill that bird? Its mother will be sad.' My mood immediately shifted from one of pride to shame; I felt that this small boy had far more humanity than I did. It was an odd sensation for a man who was the leader of a nascent guerrilla army.

45

In planning the direction and form that MK would take, we considered four types of violent activities: sabotage, guerrilla warfare, terrorism and open revolution. For a small and fledgling army, open revolution was inconceivable. Terrorism inevitably reflected poorly on those who used it, undermining any public support it might otherwise garner. Guerrilla warfare was a possibility, but since the ANC had been reluctant to embrace violence at all, it made sense to start with the form of violence that inflicted the least harm against individuals: sabotage.

Because it did not involve loss of life, it offered the best hope for reconciliation among the races afterwards. We did not want to start a blood-feud between white and black. Animosity between Afrikaner and Englishman was still sharp fifty years after the Anglo-Boer war; what would race relations be like between white and black if we provoked a civil war? Sabotage had the added virtue of requiring the least manpower.

Our strategy was to make selective forays against military installations, power plants, telephone lines and transportation links; targets that would not only hamper the military effectiveness of the state, but frighten National Party supporters, scare away foreign capital, and weaken the economy. This we hoped would bring the government to the bargaining table. Strict instructions were given to members of MK that we would countenance no loss of life. But if sabotage did not produce the results we wanted, we were prepared to move on to the next stage: guerrilla warfare and terrorism.

The structure of MK mirrored that of the parent organization. The National High Command was at the top; below it were Regional Commands in each of the provinces, and below that there were local commands and cells. Regional Commands were set up around the country, and an area like the eastern Cape had over fifty cells. The High Command determined tactics and general targets and was in charge of training and finance. Within the framework laid down by the High Command, the Regional Commands had authority to select local targets to be attacked. All MK members were forbidden to go armed into an operation and were not to endanger life in any way.

One problem we encountered early on was the question of divided loyalties between MK and the ANC. Most of our recruits were ANC members who were active in the local branches, but we found that once they were working for MK, they stopped doing the local work they had been performing before. The secretary of the local branch would find that certain men were no longer attending meetings. He might approach one and say, 'Man, why were you not at the meeting last night?' and the fellow would say, 'Ah, well, I was at another meeting.'

'What kind of meeting?' the secretary would say.

'Oh, I cannot say.'

'You cannot tell me, your own secretary?' But the secretary would soon discover the member's other loyalty. After some initial misunderstandings, we decided that if we recruited members from a branch, the secretary must be informed that one of his members was now with MK.

One warm December afternoon, while I sat in the kitchen at Liliesleaf Farm, I listened on the radio to the announcement that Chief Luthuli had been awarded the Nobel Peace Prize at a ceremony in Oslo. The government had issued him with a ten-day visa to leave the country and accept the award. I was – we all were – enormously pleased. It was, first of all, an acknowledgment of our struggle, and of the achievements of the chief as the leader of that struggle and as a man. It represented a recognition in the West that our struggle was a moral one, one too long ignored by the great powers. The award was an affront to the Nationalists, whose propaganda portrayed Luthuli as a dangerous agitator at the head of a communist conspiracy. Afrikaners were dumbfounded; to them the award was another example of the perversity of Western liberals and their bias against white South Africans. When the award was announced, the chief was in the third year of a five-year ban restricting him to the district of Stanger in Natal. He was also unwell; his heart was strained and his memory was poor. But the award cheered him and all of us as well.

The honour came at an awkward time for it was juxtaposed against an announcement that seemed to call the award itself into question. The day after Luthuli returned from Oslo, MK dramatically announced its emergence. On the orders of the MK High Command, in the early morning hours of 16 December – the day white South Africans used to celebrate as Dingane's Day – homemade bombs were exploded at electric power stations and government offices in Johannesburg, Port Elizabeth and Durban. One of our men, Petrus Molife, was inadvertently killed, the first death of an MK soldier. Death in war is unfortunate, but unavoidable. Every man who joined MK knew that he might be called on to pay the ultimate sacrifice.

At the time of the explosions, thousands of leaflets with the new MK Manifesto were circulated all over the country announcing the birth of Umkhonto we Sizwe.

Units of Umkhonto we Sizwe today carried out planned attacks against government installations, particularly those connected with the policy of apartheid and race discrimination. Umkhonto we Sizwe is a new, independent body, formed by Africans. It includes in its ranks South Africans of all races . . . Umkhonto we Sizwe will carry on the struggle for freedom and democracy by new methods, which are necessary to complement the actions of the established national liberation movement. . . .

The time comes in the life of any nation when there remain only two choices: submit or fight. That time has now come to South Africa. We shall not submit and we have no choice but to hit back by all means within our power in defence of our people, our future and our freedom. . . .

We of Umkhonto have always sought − as the liberation movement has sought − to achieve liberation without bloodshed and civil clash. We hope, even at this late hour, that our first actions will awaken everyone to a realization of the disastrous situation to which the Nationalist policy is leading. We hope that we will bring the government and its supporters to their senses before it is too late, so that both the government and its policies can be changed before matters reach the desperate stage of civil war. . . .

We chose 16 December, Dingane's Day, for a reason. That day, white South Africans celebrate the defeat of the great Zulu leader Dingane at the Battle of Blood River in 1838. Dingane, the half-brother of Shaka, then ruled the most powerful African state that ever existed south of the Limpopo River. That day, the bullets of the Boers were too much for the assegais of the Zulu *impis* and the water of the nearby river ran red with their blood. Afrikaners celebrated 16 December as the triumph of the Afrikaner over the African and the demonstration that God was on their side, while Africans mourned this day of the massacre of their people. We chose 16 December to show that the African had only begun to fight, and that we had righteousness – and dynamite – on our side.

The explosions took the government by surprise. They condemned the sabotage as heinous crimes while at the same time deriding it as the work of foolish amateurs. The explosions also shocked white South Africans into the realization that they were sitting on top of a volcano. Black South Africans realized that the ANC was no longer an organization of passive resistance, but a powerful spear that would take the struggle to the heart of white power. We planned and executed another set of explosions two weeks later on New Year's Eve. The combined sound of bells tolling and sirens wailing seemed not just a cacophonous way to ring in the new year, but a sound that symbolized a new era in our freedom struggle.

The announcement of Umkhonto spurred a vicious and unrelenting government counter-offensive on a scale that we had never before seen. The Special Branch of the police now made it their number one mission to capture members of MK, and they would spare no effort to do so. We had shown them we were not going to sit back any longer; they would show us that nothing would stop them from rooting out what they saw as the greatest threat to their own survival.

46

When Winnie visited, I had the illusion, however briefly, that the family was still intact. Her visits were becoming less frequent, as the police were becoming more vigilant. Winnie would bring Zindzi and Zenani to Rivonia, but the children were too young to know that I was in hiding. Makgatho, then eleven, was old enough to know, and he had been instructed never to reveal my real name in front of anyone. I could tell that he was determined, in his own small way, to keep my identity a secret.

But one day, towards the end of that year, he was at the farm playing with Nicholas Goldreich, Arthur's eleven-year-old son. Winnie had brought me a copy of the magazine *Drum*, and Makgatho and Nicholas stumbled upon it while they were playing. They began leafing through it when suddenly Makgatho stopped at a picture of me taken before I had gone underground. 'That's my father,' he exclaimed. Nicholas did not believe him, and his scepticism made Makgatho even keener to prove it was true. Makgatho then told his friend that my real name was Nelson Mandela. 'No, your father's name is David,' Nicholas replied. The boy then ran to his mother and asked her whether or not my name was David. She replied, 'yes, it is David.' Nicholas then explained to his mother that Makgatho had told him that his father's real name was Nelson. This alarmed Hazel, and I soon learned of this lapse. Once again I had the feeling that I had remained too long in one place. But I stayed put, for in a little over a week I was to leave on a mission that would take me to places that I had only ever dreamed of. Now, the struggle would for the first time take me outside the borders of my country.

In December the ANC received an invitation from the Pan-African Freedom Movement for East, Central and Southern Africa (PAFMECSA) to attend its conference in Addis Ababa in February 1962. PAFMECSA, which later became the Organization of African Unity, aimed to draw together the independent states of Africa and promote the liberation movements on the continent. The conference would furnish important connections for the ANC and be the first and best chance for us to enlist support, money, and training for MK.

The underground Executive asked me to lead the ANC delegation to the conference. Although I was eager to see the rest of Africa and meet freedom fighters from my own continent, I was greatly concerned that I would be violating the promise I had made not to leave the country but operate from underground. My colleagues, including Chief Luthuli, insisted that I go, but were adamant that I return immediately afterwards. I decided to make the trip.

My mission in Africa was broader than simply attending the conference; I was to arrange political and economic support for our new military force and, more important, military training for our men in as many places on the continent as possible. I was also determined to boost our reputation in the rest of Africa where we were still relatively unknown. The PAC had launched its own propaganda campaign and I was delegated to make our case wherever possible.

Before leaving, I secretly drove to Groutville to confer with the chief. Our meeting – at a safe house in town – was disconcerting. As I have related, the chief was present at the creation of MK, and was as informed as any member of the National Executive about its development. But the chief was not well and his memory was not what it had once been. He chastised me for not consulting him about the formation of MK. I attempted to remind him of the discussions that we had in Durban about taking up violence, but he did not recall them. This is in large part why the story has gained currency that Chief Luthuli was not informed about the creation of MK and was deeply opposed to the ANC taking up violence. Nothing could be further from the truth.

I had spent the night before my departure with Winnie at the house of white friends in the northern suburbs, and she brought me a new suitcase that she had packed. She was anxious about my leaving the country, but once again remained stoic. She behaved as much like a soldier as a wife.

The ANC had to arrange for me to travel to Dar es Salaam in Tanganyika, from where the flight to Addis Ababa would originate. The plan was for Walter, Kathrada, and Duma Nokwe to meet me at a secret rendezvous in Soweto and bring me my credentials for the trip. It would also be a moment for last-minute consultations before I left the country.

Ahmed Kathrada arrived at the appointed hour, but Walter and Duma were extremely late. I finally had to make alternative arrangements and Kathy managed to locate someone to drive me to Bechuanaland, where I would charter a plane. I later learned that Walter and Duma had been arrested on their way.

The drive to Bechuanaland was trying, as I was nervous both about the police and the fact that I had never crossed the boundaries of my country before. Our destination was Lobatse, near the South African border. We passed through the border without a problem and arrived in Lobatse in the late afternoon, where there was a telegram for me from Dar es Salaam postponing my trip for a fortnight. I stayed with my fellow Treason Trialist Fish Keitsing, who had since moved to Lobatse.

That afternoon I met Professor K.T. Motsete, the president of the Bechuanaland People's Party, which had been formed mainly by ex-ANC members. I now had unexpected spare time, which I used for reading, preparing my speech for the conference and hiking through the wild and beautiful hills above the town. Although I was not far outside my own country's borders, I felt as though I were in an exotic land. I was often accompanied by Max Mlonyeni, the son of a friend from the Transkei and a young member of the PAC. It was as though we were on safari, for we encountered all manner of animals, including a battalion of sprightly baboons, which I followed for some time, admiring their military-like organization and movements.

I was soon joined by Joe Matthews, who had come from Basutoland, and I insisted we should make haste for Dar es Salaam. An ANC colleague in Lobatse had recently been kidnapped by the South African police and I thought the sooner we could leave, the better. A plane was arranged, and our first destination was a town in northern Bechuanaland called Kasane, strategically situated near a point where the borders of four countries met – Bechuanaland, Northern and Southern Rhodesia, and South West Africa, as these colonies were then known. The landing strip at Kasane was waterlogged and we came in at a drier strip several miles away in the middle of the bush. The manager of a local hotel, armed with rifles, came to fetch us and reported that he had been delayed by a herd of rogue elephants. He was in an open van and Joe and I sat in the back, and I watched a lioness lazily emerge from the bush. I felt far from my home streets of Johannesburg; I was in the Africa of myth and legend for the first time.

Early the next morning we left for Mbeya, a Tanganyikan town near the Northern Rhodesian border. We flew near Victoria Falls and then headed north through a mountain range. While over the mountains, the pilot tried to contact Mbeya, but there was no answer. 'Mbeya, Mbeya!' he kept saying into the microphone. The weather had changed and the mountains were full of air pockets that made the plane bounce up and down like a cork on a rough sea. We were now flying through clouds and mists and in desperation the pilot descended and followed a twisting road through the mountains. By this time the mist had become so thick we could not see the road and when the pilot abruptly turned the plane I realized that we had narrowly missed a mountain that seemed to rear up out of nowhere. The emergency alarm went off, and I remember saying to myself, 'That's the end of us.' Even the ever-loquacious Joe was stone silent. But then just as we could see no further in the clouds and I imagined we were about to crash into a mountain, we emerged from the bad weather into a gloriously clear sky. I have never enjoyed flying much, and while this was the most frightening episode I have ever had on a plane, I am sometimes adept at appearing brave and I pretended that I was unconcerned.

We booked in a local hotel and found a crowd of blacks and whites sitting on the veranda making polite conversation. Never before had I been in a public place or hotel where there was no colour bar. We were waiting for Mr Mwakangale of the Tanganyika African National Union, a member of Parliament, and unbeknown to us he had already arrived and was looking for us. An African guest approached the white receptionist. 'Madam, did a Mr Mwakangale inquire after these two gentlemen?' he asked, pointing to us. 'I'm sorry, sir,' she replied. 'He did, but I forgot to tell them.'

'Please be careful, madam,' he said in a polite but firm tone. 'These men are our guests and we would like them to receive proper attention.' I then truly realized that I was in a country ruled by Africans. For the first time in my life, I was a free man. Though I was a fugitive and wanted in my own land, I felt the burden of oppression lifting from my shoulders. Everywhere I went in Tanganyika my skin colour was automatically accepted rather than instantly reviled. I was being judged for the first time not by the colour of my skin but by the measure of my mind and character. Although I was often homesick during my travels, I nevertheless felt as though I were truly home for the first time.

We arrived in Dar es Salaam the next day and I met Julius Nyerere, the newly independent country's first president. We talked at his house, which was not at all grand, and I recall that he drove himself in a simple car, a little Austin. This impressed me, for it suggested that he was a man of the people. Class, Nyerere always insisted, was alien to Africa; socialism indigenous.

I reviewed our situation for him, ending with an appeal for help. He was a shrewd, soft-spoken man who was well disposed to our mission, but his perception of the situation surprised and dismayed me. He suggested we postpone the armed struggle until Sobukwe came out of prison. This was the first of many occasions when I learned of the PAC's appeal in the rest of Africa. I described the weakness of the PAC, and argued that a postponement would be a setback for the struggle as a whole. He suggested I seek the favour of Emperor Haile Selassie and promised to arrange an introduction.

I was meant to meet Oliver Tambo in Dar, but because of my delay he was unable to wait and left a message for me to follow him to Lagos, where he was to attend the Lagos Conference of Independent States. On the flight to Accra I ran into Hymie Basner and his wife. Basner, who had once been my employer, had been offered a position in Accra. His radical politics and left-wing activities in South Africa had made him *persona non grata* there and he was seeking political asylum in Ghana.

The plane stopped in Khartoum and we lined up to go through customs. Joe Matthews was first, then myself, followed by Basner and his wife. Because I did not have a passport, I carried with me a rudimentary document from Tanganyika that merely said, 'This is Nelson Mandela, a citizen of the Republic of South Africa. He has permission to leave Tanganyika and return here.' I handed this paper to the old Sudanese man behind the immigration counter, and he looked up with a smile and said, 'My son, welcome to the Sudan.' He then shook my hand and stamped my document. Basner was behind me and handed the old man the same type of document. The old man looked at it for a moment, and then said in a rather agitated manner: 'What is this? What is this piece of paper? It is not official!'

Basner calmly explained that it was a document he had been given in Tanganyika because he did not have a passport. 'Not have a passport?' the immigration official said with disdain. 'How can you not have a passport – you are a white man!' Basner replied that he was persecuted in his own country because he fought for the rights of blacks. The Sudanese looked sceptical: 'But you are a white man!' Joe looked at me and knew what I was thinking: he whispered to me not to intervene, as we were guests in Sudan and did not want to offend our host's hospitality. But apart from being my employer, Basner was one of those whites who had truly taken risks on the behalf of black emancipation, and I could not desert him. Instead of leaving with Joe, I remained and stood close to the official and every time Basner said something, I simply bowed and nodded to the official as if to verify what he was saying. The old man realized what I was doing, softened his manner, and finally stamped his document and said quietly, 'Welcome to the Sudan.'

I had not seen Oliver for nearly two years, and when he met me at the airport in Accra I barely recognized him. Once clean-shaven and conservatively groomed, he now had a beard and longish hair and affected the military-style clothing characteristic of freedom fighters around the continent. (He probably had exactly the same reaction to me.) It was a happy reunion, and I complimented him on the tremendous work he had done abroad. He had already established ANC offices in Ghana, England, Egypt and Tanganyika, and had made valuable contacts for us in many other countries. Everywhere I subsequently travelled, I discovered the positive impression Oliver had made on diplomats and statesmen. He was the best possible ambassador for the organization.

The goal of the Lagos Conference of Independent States was to unite all African states, but it eventually disintegrated into bickering about which states to include or exclude. I kept a low profile and avoided the conference, for we did not want the South African government to know that I was abroad until I appeared at the PAFMECSA conference in Addis.

On the plane from Accra to Addis, we found Gaur Radebe, Peter Molotsi and other members of the PAC who were also on their way to PAFMECSA. They were all surprised to see me, and we immediately plunged into discussions concerning South Africa. The atmosphere was enjoyable and relaxed. Though I had been dismayed to learn of Gaur's leaving the ANC, that did not diminish my pleasure in seeing him. High above the ground and far from home, we had much more that united us than separated us.

We put down briefly in Khartoum, where we changed to an Ethiopian Airways flight to Addis. Here I experienced a rather strange sensation. As I was boarding the plane I saw that the pilot was black. I had never seen a black pilot before, and the instant I did I had to quell my panic. How could a black man fly a plane? But a moment later I caught myself: I had fallen into the apartheid mind-set, thinking Africans were inferior and that flying was a white man's job. I sat back in my seat, and chided myself for such thoughts. Once we were in the air, I lost my nervousness and studied the geography of Ethiopia, thinking how guerrilla forces had hidden in these very forests to fight the Italian imperialists.

47

Formerly known as Abyssinia, Ethiopia, according to tradition, was founded long before the birth of Christ, supposedly by the son of Solomon and the Queen of Sheba. Although it had been conquered dozens of times, Ethiopia was the birthplace of African nationalism. Unlike so many other African states, it had fought colonialism at every turn. Menelik had rebuffed the Italians in the last century, though Ethiopia failed to halt them in this one. In 1930 Haile Selassie became emperor and the shaping force of contemporary Ethiopian history. I was seventeen when Mussolini attacked Ethiopia, an invasion that spurred not only my hatred of that despot but of fascism in general. Although Selassie was forced to flee when the Italians conquered Ethiopia in 1936, he returned after the Allied forces drove the Italians out in 1941.

Ethiopia has always held a special place in my own imagination and the prospect of visiting Ethiopia attracted me more strongly than a trip to France, England and America combined. I felt I would be visiting my own genesis, unearthing the roots of what made me an African. Meeting the emperor himself would be like shaking hands with history.

Our first stop was Addis Ababa, the Imperial City, which did not live up to its title, for it was the opposite of grand, with only a few tarred streets, and more goats and sheep than cars. Apart from the Imperial Palace, the university and the Ras Hotel, where we stayed, there were few structures that could compare with even the least impressive buildings of Johannesburg. Contemporary Ethiopia was not a model when it came to democracy, either. There were no political parties, no popular organs of government, no separation of powers; only the emperor, who was supreme.

Before the opening of the conference, the delegates assembled at the tiny town of Debra Zaid. A grandstand had been erected in the central square and Oliver and I sat off to the side, away from the main podium. Suddenly we heard the distant music of a lone bugle and then the strains of a brass band accompanied by the steady beating of African drums. As the music came closer, I could hear – and feel – the rumbling of hundreds of marching feet. From behind a building at the edge of the square, an officer appeared brandishing a gleaming sword; at his heels marched five hundred black soldiers in ranks of four, each carrying a polished rifle against his uniformed shoulder. When the troops had marched directly in front of the grandstand, an order rang out in Amharic, and the five hundred soldiers halted as one man, spun round, and executed a precise salute to an elderly man in a dazzling uniform, His Highness the Emperor of Ethiopia, Haile Selassie, the Lion of Judah.

Here, for the first time in my life, I was witnessing black soldiers commanded by black generals applauded by black leaders who were all guests of a black head of state. It was a heady moment. I only hoped it was a vision of what lay in the future for my own country.

On the morning after the parade, Oliver and I attended a meeting where each organization had to apply for accreditation. We were unpleasantly surprised to find that our application was blocked by a delegate from Uganda who complained that we were a tribal organization of Xhosas. My impulse was to dismiss this claim contemptuously, but Oliver's notion was that we should simply explain that our organization was formed to unite Africans and our membership was drawn from all sections of the people. This I did, adding that the president of our organization, Chief Luthuli, was a Zulu. Our application was accepted. I realized that many people on the continent knew about the ANC only from the PAC's description of us.

The conference was officially opened by our host, His Imperial Majesty, who was dressed in an elaborate brocaded army uniform. I was surprised by how small the emperor appeared, but his dignity and confidence made him seem like the African giant that he was. It was the first time I had witnessed a head of state go through the formalities of his office, and I was fascinated. He stood perfectly straight, and inclined his head only slightly to indicate that he was listening. Dignity was the hallmark of all his actions.

I was scheduled to speak after the emperor, the only other speaker that morning. For the first time in many months, I flung aside the identity of David Motsamayi and became Nelson Mandela. In my speech, I reviewed the history of the freedom struggle in South Africa and listed the brutal massacres that had been committed against our people, from Bulhoek in 1921, when the army and police killed 183 unarmed peasants, to Sharpeville forty years later. I thanked the assembled nations for exerting pressure on South Africa, citing in particular Ghana, Nigeria and Tanganyika, who spearheaded the successful drive to oust South Africa from the British Commonwealth. I retraced the birth of Umkhonto we

Sizwe, explaining that all opportunities for peaceful struggle had been closed to us. 'A leadership commits a crime against its own people it if hesitates to sharpen its political weapons where they have become less effective. . . . On the night of 16 December last year, the whole of South Africa vibrated under the heavy blows of Umkhonto we Sizwe.' I had no sooner said this than the chief minister of Uganda cried out: 'Give it to them again!'

I then related my own experience:

> I have just come out of South Africa, having for the last ten months lived in my own country as an outlaw, away from family and friends. When I was compelled to lead this sort of life, I made a public statement in which I announced that I would not leave the country but would continue working underground. I meant it and I will honour that undertaking.

The announcement that I would return to South Africa was met with loud cheers. We had been encouraged to speak first so that PAFMECSA could evaluate our cause and decide how much support to give it. There was a natural reluctance among many African states to support violent struggles elsewhere, but the speech persuaded people that freedom fighters in South Africa had no alternative but to take up arms.

Oliver and I had a private discussion with Kenneth Kaunda, the leader of the United National Independence Party of Northern Rhodesia and the future president of Zambia. Like Julius Nyerere, Kaunda was worried about the lack of unity among South African freedom fighters and suggested that when Sobukwe emerged from jail, we might all join forces. Among Africans, the PAC had captured the spotlight at Sharpeville in a way that far exceeded their influence as an organization. Kaunda, who had once been a member of the ANC, told us he was concerned about our alliance with white communists and indicated that this reflected poorly on us in Africa. Communism was suspect not only in the West but in Africa. This came as something of a revelation to me, and it was a view that I was to hear over and over during my trip.

When I attempted to make the case that UNIP's support of the PAC was misguided, Kaunda put his hand on my shoulder and said, 'Nelson, speaking to me on this subject is like carrying coals to Newcastle. I am your supporter and a follower of Chief Luthuli. But I am not the sole voice of UNIP. You must speak to Simon Kapwepwe. If you persuade him, you will make my job easier.' Kapwepwe was the second in command of UNIP, and I made arrangements to see him the following day. I asked Oliver to join me but he said, 'Nel, you must see him on your own. Then you can be completely frank.'

I spent the entire day with Kapwepwe and heard from him the most astonishing tale. 'We were mightily impressed by your speech,' he said, 'and indeed by your entire ANC delegation. If we were to judge your organization by these two things, we would certainly be in your camp. But we have heard disturbing reports from the PAC to the effect that Umkhonto we Sizwe is the brainchild of the Communist Party and the Liberal Party, and that the idea of the organization is merely to use Africans as cannon fodder.'

I was nonplussed, and I blurted out that I was astounded that he could not see himself how damnably false this story was. 'First of all,' I said, 'it is well known that the Liberal Party and the Communist Party are arch-enemies and could not come together to play a game of cards. Second, I am here to tell you at the risk of immodesty that I myself was the prime mover behind MK's formation.' Finally, I said I was greatly disappointed in the PAC for spreading such lies.

By the end of the day I had converted Kapwepwe, and he said he would call a meeting and make our case himself – and he did so. But it was another example of both the lack of knowledge about South Africa in the rest of Africa and the extraordinary lengths the PAC would go to besmirch the ANC. Kapwepwe bade me good luck, for the conference was now over. It had been successful, but we had our work cut out for us.

As a student, I had fantasized about visiting Egypt, the cradle of African civilization, the treasure chest of so much beauty in art and design, about seeing the pyramids and the sphinx, and crossing the Nile, the greatest of African rivers. From Addis, Oliver, Robert Resha – who was to accompany me on the rest of my travels – and I flew to Cairo. I spent the whole morning of my first day in Cairo at the museum, looking at art, examining artifacts, making notes, learning about the type of men who founded the ancient civilization of the Nile Valley. This was not amateur archaeological interest; it is important for African nationalists to be armed with evidence to refute the fictitious claims of whites that Africans are without a civilized past that compares with that of the West. In a single morning, I discovered that Egyptians were creating great works of art and architecture when whites were still living in caves.

Egypt was an important model for us, for we could witness at firsthand the programme of socialist economic reforms being launched by President Nasser. He had reduced private ownership of land, nationalized certain sectors of the economy, pioneered rapid industrialization, democratized education and built a modern army. Many of these reforms were precisely the sorts of things that we in the ANC someday hoped to enact. At that time, however, it was more important to us that Egypt was the only African state with an army, navy and air force that could in any way compare with those of South Africa.

After a day, Oliver left for London, promising to join Robbie and me in Ghana. Before Robbie and I left on our tour, we discussed the presentation we would make in each country. My inclination was to explain the political situation as truthfully and objectively as possible and not omit the accomplishments of the PAC. In each new country, I would initially seal myself away in our hotel to familiarize myself with information about the country's policies, history and leadership. Robbie did the opposite. A natural extrovert, he would leave the hotel as soon as we arrived and hit the streets, learning by seeing and talking to people. We were an odd couple, for I affected the informal dress I had got used to underground and wore khakis and fatigues, while Robbie was always smartly turned out in a suit.

In Tunis, our first stop, we met the minister of defence, who bore a striking resemblance to Chief Luthuli. But I'm afraid that is where the similarity ended, for when I was explaining to him the situation in our country with PAC leaders such as Robert Sobukwe in jail, he interrupted me and said, 'When that chap returns, he will finish you!' Robbie raised his eyebrows at this (later he said, 'Man, you were putting the case for the PAC better than they could!'), but I insisted on giving the minister the full picture. When the following day we met President Habib Bourguiba, his response was utterly positive and immediate: he offered training for our soldiers and £5,000 for weapons.

Rabat in Morocco, our next stop, with its ancient and mysterious walls, its fashionable shops and medieval mosques, seemed a charming mixture of Africa, Europe and the Middle East. Apparently freedom fighters thought so as well, for Rabat was the crossroads of virtually every liberation movement on the continent. While there, we met freedom fighters from Mozambique, Angola, Algeria and Cape Verde. It was also the headquarters of the Algerian revolutionary army, and we spent several days with Dr Mustafa, head of the Algerian mission in Morocco, who briefed us on the history of the Algerian resistance to the French.

The situation in Algeria was the closest model to our own in that the rebels faced a large white settler community that ruled the indigenous majority. He related how the FLN had begun their struggle with a handful of guerrilla attacks in 1954, having been heartened by the defeat of the French at Dien Bien Phu in Vietnam. At first, the FLN believed they could defeat the French militarily, Dr Mustafa said, then realized that a purely military victory was impossible.

Instead, they resorted to guerrilla warfare. Guerrilla warfare, he explained, was not designed to win a military victory so much as to unleash political and economic forces that would bring down the enemy. Dr Mustafa advised us not to neglect the political side of war while planning the military effort. International public opinion, he said, is sometimes worth more than a fleet of jet fighters.

At the end of three days, he sent us to Oujda, a dusty little town just across the border from Algeria and the headquarters of the Algerian army in Morocco. We visited an army unit at the front, and at one point I took a pair of field glasses and could actually see French troops across the border. I confess I imagined that I was looking at the uniforms of the South African Defence Force.

A day or two later I was a guest at a military parade in honour of Ahmed Ben Bella, who was to become the first prime minister of independent Algeria and who had recently emerged from a French prison. A far cry from the military parade I had witnessed in Addis Ababa, this parade was not the crisp, well-drilled, handsomely uniformed force of Ethiopia but a kind of walking history of the guerrilla movement in Algeria.

At its head sauntered proud, battle-hardened veterans in turbans, long tunics and sandals, who had started the struggle many years before. They carried the weapons they had used: sabres, old flintlock rifles, battle-axes and assegais. They were followed in turn by younger soldiers, all carrying modern arms and equally proud. Some held heavy anti-tank and anti-aircraft guns. But even these soldiers did not march with the smartness and precision of the Ethiopians. This was a guerrilla force, and they were soldiers who had won their stripes in the fire of battle, who cared more about fighting and tactics than dress uniforms and parades. Inspired as I was by the troops in Addis, I knew that our own force would be more like these troops here in Oujda, and I could only hope they would fight as valiantly.

At the rear was a rather rag-tag military band that was led by a man called Sudani. Tall, well built and confident, he was as black as the night. He was swinging a ceremonial mace, and when we saw him, our whole party stood up and started clapping and cheering. I looked around and noticed others staring at us, and I realized that we were only cheering because this fellow was a black man and black faces were quite rare in Morocco. Once again I was struck by the great power of nationalism and ethnicity. We reacted instantly, for we felt as though we were seeing a brother African. Later, our hosts informed us that Sudani had been a legendary soldier, and had even reputedly captured an entire French unit single-handedly. But we were cheering him because of his colour not his exploits.

From Morocco, I flew across the Sahara to Bamako, the capital of Mali, and then on to Guinea. The flight from Mali to Guinea was more like a local bus than a plane. Chickens wandered the aisles, women walked back and forth carrying packages on their heads and selling bags of peanuts and dried vegetables. It was flying democratic-style, and I admired it very much.

My next stop was Sierre Leone and, when I arrived, I discovered that Parliament was in session and decided to attend the proceedings. I entered as any tourist would and was given a seat not far from the Speaker. The clerk of the House approached me and asked me to identify myself. I whispered to him, 'I am the representative of Chief Luthuli of South Africa.' He shook my hand warmly and proceeded to report to the Speaker. The clerk then explained that I had inadvertently been given a seat not normally allowed to visitors, but in this case it was an honour for them to make an exception.

Within an hour there was an adjournment, and as I stood among the members and dignitaries drinking tea, a queue formed in front of me and I saw to my amazement that the entire Parliament had lined up to shake hands with me. I was very gratified, until the third or fourth person in line mumbled something to the effect of, 'It is a great honour to shake the hand of the revered Chief Luthuli, winner of the Nobel Peace Prize.' I was an impostor! The clerk had misunderstood. The prime minister, Sir Milton Margai, was then brought over to meet me, and the clerk introduced me as the chief. I immediately attempted to inform the clerk that I was not Chief Luthuli, but he would have none of it, and I decided that in the interests of hospitality I would continue the charade. I later met the president, explained the case of mistaken identity, and he offered generous material assistance.

In Liberia, I met President Tubman, who not only gave me $5,000 for weapons and training, but said in a quiet voice, 'Have you any pocket money?' I confessed that I was a bit low, and instantly an aide came back with an envelope containing $400 in cash. From Liberia, I went to Ghana, where I was met by Oliver and entertained by Guinea's resident minister, Abdoulaye Diallo. When I told him that I had not seen Sekou Touré when I was in Guinea, he arranged for us to return immediately to that arid land. Oliver and I were impressed with Touré. He lived in a modest bungalow, and wore an old faded suit that could have done with a visit to the dry cleaner's. We made our case to him, explained the history of the ANC and MK, and asked for $5,000 for the support of MK. He listened very carefully, and replied in a rather formal way. 'The government and the people of Guinea,' he said, as though giving a speech, 'fully support the struggle of our brothers in South Africa, and we have made statements at the UN to that effect.' He went to the bookcase, where he removed two books of his, which he autographed to Oliver and me. He then said thank you, and we were dismissed.

Oliver and I were annoyed: we had been called back from another country, and all he gave us were signed copies of his book? We had wasted our time. A short while later, we were in our hotel room when an official from the Foreign Affairs Department knocked on our door and presented us with a suitcase. We opened it and it was filled with banknotes; Oliver and I looked at each other in glee. But then Oliver's expression changed. 'Nelson, this is Guinean currency,' he said. 'It is worthless outside here; it is just paper.' But Oliver had an idea: we took the money to the Czech embassy, where he had a friend who exchanged it for a convertible currency.

The gracefulness of the slender fishing boats that glided into the harbour in Dakar was equalled only by the elegance of the Senegalese women who sailed through the city in flowing robes and turbanned heads. I wandered through the nearby market place, intoxicated by the exotic spices and perfumes. The Senegalese are a handsome people and I enjoyed the brief time that Oliver and I spent in their country. Their society showed how disparate elements – French, Islamic and African – can mingle to create a unique and distinctive culture.

On our way to a meeting with President Léopold Senghor, Oliver suffered a severe attack of asthma. He refused to return to the hotel, and I carried him on my back up the stairs to the president's office. Senghor was greatly concerned by Oliver's condition and insisted that he be attended to by his personal physician.

I had been told to be wary of Senghor, for there were reports that Senegalese soldiers were serving with the French in Algeria, and that he was a bit too taken with the customs and charms of the *ancien régime*. There will always be, in emerging nations, an enduring attraction to the ways of the colonizer – I myself was not immune to it. President Senghor was a scholar and poet, and he told us he was collecting research material on Shaka, flattering us by asking numerous questions about that great South African warrior. We summarized the situation in South Africa and made our request for military training and money. Senghor replied that his hands were tied until Parliament met.

In the meantime, he wanted us to talk with the minister of justice, a M. Daboussier, about military training, and the president introduced me to a beautiful white French girl who, he explained, would interpret for me in my meeting with him. I said nothing, but was disturbed. I did not feel comfortable discussing the very sensitive issues of military training in front of a young woman I did not know and was not sure I could trust. Senghor sensed my uneasiness, for he said, 'Mandela, do not worry, the French here identify themselves completely with our African aspirations.'

When we reached the minister's office, we found some African secretaries in the reception area. One of the black secretaries asked the Frenchwoman what she was doing there. She said she had been sent by the president to interpret. An argument ensued and in the middle of it, one of the African secretaries turned to me and said, 'Sir, can you speak English?' I said I could, and she replied, 'The minister speaks English and you can talk with him directly. You don't need an interpreter.' The French girl, now quite miffed, stood aside as I went in to speak to the minister, who promised to fulfil our requests. In the end, although Senghor did not then provide us with what we asked for, he furnished me with a diplomatic passport and paid for our plane fares from Dakar to our next destination: London.

48

I confess to being something of an Anglophile. When I thought of Western democracy and freedom, I thought of the British parliamentary system. In so many ways, the very model of the gentleman for me was an Englishman. Despite Britain being the home of parliamentary democracy, it was that democracy that had helped to inflict a pernicious system of iniquity on my people. While I abhorred the notion of British imperialism, I never rejected the trappings of British style and manners.

I had several reasons for wanting to go to England, apart from my desire to see the country I had so long read and heard about. I was concerned about Oliver's health and wanted to persuade him to receive treatment. I very much wanted to see Adelaide, his wife, and their children, as well as Yusuf Dadoo, who was now living there and representing the Congress movement. I also knew that in London I would be able to obtain literature on guerrilla warfare that I had been unable to acquire elsewhere.

In London, I resumed my old underground ways, not wanting word to leak back to South Africa that I was there. The tentacles of South African security forces reached all the way to London. But I was not a recluse; my ten days there were divided among ANC business, seeing old friends and occasional jaunts as a conventional tourist. With Mary Benson, a British friend who had written about our struggle, Oliver and I saw the sights of the city that had once commanded nearly two-thirds of the globe: Westminster Abbey, Big Ben, the Houses of Parliament. While I gloried in the beauty of these buildings, I was ambivalent about what they represented. When we saw the statue of General Smuts near Westminster Abbey, Oliver and I joked that perhaps some day there would be a statue of us in its stead.

I had been informed by numerous people that the *Observer* newspaper, run by David Astor, had been tilting towards the PAC in its coverage, its editorials implying that the ANC was the party of the past. Oliver arranged for me to meet Astor at his house, and we talked at length about the ANC. I do not know if I had an effect on him, but the coverage certainly changed. He also recommended that I talk to a number of prominent politicians, and in the company of the Labour MP Denis Healey, I met Hugh Gaitskell, leader of the Labour Party, and Jo Grimond, leader of the Liberal Party.

It was only towards the end of my stay that I saw Yusuf, but it was not a happy reunion. Oliver and I had encountered a recurring difficulty in our travels: one African leader after another had questioned us about our relations with white and Indian communists, sometimes suggesting that they controlled the ANC. Our non-racialism would have been less of a problem had it not been for the formation of the explicitly nationalistic and anti-white PAC. In the rest of Africa, most African leaders could understand the views of the PAC better than those of the ANC. Oliver had discussed these things with Yusuf, who was unhappy about Oliver's conclusions. Oliver had resolved that the ANC had to appear more independent, taking certain actions unilaterally without the involvement of the other members of the Alliance, and I agreed.

I spent my last night in London discussing these issues with Yusuf. I explained that now that we were embarking on an armed struggle we would be relying on other African nations for money, training and support, and therefore had to take their views into account more than we did in the past. Yusuf believed that Oliver and I were changing ANC policy, that we were preparing to depart from the non-racialism that was the core of the Freedom Charter. I told him he was mistaken; we were not rejecting non-racialism; we were simply saying the ANC must stand more on its own and make statements that were not part of the Congress Alliance. Often the ANC, the South African Indian Congress and the Coloured People's Congress would make a collective statement on an issue affecting only Africans. That would have to change. Yusuf was unhappy about this. 'What about policy?' he kept asking. I told him I was not talking about policy, I was talking about image. We would still work together, only the ANC had to appear to be the first among equals.

Although I was sad to leave my friends in London, I was now embarking on what was to be the most unfamiliar part of my trip: military training. I had arranged to receive six months of training in Addis Ababa. I was met there by Foreign Minister Yefu, who warmly greeted me and took me to a suburb called Kolfe, the headquarters of the Ethiopian Riot Battalion, where I was to learn the art and science of soldiering. While I was a fair amateur boxer, I had very little knowledge of even the rudiments of combat. My trainer was a Lieutenant Wondoni Befikadu, an experienced soldier, who had fought with the underground against the Italians. Our programme was strenuous: we trained from 8 a.m. until 1 p.m. broke for a shower and lunch, and then again from 2 to 4 p.m. From 4 p.m. into the evening I was lectured on military science by Colonel Tadesse, who was also assistant commissioner of police and had been instrumental in foiling a recent coup attempt against the emperor.

I learned how to use an automatic rifle and a pistol and took target practice both in Kolfe with the Emperor's Guard and at a shooting range about fifty miles away with the entire battalion. I was taught about demolition and mortar-firing and I learned how to make small bombs and mines – and how to avoid them. I felt myself being moulded into a soldier and began to think as a soldier thinks – a far cry from the way a politician thinks.

What I enjoyed most were the 'fatigue marches' in which you are equipped with only a gun, bullets and some water, and must reach a distant point within a certain time. During these marches I got a sense of the landscape, which was very beautiful, with dense forests and spare highlands. The country was extremely backward: people used wooden ploughs and lived on a very simple diet supplemented by home-brewed beer. Their existence was similar to the life in rural South Africa; poor people everywhere are more alike than they are different.

In my study sessions, Colonel Tadesse discussed matters such as how to create a guerrilla force, how to command an army and how to enforce discipline. One evening, during supper, he said to me, 'Now, Mandela, you are creating a liberation army not a conventional capitalist army. A liberation army is an egalitarian army. You must treat your men entirely differently from how you would in a capitalist army. When you are on duty, you must exercise your authority with assurance and control. That is no different from a capitalist command. But when you are off duty, you must conduct yourself on the basis of perfect equality, even with the lowliest soldier. You must eat what they eat; you must not take your food in your office, but eat with them, drink with them, not isolate yourself.'

All this seemed admirable and sensible, but while he was talking to me, a sergeant came into the hall and asked the colonel where he could find a certain lieutenant. The colonel regarded him with ill-concealed contempt and said, 'Can't you see that I am talking to an important individual here? Don't you know not to interrupt me when I am eating? Now, get out of my sight!' Then he continued with his discussion in the same didactic tone as before.

The training course was meant to be six months long, but after eight weeks I received a telegram from the ANC urgently requesting that I return home. The internal armed struggle was escalating and they wanted the commander of MK on the scene.

Colonel Tadesse rapidly arranged for me to take an Ethiopian flight to Khartoum. Before I left, he presented me with a gift: an automatic pistol and two hundred rounds of ammunition. I was grateful, both for the gun and his instruction. Despite my fatigue marches, I found it wearying to carry around all that ammunition. A single bullet is surprisingly heavy: hauling around two hundred is like carrying a small child on one's back.

In Khartoum I was met by a British Airways official who told me that my connecting flight to Dar es Salaam would not leave until the following day and they had taken the liberty of booking me into a posh hotel in town. I was dismayed, for I would have preferred to stay in a less conspicuous third-class hotel.

When I was dropped off, I had to walk across the hotel's long and elegant veranda, where several dozen whites were sitting and drinking. This was long before metal detectors and security checks, and I was carrying my pistol in a holster inside my jacket and the two hundred rounds wrapped around my waist inside my trousers. I also had several thousand pounds in cash. I had the feeling that all these well-dressed whites had X-ray vision and that I was going to be arrested at any moment. But I was escorted safely to my room, where I ordered room service; even the footsteps of the waiters put me on edge.

From Khartoum I went direct to Dar es Salaam, where I greeted the first group of twenty-one Umkhonto recruits who were headed for Ethiopia to train as soldiers. It was a proud moment, for these men had volunteered for duty in an army I was then attempting to create. They were risking their lives in a battle that was only just beginning, a battle that would be most dangerous for those who were its first soldiers. They were young men, mainly from the cities, and they were proud and eager. We had a dinner in Addis; the men slaughtered a goat in my honour, and I addressed them about my trip and told them of the necessity of good behaviour and discipline abroad, because they were representatives of the South African freedom struggle. Military training, I said, must go hand in hand with political training, for a revolution is not just a question of pulling a trigger; its purpose is to create a fair and just society. It was the first time that I was ever saluted by my own soldiers.

President Nyerere gave me a private plane to Mbeya, and I then flew directly to Lobatse. The pilot informed me that we would be landing in Kanye. This concerned me: why was the plan altered? In Kanye, I was met by the local magistrate and a security man, both of whom were white. The magistrate approached me and asked me my name. David Motsamayi, I replied. No, he said, please tell me your real name. Again, I said David Motsamayi. The magistrate said, 'Please tell me your real name because I was given instructions to meet Mr Mandela here and provide him with help and transportation. If you are not Mr Nelson Mandela, I am afraid I will have to arrest you for you have no permit to enter the country. Are you Nelson Mandela?'

This was a quandary; I might be arrested either way. 'If you insist that I am Nelson Mandela and not David Motsamayi,' I said, 'I will not challenge you.' He smiled and said simply, 'We expected you yesterday.' He then offered me a lift to where my comrades would be waiting for me. We drove to Lobatse, where I met Joe Modise and an ANC supporter named Jonas Matlou, who was then living there. The magistrate told me that the South African police were aware that I was returning, and he suggested that I leave the next day. I thanked him for his help and advice, but when I arrived at Matlou's house, I said that I would leave that night. I was to drive back to South Africa with Cecil Williams, a white theatre director and member of MK. Posing as his chauffeur, I got behind the wheel and we left that night for Johannesburg.

PART SEVEN

———

Rivonia

49

After crossing the border, I breathed in deeply. The air of one's home always smells sweet after one has been away. It was a clear winter night and somehow even the stars looked more welcoming here than from elsewhere on the continent. Though I was leaving a world where I experienced freedom for the first time and returning to one where I was a fugitive, I was profoundly relieved to be back in the land of my birth and destiny.

Between Bechuanaland and the northwestern Transvaal, dozens of unmarked roads transverse the border, and Cecil knew just which ones to take. During the drive, he filled me in on many of the events I had missed. We drove all night, slipping across the border just after midnight and reaching Liliesleaf Farm at dawn. I was still wearing my beat-up khaki training uniform.

Once at the farm, I did not have time for rest and reflection because the following night we held a secret meeting for me to brief the Working Committee on my trip. Walter, Moses Kotane, Govan Mbeki, Dan Tloome, J.B. Marks and Duma Nokwe all arrived at the farm, a rare reunion. I first gave a general overview of my travels, itemizing the money we had received and the offers of training. At the same time, I reported in detail the reservations I had encountered about the ANC's co-operation with whites, Indians and particularly communists. Still ringing in my ears was my final meeting with the Zambian leaders, who told me that while they knew the ANC was stronger and more popular than the PAC, they understood the PAC's pure African nationalism but were bewildered by the ANC's non-racialism and communist ties. I informed them that Oliver and I believed the ANC had to appear more independent to reassure our new allies on the continent, for they were the ones who would be financing and training Umkhonto we Sizwe. I proposed reshaping the Congress Alliance so that the ANC would clearly be seen as the leader, especially on issues directly affecting Africans.

This was a serious proposition, and the entire leadership had to be consulted. The Working Committee urged me to go down to Durban and brief Chief Luthuli. All agreed except Govan Mbeki, who was not then living at Liliesleaf Farm but was present as part of the High Command of MK. He urged me to send someone else. It was simply too risky, he said, and the organization should not jeopardize my safety, especially as I was newly returned and ready to push ahead with MK. This wise advice was overruled by everyone, including myself.

I left the next night from Rivonia in the company of Cecil, again posing as his chauffeur. I had planned a series of secret meetings in Durban, the first of which was with Monty Naicker and Ismail Meer to brief them about my trip and to discuss the new proposal. Monty and Ismail were extremely close to the chief, and the chief trusted their views. I wanted to be able to tell Luthuli I had spoken to his friends and convey their reaction. Ismail and Monty, however, were disturbed by my belief that the ANC needed to take the lead among the Congress Alliance and make statements on its own concerning affairs that affected Africans. They were against anything that unravelled the Alliance.

I was taken to Groutville, where the chief lived, and we met in the house of an Indian lady in town. I explained the situation to the chief at some length, and he listened without speaking. When I was done, he said he did not like the idea of foreign politicians dictating policy to the ANC. He said we had evolved the policy of non-racialism for good reasons and he did not think that we should alter our policy because it did not suit a few foreign leaders.

I told the chief that these foreign politicians were not dictating our policy, but merely saying that they did not understand it. My plan, I told him, was simply to effect essentially cosmetic changes in order to make the ANC more intelligible – and more palatable – to our allies. I saw this as a defensive manoeuvre, for if African states decided to support the PAC, a small and weak organization could suddenly become a large and potent one.

The chief did not make decisions on the spur of the moment. I could see he wanted to think about what I had said and talk to some of his friends about it. I said farewell, and he advised me to be careful. I still had a number of clandestine meetings in the city and townships that evening. My last meeting that evening was with the MK Regional Command in Durban.

The Durban Command was led by a sabotage expert named Bruno Mtolo, whom I had never met before, but would come across again under dramatically different circumstances. I briefed them on my trip around Africa, about the support we had received and the offers of training. I explained that for the moment MK was limited to sabotage, but that if sabotage did not have the desired effect we would probably move on to guerrilla warfare.

Later that same evening, at the home of the photojournalist G. R. Naidoo, where I was staying, I was joined by Ismail and Fatima Meer, Monty Naicker, and J. N. Singh for what was a combination welcome-home and going-away party, for I was leaving the next day for Johannesburg. It was a pleasant evening and my first night of relaxation in a long while. I slept well and I met Cecil on Sunday afternoon – 5 August – for the long drive back to Johannesburg in his trusty Austin.

I wore my chauffeur's white dust-coat and sat next to Cecil as he drove. We often took turns behind the wheel. It was a clear, cool day and I revelled in the beauty of the Natal countryside; even in winter, Natal remains green. Now that I was returning to Johannesburg I would have some time to see Winnie and the children. I had often wished that Winnie could share with me the wonders of Africa, but the best I could do was to tell her what I had seen and done.

Once we left the industrial precincts of Durban, we moved through hills that offered majestic views of the surrounding valleys and the blue-black waters of the Indian Ocean. Durban is the principal port for the country's main industrial area, and the highway that leads to Johannesburg runs parallel to the railway line for a great distance. I went from contemplating the natural beauty to ruminating on the fact that the railway line, being so close to the highway, offered a convenient place for sabotage. I made a note of this in the small notebook I always carried with me.

Cecil and I were engrossed in discussions of sabotage plans as we passed through Howick, twenty miles northwest of Pietermaritzburg. At Cedara, a small town just past Howick, I noticed a Ford V-8 filled with white men shoot past us on the right. I instinctively turned round to look behind and I saw two more cars filled with white men. Suddenly, in front of us, the Ford was signalling to us to stop. I knew in that instant that my life on the run was over; my seventeen months of 'freedom' were about to end.

As Cecil slowed down, he turned to me and said, 'Who are these men?' I did not answer because we both knew very well who they were. They had chosen their hiding-spot well; to the left of us was a steep wooded bank they could have forced us into had we tried to elude them. I was in the left-hand passenger seat, and for a moment I thought about jumping out and making an escape into the woods, but I would have been shot in a matter of seconds.

When our car stopped, a tall slender man with a stern expression came directly over to the window on the passenger side. He was unshaven and it appeared that he had not slept in quite a while. I immediately assumed he had been waiting for us for several days. In a calm voice, he introduced himself as Sergeant Vorster of the Pietermaritzburg police and produced an arrest warrant. He asked me to identify myself. I told him my name was David Motsamayi. He nodded, and then, in a very proper way, he asked me a few questions about where I had been and where I was going. I parried these without giving him much information. He seemed a bit irritated and then he said, 'Ag, you're Nelson Mandela, and this is Cecil Williams, and you are under arrest!'

He informed us that a police major from the other car would accompany us back to Pietermaritzburg. The police were not yet so vigilant in those days, and Sergeant Vorster did not bother searching me. I had my loaded revolver, and again I thought of escape, but I would have been greatly outnumbered. I secretly put the revolver – and my notebook – in the upholstery between my seat and Cecil's. For some reason, the police never found the gun or the small notebook, which was fortunate, for many more people would have been arrested if they had.

At the police station I was led into Sergeant Vorster's office, where I saw a number of officers, one of whom was Warrant Officer Truter, who had testified in the Treason Trial. Truter had made a favourable impression on the accused because he had accurately explained the policy of the ANC, and had not exaggerated or lied. We greeted each other in a friendly way.

I had still not admitted to anything other than the name David Motsamayi, and Truter said to me, 'Nelson, why do you keep up this farce? You know I know who you are. We all know who you are.' I told him simply that I had given a name, and that was the name I was standing by. I asked for a lawyer and was curtly refused. I then declined to make a statement.

Cecil and I were locked in separate cells. I now had time to ruminate on my situation. I had always known that arrest was a possibility, but even freedom fighters practise denial, and in my cell that night I realized I was not prepared for the reality of capture and confinement. I was upset and agitated. Someone had tipped the police off about my whereabouts; they had known I was in Durban and that I would be returning to Johannesburg. For weeks before my return, the police believed that I was already back in the country. In June, newspaper headlines blared 'RETURN OF THE BLACK PIMPERNEL' while I was still in Addis Ababa. Perhaps that had been a bluff?

The authorities had been harassing Winnie in the belief that she would know whether I was back. I knew that they had followed her and searched the house on a number of occasions. I guessed they had figured I would visit Chief Luthuli directly upon my return, and they were correct. But I also suspected they had information that I was in Durban at that time. The movement had been infiltrated with informers, and even well-intentioned people were generally not as tight-lipped as they should have been. I had also been lax. Too many people had known I was in Durban. I had even had a party the night before I left, and I chastised myself for letting down my guard. My mind ricocheted among the possibilities. Was it an informer in Durban? Someone from Johannesburg? Someone from the movement? Or even a friend or member of the family? But such speculation about unknowns is futile, and with the combination of mental and physical exhaustion, I soon fell deeply asleep. At least on this night – 5 August 1962 – I did not have to worry about whether the police would find me. They already had.

In the morning I felt restored and braced myself for the new ordeal that lay ahead of me. I would not, under any circumstances, seem despairing or even disappointed to my captors. At 8.30 I appeared before the local magistrate and was formally remanded to Johannesburg. It was low-key, and the magistrate seemed no more concerned than if he were handling a traffic summons. The police had not taken elaborate precautions for the trip back to Johannesburg or for my security, and I merely sat in the back seat of a sedan, un-handcuffed, with two officers riding in front. My arrest had been discovered by my friends; Fatima Meer brought some food to the jail and I shared it with the two officers in the car. We even stopped at Volksrust, a town along the way, and they allowed me to take a brief walk to stretch my legs. I did not contemplate escape when people were kind to me; I did not want to take advantage of the trust they placed in me.

But as we approached Johannesburg, the atmosphere changed. I heard an announcement over the police radio of my capture and the order to fold up the roadblocks to and from Natal. At sunset, on the outskirts of Johannesburg, we were met by a sizable police escort. I was abruptly handcuffed, taken from the car, and placed in a sealed police van with small opaque windows reinforced with wire netting. The motorcade then took a circuitous and unfamiliar route to Marshall Square as if they were concerned we might be ambushed.

I was locked in a cell by myself. In the quiet, I was planning my strategy for the next day, when I heard a cough from a nearby cell. I did not realize a prisoner was close by, but more than that, there was something about this cough, something that struck me as curiously familiar. I sat up in sudden recognition and called out, 'Walter?'

'Nelson, is that you?' he said, and we laughed with an indescribable mixture of relief, surprise, disappointment and happiness. Walter, I learned, had been arrested shortly after my own arrest. We did not think that the arrests were unrelated. While this was not the most auspicious place for a meeting of the National Working Committee, it was certainly convenient, and the night sped by as I gave him a full account of my arrest, as well as my meetings in Durban.

The next day I appeared in court before a senior magistrate for formal remand. Harold Wolpe and Joe Slovo had come to court after hearing of my arrest, and we conferred in the basement. I had appeared before this magistrate on numerous occasions in my professional capacity and we had grown to respect one another. A number of attorneys were also present, some of whom I knew quite well. It is curious how one can be easily flattered in certain situations by otherwise insignificant incidents. I am by no means immune to flattery in normal circumstances, but there I was, a fugitive, No. 1 on the state's Most Wanted list, a handcuffed outlaw who had been underground for more than a year, and yet the judge, the other attorneys and the spectators all greeted me with deference and professional courtesy. They knew me as Nelson Mandela, attorney-at-law, not Nelson Mandela, outlaw. It lifted my spirits immensely.

During the proceedings, the magistrate was diffident and uneasy, and would not look at me directly. The other attorneys also seemed embarrassed, and at that moment I had something of a revelation. These men were not only uncomfortable because I was a colleague brought low, but because I was an ordinary man being punished for his beliefs. In a way I had never quite comprehended before, I realized the role I could play in court and the possibilities before me as a defendant. I was the symbol of justice in the court of the oppressor, the representative of the great ideals of freedom, fairness and democracy in a society that dishonoured those virtues. I realized then and there that I could carry on the fight even within the fortress of the enemy.

When I was asked the name of my counsel, I announced that I would represent myself, with Joe Slovo as legal adviser. By representing myself I would enhance the symbolism of my role. I would use my trial as a showcase for the ANC's moral opposition to racism. I would not attempt to defend myself so much as put the state itself on trial. That day, I answered only the questions as to my name and choice of counsel. I listened silently to the charges: inciting African workers to strike and leaving the country without valid travel documents. In apartheid South Africa, the penalties for these 'crimes' could be as much as ten years in prison. Yet the charges were something of a relief: the state clearly did not have enough evidence to link me with Umkhonto we Sizwe or I would have been charged with the far more serious crimes of treason or sabotage.

Only as I was leaving the courtroom did I see Winnie in the spectators' gallery. She looked distressed and gloomy; she was undoubtedly considering the difficult months and years ahead, of life on her own, raising two small children, in an often hard and forbidding city. It is one thing to be told of possible hardships ahead, it is entirely another to have to confront them in reality. All I could do, as I descended the steps to the basement, was to give her a wide smile, as if to show her that I was not worried and that she should not be either. I cannot imagine that it helped very much.

From the court, I was taken to the Johannesburg Fort. When I emerged from the courthouse to enter the sealed van, there was a crowd of hundreds of people cheering and shouting 'Amandla!' followed by 'Ngawethu!' a popular ANC call-and-response meaning 'Power!' and 'The power is ours!' People yelled and sang and pounded their fists on the sides of the van as the vehicle crawled out of the courthouse exit. My capture and case had made headlines in every paper: 'POLICE SWOOP ENDS TWO YEARS ON THE RUN' was one; 'NELSON MANDELA UNDER ARREST' was another. The so-called Black Pimpernel was no longer at large.

A few days later Winnie was granted permission to visit me. She had dressed up and now, at least on the face of it, appeared less glum than before. She brought me a new pair of expensive pyjamas and a lovely silk dressing gown more appropriate to a salon than a prison. I did not have the heart to tell her it was wholly inappropriate for me to wear such things in jail. I knew, however, that the parcel was a way of expressing her love and a pledge of solidarity. I thanked her, and although we did not have much time we quickly discussed family matters, especially how she would support herself and the children. I mentioned the names of friends who would help her and also clients of mine who still owed me money. I told her to tell the children the truth of my capture, and how I would be away for a long time. I said we were not the first family in this situation, and that those who underwent such hardships came out the stronger. I assured her of the strength of our cause, the loyalty of our friends, and how it would be her love and devotion that would see me through whatever transpired. The officer supervising the visit turned a blind eye, and we embraced and clung to each other with all the strength and pent-up emotion inside each of us, as if this were to be the final parting. In a way it was, for we were to be separated for much longer than either of us could then have imagined. The warrant officer allowed me to accompany Winnie part of the way to the main gate where I was able to watch her, alone and proud, disappear round the corner.

50

At the Fort I was being supervised by Colonel Minnaar, a courtly Afrikaner considered something of a liberal by his more *verkrampte* (hard-line) colleagues. He explained that he was placing me in the prison hospital because it was the most comfortable area and I would be able to have a chair and table on which I could prepare my case. While the hospital was indeed comfortable – I was able to sleep in a proper bed, something I had never done before in prison – the real reason for his generosity was that the hospital was the safest place to keep me. To reach it one had to pass through two impregnable walls, each with armed guards; and, once inside, four massive gates had to be unlocked before one even reached the area where I was kept. There was speculation in the press that the movement was going to attempt to rescue me, and the authorities were doing their utmost to prevent it.

There had also been wild speculations, in the press and within the ANC, that I had been betrayed by someone in the movement. I knew that some people blamed G. R. Naidoo, my Durban host, a suggestion I believe was unfounded. The press trumpeted the notion that I had been betrayed by white and Indian communists who were unsettled by my suggestions that the ANC must become more Africanist-oriented. But I believed these stories were planted by the government to divide the Congress movement, and I regarded it as malicious mischief. I later discussed the matter not only with Walter, Duma, Joe Slovo and Ahmed Kathrada, but Winnie, and I was gratified to see that they shared my feelings. Winnie had been invited to open the annual conference of the Transvaal Indian Youth Congress, and at my instigation she repudiated these rumours in no uncertain terms. The newspapers were filled with stories of her beauty and eloquence. 'We shall not waste time looking for evidence as to who betrayed Mandela,' she told the audience. 'Such propaganda is calculated to keep us fighting one another instead of uniting to combat Nationalist oppression.'

The most oft-cited story was that an American consular official with connections to the CIA had tipped off the authorities. This story has never been confirmed and I have never seen any reliable evidence as to the truth of it. Although the CIA has been responsible for many contemptible activities in its support of American imperialism, I cannot lay my capture at its door. In truth, I had been imprudent about maintaining the secrecy of my movements. In retrospect, I realized that the authorities could have had a myriad of ways of locating me on my trip to Durban. It was a wonder in fact that I wasn't captured sooner.

I spent only a few days in the Fort's hospital before being transferred to Pretoria. There had been no restrictions on visits in Johannesburg, and I had had a continuous stream of people coming to see me. Visitors keep one's spirits up in prison, and the absence of them can be disheartening. In transferring me to Pretoria, the authorities wanted to get me away from my home turf to a place where I would have fewer friends dropping in.

I was handcuffed and taken to Pretoria in an old van in the company of another prisoner. The inside of the van was filthy and we sat on a greasy spare tyre, which slid from side to side as the van rumbled on its way. The choice of companion was curious: his name was Nkadimeng and he was a member of one of Soweto's fiercest gangs. Normally, officials would not permit a political prisoner to share the same vehicle with a common-law criminal, but I suspect they were hoping I would be intimidated by Nkadimeng, who I assumed was a police informer. I was dirty and annoyed by the time I reached prison, and my irritation was aggravated by the fact that I was put in a single cell with this fellow. I demanded and eventually received separate space so that I could prepare my case.

I was now permitted visitors only twice a week. Despite the distance, Winnie came regularly and always brought clean clothes and delicious food. This was another way of showing her support, and every time I put on a fresh shirt I felt her love and devotion. I was aware of how difficult it must have been to get to Pretoria in the middle of the day in the middle of the week with two small children at home. I was visited by many others who brought food, including the ever-faithful Mrs Pillay who supplied me with a spicy lunch every day.

Because of the generosity of my visitors I had an embarrassment of riches and wanted to share my food with the other prisoners on my floor. This was strictly forbidden. In order to circumvent the restrictions, I offered food to the warders, who might then relent. With this in mind I presented a shiny red apple to an African warder who looked at it and stonily rebuffed me with the phrase '*Angiyifuni*' ('I don't want it'). African warders tend to be either much more sympathetic than white warders, or even more severe, as though to outdo their masters. But, a short while later, the black warder saw a white warder take the apple he had rejected, and changed his mind. Soon I was supplying all my fellow prisoners with food.

Through the prison grapevine, I learned that Walter had been brought to Pretoria as well, and although we were isolated from each other we did manage to communicate. Walter had applied for bail – a decision I fully supported. Bail had long been a sensitive issue within the ANC. There are those who believed we should always reject bail, as it could be interpreted that we were fainthearted rebels who accepted the racist strictures of the legal system. I did not think this view should be universally applied and believed we should examine the issue on a case-by-case basis. Ever since Walter had become secretary-general of the ANC, I had felt that every effort should be made to bail him out of prison. He was simply too vital to the organization to be allowed to languish in jail. In his case, bail was a practical not a theoretical issue. It was different with me. I had been underground; Walter had not. I had become a public symbol of rebellion and struggle; Walter operated behind the scenes. He agreed that no application for bail should be made for me. For one thing, it would not have been granted and I did not want to do anything that might suggest that I was not prepared for the consequences of the underground life I had chosen.

Not long after Walter and I reached this decision I was again transferred back to the hospital at the Fort. A hearing had been set for October. Little can be said in favour of prison, but enforced isolation is conducive to study. I had begun correspondence studies for my LL B degree, which allows one to practise as an advocate. One of the first things I had done after arriving at Pretoria Local was to send a letter to the authorities notifying them of my intention to study and requesting permission to purchase a copy of *The Law of Torts*, part of my syllabus.

A few days later, Colonel Aucamp, commanding officer of Pretoria Local and one of the more notorious of prison officials, marched into my cell and in a gloating manner said, 'Mandela, we have got you now!' Then he said, 'Why do you want a book about torches, man, unless you plan to use it for your damn sabotage?' I had no idea what he was talking about, until he produced my letter requesting a book about what he called 'the Law of Torches'. I smiled at this and he became angry that I was not taking him seriously. The Afrikaans word for 'torch' is *toort*, very similar to tort, and I explained to him that in English *tort* was a branch of law, not a burning stick of wood that could be used to set off a bomb. He went away in a huff.

*   *   *

One day I was in the prison courtyard at the Fort doing my daily exercises, which consisted of jogging, running on the spot, push-ups and sit-ups, when I was approached by a tall, handsome Indian fellow named Moosa Dinath whom I had known slightly as a prosperous, even flamboyant, businessman. He was serving a two-year sentence for fraud. On the outside we would have remained acquaintances, but prison is an incubator of friendship. Dinath would often accompany me on my jogs around the courtyard. One day he asked whether I would have any objection if he obtained permission from the commanding officer to be near me in the prison hospital. I told him that I would welcome it, but I thought to myself that the authorities would never permit it. I was wrong.

It was exceedingly odd that a convicted prisoner like Dinath was permitted to stay together with a political prisoner awaiting trial. But I said nothing as I was glad to have company. Dinath was wealthy and had a private payroll for the prison authorities. In return for his money, he received many privileges: he wore clothes meant for white prisoners, ate their diet and did no jail work at all.

One night, to my astonishment, I observed Colonel Minnaar, who was the head of prison and a well-known Afrikaner advocate, come to fetch him. Dinath then left prison for the night and did not come back again until the morning. If I had not seen it with my own eyes I would not have believed it.

Dinath regaled me with tales of financial shenanigans and corruption among cabinet ministers, which I found fascinating. It confirmed to me how apartheid was a poison that bred moral decay in all areas. I scrupulously avoided discussing with him any matters of a political or sensitive nature on the grounds that he might also have been an informer. He once asked me to tell him about my African trip and I simply glossed over it. In the end, Dinath pulled enough strings to speed up his release and left after serving only four months of his two-year sentence.

Escape serves a double purpose: it liberates a freedom fighter from jail so that he can continue to fight, but offers a tremendous psychological boost to the struggle and a great publicity blow against the enemy. As a prisoner, I always contemplated escape, and during my various trips to and from the commanding officer's office, I carefully surveyed the walls, the movements of the guards, the types of keys and locks used in the doors. I made a detailed sketch of the prison grounds with particular emphasis on the exact location of the prison hospital and the gates leading out of it. This map was smuggled out to the movement with instructions to destroy it immediately after it was perused.

There were two plans, one hatched by Moosa Dinath, which I ignored;

the second was conceived by the ANC and communicated to me by Joe Slovo. It involved bribes, copies of keys and even a false beard that was to be sewn into the shoulder pad of one of my jackets brought to me in prison. The idea was that I would don the beard after I had made my escape. I carefully considered the plan and concluded that it was premature, and the likelihood of its failure unacceptably high. Such a failure would be fatal to the organization. During a meeting with Joe, I passed him a note communicating my views. I wrote that MK was not ready for such an operation; even an elite and trained force would probably not be able to accomplish such a mission. I suggested that such a gambit be postponed until I was a convicted prisoner and the authorities were less cautious. At the end, I wrote, 'Please destroy this after you have finished reading it.' Joe and the others took my advice about not attempting the escape, but he decided the note should be saved as a historical document, and it later turned up at a very unfortunate time.

Sparring with Jerry
Moloi at his gym
in Orlando. *(Bob
Gosani/Bailey's)*

With Ruth First outside the court. *(Peter Magubane)*

Opposite, above: After the second trial I went underground, becoming known for a time as "the black pimpernel". *(photographer unknown)*

A triumphant moment with Moses Kotane outside the court; we had just learned that the Crown was withdrawing its indictment. But the victory was to be short-lived: three months later, in 1959, twenty-nine of us found ourselves on trial once again. *(Jurgen Schadeberg)*

Opposite, below: Oliver Tambo and Robert Resha at the Dar es Salaam airport after the banning of the ANC, 1962. *(Associated Press)*

In hiding after my
return from abroad,
1962. *(Eli Weinberg/
Camera Press Ltd.)*

At work sewing clothes in prison in Pretoria, before being sent to Robben Island. *(Archive Photos)*

The books I kept in my cell during my years on Robben Island. *(Archive Photos)*

Opposite, above: With Walter in the prison yard, 1966. *(Archive Photos)*

Opposite, below: The prison yard at Robben Island. *(Archive Photos)*

Opposite:
Walter and I had been imprisoned together on Robben Island for nearly two decades; in the Bishopscourt Gardens Residence of Archbishop Tutu in Capetown, we gave the *"Afrika"* salute and prepared to take up the battle on the outside once again. *(Gideon Mendel/ Magnum)*

Freedom. February 1990. *(Gideon Mendel/ Magnum)*

At home in Orlando. *(Peter Magubane)*

Above, left:
A private exchange between old comrades. *(Peter Magubane)*

Above:
In December of 1990 Oliver Tambo returned home to South Africa after more than thirty years in exile. *(Associated Press)*

Left:
Oliver's welcome home rally in Johannesburg. *(Associated Press)*

51

The initial hearing was set for Monday 15 October 1962. The organization had set up a Free Mandela Committee and launched a lively campaign with the slogan 'Free Mandela'. Protests were held throughout the country and the slogan began to appear scrawled on the sides of buildings. The government retaliated by banning all gatherings relating to my imprisonment, but this restriction was ignored by the liberation movement.

In preparation for Monday's hearing, the Free Mandela Committee had organized a mass demonstration at the courthouse. The plan was for people to line both sides of the road along the route my van would take. From press reports, conversations with visitors and even the remarks of prison guards, I learned that a large and vociferous turnout was expected.

On Saturday, while I was preparing myself for the Monday hearing, I was ordered to pack my things immediately: the hearing had been shifted to Pretoria. The authorities had made no announcement, and had I not managed to get word out through a sympathetic jailer, no one would have known that I had left Johannesburg.

But the movement reacted quickly, and by the time my case began on Monday morning, the Old Synagogue was packed with supporters. The synagogue was like a second home to me after four years of the Treason Trial. My legal adviser, Joe Slovo, could not be present as he was confined to Johannesburg by bans and I was ably assisted instead by Bob Hepple.

I entered the court that Monday morning wearing a traditional Xhosa leopard-skin *kaross* instead of a suit and tie. The crowd of supporters rose as one and with raised clenched fists shouted '*Amandla!*' and '*Ngawethu!*' The *kaross* electrified the spectators, many of whom were friends and family, some of whom had come all the way from the Transkei. Winnie also wore a traditional beaded headdress and an ankle-length Xhosa skirt.

I had chosen traditional dress to emphasize the symbolism that I was a black African walking into a white man's court. I was literally carrying on my back the history, culture and heritage of my people. That day, I felt myself to be the embodiment of African nationalism, the inheritor of Africa's difficult but noble past and her uncertain future. The *kaross* was also a sign of contempt for the niceties of white justice. I well knew the authorities would feel threatened by my *kaross* as so many whites feel threatened by the true culture of Africa.

When the crowd had quietened down and the case was called, I formally greeted the prosecutor, Mr Bosch, whom I had known from my attorney days, and the magistrate, Mr von Heerden, who was also familiar to me. I then immediately applied for a two-week remand on the grounds that I had been transferred to Pretoria without being given the opportunity of notifying my attorneys. I was granted a week's postponement.

When I was on my way back to my cell, a very nervous white warder said that the commanding officer, Colonel Jacobs, had ordered me to hand over the *kaross*. I said, 'You can tell him that he is not going to have it.' This warder was a weak fellow, and he started trembling. He practically begged me for it and said he would be fired if he did not bring it back. I felt sorry for him and said, 'Look, here, just tell your commanding officer that it is Mandela speaking, not you.' A short while later Colonel Jacobs himself appeared and ordered me to turn over what he referred to as my 'blanket'. I told him that he had no jurisdiction over the attire I chose to wear in court and if he tried to confiscate my *kaross* I would take the matter all the way to the Supreme Court. The colonel never again tried to take my 'blanket', but the authorities would permit me to wear it only in court, not on my way to or from court for fear it would 'incite' other prisoners.

When the case resumed a week later I was given permission to address the court before I was asked to plead. 'I hope to be able to indicate,' I explained, 'that this case is a trial of the aspirations of the African people, and because of that I thought it proper to conduct my own defence.' I wanted to make it clear to the bench, the gallery, and the press that I intended to put the state on trial. I then made application for the recusal of the magistrate on the grounds that I did not consider myself morally bound to obey laws made by a Parliament in which I had no representation. Nor was it possible to receive a fair trial from a white judge:

Why is it that in this courtroom I am facing a white magistrate, confronted by a white prosecutor, escorted by white orderlies? Can anybody honestly and seriously suggest that in this type of atmosphere the scales of justice are evenly balanced? Why is it that no African in the history of this country has ever had the honour of being tried by his own kith and kin, by his own flesh and blood? I will tell Your Worship why: the real purpose of this rigid colour bar is to ensure that the justice dispensed by the courts should conform to the policy of the country, however much that policy might be in conflict with the norms of justice accepted in judiciaries throughout the civilized world. . . . Your Worship, I hate racial discrimination most intensely and in all its manifestations. I have fought it all my life. I fight it now, and I will do so until the end of my days. I detest most intensely the set-up that surrounds me here. It makes me feel that I am a black man in a white man's court. This should not be.

During the trial the prosecutor called more than a hundred witnesses from all over the country, including the Transkei and South West Africa. They were policemen, journalists, township superintendents, printers. Most of them gave technical evidence to show that I had left the country illegally and that I had incited African workers to strike during the three-day stay-at-home in May 1961. It was indisputable – and in fact I did not dispute – that I was technically guilty of both charges.

The prosecutor had called Mr Barnard, the private secretary to the prime minister, to testify to the letter I had sent the prime minister demanding that he call a national convention and informing him that if he did not, we would organize a three-day strike. In my cross-examination of Mr Barnard I first read the court the letter I sent requesting that the prime minister call a national convention for all South Africans to write a new non-racial constitution.

NM: Did you place this letter before your prime minister?
WITNESS: Yes.
NM: Now was any reply given to this letter by the prime minister?
WITNESS: He did not reply to the writer.
NM: He did not reply to the letter. Now, will you agree that this letter raises matters of vital concern to the vast majority of the citizens of this country?
WITNESS: I do not agree.
NM: You don't agree? You don't agree that the question of human rights, of civil liberties, is a matter of vital importance to the African people?
WITNESS: Yes, that is so, indeed.
NM: Are these things mentioned here?
WITNESS: Yes, I think so.

NM: . . . You have already agreed that this letter raises questions like the rights of freedom, civil liberties, and so on?

Witness: Yes, the letter raises it.

NM: Now, you know of course that Africans don't enjoy the rights demanded in this letter? They are denied these rights of government.

Witness: Some rights.

NM: No African is a member of Parliament?

Witness: That is right.

NM: No African can be a member of the provincial council, of the municipal councils?

Witness: Yes.

NM: Africans have no vote in this country?

Witness: They have got no vote as far as Parliament is concerned.

NM: Yes, that is what I am talking about, I am talking about Parliament and other government bodies of the country, the provincial councils, the municipal councils. They have no vote?

Witness: That is right.

NM: Would you agree with me that in any civilized country in the world it would be scandalous for a prime minister to fail to reply to a letter raising vital issues affecting the majority of the citizens of that country. Would you agree with that?

Witness: I don't agree with that.

NM: You don't agree that it would be irregular for a prime minister to ignore a letter raising vital issues affecting the vast majority of the citizens of that country?

Witness: This letter has not been ignored by the prime minister.

NM: Just answer the question. Do you regard it as proper for a prime minister not to respond to pleas made in regard to vital issues by the vast majority of the citizens of the country? You say that is wrong?

Witness: The prime minister did respond to the letter.

NM: Mr Barnard, I don't want to be rude to you. Will you confine yourself to answering my questions. The question I am putting to you is, do you agree that it is most improper on the part of a prime minister not to reply to a communication raising vital issues affecting the vast majority of the country?

Mr Barnard and I never did agree. In the end, he simply said that the tone of the letter was aggressive and discourteous and for that reason the prime minister did not answer it.

*   *   *

Throughout the proceedings the prosecutor and the magistrate repeatedly inquired about the number of witnesses I intended to call. I would always reply, 'I plan to call as many witnesses as the state, if not more.' When the state finally concluded its case, there was a stillness in the courtroom in anticipation of the beginning of my defence. I rose, and instead of calling my first witness I declared quite matter-of-factly that I was not calling any witnesses at all, at which point I abruptly closed my case. There was a murmur in the courtroom and the prosecutor could not help exclaiming, 'Lord!'

I had misled the court from the beginning because I knew the charge was accurate and the state's case was solid, and I saw no point in attempting to call witnesses and defend myself. Through my cross-examination and attempts to force the judge to recuse himself, I had made the statements I wanted about the unfairness of the court. I saw no advantage in calling witnesses to try to disprove something that was incontrovertible.

The magistrate was taken by surprise by my action and asked me with some incredulity, 'Have you anything more to say?'

'Your Worship, I submit that I am guilty of no crime.'

'Is that all you have to say?'

'Your Worship, with respect, if I had something more to say I would have said it.'

The prosecutor then shuffled through his papers attempting to get ready for an address he did not expect to have to make. He briefly addressed the court and asked the magistrate to find me guilty on both counts. The court was then adjourned until the following day, when I would have a chance to address it in what is known as the plea in mitigation before the magistrate gave his sentence.

The following morning, before court was called into session, I was in an office off the courtroom talking with Bob Hepple, who had been advising me on the case, and we were praising the fact that the day before, the General Assembly of the UN had voted in favour of sanctions against South Africa for the first time. Bob also told me that acts of sabotage in Port Elizabeth and Durban had occurred, both celebrating the UN vote and in protest at my trial. We were in the midst of this discussion when the prosecutor, Mr Bosch, entered the room and then asked Bob to excuse himself.

'Mandela,' he said, after Bob had left, 'I did not want to come to court today. For the first time in my career, I despise what I am doing. It hurts me that I should be asking the court to send you to prison.' He then reached out and shook my hand, and expressed the hope that everything would turn out well for me. I thanked him for his sentiments, and assured him that I would never forget what he had said.

The authorities were on alert that day. The crowd inside the courtroom seemed even larger than on the first day of the case. All 150 'Non-European' seats were filled. Winnie was present, in Xhosa dress, as well as a number of my relatives from the Transkei. Hundreds of demonstrators stood a block from the courthouse, and there seemed to be as many policemen as spectators.

When I walked into the courtroom, I raised my right fist and called out *'Amandla!'* which was met by a mighty *'Ngawethu!'* The magistrate pounded his gavel and cried for order. When the court was quiet, he summed up the charges, after which I had my opportunity to speak.

My plea in mitigation lasted over an hour. It was not a judicial appeal at all but a political testament. I wanted to explain to the court how and why I had become the man I was, why I had done what I had done, and why, if given the chance, I would do it again.

Many years ago, when I was a boy brought up in my village in the Transkei, I listened to the elders of the tribe telling stories about the good old days before the arrival of the white man. Then our people lived peacefully, under the democratic rule of their kings and their *amapakati* [literally 'insiders', but meaning those closest in rank to the king], and moved freely and confidently up and down the country without let or hindrance. The country was our own, in name and right. We occupied the land, the forests, the rivers; we extracted the mineral wealth beneath the soil and all the riches of this beautiful country. We set up and operated our own government, we controlled our own arms and we organized our trade and commerce. The elders would tell tales of the wars fought by our ancestors in defence of the Fatherland, as well as the acts of valour by generals and soldiers during these epic days. . . .

The structure and organization of early African societies in this country fascinated me very much and greatly influenced the evolution of my political outlook. The land, then the main means of production, belonged to the whole tribe and there was no individual ownership whatsoever. There were no classes, no rich or poor and no exploitation of man by man. All men were free and equal and this was the foundation of government. Recognition of this general principle found expression in the constitution of the council, variously called 'Imbizo' or 'Pitso' or 'Kgotla', which governs the affairs of the tribe. The council was so completely democratic that all members of the tribe could participate in its deliberations. Chief and subject, warrior and medicine man, all took part and endeavoured to influence its decisions. It was so weighty and influential a body that no step of any importance could ever be taken by the tribe without reference to it.

There was much in such a society that was primitive and insecure and it certainly could never measure up to the demands of the present epoch. But in such a society are contained the seeds of revolutionary democracy in which none will be held in slavery or servitude, and in which poverty, want and insecurity shall be no more. This is the history which, even today, inspires me and my colleagues in our political struggle.

I told the court how I had joined the African National Congress and how its policy of democracy and non-racialism reflected my own deepest convictions. I explained how as a lawyer I was often forced to choose between compliance with the law or accommodating my conscience.

I would say that the whole life of any thinking African in this country drives him continuously to a conflict between his conscience on the one hand and the law on the other. This is not a conflict peculiar to this country. The conflict arises for men of conscience, for men who think and who feel deeply in every country. Recently in Britain, a peer of the realm, Earl [Bertrand] Russell, probably the most respected philosopher of the Western world, was sentenced and convicted for precisely the type of activities for which I stand before you today – for following his conscience in defiance of the law, as a protest against the nuclear weapons policy being pursued by his own government. He could do no other than to oppose the law and to suffer the consequences for it. Nor can I. Nor can many Africans in this country. The law as it is applied, the law as it has been developed over a long period of history, and especially the law as it is written and designed by the Nationalist government is a law which, in our views, is immoral, unjust and intolerable. Our consciences dictate that we must protest against it, that we must oppose it and that we must attempt to alter it. . . . Men, I think, are not capable of doing nothing, of saying nothing, of not reacting to injustice, of not protesting against oppression, of not striving for the good society and the good life in the ways they see it.

I recounted in detail the numerous times the government had used the law to hamper my life, career and political work, through bannings, restrictions and trials.

I was made, by the law, a criminal, not because of what I had done, but because of what I stood for, because of what I thought, because of my conscience. Can it be any wonder to anybody that such conditions make a man an outlaw of society? Can it be wondered that such a man, having been outlawed by the government, should be prepared to lead the life of an outlaw, as I have led for some months, according to the evidence before this court?

It has not been easy for me during the past period to separate myself from my wife and children, to say good-bye to the good old days when, at the end of a strenuous day at an office, I could look forward to joining my family at the dinner-table, and instead to take up the life of a man hunted continuously by the police, living separated from those who are closest to me, in my own country, facing continually the hazards of detection and of arrest. This has been a life infinitely more difficult than serving a prison sentence. No man in his right senses would voluntarily choose such a life in preference to the one of normal, family, social life which exists in every civilized community.

But there comes a time, as it came in my life, when a man is denied the right to live a normal life, when he can only live the life of an outlaw because the government has so decreed to use the law to impose a state of outlawry upon him. I was driven to this situation, and I do not regret having taken the decisions that I did take. Other people will be driven in the same way in this country, by this very same force of police persecution and of administrative action by the government, to follow my course, of that I am certain.

I enumerated the many times that we had brought our grievances before the government and the equal number of times that we were ignored or shunted aside. I described our stay-away of 1961 as a last resort after the government showed no signs of taking any steps to either talk with us or meet our demands. It was the government that provoked violence by employing violence to meet our non-violent demands. I explained that because of the government's actions we had taken a more militant stance. I said that I had been privileged throughout my political life to fight alongside colleagues whose abilities and contributions were far greater than my own. Many others had paid the price of their beliefs before me, and many more would do so after me.

Before sentencing, I informed the court that whatever sentence the state imposed, it would do nothing to change my devotion to the struggle.

I do not believe, Your Worship, that this court, in inflicting penalties on me for the crimes for which I am convicted should be moved by the belief that penalties will deter men from the course that they believe is right. History shows that penalties do not deter men when their conscience is aroused, nor will they deter my people or the colleagues with whom I have worked before.

I am prepared to pay the penalty even though I know how bitter and desperate is the situation of an African in the prisons of this country. I have been in these prisons and I know how gross is the discrimination, even behind the prison wall, against Africans. . . . Nevertheless these considerations do not sway me from the path that I have taken nor will they sway others like me. For to men, freedom in their own land is the pinnacle of their ambitions, from which nothing can turn men of conviction aside. More powerful than my fear of the dreadful conditions to which I might be subjected in prison is my hatred for the dreadful conditions to which my people are subjected outside prison throughout this country. . . .

Whatever sentence Your Worship sees fit to impose upon me for the crime for which I have been convicted before this court, may it rest assured that when my sentence has been completed I will still be moved, as men are always moved, by their conscience; I will still be moved by my dislike of the race discrimination against my people when I come out from serving my sentence, to take up again, as best I can, the struggle for the removal of those injustices until they are finally abolished once and for all. . . .

I have done my duty to my people and to South Africa. I have no doubt that posterity will pronounce that I was innocent and that the criminals that should have been brought before this court are the members of the government.

When I had finished, the magistrate ordered a ten-minute recess to consider the sentence. I turned and looked out at the crowd before leaving the courtroom. I had no illusions about the sentence I would receive. Exactly ten minutes later, in a courtroom heavy with tension, the magistrate pronounced sentence: three years for inciting people to strike and two years for leaving the country without a passport; five years in all, with no possibility of parole. It was a stern sentence, and there was wailing among the spectators. As the court rose, I turned to the gallery and again made a clenched fist, shouting 'Amandla!' three times. Then, on its own, the crowd began to sing our beautiful anthem, 'Nkosi Sikelel' iAfrika'. People sang and danced and the women ululated as I was led away. The uproar among the gallery made me forget for a moment that I would be going to prison to serve what was then the stiffest sentence yet imposed in South Africa for a political offence.

Downstairs, I was permitted a brief good-bye to Winnie, and on this occasion she was not at all grim: she was in high spirits and shed no tears. She seemed confident, as much a comrade as a wife. She was determined to brace me. As I was driven away in the police van I could still hear the people outside singing '*Nkosi Sikelel' iAfrika*'.

52

Prison not only robs you of your freedom, it attempts to take away your identity. Everyone wears a uniform, eats the same food, follows the same schedule. It is by definition a purely authoritarian state that tolerates no independence or individuality. As a freedom fighter and as a man, one must fight against the prison's attempt to rob one of these qualities.

From the courthouse, I was taken directly to Pretoria Local, the gloomy red-brick monstrosity that I knew so well. But I was now a convicted prisoner, not an awaiting-trial prisoner, and was treated without even the little deference that is afforded to the latter. I was stripped of my clothes and Colonel Jacobs was finally able to confiscate my *kaross*. I was issued the standard prison uniform for Africans: a pair of short trousers, a rough khaki shirt, a canvas jacket, socks, sandals and a cloth cap. Only Africans are given short trousers, for only African men are deemed 'boys' by the authorities.

I informed the authorities that I would under no circumstances wear shorts and told them I was prepared to go to court to protest. Later, when I was brought dinner, stiff cold porridge with half a teaspoonful of sugar, I refused to eat it. Colonel Jacobs pondered this and came up with a solution: I could wear long trousers and have my own food, if I agreed to be put in isolation. 'We were going to put you with the other politicals,' he said, 'but now you will be alone, man. I hope you enjoy it.' I assured him that solitary confinement would be fine as long as I could wear and eat what I chose.

For the next few weeks, I was completely and utterly isolated. I did not see the face or hear the voice of another prisoner. I was locked up for twenty-three hours a day, with thirty minutes of exercise in the morning and again in the afternoon. I had never been in isolation before, and every hour seemed like a year. There was no natural light in my cell; a single bulb burned overhead twenty-four hours a day. I did not have a wristwatch and I often thought it was the middle of the night when it was only late afternoon. I had nothing to read, nothing to write on or with, no one to talk to. The mind begins to turn in on itself, and one desperately wants something outside oneself on which to fix one's attention. I have known men who took half-a-dozen lashes in preference to being locked up alone. After a time in solitary, I relished the company even of the insects in my cell, and found myself on the verge of initiating conversations with a cockroach.

I had one middle-aged African warder whom I occasionally was able to see, and one day I tried to bribe him with an apple to get him to talk to me. '*Baba*,' I said, which means Father, and is a term of respect, 'can I give you an apple?' He turned away, and met all my subsequent overtures with silence. Finally he said, 'Man, you wanted long trousers and better food, and now you have them and you are still not happy.' He was right. Nothing is more dehumanizing than the absence of human companionship. After a few weeks I was ready to swallow my pride and tell Colonel Jacobs that I would trade my long trousers for some company.

During those weeks I had plenty of time to ponder my fate. The place of a freedom fighter is beside his people, not behind bars. The knowledge and contacts I had recently made in Africa were going to be locked away rather than used in the struggle. I cursed the fact that my expertise would not be put to use in creating a freedom army.

I soon began to protest vigorously against my circumstances and demanded to be put with the other political prisoners at Pretoria Local. Among them was Robert Sobukwe. My request was ultimately granted, accompanied by a stern warning from Colonel Jacobs that serious consequences would result if I returned to my impudent ways. I don't think I ever looked forward to eating cold mealie pap so much in my life.

Apart from my desire for company, I was keen to talk with Sobukwe and the others, most of whom were PAC, because I thought that in prison we might forge a unity that we could not on the outside. Prison conditions have a way of tempering polemics, and making individuals see more what unites them than what divides them.

When I was taken to the courtyard with the others, we greeted each other warmly. Besides Sobukwe, there was also John Gaetsewe, a leading member of the South African Congress of Trade Unions; Aaron Molete, an ANC member who worked for *New Age*; and Stephen Tefu, a prominent communist trade unionist, and PAC member. Robert asked me to give them an account of my African tour, which I did gladly. I was candid about how both the PAC and the ANC were perceived in the rest of Africa. At the end of my narrative I said there were issues that I wanted us to examine. But after initially allowing Sobukwe and me a certain proximity, the authorities took pains to keep us apart. We lived in single cells along a corridor and he and I were put at opposite ends.

Occasionally we did have a chance to talk as we sat next to each other on the ground of the prison courtyard sewing and patching up shabby old mailbags. I have always respected Sobukwe, and found him a balanced and reasonable man. But we differed markedly about the principal subject at hand: prison conditions. Sobukwe believed that to fight poor conditions would be to acknowledge the state's right to have him in prison in the first place. I responded that it was always unacceptable to live in degrading conditions and that political prisoners throughout history had considered it part of their duty to fight to improve them. Sobukwe responded that prison conditions would not change until the country changed. I completely agreed with this, but I did not see why that ought to prevent us from fighting in the only realm in which we now could fight. We never resolved this issue, but we did make some progress when we submitted a joint letter to the commanding officer setting out our complaints about prison conditions.

Sobukwe never broke in prison. But in Pretoria he was a bit sensitive and testy, and I attribute this to Stephen Tefu. Tefu had become a kind of goad to Sobukwe, teasing, taunting and challenging him. Even at the best of times, Tefu was a difficult fellow: dyspeptic, argumentative, overbearing. He was also articulate, knowledgeable, and an expert in Russian history. Above all, he was a fighter, but he would fight everyone, even his friends. Tefu and Sobukwe quarrelled every day.

I was keen to discuss policy issues with Sobukwe, and one of the matters I took up with him was the PAC slogan 'Freedom in 1963'. It was already 1963 and freedom was nowhere to be seen. 'My brother,' I said to Sobukwe, 'there is nothing so dangerous as a leader making a demand that he knows cannot be achieved. It creates false hopes among the people.'

I said this in a most respectful manner, but Tefu jumped in and started to berate Sobukwe. 'Bob,' he said, 'you have met your match with Mandela. You know he is right.' Tefu continued in this vein, annoying Sobukwe to the point where he would tell Tefu, 'Leave me alone.' But Tefu would not stop. 'Bob, the people are waiting for you. They are going to kill you because you have deceived them. You are just an amateur, Bob. You are not a real politician.'

Tefu did his best to alienate me as well. Every morning, when we were visited by the warders, he would complain to them about something –

the food, the conditions, the heat or the cold. One day an officer said to Tefu: 'Look, man, why do you complain every morning?'

'I complain because it is my duty to complain,' Steve said.

'But, look at Mandela,' the officer said, 'he does not complain every day.'

'Ah,' said Tefu with disgust, 'Mandela is a little boy who is afraid of the white man. I don't even know who he is. One morning, I woke up and found every newspaper saying, "Mandela, Mandela, Mandela", and I said to myself, "Who is this Mandela?" I will tell you who Mandela is. He is a chap built up by you people for some reason that I don't understand. That is who Mandela is!'

We were joined for two weeks by Walter Sisulu, who had been on trial in Johannesburg for incitement to strike while I had been in Pretoria. He was sentenced to six years. We had a number of opportunities to talk in jail and we discussed Walter's application for bail while his appeal was pending, a move I wholeheartedly supported. After two weeks he was released on bail, and he was instructed by the movement to go underground, from where he was to continue to lead the struggle, which he ably did.

Not long after Walter left, I was walking to the prison hospital with Sobukwe when I spotted Nana Sita in the courtyard about twenty-five yards away. Sita, the distinguished Indian campaigner who had led our defiance at Boksburg in 1952, had just been convicted by a Pretoria magistrate for refusing to vacate his house – the house he had lived in for more than forty years – which was in a neighbourhood that had been proclaimed 'white' in terms of the Group Areas Act. He was hunched over, and the fact that he was barefoot despite an acute arthritic condition made me uncomfortable in my own sandals. I wanted to go over to greet him, but we were marching under the eyes of half a dozen warders.

Suddenly and without warning, I suffered a blackout. I crumpled to the concrete and sustained a deep gash above my left eye, which required three stitches. I had been diagnosed back in the Fort with high blood pressure and had been given certain pills. The cause of the blackout was evidently an overdose of these pills; I was taken off them and put on a low-salt diet; this solved the problem.

That afternoon was my first scheduled visit from Winnie since I had been sentenced. Stitches or no stitches, I was not going to miss it. She was extremely concerned when she saw me but I assured her I was fine and explained what happened. Even so, rumours circulated that my health had broken down.

53

In October 1962, during my trial, the ANC held its first annual conference since 1959. Because the organization was illegal, the conference took place in Lobatse, just over the border in Bechuanaland. The conference was a milestone, for it explicitly linked the ANC and MK. Although the National Executive stated, 'Our emphasis still remains mass political action,' Umkhonto was referred to as the 'military wing of our struggle'. This was done in part to try to quell the more irresponsible acts of terrorism then being committed by Poqo. Poqo, Xhosa for 'independent' or 'standing alone', was loosely linked to the PAC, and their acts of terrorism targeted both African collaborators and whites. The ANC wanted the people to see its new militancy, but also to see that it was controlled and responsible.

The government had decided to accelerate the programme of 'separate development' to show the world that apartheid allowed races their individual 'freedom'. The prototype would be the Transkei. In January 1962, Verwoerd had announced that South Africa intended to grant the Transkei 'self-government'. In 1963 the Transkei became a 'self-governing' homeland. In November 1963, an election was held for the Transkei legislative assembly. But by a margin of more than three to one, Transkei voters elected members opposed to the homeland policy.

The Bantustan system was nevertheless instituted; the voters had opposed it, but participated in it simply by voting. Though I abhorred the Bantustan system, I felt the ANC should use both the system and those within it as a platform for our policies, particularly as so many of our leaders were now voiceless through imprisonment, banning or exile.

Terrorism against the Bantu Authorities increased. As acts of sabotage mounted, so did the government's vigilance. John Vorster, the new minister of justice, who had himself been detained during the Second World War for opposing the government's support of the Allies, was a man unsentimental in the extreme. For him, the iron fist was the best and only answer to subversion.

On 1 May 1963, the government enacted legislation designed 'to break the back' of Umkhonto, as Vorster put it. The General Law Amendment Act, better known as the Ninety-Day Detention Law, waived the right of habeas corpus and empowered any police officer to detain any person without a warrant on grounds of suspicion of a political crime. Those arrested could be detained without trial, charge, access to a lawyer, or protection against self-incrimination for up to ninety days. The ninety-day detention could be extended, as Vorster ominously explained, until 'this side of eternity'. The law helped to transform the country into a police state; no dictator could covet more power than the Ninety-Day Detention Law gave to the authorities. As a result, the police became more savage: prisoners were routinely beaten and we soon heard reports of electric shock, suffocation and other forms of torture. In Parliament, Helen Suzman, the representative of the liberal Progressive Party, cast the lone vote against the act.

Increased penalties were ordered for membership of illegal organizations; sentences from five years to the death penalty were instituted for 'furthering the aims' of communism or of other banned organizations. Political prisoners were redetained, as I found out in May 1963 when Sobukwe's three-year sentence was up; instead of releasing him, the government simply redetained him without charging him, and then sent him to Robben Island.

Vorster also championed the Sabotage Act of June 1962, which allowed for house arrests and more stringent bannings not subject to challenge in the court, restricting the liberties of citizens to those in the most extreme fascist dictatorships. Sabotage itself now carried a minimum penalty of five years without parole and a maximum of death. Because the wording of the act was so broad, even activities such as trespassing or illegal possession of weapons could constitute sabotage. Another act of Parliament prohibited the reproduction of any statement made by a banned person. Nothing I said or had ever said could be reported in the newspapers. *New Age* was banned at the end of 1962, and possession of a banned publication became a criminal offence, punishable by up to two years in prison. Provision was also made for house arrest, the best-known use of which was imposed on the white political activist Helen Joseph.

54

One night towards the end of May, a warder came to my cell and ordered me to pack my things. I asked him why, but he did not answer. In less than ten minutes, I was escorted down to the reception office where I found three other political prisoners: Tefu, John Gaetsewe and Aaron Molete. Colonel Aucamp curtly informed us that we were being transferred. Where? Tefu asked. Someplace very beautiful, Aucamp said. Where? said Tefu. '*Die Eiland*,' said Aucamp. The island. There was only one. Robben Island.

The four of us were shackled together and put in a windowless van that contained only a sanitary bucket. We drove all night to Cape Town, and arrived at the city's docks in the late afternoon. It is not an easy or pleasant task for men shackled together to use a sanitary bucket in a moving van.

The docks at Cape Town were swarming with armed police and nervous plain-clothed officials. We had to stand, still chained, in the hold of the old wooden ferry, which was difficult as the ship rocked in the swells off the coast. A small porthole above was the only source of light and air. The porthole served another purpose as well: the warders enjoyed urinating on us from above. It was still light when we were led on deck and we saw the island for the first time. Green and beautiful, it looked at first more like a resort than a prison.

'*Esiquithini*.' 'At the island.' That is how the Xhosa people describe the narrow, windswept outcrop of rock that lies eighteen miles off the coast of Cape Town. Everyone knows which island you are referring to. I first heard about the island as a child. Robben Island was well known among the Xhosas after Makanna (also known as Nxele), the six-foot six-inch commander of the Xhosa army in the Fourth Xhosa War, was banished there by the British after leading ten thousand warriors against Grahamstown in 1819. He tried to escape from Robben Island by boat, but drowned before reaching shore. The memory of that loss is woven into the language of my people who speak of a 'forlorn hope' by the phrase '*Ukuza kuka Nxele.*'

Makanna was not the first African hero confined on the island. In 1658, Autshumao, known to European historians as Harry the Strandloper, was banished by Jan van Riebeeck during a war between the Khoi Khoi and the Dutch. I took solace in the memory of Autshumao, for he is reputed to be the first and only man ever to escape from Robben Island, and he did so by rowing to the mainland in a small boat.

The island takes its name from the Dutch word for seal, hundreds of which once cavorted in the icy Benguela currents that wash the shores. Later the island was turned into a leper colony, a lunatic asylum and a naval base. The government had only recently turned the island back into a prison.

We were met by a group of burly white warders shouting: '*Dis die Eiland! Hier julle gaan vrek!*' ('This is the island. Here you will die!') Ahead of us was a compound flanked by a number of guardhouses. Armed guards lined the path to the compound. It was extremely tense. A tall, red-faced warder yelled at us: '*Hier ek is you baas!*' 'Here I am your boss!' He was one of the notorious Kleynhans brothers, known for their brutality to prisoners. The warders always spoke in Afrikaans. If you replied in English they would say, '*Ek verstaan nie daardie kaffirboetie se taal nie.*' ('I don't understand that kaffir-lover's language.')

As we walked towards the prison, the guards shouted 'Two-two! Two-two!' – meaning we should walk in pairs, two in front, two behind. I linked up with Tefu. The guards started screaming, '*Haak! Haak!*' The word *haak* means 'move' in Afrikaans, but it is customarily reserved for cattle.

The warders were demanding that we jog, and I turned to Tefu and under my breath said that we must set an example; if we gave in now we would be at their mercy. Tefu nodded his head in agreement. We had to show them that we were not everyday criminals but political prisoners being punished for our beliefs.

I motioned to Tefu that we two should walk in front, and we took the lead. Once in front, we actually decreased the pace, walking slowly and deliberately. The guards were incredulous. 'Listen,' Kleynhans said, 'this is not Johannesburg, this is not Pretoria, this is Robben Island, and we will tolerate no insubordination here. *Haak! Haak!*' But we continued at our stately pace. Kleynhans ordered us to halt, and stood in front of us: 'Look, man, we will kill you, we are not fooling around, your wives and children and mothers and fathers will never know what happened to you. This is the last warning. *Haak! Haak!*'

To this I said: 'You have your duty and we have ours.' I was determined that we would not give in, and we did not, for we were already at the cells. We were ushered into a rectangular stone building and taken to a large open room. The floor was covered with water a few inches deep. The guards yelled: '*Trek uit! Trek uit!*' ('Undress! Undress!') As we removed each item of clothing, the guards would grab it, search it quickly and then throw it in the water. Jacket off, searched, thrown in the water. Then the guards commanded us to get dressed, by which they meant for us to put on our soaking clothes.

Two officers entered the room. The less senior of the two was a captain whose name was Gericke. From the start, we could see that he was intent on manhandling us. The captain pointed to Aaron Molete, the youngest of the four of us and a very mild and gentle person, and said, 'Why is your hair so long?' Aaron said nothing. The captain shouted, 'I'm talking to you! Why is your hair so long? It is against regulations. Your hair should have been cut. Why is it long . . .' and then he paused and turned to look at me, and said, '. . . like this boy's?' pointing at me. I began to speak: 'Now, look here, the length of our hair is determined by the regulations . . .'

Before I could finish, he shouted in disbelief: 'Never talk to me that way, boy!' and began to advance. I was frightened; it is not a pleasant sensation to know that someone is about to hit you and you are unable to defend yourself.

When he was just a few feet from me, I said, as firmly as I could, 'If you so much as lay a hand on me, I will take you to the highest court in the land and when I finish with you, you will be as poor as a church mouse.' The moment I began speaking, he paused, and by the end of my speech he was staring at me with astonishment. I was a bit surprised myself. I had been afraid, and spoke not from courage but out of a kind of bravado. At such times, one must put up a bold front despite what one feels inside.

'Where's your ticket?' he asked, and I handed it to him. I could see he was nervous. 'What's your name?' he said. I nodded my head towards the ticket, and said, 'It is written there.' He said, 'How long are you in for?' I said again, gesturing towards the ticket, 'It is written there.' He looked down and said, 'Five years! You are in for five years and you are so arrogant! Do you know what it means to serve five years?' I said, 'That is my business. I am ready to serve five years but I am not prepared to be bullied. You must act within the law.'

No one had informed him who we were, or that we were political prisoners, or that I was a lawyer. I had not noticed it myself, but the other officer, a tall, quiet man, had vanished during our confrontation;

I later discovered that he was Colonel Steyn, the commanding officer of Robben Island. The captain then left, much quieter than he had entered.

We were then by ourselves, and Steve, his nerves jangling, could not stop speaking. 'We have provoked the Boer,' he said. 'Now we are in for a rough time.' He was in the midst of speaking when a stocky fellow named Lieutenant Pretorius walked in. To our surprise, Pretorius spoke to us in Xhosa, which he seemed to know quite well. 'We have looked at your records and they are not so bad. All except this one,' he said, nodding towards Steve. 'Your record is filthy.'

Steve exploded. 'Who are you to talk to me like that? You say I have a filthy record. You have read my files, eh? Well, you will find that all those convictions were for cases I was fighting for the rights of my people. I am not a criminal; you are the criminal.' The lieutenant then warned Steve that he would charge him if he ever addressed him in that way again. Before leaving, Pretorius said he was placing us in a single large cell with windows that faced outside and then added, rather ominously, 'But I don't want you to talk to anyone through those windows, especially you, Mandela.'

We were then taken to our cell, one of the best I had ever seen. The windows were large and within easy reach. Through those in one wall we could see other prisoners and warders as they walked past. It was spacious, certainly large enough for the four of us, and had its own toilets and showers.

It had been an exhausting day and a short while later, after a supper of cold porridge, the others went to sleep. I was lying on my blanket on the floor, when I heard a tapping at the window. I looked up and saw a white man beckoning me to come to the glass. I remembered the lieutenant's admonition and stayed put.

Then I heard the fellow whisper: 'Nelson, come here.' The fact that he knew my name intrigued me and I decided to take a chance. I went over to the window and looked at him. He must have realized that I thought he was white, because the first thing he whispered was, 'I'm a Coloured warder from Bloemfontein.' He then gave me news of my wife. There had been a report in the Johannesburg newspapers that my wife had come to see me at Pretoria Local, but that they had not informed her that I had been taken to Robben Island. I thanked him for the information.

'Do you smoke?' he said. I told him that I did not and he seemed disappointed. I then got the idea: 'Yes, but my comrades do.' He brightened at this and said he would return in a few minutes with tobacco and sandwiches. Everyone was now awake. Tefu and John Gaetsewe smoked, and I split the pouch of tobacco between them, and we all divided the sandwiches.

For the next few weeks the Coloured warder came almost every night with tobacco and sandwiches. And each night I would divide up the tobacco evenly between Tefu and Gaetsewe. The warder was taking great risks, and he warned me that he was prepared to deal directly only with me, or the arrangement was off.

When we arrived on the island we had no idea how many other prisoners were there. Within a few days we learned there were about a thousand men, all Africans, all recent arrivals. Most of these men were common-law prisoners, but I knew there would be some political prisoners among them. I wanted to contact them, but we were completely isolated. For the first few days we were kept locked in our cell and not even permitted outside. We demanded to be taken to work like the other prisoners, and this was soon granted, but we were taken out alone, supervised by Kleynhans. Our first job was covering up some newly laid pipe, and we were on a small hill and could see some of the island, which was wild and lovely.

We worked hard that first day, but on each succeeding day Kleynhans pushed us harder. He did this crudely, as one would urge on a horse or cow. '*Nee, man, Kom aan! Gaan aan!*' ('No, man. Come on. Go on.') At one point, Steve, who was older than the rest of us, put down his shovel and was immediately threatened by Kleynhans. But Steve, in Afrikaans, responded: 'You ignoramus who cannot even speak your own language properly – you cannot tell me what to do. I will work at my own rate, that is what I am prepared to do, and that is all I can do.' Then, with great dignity, he picked up his shovel and resumed work. Steve had been a teacher of Afrikaans, and he not only spoke perfect Afrikaans but its antecedent, High Dutch. Steve would speak to the warders in a condescending and grandiloquent style that they probably did not understand. But they knew better than to engage him in a verbal battle.

There were two Kleynhans brothers on the island, both reputed to have viciously assaulted prisoners. We were looked after by the older brother, who must have been warned to restrain himself, for he never touched us. The younger one was under no such constraints. One day, we were walking back from work along a road and passed a workspan of several hundred prisoners carting sand in wheelbarrows. They were non-political prisoners and both of our groups were ordered to halt while the two brothers had a chat; the younger brother ordered one of his men to polish his boots while he talked. I recognized some of the men in the other workspan as those who had been sentenced to death in the Sekhukhuneland peasant revolt of 1958, and I turned round to get a better look at them. The younger brother rudely ordered me to look the other way. I do not know how I would have reacted had I not been standing in full view of the other prisoners, but my pride was now at stake. I refused to turn round. The younger Kleynhans advanced with the obvious intent of assaulting me, but when he was a few steps away, his brother ran over, grabbed him, whispered a few words, and the incident passed.

One day we were visited by the head of prison, who was responsible for running all of Robben Island and had come to hear our complaints. Theron was a sour fellow who did not like to deal with prisoners face to face. I did not want to alienate him but I was not going to cringe. 'We are grateful that you have come to see us,' I said, speaking for the group, 'because we have a number of problems which I am certain you will be able to sort out.' I enumerated the problems, and when I finished, he said, 'I will see what I can do.'

Perhaps he thought he had given in too easily because as he was walking out he turned to Tefu, who had a large belly, and said, '*Jou groot pens sal in die plek verbruin*', Afrikaans for 'That great stomach of yours is going to disappear here in prison.' *Pens* means stomach, but is used to refer to the stomach of animals like sheep or cattle. The word for the stomach of a human being is *maag*.

Steve did not take kindly to the prison head's jibe, and he was incapable of letting an insult go unanswered. 'You know, Captain,' he said, 'there is nothing you can do to me that can truly affect me for I am a member of the most revolutionary political organization in the world, the Communist Party, which has a distinguished record of service to oppressed people around the globe. You and your poor National Party will be in the ash-heap of history while we are ruling the world. I am better known internationally than your witless state president. Who are you? A small functionary not even worth paying attention to. By the time I leave prison I won't even know your name.' Theron turned on his heel and left.

The nightly visits of our Coloured warder went a long way to mitigate the harshness of the island. But even with this luxury, Steve was still dissatisfied. Tefu was a heavy smoker; he would sometimes puff away the entire night leaving himself no tobacco for the next day. Gaetsewe, however, conserved his tobacco, and never ran out. One evening, in a particularly irritable mood, Tefu confronted me. 'Nelson,' he said, 'you are short-changing me. You are giving Gaetsewe more tobacco than me.'

This was not true, but I thought I would play a game with him. 'Very well then,' I said. 'Every night when I get the tobacco I will first divide it into two portions and then I will let you choose which one you want.' That night, and each night afterwards, I separated the tobacco into equal piles and said to Steve, 'Choose.'

Tefu would be in an agony of indecision. He would look at both piles, his head swinging back and forth between the two. Finally, in frustration, he would grab one of the piles and go off and begin to smoke. Though this process seemed to me eminently fair – and also humorous – Tefu was still unhappy. He began to hover about when the warder came to the window in order to make sure that I was not hoarding the tobacco. This made the warder uncomfortable. 'Look,' he said to me, 'I deal only with you. It is a question of security.' I said I understood, and told Tefu that he could not be around when I was dealing with the warder.

The next night, however, when the warder came to the window, Tefu strode up to the bars and said to him, 'From now on I want my own tobacco. Just give it to me directly.' The warder panicked. 'Mandela,' he said, 'you have broken our agreement. No more. I won't be bringing you these things.' I shooed Tefu away and remonstrated with the warder. I said, 'Look, man, this is an old chap,' meaning Tefu. 'And he's not very normal,' I said, pointing to my head. 'Make an exception.' So he softened and gave me the supplies, but warned if it happened again, that would be the end.

That night, I thought it necessary to punish Tefu. I said, 'Now, look, you have jeopardized our supplies. You are not going to have any tobacco or sandwiches tonight. You have almost lost us these privileges. So we're cutting you off until you improve.' Tefu was silent.

We stayed in one corner of the cell that night, eating our sandwiches and reading the paper the warder also brought for us. Tefu sat by himself in the opposite corner. Eventually we drifted off to sleep. At about midnight, I felt an arm on my shoulder, jostling me awake.

'Nelson . . . Nelson.' It was Tefu. 'Nelson,' he said, speaking softly, 'you have hit me in a weak spot. You have deprived me of my tobacco. I am an old man. I have suffered for my commitment to my people. You are the leader here in jail, and you are punishing me like this. It is not fair, Nelson.'

He had hit *me* in a weak spot. I felt as though I had abused my power. He had indeed suffered, far more than I had. I had not eaten half my sandwich, and I immediately gave it to him. I roused Gaetsewe – I had given him all the tobacco – and asked him if he would share it with Tefu. Tefu was always difficult, but from that point on he behaved much better.

Once we started working, I got some sense of what life was like for other prisoners on the island. The authorities also moved some young political prisoners from the PAC into the cells opposite ours. At night, we were able to talk with them through the barred door. Among these young men, I discovered, was Nqabeni Menye, a nephew of mine from Mqhekezweni whom I had last seen when he was a baby in 1941.

We conversed about the Transkei and caught up on family history. One night, while his friends were gathered around him, he said, 'Uncle, what organization do you belong to?' The ANC, I said, of course. My response caused consternation among those young men and suddenly their faces disappeared from the window. After some time, my nephew reappeared and asked me whether or not I had ever been a member of the PAC. I replied that I had not. He then said he had understood that I joined the PAC during my Africa tour. I told him that I had not, that I had always been a member of the ANC, and that I always would be. This again caused dismay among them and they vanished.

I later learned that PAC propaganda claimed that I had joined that organization when I was travelling elsewhere on the continent. Although I was not pleased to hear this, it did not surprise me. In politics, one can never underestimate how little people know about a situation. A short while later my nephew was back and asked me if I had met and talked with Sobukwe at Pretoria Local. I said that I had and that we had very good discussions. This pleased them, and they said good night and that was the last I saw of them.

A few hours later that same evening a captain came to our cell and commanded the four of us to pack our belongings. Within minutes my comrades were taken away, leaving me in the cell by myself. In prison, one counts oneself lucky to be able to wave good-bye to one's comrades. One can be in extraordinarily intimate circumstances with someone for months, and then never see the person again. It is dehumanizing, for it forces one to adapt by becoming more self-contained and insulated.

Now that I was alone, I was also somewhat anxious. There is sometimes safety in numbers; when you are alone, there are no witnesses. I realized I had not been served any food, and banged on the door: 'Warder, I have not received my supper.'

'You must call me *baas*,' he yelled. I went hungry that night.

Very early the next morning I was taken back to Pretoria. The Department of Prisons released a statement to the press that I had been removed from the island for my own safety because PAC prisoners were planning to assault me. This was patently false; they had brought me back to Pretoria for their own motives, which soon became clear.

I was kept in solitary confinement at Pretoria Local. But prisoners are resourceful and I was soon receiving secret notes and other communications from some of the ANC people there. I had a communication from Henry Fazzie, one of the MK cadres who had undergone military training in Ethiopia and been arrested while attempting to return to South Africa. They were among the first ANC members to be tried under the Sabotage Act.

Through the prison grapevine, I attempted to help them with their defence and suggested they contact Harold Wolpe. I later heard that Wolpe was in police detention. This was my first intimation that something had gone seriously wrong. One day, as I was being led away from the courtyard after exercise, I saw Andrew Mlangeni. I had last seen him in September 1961 when he was leaving the country for military training. Wolpe, Mlangeni – who else was under arrest?

Early in 1961, Winnie had been banned for two years. I heard from another prisoner that Winnie had recently been charged with violating her bans, which could lead to imprisonment or house arrest. Winnie was headstrong; a banning order was just the type of thing that would make her angry. I had no doubt that she violated her orders, and I would never counsel her not to do so, but it concerned me greatly that she might spend time in prison.

One morning in July 1963, as I was walking along the corridor to my cell, I saw Thomas Mashifane, who had been the foreman at Liliesleaf Farm. I greeted him warmly, though I realized that the authorities had undoubtedly led him to my corridor to see if I recognized or acknowledged him. I could not but do otherwise. His presence there could mean only one thing: the authorities had discovered Rivonia.

A day or two later I was summoned to the prison office where I found Walter; Govan Mbeki; Ahmed Kathrada; Andrew Mlangeni; Bob Hepple; Raymond Mhlaba, a member of the MK High Command who had recently returned from training in China; Elias Motsoaledi, also a member of MK; Dennis Goldberg, an engineer and a member of the Congress of Democrats; Rusty Bernstein, an architect and also a member of the COD; and Jimmy Kantor, an attorney who was Harold Wolpe's brother-in-law. We were all charged with sabotage, and scheduled to appear in court the next day. I had served just nine months of my five-year sentence.

In bits and pieces, I learned what had happened. On the afternoon of

11 July, a dry cleaner's van entered the long driveway of the farm. No one at Liliesleaf had ordered a delivery. The vehicle was stopped by a young African guard, but he was overwhelmed when dozens of armed policemen and several police dogs sprang from the vehicle. They surrounded the property and a handful of officers entered the main building and the principal outbuilding. In the latter they found a dozen men around a table discussing a document. Walter jumped out of a window but was cut off by a snarling police dog. The arrests also included Arthur Goldreich, who had driven into the farm as the police raid was in progress.

The police searched the entire farm and confiscated hundreds of documents and papers, though they found no weapons. One of the most important documents remained right on the table: Operation Mayibuye, a plan for guerrilla warfare in South Africa. In one fell swoop, the police had captured the entire High Command of Umkhonto we Sizwe. Everyone was detained under the new Ninety-Day Detention Law.

Joe Slovo and Bram Fischer were fortunately not there at the time of the raid, but they often went to the farm two or three times a day. In hindsight, it is extraordinary that Liliesleaf was not discovered sooner. The regime had become stricter and more sophisticated. Wiretaps had become common as was twenty-four-hour surveillance. The raid was a coup for the state.

On our first day in court we were not given the opportunity to instruct counsel. We were brought before a magistrate and charged with sabotage. A few days later we were allowed to meet Bram, Vernon Berrangé, Joel Joffe, George Bizos and Arthur Chaskalson, all of whom were acting for us. I was still being kept separately as I was a convicted prisoner, and these sessions were my first opportunity to talk with my colleagues.

Bram was very sombre. In his quiet voice, he told us that we were facing an extremely serious trial and that the state had formally advised him they would ask for the supreme penalty permitted by law, the death sentence. Given the climate of the times, Bram said, this result was a very real possibility. From that moment on we lived in the shadow of the gallows. The mere possibility of a death sentence changes everything. From the start, we considered it the most likely outcome of the trial. Far lesser crimes than ours had recently been punished by life sentences.

Prison officials never let you forget that you might hang. That night, a warder rapped on my cell door at bedtime. 'Mandela, you don't have to worry about sleep,' he said. 'You are going to sleep for a long, long time.' I waited a moment and said, 'All of us, you included, are going to sleep for a long, long time.' It was small consolation.

55

On 9 October 1963, we were picked up in a heavily fortified police van. It had a steel divider running along the centre, segregating the white prisoners from the Africans. We were driven to the Palace of Justice in Pretoria, where the Supreme Court sits, for the opening of 'The State versus the National High Command and others', that later become known as 'The State versus Nelson Mandela and others', and is still better known as the Rivonia Trial. Near the court stands a statue of Paul Kruger, the president of the Republic of the Transvaal who fought against British imperialism in the nineteenth century. Underneath this Afrikaner hero is a quotation from one of his speeches. The inscription reads: 'In confidence we lay our cause before the whole world. Whether we win or whether we die, freedom will rise in Africa like the sun from the morning clouds.'

Our van was in the centre of a convoy of police trucks. At the front of this motorcade were limousines carrying high police officials. The Palace of Justice was teeming with armed policemen. To avoid the enormous crowd of our supporters who had grouped in front of the building, we were driven to the rear of the building and taken in through great iron gates. All around the building police officers with machine guns stood at attention. As we descended from the van, we could hear the great crowd singing and chanting. Once inside, we were held in cells below the courtroom before the opening of what was depicted in the newspapers at home and around the world as the most significant political trial in the history of South Africa.

As we emerged from the cells, each of the accused was accompanied by two armed warders. When we entered the ornate, high-ceilinged courtroom, we each turned to the crowd and made a clenched-fist ANC salute. In the visitors' gallery our supporters shouted '*Amandla! Ngawethu!*' and '*Mayibuye Afrika!*' This was inspiring, but dangerous: the police took the names and addresses of all the spectators in the galleries, and photographed them as they left the court. The courtroom was filled with domestic and international journalists, and dozens of representatives of foreign governments.

After we filed in, a group of police officers formed a tight cordon between us and the spectators. I was disgusted to have to appear in court wearing my prison clothes of khaki shorts and flimsy sandals. As a convicted prisoner, I did not have the choice of wearing proper clothes. Many people later commented on how poorly I looked, and not just because of my wardrobe. I had been in and out of solitary confinement for months and I had lost more than twenty-five pounds. I took pains to smile at the gallery when I walked into the courtroom, and seeing our supporters was the best medicine I could have had.

Security was particularly tight as only a few weeks earlier Arthur Goldreich, Harold Wolpe, Mosie Moola and Abdulhay Jassat had bribed a young guard and escaped from jail. Arthur and Harold made their way to Swaziland disguised as priests, then flew to Tanganyika. Their escape came at a time of hysteria about the underground and was greeted with blaring newspaper headlines. It was an embarrassment to the government and a boost to our morale.

Our judge in the Rivonia Trial was Mr Quartus de Wet, judge-president of the Transvaal, who sat in his flowing red robes beneath a wooden canopy. De Wet was one of the last judges appointed by the United Party before the Nationalists came to power and was not considered a government lackey. He was a poker-faced judge who did not suffer fools gladly. The prosecutor was Dr Percy Yutar, deputy attorney general of the Transvaal, whose ambition was to become attorney general of South Africa. He was a small, bald, dapper fellow, whose voice squeaked when he became angry or emotional. He had a flair for the dramatic and for high-flown if imprecise language.

Yutar rose and addressed the court, 'My Lord, I call the case of the state against the National High Command and others.' I was accused No. 1. Yutar handed in the indictment and authorized that we be charged immediately and tried summarily. This was the first time we were given a copy of the indictment. The prosecution had kept it from us, though they gave it to the *Rand Daily Mail*, which had splashed it all over that day's edition of the paper. The indictment charged eleven of us with complicity in over two hundred acts of sabotage aimed at facilitating violent revolution and an armed invasion of the country. The state contended that we were actors in a conspiracy to overthrow the government.

We were charged with sabotage and conspiracy rather than high treason because the law does not require a long preparatory examination (which is highly useful to the defence) for sabotage and conspiracy as it does for treason. Yet the supreme penalty – death by hanging – is the same. With high treason, the state must prove its case beyond a reasonable doubt and needs two witnesses to testify to each charge. Under the Sabotage Law, the onus was on the defence to prove the accused innocent.

Bram Fischer stood up and asked the court for a remand on the grounds that the defence had not had time to prepare its case. He noted that a number of the accused had been held in solitary confinement for unconscionable lengths of time. The state had been preparing for three months, but we had only received the indictment that day. Justice de Wet gave us a three-week adjournment until 29 October.

I was disturbed to discover that first day that Winnie was unable to attend. Because of her banning and her restriction to Johannesburg, she needed police permission to come to court. She had applied and been refused. I also learned that our house had been raided and the police had detained a young relative of Winnie's. Winnie was not the only wife being harassed. Albertina Sisulu and Caroline Motsoaledi were detained under the Ninety-Day Detention Act, and Walter's young son Max was also arrested. This was one of the state's most barbarous techniques of applying pressure: imprisoning the wives and children of freedom fighters. Many men in prison were able to handle anything the authorities did to them, but the thought of the state doing the same thing to their families was almost impossible to bear.

Winnie subsequently appealed to the minister of justice, who granted her permission to attend the trial on condition that she did not wear traditional dress. Ironically, the same government that was telling us to embrace our culture in the homelands forbade Winnie to wear a Xhosa gown into court.

During the next three weeks, we were permitted to spend our days together preparing our case. I was now among my fellow accused, and the company of my colleagues was a tonic. As awaiting-trial prisoners we were entitled to two half-hour visits a week, and one meal a day could be sent in from the outside. I soon gained back my lost weight with Mrs Pillay's delicious dinners.

While we were preparing our defence, the government was trying the case in the newspapers. Normally, a case that is *sub judice* cannot be commented upon in public or in the press. But since the men arrested at Rivonia were Ninety-Day detainees, and therefore not technically charged with a crime, this judicial principle went by the wayside. We were publicly branded as violent revolutionaries by everyone from the minister of justice on down. Newspapers regularly featured headlines like 'REVOLUTION ON MILITARY BASIS'.

On 29 October, we again entered the Palace of Justice; again the crowds were large and excited; again the security was extremely tight; again the court was filled with dignitaries from many foreign embassies. After three weeks with my comrades I felt rejuvenated, and I was far more comfortable in court this time in a suit. Our attorneys had objected to our having to come to court in prison garb and we had won the right to wear our own clothes. We raised clenched fists to the gallery, and we were warned by the authorities that if we did it again, we would be forced to come to court in our prison khakis. To prevent such outbursts, the authorities reversed the normal order of the prisoners preceding the judge into the courtroom. After that first day, the judge entered first so that court would already be in session when we entered.

We went on the attack immediately – Bram Fischer criticized the state's indictment as shoddy, poorly drawn and containing absurdities such as the allegation that I had participated in certain acts of sabotage on dates when I was in Pretoria Local. Yutar was flummoxed. Judge de Wet looked to him to reply to Bram's argument, and instead of offering particulars he began to give what the judge derided as 'a political speech'. De Wet was impatient with Yutar's fumbling and told him so. 'The whole basis of your argument as I understand it, Mr Yutar, is that you are satisfied that the accused are guilty.' De Wet then quashed the indictment and gavelled the session to a close.

For that moment we were technically free, and there was pandemonium in the court. But we were rearrested even before Judge de Wet left his seat. Lieutenant Swanepoel clapped each of us on the shoulder and said, 'I am arresting you on a charge of sabotage', and we were herded back to our cells. Even so, this was a blow to the government, for it now had to go back to the drawing-board in the case it was calling the trial to end all trials.

The state redrew its indictment and we were back in court in early December. We all sensed that in the interim Justice de Wet had grown more hostile to us. We suspected his previous independence had brought down the wrath of the government and that pressure had been applied. The new charges were read: we were alleged to have recruited persons for sabotage and guerrilla warfare for the purpose of starting a violent revolution; we had allegedly conspired to aid foreign military units to invade the republic in order to support a communist revolution; and we had solicited and received funds from foreign countries for this purpose. The orders for munitions on the part of the accused, said Yutar melodramatically, were enough to blow up Johannesburg.

The registrar then requested our pleas. We had agreed not to plead in the traditional manner but to use the moment to show our disdain for the proceedings.

'Accused No. 1, Nelson Mandela, do you plead guilty or not guilty?'

I rose and said, 'My Lord, it is not I, but the government that should be in the dock. I plead not guilty.'

'Accused No. 2, Walter Sisulu, do you plead guilty or not guilty?'

Sisulu: 'The government is responsible for what has happened in this country. I plead not guilty.'

Justice de Wet said he was not interested in hearing political speeches, but that we should merely plead not guilty or guilty. His direction was ignored. Each of the accused suggested that it was the government that was criminal before pleading not guilty.

To enhance the drama of the proceedings, the state had made arrangements for a live broadcast of Yutar's speech on the South African Broadcasting System. Microphones had been placed on the prosecution table as well as in front of the judge. But just as Yutar was clearing his throat, Bram Fischer rose and made an application to the court for the removal of the microphones on the grounds that the broadcasts would unfairly prejudice the case and were not in keeping with the dignity of the court. Despite Yutar's shrill plea for their retention, Justice de Wet ordered them removed.

In his address, Yutar argued that from the time the ANC had been driven underground, the organization had embarked on a policy of violence designed to lead from sabotage through guerrilla warfare to an armed invasion of the country. He asserted that we planned to deploy thousands of trained guerrilla units throughout the country, and these units were to spearhead an uprising that would be followed by an armed invasion by military units of a foreign power. 'In the midst of the resulting chaos, turmoil and disorder,' Yutar proclaimed, 'it was planned by the accused to set up a Provisional Revolutionary Government to take over the administration and control of the country.' The engine of this grand plan was Umkhonto we Sizwe, under the political direction of the ANC and the Communist Party, and the headquarters of Umkhonto was Rivonia.

In his orotund prose, Yutar described how we recruited members for MK, how we planned our national uprising for 1963 (here he was confusing us with the PAC), how we erected a powerful radio transmitter at Rivonia, and how we were collectively responsible for 222 acts of sabotage. He said Elias Motsoaledi and Andrew Mlangeni were in charge of recruiting members and that Dennis Goldberg ran a special school for recruits in the Cape. He detailed the production of various bombs, as well as the solicitation of money abroad.

Over the next three months, the state produced 173 witnesses and entered into the record thousands of documents and photographs, including standard works on Marxism, histories of guerrilla warfare, maps, blueprints, and a passport made out to one David Motsamayi. The first witness was a police photographer who had taken pictures of Rivonia, and the next witnesses were domestic workers for the Goldreich family, who had been held in detention all this time even though they had no connection with the politics of the household. These servants identified most of us by pointing to us in the dock, but old Mr Jelliman, in a brave attempt to help me, pretended that he did not see me when he was asked to point to accused No. 1. Look again, the prosecutor said, go over all the faces carefully. 'I do not think he is here,' Jelliman said quietly.

We wondered what evidence the state had to prove my guilt. I had been out of the country and in prison while much of the planning at Rivonia had taken place. When I saw Walter in Pretoria Local just after my sentencing, I urged him to make sure that all my books and notes were removed from the farm. But during the first week of the trial, when Rusty Bernstein applied for bail, Percy Yutar dramatically produced the sketch of the Fort and the accompanying note about escape that I had made while detained there. Yutar exclaimed that this was evidence that all of the accused meant to escape. It was a sign that nothing of mine had been removed from Rivonia. Later, I was told that my colleagues at Rivonia had decided to preserve my escape note because they thought it would be historic in the future. But in the present, it cost Rusty Bernstein his bail.

The state's star witness was Bruno Mtolo, or 'Mr X' as he was known in court. In introducing 'Mr X', Yutar informed the court that the interrogation would take three days and then, in theatrical tones, he added that the witness was 'in mortal danger'. Yutar asked that the evidence be given *in camera*, but that the press be included provided that they not identify the witness.

Mtolo was a tall, well-built man with an excellent memory. A Zulu from Durban, he had become the leader of the Natal region of MK. He was an experienced saboteur, and had been to Rivonia. I had met him only once, when I addressed his group of MK cadres in Natal after my return from the continent. His evidence concerning me in particular made me realize that the state would certainly be able to convict me.

He began by saying that he was an MK saboteur who had blown up a municipal office, a power pylon and an electricity line. With impressive precision, he explained the operation of bombs, land mines and grenades, and how MK worked from underground. Mtolo said that while he had never lost faith in the ideals of the ANC, he did lose faith in the organization when he realized that it and MK were instruments of the Communist Party.

His testimony was given with simplicity and what seemed like candour, but Mtolo had gone out of his way to embellish his evidence. This was undoubtedly done on police instructions. He told the court that during my remarks to the Natal Regional Command I had stated that all MK cadres ought to be good communists but not to disclose their views publicly. In fact, I never said anything of the sort, but his testimony was meant to link me and MK to the Communist Party. His memory appeared so precise that the ordinary person would assume that it was accurate in all instances. But this was not so.

I was bewildered by Mtolo's betrayal. I never ruled out the possibility of even senior ANC men breaking down under police torture. But by all accounts, Mtolo was never touched. On the stand, he went out of his way to implicate people who were not even mentioned in the case. It is possible, I know, to have a change of heart, but to betray so many others, many of whom were quite innocent, seemed to me inexcusable.

During cross-examination we learned that Mtolo had been a petty criminal before joining MK and had been imprisoned three previous times for theft. But despite these revelations, he was an extremely damaging witness, for the judge found him reliable and believable, and his testimony incriminated nearly all of us.

The keystone of the state's case was the six-page Plan of Action confiscated in the Rivonia raid. The leaders of the High Command had had this very document before them on the table when the police stormed the farm. Operation Mayibuye sketches out in general form the plan for the possible commencement of guerrilla operations, and how it might spark a mass armed uprising against the government. It envisions an initial landing of small guerrilla forces in four different areas of South Africa and the attacking of preselected targets. The document set a goal of some 7,000 MK recruits in the country who would meet the initial outside force of 120 trained guerrillas.

The prosecution's case rested in large part on their contention that Operation Mayibuye had been approved by the ANC Executive and had become the operating plan of MK. We insisted that Operation Mayibuye had not yet been formally adopted and was still under discussion at the time of the arrests. As far as I was concerned, Operation Mayibuye was a draft document that was not only not approved, but was entirely unrealistic in its goals and plans. I did not believe that guerrilla warfare was a viable option at that stage.

The plan had been drafted in my absence, so I had very little knowledge of it. Even among the Rivonia Trialists there was disagreement as to whether the plan had been adopted as ANC policy. Govan, who had drafted the document with Joe Slovo, insisted that it had been agreed upon and felt that it was wrong for us to argue in court that it was still under discussion. But all the other accused contended that the document, while drawn up by the High Command, had not been approved by the ANC Executive or even seen by Chief Luthuli.

Although a capital trial can be quite grim, our spirits were generally high. There was a good deal of gallows humour among us. Dennis Goldberg, the youngest of the accused, had an irrepressible sense of humour and often had us laughing when we should not have been. When one of the prosecution witnesses described how Raymond Mhlaba had worn a clerical collar as a disguise, Dennis took to calling him Reverend Mhlaba.

In our consulting room downstairs, we often communicated through notes, which we would then burn and throw in the wastebasket. One of the Special Branch officers who looked after us was Lieutenant Swanepoel, a burly, red-faced fellow who was convinced we were always putting one over on him. One day, while Swanepoel was observing us from the door, Govan Mbeki began to write a note in a conspicuously secretive manner. With similar drama he handed me the note. I read it, nodded my head sagely, and passed it to Kathy, who ostentatiously took out his matches as if to burn the note when Swanepoel swooped into the room, grabbed the paper out of Kathy's hands, and said something about the dangers of lighting matches indoors. He then left the room to read his prize; a few seconds later, he stormed back saying, 'I will get all of you for this!' Govan had written in capital letters: 'ISN'T SWANEPOEL A FINE-LOOKING CHAP?'

We were locked up in prison and on trial for our lives but, outside, new life was blossoming. Jimmy Kantor's wife was to give birth any day. Jimmy was an attorney who had been roped into the trial by the state for no other reason than that he was Harold Wolpe's brother-in-law.

One morning, when we were sitting in the dock, a note was passed down to me from the other end.

Barbara and I have discussed godfathers at length and we have come to the conclusion that, whether the baby is a girl or boy, we would consider it an honour if you would agree to accept this office as an adjunct to the more disreputable positions you have held in the past.

By return mail I sent Jimmy back a note.

I would be more than delighted, and the honour is mine, not the baby's. Now they dare not hang me.

56

The state case continued during the Christmas season of 1963, ending on 29 February 1964. We had a little over a month to examine the evidence and prepare our defence. We were not all equally affected by the evidence. There was no evidence against James Kantor; he was not even a member of our organization and should not have been on trial at all. For Rusty Bernstein, Raymond Mhlaba and Ahmed Kathrada, the evidence of involvement in conspiracy was slight and we decided they should not incriminate themselves. In Rusty's case, the evidence was negligible; he had merely been found at Rivonia with the others. The remaining six of us would make admissions of guilt on certain charges.

Bram was deeply pessimistic. He avowed that even if we proved that guerrilla war had not been approved and our policy of sabotage was designed not to sacrifice human life, the state could still impose the death sentence. The defence team was divided on whether or not we should testify. Some asserted that it would hurt our case if we testified. George Bizos, though, suggested that unless we gave evidence and convinced the judge that we had not decided on guerrilla warfare, he would certainly impose the supreme penalty.

Right from the start we had made it clear that we intended to use the trial not as a test of the law but as a platform for our beliefs. We would not deny, for example, that we had been responsible for acts of sabotage. We would not deny that a group of us had turned away from non-violence. We were not concerned with getting off or lessening our punishment, but with making the trial strengthen the cause for which we were all struggling – at whatever cost to ourselves. We would not defend ourselves in a legal sense so much as in a moral sense. We saw the trial as a continuation of the struggle by other means. We would readily admit what was known by the state to be true but refuse to give away any information we thought might implicate others.

We would dispute the state's central contention that we had embarked on guerrilla warfare. We would admit that we had made contingency plans to undertake guerrilla warfare in the event of sabotage failing. But we would claim it had not yet failed, for it had not been sufficiently attempted. We would deny the claims of murder and damage to innocent bystanders that the state alleged; either these claims were outright lies, or the incidents were the work of someone else. We had never contemplated the intervention of foreign military forces. In order to make these claims, we believed we would have to explain Operation Mayibuye to the court.

In my own case, the court had sufficient evidence for a conviction. Documents in my handwriting showed that I had left the country illegally, had arranged for military training for our men and had been behind the formation of Umkhonto we Sizwe. There was also a document in my handwriting called 'How to be a good communist', which the state suggested was proof that I was a card-carrying communist. In fact the document's title was taken from the work of a Chinese theoretician named Liu Shao Chi, and was written by me to prove a point to Moses Kotane. We had been engaged in a running debate about the appeal of communism to ordinary South Africans. I had long argued that communist literature was, for the most part, dull, esoteric and Western-centred, but ought to be simple, clear and relevant to the African masses. Moses insisted it could not be done. To prove my point, I had taken Liu's essay and rewritten it for an African audience.

I would be the first witness and therefore set the tone for the defence. In South African courts, evidence from the witness box can be given only in the form of an answer to a question. I did not want to be limited to that format. We decided that instead of giving testimony, I would read a statement from the dock, while the others would testify and go through cross-examination.

Because a witness making a statement from the dock does not submit to cross-examination or questions from the bench, the statement does not have the same legal weight as ordinary testimony. Those who choose to make such a statement usually do so to avoid cross-examination. Our attorneys warned me that it would put me in a more precarious legal situation; anything I said in my statement regarding my own innocence would be discounted by the judge. But that was not our highest priority. We believed it was important to open the defence with a statement of our politics and ideals, which would establish the context for all that followed. I wanted very much to cross swords with Percy Yutar, but it was more important that I use the platform to highlight our grievances.

All of this was agreed upon in consultation, mainly through notes because the consultation room was bugged. We even used the state's eavesdropping to our advantage by supplying them with disinformation. We gave every indication that I was going to testify so that they would spend their time planning their cross-examination. In a staged conversation, I told our attorney Joel Joffe that i would need the Treason Trial record to prepare my testimony. We smiled at the notion of Yutar poring over the hundred or so volumes of Treason Trial transcripts.

I spent about a fortnight drafting my address, working mainly in my cell in the evenings. When I was finished, I read it first to my comrades and fellow accused. They approved of it, suggesting a few changes, and then I asked Bram Fischer to look it over. Bram became concerned after reading it and got a respected advocate named Hal Hanson to read it. Hanson told Bram, 'If Mandela reads this in court they will take him straight out to the back of the courthouse and string him up.' That confirmed Bram's anxieties and he came to me the next day and urged me to modify the speech. I felt we were likely to hang no matter what we said, so we might as well say what we truly believed. The atmosphere at the time was extremely grim, with newspapers routinely speculating that we would receive the death sentence. Bram begged me not to read the final paragraph, but I was adamant.

On Monday 20 April, under the tightest of security, we were taken to the Palace of Justice, this time to begin our defence. Winnie was there with my mother, and I nodded to them as we entered the court, which was again full.

Bram announced that certain parts of the state's evidence would be conceded by the accused, and there was a buzz in the court. But he went on to say that the defence would deny a number of the state's assertions, including the contention that Umkhonto we Sizwe was the military wing of the ANC. He said that the leaders of MK and the ANC 'endeavoured to keep these two organizations entirely separate. They did not always succeed in this,' he said, 'but . . . every effort was made to achieve that object.' He emphatically denied that the ANC took orders from the Communist Party. He said the defence would challenge the allegation that Goldberg, Kathrada, Bernstein and Mhlaba were members of Umkhonto. He stated that the defence would show that Umkhonto had not in fact adopted Operation Mayibuye, and that MK had not embarked on preparations for guerrilla warfare.

'That will be denied?' asked Justice de Wet incredulously.

'That will be denied,' replied Bram. 'The evidence will show that while preparations for guerrilla warfare were being made, no plan was ever adopted. It was hoped throughout that such a step could be avoided.'

Then, in his soft voice, Bram said, 'The defence case, My Lord, will commence with a statement from the dock by accused No. 1, who personally took part in the establishment of Umkhonto, and who will be able to inform the court of the beginnings of that organization.'

At this, Yutar popped up from the table and cried, 'My Lord! My Lord!' He was distressed that I would not be testifying, for he had undoubtedly prepared for my cross-examination. 'My Lord,' he said rather despondently, 'a statement from the dock does not carry the same weight as evidence under oath.'

'I think, Dr Yutar,' Justice de Wet responded drily, 'that counsel for the defence have sufficient experience to advise their clients without your assistance.' Yutar sat down.

'Neither we nor our clients are unaware of the provisions of the criminal code,' replied Bram. 'I call on Nelson Mandela.'

I rose and faced the courtroom and read slowly.

I am the first accused.

I hold a bachelor's degree in Arts, and practised as an attorney in Johannesburg for a number of years in partnership with Mr Oliver Tambo. I am a convicted prisoner, serving five years for leaving the country without a permit and for inciting people to go on strike at the end of May 1961.

I admit immediately that I was one of the persons who helped to form Umkhonto we Sizwe and that I played a prominent role in its affairs until I was arrested in August 1962.

At the outset, I want to say that the suggestion made by the state in its opening that the struggle in South Africa is under the influence of foreigners or communists is wholly incorrect. I have done whatever I did, both as an individual and as a leader of my people, because of my experience in South Africa, and my own proudly felt African background, and not because of what any outsider might have said.

In my youth in the Transkei, I listened to the elders of my tribe telling stories of the old days. Amongst the tales they related to me were those of wars fought by our ancestors in defence of the fatherland. The names of Dingane and Bambatha, Hintsa and Makanna, Squngthi and Dalasile, Moshoeshoe and Sekhukhuni were praised as the pride and glory of the entire African nation. I hoped then that life might offer me the opportunity to serve my people and make my own humble contribution to their freedom struggle. This is what has motivated me in all that I have done in relation to the charges made against me in this case.

Having said this, I must deal immediately and at some length with the question of violence. Some of the things so far told the court are true and some are untrue. I do not, however, deny that I planned sabotage. I did not plan it in a spirit of recklessness or because I have any love of violence. I planned it as a result of a calm and sober assessment of the political situation that had arisen after many years of tyranny, exploitation, and oppression of my people by whites.

I wanted to impress upon the court that we had not acted irresponsibly or without thought to the ramifications of taking up violent action. I laid particular emphasis on our resolve to cause no harm to human life.

We of the ANC have always stood for a non-racial democracy, and we shrank from any action which might drive the races further apart than they already were. But the hard facts were that fifty years of non-violence had brought the African people nothing but more repressive legislation, and fewer and fewer rights. It may not be easy for this court to understand, but it is a fact that for a long time the people had been talking of violence – of the day when they would fight the white man and win back their country, and we, the leaders of the ANC, had nevertheless always prevailed upon them to avoid violence and to use peaceful methods. While some of us discussed this in May and June 1961, it could not be denied that our policy to achieve a non-racial state by non-violence had achieved nothing, and that our followers were beginning to lose confidence in this policy and were developing disturbing ideas of terrorism. . . .

Umkhonto was formed in November 1961. When we took this decision, and subsequently formulated our plans, the ANC heritage of non-violence and racial harmony was very much with us. We felt that the country was drifting towards a civil war in which blacks and whites would fight each other. We viewed the situation with alarm. Civil war would mean the destruction of what the ANC stood for; with civil war racial peace would be more difficult than ever to achieve. We already have examples in South African history of the results of war. It has taken more than fifty years for the scars of the South African [Anglo-Boer] War to disappear. How much longer would it take to eradicate the scars of inter-racial civil war, which could not be fought without a great loss of life on both sides?

Sabotage, I said, offered the best hope for future race relations. The reaction of the white rulers to our first efforts were swift and brutal:

sabotage was declared to be a crime punishable by death. We did not want civil war, I said, but we needed to be prepared for it.

> Experience convinced us that rebellion would offer the government limitless opportunities for the indiscriminate slaughter of our people. But it was precisely because the soil of South Africa is already drenched with the blood of innocent Africans that we felt it our duty to make preparations as a long-term undertaking to use force in order to defend ourselves against force. If war were inevitable, we wanted the fight to be conducted on terms most favourable to our people. The fight which held out prospects best for us and the least risk of life to both sides was guerrilla warfare. We decided, therefore, in our preparations for the future, to make provision for the possibility of guerrilla warfare.
>
> All whites undergo compulsory military training, but no such training was given to Africans. It was in our view essential to build up a nucleus of trained men who would be able to provide the leadership which would be required if guerrilla warfare started. We had to prepare for such a situation before it became too late to make proper preparations.

I explained that at this stage in our discussions I left the country to attend the PAFMECSA conference and undergo military training. I said that I underwent training because if there was to be a guerrilla war, I wanted to be able to stand and fight beside my own people. Even so, I believed that the possibilities of sabotage were far from exhausted and should be pursued with vigour.

I told the court of the dividing line between the ANC and MK, and how we made good-faith attempts to keep the two separate. This was our policy, but in practice it was not so simple. Because of bannings and imprisonment, people often had to work in both organizations. Though this might have sometimes blurred the distinction, it did not abolish it. I disputed the allegations of the state that the aims and objects of the ANC and the Communist Party were one and the same.

> The ideological creed of the ANC is, and always has been, the creed of African Nationalism. It is not the concept of African Nationalism expressed in the cry, 'Drive the white man into the sea.' The African Nationalism for which the ANC stands is the concept of freedom and fulfilment for the African people in their own land. The most important political document ever adopted by the ANC is the Freedom Charter. It is by no means a blueprint for

a socialist state. . . . The ANC has never at any period of its history advocated a revolutionary change in the economic structure of the country, nor has it, to the best of my recollection, ever condemned capitalist society. . . .

The ANC, unlike the Communist Party, admitted Africans only as members. Its chief goal was, and is, for the African people to win unity and full political rights. The Communist Party's main aim, on the other hand, was to remove the capitalists and to replace them with a working-class government. The Communist Party sought to emphasize class distinctions whilst the ANC seeks to harmonize them.

It is true that there has often been close cooperation between the ANC and the Communist Party. But cooperation is merely proof of a common goal – in this case the removal of white supremacy – and is not proof of a complete community of interests. The history of the world is full of similar examples. Perhaps the most striking illustration is to be found in the cooperation between Great Britain, the United States of America and the Soviet Union in the fight against Hitler. Nobody but Hitler would have dared to suggest that such cooperation turned Churchill or Roosevelt into communists or communist tools, or that Britain and America were working to bring about a communist world.

It is perhaps difficult for white South Africans, with an ingrained prejudice against communism, to understand why experienced African politicians so readily accepted communists as their friends. But to us the reason is obvious. Theoretical differences amongst those fighting against oppression are a luxury we cannot afford at this stage. What is more, for many decades communists were the only political group in South Africa who were prepared to treat Africans as human beings and their equals; who were prepared to eat with us; talk with us, live with and work with us. Because of this, there are many Africans who, today, tend to equate freedom with communism.

I told the court that I was not a communist and had always regarded myself as an African patriot. I did not deny that I was attracted by the idea of a classless society, or that I had been influenced by Marxist thought. This was true of many leaders of the newly independent states of Africa, who accepted the need for some form of socialism to enable their people to catch up with the advanced countries of the West.

From my reading of Marxist literature and from conversations with

Marxists, I have gained the impression that communists regard the parliamentary system of the West as undemocratic and reactionary. But, on the contrary, I am an admirer of such a system.

The Magna Carta, the Petition of Rights and the Bill of Rights are documents which are held in veneration by democrats throughout the world. I have great respect for British political institutions, and for the country's system of justice. I regard the British Parliament as the most democratic institution in the world, and the independence and impartiality of its judiciary never fail to arouse my admiration. The American Congress, the country's doctrine of separation of powers, as well as the independence of its judiciary, arouse in me similar sentiments.

I detailed the terrible disparities between black and white life in South Africa. In education, health, income, every aspect of life, blacks were barely at a subsistence level while whites had the highest standards in the world – and aimed to keep it that way. Whites, I said, often claimed that Africans in South Africa were better off than Africans in the rest of the continent. Our complaint, I said, was not that we were poor by comparison with the people in the rest of Africa, but that we were poor by comparison with the whites in our country, and that we were prevented by legislation from righting that imbalance.

The lack of human dignity experienced by Africans is the direct result of the policy of white supremacy. White supremacy implies black inferiority. Legislation designed to preserve white supremacy entrenches this notion. Menial tasks in South Africa are invariably performed by Africans. When anything has to be carried or cleaned the white man looks around for an African to do it for him, whether the African is employed by him or not. . . .

Poverty and the breakdown of family life have secondary effects. Children wander about the streets of the townships because they have no schools to go to, or no money to enable them to go to school, or no parents at home to see that they go to school, because both parents (if there be two) have to work to keep the family alive. This leads to a breakdown in moral standards, to an alarming rise in illegitimacy and to growing violence which erupts, not only politically, but everywhere. . . .

Africans want a just share in the whole of South Africa; they want security and a stake in society. Above all, we want equal political rights, because without them our disabilities will be permanent. I know this sounds revolutionary to the whites in this country, because the majority of voters will be Africans. This makes the white man fear democracy. . . .

This then is what the ANC is fighting for. Their struggle is a truly national one. It is a struggle of the African people, inspired by their own suffering and their own experience. It is a struggle for the right to live.

I had been reading my speech, and at this point I placed my papers on the defence table, and turned to face the judge. The courtroom became extremely quiet. I did not take my eyes off Justice de Wet as I spoke from memory the final words.

During my lifetime I have dedicated myself to this struggle of the African people. I have fought against white domination, and I have fought against black domination. I have cherished the ideal of a democratic and free society in which all persons live together in harmony and with equal opportunities. It is an ideal which I hope to live for and to achieve. But if needs be, it is an ideal for which I am prepared to die.

The silence in the courtroom was now complete. At the end of the address, I simply sat down. I did not turn and face the gallery, though I felt all their eyes on me. The silence seemed to stretch for many minutes. But in fact it lasted probably no more than thirty seconds, and then from the gallery I heard what sounded like a great sigh, a deep, collective 'ummmm', followed by the cries of women.

I had read for over four hours. It was a little after 4 in the afternoon, the time court normally adjourned. But Justice de Wet, as soon as there was order in the courtroom, asked for the next witness. He was determined to lessen the impact of my statement. He did not want it to be the last and only testimony of the day. But nothing he did could weaken its effect. When I finished my address and sat down, it was the last time that Justice de Wet ever looked me in the eye.

The speech received wide publicity in both the local and foreign press, and was printed, virtually word for word, in the *Rand Daily Mail*. This despite the fact that all my words were banned. The speech both indicated our line of defence and disarmed the prosecution, which had prepared its entire case based on the expectation that I would be giving evidence denying responsibility for sabotage. It was now plain that we would not attempt to use legal niceties to avoid accepting responsibility for actions we had taken with pride and premeditation.

*   *   *

Accused No. 2, Walter Sisulu, was next. Walter had to bear the brunt of the cross-examination that Yutar had prepared for me. Walter withstood a barrage of hostile questions and rose above Yutar's petty machinations to explain our policy in clear and simple terms. He asserted that Operation Mayibuye and the policy of guerrilla warfare had not been adopted as ANC policy. In fact, Walter told the court that he had personally opposed its adoption on the grounds that it was premature.

Govan followed Walter into the witness box and proudly related to the court his longtime membership of the Communist Party. The prosecutor asked Govan why, if he admitted many of the actions in the four counts against him, he did not simply plead guilty to the four counts? 'First,' Govan said, 'I felt I should come and explain under oath some of the reasons that led me to join these organizations. There was a sense of moral duty attached to it. Secondly, for the simple reason that to plead guilty would to my mind indicate a sense of moral guilt. I do not accept there is moral guilt attached to my answers.'

Like Govan, Ahmed Kathrada and Rusty Bernstein testified to their membership of the Communist Party as well as the ANC. Although Rusty was captured at Rivonia during the raid, the only direct evidence that the state had against him was that he had assisted in the erection of a radio aerial at the farm. Kathy, in his sharp-witted testimony, denied committing acts of sabotage or inciting others to do so, but he said he supported such acts if they advanced the struggle.

We had all been surprised when accused No. 8, James Kantor, had been arrested and grouped with us. Apart from being the brother-in-law and legal partner of Harold Wolpe, who performed a number of transactions for us through his office, he had no involvement whatsoever with the ANC or MK. There was virtually no evidence against him, and I assumed the only reason the state kept up the charade of prosecuting him in prison was to intimidate progressive lawyers.

On the day that Justice de Wet was to rule on Jimmy's case, we were waiting in the cells underneath the court and I said to Jimmy, 'Let us exchange ties for good luck.' But when he saw the wide, old-fashioned tie I gave him compared to the lovely silk tie he gave me, he probably thought I was merely trying to improve my wardrobe. Jimmy was something of a clothes-horse, but he wore the tie to court and when Justice de Wet dismissed the charges against him, he lifted the tie up to me as a kind of salute and farewell.

Raymond Mhlaba was one of the leading ANC and MK figures in the eastern Cape, but because the state did not have much evidence against him, he denied he was a member of MK and that he knew anything

about sabotage. We all decided that neither Elias Motsoaledi, accused
No. 9, nor Andrew Mlangeni, accused No. 10, should testify. They were
low-level members of MK, and could not add much to what had already
been said. Elias Motsoaledi, despite having been beaten and tortured in
prison, never broke down. Andrew Mlangeni, the last accused, made an
unsworn statement admitting that he carried messages and instructions
for MK and had disguised himself as a priest to facilitate this work. He,
too, informed the court that he had been assaulted while in prison, and
subjected to electric shock treatment. Andrew was the last witness. The
defence rested. All that remained were the final arguments and then
judgment.

On 20 May, Yutar handed out a dozen blue leather-bound volumes of
his final speech to the press and one to the defence. Despite its handsome
packaging, Yutar's address was a garbled summary of the prosecution's
case and did not explain the indictment or assess the evidence. It was
filled with *ad hominem* insults. 'The deceit of the accused is amazing,' he
said at one point. 'Although they represented scarcely 1 per cent of the
Bantu population they took it upon themselves to tell the world that the
Africans in South Africa are suppressed, oppressed and depressed.' Even
Judge de Wet seemed mystified by Yutar's speech, and at one point
interrupted him to say, 'Mr Yutar, you do concede that you failed to
prove guerrilla warfare was ever decided upon, do you not?'

Yutar was stunned. He had assumed precisely the opposite. We
were surprised as well, for the judge's question gave us hope. Yutar
haltingly told the court that preparations for guerrilla warfare were
indeed made.

'Yes, I know that,' de Wet replied impatiently, 'the defence concedes
that. But they say that prior to their arrest they took no decision to engage
in guerrilla warfare. I take it that you have no evidence contradicting that
and that you accept it?'

'As Your Worship wishes,' Yutar said in a strangled voice.

Yutar finished by saying that the case was not only one of high treason
par excellence, but of murder and attempted murder – neither of which
was mentioned in the indictment. In a fit of bluster, he proclaimed, 'I
make bold to say that every particular allegation in the indictment has
been proved.' He knew, even as he uttered those words, that they were
patently false.

Defence counsel Arthur Chaskalson rose first to deal with some of the
legal questions raised by the prosecution. He rejected Yutar's statement
that the trial had anything to do with murder, and reminded the court

that MK's express policy was that there should be no loss of life. When Arthur began to explain that other organizations committed acts of sabotage for which the accused were blamed, de Wet interrupted to say he already accepted that as a fact. This was another unexpected victory.

Bram Fischer spoke next and was prepared to tackle the state's two most serious contentions: that we had undertaken guerrilla warfare and that the ANC and MK were the same. Though de Wet had said he believed that guerrilla warfare had not yet begun, we were taking no chances. But as Bram launched into his first point, de Wet interjected somewhat testily, 'I thought I made my attitude clear. I accept that no decision or date was fixed upon for guerrilla warfare.'

When Bram began his second point, de Wet again interrupted him to say that he also conceded the fact that the two organizations were separate. Bram, who was usually prepared for anything, was hardly prepared for de Wet's response. He then sat down; the judge had accepted his arguments even before he had made them. We were jubilant – that is, if men facing the death sentence can be said to be jubilant. Court was adjourned for three weeks while de Wet considered the verdict.

57

The world had been paying attention to the Rivonia Trial. Night-long vigils were held for us at St Paul's Cathedral in London. The students of the University of London elected me president of their Students' Union, *in absentia*. A group of experts at the UN pressed for a national convention for South Africa that would lead to a truly representative parliament, and recommended an amnesty for all opponents of apartheid. Two days before Judge de Wet was due to give his decision, the UN Security Council (with four abstentions, including Great Britain and the United States) urged the South African government to end the trial and grant amnesty to the defendants.

In the days before we were due to reconvene, I wrote papers for a set of University of London examinations for my LLB. It might seem odd that I was taking law exams a few days before the verdict. It certainly seemed bizarre to my guards, who said I would not need a law degree where I was going. But I had continued my studies throughout the trial and I wanted to take the examination. I was single-minded about it, and I later realized that it was a way to keep myself from thinking negatively. I knew I would not be practising law again very soon, but I did not want to consider the alternative. I passed the exams.

On Thursday 11 June we reassembled in the Palace of Justice for the verdict. We knew that for at least six of us there could be no verdict but guilty. The question was the sentence.

De Wet wasted no time in getting down to business. He spoke in low, rapid tones. 'I have recorded the reasons for the conclusions I have come to. I do not propose to read them out.

'Accused No. 1 is found guilty on all four counts. Accused No. 2 is found guilty on all four counts. Accused No. 3 is found guilty on all four counts. . . .'

De Wet pronounced each of the main accused guilty on all counts.

Kathy was found guilty on only one of four counts, and Rusty Bernstein was found not guilty and discharged.

'I do not propose to deal with the question of sentence today,' de Wet said. 'The state and the defence will be given opportunities to make any submission they want tomorrow morning at ten o'clock.' Court was then adjourned.

We had hoped that Kathy and Mhlaba might escape conviction, but it was another sign, if one was necessary, that the state was taking a harsh line. If he could convict Mhlaba on all four counts with little evidence, could the death sentence be far behind for those of us against whom the evidence was overwhelming?

That night, after a discussion among ourselves, Walter, Govan and I informed counsel that whatever sentences we received, even the death sentence, we would not appeal. Our decision stunned our lawyers. Walter, Govan and I believed an appeal would undermine the moral stance we had taken. We had from the first maintained that what we had done, we had done proudly and for moral reasons. We were not now going to suggest otherwise in an appeal. If a death sentence was passed, we did not want to hamper the mass campaign that would surely spring up. In light of the bold and defiant line we had taken all along, an appeal would seem anti-climactic and even disillusioning. Our message was that no sacrifice was too great in the struggle for freedom.

Counsel were unhappy about our decision, and wanted to talk about an appeal. But Walter, Govan and I wanted to discuss the mechanics of the sentencing procedure the next day. If we were sentenced to death, what would then happen? We were told that after de Wet pronounced the death sentence, he would ask me, as the first accused, 'Have you any reason to advance why the sentence of death should not be passed?' I told Bram, Joel and Vernon that in that case I would have quite a lot to say. I would tell de Wet that I was prepared to die secure in the knowledge that my death would be an inspiration to the cause for which I was giving my life. My death – our deaths – would not be in vain; if anything we might serve the cause better in death as martyrs than we ever could in life. Counsel said that such a speech would not be very helpful for an appeal, and I reaffirmed that we would not be appealing.

Even if – especially if – we did not receive the death penalty, there were practical reasons not to appeal. For one thing, we might lose. An appellate court might decide that de Wet had been too lenient and that we deserved the death penalty. An appeal would forestall international pressure to release us.

For the state, a death sentence would be the most practical verdict. We had heard that John Vorster, the minister of justice, had told friends that Prime Minister Smuts's greatest blunder during the Second World War was not hanging him for his treason. The Nationalists, he said, would not make the same mistake.

I was prepared for the death penalty. To be truly prepared for something, one must actually expect it. One cannot be prepared for something while secretly believing it will not happen. We were all prepared, not because we were brave but because we were realistic. I thought of the line from Shakespeare: 'Be absolute for death; for either death or life shall be the sweeter.'

58

On Friday 12 June 1964 we entered court for the last time. Nearly a year had passed since the fateful arrests at Rivonia. Security was extraordinarily high. Our convoy raced through the streets with sirens wailing. All the roads leading to the courthouse had been blocked off to normal traffic. The police checked the identification of anyone attempting to go near the Palace of Justice. They had even set up checkpoints at the local bus and railway stations. Despite the intimidation, as many as two thousand people assembled in front of the courthouse holding banners and signs such as 'WE STAND BY OUR LEADERS'. Inside, the spectators' gallery was full, and it was standing room only for the local and foreign press.

I waved hello to Winnie and my mother. It was heartening to see them there; my mother had journeyed all the way from the Transkei. It must be a very odd sensation to come to a courtroom to see whether or not your son will be sentenced to death. Though I suspect my mother did not understand all that was going on, her support never wavered. Winnie was equally stalwart, and her strength gave me strength.

The registrar called out the case: 'The State against Nelson Mandela and others.' Before sentence was passed, there were two pleas in mitigation. One was delivered by Harold Hanson and the other by the author Alan Paton, who was also national president of the Liberal Party. Hanson spoke eloquently, saying that a nation's grievances cannot be suppressed, that people will always find a way to give voice to those grievances. 'It was not their aims which had been criminal,' said Hanson, 'only the means to which they had resorted.' Hanson said the judge would do well to recall that his own people, the Afrikaners, had struggled violently for their freedom.

Though Paton did not himself support violence, he said the accused had had only two alternatives: 'to bow their heads and submit, or to resist by force'. The defendants should receive clemency, he said, otherwise the future of South Africa would be bleak.

But de Wet did not seem to be listening to either man. He neither looked up nor took any notes while they spoke. He seemed absorbed in his own thoughts. He had obviously already decided; he was merely waiting for the moment to reveal his decision.

He nodded for us to rise. I tried to catch his eye, but he was not even looking in our direction. His eyes were focused on the middle distance. His face was very pale, and he was breathing heavily. We looked at each other and seemed to know: it would be death, otherwise why was this normally calm man so nervous? And then he began to speak.

> I have heard a great deal during the course of this case about the grievances of the non-European population. The accused have told me and their counsel have told me that the accused who were all leaders of the non-European population were motivated entirely by a desire to ameliorate these grievances. I am by no means convinced that the motives of the accused were as altruistic as they wish the court to believe. People who organize a revolution usually take over the government and personal ambition cannot be excluded as a motive.

De Wet paused for a moment as if to catch his breath. His voice, which was muted before, was now barely audible.

> The function of this court, as is the function of the court in any other country, is to enforce law and order and to enforce the laws of the state within which it functions. The crime of which the accused have been convicted, that is the main crime, the crime of conspiracy, is in essence one of high treason. The state has decided not to charge the crime in this form. Bearing this in mind and giving the matter very serious consideration I have decided not to impose the supreme penalty which in a case like this would usually be the proper penalty for the crime, but consistent with my duty that is the only leniency which I can show. The sentence in the case of all the accused will be one of life imprisonment.

We looked at each other and smiled. There had been a great collective gasp in the courtroom when de Wet announced that he was not sentencing us to death. But there was consternation among some spectators because they had been unable to hear de Wet's sentence. Dennis Goldberg's wife called to him, 'Dennis, what is it?'

'Life!' he yelled back, grinning. 'Life! To live!'

I turned and smiled broadly to the gallery, searching out Winnie's face and that of my mother, but it was extremely confused in the court, with people shouting, police pushing the crowd this way and that. I could not see them. I flashed the thumbs-up ANC salute as many of the spectators were dashing outside to tell the crowd the verdict. Our police guardians began to hustle us out of the dock and towards the door leading underground, but although I looked again for Winnie's face, I was not able to see her before I ducked through the door leading to the cells below.

We were kept handcuffed in the cells underneath the courthouse. The police were extremely nervous about the crowd outside. They kept us underground for more than half an hour, hoping people would disperse. We were taken through the back of the building and entered the black van. We could hear the motorcycle escort revving up beside us. To avoid the crowd, the van took a different route, but even so, we could hear the crowd shouting 'Amandla!', and the slow beautiful rhythms of 'Nkosi Sikelel' iAfrika'. We made clenched fists through the bars of the window, hoping the crowd could see us, not knowing if they could.

All of us were now convicted prisoners. We were separated from Dennis Goldberg because he was white and was taken to a different facility. The rest of us were locked up in cells in Pretoria Local away from all the other prisoners. Instead of shouts and songs, we now heard only the clanging of doors and gates.

That night, as I lay on my mat on the floor of my cell, I ran over the reasons for de Wet's decision. The demonstrations throughout South Africa and the international pressure undoubtedly weighed on his mind. International trade unions had protested the trial. Dock-workers' unions around the world threatened not to handle South African goods. The Russian prime minister, Leonid Brezhnev, wrote to Dr Verwoerd asking for leniency. Members of the United States Congress protested. Fifty members of the British Parliament had staged a march in London. Alec Douglas-Home, the British foreign secretary, was rumoured to be working behind the scenes to help our cause. Adlai Stevenson, the US representative at the UN, wrote a letter saying that his government would do everything it could to prevent a death sentence. I thought that once de Wet had accepted that we had not yet initiated guerrilla warfare and that the ANC and MK were separate entities, it would have been difficult to impose the death penalty; it would have seemed excessive.

Verwoerd told Parliament that the judgment had not been influenced by the telegrams of protest and representations that had come in from around the world. He boasted that he had tossed into the waste-basket all the telegrams from socialist nations.

Towards the end of the proceedings, Judge de Wet had remarked in passing to Bram Fischer that the defence had generated a great deal of worldwide propaganda in the case. This was perhaps his own way of acknowledging the pressure. He knew that if we were executed, the great majority of the people would regard him as our killer.

Yet he was under even greater pressure from his own people. He was a white Afrikaner, a creature of the South African system and mind-set. He had no inclination to go against the belief system that had formed him. He had succumbed to these pressures by sentencing us to life and resisted them by not giving us death.

I was surprised and displeased by the sentences de Wet imposed on Kathrada, Motsoaledi and Mlangeni. I had expected him to discharge Kathy, and to give Elias and Andrew lighter sentences. The latter two were comparatively junior members of MK, and the combined offences of the three of them could hardly be compared with those of the rest of us. But by not appealing, we undoubtedly cost Kathy, Andrew and Elias: an appeals court might have cut down their sentences.

Every evening, in Pretoria Local, before lights were out, the jail would echo to African prisoners singing freedom songs. We too would sing in this great swelling chorus. But, each evening, seconds before the lights were dimmed, as if in obedience to some silent command, the hum of voices would stop and the entire jail would become silent. Then, from a dozen places throughout the prison, men would yell '*Amandla!*' This would be met by hundreds of voices replying '*Ngawethu!*' Often we would start this call-and-response ourselves, but that night other, nameless, prisoners took the initiative, and the voices from around the prison seemed uncommonly strong as though steeling us for what lay ahead.

PART EIGHT

———

Robben Island: The Dark Years

59

At midnight, I was awake and staring at the ceiling – images from the trial were still rattling around in my head – when I heard steps coming down the corridor. I was locked in my own cell, away from the others. There was a knock at my door and I could see Colonel Aucamp's face at the bars. 'Mandela,' he said in a husky whisper, 'are you awake?'

I told him I was. 'You are a lucky man,' he said. 'We are taking you to a place where you will have your freedom. You will be able to move around; you'll see the ocean and the sky, not just grey walls.'

He intended no sarcasm, but I well knew that the place he was referring to would not afford me the freedom I longed for. He then remarked rather cryptically, 'As long as you don't make trouble, you'll get everything you want.'

Aucamp then woke the others, all of whom were in a single cell, ordering them to pack their things. Fifteen minutes later we were making our way through the iron labyrinth of Pretoria Local, with its endless series of clanging metal doors echoing in our ears.

Once outside, the seven of us – Walter, Raymond, Govan, Kathy, Andrew, Elias and I – were handcuffed and piled into the back of a police van. It was well after midnight, but none of us was tired, and the atmosphere was not at all sombre. We sat on the dusty floor, singing and chanting, reliving the final moments of the trial. The warders provided us with sandwiches and cold drinks and Lieutenant van Wyck was perched in the back with us. He was a pleasant fellow and, during a lull in the singing, he offered his unsolicited opinion on our future. 'Well,' he said, 'you chaps won't be in prison long. The demand for your release is too strong. In a year or two, you will get out and you will return as national heroes. Crowds will cheer you, everyone will want to be your friend, women will want you. Ag, you fellows have it made.' We listened without comment, but I confess his speech cheered me considerably. Unfortunately, his prediction proved to be out by nearly three decades.

*   *   *

We were departing quietly, secretly, under a heavy police escort, in the middle of the night, and in less than half an hour we found ourselves at a small military airport outside the city. We were hustled on to a Dakota, a large military transport plane that had seen better days. There was no heat, and we shivered in the belly of the plane. Some of the others had never flown before and they seemed more anxious about our voyage than our destination; bumping up and down in a plane at fifteen thousand feet seemed far more perilous than being locked in a cell behind high walls.

After about an hour in the air, dawn lightened the terrain below. The plane had portholes, and as soon as we could see in the half-light, my comrades pressed their faces to the glass. We flew southeast, over the dry, flat plains of the Orange Free State and the green and mountainous Cape peninsula. I, too, craned to see out of the portholes, examining the scenery not as a tourist but as a strategist, looking for areas where a guerrilla army might hide itself.

There had been a running argument since the formation of MK as to whether the countryside of South Africa could support a guerrilla army. Most of the High Command thought that it could not. When we flew over a wooded, mountainous area called Matroosberg in the Cape, I yelled to my colleagues that here was terrain where we could fight. The men became excited and craned to get a better look, and indeed, the heavily forested area appeared as though it could shelter a nascent guerrilla force.

Minutes later we approached the outskirts of Cape Town. Soon, we could see the little matchbox houses of the Cape Flats, the gleaming towers of downtown, and the horizontal top of Table Mountain. Then, out in Table Bay, in the dark blue waters of the Atlantic, we could make out the misty outline of Robben Island.

We landed at an airstrip on one end of the island. It was a grim, overcast day, and when I stepped out of the plane, the cold winter wind whipped through our thin prison uniforms. We were met by guards with automatic weapons; the atmosphere was tense but quiet, unlike the boisterous reception I had received on my arrival on the island two years before.

We were driven to the old jail, an isolated stone building, where we were ordered to strip while standing outside. One of the ritual indignities of prison life is that when you are transferred from one prison to another, the first thing that happens is that you change from the garb of the old prison to that of the new. When we were undressed, we were thrown the plain khaki uniforms of Robben Island.

Apartheid's regulations extended even to clothing. All of us, except Kathy, received short trousers, an insubstantial jersey and a canvas jacket. Kathy, the one Indian among us, was given long trousers. Normally Africans would receive sandals made from car tyres, but in this instance we were given shoes. Kathy, alone, received socks. Short trousers for Africans were meant to remind us that we were 'boys'. I put on the short trousers that day, but I vowed that I would not put up with them for long.

The warders pointed with their guns to where they wanted us to go, and barked their orders in simple one-word commands: 'Move!' 'Silence!' 'Halt!' They did not threaten us in the swaggering way that I recalled from my previous stay, and betrayed no emotion.

The old jail was only temporary quarters for us. The authorities were in the process of finishing an entirely separate maximum-security structure for political prisoners. While there, we were not permitted to go outside or have any contact with other prisoners.

The fourth morning we were handcuffed and taken in a covered truck to a prison within a prison. This new structure was a one-storey rectangular stone fortress with a flat cement courtyard in the centre, about one hundred feet by thirty feet. It had cells on three of the four sides. The fourth side was a twenty-foot-high wall with a catwalk patrolled by guards with German shepherds.

The three lines of cells were known as sections A, B and C, and we were put in section B, on the easternmost side of the quadrangle. We were each given individual cells on either side of a long corridor, with half the cells facing the courtyard. There were about thirty cells in all. The total number of prisoners in the single cells was usually about twenty-four. Each cell had one window, about a foot square, covered with iron bars. The cell had two doors: a metal gate or grille with iron bars on the inside and a thick wooden door outside that. During the day, only the grille was locked; at night, the wooden door was locked as well.

The cells had been constructed hurriedly, and the walls were perpetually damp. When I mentioned this to the commanding officer, he told me our bodies would absorb the moisture. We were each issued with three blankets so flimsy and worn they were practically transparent. Our bedding consisted of a single sisal or straw mat. Later we were given a felt mat, and one placed the felt mat on top of the sisal one to provide some softness. At that time of year, the cells were so cold and the blankets provided so little warmth that we always slept fully dressed.

I was assigned a cell at the head of the corridor. It overlooked the courtyard and had a small eye-level window. I could walk the length of my cell in three paces. When I lay down, I could feel the wall with my feet and my head grazed the concrete at the other side. The width was about six feet, and the walls were at least two feet thick. Each cell had a white card posted outside it with our name and our prison service number. Mine read, 'N. Mandela 466/64', which meant I was the 466th prisoner admitted to the island in 1964. I was forty-six years old, a political prisoner with a life sentence, and that small cramped space was to be my home for I knew not how long.

We were immediately joined by a number of prisoners who had been held in the general section of the prison, a squat brick building not far from section B. The general prison, known as sections F and G, contained about a thousand mostly common-law prisoners. As many as a quarter of them were political prisoners, and a handful of those men were put with us in section B. We were isolated from the general prisoners for two reasons: we were considered risky from a security perspective, but even more dangerous from a political standpoint. The authorities were concerned that we might 'infect' the other prisoners with our political views.

Among the men put with us was George Peake, one of the founders of the South African Coloured People's Organization, a Treason Trialist, and most recently a member of the Cape Town City Council. He had been sentenced for planting explosives outside a Cape Town prison. Dennis Brutus, another Coloured political activist, was a poet and writer from Port Elizabeth imprisoned for violating his bans. We were also joined by Billy Nair, a long-time member of the Natal Indian Congress, sentenced for sabotage as a member of Umkhonto we Sizwe.

Within a few days we had more company, including Neville Alexander, a prominent Coloured intellectual and member of the Non-European Unity Movement, who had formed a tiny radical offshoot called the Yu Chi Chan Club in Cape Town which studied guerrilla warfare. Neville had a BA from the University of Cape Town and a doctorate in German literature from Tübingen University in Germany. Along with Neville, there was Fikile Bam, a law student from of the University of Cape Town and another member of the Yu Chi Chan Club, and Zephania Mothopeng, a member of the PAC National Executive. Zeph had been a teacher in Orlando, and was a staunch opponent of Bantu Education, and one of the most level-headed of the PAC's leaders. Three aged peasants from the Transkei, sentenced for plotting to assassinate K. D. Matanzima, now the chief minister of the 'self-governing' Transkei, were also imprisoned with us.

This became our core group of about twenty prisoners. Some I knew, some I had heard of, while others I did not know at all. Normally in prison one of the few festive times is seeing old friends and new faces, but the atmosphere in those first few weeks was so oppressive that we were not even able to greet each other. There were as many guards as prisoners, and they enforced every regulation with threats and intimidation.

That first week we began the work that would occupy us for the next few months. Each morning, a load of stones about the size of volleyballs was dumped by the entrance to the courtyard. Using wheelbarrows, we moved the stones to the centre of the yard. We were given either four-pound hammers, or fourteen-pound hammers for the larger stones. Our job was to crush the stones into gravel. We were divided into four rows, about a yard-and-a-half apart, and sat cross-legged on the ground. We were each given a thick rubber ring, made from tyres, in which to place the stones. The ring was meant to catch flying chips of stone, but hardly ever did so. We wore makeshift wire masks to protect our eyes.

Warders walked among us to enforce the silence. During those first few weeks, warders from other sections and even other prisons came to stare at us as if we were a collection of rare caged animals. The work was tedious and difficult; it was not strenuous enough to keep us warm but demanding enough to make all our muscles ache.

June and July were the bleakest months on Robben Island. Winter was in the air, and the rains were just beginning. It never seemed to go above 40 degrees Fahrenheit. Even in the sun, I shivered in my light khaki shirt. It was then that I first understood the cliché of feeling the cold in one's bones. At noon we would break for lunch. That first week all we were given was soup, which stank horribly. In the afternoons we were permitted to exercise for half an hour under strict supervision. We walked briskly around the courtyard in single file.

On one of our first days pounding rocks, a warder commanded Kathy to take a wheelbarrow filled with gravel to the truck parked by the entrance. Kathy was a slender fellow unused to hard physical labour. He could not shift the wheelbarrow. The warders yelled: '*Laat daardie kruiwa loop!*' ('Make that wheelbarrow move!') As Kathy managed to nudge it forward, the wheelbarrow looked as if it would tip over, and the warders began to laugh. Kathy, I could see, was determined not to give them cause for mirth. I knew how to manoeuvre the wheelbarrows, and I jumped up to help him. Before being ordered to sit down, I managed to tell Kathy to wheel it slowly, that it was a matter of balance not strength. He nodded and then carefully moved the wheelbarrow across the courtyard. The warders stopped smiling.

The next morning, the authorities placed an enormous skip in the courtyard and announced that it had to be half full by the end of the week. We worked hard, and succeeded. The following week, the warder in charge announced that we must now fill the skip three-quarters of the way. We worked with great diligence, and succeeded. The next week we were ordered to fill the skip to the top. We knew we could not tolerate this much longer, but said nothing. We even managed to fill the skip all the way, but the warders had provoked us. In stolen whispers we resolved on a policy: no quotas. The next week we initiated our first go-slow strike on the island: we would work at less than half the speed we had before to protest at the excessive and unfair demands. The guards immediately saw this and threatened us, but we would not increase our pace, and we continued this go-slow strategy for as long as we worked in the courtyard.

Robben Island had changed since I had been there for a fortnight in 1962. In 1962 there were few prisoners; the place seemed more like an experiment than a fully-fledged prison. Two years later, Robben Island was without question the harshest, most iron-fisted outpost in the South African penal system. It was a hardship station not only for the prisoners but for the prison staff. Gone were the Coloured warders who had supplied cigarettes and sympathy. The warders, now white and overwhelmingly Afrikaans-speaking, demanded a master–servant relationship. They ordered us to call them *baas*, which we refused to do. The racial divide on Robben Island was absolute: there were no black warders, and no white prisoners.

Moving from one prison to another always requires a period of adjustment. But journeying to Robben Island was like going to another country. Its isolation made it not simply another prison, but a world of its own, far removed from the one we had come from. The high spirits with which we left Pretoria had been snuffed out by its stern atmosphere; we were face to face with the realization that our life would be unredeemably grim. In Pretoria we felt connected to our supporters and our families; on the island we felt cut off, and indeed we were. We had the consolation of being with each other, but that was the only consolation. My dismay was quickly replaced by a sense that a new and different fight had begun.

From the first day, I had protested about being forced to wear short trousers. I demanded to see the head of the prison and made a list of complaints. The warders ignored my protests, but by the end of the second week, I found a pair of old khaki trousers unceremoniously dumped on the floor of my cell. No pin-striped three-piece suit has ever pleased me as much. But before putting them on I checked to see if my comrades had also been issued with trousers.

They had not, and I told the warder to take the trousers back. I insisted that all African prisoners must have long trousers. The warder grumbled,

'Mandela, you say you want long pants and then you don't want them when we give them to you.' The warder baulked at touching trousers worn by a black man, and finally the commanding officer himself came to my cell to pick them up. 'Very well, Mandela,' he said, 'you are going to have the same clothing as everyone else.' I replied that if he was willing to give me long trousers, why couldn't everyone else have them? He did not have an answer.

60

At the end of our first two weeks on the island, we were informed that our lawyers, Bram Fischer and Joel Joffe, were going to be visiting the following day. When they arrived, we were escorted to the visiting area to meet them. The purpose of their visit was twofold: to see how we had settled in, and to verify that we still did not want to appeal against our sentences. It had only been a few weeks since I had seen them, but it felt like an eternity. They seemed like visitors from another world.

We sat in an empty room, a major just outside to supervise the consultation. I felt like hugging them, but I was restrained by the presence of the major. I told them that all of us were well, and explained that we were still opposed to an appeal for all the reasons we had previously enunciated, including the fact that we did not want our appeal to interfere with the cases of other ANC defendants. Bram and Joel seemed resigned to this, though I knew Bram believed we should mount an appeal.

When we were winding up our conversation, I briefly asked Bram about Molly, his wife. No sooner had I pronounced Molly's name then Bram stood up, turned away, and abruptly walked out of the room. A few minutes later he returned, once again composed, and resumed the conversation, but without answering my question.

Our meeting ended shortly afterwards, and when we were walking back to our cells with the major, he said to me, 'Mandela, were you struck by the behaviour of Bram Fischer?' I said that I had been. He told me that Molly had died in a car accident the previous week. Bram, he said, had been driving and had swerved to avoid an animal in the road, and the car had plunged into a river. Molly had drowned.

We were devastated by the news. Molly was a wonderful woman, generous and unselfish, utterly without prejudice. She had supported Bram in more ways than it was possible to know. She had been wife, colleague and comrade. Bram had already experienced disaster in his life: his son, a diabetic, had died in adolescence.

The act of turning away when I asked about Molly was typical of Bram's character. He was a stoic, a man who never burdened his friends with his own pain and troubles. As an Afrikaner whose conscience forced him to reject his own heritage and be ostracized by his own people, he showed a level of courage and sacrifice that was in a class by itself. I fought only against injustice, not my own people.

I informed the major that I intended to write Bram a letter of condolence, and he responded that I could. The rules governing letter-writing were then extremely strict. We were permitted to write only to our immediate families, and just one letter of five hundred words every six months. I was therefore surprised and pleased when the major did not oppose my writing to Bram. But he didn't live up to his agreement. I wrote the letter and handed it over, but it was never posted.

Within a few months our life settled into a pattern. Prison life is about routine: each day like the one before; each week like the one before it, so that the months and years blend into each other. Anything that departs from this pattern upsets the authorities, for routine is the sign of a well-run prison.

Routine is also comforting for the prisoner, which is why it can be a trap. Routine can be a pleasant mistress whom it is hard to resist, for routine makes the time go faster. Watches and timepieces of any kind were barred on Robben Island, so we never knew precisely what time it was. We were dependent on bells and warders' whistles and shouts. With each week resembling the one before, one must make an effort to recall what day and month it is. One of the first things I did was to make a calendar on the wall of my cell. Losing a sense of time is an easy way to lose one's grip and even one's sanity.

Time slows down in prison; the days seem endless. The cliché of time passing slowly usually has to do with idleness and inactivity. But this was not the case on Robben Island. We were busy almost all the time with work, study, resolving disputes. Yet time nevertheless moved glacially. This is partially because things that took a few hours or days outside would take months or years in prison. A request for a new toothbrush might take six months or a year to be fulfilled. Ahmed Kathrada once said that in prison the minutes can seem like years, but the years go by like minutes. An afternoon pounding rocks in the courtyard might seem like forever, but suddenly it is the end of the year, and you do not know where all the months went.

The challenge for every prisoner, particularly every political prisoner, is how to survive prison intact, how to emerge from prison undiminished, how to conserve and even replenish one's beliefs. The first task in accomplishing that is learning exactly what one must do to survive. To that end, one must know the enemy's purpose before adopting a strategy to undermine it. Prison is designed to break one's spirit and destroy one's resolve. To do this, the authorities attempt to exploit every weakness, demolish every initiative, negate all signs of individuality – all with the idea of stamping out that spark that makes each of us human and each of us who we are.

Our survival depended on understanding what the authorities were attempting to do to us, and sharing that understanding with each other. It would be very hard, if not impossible, for one man alone to resist. I do not know that I could have done it had I been alone. But the authorities' greatest mistake was to keep us together, for together our determination was reinforced. We supported each other and gained strength from each other. Whatever we knew, whatever we learned, we shared, and by sharing we multiplied whatever courage we had individually. That is not to say that we were all alike in our responses to the hardships we suffered. Men have different capacities and react differently to stress. But the stronger ones raised up the weaker ones, and both became stronger in the process. Ultimately, we had to create our own lives in prison. In a way that even the authorities acknowledged, order in prison was preserved not by the warders but by ourselves.

As a leader, one must sometimes take actions that are unpopular, or whose results will not be known for years to come. There are victories whose glory lies only in the fact that they are known to those who win them. This is particularly true of prison, where you must find consolation in being true to your ideals, even if no one else knows of it.

I was now on the sidelines, but I also knew that I would not give up the fight. I was in a different and smaller arena, an arena for whom the only audience was ourselves and our oppressors. We regarded the struggle in prison as a microcosm of the struggle as a whole. We would fight inside as we had fought outside. The racism and repression were the same; I would simply have to fight on different terms.

Prison and the authorities conspire to rob each man of his dignity. In and of itself, that assured that I would survive, for any man or institution that tries to rob me of my dignity will lose because I will not part with it at any price or under any pressure. I never seriously considered the possibility that I would not emerge from prison one day. I never thought that a life sentence truly meant life and that I would die behind bars. Perhaps I was denying this prospect because it was too unpleasant to contemplate. But I always knew that someday I would once again feel the grass under my feet and walk in the sunshine as a free man.

I am fundamentally an optimist. Whether that comes from nature or nurture, I cannot say. Part of being optimistic is keeping one's head pointed towards the sun, one's feet moving forward. There were many dark moments when my faith in humanity was sorely tested, but I would not and could not give myself up to despair. That way lay defeat and death.

61

We were awakened at 5.30 each morning by the night warder, who clanged a brass bell at the head of our corridor and yelled, '*Word wakker! Staan op!*' ('Wake up! Get up!') I have always been an early riser and this hour was not a burden to me. Although we were roused at 5.30, we were not let out of our cells until 6.45, by which time we were meant to have cleaned our cells and rolled up our mats and blankets. We had no running water in our cells and instead of toilets had iron sanitary buckets known as 'ballies'. The ballies had a diameter of ten inches with a concave porcelain lid on the top that could contain water. The water in this lid was meant to be used for shaving and to clean our hands and faces.

At 6.45, when we were let out of our cells, the first thing we did was to empty our ballies. The ballies had to be thoroughly cleansed in the sinks at the end of the corridor or they created a stench. The only pleasant thing about cleaning one's ballie was that this was the one moment in those early days when we could have a whispered word with our colleagues. The warders did not like to linger when we cleaned them, so it was a chance to talk softly.

During those first few months, breakfast was delivered to us in our cells by prisoners from the general section. Breakfast consisted of mealie pap porridge, cereal made from maize or corn, which the general prisoners would slop in a bowl and then spin through the bars of our cells. It was a clever trick and required a deft hand so as not to spill any of the porridge.

After a few months, breakfast was delivered to us in the courtyard in old metal drums. We would help ourselves to pap using simple metal bowls. We each received a mug of what was described as coffee, but which was in fact ground-up maize, baked until it was black, and then brewed with hot water. Later, when we were able to go into the courtyard to serve ourselves, I would go out there and jog around the perimeter until breakfast arrived.

Like everything else in prison, diet is discriminatory. In general,

Coloureds and Indians received a slightly better diet than Africans, but it was not much of a distinction. The authorities liked to say that we received a balanced diet; it was indeed balanced – between the unpalatable and the inedible. Food was the source of many of our protests, but in those early days, the warders would say, 'Ag, you kaffirs are eating better in prison than you ever ate at home!'

In the midst of breakfast, the guards would yell, '*Val in! Val in!*' ('Fall in! Fall in!'), and we would stand outside our cells for inspection. Each prisoner was required to have the three buttons of his khaki jacket properly buttoned. We were required to doff our hats as the warder walked by. If our buttons were undone, our hats unremoved, or our cells untidy, we were charged with a violation of the prison code and punished with either solitary confinement or the loss of meals.

After inspection we would work in the courtyard hammering stones until noon. There were no breaks; if we slowed down, the warders would yell at us to speed up. At noon, the bell would clang for lunch and another metal drum of food would be wheeled into the courtyard. For Africans, lunch consisted of boiled mealies, that is, coarse kernels of corn. The Indians and Coloured prisoners received samp, or mealie rice, which consisted of ground mealies in a soup-like mixture. The samp was sometimes served with vegetables, whereas our mealies were served straight.

For lunch we often received *phuzamandla*, which means 'drink of strength', a powder made from mealies and a bit of yeast. It is meant to be stirred into water or milk, and when it is thick it can be tasty, but the prison authorities gave us so little of the powder that it barely coloured the water. I would usually try to save my powder for several days until I had enough to make a proper drink, but if the authorities discovered that you were hoarding food, the powder was confiscated and you were punished.

After lunch we worked until 4, when the guards blew shrill whistles and we once again lined up to be counted and inspected. We were then permitted half an hour to clean up. The bathroom at the end of our corridor had two seawater showers, a saltwater tap and three large galvanized metal buckets, which were used as bathtubs. There was no hot water. We would stand or squat in these buckets, soaping ourselves with the brackish water, rinsing off the dust from the day. To wash yourself with cold water when it is cold outside is not pleasant, but we made the best of it. We would sometimes sing while washing, which made the water seem less icy. In those early days, this was one of the only times when we could converse.

Precisely at 4.30 there would be a loud knock on the wooden door at the end of our corridor, which meant that supper had been delivered. Common-law prisoners used to dish out the food to us and we would return to our cells to eat it. We again received mealie pap porridge, sometimes with the odd carrot or piece of cabbage or beetroot thrown in – but one usually had to search for it. If we did get a vegetable, we would usually have the same one for weeks on end, until the carrots or cabbages were old and mouldy and we were thoroughly sick of them. Every other day we received a small piece of meat with our porridge. The meat was usually mostly gristle.

For supper, Coloured and Indian prisoners received a quarter loaf of bread (known as a *katkop*, that is, a cat's head, after the shape of the bread) and a slab of margarine. Africans, it was presumed, did not care for bread as it was a 'European' type of food.

Typically, we received even less than the scanty amounts stipulated in the regulations. This was because the kitchen was rife with smuggling. The cooks – all of whom were common-law prisoners – kept the best food for themselves or their friends. Often they would lay aside the tastiest morsels for the warders in exchange for favours or preferential treatment.

At 8 p.m. the night warder would lock himself in the corridor with us, passing the key through a small hole in the door to another warder outside. The warder would then walk up and down the corridor, ordering us to go to sleep. No cry of 'lights out' was ever given on Robben Island because the single mesh-covered bulb in our cell burned day and night. Later, those studying for higher degrees were permitted to read until 10 or 11 p.m.

The acoustics along the corridor were quite good, and we would try to chat a bit to each other before going to sleep. But if we could hear a whisper quite clearly, so could the warder, who would yell, '*Stilte in die gang!*' ('Quiet in the passage!') The warder would walk up and down a few times to make sure we were not reading or writing. After a few months, we would sprinkle a handful of sand along the corridor so that we could hear the warder's footsteps and have time to stop talking or hide any contraband. Only when we were quiet did he take a seat in the small office at the end of the passage where he dozed until morning.

62

One morning, several days after my meeting with Bram and Joel, we were taken to the head office. This was only about a quarter of a mile away and was a simple stone structure that resembled our own section. Once there, we were lined up to have our fingerprints taken, which was routine prison service business. But, while waiting, I noticed a warder with a camera. After our fingerprints had been taken, the chief warder ordered us to line up for photographs. I motioned to my colleagues not to move, and I addressed the warder: 'I would like you to produce the document from the commissioner of prisons authorizing our pictures to be taken.' Photographs of prisoners required such authorization.

It was always valuable to be familiar with regulation, because the warders themselves were often ignorant of them and could be intimidated by one's superior knowledge. The warder was taken aback by my request and unable to offer any explanation or produce anything in writing from the commissioner of prisons. He threatened to charge us if we did not consent to have our photographs taken, but I said that if there was no authorization, there would be no pictures, and that was where the matter remained.

As a rule, we objected to having our pictures taken in prison on the ground that it is generally demeaning to be seen as a prisoner. But there was one photograph I did consent to, the only one I ever agreed to while on Robben Island.

One morning a few weeks later, the chief warder, instead of handing us hammers for our work in the courtyard, gave us each needles and thread and a pile of worn prison jerseys. We were instructed to repair the garments, but we discovered that most of these jerseys were frayed beyond repair. This struck us as a curious task, and we wondered what had provoked the change. Later that morning, at about eleven o'clock, the front gate swung open to reveal the commanding officer with two men in suits. The CO announced that the two visitors were a reporter and photographer from the *Daily Telegraph* in London. He related this as if visiting members of the international press were a regular diversion for us.

Although these men were our first official visitors, we regarded them sceptically. First, they were brought in under the auspices of the government, and second, we were aware that the *Telegraph* was a conservative newspaper unlikely to be sympathetic to our cause. We well knew that there was great concern in the outside world about our situation and that it was in the government's interest to show that we were not being mistreated.

The two journalists walked slowly around the courtyard, surveying us. We kept our heads down, concentrating on our work. After they had made one circuit, one of the guards plucked me by the shoulder and said, 'Mandela, come, you will talk now.' In those early days I often spoke on behalf of my fellow prisoners. The prison service regulations were explicit that each prisoner was permitted to speak only for himself. This was done to negate the power of organization and to neutralize our collective strength. We objected to this rule, but made little headway. We were not even permitted to use the word *we* when we made complaints. But during the first few years, when the authorities needed one prisoner to speak on behalf of others, that individual would be me.

I talked to the reporter, whose name was Mr Newman, for about twenty minutes, and was candid about both prison and the Rivonia Trial. He was an agreeable fellow, and at the end of our talk he said he would like the photographer to take my picture. I was reluctant, but in this case relented because I knew the photograph would be published only overseas, and might serve to help our cause if the article were even the least bit friendly. I told him I would agree, provided Mr Sisulu could join me. The image shows the two of us talking in the courtyard about some matter that I can no longer remember. I never saw the article or heard anything about it. The reporters were barely out of sight when the warders removed the jerseys and gave us back our hammers.

The men from the *Telegraph* were the first of a small stream of visitors during those early months. While the Rivonia Trial still resonated in people's minds, the government was eager to show the international community that we were being treated properly. There were stories in the press about the inhuman conditions on the island, about how we were being assaulted and tortured. These allegations embarrassed the government, and to combat them they brought in a string of outsiders meant to rebut these critical stories.

We were briefly visited by a British lawyer who had argued for

Namibian independence before the World Court, after which we were informed that a Mr Hynning, a representative of the American Bar Association, would be coming to see us. Americans were then a novelty in South Africa, and I was curious to meet a representative of so august a legal organization.

On the day of Mr Hynning's visit we were called into the courtyard. The American arrived in the company of General Steyn, the commissioner of prisons, who rarely made appearances on the island. General Steyn was that unusual thing in the prison service, a polished and sophisticated man. His suits were always of a fine quality and a fashionable cut. He was courtly, and referred to us as 'gentlemen', even doffing his hat to us, something no one else in the prison service ever did. Yet General Steyn oppressed us by omission rather than commission. He basically turned a blind eye to what was happening on the island. His habitual absence emboldened the more brutal prison officials and gave them carte blanche to do whatever they wanted. In his most gracious manner, the general introduced our guest and said, 'Gentlemen, please select your spokesman.' A number of the prisoners called out my name.

General Steyn nodded in my direction, and I stood up. In contrast to General Steyn, Mr Hynning was a heavyset, unkempt man. I thanked him for visiting us and said we were honoured by his presence. I then summarized our complaints, beginning with the central and most important one, that we were political prisoners, not criminals, and that we should be treated as such. I enumerated our grievances about the food, our living conditions and the work detail. But as I was speaking, Mr Hynning kept interrupting me. When I made a point about the long hours of mindless work, he declared that as prisoners we had to work and were probably lazy to boot.

When I started to explain the problems with our cells, he interjected that the conditions in backward American prisons were far worse than on Robben Island, which was a paradise by comparison. He added that we had been justly convicted and were lucky not to have received the death penalty, which we probably deserved.

Mr Hynning perspired a great deal and there were those among us who thought he was not altogether sober. He spoke in what I assumed was a southern American accent, and had a curious habit of spitting when he talked, something none of us had ever seen before.

Finally, I had heard enough, and I interrupted him, 'No, sir, you misunderstand the points that I am making.' Hynning took offence that I was now contradicting him, while General Steyn watched and listened without comment. Under the circumstances, it was difficult to keep tempers down. The men were angered by Mr Hynning's remarks and annoyed that he had been permitted to see us at all. Normally a visit of any kind lifted our spirits, but the visit of Mr Hynning was demoralizing. Perhaps that is what the authorities wanted. To meet someone with so impressive an affiliation and so little understanding was depressing. Hynning finally just turned and walked away without so much as a good-bye. We were not sorry to see him go.

We discussed Mr Hynning for years afterwards and many of the men imitated the way he spoke to comic effect. We never heard about him again, and he certainly did not win any friends on Robben Island for the American Bar Association.

63

In jail, all prisoners are classified by the authorities as one of four categories: A, B, C or D. A is the highest classification and confers the most privileges; D is the lowest and confers the least. All political prisoners, or what the authorities called 'security prisoners', were automatically classified as D on admission. The privileges affected by these classifications included visits and letters, studies, and the opportunity to buy groceries and incidentals – all of which are the lifeblood of any prisoner. It normally took years for a political prisoner to raise his status from D to C.

We despised the classification system. It was corrupt and demeaning, another way of repressing prisoners in general and political prisoners in particular. We demanded that all political prisoners be in one category. Although we criticized it, we could not ignore it: the classification system was an inflexible feature of prison life. If you protested that, as a D group prisoner, you could receive only one letter every six months, the authorities would say, 'Improve your behaviour, become a C group prisoner, and you will be able to receive two letters every six months.' If you complained that you did not receive enough food, the authorities would remind you that if you were in A group, you would be able to receive money orders from the outside and purchase extra food at the prison tuckshop. Even a freedom fighter benefits from the ability to buy groceries and books.

The classifications generally ran parallel to the length of one's sentence. If you were sentenced to eight years, you would generally be classified as D for the first two years, C for the next two, B for the following two and A for the last two. But the prison authorities wielded the classification system as a weapon against political prisoners, threatening to lower our hard-won classifications in order to control our behaviour.

Though I had been in prison for nearly two years before I was taken to Robben Island, I was still in D group when I arrived. While I desired the privileges that came with higher classifications, I refused to compromise my conduct. The fastest way to raise one's classification was to be docile and not complain. 'Ag, Mandela, you are a troublemaker,' the warders would say. 'You will be in D group for the rest of your life.'

Every six months, prisoners were called before the prison board to have their classifications evaluated. The board was meant to assess our behaviour in terms of prison regulations, but we found that it preferred to act as a political tribunal rather than a mere evaluator of behaviour. During my first meeting with the board, the officials asked me questions about the ANC and my beliefs. Although this had nothing to do with the classification system, I was vain enough to answer and think that I might convert them to my beliefs. It was one of the few times we were treated as human beings, and I for one responded. Later I realized that this was simply a technique on the part of the authorities to glean information from us, and I had fallen for it. Shortly afterwards, we agreed among ourselves not to discuss politics with the prison board.

As a D group prisoner, I was entitled to have only one visitor, and write and receive only one letter every six months. I found this one of the most inhumane restrictions of the prison system. Communication with one's family is a human right; it should not be restricted by the artificial gradations of a prison system. But it was one of the facts of prison life.

Visits and letters were restricted to 'first degree' relatives. This was a restriction we not only found irksome but racist. The African sense of immediate family is very different from that of the European or Westerner. Our family structures are larger and more inclusive; anyone who claims descent from a common ancestor is deemed part of the same family.

In prison, the only thing worse than bad news about one's family is no news at all. It is always harder to cope with the disasters and tragedies one imagines than with the reality, however grim or disagreeable. A letter with ill tidings was always preferable to no letter at all.

But even this miserable restriction was abused by the authorities. The anticipation of mail was overwhelming. Mail-call took place once a month, and sometimes six months would go by without a letter. To be allowed one letter in six months and then not to receive it is a great blow. One wonders: What has happened to my wife and children, to my mother and my sisters? When I did not receive a letter I felt as dry and barren as the Great Karroo desert. Often the authorities would withhold mail out of spite. I can remember warders saying, 'Mandela, we have received a letter for you, but we cannot give it to you.' No explanation of why, or who the letter is from. It required all my self-discipline not to explode at such times. Afterwards, I would protest through the proper channels, and sometimes get it.

When letters did arrive, they were cherished. A letter was like the summer rain that could make even the desert bloom. When I was handed a letter by the authorities, I would not rush forward and grab it as I felt like doing, but take it in a leisurely manner. Though I yearned to tear it open and read it on the spot, I would not give the authorities the satisfaction of seeing my eagerness, and I would return slowly to my cell as though I had many things to occupy me before opening a letter from my family.

During the first few months, I received one letter from Winnie, but it was so heavily censored that not much more than the salutation was left. The island's censors would black out the offending passages in ink, but they later changed this when they realized we could wash away the ink and see what was underneath. They began to use razors to slice out whole paragraphs. Since most letters were written on both sides of a single piece of paper, the material on the other side would also be excised. They seemed to relish delivering letters in tatters. The censorship delayed the delivery of mail because the warders, some of whom were not proficient in English, might take as long as a month to censor a letter. The letters we wrote were censored as well; they were often as cut up as those we received.

At the end of August, after I had been on the island less than three months, I was informed by the authorities that I would have a visitor the following day. They would not tell me who it was. Walter was informed that he, too, would have a visitor, and I suspected, I hoped, I wished – I believed – that it would be a visit from Winnie and Albertina.

From the moment Winnie learned we had been brought to the island, she had been trying to arrange a visit. As a banned person, she had to receive a special dispensation from the minister of justice, for she was technically not permitted to communicate with me.

Even with the help of the authorities, visiting Robben Island was not an easy proposition. Visits were a maximum of thirty minutes long, and political prisoners were not permitted contact visits, in which the visitor and prisoner were in the same room.

Visits did not seem to be planned in advance by the authorities. One day, they would contact your wife and say, 'You have permission to visit your husband tomorrow.' This was enormously inconvenient, and often had the effect of making visits impossible. If a family member was able to plan a visit in advance, the authorities would sometimes deliberately delay issuing a permit until after the plane had departed. Since most of the men's families lived far from the Cape and had very little money, visits by family members were often far beyond their means. Some men who came from poor families did not see their wives for many years at a time, if at all. I knew of men who spent a decade or more on Robben Island without a single visit.

The visiting room for non-contact visits was cramped and windowless. On the prisoner's side was a row of five cubicles with small square pieces of glass that looked out on identical cubicles on the other side. One sat in a chair and looked through the thick, smudged glass that had a few small holes drilled into it to permit conversation. One had to talk very loudly to be heard. Later the authorities installed microphones and speakers in front of the glass, a marginal improvement.

Walter and I were called to the visitors' office in the late morning and took seats at the far end of the room. I waited with some anxiety, and suddenly, filling the glass on the other side of the window was Winnie's lovely face. Winnie always dressed up for prison visits, and tried to wear something new and elegant. It was tremendously frustrating not to be able to touch my wife, to speak tenderly to her, to have a private moment together. We had to conduct our relationship at a distance under the eyes of people we despised.

I could see immediately that Winnie was under tremendous strain. Seeing me in such circumstances must have been trying. Just getting to the island itself was difficult, and added to that were the harsh rituals of the prison, the undoubted indignities of the warders and the impersonality of the contact.

Winnie, I later discovered, had recently received a second banning order and had been dismissed from her job at the Child Welfare Office as a result. Her office was searched by the police shortly before she was sacked. The authorities were convinced that she was in secret communication with me. Winnie loved her job as a social worker. It was the hands-on end of the struggle: placing babies with adoptive parents, finding work for the unemployed and medical help for the uninsured. The banning and harassment of my wife greatly troubled me: I could not look after her and the children, and the state was making it difficult for her to look after herself. My powerlessness gnawed at me.

Our conversation was awkward at first, and was not made easier by the presence of two warders standing directly behind her and three behind me. Their role was not only to monitor but to intimidate. Regulations dictated that conversation had to be in either English or Afrikaans – African languages were forbidden – and could involve family matters only. Any line of talk that departed from the family and verged on the political might mean the abrupt termination of the visit. If one mentioned a name unfamiliar to the warders, they would interrupt the conversation, and ask who the person was and the nature of the relationship. This happened often, as the warders were generally unfamiliar with the variety and nature of African names. It was frustrating to spend precious minutes of one's visit explaining to a warder the different branches of one's family tree. But their ignorance also worked in our favour: it allowed us to invent code names for people we wanted to talk about and pretend that we were referring to family members.

That first visit was important, for I knew that Winnie was anxious about my health: she had heard stories that we were being physically abused. I quickly informed her that I was fine and she could see that I was fit, though a bit thinner than before. She, too, was thinner, something I always attributed to stress. After a visit in which Winnie's face looked drawn or tense, I would urge her to put on a bit of weight. She was always dieting, and I was always telling her not to. I inquired one by one about all the children, about my mother and sisters and Winnie's own family.

Suddenly, I heard the warder behind me say, 'Time up! Time up!' I turned and looked at him with incredulity. It was impossible that half an hour had passed. But, in fact, he was right; visits always seemed to go by in the blinking of an eye. For all the years that I was in prison, I never failed to be surprised when the warder called, 'Time up!' Winnie and I were both hustled from our chairs and we waved a quick farewell. I always felt like lingering after Winnie left, just to retain the sense of her presence, but I would not let the warders see such emotion. As I walked back to the cell, I reviewed in my head what we had talked about. Over the next days, weeks and months, I would return to that one visit again and again. I knew I would not be able to see my wife again for at least six months. As it turned out, Winnie was not able to visit me for another two years.

64

One morning in early January, as we lined up to be counted before beginning work in the courtyard, we were instead marched outside and ordered into a covered truck. It was the first time that we had left our compound. No announcement was made as to our destination, but I had an idea of where we were headed. A few minutes later we emerged from the truck in a place that I had first seen when I was on the island in 1962: the lime quarry.

The lime quarry looked like an enormous white crater cut into a rocky hillside. The cliffs and the base of the hillside were blindingly white. At the top of the quarry were grass and palm trees, and at the base was a clearing with a few old metal sheds.

We were met by the commanding officer, Colonel Wessels, a rather colourless fellow who cared only about strict adherence to prison regulations. We stood at attention as he told us that the work we would be doing would last six months and afterwards we would be given light tasks for the duration of our terms. His timing was considerably off. We remained at the quarry for the next thirteen years.

After the CO's speech, we were handed picks and shovels and given rudimentary instructions as to the mining of lime. Mining lime is not a simple task. That first day, we were clumsy with our new tools and extracted little. The lime itself, which is the soft, calcified residue of seashells and coral, is buried in layers of rock, and one had to break through to it with a pick, and then extract the seam of lime with a shovel. This was far more strenuous than the work in the courtyard, and after our first few days on the quarry we fell asleep immediately after our supper at 4.30 in the afternoon. We woke the next morning aching and still tired.

The authorities never explained why we had been taken from the courtyard to the quarry. They may simply have needed extra lime for the island's roads. But when we later discussed the transfer, we assumed it was another way of enforcing discipline, of showing us that we were no different from the general prisoners – who worked in the island's stone quarry – and that we had to pay for our crimes just as they did. It was an attempt to crush our spirits.

But those first few weeks at the quarry had the opposite effect on us. Despite blistered and bleeding hands, we were invigorated. I much preferred being outside in nature, being able to see grass and trees, to observe birds flitting overhead, to feel the wind blowing in from the sea. It felt good to use all one's muscles, with the sun at one's back, and there was simple gratification in building up mounds of stone and lime.

Within a few days we were walking to the quarry, rather than going by truck, and this too was a tonic. During our twenty-minute march we got a better sense of the island, and could see the dense brush and tall trees that covered our home, and smell the eucalyptus blossoms, spot the occasional springbok or kudu grazing in the distance. Although some of the men regarded the march as drudgery, I never did.

Although our work at the quarry was meant to show us that we were no different from the other prisoners, the authorities still treated us like the lepers who once populated the island. Sometimes we would see a group of common-law prisoners working by the side of the road, and their warders would order them into the bushes so they would not see us as we marched past. It was as if the mere sight of us might somehow affect their discipline. Sometimes out of the corner of an eye we could see a prisoner raise his fist in the ANC salute.

Near the quarry the dirt road diverged, and to the right the general prisoners trooped off to the rock quarry. This crossroads was later to become an important site of communication with them. Where the road branched, we could see in the brush the small white cottage where Robert Sobukwe lived. The house had been built for a black warder years before, and now Sobukwe lived in it by himself. It was a tiny plot, unkempt and overgrown, and one would not even know that anyone lived there, except for the guard who stood in front.

Sobukwe's sentence had ended in 1963, but under what became known as the Sobukwe clause of the General Law Amendment Act of 1963, the minister of justice could hold political prisoners indefinitely without charge. That is precisely what they did with Bob. For six years, Sobukwe lived a kind of half-life on the island; he was a free man who was denied his liberty. Sometimes we were able to get a glimpse of him in his garden, but that was all.

After arriving in the morning, we would fetch our picks, shovels, hammers and wheelbarrows from a zinc shed at the top of the quarry. Then we would assemble along the quarry face, usually in groups of three or four.

Warders with automatic weapons stood on raised platforms watching us. Unarmed warders walked among us, urging us to work harder. '*Gaan aan! Gaan aan!*' ('Go on! Go on!'), they would shout, as if we were oxen.

By eleven, when the sun was high in the sky, we would begin to flag. By that time I would already be drenched in sweat. The warders would then drive us even harder. '*Nee, man! Kom aan! Kom aan!*' ('No, man! Come on! Come on!') they would shout. Just before noon, when we would break for lunch, we would pile the lime into wheelbarrows and cart it over to the truck that would take it away.

At midday, a whistle would blow, and we would make our way to the bottom of the hill. We sat on makeshift seats under a simple zinc shed shielding us from the sun. The warders ate at a larger shed with tables and benches. Drums of boiled mealies were delivered to us. Hundreds of seagulls, screaming and swooping, circled above us as we ate, and a well-aimed dropping could sometimes spoil a man's lunch.

We worked until four, when we again carted the lime to the waiting truck. By the end of the day, our faces and bodies were caked with white dust. We looked like pale ghosts except where rivulets of sweat had washed away the lime. When we returned to our cells, we would scrub ourselves in the cold water, which never seemed to rinse away the dust completely.

Worse than the heat at the quarry was the light. Our backs were protected from the sun by our shirts, but the sun's rays would be reflected into our eyes by the lime itself. The glare hurt our eyes and, along with the dust, made it difficult to see. Our eyes streamed and our faces became fixed in a permanent squint. It would take a long time after each day's work for our eyes to adjust to the diminished light.

After our first few days at the quarry, we made an official request for sunglasses. The authorities refused. This was not unexpected, for we were then not even permitted reading glasses. I had previously pointed out to the commanding officer that it did not make sense to permit us to read books but not to permit us glasses to read them with.

During the following weeks and months we requested sunglasses again and again. But it was to take us almost three years before we were allowed to have them, and that was only after a sympathetic physician agreed that the glasses were necessary to preserve our eyesight. Even then, we had to purchase the glasses ourselves.

For us, such struggles – for sunglasses, long trousers, study privileges, equalized food – were corollaries to the struggle we waged outside prison. The campaign to improve conditions in prison was part of the apartheid struggle. It was, in that sense, all the same; we fought injustice wherever we found it, no matter how large or how small, and we fought injustice to preserve our own humanity.

Shortly after we started working at the quarry, we were joined in section B by a number of other prominent political prisoners. Several were MK men who had been arrested in July 1964 and convicted of more than fifty acts of sabotage in what became known as the 'little Rivonia Trial'. These included Mac Maharaj, a member of the SACP and one of the sharpest minds in the struggle; Laloo Chiba, also a member of the MK high command and a stalwart colleague who proved a great asset in prison; and Wilton Mkwayi, the Treason Trialist who had been mistakenly let go during a moment of confusion when the State of Emergency was declared in 1960. He had left South Africa secretly, received military training and became commander-in-chief of MK after the Rivonia Trial. We were also joined by Eddie Daniels, a Coloured member of the Liberal Party, who had been convicted for sabotage operations undertaken by the African Resistance Movement, a small sabotage group composed of members of the Liberal Party. Eddie was to become one of my greatest friends in prison.

To counterbalance the effect of these new political allies, the authorities also put a handful of common-law prisoners in our section. These men were hardened criminals, convicted of murder, rape and armed robbery. They were members of the island's notorious criminal gangs, either the Big Fives or the Twenty-Eights, which terrorized other prisoners. They were brawny and surly, and their faces bore the scars of the knife fights that were common among gang members. Their role was to act as *agents provocateurs*, and they would attempt to push us around, take our food and inhibit any political discussions we tried to have. One of these fellows was known as Bogart, after the American tough-guy movie actor. He had a cell opposite Walter's and Walter used to complain that he would demand Walter's breakfast from him each morning, and that he was too scared to refuse.

The gang members worked in their own group apart from us at the quarry. One day, they began singing what sounded like a work song. In fact, it was a famous work song, with their own adapted lyrics: '*Benifunani eRivonia?*' which means 'What did you want at Rivonia?' The next line was something like 'Did you think that you would become the government?' They sang exuberantly and with a mocking tone. They had obviously been encouraged by the warders, who were hoping that the song would provoke us.

Although the more hotheaded among us wanted to confront them, we decided to fight fire with fire. We had far more and better singers among us than they had, and we huddled together and planned our response. Within a few minutes, we were all singing the song '*Stimela*', a rousing anthem about a train making its way down from Southern Rhodesia. '*Stimela*' is not a political song but, in the context, it became one, for the implication was that the train contained guerrillas coming down to fight the South African army.

For a number of weeks our two groups sang as we worked, adding songs and changing lyrics. Our repertoire increased, and we were soon singing overt political songs, such as '*Amajoni*', a song about guerrilla soldiers, the title of which was a corruption of the English slang word for soldier, Johnny, and '*Tshotsholoza*', a song that compares the struggle to the motion of an oncoming train. (If you say the title over and over, it mimics the sound of the train.) We sang a song about the Freedom Charter, and another about the Transkei, with the lyrics, 'There are two roads, one road is the Matanzima road, and one road is the Mandela road, which one will you take?'

The singing made the work lighter. A few of the fellows had extra-ordinary voices, and I often felt like putting my pick down and simply listening. The gang members were no competition for us; they soon became quiet while we continued singing. But one of the warders was fluent in Xhosa and understood the content of our songs, and we were soon ordered to stop singing. (Whistling was also banned.) From that day on we worked in silence.

I saw the gang members not as rivals but as raw material to be converted. There was a non-political prisoner among us nicknamed 'Joe My Baby' who later joined the ANC and proved invaluable in helping us smuggle material in and out of prison.

One day we heard that Bogart had been savagely beaten by a warder at the quarry. I did not see the assault, but I saw the results. His face was cut and badly bruised. Bogart approached me in our corridor and asked for help. I immediately agreed to take up his case.

We were always looking for ways to stand up to the authorities, and the report of a beating was the kind of incident we could raise with head office. Shortly before this, we had learned that a certain PAC man named Ganya had been beaten by a warder. In my role as an attorney, I wrote a letter to the commissioner of prisons protesting on behalf of Ganya. I was brought to head office, where I was confronted by prison officials. In the same breath they denied that the beating had occurred and wanted to know how I had heard about it. I insisted that the warder who had beaten Ganya be removed from the island. They refused, saying there was no evidence against him.

But shortly afterwards the warder in question was transferred off the island.

I had been emboldened by this case, so when Bogart asked for help I immediately demanded to see the commanding officer. The next day I was summoned to head office, where the commander blandly informed me that the case had been investigated and dismissed. 'That's a violation of regulations,' I said. 'The case must be tried.'

'No,' he said, 'we have attempted to interview the so-called complainant and he denies that he was ever assaulted.'

'That's impossible,' I said. 'I spoke to him only yesterday.'

The commander gestured to a lieutenant and said, 'Then see for yourself.' The lieutenant led Bogart into the room. His face was covered with bandages. The commander asked him whether or not he had been beaten. 'No, *baas*,' he said quietly, without meeting my gaze, 'I was never assaulted.' He was then dismissed.

'Well, Mandela,' the commander said, 'the case is closed.' The commander had succeeded in humiliating me. He had obviously bribed Bogart with extra food and tobacco to drop his charges. From that point on, I demanded a signed and written statement from a prisoner before I agreed to take up his case.

65

One day in the summer of 1965 we discovered some fat glistening on our porridge at breakfast and chunks of fresh meat with our pap at supper. The next day some of the men received new shirts. The guards at the quarry and the warders in our section seemed a bit more deferential. All of us were suspicious; in prison, no improvement happens without a reason. A day later we were notified that the International Red Cross would be arriving the following day.

This was a crucial occasion, more important than that of any of our previous visitors. The International Red Cross was responsible and independent, an international organization to whom the Western powers and the United Nations paid attention. The prison authorities respected the International Red Cross – and by respected, I mean feared, for the authorities respected only what they were afraid of. The prison service distrusted all organizations that could affect world opinion, and regarded them not as legitimate investigators to be dealt with honestly but as meddling interlopers to be hoodwinked if possible. Avoiding international condemnation was the authorities' principal goal.

In those early years, the International Red Cross was the only organization that both listened to our complaints and responded to them. This was vital, because the authorities ignored us. Regulations required that the authorities provide some official procedure for acknowledging our complaints. They did so, but only in the most perfunctory manner. Every Saturday morning, the chief warder would come into our section and call out, '*Klagtes and Versoeke! Klagtes and Versoeke!*' ('Complaints and requests! Complaints and requests!') Those of us with *klagtes* and *versoeke* – which was nearly everyone – lined up to see the chief warder. One by one, we would make formal complaints about food, or clothing, or visits. To each, the chief warder would nod his head and simply say, '*Ja, ja,*' and then, 'Next!' He did not even write down what we said. If we tried to speak for our organizations, the warders would yell, 'No ANC or PAC here! *Verstaan?*' ('Understand?')

*   *   *

Shortly before the International Red Cross visit we had submitted a formal list of complaints to the commissioner of prisons. At the time we were permitted paper and pencil only to write letters. We had secretly consulted with each other at the quarry and in the lavatory, and put together a list. We submitted it to our chief warder, who did not want to take it and accused us of violating regulations by making such a list. One of our complaints to the International Red Cross would be that the authorities did not listen to our grievances.

On the day of their visit, I was called to head office to meet the International Red Cross representative. That year, and for the following few years, the representative was a Mr Senn, a former director of prisons in his native Sweden who had emigrated to Rhodesia. Senn was a quiet, rather nervous man in his mid-fifties who did not seem at all comfortable in his surroundings.

The meeting was not monitored, a critical difference from nearly all of our other visitors. He asked to hear all of our complaints and grievances, and listened very carefully, taking extensive notes. He was very courteous and thanked me for all that I told him. Even so, that first visit was rather tense. Neither of us yet knew what to expect from the other.

I complained quite vociferously about our clothing, affirming that we did not want to wear short trousers and needed proper clothing including socks and underwear, which we were not then given. I recounted our grievances regarding food, visits, letters, studies, exercise, hard labour and the behaviour of the warders. I made certain requests I knew the authorities would never satisfy, such as our desire to be transferred to prisons nearer our homes.

After our session, Senn met the commissioner of prisons and his staff while I waited. I assumed that he relayed our complaints to the authorities, indicating the ones he thought were reasonable. Not long after Senn's visit our clothing did improve and we were given long trousers. But Senn was not a progressive fellow by any means; his years in Rhodesia seemed to have acclimatized him to racism. Before I returned to my cell, I reminded him of our complaint that African prisoners did not receive bread. Mr Senn appeared flustered, and glanced over at the colonel, who was head of the prison. 'Bread is very bad for your teeth, you know, Mandela,' Mr Senn said. 'Mealies are much better for you. They make your teeth strong.'

In later years, the International Red Cross sent more liberal men who wholeheartedly fought for improvements. The organization also played a critical role in an area that was less obvious but no less important to us. They often provided money to wives and relatives who would not otherwise have been able to visit us on the island.

*   *   *

After we had been sent to Robben Island, there was concern among our supporters that we would not be permitted to study. Within a few months of our arrival, the authorities announced that those who wanted to study could apply for permission. Most of the men did so, and even though they were D group prisoners, permission was granted. The state, after the Rivonia Trial, was feeling confident and thought giving us study privileges would be harmless. Later, they came to regret it. Postgraduate study was not permitted, but they made an exception in my case because I had established a precedent when I was in Pretoria.

Very few of the men in our section had BAs and many registered for university-level courses. Quite a few did not have high school certificates and chose courses to qualify for them. Some of the men were already well educated, like Govan Mbeki and Neville Alexander, but others had not gone past Standard V or VI. Within months, virtually all of us were studying for one qualification or another. At night, our cell block seemed more like a study hall than a prison.

But the privilege of studying came with a host of conditions. Certain subjects, such as politics or military history, were prohibited. For years, we were not permitted to receive funds except from our families, so that poor prisoners rarely had money for books or tuition. This made the opportunity to study a function of how much money one had. Nor were we permitted to lend books to other prisoners, which would have enabled our poorer colleagues to study.

There was always controversy about whether or not we should accept study privileges. Some members of the Unity Movement at first felt that we were accepting a handout from the government, which compromised our integrity. They argued that studying should not be a conditional privilege but an unfettered right. While I agreed, I could not accept that we should therefore refuse studying. As freedom fighters and political prisoners, we had an obligation to improve and strengthen ourselves, and study was one of the few opportunities to do so.

Prisoners were permitted to enrol at either the University of South Africa (UNISA) or the Rapid Results College, which was for those studying for their high school qualification. In my own case, studying under the auspices of the University of London was a mixed blessing. On the one hand I was assigned the sorts of stimulating books that would not have been on a South African reading list; on the other, the authorities inevitably regarded many of them as unsuitable and thus banned them.

Receiving books at all was often a challenge. You might make an application to a South African library for a book on contract law. They would process your request and then send you the book by post. But because of the vagaries of the mail system, the remoteness of the island and the often deliberate slowness of the censors, the book would reach you after the date by which it needed to be returned. If the date had passed, the warders would typically send the book back without even showing it to you. Given the nature of the system, you might receive a late fine without ever having received the book.

In addition to books, we were permitted to order publications necessary to our studies. The authorities were extremely strict about this and the only kind of publication that would pass muster might be a quarterly on actuarial science for a prisoner studying accounting. But one day Mac Maharaj told a comrade who was studying economics to request the *Economist*. We laughed and said we might as well ask for *Time* magazine, because the *Economist* was also a newsweekly. But Mac simply smiled and said the authorities wouldn't know that; they judged a book by its title. Within a month, we were receiving the *Economist* and reading the news we hungered for. But the authorities soon discovered their mistake and ended the subscription.

Once most of the men began to study, we complained that we did not even have the minimum facilities necessary for studying, such as desks and chairs. I made this complaint to the International Red Cross. Finally, the authorities built in each cell a kind of stand-up desk, a simple wooden board that jutted out from the wall at about chest-level.

This was not precisely what we had envisaged. After a tedious day at the quarry, one did not much feel like working at a stand-up desk. A number of us complained about the desks, and Kathy was the most vociferous. He informed the commanding officer that not only was it an imposition to have stand-up desks, but that they sloped so steeply that the books fell off. The commanding officer made a surprise visit to Kathy's cell, asked for a book, and plonked it on his desk. It did not move. He asked Kathy for another and placed it on top of the first one; again, nothing happened. Finally, after placing four books on the desk, he turned to a sheepish Kathy and said, 'Ag, there's nothing wrong with these desks,' and walked out. But about six months later the authorities relented and we were given three-legged wooden stools and the stand-up desks were lowered.

One complaint I voiced to the International Red Cross concerned the arbitrary way in which we were charged by the warders. To be 'charged' meant that a warder claimed that a prisoner had violated a specific regulation, which could be punished by isolation or by loss of meals and privileges. Warders generally did not treat this lightly, for when a prisoner was charged he was allowed a judicial hearing and, depending on the seriousness of the offence, a magistrate was brought in from Cape Town. At the time, the authorities were refusing to permit hearings. When I complained to the International Red Cross about this, I had yet to experience the problem myself. But that situation was soon altered.

At weekends, during our first year on the island, we were kept inside our cells all day except for half an hour of exercise. One Saturday, after returning from exercise in the courtyard, I noticed that a warder had left a newspaper on the bench at the end of the corridor. He had become rather friendly to us, and I assumed that he had not left the newspaper there by accident.

Newspapers are more valuable to political prisoners than gold or diamonds, more hungered for than food or tobacco; they were the most precious contraband on Robben Island. News was the intellectual raw material of the struggle. We were not allowed any news at all, and we craved it. Walter, even more than myself, seemed bereft without news. The authorities attempted to impose a complete blackout; they did not want us to learn anything that might raise our morale or reassure us that people on the outside were still thinking about us.

We regarded it as our duty to keep ourselves up to date with the politics of the country and fought long and hard for the right to have newspapers. Over the years we devised many ways of obtaining them, but at that time we were not so adept. One of the advantages of going to the quarry was that warders' sandwiches were wrapped in newspaper and they would often discard these newsprint wrappers in the rubbish, where we secretly retrieved them. We would distract the warders' attention, pluck the papers out of the bin and slide them into our shirts.

One of the most reliable ways to acquire papers was through bribery, and this was the only area where I tolerated what were often unethical means of obtaining information. The warders always seemed to be short of money, and their poverty was our opportunity.

When we did get hold of a paper, it was far too risky to pass around. Possession of a newspaper was a serious charge. Instead, one person would read the paper, usually Kathy or, later, Mac Maharaj. Kathy was in charge of communications, and he had thought of ingenious ways for us to pass information. Kathy would go through the paper and make cuttings of relevant stories, which were then secretly distributed to the rest of us. Each of us would write out a summary of the story we were given; these summaries were then passed among us, and later smuggled to the general section. When the authorities were particularly vigilant, Kathy or Mac would write out his summary of the news and then destroy the paper, usually by tearing it into small pieces and placing it in his ballie, which the warders never inspected.

*   *   *

When I noticed the newspaper lying on the bench, I quickly left my cell, walked to the end of the corridor, looked in both directions and then plucked it off the bench and slipped it into my shirt. Normally, I would have hidden the newspaper somewhere in my cell and taken it out only after bedtime. But like a child who eats his pudding before his main course, I was so eager for news that I opened the paper in my cell immediately.

I don't know how long I was reading; I was so engrossed in the paper that I did not hear any footsteps. Suddenly an officer and two other warders appeared, and I did not even have time to slide the paper under my bed. I was caught black-and-white-handed, so to speak. 'Mandela,' the officer said, 'we are charging you for possession of contraband, and you will pay for this.' The two warders then began a thorough search of my cell to see if they could turn up anything else.

Within a day or two a magistrate was brought in from Cape Town and I was taken to the room at headquarters that was used as the island's court. In this instance, the authorities were willing to call in an outside magistrate because they knew they had an open-and-shut case. I offered no defence, and was sentenced to three days in isolation and deprivation of meals.

I do not think that I was set up by the warder who left the newspaper on the bench, though some assumed I had been. At the hearing, the authorities grilled me as to how I got the newspaper, and I refused to answer. If I had been railroaded, the authorities would have known how I'd got it.

The isolation cells were in our same complex, but in another wing. Although just across the courtyard, they felt enormously distant. In isolation, one was deprived of company, exercise and even food: one received only rice water three times a day for three days. (Rice water is simply water in which rice has been boiled.) By comparison, our normal ration of pap seemed like a feast.

The first day in isolation was always the most painful. One grows accustomed to eating regularly and the body is not used to being deprived. I found that by the second day I had more or less adjusted to the absence of food, and the third passed without much craving at all. Such deprivation was not uncommon among Africans in everyday life. I myself had gone without food for days at a time in my early years in Johannesburg.

As I have already mentioned, I found solitary confinement the most forbidding aspect of prison life. There was no end and no beginning;

there is only one's own mind, which can begin to play tricks. Was that a dream or did it really happen? One begins to question everything. Did I make the right decision, was my sacrifice worth it? In solitary, there is no distraction from these haunting questions.

But the human body has an enormous capacity for adjusting to trying circumstances. I have found that one can bear the unbearable if one can keep one's spirits strong even when one's body is being tested. Strong convictions are the secret of surviving deprivation; your spirit can be full even when your stomach is empty.

In those early years, isolation became a habit. We were routinely charged for the smallest infractions and sentenced to isolation. A man might lose his meals for a sidelong glance or be sentenced for failing to stand when a warder entered the room. Some PAC prisoners, who often flouted the rules simply for the sake of doing so, spent a great deal of time in isolation. The authorities believed that isolation was the cure for our defiance and rebelliousness.

The second time I was charged and spent time in isolation occurred shortly after the first. As I have mentioned, we were having great difficulty making our complaints heard. The remoteness of the prison made the authorities feel they could ignore us with impunity. They believed that if they turned a deaf ear, we would give up in frustration and the people on the outside would forget about us.

One day we were working at the lime quarry when the commanding officer came to observe us, accompanied by a gentleman whom we at first did not recognize. One of my colleagues whispered to me that it was Brigadier Aucamp* from Head Office, our commanding officer's commanding officer. The two men stood at a distance, watching us.

Aucamp was a short, heavyset fellow in a suit rather than a military uniform. He normally came to the island on biannual inspections. On those occasions we were ordered to stand to attention at the grille of our cells and hold up our prison cards as he walked by.

I decided that Aucamp's unexpected appearance was a singular opportunity to present our grievances to the man who had the power to remedy them. I put down my pick and began to walk over to them. The warders immediately became alarmed and moved towards me. I knew that I was violating regulations, but I hoped the warders would be so surprised by the novelty of my action that they would do nothing to stop me. That proved to be the case.

* He is not to be confused with the officer with the same name at Pretoria Local, who looked after us during the Rivonia Trial.

When I reached the two men, the commanding officer said bluntly, 'Mandela, go back to your place. No one called you.' I disregarded him and addressed Aucamp, saying I had taken this extraordinary action because our complaints were being ignored. The CO interrupted me: 'Mandela, I order you back to your place.' I turned to him and said in a measured tone, 'I am here already, I will not go back.' I was hoping that Aucamp would agree to hear me out, but he studied me coldly and then turned to the warders and said calmly, 'Charge him.'

I continued to speak as the guards led me away. 'Take him back to the cells,' the CO said. I was charged and, once again, I had no defence. The punishment this time was four days in isolation. There was a lesson in what I had done, a lesson I already knew but had disobeyed out of desperation. No one, least of all a prison official, ever likes to have his authority publicly challenged. In order to respond to me, Aucamp would have had to humiliate his subordinate. Prison officials responded much better to private overtures. The best way to effect change on Robben Island was to attempt to influence officials privately rather than publicly. I was sometimes condemned for appearing to be too accommodating to prison officials, but I was willing to accept the criticism in exchange for the improvement.

66

The most important person in any prisoner's life is not the minister of justice, not the commissioner of prisons, not even the head of prison, but the warder in one's section. If you are cold and want an extra blanket, you might petition the minister of justice, but you will get no response. If you go to the commissioner of prisons, he will say, 'Sorry, it is against regulations.' The head of prison will say, 'If I give you an extra blanket, I must give one to everyone.' But if you approach the warder in your corridor, and you are on good terms with him, he will simply go to the stockroom and fetch a blanket.

I always tried to be decent to the warders in my section; hostility was usually self-defeating. There was no point in having a permanent enemy among the warders. It was ANC policy to try to educate all people, even our enemies: we believed that all men, even prison service warders, were capable of change, and we did our utmost to try to sway them.

In general we treated the warders as they treated us. If a man was considerate, we were considerate in return. Not all of our warders were ogres. We noticed right from the start that there were some among them who believed in fairness. Yet being friendly with warders was not an easy proposition, for they generally found the idea of being courteous to a black man abhorrent. Because it was useful to have warders who were well disposed towards us, I often asked certain men to make overtures to selected warders. No one liked to take on such a job.

We had one warder at the quarry who seemed particularly hostile to us. This was troublesome, for at the quarry we would hold discussions among ourselves, and a warder who did not permit us to talk was a great hindrance. I asked a certain comrade to befriend this fellow so that he would not interrupt our talks. The warder was quite crude, but he soon began to relax a bit around this one prisoner. One day, the warder asked this comrade for his jacket so that he could lay it on the grass and sit on it. Even though I knew it went against the comrade's grain, I nodded to him to do it.

A few days later, we were having our lunch under the shed when this warder wandered over. The warder had an extra sandwich, and he threw it on the grass near us and said, 'Here.' That was his way of showing friendship.

This presented us with a dilemma. On the one hand, he was treating us as animals to whom he could toss a bit of slop, and I felt it would undermine our dignity to take the sandwich. On the other hand, we were hungry, and to reject the gesture altogether would humiliate the warder we were trying to befriend. I could see that the comrade who had befriended the warder wanted the sandwich, and I nodded for him to take it.

The strategy worked, for this warder became less wary around us. He even began to ask questions about the ANC. By definition, if a man worked for the prison service he was probably brainwashed by the government's propaganda. He would have believed that we were terrorists and communists who wanted to drive the white man into the sea. But as we quietly explained to him our non-racialism, our desire for equal rights and our plans for the redistribution of wealth, he scratched his head and said, 'It makes more bloody sense than the Nats.'

Having sympathetic warders facilitated one of our most vital tasks on Robben Island: communication. We regarded it as our duty to stay in touch with our men in groups F and G, which was where the general prisoners were kept. As politicians, we were just as intent on fortifying our organization in prison as we had been outside. Communication was essential if we were to coordinate our protests and complaints. Because of the greater numbers of prisoners coming and going in the general section, the men in F and G tended to have more recent information about not only what was happening in the movement, but about our friends and families.

Communication between sections was a serious violation of regulations. We found many effective ways around the ban. The men who delivered our drums of food were from the general section, and in the early months we managed to have whispered conversations with them in which we conveyed brief messages. We formed a clandestine communications committee, composed of Kathy, Mac Maharaj, Laloo Chiba and several others, and their job was to organize all such practices.

One of the first techniques was engineered by Kathy and Mac, who had noticed that, on our walks to the quarry, the warders often tossed away empty matchboxes. They began secretly collecting them, and Mac had the idea of constructing a false bottom to the box and placing in it a tiny written message. Laloo Chiba, who once trained as a tailor, wrote out minuscule coded messages that would be placed in the converted matchbox. Joe Gqabi, another MK soldier who was with us, would carry the matchboxes on our walks to the quarry and drop them at a strategic crossing where we knew the general prisoners would pass. Through whispered conversations at food deliveries, we explained the plan. Designated prisoners from F and G would pick up the matchboxes on their walks, and we retrieved messages in the same fashion. It was far from perfect, and we could easily be foiled by something as simple as the rain. We soon evolved more efficient methods.

We looked for moments when the warders were inattentive. One such time was during and after meals. We helped ourselves to our food, and we worked out a scheme whereby comrades from the general section who worked in the kitchen began placing letters and notes wrapped in plastic at the bottom of the food drums. We sent return communications in a similar way, wrapping notes in the same plastic and placing them at the bottom of the mounds of dirty dishes that were routed back to the kitchen. We would do our best to create a mess, scattering food all over the plates. The warders even complained about the disarray, but never bothered to investigate.

Our toilets and showers were adjacent to the isolation section. Prisoners from the general section were often sentenced to isolation there and would use the same set of toilets we did, though at different times. Mac devised a method of wrapping notes in plastic and then taping them inside the rim of the toilet bowl. We encouraged our political comrades in the general section to be charged and placed in isolation so that they could retrieve these notes and send replies. The warders never bothered to search there.

In order not to have our notes read or understood by the authorities if they were found, we devised ways of writing that could not easily be seen or deciphered. One way was to write messages with milk. The milk would dry almost immediately, and the paper would look blank. But the disinfectant we were given to clean our cells, when sprayed on the dried milk, made the writing reappear. Unfortunately we did not regularly receive milk. After one of us was diagnosed with an ulcer, we used his.

Another technique was to write in tiny coded script on toilet paper. The paper was so small and easily hidden that this became a popular way of smuggling out messages. When the authorities discovered a number of these communications, they took the extraordinary measure of rationing toilet paper. Govan was then ill and not going to the quarry, and he was given the task of counting out eight squares of toilet paper for each prisoner per day.

But even with all these ingenious methods, one of the best ways was also the easiest: getting sent to the prison hospital. The island had one hospital, and it was difficult to segregate us from the general prisoners while we were there. Sometimes prisoners from the different sections even shared the same wards, and men from section B and prisoners from F and G mingled and exchanged information about political organizations, strikes, go-slows, whatever the current prison issues were.

Communication with the outside world was accomplished in two ways: through prisoners whose sentences were completed and who were leaving the island, and through contact with visitors. Prisoners who were leaving would smuggle out letters in their clothes or baggage. With outside visitors, the situation was even more dangerous, because the risks were also borne by the visitor. When lawyers visited us, warders were not permitted in the room and we would sometimes pass a letter to the lawyer to be taken out. Lawyers were not searched. In these meetings, we could also communicate by writing as we had during the Rivonia Trial. Because the room was bugged, we might say, 'Please tell . . .' and then pause and write 'O.T.,' meaning Oliver Tambo, on a piece of paper, 'that we approve of his plan to cut down the size of the . . .' and then write 'National Executive'.

Through a plastic-wrapped note hidden in our food drum, we learned in July 1966 that the men in the general section had embarked on a hunger strike to protest at the poor conditions. The note was imprecise, and we did not know exactly when the strike had started or exactly what it was about. But we would support any strike of prisoners for whatever reason they were striking. Word was passed among us, and we resolved to initiate a sympathetic strike beginning with our next meal. A hunger strike consists of one thing: not eating.

Because of the time-lag in communication, the general prisoners probably did not learn of our participation for a day or so. But we knew that the news would hearten them. The authorities would be telling them that we were not participating in the strike, that we were gorging ourselves on gourmet meals. This was standard operating procedure; in a crisis, the authorities inevitably started a disinformation campaign to play off one section against the other. In this case, while the ANC unanimously supported the strike, some PAC men in the general section did not.

During the first day of our strike, we were served our normal rations and refused to take them. On the second day, we noticed that our portions were larger and a few more vegetables accompanied our pap. On the third day, juicy pieces of meat were served with supper. By the fourth day, the porridge was glistening with fat, and great hunks of meat and colourful vegetables were steaming on top. The food was positively mouthwatering.

The warders smiled when we refused the food. The temptation was great, but we resisted, even though we were being driven especially hard at the quarry. We heard that in the main section, prisoners were collapsing and being taken away in wheelbarrows.

I was called to head office for an interview with Colonel Wessels. Such sessions were delicate, as my fellow prisoners knew that the authorities would attempt to influence me to call off the strike. Wessels was a direct man and demanded to know why we were on hunger strike. I explained that as political prisoners we saw protest to alter prison conditions as an extension of the anti-apartheid struggle. 'But you don't even know why they are striking in F and G,' he said. I said that did not matter, that the men in F and G were our brothers and that our struggle was indivisible. He snorted, and dismissed me.

The following day we learned of an extraordinary course of events: the warders had gone on their own food boycott, refusing to go to their own cafeteria. They were not striking in support of us, but had decided that if we could do such a thing, why couldn't they? They were demanding better food and improved living conditions. The combination of the two strikes was too much for the authorities. They settled with the warders and then, a day or two later, we learned the authorities had gone to the general section and asked for three representatives to negotiate changes. The general prisoners declared victory and called off the hunger strike. We followed suit a day later.

That was the first and most successful of the hunger strikes on the island. As a form of protest, they did not have a high success rate and the rationale behind them always struck me as quixotic. In order for a hunger strike to succeed, the outside world must learn of it. Otherwise, prisoners will simply starve themselves to death and no one will know. Smuggled-out information that we were on a hunger strike would elicit newspaper stories, which in turn would generate pressure from support groups. The problem, particularly in the early years, was that it was next to impossible to alert people on the outside that we were waging a hunger strike inside.

For me, hunger strikes were altogether too passive. We who were already suffering were threatening our health, even courting death. I have always favoured a more active, militant style of protest such as work strikes, go-slow strikes, or refusing to clean up; actions that punished the authorities, not ourselves. They wanted gravel and we produced no gravel. They wanted the prison yard clean, and it was untidy. This kind of behaviour distressed and exasperated them, whereas I think they secretly enjoyed watching us go hungry.

But when it came to a decision, I was often outvoted. My colleagues even jokingly accused me of not wanting to miss a meal. The advocates of hunger strikes argued that it was a traditionally accepted form of protest that had been waged all over the world by such prominent leaders as Mahatma Gandhi. Once the decision was taken, however, I would support it as wholeheartedly as any of its advocates. In fact, during the strikes I was often in the position of remonstrating with some of my more wayward colleagues who did not want to abide by our agreement. 'Madiba, I want my food,' I remember one man saying. 'I don't see why I should go without. I have served the struggle for many years.'

Comrades would sometimes eat on the sly. We knew this for a simple reason: by the second day of a hunger strike, no one needs to use the toilet. Yet one morning you might see a fellow going to the toilet. We had our own internal intelligence service because we knew that certain men were weak in this regard.

67

In the midst of the July 1966 hunger strike I had my second visit from my wife. It was almost exactly two years after the first, and it nearly did not happen at all. Winnie had been under constant harassment since her first visit in 1964. Her sisters and brother were persecuted by the police, and the authorities attempted to forbid anyone in her family from living with her. Some of this I learned at the time, much of it I found out later. Some of the nastiest items were known to me because when I would return from the quarry, I would often find neatly cut clippings about Winnie that had been anonymously placed on my bed by the warders.

In small and spiteful ways, the authorities did their best to make Winnie's journeys as unpleasant as possible. For the previous two years, her visits had been stymied by local magistrates and by the repeated bannings that prevented her from travelling. I had recently heard through counsel that Winnie had been informed by the police that she could visit me only if she carried a pass. Winnie, who had been protesting against the government's policy regarding women's passes since the 1950s, rightly refused to carry the hated document. The authorities were clearly attempting to humiliate her and me. But I thought it was more important that we see each other than to resist the petty machinations of the authorities, and Winnie consented to carry a pass. I missed her enormously and needed the reassurance of seeing her, and we also had vital family matters to discuss.

The regulations governing each of Winnie's visits were long and complicated. She was barred from taking a train or car and had to fly, making the trip much more expensive. She was required to take the shortest route from the airport to Caledon Square, the Cape Town police station, where she was required to sign various documents. She had to report to the same station on the way back and sign more documents.

I had also learned from a newspaper clipping that a Special Branch officer broke into our Orlando house while Winnie was dressing and she reacted angrily, pushing the officer out of the bedroom. The lieutenant laid a charge of assault against her, and I asked my friend and colleague George Bizos to defend her, which he ably did. We had seen stories about this in the newspapers, and some of the men even joked with me about Winnie's bellicosity. 'You are not the only boxer in the family, Madiba,' they said.

This second visit was for only half an hour, and we had much to discuss. Winnie was a bit agitated from the rough treatment in Cape Town and the fact that, as always, she had to travel in the hold of the ferry where the fumes from the engine made her ill. She had taken pains to dress up for me, but she looked thin and drawn.

We reviewed the education of the children, the health of my mother, which was not very good, and our finances. A critical issue was the education of Zeni and Zindzi. Winnie had placed the girls in a school designated as Indian, and the authorities were harassing the principal on the grounds that it was a violation of the law for the school to accept 'African' pupils. We made the difficult decision to send Zeni and Zindzi to boarding school in Swaziland. This was hard on Winnie, who found her greatest support in the two girls. I was consoled by the fact that their education would probably be superior there, but I worried about Winnie. She would be lonely and a prey for people who sought to undermine her under the guise of being her friends. If anything, Winnie was too trusting of people's motives.

To get around the restrictions on discussing non-family matters, we used names whose meaning was clear to us, but not to the warders. If I wanted to know how Winnie was really doing, I might say, 'Have you heard about Ngutyana recently; is she all right?' Ngutyana is one of Winnie's clan names, but the authorities were unaware of that. Then Winnie could talk about how and what Ngutyana was doing. If the warder asked who Ngutyana was, we would say she was a cousin. If I wanted to know about how the external mission of the ANC was faring, I would ask, 'How is the church?' Winnie would discuss 'the church' in appropriate terms, and I might then ask, 'How are the priests? Are there any new sermons?' We improvised and managed to exchange a great deal of information that way.

As always, when the warder yelled 'Time up!', I thought only a few minutes had passed. I wanted to kiss the glass barrier good-bye, but restrained myself. I always preferred Winnie to leave first so that she would not have to see me led away, and I watched as she whispered a good-bye, hiding her pain from the warders.

After the visit I replayed all the details in my mind, what Winnie wore, what she said, what I said. I then wrote her a letter going over some of what we had discussed, and reminding her of how much I cared for her, how unshakable our bond was, how courageous she was. I saw my letters to her both as love letters and as the only way I could give her the emotional support she needed.

Soon after the visit, I learned that Winnie had been charged for failing to report to the police on her arrival in Cape Town as well as refusing to furnish the police with her address when she left. Having already given her address at the ferry, she was asked again when she returned, and refused, saying she had done so earlier.

Winnie was arrested and released on bail. She was tried and sentenced to a year's imprisonment, which was suspended except for four days. Winnie was subsequently dismissed from her second job as a social worker because of the incident, and lost her main source of income.

The state did its utmost to harass me in ways they thought I would be powerless to resist. Towards the end of 1966 the Transvaal Law Society, at the instigation of the minister of justice, made a motion to strike me off the roll of practising attorneys as a result of my conviction in the Rivonia Trial. Apparently they were not discouraged by the earlier unsuccessful attempt to remove my name from the roll because of my conviction in the Defiance Campaign.

I found out about the Law Society's action only after it had been initiated. The Transvaal Law Society was an extremely conservative organization, and it was seeking to punish me at a time when it assumed I would be unable to defend myself. It is not easy for a prisoner on Robben Island to defend himself in court, but that is precisely what I intended to do.

I informed the authorities that I planned to contest the action and would prepare my own defence. I told prison officials that in order to prepare adequately, I would need to be exempt from going to the quarry and would also require a proper table, chair and reading light to work on my brief. I said I needed access to a law library and demanded to be taken to Pretoria.

My strategy was to overwhelm the prison authorities and the courts with legitimate requests, which I knew they would have a difficult time satisfying. The authorities always found it distressing when I wanted to defend myself in court because the accompanying publicity would show that I was still fighting for the same values I always had.

Their first response was 'Mandela, why don't you retain a lawyer to defend you? He will be able to handle the case properly. Why put yourself out?' I went ahead and applied to the registrar of the Supreme Court for the records, documents and books that I would need. I also requested a list of the state's witnesses and summaries of their prospective testimony.

I received a letter stating that before the registrar would grant my requests he would need to know the nature of my defence. This was extraordinary. To ask the nature of a lawyer's defence before the trial? No defendant can be compelled to reveal his defence before he is actually in court. I wrote back to tell him that the nature of my defence would become clear when I filed my papers – and not until then.

This was the beginning of a flurry of correspondence between me and the registrar as well as the state attorney, who was representing the Law Society. I would not back down on any of my requests. The authorities were equally intransigent: I could not be taken off quarry detail, I could not have a table and chair, and under no circumstances would I be able to go to Pretoria to use the law library.

I continued to bedevil the Law Society and registrar with demands, which they continued to deflect. Finally, several months and many letters later, without any fanfare and with just a cursory notification to me, they dropped the entire matter. The case was becoming more than they had bargained for. They had reckoned I would not have the initiative or wherewithal to defend myself; they were mistaken.

I was able to read in detail about the official reactions to my opposition to the Law Society's actions because we were receiving a daily newspaper just as if it were delivered to our door. In effect, it was.

The warder who supervised us at night was a quiet, elderly Jehovah's Witness whom Mac Maharaj had befriended. One night he wandered over to Mac's cell and told him that he wanted to enter a newspaper contest that required an essay. Would Mac, he wondered, be willing to assist him in writing it? The old warder hinted that if Mac helped him, there would be a reward. Mac agreed, and duly wrote the essay. A fortnight later, the old man came to Mac very excited. He was now a finalist in the competition; would Mac write him another essay? The warder promised Mac a cooked chicken in return. Mac told the old warder that he would think about it.

The next day Mac came to Walter and me and explained the situation. While Walter encouraged Mac to accept the food, I appreciated his reluctance to do so, because it would appear that he was getting special treatment. That night, he told the warder he would write the essay in exchange for a pack of cigarettes. The old warder agreed, and the following evening presented Mac with a newly bought pack of cigarettes.

The next day Mac told us that he now had the leverage he wanted over the old warder. How? we asked. 'Because I have his fingerprints on the cigarette pack,' Mac said, 'and I can blackmail him.' Walter exclaimed that that was immoral. I did not criticize Mac, but asked what he would blackmail him for. Mac raised his eyebrows. 'Newspapers,' he said. Walter and I looked at each other. I think Walter was the only man on Robben Island who relished newspapers as much as I did. Mac had already discussed his plan with the communications committee, and although we both had reservations about Mac's technique, we did not stop him.

That night Mac told the warder that he had his fingerprints on the pack of cigarettes and that if he did not cooperate, he would expose him to the commanding officer. Terrified of being sacked and losing his pension, the warder agreed to do whatever Mac wanted. For the next six months, until the warder was transferred, the old man would smuggle that day's newspaper to Mac. Mac would then summarize the news and reduce it to a single small piece of paper, which would circulate among us. The unfortunate warder did not win the contest, either.

It would be hard to say what we did more of at the quarry: mine lime or talk. By 1966, the warders had adopted a laissez-faire attitude: we could talk as much as we wanted as long as we worked. We would cluster in small groups, four or five men in a rough circle, and talk all day long, about every subject under the sun. We were in a perpetual conversation with each other on topics both solemn and trifling.

There is no prospect about prison which pleases – with the possible exception of one. One has time to think. In the vortex of the struggle, when one is constantly reacting to changing circumstances, one rarely has the chance to consider carefully all the ramifications of one's decisions or policies. Prison provided the time – much more than enough time – to reflect on what one had done and not done.

We were constantly engaged in political debates. Some were dispatched in a day; others were disputed for years. I have always enjoyed the cut-and-thrust of debating, and was a ready participant. One of our earliest and longest debates concerned the relationship between the ANC and the Communist Party. Some of the men, especially those MK soldiers who had been trained in socialist countries, believed that the ANC and the party were one and the same. Even some very senior ANC colleagues, such as Govan Mbeki and Harry Gwala, subscribed to this theory.

The party did not exist as a separate entity on Robben Island. In prison, there was no point in making the distinction between the ANC and the party that existed on the outside. My own views on the subject had not altered in many years. The ANC was a mass liberation movement that welcomed all those with the same objectives.

Over time, the debate concerning the ANC and the party grew progressively acrimonious. A number of us proposed one way to resolve it: we would write to the ANC in exile in Lusaka. We prepared a secret twenty-two-page document on the subject with a covering letter from myself to be sent to Lusaka. It was a risky manoeuvre to prepare and smuggle out such a document. In the end, Lusaka confirmed the separation of the ANC and the party and the argument eventually withered away.

Another recurrent political discussion was whether or not the ANC leadership should come exclusively from the working class. Some argued that because the ANC was a mass organization made up mainly of ordinary workers, the leadership should come from those same ranks. My argument was that it was as undemocratic to specify that the leaders had to be from the working class as to declare that they should be bourgeois intellectuals. If the movement had insisted on such a rule, most of its leaders, men such as Chief Luthuli, Moses Kotane, Dr Dadoo, would have been ineligible. Revolutionaries are drawn from every class.

Not all debates were political. One issue that provoked much discussion was circumcision. Some among us maintained that circumcision as practised by the Xhosa and other tribes was not only an unnecessary mutilation of the body but a reversion to the type of tribalism that the ANC was seeking to overthrow. It was not an unreasonable argument, but the prevailing view, with which I agreed, was that circumcision was a cultural ritual that had not only a salutary health benefit but an important psychological effect. It was a rite that strengthened group identification and inculcated positive values.

The debate continued for years, and a number of men voted in favour of circumcision in a very direct way. A prisoner working in the hospital who had formerly practised as an *ingcibi* set up a secret circumcision school, and a number of the younger prisoners from our section were circumcised there. Afterwards, we would organize a small party of tea and biscuits for the men, and they would spend a day or two walking around in blankets, as was the custom.

One subject we harkened back to again and again was whether there were tigers in Africa. Some argued that although it was popularly assumed that tigers lived in Africa, this was a myth and that they were native to Asia and the Indian subcontinent. Africa had leopards in abundance, but no tigers. The other side argued that tigers were native to Africa and some still lived there. Some claimed to have seen with their own eyes this most powerful and beautiful of cats in the jungles of Africa.

I maintained that while there were no tigers to be found in contemporary Africa, there was a Xhosa word for tiger, a word different from the one for leopard, and that if the word existed in our language, the creature must have once existed in Africa. Otherwise, why would there be a name for it? This argument went round and round, and I remember Mac retorting that hundreds of years ago there was a Hindi word for a craft that flew in the air, long before the aeroplane was invented, but that did not mean that aeroplanes existed in ancient India.

68

'Zithulele', the Quiet One, was what we called the tolerant, soft-spoken warder in charge of us at the quarry. He routinely stood a great distance from us while we worked and did not appear to care what we did as long as we were orderly. He never berated us when he found us leaning on our spades and talking.

We responded in kind. One day in 1966 he came to us and said, 'Gentlemen, the rains have washed away the lines on the roads; we need twenty kilos of lime today. Can you help?' Although we were working very little at the time, he had approached us as human beings, and we agreed to assist him.

That spring, we had felt a certain thawing on the part of the authorities, a relaxation of the iron-fisted discipline that had prevailed on the island. The tension between prisoners and warders had lessened somewhat.

But this lull proved to be short-lived and it came to an abrupt end one morning in September. We had just put down our picks and shovels on the quarry face and were walking to the shed for lunch. As one of the general prisoners wheeled a drum of food towards us, he whispered, 'Verwoerd is dead.' That was all. The news quickly passed among us. We looked at each other in disbelief and glanced over at the warders, who seemed unaware that anything momentous had occurred.

We did not know how the prime minister had died. Later, we heard about the obscure white parliamentary messenger who stabbed Verwoerd to death, and we wondered at his motives. Although Verwoerd thought Africans were lower than animals, his death did not yield us any pleasure. Political assassination is not something I or the ANC have ever supported. It is a primitive way of contending with an opponent.

Verwoerd had proved to be both the chief theorist and master builder of grand apartheid. He had championed the creation of the Bantustans and Bantu Education. Shortly before his death he had led the Nationalists in the general election of 1966, in which the party of apartheid had increased its majority, winning 126 seats to the 39 achieved by the United Party, and the single seat won by the Progressive Party.

As often happened on the island, we had learned significant political news before our own guards. But by the following day it was obvious the warders knew, for they took out their anger on us. The tension that had taken months to abate was suddenly at full force. The authorities began a crackdown against political prisoners as though we had held the knife that stabbed Verwoerd.

The authorities always imagined that we were secretly linked with all kinds of powerful forces on the outside. The spate of successful guerrilla attacks against the South African police forces in Namibia by the South West African People's Organization (SWAPO) – an ally of the ANC – had also unnerved them. I suppose we should have been flattered that the government thought our nascent military ability was sophisticated enough to eliminate successfully their head of state. But their suspicions merely reflected the insecurities of narrow, shortsighted men who blamed their problems not on their own misguided policies but on an opponent by the name of the ANC.

The punishment against us was never spelled out as an official policy, but it was a renewal of the harsh atmosphere that had prevailed upon our arrival on the island. The Quiet One was replaced by a man who was a vicious martinet. His name was van Rensburg and he had been flown to the island at twenty-four hours' notice after the assassination. His reputation preceded him, for his name was a byword among prisoners for brutality.

Van Rensburg was a big, clumsy, brutish fellow who did not speak but shouted. During his first day on the job we noticed he had a small swastika tattooed on his wrist. But he did not need this offensive symbol to prove his cruelty. His job was to make our lives as wretched as possible, and he pursued that goal with great enthusiasm.

Each day over the next few months, van Rensburg would charge one of us for insubordination or malingering. Each morning, he and the other warders would discuss who would be charged that afternoon. It was a policy of selective intimidation, and the decision on who would be charged was taken regardless of how hard that prisoner had worked that day. When we were trudging back to our cells, van Rensburg would read from a list, 'Mandela [or Sisulu or Kathrada], I want to see you immediately in front of the head of prison.'

The island's administrative court began working overtime. In response, we formed our own legal committee made up of myself, Fikile Bam and Mac Maharaj. Mac had studied law and was adept at putting the authorities on the defensive. Fiks, who was working towards a law degree, was a vigilant, resourceful fellow who had become the head of the prisoners' committee in our section. The job of our legal committee was to advise our comrades on how to conduct themselves in the island's administrative court.

Van Rensburg was not a clever fellow, and while he would lord it over us at the quarry, we could outwit him in court. Our strategy was not to argue with him in the field, but to contest the charges in court where we would have a chance to make our case before slightly more enlightened officers. In the administrative court, the charge would be read by the presiding magistrate. 'Malingering at the quarry,' he might say, at which van Rensburg would look smug. After the charge had been read in full, I always advised my colleagues to do one thing and one thing only: ask the court for 'further particulars'. This was one's right as a defendant, and though the request became a regular occurrence, van Rensburg would almost always be stumped. Court would then have to be adjourned while van Rensburg went out to gather 'further particulars'.

Van Rensburg was vindictive in large ways and small. When our lunch arrived at the quarry and we would sit down to eat – we now had a simple wooden table – van Rensburg would inevitably choose that moment to urinate next to our food. I suppose we should have been grateful that he did not urinate directly on our food, but we lodged a protest against the practice anyway.

One of the few ways prisoners can take their revenge on warders is through humour, and van Rensburg became the butt of many of our jokes. Among ourselves we called him 'Suitcase'. Warders' lunch boxes were known as 'suitcases' and normally a warder would designate a prisoner, usually his favourite, to carry his 'suitcase' and then reward him with half a sandwich. But we always refused to carry van Rensburg's 'suitcase', hence the nickname. It was humiliating for a warder to carry his own lunch box.

One day Wilton Mkwayi inadvertently referred to 'Suitcase' within van Rensburg's hearing. 'Who is Suitcase?' van Rensburg bellowed. Wilton paused for a moment and then blurted out, 'It's you!'

'Why do you call me Suitcase?' van Rensburg asked. Wilton paused. 'Come, man,' van Rensburg said. 'Because you carry your own "suitcase",' Wilton replied tentatively. 'The general prisoners carry the "suitcases" of their warders, but we won't carry yours – so we call you Suitcase.'

Van Rensburg considered this for a moment and, instead of getting angry, announced, 'My name is not Suitcase, it's Dik Nek.' There was silence for a moment, and then all of us burst into laughter. In Afrikaans, 'Dik Nek' literally means 'thick neck'; it suggests someone who is stubborn and unyielding. Suitcase, I suspect, was too thick to know that he had been insulted.

One day at the quarry, we resumed our discussion of whether the tiger was native to Africa. We were not able to talk as freely during van Rensburg's tenure as we had been before, but we were able to talk nonetheless while we worked.

The principal advocate of those who argued that the tiger was not native to Africa was Andrew Masondo, an ANC leader from the Cape who had also been a lecturer at Fort Hare. Masondo could be a volatile fellow, and he was vehement in his assertion that no tigers had ever been found in Africa. The argument was going back and forth and the men had put down their picks and shovels in the heat of the debate. This attracted the attention of the warders, and they shouted at us to get back to work. But we were so absorbed in the argument that we ignored them. A few of the lower-ranking warders ordered us to go back to work, but we paid them no attention. Finally, Suitcase marched over and bellowed at us in English, a language in which he was not expert: 'You talk too much, but you work too few!'

The men now did not pick up their tools because they were bent over in laughter. Suitcase's grammatical mistake struck everyone as extremely comical. But Suitcase was not at all amused. He immediately sent for Major Kellerman, the commanding officer.

Kellerman arrived on the scene a few minutes later to find us in much the same state as we had been before. He was relatively new to the island, and was determined to set the right tone. One of the warders then reported to Kellerman that Andrew Masondo and I had not been working, and we were to be charged with malingering and insubordination. Under Kellerman's authority, we were then led away handcuffed and put in isolation.

From that point on, Suitcase seemed to hold a special grudge against me. One day, while he was supervising us, I was working next to Fikile Bam. We were by ourselves, on the far side of the quarry. We worked diligently, but since we were both studying law at the time, we were discussing what we had read the night before. At the end of the day, van Rensburg stood in front of us and said, 'Fikile Bam and Nelson Mandela, I want to see you in front of the head of prison.'

We were brought before the lieutenant who was the head of prison, and van Rensburg announced, 'These men did not work the whole day.

I'm charging them with defying orders.' The lieutenant asked if we had anything to say. 'Lieutenant,' I responded, 'we dispute the charge. We have been working and, in fact, we have evidence that we have been working, and it is essential to our defence.' The lieutenant scoffed at this. 'All you men work in the same area,' he said. 'How is it possible to have evidence?' I explained that Fiks and I had been working apart from the others and that we could show exactly how much work we had done. Suitcase naively confirmed that we had been off by ourselves, and the lieutenant agreed to have a look. We drove back to the quarry.

Once there, Fiks and I walked to the area where we had been working. I pointed to the considerable pile of rocks and lime that we had built up, and said, 'There, that is what we have done today.' Suitcase had never even bothered to examine our work and was rattled by the quantity of it. 'No,' he said to the lieutenant, 'that is the result of a week's work.' The lieutenant was sceptical. 'All right, then,' he said to Suitcase, 'show me the small pile that Mandela and Bam put together today.' Suitcase had no reply, and the lieutenant did something I have rarely seen a superior officer do: he chastised his subordinate in the presence of prisoners. 'You are telling lies,' he said, and dismissed the charges on the spot.

One morning in early 1967, during Suitcase's tenure, we were preparing to walk to the quarry when Suitcase informed us that an order had come down from Major Kellerman forbidding us to talk. Not only was conversation banned on our walks; henceforth, there would be no conversation permitted at the quarry. 'From now on, silence!' he yelled.

This command was greeted by profound dismay and outrage. Talking and discussing issues were the only things that made the work at the quarry tolerable. Of course we could not discuss this problem on the way to the quarry because we were ordered not to talk, but during our lunch break the ANC leadership and the heads of the other political groups managed secretly to work out a plan.

While we were surreptitiously hatching our plan, Major Kellerman himself appeared and walked into our lunch shed. This was highly unusual; we had never had such a high-ranking visitor in our lowly shed. With a cough of embarrassment, he announced that his order had been a mistake and that we could resume talking at the quarry, just as long as we did it quietly. He then told us to carry on, and turned on his heel and was gone. We were glad the order was rescinded, but suspicious as to why.

For the remainder of the day, we were not forced to work very hard. Suitcase did his best to be friendly, and said that as a gesture of goodwill he had decided to withdraw all pending charges against us.

That afternoon, I discovered that my cell had been moved from No. 4, near the entrance of the passage, to No. 18, at the back. All my belongings had been dumped in the new cell. As always, there was no explanation.

We guessed that we were to have a visitor and I had been moved because the authorities did not want me to be the first among the prisoners to talk to whoever was coming. If each prisoner in turn voiced his complaints, the authorities could yell 'Time up!' before a visitor reached cell No. 18. We resolved that in the interest of unity, each individual along the passage would inform any visitor that while everyone had individual complaints, the prisoner in No. 18 would speak for all.

The following morning after breakfast, we were informed by Suitcase that we would not be going to the quarry. Then Major Kellerman appeared to say that Mrs Helen Suzman, the only member of the liberal Progressive Party in Parliament and the lone parliamentary voice of true opposition to the Nationalists, would be arriving shortly. In less than fifteen minutes, Mrs Suzman – all five feet two inches of her – came through the door of our corridor, accompanied by General Steyn, the commissioner of prisons. As she was introduced to each prisoner, she asked him whether he had any complaints. Each man replied in the same way: 'I have many complaints, but our spokesman is Mr Nelson Mandela at the end of the corridor.' To General Steyn's dismay, Mrs Suzman was soon at my cell. She firmly shook my hand and cordially introduced herself.

Unlike judges and magistrates, who were automatically permitted access to prisons, members of Parliament had to request permission to visit a prison. Mrs Suzman was one of the few, if not the only, member of Parliament who took an interest in the plight of political prisoners. Many stories were circulating about Robben Island, and Mrs Suzman had come to investigate for herself.

As this was Mrs Suzman's first visit to Robben Island, I attempted to put her at ease. But she was remarkably confident and utterly unfazed by her surroundings, and proposed that we get down to business right away. General Steyn and the commanding officer stood by her, but I did not mince words. I told her of our desire to have the food improved and equalized and to have better clothing, the need for facilities for studying, our lack of rights to information such as newspapers and many more things. I told her of the harshness of the warders, and mentioned van Rensburg in particular. I pointed out that he had a swastika tattooed on his forearm. Helen reacted like a lawyer. 'Well, Mr Mandela,' she said, 'we must not take that too far because we don't know when it was done. Perhaps, for example, his parents had it tattooed on him?' I assured her that was not the case.

Normally I would not complain about an individual warder. One learns in prison that it is better to fight for general principles than to battle each individual case. However callous a warder may be, he is usually just carrying out prison policy. But van Rensburg was in a class by himself, and we believed that if he were gone, it would make a disproportionate difference to all of us.

Mrs Suzman listened attentively, jotting down what I said in a small notebook, and promised to take these matters up with the minister of justice. She then made an inspection of our cells, and talked a bit with some of the other men. It was an odd and wonderful sight to see this courageous woman peering into our cells and strolling around our courtyard. She was the first and only woman ever to grace our cells.

Van Rensburg was exceedingly nervous during Mrs Suzman's visit. According to Kathy, while Mrs Suzman and I were talking, van Rensburg apologized for all his past actions. But his contrition did not last long, for the next day he informed us that he was reinstating all the charges against us. We later learned that Mrs Suzman had taken up our case in Parliament, and within a few weeks of her visit, Suitcase was transferred off the island.

69

I never imagined the struggle would be either short or easy. The first few years on the island were difficult times both for the organization outside and those of us in prison. After Rivonia, much of the movement's underground machinery had been destroyed. Our structures had been discovered and uprooted; those who were not captured were scrambling to stay one step ahead of the enemy. Virtually every one of the ANC's senior leaders was either in jail or in exile.

In the years after Rivonia, the ANC's External Mission, formerly responsible for fund-raising, diplomacy and establishing a military training programme, took up the reins of the organization as a whole. The External Mission not only had to create an organization in exile, but had the even more formidable task of trying to revitalize the underground ANC inside South Africa.

The state had grown stronger. The police had become more powerful, their methods more ruthless, their techniques more sophisticated. The South African Defence Force was expanding. The economy was stable, the white electorate untroubled. The South African government had powerful allies in Great Britain and the United States who were content to maintain the status quo.

But elsewhere the struggle against imperialism was on the march. In the middle to late 1960s armed struggles were being fought throughout southern Africa. In Namibia (then South West Africa), SWAPO was making its first incursions into the Caprivi Strip; in Mozambique and Angola the guerrilla movement was growing and spreading. In Zimbabwe (then Rhodesia), the battle against white minority rule was advancing. Ian Smith's white government was bolstered by the South African Defence Force, and the ANC regarded the battle in Zimbabwe as an extension of our struggle at home. In 1967 we learned that the ANC had forged an alliance with the Zimbabwe African People's Union (ZAPU), which had been formed by Joshua Nkomo.

That year, a group of MK soldiers who had been training in Tanzania and Zambia crossed the Zambezi River into Rhodesia with the intention of making their way home. This first group of MK soldiers was christened the Luthuli Detachment and they were the spearhead of the armed struggle. In August, as the Luthuli Detachment, accompanied by ZAPU troops, moved southward, they were spotted by the Rhodesian army. Over the next few weeks, fierce battles were fought and both sides sustained casualties. Finally, our troops were overpowered by the superior numbers of the Rhodesian forces. Some were captured, and others retreated into Bechuanaland – which had become independent Botswana. By the beginning of 1968 another, larger, ANC detachment had entered Rhodesia and fought not only the Rhodesian army but South African policemen who had been posted to Rhodesia.

We heard of this months later by rumour, but did not learn the full story until some of the men who had fought there were imprisoned with us. Though our forces were not victorious, we quietly celebrated the fact that our MK cadres had engaged the enemy in combat on their own terms. It was a milestone in the struggle. 'Justice' Panza, one of the commanders of the Luthuli Detachment, was later imprisoned with us. He briefed us on the detachment's military training, political education and valour in the field. As a former commander-in-chief of MK, I was terribly proud of our soldiers.

Before receiving the news of MK's battles abroad, we also learned of Chief Luthuli's death at home in July 1967. The circumstances were curious: he had been hit by a train in an area near his farm where he often walked. I was granted permission to write a letter to his widow. Luthuli's death left a great vacuum in the organization; the chief was a Nobel Prize winner, a distinguished, internationally known figure, a man who commanded respect from both black and white. For these reasons, he was irreplaceable. Yet in Oliver Tambo, who was acting president-general of the ANC, the organization found a man who could fill the chief's shoes. Like Luthuli, he was articulate yet not showy, confident but humble. He too epitomized Chief Luthuli's precept: 'Let your courage rise with danger.'

We organized a small memorial service for the chief in section B and permitted everyone who wanted to say something to do so. It was a quiet, respectful service with only one sour note. When Neville Alexander of the Non-European Unity Movement rose to speak, it was apparent that he had come not to praise the chief but to bury him. Without even perfunctory regrets at the man's passing, he accused Luthuli of being a stooge of the white man, mainly on the ground that the chief had accepted the Nobel Peace Prize.

Apart from its wrong-headedness, Neville's speech was entirely contrary to the climate of cooperation between organizations we were trying to create on the island. From the moment I had arrived, I had made it my mission to seek some accommodation with our rivals in the struggle. I saw Robben Island as an opportunity to patch up the long and often bitter differences between the PAC and the ANC. If we could unite the two organizations on the island, that could set a precedent for uniting them in the liberation struggle as a whole.

Yet, from the beginning, relations with the PAC had been more competitive than cooperative. Some of the PAC men were already on the island, and saw our arrival as an encroachment on their territory. We heard from some of our men that the most senior PAC prisoners had expressed regret that we had not been hanged.

In 1962, on my first stay on the island, the PAC had greatly outnumbered the ANC. In 1967 the numbers were reversed. Yet this seemed to harden the PAC in their positions. They were unashamedly anti-communist and anti-Indian. In the early years, I had talks with Zeph Mothopeng, who had been on the PAC's National Executive Committee. Zeph argued that the PAC was more militant than the ANC, and that in prison, the ANC should follow the PAC's lead. The PAC maintained that negotiations with the authorities were a betrayal, but that did not stop them from taking advantage of the benefits that resulted from negotiations. In 1967 I held talks with Selby Ngendane on the question of unity. Outside prison, Ngendane had been violently opposed to the Freedom Charter, but in prison, particularly when sent to our section, Selby mellowed. We eventually wrote separate letters to our respective organizations in the general section advocating the idea of unity. The ANC also worked well with Clarence Makwetu, who later became president of the PAC. Makwetu, who had once been a member of the ANC Youth League, was in our section and was a balanced, sensible man. We had many fruitful discussions about the unity of our two organizations, but after Makwetu was released and was succeeded in the PAC leadership on Robben Island by John Pokela, the talks foundered.

The PAC's insecurity occasionally had comical results. At one point, an order came from Pretoria that I was to be isolated from all other prisoners at the quarry. I would work separately, eat separately and have my own guard. We noticed that this new ruling caused some agitation among the PAC. Several days later, the PAC decided that their leader, Zeph Mothopeng, would also be isolated, and on their own they made him work and eat separately for as long as I did.

The PAC often refused to participate in meetings that had no overt party affiliation. When we called meetings to discuss our grievances and later had news sessions to discuss what we had learned from the paper, the PAC boycotted these gatherings. I found this greatly annoying. The PAC, we learned, were ignorant of changes in their own organization on the outside. At the time, the PAC members on the island refused to believe our claims that the PAC in exile had opened its doors to whites and Indians as members. That was heresy. Yet we had read in the paper that the white activist Patrick Duncan had become a member of the PAC Executive. The PAC members derided this at the time as ANC propaganda.

The ANC formed its own internal organization on Robben Island. Known as the High Command or, more officially, the High Organ, it consisted of the most senior ANC leaders on the island, the men who had been members of the National Executive: Walter Sisulu, Govan Mbeki, Raymond Mhlaba and me. I served as the head of the High Organ.

From its inception, we decided the High Organ would not try to influence external ANC policy. We had no reliable way of evaluating the situation in the country, and concluded it would be neither fair nor wise for us to offer guidance on matters about which we were uninformed. Instead, we made decisions about such matters as prisoners' complaints, strikes, mail, food – all the day-to-day concerns of prison life. We would, when possible, convene a general members' meeting, which we regarded as vital to the health of our organization. But as these meetings were extremely dangerous and thus infrequent, the High Organ would often take decisions that were then communicated to all the other members. The High Organ also operated a cell system, with each cell consisting of three members.

In the first few years on the island, the High Organ also acted as a representative committee for all the political prisoners in our section. In 1967 we organized a petition demanding better treatment that was signed by virtually everyone, including members of the PAC, the Unity Movement and the Liberal Party, represented by Eddie Daniels. This arrangement was acceptable to all until Neville Alexander complained that the High Organ was neither democratic nor truly representative, and that some other body ought to be created.

Neville's original suggestion eventually turned into a prisoners' committee composed of people from all political parties. There was fear among the other organizations that the ANC would attempt to dominate it, and the committee's rules were crafted so that its powers were purely consultative and its decisions not binding. Even so, it was still difficult to agree on a common approach to problems. We suggested that Fikile Bam, a member of the Yu Chi Chan Club, preside over meetings. Later, the committee leadership would rotate. Eventually the committee became known as Ulundi, and acted as a disciplinary committee for all political prisoners.

The High Organ was the source of some controversy because of its ethnic composition: all four permanent members were from Xhosa backgrounds. This was a matter of coincidence rather than design; the senior ANC leadership on the island, the only four to have served on the National Executive Committee, happened to be Xhosa. It would not have been proper to take a less senior comrade and put him on the High Organ simply because he was not a Xhosa. But the fact that the High Organ was Xhosa-dominated disturbed me because it seemed to reinforce the mistaken perception that we were a Xhosa organization.

I have always found this criticism to be vexing and based on both ignorance of ANC history and maliciousness. I would refute it by noting that the presidents of the ANC have been Zulus, Mosothos, Pedis and Tswanas, and the Executive has always been a mixture of tribal groups. I recall once working in our courtyard on a sunny afternoon while some men from the general section were working on the roof above me. They shouted at me, 'Mdala! [Old man!], why do you talk only to Xhosas?' The accusation stung me. I looked up and said, 'How can you accuse me of discrimination? We are one people.' They seemed satisfied by that, but their perception stuck in my mind. From then on, whenever I knew I would be walking in front of men from the general section, I would try to converse with Kathy or Eddie Daniels, or someone who was not a Xhosa.

We subsequently decided that there should be a fifth, rotating, member of the High Organ. He was usually not a Xhosa: Kathy, for example, was the fifth member of the High Organ for more than five years. Laloo Chiba also served for a time and, in the end, the criticism died a slow and unremarkable death.

I did not by any means dominate the High Organ, and in fact, a number of proposals that I felt strongly about were rejected. This was as it should be, but I sometimes found it frustrating. There were two issues regarding the authorities about which I could never persuade my colleagues. Prison regulations stated that prisoners must stand in the presence of a senior officer. I advocated that we should remain seated, as it was demeaning to have to recognize the enemy when he did not recognize us as political prisoners. My comrades believed this was a trivial matter and the negative consequences of resistance would outweigh any benefits.

The second issue was rejected by the High Organ on similar grounds. The warders either called us by our surnames or our Christian names.

Each, I felt, was degrading, and I thought we should insist on the honorific 'Mr'. I pressed for this for many years, without success. Later, it even became a source of humour as my colleagues would occasionally call me 'Mr' Mandela.

70

Time may seem to stand still for those of us in prison, but it did not halt for those outside. I was reminded of this when I was visited by my mother in spring 1968. I had not seen her since the end of the Rivonia Trial. Change is gradual and incremental, and when one lives in the midst of one's family, one rarely notices differences in them. But when one doesn't see one's family for many years at a time, the transformation can be striking. My mother suddenly seemed very old.

She had journeyed all the way from the Transkei, accompanied by my son Makgatho, my daughter Makaziwe and my sister Mabel. Because I had four visitors and they had come a great distance, the authorities extended the visiting time from half an hour to forty-five minutes.

I had not seen my son and daughter since before the trial and they had become adults in the interim, growing up without me. I looked at them with amazement and pride. But though they had grown up, I am afraid I still treated them more or less as the children they had been when I went to prison. They may have changed, but I hadn't.

My mother had lost a great deal of weight, which concerned me. Her face appeared haggard. Only my sister Mabel seemed unchanged. While it was a great pleasure to see all of them and to discuss family issues, I was uneasy about my mother's health.

I spoke to Makgatho and Maki about my desire for them both to pursue further schooling and asked Mabel about relatives in the Transkei. The time passed far too quickly. As with most visits, the greatest pleasure often lies in the recollection of it, but this time, I could not stop worrying about my mother. I feared that it would be the last time I would ever see her.

Several weeks later, after returning from the quarry, I was told to go to head office to collect a telegram. It was from Makgatho, informing me that my mother had died of a heart attack. I immediately made a request to the commanding officer to be permitted to attend her funeral in the Transkei, which he turned down. 'Mandela,' he said, 'while I know you are a man of your word and would not try to escape, I cannot trust your own people, and we fear that they would try to kidnap you.' It added to my grief that I was not able to bury my mother, which was my responsibility as her eldest child and only son.

Over the next few months I thought about her a great deal. Her life had been far from easy. I had been able to support her when I was practising as an attorney but, once I went to prison, I was unable to help her. I had never been as attentive as I should have been.

A mother's death causes a man to look back on and evaluate his own life. Her difficulties, her poverty, made me question once again whether I had taken the right path. That was always the conundrum: Had I made the right choice in putting the people's welfare even before that of my own family? For a long time, my mother had not understood my commitment to the struggle. My family had not asked for or even wanted to be involved in the struggle, but my involvement penalized them.

But I came back to the same answer. In South Africa it is hard for a man to ignore the needs of the people, even at the expense of his own family. I had made my choice and, in the end, she had supported it. But that did not lessen the sadness I felt at not being able to make her life more comfortable, or the pain of not being able to lay her to rest.

In the early hours of the morning of 12 May 1969 the security police woke Winnie at our home in Orlando and detained her without charge under the 1967 Terrorism Act, which gave the government unprecedented powers of arrest and detention without trial. The raid, I later learned, was part of a nationwide crackdown in which dozens of others were detained, including Winnie's sister. The police dragged Winnie away while Zeni and Zindzi clung to her skirts. She was placed in solitary confinement in Pretoria, where she was denied bail and visitors; over the next weeks and months she was relentlessly and brutally interrogated.

When Winnie was finally charged – six months later – I managed to send instructions for her to be represented by Joel Carlson, a long-time anti-apartheid lawyer. Winnie and twenty-two others were charged under the Suppression of Communism Act for attempting to revive the ANC. Later, George Bizos and Arthur Chaskalson, both members of the Rivonia team, joined the defence. In October, seventeen months after her arrest, the state withdrew its case without explanation, and Winnie was released. Within two weeks, she was again banned, and placed under house arrest. She immediately applied for permission to visit me but was rebuffed.

There was nothing I found so agonizing in prison as the thought that Winnie was in prison too. I put a brave face on the situation, but inwardly I was deeply disturbed and worried. Nothing tested my inner equilibrium as much as the time that Winnie was in solitary confinement. Although

I often urged others not to worry about what they could not control, I was unable to take my own advice. I had many sleepless nights. What were the authorities doing to my wife? How would she bear up? Who was looking after our daughters? Who would pay the bills? It is a form of mental torture to be constantly plagued by such questions and not have the means to answer them.

Brigadier Aucamp allowed me to send letters to Winnie, and relayed one or two from her. Normally, prisoners awaiting trial are not permitted mail, but Aucamp permitted it as a favour to me. I was grateful, but knew the authorities had not granted permission out of altruism: they were reading our letters, hoping to glean some information that would assist their case against Winnie.

During this time I experienced another grievous loss. One cold morning in July 1969, three months after I learned of Winnie's incarceration, I was called to the main office on Robben Island and handed a telegram. It was from my youngest son, Makgatho, and only a sentence long. He informed me that his elder brother, my first and oldest son, Madiba Thembekile, whom we called Thembi, had been killed in a motor accident in the Transkei. Thembi was then twenty-five, and the father of two small children.

What can one say about such a tragedy? I was already overwrought about my wife, I was still grieving for my mother, and then to hear such news . . . I do not have words to express the sorrow, or the loss I felt. It left a hole in my heart that can never be filled.

I returned to my cell and lay on my bed. I do not know how long I stayed there, but I did not emerge for dinner. Some of the men looked in, but I said nothing. Finally, Walter came to me and knelt beside my bed, and I handed him the telegram. He said nothing, but only held my hand. I do not know how long he remained with me. There is nothing that one man can say to another at such a time.

I asked the authorities for permission to attend my son's funeral. As a father, it was my responsibility to make sure that my son's spirit would rest peacefully. I told them they could send a security cordon with me, and that I would give my word that I would return. Permission was denied. All I was permitted to do was write a letter to Thembi's mother, Evelyn, in which I did my best to comfort her and tell her that I shared her suffering.

I thought back to one afternoon when Thembi was a boy and he came to visit me at a safe house in Cyrildene that I used for secret ANC work. Between my underground political work and legal cases, I had not been able to see him for some time. I surprised him at home and found him wearing an old jacket of mine that came to his knees. He must have taken some comfort and pride in wearing his father's clothing, just as I once did with my own father's. When I had to say good-bye again, he stood up tall, as if he were already grown, and said, 'I shall look after the family while you are gone.'

PART NINE

———

Robben Island:
Beginning to Hope

71

The graph of improvement in prison was never steady. Progress was halting, and typically accompanied by setbacks. An advancement might take years to win, and then be rescinded in a day. We would push the rock up the hill, only to have it tumble down again. But conditions did improve. We had won a host of small battles that added up to a change in the atmosphere of the island. While we did not run it, the authorities could not run it without us, and in the aftermath of van Rensburg's departure, our life became more tolerable.

Within our first three years on the island we were all given long trousers. By 1969, we received our own individual prison uniforms instead of being issued a different set each week. These uniforms actually fitted us and we were allowed to wash them ourselves. We were permitted out in the courtyard at all hours during the weekend. Although our food was not yet equalized, African prisoners would occasionally receive bread in the morning. We were allowed to pool our food anyway, so that the differences did not matter. We had been given board games and cards, which we often played on Saturdays and Sundays. At the quarry, our talk was rarely interrupted. If the commanding officer was coming, the warders on duty would blow a whistle to warn us to pick up our tools. We had neutralized the worst warders and befriended the more reasonable ones, though the authorities realized this and rotated warders every few months.

We were able to meet among ourselves virtually whenever we wanted. Meetings of the High Organ, general members' meetings and meetings of Ulundi were generally not broken up unless they were too conspicuous. The inmates, not the authorities, seemed to be running the prison.

Stern and God-fearing, the Afrikaner takes his religion seriously. The one inflexible event in our weekly schedule was Sunday morning religious services. This was an observance the authorities considered mandatory. It was as though they believed their own mortal souls would be in peril if they did not give us the benefit of worship on Sunday.

Every Sunday morning a minister from a different denomination would preach to us. One Sunday it would be an Anglican priest, the next a Dutch Reformed predicant, the next a Methodist minister. The clerics were recruited by the prison service, whose one edict was that they must preach exclusively on religious matters. Warders were present at all services, and if the minister strayed from religion he was not invited back.

During the first two years on the island, we were not allowed to leave our cells even for Sunday services. The minister would preach from the head of our corridor. By our third year, services were held in the courtyard, which we preferred. In those years, this was the only time we were permitted in the courtyard on Sunday, except for our half hour of exercise. Few of our men were religious, but no one minded long sermons; we enjoyed being outside.

Once services were held outside, we were given the option of attending. Some men attended services only in their own denomination. Though I am a Methodist, I would attend each different religious service.

One of our first ministers was an Anglican priest by the name of Father Hughes, a gruff, burly Welshman who had served as a chaplain in the submarine corps during the Second World War. When he first arrived, he was perturbed by having to preach in the corridor, which he found inimical to the contemplation of God. On his first visit, instead of preaching to us, he recited passages of Winston Churchill's wartime radio addresses in his beautiful baritone: 'We shall fight on the beaches, we shall fight on the landing grounds, we shall fight in the fields and in the streets, we shall fight in the hills; we shall never surrender.'

Father Hughes soon preached to us in the courtyard and we found his sermons splendid. He made a point of discreetly inserting bit and pieces of news into his sermons, something we appreciated. He might say, for example, that like the pharaoh of ancient Egypt, the prime minister of South Africa was raising an army.

We always sang hymns at the end of services, and I think Father Hughes visited us so frequently just to hear us sing. He brought along a portable organ, and he would play for us. He praised our singing, saying that it was the only singing that matched the choirs in his native Wales.

The Methodist minister was a Reverend Jones, a nervous and gloomy fellow who had been based in the Congo during its revolution. His experience there seemed to be the source of his melancholy. Over and over, he preached the importance of reconciliation – implying that it was we who needed to reconcile ourselves to the whites.

One Sunday, during the Methodist's one-sided message, I noticed

Eddie Daniels shifting uneasily. Finally, Eddie could take it no longer. 'You're preaching reconciliation to the wrong people,' he called out. 'We've been seeking reconciliation for the last seventy-five years.' This was enough for Reverend Jones, and we never saw him again.

Reverend Jones was not the only minister Eddie scared away. We were visited by a Coloured minister known as Brother September. One Sunday, a prisoner named Hennie Ferris, who was an eloquent speaker, volunteered to lead a prayer. Brother September was pleased to recognize such devotion. Hennie began speaking in lofty language and, at one point, asked the congregation to close its eyes and pray. Everyone, including Brother September, obliged. Eddie then tiptoed to the front, opened Brother September's briefcase, and removed the *Sunday Times* of that day. No one suspected anything at the time, but Brother September never brought newspapers again.

The Reverend André Scheffer was a minister of the Dutch Reformed Mission Church in Africa, a sister church of the Dutch Reformed Church, the faith of nearly all the Afrikaner people. The Mission Church catered only to Africans. Reverend Scheffer was a crusty, conservative fellow who usually preached to the general prisoners. One Sunday, he wandered over to our section and we asked him why he didn't preach to us. 'You men think you are freedom fighters,' he said contemptuously. 'You must have been drunk on liquor or high on *dagga* [marijuana] when you were arrested. Freedom fighters, my foot!' But we challenged him to come to preach to us and, eventually, in the late 1960s, he responded.

Reverend Scheffer was unorthodox in one respect: he took a scientific approach to religion. I found this very appealing. Many people use science to debunk religion, but he enlisted science to bolster his beliefs. I recall one sermon in which he talked about the Three Wise Men from the East who followed a star until it led them to Bethlehem. 'This is not just a superstition or a myth,' he said, and then cited evidence from astronomers that at that time in history there was a comet that followed the path outlined in the Bible.

As Reverend Scheffer became familiar with us, he became more sympathetic. He had a dry sense of humour and liked to poke fun at us. 'You know,' he would say, 'the white man has a more difficult task than the black man in this country. Whenever there is a problem, we have to find a solution. But whenever you blacks have a problem, you have an excuse. You can simply say, "*Ingabilungu*".' We burst into laughter not only because his pronunciation was unintentionally comical, but also because we were amused by the idea. *Ngabelungu* is a Xhosa expression that means 'It is the whites.' He was saying that we could always blame all our troubles on the white man. His message was that we must also look within ourselves and become responsible for our actions – sentiments with which I wholeheartedly agreed.

What Sundays were to the rest of the week, Christmas was to the rest of the year. It was the one day on which the authorities showed any goodwill towards men. We did not have to go to the quarry on Christmas Day, and we were permitted to purchase a small quantity of sweets. We did not have a traditional Christmas meal, but we were given an extra mug of coffee for supper.

The authorities permitted us to organize a concert, hold competitions and put on a play. The concert was the centrepiece. Our choirmaster was Selby Ngendane of the PAC. Selby had been a member of the ANC Youth League before switching allegiance to the Pan-Africanist Congress. He was a natural entertainer with a lovely voice and a fine ear.

Selby chose the songs, arranged the harmonies, selected the soloists and conducted the performance. The concert took place on Christmas morning in the courtyard. We would mix traditional English Christmas songs with African ones, and include a few protest songs – the authorities did not seem to mind or know the difference. The warders were our audience, and they enjoyed our singing as much as we did.

Before coming to prison, Selby was perceived as something of a political lightweight. But in prison, he showed his mettle. In prison, one likes to be around men who have a sunny disposition, and Selby had one.

Prison was a kind of crucible that tested a man's character. Some men, under the pressure of incarceration, showed true mettle, while others revealed themselves as less than what they had appeared to be.

In addition to the concerts, we held a chess and draughts tournament, and also played Scrabble and bridge. Every year I competed in the draughts competition, and some years I won the grand prize, which was usually a candy bar. My style of play was slow and deliberate; my strategy conservative. I carefully considered the ramifications of every option and took a long time between moves. I resist such analogies, but it is my preferred mode of operating not only in draughts but in politics.

Most of my opponents played more swiftly, and often lost patience with my manner of play. One of my most frequent opponents was Don Davis. A member of the Non-European Unity Movement, Don had grown up in the diamond-mining area of Kimberley and was a rugged, fearless fellow who was also highly strung. Don was an excellent draughts player, but his style contrasted with mine. When he played, perspiration would flow down his face. He became tense and agitated as he played, and made his moves rapidly as though points were awarded for speed. Several times he and I found ourselves in the finals of the annual tournament.

Don called me Qhipu because of a habit I had when playing draughts. I would ponder each possibility, and then when I was about to move I would call out, '*Qhipu!*' – which means 'I strike!' – and then move the piece. Don found this frustrating and he called me Qhipu more in irritation than in amiability.

Don and I played in many tournaments and, even if he won, he would come back within a few minutes, challenging me to another match. Don always wanted to play draughts, and did not seem satisfied until I responded. Soon I was spending so much time playing with Don that my other pursuits languished. When I once failed to pass an exam in my studies, a few colleagues asked me why, and I responded, to much laughter, 'Don Davis!'

Our amateur drama society made its yearly offering at Christmas. My thespian career, which had lain dormant since I played John Wilkes Booth while at Fort Hare, had a modest revival on Robben Island. Our productions were what might now be called minimalist: no stage, no scenery, no costumes. All we had was the text of the play.

I performed in only a few dramas, but I had one memorable role: that of Creon, the king of Thebes, in Sophocles' *Antigone*. I had read some of the classic Greek plays in prison, and found them enormously elevating. What I took out of them was that character was measured by facing up to difficult situations and that a hero was a man who would not break down even under the most trying circumstances.

When *Antigone* was chosen as the play I volunteered my services, and was asked to play Creon, an elderly king fighting a civil war over the throne of his beloved city-state. At the outset, Creon is sincere and patriotic, and there is wisdom in his early speeches when he suggests that experience is the foundation of leadership and that obligations to the people take precedence over loyalty to an individual.

> Of course you cannot know a man completely, his character, his principles, sense of judgment, not till he's shown his colours, ruling the people, making laws. Experience, there's the test.

But Creon deals with his enemies mercilessly. He has decreed that the body of Polynices, Antigone's brother, who had rebelled against the city, does not deserve a proper burial. Antigone rebels, on the grounds that there is a higher law than that of the state. Creon will not listen to Antigone, neither does he listen to anyone but his own inner demons.

His inflexibility and blindness ill become a leader, for a leader must temper justice with mercy. It was Antigone who symbolized our struggle; she was, in her own way, a freedom fighter, for she defied the law on the ground that it was unjust.

72

Some of the warders began to engage us in conversation. I never initiated conversations with warders, but if they addressed a question to me, I tried to answer. It is easier to educate a man when he wants to learn. Usually, these questions were posed with a kind of exasperation: 'All right, Mandela, what is it you really want?' Or, 'Look, you have a roof over your head and enough food, why are you causing so much trouble?' I would then calmly explain our policies to the warders. I wanted to demystify the ANC for them, to peel away their prejudices.

In 1969 a young warder arrived who seemed particularly eager to get to know me. I had heard rumours that our people on the outside were organizing an escape for me, and had infiltrated a warder on to the island who would assist me. Gradually, this fellow communicated to me that he was planning my escape.

In bit and pieces he explained the plan: one night, he would drug the warders on duty at the lighthouse to allow for the landing of a boat on the beach. He would furnish me with a key to get out of our section so that I could meet the boat. On the boat I was to be equipped with underwater diving gear, which I would use to swim into the harbour at Cape Town. From Cape Town I would be taken to a local airport and flown out of the country.

I listened to the plan in its entirety and did not reveal to him how far-fetched and unreliable it sounded. I consulted Walter, and we agreed that this fellow was not to be trusted. I never told him that I would not do it, but I never took any of the actions required to implement the plan. He must have got the message, for he was soon transferred off the island.

As it turned out, my mistrust was justified, for we later learned that the warder was an agent of the Bureau of State Security (BOSS), South Africa's secret intelligence agency. The plot was that I was to be successfully taken off the island, but killed in a dramatic shoot-out with security forces at the airport as I tried to leave the country. The entire plan had been dreamed up by BOSS, even the rumours that reached me about the ANC's planning an escape. It was not the last time they would try to eliminate me.

The term of a commanding officer was usually no more than three years, and we had been through several by 1970. That year, Robben Island's CO was Colonel van Aarde, a rather amiable, harmless fellow who allowed us a free rein. But at the end of the year, the authorities concluded that they wanted a different atmosphere on the island, and Colonel Piet Badenhorst was named the new CO.

This was an ominous development. Badenhorst was reputed to be one of the most brutal and authoritarian officers in the entire prison service. His appointment indicated one thing: the government believed that discipline on the island was too lax, and that a strong hand was needed to keep us in line. Badenhorst would supposedly make us yearn for the days of Suitcase.

Whenever a new commanding officer was appointed, I requested a meeting with him. I did this in order to impress upon him the seriousness of our cause and also to evaluate his character. I requested a meeting with Colonel Badenhorst and was turned down. He was the first CO to spurn such a meeting.

We felt the effects of his regime before we ever saw him. A number of the newer regulations regarding study and free time were immediately rescinded. It was obvious that he intended to roll back every privilege we had won over the years. Our old warders were transferred off the island and replaced by Badenhorst's handpicked guards. They were younger, coarser men who enforced every niggling regulation, whose job was to harass and demoralize us. Within days of Badenhorst's appointment, our cells were raided and searched, books and papers were confiscated, meals were suspended without warning and men were jostled on the way to the quarry.

Badenhorst attempted to turn back the clock to the way the island was in the early 1960s. The answer to every question was always no. Prisoners who requested to see their lawyers were given solitary confinement instead. Complaints were completely ignored. Visits were cancelled without explanation. The food deteriorated. Censorship increased.

About a week after Badenhorst arrived, we were working at the quarry one morning when, without introduction or fanfare, he and his driver pulled up in the commander's car. He got out and surveyed us from a distance. We paused to look at our new commander. Badenhorst returned my glance and called out, 'Mandela, *Jy moet jou vinger uit jou gat trek*' ('You must pull your finger out of your arse'). I did not care for this expression at all, and without thinking, I started advancing towards Badenhorst. He was still some distance away, and before I got close he had returned to his car and driven off.

From his car, Badenhorst radioed a command to his staff, and within minutes a truck had arrived to transport us back to section B. We were commanded to be silent in the truck, and when we arrived at the courtyard we were ordered to stand at attention. Badenhorst appeared in front of us, pacing back and forth. He seemed incapable of uttering a sentence without including an oath or swear-word. '*Jou ma se moer*', was his favourite expression. 'Your mother is a *moer*' – *moer* being a vulgar term for an intimate part of a woman's anatomy.

In his guttural voice, he told us he was disgusted to have observed our laziness at the quarry. As a result, he said, he was arbitrarily dropping all our classifications by one notch. Though we despised the classification system, most of the men had by that time risen to at least C level, where they were permitted to study. D level prisoners were not allowed to study. The authorities rued the fact that they had allowed us study privileges, and Badenhorst was determined to rectify that mistake.

Later, after my anger abated, I realized that Badenhorst's crude remark to me at the quarry was a calculated one. He had been brought to Robben Island to restore order, and he had singled out the individual he assumed was the source of the disorder. Like a teacher who takes over a rowdy class, he sought to discipline the student he regarded as the principal troublemaker.

73

In late May 1971 a number of men from SWAPO (the South West African People's Organization), an ally of the ANC fighting for independence in Namibia, were brought to the isolation section. They were led by Andimba Toivo ja Toivo, a founder of SWAPO and a formidable freedom fighter. We learned that they had embarked on a hunger strike to protest against their isolation, and we immediately decided to join in. This angered Badenhorst and the authorities, who regarded this as unacceptable insubordination.

Late on the night of 28 May we were woken by shouts and fierce knocking on our cell doors. 'Get up! Get up!' the warders yelled. We were ordered to strip and then line up against the wall of the courtyard. The warders were obviously drunk and were yelling and taunting us. They were led by a sadistic fellow named Fourie, whom we privately called Gangster.

It was a bitterly cold night, and for the next hour, while we stood to attention naked and shivering, our cells were searched one by one. Warders kept up their abuse for the entire time. Towards the end of the hour, Govan experienced severe chest pains and collapsed. This seemed to scare Fourie, and he ordered us to return to our cells.

The warders searched high and low, and found nothing. But the search seemed only an excuse for Fourie's sadistic impulses. Only later did we learn that he was reputed to have molested prisoners in the general section. The following day we discovered that the warders had brutally beaten some general prisoners before they came to us, and afterwards assaulted Toivo ja Toivo, who hit back and knocked down the warder who was beating him. Toivo was severely punished for this.

We filed a formal complaint about our treatment, but it was ignored. The incident stands out in my memory, but it was by no means unique: incidents like it were the rule rather than the exception under Badenhorst's command.

*   *   *

We were determined not to let conditions deteriorate entirely under Badenhorst. We smuggled messages to our people on the outside to agitate for his dismissal. At the same time, we resolved to create a delegation among ourselves to see Badenhorst. We discussed this for months and gradually decided on its composition; Walter and I represented the ANC, and each of the other parties had two representatives as well.

Badenhorst agreed to meet us, and at our parley we threatened work stoppages, go-slows, hunger strikes – every weapon at our disposal – unless he reformed his ways and restored many of the privileges that he had rescinded. He merely said he would take what we said into consideration. We regarded this confrontation as a victory, for he was wary of us and knew that we had alerted people on the outside to our complaints. These efforts soon produced a response.

A few weeks later, we knew an important visit must be imminent because when it rained that day at the quarry we were allowed to take shelter instead of continuing working. The following day we were informed that a troika of judges was coming to the island. The authorities asked us to nominate a spokesman to express our grievances, and I was chosen.

As I was preparing for my meeting with the judges, I was informed by a reliable source that a prisoner in the general section had recently been severely beaten by a guard. The three judges were Justices Jan Steyn, M.E. Theron and Michael Corbett of the Cape provincial division of the Supreme Court. They were escorted by the commissioner of prisons, General Steyn, and accompanied by Colonel Badenhorst. I met them that day outside, where we were working.

General Steyn introduced me to the judges and explained that I had been selected to represent the other prisoners. The judges then indicated that as a matter of course they would talk with me privately. I replied that I had nothing to hide and that in fact I welcomed the presence of General Steyn and the colonel. I could see that they were taken aback by my statement, and I added that it would be only proper for them to have the opportunity to reply to my charges. The judges reluctantly acquiesced.

I began by recounting the recent assault in the general section. I told them the details that had been reported to me, the viciousness of the beating and the cover-up of the crime. I had barely begun to speak when I noticed Badenhorst shifting uncomfortably. When I had finished describing the incident, he interjected in a gruff, aggressive manner: 'Did you actually witness this assault?' I replied calmly that I had not but that I trusted the people who had told me of it. He snorted and wagged his finger in my face. 'Be careful, Mandela,' he said. 'If you talk about things you haven't seen, you will get yourself into trouble. You know what I mean.'

I ignored Badenhorst's remarks and turned to the judges and said, 'Gentlemen, you can see for yourselves the type of man we are dealing with as commanding officer. If he can threaten me here, in your presence, you can imagine what he does when you are not here.' Judge Corbett then turned to the others and said, 'The prisoner is quite right.'

I spent the remainder of the meeting enumerating complaints about our diet, work and studying. Inwardly Badenhorst must have been fuming, but outwardly he seemed chastened. At the end of the session, the judges thanked me, and I bade them good-bye.

I have no idea what the judges said or did after the meeting, but over the next few months Badenhorst seemed to have his hands tied. The harshness abated, and within three months of the judges' visit, we received word that he was to be transferred.

A few days before Badenhorst's departure, I was called to the main office. General Steyn was visiting the island and wanted to know if we had any complaints. Badenhorst was there as I went through a list of demands. When I had finished, Badenhorst spoke to me directly. He told me that he would be leaving the island, and added, 'I just want to wish you people good luck.' I do not know if I looked dumbfounded, but I was amazed. He spoke these words like a human being, and showed a side of himself we had never seen before. I thanked him for his good wishes, and wished him luck in his endeavours.

I thought about this moment for a long time afterwards. Badenhorst had perhaps been the most callous and barbaric commanding officer we had had on Robben Island. But that day in the office, he had revealed that there was another side to his nature, a side that had been obscured but that still existed. It was a useful reminder that all men, even the most seemingly cold-blooded, have a core of decency, and that if their hearts are touched, they are capable of changing. Ultimately, Badenhorst was not evil; his inhumanity had been foisted upon him by an inhuman system. He behaved like a brute because he was rewarded for brutish behaviour.

74

It was announced that Colonel Willemse would succeed Colonel Badenhorst as commanding officer. I requested a meeting with the colonel after
his appointment and visited him shortly after his arrival. While he was
obviously not a progressive man, he was courteous and reasonable, in
marked contrast to his predecessor. Badenhorst's tenure, we hoped,
would simply be a dip on the graph of the steady improvement of our
conditions.

The aggressive young warders departed with Badenhorst as well, and
we quickly resumed our customary behaviour at the quarry and in our
section. Willemse might have been a reasonable man, but when he saw
that we spent more time at the quarry talking than working, he was
shocked.

He had been on the island for only a few weeks when I was summoned
to his office. 'Mandela,' he said frankly, 'you must help me.' I asked him
how. 'Your men are not working. They don't listen to orders. They only
do what they want to do. This is a prison. There must be some discipline.
It is not only good for us but good for you. We must have some order or
they will bring back someone like the previous head of prison.'

What the colonel said made sense. I listened and told him that his
request was a legitimate one, but before I could respond to him, I would
need to have a meeting with all my men. At that time, a meeting of all
prisoners in the single cells was something that was expressly forbidden.
By asking him to permit this, I was asking him for a significant extension
of the rules. He knew this as well as I did, and he wanted some time to
consider it.

Within days, I received a communication from Willemse saying he
would allow it. All of us met one afternoon in the courtyard, without
guards watching over us. I told the men what Willemse had said,
and noted that by compromising a bit now, we would be making our
conditions better in the long run. We decided that we would at least
appear to be working, but what work we did would be at a pace that

suited us. From then on, that is what we did, and we heard no more complaints from the commanding officer.

During the early part of Willemse's tenure, in 1971–2, there was a steady influx of captured MK soldiers. These men had seen combat, and were well informed about the state of the movement in exile. While I was never happy to see ANC men imprisoned, I was keen to debrief them after they arrived. I was extremely eager to know about Oliver, about the training camps, about MK's successes and failures.

The men were extremely militant, and they did not take to prison life easily. One of the first of them was Jimmy April, an MK officer who had trained under Joe Slovo, and had fought against the enemy in Rhodesia. MK had been slowly infiltrating men back into the country with forged identity documents. Jimmy had been one of them and he was arrested in South Africa.

Jimmy regaled us with war stories, but I also took him aside and asked him about MK's problems. As I was founder of MK and its first commander-in-chief, Jimmy and the others were more candid with me than with the others. He told me stories of discontent in the camps, and of abuses by MK officers. I asked him to keep the matter to himself, and managed to smuggle a letter out to Oliver suggesting that some reforms must be made in the camps.

One day I was at head office, meeting Colonel Willemse, when I saw Jimmy outside the office of another official. He turned to me and said in some agitation, 'They are refusing to give me my letter.'

'On what ground?' I replied.

'They claim it contains matter which I am not allowed to see,' he said. I entered the official's room to discuss the point, but before I could even open my mouth, Jimmy had barged in and loudly said to him, 'Give me my letter!' Jimmy began to push me aside to get to the officer's desk and take the letter himself. At this point, the officer took the letter and moved behind me as if for protection from Jimmy. It might have been a comical scene in a film, but at the time it was nerve-racking. I turned to Jimmy and said quietly but sternly, 'Please don't do this. Calm down. I'll sort out this matter and see that you get your letter. Now, please leave.'

My speech had the intended effect, and Jimmy left the room. I then turned to the officer, who was extremely rattled. It was, for me, an odd position. I was not opposing the authorities but mediating between my own people and the men I had so long fought against. The militancy of those who were coming to the island put me in this position more and more frequently. While we were encouraged by their radicalism, these men sometimes made our day-to-day life more burdensome.

Within a week, the officer handed me Jimmy's letter.

75

One morning, instead of walking to the quarry, we were ordered into the back of a truck. It rumbled off in a new direction, and fifteen minutes later we were ordered to jump out. There in front of us, glinting in the morning light, we saw the ocean, the rocky shore, and in the distance, winking in the sunshine, the glass towers of Cape Town. Although it was surely an illusion, the city, with Table Mountain looming behind it, looked agonizingly close, as though one could almost reach out and grasp it.

The senior officer explained that we had been brought to the shore to collect seaweed. We were instructed to pick up the large pieces that had washed up on the beach, and wade out to collect weed attached to rocks or coral. The seaweed itself was long and slimy and brownish-green in colour. Sometimes the pieces were six to eight feet in length and thirty pounds in weight. After fishing out the seaweed from the shallows, we lined it up in rows on the beach. When it was dry, we loaded it into the back of the truck. We were told it was then shipped to Japan, where it was used as a fertilizer.

The work did not seem too taxing to us that day, but in the coming weeks and months we found it could be quite strenuous. But that hardly mattered because we had the pleasures and distractions of such a panoramic tableau: we watched ships trawling, stately oil tankers moving slowly across the horizon; we saw gulls spearing fish from the sea and seals cavorting on the waves; we laughed at the colony of penguins, which resembled a brigade of clumsy, flat-footed soldiers; and we marvelled at the daily drama of the weather over Table Mountain, with its shifting canopy of clouds and sun.

In the summer the water felt wonderful, but in winter the icy Benguela Current made wading out into the waves a torture. The rocks on and around the shore were jagged, and we often cut and scraped our legs as we worked. But we preferred the sea to the quarry, although we never spent more than a few days there at a time.

*　　*　　*

The ocean proved to be a treasure chest. I found beautiful pieces of coral and elaborate shells, which I sometimes brought back to my cell. Once someone discovered a bottle of wine stuck in the sand that was still corked. I am told it tasted like vinegar. Jeff Masemola of the PAC was an extremely talented artist and sculptor and the authorities allowed him to harvest pieces of driftwood, which he carved into fantastic figures, some of which the warders offered to buy. He constructed a bookcase for me, which I used for many years. The authorities told visitors that they had provided me with it.

The atmosphere at the shore was more relaxed than at the quarry. We also relished the seaside because we ate extremely well there. Each morning when we went to the shore, we would take a large drum of fresh water. Later we would bring along a second drum, which we would use to make a kind of Robben Island seafood stew. For our stew we would pick up clams and mussels. We also caught crayfish, which hid in the crevices of rocks. Capturing a crayfish was tricky; one had to grab it firmly between its head and tail or it would wriggle free.

Abalone, or what we call *perlemoen*, were my favourite. Abalone are molluscs that cling tenaciously to rocks, and one had to prise them loose. They were stubborn creatures, difficult to open, and if they were the slightest bit overcooked, they were too tough to eat.

We would take our catch and pile it into the second drum. Wilton Mkwayi, the chef among us, would concoct the stew. When it was ready, the warders would join us and we would all sit down on the beach and have a kind of picnic lunch. In 1973, in a smuggled newspaper, we read about the wedding of Princess Anne and Mark Phillips, and the story detailed the bridal luncheon of rare and delicate dishes. The menu included mussels, crayfish and abalone, which made us laugh; we were dining on such delicacies every day.

One afternoon, we were sitting on the beach eating our stew when Lieutenant Terblanche, who was then head of prison, made a surprise visit. We quickly pretended to be working, but we had not fooled him. He soon discovered the second drum containing a mussel stew bubbling over the fire. The lieutenant opened the pot and looked inside. He then speared a mussel, ate it, and pronounced it '*smaaklik*', Afrikaans for 'tasty'.

76

In the struggle, Robben Island was known as 'the University'. This was not only because of what we learned from books, or because prisoners studied English, Afrikaans, art, geography and mathematics, or because so many of our men like Billy Nair, Ahmed Kathrada, Mike Dingake and Eddie Daniels earned multiple degrees. Robben Island was known as 'the University' because of what we learned from each other. We became our own faculty, with our own professors, our own curriculum, our own courses. We made a distinction between academic studies, which were official, and political studies, which were not.

Our university grew up partly out of necessity. As young men came to the island, we realized that they knew very little about the history of the ANC. Walter, perhaps the greatest living historian of the ANC, began to tell them about the genesis of the organization and its early days. His teaching was wise and full of understanding. Gradually this informal history grew into a course of study, constructed by the High Organ, which became known as Syllabus A, involving two years of lectures on the ANC and the liberation struggle. Syllabus A included a course taught by Kathy, 'A History of the Indian Struggle'. Another comrade added a history of the Coloured people. Mac, who had studied in the German Democratic Republic, taught a course on Marxism.

Teaching conditions were not ideal. Study groups would work together at the quarry and station themselves in a circle around the leader of the seminar. The style of teaching was Socratic in nature; ideas and theories were elucidated through the leaders asking and answering questions.

It was Walter's course that was at the heart of all our education. Many of the young ANC members who came to the island had no idea that the organization had even been in existence in the 1920s and 1930s. Walter guided them from the founding of the ANC in 1912, through to the present day. For many of these young men, it was the only political education they had ever received.

As these courses became known in the general section, we began to get queries from our men on the other side. This started what became a kind of correspondence course with the prisoners in the general section. The teachers would smuggle lectures over to them and they would respond with questions and comments.

This was beneficial for us as well as for them. These men had little formal education, but a great knowledge of the hardships of the world. Their concerns tended to be practical rather than philosophical. If one of the lectures stated that a tenet of socialism is 'From each according to his ability, to each according to his need', we might receive a question back that said, 'Yes, but what does that mean in practice? If I have land and no money, and my friend has money but no land, which of us has a greater need?' Such questions were immensely valuable and forced us to think hard about our views.

For a number of years, I taught a course in political economy. In it, I attempted to trace the evolution of economic man from the earliest times up to the present, sketching out the path from ancient communal societies to feudalism to capitalism and socialism. I am by no means a scholar and not much of a teacher, and I would generally prefer to be asked questions than to lecture. My approach was not ideological, but it was biased in favour of socialism, which I saw as the most advanced stage of economic life then evolved by man.

In addition to my informal studies, my legal work continued. I sometimes considered hanging a name-plate outside my cell, because I was spending so many hours a week preparing judicial appeals for other prisoners, though this was forbidden under prison service regulations. Prisoners with very different political ideas sought my help.

South African law does not guarantee a defendant the right to legal representation, and thousands upon thousands of indigent men and women went to prison every year for lack of such representation. Few Africans could afford a lawyer, and most had no choice but to accept whatever verdict the court handed down. Many men in the general section had been sentenced without benefit of counsel, and a number of them sought me out to make an appeal. For most of these men, it was the first time they had ever dealt with an attorney.

I would receive a smuggled note from a prisoner in F or G asking for help. I would then request the particulars of the case, the charge, the evidence and the testimony. Because of the clandestine nature of these exchanges, information would come slowly in bits and pieces. A consultation that would last no more than half an hour in my old Mandela and Tambo office might take a year or more on the island.

I advised my 'clients' to write a letter to the registrar of the Supreme Court asking for a record of the case. I told the prisoner to inform the registrar that he had limited funds and would like the record at no charge. Sometimes the registrars were kind enough to supply that material gratis.

Once I had the record of the case, I could put together an appeal, usually based on some judicial irregularity such as bias, incorrect procedure or insufficient evidence. I drafted a letter to the judge or magistrate in my own handwriting, and then sent it to the other side. Because it was a violation of regulations for me to prepare a man's case, I would instruct the prisoner to copy the document in his own hand. If he could not write, and many prisoners could not, I told him to find someone who could.

I enjoyed keeping my legal skills sharp, and in a few cases verdicts were overturned and sentences reduced. These were gratifying victories; prison is contrived to make one feel powerless, and this was one of the few ways to move the system. Often I never met the men I worked for, and sometimes, out of the blue, a man who was serving us pap for lunch would whisper a thank you to me for the work I had done on his behalf.

77

The oppression of my wife did not let up. In 1972, security policemen kicked down the door of No. 8115 Orlando West. Bricks were hurled through the window. Gunshots were fired at the front door. In 1974 Winnie was charged with violating her banning orders, which restricted her from having any visitors apart from her children and her doctor. She was then working at a lawyer's office, and a friend brought Zeni and Zindzi to see her during her lunch hour. For this, Winnie was charged and then sentenced to six months' imprisonment. She was put in Kroonstad Prison in the Orange Free State, but her experience there was not as horrendous as her previous stay in Pretoria. Winnie wrote to me that she felt liberated in prison this time, and it served to reaffirm her commitment to the struggle. The authorities permitted Zindzi and Zeni to visit her on Sundays.

When Winnie was released in 1975, we managed, through letters and communications with our lawyers, to work out a plan for me to see Zindzi. Prison regulations stated that no child between the ages of two and sixteen might visit a prisoner. When I went to Robben Island, all my children were in this legal limbo of age restrictions. The reasoning behind the rule was not pernicious: the lawmakers presumed that a prison visit would negatively affect the sensitive psyches of children. But the effect on prisoners was perhaps equally damaging; it is a source of deep sorrow not to be able to see one's children.

In 1975, Zindzi turned fifteen. The plan was for her mother to alter her birth documents to show that she was turning sixteen, not fifteen, and therefore able to see me. Birth records are not kept in a very uniform or organized way for Africans, and Winnie found that it was not hard to modify her documents to show that Zindzi was born a year earlier. She applied for a permit, and it was approved.

A few weeks before Zindzi's scheduled visit in December, I had a previously arranged visit from Winnie's mother. When I was seated across from her in the visiting area, I said to her, 'Well, Ma, I'm very excited because I'm going to see Zindzi.' My mother-in-law, who was a former teacher, regarded me with some surprise and then said in a rather peevish way, 'No, Zindzi cannot come and see you because she is not yet sixteen.'

I realized immediately that no one had told her about our gambit. There was a warder behind each of us, and I decided I would simply gloss over what she had said, and mumbled, 'Ah, well, Ma, it is nothing.'

But my mother-in-law is a stubborn woman and she did not let it pass. 'Well, Mkonyanisi' – an affectionate term for 'son-in-law' in Xhosa, which is what she called me – 'you have made a serious error because Zindzi is only fifteen.'

I widened my eyes in a gesture of alarm and she must have got the message, because she did not mention Zindzi again.

I had not seen Zindzi since she was three years old. She was a daughter who knew her father from old photographs rather than memory. I put on a fresh shirt that morning, and took more trouble than usual with my appearance: it is my own vanity, but I did not want to look like an old man for my youngest daughter.

I had not seen Winnie for over a year, and I was pleased to find that she looked well. But I was delighted to behold what a beautiful woman my youngest daughter had become and how closely she resembled her equally beautiful mother.

Zindzi was shy and hesitant at first. I am sure it was not easy for her finally to see a father she had never really known, a father who could love her only from a distance, who seemed to belong not to her but to the people. Somewhere deep inside she must have harboured resentment and anger for a father who was absent during her childhood and adolescence. I could see right away that she was a strong and fiery young woman like her own mother had been when she was Zindzi's age.

I knew she would be feeling uncomfortable, and I did my best to lighten the atmosphere. When she arrived I said to her, 'Have you met my guard of honour?', gesturing to the warders who followed me everywhere. I asked her questions about her life, her schooling and her friends, and then tried to take her back to the old days that she hardly remembered. I told her how I often recalled Sunday mornings at home when I dandled her on my knee while Mum was in the kitchen preparing a roast. I recollected small incidents and adventures in Orlando when she was a baby, and how she had rarely cried even when she was small. Through the glass, I could see her holding back her tears as I talked.

*   *   *

The one tragic note of the visit was when I learned from Winnie that Bram Fischer had died of cancer shortly after being let out of prison. Bram's death affected me deeply. Although the government left no fingerprints on Bram's body, it was the state's relentless harassment of him that brought on the final illness that took him too soon. They hounded him even after death – the state confiscated his ashes after his cremation.

Bram was a purist, and after the Rivonia Trial he decided he could best serve the struggle by going underground and living the life of an outlaw. It burdened him that the men whom he was representing in court were going to prison while he lived freely. During the trial, I advised Bram not to take this route, stressing that he served the struggle best in the courtroom, where people could see this Afrikaner son of a judge president fighting for the rights of the powerless. But he could not let others suffer while he remained free. Like the general who fights side by side with his troops at the front, Bram did not want to ask others to make a sacrifice that he was unwilling to make himself.

Bram went underground while out on bail and was captured in 1965, and sentenced to life imprisonment for conspiracy to commit sabotage. I had tried to write to him in prison, but regulations forbade prisoners to correspond with each other. After he had been diagnosed with cancer, a newspaper campaign calling for his release on humanitarian grounds had influenced the government. Just a few weeks after the authorities released him to his brother's house in Bloemfontein, still under house arrest, he died.

In many ways, Bram Fischer, the grandson of the prime minister of the Orange River Colony, had made the greatest sacrifice of all. No matter what I suffered in my pursuit of freedom, I always took strength from the fact that I was fighting with and for my own people. Bram was a free man who fought against his own people to ensure the freedom of others.

A month after this visit I received word from Winnie that her most recent request for a visit had been turned down by the authorities on the absurd grounds that I did not wish to see her. I immediately made an appointment with Lieutenant Prins, who was then head of prison, to lodge a protest.

Prins was not what one would call a sophisticated man. When I went in to see him I explained the situation evenly and without animosity. But I said the situation as it stood was unacceptable and that my wife must be permitted to visit.

Prins did not appear to be listening, and when I had finished he said, 'Ag, Mandela, your wife is only seeking publicity.' I told him that I resented his remark, and before I had even finished, he uttered something so offensive and uncomplimentary about my wife that I immediately lost my temper.

I rose from my chair and started to move around the desk towards him. Prins began to retreat, but I soon checked myself. Instead of assaulting him with my fists, as I felt like doing, I pummelled him with words. I am not a man who approves of oaths or curses, but that day I violated my own principle. I finished by telling him that he was a contemptible man without honour, and that if he ever repeated those same words I would not hold myself back as I had that day.

When I had finished, I turned and stormed out of his office. As I was leaving, I saw Kathy and Eddie Daniels outside, but I did not even greet them as I walked back to my cell. Even though I had silenced Prins, he had caused me to violate my self-control and I considered that a defeat at the hands of my opponent.

After breakfast the following morning, two warders entered my cell and said I was wanted at head office. When I reached the office, I was surrounded by half a dozen armed warders. Off to one side was Lieutenant Prins and in the centre of this circle was a warrant officer who was the prison prosecutor. The atmosphere was tense.

'Well, Mandela,' the prosecutor said, 'I hear you had a nice time yesterday, but today will not be so pleasant. I am charging you for having insulted and threatened the head of prison. It is a grave charge.' He then handed me the summons.

'Do you have anything to say?' he asked.

'No,' I replied. 'You can speak to my attorney.' I then asked to be taken back to my cell. Prins did not say a word.

I knew immediately what I would do: prepare a counter suit charging everyone from the lieutenant all the way up to the minister of justice with misconduct. I would indict the prison system as a whole as a racist institution that sought to perpetuate white supremacy. I would make the case a *cause célèbre*, and make them regret they had ever charged me in the first place.

I asked George Bizos to represent me, and a meeting was soon arranged. Before George's visit I informed the authorities that I would be giving him written instructions. They asked me why, and I replied candidly that I assumed the consultation room was bugged. The authorities then refused permission for me to give a written statement; I must make an oral one. I told them that they had no right to withhold permission, and the fact that they did only confirmed my suspicions.

The truth was that the authorities were afraid George would leak a written statement to the press. This was indeed part of our strategy. They were also concerned that I was using George as a conduit to communicate with Oliver Tambo in Lusaka, and assumed that the written statement would contain sensitive information. I had previously used George for such purposes, but the document in question did not contain such material.

A date was set for the island's disciplinary court, and a magistrate from Cape Town was assigned. A day before the hearing, I was told that my attorney would be arriving the following day and I would be free to give him my written statement. I met George at head office in the morning and we briefly consulted before court was called into session. But the hearing had no sooner started than the prosecutor announced that the prison was withdrawing its case. The judge gavelled the session to a close and abruptly left the room. George and I looked at each other in surprise and we congratulated one another on an apparent victory. I was putting away my papers when another warrant officer came over and, pointing to my written statement, said, 'Hand me that file.'

I refused, saying it was a confidential matter between me and my attorney. I called over the prosecutor and said: 'Inform this man that these documents are protected by attorney–client privilege, and that I do not have to turn them over.' The prosecutor replied that they were, but that the case was over, court was no longer in session, and the only authority in the room was that of the warrant officer. The officer plucked the documents off the table. There was nothing I could do to stop him. I believe the authorities dropped the case simply to get hold of the documents – which, as they discovered, contained nothing they did not already know.

Unlikely a prospect as it might have seemed, I nevertheless thought about escape the entire time I was on the island. Mac Maharaj and Eddie Daniels, both brave and resourceful men, were always hatching plans and discussing possibilities. Most were far too risky, but that did not stop us from considering them.

We had made certain advances. Jeff Masemola, our master craftsman, had managed to make a passkey that unlocked most of the doors in and around our section. One day, a warder had left his key on the desk in the office at the end of our corridor. Jeff took a piece of soap and made an imprint of the key. Using that outline, he took a piece of metal and filed it into the shape of the key. This gave us access to some of the storerooms behind our cells as well as to the isolation section. But we never used it to leave our section. It was the sea, after all, that was the uncrossable moat around Robben Island.

In 1974 Mac had an idea how to cross that barrier. He had recently been taken to the dentist in Cape Town and discovered that the dentist himself was related by marriage to a well-known political prisoner. The dentist was sympathetic; he had refused to treat Mac unless Mac's leg irons were first removed. Mac had also noticed that the window in the dentist's second-floor waiting room was just a short drop to a small side-street where we might make a run for it.

When Mac returned, he met a few of us and urged us to make appointments at the dentist. We did so, and learned that a day had been arranged for Mac, Wilton Mkwayi, me, and one other prisoner to go to Cape Town. The three of us were willing to make the attempt, but when Mac contacted the fourth man, he refused to come with us. We had doubts about this man's loyalty, and it concerned me that he knew what we were planning.

The three of us were taken by boat to Cape Town and then to the dentist's office under heavy guard. All three of us had trained as soldiers and we probably had the best chance of actually executing an escape. Mac was also carrying a knife, and was prepared to use it. At the dentist's office, the guards first cleared away all the other patients. We demanded to have our leg irons removed, and with the support of the dentist, our guards took them off.

Mac led us over to the window and pointed out the street that was our escape route. But something about the street bothered him as soon as he saw it: we were in the centre of Cape Town in the middle of the day, and yet the street was empty. When he had been here before, the street had been filled with traffic. 'It's a trap,' Mac whispered. I, too, had the sense that something was not right. Wilton, whose adrenaline was flowing, said Mac was talking nonsense. 'Madiba, you're losing your nerve,' he said. But I agreed with Mac, and the three of us simply ended up having our teeth examined. The dentist was curious as to why I had come, because my teeth were fine.

While Mac considered the most practical escape plans, Eddie Daniels hatched the most imaginative ones. During the early years, aeroplanes were not permitted to fly over the island. But by the mid-1970s, we noticed that not only were planes flying over our heads, but helicopters on their way to and from the tankers that sailed off the coast. Eddie came to me with a plan that would involve the organization using a helicopter, painted with the South African military colours, to pick me up on the island and then deposit me on the roof of a friendly foreign embassy in Cape Town where I would seek asylum. It was not an ill-conceived plan, and I told Eddie he should smuggle out the suggestion to Oliver in Lusaka. Eddie did manage to get his idea to Lusaka, but we never received a response.

78

Birthdays celebrations were bare-bone affairs on Robben Island. In lieu of cake and gifts, we would pool our food and present an extra slice of bread or cup of coffee to the birthday honouree. Fikile Bam and I were born on the same date, 18 July, and I would save a few sweets that I had purchased at Christmas for the two of us to share on our common anniversary. My fiftieth birthday had passed without much notice in 1968, but in 1975, when I turned fifty-seven, Walter and Kathy approached me with a long-term plan that would make my sixtieth birthday rather more memorable.

One of the issues that always concerned us was how to keep the idea of the struggle before the people. During the previous decade, the government had silenced most of the radical press, and there remained a proscription on publishing the words or pictures of any banned or imprisoned individuals. An editor could go to jail and his newspaper be closed down for publishing so much as a snapshot of me or my colleagues.

One day, Kathy, Walter and I were talking in the courtyard when they suggested that I ought to write my memoirs. Kathy noted that the perfect time for such a book to be published would be on my sixtieth birthday. Walter said that such a story, if told truly and fairly, would serve to remind people of what we had fought and were still fighting for. He added that it could become a source of inspiration for young freedom fighters. The idea appealed to me, and during a subsequent discussion, I agreed to go ahead.

When I decide to do something, I like to start immediately, and I threw myself into this new project. I adopted a rather unorthodox work schedule: I would write most of the night and sleep during the day. During the first week or two I would take a nap after dinner, wake at 10 p.m. and then write until it was time for breakfast. After working at the quarry, I would then sleep until dinner, and the process would begin again. After a few weeks of this, I notified the authorities that I was not feeling well and would not be going to the quarry. They did not seem to care, and from then on I was able to sleep most of the day.

We created an assembly line to process the manuscript. Each day I passed what I wrote to Kathy, who reviewed it and then read it to Walter. Kathy then wrote their comments in the margins. Walter and Kathy have never hesitated to criticize me, and I took their suggestions to heart, often incorporating their changes. This marked-up manuscript was then given to Laloo Chiba, who spent the next night transferring my writing to his own almost microscopic shorthand, reducing ten pages of foolscap to a single small piece of paper. It would be Mac's job to smuggle the manuscript to the outside world.

The warders grew suspicious. They went to Mac and said, 'What is Mandela up to? Why is he sitting up late at night?' But Mac merely shrugged his shoulders and said he had no idea. I wrote rapidly, completing a draft in four months. I did not hesitate over choosing a word or phrase. I covered the period from my birth through to the Rivonia Trial, and ended with some notes about Robben Island.

I relived my experiences as I wrote about them. Those nights, as I wrote in silence, I could once again experience the sights and sounds of my youth in Qunu and Mqhekezweni; the excitement and fear of coming to Johannesburg; the tempests of the Youth League; the endless delays of the Treason Trial; the drama of Rivonia. It was like a waking dream and I attempted to transfer it to paper as simply and truthfully as I could.

Mac ingeniously hid the transcribed version of the manuscript inside the binding of a number of notebooks he used for his studies. In this way, he was able to conceal the entire text from the authorities and smuggle it out when he was released in 1976. The arrangement was that Mac would secretly communicate when the manuscript was safely out of the country; only then would we destroy the original. In the meantime, we still had to dispose of a five-hundred-page manuscript. We did the only thing we thought we could do: we buried it in the garden in the courtyard. Surveillance in the courtyard had become careless and sporadic. The warders usually sat talking in an office at the northern end. From that office, they could not see the southern end next to the isolation area where there was a small garden. I had casually inspected this area on my early morning walks, and it was there that I decided to bury the manuscript.

In order not to have to dig a great hole, we decided to bury the manuscript in three separate places. We divided it into two smaller segments and one larger one, each wrapped in plastic, and placed them inside empty cocoa containers. The work would have to be done quickly, and I asked Jeff Masemola to fashion some digging tools. Within a few days I was equipped with several sharp iron stakes.

One morning after breakfast, Kathy, Walter, Eddie Daniels and I drifted over to the garden at the southern end of the courtyard where we appeared to be having a political discussion. We were each hiding portions of the manuscript in our shirts. At a signal from me, we bent down and began digging. I dug in the centre, near a manhole cover that led to a drainpipe. When I reached the pipe, I carved out a space beneath it, and it was there that I placed the largest of the three containers. The others dug two shallower holes for their portions.

We finished just in time to line up for our march to the quarry. As I walked that morning, I felt a sense of relief that the manuscript was safely hidden. I then thought no more about it.

A few weeks later, just after our wake-up call, I heard a sound in the courtyard that made me uneasy: it was the thud of picks and shovels on the ground. When we were allowed out of our cells to wash, I walked to the end of the corridor and managed to peer out of the door and around the corner. There, at the south end of the courtyard was a work crew from the general section. To my alarm, they were digging in the area where the manuscript was buried.

The authorities had decided to build a wall in front of the isolation section because they had discovered that the prisoners in isolation were able to communicate with us in the courtyard. The work crew was digging a shallow trench for the concrete foundation of the wall.

While washing, I managed to inform Walter and Kathy about the digging outside. Kathy thought that the main part of the manuscript, which was buried under the pipe, would probably be safe, but that the other two were vulnerable. When the drums of breakfast porridge were wheeled into the courtyard, the warders in charge of the work crew ordered the men out of the yard. This was done to prevent any fraternization with the political prisoners.

With our bowls of porridge in hand, I led Walter and Kathy over to the south end of the courtyard as though I wanted to confer with them privately. The beginnings of the trench were already perilously close to the two smaller containers. At the same time we were joined by Eddie Daniels, who immediately recognized the problem.

There was only one thing to do: as inconspicuously as possible, the four of us began digging in the area where the two smaller pieces of manuscript would be. We managed to unearth the two containers fairly quickly, and covered the area again with soil. To rescue the chunk of manuscript under the pipe would require more time, but we were confident that they would not find it because they would not have to dislodge the pipe in order to build the wall.

We hid the manuscript in our shirts as we walked back to our cells. Eddie was not going to the quarry that day, and we gave the containers to him, instructing him to destroy them as soon as possible. At great personal risk, Eddie agreed to do so. I breathed more easily knowing that we had salvaged the two containers, and tried not to dwell on the remaining piece of manuscript as I worked that day.

When we returned from the quarry that afternoon, instead of washing, which I normally did, I strolled over to the far end of the courtyard. I attempted to appear as casual as possible, but I was alarmed by what I saw. The prisoners had dug a trench that ran parallel to the wall of the isolation section and had actually removed the pipe altogether. They could not help but to have uncovered the manuscript.

I must have flinched or reacted in some way that was noticeable. Unknown to me, I was being watched by a number of warders, who later said that my reaction confirmed that I knew something had been hidden there. I returned to the corridor to wash, and told Walter and Kathy that I suspected the manuscript had been discovered. Eddie had meanwhile successfully disposed of the other two pieces.

Early the next morning, I was summoned to the office to see the commanding officer. Next to him stood a high prison official who had just arrived from Pretoria. Without any greeting whatsoever, the commanding officer announced: 'Mandela, we have found your manuscript.'

I did not reply. The commanding officer then reached behind his desk and produced a sheaf of papers.

'This is your handwriting, is it not?' he demanded. Again, I remained silent. 'Mandela,' the commander said in some exasperation. 'We know this is your work.'

'Well,' I replied, 'you must produce some proof of that.'

They scoffed at this, and said they knew the notations in the margin had been made by Walter Sisulu and Ahmed Kathrada. Again, I said that they must furnish evidence if they were going to impose any penalties.

'We do not need evidence,' the commander said. 'We have the evidence.'

Although he did not impose a penalty that day, a short while later Walter, Kathy and I were called before General Rue, the deputy commissioner of prisons, who told us that we had abused our study privileges in order to write the manuscript illegally. For that offence, our study privileges were being suspended indefinitely. As it turned out, we lost study privileges for four years.

*   *   *

After Mac was released in December, he sent the notebooks overseas to England. He spent the next six months under house arrest in South Africa before slipping out of the country and going first to Lusaka to see Oliver Tambo, and then to London. He stayed there for six months; with a typist, he reconstructed the manuscript and put together a typescript. He then returned to Lusaka and presented Oliver with a copy.

From there, the trail grows cold. I heard nothing from Lusaka about the manuscript and still don't know precisely what Oliver did with it. Although it was not published while I was in prison, it forms the basis of this memoir.

79

In 1976 I received an extraordinary visit: Jimmy Kruger, the minister of prisons, a prominent member of the prime minister's cabinet, came to see me. Kruger was not only influential about prisons policy but was critical of the government's handling of the liberation struggle.

I had an inkling as to why he had come. The government was then engaged in a massive effort to make a success of its separate development policy, and the 'quasi-independent' homelands. The showpiece of separate development was the Transkei, led by my nephew and one-time benefactor, K.D. Matanzima, who had successfully repressed almost all legitimate opposition to his rule. I recalled that the commanding officer had recently said to me in a bantering way, 'Mandela, you ought to retire to the Transkei and take a good long rest.'

As it turned out, that was precisely what Jimmy Kruger was proposing as well. He was a stout, blunt man, not nearly as polished as I would have expected from a cabinet minister. I approached the meeting as another opportunity to present our grievances, and at first he seemed content to listen. I began by reminding him of the letter we had sent him in 1969, which had gone unanswered. He merely shrugged. I then detailed the poor conditions on the island, reiterating once more that we were political prisoners, not criminals, and expected to be treated as such. But Kruger scoffed at this, saying, 'Nah, you are all violent communists!'

I then began to tell him a bit about the history of our organization and why we had turned to violence. It was clear that he knew almost nothing about the ANC, and what he did know was gleaned from the propaganda of the right-wing press. When I told him the organization was far older than the National Party, he was dumbfounded. I said that if he considered us to be communists, he should reread the Freedom Charter. He looked at me blankly. He had never heard of the Freedom Charter. I found it extraordinary that a cabinet minister should be so uninformed. Yet I should not have been surprised; Nationalist politicians routinely condemned what they didn't understand.

I raised the question of our release and reminded him of the case of the 1914 Afrikaner rebels, who had resorted to violence although they were represented in Parliament, could hold meetings and could even vote. Even though General de Wet and Major Kemp had led a force of twelve thousand and occupied towns and caused many deaths, they were both released soon after their convictions for high treason. I mentioned the case of Robey Leibbrandt, who set up an underground organization during the Second World War to oppose South Africa's support for the Allies, who was sentenced to life imprisonment but soon pardoned. Kruger seemed as ignorant of these episodes in the history of his own people as he was of the Freedom Charter. It is difficult to negotiate with those who do not share the same frame of reference.

Kruger waved all of this aside. 'That is ancient history,' he said. He came armed with a specific offer. Despite his reputation for brusqueness, he made his proposal in a deferential manner. He stated the matter simply: if I recognized the legitimacy of the Transkei government and was willing to move there, my sentence would be dramatically reduced.

I listened respectfully until he had finished. First, I said, I wholly rejected the Bantustan policy and would do nothing to support it, and second, I was from Johannesburg, and it was to Johannesburg that I would return. Kruger remonstrated with me, but to no avail. A month later he returned with the same proposal, and again I turned him down. It was an offer only a turncoat could accept.

80

Diligent as we were in gathering news and information, our knowledge of current events was always sketchy. Happenings in the outside world were muffled by the fact that we heard of them first through rumour; only later might they be confirmed by a newspaper account or an outside visitor.

In June 1976 we began to hear vague reports of a great uprising in the country. The whispers were fanciful and improbable: the youth of Soweto had overthrown the military and the soldiers had dropped their guns and fled. It was only when the first young prisoners who had been involved in the 16 June uprising began to arrive on Robben Island in August that we learned what had truly happened.

On 16 June 1976 fifteen thousand schoolchildren gathered in Soweto to protest at the government's ruling that half of all classes in secondary schools must be taught in Afrikaans. Students did not want to learn and teachers did not want to teach in the language of the oppressor. Pleadings and petitions by parents and teachers had fallen on deaf ears. A detachment of police confronted this army of earnest schoolchildren and without warning opened fire, killing thirteen-year-old Hector Pieterson and many others. The children fought with sticks and stones, and mass chaos ensued, with hundreds of children wounded and killed and two white men stoned to death.

The events of that day reverberated in every town and township of South Africa. The uprising triggered riots and violence across the country. Mass funerals for the victims of state violence became national rallying points. Suddenly the young people of South Africa were fired with the spirit of protest and rebellion. Students boycotted schools all across the country. ANC organizers joined with students to actively support the protest. Bantu Education had come back to haunt its creators, for these angry and audacious young people were its progeny.

In September, the isolation section was filled with young men who had been arrested in the aftermath of the uprising. Through whispered

With Walter and
Winnie in 1990.
*(Gideon Mendel/
Magnum)*

Cyril Ramaphosa
and Joe Slovo in
Johannesburg, during
preparatory talks for
a new constitution.
(Associated Press)

Left: At the Chris Hani memorial at Orlando Stadium, Soweto, with Tokyo Sexwale (right) and Charles Ngekule (left). *(Magnum)*

Below: In 1993, I revisited Robben Island. *(Copyright Island Pictures)*

Opposite, above: The cell in which I lived for eighteen of my twenty-seven years in prison. *(Copyright Island Pictures)*

Opposite, below: The waters of Table Bay separate Robben Island from Cape Town. In the distance is Table Mountain. *(Copyright Island Pictures)*

With Archbishop
Tutu. *(Peter
Magubane)*

With F. W. de Klerk.
(Peter Magubane)

Casting my vote in
South Africa's first
general election.
(Peter Magubane)

Singing the national
anthem at my
inauguration with
Thabo Mbeki and
my daughter Zenani.
(Ian Berry/Magnum)

A warm embrace
with Bishop Tutu
after the ceremony.
(Ian Berry/Magnum)

With my children
Zindzi, Zenani,
Makaziwe, and
Makgatho. *(Peter
Magubane)*

Left:
With my great-granddaughter in September 1994. *(Peter Magubane)*

My family. *(Peter Magubane)*

With my grandson
Bambata. *(Peter Magubane)*

conversations in an adjacent corridor we learned first-hand what had taken place. My comrades and I were enormously cheered; the spirit of mass protest that had seemed dormant during the 1960s was erupting in the 1970s. Many of these young people had left the country to join our own military movement, and then smuggled themselves back. Thousands of them were trained in our camps in Tanzania, Angola and Mozambique. There is nothing so encouraging in prison as learning that the people outside are supporting the cause for which you are inside.

These young men were a different breed of prisoner from those we had seen before. They were brave, hostile and aggressive; they would not take orders, and shouted '*Amandla!*' at every opportunity. Their instinct was to confront rather than cooperate. The authorities did not know how to handle them, and they turned the island upside down. During the Rivonia Trial, I remarked to a security policeman that if the government did not reform itself, the freedom fighters who would take our place would some- day make the authorities yearn for us. That day had indeed come on Robben Island.

In these young men we saw the angry revolutionary spirit of the times. I had had some warning. On a visit with Winnie a few months before, she had managed to tell me through our coded conversation that there was a rising class of discontented youths who were militant and Africanist in orientation. She said they were changing the nature of the struggle and that I should be aware of them.

The new prisoners were appalled by what they considered the barbaric conditions of the island, and said they could not understand how we could live in such a way. We told them that they should have seen the island in 1964. But they were almost as sceptical of us as they were of the authorities. They chose to ignore our calls for discipline and thought our advice feeble and unassertive.

It was obvious that they regarded us, the Rivonia Trialists, as moderates. After so many years of being branded a radical revolutionary, to be perceived as a moderate was a novel and not altogether pleasant feeling. I knew that I could react in one of two ways: I could scold them for their impertinence or I could listen to what they were saying. I chose the latter.

When some of these men, such as Strini Moodley of the South African Students' Organization and Saths Cooper of the Black People's Convention, came into our section, I asked them to give us papers on their movement and philosophy. I wanted to know what had brought them to the struggle, what motivated them, what their ideas were for the future.

Shortly after their arrival on the island, the commanding officer came to me and asked me as a favour to address the young men. He wanted me to tell them to restrain themselves, to recognize the fact that they were in prison and to accept the discipline of prison life. I told him that I was not prepared to do that. Under the circumstances, they would have regarded me as a collaborator of the oppressor.

These fellows refused to conform to even basic prison regulations. One day I was at head office conferring with the commanding officer. As I was walking out with the major, we came upon a young prisoner being interviewed by a prison official. The young man, who was no more than eighteen, was wearing his prison cap in the presence of senior officers, a violation of regulations. Nor did he stand up when the major entered the room, another violation.

The major looked at him and said, 'Please take off your cap.' The prisoner ignored him. Then in an irritated tone, the major said, 'Take off your cap.' The prisoner turned and looked at the major and said, 'What for?'

I could hardly believe what I had just heard. It was a revolutionary question: What for? The major also seemed taken aback, but managed a reply. 'It is against regulations,' he said. The young prisoner responded, 'Why do you have this regulation? What is the purpose of it?' This questioning on the part of the prisoner was too much for the major, and he stomped out of the room, saying, 'Mandela, you talk to him.' But I would not intervene on his behalf, and simply bowed in the direction of the prisoner to let him know that I was on his side.

This was our first exposure to the Black Consciousness Movement. With the banning of the ANC, PAC and Communist Party, the Black Consciousness Movement helped fill a vacuum among young people. Black Consciousness was less a movement than a philosophy and grew out of the idea that blacks must first liberate themselves from the sense of psychological inferiority bred by three centuries of white rule. Only then could the people rise in confidence and truly liberate themselves from repression. While the Black Consciousness Movement advocated a non-racial society, they excluded whites from playing a role in achieving that society.

These concepts were not unfamiliar to me: they closely mirrored ideas I myself had held at the time of the founding of the ANC Youth League a quarter of a century before. We, too, were Africanists; we, too, stressed ethnic pride and racial self-confidence; we, too, rejected white assistance in the struggle. In many ways, Black Consciousness represented the same response to the same problem that had never gone away.

But just as we had outgrown our Youth League outlook, I was confident that these young men would transcend some of the strictures of Black Consciousness. While I was encouraged by their militancy, I thought that their philosophy, in its concentration on blackness, was sectarian, and represented an intermediate view that was not fully mature. I saw my role as an elder statesman who might help them move on to the more inclusive ideas of the Congress Movement. I knew also that these young men would eventually become frustrated because Black Consciousness offered no programme of action, no outlet for their protest.

Although we viewed the ranks of the BCM as a fertile ground for the ANC, we did not attempt to recruit these men. We knew that this would alienate both them and the other parties on the island. Our policy was to be friendly, to take an interest, to compliment them on their achievements, but not to proselytize. If they came to us and asked questions – 'What is the ANC policy on the Bantustans?' 'What does the Freedom Charter say about nationalization?' – we would answer them, and a great many of them did come to us with questions.

I myself contacted some of these men through smuggled notes. I spoke with some who were from the Transkei and asked questions about my old home. Some of the men who arrived were already well known in the struggle. I had heard reports of the bravery of Patrick 'Terror' Lekota, a leader of the South African Students' Association, and sent him a note of welcome to Robben Island.

Terror's nickname came from his prowess on the soccer field, but he was just as formidable in a debate. He disagreed with some of his colleagues on the issue of racial exclusiveness and inched closer to the ideas of the ANC. Once on the island, Terror decided that he wanted to join us, but we discouraged him – not because we did not want him but because we thought such a manoeuvre would create tensions in the general section.

But Terror would not take no for an answer and publicly switched his allegiance to the ANC. One day, not long afterwards, he was assaulted with a garden fork by disgruntled BCM members. After he was treated, the authorities charged the attackers and planned to put them on trial. But in the interest of harmony, we advised Terror not to lodge a complaint. He agreed, and refused to testify against those who had hurt him. The case was dropped. Such a trial, I felt, would only play into the hands of the authorities. I wanted these young men to see that the ANC was a great tent that could accommodate many different views and affiliations.

After that incident, the floodgates seemed to open and dozens of BCM men decided to join the ANC, including some of those who had planned the attack on Terror. Terror rose to the top of the ANC hierarchy in the general section, and was soon teaching ANC policies to other prisoners.

The courage and vision of men like him confirmed to us that our views remained potent, and still represented the best hope for unifying the liberation struggle as a whole.

Political feuding continued in sections F and G. We learned of a clash among the ANC, the PAC and the BCM in the general section. A number of ANC people had been beaten. A large number of ANC members were charged by the authorities, and a trial was set for the island's administrative court. The ANC men brought in an outside lawyer to handle the case. Although I had not witnessed the fight, I was asked to be a character witness. This was a troubling prospect. While I was more than willing to give testimonials for my comrades, I did not want to take any action that would heighten the bitterness between the ANC, the PAC and the BCM.

I regarded my role in prison as not just the leader of the ANC, but as a promoter of unity, an honest broker, a peacemaker, and I was reluctant to take a side in this dispute, even if it was the side of my own organization. If I testified on behalf of the ANC, I would jeopardize my chances of bringing about reconciliation among the different groups. If I preached unity, I must act like a unifier, even at the risk of perhaps alienating some of my own colleagues.

I decided not to testify. This disappointed some of my colleagues, but I thought the issue was serious enough to risk their displeasure. It was more important to show the young Black Consciousness men that the struggle was indivisible and that we all had the same enemy.

81

In their anxiousness to deal with these young lions, the authorities more or less let us fend for ourselves. We were in the second year of a go-slow strike at the quarry, demanding a complete end to all manual labour. Our requirement was for the right to do something useful with our days, such as studying or learning a trade. We no longer even went through the motions of working at the quarry; we simply talked among ourselves. In early 1977, the authorities announced the end of manual labour. Instead, we could spend our days in our section. They arranged some type of work for us to do in the courtyard, but it was merely a figleaf to hide their capitulation.

This victory was the combined result of our own unceasing protests and simple logistics. The authorities normally preferred to have a ratio of one warder for every three prisoners. Even before the arrival of the post-Soweto prisoners, there was a shortage of warders, and the rebellious young men required even greater supervision. They were so bold that each man seemed to require his own warder. If we remained in our section, we required less supervision.

The end of manual labour was liberating. I could now spend the day reading, writing letters, discussing issues with my comrades or formulating legal briefs. The free time allowed me to pursue what became two of my favourite hobbies on Robben Island: gardening and tennis.

To survive in prison, one must develop ways to take satisfaction in one's daily life. One can feel fulfilled by washing one's clothes so that they are particularly clean, by sweeping a corridor so that it is free of dust, by organizing one's cell to conserve as much space as possible. The same pride one takes in more consequential tasks outside prison one can find in doing small things inside prison.

Almost from the beginning of my sentence on Robben Island, I asked the authorities for permission to start a garden in the courtyard. For years, they refused without offering a reason. But eventually they relented, and we were able to cut out a small garden on a narrow patch of earth against the far wall.

The soil in the courtyard was dry and rocky. The courtyard had been constructed over a landfill, and in order to start my garden I had to excavate a great many rocks to allow the plants room to grow. At the time, some of my comrades jested that I was a miner at heart, for I spent my days at the quarry and my free time digging in the courtyard.

The authorities supplied me with seeds. I initially sowed tomatoes, chillies and onions – hardy plants that did not require rich earth or constant care. The early harvests were poor, but they soon improved. The authorities did not regret giving permission, for once the garden began to flourish, I often provided the warders with some of my best tomatoes and onions.

While I have always enjoyed gardening, it was not until I was behind bars that I was able to tend my own plot. My first experience in a garden was at Fort Hare where, as part of the university's manual labour requirement, I worked in the garden of one of my professors and enjoyed the contact with the soil as an antidote to my intellectual labours. Once I was in Johannesburg studying and then working, I had neither the time nor the space to cultivate a garden.

I began to order books on gardening and horticulture. I studied different gardening techniques and types of fertilizer. I did not have many of the materials that the books discussed, but I learned through trial and error. For a time I attempted to grow peanuts, and used different soils and fertilizers, but finally I gave up. It was one of my only failures.

A garden was one of the few things in prison that one could control. To plant a seed, watch it grow, to tend it and then harvest it offered a simple but enduring satisfaction. The sense of being the custodian of this small patch of earth offered a small taste of freedom.

In some ways, I saw the garden as a metaphor for certain aspects of my life. A leader must also tend his garden; he, too, sows seeds, and then watches, cultivates and harvests the result. Like the gardener, a leader must take responsibility for what he cultivates; he must mind his work, try to repel enemies, preserve what can be preserved and eliminate what cannot succeed.

I wrote Winnie two letters about a particularly beautiful tomato plant, how I coaxed it from a tender seedling to a robust plant that produced deep red fruit. But, then, either through some mistake or lack of care, the plant began to wither and decline, and nothing I did would bring it back to health. When it finally died, I removed the roots from the soil, washed them and buried them in a corner of the garden.

I narrated this small story at great length. I do not know what she read into that letter, but when I wrote it I had a mixture of feelings: I did not want our relationship to go the way of that plant, and yet I felt that I had been unable to nourish many of the most important relationships in my life. Sometimes there is nothing one can do to save something that must die.

One unanticipated result of ending manual labour was that I began to gain weight. Though we were doing barely enough at the quarry to work up a sweat, the walk there and back was enough to keep me trim.

I have always believed that exercise is a key not only to physical health but to peace of mind. Many times in the old days I unleashed my anger and frustration on a punchbag rather than taking it out on a comrade or even a policeman. Exercise dissipates tension, and tension is the enemy of serenity. I found that I worked better and thought more clearly when I was in good physical condition, and so training became one of the inflexible disciplines of my life. In prison, having an outlet for my frustrations was absolutely essential.

Even on the island, I attempted to follow my old boxing routine of doing roadwork and muscle-building from Monday to Thursday and then resting for the next three days. On Mondays to Thursdays I would run on the spot in my cell in the morning for up to forty-five minutes. I would also perform a hundred fingertip push-ups, two hundred sit-ups, fifty deep knee-bends and various other callisthenics.

In my letters to my children, I regularly urged them to exercise, to play some fast-moving sport like basketball, soccer or tennis to take their mind off whatever might be bothering them. While I was not always successful with my children, I did manage to influence some of my more sedentary colleagues. Exercise was unusual for African men of my age and generation. After a while even Walter began to take a few turns around the courtyard in the morning. I know that some of my younger comrades looked at me and said to themselves, 'If that old man can do it, why can't I?' They, too, began to exercise.

From the very first meetings I had with outside visitors and the International Red Cross, I stressed the importance of having the time and facilities for proper exercise. Only in the mid-1970s, under the auspices of the International Red Cross, did we begin to receive things like volleyball equipment and a ping-pong table.

At roughly the same time as we stopped working at the quarry, one of the warders had the idea of converting our courtyard into a tennis court. Its dimensions were almost exact. Prisoners from the general section painted the cement surface green and then fashioned the traditional configuration of white lines. A few days later a net was put up and suddenly we had our own Wimbledon in our front yard.

I had played a bit of tennis when I was at Fort Hare, but I was by no means an expert. My forehand was relatively strong, my backhand regrettably weak. But I pursued the sport for exercise, not style; it was the best and only replacement for the walks to and from the quarry. I was one of the first in our section to play regularly. I was a back-court player, only rushing the net when I had a clean slam.

Once manual labour ended, I had much more time for reading, but the books I had been using were now out of bounds. When my studies were cancelled, I was still in the midst of pursuing my LLB at the University of London. I had started studying for the degree during the Rivonia Trial and the suspension of study privileges for four years would undoubtedly assure me the university record for taking the longest time in pursuit of that degree.

But the suspension of study privileges had an unintended benefit, and that was that I began to read many books that I would not otherwise have come across. Instead of poring over tomes about contract law, I was now absorbed by novels.

I did not have an unlimited library to choose from on Robben Island. We had access to many unmemorable mysteries and detective novels and all the works of Daphne du Maurier, but little more. Political books were off limits. Any book about socialism or communism was definitely out. A request for a book with the word *red* in the title, even if it was *Little Red Riding Hood*, would be rejected by the censors. *The War of the Worlds* by H. G. Wells, though it is a work of science fiction, would be turned down because the word *war* appeared in its title.

From the first, I tried to read books about South Africa or by South African writers. I read all the unbanned novels of Nadine Gordimer and learned a great deal about the white liberal sensibility. I read many American novels, and recall especially John Steinbeck's *The Grapes of Wrath*, in which I found many similarities between the plight of the migrant workers in that novel and our own labourers and farmworkers.

One book that I returned to many times was Tolstoy's great work, *War and Peace*. (Although the word *war* was in the title, this book was permitted.) I was particularly taken with the portrait of General Kutuzov, whom everyone at the Russian court underestimated. Kutuzov defeated Napoleon precisely because he was not swayed by the ephemeral and superficial values of the court, and made his decisions on a visceral understanding of his men and his people. It reminded me once again that truly to lead one's people one must also truly know them.

82

In the wake of the Soweto student uprising, I learned that Winnie, along with my old friend and physician, Dr Nthatho Motlana, had become involved with the Black Parents' Association, an organization of concerned local professionals and church leaders who acted as a guiding hand and intermediary for the students. The authorities seemed to be equally wary of the parents association and the young rebels. In August, less than two months after the student revolt, Winnie was detained under the Internal Security Act and imprisoned without charge in the Fort in Johannesburg, where she was held for five months. During that time I was able to write to her and my daughters, who were at boarding school in Swaziland, expressing support and solidarity. I was greatly distressed by her imprisonment, though she was apparently not mistreated this time and emerged from jail in December even firmer in her commitment to the struggle.

Though banned, Winnie picked up where she left off, and the authorities were dismayed about her popularity with the young radicals of Soweto. They were determined to lessen her influence and did it with a brazen and shameless act: they sent her into internal exile. On the night of 16 May 1977 police cars and a truck pulled up outside the house in Orlando West and began loading furniture and clothing into the back of the truck. This time Winnie was not being arrested, detained or interrogated; she was being banished to a remote township in the Free State called Brandfort. I discovered the details from Kathy, who had been given the information from a visiting Hindu priest.

Brandfort is about two hundred and fifty miles southwest of Johannesburg, just north of Bloemfontein, in the Free State. After a long and rough ride, Winnie, Zindzi and all their possessions were dumped in front of a three-room tin-roofed shack in Brandfort's bleak African township, a desperately poor and backward place where the people were under the thumb of the local white farmers. Winnie was regarded with wariness and trepidation. The local language was Sesotho, which Winnie did not speak.

Her new circumstance's saddened and angered me. At least when she was home in Soweto, I could picture her cooking in the kitchen or reading in the lounge; I could imagine her waking up in the house I knew so well. That was a source of comfort to me. In Soweto, even if she was banned, there were friends and family near by. In Brandfort she and Zindzi would be alone.

I had passed through this township once on my way to Bloemfontein, and took no notice of it. There was nothing memorable in its all too typical poverty and desolation. I did not know at the time how familiar the address – house No. 802, Brandfort – would one day become to me. Once again, I felt as though Winnie and I were in prison at the same time.

Life in Brandfort was hard, as I learned from Winnie's letters. They had no heat, no toilet, no running water. The township had no shops and the stores in town were hostile to African customers. The whites for the most part were Afrikaans-speaking and deeply conservative.

Winnie and Zindzi were under constant police surveillance and intermittent harassment. Within a few months Zindzi – who was not banned – was upset by the security police's intimidation. In September, with the help of Winnie's lawyers, I brought an urgent application for an interdict against the local Brandfort security police to restrain them from harassing my daughter. Affidavits filed before the judge described policemen bursting into the house and threatening Zindzi. The judge ruled that Zindzi could receive visitors in peace.

Winnie is a resilient person, and within a relatively short time she had won over the people of the township, including some sympathetic whites in the vicinity. She supplied food to the people in the township with the help of Operation Hunger, started a crèche for the township's children and raised funds to create a medical clinic in a place where few people had ever seen a doctor.

In 1978 Zeni, my second-youngest daughter and my first child with Winnie, married Prince Thumbumuzi, a son of King Sobhuza of Swaziland. They had met while Zeni was away at school. Being in prison, I was not able to fulfil the father's traditional duties. In our culture, the father of the bride must interview the prospective groom and assess his prospects. He must also determine *lobola*, the brideprice, which is paid by the groom to the bride's family. On the wedding day itself, the father gives away his daughter. Although I had no doubts about the young man, I asked my friend and legal adviser George Bizos to stand in for me. I instructed George to interview the prince about how he intended to look after my daughter.

George met the prince in his office and then arranged to have a consultation with me on Robben Island. Because Zeni was under twenty-one, it was necessary for me to give my legal consent for her to marry. I met George in the consulting room and he was surprised to find a warder in the room with us. I explained that it was according to regulations because this was considered a family visit, not a legal one. I jestingly reassured George by saying that I had no secrets from my guards.

George reported how much the two children loved one another and the bright prospects of my future son-in-law. His father, King Sobhuza, was an enlightened traditional leader and also a member of the ANC. As George relayed to me some of the requirements made by the young man's family, he was at pains to point out that the boy was a Swazi prince. I told George to tell the young man that he was getting a Thembu princess.

There was a tremendous advantage in Zeni becoming a member of the Swazi royal family: she was immediately granted diplomatic privileges and could visit me virtually at will. That winter, after she and Thumbumuzi were married, they came to see me, along with their newborn baby daughter. Because of the prince's status, we were allowed to meet one another in the consulting room, not the normal visiting area where one is separated from one's family by thick walls and glass. I waited for them with some nervousness.

It was a truly wondrous moment when they came into the room. I stood up, and when Zeni saw me, she practically tossed her tiny daughter to her husband and ran across the room to embrace me. I had not held my now grown-up daughter since she was about her own daughter's age. It was a dizzying experience, as though time had sped forward in a science fiction novel, suddenly to hug one's fully grown child. I then embraced my new son and he handed me my tiny granddaughter, whom I did not let go of for the entire visit. To hold a newborn baby, so vulnerable and soft in my rough hands, hands that for too long had held only picks and shovels, was a profound joy. I don't think a man was ever happier to hold a baby than I was that day.

The visit had a more official purpose and that was for me to choose a name for the child. It is the custom for the grandfather to select a name, and the one I had chosen was Zaziwe – which means 'Hope'. The name had a special meaning for me, for during all my years in prison hope never left me – and now it never would. I was convinced that this child would be a part of a new generation of South Africans for whom apartheid would be a distant memory – that was my dream.

83

I do not know whether it was the upheaval inside the prison after the Soweto uprising or the upheaval in my family's life outside prison, but in the year or two following 1976 I was in a dreamy, nostalgic state of mind. In prison, one has time to review the past, and memory becomes both a friend and a foe. My memory transported me into moments of both great joy and sadness. My dream life became very rich, and I seemed to pass entire nights reliving the high and low times of the old days.

I had one recurring nightmare. In the dream, I had just been released from prison – only it was not Robben Island, but a jail in Johannesburg. I walked outside the gates into the city and found no one to meet me. In fact there was no one there at all, no people, no cars, no taxis. I would then set out on foot towards Soweto. I walked for many hours before arriving in Orlando West, and then turned the corner towards, No. 8115. Finally I would see my home, but it turned out to be empty, a ghost house, with all the doors and windows open but no one there at all.

But not all my dreams of release were so dark. In 1976 I wrote to Winnie of a happier vision:

> The night of 24 February, I dreamt of arriving at No. 8115, finding the house full of youth dancing away a mixture of jive and *infiba*. I caught all of them by surprise as I walked in unexpectedly. Some greeted me warmly, whilst others simply melted away shyly. I found the bedroom equally full with members of the family and close friends. You were relaxing in bed, with Kgatho [my son Makgatho], looking young and sleeping against the opposite wall.
>
> Perhaps in that dream I was recalling the two weeks in December 1956 when he was six and when I left Makhulu [Evelyn's mother] alone in the house. He was living with his mother in OE [Orlando East] then, but a few days before I came back he joined Makhulu and slept in my bed. He was missing me very much and using the bed must have relieved the feeling of longing a bit.

While I took joy from dwelling on happy moments, I rued the pain I had often caused my family through my absence. Here is another letter from 1976:

> As I woke up on the morning of 25 February I was missing you and the children a great deal as always. These days I spend quite some time thinking of you both as Dadewethu [Sister], Mum, pal and mentor. What you perhaps don't know is how I often think and actually picture in my mind all that makes you up physically and spiritually – the loving remarks which came daily and the blind eye you've always turned against those numerous irritations that would have frustrated another woman . . . I even remember a day when you were bulging with Zindzi, struggling to cut your nails. I now recall those incidents with a sense of shame. I could have done it for you. Whether or not I was conscious of it, my attitude was: I've done my duty, a second brat is on the way, the difficulties you are now facing as a result of your physical condition are all yours. My only consolation is the knowledge that I then led a life where I'd hardly enough time even to think. Only I wonder what it'll be like when I return . . .
>
> Your beautiful photo still stands about two feet above my left shoulder as I write this note. I dust it carefully every morning, for to do so gives me the pleasant feeling that I'm caressing you as in the old days. I even touch your nose with mine to recapture the electric current that used to flush through my blood whenever I did so. Nolitha stands on the table directly opposite me. How can my spirits ever be down when I enjoy the fond attentions of such wonderful ladies.

Nolitha was the one person who was not a member of the family whose photo I kept. I revealed the secret of her identity to my daughter Zindzi in another letter from 1976:

> By the way, has Mum ever told you about Nolitha, the other lady in my cell from the Andaman Islands? She keeps you, Zeni, Ndindi and Nandi, Mandla [these last three are grandchildren], Maki and Mum company. It's one matter over which Mum's comments are surprisingly economic. She regards the pygmy beauty as some sort of rival and hardly suspects that I took her picture out of the *National Geographic*.

I thought continually of the day when I would walk free. Over and over,

I fantasized about what I would like to do. This was one of the pleasantest ways to pass the time. I put my daydreams on paper, again in 1976.

I wish I could drive you on a long, long journey just as I did on 12/6/58, with the one difference that this time I'd prefer us to be alone. I've been away from you for so long that the very first thing I would like to do on my return would be to take you away from that suffocating atmosphere, drive you along carefully, so that you could have the opportunity of breathing fresh and clean air, seeing the beauty spots of South Africa, its green grass and trees, colourful wild flowers, sparkling streams, animals grazing in the veld and be able to talk to the simple people we meet along the road. Our first stop would be to the place where Ma Radebe and CK [Winnie's mother and father] sleep. I hope they lie next to each other. Then I would be able to pay my respects to those who have made it possible for me to be as happy and free as I am now. Perhaps the stories I've so much wanted to tell you all these years would begin there. The atmosphere should probably sharpen your ears and restrain me to concentrate on those aspects which are tasty, edifying and constructive. Thereafter, we would adjourn and resume next to Mphakanyiswa and Nosekeni [my parents] where the environment would be similar. I believe we would then be fresh and solid as we drive back to No. 8115.

When the authorities began to allow us to receive photographs of immediate family members in the early 1970s, Winnie sent me an album. Whenever I received a photograph of Winnie, the children or the grandchildren, I would carefully paste it in. I cherished this album; it was the one way that I could see those I loved whenever I wanted.

But in prison no privilege comes without some accompanying pain. Though I was permitted to receive pictures and to keep the album, warders would often search my cell and confiscate pictures of Winnie. Eventually, however, the practice of seizing pictures ceased, and I built up my album so that it was thick with pictures of my entire family.

I do not remember who first asked to borrow my photo album, but it was undoubtedly someone in my section. I happily lent it, and someone else asked, and then someone else. Soon it became so widely known that I possessed a photo album that I was receiving requests from men in F and G.

The men of F and G rarely received visitors or even letters, and it would have been ungenerous to deny them this window on the world. But before long I found that my precious photo album was in tatters, and that many of my irreplaceable photographs had been removed. These men were desperate to have something personal in their cells and could not help themselves. Each time this happened, I resolved to build up my album once more.

Sometimes men would just ask me for a photograph rather than the album. I recall one day when a young BCM fellow from the general section who was bringing us food took me aside and said, 'Madiba, I would like a photograph.' I said fine, I would send him one. 'When?' he said rather brusquely. I replied that I would try to send it that weekend. This seemed to satisfy him, and he began to walk away, but suddenly he turned round and said, 'Look, don't send me a photograph of the old lady. Send me one of the young girls, Zindzi or Zeni – remember, not the old lady!'

84

In 1978, after we had spent almost fifteen years agitating for the right to receive news, the authorities offered us a compromise. Instead of permitting us to receive newspapers or listen to radio, they started their own radio news service, which consisted of a daily canned summary of the news read over the prison's intercom system.

The broadcasts were far from objective or comprehensive. Several of the island's censors would compile a brief news digest from other daily radio bulletins. The broadcasts consisted of good news for the government and bad news for all its opponents.

The first broadcast opened with a report about the death of Robert Sobukwe. Other early reports concerned the victories of Ian Smith's troops in Rhodesia and detentions of government opponents in South Africa. Despite the slanted nature of the news, we were glad to have it, and prided ourselves on reading between the lines and making educated guesses based on the obvious omissions.

That year, we learned via the intercom that P. W. Botha had succeeded John Vorster as prime minister. What the warders did not tell us was that Vorster resigned as a result of press revelations about the Department of Information's misuse of government funds. I knew little about Botha apart from the fact that he had been an aggressive defence minister and had supported a military strike into Angola in 1975. We had no sense that he would be a reformer in any way.

I had recently read an authorized biography of Vorster (this was one of the books the prison library did have) and found that he was a man willing to pay for his beliefs; he went to prison for his support of Germany during the Second World War. We were not sorry to see Vorster go. He had escalated the battle against freedom to new heights of repression.

But even without our expurgated radio broadcasts, we had learned what the authorities did not want us to know. We learned of the successful liberation struggles in Mozambique and Angola in 1975 and their emergence as independent states with revolutionary governments. The tide was turning our way.

In keeping with the increased openness on the island, we now had our own cinema. Almost every week we watched films on a sheet in a large room adjacent to our corridor. Later, we had a proper screen. The films were a wonderful diversion, a vivid escape from the bleakness of prison life.

The first films we saw were silent, black-and-white Hollywood action movies and Westerns that were made before even my time. I recall one of the first ones was *The Mark of Zorro*, with the swashbuckling Douglas Fairbanks, a movie that was made in 1920. The authorities seemed to have a weakness for historical films, particularly ones with a stern moral message. Among the early films we saw – now in colour, with dialogue – were *The Ten Commandments* with Charlton Heston as Moses, *The King and I* with Yul Brynner and *Cleopatra* with Richard Burton and Elizabeth Taylor.

We were intrigued by *The King and I*, for to us it depicted the clash between the values of East and West, and seemed to suggest that the West had much to learn from the East. *Cleopatra* proved controversial; many of my comrades took exception to the fact that the queen of Egypt was depicted by a raven-haired, violet-eyed American actress, however beautiful. The detractors asserted that the movie was an example of Western propaganda that sought to erase the fact that Cleopatra was an African woman. I related how on my trip to Egypt I had seen a splendid sculpture of a young ebony-skinned Cleopatra.

Later, we also saw local South African films with black stars whom we all knew from the old days. On those nights, our little makeshift theatre echoed with the shouts, whistles and cheers that greeted the appearance of an old friend on screen. Later, we were permitted to select documentaries – a form that I preferred – and I began to skip the conventional films. (Although I would never miss a movie with Sophia Loren in it.) The documentaries were ordered from the state library and usually selected by Ahmed Kathrada, who was our section's librarian. I was particularly affected by a documentary we saw about the great naval battles of the Second World War, which showed newsreel footage of the sinking of HMS *Prince of Wales* by the Japanese. What moved me most was a brief image of Winston Churchill weeping after he heard the news of the loss of the British vessel. The image stayed in my memory a long time, and demonstrated to me that there are times when a leader can show sorrow in public, and that it will not diminish him in the eyes of his people.

*   *   *

One of the documentaries we watched concerned a controversial American motorcycle group, the Hell's Angels. The film depicted them as reckless, violent and antisocial, and the police as decent, upstanding and trustworthy. When the film ended, we immediately began to discuss its meaning. Almost without exception the men criticized the Hell's Angels for their lawless ways. But then Strini Moodley, a bright young Black Consciousness member, stood up and accused the assembled group of being out of touch with the times, for the bikers represented the equivalent of the Soweto students of 1976 who rebelled against the authorities. He reproached us for being elderly middle-class intellectuals who identified with the movie's right-wing authorities instead of the bikers.

Strini's accusations caused a furore, and a number of men rose to speak against him, saying the Hell's Angels were indefensible and it was an insult to compare our struggle with this band of amoral sociopaths. But I considered what Strini said, and while I did not agree with him, I came to his defence. Even though the Hell's Angels were unsympathetic, they were rebels against the authorities, unsavoury rebels though they were.

I was not interested in the Hell's Angels, but the larger question that concerned me was whether we had, as Strini suggested, become stuck in a mind-set that was no longer revolutionary. We had been jailed for more than fifteen years; I had been in prison for nearly eighteen. The world that we left was long gone. The danger was that our ideas had become frozen in time. Prison is a still point in a turning world, and it is very easy to remain in the same place in jail while the world moves on.

I had always attempted to remain open to new ideas, not to reject a position because it was new or different. During our years on the island we kept up a continuing dialogue about our beliefs and ideas; we debated them, questioned them and thereby refined them. I did not think we had stayed in one place; I believed we had evolved.

Although Robben Island was becoming more open, there was as yet no sign that the state was reforming its views. Even so, I did not doubt that I would some day be a free man. We might have been stuck in one place, but I was confident that the world was moving towards our position, not away from it. The movie reminded me once again that on the day I did walk out of prison, I did not want to appear to be a political fossil from an age long past.

It took fifteen years, but in 1979 the authorities announced over the intercom system that the diet for African, Coloured and Indian prisoners would henceforth be the same. But just as justice delayed is justice denied, a reform so long postponed and so grudgingly enacted was hardly worth celebrating.

All prisoners were to receive the same amount of sugar in the morning: a spoonful and a half. But instead of simply increasing the African quota, the authorities reduced the amount of sugar that Coloured and Indian prisoners received by half a spoonful, while adding that amount for African prisoners. A while before, African prisoners had begun to receive bread in the morning, but that made little difference. We had been pooling bread for years.

Our food had already improved in the previous two years, but not because of the authorities. In the wake of the Soweto uprising, the authorities had decided that the island would become the exclusive home of South Africa's 'security prisoners'. The number of general prisoners had been drastically reduced. As a result, political prisoners were recruited to work in the kitchen for the first time. Once political prisoners were in the kitchen, our diet improved dramatically. This was not because they were better chefs, but because the smuggling of food immediately stopped. Instead of siphoning off food for themselves or to bribe the warders, the new cooks used all the food allotted to us. Vegetables became more abundant, and chunks of meat began to appear in our soups and stews. Only then did we realize we should have been eating such food for years.

85

In the summer of 1979, I was playing tennis in the courtyard when my opponent hit a cross-court shot that I strained to reach. As I ran across the court, I felt a pain in my right heel so intense that I had to stop playing. For the next few days I walked with a severe limp.

I was examined by a doctor on the island who decided I should go to Cape Town to see a specialist. The authorities had become more solicitous of our health, afraid that if we died in prison they would be condemned by the international community.

Although under normal circumstances I and the other men would relish a visit to Cape Town, going as a prisoner was altogether different. I was handcuffed and kept in a remote corner of the boat surrounded by five armed warders. The sea was rough that day, and the boat shuddered at every wave. About midway between the island and Cape Town, I thought we were in danger of capsizing. I spied a lifejacket behind two warders young enough to be my grandsons. I said to myself, 'If this boat goes under, I will commit my last sin on earth and run over those two boys to get that lifejacket.' But in the end, it was unnecessary.

On the docks, we were met by more armed guards and a small crowd. It is a humiliating experience to watch the fear and disgust on ordinary citizens' faces when they watch a convict go by. My inclination was to duck down and hide, but one could not do that.

I was examined by a young surgeon, who asked if I had ever before injured my heel. In fact, I had when I was at Fort Hare. One afternoon, I was playing soccer when I attempted to steal the ball and felt a searing pain in my heel. I was taken to the local hospital, the first time in my life I had ever been to a hospital or seen a doctor. Where I grew up, there was no such thing as an African doctor, and going to see a white doctor was unheard of.

The Fort Hare doctor had examined my heel and said he would need to operate. The diagnosis alarmed me, and I abruptly told him that I did not want him to touch me. At that stage in my life I regarded seeing a doctor as unmanly, and having any medical procedure seemed even worse. 'Suit yourself,' he said, 'but when you are old this thing will worry you.'

The Cape Town surgeon X-rayed my heel and discovered bone fragments that had probably been there since Fort Hare. He said he could remove them in his surgery with a local anaesthetic. I immediately agreed.

The surgery went well, and when it was over, the doctor was explaining how to care for my heel. He was abruptly interrupted by the head warder, who said that I had to return immediately to Robben Island. The surgeon was incensed by this and in his most authoritative manner said that it was necessary for Mr Mandela to remain in hospital overnight and that he would not release me under any circumstances. The warder was intimidated and acquiesced.

My first night in a proper hospital turned out to be quite pleasant. The nurses fussed over me a good deal. I slept very well, and in the morning a group of nurses came in and said that I should keep the pyjamas and dressing gown I had been given. I thanked them and told them that I would be the envy of all my comrades.

I found the trip instructive in another way because in that hospital I sensed a thawing in the relationship between black and white. The doctor and nurses had treated me in a natural way as though they had been dealing with blacks on a basis of equality all their lives. This was something new and different to me, and an encouraging sign. It reaffirmed my long-held belief that education was the enemy of prejudice. These were men and women of science, and science had no room for racism.

My only regret was that I did not have the opportunity to contact Winnie before I went into hospital. Rumours had appeared in newspapers that I was at death's door, and she had become quite concerned. But when I returned, I wrote to her to dispel her fears.

In 1980 we were granted the right to buy newspapers. This was a victory but, as always, each new privilege contained within it a catch. The new regulation stated that A group prisoners were granted the right to buy one English-language newspaper and one Afrikaans newspaper a day. But the annoying caveat was that any A group prisoner found sharing his newspaper with a non-A group prisoner would lose his newspaper privileges. We protested against this restriction, but to no avail.

We received two daily newspapers: *Cape Times* and *Die Burger*. Both were conservative papers, especially the latter. Yet the prison censors went through each of those newspapers every day with scissors, clipping out articles that they deemed unsafe for us to see. By the time we received them, they were filled with holes. We were soon able to supplement these papers with copies of the *Star*, the *Rand Daily Mail* and the *Sunday Times*, but these papers were even more heavily censored.

One story I was certainly not able to read was in the *Johannesburg Sunday Post* in March 1980. The headline was 'FREE MANDELA!' Inside was a petition that people could sign to ask for my release and that of my fellow political prisoners. While newspapers were still barred from printing my picture or any words I had ever said or written, the *Post*'s campaign ignited a public discussion of our release.

The idea had been conceived in Lusaka by Oliver Tambo and the ANC, and the campaign was the cornerstone of a new strategy that would put our cause in the forefront of people's minds. The ANC had decided to personalize the quest for our release by centring the campaign on a single figure. There is no doubt that the millions of people who subsequently became supporters of this campaign had no idea of precisely who Nelson Mandela was. (I am told that when 'Free Mandela' posters went up in London, most young people thought my Christian name was 'Free'.) There was a handful of dissenting voices on the island who felt that personalizing the campaign was a betrayal of the collectivity of the organization, but most people realized that it was a technique to rouse the people.

The previous year I had been awarded the Jawaharlal Nehru Human Rights Award in India, another piece of evidence of the resurgence of the struggle. I was of course refused permission to attend the ceremony, as was Winnie, but Oliver accepted the award in my absence. We had a sense of a reviving ANC. Umkhonto we Sizwe was stepping up its sabotage campaign, which had become far more sophisticated. In June, MK men set off bombs at the vast Sasolburg refinery just south of Johannesburg. MK was orchestrating an explosion a week at some strategic site or another. Bombs exploded at power stations in the eastern Transvaal, at police stations in Germiston, Daveyton, New Brighton and elsewhere, and at the Voortrekkerhoogte military base outside Pretoria. These were all strategically significant locations, places that would attract attention and worry the state. The defence minister, General Magnus Malan, backed by P. W. Botha, introduced a policy known as 'total onslaught', which was a militarization of the country to combat the liberation struggle.

The Free Mandela campaign had its lighter side as well. In 1981 I learned that the students at the University of London had nominated me as a candidate for the honorific post of university chancellor. This was a wonderful honour, to be sure, and my rivals were none other than Princess Anne and the trade union leader Jack Jones. In the end, I polled 7,199 votes and lost to the daughter of the Queen. I wrote to

Winnie in Brandfort that I hoped the voting might have for a moment turned her humble shack into a castle, making its tiny rooms as grand as the ballroom at Windsor.

The campaign for our release rekindled our hopes. During the harsh days of the early 1970s, when the ANC seemed to sink into the shadows, we had to force ourselves not to give in to despair. In many ways we had miscalculated; we had thought that by the 1970s we would be living in a democratic, non-racial South Africa. Yet as we entered the new decade my hopes for that South Africa rose once again. Some mornings I walked out into the courtyard and every living thing there, the seagulls and wagtails, the small trees, and even the stray blades of grass seemed to smile and shine in the sun. It was at such times, when I perceived the beauty of even this small, closed-in corner of the world, that I knew that some day my people and I would be free.

86

Like my father before me, I had been groomed to be a counsellor to the king of the Thembu. Although I had chosen a different path, I tried in my own fashion to live up to the responsibilities of the role for which I had been schooled. From prison, I did my best to remain in contact with the king and advise him as best I could. As I grew older, my thoughts turned more and more often to the green hills of the Transkei. Although I would never move there under the government's auspices, I dreamed of one day returning to a free Transkei. Thus it was with great dismay that I learned in 1980 that the king, Sabata Dalindyebo, the paramount chief of the Thembu, had been deposed by my nephew, K.D. Matanzima, the prime minister of the Transkei.

A group of Thembu chiefs requested an urgent visit with me, which was approved by the authorities, who were usually willing to countenance visits by traditional leaders – believing that the more involved I was in tribal and Transkei matters, the less committed I would be to the struggle.

The government promoted the power of traditional leaders as a counterpoint to the ANC. While many of my comrades thought we should disclaim those leaders, my inclination was to reach out to them. There is no contradiction between being a traditional leader and a member of the ANC. This spurred one of the longest and most delicate debates we had on the island: whether or not the ANC should participate in government-sponsored institutions. Many of the men considered this collaborationist. Once again, I thought it necessary to draw a distinction between principle and tactics. To me, the critical question was a tactical one: Will our organization emerge stronger through participating in these organizations or by boycotting them? In this case, I thought we would emerge stronger by participating.

I met the chiefs in a large room in the visiting area, and they explained their dilemma. Although their hearts were with Sabata, they feared

Matanzima. After listening to their presentation, I advised them to support Sabata against Matanzima, who was illegally and shamefully usurping power from the king. I sympathized with their situation, but I could not condone Matanzima's actions. I asked them to convey my support to Sabata and my disapproval to Matanzima.

Matanzima had also proposed a visit to discuss Sabata and family matters. As my nephew, he had actually been requesting such a visit for a number of years. Although Matanzima claimed to want to discuss family matters, such a visit would have political consequences. From the moment of Matanzima's first request, I referred the matter to the High Organ and the ANC men in our section. Some simply shrugged their shoulders and said, 'He's your nephew; he has a right to visit.' Raymond, Govan and Kathy, however, insisted that although such a visit could be explained away as a family matter, it would be interpreted by many people inside and outside as a sign of my endorsement of the man and his policies. That was the reason why Matanzima wanted to see me, and the reason such a visit was unacceptable.

I understood and in large part agreed with their arguments, but I wanted to meet my nephew. I have always had perhaps too high a regard for the importance of face-to-face meetings and of my own ability in such a meeting to persuade men to change their views. I was hoping I could convince Matanzima to modify his policies.

Eventually the ANC men in our section decided not to object to a visit. In the interests of democracy, we then consulted with our men in F and G on the matter, and they were adamantly opposed. Steve Tshwete, who was one of the leading ANC figures in the general section, said such a visit would help Matanzima politically and was therefore out of the question. Many of them noted that Matanzima had already tried to coopt my approval by appointing Winnie's father, Columbus Madikizela, the minister of agriculture in his government. This was bad enough, they said, without Madiba agreeing to see him. I bowed to the views of the membership in the general section and regretfully informed the authorities that I would not accept a visit from my nephew.

In March 1982, I was told by the prison authorities that my wife had been in a car accident, and that she was in hospital. They had very little information, and I had no idea of her condition or what her circumstances were. I accused the authorities of holding back information, and made an urgent application for my attorney to visit me. The authorities used information as a weapon, and it was a successful one. I was preoccupied with my wife's health until I was visited on 31 March by Winnie's attorney and my friend Dullah Omar.

Dullah quickly eased my mind about Winnie. She had been in a car that had overturned, but she was all right. Our visit was brief, and as I was led back to section B my mind was still dwelling on Winnie, and I was plagued by the feeling of powerlessness and my inability to help her.

I had not been in my cell long when I was visited by the commanding officer and a number of other prison officials. This was highly unusual; the CO did not generally pay calls on prisoners in their cells. I stood up when they arrived, and the commander actually entered my cell. There was barely room for the two of us.

'Mandela,' he said, 'I want you to pack up your things.'

I asked him why.

'We are transferring you,' he said simply.

Where?

'I cannot say,' he replied.

I demanded to know why. He told me only that he had received instructions from Pretoria that I was to be transferred off the island immediately. The commanding officer left and went in turn to the cells of Walter, Raymond Mhlaba and Andrew Mlangeni and gave them the same order.

I was disturbed and unsettled. What did it mean? Where were we going? In prison, one can only question and resist an order to a certain point, then one must succumb. We had no warning, no preparation. I had been on the island for over eighteen years, and to leave so abruptly?

We were each given several large cardboard boxes in which to pack our things. Everything that I had accumulated in nearly two decades could fit into these few boxes. We packed in little more than half an hour.

There was a commotion in the corridor when the other men learned we were leaving, but we had no time to say a proper good-bye to our comrades of many years. This is another one of the indignities of prison. The bonds of friendship and loyalty with other prisoners count for nothing with the authorities.

Within minutes we were on board the ferry headed for Cape Town. I looked back at the island as the light was fading, not knowing whether I would ever see it again. A man can get used to anything, and I had grown used to Robben Island. I had lived there for almost two decades and while it was never a home – my home was in Johannesburg – it had become a place where I felt comfortable. I have always found change difficult, and leaving Robben Island, however grim it had been at times, was no exception. I had no idea what to look forward to.

At the docks, surrounded by armed guards, we were hustled into a windowless truck. The four of us stood in the dark while the truck drove for what seemed considerably more than an hour. We passed through various checkpoints, and finally came to a stop. The back doors swung open, and in the dark we were marched up some concrete steps and through metal doors into another security facility. I managed to ask a guard where we were.

'Pollsmoor Prison', he said.

PART TEN

————

Talking with the Enemy

87

Pollsmoor maximum security prison is located on the edge of a prosperous white suburb of green lawns and tidy houses called Tokai, a few miles southeast of Cape Town. The prison itself is set amid the strikingly beautiful scenery of the Cape, between the mountains of Constantiaberge to the north and hundreds of acres of vineyards to the south. But this natural beauty was invisible to us behind Pollsmoor's high concrete walls. At Pollsmoor I first understood the truth of Oscar Wilde's haunting line about the tent of blue that prisoners call the sky.

Pollsmoor had a modern face but a primitive heart. The buildings, particularly the ones for the prison staff, were clean and contemporary; but the housing for the prisoners was archaic and dirty. With the exception of ourselves, all men at Pollsmoor were common-law prisoners and their treatment was oppressive. We were kept separately from them and treated differently.

It was not until the next morning that we got a proper sense of our surroundings. The four of us had been given what was in effect the prison's penthouse: a spacious room on the third and topmost floor. We were the only prisoners on the entire floor. The main room was clean, modern and rectangular, about fifty by thirty feet and had a separate section with a toilet, urinal, two basins and two showers. There were four proper beds, with sheets, and towels, a great luxury for men who had spent much of the last eighteen years sleeping on thin mats on a stone floor. Compared with Robben Island, we were in a five-star hotel.

We also had our own L-shaped terrace, an open, outdoor section that was as long as half a soccer field, where we were allowed out during the day. It had white concrete walls about twelve feet high, so that we could see only the sky, except in one corner where we could make out the ridges of the Constantiaberge mountains, in particular a section known as the Elephant's Eye. I sometimes thought of this bit of mountain as the tip of the iceberg of the rest of the world.

It was greatly disorienting to be uprooted so suddenly and without explanation. One must be prepared for precipitate movements in prison, but one does not ever get used to them. Though we were now on the mainland, we felt more isolated. For us, the island had become the locus of the struggle. We took solace in each other's company, and spent those early weeks speculating on why we had been transferred. We knew the authorities had long resented and feared the influence we had on younger prisoners. But the reason seemed to be more strategic: we believed the authorities were attempting to cut off the head of the ANC on the island by removing its leadership. Robben Island itself was becoming a sustaining myth in the struggle, and they wanted to rob it of some of its symbolic import by removing us. Walter, Raymond and I were members of the High Organ, but the one piece that did not fit was the presence of Mlangeni. Andrew was not a member of the High Organ and had not been in the forefront of the island leadership, although we considered the possibility that the authorities did not know this. Their intelligence about the organization was often inexact.

One of our hypotheses seemed to be confirmed a few months later when we were joined by Kathy, who had indeed been a member of the High Organ. More important, Kathy had been our chief of communications, and it was because of his work that we were able to communicate with new young prisoners.

A few weeks after Kathy arrived, we were also joined by a man we did not know who had not even come from Robben Island. Patrick Maqubela was a young lawyer and ANC member from the eastern Cape. He had been articled to Griffiths Mxenge, a highly respected attorney who had appeared for many detained ANC men and who had been assassinated near Durban the year before. Maqubela was serving a twenty-year sentence for treason and had been transferred to Pollsmoor from Diepkloof in Johannesburg, where he had made waves by organizing prisoners.

At first, we were sceptical about this new arrival, and wondered if he could perhaps be a security plant by the authorities. But we soon saw that this was not the case. Patrick was a bright, amiable, undaunted fellow with whom we got along very well. It could not have been easy for him bunking in with a group of old men set in their ways who had been together for the previous two decades.

We were now in a world of concrete. I missed the natural splendour of Robben Island. But our new home had many consolations. For one thing, the food at Pollsmoor was far superior; after years of eating pap three meals a day, Pollsmoor's dinners of proper meat and vegetables were like a feast. We were permitted a fairly wide range of newspapers and magazines, and could receive such previously contraband publications as *Time* magazine and the *Guardian Weekly* from London. This gave us a window on the wider world. We also had a radio, but one that received only local stations and not what we really wanted: the BBC World Service. We were allowed out on our terrace all day long, except between twelve and two when the warders had their lunch. There was not even a pretence that we had to work. I had a small cell near our large one that functioned as a study, with a chair, desk and bookshelves, where I could read and write during the day.

On Robben Island I would do my exercises in my own cramped cell, but now I had room to stretch out. At Pollsmoor I would wake up at five and do an hour and a half of exercise in our communal cell. I followed my usual regimen of stationary running, skipping, sit-ups, fingertip press-ups. My comrades were not early risers and my programme soon made me a very unpopular fellow in our cell.

I was visited by Winnie shortly after arriving at Pollsmoor and was pleased to find that the visiting area was far better and more modern than the one on Robben Island. We had a large glass barrier through which one could see the visitor from the waist up and far more sophisticated microphones so that we did not have to strain to hear. The window gave at least the illusion of greater intimacy, and in prison, illusions can offer comfort.

It was far easier for my wife and family to get to Pollsmoor than to Robben Island, and this made a tremendous difference. The supervision of visits also became more humane. Often, Winnie's visits were overseen by Warrant Officer James Gregory, who had been a censor on Robben Island. I had not known him terribly well, but he knew us, because he had been responsible for reviewing our incoming and outgoing mail.

At Pollsmoor I got to know Gregory better and found him a welcome contrast to the typical warder. He was polished and soft-spoken, and treated Winnie with courtesy and deference. Instead of barking, 'Time up!' he would say, 'Mrs Mandela, you have five more minutes.'

The Bible tells us that gardens preceded gardeners, but that was not the case at Pollsmoor, where I cultivated a garden that became one of my happiest diversions. It was my way of escaping from the monolithic concrete world that surrounded us. Within a few weeks of surveying all the empty space we had on the building's roof and how it was bathed in sun the whole day, I decided to start a garden and received permission to do so from the commanding officer. I requested that the prison service supply me with sixteen forty-four-gallon oil drums that they sliced in half for me. The authorities then filled each half with rich, moist soil, creating in effect thirty-two giant flowerpots.

I grew onions, aubergines, cabbage, cauliflower, beans, spinach, carrots, cucumbers, broccoli, beetroot, lettuce, tomatoes, peppers, strawberries, and much more. At its height, I had a small farm with nearly nine hundred plants; a garden far grander than the one I had on Robben Island.

Some of the seeds I purchased and some – for example, broccoli and carrots – were given to me by the commanding officer, Brigadier Munro, who was particularly fond of these vegetables. Warders also gave me seeds of vegetables they liked, and I was supplied with excellent manure to use as fertilizer.

Each morning, I put on a straw hat and rough gloves and worked in the garden for two hours. Every Sunday I would supply vegetables to the kitchen so that they could cook a special meal for the common-law prisoners. I also gave quite a lot of my harvest to the warders, who used to bring satchels to take away their fresh vegetables.

At Pollsmoor, our problems tended to be less consequential than those we experienced on Robben Island. Brigadier Munro was a decent, helpful man, who took extra pains to make sure we had what we wanted. Nevertheless, small problems sometimes got blown up out of proportion. In 1983, during a visit from Winnie and Zindzi, I mentioned to my wife that I had been given shoes that were a size too small and were pinching my toe. Winnie was concerned, and I soon learned that there were press reports that I was having a toe amputated. Because of the difficulty of communication, information from prison often becomes exaggerated in the outside world. If I had simply been able to telephone my wife and tell her that my foot was fine, such confusion would not have happened. A short while later, Helen Suzman was permitted to visit, and she inquired about my toe. I thought the best answer was a demonstration: I took off my socks, held my bare foot up to the glass, and wiggled my toes.

We complained about the dampness in our cell, which was causing us to catch colds. Later, I heard reports that South African newspapers were writing that our cell was flooded. We asked for contact with other prisoners, and in general made the same basic complaint that we always had: to be treated as political prisoners.

In May 1984, I found some consolation that seemed to make up for all the discomforts. On a scheduled visit from Winnie, Zeni and her youngest daughter, I was escorted by Warrant Officer Gregory who, instead of taking me to the normal visiting area, ushered me into a separate room where there was only a small table, and no dividers of any kind. He very softly said to me that the authorities had made a change. That day was the beginning of what were known as 'contact' visits.

He then went outside to see my wife and daughter and asked to speak to Winnie privately. Winnie actually got a fright when Gregory took her aside, thinking that I was perhaps ill. But Gregory escorted her around the door and before either of us knew it, we were in the same room and in each other's arms. I kissed and held my wife for the first time in all these many years. It was a moment I had dreamed about a thousand times. It was as if I were still dreaming. I held her to me for what seemed like an eternity. We were still and silent except for the sound of our hearts. I did not want to let go of her at all, but I broke free and embraced my daughter and then took her child onto my lap. It had been twenty-one years since I had even touched my wife's hand.

88

At Pollsmoor, we were more connected to outside events. We were aware that the struggle was intensifying, and that the efforts of the enemy were similarly increasing. In 1981, the South African Defence Force launched a raid on ANC offices in Maputo, Mozambique, killing thirteen of our people, including women and children. In December 1982, MK set off explosions at the unfinished Koeberg nuclear power plant outside Cape Town and placed bombs at many other military and apartheid targets around the country. That same month, the South African military again attacked an ANC outpost in Maseru, Lesotho, killing forty-two people, including a dozen women and children.

In August 1982 the activist Ruth First was opening her post in Maputo, where she was living in exile, when she was murdered by a letter bomb. Ruth, the wife of Joe Slovo, was a brave anti-apartheid activist who had spent a number of months in prison. She was a forceful, engaging woman whom I first met when I was studying at Wits, and her death revealed the extent of the state's cruelty in combating our struggle.

MK's first car bomb attack took place in May 1983, and was aimed at an air force and military intelligence office in the heart of Pretoria. This was an effort to retaliate for the unprovoked attacks the military had launched on the ANC in Maseru and elsewhere and was a clear escalation of the armed struggle. Nineteen people were killed and more than two hundred injured.

The killing of civilians was a tragic accident, and I felt a profound horror at the death toll. But disturbed as I was by these casualties, I knew that such accidents were the inevitable consequence of the decision to embark on a military struggle. Human fallibility is always a part of war, and the price of it is always high. It was precisely because we knew that such incidents would occur that our decision to take up arms had been so grave and reluctant. But as Oliver said at the time of the bombing, the armed struggle was imposed upon us by the violence of the apartheid regime.

Both the government and the ANC were working on two tracks: military and political. On the political front, the government was pursuing its standard divide-and-rule strategy in attempting to separate Africans from Coloureds and Indians. In a referendum in November 1983, the white electorate endorsed P.W. Botha's plan to create a so-called tricameral Parliament, with Indian and Coloured chambers in addition to the white Parliament. This was an effort to lure Indians and Coloureds into the system, and divide them from Africans. But the offer was merely a 'toy telephone', as all parliamentary action by Indians and Coloureds was subject to a white veto. It was also a way of fooling the outside world into thinking that the government was reforming apartheid. Botha's ruse did not deceive the people, as more than 80 per cent of eligible Indian and Coloured voters boycotted the election to the new houses of Parliament in 1984.

Powerful grassroots political movements were being formed inside the country that had firm links to the ANC, the principal one being the United Democratic Front, of which I was named a patron. The UDF had been created to coordinate protest against the new apartheid constitution in 1983, and the first elections to the segregated tricameral Parliament in 1984. The UDF soon blossomed into a powerful organization that united over six hundred anti-apartheid organizations – trade unions, community groups, church groups, student associations.

The ANC was experiencing a new birth of popularity. Opinion polls showed that the Congress was far and away the most popular political organization among Africans even though it had been banned for a quarter of a century. The anti-apartheid struggle as a whole had captured the attention of the world; in 1984 Bishop Desmond Tutu was awarded the Nobel Peace Prize. (The authorities refused to send Bishop Tutu my letter of congratulations.) The South African government was under growing international pressure, as nations all across the globe began to impose economic sanctions on Pretoria.

The government had sent 'feelers' to me over the years, beginning with Minister Kruger's efforts to persuade me to move to the Transkei. These were not efforts to negotiate, but attempts to isolate me from my organization. On several other occasions, Kruger said to me: 'Mandela, we can work with you, but not your colleagues. Be reasonable.' Although I did not respond to these overtures, the mere fact that they were talking rather than attacking could be seen as a prelude to genuine negotiations.

The government was testing the waters. In late 1984 and early 1985 I had visits from two prominent Western statesmen, Lord Nicholas Bethell, a member of the British House of Lords and the European Parliament,

and Samuel Dash, a professor of law at Georgetown University and a
former counsel to the US Senate Watergate Committee. Both visits were
authorized by the new minister of justice, Kobie Coetsee, who appeared
to be a new sort of Afrikaner leader.

I met Lord Bethell in the prison commander's office, which was
dominated by a large photograph of a glowering President Botha.
Bethell was a jovial, rotund man and when I first met him, I teased
him about his stoutness. 'You look as though you are related to Winston
Churchill,' I said as we shook hands, and he laughed.

Lord Bethell wanted to know about our conditions at Pollsmoor and
I told him. We discussed the armed struggle and I explained to him it
was not up to us to renounce violence, but the government. I reaffirmed
that we aimed for hard military targets, not people. 'I would not want
our men to assassinate, for instance, the major here,' I said, pointing
to Major Fritz van Sittert, who was monitoring the talks. Van Sittert
was a good-natured fellow who did not say much, but he started at my
remark.

In my visit from Professor Dash, which quickly followed that of Lord
Bethell, I laid out what I saw as the minimum for a future non-racial
South Africa: a unitary state without homelands, non-racial elections
for the central Parliament and one-person one-vote. Professor Dash
asked me whether I took any encouragement from the government's
stated intention of repealing the mixed-marriage laws and certain other
apartheid statutes. 'This is a pinprick,' I said. 'It is not my ambition to
marry a white woman or swim in a white pool. It is political equality
that we want.' I told Dash quite candidly that at the moment we could
not defeat the government on the battlefield, but could make governing
difficult for them.

I had one not-so-pleasant visit from two Americans, editors of the
conservative newspaper the *Washington Times*. They seemed less intent
on finding out my views than on proving that I was a communist and
a terrorist. All their questions were slanted in that direction, and when I
reiterated that I was neither a communist nor a terrorist, they attempted
to show that I was not a Christian either by asserting that the Reverend
Martin Luther King never resorted to violence. I told them that the
conditions in which Martin Luther King struggled were totally different
from my own: the United States was a democracy with constitutional
guarantees of equal rights that protected non-violent protest (though there
was still prejudice against blacks); South Africa was a police state with
a constitution that enshrined inequality and an army that responded to
non-violence with force. I told them that I was a Christian and had always
been a Christian. Even Christ, I said, when he was left with no alternative,

used force to expel the moneylenders from the temple. He was not a man of violence, but had no choice but to use force against evil. I do not think I persuaded them.

Faced with trouble at home and pressure from abroad, P. W. Botha offered a tepid, halfway measure. On 31 January 1985, in a debate in Parliament, the state president publicly offered me my freedom if I 'unconditionally rejected violence as a political instrument'. This offer was extended to all political prisoners. Then, as though he were staking me to a public challenge, he added, 'It is therefore not the South African government which now stands in the way of Mr Mandela's freedom. It is he himself.'

I had been warned by the authorities that the government was going to make a proposal involving my freedom, but I had not been prepared for the fact that it would be made in Parliament by the state president. By my reckoning, it was the sixth conditional offer the government had made for my release in the past ten years. After I listened to the speech on the radio, I made a request to the commander of the prison for an urgent visit by my wife and my lawyer, Ismail Ayob, so that I could dictate my response to the state president's offer.

Winnie and Ismail were not given permission to visit for a week, and in the meantime I wrote a letter to the foreign minister, Pik Botha, rejecting the conditions for my release, while also preparing a public response. I was keen to do a number of things in this response, because Botha's offer was an attempt to drive a wedge between me and my colleagues by tempting me to accept a policy the ANC rejected. I wanted to reassure the ANC in general and Oliver Tambo in particular that my loyalty to the organization was beyond question. I also wished to send a message to the government that while I rejected its offer because of the conditions attached to it, I nevertheless thought negotiation, not war, was the path to a solution.

Botha wanted the onus of violence to rest on my shoulders and I wanted to reaffirm to the world that we were only responding to the violence done to us. I intended to make it clear that if I emerged from prison into the same circumstances under which I was arrested, I would be forced to resume the same activities for which I was arrested.

I met Winnie and Ismail on a Friday; on Sunday, a UDF rally was to be held in Soweto's Jabulani Stadium, where my response would be made public. Some guards with whom I was not familiar supervised the visit, and as we began discussing my response to the state president, one of the warders, a relatively young fellow, interrupted to say that only family matters were permitted to be discussed. I ignored him, and he returned minutes later with a senior warder whom I barely knew. This warder said that I must cease discussing politics, and I told him that I was dealing with a matter of national importance involving an offer from the state president. I warned him that if he wanted to halt the discussion he must get direct orders from the state president himself. 'If you are not willing to telephone the state president to get those orders,' I said coldly, 'then kindly do not interrupt us again.' He did not.

I gave Ismail and Winnie the speech I had prepared. In addition to responding to the government, I wanted to thank publicly the UDF for its fine work and to congratulate Archbishop Tutu on his prize, adding that his award belonged to all the people. On Sunday 10 February 1985, my daughter Zindzi read my response to a cheering crowd of people who had not been able to hear my words legally anywhere in South Africa for more than twenty years.

Zindzi was a dynamic speaker like her mother, and said that her father should be at the stadium to speak the words himself. I was proud to know that it was she who spoke my words.

I am a member of the African National Congress. I have always been a member of the African National Congress and I will remain a member of the African National Congress until the day I die. Oliver Tambo is more than a brother to me. He is my greatest friend and comrade for nearly fifty years. If there is any one amongst you who cherishes my freedom, Oliver Tambo cherishes it more, and I know that he would give his life to see me free . . .

I am surprised at the conditions that the government wants to impose on me. I am not a violent man . . . It was only then, when all other forms of resistance were no longer open to us, that we turned to armed struggle. Let Botha show that he is different to Malan, Strijdom and Verwoerd. Let him renounce violence. Let him say that he will dismantle apartheid. Let him unban the people's organization, the African National Congress. Let him free all who have been imprisoned, banished or exiled for their opposition to apartheid. Let him guarantee free political activity so that people may decide who will govern them.

I cherish my own freedom dearly, but I care even more for your freedom. Too many have died since I went to prison. Too many have suffered for the love of freedom. I owe it to their widows, to their orphans, to their mothers and to their fathers who have grieved and wept for them. Not only I have suffered during these long, lonely, wasted years. I am not less life-loving than you are. But

I cannot sell my birthright, nor am I prepared to sell the birthright of the people to be free . . .

What freedom am I being offered while the organization of the people remains banned? What freedom am I being offered when I may be arrested on a pass offence? What freedom am I being offered to live my life as a family with my dear wife who remains in banishment in Brandfort? What freedom am I being offered when I must ask for permission to live in an urban area? . . . What freedom am I being offered when my very South African citizenship is not respected?

Only free men can negotiate. Prisoners cannot enter into contracts . . . I cannot and will not give any undertaking at a time when I and you, the people, are not free. Your freedom and mine cannot be separated. I will return.

89

In 1985 after a routine medical examination from the prison doctor, I was referred to a urologist, who diagnosed an enlarged prostate gland and recommended surgery. He said the procedure was routine. I consulted with my family and decided to go ahead with the operation.

I was taken to Volks Hospital in Cape Town under heavy security. Winnie flew down and was able to see me prior to the surgery. But I had another visitor, a surprising and unexpected one: Kobie Coetsee, the minister of justice. Not long before, I had written to Coetsee pressing him for a meeting to discuss talks between the ANC and the government. He did not respond. But that morning, he dropped by the hospital unannounced as if he were visiting an old friend who was laid up for a few days. He was altogether gracious and cordial, and for the most part we simply made pleasantries. Though I acted as though this was the most normal thing in the world, I was amazed. The government, in its slow and tentative way, was reckoning that they had to come to some accommodation with the ANC. Coetsee's visit was an olive branch.

Although we did not discuss politics, I did bring up one sensitive issue, and that was the status of my wife. In August, shortly before I entered hospital, Winnie had gone to Johannesburg to receive medical treatment. The only trips she was permitted from Brandfort was to visit either me or her doctor. While in Johannesburg, her house in Brandfort and the clinic behind it were firebombed and destroyed. Winnie had no place in which to reside, and she decided to remain in Johannesburg despite the fact that the city was off-limits to her. Nothing happened for a few weeks, and then the security police wrote to inform her that the house in Brandfort had been repaired and she must return. But she refused to do so. I asked Coetsee to allow Winnie to remain in Johannesburg and not force her to return to Brandfort. He said he could promise nothing, but he would indeed look into it. I thanked him.

I spent several days in hospital recuperating from the surgery. When I was discharged, I was collected from the hospital by Brigadier Munro. Commanding officers do not usually pick up prisoners from hospitals, so my suspicions were immediately aroused.

On the ride back, Brigadier Munro said to me in a casual way, as though he were simply making conversation, 'Mandela, we are not taking you back to your friends now.' I asked him what he meant. 'From now on, you are going to be alone.' I asked him why. He shook his head. 'I don't know. I've just been given these instructions from headquarters.' Once again, there was no warning and no explanation.

Upon my return to Pollsmoor I was taken to a new cell on the ground floor of the prison, three floors below and in an entirely different wing. I was given three rooms and a separate toilet, with one room to be used for sleeping, one across the hall for studying, and another for exercise. By prison standards, this was palatial, but the rooms were damp and musty and received very little natural light. I said nothing to the brigadier, for I knew the decision had not been his. I wanted time to consider the implications of the move. Why had the state taken this step?

It would be too strong to call it a revelation, but over the next few days and weeks I came to a realization about my new circumstances. The change, I decided, was not a liability but an opportunity. I was not happy to be separated from my colleagues and I missed my garden and the sunny terrace on the third floor. But my solitude gave me a certain liberty, and I resolved to use it to do something I had been pondering for a long while: begin discussions with the government. I had concluded that the time had come when the struggle could best be pushed forward through negotiations. If we did not start a dialogue soon, both sides would soon be plunged into a dark night of oppression, violence and war. My solitude would give me an opportunity to take the first steps in that direction, without the kind of scrutiny that might destroy such efforts.

We had been fighting against white minority rule for three-quarters of a century. We had been engaged in the armed struggle for more than two decades. Many people on both sides had already died. The enemy was strong and resolute. Yet even with all their bombers and tanks, they must have sensed they were on the wrong side of history. We had right on our side, but not yet might. It was clear to me that a military victory was a distant if not impossible dream. It simply did not make sense for both sides to lose thousands if not millions of lives in a conflict that was unnecessary. They must have known this as well. It was time to talk.

This would be extremely sensitive. Both sides regarded discussions as a sign of weakness and betrayal. Neither would come to the table until the other made significant concessions. The government asserted over and over that we were a terrorist organization of communists, and that they would never talk to terrorists or communists. This was National Party dogma. The ANC asserted over and over that the government were fascistic and racist and that there was nothing to talk about until they unbanned the ANC, unconditionally released all political prisoners and removed the troops from the townships.

A decision to talk to the government was of such importance that it should only have been made in Lusaka. But I felt that the process needed to begin, and I had neither the time nor the means to communicate fully with Oliver. Someone from our side needed to take the first step, and my new isolation gave me both the freedom to do so and the assurance, at least for a while, of the confidentiality of my efforts.

I was now in a kind of splendid isolation. Though my colleagues were only three floors above me, they might as well have been in Johannesburg. In order to see them, I had to put in a formal request for a visit, which had to be approved by the head office in Pretoria. It often took weeks to receive a response. If it was approved, I would then meet them in the visiting area. This was a novel experience: my comrades and fellow prisoners were now official visitors. For years we had been able to talk for hours a day, now we had to make official requests and appointments, and our conversations were monitored.

After I had been in my new cell for a few days, I asked the commanding officer to arrange such a meeting. He did so, and the four of us discussed the issue of my transfer. Walter, Kathy and Ray were angry that we had been separated. They wanted to lodge a strong protest, and demand that we be reunited. My response was not what they expected. 'Look, chaps,' I said, 'I don't think we should oppose this thing.' I mentioned that my new accommodation was superior, and maybe this would set a precedent for all political prisoners. I then added somewhat ambiguously, 'Perhaps something good will come of this. I'm now in a position where the government can make an approach to us.' They did not care too much for this latter explanation, as I knew they would not.

I chose to tell no one what I was about to do. Not my colleagues upstairs nor those in Lusaka. The ANC is a collective, but the government had made collectivity in this case impossible. I did not have the security or the time to discuss these issues with my organization. I knew that my colleagues upstairs would condemn my proposal, and that would kill my initiative even before it was born. There are times when a leader must move out ahead of the flock, go off in a new direction, confident that he is leading his people the right way. Finally, my isolation furnished my organization with an excuse in case matters went awry: the old man was alone and completely cut off, and his actions were taken by him as an individual, not a representative of the ANC.

90

Within a few weeks of my move, I wrote to Kobie Coetsee to propose talks about talks. As before, I received no response. I wrote once more, and again there was no response. I found this peculiar and demoralizing, and I realized I had to look for another opportunity to be heard. That came in early 1986.

At a meeting of the British Commonwealth in Nassau in October 1985, the leaders could not reach agreement on whether to participate in international sanctions against South Africa. This was mainly because British Prime Minister Margaret Thatcher was adamantly opposed. To resolve the deadlock, the assembled nations agreed that a delegation of 'eminent persons' would visit South Africa and report back on whether sanctions were the appropriate tool to help bring about the end of apartheid. In early 1986 the seven-member Eminent Persons Group, led by General Olusegun Obasanjo, the former military leader of Nigeria, and the former Australian Prime Minister Malcolm Fraser, arrived in South Africa on their fact-finding mission.

In February, I was visited by General Obasanjo to discuss the nature of the delegation's brief. He was eager to facilitate a meeting between me and the full group. With the government's permission, such a meeting was scheduled for May. The group would be talking with the cabinet after they had seen me, and I viewed this as a chance to raise the subject of negotiations.

The government regarded my session with the group as something extraordinary. Two days before the meeting I was visited by Brigadier Munro, who had brought along a tailor. 'Mandela,' the commander said, 'we want you to see these people on an equal footing. We don't want you to wear those old prison clothes, so this tailor will take your measurements and outfit you with a proper suit.' The tailor must have been some kind of wizard, for the very next day I tried on a pinstriped suit that fitted me like a glove. I was also given a shirt, tie, shoes, socks and underwear. The commander admired my new attire.

'Mandela, you look like a prime minister now, not a prisoner,' he said and smiled.

At the meeting between me and the Eminent Persons Group, we were joined by two significant observers: Kobie Coetsee, and Lieutenant General W. H. Willemse, the commissioner of prisons. Like the tailor, these two men were there to take my measure. But, curiously, they left shortly after the session started. I pressed them to remain, saying I had nothing to hide, but they left anyway. Before they took their leave, I told them the time had come for negotiations, not fighting, and that the government and the ANC should sit down and talk.

The Eminent Persons Group had come with many questions involving the issues of violence, negotiations and international sanctions. At the outset, I set the ground rules for our discussions. 'I am not the head of the movement,' I told them. 'The head of the movement is Oliver Tambo in Lusaka. You must go and see him. You can tell him what my views are, but they are my personal views alone. They don't even represent the views of my colleagues here in prison. All that being said, I favour the ANC beginning discussions with the government.'

Various members of the group had concerns about my political ideology and what a South Africa under ANC leadership might look like. I told them I was a South African nationalist, not a communist, that nationalists came in every hue and colour, and that I was firmly committed to a non-racial society. I told them I believed in the Freedom Charter, that the charter embodied principles of democracy and human rights, and that it was not a blueprint for socialism. I spoke of my concern that the white minority should feel a sense of security in any new South Africa. I told them I thought many of our problems were a result of lack of communication between the government and the ANC, and that some of these could be resolved through actual talks.

They questioned me extensively on the issue of violence, and while I was not yet willing to renounce violence, I affirmed in the strongest possible terms that violence could never be the ultimate solution to the situation in South Africa and that men and women by their very nature required some kind of negotiated understanding. While I once again reiterated that these were my views and not those of the ANC, I suggested that if the government withdrew the army and the police from the townships, the ANC might agree to a suspension of the armed struggle as a prelude to talks. I told them that my release alone would not stem the violence in the country or stimulate negotiations.

After the group had finished with me, they planned to see both Oliver in Lusaka and government officials in Pretoria. In my remarks, I had sent messages to both places. I wanted the government to see that under the right circumstances we would talk, and I wanted Oliver to know that my position and his were the same.

In May, the Eminent Persons Group was scheduled to see me one last time. I was optimistic, as they had been to both Lusaka and Pretoria, and I hoped that the seed of negotiations had been sown. But the day before we were to meet, the South African government took a step that sabotaged whatever goodwill had been engendered by the Commonwealth visitors. On the day the Eminent Persons Group was scheduled to meet cabinet ministers, the South African Defence Force, under the orders of President Botha, launched air raid and commando attacks on ANC bases in Botswana, Zambia and Zimbabwe. This utterly poisoned the talks, and the Eminent Persons Group immediately left South Africa. Once again, I felt my efforts to move negotiations forward had stalled.

Oliver Tambo and the ANC had called for the people of South Africa to render the country ungovernable, and the people were obliging. The state of unrest and political violence was reaching new heights. The anger of the masses was unrestrained; the townships were in upheaval. International pressure was growing stronger every day. On 12 June 1986 the government imposed a State of Emergency in an attempt to keep a lid on protest. In every outward way, the time seemed inauspicious for negotiations. But often, the most discouraging moments are precisely the time to launch an initiative. At such times people are searching for a way out of their dilemma. That month I wrote a very simple letter to General Willemse, the commissioner of prisons, saying merely, 'I wish to see you on a matter of national importance.' I handed the letter to Brigadier Munro on a Wednesday.

That weekend, I was told by the commanding officer to be prepared to see General Willemse, who was coming down from Pretoria. This meeting was not treated in the usual fashion. Instead of conferring with the general in the visiting area, I was taken to his residence in the grounds of Pollsmoor itself.

Willemse is a direct fellow and we got down to business immediately. I told him I wanted to see Kobie Coetsee, the minister of justice. He asked me why. I hesitated for a moment, reluctant to discuss political matters with a prison official. But I responded with frankness: 'I want to see the minister in order to raise the question of talks between the government and the ANC.'

He pondered this for a moment, and then said, 'Mandela, as you know, I am not a politician. I cannot discuss such issues myself, for they are beyond my authority.' He then paused, as if something had just occurred to him. 'It just so happens,' he said, 'that the minister of justice is in Cape Town. Perhaps you can see him. I will find out.'

The general then telephoned the minister and the two spoke for a few moments. After putting down the phone, the general turned to me and said, 'The minister said, "Bring him round."' Minutes later, we left the general's residence in his car bound for the minister's house in Cape Town. Security was light; only one other car accompanied the general's vehicle. The ease and rapidity with which this meeting was set up made me suspect that the government might have planned this rendezvous in advance. Whether they had or not was immaterial; it was an opportunity to take the first step towards negotiations.

At his official residence in the city, Coetsee greeted me warmly and we settled down on comfortable chairs in his lounge. He apologized that I had not had a chance to change out of my prison clothes. I spent three hours in conversation with him and was struck by his sophistication and willingness to listen. He asked knowledgeable and relevant questions – questions that reflected a familiarity with the issues that divided the government and the ANC. He asked me under what circumstances we would suspend the armed struggle; whether or not I spoke for the ANC as a whole; whether I envisioned any constitutional guarantees for minorities in a new South Africa. His questions went to the heart of the issues dividing the government and the ANC.

After responding in much the same way as I did to the Eminent Persons Group, I sensed that Coetsee wanted some resolution. 'What is the next step?' he asked. I told him I wanted to see the state president and the foreign minister, Pik Botha. Coetsee noted this on a small pad he had kept beside him, and said he would send my request through the proper channels. We then shook hands, and I was driven back to my solitary cell on the ground floor of Pollsmoor prison.

I was greatly encouraged. I sensed the government was anxious to overcome the impasse in the country, that they were now convinced they had to depart from their old positions. In ghostly outline, I saw the beginnings of a compromise.

I told no one of my encounter. I wanted the process to be under way before I informed anyone. Sometimes it is necessary to present one's colleagues with a policy that is already a *fait accompli*. I knew that once they examined the situation carefully, my colleagues at Pollsmoor and in Lusaka would support me. But again, after this promising start, nothing happened. Weeks and then months passed without a word from Coetsee. In some frustration, I wrote him another letter.

91

Although I did not get a direct response from Kobie Coetsee, there were other signs that the government was preparing me for a different kind of existence. On the day before Christmas, Lieutenant Colonel Gawie Marx, the deputy commander of Pollsmoor, wandered by my cell after breakfast and said quite casually, 'Mandela, would you like to see the city?' I was not exactly certain what he had in mind, but I thought there was no harm in saying yes. Good, he said, come along. I walked with the colonel through the fifteen locked metal doors between my cell and the entrance, and when we emerged, I found his car waiting for us.

We drove into Cape Town along the lovely road that runs parallel to the coast. He had no destination in mind and we simply meandered around the city in a leisurely fashion. It was absolutely riveting to watch the simple activities of people out in the world: old men sitting in the sun, women doing their shopping, people walking their dogs. It is precisely those mundane activities of daily life that one misses most in prison. I felt like a curious tourist in a strange and remarkable land.

After an hour or so, Colonel Marx stopped the car in front of a small shop in a quiet street. 'Would you like a cold drink?' he asked. I nodded, and he disappeared inside the shop. I sat there alone. For the first few moments, I did not think about my situation, but as the seconds ticked away, I became more and more agitated. For the first time in twenty-two years, I was out in the world and unguarded. I had a vision of opening the door, jumping out, and then running and running until I was out of sight. Something inside was urging me to do just that. I noticed a wooded area near the road where I could hide. I was extremely tense and began to perspire. Where was the colonel? But then I took control of myself; such an action would be unwise and irresponsible, not to mention dangerous. It was possible that the whole situation was contrived to try to get me to escape, though I do not think that was the case. I was greatly relieved a few moments later when I saw the colonel walking back to the car with two cans of Coca-Cola.

As it turned out, that day in Cape Town was the first of many excursions. Over the next few months, I went out again with the colonel not only to Cape Town but to some of the sights around the city, its beautiful beaches and lovely cool mountains. Soon, more junior officers were permitted to take me around. One of the places I regularly visited with these junior officers was known as the 'gardens', a series of smallholdings on the edge of the prison grounds where crops were grown for the prison kitchen. I enjoyed being out in nature, being able to see the horizon and feel the sun on my shoulders.

One day I went to the gardens with a captain, and after walking in the fields we strolled over to the stables. There were two young white men in overalls working with the horses. I walked over to them, praised one of the animals, and said to the fellow, 'Now, what is this horse's name?' The young man seemed quite nervous and did not look at me. He then mumbled the name of the horse, but to the captain, not to me. I then asked the other fellow in turn what the name of his horse was, and he had precisely the same reaction.

As I was walking back to the prison with the captain, I commented on what I thought was the curious behaviour of the two young men. The captain laughed. 'Mandela, don't you know what those two chaps were?' I said I did not. 'They were white prisoners. They had never been questioned by a native prisoner in the presence of a white officer before.'

Some of the younger warders took me quite far afield, and we would walk on the beach and even stop at a café and have tea. At such places I often tried to see if people recognized me, but no one ever did; the last published picture of me had been taken in 1962.

These trips were instructive on a number of levels. I saw how life had changed in the time I had been away, and because we mainly went to white areas, I saw the extraordinary wealth and ease that whites enjoyed. Though the country was in upheaval and the townships were on the brink of open warfare, white life went on placidly and undisturbed. Their lives were unaffected. Once, one of the warders, a very pleasant young man named Warrant Officer Brand, actually took me to his family's flat and introduced me to his wife and children. From then on, I sent his children Christmas cards every year.

Much as I enjoyed these little adventures, I well knew that the authorities had a motive other than keeping me diverted. I sensed that they wanted to acclimatize me to life in South Africa and perhaps at the same time, get me so used to the pleasures of small freedoms that I might be willing to compromise in order to have complete freedom.

92

In 1987 I resumed contact with Kobie Coetsee. I had several private meetings with him at his residence, and later that year the government made its first concrete proposal. Coetsee said the government would like to appoint a committee of senior officials to conduct private discussions with me. This would be done with the full knowledge of the state president, Coetsee said. He himself would be head of the committee, and it would include General Willemse, the commissioner of prisons, Fanie van der Merwe, director general of the Prisons Department and Dr Niel Barnard, a former academic who was then head of the National Intelligence Service. The first three individuals were associated with the prison system, so if talks foundered or were leaked to the press, both sides would be able to cover up and say we were discussing prison conditions and nothing more.

The presence of Dr Barnard, however, disturbed me. He was the head of South Africa's equivalent of the CIA, and was also involved with military intelligence. I could justify to my organization discussions with the other officials, but not Barnard. His presence made the talks more problematic and suggested a larger agenda. I told Coetsee that I would like to think about the proposal overnight.

That night I considered all the ramifications. I knew that P. W. Botha had created something called the State Security Council, a shadowy secretariat of security experts and intelligence officials. He had done this, according to the press, to circumvent the authority of the cabinet and increase his own power. Dr Barnard was a key player in this inner council and was said to be a protégé of the president. I thought that my refusing Barnard would alienate Botha, and decided that such a tack was too risky. If the state president was not brought on board, nothing would happen. In the morning, I sent word to Coetsee that I accepted his offer.

I knew that I had three crucial matters that I needed to address: first, I wanted to sound out my colleagues on the third floor before

I proceeded any further, second, it was essential to communicate with Oliver in Lusaka about what was taking place and, finally, I intended to draft a memorandum to P. W. Botha laying out my views and those of the ANC on the vital issues before the country. This memorandum would create talking points for any future discussion.

I requested a meeting with my colleagues, and to my surprise, the authorities summarily refused. This was remarkable, and I assumed it reflected a great deal of nervousness about the prospect of secret talks between myself and the government. I took my complaints to more senior officials. Finally the request was approved, with the proviso that I could see my colleagues one by one, not together.

I met them in the visiting area. I had resolved to leave out a few details; I would seek their counsel about the idea of having talks with the government without mentioning that an actual committee had been formed. Walter was first. I told him about my letter to the commissioner of prisons and my meeting with Coetsee. I said that I had discussed with Coetsee the idea of beginning talks with the government and that the government seemed interested. What were his views on the matter?

I have been through thick and thin with Walter. He was a man of reason and wisdom, and no man knew me better than he did. There was no one whose opinion I trusted or valued more. Walter considered what I told him. I could see he was uncomfortable and, at best, lukewarm. 'In principle,' he said, 'I am not against negotiations. But I would have wished that the government initiated talks with us rather than our initiating talks with them.'

I replied that if he was not against negotiations in principle, what did it matter who initiated them? What mattered was what they achieved, not how they started. I told Walter that I thought we should move forward with negotiations and not worry about who knocked on the door first. Walter saw that my mind was made up and he said he would not stop me, but that he hoped I knew what I was doing.

Next was Raymond Mhlaba. I explained the entire situation to him as I had to Walter. Ray was always a man of few words, and for several moments he digested what I had said. He then looked at me and said, 'Madiba, what have you been waiting for? We should have started this years ago.' Andrew Mlangeni's reaction was virtually the same as Ray's. The last man was Kathy. His response was negative; he was as resolutely against what I was suggesting as Raymond and Andrew were in favour. Even more strongly than Walter, he felt that by initiating talks it would appear that we were capitulating. Like Walter, he said he was not against negotiations in principle, and I responded exactly as I had with Walter. But Kathy was adamant; he felt I was going down the wrong path. But, despite his misgivings, he said he would not stand in my way.

Not long after this I received a note from Oliver Tambo that was smuggled to me by one of my lawyers. He had heard reports that I was having secret discussions with the government and he was concerned. He said he knew I had been alone for some time and separated from my colleagues. He must have been wondering: what is going on with Mandela? Oliver's note was brief and to the point: what, he wanted to know, was I discussing with the government? Oliver could not have believed that I was selling out, but he might have thought I was making an error in judgment. In fact, the tenor of his note suggested that.

I replied to Oliver in a very terse letter saying that I was talking to the government about one thing and one thing only: a meeting between the National Executive of the ANC and the South African government. I would not spell out the details, for I could not trust the confidentiality of the communication. I simply said the time had come for such talks and that I would not compromise the organization in any way.

Although the ANC had called for talks with the government for decades, we had never been confronted with the actual prospect of such talks. It is one thing to consider them in theory, and quite another to engage in them. As I was writing my response to Oliver, I was also beginning to draft my memorandum to P. W. Botha. I would make sure that Oliver saw this as well. I knew that when Oliver and the National Executive read my memo, their fears that I had gone off the road would be allayed.

93

The first formal meeting of the secret working group took place in May 1988, at a posh officers' club within the precincts of Pollsmoor. While I knew both Coetsee and Willemse, I had never before met van der Merwe and Dr Barnard. Van der Merwe was a quiet, even-handed man who spoke only when he had something important to say. Dr Barnard was in his mid-thirties and was exceedingly bright, a man of controlled intelligence and self-discipline.

The initial meeting was quite stiff, but in subsequent sessions we were able to talk more freely and directly. I met them almost every week for a few months, and then the meetings occurred at irregular intervals, sometimes not for a month, and then suddenly every week. The meetings were usually scheduled by the government, but sometimes I would request a session.

During our early meetings, I discovered that my new colleagues, with the exception of Dr Barnard, knew little about the ANC. They were all sophisticated Afrikaners, and far more open-minded than nearly all of their brethren. But they were the victims of so much propaganda that it was necessary to straighten them out about certain facts. Even Dr Barnard, who had made a study of the ANC, had received most of his information from police and intelligence files, which were in the main inaccurate and sullied by the prejudices of the men who had gathered them. He could not help but be infected by the same biases.

I spent some time in the beginning sketching out the history of the ANC and then explaining our positions on the primary issues that divided the organization from the government. After these preliminaries, we focused on the critical issues: the armed struggle, the ANC's alliance with the Communist Party, the goal of majority rule and the idea of racial reconciliation.

The first issue to arise was in many ways the most crucial, and that was the armed struggle. We spent a number of months discussing it. They insisted that the ANC must renounce violence and give up the armed struggle before the government would agree to negotiations – and before I could meet President Botha. Their contention was that violence was nothing more than criminal behaviour that could not be tolerated by the state.

I responded that the state was responsible for the violence and that it is always the oppressor, not the oppressed, who dictates the form of the struggle. If the oppressor uses violence, the oppressed have no alternative but to respond violently. In our case it was simply a legitimate form of self-defence. I ventured that if the state decided to use peaceful methods, the ANC would also use peaceful means. 'It is up to you,' I said, 'not us, to renounce violence.'

I think I advanced their understanding on this point, but the issue soon moved from a philosophical question to a practical one. As Minister Coetsee and Dr Barnard pointed out, the National Party had repeatedly stated that it would not negotiate with any organization that advocated violence: therefore, how could it suddenly announce talks with the ANC without losing its credibility? In order for us to begin talks, they said, the ANC must make some compromise so that the government would not lose face with its own people.

It was a fair point and one that I could well understand, but I would not offer them a way out. 'Gentlemen,' I said, 'it is not my job to resolve your dilemma for you.' I simply told them that they must tell their people that there could be no peace and no solution to the situation in South Africa without sitting down with the ANC. 'People will understand,' I said.

The ANC's alliance with the Communist Party seemed to trouble them almost as much as the armed struggle. The National Party accepted the most hide-bound of 1950s cold war ideology and regarded the Soviet Union as the evil empire and communism as the work of the devil. There was nothing that one could do to disabuse them of this notion. They maintained that the Communist Party dominated and controlled the ANC and that in order for negotiations to begin we must break from the party.

First of all, I said, no self-respecting freedom fighter would take orders from the government he is fighting against or jettison a longtime ally in the interest of pleasing an antagonist. I then explained at great length that the party and the ANC were separate and distinct organizations that shared the same short-term objectives, the overthrow of racial oppression and the birth of a non-racial South Africa, but that our long-term interests were not the same.

This discussion went on for months. Like most Afrikaners, they thought that because many of the communists in the ANC were white or Indian, they were controlling the blacks in the ANC. I cited many occasions when the ANC and the CP had differed on policy and the ANC had prevailed, but this did not seem to impress them. Finally, in exasperation, I said to them, 'You gentlemen consider yourselves intelligent, do you not? You consider yourselves forceful and persuasive, do you not? Well, there are four of you and only one of me, and you cannot control me or get me to change my mind. What makes you think the communists can succeed where you have failed?'

They were also concerned about the idea of nationalization, insisting that the ANC and the Freedom Charter supported the wholesale nationalization of the South African economy. I explained that we were for a more even distribution of the rewards of certain industries, industries that were already monopolies, and that nationalization might occur in some of those areas. But I referred them to an article I wrote in 1956 for *Liberation* in which I said that the Freedom Charter was not a blueprint for socialism but for African-style capitalism. I told them I had not changed my mind since then.

The other main area of discussion was the issue of majority rule. They felt that if there was majority rule, the rights of minorities would be trampled. How would the ANC protect the rights of the white minority? they wanted to know. I said that there was no organization in the history of South Africa to compare with the ANC in terms of trying to unite all the people and races of South Africa. I referred them to the preamble of the Freedom Charter: 'South Africa belongs to all who live in it, black and white.' I told them that whites were Africans as well, and that in any future dispensation the majority would need the minority. 'We do not want to drive you into the sea,' I said.

94

The meetings had a positive effect: I was told in the winter of 1988 that President Botha was planning to see me before the end of August. The country was still in turmoil. The government had reimposed a State of Emergency in both 1987 and 1988. International pressure mounted. More companies left South Africa. The American Congress had passed a sweeping sanctions bill.

In 1987, the ANC celebrated its seventy-fifth anniversary and held a conference at the end of the year in Tanzania attended by delegates from more than fifty nations. Oliver declared that the armed struggle would intensify until the government was prepared to negotiate the abolition of apartheid. Two years before, at the ANC's Kabwe conference in Zambia marking the thirtieth anniversary of the Freedom Charter, members of other races were elected to the National Executive Committee for the first time, and the NEC pledged that no discussions with the government could be held until all ANC leaders were released from prison.

Although violence was still pervasive, the National Party had never been stronger. In the white general election of May 1987, the Nationalists won an overwhelming majority. Worse still, the liberal Progressive Federal Party had been replaced as the official opposition by the Conservative Party, which was to the right of the Nationalists and campaigned on the theme that the government was too lenient with the black opposition.

Despite my optimism about the secret talks, it was a difficult time. I had recently had a visit from Winnie and I learned that No. 8115 Orlando West, the house in which we had been married and which I considered home, had been burned down by arsonists. We had lost invaluable family records, photographs and keepsakes – even the slice of wedding cake Winnie was saving for my release. I had always thought that some day when I left prison I would be able to recapture the past when looking over those pictures and letters, and now they were gone. Prison had robbed me of my freedom but not my memories, and now I felt some enemies of the struggle had tried to rob me of even those.

I was also suffering from a bad cough that I could not seem to shake off, and I often felt too weak to exercise. I had continued to complain about the dampness of my cell, but nothing had been done about it. One day, during a meeting in the visiting area with my attorney, Ismail Ayob, I felt ill and vomited. I was taken back to my cell, examined by a doctor, and soon recovered. A few days later, however, I was in my cell after dinner when a number of warders and a doctor arrived. The physician gave me a cursory examination, and then one of the warders told me to get dressed. 'We are taking you to hospital in Cape Town,' I was told. Security was tight; I went in a convoy of cars and military vehicles accompanied by at least a dozen warders.

I was taken to Tygerberg Hospital, on the campus of the University of Stellenbosch in a rich and verdant area of the Cape. As I later discovered, they had nearly chosen a different facility because the authorities feared I might attract sympathetic attention at a university hospital. The warders went in first and cleared everyone out of the entrance area. I was then escorted up to a floor that had been entirely emptied; the hall was lined with more than a dozen armed guards.

While sitting on a table in the examining room, I was looked at by a young and amiable doctor who was also a professor at the university medical school. He inspected my throat, tapped my chest, took some cultures and in no time pronounced me fit. 'There is nothing wrong with you,' he said with a smile. 'We should be able to release you tomorrow.' I was anxious not to be diverted from my talks with the government, so I was pleased with his diagnosis.

After the examination, the doctor asked me if I would like some tea. I said I would, and a few minutes later a tall young Coloured nurse came in with a tray. The presence of all the armed guards and warders so frightened her that she dropped the tray on my bed, spilling the tea, before rushing out.

I spent the night in the empty ward under heavy guard. The first thing next morning, even before I had breakfasted, I was visited by an older doctor who was head of internal medicine at the hospital. He was a no-nonsense fellow and had far less of a bedside manner than the cordial young physician of the night before. Without any preliminaries, he tapped me roughly on my chest and then said gruffly, 'There is water in your lung.' I told him that the previous doctor had done tests and said I was fine. With a hint of annoyance, he said, 'Mandela, take a look at your chest.' He pointed out that one side of my chest was actually larger than the other, and said that it was probably filled with water.

He asked a nurse to bring him a syringe, and without further ado he poked it into my chest and drew out some brownish liquid. 'Have you had breakfast?' he said. No, I replied. 'Good,' he said, 'we are taking you to the operating theatre immediately.' He told me I had a great deal of fluid on my lung and he wanted to draw it out right away.

In the operating room I was anaesthetized, and the next thing I recalled was waking up in a room with the doctor present. I was groggy, but I concentrated on what he said: he had removed two litres of fluid from my chest and when the liquid was analysed, tuberculosis had been discovered. He said it was in the very early stages of the illness, and that there was no damage to the lung. While full-blown tuberculosis normally took six months to cure, he said, I should be better in two months. The doctor agreed that it was probably the damp cell that had helped to cause my illness.

I spent the next six weeks at Tygerberg recuperating and receiving treatment. In December, I was moved to the Constantiaberge Clinic, a luxurious facility near Pollsmoor that had never had a black patient before. My first morning there, I had an early visit from Kobie Coetsee, who was accompanied by Major Marais, a deputy commander responsible for looking after me. We had barely exchanged greetings when the orderly brought in my breakfast.

Because of my recent illness and my history of high blood pressure, I had been put on a strict low-cholesterol diet. That order had apparently not yet been conveyed to the clinic's kitchen, for the breakfast tray contained scrambled eggs, three rashers of bacon and several pieces of buttered toast. I could not remember the last time I had tasted bacon and eggs and I was ravenous. Just as I was about to take a delicious forkful of egg, Major Marais said, 'No, Mandela, that is against the orders of your physician,' and he reached over to take the tray. I held it tightly, and said, 'Major, I am sorry. If this breakfast will kill me, then today I am prepared to die.'

Once I was ensconced at Constantiaberge, I again began to meet Kobie Coetsee and the secret committee. While I was still at the clinic Coetsee said he wanted to put me in a situation that was halfway between confinement and freedom. While he did not spell out what this meant, I had a notion of what he was talking about, and I merely nodded. I would not be so naive as to consider his proposal to be freedom, but I knew that it was a step in that direction.

In the meantime, the clinic was extremely comfortable and for the first time I actually enjoyed a hospital convalescence. The nurses – who were white or Coloured; no black nurses were permitted – spoiled me; they brought extra desserts and pillows and were constantly visiting, even during their time off.

One day, one of the nurses came and said, 'Mr Mandela, we are having a party tonight and we would like you to come.' I said I'd be honoured to attend, but that the authorities would undoubtedly have something to say about it. The prison authorities refused permission for me to go, which nettled the nurses, and as a result they decided to hold their party in my room, insisting they could not have it without me.

That night, a dozen or so of these young ladies in party frocks descended on my room with cake and punch and gifts. The guards seemed befuddled, but they could hardly consider these vivacious young girls a security risk. In fact, when one of the guards attempted to prevent some of the nurses from entering my room, I jestingly accused him of being jealous of an old man receiving so much attention from such beautiful young ladies.

95

In early December 1988, security on my ward was tightened and the officers on duty were more alert than usual. Some change was imminent. On the evening of 9 December, Major Marais came into my room and told me to prepare to leave. 'Where to?' I asked him. He could not say. I packed my things and looked around for some of my loyal nurses; I was disappointed at not being able to thank them and bid them farewell.

We left in a rush, and after about an hour on the road we entered a prison whose name I recognized: Victor Verster. Located in the lovely old Cape Dutch town of Paarl, Victor Verster is thirty-five miles northeast of Cape Town in the province's wine-growing region. The prison had the reputation of being a model facility. We drove through its entire length, and then along a winding dirt road through a rather wild, wooded area at the rear of the property. At the end of the road we came to an isolated whitewashed one-storey cottage set behind a concrete wall and shaded by tall fir trees.

I was ushered into the house by Major Marais and found a spacious lounge next to a large kitchen, with an even larger bedroom at the back. The place was sparsely but comfortably furnished. It had not been cleaned or swept before my arrival, and the bedroom and living room were teeming with all kinds of exotic insects, centipedes, monkey spiders and the like, some of which I had never seen before. That night, I swept the insects off my bed and windowsill and slept extremely well in what was to be my new home.

The next morning I surveyed my new abode and discovered a swimming pool in the back yard, and two smaller bedrooms. I walked outside and admired the trees that shaded the house and kept it cool. The entire place felt removed, isolated. The only thing spoiling the idyllic picture was that the walls were topped with razor wire, and there were guards at the entrance to the house. Even so, it was a lovely place and situation; a halfway house between prison and freedom.

That afternoon I was visited by Kobie Coetsee, who brought a case of Cape wine as a housewarming gift. The irony of a jailer bringing his prisoner such a gift was not lost on either of us. He was extremely solicitous and wanted to make sure that I liked my new home. He surveyed the house himself, and the only thing he recommended was that the walls outside the house be raised – for my privacy, he said. He told me that the cottage at Victor Verster would be my last home before becoming a free man. The reason behind this move, he said, was that I should have a place where I could hold discussions in privacy and comfort.

The cottage did in fact give me the illusion of freedom. I could go to sleep and wake up as I pleased, swim whenever I wanted, eat when I was hungry – all were delicious sensations. Simply to be able to go outside during the day and take a walk when I desired was a moment of private glory. There were no bars on the windows, no jangling keys, no doors to lock or unlock. It was altogether pleasant, but I never forgot that it was a gilded cage.

The prison service provided me with a cook, Warrant Officer Swart, a tall, quiet Afrikaner who had once been a warder on Robben Island. I did not remember him, but he said he sometimes drove us to the quarry and purposely steered the truck over bumps to give us a rocky ride. 'I did that to you,' he said sheepishly, and I laughed. He was a decent, sweet-tempered fellow without any prejudice and he became like a younger brother to me.

He arrived at seven in the morning and left at four, and would make my breakfast, lunch and dinner. I had a diet outlined by my physician and he would follow it in his preparations. He was a lovely cook, and when he went home, he would leave my supper to heat up in the microwave oven, a device that was new to me.

Warrant Officer Swart baked bread, made home-brewed ginger-beer and assorted other delicacies. When I had visitors, which was increasingly often, he would prepare gourmet meals. They always praised the food and I dare say my chef was the envy of all my visitors. When the authorities began to permit some of my ANC comrades and members of the United Democratic Front (UDF) and the Mass Democratic Movement (MDM) to visit, I accused them of coming only for the food.

One day, after a delicious meal prepared by Mr Swart, I went into the kitchen to wash the dishes. 'No,' he said, 'that is my duty. You must return to the sitting room.' I insisted that I had to do something, and that if he cooked, it was only fair for me to do the dishes. Mr Swart protested, but finally gave in. He also objected to the fact that I would make my bed in the morning, saying it was his responsibility to do so.

But I had been making my own bed for so long that it had become a reflex.

We also swapped favours in another respect. Like many Afrikaans-speaking warders, he was keen to improve his English. I was always looking for ways to improve my Afrikaans. We made an agreement: he would speak to me in English and I would answer in Afrikaans, and in that way we both practised the language at which we were weakest.

I would occasionally ask him to make certain dishes. I sometimes requested samp and beans, which I used to eat as a boy. One day, I asked, 'You know, I would like you to cook me some brown rice.' To my astonishment, he said, 'What is brown rice?' Swart was a young man, and I explained to him that brown rice was the unrefined rice kernel that we used to eat during the war when white rice was unavailable. I said it was far healthier than white rice. He was sceptical, but managed to find me some. He cooked it and I enjoyed it very much. But Mr Swart could not abide the taste and vowed that if I ever wanted it again, I would have to cook it myself.

Even though I was not a drinker, I wanted to be a proper host and serve wine to my guests. I would occasionally take a sip in order to make my guests feel comfortable, but the only wine I can stomach is a South African 'semi-sweet' wine, which is actually very sweet.

Before my guests came I would ask Mr Swart to get a certain type of Nederburg wine, which I had tasted before and knew was a semi-sweet. One day, I was expecting my friends and lawyers, Dullah Omar, George Bizos and Ismail Ayob, for lunch and asked Mr Swart to purchase some Nederburg wine should George Bizos, not a Muslim, want some with his meal. I noticed that he grimaced when I said this, and asked him what was wrong.

'Mr Mandela,' he said. 'I always buy that wine for you because you ask me to, but it is cheap stuff and not very nice.' I reminded him that I did not like dry wines and I was sure George could not tell the difference anyway. Mr Swart smiled at this and proposed a compromise: he would go out and buy two bottles, a dry wine and my Nederburg, and then he would ask my guest which he preferred. 'Fine,' I said, 'let us try your experiment.'

When all four of us were seated for lunch, Swart came out holding the two bottles and turned to the guests and said, 'Gentlemen, which wine would you like?' Without even looking at me, George pointed to the bottle of dry white. Warrant Officer Swart just smiled.

96

The meetings with the committee continued, but we stalled on the same issues that had always prevented us from moving forward: the armed struggle, the Communist Party, and majority rule. I was still pressing Coetsee for a meeting with P. W. Botha. By this time, the authorities permitted me to have rudimentary communications with my comrades at Pollsmoor and Robben Island and also the ANC in Lusaka. Although I knew I was going ahead of my colleagues, I did not want to go too far, and find that I was all alone.

In January 1989, I was visited by my four comrades from Pollsmoor and we discussed the memorandum I was planning to send to the state president. It reiterated most of the points I had made in our secret committee meetings, but I wanted to make sure the state president heard them directly from me. He would see that we were not wild-eyed terrorists, but reasonable men.

'I am disturbed,' I wrote to Mr Botha in the memorandum sent to him in March, 'as many other South Africans no doubt are, by the spectre of a South Africa split into two hostile camps – blacks on one side . . . and whites on the other, slaughtering one another.' To avert this and prepare the groundwork for negotiations, I proposed to deal with the three demands made of the ANC by the government as a precondition to negotiations: renouncing violence; breaking with the SACP; and abandoning the call for majority rule.

On the question of violence I wrote that the refusal of the ANC to renounce violence was not the problem: 'The truth is that the government is not yet ready . . . for the sharing of political power with blacks.' I explained our unwillingness to cast aside the SACP, and reiterated that we were not under its control. 'Which man of honour,' I wrote, 'will desert a life-long friend at the insistence of a common opponent and still retain a measure of credibility with his people?' I said the rejection of majority rule by the government was a poorly disguised attempt to preserve power. I suggested he must face reality. 'Majority rule and internal peace are like the two sides of a single coin, and white South Africa simply has to accept that there will never be peace and stability in this country until the principle is fully applied.'

At the end of the letter, I offered a very rough framework for negotiations.

> Two political issues will have to be addressed; firstly, the demand for majority rule in a unitary state; secondly, the concern of white South Africa over this demand, as well as the insistence of whites on structural guarantees that majority rule will not mean domination of the white minority by blacks. The most crucial tasks which will face the government and the ANC will be to reconcile these two positions.

I proposed that this be done in two stages, the first being a discussion to create the proper conditions for negotiations, the second being the actual negotiations themselves. 'I must point out that the move I have taken provides you with the opportunity to overcome the current deadlock, and to normalize the country's political situation. I hope you will seize it without delay.'

But delay there was. In January, P. W. Botha suffered a stroke. While it did not incapacitate the president, it did weaken him and, according to his cabinet, made him even more irascible. In February Botha unexpectedly resigned as head of the National Party, but kept his position as state president. This was an unparalleled situation in the country's history: in the South African parliamentary system, the leader of the majority party becomes the head of state. President Botha was now head of state but not of his own party. Some saw this as a positive development: that Botha wanted to be 'above party politics' in order to bring about true change in South Africa.

Political violence and international pressure both continued to intensify. Political detainees all across the country had held a successful hunger strike, persuading the minister of law and order to release over nine hundred detainees. In 1989 the UDF formed an alliance with the Congress of South African Trade Unions (COSATU) to form the Mass Democratic Movement (MDM), which then began organizing a countrywide 'defiance campaign' of civil disobedience to challenge apartheid institutions. On the international front, Oliver Tambo held talks with the governments of Great Britain and the Soviet Union, and in January 1987 met the US secretary of state, George Shultz, in Washington. The Americans recognized the ANC as an indispensable element of any solution in South Africa. Sanctions against South Africa remained in force and even increased.

Political violence also had its tragic side. As the violence in Soweto intensified, my wife permitted a group of young men to act as her bodyguards as she moved around the township. These young men were untrained and undisciplined and became involved in activities that were unbecoming to a liberation struggle. Winnie subsequently became legally entangled in the trial of one of her bodyguards who was convicted of murdering a young comrade. This situation was deeply disconcerting to me, for such a scandal only served to divide the movement at a time when unity was essential. I wholly supported my wife and maintained that while she had shown poor judgment, she was innocent of any serious charges.

That July, for my seventy-first birthday, I was visited at the cottage at Victor Verster by nearly my entire family. It was the first time I had ever had my wife and children and grandchildren all in one place, and it was a grand and happy occasion. Warrant Officer Swart outdid himself in preparing a feast, and he did not even get upset when I let some of the grandchildren eat their puddings before their main courses. After the meal, the grandchildren went into my bedroom to watch a video of a horror movie while the adults stayed outside gossiping in the lounge. It was a deep, deep pleasure to have my whole family around me, and the only pain was the knowledge that I had missed such occasions for so many years.

97

On 4 July I was visited by General Willemse who informed me that I was being taken to see President Botha the following day. He described the visit as a 'courtesy call', and I was told to be ready to leave at 5.30 a.m. I told the general that while I was looking forward to the meeting, I thought I ought to have a suit and tie in which to see Mr Botha. (The suit from the visit of the Eminent Persons Group had long since vanished.) The general agreed, and a short while later a tailor appeared to take my measurements. That afternoon I received a new suit, tie, shirt and shoes. Before leaving, the general also asked me my blood type, just in case anything untoward should happen the following day.

I prepared as best I could for the meeting. I reviewed my memo and the extensive notes I had made for it. I looked at as many newspapers and publications as I could to make sure I was up to date. After President Botha's resignation as head of the National Party, F. W. de Klerk had been elected in his place, and there was said to be considerable jockeying between the two men. Some might interpret Botha's willingness to meet me as his way of stealing the thunder from his rival, but that did not concern me. I rehearsed the arguments that the state president might make and the ones I would put in return. In every meeting with an adversary, you must make sure you have conveyed precisely the impression you intend to.

I was tense about seeing Mr Botha. He was known as *'die Groot Krokodil'* – 'the Great Crocodile' – and I had heard many accounts of his ferocious temper. He seemed to me to be the very model of the old-fashioned, stiff-necked, stubborn Afrikaner who did not so much discuss matters with black leaders as dictate to them. His recent stroke had apparently only exacerbated this tendency. I resolved that if he acted in that finger-wagging fashion with me, I would have to inform him that I found such behaviour unacceptable, and I would then stand up and adjourn the meeting.

*   *   *

At precisely 5.30 in the morning Major Marais, the commander of Victor Verster, arrived at my cottage. He came into the lounge where I stood in front of him in my new suit for inspection. He walked around me, and then shook his head from side to side.

'No, Mandela, your tie,' he said. I did not have much use for ties in prison, and I realized that morning when I was putting it on that I had forgotten how to tie it properly. I made a knot as best I could and hoped no one would notice. Major Marais unbuttoned my collar, loosened and then removed my tie, and then, standing behind me, tied it in a double Windsor knot. He then stood back to admire his handiwork. 'Much better,' he said.

We drove from Victor Verster to Pollsmoor, to the home of General Willemse, where we were served breakfast by the general's wife. After breakfast, in a small convoy, we drove to Tuynhuys, the official presidential office, and parked in an underground garage where we would not be seen. Tuynhuys is a graceful, nineteenth-century Cape-Dutch-style building, but I did not get a proper look at it that day. I was essentially smuggled into the presidential suite.

We took a lift to the ground floor and emerged in a grand wood-panelled lobby in front of the president's office. There we were met by Kobie Coetsee, Niel Barnard and a retinue of prison officials. I had spoken extensively with both Coetsee and Dr Barnard about this meeting, and they had always advised me to avoid controversial issues with the president. While we were waiting, Dr Barnard looked down and noticed that my shoelaces were not properly tied and he quickly knelt down to tie them for me. I realized just how nervous they were, and that did not make me any calmer. The door then opened and I walked in expecting the worst.

From the opposite side of his grand office, P.W. Botha walked towards me. He had planned his march perfectly, for we met exactly halfway. He had his hand out and was smiling broadly, and in fact, from that very first moment, he completely disarmed me. He was unfailingly courteous, deferential and friendly.

We very quickly posed for a photograph of the two of us shaking hands, and then were joined at a long table by Kobie Coetsee, General Willemse and Dr Barnard. Tea was served and we began to talk. From the first, it was not as though we were engaged in tense political arguments but a lively and interesting tutorial. We did not discuss substantive issues so much as history and South African culture. I mentioned that I had recently read an article in an Afrikaans magazine about the 1914 Afrikaner Rebellion, and mentioned how they had occupied towns in the Free State. I said I saw our struggle as a parallel to this famous rebellion, and we discussed this historical episode for quite a while. South African history, of course, looks very different to the black man and the white man. Their view was that the rebellion had been a quarrel between brothers, whereas my struggle was a revolutionary one. I said that it could also be seen as a struggle between brothers who happen to be different colours.

The meeting was not even half an hour long, and was friendly and breezy until the end. It was then that I raised a serious issue. I asked Mr Botha to release unconditionally all political prisoners, including myself. That was the only tense moment in the meeting, and Mr Botha said that he was afraid that he could not do that.

There was then a brief discussion as to what we should say if news of the meeting leaked out. We very quickly drafted a bland statement saying that we had met for tea in an effort to promote peace in the country. Once this was agreed upon, Mr Botha rose and shook my hand, saying what a pleasure it had been. Indeed, it had been. I thanked him, and left the way I had come.

While the meeting was not a breakthrough in terms of negotiations, it was one in another sense. Mr Botha had long talked about the need to cross the Rubicon, but he never did it himself until that morning at Tuynhuys. Now, I felt, there was no turning back.

A little more than a month later, in August 1989, P.W. Botha went on national television to announce his resignation as state president. In a curiously rambling farewell address, he accused cabinet members of a breach of trust, of ignoring him and of playing into the hands of the African National Congress. The following day, F.W. de Klerk was sworn in as acting president and affirmed his commitment to change and reform.

To us, Mr de Klerk was a cipher. When he became head of the National Party, he seemed to be the quintessential party man, nothing more and nothing less. Nothing in his past seemed to hint at a spirit of reform. As education minister, he had attempted to keep black students out of white universities. But as soon as he took over the National Party, I began to follow him closely. I read all of his speeches, listened to what he said and began to see that he represented a genuine departure from his predecessor. He was not an ideologue but a pragmatist, a man who saw change as necessary and inevitable. On the day he was sworn in, I wrote him a letter requesting a meeting.

In his inaugural address, Mr de Klerk said his government was committed to peace and that it would negotiate with any other group committed to peace. But his commitment to a new order was demonstrated only after his inauguration when a march was planned in Cape Town to protest at police brutality. It was to be led by Bishop Tutu and the Reverend Allan Boesak. Under President Botha, the march would have been banned, marchers would have defied that ban and violence would have resulted. The new president lived up to his promise to ease restrictions on political gatherings and permitted the march to take place, only asking that the demonstrators remain peaceful. A new and different hand was on the tiller.

98

Even as de Klerk became president, I continued to meet the secret negotiating committee. We were joined by Gerrit Viljoen, the minister of constitutional development, a brilliant man with a doctorate in Classics, whose role was to bring our discussions into a constitutional framework. I pressed the government to display evidence of its good intentions, urging the state to show its bona fides by releasing my fellow political prisoners at Pollsmoor and Robben Island. While I told the committee that my colleagues had to be released unconditionally, I said the government could expect disciplined behaviour from them after their release. That was demonstrated by the conduct of Govan Mbeki, who had been unconditionally released at the end of 1987.

On 10 October 1989, President de Klerk announced that Walter Sisulu and seven of my former Robben Island comrades, Raymond Mhlaba, Ahmed Kathrada, Andrew Mlangeni, Elias Motsoaledi, Jeff Masemola, Wilton Mkwayi and Oscar Mpetha, were to be released. That morning, I had been visited by Walter, Kathy, Ray and Andrew, who were still at Pollsmoor, and I was able to say good-bye. It was an emotional moment, but I knew I would not be too far behind. The men were released five days later from Johannesburg Prison. It was an action that rightly evoked praise here and abroad, and I conveyed my appreciation to Mr de Klerk.

But my gratitude paled compared with my unalloyed joy that Walter and the others were free. It was a day we had yearned for and fought for over so many years. De Klerk had lived up to his promise, and the men were released under no bans; they could speak in the name of the ANC. It was clear that the ban on the organization had effectively expired, a vindication of our long struggle and our resolute adherence to principle.

De Klerk began a systematic dismantling of many of the building blocks of apartheid. He opened South African beaches to people of all colours, and stated that the Reservation of Separate Amenities Act would soon be repealed. Since 1953 this act had enforced what was known as 'petty apartheid', segregating parks, theatres, restaurants, buses, libraries, toilets and other public facilities according to race. In November, he announced that the National Security Management System, a secret structure set up under P.W. Botha to combat anti-apartheid forces, would be dissolved.

In early December I was informed that a meeting with de Klerk was set for the twelfth of that month. By this time I was able to consult my colleagues new and old, and had meetings at the cottage with my old colleagues and the leaders of the Mass Democratic Movement and the UDF. I received ANC people from all of the regions, as well as delegates from the UDF and COSATU. One of these young men was Cyril Ramaphosa, the general secretary of the National Mine Workers' Union and one of the ablest of the new generation of leadership. I also had visits from colleagues of mine from Robben Island, including Terror Lekota and Tokyo Sexwale, who stayed for lunch. They are both men with large appetites, and the only complaint I heard about them was from Warrant Officer Swart, who said, 'Those fellows will eat us out of house and home!'

With guidance from a number of colleagues, I then drafted a letter to de Klerk not unlike the one I had sent to P. W. Botha. The subject was talks between the government and the ANC. I told the president that the current conflict was draining South Africa's lifeblood and that talks were the only solution. I said the ANC would accept no preconditions to talks, especially not the precondition that the government wanted: the suspension of the armed struggle. The government asked for an 'honest commitment to peace' and I pointed out that our readiness to negotiate was exactly that.

I told Mr de Klerk how impressed I was by his emphasis on reconciliation, enunciated in his inaugural address. His words had imbued millions of South Africans and people around the world with the hope that a new South Africa was about to be born. The very first step on the road to reconciliation, I said, would be the complete dismantling of apartheid and all the measures used to enforce it.

But I said that the spirit of that speech had not been much in evidence of late. The government's policies were perceived by many as a continuation of apartheid by other means. The government, I said, had spent too much time talking with black homeland leaders and others co-opted by the system; these men, I asserted, were the agents of an oppressive past that the mass of black South Africans rejected.

I reiterated my proposal that talks take place in two stages. I told him I fully supported the guidelines the ANC had adopted in the

Harare Declaration of 1989, which put the onus on the government to eliminate the obstacles to negotiations that the state itself had created. Those demands included the release of all political prisoners, the lifting of all bans on restricted organizations and persons, the ending of the State of Emergency and the removal of all troops from the townships. I stressed that a mutually agreed-upon cease-fire to end hostilities ought to be the first order of business, for without that, no business could be conducted. The day before our meeting the letter was delivered to Mr de Klerk.

On the morning of 13 December I was again taken to Tuynhuys. I met de Klerk in the same room where I had had tea with his predecessor. He was accompanied by Kobie Coetsee, General Willemse, Dr Barnard and his colleague Mike Louw. I congratulated Mr de Klerk on becoming president and expressed the hope that we would be able to work together. He was extremely cordial and reciprocated these sentiments.

From the first I noticed that Mr de Klerk listened to what I had to say. This was a novel experience. National Party leaders generally heard what they wanted to hear in discussions with black leaders, but Mr de Klerk seemed to be making a real attempt to listen and understand.

One of the issues I emphasized that day was the National Party's recently introduced five-year plan, which contained the concept of 'group rights'. The idea of 'group rights' was that no racial or ethnic group could take precedence over any other. Although they defined 'group rights' as a way of protecting the freedom of minorities in a new South Africa, in fact their proposal was a means of preserving white domination. I told Mr de Klerk that this was unacceptable to the ANC.

I added that it was not in his interest to retain this concept, for it gave the impression that he wanted to modernize apartheid without abandoning it; this was damaging his image and that of the National Party in the eyes of the progressive forces in this country and around the world. An oppressive system cannot be reformed, I said; it must be entirely cast aside. I mentioned an editorial that I had recently read in Die Burger, the mouthpiece of the National Party in the Cape, implying that the group rights concept was conceived as an attempt to bring back apartheid through the back door. I told Mr de Klerk that if that was how his party's paper perceived group rights, how did he think we regarded it? I added that the ANC had not struggled against apartheid for seventy-five years only to yield to a disguised form of it, and that if it was his true intention to preserve apartheid through the Trojan horse of group rights, then he did not truly believe in ending apartheid.

Mr de Klerk, I saw that day, does not react quickly to things. It was a mark of the man that he listened to what I had to say and did not argue with me. 'You know,' he said, 'my aim is no different than yours. Your memo to P. W. Botha said the ANC and the government should work together to deal with white fears of black domination, and the idea of "group rights" is how we propose to deal with it.' I was impressed with this response, but said that the idea of 'group rights' did more to increase black fears than allay white ones. De Klerk then said, 'We will have to change it, then.'

I then brought up the question of my freedom and said that if he expected me to go out to pasture upon my release he was greatly mistaken. I reaffirmed that if I was released into the same conditions under which I had been arrested I would go back to doing precisely those things for which I had been imprisoned. I made the case to him that the best way to move forward was to unban the ANC and all other political organizations, to lift the State of Emergency, to release political prisoners and to allow the exiles to return. If the government did not unban the ANC, as soon as I was out of prison I would be working for an illegal organization. 'Then,' I said, 'you must simply rearrest me after I walk through those gates.'

Again, he listened carefully to what I had to say. My suggestions certainly came as no surprise to him. He said he would take all I said into consideration, but that he would make no promises. The meeting was an exploratory one and I understood that nothing was going to be resolved that day. But it was extremely useful, for I had taken the measure of Mr de Klerk just as I had with new prison commanders when I was on Robben Island. I was able to write to our people in Lusaka that Mr de Klerk seemed to represent a true departure from the National Party politicians of the past. Mr de Klerk, I said, echoing Mrs Thatcher's famous description of Mr Gorbachev, was a man we could do business with.

99

On 2 February 1990 F.W. de Klerk stood before Parliament to make the traditional opening speech and did something no other South African head of state had ever done: he truly began to dismantle the apartheid system and lay the groundwork for a democratic South Africa. In dramatic fashion, he announced the lifting of the bans on the ANC, the PAC, the South African Communist Party and thirty-one other illegal organizations; the freeing of political prisoners incarcerated for non-violent activities; the suspension of capital punishment; and the lifting of various restrictions imposed by the State of Emergency. 'The time for negotiation has arrived,' he said.

It was a breathtaking moment, for in one sweeping action he had virtually normalized the situation in South Africa. Our world had changed overnight. After forty years of persecution and banishment, the ANC was now a legal organization. I and all my comrades could no longer be arrested for being a member of the ANC, for carrying its green, yellow and black banner, for speaking its name. For the first time in almost thirty years, my picture and my words, and those of all my banned comrades, could appear in South African newspapers. The international community applauded de Klerk's bold actions. Amid all the good news, however, the ANC objected to the fact that Mr de Klerk had not completely lifted the State of Emergency or ordered the troops out of the townships.

On 9 February, seven days after Mr de Klerk's speech opening Parliament, I was informed that I was again going to Tuynhuys. I arrived at six o'clock in the evening. I met a smiling Mr de Klerk in his office and, as we shook hands, he informed me that he was going to release me from prison the following day. Although the press in South Africa and around the world had been speculating for weeks that my release was imminent, the announcement nevertheless came as a surprise to me. I had not been told that the reason de Klerk wanted to see me was to tell me that he was making me a free man.

I felt a conflict between my blood and my brain. I deeply wanted to leave prison as soon as I could, but to do so on such short notice would not be wise. I thanked Mr de Klerk, and then said that at the risk of appearing ungrateful I would prefer to have a week's notice in order that my family and my organization could be prepared for my release. Simply to walk out tomorrow, I said, would cause chaos. I asked de Klerk to release me a week from that day. After waiting twenty-seven years, I could certainly wait another seven days.

De Klerk was taken aback by my response. Instead of replying, he continued to relate the plan for my release. He said that the government would fly me to Johannesburg and officially release me there. Before he went any further, I told him that I strongly objected to that. I wanted to walk out of the gates of Victor Verster and be able to thank those who looked after me and greet the people of Cape Town. Though I was from Johannesburg, Cape Town had been my home for nearly three decades. I would make my way back to Johannesburg, but when I chose to, not when the government wanted me to. 'Once I am free,' I said, 'I will look after myself.'

De Klerk was again nonplussed. But this time my objections caused a reaction. He excused himself and left his office to consult with others. After ten minutes he returned with a rather long face and said, 'Mr Mandela, it is too late to change the plan now.' I replied that the plan was unacceptable and that I wanted to be released a week hence and at Victor Verster, not Johannesburg. It was a tense moment and, at the time, neither of us saw any irony in a prisoner asking not be released and his jailer attempting to release him.

De Klerk again excused himself and left the room. After ten minutes he returned with a compromise: yes, I could be released at Victor Verster, but, no, the release could not be postponed. The government had already informed the foreign press that I was to be set free the next day and felt they could not renege on that statement. I felt I could not argue with that. In the end, we agreed on the compromise, and Mr de Klerk poured a tumbler of whisky for each of us to drink in celebration. I raised the glass in a toast, but only pretended to drink; such spirits are too strong for me.

I did not get back to my cottage until shortly before midnight, whereupon I immediately sent word to my colleagues in Cape Town that I was to be released the following day. I managed to get a message to Winnie, and telephoned Walter in Johannesburg. They would all fly in on a chartered plane the next day. That evening, a number of ANC people on what was known as the National Reception Committee came to the cottage to draft a statement that I would make the following day. They left in the early hours of the morning and, despite my excitement, I had no trouble falling asleep.

PART ELEVEN

———

Freedom

100

I awoke on the day of my release after only a few hours' sleep at 4.30
a.m. 11 February was a cloudless, end-of-summer Cape Town day. I
did a shortened version of my usual exercise regimen, washed and ate
breakfast. I then telephoned a number of people from the ANC and the
UDF in Cape Town to come to the cottage to prepare for my release
and work on my speech. The prison doctor came by to give me a
brief check-up. I did not dwell on the prospect of my release, but on
all the many things I had to do before then. As so often happens in
life, the momentousness of an occasion is lost in the welter of a thousand
details.

There were numerous matters that had to be discussed and resolved
with very little time to do so. A number of comrades from the Reception
Committee, including Cyril Ramaphosa and Trevor Manuel, were at the
house bright and early. I wanted initially to address the people of Paarl,
who had been very kind to me during my incarceration, but the reception
committee was adamant that that would not be a good idea: it would
look curious if I gave my first speech to the prosperous white burghers
of Paarl. Instead, as planned, I would speak first to the people of Cape
Town at the Grand Parade in Cape Town.

One of the first questions to be resolved was where I would spend my
first night of freedom. My inclination was to spend the night in the Cape
Flats, the bustling black and Coloured townships of Cape Town, in order
to show my solidarity with the people. But my colleagues and, later, my
wife argued that for security reasons I should stay with Archbishop
Desmond Tutu in Bishopscourt, a plush residence in a white suburb.
It was not an area where I would have been permitted to live before I
went to prison, and I thought it would send the wrong signal to spend my
first night of freedom in a posh white area. But the committee explained
that Bishopscourt had become multi-racial under Tutu's tenure, and
symbolized an open, generous non-racialism.

The prison service supplied me with boxes and crates for packing.

During my first twenty or so years in prison, I accumulated very few possessions, but in the last few years I had amassed enough property – mainly books and papers – to make up for previous decades. I filled over a dozen crates and boxes.

My actual release time was set for 3 p.m., but Winnie and Walter and the other passengers from the chartered flight from Johannesburg did not arrive until after two. There were already dozens of people at the house, and the entire scene took on the aspect of a celebration. Warrant Officer Swart prepared a final meal for all of us and I thanked him not only for the food he had provided for the last two years but also the companionship. Warrant Officer James Gregory was also there at the house, and I embraced him warmly. In the years that he had looked after me from Pollsmoor to Victor Verster, we had never discussed politics, but our bond was an unspoken one and I would miss his soothing presence. Men like Swart, Gregory and Warrant Officer Brand reinforced my belief in the essential humanity even of those who had kept me behind bars for the previous twenty-seven and a half years.

There was little time for lengthy farewells. The plan was that Winnie and I would be driven in a car to the front gate of the prison. I had told the authorities that I wanted to be able to say good-bye to the guards and warders who had looked after me and I asked that they and their families wait for me at the front gate, where I would be able to thank them individually.

At a few minutes after three, I was telephoned by a well-known SABC presenter who requested that I get out of the car a few hundred feet before the gate so that they could film me walking towards freedom. This seemed reasonable, and I agreed. This was my first inkling that things might not go as smoothly as I had imagined.

By 3.30, I began to get restless, as we were already behind schedule. I told the members of the Reception Committee that my people had been waiting for me for twenty-seven years and I did not want to keep them waiting any longer. Shortly before four, we left in a small motorcade from the cottage. About a quarter of a mile in front of the gate, the car slowed to a stop and Winnie and I got out and began to walk towards the prison gate.

At first I could not really make out what was going on in front of us, but when I was within 150 feet or so, I saw a tremendous commotion and a great crowd of people: hundreds of photographers and television cameras and newspeople as well as several thousand well-wishers. I was astounded and a little bit alarmed. I had truly not expected such a scene; at most, I had imagined that there would be several dozen people, mainly the warders and their families. But this proved to be only the beginning; I realized we had not thoroughly prepared for all that was about to happen.

Within twenty feet or so of the gate, the cameras started clicking, a noise that sounded like some great herd of metallic beasts. Reporters started shouting questions; television crews began crowding in; ANC supporters were yelling and cheering. It was a happy, if slightly disorienting, chaos. When a television crew thrust a long, dark and furry object at me, I recoiled slightly, wondering if it were some newfangled weapon developed while I was in prison. Winnie informed me that it was a microphone.

When I was among the crowd I raised my right fist, and there was a roar. I had not been able to do that for twenty-seven years and it gave me a surge of strength and joy. We stayed among the crowd for only a few minutes before jumping back into the car for the drive to Cape Town. Although I was pleased to have such a reception, I was greatly vexed by the fact that I did not have a chance to say good bye to the prison staff. As I finally walked through those gates to enter a car on the other side, I felt – even at the age of seventy-one – that my life was beginning anew. My ten thousand days of imprisonment were at last over.

Cape Town was thirty-five miles to the southwest, but because of the unexpected crowds at the gate, the driver elected to take a different path to the city. We drove round to the back of the prison, and our convoy took small roads and byways into town. We drove through beautiful green vineyards and manicured farms, and I relished the scenery around me.

The countryside was lush and well cared for, but what surprised me was how many white families were standing beside the road to get a glimpse of our motorcade. They had heard on the radio that we were taking an alternative route. Some, perhaps a dozen, even raised their clenched right fists in what had become the ANC power salute. This astonished me; I was tremendously encouraged by these few brave souls from a conservative farming area who expressed their solidarity. At one point I stopped and got out of the car to greet and thank one such white family and tell them how inspired I was by their support. It made me think that the South Africa I was returning to was far different from the one I had left.

As we entered the outskirts of the city, I could see people streaming towards the centre. The Reception Committee had organized a rally at the Grand Parade in Cape Town, a great open square that stretched out in front of the old City Hall. I would speak to the crowd from the balcony of that building, which overlooked the entire area. We had heard sketchy reports that a great sea of people had been waiting there since morning. The plan was for our motorcade to avoid the crowd and drive round to the back of City Hall, where I would quietly enter the building.

The drive to Cape Town took forty-five minutes, and as we neared the Grand Parade we could see an enormous crowd. The driver was meant to turn right and skirt its edges, but instead he inexplicably plunged straight into the sea of people. Immediately the crowd surged forward and enveloped the car. We inched forward for a minute or two but were then forced to stop by the sheer press of bodies. People began knocking on the windows, and then on the boot and the bonnet. Inside, it sounded like a massive hailstorm. Then people began to jump on the car in their excitement. Others began to shake it and at that moment I began to worry. I felt as though the crowd might very well kill us with their love.

The driver was even more anxious than Winnie and I, and he was clamouring to jump out of the car. I told him to stay calm and remain inside, that others from the cars behind us would come to our rescue. Allan Boesak and others began to attempt to clear a way for our vehicle and push the people off the car; but with little success. We sat inside – it would have been futile even to attempt to open the door, so many people were pressing on it – for more than an hour, imprisoned by thousands of our own supporters. The time for the scheduled beginning of the speech had long passed.

Several dozen marshals eventually came to the rescue and managed slowly to clear an exit path. When we finally broke free, the driver set off at great speed in the opposite direction from the City Hall. 'Man, where are you going?' I asked him in some agitation. 'I don't know!' he said, his voice tense with anxiety. 'I've never experienced anything like this before,' he said, and then continued driving without any destination in mind.

When he began to calm down I gave him directions to the house of my friend and attorney Dullah Omar, who lived in the Indian area of the city. We could go there, I said, and relax for a few minutes. This appealed to him. Fortunately, Dullah and his family were home, but they were more than a bit surprised to see us. I was a free man for the first time in twenty-seven years, but instead of greeting me, they said with some concern, 'Aren't you meant to be at the Grand Parade?'

We were able to have some cold drinks at Dullah's, but we had only been there a few minutes when Archbishop Tutu telephoned. How he knew we were there I do not know. He was quite distressed, and said,

'Nelson, you must come back to the Grand Parade immediately. The people are growing restless. If you do not return straightaway, I cannot vouch for what will happen. I think there might be an uprising!' I said I would return at once.

Our problem was the driver: he was deeply reluctant to return to the Grand Parade. But I remonstrated with him and soon we were on our way back to City Hall. The building was surrounded by people on all sides, but it was not as dense at the back, and the driver managed to make his way through to the rear entrance. It was almost dusk when I was led up to the top floor of this stately building whose halls had always been filled with shuffling white functionaries. I walked out on to the balcony and saw a boundless sea of people cheering, holding flags and banners, clapping and laughing.

I raised my fist to the crowd, and the crowd responded with an enormous cheer. Those cheers fired me anew with the spirit of the struggle. '*Amandla!*' I called out. '*Ngawethu!*' they responded. '*iAfrika!*' I yelled; '*Mayibuye!*' they answered. Finally, when the crowd had started to settle down, I took out my speech and then reached into my breast pocket for my glasses. They were not there; I had left them at Victor Verster. I knew Winnie's glasses had a similar prescription, and I borrowed hers.

> Friends, comrades and fellow South Africans. I greet you all in the name of peace, democracy and freedom for all! I stand here before you not as a prophet but as a humble servant of you, the people. Your tireless and heroic sacrifices have made it possible for me to be here today. I therefore place the remaining years of my life in your hands.

I spoke from the heart. I wanted first of all to tell the people that I was not a messiah, but an ordinary man who had become a leader because of extraordinary circumstances. I wanted immediately to thank the people all over the world who had campaigned for my release. I thanked the people of Cape Town, and I saluted Oliver Tambo and the African National Congress, Umkhonto we Sizwe, the South African Communist Party, the UDF, the South African Youth Congress, COSATU, the Mass Democratic Movement, the National Union of South African Students, and the Black Sash, a group formed by women that had long been a voice of conscience. I also publicly expressed my gratitude to my wife and family, saying, 'I am convinced that [their] pain and suffering was far greater than my own.'

I told the crowd in no uncertain terms that apartheid had no future in South Africa, and that the people must not scale down their campaign of mass action. 'The sight of freedom looming on the horizon should encourage us to redouble our efforts.' I felt it was important publicly to explain my talks with the government. 'Today,' I said, 'I wish to report to you that my talks with the government have been aimed at normalizing the political situation in the country. I wish to stress that I myself have at no time entered into negotiations about the future of our country except to insist on a meeting between the ANC and the government.'

I said I hoped that a climate conducive to a negotiated settlement could soon be achieved, ending the need for the armed struggle. The steps to achieving such a climate, I said, had been outlined in the ANC's 1989 Harare Declaration. As a condition to real negotiations, I said, the government must immediately end the State of Emergency and free all political prisoners.

I told the people that de Klerk had gone further than any other Nationalist leader to normalize the situation and then, in words that came back to haunt me, I called Mr de Klerk 'a man of integrity'. These words were flung back at me many times when Mr de Klerk seemed not to live up to them.

It was vital for me to show my people and the government that I was unbroken and unbowed, and that the struggle was not over for me but beginning anew in a different form. I affirmed that I was 'a loyal and disciplined member of the African National Congress'. I encouraged the people to return to the barricades, to intensify the struggle, and we would walk the last mile together.

It was evening by the time my speech was finished, and we were hustled back into our cars for the trip to Bishopscourt. As we entered its pristine environs, I saw hundreds of black faces waiting to greet me. When they saw us, the people burst into song. When I greeted Archbishop Tutu, I enveloped him in a great hug; here was a man who had inspired an entire nation with his words and his courage, who had revived the people's hope during the darkest of times. We were led inside the house, where more family and friends met us but, for me, the most wonderful moment was when I was told that I had a telephone call from Stockholm. I knew immediately who it was. Oliver Tambo's voice was weak but unmistakable, and to hear him after all those years filled me with great joy. Oliver was in Sweden recuperating from a debilitating stroke he had suffered in August 1989. We agreed to meet as soon as possible.

My dream upon leaving prison was to take a leisurely drive down to the Transkei and visit my birthplace, the hills and streams where I had played as a boy, and the burial ground of my mother, which I had never seen. But my dream had to be deferred, for I learned very quickly of the extensive plans that the ANC had for me, and none of them involved a relaxing journey to the Transkei.

101

I was scheduled to hold a press conference the afternoon after my release, and in the morning I met a number of my colleagues to talk about scheduling and strategy. A small mountain of telegrams and messages of congratulations had arrived, and I tried to review as many of these as possible. They came from all over the world, from presidents and prime ministers, but I remember one in particular from a white Cape Town housewife that amused me greatly. It read: 'I am very glad that you are free, and that you are back among your friends and family, but your speech yesterday was very boring.'

Before I went to prison I had never held such a press conference as I did that day. In the old days there were no television cameras, and most ANC press conferences were conducted clandestinely. That afternoon, there were so many journalists, from so many different countries, I did not know whom to speak to. I was pleased to see a high percentage of black journalists among the throng. At the press conference I was once again keen to reassert a number of themes: first, that I was a loyal and disciplined member of the ANC. I was mindful of the fact that the most senior ANC people would be watching my release from abroad, and attempting to gauge my fidelity from a distance. I was aware that they had heard rumours that I had strayed from the organization, that I was compromised, so at every turn I sought to reassure them. When asked what role I would play in the organization, I told the press that I would play whatever role the ANC ordered.

I told the reporters that there was no contradiction between my continuing support for the armed struggle and my advocating negotiations. It was the reality and the threat of the armed struggle that had brought the government to the verge of negotiations. I added that when the state stopped inflicting violence on the ANC, the ANC would reciprocate with peace. Asked about sanctions, I said the ANC could not yet call for the relaxation of sanctions, because the situation that caused sanctions in the first place – the absence of political rights for blacks

– was still the status quo. I might be out of jail, I said, but I was not yet free.

I was asked as well about the fears of whites. I knew that people expected me to harbour anger towards whites. But I had none. In prison, my anger towards whites decreased, but my hatred for the system grew. I wanted South Africa to see that I loved even my enemies while I hated the system that turned us against one another.

I wanted to impress upon the reporters the critical role of whites in any new dispensation. I have tried never to lose sight of this. We did not want to destroy the country before we freed it, and to drive the whites away would devastate the nation. I said that there was a middle ground between white fears and black hopes, and we in the ANC would find it. 'Whites are fellow South Africans,' I said, 'and we want them to feel safe and to know that we appreciate the contribution that they have made towards the development of this country.' Any man or woman who abandons apartheid will be embraced in our struggle for a democratic, non-racial South Africa; we must do everything we could to persuade our white compatriots that a new, non-racial South Africa would be a better place for all.

From my very first press conference I noticed that journalists were as eager to learn about my personal feelings and relationships as my political thoughts. This was new to me; when I went to prison, a journalist would never have thought of asking questions about one's wife and family, one's emotions, one's most intimate moments. While it was understandable that the press might be interested in these things, I nevertheless found their curiosity difficult to satisfy. I am not and never have been a man who finds it easy to talk about his feelings in public. I was often asked by reporters how it felt to be free, and I did my best to describe the indescribable, and usually failed.

After the press conference, Archbishop Tutu's wife telephoned us from Johannesburg to say that we must fly there straightaway. Winnie and I had hoped to spend a few days in Cape Town relaxing, but the message we were receiving was that the people of Johannesburg were getting restless and there might be chaos if I did not return at once. We flew to Johannesburg that evening, but I was informed that there were thousands of people surrounding our old home, No. 8115 Orlando West, which had been reconstructed, and that it would be unwise to go there. I reluctantly acceded; I yearned to spend my second night of freedom under my own roof. Instead, Winnie and I stayed in the northern suburbs at the home of an ANC supporter.

The following morning we flew by helicopter to the First National Bank stadium in Soweto. We were able to make an aerial tour of Soweto, the teeming metropolis of matchbox houses, tin shanties and dirt roads, the mother city of black urban South Africa, the only home I ever knew as a man before I went to prison. While Soweto had grown, and in some places prospered, the overwhelming majority of the people remained dreadfully poor, without electricity or running water, eking out an existence that was shameful in a nation as wealthy as South Africa. In many places, the poverty was far worse than when I went to prison.

We circled over the stadium, overflowing with 120,000 people, and landed in the centre. The stadium was so crowded, with people sitting or standing in every inch of space, that it looked as though it would burst. I expressed my delight to be back among them, but I then scolded the people for some of the crippling problems of urban black life. Students, I said, must return to school. Crime must be brought under control. I told them that I had heard of criminals masquerading as freedom fighters, harassing innocent people and setting alight vehicles; these rogues had no place in the struggle. Freedom without civility, freedom without the ability to live in peace, was not true freedom at all.

> Today, my return to Soweto fills my heart with joy. At the same time I also return with a deep sense of sadness. Sadness to learn that you are still suffering under an inhuman system. The housing shortage, the schools crisis, unemployment and the crime rate still remain . . . Proud as I am to be part of the Soweto community, I have been greatly disturbed by the statistics of crime that I read in the newspapers. Although I understand the deprivations our people suffer, I must make it clear that the level of crime in the township is unhealthy and must be eliminated as a matter of urgency.

I ended by opening my arms to all South Africans of goodwill and good intentions, saying that 'no man or woman who has abandoned apartheid will be excluded from our movement towards a non-racial, united and democratic South Africa based on one-person one-vote on a common voters' roll.' That was the ANC's mission, the goal that I had always kept before me during the many lonely years in prison, the goal that I would work towards during the remaining years of my life. It was the dream I cherished when I entered prison at the age of forty-four, but I was no longer a young man, I was seventy-one, and I could not afford to waste any time.

That night, I returned with Winnie to No. 8115 in Orlando West. It was only then that I knew in my heart that I had left prison. For me,

No. 8115 was the centrepoint of my world, the place marked with an X in my mental geography. The four-roomed house had been soundly rebuilt after the fire. When I saw it, I was surprised by how much smaller and humbler it was than I remembered it being. Compared with my cottage at Victor Verster, No. 8115 could have been the servants' quarters at the back. But any house in which a man is free is a castle when compared with even the plushest prison.

That night, happy as I was to be home, I had a sense that what I most wanted and longed for was going to be denied me. I yearned to resume a normal and ordinary life, to pick up some of the old threads from my life as a young man, to be able to go to my office in the morning and return to my family in the evening, to be able to pop out and buy some toothpaste at the pharmacy, to visit old friends in the evening. These ordinary things are what one misses most in prison, and dreams about doing when one is free. But I quickly realized that such things were not going to be possible. That night, and every night for the next weeks and months, the house was surrounded by hundreds of well-wishers. People sang and danced and called out, and their joy was infectious. These were my people, and I had no right and no desire to deny myself to them. But in giving myself to my people, I could see that I was once again taking myself away from my family.

We did not sleep much that night, as the singing continued until the early hours, when members of the ANC and UDF who were guarding the house begged the crowd to remain quiet and allow us to rest. There were many in the ANC who advised me to move to the home a few blocks away, in Diepkloof extension, that Winnie had built while I was in prison. It was a grand place by Soweto standards, but it was a house that held no meaning or memories for me. Moreover, it was a house that because of its size and expense seemed somehow inappropriate for a leader of the people. I rejected that advice as long as I could. I wanted to live not only among my people, but like them.

102

My first responsibility was to report to the leadership of the ANC, and on 27 February, when I had been out of prison a little over two weeks, I flew to Lusaka for a meeting of the National Executive Committee. It was a wonderful reunion to be with old comrades whom I had not seen in decades. A number of African heads of state were also in attendance, and I had brief talks with Robert Mugabe of Zimbabwe, Kenneth Kaunda of Zambia, Quett Masire of Botswana, Joaquim Chissano of Mozambique, José Eduardo Dos Santos of Angola, and Yoweri Musaveni of Uganda.

While the members of the Executive were pleased that I had been freed, they were also eager to evaluate the man who had been released. I could see the questions in their eyes. Was Mandela the same man who went to prison twenty-seven years before, or was this a different Mandela, a reformed Mandela? Had he survived or had he been broken? They had heard reports of my conversations with the government and they were rightly concerned. I had not only been out of touch with the situation on the ground – since 1984 I had not been able to communicate even with my colleagues in prison.

I carefully and soberly explained the nature of my talks with the government. I described the demands I had made, and the progress that had been achieved. They had seen the memoranda I had written to Botha and de Klerk, and knew that these documents adhered to ANC policy. I knew that over the previous few years some of the men who had been released had gone to Lusaka and whispered, 'Madiba has become soft. He has been bought off by the authorities. He is wearing three-piece suits, drinking wine and eating fine food.' I knew of these whispers, and I intended to refute them. I knew that the best way to disprove them was simply to be direct and honest about everything that I had done.

At that session of the NEC I was elected deputy president of the organization while Alfred Nzo, the organization's secretary-general, was named acting president while Oliver was recuperating. At a press conference after our meeting, I was asked about a suggestion made by Dr Kaunda, the president of Zambia and a long-time supporter of the Congress, that the ANC should suspend armed operations inside South Africa now that I had been released. I replied that while we valued Dr Kaunda's wisdom and support, it was too soon to suspend the armed struggle, for we had not yet achieved the goal for which we had taken up arms; it was not the ANC's job, I said, to help Mr de Klerk to placate his right-wing supporters.

I began a tour of Africa, which included many countries. During the first six months after my release, I spent more time abroad than at home. Nearly everywhere I went there were great enthusiastic crowds so that even if I felt weary, the people buoyed me. In Dar es Salaam I was met by a crowd estimated at half a million.

I enjoyed my travels immensely. I wanted to see new – and old – sights, taste different foods, speak with all manner of people. I very quickly had to acclimatize myself to a world radically different from the one I had left. With changes in travel, communication and mass media, the world had accelerated; things now happened so fast that it was sometimes difficult to keep up with them. Winnie tried to get me to slow down, but there was simply too much to do; the organization wanted to make sure we took advantage of the euphoria generated by my release.

In Cairo, the day after a private meeting with the Egyptian president, Hosni Mubarak, I was scheduled to address a large meeting in a local hall. When I arrived, the crowd seemed to be spilling out of the building and there was precious little security. I mentioned to a policeman that I thought he needed reinforcements, but he merely shrugged. Winnie and I waited in a room behind the hall, and at the appointed hour a policeman motioned for me to go in. I told him to escort the rest of my delegation in first because I feared that when I went in there would be pandemonium and they would be cut off. But the policeman urged me to go first, and indeed as soon as I was in the hall, the crowd surged forward and overcame the cordon of policemen. In their enthusiasm, I was jostled and a bit shaken, and at one point I lost my shoe in the general confusion. When things began to calm down a few minutes later, I found that neither my shoe nor my wife could be located. Finally, after nearly half an hour, Winnie was brought on to the stage with me, quite cross that she had been lost. I was not even able to address the crowd, for they were shouting 'Mandela! Mandela!' so furiously that I could not be heard above the din, and finally I left, without my shoe and with an uncharacteristically silent wife.

While in Cairo I held a press conference in which I said the ANC was 'prepared to consider a cessation of hostilities'. This was a signal to the government. Both the ANC and the government were engaged in creating a climate whereby negotiations would succeed. While the ANC was demanding that the government normalize the situation in the country by ending the State of Emergency, releasing all political prisoners and repealing all apartheid laws, the government was intent on first persuading the ANC to suspend the armed struggle. While we were not yet ready to announce such a suspension, we wanted to provide Mr de Klerk with enough encouragement to pursue his reformist strategies. We knew that eventually we would suspend the armed struggle, in part to facilitate more serious negotiations and in part to allow Mr de Klerk to go to his own constituency, the white voters of South Africa, and say, 'Look, here are the fruits of my policy.'

After my last stop in Africa, I flew to Stockholm to visit Oliver. Seeing my old friend and law partner was the reunion I most looked forward to. Oliver was not well, but when we met we were like two young boys in the veld who took strength from our love for each other. We began by talking of old times, but when we were alone, the first subject he raised was the leadership of the organization. 'Nelson,' he said, 'you must now take over as president of the ANC. I have been merely keeping the job warm for you.' I refused, telling him that he had led the organization in exile far better than I ever could have. It was neither fair nor democratic for a transfer to occur in such a manner. 'You have been elected by the organization as the president,' I said. 'Let us wait for an election; then the organization can decide.' Oliver protested, but I would not budge. It was a sign of his humility and selflessness that he wanted to appoint me president, but it was not in keeping with the principles of the ANC.

In April 1990, I flew to London to attend a concert at Wembley, held in my honour. Many international artists, most of whom I didn't know, were performing and the event was to be televised worldwide. I took advantage of this to thank the world's anti-apartheid forces for the tremendous work they had done in pressurising for sanctions, for the release of myself and fellow political prisoners, and for the genuine support and solidarity they had shown the oppressed people of my country.

103

When I emerged from prison, Chief Mangosuthu Buthelezi, head of the Inkatha Freedom Party and the chief minister of KwaZulu, was one of the premier players on the South African political stage. But within ANC circles, he was a far from popular figure. Chief Buthelezi was descended from the great Zulu king Cetywayo, who had defeated the British at the Battle of Isandlwana in 1879. As a young man, he attended Fort Hare and then joined the ANC Youth League. I saw him as one of the movement's upcoming young leaders. He had become chief minister of the KwaZulu homeland with the tacit support of the ANC, and even his launching of Inkatha as a Zulu cultural organization was unopposed by the organization. But, over the years, Chief Buthelezi drifted away from the ANC. Though he resolutely opposed apartheid and refused to allow KwaZulu to become an 'independent' homeland as the government wished, he was a thorn in the side of the democratic movement. He opposed the armed struggle. He criticized the 1976 Soweto uprising. He campaigned against international sanctions. He challenged the idea of a unitary state of South Africa. Yet Chief Buthelezi had consistently called for my release and refused to negotiate with the government until I and other political prisoners were liberated.

Chief Buthelezi was one of the first people I telephoned after my release to thank him for his long-standing support. My inclination was to meet the chief as soon as possible to try to resolve our differences. During my initial visit to Lusaka I brought up the idea of such a meeting, and it was voted down. While I was at Victor Verster, Walter had been invited by the Zulu king, Goodwill Zwelithini, to visit him in Ulundi, KwaZulu's capital, and I urged him to accept. I thought it was an excellent opportunity to influence the head of one of the most respected and powerful royal families in the country. The visit was tentatively approved by the NEC, provided Walter went to the king's palace in Nongoma; it was thought that going to Ulundi would suggest recognition of the authority of the homeland.

When I returned from Lusaka I phoned both Chief Buthelezi and the king, and explained that Walter would be coming to see the king, not in Ulundi but in Nongoma. The king said he would not accept Walter coming to see him anywhere but in the capital. 'I am the king,' he said. 'I have invited him to see me in Ulundi, and he has no right to say I will see you elsewhere.' 'Your Majesty,' I said, 'we are facing a wall of opposition from our membership who did not want Mr Sisulu to go to KwaZulu at all. We managed to get this compromise approved; surely you can bend as well?' But he could not, and he refused to see Walter.

Relations deteriorated after this, and in May I persuaded the ANC of the need for me to make a visit to the king and Buthelezi. The king approved, but a week or so before the visit I received a letter from him to say I must come alone. This proved to be the last straw, and the NEC would not give in to such a demand. I told the king that I could not come unless I was accompanied by my colleagues; the king regarded this as another slight and cancelled the visit.

My goal was to forge an independent relationship with the king, separate from my relationship with Chief Buthelezi. The king was the true hereditary leader of the Zulus, who loved and respected him. Fidelity to the king was far more widespread in KwaZulu than allegiance to Inkatha.

In the meantime, Natal became a killing-ground. Heavily armed Inkatha supporters had in effect declared war on ANC strongholds across the Natal Midlands region and around Pietermaritzburg. Entire villages were set alight, dozens of people were killed, hundreds were wounded and thousands became refugees. In March 1990 alone, 230 people lost their lives in this internecine violence. In Natal, Zulu was murdering Zulu, for Inkatha members and ANC partisans are Zulus. In February, only two weeks after my release, I went to Durban and spoke to a crowd of over 100,000 people at King's Park, almost all of whom were Zulus. I pleaded with them to lay down their arms, to take each other's hands in peace: 'Take your guns, your knives and your pangas, and throw them into the sea! Close down the death factories. End this war now!' But my call fell on deaf ears. The fighting and dying continued.

I was so concerned that I was willing to go to great lengths to meet Chief Buthelezi. In March, after one particularly horrifying spasm of violence, I announced on my own that I would meet him at a mountain hamlet outside Pietermaritzburg. On a personal level, my relations with the chief were close and respectful, and I hoped to capitalize on that. But I found that such a meeting was anathema to the ANC leaders in Natal. They considered it dangerous, and vetoed my meeting. I did go to Pietermaritzburg, where I saw the burned remains of ANC supporters and tried to comfort their grieving families, but I did not see Chief Buthelezi.

104

In March, after much negotiation within our respective parties, we scheduled our first face-to-face meeting with Mr de Klerk and the government. These were to be 'talks about talks', and the meetings were to begin in early April. But on 26 March, in Sebokeng township, about thirty miles south of Johannesburg, the police opened fire without warning on a crowd of ANC demonstrators, killing twelve and wounding hundreds more, most of them shot in the back as they were fleeing. Police had used live ammunition in dealing with the demonstrators, which was intolerable. The police claimed that their lives were endangered, but many demonstrators who were shot in the back had no weapons. You cannot be in danger from an unarmed man who is running away from you. The right to assemble and demonstrate in support of our just demands was not a favour to be granted by the government at its discretion. This sort of action angered me like no other, and I told the press that every white policeman in South Africa regarded every black person as a military target. After consultation with the NEC, I announced the suspension of our talks and warned Mr de Klerk that he could not 'talk about negotiations on the one hand and murder our people on the other'.

But despite the suspension of our official talks, with the approval of the leadership, I met privately with Mr de Klerk in Cape Town in order to keep up the momentum for negotiations. Our discussions centred primarily on a new date, and we agreed on early May. I brought up the appalling behaviour at Sebokeng and the police's unequal treatment of blacks and whites; police used live ammunition on black demonstrators, while they never unsheathed their guns at white right-wing protests.

The government was in no great rush to begin negotiations; they were counting on the euphoria that greeted my release to die down. They wanted to allow time for me to fall on my face and show that the former prisoner hailed as a saviour was a highly fallible man who had lost touch with the present situation.

Despite his seemingly progressive actions, Mr de Klerk was by no means the great emancipator. He was a gradualist, a careful pragmatist. He did not make any of his reforms with the intention of putting himself out of power. He made them for precisely the opposite reason: to ensure power for the Afrikaner in a new dispensation. He was not prepared to negotiate the end of white rule.

His goal was to create a system of power-sharing based on group rights, which would preserve a modified form of minority power in South Africa. He was decidedly opposed to majority rule, or 'simple majoritarianism', as he sometimes called it, because that would end white domination in a single stroke. We knew early on that the government was fiercely opposed to a winner-take-all Westminster parliamentary system, and advocated instead a system of proportional representation with built-in structural guarantees for the white minority. Although he was prepared to allow the black majority to vote and create legislation, he wanted to retain a minority veto. From the start I would have no truck with this plan. I described it to Mr de Klerk as apartheid in disguise, a 'loser-takes-all' system.

The Nationalists' long-term strategy to overcome our strength was to build an anti-ANC alliance with the Inkatha Freedom Party and to lure the Coloured Afrikaans-speaking voters of the Cape into a new National Party. From the moment of my release, they began wooing both Buthelezi and the Coloured voters of the Cape. The government attempted to scare the Coloured population into thinking the ANC was anti-Coloured. They supported Chief Buthelezi's desire to retain Zulu power and identity in a new South Africa by preaching to him the doctrine of group rights and federalism.

The first round of talks with the government was held over three days in early May. Our delegation consisted of Walter Sisulu, Joe Slovo, Alfred Nzo, Thabo Mbeki, Ahmed Kathrada, Joe Modise, Ruth Mompati, Archie Gumede, the Reverend Beyers Naude, Cheryl Carolus and me. The setting was Groote Schuur, the Cape-Dutch-style mansion that was the residence of South Africa's first colonial governors, among them Cecil Rhodes. Some of our delegation joked that we were being led into an ambush on the enemy's ground.

But the talks, contrary to expectation, were conducted with seriousness and good humour. Historic enemies who had been fighting each other for three centuries met and shook hands. Many wondered out loud why such discussions had not taken place long before. The government had granted temporary indemnities to Joe Slovo, the general secretary of the Communist Party, and Joe Modise, the commander of MK, and to see these two men shaking hands with the National Party leaders who had demonized them for decades was extraordinary. As Thabo Mbeki later said to reporters, each side had discovered that the other did not have horns.

The very fact of the talks themselves was a significant milestone in the history of our country; as I pointed out, the meeting represented not only what the ANC had been seeking for so many years, but an end to the master/servant relationship that characterized black and white relations in South Africa. We had come to the meeting not as supplicants or petitioners, but as fellow South Africans who merited an equal place at the table.

The first day was more or less a history lesson. I explained to our counterparts that the ANC from its inception in 1912 had always sought negotiations with the government in power. Mr de Klerk, for his part, suggested that the system of separate development had been conceived as a benign idea, but had not worked in practice. For that, he said, he was sorry, and hoped the negotiations would make amends. It was not an apology for apartheid, but he went further than any other National Party leader ever had.

The primary issue discussed was the definition of political prisoners and political exiles. The government argued for a narrow definition, wanting to restrict the number of our people who would qualify for an indemnity. We argued for the broadest possible definition and said that any person who was convicted of an offence that was politically motivated should qualify for an indemnity. We could not agree on a mutually satisfactory definition of 'politically motivated' crimes, and this would be an issue that would bedevil us for quite a while to come.

At the end of the three-day meeting, we agreed on what became known as the Groote Schuur Minute, pledging both sides to a peaceful process of negotiations and committing the government to lifting the State of Emergency, which they shortly did everywhere except for the violence-ridden province of Natal. We agreed to set up a joint working group to resolve the many obstacles that still stood in our way.

When it came to constitutional issues, we told the government we were demanding an elected constituent assembly to draw up a new constitution; we believed that the men and women creating the constitution should be the choice of the people themselves. But before the election of an assembly, it was necessary to have an interim government that could oversee the transition until a new government was elected. The government could not be both player and referee, as it was now. We advocated the creation of a multi-party negotiating conference to set up the interim government and set out the guiding principles for the functioning of a constituent assembly.

105

Although I had wanted to go to Qunu immediately after my release from prison, it was not until April that I was able to travel. I could not pick up and leave whenever I wanted; security had to be arranged, as well as speeches prepared for local organizations. By April, the ANC and General Bantu Holomisa, the military leader of the Transkei and an ANC loyalist, had arranged for a visit. But what was foremost in my mind and heart was paying my respects to my mother's grave.

I went first to Qunu and the site where my mother was buried. Her grave was simple and unadorned, covered only by a few stones and some upturned bricks, no different from the other graves at Qunu. I find it difficult to describe my feelings: I felt regret that I had been unable to be with her when she died, remorse that I had not been able to look after her properly during her life and a longing for what might have been had I chosen to live my life differently.

In seeing my village again after so many years, I was greatly struck by what had changed and what had not. When I had been young, the people of Qunu were not at all political; they were unaware of the struggle for African rights. People accepted life as it was and did not dream of changing it. But, when I returned, I heard the schoolchildren of Qunu singing songs about Oliver Tambo and Umkhonto we Sizwe, and I marvelled at how knowledge of the struggle had by then seeped into every corner of African society.

What had endured was the warmth and simplicity of the community, which took me back to my days as a boy. But what disturbed me was that the villagers seemed as poor if not poorer than they had been then. Most people still lived in simple huts with dirt floors, with no electricity and no running water. When I was young, the village was tidy, the water pure and the grass green and unsullied as far as the eye could see. Kraals were swept, the topsoil was conserved, fields were neatly divided. But now the village was unswept, the water polluted and the countryside littered with plastic bags and wrappers. We had not known of plastic when I was a boy, and though it surely improved life in some ways, its presence in Qunu appeared to me to be a kind of blight. Pride in the community seemed to have vanished.

That month I had another homecoming: I returned to Robben Island in order to persuade twenty-five MK political prisoners to accept the government's offer of an amnesty and leave the island. Though I had left the island eight years before, my memories of prison were still fresh and untinged by nostalgia. After all the years of being visited by others, it was a curious sensation to be a visitor on Robben Island.

But that day I did not have much opportunity to sightsee, for I immediately met the men protesting at the government's offer of an amnesty. They maintained that they would leave only after a victory on the battlefield, not the negotiating table. They were fiercely opposed to this particular settlement, in which they had to enumerate their crimes before receiving indemnity. They accused the ANC of retreating from the Harare Declaration demand for an unconditional, blanket amnesty covering political prisoners and exiles. One man said, 'Madiba, I have been fighting the government all my life, and now I have to ask for a pardon from them.'

I could sympathize with their arguments, but they were being unrealistic. Every soldier would like to defeat his enemy on the field but, in this case, such a victory was out of reach. The struggle was now at the negotiating table. I argued that they were not advancing the cause by remaining in jail. They could be of greater service outside than inside. In the end, they agreed to accept the government's offer.

In early June I was scheduled to leave on a six-week tour of Europe and North America. Before going, I privately met Mr de Klerk, who wanted to discuss the issue of sanctions. Based on the changes he had made in South Africa, he asked me to modify the call for the continuation of international sanctions. While we were mindful of what Mr de Klerk had done, in our view sanctions remained the best lever to force him to do more. I was aware that the European Community and the USA were inclined to relax sanctions based on Mr de Klerk's reforms. I explained to Mr de Klerk that we could not tell our supporters to do so until he had completely dismantled apartheid and a transitional government was in place. While he was disappointed at my response, he was not surprised.

The first leg of the trip took Winnie and me to Paris, where we were treated in very grand style by François Mitterrand and his charming wife Danielle, a long-time ANC supporter. This was not my first trip to the continental mainland, but I was still entranced by the beauties of the Old

World. Although I do not want to decry the loveliness of the City of Light, the most important event that occurred while I was in France was that the government announced the suspension of the State of Emergency. I was pleased, but well aware that they had taken this action while I was in Europe in order to undermine my call for sanctions.

After stops in Switzerland, Italy and the Netherlands, I went to England, where I spent two days on a visit to Oliver and Adelaide. My next stop was the United States, but I would be returning to England on my way back to South Africa, which is when I was scheduled to meet Mrs Thatcher. As a courtesy, however, I phoned her before I left, and she proceeded to give me a stern but well-meaning lecture: she said she had been following my travels and noting how many events I attended each day. 'Mr Mandela, before we discuss any issues,' she said, 'I must warn you that your schedule is too heavy. You must cut it in half. Even a man half your age would have trouble meeting the demands that are being made on you. If you keep this up, you will not come out of America alive. That is my advice to you.'

I had read about New York City since I was a young man, and finally to see it from the bottom of its great glass-and-concrete canyons while millions upon millions of pieces of ticker tape came floating down was a breathtaking experience. It was reported that as many as a million people personally witnessed our procession through the city, and to see the support and enthusiasm they gave to the anti-apartheid struggle was truly humbling. I had always read that New York was a hard-hearted place, but I felt the very opposite of that on my first full day in the city.

The following day I went up to Harlem, an area that had assumed legendary proportions in my mind since the 1950s when I watched young men in Soweto emulate the sharp fashions of Harlem dandies. Harlem, as my wife said, was the Soweto of America. I spoke to a great crowd at Yankee Stadium, telling them that an unbreakable umbilical cord connected black South Africans and black Americans, for we were together children of Africa. There was a kinship between the two, I said, that had been inspired by such great Americans as W.E.B. Du Bois, Marcus Garvey and Martin Luther King Jr. As a young man, I idolized the Brown Bomber, Joe Louis, who took on not only his opponents in the ring but racists outside it. In prison, I followed the struggle of black Americans against racism, discrimination and economic inequality. To us, Harlem symbolized the strength of resistance and the beauty of black pride. This was brought home to me by a young man I had seen the previous day who wore a T-shirt that read, 'BLACK BY NATURE, PROUD BY CHOICE'.

We were linked by nature, I said, but we were proud of each other by choice.

After journeying to Memphis and Boston, I went to Washington to address a joint session of Congress and attend a private meeting with President Bush. I thanked the US Congress for its anti-apartheid legislation and said the new South Africa hoped to live up to the values that had created the two chambers before which I spoke. I said that as freedom fighters we could not have known of such men as George Washington, Abraham Lincoln and Thomas Jefferson 'and not been moved to act as they were moved to act'. I also delivered a strong message on sanctions, for I knew that the Bush administration felt it was time to loosen them. I urged Congress not to do so.

Even before meeting George Bush, I had formed a positive impression of him, for he was the first world leader to telephone me with congratulations after I left prison. From that point on, President Bush included me on his short list of world leaders whom he briefed on important issues. In person, he was just as warm and thoughtful, though we differed markedly on the issues of the armed struggle and sanctions. He was a man with whom one could disagree and then shake hands.

From the United States I proceeded to Canada, where I had a meeting with Prime Minister Mulroney and also addressed their Parliament. We were due to go to Ireland next, and before crossing the Atlantic, our plane, a small jet, stopped for refuelling in a remote place north of the Arctic Circle called Goose Bay. I felt like having a walk in the brisk air, and as I was strolling on the tarmac, I noticed some people standing by the airport fence. I asked a Canadian official who they were. 'Eskimos,' he said.

In my seventy-two years on earth I had never met an Innuit, and never imagined that I would. I headed over to that fence and found a dozen or so young people in their late teens who had come out to the airport because they had heard our plane was going to stop there. As a boy I had read about the Innuit (the name 'Eskimo' was given to them by the colonists), and the impression I received from the racist colonialist texts was that they were a very backward people.

But in talking with these bright young people, I learned that they had watched my release on television and were familiar with events in South Africa. 'Viva ANC!' one of them said. The Innuit are an aboriginal people historically mistreated by a white settler population; there were parallels between the plights of black South Africans and the Innuit people. What struck me so forcefully was how small the planet had become during my decades in prison; it was amazing to me that a teenage Innuit living at the roof of the world could watch the release of a political prisoner on the southern tip of Africa. Television had shrunk the world, and had in the process become a great weapon for eradicating ignorance and promoting democracy.

After Dublin I went to London, where I had a three-hour meeting with Mrs Thatcher. Standing out in the cold talking with the young Innuits had given me a chill. On the day I was to see Mrs Thatcher it was wintry and raining and, as we were leaving, Winnie told me I must take a raincoat. We were already in the lobby of the hotel, and if I went back for my coat we would be late. I am a stickler about punctuality, not only because I think it is a sign of respect to the person you are meeting but in order to combat the Western stereotype of Africans as being notoriously tardy. I told Winnie we did not have time, and instead I stood out in the rain signing autographs for some children. By the time I got to Mrs Thatcher I was feeling poorly, and was later diagnosed as having a mild case of pneumonia.

But it did not interfere with our meeting, except that she chided me like a schoolmarm for not taking her advice and cutting down on my schedule. Even though Mrs Thatcher was on the opposite side of the ANC on many issues such as sanctions, she was always a forthright and solicitous lady. In our meeting that day, though, I could not make the slightest bit of headway with her on the question of sanctions.

106

When I returned to South Africa in July, after brief trips to Uganda, Kenya and Mozambique, I requested a meeting with Mr de Klerk. Violence in the country was worsening; the death toll in 1990 was already over fifteen hundred, more than all the political deaths of the previous year. After conferring with my colleagues, I felt it necessary to speed up the process of normalization. Our country was bleeding to death, and we had to move ahead faster.

Mr de Klerk's lifting of the State of Emergency in June seemed to set the stage for a resumption of talks, but in July government security forces arrested about forty members of the ANC, including Mac Maharaj, Pravin Gordhan, Siphiwe Nyanda and Billy Nair, claiming that they were part of a Communist Party plot called Operation Vula to overthrow the government. De Klerk called for an urgent meeting with me and read to me from documents he claimed had been confiscated in the raid. I was taken aback because I knew nothing about it.

After the meeting I wanted an explanation, and called Joe Slovo. Joe explained that the passages read by Mr de Klerk had been taken out of context and that Vula was a moribund operation. But the government was intent on using this discovery to try to prise the ANC away from the SACP and keep Joe Slovo out of the negotiations. I went back to Mr de Klerk and told him that he had been misled by his own police and that we had no intention of parting ways with the SACP or dropping Joe Slovo from our negotiating team.

In the middle of July, shortly before a scheduled meeting of the National Executive Committee, Joe Slovo came to me privately with a proposition. He suggested we voluntarily suspend the armed struggle in order to create the right climate to move the negotiation process forward. Mr de Klerk, he said, needed to show his supporters that his policy had brought benefits to the country. My first reaction was negative; I did not think the time was ripe.

But the more I thought about it, the more I realized that we had to take the initiative and this was the best way to do it. I also recognized that Joe, whose credentials as a radical were above dispute, was precisely the right person to make the proposal. He could not be accused of being a dupe of the government or of having gone soft. The following day I told Joe that if he brought up the idea in the NEC, I would support him.

When Joe raised the idea in the NEC the next day there were some who firmly objected, claiming that we were giving de Klerk's supporters a reward, but not our own people. But I defended the proposal, saying the purpose of the armed struggle was always to bring the government to the negotiating table, and now we had done so. I argued that the suspension could always be withdrawn, but it was necessary to show our good faith. After several hours, our view prevailed.

This was a controversial move within the ANC. Although MK was not active, the aura of the armed struggle had great meaning for many people. Even when cited merely as a rhetorical device, the armed struggle was a sign that we were actively fighting the enemy. As a result, it had a popularity out of proportion to what it had achieved on the ground.

On 6 August in Pretoria, the ANC and the government signed what became known as the Pretoria Minute in which we agreed to suspend the armed struggle. As I was to say over and over to our followers, although we had suspended armed action, we had not terminated the armed struggle. The agreement also set forth target dates for the release of political prisoners and the granting of certain types of indemnity. The process of indemnity was scheduled to be completed by May 1991, and the government also agreed to review the Internal Security Act.

Of all the issues that hindered the peace process, none was more devastating and frustrating than the escalation of violence in the country. We had all hoped that as negotiations got under way, violence would decrease. But in fact the opposite happened. The police and security forces were making very few arrests. People in the townships were accusing them of aiding and abetting the violence. It was becoming more and more clear to me that there was connivance on the part of the security forces. Many of the incidents indicated to me that the police, rather than quelling violence, were fomenting it.

Over the next few months, I visited townships all across the violence-racked Vaal Triangle south of Johannesburg, comforting wounded people and grieving families. Over and over again I heard the same story: the police and the defence force were destabilizing the area. I was told of the police confiscating weapons one day in one area, and then Inkatha forces attacking our people with those stolen weapons the next day. We heard stories of the police escorting Inkatha members to meetings and on their attacks.

In September I gave a speech in which I said there was a hidden hand behind the violence and suggested that there was a mysterious 'Third Force', which consisted of renegade men from the security forces who were attempting to disrupt the negotiations. I could not say who the members of the Third Force were, for I did not know myself, but I was certain that they existed and that they were murderously effective in their targeting of the ANC and the liberation struggle.

I came to this conclusion after becoming personally involved in two specific incidents. In July 1990 the ANC received information that hostel-dwellers belonging to the Inkatha Freedom Party were planning a major attack on ANC members in Sebokeng township in the Vaal Triangle on 22 July. Through our attorneys, we notified the minister of law and order, the commissioner of police and the regional commissioner, warning them of the impending attacks and urging them to take the proper action. We asked the police to prevent armed Inkatha members from entering the township to attend an Inkatha rally.

On 22 July busloads of armed Inkatha members, escorted by police vehicles, entered Sebokeng in broad daylight. A rally was held, after which the armed men went on a rampage, murdering approximately thirty people in a dreadful and grisly attack. I visited the area the next day and witnessed scenes I have never before seen and hope never to see again. At the morgue were bodies of people who had been hacked to death; a woman had both her breasts cut off with a machete. Whoever these killers were, they were animals.

I requested a meeting with Mr de Klerk the following day. When I saw him, I angrily demanded an explanation. 'You were warned in advance,' I told him, 'and yet did nothing. Why is that? Why is it that there have been no arrests? Why have the police sat on their hands?' I then told him that in any other nation where there was a tragedy of this magnitude, when more than thirty people had been slain, the head of state would make some statement of condolence, yet he had not uttered a word. He had no reply to what I said. I asked de Klerk to furnish me with an explanation, and he never did.

The second incident occurred in November, when a group of Inkatha members entered a squatters' camp known as Zonkizizwe (Zulu for 'the place where all nations are welcome') outside the city of Germiston, east of Johannesburg, and drove ANC people out, killing a number of them in the process. Inkatha members then proceeded to occupy the abandoned shacks and confiscate all the property. Residents of the area said that the Inkatha members were accompanied by the police. Once again, in the wake of this tragedy, the police and the government took no action. Black life in South Africa had never been so cheap.

Again, I met Mr de Klerk and his minister of law and order, Adriaan Vlok. Again, I asked Mr de Klerk why no action had been taken by the police in the aftermath of these crimes. I said the attackers could easily be found because they were now occupying the shacks of the people they had killed. Mr de Klerk asked Mr Vlok for an explanation and then Vlok, in a rather rude tone, asked me on whose property the shacks were located, the implication being that these people were squatters and therefore had no rights. In fact, I told him, the land had been made available to these people by the local authorities. His attitude was that of many Afrikaners who simply believed that black tribes had been killing each other since time immemorial. Mr de Klerk again told me he would investigate and respond, but never did.

During this time, the government took another action that added fuel to the flames. It introduced a regulation permitting Zulus to carry so-called 'traditional weapons' to political rallies and meetings in Natal and elsewhere. These weapons, assegais, which are spears, and knobkerries, wooden sticks with a heavy wooden head, are actual weapons with which Inkatha members killed ANC members. This gave me grave doubts about Mr de Klerk's peaceful intentions.

Those opposed to negotiations benefited from the violence, which always seemed to flare up when the government and the ANC were moving towards an agreement. These forces sought to ignite a war between the ANC and Inkatha, and I believe many members of Inkatha connived at this as well. Many in the government, including Mr de Klerk, chose to look the other way or ignore what they knew was going on under their noses. We had no doubts that men at the highest levels of the police and the security forces were aiding the Third Force. These suspicions were later confirmed by newspaper reports disclosing that the South African police had secretly funded Inkatha.

As the violence continued to spiral, I began to have second thoughts about the suspension of the armed struggle. Many of the people in the ANC were restive, and in September, at a press conference, I said that the continuing violence might necessitate taking up arms once more. The situation looked very grim, and any understanding that had been achieved with the government seemed lost.

107

In December 1990 Oliver returned to South Africa, having been in exile from his native land for three decades. It was wonderful to have him near. He returned for an ANC consultative conference in Johannesburg, which was attended by over fifteen hundred delegates from forty-five different regions, from home and abroad.

At the meeting I spoke in tribute to Oliver as the man who had led the ANC during its darkest hours and never let the flame go out. Now, he had ushered us to the brink of a future that looked bright and hopeful. During the twenty-seven years that I was in prison, it was Oliver who saved the ANC and then built it into an international organization with power and influence. He took up the reins when most of its leaders were either in prison or in exile. He was a soldier, a diplomat, a statesman.

Although I criticized the government for its orchestrated campaign of counter-revolutionary activities, it was Oliver's address that created a storm. He opened the meeting with a controversial speech in which he called for our sanctions policy to be re-evaluated. The ANC, he maintained, faced 'international marginalization' unless it took the initiative to de-escalate sanctions. The European Community had already begun to scale down sanctions. The countries in the West, particularly the United Kingdom and the United States, wanted to reward Mr de Klerk for his reforms, believing that this would encourage him to go further. We felt this was the wrong strategy, but we had to recognize international realities.

Although Oliver's speech had been discussed and approved by the NEC, his proposal was met with indignation by ANC militants, who insisted that sanctions must be maintained unchanged. The conference decided to retain the sanctions policy as it was.

I myself was the target of complaints by those who charged that the negotiators were out of touch with the grass roots and that we spent more time with National Party leaders than with our own people. I was also criticized at the conference for engaging in 'personal diplomacy' and not keeping the rank-and-file of the organization informed. As a leader of a mass organization, one must listen to the people, and I agreed that we had been remiss in not keeping the entire organization informed about the course of the negotiations. But I also knew the delicacy of our talks with the government; any agreements that we arrived at depended in part on their confidentiality. Although I accepted the criticism, I believed we had no alternative but to advance on the same course. I knew that I had to be more inclusive, brief more people as to our progress, and I proceeded with that in mind.

Each day, each weekend, the newspapers were filled with fresh reports of new and bloody violence in our communities and townships. It was clear that violence was the number one issue in the country. In many communities in Natal and on the Reef around Johannesburg, a poisonous mixture of crime, political rivalries, police brutality and shadowy death squads made life brutish and untenable. As long as the violence was not dealt with, the progress to a new dispensation would remain uneven and uncertain.

To try to arrest the spiral of violence, I contacted Chief Buthelezi to arrange a meeting. We met at Durban's Royal Hotel in January. Chief Buthelezi spoke first to assembled delegates and the media, and in the process opened old wounds rather than healing them. He catalogued the verbal attacks the ANC had made on him and criticized the ANC's negotiating demands. When it was my turn to speak, I chose not to respond to his remarks but to thank him for his efforts over many years to secure my release from prison. I cited our long relationship and underlined the many matters that united our two organizations rather than divided us.

Progress was made during our private talks, and Chief Buthelezi and I signed an agreement that contained a code of conduct covering the behaviour of our two organizations. It was a fair accord, and I suspect that if it had been implemented it would indeed have helped to staunch the bloodletting. But, as far as I could tell, Inkatha never made any effort to implement the accord, and there were also violations on our own side.

The violence continued between our two organizations. Each month people were dying by the hundreds. In March, Inkatha members launched an attack in Alexandra township north of Johannesburg in which forty-five people were killed over three days of fighting. Again, no one was arrested.

I could not sit idly by as the violence continued, and I sought another meeting with Chief Buthelezi. In April I went down to Durban, and we again made strong statements and signed another agreement. But, again, the ink was no sooner dry than it was drenched in blood. I was more convinced than ever that the government was behind much of the violence and that the violence was impeding the negotiations. Mr de Klerk's failure to respond put our own relationship in jeopardy.

In April, at a two-day meeting of the National Executive Committee, I discussed my doubts about Mr de Klerk. The NEC believed that the government was behind the violence and that the violence was upsetting the climate for negotiations. In an open letter to the government, we called for the dismissal of Magnus Malan, the minister of defence, and Adriaan Vlok, the minister of law and order; the banning of the carrying of traditional weapons in public; the phasing out of the migrant-worker hostels, where so many Inkatha members lived in the townships around Johannesburg; the dismantling of secret government counter-insurgency units; and the appointment of an independent commission to probe complaints of misconduct on the part of the security forces.

We gave the government until May to meet our demands. Mr de Klerk responded by calling for a multiparty conference on violence to be held in May but I replied that this was pointless, since the government knew precisely what it had to do to end the violence. In May we announced the suspension of talks with the government.

In July 1991 the ANC held its first annual conference inside South Africa in thirty years. The conference was attended by 2,244 voting delegates who were democratically elected at ANC branches at home and abroad. At the conference I was elected president of the ANC without opposition. Cyril Ramaphosa was elected secretary-general, evidence that the torch was being passed from an older generation of leadership to a younger one. Cyril, whom I met only upon my release from prison, was a worthy successor to a long line of notable ANC leaders. He was probably the most accomplished negotiator in the ranks of the ANC, a skill he honed as general secretary of the National Mine Workers' Union.

In my speech I expressed my appreciation for the great honour that had been bestowed on me, and spoke of how difficult it would be to follow in the great footsteps of my predecessor, Oliver Tambo. Though we were then at loggerheads with the government, negotiations in and of themselves, I said, constituted a victory. The mere fact that the government was engaged in negotiations at all was a sign that they did not have the strength to sustain apartheid. I reiterated that the process would not be smooth, as we were dealing with politicians who do not want to negotiate themselves out of power. 'The point which must be clearly understood is that the struggle is not over, and negotiations themselves are a theatre of struggle, subject to advances and reverses as any other form of struggle.'

But negotiations could not wait. It was never in our interest to prolong the agony of apartheid for any reason. It was necessary, I said, to create a transitional government as soon as possible.

The conference underlined one of the most important and demanding tasks before the ANC: to transform an illegal underground liberation movement into a legal mass political party. For thirty years the ANC had functioned clandestinely in South Africa; those habits and techniques were deeply ingrained. We had to reconstruct an entire organization, from the smallest local branch to the National Executive. And we had to do so in a matter of months during a period of extraordinary change.

A large part of the ANC and Communist Party leadership had been in exile. Most of them had returned for the conference in July. They were unfamiliar with present-day South Africa; it was a new-found land for them as well as me. There was, however, an extraordinary crop of young leaders of the United Democratic Front and COSATU who had remained in the country, who knew the political situation in a way that we did not. These organizations had in some measure been surrogates for the ANC inside South Africa during the 1980s. The ANC had to integrate these men and women into the organization as well.

We faced not only logistical problems but philosophical ones. It is a relatively simple proposition to keep a movement together when you are fighting a common enemy. But creating a policy when that enemy is across the negotiating table is another matter altogether. In the new ANC, we had to integrate not only many different groups, but many different points of view. We needed to unite the organization around the idea of negotiations.

In the first seventeen months of legal activity, the ANC had recruited 700,000 members. This was impressive, but there was no room for complacency. A proportionately low number of these members were from the rural areas, the regions where the ANC had historically been weakest. At the same time, the National Party was throwing open its doors to non-whites and was busily recruiting disaffected Coloureds and Indians.

Ever since my release from prison, the state had continued its campaign to discredit my wife. After the alleged kidnapping of four youths who were staying in the Diepkloof house and the death of one of them, Winnie had first been vilified by a whispering campaign and was then charged with four counts of kidnapping and one of assault. The continuing aspersions cast on her character were such that both Winnie and I were eager for her to have her day in court and prove her innocence of the charges.

My wife's formal trial began in February in the Rand Supreme Court in Johannesburg. I attended on the first day, as did many senior figures in the ANC, and I continued to attend as often as I could. I did this both to support my wife and to show my belief in her innocence. She was ably defended by George Bizos, who attempted to demonstrate that Winnie had had no involvement with either the kidnappings or beatings.

After three and a half months, the court found her guilty of kidnapping charges and being an accessory to assault. The judge, however, acknowledged that she had not taken part in any assault herself. She was sentenced to six years in prison, but was released on bail pending her appeal. As far as I was concerned, verdict or no verdict, her innocence was not in doubt.

108

On 20 December 1991, after more than a year and a half of talks about talks, the real talks began: CODESA – the Convention for a Democratic South Africa – represented the first formal negotiations forum between the government, the ANC and other South African parties. All our previous bilateral discussions had been laying the groundwork for these talks, which took place at the World Trade Centre, a modern exhibition centre near Jan Smuts airport in Johannesburg. CODESA comprised eighteen delegations covering the gamut of South African politics, plus observers from the United Nations, the Commonwealth, the European Community and the Organization of African Unity. It was the widest cross-section of political groups ever gathered in one place in South Africa.

The opening of such talks was a historic occasion, certainly the most important constitutional convention since that of 1909 when the former British colonies of the Cape and Natal and the Boer republics of the Transvaal and the Orange Free State agreed to form a single union. Of course, that convention was not a tribute to democracy but a betrayal of it, for none of the representatives there that day was black. In 1991, the majority of them were.

Our planning delegation, led by Cyril Ramaphosa and including Joe Slovo and Valli Moosa, had been engaged in weekly discussions with the government on the issues of elections, the constitution, a constituent assembly and a transitional government. Delegates from twenty different parties including the homeland governments had already agreed on the ground rules for the convention.

The optimism at the opening of the talks could not be dampened even by a few spoilers. The PAC decided to boycott the talks, accusing the ANC and the National Party of conspiring together to set up a multi-racial government. This occurred despite the formation, a month before, of the Patriotic Front, an alliance of the ANC, the PAC and the Azanian People's Organization around a declaration of common goals.

The PAC feared democratic elections because they knew that such a vote would expose their meagre popular support. Chief Buthelezi also boycotted the talks on the ground that he was not permitted three delegations: for Inkatha, the KwaZulu government and King Zwelithini. We argued that the king should be above politics, and that if he were included then every tribe in South Africa should be able to send their paramount chief.

There was not only a sense of history at the World Trade Centre, but of self-reliance. Unlike the negotiations preceding new dispensations in African states like Zimbabwe and Angola, which required outside mediators, we in South Africa were settling our differences among ourselves. Mr de Klerk talked about the need for a transitional, 'power-sharing' government on a democratic basis. The National Party's chief delegate to the talks, Dawie de Villiers, even offered an apology for apartheid.

In my own opening remarks I said that, with the dawn of CODESA, progress in South Africa had at last become irreversible. Governments, I said, derive their authority and legitimacy from the consent of the governed, and we had assembled to create such a legitimate authority. I said that CODESA marked the beginning of the road to an elected assembly that would write a new constitution, and I did not see any reason why an election for such a constituent assembly could not occur in 1992. I called on the government to usher in an interim government of national unity to supervise such an election, control the state media and the military and generally oversee the transition to a new, non-racial, democratic South Africa.

On the convention's first day, the lion's share of the participating parties, including the National Party and the ANC, endorsed a Declaration of Intent, which committed all parties to support an undivided South Africa whose supreme law would be a constitution safeguarded by an independent judiciary. The country's legal system would guarantee equality before the law, and a bill of rights would be drawn up to protect civil liberties. In short there would be a multi-party democracy based on universal adult suffrage on a common voters' roll. As far as we were concerned, this was the minimum acceptable constitutional threshold for a new South Africa. Inkatha refused to sign on the ground that the phrase an 'undivided' South Africa implied that a federal system was off limits.

The convention created five working groups that would meet in early 1992 to prepare the way for the second round of CODESA scheduled for May 1992. The groups would explore the question of creating a free political climate, the future of the homelands, the restructuring of the South African Broadcasting Corporation, the examination of various constitutional principles such as federalism, and the creation and installation of an interim government. The parties agreed that decisions would be taken by 'sufficient consensus', which was never defined, but in practice meant an agreement between the government and the ANC and a majority of the other parties.

The first day of CODESA 1 was uneventful, until it came to a close. The night before the convention I had been negotiating with Mr de Klerk on the telephone until after 8 in the evening. Mr de Klerk asked me whether or not I would agree to permit him to be the final speaker the next day. Though I was scheduled to give the concluding remarks, I told him that I would take up the matter with our National Executive. I did so that evening and, despite their misgivins, I persuaded them to permit Mr de Klerk to have the last word. I did not see the issue as a vital one, and I was prepared to do Mr de Klerk the favour.

At the end of the session, all seemed well; I spoke about the importance of the talks and I was followed by Mr de Klerk. He proceeded to underline the historic significance of the occasion and discussed the need for overcoming mutual distrust. But then he did a curious thing. He began to attack the ANC for not adhering to the agreements that we had made with the government. He began to speak to us like a schoolmaster admonishing a naughty child. He berated the ANC for failing to disclose the location of arms caches and then rebuked us for maintaining a 'private army', Umkhonto we Sizwe, in violation of the National Peace Accord of September 1991. In intemperate language, he questioned whether the ANC was honourable enough to abide by any agreements it signed.

This was more than I could tolerate and I would now be damned if I would permit Mr de Klerk to have the last word. When he finished, the meeting was meant to be over. But the room had grown very quiet; instead of allowing the session to end, I walked to the podium. I could not let his remarks go unchallenged. My voice betrayed my anger.

I am gravely concerned about the behaviour of Mr de Klerk today. He has launched an attack on the ANC and in doing so he has been less than frank. Even the head of an illegitimate, discredited minority regime, as his is, has certain moral standards to uphold. He has no excuse just because he is the head of such a discredited regime not to uphold moral standards . . . If a man can come to a conference of this nature and play the type of politics he has played – very few people would like to deal with such a man.

The members of the government persuaded us to allow them to speak last. They were very keen to say the last word here. It is now clear why they did so. He has abused his position, because he hoped that I would not respond. He was completely mistaken. I respond now.

I said it was unacceptable for Mr de Klerk to speak to us in such language. I reiterated that it was the ANC, not the government, that started the initiative of peace discussions, and it was the government, not the ANC, who time and again failed to live up to its agreements. I had told Mr de Klerk before that it served no useful purpose to attack the ANC publicly, yet he continued to do so. I noted that we had suspended our armed struggle to show our commitment to peace, yet the government was still colluding with those waging war. We told him that we would turn in our weapons only when we were a part of the government collecting those weapons, and not until then.

I added that it was apparent the government had a double agenda. They were using the negotiations not to achieve peace, but to score their own petty political gains. Even while negotiating, they were secretly funding covert organizations that committed violence against us. I mentioned the recent revelations about million-rand pay-offs to Inkatha that Mr de Klerk claimed not to have known about. I stated that if a man in his position 'doesn't know about such things, then he is not fit to be the head of government'.

I knew I had been harsh, but I did not want to capsize the whole ship of negotiations, and I ended on a more conciliatory note.

> I ask him to place his cards on the table face upwards. Let us work together openly. Let there be no secret agendas. Let him not persuade us that he would be the last speaker because he wants to abuse that privilege and attack us in the hope that we won't respond. I am prepared to work with him in spite of all his mistakes.

CODESA convened the following day for its final session, and both Mr de Klerk and I took pains to show that no irreparable harm had been done. At the beginning of the session, he and I publicly shook hands and said we would work together. But much trust had been lost, and the negotiations were now in a state of disarray.

Six weeks after the opening of CODESA 1, the National Party contested an important by-election in Potchefstroom, a conservative university town in the Transvaal, traditionally the party's stronghold. In a stunning upset, the Nationalists were defeated by the candidate of the right-wing Conservative Party. The Conservatives resolutely opposed the government's policy of negotiations with the ANC, and were composed mainly of Afrikaners who felt that Mr de Klerk was giving away the store. The election result seemed to cast doubt on Mr de Klerk's policy of reform and negotiations. The National Party was alarmed; these were their own voters in their own heartland rejecting their policies.

Mr de Klerk decided to gamble. He announced that as a result of the by-election in Potchefstroom he would call a nationwide all-white referendum for 17 March so that the people of South Africa could vote on his reform policy and on negotiations with the ANC. He stated that if the referendum was defeated, he would resign from office. The referendum asked a plain and direct question of all white voters over the age of eighteen: 'Do you support the continuation of the reform process which the state president began on 2 February 1990 which is aimed at a new constitution through negotiation?'

The ANC opposed the referendum on the principle that it was a vote that excluded all non-whites. At the same time, we were realistic: we certainly did not want white voters to rebuff Mr de Klerk's efforts to pursue negotiations. Though we disdained the election on principle, we urged whites to vote 'yes'. We saw such a vote as a signal of support for negotiations, not necessarily for de Klerk.

We watched Mr de Klerk's campaign with interest and some consternation. He and the National Party conducted a sophisticated, expensive, American-style political campaign accompanied by extensive newspaper and television advertisements, bumper stickers and colourful rallies. We saw this as a dress rehearsal for the campaign Mr de Klerk would wage against us.

In the end, 69 per cent of the white voters supported negotiations, giving de Klerk a great victory. He felt vindicated; I think the margin even swelled his head a bit. His hand was strengthened, and as a result, the Nationalists toughened their negotiating positions. This was a dangerous strategy.

109

On 13 April 1992 at a press conference in Johannesburg, flanked by my two oldest friends and comrades, Walter and Oliver, I announced my separation from my wife. The situation had grown so difficult that I felt that it was in the best interests of all concerned – the ANC, the family and Winnie – that we part. Although I discussed the matter with the ANC, the separation itself was made for personal reasons.

I read the following statement:

> The relationship between myself and my wife, Comrade Nomzamo Winnie Mandela, has become the subject of much media speculation. I am issuing this statement to clarify the position and in the hope that it will bring an end to further conjecture.
>
> Comrade Nomzamo and myself contracted our marriage at a critical time in the struggle for liberation in our country. Owing to the pressures of our shared commitment to the ANC and the struggle to end apartheid, we were unable to enjoy a normal family life. Despite these pressures our love for each other and our devotion to our marriage grew and intensified. . . .
>
> During the two decades I spent on Robben Island she was an indispensable pillar of support and comfort to myself personally. . . . Comrade Nomzamo accepted the onerous burden of raising our children on her own. . . . She endured the persecutions heaped upon her by the Government with exemplary fortitude and never wavered from her commitment to the freedom struggle. Her tenacity reinforced my personal respect, love and growing affection. It also attracted the admiration of the world at large. My love for her remains undiminished.
>
> However, in view of the tensions that have arisen owing to differences between ourselves on a number of issues in recent months, we have mutually agreed that a separation would be best for each of us. My action was not prompted by the current

allegations being made against her in the media. . . . Comrade Nomzamo has and can continue to rely on my unstinting support during these trying moments in her life.

I shall personally never regret the life Comrade Nomzamo and I tried to share together. Circumstances beyond our control however dictated it should be otherwise. I part from my wife with no recriminations. I embrace her with all the love and affection I have nursed for her inside and outside prison from the moment I first met her. Ladies and gentlemen, I hope you will appreciate the pain I have gone through.

Perhaps I was blinded to certain things because of the pain I felt for not being able to fulfil my role as a husband to my wife and a father to my children. But just as I am convinced that my wife's life while I was in prison was more difficult than mine, my own return was also more difficult for her than it was for me. She married a man who soon left her; that man became a myth; and then that myth returned home and proved to be just a man after all.

As I later said at my daughter Zindzi's wedding, it seems to be the destiny of freedom fighters to have unstable personal lives. When your life is the struggle, as mine was, there is little room left for family. That has always been my greatest regret, and the most painful aspect of the choice I made.

'We watched our children growing without our guidance,' I said at the wedding, 'and when we did come out [of prison], my children said, "We thought we had a father and one day he'd come back. But to our dismay, our father came back and he left us alone because he has now become the father of the nation."' To be the father of a nation is a great honour, but to be the father of a family is a greater joy. But it was a joy I had far too little of.

110

In May 1992, after a four-month interruption, the multi-party conference held its second plenary session at the World Trade Centre. Known as CODESA 2, the talks had been prepared by secret meetings between negotiators from both the ANC and the government as well as discussions between the ANC and other parties. These meetings culminated in a final session between Mr de Klerk and me the day before the opening of CODESA 2, the first time the two of us had met since before CODESA 1.

Only days before CODESA 2 was to begin, the government was hit by two scandals. The first involved the revelation of massive corruption and bribery at the Department of Development Aid, which was responsible for improving black life in the homelands, and the second was the implication of high government security officials in the 1985 murder of four of the UDF, the best known of whom was Matthew Goniwe. These revelations were added to the recent evidence implicating the police in murders in Natal and suspicions that the Department of Military Intelligence was conducting covert operations against the ANC. These two scandals coming together undermined the credibility of the government and strengthened our hand.

Over the previous months, the government had made numerous proposals that fell by the wayside. Most of them, like the idea of a rotating presidency, sought to preserve their power. But through negotiations over the past months, the ANC and government teams had put together a tentative agreement involving a two-stage transitional period to a fully democratic South Africa. In the first stage, a multi-party 'transitional executive council' would be appointed from the CODESA delegations to function as a temporary government in order to 'level the playing-field' for all parties and create an interim constitution. In the second stage, general elections would be held for a constituent assembly and legislature in which all political parties winning 5 per cent or more of the vote would participate in the cabinet. Half the members of the assembly would be elected on a national basis and half on a regional one, and the assembly would be empowered both to write a new constitution and to pass legislation. An independent commission would preside over the election and make sure it was free and fair.

Yet there were many matters on which the ANC and the government could not reach agreement, such as the percentage of voting necessary in the assembly to decide constitutional issues and to agree on a bill of rights. Only days before CODESA 2, the government proposed a second body, a senate, composed of regional representatives, as a way of ensuring a minority veto. They also proposed that, before all this, CODESA 2 first agree on an interim constitution, which would take months to draw up.

All of this bargaining was going on behind the scenes, and by the time CODESA 2 opened on 15 May 1992, the prospects for agreement looked bleak. What we disagreed about was threatening all that we had agreed upon. Mr de Klerk and I had not managed to find a consensus on most of the outstanding issues. The government seemed prepared to wait indefinitely; their thinking was that the longer we waited, the more support we would lose.

The convention was deadlocked at the end of the first day. At that time, the two judges presiding over the talks told Mr de Klerk and me to meet that evening to attempt to find a compromise. We did meet that night over coffee, and though we did not find a way out of the impasse, we agreed that the negotiations must not founder. 'The whole of South Africa and the world is looking at you and me,' I told Mr de Klerk. 'Let us save the peace process. Let us reach some kind of agreement. Let us at least fix a date for the next round of talks.' We decided that we would each speak the following day in a spirit of constructive compromise.

The next afternoon we spoke in the reverse order that we had agreed to at CODESA 1: Mr de Klerk first, and I last. In his remarks, Mr de Klerk insisted that the National Party did not seek a 'minority veto', but that he did want a system of 'checks and balances' so that the majority would not be able 'to misuse its power'. Although this certainly sounded to me like outright opposition to the idea of majority rule, when I spoke after Mr de Klerk I merely said we needed to work in a constructive manner and dispel the tensions around the negotiations.

Despite our attempts to put a positive face on the matter, the convention ended the second day in a stalemate. The impasse, as I saw it, was caused by the National Party's continuing reluctance to submit their fate to the will of the majority. They simply could not cross that hurdle.

Ultimately, CODESA 2 broke down on four fundamental issues: the government's insistence on an unacceptably high percentage of votes in the assembly to approve the constitution (essentially a back-door veto); entrenched regional powers that would be binding on a future constitution; an undemocratic and unelected senate that had veto power over legislation from the main chamber; and a determination to make an interim constitution negotiated by the convention into a permanent constitution.

These were all difficult issues, but not insoluble ones, and I was determined not to let the deadlock at CODESA 2 subvert the negotiation process. The government and the ANC agreed to continue bilateral talks to work towards a solution. But, then, other matters intruded to render this impossible.

With negotiations stalled, the ANC and its allies agreed on a policy of 'rolling mass action', which would display to the government the extent of our support around the country and show that the people of South Africa were not prepared to wait forever for their freedom. The mass action consisted of strikes, demonstrations and boycotts. The date chosen for the start of mass action was 16 June 1992, the anniversary of the 1976 Soweto revolt, and the campaign was meant to culminate in a two-day national strike set for 3 and 4 August.

But before that happened, another event occurred that drove the ANC and the government even further apart. On the night of 17 June 1992, a heavily armed force of Inkatha members secretly raided the Vaal township of Boipatong and killed forty-six people. Most of the dead were women and children. It was the fourth mass killing of ANC people that week. People across the country were horrified by the violence and charged the government with complicity. The police did nothing to stop the criminals and nothing to find them; no arrests were made, no investigation began. Mr de Klerk said nothing. I found this to be the last straw, and my patience snapped. The government was blocking the negotiations and at the same waging a covert war against our people. Why then were we continuing to talk with them?

Four days after the murders, I addressed a crowd of twenty thousand angry ANC supporters and told them I had instructed the ANC secretary-general Cyril Ramaphosa to suspend direct dealings with the government. I also announced an urgent meeting of the National Executive Committee to examine our options. It was as if we had returned to the dark days of Sharpeville. I likened the behaviour of the National Party to the Nazis in Germany, and publicly warned de Klerk that if he sought to impose new measures to restrict demonstrations or free expression, the ANC would launch a nationwide defiance campaign with myself as the first volunteer.

At the rally, I saw signs that read, 'MANDELA, GIVE US GUNS' and 'VICTORY THROUGH BATTLE NOT TALK'. I understood such sentiments; the people were frustrated. They saw no positive results of the negotiations. They were beginning to think that the only way to overthrow apartheid was through the barrel of a gun. After Boipatong, there were those in the NEC who said, 'Why did we abandon the armed struggle? We should abandon negotiations instead; they will never advance us to our goal.' I was initially sympathetic to this group of hardliners, but gradually realized that there was no alternative to the process. It was what I had been urging for so many years, and I would not turn my back on negotiations. But it was time to cool things down. Mass action in this case was a middle course between armed struggle and negotiations. The people must have an outlet for their anger and frustration, and a mass action campaign was the best way to channel those emotions.

When we informed the government that we were suspending talks, we sent Mr de Klerk a memo outlining the reasons for our withdrawal. In addition to resolving the constitutional deadlocks at CODESA 2, we demanded that the people responsible for the violence be tracked down and brought to justice and that some mechanism be found for fencing in and policing the hostels, the seedbeds of so much violence. Mr de Klerk sent us back a memo asking for a face-to-face meeting with me, which we rebuffed. I felt such a meeting would suggest that we had something to talk about, and at the time we did not.

The mass action campaign culminated in a general strike on 3 and 4 August in support of the ANC's negotiation demands and in protest against state-supported violence. More than four million workers stayed at home in what was the largest political strike in South African history. The centrepiece of the strike was a march of one hundred thousand people to the Union Buildings in Pretoria, the imposing seat of the South African government, where we held an enormous outdoor rally on the great lawn in front of the buildings. I told the crowd that one day we would occupy these buildings, as the first democratically elected government of South Africa.

In the face of this mass action, Mr de Klerk said that if the ANC made the country ungovernable, the government might be forced to consider some unpleasant options. I warned Mr de Klerk that any anti-democratic actions would have serious repercussions. It was because of such threats, I said, that it was absolutely critical to set up a transitional government.

Inspired by the success of the mass action campaign, a group within the ANC decided to march on Bisho, the capital of the Ciskei homeland in the eastern Cape, a Bantustan led by Brigadier General Oupa Gqozo. The Ciskei had a history of repression against the ANC and in 1991 Brigadier Gqozo had declared a State of Emergency in the homeland to curtail what he called ANC-sponsored terrorism. On the morning of 7 September 1992, seventy thousand protesters set out on a march to Bisho's main stadium. When a group of marchers attempted to run through an opening in a fence and take a different path to town, the poorly trained homeland troops opened fire on the marchers and killed twenty-nine people, wounding over two hundred. Now Bisho joined Boipatong as a byword for brutality.

Like the old proverb that says the darkest hour is before the dawn, the tragedy of Bisho led to a new opening in the negotiations. I met de Klerk in order to find common ground and avoid a repetition of another tragedy like Bisho. Our respective negotiators began meeting regularly. Both sides were making an effort in good faith to get the negotiations back on track, and on 26 September de Klerk and I met for an official summit.

On that day he and I signed the Record of Understanding, an agreement which set the mould for all the negotiations that followed. The agreement established an independent body to review police actions, created a mechanism to fence in the hostels and banned the display of 'traditional weapons' at rallies. But the real importance of the Record of Understanding was that it broke the constitutional deadlock of CODESA 2. The government finally agreed to accept a single, elected constitutional assembly, which would adopt a new constitution and serve as a transitional legislature for the new government. All that was left to negotiate was a date for the election of the assembly and the percentage of majorities necessary for it to reach its decisions. We were now aligned on the basic framework that would take the country into a democratic future.

The Record of Understanding prompted Inkatha to announce its withdrawal from all negotiations involving the government and the ANC. The agreement infuriated Chief Buthelezi, who severed relations with the NP and formed an alliance with a group of discredited homeland leaders and white right-wing parties solely concerned with obtaining an Afrikaner homeland. Chief Buthelezi called for the abolition of the Record of Understanding, the ending of CODESA and the disbanding of Umkhonto we Sizwe.

Just as Joe Slovo had taken the initiative concerning the suspension of the armed struggle, he again took the lead in making another controversial proposal: a government of national unity. In October, Joe published a paper in which he wrote that negotiations with the government were not armistice talks in which we could dictate terms to a defeated enemy. It would probably take years for the ANC to control the levers of government, even after an election. An ANC government would still require much of the present civil service to run the country. Joe proposed a 'sunset clause' providing for a government of national unity that would include power-sharing with the National Party for a fixed period of time, an amnesty for security officers and the honouring of contracts of civil servants. 'Power-sharing' was a debased term within the ANC, considered a code-phrase for the government's quest for a minority veto. But in this context it merely meant that the National Party would be part of any popularly elected government, provided it polled enough votes.

After much discussion, I supported Joe's proposal and it was endorsed by the National Executive on 18 November. The NEC agreed to support power-sharing, provided the minority parties did not have a veto. In December we began a new round of secret bilateral talks with the government. These were held over a five-day period at a game lodge in the bush. The talks proved to be critical, for they built on the foundation established in the Record of Understanding. At this bush meeting we agreed in principle on a five-year government of national unity in which all parties polling over 5 per cent in a general election would be proportionally represented in the cabinet. After five years, the government of national unity would become a simple majority-rule government. In February the ANC and the government announced an agreement in principle on the five-year government of national unity, a multi-party cabinet and the creation of a transitional executive council. Elections would be held as early as the end of 1993.

111

I have always believed that a man should have a home within sight of the house where he was born. After being released from prison, I set about plans to build a country house for myself in Qunu. By autumn 1993, the house was complete. It was based on the floor plan of the house I had lived in at Victor Verster. People often commented on this, but the answer was simple: the Victor Verster house was the first spacious and comfortable home I ever stayed in, and I liked it very much. I was familiar with its dimensions, so at Qunu I would not have to wander at night looking for the kitchen.

In April, I was at my house in the Transkei on a brief holiday. On the morning of 10 April I had just gone outside to greet some members of the Transkei police rugby team when my housekeeper ran out and informed me of an urgent telephone call. She was weeping. I excused myself from the young men and learned from a colleague that Chris Hani, the secretary-general of the SACP, the former chief of staff of MK and one of the most popular figures in the ANC, had been shot at point-blank range in front of his home in Boksburg, Johannesburg, a mostly white working-class suburb that Chris was seeking to integrate.

Chris's death was a blow to me personally and to the movement. He was a soldier and patriot, for whom no task was too small. He was a great hero among the youth of South Africa, a man who spoke their language and to whom they listened. If anyone could mobilize the unruly youth behind a negotiated solution, it was Chris. South Africa was now deprived of one of its greatest sons, a man who would have been invaluable in transforming the country into a new nation.

The country was fragile. There were concerns that Hani's death might trigger a racial war, with the youth deciding that their hero should become a martyr for whom they would lay down their own lives. I first flew via helicopter to pay my respects to Chris's eighty-two-year-old father in Sabalele, a tiny, dusty town in the Cofimvaba district in the Transkei, a place well known to me because it was the home region of the Matanzima family. As I arrived in this village with no running water or electricity, I marvelled at how this poor and tiny place could produce a man like Chris Hani, a man who stirred the entire nation with his passion and ability. His concern for the rural poor came from his childhood in Sabalele, for his roots were deep and true, and he never lost them. Chris's father spoke eloquently of the pain of losing a son, but with satisfaction that he had died in the struggle.

Upon my return to Johannesburg I learned that the police had arrested a member of the militant right-wing Afrikaner Weerstandsbeweging (AWB), a Polish immigrant to South Africa who had been captured after a courageous Afrikaner woman had phoned the police with the killer's licence-plate number. The murder was an act of mad desperation, an attempt to derail the negotiation process. I was asked to speak on the SABC that night to address the nation. In this instance, it was the ANC, not the government, that sought to calm the people.

I said that the process of peace and negotiations could not be halted. With all the authority at my command, I said, 'I appeal to all our people to remain calm and to honour the memory of Chris Hani by remaining a disciplined force for peace.'

> Tonight I am reaching out to every single South African, black and white, from the very depths of my being. A white man, full of prejudice and hate, came to our country and committed a deed so foul that our whole nation now teeters on the brink of disaster. A white woman, of Afrikaner origin, risked her life so that we may know, and bring to justice, this assassin. . . . Now is the time for all South Africans to stand together against those who, from any quarter, wish to destroy what Chris Hani gave his life for – the freedom of all of us.

The assassination of Chris was an attempt by white supremacists to arrest the inevitable. They preferred that the country descend into civil war rather than have majority rule by peaceful means.

We adopted a strategy to deal with our own constituency in the ANC. In order to forestall outbreaks of retaliatory violence, we arranged a week-long series of mass rallies and demonstrations throughout the country. This would give people a means of expressing their frustration without resorting to violence. Mr de Klerk and I spoke privately and agreed that we would not let Hani's murder derail the negotiations.

We learned within days that a member of the Conservative Party, Clive Derby-Lewis, had been arrested in connection with the murder. More confirmation of a Third Force. It was Chris himself who had criticized a recent theft of weapons from an air force base; preliminary police reports suggested that the gun that killed him had come from that stockpile.

Exactly two weeks later, there was another significant passing. This one did not shake the nation as Chris's had, but it shook me. Oliver Tambo had not been well for a long time, but the stroke that killed him occurred suddenly and without warning. His wife Adelaide phoned me early in the morning and I rushed to Oliver's bedside. I did not have a chance to say a proper good-bye, for he was already gone.

In Plato's allegory of the metals, the philosopher classifies men into groups of gold, silver and lead. Oliver was pure gold; there was gold in his intellectual brilliance, gold in his warmth and humanity, gold in his tolerance and generosity, gold in his unfailing loyalty and self-sacrifice. As much as I respected him as a leader, that is how much I loved him as a man.

Though we had been apart for all the years that I was in prison, Oliver was never far from my thoughts. In many ways, even though we were separated, I kept up a life-long conversation with him in my head. Perhaps that is why I felt so bereft when he died. I felt, as I told one colleague, like the loneliest man in the world. It was as though he had been snatched away from me just as we had finally been reunited. When I looked at him in his coffin, it was as if a part of myself had died.

Though we were not yet in power, I wanted Oliver to have a state funeral, and that is what the ANC gave him. At a mass rally at a stadium in Soweto, hundreds of dignitaries from foreign governments gathered to pay their respects to the man who kept the ANC alive during its years of exile. MK troops marched in his honour and a twenty-one-gun salute was given at his graveside. Oliver had lived to see the prisoners released and the exiles return, but he had not lived to cast his vote in a free and democratic South Africa. That was what remained to be accomplished.

112

Although few people will remember 3 June 1993, it was a landmark in South African history. On that day, after months of negotiations at the World Trade Centre, the multi-party forum voted to set a date for the country's first national, non-racial, one-person-one-vote election: 27 April 1994. For the first time in South African history, the black majority would go to the polls to elect their own leaders. The agreement was that voters would elect four hundred representatives to a constituent assembly, which would both write a new constitution and serve as a parliament. After convening, the first order of business for the assembly would be to elect a president.

The talks had reconvened in April. This time, the twenty-six parties included Inkatha, the Pan-Africanist Congress and the Conservative Party. We had been pressing the government to establish a date for months, and they had been stalling. But now the date was written in stone.

A month later, in July, the multi-party forum agreed on a first draft of an interim constitution. It provided for a bicameral parliament with a four-hundred-member national assembly elected by proportional representation from national and regional party lists, and a senate elected indirectly by regional legislatures.

Elections to regional legislatures would take place at the same time as national elections, and the regional bodies could draw up their own constitutions consistent with the national constitution.

Chief Buthelezi wanted a constitution drawn up before the election and walked out in protest against the setting of an election date before a constitution was finalized. A second draft interim constitution in August gave greater powers to the regions, but this did not placate either Chief Buthelezi or the Conservative Party. The Conservative Party described the resolutions as hostile to Afrikaner interests. A group called the Afrikaner Volksfront, led by General Constand Viljoen, a former chief of the South African Defence Force, was formed to unite conservative white organizations around the idea of a *volkstaat*, a white homeland

Just after midnight on 18 November an interim constitution was approved by a plenary session of the multiparty conference. The government and the ANC had cleared the remaining hurdles. The new cabinet would be composed of those winning more than 5 per cent of the vote and would make decisions by consensus, rather than the two-thirds majority proposed by the government; national elections would not take place until 1999, so that the government of national unity would serve for five years; finally, the government gave way on our insistence on a single ballot paper for the election, rather than separate ballots for national and provincial legislatures. Two ballot papers would only confuse a majority of voters, most of whom would be voting for the first time in their lives. In the period leading up to the election, a Transitional Executive Council with members from each party would ensure the right climate for the elections. In effect, the TEC would be the government between 22 December and the election on 27 April. An Independent Electoral Commission with extensive powers would be responsible for the administration of the election. We were truly on the threshold of a new era.

I have never cared very much for personal prizes. A man does not become a freedom fighter in the hope of winning awards, but when I was notified that I had won the 1993 Nobel Peace Prize jointly with Mr de Klerk, I was deeply moved. The Nobel Peace Prize had a special meaning to me because of its involvement with South African history.

I was the third South African since the end of the Second World War to be so honoured by the Nobel Committee. Chief Albert Luthuli was awarded the prize in 1960. The second was Archbishop Desmond Tutu, who selflessly fought the evils of racism during the most terrible days of apartheid, and won the prize in 1984.

The award was a tribute to all South Africans and especially to those who had fought in the struggle; I would accept it on their behalf. But the Nobel award was one I had never thought about. Even during the bleakest years on Robben Island, Amnesty International would not campaign for us on the ground that we had pursued an armed struggle, and their organization would not represent anyone who had embraced violence. It was for that reason that I assumed the Nobel Committee would never consider for the peace prize the man who had started Umkhonto we Sizwe.

I had tremendous respect for the nations of Norway and Sweden. In the 1950s and 1960s, when we went to Western governments seeking contributions to the ANC, we were turned down flat. But in Norway and Sweden we were greeted with open arms and given assistance and scholarships and money for legal defence and humanitarian aid for political prisoners.

I used my speech in Norway not only to thank the Nobel Committee and sketch out a vision of a future South Africa that was just and equitable, but to pay tribute to my fellow laureate, Mr F.W. de Klerk.

> He had the courage to admit that a terrible wrong had been done to our country and people through the imposition of the system of apartheid. He had the foresight to understand and accept that all the people of South Africa must, through negotiations and as equal participants in the process, together determine what they want to make of their future.

I was often asked how I could accept the award jointly with Mr de Klerk after I had criticized him so severely. Although I would not take back my criticisms, I could say that he had made a genuine and indispensable contribution to the peace process. I never sought to undermine Mr de Klerk, for the practical reason that the weaker he was, the weaker the negotiations process. To make peace with an enemy, one must work with that enemy, and that enemy becomes your partner.

Although the official campaign for the national assembly was not scheduled to begin until February 1994, we started to campaign in earnest after the new constitution was ratified. That did not give us a head start; the National Party began its campaign the day they released me from prison.

Although the polls showed the ANC with a healthy margin, we never took victory for granted. I counselled everyone against over-optimism. We had all read dozens of accounts of parties favoured to win who subsequently came in second. We faced an experienced, well-organized and well-financed rival.

Our campaign was under the capable leadership of Popo Molefe, Terror Lekota and Ketso Gordhan, all veteran UDF activists adept at mass mobilization. The task was a formidable one. We estimated that there would be over twenty million people going to the polls, most of them voting for the first time. Many of our voters were illiterate, and were likely to be intimidated by the mere idea of voting. According to the Independent Electoral Commission, there would be ten thousand polling stations around the country. We sought to train over a hundred thousand people to assist with voter education.

The first stage of our election effort was what were known as People's

Forums. ANC candidates would travel all over the country and hold meetings in towns and villages in order to listen to the hopes and fears, the ideas and complaints, of our people. The People's Forums were similar to the town meetings that candidate Bill Clinton held in America on his way to the presidency. The forums were parliaments of the people, not unlike the meetings of chiefs at the Great Place that I witnessed as a boy.

I revelled in the People's Forums. I began in Natal in November, and then went to the PWV area, the northern Transvaal and the Orange Free State. I attended as many as three or four forums in a day. The people themselves enjoyed them immensely. No one had ever come to solicit their opinion on what should be done in their own country.

After incorporating the suggestions from the forums, we travelled the country delivering our message to the people. Some in the ANC wanted to make the campaign simply a liberation election, and tell the people: Vote for us because we set you free. We decided instead to offer them a vision of the South Africa we hoped to create. We wanted people to vote for the ANC not simply because we had fought apartheid for eighty years, but because we were best qualified to bring about the kind of South Africa they hoped to live in. I felt that our campaign should be about the future, not the past.

The ANC drafted a 150-page document known as the Reconstruction and Development Programme, which outlined our plan to create jobs through public works; to build a million new houses with electricity and flush toilets; to extend primary health care and provide ten years of free education to all South Africans; to redistribute land through a land claims court; and to end the value-added tax on basic foodstuffs. We were also committed to extensive affirmative action measures in both the private and public sectors. This document was translated into a simpler manifesto called 'A Better Life for All', which in turn became the ANC's campaign slogan.

Just as we told the people what we would do, I felt we must also tell them what we could not do. Many people felt life would change overnight after a free and democratic election, but that would be far from the case. Often, I said to the crowds, 'Do not expect to be driving a Mercedes the day after the election or swimming in your own backyard pool.' I told our supporters, 'Life will not change dramatically, except that you will have increased your self-esteem and become a citizen in your own land. You must have patience. You might have to wait five years for results to show.' I challenged them; I did not patronize them: 'If you want to continue living in poverty without clothes and food,' I told them, 'then go and drink in the shebeens. But if you want better things, you must work hard. We cannot do it all for you; you must do it yourselves.'

I told white audiences that we needed them and did not want them to leave the country. They were South Africans just like ourselves and this was their land, too. I would not mince words about the horrors of apartheid, but I said, over and over, that we should forget the past and concentrate on building a better future for all.

Each rally was also designed to teach people how to vote. The ballot itself was a long, narrow piece of paper with the parties listed in descending order to the left, and then the symbol of the party and a picture of its leader to the right. Voters were to place an X in the box next to the party of their choice. I would tell audiences, 'On election day, look down your ballot and when you see the face of a young and handsome man, mark an X.'

113

The road to freedom was far from smooth. Although the Transitional Executive Council began functioning in the new year, some parties opted out. Inkatha rejected participation in the election and gave itself over to the politics of resistance. King Zwelithini, supported by Chief Buthelezi, called for an autonomous and sovereign KwaZulu, and discouraged everyone in his province from voting. The white right called the elections a betrayal and clamoured for a *volkstaat*, yet they still had not proposed where it would be located or how it would work. There was no magisterial district in the whole of South Africa where whites constituted a majority of residents.

12 February 1994 was the deadline for registration of all parties, and on that day Inkatha, the Conservative Party and the Afrikaner Volksfront failed to sign. The government of the Bophuthatswana homeland also refused to participate and resisted reincorporation into a united South Africa. I was disturbed that these important groups were choosing not to participate. To bring them on board, we proposed certain significant compromises: we agreed to the use of double ballots for provincial and national legislatures; guarantees of greater provincial powers; the renaming of Natal province as KwaZulu/Natal; and the affirmation that a principle of 'internal' self-determination would be included in the constitution for groups sharing a common cultural and language heritage.

I arranged to meet Chief Buthelezi in Durban on 1 March. 'I will go down on my knees to beg those who want to drag our country into bloodshed,' I told a rally before this meeting. Chief Buthelezi agreed to register provisionally for the elections in exchange for a promise to subject our differences over constitutional issues to international mediation. To this I gladly assented. Before the final registration deadline, General Viljoen also registered under a new party known as the Freedom Front.

Though Lucas Mangope, the president of Bophuthatswana, had

chosen to keep his homeland out of the election, the tide of events soon altered the situation. I spoke to him on a number of occasions urging him to let his people decide, but he would not listen. Those who wanted to participate launched mass demonstrations and strikes, which soon spread to the Bophuthatswana civil service. The radio and television networks went off the air. On the streets of Mafikeng, battles broke out between the homeland police and striking workers and students. Mangope called in military help from his white right-wing allies. Soon his own forces deserted him and he was ousted in a coup in early March. A few weeks later, Brigadier Gqozo in the Ciskei capitulated and asked South Africa to take over the homeland.

Violence in Natal worsened. Inkatha supporters were blocking our efforts to campaign in Natal. Fifteen ANC election workers were shot and hacked to death after putting up ANC posters. In March, Judge Johann Kriegler reported to me and Mr de Klerk that because of the lack of cooperation from the KwaZulu government, free elections could not be held there without direct political intervention. To demonstrate our strength in Natal, the ANC held a mass march through the centre of Durban. Then Inkatha attempted to do the same in Johannesburg, with dire results.

On 28 March thousands of Inkatha members brandishing spears and knobkerries marched through Johannesburg to a rally in the centre of town. At the same time an armed Inkatha group attempted to enter Shell House, the ANC headquarters, but was repulsed by armed guards. Shots by unidentified gunmen were also fired in the city centre, and altogether fifty-three people died. It was a grisly spectacle that made South Africa appear as if it was on the brink of internal war. Inkatha was attempting to postpone the election, but neither Mr de Klerk nor I would budge. That day was sacrosanct.

I had agreed to international mediation, and on 13 April a delegation arrived led by Lord Carrington, the former British foreign secretary, and Henry Kissinger, the former American secretary of state. But when Inkatha was informed that the election date was not subject to mediation, they refused to see the mediators, who left without talking to anyone. Now Chief Buthelezi knew the election would take place no matter what. On 19 April Chief Buthelezi accepted the offer of a constitutional role for the Zulu monarchy and agreed to participate.

Ten days before the vote, Mr de Klerk and I held our single television debate. I had been a fair debater at Fort Hare, and in my early years in the organization I had engaged in many impassioned debates on the platform. On Robben Island we had honed our debating skills while we chipped away at limestone. I was confident, but the day before, we held a mock debate in which the journalist Allister Sparks ably performed as Mr de Klerk. Too ably, according to my campaign advisers, for they chided me for speaking too slowly and not aggressively enough.

When the time came for the actual debate, however, I attacked the National Party quite firmly. I accused the National Party of fanning race hatred between Coloureds and Africans in the Cape by distributing an inflammatory comic book that said the ANC's slogan was 'Kill a Coloured, kill a farmer'. 'There is no organization in this country as divisive as the new National Party,' I declared. When Mr de Klerk criticized the ANC's plan to spend billions of dollars on housing and social programmes, I scolded him, saying he was alarmed that we would have to devote so many of our resources to blacks.

But as the debate was nearing an end, I felt I had been too harsh with the man who would be my partner in a government of national unity. In summation, I said, 'The exchanges between Mr de Klerk and me should not obscure one important fact. I think we are a shining example to the entire world of people drawn from different racial groups who have a common loyalty, a common love, to their common country. . . . In spite of criticism of Mr de Klerk,' I said, and then looked over at him, 'sir, you are one of those I rely upon. We are going to face the problem of this country together.' At which point I reached over to take his hand and said, 'I am proud to hold your hand for us to go forward.' Mr de Klerk seemed surprised, but pleased.

114

I voted on 27 April, the second of the four days of voting [certain categories including the elderly, the disabled and South Africans voting abroad were allowed to vote on 26 April]. I chose to vote in Natal to show the people in that divided province that there was no danger in going to the polling stations. I voted at Ohlange High School in Inanda, a green and hilly township just north of Durban, for it was there that John Dube, the first president of the ANC, was buried. This African patriot had helped found the organization in 1912, and casting my vote near his graveside brought history full circle, for the mission he began eighty-two years before was about to be achieved.

As I stood over his grave, on a rise above the small school below, I thought not of the present but of the past. When I walked to the voting station, my mind dwelt on the heroes who had fallen so that I might be where I was that day, the men and women who had made the ultimate sacrifice for a cause that was now finally succeeding. I thought of Oliver Tambo, Chris Hani, Chief Luthuli and Bram Fischer. I thought of our great African heroes, who had made great sacrifices so that millions of South Africans could be voting on that very day; I thought of Josiah Gumede, G. M. Naicker, Dr Abdullah Abdurahman, Lilian Ngoyi, Helen Joseph, Yusuf Dadoo, Moses Kotane. I did not go into that voting station alone on 27 April; I was casting my vote with all of them.

Before I entered the polling station, an irreverent member of the press called out, 'Mr Mandela, who are you voting for?' I laughed. 'You know,' I said, 'I have been agonizing over that choice all morning.' I marked an X in the box next to the letters ANC and then slipped my folded ballot paper into a simple wooden box; I had cast the first vote of my life.

The images of South Africans going to the polls that day are burned in my memory. Great lines of patient people snaking through the dirt roads and streets of towns and cities; old women who had waited half a century to cast their first vote saying that they felt like human beings for the first time in their lives; white men and women saying they were proud to live in a free country at last. The mood of the nation during those days of voting was buoyant. The violence and bombings ceased, and it was as though we were a nation reborn. Even the logistical difficulties of the voting, misplaced ballots, pirate voting stations and rumours of fraud in certain places could not dim the overwhelming victory for democracy and justice.

It took several days for the results to be counted. We polled 62.6 per cent of the national vote, slightly short of the two-thirds needed had we wished to push through a final constitution without support from other parties. That percentage qualified us for 252 of 400 seats in the national assembly. The ANC thoroughly dominated the northern and eastern Transvaal, the northwest, the eastern Cape and the Free State. We won 33 per cent of the vote in the western Cape, which was won by the National Party, which did extremely well among Coloured voters. We captured 32 per cent in KwaZulu/Natal, which was won by Inkatha. In Natal, fear of violence and intimidation kept many of our voters at home. There were charges, as well, of vote fraud and vote rigging. But, in the end, that did not matter. We had underestimated Inkatha's strength in KwaZulu, and they had demonstrated it on election day.

Some in the ANC were disappointed that we did not cross the two-thirds threshold, but I was not one of them. In fact I was relieved; had we won two-thirds of the vote and been able to write a constitution unfettered by input from others, people would argue that we had created an ANC constitution, not a South African constitution. I wanted a true government of national unity.

On the evening of 2 May Mr de Klerk made a gracious concession speech. After more than three centuries of rule, the white minority was conceding defeat and turning over power to the black majority. That evening the ANC was planning a victory celebration at the ballroom of the Carlton Hotel in downtown Johannesburg. I was suffering from a bad case of flu and my doctors ordered me to remain at home. But there was nothing that could keep me away from that party. I went on stage at about nine o'clock and faced a crowd of happy, smiling, cheering faces.

I explained to the crowd that my voice was hoarse from a cold and that my physician had advised me not to attend. 'I hope that you will not disclose to him that I have violated his instructions,' I told them. I congratulated Mr de Klerk for his strong showing. I thanked all those in the ANC and the democratic movement who had worked so hard for so long. Mrs Coretta Scott King, the wife of the great freedom fighter Martin Luther King Jr, was on the podium that night, and I looked over to her as I made reference to her husband's immortal words.

This is one of the most important moments in the life of our country. I stand here before you filled with deep pride and joy – pride in the ordinary, humble people of this country. You have shown such a calm, patient determination to reclaim this country as your own, and now the joy that we can loudly proclaim from the rooftops – Free at last! Free at last! I stand before you humbled by your courage, with a heart full of love for all of you. I regard it as the highest honour to lead the ANC at this moment in our history. I am your servant. . . . It is not the individuals that matter, but the collective. . . . This is a time to heal the old wounds and build a new South Africa.

From the moment the results were in and it was apparent that the ANC was to form the government, I saw my mission as one of preaching reconciliation, of binding the wounds of the country, of engendering trust and confidence. I knew that many people, particularly the minorities, whites, Coloureds and Indians, would be feeling anxious about the future, and I wanted them to feel secure. I reminded people again and again that the liberation struggle was not a battle against any one group or colour, but a fight against a system of repression. At every opportunity, I said all South Africans must now unite and join hands and say we are one country, one nation, one people, marching together into the future.

115

10 May dawned bright and clear. For the past few days I had been pleasantly besieged by dignitaries and world leaders who were coming to pay their respects before the inauguration. The inauguration would be the largest gathering ever of international leaders on South African soil.

The ceremonies took place in the lovely sandstone amphitheatre formed by the Union Buildings in Pretoria. For decades this had been the seat of white supremacy, and now it was the site of a rainbow gathering of different colours and nations for the installation of South Africa's first democratic, non-racial government.

On that lovely autumn day I was accompanied by my daughter Zenani. On the podium, Mr de Klerk was first sworn in as second deputy president. Then Thabo Mbeki was sworn in as first deputy president. When it was my turn, I pledged to obey and uphold the constitution and to devote myself to the well-being of the republic and its people. To the assembled guests and the watching world, I said:

> Today, all of us do, by our presence here . . . confer glory and hope to newborn liberty. Out of the experience of an extraordinary human disaster that lasted too long, must be born a society of which all humanity will be proud.
>
> . . . We, who were outlaws not so long ago, have today been given the rare privilege to be host to the nations of the world on our own soil. We thank all of our distinguished international guests for having come to take possession with the people of our country of what is, after all, a common victory for justice, for peace, for human dignity.
>
> We have, at last, achieved our political emancipation. We pledge ourselves to liberate all our people from the continuing bondage of poverty, deprivation, suffering, gender and other discrimination.
>
> Never, never, and never again shall it be that this beautiful land

will again experience the oppression of one by another. . . . The sun shall never set on so glorious a human achievement.

Let freedom reign. God bless Africa!

A few moments later we all lifted our eyes in awe as a spectacular array of South African jets, helicopters and troop carriers roared in perfect formation over the Union Buildings. It was not only a display of pinpoint precision and military force, but a demonstration of the military's loyalty to democracy, to a new government that had been freely and fairly elected. Only moments before, the highest generals of the South African Defence Force and police, their chests bedecked with ribbons and medals from days gone by, saluted me and pledged their loyalty. I was not unmindful of the fact that not so many years before they would not have saluted but arrested me. Finally a chevron of Impala jets left a smoke trail of the black, red, green, blue and gold of the new South African flag.

The day was symbolized for me by the playing of our two national anthems, and the vision of whites singing 'Nkosi Sikelel' iAfrika' and blacks singing 'Die Stem', the old anthem of the republic. Although that day neither group knew the lyrics of the anthem they once despised, they would soon know the words by heart.

On the day of the inauguration, I was overwhelmed with a sense of history. In the first decade of the twentieth century, a few years after the bitter Anglo-Boer war and before my own birth, the white-skinned peoples of South Africa patched up their differences and erected a system of racial domination against the dark-skinned peoples of their own land. The structure they created formed the basis of one of the harshest, most inhumane, societies the world has ever known. Now, in the last decade of the twentieth century, and my own eighth decade as a man, that system had been overturned forever and replaced by one that recognized the rights and freedoms of all peoples regardless of the colour of their skin.

That day had come about through the unimaginable sacrifices of thousands of my people, people whose suffering and courage can never be counted or repaid. I felt that day, as I have on so many other days, that I was simply the sum of all those African patriots who had gone before me. That long and noble line ended and now began again with me. I was pained that I was not able to thank them and that they were not able to see what their sacrifices had wrought.

The policy of apartheid created a deep and lasting wound in my country and my people. All of us will spend many years, if not generations, recovering from that profound hurt. But the decades of oppression and brutality had another, unintended, effect, and that was that it produced the Oliver Tambos, the Walter Sisulus, the Chief Luthulis, the Yusuf Dadoos, the Bram Fischers, the Robert Sobukwes of our time – men of such extraordinary courage, wisdom and generosity that their like may never be known again. Perhaps it requires such depths of oppression to create such heights of character. My country is rich in the minerals and gems that lie beneath its soil, but I have always known that its greatest wealth is its people, finer and truer than the purest diamonds.

It is from these comrades in the struggle that I learned the meaning of courage. Time and again, I have seen men and women risk and give their lives for an idea. I have seen men stand up to attacks and torture without breaking, showing a strength and resilience that defies the imagination. I learned that courage was not the absence of fear, but the triumph over it. I felt fear myself more times than I can remember, but I hid it behind a mask of boldness. The brave man is not he who does not feel afraid, but he who conquers that fear.

I never lost hope that this great transformation would occur. Not only because of the great heroes I have already cited, but because of the courage of the ordinary men and women of my country. I always knew that deep down in every human heart, there was mercy and generosity. No one is born hating another person because of the colour of his skin, or his background, or his religion. People must learn to hate, and if they can learn to hate, they can be taught to love, for love comes more naturally to the human heart than its opposite. Even in the grimmest times in prison, when my comrades and I were pushed to our limits, I would see a glimmer of humanity in one of the guards, perhaps just for a second, but it was enough to reassure me and keep me going. Man's goodness is a flame that can be hidden but never extinguished.

We took up the struggle with our eyes wide open, under no illusion that the path would be an easy one. As a young man, when I joined the African National Congress, I saw the price my comrades paid for their beliefs, and it was high. For myself, I have never regretted my commitment to the struggle, and I was always prepared to face the hardships that affected me personally. But my family paid a terrible price, perhaps too dear a price, for my commitment.

In life, every man has twin obligations – obligations to his family, to his parents, to his wife and children; and he has an obligation to his people, his community, his country. In a civil and humane society, each man is able to fulfil those obligations according to his own inclinations and abilities. But in a country like South Africa, it was almost impossible for a man of my birth and colour to fulfil both of those obligations. In South Africa, a man of colour who attempted to live as a human being was punished and isolated. In South Africa, a man who tried to fulfil his duty to his people was inevitably ripped from his family and his home and was forced to live a life apart, a twilight existence of secrecy and rebellion. I did not in the beginning choose to place my people above my family, but in attempting to serve my people, I found that I was prevented from fulfilling my obligations as a son, a brother, a father and a husband.

In that way, my commitment to my people, to the millions of South Africans I would never know or meet, was at the expense of the people I knew best and loved most. It was as simple and yet as incomprehensible as the moment a small child asks her father, 'Why can you not be with us?' And the father must utter the terrible words: 'There are other children like you, a great many of them . . .' and then one's voice trails off.

I was not born with a hunger to be free. I was born free – free in every way that I could know. Free to run in the fields near my mother's hut, free to swim in the clear stream that ran through my village, free to roast mealies under the stars and ride the broad backs of slow-moving bulls. As long as I obeyed my father and abided by the customs of my tribe, I was not troubled by the laws of man or God.

It was only when I began to learn that my boyhood freedom was an illusion, when I discovered as a young man that my freedom had already been taken from me, that I began to hunger for it. At first, as a student, I wanted freedom only for myself, the transitory freedoms of being able to stay out at night, read what I pleased and go where I chose. Later, as a young man in Johannesburg, I yearned for the basic and honourable freedoms of achieving my potential, of earning my keep, of marrying and having a family – the freedom not to be obstructed in a lawful life.

But then I slowly saw that not only was I not free, but my brothers and sisters were not free. I saw that it was not just my freedom that was curtailed, but the freedom of everyone who looked like I did. That is when I joined the African National Congress, and that is when the hunger for my own freedom became the greater hunger for the freedom of my people. It was this desire for the freedom of my people to live their lives with dignity and self-respect that animated my life, that transformed a frightened young man into a bold one, that drove a law-abiding attorney to become a criminal, that turned a family-loving husband into a man without a home, that forced a life-loving man to live like a monk. I am no more virtuous or self-sacrificing than the next man, but I found that I could not even enjoy the poor and limited freedoms I was allowed when I knew my people were not free. Freedom is indivisible; the chains on any one of my people were the chains on all of them, the chains on all of my people were the chains on me.

It was during those long and lonely years that my hunger for the freedom of my own people became a hunger for the freedom of all people, white and black. I knew as well as I knew anything that the oppressor must be liberated just as surely as the oppressed. A man who takes away another man's freedom is a prisoner of hatred, he is locked behind the bars of prejudice and narrow-mindedness. I am not truly free if I am taking away someone else's freedom, just as surely as I am not free when my freedom is taken from me. The oppressed and the oppressor alike are robbed of their humanity.

When I walked out of prison, that was my mission, to liberate the oppressed and the oppressor both. Some say that has now been achieved. But I know that that is not the case. The truth is that we are not yet free; we have merely achieved the freedom to be free, the right not to be oppressed. We have not taken the final step of our journey, but the first step on a longer and even more difficult road. For to be free is not merely to cast off one's chains, but to live in a way that respects and enhances the freedom of others. The true test of our devotion to freedom is just beginning.

I have walked that long road to freedom. I have tried not to falter; I have made missteps along the way. But I have discovered the secret that after climbing a great hill, one only finds that there are many more hills to climb. I have taken a moment here to rest, to steal a view of the glorious vista that surrounds me, to look back on the distance I have come. But I can rest only for a moment, for with freedom come responsibilities, and I dare not linger, for my long walk is not yet ended.

INDEX